SHARE YOUR LOVE OF READING

Gift a Book!

Purchase of this book

was made possible by a

Generous Borrower

December 2020

South Shore
Public Libraries

ALSO EDITED BY OTTO PENZLER

THE BIG BOOK OF
ESPIONAGE

EDITED AND WITH AN INTRODUCTION BY
OTTO PENZLER

VINTAGE CRIME/BLACK LIZARD
VINTAGE BOOKS
A DIVISION OF PENGUIN RANDOM HOUSE LLC
NEW YORK

A VINTAGE CRIME/BLACK LIZARD ORIGINAL, NOVEMBER 2020

Copyright © 2020 by Otto Penzler

Due to limitations of space, permissions to reprint previously
published material can be found on pages 815–17.

Cataloging-in-Publication Data is available at the Library of Congress.

Vintage Crime/Black Lizard Trade Paperback ISBN: 978-1-9848-9805-0
eBook ISBN: 978-1-9848-9806-7

Book design by Christopher M. Zucker

www.vintagebooks.com

Printed in the United States of America
10 9 8 7 6 5 4 3 2 1

For Morgan Entrekin
It's been a joy and an honor to be your partner.

CONTENTS

Introduction by Otto Penzler xi

INTRODUCTION

ESPIONAGE HAS BEEN called the second-oldest profession, and with good reason. Sun Tzu's *The Art of War*, a famous textbook on waging an effective war, devoted a great deal of significance to espionage and the creation of a secret spy network. All warfare is deception, he stated, and "Be subtle! Be subtle!" he intoned, and "use your spies for every kind of business." It was published in 510 BC.

The craft of espionage has fascinated people ever since stories were told, whether orally, on the printed page as journalism or fiction, or on a screen. The secrecy, manipulation, deception, and potential danger combine to produce an aura of romance and adventure to the enterprise.

Those who are actually involved in the world of espionage and counterespionage have quite a different view, recognizing and accepting the fact that it is mostly boring work, gathering information from technical journals, computers, overlong reports, and often self-serving memos, then analyzing the staggering mountain of information in order to filter out the tiny nuggets of data that may add a worthwhile grain of gold to a dossier that may never be used for any serious purpose.

Of course, once espionage stories get into the hands of creative authors, much of the dull day-to-day grind is ignored and whatever color there may be in the week is highlighted and embellished. Just as characters rarely make bathroom visits in fiction or, thankfully, in motion pictures and television programs, spy novels do not dwell on the filling-out of expense vouchers, the writing of countless memos arranging tedious meetings, and the telephone calls to spouses that entail making stops at the grocery store for milk and toothpaste.

There was a time when espionage fiction was far more exciting and flamboyant than it is today, mainly because it bore no connection to reality. The many thrilling spy stories of E. Phillips Oppenheim, H. C. McNeile's "Bulldog" Drummond adventures, John Buchan's Richard Hannay thrillers, Baroness Orczy's novels about the Scarlet Pimpernel, and William Le Queux's tales were aimed at entertaining readers with the rip-roaring exploits of characters whose lives were far more enthralling than their own. Virtually all the stories were set among the wealthy and fabulous. Clandestine meetings, romantic trysts, and the surreptitious handing-over of stolen documents were done in palaces, mansions, and castles, as well as on yachts. The women in these books were all young and beautiful or old and eccentric, and the heroes were unfailingly handsome, patriotic, courageous, and honorable.

The notion of honor among spies was highly regarded and perhaps carried out to a perplexing degree in an earlier time. Its apotheosis came in the form of Henry Stimson, the newly appointed secretary of state, who shut down the Cipher Bureau because he thought it was unethical. "Gentlemen do not read each other's mail," he stated, defining his peculiar foreign policy.

The vast majority of these espionage stories and novels were not espionage fiction at all but, rather, were counterespionage adventures. The excitement would erupt when a plot against Western countries or ruling governments by Eastern powers, anarchists, secret societies, or criminals was discovered and thwarted.

This wholly fantastical world of spy thrillers began to see the kernel of its demise when W. Somerset Maugham wrote *Ashenden; or, The British Agent* in 1928. This volume of connected episodes marked the birth of the realistic espionage story in which ordinary people are caught up in extraordinary circumstances and simply try their best to cope.

Buchan, Oppenheim, and others continued to write their swashbucklers for a time (and make no mistake, realistic or not, many of them were fabulously entertaining and thrilling), but the seed had been planted and the coup d'état (to mix a metaphor) occurred when Eric Ambler wrote his spy novels in the late 1930s. Largely dark and pessimistic, his primary characters were common people who preferred to do the right thing but didn't make it their life's calling or brag about it. When credited with helping to change the espionage novel from a romance to a realist work, Ambler gave credit to Maugham, whose work had been so influential to him. "The breakthrough was entirely Mr. Maugham's," he said, while noting other influences. "There

is, after all, a lot of Simenon and a satisfactory quantity of W. R. Burnett, but only one *Ashenden*."

The conclusion of World War I impelled a large number of British authors to write espionage stories about the Kaiser's evil intent and the relentless fortitude and intelligence of various spy heroes to outwit him. These postwar thrillers soon morphed into predictive anti-Nazi counterespionage tales that continued to elevate the level of verisimilitude, particularly among British authors, many of whom enjoyed great success, such as Graham Greene and Henry Patterson (best-known under his Jack Higgins pseudonym).

The Cold War inspired more and more complex novels and a greater requirement for accuracy as the reading public became more sophisticated. Newspapers no longer fabricated articles extolling the bravery and brilliance of one side as it trounced the buffoons on the other. Statistics and other data were reported in magazines and newspapers, and television provided images that were irrefutable. Additionally, there was a greater willingness on the part of news media and fiction writers to accept a higher level of moral ambiguity than had existed in other wars. It was rare to find a kind, generous, and intelligent Nazi in literature, while they abounded among Soviet Communists.

Many authors, both British and American, presented the Cold War as a nuanced game played between two powers who employed the same tactics, its spies and counterspies equally ruthless but also just human beings working for their respective countries.

The greatest of these authors was John le Carré (the pseudonym of David John Moore Cornwell), whose breakout novel was *The Spy Who Came in from the Cold* (1963), the dark tale that posited (and illustrated) that the British were perfectly comfortable sacrificing one of their spies. The Americans James Grady and Brian Garfield went a step further by demonstrating that it was quite all right for members of the Central Intelligence Agency to assassinate their colleagues, in *Six Days of the Condor* (1974) and *Hopscotch* (1975), respectively.

Charles McCarry, arguably the greatest American writer of espionage who ever lived, maintained a clearer vision, primarily through his series character Paul Christopher, recognizing that the West, most notably the United States, was in a just battle against totalitarianism. A deep undercover agent for the CIA for eleven years, he brought a level of accuracy and believable detail to his work that would have been impossible for any author without that background.

If a single author can be said to have bridged the era of the ultraheroic, extravagantly colorful patriot, it is Ian Fleming, whose James Bond character may have challenged Sherlock Holmes as the world's most recognizable crime fighter. Bond's extraordinary set of skills and attractiveness to women were never designed to appear totally realistic, which was fine with his readers and the millions who flocked to his cinematic adventures. Although Bond (like Fleming) despised the Soviet Union, his villains seldom had ideologies that transcended their thirst for massive fortunes or total world conquest—an acceptable substitute for fascism and communism.

The latest enemy of democracy in espionage stories is Islamic terrorism. Counterterrorism plays a vital role in contemporary thrillers (and in real life) as various secret service agencies are kept busy thwarting potential attacks on political leaders, military personnel, ordinary citizens, and even ancient landmarks that somehow offend the sensibilities of jihadists.

As the modern spy novel has become ultrarealistic, relying more on technology than on colorful espionage agents, one might think that the genre would be in danger of becoming tedious, bogged down with computers and other futuristically developed machinery that removes the human factor from these adventures. Fortunately, the talent and finely honed skill of most modern practitioners make this a fear to be discarded. As long as Nelson DeMille, Lee Child, Daniel Silva, Stephen Hunter, and others continue to work in the field (even if only occasionally), the future for those of us who love the battle between Good and Evil is assured.

—*Otto Penzler*

THE
GREAT WAR

THE HAIRLESS MEXICAN

W. SOMERSET MAUGHAM

ONE OF THE MOST popular and successful authors of the twentieth century and the most highly paid author of the 1930s, William Somerset Maugham (1874–1965) is still read for pleasure today, though his misanthropic work is notorious for its cruel and malicious portrayal of people. He was an important historical figure in the world of mystery and thriller fiction as his groundbreaking work, *Ashenden; or, The British Agent* (1928), variously called a novel (inaccurate) and a short story collection, is generally regarded as the first modern book of espionage fiction.

In *Ashenden*, secret agents are portrayed as ordinary people in unusual circumstances, not as dashing heroes whose lives are filled with beautiful, compliant women, secret societies, and cliff-hanging adventures.

It was Maugham's World War I experience with British Intelligence that provided him with material for the connected stories about Richard Ashenden, a well-known author who meets a British colonel known to the Intelligence Department only as R., who asks Ashenden to work as a secret agent.

It is thought that his profession as a writer will allow him to travel freely without causing suspicion and that his knowledge of European languages will prove useful. The last advice that R. gives to Ashenden before his first assignment impresses the author: "If you do well you'll get no thanks and if you get into trouble you'll get no help."

Ashenden admires goodness in others but has learned to live with evil. His interest in other people goes no further than the scientist's feelings for experimental rabbits. They are source material for future books and he is as realistic about their bad points as he is about their good qualities. Never bored, he believes that only stupid people require external stimulation to be amused; a man of intellect can avoid boredom by using his own resources.

Ashenden, a quiet, gentlemanly figure, was to a degree based on the exceptionally shy Maugham himself, and is said to have inspired some of the characteristics of Ian Fleming's espionage agent, James Bond—though only *some*, as it would be difficult to think of 007 as shy.

"The Hairless Mexican" was originally published in the December 1927 issue of *Cosmopolitan;* it was first collected in *Ashenden; or, The British Agent* (London, Heinemann, 1928).

THE HAIRLESS MEXICAN

W. SOMERSET MAUGHAM

"DO YOU LIKE MACARONI?" said R.

"What do you mean by macaroni?" answered Ashenden. "It is like asking me if I like poetry. I like Keats and Wordsworth and Verlaine and Goethe. When you say macaroni, do you mean *spaghetti, tagliatelli, rigatoni, vermicelli, fettucini, tufali, farfalli,* or just macaroni?"

"Macaroni," replied R., a man of few words.

"I like all simple things, boiled eggs, oysters and caviare, *truite au bleu*, grilled salmon, roast lamb (the saddle by preference), cold grouse, treacle tart, and rice pudding. But of all simple things the only one I can eat day in and day out, not only without disgust but with the eagerness of an appetite unimpaired by excess, is macaroni."

"I am glad of that because I want you to go down to Italy."

Ashenden had come from Geneva to meet R. at Lyons and having got there before him had spent the afternoon wandering about the dull, busy, and prosaic streets of that thriving city. They were sitting now in a restaurant on the *place* to which Ashenden had taken R. on his arrival because it was reputed to give you the best food in that part of France. But since in so crowded a resort (for the Lyonese like a good dinner) you never knew what inquisitive ears

were pricked up to catch any useful piece of information that might fall from your lips, they had contented themselves with talking of indifferent things. They had reached the end of an admirable repast.

"Have another glass of brandy?" said R.

"No, thank you," answered Ashenden, who was of an abstemious turn.

"One should do what one can to mitigate the rigours of war," remarked R. as he took the bottle and poured out a glass for himself and another for Ashenden.

Ashenden, thinking it would be affectation to protest, let the gesture pass, but felt bound to remonstrate with his chief on the unseemly manner in which he held the bottle.

"In my youth I was always taught that you should take a woman by the waist and a bottle by the neck," he murmured.

"I am glad you told me. I shall continue to hold a bottle by the waist and give women a wide berth."

Ashenden did not know what to reply to this and so remained silent. He sipped his brandy and R. called for his bill. It was true that he was an important person, with power to make or mar quite a large number of his fellows, and

4

his opinions were listened to by those who held in their hands the fate of empires; but he could never face the business of tipping a waiter without an embarrassment that was obvious in his demeanour. He was tortured by the fear of making a fool of himself by giving too much or of exciting the waiter's icy scorn by giving too little. When the bill came he passed some hundred-franc notes over to Ashenden and said:

"Pay him, will you? I can never understand French figures."

The groom brought them their hats and coats.

"Would you like to go back to the hotel?" asked Ashenden.

"We might as well."

It was early in the year, but the weather had suddenly turned warm, and they walked with their coats over their arms. Ashenden knowing that R. liked a sitting-room had engaged one for him and to this, when they reached the hotel, they went. The hotel was old-fashioned and the sitting-room was vast. It was furnished with a heavy mahogany suite upholstered in green velvet and the chairs were set primly round a large table. On the walls, covered with a dingy paper, were large steel engravings of the battles of Napoleon, and from the ceiling hung an enormous chandelier once used for gas, but now fitted with electric bulbs. It flooded the cheerless room with a cold, hard light.

"This is very nice," said R., as they went in.

"Not exactly cosy," suggested Ashenden.

"No, but it looks as though it were the best room in the place. It all looks very *good* to me."

He drew one of the green velvet chairs away from the table and, sitting down, lit a cigar. He loosened his belt and unbuttoned his tunic.

"I always thought I liked a cheroot better than anything," he said, "but since the war I've taken quite a fancy to Havanas. Oh, well, I suppose it can't last for ever." The corners of his mouth flickered with the beginning of a smile. "It's an ill wind that blows nobody any good."

Ashenden took two chairs, one to sit on and one for his feet, and when R. saw him said:

"That's not a bad idea," and swinging another chair out from the table with a sigh of relief put his boots on it.

"What room is that next door?" he asked.

"That's your bedroom."

"And on the other side?"

"A banqueting hall."

R. got up and strolled slowly about the room and when he passed the windows, as though in idle curiosity, peeped through the heavy rep curtains that covered them, and then returning to his chair once more comfortably put his feet up.

"It's just as well not to take any more risk than one need," he said.

He looked at Ashenden reflectively. There was a slight smile on his thin lips, but the pale eyes, too closely set together, remained cold and steely. R.'s stare would have been embarrassing if Ashenden had not been used to it. He knew that R. was considering how he would broach the subject that he had in mind. The silence must have lasted for two or three minutes.

"I'm expecting a fellow to come and see me tonight," he said at last. "His train gets in about ten." He gave his wrist-watch a glance. "He's known as the Hairless Mexican."

"Why?"

"Because he's hairless and because he's a Mexican."

"The explanation seems perfectly satisfactory," said Ashenden.

"He'll tell you all about himself. He talks nineteen to the dozen. He was on his uppers when I came across him. It appears that he was mixed up in some revolution in Mexico and had to get out with nothing but the clothes he stood up in. They were rather the worse for wear when I found him. If you want to please him you call him General. He claims to have been a general in Huerta's army, at least I think it was Huerta; anyhow he says that if things had gone right he would be minister of war now and no end of a big bug. I've found him very useful. Not a bad chap. The only thing I really have against him is that he will use scent."

"And where do I come in?" asked Ashenden.

"He's going down to Italy. I've got rather a ticklish job for him to do and I want you to stand by. I'm not keen on trusting him with a lot of money. He's a gambler and he's a bit too fond of the girls. I suppose you came from Geneva on your Ashenden passport."

"Yes."

"I've got another for you, a diplomatic one, by the way, in the name of Somerville with visas for France and Italy. I think you and he had better travel together. He's an amusing cove when he gets going, and I think you ought to get to know one another."

"What is the job?"

"I haven't yet quite made up my mind how much it's desirable for you to know about it."

Ashenden did not reply. They eyed one another in a detached manner, as though they were strangers who sat together in a railway carriage and each wondered who and what the other was.

"In your place I'd leave the General to do most of the talking. I wouldn't tell him more about yourself than you find absolutely necessary. He won't ask you any questions, I can promise you that, I think he's by way of being a gentleman after his own fashion."

"By the way, what is his real name?"

"I always call him Manuel, I don't know that he likes it very much, his name is Manuel Carmona."

"I gather by what you have not said that he's an unmitigated scoundrel."

R. smiled with his pale blue eyes.

"I don't know that I'd go quite so far as that. He hasn't had the advantages of a public-school education. His ideas of playing the game are not quite the same as yours or mine. I don't know that I'd leave a gold cigarette case about when he was in the neighbourhood, but if he lost money to you at poker and had pinched your cigarette case he would immediately pawn it to pay you. If he had half a chance he'd seduce your wife, but if you were up against it he'd share his last crust with you. The tears will run down his face when he hears Gounod's 'Ave Maria' on the gramo-phone, but if you insult his dignity he'll shoot you like a dog. It appears that in Mexico it's an insult to get between a man and his drink and he told me himself that once when a Dutchman who didn't know passed between him and the bar he whipped out his revolver and shot him dead."

"Did nothing happen to him?"

"No, it appears that he belongs to one of the best families. The matter was hushed up and it was announced in the papers that the Dutch-man had committed suicide. He did practically. I don't believe the Hairless Mexican has a great respect for human life."

Ashenden who had been looking intently at R. started a little and he watched more carefully than ever his chief's tired, lined, and yellow face. He knew that he did not make this remark for nothing.

"Of course a lot of nonsense is talked about the value of human life. You might just as well say that the counters you use at poker have an intrin-sic value, their value is what you like to make it; for a general giving battle men are merely coun-ters and he's a fool if he allows himself for sen-timental reasons to look upon them as human beings."

"But, you see, they're counters that feel and think and if they believe they're being squan-dered they are quite capable of refusing to be used any more."

"Anyhow that's neither here nor there. We've had information that a man called Constantine Andreadi is on his way from Constantinople with certain documents that we want to get hold of. He's a Greek. He's an agent of Enver Pasha and Enver has great confidence in him. He's given him verbal messages that are too secret and too important to be put on paper. He's sail-ing from the Piraeus, on a boat called the *Ithaca*, and will land at Brindisi on his way to Rome. He's to deliver his dispatches at the German embassy and impart what he has to say person-ally to the ambassador."

"I see."

At this time Italy was still neutral; the Cen-tral Powers were straining every nerve to keep her so; the Allies were doing what they could to induce her to declare war on their side.

"We don't want to get into any trouble with the Italian authorities, it might be fatal, but we've got to prevent Andreadi from getting to Rome."

"At any cost?" asked Ashenden.

"Money's no object," answered R., his lips twisting into a sardonic smile.

"What do you propose to do?"

"I don't think you need bother your head about that."

"I have a fertile imagination," said Ashenden.

"I want you to go down to Naples with the Hairless Mexican. He's very keen on getting back to Cuba. It appears that his friends are organizing a show and he wants to be as near at hand as possible so that he can hop over to Mexico when things are ripe. He needs cash. I've brought money down with me, in American dollars, and I shall give it to you to-night. You'd better carry it on your person."

"Is it much?"

"It's a good deal, but I thought it would be easier for you if it wasn't bulky, so I've got it in thousand dollar notes. You will give the Hairless Mexican the notes in return for the documents that Andreadi is bringing."

A question sprang to Ashenden's lips, but he did not ask it. He asked another instead.

"Does this fellow understand what he has to do?"

"Perfectly."

There was a knock at the door. It opened and the Hairless Mexican stood before them.

"I have arrived. Good evening, Colonel. I am enchanted to see you."

R. got up.

"Had a nice journey, Manuel? This is Mr. Somerville who's going to Naples with you. General Carmona."

"Pleased to meet you, sir."

He shook Ashenden's hand with such force that he winced.

"Your hands are like iron, General," he murmured.

The Mexican gave them a glance.

"I had them manicured this morning. I do not think they were very well done. I like my nails much more highly polished."

They were cut to a point, stained bright red, and to Ashenden's mind shone like mirrors. Though it was not cold the General wore a fur-coat with an astrakhan collar and with his every movement a wave of perfume was wafted to your nose.

"Take off your coat, General, and have a cigar," said R.

The Hairless Mexican was a tall man, and though thinnish gave you the impression of being very powerful; he was smartly dressed in a blue serge suit, with a silk handkerchief neatly tucked in the breast pocket of his coat, and he wore a gold bracelet on his wrist. His features were good, but a little larger than life-size, and his eyes were brown and lustrous. He was quite hairless. His yellow skin had the smoothness of a woman's and he had no eyebrows nor eyelashes; he wore a pale brown wig, rather long, and the locks were arranged in artistic disorder. This and the unwrinkled sallow face, combined with his dandified dress, gave him an appearance that was at first glance a trifle horrifying. He was repulsive and ridiculous, but you could not take your eyes from him. There was a sinister fascination in his strangeness.

He sat down and hitched up his trousers so that they should not bag at the knee.

"Well, Manuel, have you been breaking any hearts to-day?" said R. with his sardonic joviality.

The General turned to Ashenden.

"Our good friend, the Colonel, envies me my successes with the fair sex. I tell him he can have just as many as I if he will only listen to me. Confidence, that is all you need. If you never fear a rebuff you will never have one."

"Nonsense, Manuel, one has to have your way with the girls. There's something about you that they can't resist."

The Hairless Mexican laughed with a self-satisfaction that he did not try to disguise. He spoke English very well, with a Spanish accent, but with an American intonation.

"But since you ask me, Colonel, I don't mind telling you that I got into conversation on the train with a little woman who was coming to Lyons to see her mother-in-law. She was not very young and she was thinner than I like a woman to be, but she was possible, and she helped me to pass an agreeable hour."

"Well, let's get to business," said R.

"I am at your service, Colonel." He gave Ashenden a glance. "Is Mr. Somerville a military man?"

"No," said R., "he's an author."

"It takes all sorts to make a world, as you say. I am happy to make your acquaintance, Mr. Somerville. I can tell you many stories that will interest you; I am sure that we shall get on well together. You have a sympathetic air. I am very sensitive to that. To tell you the truth I am nothing but a bundle of nerves and if I am with a person who is antipathetic to me I go all to pieces."

"I hope we shall have a pleasant journey," said Ashenden.

"When does our friend arrive at Brindisi?" asked the Mexican, turning to R.

"He sails from the Piraeus in the *Ithaca* on the fourteenth. It's probably some old tub, but you'd better get down to Brindisi in good time."

"I agree with you."

R. got up and with his hands in his pockets sat on the edge of the table. In his rather shabby uniform, his tunic unbuttoned, he looked a slovenly creature beside the neat and well-dressed Mexican.

"Mr. Somerville knows practically nothing of the errand on which you are going and I do not desire you to tell him anything. I think you had much better keep your own counsel. He is instructed to give you the funds you need for your work, but your actions are your own affair. If you need his advice of course you can ask for it."

"I seldom ask other people's advice and never take it."

"And should you make a mess of things I trust you to keep Mr. Somerville out of it. He must on no account be compromised."

"I am a man of honour, Colonel," answered the Hairless Mexican with dignity, "and I would sooner let myself be cut in a thousand pieces than betray my friends."

"That is what I have already told Mr. Somerville. On the other hand if everything pans out okay Mr. Somerville is instructed to give you the sum we agreed on in return for the papers I spoke to you about. In what manner you get them is no business of his."

"That goes without saying. There is only one thing I wish to make quite plain; Mr. Somerville understands of course that I have not accepted the mission with which you have entrusted me on account of the money?"

"Quite," replied R., gravely, looking him straight in the eyes.

"I am with the Allies body and soul, I cannot forgive the Germans for outraging the neutrality of Belgium, and if I accept the money that you have offered me it is because I am first and foremost a patriot. I can trust Mr. Somerville implicitly, I suppose?"

R. nodded. The Mexican turned to Ashenden.

"An expedition is being arranged to free my unhappy country from the tyrants that exploit and ruin it and every penny that I receive will go on guns and cartridges. For myself I have no need of money; I am a soldier and I can live on a crust and a few olives. There are only three occupations that befit a gentleman, war, cards, and women; it costs nothing to sling a rifle over your shoulder and take to the mountains—and that is real warfare, not this manoeuvring of battalions and firing of great guns—women love me for myself, and I generally win at cards."

Ashenden found the flamboyance of this strange creature, with his scented handkerchief and his gold bracelet, very much to his taste. This was far from being just the man in the street (whose tyranny we rail at but in the end submit to) and to the amateur of the baroque in human nature he was a rarity to be considered with delight. He was a purple patch on two legs. Notwithstanding his wig and his hairless big face he had undoubtedly an air; he was absurd, but he did not give you the impression that he was a man to be trifled with. His self-complacency was magnificent.

"Where is your kit, Manuel?" asked R.

It was possible that a frown for an instant darkened the Mexican's brow at the abrupt question that seemed a little contemptuously to brush to one side his eloquent statement, but he gave no other sign of displeasure. Ashenden suspected that he thought the Colonel a barbarian insensitive to the finer emotions.

"I left it at the station."

"Mr. Somerville has a diplomatic passport so that he can get it through with his own things at the frontier without examination if you like."

"I have very little, a few suits and some linen, but perhaps it would be as well if Mr. Somerville would take charge of it. I bought half a dozen suits of silk pyjamas before I left Paris."

"And what about you?" asked R., turning to Ashenden.

"I've only got one bag. It's in my room."

"You'd better have it taken to the station while there's someone about. Your train goes at one ten."

"Oh?"

This was the first Ashenden had heard that they were to start that night.

"I think you'd better get down to Naples as soon as possible."

"Very well."

R. got up.

"I'm going to bed. I don't know what you fellows want to do."

"I shall take a walk about Lyons," said the Hairless Mexican. "I am interested in life. Lend me a hundred francs, Colonel, will you? I have no change on me."

R. took out his pocket-book and gave the General the note he asked for. Then to Ashenden:

"What are you going to do? Wait here?"

"No," said Ashenden, "I shall go to the station and read."

"You'd both of you better have a whisky and soda before you go, hadn't you? What about it, Manuel?"

"It is very kind of you, but I never drink anything but champagne and brandy."

"Mixed?" asked R. drily.

"Not necessarily," returned the other with gravity.

R. ordered brandy and soda and when it came, whereas he and Ashenden helped themselves to both, the Hairless Mexican poured himself out three parts of a tumbler of neat brandy and swallowed it in two noisy gulps. He rose to his feet and put on his coat with the astrakhan collar, seized in one hand his bold black hat and, with the gesture of a romantic actor giving up the girl he loved to one more worthy of her, held out the other to R.

"Well, Colonel, I will bid you good night and pleasant dreams. I do not expect that we shall meet again so soon."

"Don't make a hash of things, Manuel, and if you do keep your mouth shut."

"They tell me that in one of your colleges where the sons of gentlemen are trained to become naval officers it is written in letters of gold: there is no such word as impossible in the British Navy. I do not know the meaning of the word failure."

"It has a good many synonyms," retorted R.

"I will meet you at the station, Mr. Somerville," said the Hairless Mexican, and with a flourish left them.

R. looked at Ashenden with that little smile of his that always made his face look so dangerously shrewd.

"Well, what d'you think of him?"

"You've got me beat," said Ashenden. "Is he a mountebank? He seems as vain as a peacock. And with that frightful appearance can he really be the lady's man he pretends? What makes you think you can trust him?"

R. gave a low chuckle and he washed his thin, old hands with imaginary soap.

"I thought you'd like him. He's quite a character, isn't he? I think we can trust him." R.'s eyes suddenly grew opaque. "I don't believe it would pay him to double-cross us." He paused for a moment. "Anyhow we've got to risk it. I'll give you the tickets and the money and then you can take yourself off; I'm all in and I want to go to bed."

Ten minutes later Ashenden set out for the station with his bag on a porter's shoulder.

Having nearly two hours to wait he made himself comfortable in the waiting-room. The light was good and he read a novel. When the time drew near for the arrival of the train from Paris that was to take them direct to Rome and the Hairless Mexican did not appear Ashenden, beginning to grow a trifle anxious, went out on the platform to look for him. Ashenden suffered from that distressing malady known as train fever: an hour before his train was due he began to have apprehensions lest he should miss it; he was impatient with the porters who would never bring his luggage down from his room in time and he could not understand why the hotel bus cut it so fine; a block in the street would drive him to frenzy and the languid movements of the station porters infuriate him. The whole world seemed in a horrid plot to delay him; people got in his way as he passed through the barriers; others, a long string of them, were at the ticket-office getting tickets for other trains than his and they counted their change with exasperating care; his luggage took an interminable time to register; and then if he was travelling with friends they would go to buy newspapers, or would take a walk along the platform and he was certain they would be left behind, they would stop to talk to a casual stranger or suddenly be seized with a desire to telephone and disappear at a run. In fact the universe conspired to make him miss every train he wanted to take and he was not happy unless he was settled in his corner, his things on the rack above him, with a good half hour to spare. Sometimes by arriving at the station too soon he had caught an earlier train than the one he had meant to, but that was nerve-racking and caused him all the anguish of very nearly missing it.

The Rome express was signalled and there was no sign of the Hairless Mexican, it came in and he was not to be seen. Ashenden became more and more harassed. He walked quickly up and down the platform, looked in all the waiting-rooms, went to the *consigne* where the luggage was left; he could not find him. There were no sleeping-cars, but a number of people got out and he took two seats in a first-class carriage. He stood at the door, looking up and down the platform and up at the clock; it was useless to go if his travelling companion did not turn up and Ashenden made up his mind to take his things out of the carriage as the porter cried *en voiture*; but, by George! he would give the brute hell when he found him. There were three minutes more, then two minutes, then one; at that late hour there were few persons about and all who were travelling had taken their seats. Then he saw the Hairless Mexican, followed by two porters with his luggage and accompanied by a man in a bowler-hat, walk leisurely onto the platform. He caught sight of Ashenden and waved to him.

"Ah, my dear fellow, there you are, I wondered what had become of you."

"Good God, man, hurry up or we shall miss the train."

"I never miss a train. Have you got good seats? The *chef de gare* has gone for the night; this is his assistant."

The man in the bowler-hat took it off when Ashenden nodded to him.

"But this is an ordinary carriage. I am afraid I could not travel in that." He turned to the station-master's assistant with an affable smile. "You must do better for me than that, *mon cher.*"

"*Certainement, mon général*, I will put you into a *salon-lit*. Of course."

The assistant station-master led them along the train and put them in an empty compartment where there were two beds. The Mexican eyed it with satisfaction and watched the porters arrange the luggage.

"That will do very well. I am much obliged to you." He held out his hand to the man in the

10

bowler-hat. "I shall not forget you and next time I see the Minister I will tell him with what civility you have treated me."

"You are too good, General. I shall be very grateful."

A whistle was blown and the train started.

"This is better than an ordinary first-class carriage, I think, Mr. Somerville," said the Mexican. "A good traveller should learn how to make the best of things."

But Ashenden was still extremely cross.

"I don't know why the devil you wanted to cut it so fine. We should have looked a pair of damned fools if we'd missed the train."

"My dear fellow, there was never the smallest chance of that. When I arrived I told the station-master that I was General Carmona, Commander-in-Chief of the Mexican Army, and that I had to stop off in Lyons for a few hours to hold a conference with the British Field-Marshal. I asked him to hold the train for me if I was delayed and suggested that my government might see its way to conferring an order on him. I have been to Lyons before, I like the girls here; they have not the *chic* of the Parisians, but they have something, there is no denying that they have something. Will you have a mouthful of brandy before you go to sleep?"

"No, thank you," said Ashenden morosely.

"I always drink a glass before going to bed, it settles the nerves."

He looked in his suit-case and without difficulty found a bottle. He put it to his lips and had a long drink, wiped his mouth with the back of his hand and lit a cigarette. Then he took off his boots and lay down. Ashenden dimmed the light.

"I have never yet made up my mind," said the Hairless Mexican reflectively, "whether it is pleasanter to go to sleep with the kisses of a beautiful woman on your mouth or with a cigarette between your lips. Have you ever been to Mexico? I will tell you about Mexico to-morrow. Good night."

Presently Ashenden heard from his steady breathing that he was asleep and in a little while himself dozed off. Presently he woke. The Mexican, deep in slumber, lay motionless; he had taken off his fur coat and was using it as a blanket; he still wore his wig. Suddenly there was a jolt and the train with a noisy grinding of brakes stopped; in the twinkling of an eye, before Ashenden could realize that anything had happened, the Mexican was on his feet with his hand to his hip.

"What is it?" he cried.

"Nothing. Probably only a signal against us."

The Mexican sat down heavily on his bed. Ashenden turned on the light.

"You wake quickly for such a sound sleeper," he said.

"You have to in my profession."

Ashenden would have liked to ask him whether this was murder, conspiracy, or commanding armies, but was not sure that it would be discreet. The General opened his bag and took out the bottle.

"Will you have a nip?" he asked. "There is nothing like it when you wake suddenly in the night."

When Ashenden refused he put the bottle once more to his lips and poured a considerable quantity of liquor down his throat. He sighed and lit a cigarette. Although Ashenden had seen him now drink nearly a bottle of brandy and it was probable that he had had a good deal more when he was going about the town he was certainly quite sober. Neither in his manner nor in his speech was there any indication that he had drunk during the evening anything but lemonade.

The train started and soon Ashenden again fell asleep. When he awoke it was morning and turning round lazily he saw that the Mexican was awake too. He was smoking a cigarette. The floor by his side was strewn with burnt-out butts and the air was thick and grey. He had begged Ashenden not to insist on opening a window, for he said the night air was dangerous.

"I did not get up, because I was afraid of waking you. Will you do your toilet first or shall I?"

"I'm in no hurry," said Ashenden.

"I am an old campaigner, it will not take me long. Do you wash your teeth every day?"

"Yes," said Ashenden.

"So do I. It is a habit I learned in New York. I always think that a fine set of teeth are an adornment to a man."

There was a wash-basin in the compartment and the General scrubbed his teeth, with gurglings and garglings, energetically. Then he got a bottle of eau-de-cologne from his bag, poured some of it on a towel and rubbed it over his face and hands. He took a comb and carefully arranged his wig; either it had not moved in the night or else he had set it straight before Ashenden awoke. He got another bottle out of his bag, with a spray attached to it, and squeezing a bulb covered his shirt and coat with a fine cloud of scent, did the same to his handkerchief, and then with a beaming face, like a man who has done his duty by the world and is well pleased, turned to Ashenden and said:

"Now I am ready to brave the day. I will leave my things for you, you need not be afraid of the eau-de-cologne, it is the best you can get in Paris."

"Thank you very much," said Ashenden. "All I want is soap and water."

"Water? I never use water except when I have a bath. Nothing can be worse for the skin."

When they approached the frontier, Ashenden, remembering the General's instructive gesture when he was suddenly awakened in the night, said to him:

"If you've got a revolver on you I think you'd better give it to me. With my diplomatic passport they're not likely to search me, but they might take it into their heads to go through you and we don't want to have any bothers."

"It is hardly a weapon, it is only a toy," returned the Mexican, taking out of his hip-pocket a fully loaded revolver of formidable dimensions. "I do not like parting with it even for an hour, it gives me the feeling that I am not fully dressed. But you are quite right, we do not want to take any risks; I will give you my knife as well. I would always rather use a knife than a revolver; I think it is a more elegant weapon."

"I daresay it is only a matter of habit," answered Ashenden. "Perhaps you are more at home with a knife."

"Anyone can pull a trigger, but it needs a man to use a knife."

To Ashenden it looked as though it were in a single movement that he tore open his waistcoat and from his belt snatched and opened a long knife of murderous aspect. He handed it to Ashenden with a pleased smile on his large, ugly, and naked face.

"There's a pretty piece of work for you, Mr. Somerville. I've never seen a better bit of steel in my life, it takes an edge like a razor and it's strong; you can cut a cigarette-paper with it and you can hew down an oak. There is nothing to get out of order and when it is closed it might be the knife a schoolboy uses to cut notches in his desk."

He shut it with a click and Ashenden put it along with the revolver in his pocket.

"Have you anything else?"

"My hands," replied the Mexican with arrogance, "but those I daresay the custom officials will not make trouble about."

Ashenden remembered the iron grip he had given him when they shook hands and slightly shuddered. They were large and long and smooth; there was not a hair on them or on the wrists, and with the pointed, rosy, manicured nails there was really something sinister about them.

SOMEWHERE IN FRANCE

RICHARD HARDING DAVIS

THE FEARLESS WAR CORRESPONDENT par excellence Richard Harding Davis (1864–1916) was the most successful reporter of his time, working for *The Evening Sun* (New York), *The New York Herald*, *Harper's Weekly*, and *Scribner's Magazine*, among others. He was the first journalist to cover the Spanish–American War and, as a close friend of Theodore Roosevelt, helped create the image and legend of the future president as the leading light of the Rough Riders. He was an adventurer as well as a journalist, often going to the front lines to cover stories while wearing pistols and wielding other weapons.

Very popular with other writers and journalists, the handsome, square-jawed Davis is reputed to have served as the model for the famous American illustrator Charles Dana Gibson's "Gibson Man," the male equivalent of the "Gibson Girl" as the personification of American beauty. He was the prime catalyst for American men to adopt the clean-shaven look at the end of the nineteenth century.

A prolific writer, Davis produced more than thirty-five books of fiction, biography, history, and memoir. His best-known book was probably *Soldiers of Fortune* (1897), which he later turned into a successful play. In the mystery field, his most widely read book is the often-reprinted *In the Fog* (1901), composed of three connected short stories in the style of Robert Louis Stevenson's *New Arabian Nights* (1882); it contains two surprise endings.

As a sophisticated journalist familiar with world politics, Davis demonstrated that strength when he brought it to his fiction, notably "Somewhere in France." World War I was only months old when he wrote this story of the simmering hostilities between Germany and France. The story served as the basis for a silent black-and-white film released in 1916.

"Somewhere in France" was first published in the June 1915 issue of *Metropolitan Magazine;* it was first collected in *Somewhere in France* (New York, Charles Scribner's Sons, 1915).

SOMEWHERE IN FRANCE

RICHARD HARDING DAVIS

MARIE GESSLER, known as Marie Chaumontel, Jeanne d'Avrechy, the Countess d'Aurillac, was German. Her father, who served through the Franco-Prussian War, was a German spy. It was from her mother she learned to speak French sufficiently well to satisfy even an Academician and, among Parisians, to pass as one. Both her parents were dead. Before they departed, knowing they could leave their daughter nothing save their debts, they had had her trained as a nurse. But when they were gone, Marie in the Berlin hospitals played politics, intrigued, indiscriminately misued the appealing, violet eyes. There was a scandal; several scandals. At the age of twenty-five she was dismissed from the Municipal Hospital, and as now—save for the violet eyes—she was without resources, as a *compagnon de voyage* with a German doctor she travelled to Monte Carlo. There she abandoned the doctor for Henri Ravignac, a captain in the French Aviation Corps, who, when his leave ended, escorted her to Paris.

The duties of Captain Ravignac kept him in barracks near the aviation field, but Marie he established in his apartments on the Boulevard Haussmann. One day he brought from the barracks a roll of blue-prints, and as he was locking them in a drawer, said: "The Germans would pay through the nose for those!" The remark was indiscreet, but then Marie had told him she was French, and any one would have believed her.

The next morning the same spirit of adventure that had exiled her from the Berlin hospitals carried her with the blue-prints to the German embassy. There, greatly shocked, they first wrote down her name and address, and then, indignant at her proposition, ordered her out. But the day following a strange young German who was not at all indignant, but, on the contrary, quite charming, called upon Marie. For the blue-prints he offered her a very large sum, and that same hour with them and Marie departed for Berlin. Marie did not need the money. Nor did the argument that she was serving her country greatly impress her. It was rather that she loved intrigue. And so she became a spy.

Henri Ravignac, the man she had robbed of the blue-prints, was tried by court-martial. The charge was treason, but Charles Ravignac, his younger brother, promised to prove that the guilty one was the girl, and to that end obtained leave of absence and spent much time and money. At the trial he was able to show the record of Marie in Berlin and Monte Carlo; that she was the daughter of a German secret agent; that on the afternoon the prints disappeared Marie, with an agent of the German embassy, had left Paris for Berlin. In consequence of this the charge of selling military secrets was altered to one of "gross neglect," and Henri Ravignac was sentenced to two years in the military prison at Tours. But he was of an ancient and noble family, and when they came to take him from his cell in the Cherche-Midi, he was dead. Charles, his brother, disappeared. It was said he also had killed himself; that he had been appointed a military attaché in South America; that to revenge his brother he had entered the secret service; but whatever became of him no one knew. All that was certain was that, thanks to the act of Marie Gessler, on the rolls of the French army the ancient and noble name of Ravignac no longer appeared.

In her chosen profession Marie Gessler found nothing discreditable. Of herself her opinion was not high, and her opinion of men was lower. For her smiles she had watched several sacrifice honor, duty, loyalty; and she held them and their kind in contempt. To lie, to cajole, to rob men of secrets they thought important, and of secrets the importance of which they did not even guess, was to her merely an intricate and exciting game.

She played it very well. So well that in the service her advance was rapid. On important missions she was sent to Russia, through the Balkans; even to the United States. There, with credentials as an army nurse, she inspected our military hospitals and unobtrusively asked many innocent questions.

When she begged to be allowed to work in her beloved Paris, "they" told her when war came "they" intended to plant her inside that city, and that, until then, the less Paris knew of her the better.

But just before the great war broke, to report on which way Italy might jump, she was sent to Rome, and it was not until September she was recalled. The telegram informed her that her Aunt Elizabeth was ill, and that at once she must return to Berlin. This, she learned from

the code book wrapped under the cover of her thermos bottle, meant that she was to report to the general commanding the German forces at Soissons.

From Italy she passed through Switzerland, and, after leaving Basle, on military trains was rushed north to Luxemburg, and then west to Laon. She was accompanied by her companion, Bertha, an elderly and respectable, even distinguished-looking female. In the secret service her number was 528. Their passes from the war office described them as nurses of the German Red Cross. Only the Intelligence Department knew their real mission. With her, also, as her chauffeur, was a young Italian soldier of fortune, Paul Anfossi. He had served in the Belgian Congo, in the French Foreign Legion in Algiers, and spoke all the European languages. In Rome, where as a wireless operator he was serving a commercial company, in selling Marie copies of messages he had memorized, Marie had found him useful, and when war came she obtained for him, from the Wilhelmstrasse, the number 292. From Laon, in one of the automobiles of the General Staff, the three spies were driven first to Soissons, and then along the road to Meaux and Paris, to the village of Neufchelles. They arrived at midnight, and in a château of one of the Champagne princes, found the colonel commanding the Intelligence Bureau. He accepted their credentials, destroyed them, and replaced them with a *laissez passer* signed by the mayor of Laon. That dignitary, the colonel explained, to citizens of Laon fleeing to Paris and the coast had issued many passes. But as now between Laon and Paris there were three German armies, the refugees had been turned back and their passes confiscated.

"From among them," said the officer, "we have selected one for you. It is issued to the wife of Count d'Aurillac, a captain of reserves, and her aunt, Madame Benet. It asks for those ladies and their chauffeur, Briand, a safe-conduct through the French military lines. If it gets you into Paris you will destroy it and assume another name. The Count d'Aurillac is now with his regiment in that city. If he learned of the presence there of his wife, he would seek her, and that would not be good for you. So, if you reach Paris, you will become a Belgian refugee. You are high-born and rich. Your château has been destroyed. But you have money. You will give liberally to the Red Cross. You will volunteer to nurse in the hospitals. With your sad story of ill treatment by us, with your high birth, and your knowledge of nursing, which you acquired, of course, only as an amateur, you should not find it difficult to join the Ladies of France, or the American Ambulance. What you learn from the wounded English and French officers and the French doctors you will send us through the usual channels."

"When do I start?" asked the woman.

"For a few days," explained the officer, "you remain in this château. You will keep us informed of what is going forward after we withdraw."

"Withdraw?" It was more of an exclamation than a question. Marie was too well trained to ask questions.

"We are taking up a new position," said the officer, "on the Aisne."

The woman, incredulous, stared.

"And we do not enter Paris?"

"*You* do," returned the officer. "That is all that concerns you. We will join you later—in the spring. Meanwhile, for the winter we intrench ourselves along the Aisne. In a chimney of this château we have set up a wireless outfit. We are leaving it intact. The chauffeur Briand—who, you must explain to the French, you brought with you from Laon, and who has been long in your service—will transmit whatever you discover. We wish especially to know of any movement toward our left. If they attack in front from Soissons, we are prepared; but of any attempt to cross the Oise and take us in flank you must warn us."

The officer rose and hung upon himself his field-glasses, map-cases, and side-arms.

"We leave you now," he said. "When the French arrive you will tell them your reason for halting at this château was that the owner, Monsieur Iverney, and his family are friends of your husband. You found us here, and we detained you. And so long as you can use the wireless, make excuses to remain. If they offer to send you on to Paris, tell them your aunt is too ill to travel."

"But they will find the wireless," said the woman. "They are sure to use the towers for observation, and they will find it."

"In that case," said the officer, "you will suggest to them that we fled in such haste we had no time to dismantle it. Of course, you had no knowledge that it existed, or, as a loyal French woman, you would have at once told them." To emphasize his next words the officer pointed at her: "Under no circumstances," he continued, "must you be suspected. If they should take Briand in the act, should they have even the least doubt concerning him, you must repudiate him entirely. If necessary, to keep your own skirts clear, it would be your duty yourself to denounce him as a spy."

"Your first orders," said the woman, "were to tell them Briand had been long in my service; that I brought him from my home in Laon."

"He might be in your service for years," returned the colonel, "and you not know he was a German agent."

"If to save myself I inform upon him," said Marie, "of course you know you will lose him."

The officer shrugged his shoulders. "A wireless operator," he retorted, "we can replace. But for you, and for the service you are to render in Paris, we have no substitute. *You* must not be found out. You are invaluable."

The spy inclined her head. "I thank you," she said.

The officer sputtered indignantly.

"It is not a compliment," he exclaimed; "it is an order. You must not be found out!"

Withdrawn some two hundred yards from the Paris road, the château stood upon a wooded hill. Except directly in front, trees of great height surrounded it. The tips of their branches brushed the windows; interlacing, they continued until they overhung the wall of the estate.

Where it ran with the road the wall gave way to a lofty gate and iron fence, through which those passing could see a stretch of noble turf, as wide as a polofield, borders of flowers disappearing under the shadows of the trees; and the château itself, with its terrace, its many windows, its high-pitched, sloping roof, broken by towers and turrets.

Through the remainder of the night there came from the road to those in the château the roar and rumbling of the army in retreat. It moved without panic, disorder, or haste, but unceasingly. Not for an instant was there a breathing-spell. And when the sun rose, the three spies—the two women and the chauffeur—who in the great château were now alone, could see as well as hear the gray column of steel rolling past below them.

The spies knew that the gray column had reached Claye, had stood within fifteen miles of Paris, and then upon Paris had turned its back. They knew also that the reverberations from the direction of Meaux, that each moment grew more loud and savage, were the French "seventy-fives" whipping the gray column forward. Of what they felt the Germans did not speak. In silence they looked at each other, and in the eyes of Marie was bitterness and resolve.

Toward noon Marie met Anfossi in the great drawing-room that stretched the length of the terrace and from the windows of which, through the park gates, they could see the Paris road.

"This, that is passing now," said Marie, "is the last of our rear-guard. Go to your tower," she ordered, "and send word that except for stragglers and the wounded our column has just passed through Neufchelles, and that any moment we expect the French." She raised her hand impressively. "From now," she warned, "we speak French, we think French, we *are* French!"

Anfossi, or Briand, as now he called himself, addressed her in that language. His tone was bitter. "Pardon my lese-majesty," he said, "but this chief of your Intelligence Department is a *dummer Mensch*. He is throwing away a valuable life."

Marie exclaimed in dismay. She placed her hand upon his arm, and the violet eyes filled with concern.

"Not yours!" she protested.

"Absolutely!" returned the Italian. "I can send nothing by this knapsack wireless that they will not learn from others; from airmen, Uhlans, the peasants in the fields. And certainly I will be caught. Dead I am dead, but alive and in Paris the opportunities are unending. From the French Legion Etranger I have my honorable discharge. I am an expert wireless operator and in their Signal Corps I can easily find a place. Imagine me, then, on the Eiffel Tower. From the air I snatch news from all of France, from the Channel, the North Sea. You and I could work together, as in Rome. But here, between the lines, with a pass from a village *sous-préfet*, it is ridiculous. I am not afraid to die. But to die because some one else is stupid, that is hard."

Marie clasped his hands in both of hers.

"You must not speak of death," she cried; "you know I must carry out my orders, that I must force you to take this risk. And you know that thought of harm to you tortures me!"

Quickly the young man disengaged his hand. The woman exclaimed with anger.

"Why do you doubt me?" she cried.

Briand protested vehemently.

"I do not doubt you."

"My affection, then?" In a whisper that carried with it the feeling of a caress Marie added softly: "My love?"

The young man protested miserably. "You make it very hard, mademoiselle," he cried. "You are my superior officer, I am your servant. Who am I that I should share with others——"

The woman interrupted eagerly.

"Ah, you are jealous!" she cried. "Is that why you are so cruel? But when I *tell* you I love you, and only you, can you not *feel* it is the truth?"

The young man frowned unhappily.

"My duty, mademoiselle!" he stammered.

With an exclamation of anger Marie left him. As the door slammed behind her, the young man drew a deep breath. On his face was the expression of ineffable relief.

In the hall Marie met her elderly companion, Bertha, now her aunt, Madame Benet.

"I heard you quarrelling," Bertha protested. "It is most indiscreet. It is not in the part of the Countess d'Aurillac that she makes love to her chauffeur."

Marie laughed noiselessly and drew her farther down the hall. "He is imbecile!" she exclaimed. "He will kill me with his solemn face and his conceit. I make love to him—yes—that he may work the more willingly. But he will have none of it. He is jealous of the others."

Madame Benet frowned.

"He resents the others," she corrected. "I do not blame him. He is a gentleman!"

"And the others," demanded Marie; "were they not of the most noble families of Rome?"

"I am old and I am ugly," said Bertha, "but to me Anfossi is always as considerate as he is to you who are so beautiful."

"An Italian gentleman," returned Marie, "does not serve in Belgian Congo unless it is the choice of that or the marble quarries."

"I do not know what his past may be," sighed Madame Benet, "nor do I ask. He is only a number, as you and I are only numbers. And I beg you to let us work in harmony. At such a time your love-affairs threaten our safety. You must wait."

Marie laughed insolently. "With the Du Barry," she protested, "I can boast that I wait for no man."

"No," replied the older woman; "you pursue him!"

Marie would have answered sharply, but on the instant her interest was diverted. For one week, by day and night, she had lived in a world peopled only by German soldiers. Beside her in the railroad carriage, on the station platforms, at the windows of the trains that passed the one in which she rode, at the grade crossings, on the bridges, in the roads that paralleled the tracks, choking the streets of the villages and spread over the fields of grain, she had seen only the gray-green uniforms. Even her professional eye no longer distinguished regiment

from regiment, dragoon from grenadier, Uhlan from Hussar or Landsturm. Stripes, insignia, numerals, badges of rank, had lost their meaning. Those who wore them no longer were individuals. They were not even human. During the three last days the automobile, like a motor-boat fighting the tide, had crept through a gray-green river of men, stained, as though from the banks, by mud and yellow clay. And for hours, while the car was blocked, and in fury the engine raced and purred, the gray-green river had rolled past her, slowly but as inevitably as lava down the slope of a volcano, bearing on its surface faces with staring eyes, thousands and thousands of eyes, some fierce and bloodshot, others filled with weariness, homesickness, pain. At night she still saw them: the white faces under the sweat and dust, the eyes dumb, inarticulate, asking the answer. She had been suffocated by German soldiers, by the mass of them, engulfed and smothered; she had stifled in a land inhabited only by gray-green ghosts.

And suddenly, as though a miracle had been wrought, she saw upon the lawn, riding toward her, a man in scarlet, blue, and silver. One man riding alone.

Approaching with confidence, but alert; his reins fallen, his hands nursing his carbine, his eyes searched the shadows of the trees, the empty windows, even the sun-swept sky. His was the new face at the door, the new step on the floor. And the spy knew had she beheld an army corps it would have been no more significant, no more menacing, than the solitary *chasseur à cheval* scouting in advance of the enemy.

"We are saved!" exclaimed Marie, with irony. "Go quickly," she commanded, "to the bedroom on the second floor that opens upon the staircase, so that you can see all who pass. You are too ill to travel. They must find you in bed."

"And you?" said Bertha.

"I," cried Marie rapturously, "hasten to welcome our preserver!"

The preserver was a peasant lad. Under the white dust his cheeks were burned a brown-red, his eyes, honest and blue, through much staring at the skies and at horizon lines, were puckered and encircled with tiny wrinkles. Responsibility had made him older than his years, and in speech brief. With the beautiful lady who with tears of joy ran to greet him, and who in an ecstasy of happiness pressed her cheek against the nose of his horse, he was unimpressed. He returned to her her papers and gravely echoed her answers to his questions. "This château," he repeated, "was occupied by their General Staff; they have left no wounded here; you saw the last of them pass a half-hour since." He gathered up his reins.

Marie shrieked in alarm. "You will not leave us?" she cried.

For the first time the young man permitted himself to smile. "Others arrive soon," he said.

He touched his shako, wheeled his horse in the direction from which he had come, and a minute later Marie heard the hoofs echoing through the empty village.

When they came, the others were more sympathetic. Even in times of war a beautiful woman is still a beautiful woman. And the staff officers who moved into the quarters so lately occupied by the enemy found in the presence of the Countess d'Aurillac nothing to distress them. In the absence of her dear friend, Madame Iverney, the chatelaine of the château, she acted as their hostess. Her chauffeur showed the company cooks the way to the kitchen, the larder, and the charcoal-box. She, herself, in the hands of General Andre placed the keys of the famous wine-cellar, and to the surgeon, that the wounded might be freshly bandaged, intrusted those of the linen-closet. After the indignities she had suffered while "detained" by *les Boches*, her delight and relief at again finding herself under the protection of her own people would have touched a heart of stone. And the hearts of the staff were not of stone. It was with regret they gave the countess permission to continue on her way. At this she exclaimed with gratitude. She assured them, were her aunt able to travel, she would immediately depart.

"In Paris she will be more comfortable than here," said the kind surgeon. He was a reservist, and in times of peace a fashionable physician and as much at his ease in a boudoir as in a field hospital. "Perhaps if I saw Madame Benet?"

At the suggestion the countess was overjoyed. But they found Madame Benet in a state of complete collapse. The conduct of the Germans had brought about a nervous breakdown. "Though the bridges are destroyed at Meaux," urged the surgeon, "even with a détour, you can be in Paris in four hours. I think it is worth the effort."

But the mere thought of the journey threw Madame Benet into hysterics. She asked only to rest, she begged for an opiate to make her sleep. She begged also that they would leave the door open, so that when she dreamed she was still in the hands of the Germans, and woke in terror, the sound of the dear French voices and the sight of the beloved French uniforms might reassure her. She played her part well. Concerning her Marie felt not the least anxiety. But toward Briand, the chauffeur, the new arrivals were less easily satisfied.

The general sent his adjutant for the countess. When the adjutant had closed the door General Andre began abruptly:

"The chauffeur Briand," he asked, "you know him; you can vouch for him?"

"But certainly!" protested Marie. "He is an Italian."

As though with sudden enlightenment, Marie laughed. It was as if now in the suspicion of the officer she saw a certain reasonableness. "Briand was so long in the Foreign Legion in Algiers," she explained, "where my husband found him, that we have come to think of him as French. As much French as ourselves, I assure you."

The general and his adjutant were regarding each other questioningly.

"Perhaps I should tell the countess," began the general, "that we have learned——"

The signal from the adjutant was so slight, so swift, that Marie barely intercepted it.

The lips of the general shut together like the leaves of a book. To show the interview was at an end, he reached for a pen.

"I thank you," he said.

"Of course," prompted the adjutant, "Madame d'Aurillac understands the man must not know we inquired concerning him."

General Andre frowned at Marie.

"Certainly not!" he commanded. "The honest fellow must not know that even for a moment he was doubted."

Marie raised the violet eyes reprovingly.

"I trust," she said with reproach, "I too well understand the feelings of a French soldier to let him know his loyalty is questioned."

With a murmur of appreciation the officers bowed and with a gesture of gracious pardon Marie left them.

Outside in the hall, with none but orderlies to observe, like a cloak the graciousness fell from her. She was drawn two ways. In her work Anfossi was valuable. But Anfossi suspected was less than of no value; he became a menace, a death-warrant.

General Andre had said, "We have learned—" and the adjutant had halted him. What had he learned? To know that, Marie would have given much. Still, one important fact comforted her. Anfossi alone was suspected. Had there been concerning herself the slightest doubt, they certainly would not have allowed her to guess her companion was under surveillance; they would not have asked one who was herself suspected to vouch for the innocence of a fellow conspirator. Marie found the course to follow difficult. With Anfossi under suspicion his usefulness was for the moment at an end; and to accept the chance offered her to continue on to Paris seemed most wise. On the other hand, if, concerning Anfossi, she had succeeded in allaying their doubts, the results most to be desired could be attained only by remaining where they were.

Their position inside the lines was of the greatest strategic value. The rooms of the servants were under the roof, and that Briand should sleep in one of them was natural. That to reach or leave his room he should constantly be ascending or descending the stairs also was nat-ural. The field-wireless outfit, or, as he had disdainfully described it, the "knapsack" wireless, was situated not in the bedroom he had selected for himself, but in one adjoining. At other times this was occupied by the maid of Madame Iverney. To summon her maid Madame Iverney, from her apartment on the second floor, had but to press a button. And it was in the apartment of Madame Iverney, and on the bed of that lady, that Madame Benet now reclined. When through the open door she saw an officer or soldier mount the stairs, she pressed the button that rang a bell in the room of the maid. In this way, long before whoever was ascending the stairs could reach the top floor, warning of his approach came to Anfossi. It gave him time to replace the dust-board over the fireplace in which the wireless was concealed and to escape into his own bedroom. The arrangement was ideal. And already information picked up in the halls below by Marie had been conveyed to Anfossi to relay in a French cipher to the German General Staff at Rheims.

Marie made an alert and charming hostess. To all who saw her it was evident that her mind was intent only upon the comfort of her guests. Throughout the day many came and went, but each she made welcome; to each as he departed she called "*bonne chance.*" Efficient, tireless, tactful, she was everywhere: in the dining-room, in the kitchen, in the bedrooms, for the wounded finding mattresses to spread in the gorgeous salons of the Champagne prince; for the soldier-chauffeurs carrying wine into the courtyard, where the automobiles panted and growled, and the arriving and departing shrieked for right of way. At all times an alluring person, now the one woman in a tumult of men, her smart frock covered by an apron, her head and arms bare, undismayed by the sight of the wounded or by the distant rumble of the guns, the Countess d'Aurillac was an inspiring and beautiful picture. The eyes of the officers, young and old, informed her of that fact, one of which already she was well aware. By the morning of the next day she was accepted as the owner of the château. And though continually she reminded the staff she was present only as the friend of her schoolmate, Madame Iverney, they deferred to her as to a hostess. Many of them she already saluted by name, and to those who with messages were constantly motoring to and from the front at Soissons she was particularly kind. Overnight the legend of her charm, of her devotion to the soldiers of all ranks, had spread from Soissons to Meaux, and from Meaux to Paris. It was noon of that day when from the window of the second story Marie saw an armored automobile sweep into the courtyard. It was driven by an officer, young and appallingly good-looking, and, as was obvious by the way he spun his car, one who held in contempt both the law of gravity and death. That he was some one of importance seemed evident. Before he could alight the adjutant had raced to meet him. With her eye for detail Marie observed that the young officer, instead of imparting information, received it. He must, she guessed, have just arrived from Paris, and his brother officer either was telling him the news or giving him his orders. Whichever it might be, in what was told him the new arrival was greatly interested. One instant in indignation his gauntleted fist beat upon the steering wheel, the next he smiled with pleasure. To interpret this pantomime was difficult; and, the better to inform herself, Marie descended the stairs.

As she reached the lower hall the two officers entered. To the spy the man last to arrive was always the one of greatest importance; and Marie assured herself that through her friend, the adjutant, to meet with this one would prove easy.

But the chauffeur-commander of the armored car made it most difficult. At sight of Marie, much to her alarm, as though greeting a dear friend, he snatched his kept from his head and sprang toward her.

"The major," he cried, "told me you were here, that you are Madame d'Aurillac." His eyes spoke his admiration. In delight he beamed upon her. "I might have known it!" he murmured. With the confidence of one who is sure he brings good news, he laughed happily. "And I," he cried, "am 'Pierrot'!"

Who the devil "Pierrot" might be the spy could not guess. She knew only that she wished by a German shell "Pierrot" and his car had been blown to tiny fragments. Was it a trap, she asked herself, or was the handsome youth really some one the Countess d'Aurillac should know. But, as from his introducing himself it was evident he could not know that lady very well, Marie took courage and smiled.

"'*Which Pierrot*'" she parried.

"Pierre Thierry!" cried the youth.

To the relief of Marie he turned upon the adjutant and to him explained who Pierre Thierry might be.

"Paul d'Aurillac," he said, "is my dearest friend. When he married this charming lady I was stationed in Algiers, and but for the war I might never have met her."

To Marie, with his hand on his heart in a most charming manner, he bowed. His admiration he made no effort to conceal.

"And so," he said, "I know why there is war!"

The adjutant smiled indulgently, and departed on his duties, leaving them alone. The handsome eyes of Captain Thierry were raised to the violet eyes of Marie. They appraised her boldly and as boldly expressed their approval.

In burlesque the young man exclaimed indignantly: "Paul deceived me!" he cried. "He told me he had married the most beautiful woman in Laon. He has married the most beautiful woman in France!"

To Marie this was not impertinence, but gallantry.

This was a language she understood, and this was the type of man, because he was the least difficult to manage, she held most in contempt.

"But about you Paul did not deceive me," she retorted. In apparent confusion her eyes refused to meet his. "He told me 'Pierrot' was a most dangerous man!"

She continued hurriedly. With wifely solicitude she asked concerning Paul. She explained that for a week she had been a prisoner in the château, and, since the mobilization, of her husband save that he was with his regiment in Paris she had heard nothing. Captain Thierry was able to give her later news. Only the day previous, on the boulevards, he had met Count d'Aurillac. He was at the Grand Hôtel, and as Thierry was at once motoring back to Paris he would give Paul news of their meeting. He hoped he might tell him that soon his wife also would be in Paris. Marie explained that only the illness of her aunt prevented her from that same day joining her husband. Her manner became serious.

"And what other news have you?" she asked. "Here on the firing-line we know less of what is going forward than you in Paris."

So Pierre Thierry told her all he knew. They were preparing despatches he was at once to carry back to the General Staff, and, for the moment, his time was his own. How could he better employ it than in talking of the war with a patriotic and charming French woman?

In consequence Marie acquired a mass of facts, gossip, and guesses. From these she mentally selected such information as, to her employers across the Aisne, would be of vital interest.

And to rid herself of Thierry and on the fourth floor seek Anfossi was now her only wish. But, in attempting this, by the return of the adjutant she was delayed. To Thierry the adjutant gave a sealed envelope.

"Thirty-one, Boulevard des Invalides," he said. With a smile he turned to Marie. "And you will accompany him!"

"I!" exclaimed Marie. She was sick with sudden terror.

But the tolerant smile of the adjutant reassured her.

"The count, your husband," he explained, "has learned of your detention here by the enemy, and he has besieged the General Staff to have you convoyed safely to Paris." The adjutant glanced at a field telegram he held open in his hand. "He asks," he continued, "that you be permitted to return in the car of his friend, Captain Thierry, and that on arriving you join him at the Grand Hôtel."

Thierry exclaimed with delight.

"But how charming!" he cried. "To-night you must both dine with me at La Rue's." He saluted his superior officer. "Some petrol, sir," he said. "And I am ready." To Marie he added: "The car will be at the steps in five minutes." He turned and left them.

The thoughts of Marie, snatching at an excuse for delay, raced madly. The danger of meeting the Count d'Aurillac, her supposed husband, did not alarm her. The Grand Hôtel has many exits, and, even before they reached it, for leaving the car she could invent an excuse that the gallant Thierry would not suspect. But what now concerned her was how, before she was whisked away to Paris, she could convey to Anfossi the information she had gathered from Thierry. First, of a woman overcome with delight at being reunited with her husband she gave an excellent imitation; then she exclaimed in distress: "But my aunt, Madame Benet!" she cried. "I cannot leave her!"

"The Sisters of St. Francis," said the adjutant, "arrive within an hour to nurse the wounded. They will care also for your aunt."

Marie concealed her chagrin. "Then I will at once prepare to go," she said.

The adjutant handed her a slip of paper. "Your *laissez-passer* to Paris," he said. "You leave in five minutes, madame!"

As temporary hostess of the château Marie was free to visit any part of it, and as she passed her door a signal from Madame Benet told her that Anfossi was on the fourth floor, that he was at work, and that the coast was clear. Softly, in the felt slippers she always wore, as she explained, in order not to disturb the wounded, she mounted the staircase. In her hand she carried the housekeeper's keys, and as an excuse it was her plan to return with an armful of linen for the arriving Sisters. But Marie never reached the top of the stairs. When her eyes rose to the level of the fourth floor she came to a sudden halt. At what she saw terror gripped her, bound her hand and foot, and turned her blood to ice.

At her post for an instant Madame Benet had slept, and an officer of the staff, led by curiosity, chance, or suspicion, had, unobserved and unannounced, mounted to the fourth floor. When Marie saw him he was in front of the room that held the wireless. His back was toward her, but she saw that he was holding the door to the room ajar, that his eye was pressed to the opening, and that through it he had pushed the muzzle of his automatic. What would be the fate of Anfossi Marie knew. Nor did she for an instant consider it. Her thoughts were of her own safety; that she might live. Not that she might still serve the Wilhelmstrasse, the Kaiser, or the Fatherland; but that she might live. In a moment Anfossi would be denounced, the château would ring with the alarm, and, though she knew Anfossi would not betray her, by others she might be accused. To avert suspicion from herself she saw only one way open. She must be the first to denounce Anfossi.

Like a deer, she leaped down the marble stairs and, in a panic she had no need to assume, burst into the presence of the staff.

"Gentlemen!" she gasped, "my servant—the chauffeur—Briand is a spy! There is a German wireless in the château. He is using it! I have seen him." With exclamations, the officers rose to their feet. General Andre alone remained seated. General Andre was a veteran of many Colonial wars: Cochin-China, Algiers, Morocco. The great war, when it came, found him on duty in the Intelligence Department. His aquiline nose, bristling white eyebrows, and flashing, restless eyes gave him his nickname of *l'Aigle*.

In amazement, the flashing eyes were now turned upon Marie. He glared at her as though he thought she suddenly had flown mad.

"A German wireless!" he protested. "It is impossible!"

"I was on the fourth floor," panted Marie, "collecting linen for the Sisters. In the room next to the linen-closet I heard a strange buzzing sound. I opened the door softly. I saw Bri-

and with his back to me seated by an instrument. There were receivers clamped to his ears! My God! The disgrace! The disgrace to my husband and to me, who vouched for him to you!" Apparently in an agony of remorse, the fingers of the woman laced and interlaced. "I cannot forgive myself!"

The officers moved toward the door, but General Andre halted them. Still in a tone of incredulity, he demanded: "When did you see this?"

Marie knew the question was coming, knew she must explain how she saw Briand, and yet did not see the staff officer who, with his prisoner, might now at any instant appear. She must make it plain she had discovered the spy and left the upper part of the house before the officer had visited it. When that was she could not know, but the chance was that he had preceded her by only a few minutes.

"When did you see this?" repeated the general.

"But just now," cried Marie; "not ten minutes since."

"Why did you not come to me at once?"

"I was afraid," replied Marie. "If I moved I was afraid he might hear me, and he, knowing I would expose him, would kill me—and so *escape you!*" There was an eager whisper of approval. For silence, General Andre slapped his hand upon the table.

"Then," continued Marie, "I understood with the receivers on his ears he could not have heard me open the door, nor could he hear me leave, and I ran to my aunt. The thought that we had harbored such an animal sickened me, and I was weak enough to feel faint. But only for an instant. Then I came here." She moved swiftly to the door. "Let me show you the room," she begged; "you can take him in the act." Her eyes, wild with the excitement of the chase, swept the circle. "Will you come?" she begged.

Unconscious of the crisis he interrupted, the orderly on duty opened the door.

"Captain Thierry's compliments," he recited mechanically, "and is he to delay longer for Madame d'Aurillac?"

With a sharp gesture General Andre waved Marie toward the door. Without rising, he inclined his head. "Adieu, madame," he said. "We act at once upon your information. I thank you!"

As she crossed from the hall to the terrace, the ears of the spy were assaulted by a sudden tumult of voices. They were raised in threats and curses. Looking back, she saw Anfossi descending the stairs. His hands were held above his head; behind him, with his automatic, the staff officer she had surprised on the fourth floor was driving him forward. Above the clinched fists of the soldiers that ran to meet him, the eyes of Anfossi were turned toward her. His face was expressionless. His eyes neither accused nor reproached. And with the joy of one who has looked upon and then escaped the guillotine, Marie ran down the steps to the waiting automobile. With a pretty cry of pleasure she leaped into the seat beside Thierry. Gayly she threw out her arms. "To Paris!" she commanded. The handsome eyes of Thierry, eloquent with admiration, looked back into hers. He stooped, threw in the clutch, and the great gray car, with the machine gun and its crew of privates guarding the rear, plunged through the park.

"To Paris!" echoed Thierry.

In the order in which Marie had last seen them, Anfossi and the staff officer entered the room of General Andre, and upon the soldiers in the hall the door was shut. The face of the staff officer was grave, but his voice could not conceal his elation.

"My general," he reported, "I found this man in the act of giving information to the enemy. There is wireless——"

General Andre rose slowly. He looked neither at the officer nor at his prisoner. With frowning eyes he stared down at the maps upon his table.

"I know," he interrupted. "Some one has already told me." He paused, and then, as though recalling his manners, but still without raising his eyes, he added: "You have done well, sir."

In silence the officers of the staff stood motionless. With surprise they noted that, as yet, neither in anger nor curiosity had General Andre glanced at the prisoner. But of the presence of the general the spy was most acutely conscious. He stood erect, his arms still raised, but his body strained forward, and on the averted eyes of the general his own were fixed.

In an agony of supplication they asked a question.

At last, as though against his wish, toward the spy the general turned his head, and their eyes met. And still General Andre was silent. Then the arms of the spy, like those of a runner who has finished his race and breasts the tape exhausted, fell to his sides. In a voice low and vibrant he spoke his question.

"It has been so long, sir," he pleaded. "May I not come home?"

General Andre turned to the astonished group surrounding him. His voice was hushed like that of one who speaks across an open grave.

"Gentlemen," he began, "my children," he added. "A German spy, a woman, involved in a scandal your brother in arms, Henri Ravignac. His honor, he thought, was concerned, and without honor he refused to live. To prove him guiltless his younger brother Charles asked leave to seek out the woman who had betrayed Henri, and by us was detailed on secret service. He gave up home, family, friends. He lived in exile, in poverty, at all times in danger of a swift and ignoble death. In the War Office we know him as one who has given to his country services she cannot hope to reward. For she cannot return to him the years he has lost. She cannot return to him his brother. But she can and will clear the name of Henri Ravignac, and upon his brother Charles bestow promotion and honors."

The general turned and embraced the spy. "My children," he said, "welcome your brother. He has come home."

Before the car had reached the fortifications, Marie Gessler had arranged her plan of escape. She had departed from the château without even a hand-bag, and she would say that before the shops closed she must make purchases.

Le Printemps lay in their way, and she asked

that, when they reached it, for a moment she might alight. Captain Thierry readily gave permission.

From the department store it would be most easy to disappear, and in anticipation Marie smiled covertly. Nor was the picture of Captain Thierry impatiently waiting outside unamusing.

But before Le Printemps was approached, the car turned sharply down a narrow street. On one side, along its entire length, ran a high gray wall, grim and forbidding. In it was a green gate studded with iron bolts. Before this the automobile drew suddenly to a halt. The crew of the armored car tumbled off the rear seat, and one of them beat upon the green gate. Marie felt a hand of ice clutch at her throat. But she controlled herself.

"And what is this?" she cried gayly.

At her side Captain Thierry was smiling down at her, but his smile was hateful.

"It is the prison of St. Lazare," he said. "It is not becoming," he added sternly, "that the name of the Countess d'Aurillac should be made common as the Paris road!"

Fighting for her life, Marie thrust herself against him; her arm that throughout the journey had rested on the back of the driving-seat caressed his shoulders; her lips and the violet eyes were close to his.

"Why should you care?" she whispered fiercely. "You have *me*! Let the Count d'Aurillac look after the honor of his wife himself."

The charming Thierry laughed at her mockingly.

"He means to," he said. "I *am* the Count d'Aurillac!"

GAS ATTACK!

MARTHE McKENNA

THE BELGIAN-BORN Marthe Mathilde Cnockaert (1892–1969) was a nurse who became a spy for the British and its allies during World War I. First, however, she received the German Iron Cross for her work with injured soldiers—the same soldiers that had destroyed her village in West Flanders.

When she was moved to a German military hospital in Roulers, she was recruited by a family friend to become a spy, which she did so valiantly and proficiently that she was showered with honors at the end of the war, including being made a member of the French and Belgian Legions of Honor. Winston Churchill personally handed her a certificate for gallantry.

She took the name of her husband when she married John "Jock" McKenna, a British officer, who ghostwrote her memoir, *I Was a Spy* (1932), for which Churchill provided the foreword. It enjoyed great success and was bought for the movies, made quickly, and released in 1933 by Gaumont British Pictures. Madeleine Carroll played Marthe, Herbert Marshall played the hospital worker who had persuaded her to become a spy (though in real life it was a female friend), and Conrad Veidt played the commandant, one of approximately three million times he was cast in that role. The lovable Edmund Gwenn was the burgomaster and the great stage actor Gerald du Maurier played the doctor; Victor Saville directed.

The success of the memoir inspired publishers to suggest that McKenna write fictional accounts of spies, which she agreed to do, though it is almost certain that her husband was the actual author of the thirteen novels that were published between 1935 and 1950. When the marriage ended in 1951, there were no more books. One of the novels found its way to the big screen when *Lancer Spy* (1937) was released by Twentieth Century-Fox the same year; the movie starred Dolores del Rio, George Sanders, and Peter Lorre, and was directed by Gregory Ratoff.

"Gas Attack!" was originally published in *Drums Never Beat* (London, Jarrolds, 1936).

GAS ATTACK!

MARTHE McKENNA

EARLY IN JANUARY the battle flared up anew and the British stubbornly crept ever closer and closer until shells rained constantly in the village. Two of the women were slightly wounded, and several times I had narrow escapes.

One day after an intensive bombardment the town commandant sent for me and said: "Fräulein, I have given orders that all you women are to be evacuated to Roulers. In your case, both the medical officer and myself will strongly recommend you to the hospital authorities at Roulers."

Under escort next day, and with our few miserable belongings, we took our last look on the beautiful village of our childhood dreams, for its disappearance was to be utter and complete.

Two events of supreme importance were quickly to happen to me after my arrival in Roulers.

Gratefully the hospital authorities accepted my offer of help, and I began nursing in earnest. Then the mysterious reappearance of Lucelle Deldonch and my promise to her to spy and work for the British Intelligence. Of the instant success and luck of my initial attempts in this dangerous undertaking I need not speak here, but these first successes spurred me on

to greater efforts, and very soon I was to discover intrepid allies in this dangerous work. Of the normal routine of transmitting less important secret information, such as the arrival and departure of troops, identity and destination of German regiments, and the like, I shall make no mention, because it would become tedious, and the reader will no doubt take this detail work for granted.

It is more the outstanding episodes that concern us here. In the middle of March, 1915, my father, who had joyfully welcomed Mother and me in Roulers, was offered the proprietorship of the Café Carillon by its owner, who, with his family, was going to a town farther behind the lines. The café nestled in the shadow of the tall grey church of Roulers on the Grande Place, and this incidentally sheltered the café to some extent from Allied shell-fire.

Wide steps led up from the Grande Place to a beautiful façade of old Flemish style, and through this one passed into a large room with a counter which was used as the café.

The two upper stories at the back of the house had been demolished by a bomb and were nothing but bricks, rubble, and splintered beams, but for all that there was ample accommodation. My mother and I pondered for long over this offer. It certainly presented many advantages, being reasonably safe, with spacious cellars, and the income would greatly help the *ménage*, for the war had sadly curtailed Father's assets.

Men will talk, I reasoned, and boast over strong liquor, and I realized that much useful information might be garnered in such a café. But on the other hand, the thought persisted: Was it too obvious? In actual practice should I be placing myself in a too-prominent and dangerous position? At that time there were many exaggerated stories current among the Germans in Belgium of the "café girls" and the way they had suffered for trying to make the troops talk. Although I feared these tales might throw suspicion upon me, I decided in the end that the advantages would prove worth the risk.

As I should no longer have to come in contact merely with the hospital staff, with whom I was on the best of terms, but with all kinds of officers and men who would probably frequent the café, I made up my mind to adopt a definite attitude to the invader. Frequently I acted as spokesman and go-between for the townsfolk in their dealings with the town commandant. I was, therefore, to some extent in the good books of the authorities, and without presuming on this, or overstepping the bounds, I must, above all else, keep this goodwill. A too-friendly attitude on the surface would almost certainly arouse the suspicion of the German Secret Service, who were by no means fools. But at the same time I must contrive to be popular in a detached way and to gain the confidence of the men so that I was the very last person in the world they would suspect.

Then, again, a too-sympathetic attitude to the invader would call down the wrath of my own compatriots, who rightfully looked on friendliness with the detested German as a treachery to Belgium.

In a terribly difficult position, therefore, I bore myself as an aloof, rather detached girl who was quite honestly and openly in sympathy with the Allied cause and the sorrows of downtrodden Belgium, but as one nevertheless who held no ill-feeling against individual fighting-men so long as they behaved themselves.

I made a point of bestowing my smiles on regular clients, and I readily arranged for washing, mending, and other small jobs to be done for them. *Never encourage anyone, never speak to anybody; just let them know you are there, and wait for them to make the overtures*, became the essence of my policy.

It was amazing how well this attitude worked, and within a very short time it began to show startling results.

Only three persons in our immediate circle knew the Intelligence *nom de guerre* "Laura" by which I was known. My mother, of course, knew I was "Laura." Canteen Ma, the intrepid vegetable-woman and the mysterious No. 63 who took my messages and dispatched them over the frontier, were the other two who were in the secret.

So we moved into the new life during March, and from the first the café was not only well patronized by the military but was also extensively used by civilians.

One large room on the first floor which overlooked the Grande Place we reserved as a private room to be used for dinner-parties and special entertainments. When not in use for other purposes it was used as a lounge for officers, and at nights this place usually quickly filled, when cigar-smoke and restless chatter and argument made a lively scene. When it was my turn to be home for evenings from the hospital I made it a practice to help wait on our clients, reinforcing the two maids we kept.

A week after we had taken over the café I returned from the hospital rather earlier than usual and was met by Bertha, one of our serving-maids. Her face was very concerned as she told me there were three officers, just arrived, who had announced their intention of billeting upon us. This was the last thing I wanted, being afraid that this proximity in the house might curtail my activities. But there was no help for it, as the town was packed with troops, and the three had the yellow slips of billeting requisitions.

The lounge had not yet filled, and when the handbell rang I went to ask for orders, anxious to see what sort of men were to live the daily round with us.

Three officers sat round the oak table in the centre of the room, gazing over empty wine-glasses. They had flung their equipment in a pile on the floor. Two Hauptmanns leaned back with tunics undone and puffed black cigars. The other, a fair Leutnant, very neat and tightly buttoned up, watched me, elbows on table and chin on hands. When I had brought the wine they had ordered, the large florid Hauptmann with red hair raised his glass.

"Fräulein, won't you do us the honour to drink a glass with us?" he commenced. Then, rising to his feet: "Drink to our trip to Paris." He looked across at the others in a very knowing way.

"Thank you, Herr," I returned, "but I have had a very trying day at the hospital, and there are times when I feel that I do not require a drink."

I was, however, decidedly intrigued with that queer look he had flashed at the others when he mentioned the "trip to Paris." It was perhaps merely a fatuous remark born of a fervent wish, but that acute, inexplicable sense of being on the track of a secret was beginning to develop in me even in those early days.

"So you are from the big hospital on the Menin Road?" rumbled the red-haired man, as though I had committed some crime.

"Really, Red Carl," interposed a cherubic young voice, "you haven't been sent here to court-martial this Fräulein, you know." I noticed the speaker's wavy golden hair and his lively eyes. He appeared a very attractive, boyish kind of officer.

The other Hauptmann, a long, cadaverous man of middle age, with hair so closely cropped that his head appeared shaved, examined me through large spectacles whilst a cold smile played on his face.

"Perhaps the Fräulein will be kind enough to show us our quarters," he suggested in a strangely quiet voice. There was something intense and queer about this man which made me feel he was a dangerous type of individual to cross.

The trio followed me silently. I intended to give the spectacled Hauptmann a room to himself, as obviously he was the senior, and allot the only remaining room we had to be shared by the other two. But the spectacled one turned to me.

"Fräulein," he said, "I shall share with the Herr Hauptmann. We have work which we must carry on together," and his eyes glinted behind his glasses. "The Herr Leutnant can take my room."

"Splendid!" chuckled the Leutnant. "Red Carl, if you snore as thunderously to-night as you did in the train last night, I think at the Hauptmann's hands you will die a nasty, sticky death."

"Oh no . . . you wouldn't kill me, would you . . . you sinister old devil?" Red Carl returned with a great guffaw. "I'm too damned valuable to you, eh?"

I showed the two into their room and then went back to the Leutnant, who had called.

"Queer couple, those two, aren't they, Fräulein?" he opened. "Possibly you think them a trifle rude and surly . . . not the usual type of our Army officer?"

"Yes," I agreed. "But they appear to be ill assorted, yet very friendly. What are they?"

I had immediately noticed that neither of the Hauptmanns were of the Army of Würtemberg, that they wore the badges of some special unit which I failed to recognize.

"Just two representatives whom we have sent ahead to arrange our trip to Paris," he laughed cryptically.

I knew it would be imprudent to press the matter further, but I was convinced there was some deep mystery here which needed probing. The Leutnant told me his name was Otto von Promft. He lighted an expensive cigarette, and offered me his case.

Perhaps, I thought, as I stood there smoking, a little easy flattery might open his confidences. "You were a student, I see," I remarked.

"So you noticed my duelling-scar, Fräulein," he responded with great pride. "I left Stuttgart six months ago."

Then he suddenly broke into fluent French. He told me he had lived in Paris most of his life until the war.

"I have been in various parts of Belgium," he told me during the conversation. "Everywhere it is the custom of you Belgians to bewail the terrible conditions under which you are forced to live, but I have recently returned from leave, and I dare say you will be surprised to hear that in Berlin the regulations are just as severe as those you know in Belgium." He went on to paint a distressing picture, and appeared absolutely frank, and open in all he said.

I remained wary, however, thinking perhaps his apparent frankness might be a ruse to draw me.

"But we Germans," he finished with a sigh, "know how to put up with a lot, so it does not greatly matter. . . . We are bound to win."

"You may win great victories," I mildly observed, unable to let this confident prophecy pass, "but I do not believe you will emerge from this war the victors."

"Fräulein," he returned with perfect good humour, "as yet Germany is not even tried . . . but a victory, sudden, overwhelming victory is coming . . . and coming very soon!"

Some officers came into the lounge and were ringing the bell impatiently, so I told the Leutnant I must go. Altogether we had been speaking for more than half an hour. I was a little uncertain of the cherubic Otto, but those frank eyes of his somehow gave you the impression that he genuinely liked you. Would this be a well at which one could pump? I decided to make the better acquaintance of Leutnant Otto. In my hospital ward there were two wounded British prisoners. They were put there because I spoke English. The time was rapidly approaching when they would be moved to a prisoners-of-war camp. I had racked my brains and made anxious tentative inquiries with a view to getting the lovable pair

over the frontier. I knew there were intrepid and brave men amongst my compatriots who were only too willing to act as guides, but I had frankly admitted to myself it were best in all the circumstances to hide as far as possible the nature of my undertakings, and not to become mixed up with daredevil "runners" who undoubtedly carried on their hair-raising work at the risk of a firing-squad.

But I had become very good friends with the two prisoners, and my heart bled when I thought of the sufferings in store for them when they were imprisoned in one of those degrading camps. Harrowing stories had already reached us, and I was determined that two Britishers at least would have their chance of freedom. One of the men was a tall Highlander who wore a kilt, the other was a diminutive, talkative soldier, and both belonged to Canadian units. Jimmie was a common little man, originally emanating from a London slum. He possessed all the ever-ready wit and good humour of his class, and was always cheerful. He made a joke when we put him on the operating-table, and followed it with another one before he was violently sick when he woke up after we had done with him.

I eventually found I was able to understand the Highlander's Scotch *patois*. He had been a miner in civil life, and was self-educated, with a serious but argumentative outlook on life. He had taught himself quite a fair knowledge of French, and I used to lend him books in that language.

"It has always bin ma weish, leddie," he confided to me one night, "if A could but acquire the learrnin', to become a meenister."

His meaning rather puzzled me at first, for ministers are associated in our minds with high politics, but when I did understand I could not help smiling at the thought of this gaunt giant who decorated every tenth word with "Jesus Christ" ministering to his flock in a black suit.

His name was Arthur.

One morning I entered the ward to hear Jimmie and Arthur in fierce dispute—a not uncommon occurrence.

"Have ye no bin to schule, mon . . . do ye ken nothing?" expostulated Arthur mournfully to his grinning mate, who had just remarked something about a "b—— liar."

"Arthur." At my intense whisper he turned his head. As I slipped close to his bed an eager look lighted his face. At intervals we had talked together in the hospital grounds on their daily airing, and I had vaguely hinted at assisting them to escape.

On the pretext of tucking in his sheets, I whispered rapidly: "Here are a few hundred francs for you and Jimmie. When you are out walking in the grounds this evening, look out for a small Belgian with a squint. He will be standing near the civilian workers' annexe. Slip through the door. You will be found civilian clothes . . . and trust your guide . . . he will get you over the frontier."

Then I was gone, leaving Arthur gasping. Both were in the convalescent stage, and their wounds might, with care, stand the thirty-mile trip to the Dutch frontier. In any event the attempt must be now, as any day the order for their removal might arrive.

The money was all I could raise at the moment, but Pierre—the Belgian civilian—would also help if it were necessary. The rest of the day I was on tenterhooks. Had a clue been left by which, if the lads were caught, I could be traced? I knew they would never betray me, no matter what happened. But of Pierre I was not so certain.

Before the war he had been known as one of the worst characters in Roulers, had been a drunkard, and had rarely worked. Prison had known him numberless times for petty theft. But he was a cheery old ruffian with a squint eye and a detestation for the invader which no amount of punishment seemed to suppress. It was he who had broached the idea of the escape when I had spoken to him a fortnight before while he was pruning rose-bushes in the hospital garden. I was

chary of using such a notorious character, but short of pushing inquiries through other channels I had no other way for the terribly short time at my disposal. So Pierre, I had decided, must be the medium.

Soon after giving these whispered instructions to the two Canadians a wire came through that two ambulance convoys were to be expected, and in the rush of work the matter slipped my mind. At six o'clock I went off duty, ate a hasty meal, and then tried to read. The printed words ran meaninglessly in front of me as I pictured the two poor wounded fugitives making the desperate attempt for freedom.

It must have been eight o'clock when there was a sudden ringing of the alarm-bell from the hospital. I hurried over to my ward. Orderlies were rushing about and waving their arms, and when I glanced over to the corner I saw Jimmie's bed was empty, as was Arthur's.

"What do you know of this, Nurse?" an irate Feldwebel roared at me. "Two prisoner patients from your ward walk off right under your nose. When did you see them last? Have they got civilian clothes, or money?"

I professed complete ignorance of the whole affair. I had been off duty and had seen nothing.

"In any case," I volunteered, "I am certain they cannot get far, because their wounds are bound to burst with any extra exertion."

This remark seemed to appease the Feldwebel and the listening orderlies, and presently I managed to slip into the civilians' annexe, where some workmen lived and assisted in ambulance work. In the doorway I met a man I had never seen before, a big bearded fellow with flaxen hair, dressed in rough clothes, but who spoke with a cultured accent.

"Good evening, Sister. A good friend of mine asked me to give you a message. His friends are leaving and will be in Holland by midnight."

That was all, and the man slunk away. I breathed freely again. The squint-eyed Pierre had done the trick.

When I returned I passed directly into the

kitchen and my mother informed me that two soldiers were in the sitting-room and had asked twice to see me. She told me she knew the pair by sight; they were evidently soldiers billeted in the town. Such men I avoided as much as possible, because as a rule, they knew less than the civilians, so there was no point in cultivating friendliness.

It was, therefore, with no little trepidation I walked into the sitting-room to interview the insistent callers.

"Alphonse—Stephan!" I ejaculated in surprise, as I caught sight of the grim-looking soldiers.

Alphonse was an Alsatian, driver of a Red Cross ambulance, and one who by unfailing courtesies had given me the impression of being not only friendly but sympathetic towards my country.

Stephan, his friend, was a Pole, employed as a clerk in the Brigade orderly-room, who sported a thin, dark moustache, and appeared rather a delicate young man. Both had been most friendly to me. They were eyeing me queerly now. . . . Could they be German agents . . . decoys? flashed through my mind. I was a fool not to have connected them with counterespionage work—they were just the type the Germans would employ—and no doubt they had got wind of this escape of the two British prisoners. The palms of my hands grew clammy at the thought. . . . Was my masquerade finished?

"Alphonse has cut his finger, repairing the engine of his car. . . . Nothing serious, Sister, but as we were passing . . ." explained Stephan quietly.

"Of course," I said, my heart beating wildly. "Of course I will dress it for him. . . . Sit down, won't you, whilst I fetch my bandages." I ran upstairs to my room in an agony of apprehension, at once destroyed several notes I had there and a roll of Japanese writing-paper. How long had they been in the house? Why had they called? The thin excuse of the cut finger was too stupid for words. *If indeed the wound required dressing*, Stephan could have dressed it him-

self. Had they really discovered my dual role? All these questions, then, and a hundred wild suppositions hammered at my brain as I picked up my little work-basket and bandages and descended to the room again.

Stephan was sitting on the table when I entered and Alphonse was pretending to examine the pictures on the walls. I tried to persuade myself that everything was all right, that their visit after all was perfectly natural. Yet it was only with a great effort I managed to steady myself and appear quite unperturbed.

"Now, Alphonse," I said, "where is this cut?" And then, as I was bending over a small gash in his finger, which he might easily have bandaged himself, he asked in a grave, still voice: "*How do you like your double job, Sister?*"

I felt myself go as pale as death, but kept my head down so that he could not observe my agitation, and, clenching my teeth, willed my hands not to tremble.

"Perhaps you would like a pin to fasten the bandage?" he suggested as he saw me finishing. "A safety-pin perhaps."

My heart bounded with joy, and the relief was almost too great as slowly I gazed up at him.

"Have you a small one handy?" I inquired huskily.

He lifted the lapel of his great-coat, showing two diagonal safety-pins. With a great gasp of relief I smiled and looked with swimming eyes at Stephan. He too disclosed the emblem by which we were to know friends and fellow-workers for freedom in our sector.

"So you see, Sister, we all serve together, eh?" queried Alphonse, using this remark so as to give me time to cover up my emotion.

"How did you get to know?" I demanded after a while.

"The sergeant-major of the canteen told us to visit you, Sister."

"What!" I gasped, horrified. "That German!"

"He is not a German, Sister," smiled Alphonse. "Not many years ago that ranting sergeant-major was a cadet at the military college of Sandhurst, England. . . . He was sent to Germany before the war!"

"And he sent you to me?" I asked, still mystified.

"Yes. He was worked very closely with Canteen Ma, and until yesterday was our channel of communication, but unfortunately he has been transferred to Lille. Stephan, here, works at Brigade Headquarters, so you can understand he sometimes learns things that are most interesting . . . and as I myself frequently go up the line, and also manage to pick up a thing or two, we had a compact little system . . . but this transfer for the moment seemed to end matters as far as we were concerned. . . . We were told, however, that our messages must be handed to 'Laura,' and when we knew who 'Laura' was, you could have knocked us down with less than a feather."

"You have information for me?" I asked quickly, vowing at the same time never to let a guilty conscience master me again.

"First of all, Sister, let us speak of another matter that is certainly of immediate importance to you. . . ." It was the pale Stephan who was speaking as he nervously fingered one end of his moustache. "There is billeted in this café a young officer named Otto von Promft?"

"That is so," I replied.

"You like him?" was the surprising question.

"What has that to do with it?" I demanded. "He appears an agreeable boy, and better than most Germans."

"Ah . . . that is the line they take," drawled Stephan, shaking his head grimly. "The charming Otto has been sent to this area as a decoy."

"Then, as he has been placed here, I am suspected?" I asked breathlessly. "How do you know this?" I gasped.

"They do not necessarily suspect you, Sister. . . . The Germans suspect all Belgians unless they are imbeciles, or on their deathbeds, but there is a chance that you are to be kept under surveillance, and it might be very necessary for you to be watchful in return. I will tell you how I discovered about this bright Otto.

"It is one of my duties at Brigade H.Q. to assist the Censor Officer. I open the letters of the troops, place them before him, and close them for posting when he has finished censoring. Sometimes the Censor arrives late—he always takes a long time over his meals—it is not therefore difficult for me to find opportunities to examine many letters . . . and often before the Censor has attacked them with his blue pencil. . . . The mail of officers usually arrives at H.Q. in separate packages, and these I naturally consider most likely to yield matter of value.

"It was last week in one of these packages I came upon the letter of a certain Leutnant Otto von Promft. He was telling his mother that the special work which he had been detailed for in Roulers was both agreeable and interesting, and allowed him much freedom and leisure, and that if he were successful in his mission—which he had every hope in the end he would be—he would no doubt be installed in a cushy job in Berlin. This letter was both interesting and unusual, and after careful inquiries I found the charming Otto was billeted at this café, was friendly to everyone, and was employed neither regimentally nor by the police, nor indeed in any normal branch of the staff. . . . He is employed by the Army Group Secret Service on a special mission."

"I am more than grateful to you," I assured Stephan, mentally stabbing the deceitful Otto. I was not so much frightened at the moment as furiously indignant with him for singling me out for notice, and for the fact that I had placed him on the same plane as Corporal-dresser Evandan—as a German one could abide.

"Now, have you information for me to pass on?" I asked.

"Perhaps we could have a little wine over which to discuss it, Sister, for it is a puzzler, I can assure you," said Alphonse, tickling the back of his close-cropped head.

I went to fetch the wine, and at the foot of the stairs I came face to face with the deceitful Otto.

"I hope you will find time to join me later, Fräulein. . . . I——"

"Not this evening, Herr Leutnant," I excused myself. "I am tired. . . . Perhaps to-morrow."

It is strange that when you know the true character of a person the face often seems to change from that which you have previously known. This happened with Leutnant Otto. The boyish lineaments appeared to have given place to a cunning, foxy expression. It was imperative, however, to keep up my friendly footing, hoping that he did not, and would not, suspect.

When I returned to my two new conspirators, Stephan began to talk rapidly. In the last ammunition-train to arrive, he explained, besides the usual freight were several trucks containing long metal cylinders. He had not been able by any means to discover for what they were intended, and he was doubtful even if the German Brigade Headquarters knew themselves.

"Whatever they are intended for," he said, "I think perhaps a bomb would do them a bit of good, so the sooner you inform our relations over the border, the better. . . . The British might think them intriguing enough to send over a couple of bombing-'planes."

"I shall send the information over to-night," I promised. "Meanwhile, do your utmost to find out from Brigade what these cylinders contain."

"I too have some unusual information for you, Sister," interposed Alphonse. "Yesterday afternoon, when normally I should have been off duty, I and another ambulance-driver were sent on several trips to and from the station, bringing bales of cotton-wool swabs to the hospital store. They were not dressing-pads for wounds, as they have pieces of elastic and a catch attached to them. . . . I have never seen anything like them before."

"Was there no sort of descriptive label on the bales?" I asked.

"There was no label describing what they were for, but this is the strangest part of all: the consignment was not addressed to the Medical Officer of the hospital, or even to any officer of the Medical Corps. . . . The label simply stated that the consignment was to be held at the disposal of a certain Hauptmann Reichmann."

"Hauptmann Reichmann!" I ejaculated with astonishment. "He is billeted here."

"Yes, we know that, Sister, Stephan discovered it from the Brigade register; but he appears to belong to no unit, and nothing there is known about him. . . ."

"But he has visited Brigade three times, and each time had long private conferences with the Brigadier himself," interrupted Stephan.

"Sister, I think you should take every opportunity of watching this officer, for obviously there is something of importance developing," suggested Alphonse.

Presently the two of them bade me good night. We had agreed that in future dealings only two of us must ever be seen together at the same time, and that we must not seem to be anything but casual acquaintances to outsiders.

It was late, and most of our clients had left, some a trifle noisily, for their sleeping-quarters. As there might be nothing in the matter, there was no point in informing the British about our cadaverous guest, Reichmann, but to myself I determined to keep my eyes wide open. In my room then that night I described the arrival of the cylinders and the mysterious swabs. When written, the warning looked enigmatic, even comical, but it was not my business to ponder the solution; that was the job of the jig-saw readers in London. The key to the riddle might fall into their hands from an altogether different source.

I put the message in my hair and slipped down the darkened stairs, then into the silent streets. My hospital night-pass allowed me perfect freedom, but I shrank away into the shadows as the gruff voices of a patrol and the clink of metal reached me from the other side of the square. It was very dark, but presently I arrived at the silent alleyway which harboured the mysterious No. 63. At the fifth window on the left-hand side I tapped according to the signal, once—a pause—then a rapid double knock. The frame slid up without a sound, the mysterious hand appeared, and into it I pushed my precious notes, then, as though the Evil One himself was after me, I sped away from the alley.

A few mornings later I saw Canteen Ma in the Grande Place. She was, as usual, surrounded by laughing soldiers, giving a joke and taking some good-humoured chaff as she sold the fruit and vegetables from her cart. She had been named Canteen Ma since the day the Roulers canteen sergeant-major had taken the whole of his supplies from her. In her he had discovered a shrewd, clever spy of indomitable courage, and one who in the capacity of vegetable-hawker covered a wide and vital area. Besides the incredibly important items of news she managed to pick up, she had organized a gang of desperate runners who, fearing nothing, kept up an uninterrupted line of communication with the Dutch frontier. It was through this heroic woman I received my instructions from British Intelligence.

As her shrewd eyes met mine they glittered, and she made a sign to me indicating she wanted to speak. I contrived to move close to her, and she whispered: "Martha, there is something in the air . . . too much talk of sweeping victory amongst the men for things to be normal. . . . Yet nobody seems to know anything."

She brushed a few grinning soldiers away from her cart, then turned to me again and asked:

"Have you heard anything?"

"No," I returned, "but I have heard the same talk amongst the officers billeted with us."

"We must keep our eyes and ears open, Martha," she enjoined anxiously as she moved away.

That same evening Stephan supplied another piece of the puzzle. He said that Reichmann had started sending in weather reports to Brigade twice a day. The variations of the wind were graphed. The district comprised the Roulers-Menin and Poelcappelle-Passchendaele Roads. Red Carl had several times been up in an aeroplane taking observations, and twice in an observation balloon on the Menin Road. I came to the conclusion that Hauptmann Reichmann might have some papers in his room which would perhaps supply a clue. Accordingly I asked my mother to help make beds with the maids and to keep her eyes open. She quickly told me that

Reichmann filed duplicate copies of strange graphs on his table, and that he was also keeping a sort of log of the weather, and wind movements.

I determined then to search the room myself.

Next morning I sent to the hospital saying I was unwell, and when I saw Red Carl, Hauptmann Reichmann, and Leutnant Otto depart, I crept from my room into Reichmann's and examined the documents on his table. Sure enough, there was the weather log, along with its movements and the wind graphs; but there was nothing else. I also tried the papers of Red Carl, but there again I found nothing of any interest, only strange calculations and figures of which I could not make head nor tail. I left the room as mystified as I went in. But again that night I informed the British by the hand of "63," insisting that something mysterious was afoot.

A few days later Canteen Ma called, and in the small pin-cushion she left which contained my messages I found this screed in code:

Do not worry about weather reports. Troop movements, designation of units, and destination of trains, etc., etc., of more value.

But for all that I did continue to worry. And that night I found myself going to bed even more puzzled.

Red Carl was sitting in a corner of the smoky lounge by himself. He looked slightly the worse for drink, and appeared to want someone to talk to. He beckoned to me, so I crossed and stood awhile by his side.

"Have you ever been to Germany, Fräulein?" he asked, offering me a cigarette and lighting it with a rather shaky hand.

"No, Herr," I replied, perhaps a little too shortly.

"You do not like the Germans—*hein?*"

"Well, you could not expect us exactly to love them after what we have suffered, and after the shambles they have made of our country, could you, Herr Hauptmann?"

"*Ach!* Never mind, Fräulein . . . you will like us better when you understand us . . . and even if we don't win the war soon we shall have pressed so far into France that Roulers will hardly know a German soldier except for a patrol now and then. *Nach Paris! Nach Calais!*" He banged his empty glass so hard I was surprised it did not break in his hand. Then ensued a little pause while he sat dreaming heroically in a mirage of alcoholic glory.

"You Germans are good at that story," I taunted quietly. "I could tell you the names of several officers who used the same war-cry last year. *Nach Paris! Nach Calais!* is as great a dream as ever."

"*Ach*, you may think so, Fräulein; you may all think we are slow, but I know. . . ." And in his deep way he chuckled. "And yet it's all funny, *mein Fräulein* . . . damned funny! Here I am . . . Carl Sturmo, a despised chemist, and a man whom these snobs of generals, with their choker collars, their eyeglasses and brass hats, would in the old days have regarded with as much respect as they did the cobble-stones under their feet, but who is now going to play a bigger hand in winning the mightiest war the world has ever seen than they themselves, for all their swaggering militarism."

He continued chuckling to himself drunkenly, until some friends came up to him, when I left him. But all the evening he kept them laughing with a continual flow of tipsy bragging, and through my mind the news for some unaccountable reason kept drumming.

Carl, the chemist. . . . Red Carl, a chemist, a disgruntled officer with no sort of recognition . . . a braggart who boasted in his cups of sweeping victory by some mysterious means. He was so cocksure, I told myself, there must be a grain of sense among all the chaff. But where? Where was it? I went to bed racking my brains seeking an answer to the riddle.

The following day I managed to find an opportunity to tell both Stephan and Alphonse what Carl had said the night before. Alphonse thought that Carl had invented some new type of artillery, and that the calculations and wind graphs might have something to do with accurate firing.

Stephan suggested that if there was to be a great advance in that area, as was apparently the case, the authorities might be considering Roulers as a Zeppelin base, as there was no doubt the town and the environs were ideally situated for such a base.

I did not feel satisfied with either of these suppositions, but decided to mention both in my next message.

Alphonse had another piece of news for me. He said he had been told by a man in charge of the dump of metal cylinders that they contained chlorine, but still he did not know what use was to be made of them. I was not, as a matter of fact, inclined to pay much attention to the cylinders. On the way home, however, the analogy between *chemist* and *chlorine* suddenly struck me. Could Red Carl have anything to do with those cylinders? Red Carl had said strange things . . . and it was my duty to report everything that came under my notice. Perhaps it all seemed a little far-fetched trying to associate Red Carl and Hauptmann Reichmann with swabs, wind graphs, and chlorine, but I risked a snub from Intelligence. I sent over everything, giving my reasons and suggestions. It was my job to report. It was the job of British Intelligence to unravel the puzzle from the clues sent to them, and I contented myself with this thought.

Three days later back came the message:

Recent reports from you of a highly speculative nature. Repeat, troop movements, designation of units, trains, and dumps, etc., etc., of more value.

So they evidently thought me an imaginative girl who conjured molehills into mountains!

I was not discouraged. The weather-watchers continued to submit their reports day after day, and I made one new discovery. I talked to the gaunt Reichmann one evening and drew him on to speak of his life in pre-war days and of his home. He had been a professor of a big university. It was not difficult to guess what he had been a professor of when one remembered his association with Carl and, a fact which I subsequently noticed, that he received regularly periodicals of a scientific character by home mail.

The mysterious rumour of "victory before summer" seemed to have become an obsession among the Germans. The inspired Press helped matters on, and grotesque, ribald and indecent cartoons depicting Allied soldiers in all kinds of degrading situations flooded every journal.

One morning in April I reached the hospital to find it full of bustle. All possible cases that could be moved were to be evacuated at once. A civilian medical station was to be opened in the town itself so as to relieve the hospital of this branch of work, which was sometimes considerable.

"Ah, Fräulein," greeted the Oberartz in his genial voice, "I think we are in for a big advance. All stations this side of Ghent have been warned to evacuate all wounded immediately."

Repressing my burning interest, I remained silent, expecting to hear some further information and perhaps the key to the mystery; but to my disappointment he passed on without another word.

This was important news in any case.

Evacuation of hospitals close to the Front meant attack!

Empty hospitals to receive the broken wretches who would return. That night I got my urgent report away by No. 63. Then anxiously I waited and watched for the flood of reinforcements. But day followed day, and no further troops arrived. The 26th and 27th Corps of the Würtemberg Army held the sector, front and reserve lines.

The Army carried out its reliefs as usual; not an extra gun or an extra soldier passed up the line. We were all completely mystified. In talking the conundrum over with Alphonse, he thought perhaps it might mean a feint at this part of the salient to cover some determined attack at another point. I had grave misgivings, and I could only comfort myself with the thought that we had done everything possible. I had faithfully recorded every clue that had come under my notice.

Then a short week later the solution fell with a blinding crash. The 22nd of April, 1915,

I well remember, was a beautiful day with gentle spring breezes bringing promise of early summer—but from the slopes of the Passchendaele ridges another kind of breeze—a devil's wind—had been slowly creeping over No Man's Land enveloping the Allied trenches about Poelcappelle and Langemarck in a mysterious haze of death.

Soon after dawn on the 23rd I received an urgent message from the hospital to be in attendance immediately. I hurried there, and almost at once the stream of ambulances with the unfortunate prisoners began to arrive. At first scores, then later hundreds, of broken men, gasping, screaming, choking. The hospital became packed with French and British soldiers beating and fighting the air for breath. Dozens of men died like flies under our eyes, their clothes and uniforms rent to ribbons in their agony, their faces a horrible sickly green contorted out of all human shape. Tunics and brass buttons turned a greyish green, and a pungent, suffocating smell hung around them. When no more room could be found along the hospital corridors, the stretcher-bearers laid the unfortunate gasping pieces of humanity out on the footpaths on the open streets surrounding the building.

"What is it? . . . What is it?" kept pounding in my brain. "What devil's work is this?"—as I worked amid that hellish scene striving to soothe and quieten the stricken. And still the ambulances came packed with tortured prisoners . . . more and more forms struggled and tossed in the roadway.

My heart bleeding with pity, I bent over a young British soldier, a Canadian, and whispered:

"What has happened, brother?"

He looked up with inflamed, swollen eyes almost bursting from their sockets; but he could not speak, only painfully shake his head as he tried to prop himself up in my arms, and then, coughing and spitting and choking, he fell back dead.

As the number of prisoners grew, the civilian population had gathered at both ends of the

street. A section of German soldiers was trying to keep them back with the butts of their
rifles . . . when suddenly a voice from the crowd
cried: "*Vive la France! . . . Vive l'Angleterre!*"

That is a moment that will live for ever in my
memory, for the cry burst from every throat until
it swelled to a mad, indignant roar. Even the poor
gassed prisoners tried to sit up and join in the
cry: "*Vive la France! Vive l'Angleterre!*" as a last
defiant battle-cry to their implacable foes.

Blinded with tears, the civilians pressed ever
forward and showered useless cigarettes, bread,
and chocolate on the stricken soldiers. God only
knows where it came from, for all were fearfully
short and hungry in those days. The savage
crowd was getting out of hand, and several soldiers had been roughly treated, when suddenly
there came the clatter of hooves and a posse of
mounted gendarmes trotted rapidly up the road.
They put their horses into the crowd and started
to force them away.

. . . The riddle of the wind graphs had been
answered. . . . It is for the historian to tell how
the Allied line was shattered and bent, how near
the Germans were to a crushing victory, but
how the comrades of those stricken wretches
who could still cry out "*Vive la France! Vive
l'Angleterre!*" withstood the shock and desperately won their way back through a hell of carnage.

Nor will the historian forget those heroic victims who died under the first gas attack.

THE LOATHLY OPPOSITE

JOHN BUCHAN

JOHN BUCHAN, 1st Baron Tweedsmuir (1875–1940) was a Scottish diplomat, journalist, publisher, and author of historical works and espionage and adventure fiction, some of which features his famous hero Richard Hannay and his activities for British Intelligence. More than half of his literary output was nonfiction, including his first book, a biography titled *Sir Quixote of the Moors* (1895), published when he was only twenty years old. But Buchan is most remembered today for his thrillers, particularly those involving Hannay.

Modeled after one of Buchan's military idols, General Edmund "Tiny" Ironside, Hannay's first adventure was the classic *The Thirty-Nine Steps* (1915), set just before the outbreak of World War I. The success of this novel spurred the sequels *Greenmantle* (1916), *Mr. Standfast* (1919), *The Three Hostages* (1924), and *The Island of Sheep* (1936).

The enduring popularity of *The 39 Steps* is partially due to the outstanding 1935 film directed by Alfred Hitchcock that starred Robert Donat (as Hannay) and Madeleine Carroll. The motion picture version is considerably different from the novel, which did not have a female character in a major role. It was changed into mostly a chase film with the British police hunting Hannay because they believe he killed an American spy. Foreign spies also want to capture him because they believe he has information that they want to prevent from being delivered to the British government. It was remade in a forgettable 1959 production with Kenneth More and Taina Elg.

Buchan had a career in journalism as a war correspondent in France in 1915 and was for a time the executive deputy chairman of the Reuters news agency. He also was a partner in the publishing firm Thomas Nelson & Sons, Ltd., discovering E. C. Bentley's *Trent's Last Case* (1913) and other major works. His interest in politics impelled him to run for Parliament and he was elected as a Conservative in a 1927 landslide.

"The Loathly Opposite" was originally published in the October 1927 issue of *The Pall Mall Magazine;* its first book publication was in the short story collection *The Runagates Club* (London, Hodder & Stoughton, 1928).

THE LOATHLY OPPOSITE

JOHN BUCHAN

OLIVER PUGH'S STORY

How loathly opposite I stood
To his unnatural purpose.
KING LEAR

BURMINSTER HAD BEEN to a Guild-hall dinner the night before, which had been attended by many—to him—unfamiliar celebrities. He had seen for the first time in the flesh people whom he had long known by reputation, and he declared that in every case the picture he had formed of them had been cruelly shattered. An eminent poet, he said, had looked like a starting-price bookmaker, and a financier of world-wide fame had been exactly like the music-master at his preparatory school. Wherefore Burminster made the profound deduction that things were never what they seemed.

"That's only because you have a feeble imagination," said Sandy Arbuthnot. "If you had really understood Timson's poetry you would have realised that it went with close-cropped red hair and a fat body, and you should have known that Macintyre (this was the financier) had the music-and-metaphysics type of mind. That's why he puzzles the City so. If you understand a man's work well enough you can guess pretty accurately what he'll look like. I don't mean the colour of his eyes and his hair, but the general atmosphere of him."

It was Sandy's agreeable habit to fling an occasional paradox at the table with the view of

starting an argument. This time he stirred up Pugh, who had come to the War Office from the Indian Staff Corps. Pugh had been a great figure in Secret Service work in the East, but he did not look the part, for he had the air of a polo-playing cavalry subaltern. The skin was stretched as tight over his cheekbones as over the knuckles of a clenched fist, and was so dark that it had the appearance of beaten bronze. He had black hair, rather beady black eyes, and the hooky nose which in the Celt often goes with that colouring. He was himself a very good refutation of Sandy's theory.

"I don't agree," Pugh said. "At least not as a general principle. One piece of humanity whose work I studied with the microscope for two aching years upset all my notions when I came to meet it."

Then he told us this story.

"When I was brought to England in November '17 and given a 'hush' department on three floors of an eighteenth-century house in a back street, I had a good deal to learn about my business. That I learned it in reasonable time was due to the extraordinarily fine staff that I found provided for me. Not one of them was a regular soldier. They were all educated men—they had to be in that job—but they came out of every sort of environment. One of the best was a Shetland laird, another was an Admiralty Court K.C., and I had besides a metallurgical chemist, a golf champion, a leader-writer, a popular dramatist, several actuaries, and an East-end curate. None of them thought of anything but his job, and at the end of the war when some ass proposed to make them OBEs, there was a very fair imitation of a riot. A more loyal crowd never existed, and they accepted me as their chief as unquestioningly as if I had been with them since 1914.

"To the war in the ordinary sense they scarcely gave thought. You found the same thing in a lot of other behind-the-lines departments, and I daresay it was a good thing—it kept their nerves quiet and their minds concentrated. After all, our business was only to decode and decypher German messages; we had nothing to do with the use which was made of them. It was a curious little nest, and when the Armistice came my people were flabbergasted—they hadn't realised that their job was bound up with the war.

"The one who most interested me was my second-in-command, Philip Channell. He was a man of forty-three, about five-foot-four in height, weighing, I fancy, under nine stones and almost as blind as an owl. He was good enough at papers with his double glasses, but he could hardly recognise you three yards off. He had been a professor at some Midland college—mathematics or physics, I think—and as soon as the war began he had tried to enlist. Of course they wouldn't have him—he was about E5 in any physical classification, besides being well over age—but he would take no refusal, and presently he worried his way into the Government service. Fortunately he found a job which he could do superlatively well, for I do not believe there was a man alive with more natural genius for cryptography.

"I don't know if any of you have ever given your mind to that heart-breaking subject. Anyhow you know that secret writing falls under two heads—codes and cyphers, and that codes are combinations of words and cyphers of numerals. I remember how one used to be told that no code or cypher which was practically useful was really undiscoverable, and in a sense that is true, especially of codes. A system of communication which is in constant use must obviously not be too intricate, and a working code, if you get long enough for the job, can generally be read. That is why a code is periodically changed by the users. There are rules in worrying out the permutations and combinations of letters in most codes, for human ingenuity seems to run in certain channels, and a man who has been a long time at the business gets surprisingly clever at it. You begin by finding out a little bit, and then empirically building up the rules of decoding, till in a week or two you get the whole thing. Then, when you are happily engaged in reading enemy messages, the code is changed suddenly, and you have to start again from the beginning. . . . You can make a code, of course, that it is simply impossible to read except by accident—the key to which is a page of some book, for example—but fortunately that kind is not of much general use.

"Well, we got on pretty well with the codes, and read the intercepted enemy messages, cables and wireless, with considerable ease and precision. It was mostly diplomatic stuff, and not very important. The more valuable stuff was in cypher, and that was another pair of shoes. With a code you can build up the interpretation by degrees, but with a cypher you either know it or you don't—there are no half-way houses. A cypher, since it deals with numbers, is a horrible field for mathematical ingenuity. Once you have written out the letters of a message in numerals there are many means by which you can lock it and double-lock it. The two main devices, as you know, are transposition and substitution, and there is no limit to the ways one or other or both can be used. There is nothing to prevent a cypher having a double meaning, produced by two different methods, and, as a practical question, you have to decide which meaning is intended. By way of an extra complication, too, the message, when de-cyphered, may turn out to be itself in a difficult code. I can tell you our job wasn't exactly a rest cure."

Burminster, looking puzzled, inquired as to the locking of cyphers.

"It would take too long to explain. Roughly, you write out a message horizontally in numerals; then you pour it into vertical columns, the number and order of which are determined by a keyword; then you write out the contents of the columns horizontally, following the lines across. To unlock it you have to have the key word, so as to put it back into the vertical columns, and then into the original horizontal form."

Burminster cried out like one in pain. "It can't be done. Don't tell me that any human brain could solve such an acrostic."

"It was frequently done," said Pugh.

"By you?"

"Lord bless you, not by me. I can't do a simple crossword puzzle. By my people."

"Give me the trenches," said Burminster in a hollow voice. "Give me the trenches any day. Do you seriously mean to tell me that you could sit down before a muddle of numbers and travel back the way they had been muddled to an original that made sense?"

"I couldn't, but Channell could—in most cases. You see, we didn't begin entirely in the dark. We already knew the kind of intricacies that the enemy favoured, and the way we worked was by trying a variety of clues till we hit on the right one."

"Well, I'm blessed! Go on about your man Channell."

"This isn't Channell's story," said Pugh. "He only comes into it accidentally. . . . There was one cypher which always defeated us, a cypher used between the German General Staff and their forces in the East. It was a locked cypher, and Channell had given more time to it than to any dozen of the others, for it put him on his mettle. But he confessed himself absolutely beaten. He wouldn't admit that it was insoluble, but he declared that he would need a bit of real luck to solve it. I asked him what kind of luck, and he said a mistake and a repetition. That, he said, might give him a chance of establishing equations.

"We called this particular cypher 'PY,' and we hated it poisonously. We felt like pygmies battering at the base of a high stone tower. Dislike of the thing soon became dislike of the man who had conceived it. Channell and I used to—I won't say amuse, for it was too dashed serious—but torment ourselves by trying to picture the fellow who owned the brain that was responsible for PY. We had a pretty complete dossier of the German Intelligence Staff, but of course we couldn't know who was responsible for this particular cypher. We knew no more than his code name, Reinmar, with which he signed the simpler messages to the East, and Channell, who was a romantic little chap for all his science, had got it into his head that it was a woman. He used to describe her to me as if he had seen her—a she-devil, young, beautiful, with a much-painted white face, and eyes like a cobra's. I fancy he read a rather low class of novel in his off-time.

"My picture was different. At first I thought of the histrionic type of scientist, the 'ruthless brain' type, with a high forehead and a jaw puckered like a chimpanzee. But that didn't seem to work, and I settled on a picture of a first-class *Generalstaboffizier*, as handsome as Falkenhayn, trained to the last decimal, absolutely passionless, with a mind that worked with the relentless precision of a fine machine. We all of us at the time suffered from the bogy of this kind of German, and, when things were going badly, as in March '18, I couldn't sleep for hating him. The infernal fellow was so water-tight and armour-plated, a Goliath who scorned the pebbles from our feeble slings.

"Well, to make a long story short, there came a moment in September '18 when PY was about the most important thing in the world. It mattered enormously what Germany was doing in Syria, and we knew that it was all in PY. Every morning a pile of the intercepted German wireless messages lay on Channell's table, which were as meaningless to him as a child's scrawl. I was prodded by my chiefs and in turn I prodded Channell. We had a week to find the key to the cypher, after which things must go on without us, and if we had failed to make anything of it in eighteen months of quiet work, it didn't seem likely that we would succeed in seven feverish days. Channell nearly went off his head with overwork and anxiety. I used to visit his dingy little room and find him fairly grizzled and shrunken with fatigue.

"This isn't a story about him, though there is a good story which I may tell you another time. As a matter of fact we won on the post. PY made a mistake. One morning we got a long message dated *en clair*, then a very short message, and then a third message almost the same as the first. The second must mean 'Your message of today's date unintelligible, please repeat,' the regular formula. This gave us a translation of a bit of the cypher. Even that would not have brought it out, and for twelve hours Channell was on the verge of lunacy, till it occurred to him that Reinmar might have signed the long message with his name, as we used to do sometimes in cases of extreme urgency. He was right, and, within three hours of the last moment Operations could give us, we had the whole thing pat. As I have said, that is a story worth telling, but it is not this one.

"We both finished the war too tired to think of much except that the darned thing was over. But Reinmar had been so long our unseen but constantly pictured opponent that we kept up a certain interest in him. We would like to have seen how he took the licking, for he must have known that we had licked him. Mostly when you lick a man at a game you rather like him, but I didn't like Reinmar. In fact I made him a sort of compost of everything I had ever disliked in a German. Channell stuck to his she-devil theory, but I was pretty certain that he was a youngish man with an intellectual arrogance which his country's débâcle would in no way lessen. He

would never acknowledge defeat. It was highly improbable that I should ever find out who he was, but I felt that if I did, and met him face to face, my dislike would be abundantly justified.

"As you know, for a year or two after the Armistice I was a pretty sick man. Most of us were. We hadn't the fillip of getting back to civilised comforts, like the men in the trenches. We had always been comfortable enough in body, but our minds were fagged out, and there is no easy cure for that. My digestion went nobly to pieces, and I endured a miserable space of lying in bed and living on milk and olive-oil. After that I went back to work, but the darned thing always returned, and every leech had a different regime to advise. I tried them all—dry meals, a snack every two hours, lemon juice, sour milk, starvation, knocking off tobacco—but nothing got me more than half-way out of the trough. I was a burden to myself and a nuisance to others, dragging my wing through life, with a constant pain in my tummy.

"More than one doctor advised an operation, but I was chary about that, for I had seen several of my friends operated on for the same mischief and left as sick as before. Then a man told me about a German fellow called Christoph, who was said to be very good at handling my trouble. The best hand at diagnosis in the world, my informant said—no fads—treated every case on its merits—a really original mind. Dr. Christoph had a modest Kurhaus at a place called Rosensee in the Sächischen Sweitz. By this time I was getting pretty desperate, so I packed a bag and set off for Rosensee.

"It was a quiet little town at the mouth of a narrow valley, tucked in under wooded hills, a clean fresh place with open channels of running water in the streets. There was a big church with an onion spire, a Catholic seminary, and a small tanning industry. The Kurhaus was half-way up a hill, and I felt better as soon as I saw my bedroom, with its bare scrubbed floors and its wide verandah looking up into a forest glade. I felt still better when I saw Dr. Christoph. He was

a small man with a grizzled beard, a high forehead, and a limp, rather like what I imagine the
Apostle Paul must have been. He looked wise,
as wise as an old owl. His English was atrocious,
but even when he found that I talked German
fairly well he didn't expand in speech. He would
deliver no opinion of any kind until he had had
me at least a week under observation; but somehow I felt comforted, for I concluded that a first-
class brain had got to work on me.

"The other patients were mostly Germans
with a sprinkling of Spaniards, but to my delight
I found Channell. He also had been having
a thin time since we parted. Nerves were his
trouble—general nervous debility and perpetual insomnia, and his college had given him six
months' leave of absence to try to get well. The
poor chap was as lean as a sparrow, and he had
the large dull eyes and the dry lips of the sleepless. He had arrived a week before me, and like
me was under observation. But his vetting was
different from mine, for he was a mental case,
and Dr. Christoph used to devote hours to trying to unriddle his nervous tangles. 'He is a good
man for a German,' said Channell, 'but he is on
the wrong tack. There's nothing wrong with my
mind. I wish he'd stick to violet rays and massage, instead of asking me silly questions about
my great-grandmother.'

"Channell and I used to go for invalidish
walks in the woods and we naturally talked about
the years we had worked together. He was living mainly in the past, for the war had been the
great thing in his life, and his professorial duties
seemed trivial by comparison. As we tramped
among the withered bracken and heather his
mind was always harking back to the dingy little
room where he had smoked cheap cigarettes and
worked fourteen hours out of the twenty-four.
In particular he was as eagerly curious about our
old antagonist, Reinmar, as he had been in 1918.
He was more positive than ever that she was a
woman, and I believe that one of the reasons that
had induced him to try a cure in Germany was
a vague hope that he might get on her track. I
had almost forgotten about the thing, and I was

amused by Channell in the part of the untiring
sleuth-hound.

"'You won't find her in the Kurhaus,' I said.
'Perhaps she is in some old Schloss in the neigh-
bourhood, waiting for you like the Sleeping
Beauty.'

"'I'm serious,' he said plaintively. 'It is purely
a matter of intellectual curiosity, but I confess I
would give a great deal to see her face to face.
After I leave here, I thought of going to Berlin to
make some inquiries. But I'm handicapped for
I know nobody and I have no credentials. Why
don't you, who have a large acquaintance and far
more authority, take the thing up?'

"I told him that my interest in the matter
had flagged and that I wasn't keen on digging
into the past, but I promised to give him a line
to our Military Attaché if he thought of going to
Berlin. I rather discouraged him from letting his
mind dwell too much on events in the War. I said
that he ought to try to bolt the door on all that
had contributed to his present breakdown.

"'That is not Dr. Christoph's opinion,' he
said emphatically. 'He encourages me to talk
about it. You see, with me it is a purely intellectual interest. I have no emotion in the matter.
I feel quite friendly towards Reinmar, whoever
she may be. It is, if you like, a piece of romance.
I haven't had so many romantic events in my life
that I want to forget this.'

"'Have you told Dr. Christoph about Reinmar?' I asked.

"'Yes,' he said, 'and he was mildly interested.
You know the way he looks at you with his solemn grey eyes. I doubt if he quite understood
what I meant, for a little provincial doctor, even
though he is a genius in his own line, is not likely
to know much about the ways of the Great General Staff. . . . I had to tell him, for I have to tell
him all my dreams, and lately I have taken to
dreaming about Reinmar.'

"'What's she like?' I asked.

"'Oh, a most remarkable figure. Very beautiful, but uncanny. She has long fair hair down to
her knees.'

"Of course I laughed. 'You're mixing her up

with the Valkyries,' I said. 'Lord, it would be an awkward business if you met that she-dragon in the flesh.'

"But he was quite solemn about it, and declared that his waking picture of her was not in the least like his dreams. He rather agreed with my nonsense about the old Schloss. He thought that she was probably some penniless grandee, living solitary in a moated grange, with nothing now to exercise her marvellous brain on, and eating her heart out with regret and shame. He drew so attractive a character of her that I began to think that Channell was in love with a being of his own creation, till he ended with, 'But all the same she's utterly damnable. She must be, you know.'

"After a fortnight I began to feel a different man. Dr. Christoph thought that he had got on the track of the mischief, and certainly, with his deep massage and a few simple drugs, I had more internal comfort than I had known for three years. He was so pleased with my progress that he refused to treat me as an invalid. He encouraged me to take long walks into the hills, and presently he arranged for me to go out roebuck-shooting with some of the local junkers.

"I used to start before daybreak on the chilly November mornings and drive to the top of one of the ridges, where I would meet a collection of sportsmen and beaters, shepherded by a fellow in a green uniform. We lined out along the ridge, and the beaters, assisted by a marvellous collection of dogs, including the sporting dachshund, drove the roe towards us. It wasn't very cleverly managed, for the deer generally broke back, and it was chilly waiting in the first hours with a powdering of snow on the ground and the fir boughs heavy with frost crystals. But later, when the sun grew stronger, it was a very pleasant mode of spending a day. There was not much of a bag, but whenever a roe or a capercailzie fell all the guns would assemble and drink little glasses of *Kirschwasser*. I had been lent a rifle, one of those appalling contraptions which are double-barrelled shot-guns and rifles in one, and to transpose from one form to the other requires

a mathematical calculation. The rifle had a hair trigger too, and when I first used it I was nearly the death of a respectable Saxon peasant.

"We all ate our midday meal together and in the evening, before going home, we had coffee and cakes in one or other of the farms. The party was an odd mixture, big farmers and small squires, an hotel-keeper or two, a local doctor, and a couple of lawyers from the town. At first they were a little shy of me, but presently they thawed, and after the first day we were good friends. They spoke quite frankly about the war, in which every one of them had had a share, and with a great deal of dignity and good sense.

"I learned to walk in Sikkim, and the little Saxon hills seemed to me inconsiderable. But they were too much for most of the guns, and instead of going straight up or down a slope they always chose a circuit, which gave them an easy gradient. One evening, when we were separating as usual, the beaters taking a short cut and the guns a circuit, I felt that I wanted exercise, so I raced the beaters downhill, beat them soundly, and had the better part of an hour to wait for my companions, before we adjourned to the farm for refreshment. The beaters must have talked about my pace, for as we walked away one of the guns, a lawyer called Meissen, asked me why I was visiting Rosensee at a time of year when few foreigners came. I said I was staying with Dr. Christoph.

"'Is he then a private friend of yours?' he asked.

"I told him No, that I had come to his Kurhaus for treatment, being sick. His eyes expressed polite scepticism. He was not prepared to regard as an invalid a man who went down a hill like an avalanche.

"But, as we walked in the frosty dusk, he was led to speak of Dr. Christoph, of whom he had no personal knowledge, and I learned how little honour a prophet may have in his own country. Rosensee scarcely knew him, except as a doctor who had an inexplicable attraction for foreign patients. Meissen was curious about his methods and the exact diseases in which he specialised.

'Perhaps he may yet save me a journey to Homburg?' he laughed. 'It is well to have a skilled physician at one's doorstep. The doctor is something of a hermit, and except for his patients does not appear to welcome his kind. Yet he is a good man, beyond doubt, and there are those who say that in the war he was a hero.'

"This surprised me, for I could not imagine Dr. Christoph in any fighting capacity, apart from the fact that he must have been too old. I thought that Meissen might refer to work in the base hospitals. But he was positive; Dr. Christoph had been in the trenches; the limping leg was a war wound.

"I had had very little talk with the doctor, owing to my case being free from nervous complications. He would say a word to me morning and evening about my diet, and pass the time of day when we met, but it was not till the very eve of my departure that we had anything like a real conversation. He sent a message that he wanted to see me for not less than one hour, and he arrived with a batch of notes from which he delivered a kind of lecture on my case. Then I realised what an immense amount of care and solid thought he had expended on me. He had decided that his diagnosis was right—my rapid improvement suggested that—but it was necessary for some time to observe a simple regime, and to keep an eye on certain symptoms. So he took a sheet of notepaper from the table and in his small precise hand wrote down for me a few plain commandments.

"There was something about him, the honest eyes, the mouth which looked as if it had been often compressed in suffering, the air of grave goodwill, which I found curiously attractive. I wished that I had been a mental case like Channell, and had had more of his society. I detained him in talk, and he seemed not unwilling. By and by we drifted to the war and it turned out that Meissen was right.

"Dr. Christoph had gone as medical officer in November '14 to the Ypres Salient with a Saxon regiment, and had spent the winter there. In '15 he had been in Champagne, and

in the early months of '16 at Verdun, till he was invalided with rheumatic fever. That is to say, he had had about seventeen months of consecutive fighting in the worst areas with scarcely a holiday. A pretty good record for a frail little middle-aged man!

"His family was then at Stuttgart, his wife and one little boy. He took a long time to recover from the fever, and after that was put on home duty. 'Till the war was almost over,' he said, 'almost over, but not quite. There was just time for me to go back to the front and get my foolish leg hurt.' I must tell you that whenever he mentioned his war experience it was with a comical deprecating smile, as if he agreed with anyone who might think that gravity like this should have remained in bed.

"I assumed that this home duty was medical, until he said something about getting rusty in his professional work. Then it appeared that it had been some job connected with Intelligence. 'I am reputed to have a little talent for mathematics,' he said. 'No. I am no mathematical scholar, but, if you understand me, I have a certain mathematical aptitude. My mind has always moved happily among numbers. Therefore I was set to construct and to interpret cyphers, a strange interlude in the noise of war. I sat in a little room and excluded the world, and for a little I was happy.'

"He went on to speak of the enclave of peace in which he had found himself, and as I listened to his gentle monotonous voice, I had a sudden inspiration.

"I took a sheet of notepaper from the stand, scribbled the word *Reinmar* on it, and shoved it towards him. I had a notion, you see, that I might surprise him into helping Channell's researches.

"But it was I who got the big surprise. He stopped thunderstruck, as soon as his eye caught the word, blushed scarlet over every inch of face and bald forehead, seemed to have difficulty in swallowing, and then gasped. 'How did you know?'

"I hadn't known, and now that I did, the knowledge left me speechless. This was the loathly opposite for which Channell and I had nursed our hatred. When I came out of my stupefaction I found that he had recovered his balance and was speaking slowly and distinctly, as if he were making a formal confession.

"'You were among my opponents . . . that interests me deeply. . . . I often wondered. . . . You beat me in the end. You are aware of that?'

"I nodded. 'Only because you made a slip,' I said.

"'Yes, I made a slip. I was to blame—very gravely to blame for I let my private grief cloud my mind.'

"He seemed to hesitate, as if he were loath to stir something very tragic in his memory.

"'I think I will tell you,' he said at last. 'I have often wished—it is a childish wish—to justify my failure to those who profited by it. My chiefs understood, of course, but my opponents could not. In that month when I failed I was in deep sorrow. I had a little son—his name was Reinmar—you remember that I took that name for my code signature?'

"His eyes were looking beyond me into some vision of the past.

"'He was, as you say, my mascot. He was all my family, and I adored him. But in those days food was not plentiful. We were no worse off than many million Germans, but the child was frail. In the last summer of the war he developed phthisis due to malnutrition, and in September he died. Then I failed my country, for with him some virtue seemed to depart from my mind. You see, my work was, so to speak, his also, as my name was his, and when he left me he took my power with him. . . . So I stumbled. The rest is known to you.'

"He sat staring beyond me, so small and lonely, that I could have howled. I remember putting my hand on his shoulder, and stammering some platitude about being sorry. We sat quite still for a minute or two, and then I remembered Channell. Channell must have poured his views of Reinmar into Dr. Christoph's ear. I asked him if Channell knew.

"A flicker of a smile crossed his face.

"'Indeed no. And I will exact from you a promise never to breathe to him what I have told you. He is my patient, and I must first consider his case. At present he thinks that Reinmar is a wicked and beautiful lady whom he may some day meet. That is romance, and it is good for him to think so. . . . If he were told the truth, he would be pitiful, and in Herr Channell's condition it is important that he should not be vexed with such emotions as pity.'"

STACY AUMONIER

THE LARGELY FORGOTTEN Stacy Aumonier (1877–1928) had suc-
cess in several careers before his death from tuberculosis. Born in London, he
was a highly regarded landscape painter, his work being exhibited at the Royal
Academy. Unusually, he also was the subject of numerous works by other artists with several portraits of him (generally dressed in elegant evening clothes)
hanging in the National Portrait Gallery. He also was well known as an enter-
tainer, appearing at the Criterion and other distinguished theaters, and was
lauded for one-man shows that he wrote as well as performed. *The Observer*
noted "he could walk out alone before any audience, from the simplest to the
most sophisticated, and make it laugh or cry at will."

This remarkable skill on the stage translated well to the page, especially his
short stories. While his six novels are not particularly distinguished, many of
his nearly one hundred short stories were regarded as masterpieces by some of
his contemporaries, including the Nobel laureate John Galsworthy, who averred
that Aumonier was "one of the best short-story writers of all time" and that
he would "outlive all the writers of his day." James Hilton, the author of *Lost
Horizon, Goodbye, Mr. Chips, Random Harvest*, and other massive bestsellers,
selected Aumonier's "The Octave of Jealousy" as his favorite story of all time.

"Miss Bracegirdle Does Her Duty," collected in *Miss Bracegirdle and Others*
(1923), is probably his best-known story. A shy, conservative woman closes the
door to her room and sees a man on her bed, apparently asleep but actually dead.
Realizing she is in the wrong room, she seeks to escape but the door handle has
broken and she winds up hiding beneath his bed. It served as the basis for a short
film of the same title, released in 1926 with Janet Alexander starring as Milli-
cent Bracegirdle. It was made again in 1936 with Elsa Lanchester. Finally, it was
filmed as an episode on the third season of *Alfred Hitchcock Presents*, airing on
February 2, 1958, with Mildred Natwick as the unfortunate Miss Bracegirdle.

The 1940 motion picture *Spy for a Day* (also released as *The White Flower of
a Blameless Life*) was inspired by "A Source of Irritation," but largely reimag-
ined as a comedy, starring Douglas Wakefield, Paddy Browne, and Jack Allen.
It also was produced as an episode of *Studio 57* in 1958, with Joel Aldrich, John
Banner, and Helmut Dantine.

"A Source of Irritation" was originally published in the January 1918 issue
of *The Century Magazine;* it was first collected in *The Love-a-Duck and Other
Stories* (London, Hutchinson, 1921).

A SOURCE OF IRRITATION

STACY AUMONIER

TO LOOK AT old Sam Gates you would never suspect him of having nerves. His sixty-nine years of close application to the needs of the soil had given him a certain earthy stolidity. To observe him hoeing, or thinning out a broad field of turnips, hardly attracted one's attention, he seemed so much part and parcel of the whole scheme. He blended into the soil like a glorified swede. Nevertheless, the half-dozen people who claimed his acquaintance knew him to be a man who suffered from little moods of irritability.

And on this glorious morning a little incident annoyed him unreasonably. It concerned his niece Aggie. She was a plump girl with clear, blue eyes, and a face as round and inexpressive as the dumplings for which the county was famous. She came slowly across the long sweep of the downland and, putting down the bundle wrapped in a red handkerchief which contained his breakfast and dinner, she said:

"Well, Uncle, is there any noos?"

Now, this may not appear to the casual reader to be a remark likely to cause irritation, but it affected old Sam Gates as a very silly and unnecessary question. It was, moreover, the constant repetition of it which was beginning to anger him. He met his niece twice a day. In the morn-

ing she brought his bundle of food at seven, and when he passed his sister's cottage on the way home to tea at five she was invariably hanging about the gate, and she always said in the same voice:

"Well, Uncle, is there any noos?"

Noos! What noos should there be? For sixty-nine years he had never lived farther than five miles from Halvesham. For nearly sixty of those years he had bent his back above the soil. There were, indeed, historic occasions. Once, for instance, when he had married Annie Hachet. And there was the birth of his daughter. There was also a famous occasion when he had visited London. Once he had been to a flowershow at Market Roughborough. He either went or didn't go to church on Sundays. He had many interesting chats with Mr. James at the Cowman, and three years ago had sold a pig to Mrs. Way. But he couldn't always have interesting noos of this sort up his sleeve. Didn't the silly zany know that for the last three weeks he had been hoeing and thinning out turnips for Mr. Hodge on this very same field? What noos could there be?

He blinked at his niece, and didn't answer. She undid the parcel and said:

"Mrs. Goping's fowl got out again last night."

"Ah," he replied in a non-committal manner and began to munch his bread and bacon. His niece picked up the handkerchief and, humming to herself, walked back across the field.

It was a glorious morning, and a white sea mist added to the promise of a hot day. He sat there munching, thinking of nothing in particular, but gradually subsiding into a mood of placid content. He noticed the back of Aggie disappear in the distance. It was a mile to the cottage and a mile and a half to Halvesham. Silly things, girls. They were all alike. One had to make allowances. He dismissed her from his thoughts, and took a long swig of tea out of a bottle. Insects buzzed lazily. He tapped his pocket to assure himself that his pouch of shag was there, and then he continued munching. When he had finished, he lighted his pipe and stretched himself comfortably. He looked along the line of turnips he had thinned and then across the adjoining field of swedes, Silver streaks appeared on the sea below the mist. In some dim way he felt happy in his solitude amidst this sweeping immensity of earth and sea and sky.

And then something else came to irritate him: it was one of "these dratted airyplanes." "Airyplanes" were his pet aversion. He could find nothing to be said in their favor. Nasty, noisy, disfiguring things that seared the heavens and made the earth dangerous. And every day there seemed to be more and more of them. Of course "this old war" was responsible for a lot of them, he knew. The war was a "plaguy noosance." They were short-handed on the farm, beer and tobacco were dear, and Mrs. Steven's nephew had been and got wounded in the foot.

He turned his attention once more to the turnips; but an "airyplane" has an annoying genius for gripping one's attention. When it appears on the scene, however much we dislike it, it has a way of taking the stage-center. We cannot help constantly looking at it. And so it was with old Sam Gates. He spat on his hands and blinked up at the sky. And suddenly the aeroplane behaved in a very extraordinary manner. It was well over

the sea when it seemed to lurch drunkenly and skimmed the water. Then it shot up at a dangerous angle and zig-zagged. It started to go farther out, and then turned and made for the land. The engines were making a curious grating noise. It rose once more, and then suddenly dived downward, and came plump down right in the middle of Mr. Hodge's field of swedes.

And then, as if not content with this desecration, it ran along the ground, ripping and tearing up twenty-five yards of good swedes, and then came to a stop.

Old Sam Gates was in a terrible state. The aeroplane was more than a hundred yards away, but he waved his arms and called out:

"Hi, you there, you mustn't land in they swedes! They're Mister Hodge's."

The instant the aeroplane stopped, a man leaped out and gazed quickly round. He glanced at Sam Gates, and seemed uncertain whether to address him or whether to concentrate his attention on the flying-machine. The latter arrangement appeared to be his ultimate decision. He dived under the engine and became frantically busy. Sam had never seen any one work with such furious energy; but all the same it was not to be tolerated. It was disgraceful. Sam started out across the field, almost hurrying in his indignation. When he appeared within earshot of the aviator he cried out again:

"Hi! you mustn't rest your old airyplane here! You've kicked up all Mr. Hodge's swedes. A noice thing you've done!"

He was within five yards when suddenly the aviator turned and covered him with a revolver! And speaking in a sharp, staccato voice, he said:

"Old Grandfather, you must sit down. I am very much occupied. If you interfere or attempt to go away, I shoot you. So!"

Sam gazed at the horrid, glittering little barrel and gasped. Well, he never! To be threatened with murder when you're doing your duty in your employer's private property! But, still, perhaps the man was mad. A man must be more or less mad to go up in one of those crazy things.

And life was very sweet on that summer morning despite sixty-nine years. He sat down among the swedes.

The aviator was so busy with his cranks and machinery that he hardly deigned to pay him any attention except to keep the revolver handy. He worked feverishly, and Sam sat watching him. At the end of ten minutes he appeared to have solved his troubles with the machine, but he still seemed very scared. He kept on glancing around and out to sea. When his repairs were complete he straightened his back and wiped the perspiration from his brow. He was apparently on the point of springing back into the machine and going off when a sudden mood of facetiousness, caused by relief from the strain he had endured, came to him. He turned to old Sam and smiled, at the same time remarking:

"Well, old Grandfather, and now we shall be all right, isn't it?"

He came close up to Sam, and then suddenly started back.

"*Gott!*" he cried, "Paul Jouperts!"

Bewildered, Sam gazed at him, and the madman started talking to him in some foreign tongue. Sam shook his head.

"You no right," he remarked, "to come bargin' through they swedes of Mr. Hodge's."

And then the aviator behaved in a most peculiar manner. He came up and examined Sam's face very closely, and gave a sudden tug at his beard and hair, as if to see whether they were real or false.

"What is your name, old man?" he said.

"Sam Gates."

The aviator muttered some words that sounded something like "mare vudish," and then turned to his machine. He appeared to be dazed and in a great state of doubt. He fumbled with some cranks, but kept glancing at old Sam. At last he got into the car and strapped himself in. Then he stopped, and sat there deep in thought. At last he suddenly unstrapped himself and sprang out again and, approaching Sam, said very deliberately:

"Old Grandfather, I shall require you to accompany me."

Sam gasped.

"Eh!" he said. "What be talkin' about? 'Company? I got these 'ere loines o' turnips—I be already behoind—" The disgusting little revolver once more flashed before his eyes.

"There must be no discussion," came the voice. "It is necessary that you mount the seat of the car without delay. Otherwise I shoot you like the dog you are. So!"

Old Sam was hale and hearty. He had no desire to die so ignominiously. The pleasant smell of the Norfolk downland was in his nostrils; his foot was on his native heath. He mounted the seat of the car, contenting himself with a mutter:

"Well, that be a noice thing, I must say! Flyin' about the country with all they turnips on'y half thinned!"

He found himself strapped in. The aviator was in a fever of anxiety to get away. The engines made a ghastly splutter and noise. The thing started running along the ground. Suddenly it shot upward, giving the swedes a last contemptuous kick. At twenty minutes to eight that morning old Sam found himself being borne right up above his fields and out to sea! His breath came quickly. He was a little frightened.

"God forgive me!" he murmured.

The thing was so fantastic and sudden that his mind could not grasp it. He only felt in some vague way that he was going to die, and he struggled to attune his mind to the change. He offered up a mild prayer to God, Who, he felt, must be very near, somewhere up in these clouds. Automatically he thought of the vicar at Halvesham, and a certain sense of comfort came to him at the reflection that on the previous day he had taken a "cooking of runner beans" to God's representative in that village. He felt calmer after that, but the horrid machine seemed to go higher and higher. He could not turn in his seat and he could see nothing but sea and sky. Of course the man was mad, mad as a March hare. Of what earthly use could *he* be to any one? Besides, he had talked pure gibberish, and called him Paul something, when he had already told him that his name was Sam. The thing would fall down into the sea soon, and they would both be drowned. Well, well, he had almost reached three-score years and ten. He was protected by a screen, but it seemed very cold. What on earth would Mr. Hodge say? There was no one left to work the land but a fool of a boy named Billy Whitehead at Dene's Cross. On, on, on they went at a furious pace. His thoughts danced disconnectedly from incidents of his youth, conversations with the vicar, hearty meals in the open, a frock his sister wore on the day of the postman's wedding, the drone of psalm, the illness of some ewes belonging to Mr. Hodge. Everything seemed to be moving very rapidly, upsetting his sense of time. He felt outraged, and yet at moments there was something entrancing in the wild experience. He seemed to be living at an incredible pace. Perhaps he was really dead and on his way to the kingdom of God. Perhaps this was the way they took people.

After some indefinite period he suddenly caught sight of a long strip of land. Was this a foreign country, or were they returning? He had by this time lost all feeling of fear. He became interested and almost disappointed. The "airy-plane" was not such a fool as it looked. It was very wonderful to be right up in the sky like this. His dreams were suddenly disturbed by a fearful noise. He thought the machine was blown to pieces. It dived and ducked through the air, and things were bursting all around it and making an awful din, and then it went up higher and higher. After a while these noises ceased, and he felt the machine gliding downward. They were really right above solid land—trees, fields, streams, and white villages. Down, down, down they glided. This was a foreign country. There were straight avenues of poplars and canals. This was not Halvesham. He felt the thing glide gently and bump into a field. Some men ran forward and approached them, and the mad aviator called out to them. They were mostly fat men in gray uniforms, and they all spoke this foreign gibberish. Some one came and unstrapped him. He was very stiff and could hardly move. An exceptionally gross-looking man punched him in the ribs and roared with laughter. They all stood round and laughed at him, while the mad aviator talked to them and kept pointing at him. Then he said:

"Old Grandfather, you must come with me."

He was led to an iron-roofed building and shut in a little room. There were guards outside with fixed bayonets. After a while the mad aviator appeared again, accompanied by two soldiers. He beckoned him to follow. They marched through a quadrangle and entered another building. They went straight into an office where a very important-looking man, covered with medals, sat in an easy-chair. There was a lot of saluting and clicking of heels. The aviator pointed at Sam and said something, and the man with the medals started at sight of him, and then came up and spoke to him in English.

"What is your name? Where do you come from? Your age? The name and birthplace of your parents?"

He seemed intensely interested, and also pulled his hair and beard to see if they came off. So well and naturally did he and the aviator speak English that after a voluble examination they drew apart, and continued the conversation in that language. And the extraordinary conversation was of this nature:

"It is a most remarkable resemblance," said the man with medals. "*Unglaublich!* But what do you want me to do with him, Hausemann?"

"The idea came to me suddenly, Excellency," replied the aviator, "and you may consider it worthless. It is just this. The resemblance is so amazing. Paul Jouperts has given us more valuable information than any one at present in our service, and the English know that. There is an award of five thousand francs on his head. Twice they have captured him, and each time he escaped. All the company commanders and their staff have his photograph. He is a serious thorn in their flesh."

"Well?" replied the man with the medals.

The aviator whispered confidentially:

"Suppose, your Excellency, that they found the dead body of Paul Jouperts?"

"Well?" replied the big man.

"My suggestion is this. Tomorrow, as you know, the English are attacking Hill 701, which for tactical reasons we have decided to evacuate. If after the attack they find the dead body of Paul Jouperts in, say, the second line, they will take no further trouble in the matter. You know their lack of thoroughness. Pardon me, I was two years at Oxford University. And consequently Paul Jouperts will be able to prosecute his labors undisturbed."

The man with the medals twirled his mustache and looked thoughtfully at his colleague.

"Where is Paul at the moment?" he asked.

"He is acting as a gardener at the Convent of St. Eloise, at Mailleton-en-haut, which, as you know, is one hundred meters from the headquarters of the British central army staff."

The man with the medals took two or three rapid turns up and down the room, then he said:

"Your plan is excellent, Hausemann. The only point of difficulty is that the attack started this morning."

"This morning?" exclaimed the other.

"Yes; the English attacked unexpectedly at dawn. We have already evacuated the first line. We shall evacuate the second line at eleven-fifty. It is now ten-fifteen. There may be just time."

He looked suddenly at old Sam in the way that a butcher might look at a prize heifer at an agricultural show and remarked casually:

"Yes, it is a remarkable resemblance. It seems a pity not to—do something with it."

Then, speaking in German, he added:

"It is worth trying. And if it succeeds the higher authorities shall hear of your lucky accident and inspiration, Herr Hausemann. Instruct *Oberleutnant* Schultz to send the old fool by two orderlies to the east extremity of Trench 38. Keep him there till the order of evacuation is given, then shoot him, but don't disfigure him, and lay him out face upward."

The aviator saluted and withdrew, accompanied by his victim. Old Sam had not understood the latter part of the conversation, and he did not catch quite all that was said in English; but he felt that somehow things were not becoming too promising, and it was time to assert himself. So he remarked when they got outside:

"Now, look 'ee 'ere, Mister, when am I goin' to get back to my turnips?"

And the aviator replied, with a pleasant smile:

"Do not be disturbed, old Grandfather. You shall get back to the soil quite soon."

In a few moments he found himself in a large gray car, accompanied by four soldiers. The aviator left him. The country was barren and horrible, full of great pits and rents, and he could hear the roar of the artillery and the shriek of shells. Overhead, aeroplanes were buzzing angrily. He seemed to be suddenly transported from the kingdom of God to the pit of darkness. He wondered whether the vicar had enjoyed the runner beans. He could not imagine runner beans growing here; runner beans, aye, or anything else. If this was a foreign country, give him dear old England!

Gr-r-r! bang! Something exploded just at the rear of the car. The soldiers ducked, and one of them pushed him in the stomach and swore.

"An ugly-looking lout," he thought. "If I wor twenty years younger, I'd give him a punch in the eye that 'u'd make him sit up."

The car came to a halt by a broken wall. The party hurried out and dived behind a mound. He was pulled down a kind of shaft, and found himself in a room buried right underground, where three officers were drinking and smoking. The soldiers saluted and handed them a type-written despatch. The officers looked at him drunkenly, and one came up and pulled his beard and spat in his face and called him "an old English swine." He then shouted out some instructions to the soldiers, and they led him out into the narrow trench. One walked behind him, and occasionally prodded him with the butt-end of a gun. The trenches were half full of water and reeked of gases, powder, and decaying matter. Shells were constantly bursting overhead, and in places the trenches had crumbled and were nearly blocked up. They stumbled on, sometimes falling, sometimes dodging moving masses, and occasionally crawling over the dead bodies of men. At last they reached a deserted-looking trench, and one of the soldiers pushed him into the corner of it and growled something, and then disappeared round the angle. Old Sam was exhausted. He leaned panting against the mud wall, expecting every minute to be blown to pieces by one of those infernal things that seemed to be getting more and more insistent. The din went on for nearly twenty minutes, and he was alone in the trench. He fancied he heard a whistle amidst the din. Suddenly one of the soldiers who had accompanied him came stealthily round the corner, and there was a look in his eye old Sam did not like. When he was within five yards the soldier raised his rifle and pointed it at Sam's body. Some instinct impelled the old man at that instant to throw himself forward on his face. As he did so he was aware of a terrible explosion, and he had just time to observe the soldier falling in a heap near him, and then he lost consciousness.

His consciousness appeared to return to him with a snap. He was lying on a plank in a building, and he heard some one say:

"I believe the old boy's English."

He looked round. There were a lot of men lying there, and others in khaki and white overalls were busy among them. He sat up, rubbed his head, and said:

"Hi, Mister, where be I now?"

Some one laughed, and a young man came up and said:

"Well, old man, you were very nearly in hell. Who the devil are you?"

Some one came up, and two of them were discussing him. One of them said:

"He's quite all right. He was only knocked out. Better take him in to the colonel. He may be a spy."

The other came up, touched his shoulder, and remarked:

"Can you walk, Uncle?"

He replied:

"Aye, I can walk all roight."

"That's an old sport!"

The young man took his arm and helped him out of the room into a courtyard. They entered another room where an elderly, kind-faced officer was seated at a desk. The officer looked up and exclaimed:

"Good God! Bradshaw, do you know who you've got there?"

The younger one said:

"No. Who, sir?"

"It's Paul Jouperts!" exclaimed the colonel.

"Paul Jouperts! Great Scott!"

The older officer addressed himself to Sam. He said:

"Well, we've got you once more, Paul. We shall have to be a little more careful this time."

The young officer said:

"Shall I detail a squad, sir?"

"We can't shoot him without a courtmartial," replied the kind-faced senior.

Then Sam interpolated:

"Look 'ee 'ere, sir, I'm fair' sick of all this. My name bean't Paul. My name's Sam. I was a-thinnin' a loine o' turnips—"

Both officers burst out laughing, and the younger one said:

"Good! damn good! Isn't it amazing, sir, the way they not only learn the language, but even take the trouble to learn a dialect!"

The older man busied himself with some papers.

"Well, Sam," he remarked, "you shall be given a chance to prove your identity. Our methods are less drastic than those of your *Boche* masters. What part of England are you supposed to come from? Let's see how much you can bluff us with your topographical knowledge."

"I was a-thinnin' a loine o' turnips this mornin' at 'alf-past seven on Mr. Hodge's farm at Halvesham when one o' these 'ere airyplanes came down among the swedes. I tells 'e to get clear o' that, when the feller what gets out o' the car 'e drahs a revowlver and 'e says, 'you must 'company I—'"

"Yes, yes," interrupted the senior officer, "that's all very good. Now tell me—where is Halvesham? What is the name of the local vicar? I'm sure you'd know that."

Old Sam rubbed his chin.

"I sits under the Reverend David Pryce, Mister, and a good, God-fearin' man he be. I took him a cookin' o' runner beans on'y yesterday. I works for Mr. Hodge, what owns Greenway Manor and 'as a stud-farm at Newmarket, they say."

"Charles Hodge?" asked the young officer.

"Aye, Charlie Hodge. You write and ask un if he knows old Sam Gates."

The two officers looked at each other, and the older one looked at Sam more closely.

"It's very extraordinary," he remarked.

"Everybody knows Charlie Hodge," added the younger officer.

It was at that moment that a wave of genius swept over old Sam. He put his hand to his head and suddenly jerked out:

"What's more, I can tell 'ee where this yere Paul is. He's actin' a gardener in a convent—" He puckered up his brows, fumbled with his hat, and then got out, "Mighteno."

The older officer gasped.

"Mailleton-en-haut! Good God! what makes you say that, old man?"

Sam tried to give an account of his experience and the things he had heard said by the German officers; but he was getting tired, and he broke off in the middle to say:

"Ye haven't a bite o' somethin' to eat, I suppose, Mister; or a glass o' beer? I usually 'as my dinner at twelve o'clock."

Both the officers laughed, and the older said:

"Get him some food, Bradshaw, and a bottle of beer from the mess. We'll keep this old man here. He interests me."

While the younger man was doing this, the chief pressed a button and summoned another junior officer.

"Gateshead," he remarked, "ring up the G.H.Q. and instruct them to arrest the gardener in that convent at the top of the hill and then to report."

The officer saluted and went out, and in a few minutes a tray of hot food and a large bottle of beer were brought to the old man, and he was left alone in the corner of the room to negotiate his welcome compensation. And in the execution he did himself and his country credit. In the meanwhile the officers were very busy. People were coming and going and examining maps, and telephone bells were ringing furiously. They did not disturb old Sam's gastric operations. He cleaned up the mess tins and finished the last drop of beer. The senior officer found time to offer him a cigarette, but he replied:

"Thank 'ee kindly, sir, but I'd rather smoke my pipe."

The colonel smiled and said:

"Oh, all right; smoke away."

He lighted up, and the fumes of the shag permeated the room. Someone opened another window, and the young officer who had addressed him at first suddenly looked at him and exclaimed:

"Innocent, by God! You couldn't get shag like that anywhere but in Norfolk."

It must have been an hour later when another officer entered and saluted.

"Message from the G.H.Q., sir," he said.

"Well?"

"They have arrested the gardener at the convent of St. Eloise, and they have every reason to believe that he is the notorious Paul Jouperts."

The colonel stood up, and his eyes beamed. He came over to old Sam and shook his hand.

"Mr. Gates," he said, "you are an old brick. You will probably hear more of this. You have probably been the means of delivering something very useful into our hands. Your own honor is vindicated. A loving Government will probably award you five shillings or a Victoria Cross or something of that sort. In the meantime, what can I do for you?"

Old Sam scratched his chin.

"I want to get back 'ome," he said.

"Well, even that might be arranged."

"I want to get back 'ome in toime for tea."

"What time do you have tea?"

"Foive o'clock or thereabouts."

"I see."

A kindly smile came into the eyes of the colonel. He turned to another officer standing by the table and said:

"Raikes, is any one going across this afternoon with despatches?"

"Yes, sir," replied the other officer. "Commander Jennings is leaving at three o'clock."

"You might ask him if he could see me."

Within ten minutes, a young man in a flight-commander's uniform entered.

"Ah, Jennings," said the colonel, "here is a little affair which concerns the honor of the British army. My friend here, Sam Gates, has come over from Halvesham, in Norfolk, in order to give us valuable information. I have promised him that he shall get home to tea at five o'clock. Can you take a passenger?"

The young man threw back his head and laughed.

"Lord!" he exclaimed, "what an old sport! Yes, I expect I can manage it. Where is the God-forsaken place?"

A large ordnance-map of Norfolk (which had been captured from a German officer) was produced, and the young man studied it closely.

At three o'clock precisely old Sam, finding himself something of a hero and quite glad to escape from the embarrassment which the position entailed upon him, once more sped skyward in a "dratted airyplane."

At twenty minutes to five he landed once more among Mr. Hodge's swedes. The breezy young airman shook hands with him and departed inland. Old Sam sat down and surveyed the familiar field of turnips.

"A noice thing, I must say!" he muttered to himself as he looked along the lines of unthinned turnips. He still had twenty minutes, and so he went slowly along and completed a line which he had begun in the morning. He then deliberately packed up his dinner-things and his tools and started out for home.

As he came round the corner of Stillway's meadow and the cottage came in view, his niece stepped out of the copse with a basket on her arm.

"Well, Uncle," she said, "is there any noos?"

It was then that old Sam really lost his temper.

"Noos!" he said. "Noos! Drat the girl! What noos should there be? Sixty-nine year' I live in these 'ere parts, hoein' and weedin' and thinnin', and mindin' Charlie Hodge's sheep. Am I one o' these 'ere storybook folk havin' noos 'appen to me all the time? Ain't it enough, ye silly, dab-faced zany, to earn enough to buy a bite o' some'at to eat and a glass o' beer and a place to rest a's head o' night without always wantin' noos, noos, noos! I tell 'ee it's this that leads 'ee to 'alf the troubles in the world. Devil take the noos!"

And turning his back on her, he went fuming up the hill.

A PATRIOT

JOHN GALSWORTHY

HIS REPUTATION may have diminished some after his death, but John Galsworthy's (1867–1933) place in the history of English literature is assured. After a short story collection and three immature novels were published under the pen name John Sinjohn between 1897 and 1901, he had learned his craft and began to release books under his own name, which, most significantly, illustrated his view of life. Patrician by birth and education, he was nonetheless aware of and sympathetic to the poor and victims of cruelty and injustice, a philosophy evident in all his work.

In 1903 he began to write the first volume of what became known as "The Forsyte Saga." *The Man of Property* (1906) introduced his most fully developed character, Soames Forsyte. The novels and stories about the Forsytes showed Galsworthy's contempt for the privileged and propertied, who carried their unthinking distaste for the underclasses so comfortably.

It was as a playwright that Galsworthy first achieved success, beginning with *The Silver Box* (1906), which showed the different ways that justice was meted out to the rich and the poor. *Strife* (1909) brought the challenges of the new industrial age out of the realm of statistics to its effect on individuals. *Justice* (1910) depicted the horrors of prison life so powerfully that it impelled several reforms.

The immeasurable success of "The Forsyte Saga" resulted in the offer of a knighthood, which he declined, declaring that a writer's reward was the writing itself. He did accept the Order of Merit in 1929, often regarded as the greatest of British honors. In 1932, the Nobel Prize for Literature was awarded to him but he was too ill to attend the ceremony and he died seven weeks later. The fame and success of the three major novels in "The Forsyte Saga," along with the short stories and cameo appearances of members of the Forsyte family in other works, did not outlast Galsworthy's life until Granada Television produced a miniseries that was shown on America's PBS stations in 2002–2003. *The Forsyte Saga* starred Damian Lewis as Soames, Rupert Graves as Jolyon Forsyte, and Gina McKee as Irene Forsyte. Emmy-winning, the ten-part drama became must-watch television and was once ranked as the second most popular program in the history of *Masterpiece Theater.* Galsworthy's series has also served as the basis for *That*

Forsyte Woman (1949), which starred Errol Flynn, Greer Garson, Walter Pidgeon, and Robert Young, and for a 1967 BBC twenty-six-episode series that starred Eric Porter, Margaret Tyzack, Nyree Dawn Porter, and Kenneth More.

"A Patriot" was originally published in *Forsytes, Pendyces and Others* (London, William Heinemann, 1935).

A PATRIOT

JOHN GALSWORTHY

THE OTHER DAY I was told a true story, which I remember vaguely hearing or reading about during the war, but which is worth retelling for those who missed it, for it has certain valuable ironic implications and a sort of grandeur. it concerns one of those beings who, when they spy upon us, are known by that word of three letters, as offensive as any in the language, and when they spy for us are dignified by the expression "Secret Service," and looked on as heroes of at least second water.

You will recollect that when the war broke out, the fifteen hundred persons engaged in supplying Germany with information, mainly trivial and mostly erroneous, concerning our condition and arrangements, were all known by the authorities and were put out of action at a single swoop. From that moment there was not one discovered case of espionage by spies already resident in England when war was declared. There were, however, a few and, I am told, unimportant discovered cases of espionage by persons who developed the practice or went into England for the purpose, during the war. This story concerns one of the latter.

In August 1914 there was living in America a business man of German birth and American citizenship, called—let us say, for it was not his name—Lichtfelder, who had once been an officer in the German Army; a man of about fifty, of square and still military appearance, with rather short stiff hair, a straight back to his head, and a patriotic conscience too strong for his American citizenship. It was not long then before an American called Lightfield landed in Genoa and emerged as Lichtfelder at the German headquarters of his old regiment, offering his services.

"No," they said to him, "you are no longer a young and active man, and you are an American citizen. We are very disappointed with our Secret Service in England; something seems to have gone wrong. You can be of much greater service to the Fatherland if, having learned our codes, you will go to England as an American citizen and send us all the information you can acquire."

Lichtfelder's soul was with his old regiment; but, being a patriot, he consented. During the next two months he made himself acquainted with all the tricks of his new trade, took ship again at Genoa, and reappeared as Lightfield in the United States. Soon after this he sailed for

Liverpool, well stocked with business addresses and samples, and supplied with his legitimate American passport in his own American name.

He spent the first day of his "Secret Service" wandering about the docks of a town which, in his view—if not in that of other people—was a naval station of importance; he also noted carefully the half-militarized appearance of the khaki figures in the streets; and in the evening he penned a business letter to a gentleman in Rotterdam, between the lines of which, devoted to the more enlightened forms of—shall we say?—plumbing, he wrote down in invisible ink all he had seen—such and such ships arrived or about to sail; such and such "khaki" drilling or wandering about the streets; all of which had importance in his view, if not in fact. He ended with the words: "Morgens Dublin Lichtfelder," and posted the letter.

Now, unfortunately for this poor but simple patriot, there was a young lady in the General Post Office who was spending her days in opening all letters with suspected foreign addresses, and submitting them to the test for invisible ink. To her joy—for she was weary at the dearth of that useful commodity—between the lines of this commercial screed, which purported to be concerned with the refinements of plumbing, out sprang the guilty ink. To a certain Department were telephoned the incautious "Morgens Dublin Lichtfelder." Now, no alien in those days was suffered to leave for Ireland save through a bottle-neck at Holyhead. To the bottle-neck then went the message: "Did man called Lichtfelder travel yesterday to Dublin?" The answer came quickly: "American called Lightfield went Dublin yesterday returned last night, is now on train for Euston." At Euston our patriot, after precisely three days of secret service, was arrested, and lodged wherever they were then lodged.

"I am," he said, "an American citizen called Lightfield."

"That," said the British Cabinet, not without disagreement, "makes a difference. You shall be tried by ordinary process of law, and defended by counsel chosen by the American Embassy at our expense, instead of by court martial."

Speedily—for in those days the law's delays were short—the American citizen called Lightfield, alias Lichtfelder, was put on his trial for supplying information to the enemy; and for three days, at the Government's expense, a certain eminent counsel gave the utmost of his wits to preparing his defense. But a certain great advocate, whose business it was to prosecute, had given the utmost of his wits to considering with what question he should open his cross-examination, since it is well known how important is the first question; and there had come to him an inspiration.

"Mr. Lichtfelder," he said, fixedly regarding that upright figure in the dock, "tell me: have you not been an officer in the German Army?"

The hands of the American citizen went to his sides, and his figure stiffened. For hours he had been telling the Court how entirely concerned he was with business, giving his references, showing his samples, explaining that—as for the lines in invisible ink in this letter, which he admitted sending—well, it was simply that he had met a Dutch journalist on board the ship coming out, who had said to him: "You know, we can get no news at all, we neutrals—do send us *something*—not, of course, harmful to England, but *something* we can say." And he had sent it. Was it harmful? It was nothing but trifles he had sent. And now, at that first question, he was standing suddenly a little more erect, and—silent.

And the great advocate said:

"I won't press you now, Mr. Lichtfelder: we will go on to other matters. But I should like you to think that question over, because it is not only the first question that I ask you—it will also be the last."

And the Court adjourned, the cross-examination not yet over, with that question not yet asked again.

In the early morning of the following day, when the warder went to the cell of Lichtfelder, there, by his muffler, dangled his body from the grating. Beneath the dead feet the cell Bible had been kicked away; but since, with the stretching of the muffler, those feet had still been able to rest on the ground, the patriot had drawn them up, until he was choked to death. He had waited till the dawn, for on the cell slate was written this:

I am a soldier with rank I do not desire to mention . . . I have had a fair trial of the United Kingdom. I am not dying as a spy, but as a soldier. My fate I stood as a man, but I can't be a liar and perjure myself. . . . What I have done I have done for my country. I shall express my thanks, and may the Lord bless you all.

And from the ten lawyers—eight English and two American—who, with me, heard the story told, there came, as it were, one murmur: "Jolly fine!"

And so it was!

JUDITH

C. E. MONTAGUE

BETTER KNOWN AS A JOURNALIST than as a fiction writer, Charles Edward Montague (1867–1928) still managed to produce several outstanding novels and short stories, mostly about World War I.

Soon after his graduation from Balliol College, Oxford University, he went to work for *The Manchester Guardian*, working as the newspaper's editorial writer and drama critic. When C. P. Scott, the paper's editor, was elected to Parliament, Montague took over as the editor from 1895 to 1906. He was politically active in the areas of Irish Home Rule and pacifism, speaking and writing powerfully against British involvement in World War I, as Scott did.

Once war became inevitable because of German aggression, however, he accepted the reality that German militarism needed to be thwarted and joined the army, serving in the Royal Fusiliers, dyeing his gray hair to black in order to gull the recruiter into thinking he was younger than his forty-seven years. He served well, moving through the ranks quickly, ending as a captain in British Intelligence by 1915.

He returned to the *Guardian* after the war and resumed his antiwar writings, most notably his collection of newspaper articles titled *Disenchantment* (1922). His most memorable line is undoubtedly "War hath no fury like a noncombatant." He also wrote satire and literary pieces until 1925, when he retired to devote himself full-time to writing fiction, producing several books in quick succession: *Rough Justice* (1926), *Right Off the Map* (1927), and *Action and Other Stories* (1928).

"Judith" was originally published in the September 1928 issue of *The Red Book Magazine;* it was first collected in *Action and Other Stories* by C. E. Montague (London, Chatto & Windus, 1928).

JUDITH

C. E. MONTAGUE

The average youth of twenty may expect to live for some thirty-six years. But if he was an infantry subaltern marching up into the Somme battle front in the Summer of 1916, his expectation of life was thirteen days and a bit. Some men took this contracted horizon in one way, and some in another. One virgin youth would think, "Only a fortnight? Wouldn't do to chuck it in the straight." Another would think, "Only a fortnight? And life scarcely tasted! I must gather a rose while I can."

Phil Gresson thought that he was, on the whole, for the rose. So he got a night's leave from Daours, where his Company lay for two days on its way to the mincing machine at Pozières. Then he borrowed the winking Medical Officer's horse and trotted off into Amiens, pondering what sort of wine to have with his dinner at Gobert's famed restaurant. Burgundy, he concluded: Burgundy was the winiest wine, the central, essential, and typical wine, the soul and greatest common measure of all the kindly wines of the earth, the wine that ought to be allowed to survive if it were ever decreed that, after thirteen days and a bit, only one single wine was to be left alive to do the entire work of the whole heart-gladdening lot. He thought it all out very sagely.

Gobert's was full: Gresson just bagged the last single table. Soon the rising buzz of talk drew its light screen of sound in front of the endless slow thud of the guns in the East. Soon, too, the good Burgundy did its kind office, and Phil's friendly soul was no longer alone: all the voices at the other tables had melted into one mellow voice: he recognized it as the genial voice of the whole of mankind, at its admirable best—not stiff, or cold, or forbidding, as some voices seemed at some times. It set him all a-swim in a delicious reverie about the poignant beauty of this extreme brevity that had come upon life. Thirteen days and a bit—and then all love, all liking, all delight to lie drowned for ever at the bottom of an endless night. Lovely, lovely. The individual life just a mere wisp of an eddy formed and re-formed on the face of a stream, and then smoothed away. Oh! it was good Burgundy. And Phil, a modest and a sober youth, drank more of it than he had ever drunk of any wine at a sitting.

At ten he strolled out of Gobert's, full of beautiful thoughts, and decided first to have a look at the celebrated Cathedral. He was quite an intelligent boy and had read that the great Ruskin thought it, all round, the most topping cathedral in France. So he worked northward, along the Rue St. Denis, to its end and then to the left, to reach the West Front. The West Front looked all right, as far as he could see. But it was a very dark night; no moon, no lamps lit in the streets, all the shops shut. And not many people about. Far over the southern suburbs one enemy aeroplane was on duty after another, bombing the railway; and bombs addressed to a railway may be delivered anywhere else.

One ancient trade, all the same, did not slacken, bombs or no bombs. Wherever a British soldier walked, after dark, in the streets of Amiens in that year, a kind of fire-fly lamps would kindle their tiny electric lights in his path; and out of the deepened darkness that each of these made in its rear there would come a whispered assurance that some rose was there and only asked to be gathered.

In the ears of the undebauched Gresson most of these voices were more like curbs than spurs to the promptings of youth. But just as he turned from the Place Notre Dame, to go back to the Rue du Soleil, the sudden casting of one of the wee jets of electric light on his uniform and his face was followed by an English greeting that pulled him up with a jerk: "Alone! At this late hour! What would Mother say?"

The mere words were nothing: their jaunty jocosity was the common slang of a trade. Nor was it anything out of the way that the words were spoken in English: half the sisterhood did that in France. What made him stop and say "Hullo!" was the quality of the voice. It was everything that nobody could expect from the tongue of a street-walker hawking her person to any chance ruffian a foreign army might throw in her way. It had depths and reserves. Like some rare and gifted woman's most furtive looks, it seemed subtly to index and vouch for many old forces and causes, of slow growth and long operation—character, race, a culture carefully sheltered and long in the building. Besides, the brazen facetiousness had come out, as it were, in spite of some revolt in the speaker. And yet, as he gasped his "Hullo!" she acted the courtesan with a will. She flashed her lamp on her own face, her hair, her bust, as if to say. "There! See the goods, before buying."

Gresson gasped again. The woman was a Juno; no, a Tragic Muse—tall, deep-bosomed, the regular features grave with a deep and ample expressiveness, the face of one of those most beautiful women who have achieved an intense absorption in some other thing than their own beauty. And she doing this!—she that, to see or to hear, made you feel how gloriously far a woman may be from a mere slave or a mere animal. There must be some enormous mistake somewhere, some sort of fantastic illusion. All the ardent, super-rational respect of clean-minded boys for womankind in the mass was tingling in the voice of Gresson when he made shift to answer politely, in his bad French, "And you, Madame! Under enemy fire!"

"Enemy? German?" she asked.

He explained that the dry buzz which was then growing louder was more smoothly continuous than the hum of any British aeroplane. "He's coming this way," he said. "Look!"

He pointed upwards at a white patch that had just broken out on the under-side of a cloud almost directly above them. At that place the fiery stares of two British ground searchlights had just rushed together. They had been searching the sky for the raider, each light working on its own, as two town policemen search a suspected backyard with their lanterns. Now one of them had found, and the other had instantly wheeled round to share in the find and to help keep the quarry in sight. Like a fly walking on a high ceiling, a black speck was scudding across the disk that the searchlights had painted in luminous fresco on the black dome of night. But the disk moved with the speck: wherever the speck went, its halo of brilliance was round it.

The girl gazed up eagerly. When she sighted the thing that was ranging the sky, with its glory all about it, she let out an "Ah!" that made Gresson feel sure she was not funked at all, and yet that she was decidedly stirred.

"Like God!" she muttered. It made Gresson start. The words had an aptness, no doubt, to that enskyed engine of wrath, remote, alone, girdled with light, throbbing with power, like a Jehovah of old when he floated out on black wings over a culpable earth, with his bolt in his hand. But, Gosh! what a woman, to see it like that! French, and yet able to stand off and see a Boche bomber busy above her as anything but a foul vampire bat let out of Hell for an hour. Our Tommies might think in that detached way about enemies. But a civilian!—a woman!—a French one at that! She must be a genius.

While Gresson digested this latest course of the full meal of surprise that the evening had brought him, Jehovah let fly, to some purpose. When a bomb of some size falls anywhere near in the dark, it feels as if the big splash of flame from the burst were all round you. The sound, too, fills your whole world for a moment. Then there comes, just for a second, a quite remarkable silence, and then certain smaller noises consequent on the original smash, begin to rise clear of the silence. When Gresson's eyes and ears came to themselves, a large broken branch of a tree was settling down to the ground with a soft leafy crash of crushed boughs, some man up the street was screaming with pain, and the singular girl was a blob of black daubed anyhow on the blackish grey of the pavement. The metal of her little flash-lamp tinkled on the stone as it fell out of her slackening hand.

He grabbed the lamp and looked at her. She was alive: her eye flinched under the light. She had no obvious wound. But she had the look that Gresson, a youth now well versed in bloodshed, liked least of all the looks painted on faces and bodies by the queer artistry of scientific slaughter. It was the battered, bullied look of a mouse kicked to death in the dust. As often happened through the caprices of shell-fire, she was stripped half-naked; her hat, with its flowers, was tumbled and spoilt, the little gewgaws of her pitiful occupation were all disordered. What remained of her clothing was knocked about, dirtied and torn.

That grotesque and cruel disarraying moved the young expert in carnage more than he could have believed until he felt it. All thought of sex was gone in a moment. Now she was only a sort of poor human rag-doll that had been used as a football—that or a child caught and horribly mauled by some brute of a force while trundling her little soiled hoop through the mud. He laid her easy and straightened her dishevelled clothes as well as he could and then waited a minute, wondering whether a flake of the bomb had done her business for good, or only grazed and badly shocked her. In either case, what must he do? Get her to a hospital, he supposed. While he leant over her, thinking, she suddenly spoke, faintly but in the most earnest entreaty, as though she had detected his thought. "Not to a hospital. No."

"All right," he assured her. "Don't worry."

She took a moment of rest and then said, in a voice that tried to be firm, "Will you help me to rise?"

He tried, and she made a game effort. It was hopeless. One knee was clean out of action. When she attempted to use it her whole weight came upon him at once. "Madame," he urged, "may I carry you to the hospital? It is two hundred yards only."

She said, "No, no, I beg you, for the love of God," so piteously that he was silenced. "You don't know," she said in a passionate whisper, "the way French hospital people would treat a—a woman like me."

That brought him a new pang of compassion. He couldn't do what she dreaded so much. But, Lord! how his mess would guffaw, could they see him there now, stuck and perplexed, with the head and neck of a Midianitish tragedy queen sustained in his arms! "But, Madame, what to do?" he said, in a voice almost as imploring as hers.

"You'll help me?—no?" she entreated, always in English. "I live—oh, not very far off, with you helping me. I have a friend there—I'll be all right there if, with your infinite goodness——"

But no mere helping would do it. Shyly and carefully he lifted her up in his arms, said,

"You must tell me the way," and so set off, he knew not whither, through the empty and echoing streets. She steered him up the Street of St. Denis, along the Street of the Three Pebbles—the Regent Street or Broadway of Amiens—and down the smaller Street of the Three Naked Bodies without Heads to an unlighted house at its far end.

Not a soul did they meet on this picturesque progress except a corporal's party of English Military Police, out upon their everlasting quest of drunks and strays. As a matter of form, the corporal challenged the odd caravan. He was not scandalized seriously. Any natural gift for wonder with which a British soldier-policeman set out to scour the streets of Amiens in those days was much assisted to wear itself out. Even the sight of a second lieutenant bearing away a pallid Aspasia, with blood dripping from the long heels of her shoes, did not astonish. "Pass, British officer, and all's correct" was the formula that the corporal used to disclaim further interest in the incident.

Gresson could have wished that the words described the case better. Correct! Why, not to speak of its more general lack of correctness, the girl had moved convulsively in his arms at the corporal's challenge; one of her hands had plunged somewhere into her dress and had not altogether come out again, but he could have sworn that between its half-hidden fingers he saw the shine of a silvery little pistol—the miniature kind that can give you an adequate dose, and yet have a remarkably small displacement of air in a pocket.

"I shouldn't bring that any further out if I were you," Gresson had said at the moment—in his bad French, but in the fatherly tone that an old professional handler of arms of precision may permit himself in explaining the etiquette of their use to an inexperienced young woman. And she had taken it so—had left the firearm in its lair and had brought the hand out and shown him its palm, open and empty, and said, "See! I am *sage*," like a French child when it vows to be good. But why pistols at all?

And why the queer mode of their entry into the dark little house in the Street of the Three Naked Bodies? He was for ringing the bell, but she said, "No. Please bring me near. I will knock," and then she beat a curious little tattoo on the glass panel with a big ring that she wore. It was as if somebody had been standing just on the other side of the door, waiting in the dark for that tattoo, so immediately did a dim light appear within and the door open. Its opener was a staid woman of thirty or so, in the rig of a hospital nurse, who lost her composure at once, gave a cry of horror and flung herself on the patient with a wild outburst of sorrow and tenderness.

"She's hurt. Can't walk. A bomb, you know," said Gresson, in his bad French. "Permit me to carry her to her room."

The nurse, gulping sobs and alternately charging ahead a few steps and looking anxiously back, gave him a lead up the stairs. Concerned as he still was, it was a relief to be out of the streets. Here would he see, at any rate, no British corporal. Sheltered from public derision, he could take notice of things. And what a house it was! Every lamp, every hanging, every fireplace and chair had the grim, cold, dully classical look common in French bourgeois interiors. He had been billeted in such houses. But the home of the stodgiest trader, the steeliest country attorney, had looked less drearily loyal to the conventions than this. And it an arbour for Venus, a Paphian bower! Why, it was enough to freeze a Bacchante.

These women, too! A dim lamp overhead will make almost any face appear grave, but neither of theirs needed that. They made him feel he had gained their goodwill, but also that there was something about them which he was utterly "out of"—far outside it, and never to come any nearer, and yet unaccountably warmly regarded. Could that be common in women for whom the bedevilment of their womanhood had become a career? And how the damaged one had stuck the torments that his joggly walk must have inflicted! A Joan of Arc, begad!

He laid her reverentially down on her bed

that the other showed him. Then he put on the right cheerful tone, as he thought, for the sick, and said farewell in his decentest French. "Eh, bien, au revoir, Mesdames."

With a most friendly earnestness the wounded woman said, "No. Never. Never. If you should ever meet me again, by an accident, you are to think only this—that you are in danger, and go away very quickly, without looking or speaking. Please do not think me ungrateful. I was not unconscious, not for one little moment, tonight. I know all your courage and kindness and strength and your clean and delicate heart when I was abased. I only say 'Never' because this is the one kind thing I can say without a disloyalty."

She spoke with feeling, as if there were really some dreadful danger, as in the old romances, from which he was to be guarded. Well, he supposed that a "woman of pleasure," with all that she knew, must want to warn any man, to whom she wished well—to warn him off her own world with its expense of spirit and its wastes of pain. He looked across at the older woman, as if in appeal against a judgement too drastic.

Between the two women there seemed to pass glances that questioned and answered, and then the elder one shook her head too, always with that blended expression of reticence and benevolence.

He couldn't help jibbing, at the last moment, against this decree of finality in his severance from an enigma so beautiful. "Madame," he said rather pleadingly, "may I not have even a name to remember?"

She turned her dead-white face on the pillow and looked at his eager ingenuous one—the face of the English "nice boy," at its nicest—with a sort of fierce kindness. "Yes," she said, "Judith. Remember it carefully."

She closed her eyes, and the other woman let him out of the house.

He went off straight to ring at the Hôtel du Rhin and get a bed. He felt, in a way, a little discomfited. Had he not gone forth, like others, to see life and have a good time, as they say? Had not the Medical Officer winked when he bor-

rowed the horse? What would they say in the mess when he went back and avowed that he still had his ridiculous innocence? Wouldn't they laugh? And yet he was elated, too. He hadn't got what they thought so much of. But he had got what, somehow, was bigger. The skirts of something high and passionate had brushed him as it passed. In some indefinable way there was more in the world than before: life was a taller adventure.

II

An average, however accurately drawn, is only an average. It isn't a maximum. Not through any precaution of his, Gresson survived the next fortnight. He did well in a futile attack and under a smashing counter-attack. When the rags that were left of the Division were taken out of the line, he was the only officer left in his Company. So he was now the acting commander of all the thirty-seven NCOs and men that were left on their legs.

Through Albert and Amiens the dog-tired remnant trailed back at his heels to Ailly, on the Somme, to rest and re-fit, and one of its many long halts was made under the trees of the Boulevard du Mail at Amiens, a few minutes' walk from the Street of the Three Naked Bodies. Gresson's own legs felt like sackfuls of lead, but he plodded off to get a daylight glimpse of the casket containing the mystery. All its mystery was gone. A fly-blown "House to Let" bill was stuck in a window: the shutters were closed.

So that was to be the absolute end of his one Arabian night's entertainment. He stumped back to the men who were lolling and chaffing under the dusty leaves, and in ten minutes more they tramped off for Picquigny and Ailly.

Gresson asked nothing more of God and the great and wise among men than that his acting command should be made substantive. But the ways of Higher Commands are not a subaltern's ways, nor are his wishes theirs. Just when the men were getting comfortably settled in and playing football rapturously in the August dust, orders came to Ailly from on high for Gresson to report at once to Colonel Mallom, of Intelligence, at GHQ.

He found this red-tabbed Colonel refreshingly unregimental. He talked to a fellow as if such things as ranks did not exist. So Gresson, he said—he seemed to know all about Gresson—had taken an engineering course at Charlottenburg, before 1914. Yes, a two-year course. Did Gresson know Germany well? Some bits of it—yes—Dusseldorf, Cologne, Bonn, Frankfort—most of the Rhineland. Did he speak German well? Even the humble-hearted Gresson couldn't deny it as flatly as he could deny any imputation of speaking good French. Hadn't he and his sister had a beloved Hanoverian governess all the days of their childhood? Anyhow, the Colonel cut out any modest shilly-shally by speaking himself, from that point onward, in German of a perfection that Gresson observed with respectful, though silent, astonishment. Gresson, in turn, seemed to make a handsome impression. "Gad!" said the Colonel, reverting to English at last. "Some linguist! *You* won't be a Second Loot long."

"I'm in acting command of a Company, sir," Gresson replied, with some pride.

"And that's a damn fine thing to be," said Mallom cordially. "I've tried it. I've tried only one thing that's finer. D'you guess what it is?"

"I don't, sir," said Gresson. In fact he doubted whether the world contained such a jewel.

"It's a game," said the Colonel, "with much the same risk, only you take it alone, and you take it dead cold—no one within fifty miles who isn't an enemy."

"I see it now, sir," said Gresson.

"Of course it's a volunteer's job. I don't press you to go into Germany—don't even advise you. All I say is that, with your local knowledge and very exceptional German and—if you'll excuse me—your very ingenious mug, you might do Intelligence work of deuced high value. Feel like it?"

Gresson's heart was jumping with glee. Why, here he was, at the very heart of the rose, let into the last, inmost mystery and thrill of glorious war. "Who wouldn't, sir?" he said.

III

In a snug country house in Artois a party of British officers seemed to be living a nice peaceful life of their own for a good part of the war. They did not dine out, but men from neighbouring messes would see two or three of them on the road and would think what an odd lot they were, and how fresh and unweathered the coveted ribbons that most of them wore, and what indoor people some of them looked, and how much time they all seemed to have on their hands for a walk or a ride. Some wag suggested that they had founded a sort of male convent, the latest wonder of the war, where all the official rewards of combatant valour were gained by an innocent life of fasting and prayer. Probably none of the neighbours noticed that now and then one of these persons of leisure would disappear for a few days, or a month, or altogether, nor knew that one of her hermits had just been listed in the *Gazette* as "Missing": believed to have died in enemy hands.

In this shy place and in other purlieus of Intelligence the ingenious Gresson now went to school. He learnt the whole system and structure of espionage and of counter-espionage, its twin sister. He got up the "Underground Railway"—the routes by which escaped British prisoners of war or hunted spies were guided, and passed on from guide to guide, till a "ferry" across the enemy line had been reached and the final rush must be risked. He heard about the pigeon post and the little fire-balloons that sailed off eastward on west winds with a pigeon or two in the basket hanging below, and the little flame nicely adjusted to let the balloon down where friends would expect it, about the right distance behind the enemy's front. His mind came to see Germany and the occupied parts of Belgium and

France as a map speckled thickly with infinitesimal spots of sound British red—eyes and ears of British Intelligence, noting each movement of German troops, guns, supplies, railway metal, and hospital outfit.

Those were the local agents, and now and then they had to be visited, as a merchant in New York or London visits his outlying agents in China or Africa, just to judge their efficiency and devotion, hearten them up, coach them in the latest modes of publicity, transport and salesmanship, and instil the inspiring faith that good work never passes unseen by the Olympian eyes of the firm and that shining guerdons await the virtuous. Oh! plenty to learn. And, presently, plenty to do, not obtrusively.

IV

He had become, in two years, a neat hand at the trick, and a Major with good marks to his name, when an airman still more boyish than himself put him down in the dusk of a winter evening on a great frozen field in the bend of the Rhine between Godorf and Cologne.

In the eye of reason such a descent was not possible. It was almost as if a German plane had set down passengers in Richmond Park. But some bluffs depend for success upon their very absurdity. They are too mad to be guarded against. Major Gresson's pink-faced pilot had plenty of time to bid the impudent farewell, "So long, old son," and then to rise cannily from the petrified mud and rough grass of the field, and to wind up his steep spiral staircase of air to the height he wanted, before every searchlight from Bonn to Cologne was groping for him all over the sky.

A German anti-aircraft gun on a fast motor lorry was on the spot in five minutes, eagerly guided for the last few hundred yards by a discharged Bavarian soldier, who had seen everything. "A single seater, Sergeant. A small biplane," he informed the NCO in charge of the gun. "I think the swine had engine trouble.

My God! if I'd had my old rifle! But ach! this for-ever-damned leg! I couldn't even get near him in time."

The poor man did, indeed, walk very lame from the knee wound that had ended his soldiering days and sent him tramping the roads of the Rhineland in his old Army tunic and boots, with the interval filled by a pair of the reach-me-down trousers of peace. He also wore the Iron Cross and he made no secret of a pocketful of chits redounding enviably to his military honour. His face was young, fair and ingenious, but he took a good look at the red-worsted regimental number on the sergeant's shoulder-strap before he said much about his own regiment.

The little flutter was soon over. The sergeant presented the youthful veteran with a cigar and took himself off with his gun and its crew. Then the lame Bavarian hobbled off briskly along the high road running into the north, where a turbid red glow on the underside of a cloud marked the site of Cologne. The twilight was all but night now; a thin whistling wind stung the Bavarian's face; the black frost was hardening.

About every half mile the Bavarian stopped dead and listened carefully. Not a boot except his own was ringing on the road. After each time that he thus made sure of being alone, he had much less of a limp, and went much faster, till it was getting near time to listen again. When the few bleared window-lights of the village of Roden came into sight he limped very badly again.

That was a Tuesday evening. In the evening dusk of the following Monday the super-boyish pilot, with nobody in the observer's seat, was to turn off his engine, at some immense height in the sky and great distance away, and slope silently down to the very spot where he had made his first landing. There, if still alive, a German ex-soldier was to be blowing his nose with a white hanky and whistling "The Watch on the Rhine," with some slight variations, but always fortissimo.

This, you perceive, was a thoroughly reasoned arrangement. Having been caught asleep there, only six days before, the Germans were sure to be on the watch at that point—so sure that it was also sure that no British pilot would be such a fool as to take liberties there for a long time to come. So sure of this were the Germans certain to be, that it was quite a sound spec for the British Air Staff to assume that no place could be safer for that boy to land on, next week. You see, we all grew into psychologists during the war. We probed into layer below layer of our enemy's thoughts, second thoughts, counter-thoughts, forethoughts and afterthoughts. Sometimes we brought off grand strokes in this way. And sometimes we didn't.

V

Gresson's long tour of calls on the agents was finished before noon on the Sunday. He was enormously glad of it. Each call had been a separate danger. For many spies are in the pay of both sides. It means double money, and also protection behind either front and lots of news to be got on each side and sold on the other. Their double game is often known to one or both of their employers; but, even then, they may be thought to be useful. Bits of false news may be deftly put in a double spy's way, for him to snap up and convey to his second paymaster.

But even a double spy may have other and more intractable passions to clash with his deep thirst for coin. He may really be backing one side: he may secretly want it to win: and it *may* not be the right one. A spy has been known to make a quite dramatic final break with one of his two clients in business. The last time that one capital spy, as he had been thought, was dropped behind the German front he took a shot with his revolver at the English aeroplane that had just dropped him. Others "declare to win," as we say on the turf, by denouncing a fellow-spy whom they meet in the country of their choice.

Gresson knew all this. And whatever people may say of the thrills and fine savours of peril, it was never with any flawless and whole-hearted enjoyment that he went into the house of some venal scrub who at any moment might throw up the window and yell for a policeman to lead Gresson off to the slaughter. Between each of these calls and the next he would rest from fear for a little and look into shop windows, or at the scenery, till he felt he could do with another dose of blue funk. By midday on Sunday he was as tired of the hard labour of holding down his apprehensions as you might be if you had been shaved thirty times in a week by a person who might or might not feel like cutting your throat—about even betting each way.

Now, Gresson, although he was getting on very well as a serpent—in a professional way and for the good of his country—was still a bit of a dove in some other ways. He was simple: he did not keep up with the more brisk-minded youth of his day; he was a poor hand at sneering; it never occurred to him that a thing must needs be wholly rubbish if other people had treasured it for a few hundred years. In fact he was unconventional, and he did and thought what he liked, without shouting about it. This careless disrespect for current fashion was privately carried so far that he went quite often to church, merely because he liked going. And, though he had no genius for prayer, as some people have, he had a private hobby of glowing, when he was in church, with intense and humble longings for things, of the more decent sort, that he specially valued or admired, and also of working up a fervent sort of gratefulness—to whom, he couldn't say—for everything that had lately gone well with him. So it occurred to him now that, having half a day free in Cologne, he would go to the afternoon service in the Cathedral.

He found an empty seat in the inner South aisle, near a pillar and slightly turned to the left, so that it gave him a view of all the huge nave. There was scarcely another man in the place. All the thousands of women who filled it were wearing dead black, and most of them the dress of widows—half a furlong of widows. Some of the faces were veiled and some not. Even of the veilless women many were soundlessly weeping: many other faces were marred with the salt scald of more secret tears.

The winter daylight was failing; the lamp-light was meagre; opposite Gresson, in the North windows, the prelates and saints and heraldic blazonments were sinking into mere lustrous darkness. The dim religious light was its most sombre self: the Gothic forest gloom, the death of the short, bitter day, the shadows in the hearts of all these smitten women, the great cloud blackening over a falling nation—Gresson felt them all press in upon him together and quiet and soften him.

As the service went on, he insensibly gave himself up to it more and more wholly. He let it work upon him as it would. Soon he lost all consciousness of his disguise and his danger—indeed, of everything but the rite, the chanting, the figure implied and evoked by it all, the figure of youth and its gifts, even the gift of the clean soul's inner serenity, given up freely for love of something undeservedly beloved. Just to hold alive in his mind the idea of that was an ecstasy to be prolonged at the full height and heat of its joy by gazing intently at something, anything, the flame of a tall candle, the gleam of a lectern of brass. So he gazed level, along a row of the ranged faces, at a light burning beyond, till a trivial movement in front of him broke the precarious spell of this highly strung reverie. One of the faces had made a half-turn towards his own, as though the intensity of his gaze had emitted a jet of some sort that could brush past a cheek and be felt. A woman was gazing at him steadily with an air of utter astonishment.

He knew her at once. She wore widow's clothes: her features were thinner: some force would seem to have taken them when they were softer than now and moulded them into a fixed tragic mask: if all the lost hopes in the world had been shovelled into one grave, such a mask might have been put at its head. Yet he knew her at once. No other face, he was sure, could have had just that proud sculpturing of the brows and the chin, or the poised self-control of the lips and eyes that he had carried, in all their harlotry kit, through the streets of Amiens.

But she here! Why, of course—she, too, must be here as a spy. Not in the regular way, for she would have been on his list. Perhaps she was one of the fearful women of legend, queenly and monstrous Delilahs, the vessels of sadic vengeance that have delighted to turn an enemy's lusts into gins and knives to trap him and stab him. He fancied that France had given birth to such women before. The Medical Officer had told him so.

The service was ending, women rising wearily from their knees, shaking their skirts a little and streaming away. The chimera woman waited a little. Gresson waited too, till she gave him a look or gesture—he wasn't sure which, but he knew that he was being bidden to follow her out. As she moved towards the West door he fell in behind her.

Where a weak lamp burned under the porch she stopped, turned and said, "So? It is you!" in the German that all must speak there.

"I trust you recovered," he said, "without very bad pain."

"Pain!" she seemed to reject the idea that such pains could matter. She looked at his motley get-up as a disabled soldier, discharged, and wearing out bits of his old uniform. Her eyes softened a little. "And so," she said, "all the time, you were one of us—and on duty, like me, in that horrible city—horrible!"

"Us!" His word was little more than a gasp—the escape that must come when the breath has been taken away by some smashing news or strange vision. "May we walk on?" he said. "There?" He pointed to the wide flagged space, east of the Domhof, where nobody used to walk then.

She nodded and walked on beside him. He used every second of silence to think the case out in his head and to plan an escape for himself. So that was what she had been—the seductress-spy of all ages—and he the British fool-officer who was to babble in her arms. She might have caught him too. Thank God for that bomb! But now she had him—caught, done for, the moment his German slipped up or he let out a fact that gave him away.

They had reached the big vacant flagged square when she asked abruptly, "You knew what I was when you saved me? You knew I was dead if they once got me into a hospital, with the papers I had in my clothes?"

He didn't answer. He asked his own question. "Papers, Madam? British papers? Army ones?"

"Of course. Every shred I had got on that journey in France."

"From British officers? Whom you had——?" Imprudent but uncontrollable anger was flaming up in his mind. To think of poor devils, perhaps his own friends, under their sentence of death, trying to get their last gulp of pleasure out of this world, and then tricked by this dignified harlot into betraying the lives of their men! And yet it was part of his nature to pull in his tongue before it could say the most venomous word.

But she understood, partly. "No," she said. "Yours was the first British uniform I had approached—in that way. That was the miracle. God put a German inside it, to guard me—a true German, pure-minded, brave. Yes, it was a miracle—I was like Abraham. I had risked what was most precious to me, and at the last moment my sacrifice had been spared me, and you were the last man, as well as the first, to whom I was to offer my body."

Amazement was quenching his anger. It shouldn't have done so. It wasn't his job to be moved, or to admire. It wasn't the way to get home and bring the goods with him. And yet he was moved. There are times when you feel not to yield admiration, even to enemies, would be treason to all that is finest in life. He murmured, "You offered that sacrifice!"

"What woman wouldn't—for Germany—if she knew all that I knew?" Her voice was not loud, but it had the brooding fervour that some women's have when they bend and doat in ecstasy over a child. They stopped short on the flags. "Only listen!" she said, and he felt a detaining finger placed on his sleeve.

The unlighted streets had emptied. Silence was almost complete. Through it there rose to their ears the urgent whisper of a great river busy at its work, brushing a hundred piers and quays with the insistent swish of its voluminous stream. "The Rhine!" As she breathed the word she seemed to cling to it and caress it, as if just to utter it were a key giving entrance to gardens of felicity. "The Rhine and the vines and the forests and all the old, kind, simple life of brown, hard-working people in villages, and the songs and dear ways of our own."

He muttered, "How could you do it?" He had a sister who would have done much for England, but some things were almost unthinkable.

"See," she said more quietly, as a friend reasons with a friend. "My husband was killed in the month of our marriage. My two brothers were killed. I had no sister. My father and mother were dead. And we were losing the war, and my husband had said you could win any war if you only knew what your enemy had in his mind. And Judith had won a great war in that fearful way, and why shouldn't I? But, oh! the horror of it—yes, you're right, you understand—the thought of some foul lusting boar half-drunk, with his slobbery tusks. And then the miracle came and you were courteous and noble and delicate in your heart and your hands. Do you know what I wished—in my mind, secretly, when I thought you were English, I wished, with all the strength of my heart—of course, it was only a wild, fantastical wish—that some day that one Englishman—only just he—might be in a danger as deadly as mine was, and I then to help him."

"You *would* have helped him?"

"Yes."

"Even if his were the very same danger as yours?"

"You mean, if he——?"

"Yes—if he were in Germany, doing what you did in France? If you met him here, now, skulking about in disguise, and you suddenly saw who it was?" Some thirty paces away, across the dark square, a sentry in front of a building paced up and down on his post, with a smart little stamp of a foot at each about turn. "Would you call out to that sentry?" said Gresson.

He didn't know why he was putting it to the touch and taking her at her word. We don't know why we do many things that we do. Something other than reason, something below it, emits an imperious impulse that comes to the top like a bubble of air from the invisible bed of a pool. It must burst into action.

She saw in a moment what he was avowing. She stopped dead; she seemed to grow taller. He felt he had lost the great throw; he was done for—had tried to strike on something that might be responsible in her ferocious and generous mind, and had struck on the ferocity only. In the dark he could see her eyes burn at him like those of a beast crouching back in a cave. "You dared!" she said, with an intense quiet fury. "You dared to prostitute that uniform!—that Cross!"

The game was all but up. And one thing he could swear would not help him with her, and that was to whine. "You dared worse, you brave woman," he said. "You were shameless."

For a second or two she said nothing, under his taunt. She stood perfectly still. The queer clear calm which extreme danger brings to some men had come on him now. He wondered almost tranquilly—was anything within her mind struggling with anything else? Had he a single friend left in that redoubtable citadel?

When she did speak, it was low and resentfully. "Why to God did you tell me?"

"God knows. I don't," he said, quite sincerely. "Perhaps because you had said things about yourself—frightfully intimate things. It feels better to give a bit back, in the confidence line, and not do all the taking. Sort of vanity, probably. Well, aren't you calling that sentry?" He asked almost sharply, prompted by some inarticulate guide like a wrestler's perception of when to shift his grip, or strain harder, or give for a moment.

She made some gesture—he couldn't see what it was: he guessed it to mean she put off, for a few minutes more, his sentence of death. Her voice, when it did come, was almost a wail. "What possessed you to come? You!—a man, with clean fighting to do! A woman has nothing to use but cunning and sex. But a man! What need had *you* to turn spy? What devil possessed you?"

He did not weigh the words of his answer. A hare with the breath of a greyhound hot on her thighs does not weigh this and that. Some god gives her the tip when to double, and which way to go, and she does it. "Listen again," he said in his turn, and so pressingly that she too held her breath and the Rhine could again be heard whispering earnestly. "Listen to it—you," he said in a low voice as earnest as its. "You think *I* have got nothing like that in my ears? I live in a house on the Thames, near a weir. When I was a boy I went off to sleep every night to the sound of the lasher—water tumbling about at the end of our garden—always the same and always changing, like somebody's voice. Well, that's *my* Rhine. That's the voice of *my* country, to *me*. It's what told me to put on this kit and come here. When I lie down in your prison tonight, I shall hear it until I'm asleep. I don't suppose all this is rational. Your Germany may be a much finer country than ours. It's love, though. Isn't that the thing to go by? Doesn't it make everything right that's done for it—even what you were going to do for it—even what I'm doing here?"

"Go quickly," she said, "before I remember my duty."

He made out that she was extending a hand in farewell. He found it ungloved and kissed the back of it twice. "You are even more splendid," he said, before letting it go, "than I thought you, that night in Amiens."

"And you," she said, "have the great heart that I saw in you then."

She hurried off towards the riverside quarter beyond the black bulk of the Cathedral, and Gresson hurried off, almost forgetting to limp, the opposite way, to hide in the thronged Hohe Strasse and make for the old Severin Gate in the

South. Cologne was a sizeable city, but not big enough to hold that magnificent woman and him.

VI

As punctual as a constitutional King the plane glided silently down the long slant from the clouds to the field in the bend of the Rhine. "Not nabbed, sir, yet?" the cheerful boy said airily, as Gresson scrambled in. "Simple souls, these Germans."

Gresson wasn't so sure. But there was no need to answer. The whirling blast from the propeller had begun to blow the hoar-frost off the turf under the plane. Nothing more could be said without effort, or easily heard, until the many-coloured lights of their home port came rushing forward and upward to bring the frozen traveller in.

A. E. W. MASON

THE PROLIFIC and distinguished writing career of Alfred Edward Woodley Mason (1865–1948) brought success in several genres, most notably mystery fiction and historical novels.

As the author of mysteries, his major contribution to the genre was the creation of Inspector Hanaud, the first official policeman of importance in twentieth-century detective literature. Like most French detectives portrayed in English mysteries, he is a comic character, though not drawn quite as broadly as John Dickson Carr's Henri Bencolin or Agatha Christie's Hercule Poirot (who is technically Belgian). It has been widely recognized that Christie, a dedicated reader of mystery fiction, largely based her famous character on Hanaud, who appeared in six novels that were so highly regarded that the first two, *At the Villa Rose* (1910) and *The House of the Arrow* (1924), were selected for the prestigious Howard Haycraft–Ellery Queen list of cornerstone works in the history of the genre.

Equal success was accorded Mason for his adventure and historical novels, the most famous of which is *The Four Feathers* (1902), the classic about a soldier handed a white feather, the symbol of cowardice, who is then shunned by his friends, family, and fellow soldiers, and the trials he endures to prove them wrong. Of the many film versions produced of *The Four Feathers*, the 1939 version starring Ralph Richardson and John Clements is the best and remains a staple of late-night television.

Numerous films were made from Mason's prodigious output of fiction, which was both commercially successful and critically acclaimed. His writing style was smooth, his characters believable, his moods convincing, and, above all, his stories were excellent. Meticulous about realistic detail, Mason often used personal experiences in his books. His tenure in Parliament resulted in a political novel, his role as civilian chief of British Naval Intelligence during World War I provided material for his espionage novels, and his travels in the Mideast informed the authentic background for some of his adventure fiction.

"Peiffer" was originally published in the June 1916 issue of *The Story-Teller;* it was first collected in *The Four Corners of the World* by A. E. W. Mason (London, Hodder & Stoughton, 1917).

PEIFFER

A. E. W. MASON

FOR A MOMENT I was surprised to see the stout and rubicund Slingsby in Lisbon. He was drinking a vermouth and seltzer at five o'clock in the afternoon at a café close to the big hotel. But at that time Portugal was still a neutral country and a happy hunting ground for a good many thousand Germans. Slingsby was lolling in his chair with such exceeding indolence that I could not doubt his business was pressing and serious. I accordingly passed him by as if I had never seen him in my life before. But he called out to me. So I took a seat at his table.

Of what we talked about I have not the least recollection, for my eyes were quite captivated by a strange being who sat alone fairly close to Slingsby, at one side and a little behind him. This was a man of middle age, with reddish hair, a red, square, inflamed face and a bristly moustache. He was dressed in a dirty suit of grey flannel; he wore a battered Panama pressed down upon his head; he carried pince-nez on the bridge of his nose, and he sat with a big bock of German beer in front of him. But I never saw him touch the beer. He sat in a studied attitude of ferocity, his elbow on the table, his chin propped on the palm of his hand, his head

pushed aggressively forward, and he glared at Slingsby through his glasses with the fixed stare of hatred and fury which a master workman in wax might give to a figure in a Chamber of Horrors. Indeed, it seemed to me that he must have rehearsed his bearing in some such quarter, for there was nothing natural or convinced in him from the brim of his Panama to the black patent leather tips of his white canvas shoes.

I touched Slingsby on the arm.

"Who is that man, and what have you done to him?"

Slingsby looked round unconcernedly.

"Oh, that's only Peiffer," he replied. "Peiffer making frightfulness."

"Peiffer?"

The name was quite strange to me.

"Yes. Don't you know him? He's a product of 1914," and Slingsby leaned towards me a little. "Peiffer is an officer in the German Navy. You would hardly guess it, but he is. Now that their country is at war, officers in the German Navy have a marked amount of spare time which they never had before. So Peiffer went to a wonderful Government school in Hamburg, where in twenty lessons they teach the gentle art of espionage, a sort of Berlitz school. Peiffer ate his dinners and got his degrees, so to speak, and now he's at Lisbon putting obi on me."

"It seems rather infantile, and must be annoying," I said; but Slingsby would only accept half the statement.

"Infantile, yes. Annoying, not at all. For so long as Peiffer is near me, being frightful, I know he's not up to mischief."

"Mischief!" I cried. "That fellow? What mischief can he do?"

Slingsby viciously crushed the stub of his cigarette in the ashtray.

"A deuce of a lot, my friend. Don't make any mistake. Peiffer's methods are infantile and barbaric, but he has a low and fertile cunning in the matter of ideas. I know. I have had some."

And Slingsby was to have more, very much more: in the shape of a great many sleepless nights, during which he wrestled with a dreadful uncertainty to get behind that square red face and those shining pince-nez, and reach the dark places of Peiffer's mind.

The first faint wisp of cloud began to show six weeks later, when Slingsby happened to be in Spain.

"Something's up," he said, scratching his head. "But I'm hanged if I can guess what it is. See what you can make of it"; and here is the story which he told.

Three Germans dressed in the black velvet corduroy, the white stockings and the rope-soled white shoes of the Spanish peasant, arrived suddenly in the town of Cartagena, and put up at an inn in a side-street near the harbour. Cartagena, for all that it is one of the chief naval ports of Spain, is a small place, and the life of it ebbs and flows in one narrow street, the Calle Mayor; so that very little can happen which is not immediately known and discussed. The arrival of the three mysterious Germans provoked, consequently, a deal of gossip and curiosity, and the curiosity was increased when the German Consul sitting in front of the Casino loudly professed complete ignorance of these very doubtful compatriots of his, and an exceeding great contempt for them. The next morning, however, brought a new development. The three Germans complained publicly to the Alcalde. They had walked through Valencia, Alicante, and Murcia in search of work, and everywhere they had been pestered and shadowed by the police.

"Our Consul will do nothing for us," they protested indignantly. "He will not receive us, nor will any German in Cartagena. We are poor people." And having protested, they disappeared in the night.

But a few days later the three had emerged again at Almeria, and at a mean café in one of the narrow, blue-washed Moorish streets of the old town. Peiffer was identified as one of the three—not the Peiffer who had practised frightfulness in Lisbon, but a new and wonderful Peiffer, who inveighed against the shamelessness of German officials on the coasts of Spain. At Almeria, in fact, Peiffer made a scene at the German Vice-Consulate, and, having been handed over to the police, was fined and threatened with imprisonment. At this point the story ended.

"What do you make of it?" asked Slingsby.

"First, that Peiffer is working south; and, secondly, that he is quarrelling with his own officials."

"Yes, but quarrelling with marked publicity," said Slingsby. "That, I think we shall find, is the point of real importance. Peiffer's methods are not merely infantile; they are elaborate. He is working down South. I think that I will go to Gibraltar. I have always wished to see it."

Whether Slingsby was speaking the truth, I had not an idea. But he went to Gibraltar, and there an astonishing thing happened to him. He received a letter, and the letter came from Peiffer. Peiffer was at Algeciras, just across the bay in Spain, and he wanted an interview. He wrote for it with the most brazen impertinence.

"I cannot, owing to this with-wisdom-so-easily-to-have-been-avoided war, come myself to Gibraltar, but I will remain at your disposition here."

"*That*," said Slingsby, "from the man who was making frightfulness at me a few weeks ago, is a proof of some nerve. We will go and see Peiffer. We will stay at Algeciras from Saturday to Monday, and we will hear what he has to say."

A polite note was accordingly dispatched, and on Sunday morning Peiffer, decently clothed in a suit of serge, was shown into Slingsby's private sitting-room. He plunged at once into the story of his wanderings. We listened to it without a sign that we knew anything about it.

"So?" from time to time said Slingsby, with inflections of increasing surprise, but that was all. Then Peiffer went on to his grievances.

"Perhaps you have heard how I was treated by the Consuls?" he interrupted himself to ask suddenly.

"No," Slingsby replied calmly. "Continue!"

Peiffer wiped his forehead and his glasses. We were each one, in his way, all working for our respective countries. The work was honourable. But there were limits to endurance. All his fatigue and perils went for nothing in the eyes of comfortable officials sure of their salary. He had been fined; he had been threatened with imprisonment. It was *unverschämt* the way he had been treated.

"So?" said Slingsby firmly. There are fine inflections by which that simple word may be made to express most of the emotions. Slingsby's "So?" expressed a passionate agreement with the downtrodden Peiffer.

"Flesh and blood can stand it no longer," cried Peiffer, "and my heart is flesh. No, I have had enough."

Throughout the whole violent tirade, in his eyes, in his voice, in his gestures, there ran an eager, wistful plea that we should take him at his face value and believe every word he said.

"So I came to you," he said at last, slapping his knee and throwing out his hand afterwards like a man who has taken a mighty resolution. "Yes. I have no money, nothing. And they will give me none. It is *unverschämt*. So," and he screwed up his little eyes and wagged a podgy

forefinger—"so the service I had begun for my Government I will now finish for you."

Slingsby examined the carpet curiously.

"Well, there are possibly some shillings to be had if the service is good enough. I do not know. But I cannot deal in the dark. What sort of a service is it?"

"Ah!"

Peiffer hitched his chair nearer.

"It is a question of rifles—rifles for over there," and, looking out through the window he nodded towards Gibel Musa and the coast of Morocco.

Slingsby did not so much as flinch. I almost groaned aloud. We were to be treated to the stock legend of the ports, the new edition of the Spanish prisoner story. I, the mere tourist in search of health, could have gone on with Peiffer's story myself, even to the exact number of the rifles.

"It was a great plan," Peiffer continued. "Fifty thousand rifles, no less." There always were fifty thousand rifles. "They are buried—near the sea." They always were buried either near the sea or on the frontier of Portugal. "With ammunition. They are to be landed outside Melilla, where I have been about this very affair, and distributed amongst the Moors in the unsubdued country on the edge of the French zone."

"So?" exclaimed Slingsby with the most admirable imitation of consternation.

"Yes, but you need not fear. You shall have the rifles—when I know exactly where they are buried."

"Ah!" said Slingsby.

He had listened to the familiar rigmarole, certain that behind it there was something real and sinister which he did not know—something which he was desperately anxious to find out.

"Then you do not know where they are buried?"

"No, but I shall know if—I am allowed to go into Gibraltar. Yes, there is some one there. I must put myself into relations with him. Then I shall know, and so shall you."

So here was some part of the truth, at all events. Peiffer wanted to get into Gibraltar. His disappearance from Lisbon, his reappearance in corduroys, his quarrelsome progress down the east coast, his letter to Slingsby, and his story, were all just the items of an elaborate piece of machinery invented to open the gates of that fortress to him. Slingsby's only movement was to take his cigarette-case lazily from his pocket.

"But why in the world," he asked, "can't you get your man in Gibraltar to come out here and see you?"

Peiffer shook his head.

"He would not come. He has been told to expect me, and I shall give him certain tokens from which he can guess my trustworthiness. If I write to him, 'Come to me,' he will say 'This is a trap.'"

Slingsby raised another objection:

"But I shouldn't think that you can expect the authorities to give you a safe conduct into Gibraltar upon your story."

Peiffer swept that argument aside with a contemptuous wave of his hand.

"I have a Danish passport. See!" and he took the document from his breast pocket. It was complete, to his photograph.

"Yes, you can certainly come in on that," said Slingsby. He reflected for a moment before he added: "I have no power, of course. But I have some friends. I think you may reasonably reckon that you won't be molested."

I saw Peiffer's eyes glitter behind his glasses.

"But there's a condition," Slingsby continued sharply. "You must not leave Gibraltar without coming personally to me and giving me twenty-four hours' notice."

Peiffer was all smiles and agreement.

"But of course. We shall have matters to talk over—terms to arrange. I must see you."

"Exactly. Cross by the nine-fifty steamer tomorrow morning. Is that understood?"

"Yes, sir." And suddenly Peiffer stood up and actually saluted, as though he had now taken service under Slingsby's command.

The unexpected movement almost made me vomit. Slingsby himself moved quickly away, and his face lost for a second the mask of impassivity. He stood at the window and looked across the water to the city of Gibraltar.

Slingsby had been wounded in the early days of the war, and ever since he had been greatly troubled because he was not still in the trenches in Flanders. The casualty lists filled him with shame and discontent. So many of his friends, the men who had trained and marched with him, were laying down their gallant lives. He should have been with them. But during the last few days a new knowledge and inspiration had come to him. Gibraltar! A tedious, little, unlovely town of yellow houses and coal sheds, with an undesirable climate. Yes. But above it was the Rock, the heart of a thousand memories and traditions which made it beautiful. He looked at it now with its steep wooded slopes, scarred by roads and catchments and the emplacements of guns. How much of England was recorded there! To how many British sailing on great ships from far dominions this huge buttress towering to its needle-ridge was the first outpost of the homeland! And for the moment he seemed to be its particular guardian, the ear which must listen night and day lest harm come to it. Harm the Rock, and all the Empire, built with such proud and arduous labour, would stagger under the blow, from St. Kilda to distant Lyttelton. He looked across the water and imagined Gibraltar as it looked at night, its house-lights twinkling like a crowded zone of stars, and its great search-beams turning the ships in the harbour and the stone of the moles into gleaming silver, and travelling far over the dark waters. No harm must come to Gibraltar. His honour was all bound up in that. This was his service, and as he thought upon it he was filled with a cold fury against the traitor who thought it so easy to make him fail. But every hint of his anger had passed from his face as he turned back into the room.

"If you bring me good information, why, we can do business," he said; and Peiffer went away.

I was extremely irritated by the whole interview, and could hardly wait for the door to close.

"What knocks me over," I cried, "is the impertinence of the man. Does he really think that any old yarn like the fifty thousand rifles is going to deceive you?"

Slingsby lit a cigarette.

"Peiffer's true to type, that's all," he answered imperturbably. "They are vain, and vanity makes them think that you will at once believe what they want you to believe. So their deceits are a little crude." Then a smile broke over his face, and to some tune with which I was unfamiliar he sang softly: "But he's coming to Gibraltar in the morning."

"You think he will?"

"I am sure of it."

"And," I added doubtfully—it was not my business to criticize—"on conditions he can walk out again?"

Slingsby's smile became a broad grin.

"His business in Gibraltar, my friend, is not with me. He will not want to meet us any more; as soon as he has done what he came for he will go—or try to go. He thinks we are fools, you see."

And in the end it seemed almost as though Peiffer was justified of his belief. He crossed the next morning. He went to a hotel of the second class; he slept in the hotel, and next morning he vanished. Suddenly there was no more Peiffer. Peiffer was not. For six hours Peiffer was not; and then at half-past five in the afternoon the telephone bell rang in an office where Slingsby was waiting. He rushed to the instrument.

"Who is it?" he cried, and I saw a wave of relief surge into his face. Peiffer had been caught outside the gates and within a hundred yards of the neutral zone. He had strolled out in the thick of the dockyard workmen going home to Linea in Spain.

"Search him and bring him up here at once," said Slingsby, and he dropped into his chair and wiped his forehead. "Phew! Thirty seconds more and he might have snapped his fingers at us." He turned to me. "I shall want a prisoner's escort here in half an hour."

I went about that business and returned in time to see Slingsby giving an admirable imitation of a Prussian police official.

"So, Peiffer," he cried sternly, "you broke your word. Do not deny it. It will be useless."

The habit of a lifetime asserted itself in Peiffer. He quailed before authority when authority began to bully.

"I did not know I was outside the walls," he faltered. "I was taking a walk. No one stopped me."

"So!" Slingsby snorted. "And these, Peiffer—what have you to say of these?"

There were four separate passports which had been found in Peiffer's pockets. He could be a Dane of Esbjerg, a Swede of Stockholm, a Norwegian of Christiania, or a Dutchman from Amsterdam. All four nationalities were open to Peiffer to select from.

"They provide you with these, no doubt, in your school at Hamburg," and Slingsby paused to collect his best German. "You are a prisoner of war. *Das ist genug*," he cried, and Peiffer climbed to the internment camp.

So far so good. Slingsby had annexed Peiffer, but more important than Peiffer was Peiffer's little plot, and that he had not got. Nor did the most careful enquiry disclose what Peiffer had done and where he had been during the time when he was not. For six hours Peiffer had been loose in Gibraltar, and Slingsby began to get troubled. He tried to assume the mentality of Peiffer, and so reach his intention, but that did not help. He got out all the reports in which Peiffer's name was mentioned and read them over again.

I saw him sit back in his chair and remain looking straight in front of him.

"Yes," he said thoughtfully, and he turned over the report to me, pointing to a passage. It was written some months before, at Melilla, on the African side of the Mediterranean, and it ran like this:

Peiffer frequents the low houses and cafés, where he spends a good deal of money and sometimes gets drunk. When drunk he gets very arrogant, and has been known to boast that he has been three times in Bordeaux since the war began, and, thanks to his passports, can travel as easily as if the world were at peace. On such occasions he expresses the utmost contempt for neutral nations. I myself have heard him burst out: "Wait until we have settled with our enemies. Then we will deal properly with the neutral nations. They shall explain to us on their knees. Meanwhile," and he thumped the table, making the glasses rattle, "let them keep quiet and hold their tongues. We shall do what we like in neutral countries."

I read the passage.

"Do you see that last sentence? 'We shall do what we like in neutral countries.' No man ever spoke the mind of his nation better than Peiffer did that night in a squalid café in Melilla."

Slingsby looked out over the harbour to where the sun was setting on the sierras. He would have given an arm to be sure of what Peiffer had set on foot behind those hills.

"I wonder," he said uneasily, and from that day he began to sleep badly.

Then came another and a most disquieting phase of the affair. Peiffer began to write letters to Slingsby. He was not comfortable. He was not being treated as an officer should be. He had no amusements, and his food was too plain. Moreover, there were Germans and Austrians up in the camp who turned up their noses at him because their birth was better than his.

"You see what these letters mean?" said Slingsby. "Peiffer wants to be sent away from the Rock."

"You are reading your own ideas into them," I replied.

But Slingsby was right. Each letter under its simple and foolish excuses was a prayer for translation to a less dangerous place. For as the days passed and no answer was vouchsafed, the prayer became a real cry of fear.

"I claim to be sent to England without any delay. I must be sent," he wrote frankly and frantically.

Slingsby set his teeth with a grim satisfaction.

"No, my friend, you shall stay while the danger lasts. If it's a year, if you are alone in the camp, still you shall stay. The horrors you have planned you shall share with every man, woman, and child in the town."

We were in this horrible and strange predicament. The whole colony was menaced, and from the Lines to Europa Point only two men knew of the peril. Of those two, one, in an office down by the harbour, ceaselessly and vainly, with a dreadful anxiety, asked "When?" The other, the prisoner, knew the very hour and minute of the catastrophe, and waited for it with the sinking fear of a criminal awaiting the fixed moment of his execution.

Thus another week passed.

Slingsby became a thing of broken nerves. If you shut the door noisily he cursed; if you came in noiselessly he cursed yet louder, and one evening he reached the stage when the sunset gun made him jump.

"That's enough," I said sternly. "Today is Saturday. Tomorrow we borrow the car"—there is only one worth talking about on the Rock—"and we drive out."

"I can't do it," he cried.

I continued:

"We will lunch somewhere by the road, and we will go on to the country house of the Claytons, who will give us tea. Then in the afternoon we will return."

Slingsby hesitated. It is curious to remember on how small a matter so much depended. I believe he would have refused, but at that moment the sunset gun went off and he jumped out of his chair.

"Yes, I am fairly rocky," he admitted. "I will take a day off."

I borrowed the car, and we set off and lunched according to our programme. It was perhaps half an hour afterwards when we were going slowly over a remarkably bad road. A powerful car, driven at a furious pace, rushed round a corner towards us, swayed, lurched, and swept past us with a couple of inches to spare, whilst a young man seated at the wheel shouted a greeting and waved his hand.

"Who the dickens was that?" I asked.

"I know," replied Slingsby. "It's Morano. He's a count, and will be a marquis and no end of a swell if he doesn't get killed motoring. Which, after all, seems likely."

I thought no more of the man until his name cropped up whilst we were sitting at tea on the Claytons' veranda.

"We passed Morano," said Slingsby. And Mrs. Clayton said with some pride—she was a pretty, kindly woman, but she rather affected the Spanish nobility:

"He lunched with us today. You know he is staying in Gibraltar."

"Yes, I know that," said Slingsby. "For I met him a little time ago. He wanted to know if there was a good Government launch for sale."

Mrs. Clayton raised her eyebrows in surprise.

"A launch? Surely you are wrong. He is devoting himself to aviation."

"Is he?" said Slingsby, and a curious look flickered for a moment over his face.

We left the house half an hour afterwards, and as soon as we were out of sight of it Slingsby opened his hand. He was holding a visiting card.

"I stole this off the hall table," he said. "Mrs. Clayton will never forgive me. Just look at it."

His face had become extraordinarily grave. The card was Morano's, and it was engraved after the Spanish custom. In Spain, when a woman marries she does not lose her name. She may be in appearance more subject to her husband than the women of other countries, though you will find many good judges to tell you that women rule Spain. In any case her name is not lost in that of her husband; the children will bear it as well as their father's, and will have it printed on their cards. Thus, Mr. Jones will call on you, but on the card he leaves he will be styled:

MR. JONES AND ROBINSON,

if Robinson happens to be his mother's name, and if you are scrupulous in your etiquette you will so address him.

Now, on the card which Slingsby had stolen, the Count Morano was described:

MORANO Y GOLTZ.

"I see," I replied. "Morano had a German mother."

I was interested. There might be nothing in it, of course. A noble of Spain might have a German mother and still not intrigue for the Germans against the owners of Gibraltar. But no sane man would take a bet about it.

"The point is," said Slingsby, "I am pretty sure that is not the card which he sent in to me when he came to ask about a launch. We will go straight to the office and make sure."

By the time we got there we were both somewhat excited, and we searched feverishly in the drawers of Slingsby's writing-table.

"I shouldn't be such an ass as to throw it away," he said, turning over his letters. "No! Here it is!" and a sharp exclamation burst from his lips. "Look!"

He laid the card he had stolen side by side with the card which he had just found, and between the two there was a difference—to both of us a veritable world of difference. For from the second card the "y Goltz," the evidence that Morano was half-German, had disappeared.

"And it's not engraved," said Slingsby, bending down over the table. "It's just printed—printed in order to mislead us."

Slingsby sat down in his chair. A great hope was bringing the life back to his tired face, but he would not give the reins to his hope.

"Let us go slow," he said, warned by the experience of a hundred disappointments. "Let us see how it works out. Morano comes to Gibraltar and makes a prolonged stay in a hotel. Not being a fool, he is aware that I know who is in

Gibraltar and who is not. Therefore he visits me with a plausible excuse for being in Gibraltar. But he takes the precaution to have this card specially printed. Why, if he is playing straight? He pretends he wants a launch, but he is really devoting himself to aviation. Is it possible that the Count Morano, not forgetting Goltz, knows exactly how the good Peiffer spent the six hours we can't account for, and what his little plan is?"

I sprang up. It did seem that Slingsby was getting at last to the heart of Peiffer's secret.

"We will now take steps," said Slingsby, and telegrams began to fly over the wires. In three days' time the answers trickled in.

An agent of Morano's had bought a German aeroplane in Lisbon. A German aviator was actually at the hotel there. Slingsby struck the table with his fist.

"What a fool I am!" he cried. "Give me a newspaper."

I handed him one of that morning's date. Slingsby turned it feverishly over, searching down the columns of the provincial news until he came to the heading "Portugal."

"Here it is!" he cried, and he read aloud.

"'The great feature of the Festival week this year will be, of course, the aviation race from Villa Real to Seville. Amongst those who have entered machines is the Count Morano y Goltz.'"

He leaned back and lit a cigarette.

"We have got it! Morano's machine, driven by the German aviator, rises from the aerodrome at Villa Real in Portugal with the others, heads for Seville, drops behind, turns and makes a bee-line for the Rock, Peiffer having already arranged with Morano for signals to be made where bombs should be dropped. When is the race to be?"

I took the newspaper.

"Ten days from now."

"Good!"

Once more the telegrams began to fly. A week later Slingsby told me the result.

"Owing to unforeseen difficulties, the Festival committee at Villa Real has reorganized its arrangements, and there will be no aviation race. Oh, they'll do what they like in neutral countries, will they? But Peiffer shan't know," he added, with a grin. "Peiffer shall eat of his own frightfulness."

THE DONVERS CASE

E. PHILLIPS OPPENHEIM

KNOWN AS "The Prince of Storytellers" to the reading public (encouraged by his publishers), Edward Phillips Oppenheim (1866–1946) was a prolific author who gave his readers exactly what they hoped for: thrilling, fast-paced stories that gave them a glimpse of the lives of the rich and famous. He was the right man for the job, as his bestselling books made him both fabulously rich and happy to enjoy every shilling of that wealth.

In addition to his one hundred fifteen novels (including five under the pseudonym Anthony Partridge), Oppenheim produced hundreds of short stories that were published in top magazines for top dollar, all of them being collected in forty-four volumes. His staggering output was achieved by dictating to a secretary (whom he then allowed to edit his work and send it off, commonly not bothering to review it)—but not past the cocktail hour, which frequently meant a party for a hundred people or more aboard the yacht on which he lived.

After leaving school at an early age to work in his father's leather business, he worked all day and then wrote until late at night. He had thirty books published by the time he turned forty and sold the business to devote full time to writing novels of international intrigue, mystery, and crime. The plot-driven stories feature beautiful, glamorous, mainly vacuous young women, while the men are often heroic, though there is little to distinguish them from one another.

Oppenheim's most important book is *The Great Impersonation* (1920), a Haycraft-Queen cornerstone title in which a disgraced English aristocrat overcomes his alcoholism when England needs him to outwit the Germans as the First World War looms. It was filmed three times, all with the same title as the book: it was released in 1921, as a silent starring James Kirkwood; in 1935, starring Edmund Lowe and Valerie Hobson; and in 1942, updating the story line to focus on events leading to World War II, starring Ralph Bellamy and Evelyn Ankers.

In addition to his international espionage stories, Oppenheim was taken with roguery and produced novels and short stories that featured those who stood just on the other side of the law. Among the many crooks whose adventures he recounted were stories about Joseph P. Cray, an utterly charming gentleman who managed to steal in order to help a friend or to line his pockets at the expense of those who deserved to have their wallets lightened.

"The Donvers Case" was originally published in the November 1920 issue of *The Strand Magazine;* it was first collected in *The Adventures of Mr. Joseph P. Cray* (London, Hodder & Stoughton, 1925).

THE DONVERS CASE

E. PHILLIPS OPPENHEIM

I

The long Continental train drew slowly into Victoria Station, and through a long vista of wide-flung doors a heterogeneous stream of demobilised soldiers, nurses, "Wrafs," and other of the picturesque accompaniments of a concluded war, flowed out on to the platform. The majority lingered about to exchange greetings with friends and to search for their luggage. Not so Mr. Joseph P. Cray. Before the train had come to a standstill, he was on his way to the barrier.

"Luggage, sir?" inquired a porter, attracted by the benevolent appearance of this robust-looking, middle-aged gentleman in the uniform of the American Y.M.C.A.

"Checked my baggage right through," Mr. Cray replied, without slackening speed. "What I need is a taxi. What you need is five shillings. Let's get together."

Whether he was serving a lunatic or not, the five shillings was good money and the porter earned it. In exactly two minutes after the arrival of the train, Mr. Cray was on his way to the Milan Hotel. The streets were not overcrowded. The driver had seen the passing of that munificent tip and gathered that his fare was in a hurry.

They reached the Milan in exactly nine minutes. Even then Mr. Cray had the strained appearance of a man looking into futurity.

He stopped the driver at the Court entrance, fulfilled the latter's wildest dreams with regard to emolument, and presented himself eagerly before the little counter.

"Key of 89, Johnson," he demanded. "Get a slither on."

"Why, it's Mr. Cray!" the hall-porter exclaimed, after a single startled gaze at the new-comer's uniform. "Glad to see you back again, sir. Here's your key, sent over half-an-hour ago."

Mr. Cray snatched at it.

"Any packages?" he demanded over his shoulder, as he made for the lift.

"A whole heap of them, sir," was the reassuring reply. "All in your room."

Mr. Cray slipped half-a-crown into the lift-man's hand, made pantomimic signs with his palm, and they shot upwards without reference to the slow approach of a little party of intended passengers. Out stepped Mr. Cray on the fourth floor, and his face beamed as he recognised the valet standing before number eighty-nine.

"Hot bath, James," he shouted. "Set her going."

"Certainly, Mr. Cray, sir," the man replied, disappearing. "Glad to see you back again."

"Gee, it's good!" the new-comer exclaimed, dashing into the bedroom. "Off with the ornaments."

No convict ever doffed his prison garb with more haste and greater joy than did Mr. Joseph P. Cray divest himself of the honourable though somewhat unsuitable garments for a man of his build which he had worn for the last two years. The absurd little tunic looked shorter still as it lay upon the bed, his cow-puncher hat more shapeless than ever, his ample breeches—they needed to be ample, for Mr. Cray's figure was rotund—collapsed in strange fashion as they sank shamelessly upon the floor. Naked as the day on which he was born, Mr. Cray strode unabashed into the bathroom.

"Get me some clothes ready out of those packages, James," he directed. "Bring a dressing-gown and underclothes in here. Get busy."

Then for a quarter of an hour Mr. Cray steamed and gurgled, splashed and grunted. His ablutions completed, he dried himself, thrust his legs into some white silk pants, drew a vest to match over his chest, and trotted into the next room. He was still in a hurry.

"Dinner clothes, James," he ordered. "Slip over a white shirt. Speed's the one and only."

"You're in a hurry, Mr. Cray," the man observed, smiling, as he handed him his garments.

"I've been in a hurry for twelve months," was the feeling reply.

Ten minutes later, Mr. Cray left the room. The strained expression was still in his face. He rang for the lift, descended like a man absorbed with great thoughts, walked through the grill-room, climbed the stairs, passed through the smoke-room, and stood before the bar before he slackened speed.

"Why, it's Mr. Cray!" one of the young ladies declared.

"Two dry Martinis in one glass," Mr. Cray directed reverently. "Just a squeeze of lemon in, no absinthe, shake it till it froths."

The young lady chatted as she obeyed instructions. Mr. Cray, though a polite man, appeared suddenly deaf. Presently the foaming glass was held out to him. He raised it to his lips, closed his eyes and swallowed. When he set it down, that look had passed from his face. In its place shone the light of an ineffable and beatific contentment.

"First drink in twelve months," he explained. "Just mix up another kind of quietly, will you? I'll sit around for a bit."

"Mr. Cray! . . . Mr. Cray! . . . Mr. Joseph P. Cray!"

Mr. Cray, who was engaged in a lively conversation with a little group of old and new acquaintances, broke off suddenly in the midst of an animated chapter of reminiscences.

"Say, boy," he called out, "who's wanting me?"

The boy advanced.

"Lady to see you, sir, in the hall," he announced.

"Have you got that right, my child?" Mr. Cray asked incredulously.

"Mr. Joseph P. Cray, to arrive from France this evening," was the confident reply.

"That's me, sure," the person designated, admitted, rising to his feet and brushing the ash from his waistcoat. "See you later, boys. The next round is on me."

Mr. Cray made his contented but wondering way into the lounge. A tall and very elegant-looking young woman rose to her feet and came to meet him. Mr. Cray's eyes shone and his smile was wonderful.

"Sara!" he gasped. "Gee, this is great!"

"Dad!" she replied, saluting him on both cheeks. "You old dear!"

They went off arm in arm to a corner.

"To think of your being here to welcome me!" Mr. Cray murmured ecstatically.

"And why not?" the young lady replied. "If ever any one deserved a welcome home, it's you. Twelve months' work in a Y.M.C.A. hut in France is scarcely a holiday."

"And never a single drink," Mr. Cray interrupted solemnly.

"Marvellous!" she exclaimed. "But was that necessary, dad?"

"Well, I don't know," he admitted. "I guess they don't all know how to use liquor as I do. Some of the lads out there get gay on nothing at all. So the day I put the uniform on, I went on the water waggon. I took it off," he murmured, with a reminiscent smile of joy, "an hour and a half ago. . . . Where's George?"

"Sailed for the States yesterday."

"You don't say!"

Sara nodded.

"He's gone out to Washington on a Government commission. He'd have been here—sent all sorts of messages to you."

"Not ashamed of his disreputable old father-in-law, eh?"

"Don't be silly, dad. We're all proud of you. George has said often that he thinks it fine of a man of your age and tastes to go and work like that. What are you going to do, dad, now?"

"Order dinner for us two, I hope, dear."

"Just what I hoped for," she declared. "I think it's wonderful to have your first evening together. What are your plans, dad—stay over here for a time?"

"Why, I should say so," was the prompt reply. "You've heard what's got the old country?"

"You mean about Wilson?"

"Gone dry!" Mr. Cray exclaimed, in a tone of horror. "All the bars selling soft drinks. Tea-fights at the saloons, and bad spirits at the chemist's. That's what the old women we left at home did while we were out fighting."

"I'm afraid mother was one of them," Sara observed.

"Your mother's crazy about it," Mr. Cray acknowledged. "She's president of half-a-dozen prohibition societies. She's now working the anti-tobacco stunt."

"She doesn't say anything about coming over, I suppose?" the young woman asked, a little timidly.

"I should say not," Mr. Cray replied, with little shiver. "She's too busy over there."

Sara slipped her hand through her father's arm.

"We'll have a lovely time for a month or two," she said. "You know how happy I am with George, but this English life is just a little cramped. I suppose I must have some of your wandering spirit in me, dad. Anyhow, for just these few months let's see a lot of one another. You're just as fond of adventures as ever, aren't you?"

A slow smile parted Mr. Cray's lips, a fervid light shone in his eyes.

"Sara," he whispered, "after the last twelve months I'm spoiling for some fun. But you, my dear—you're Lady Sittingbourne, you know. Got your husband's position to consider and all that."

She laughed in his face.

"You can cut that out, dad, for a time," she said. "Come along, now. We'll talk over dinner. I'm nearly starving, and I want to know if you've forgotten how to order."

As they took their places at a table in the corner of the restaurant, Sara exchanged friendly greetings with a girl a short distance away, who was dining alone with a man.

"Lydia Donvers," she whispered to her father. "Lydia's rather a dear. She was at that wonderful school you sent me to at Paris. She's only been married a year."

"They don't seem to be living on a bed of roses exactly," Mr. Cray commented, glancing at the young man. "Seems all on wires, doesn't he? Has he had shell-shock?"

Sara shook her head.

"I don't think he did any soldiering at all," she replied. "He volunteered once or twice, I know, but he couldn't pass the medical examination. He was in one of the Ministries at home."

Cray's interest in the couple evaporated. Without being a gourmand, he loved good cooking, civilisation, the thousand luxuries of a restaurant de luxe. He ordered his dinner as he ate it, slowly and with obvious enjoyment.

Nevertheless, he happened to be looking across the room when a small page-boy in black livery approached the adjoining table and presented a note to Donvers. He saw the look in the young man's face as he received the envelope, tore it open and glanced at the card inside. Mr. Cray forgot his dinner just then. It was as though tragedy had been brought into their midst. The young man spoke to the girl, hesitatingly, almost apologetically. She answered with pleading, at last almost with anger. Their dinner remained untasted. In the end, the man rose to his feet and followed the boy from the room. The girl stayed behind.

"Queer little scene, that," Mr. Cray whispered.

Sara nodded.

"I can't think what's the matter with Lydia," she said.

"Kind of annoyed at having their little feast broken into, I guess," her father murmured soothingly.

Sara said nothing and for some moments her father sought and found oblivion in the slow consumption of a perfectly cooked sole colbert.

"Gee, this fellow is the goods!" he murmured appreciatively. "If you'd seen what they've been giving us over there, good solid tack enough, but after the first month everything tasted alike. Thought I'd got paralysis of the palate!"

"And nothing to drink, dad?"

"Not a spot," declared Mr. Cray, with frenzied exaltation.

"I'm worried about Lydia," Sara confided.

"She does look struck all of a heap," Mr. Cray assented.

"I'm going across to speak to her, if you don't mind."

"Sure!" Mr. Cray assented, with his eye fixed almost reverently upon the grouse which the maître d'hôtel was tendering for his inspection.

"Don't wait for me, dad," she begged.

"I won't," Mr. Cray promised. . . .

Mr. Cray ate his grouse with the deliberate and fervid appreciation of the epicure, an appreciation unaffected by the fact that within a few yards his quick sensibility told him that words of tragedy were being spoken. It was obvious that Sara's friend was confiding in her, and it was obvious that the confidence was of tragical interest. In the midst of it all, the young man who had been called away returned. He had the look of a man making a strong effort to control his feelings. Mr. Cray, who had seen much of life during the last two years, recognised the signs. Not a word was audible, but when Sara, after her friend's husband had been presented to her, engaged him in earnest conversation, Mr. Cray began to understand.

"A little job for me," he murmured to himself, as he sipped his champagne. "Pity about Sara's grouse, though."

She returned presently, and it was obvious that she had much to say. Mr. Cray was firm.

"Not a word, Sara," he insisted, "until you have eaten your portion of grouse. Charles here has kept it hot for you. Not a word! I'm the stern father about that bird. What you've got to say will keep ten minutes."

Sara obeyed. She generally obeyed when her father was in earnest. It was not until she found herself trifling with a *soufflé*, a dish for which her companion had no respect whatever, that she was permitted to unburden herself.

"Lydia is in great trouble, dad," she confided. "There is something wrong with her husband. She doesn't know what it is, but he came home, a fortnight ago, looking as though he had received a shock, and has never been the same man since. This is the third time he has been fetched away from a restaurant by a page in that same livery."

"I saw you talking to him when he came back."

She nodded.

"I asked him right out what was the matter with him, and I told him about you, dad, told him how clever you were at getting people out of difficulties, and how you didn't mind a little risk if there was an adventure at the back of it. I think I impressed him. He says he can promise you all the adventure you want, and they are coming here to take their coffee."

"If this isn't some little burg!" Mr. Cray murmured ecstatically. "Just two hours under the fogs and the wheel begins to turn!"

The arrival of Gerald Donvers and his wife, just as coffee was being served, did not seem likely to contribute in any way towards the gaiety of Mr. Cray's evening. The young man at close quarters seemed more distraught than ever. He ignored his coffee, but drank two glasses of liqueur brandy quickly. His wife scarcely took her eyes off him, and Sara's attempts to inaugurate a little general conversation were pitifully unsuccessful. Mr. Cray took the bull by the horns.

"Say, Mr. Donvers," he began, "Sara here tells me that you're up against a snag somewhere. If there's any way I can be of service, just open out. You and I are strangers, but anything my daughter says goes, so you can count on me as though I were an old friend."

"You are very good," the young man replied without enthusiasm. "I am in a very terrible position—through my own fault, too. I am to attend a sort of investigation to-night, and I am invited to bring any friend I like who isn't connected with any of the Services. If you'll come along, I'll be glad, but I tell you frankly that I don't think the shrewdest man in the kingdom would be of any service to me."

"That sounds hard," Mr. Cray observed, "but if I'm not butting in I'll come along, with pleasure. What time is this show down?"

"We shall have to leave in five minutes," the young man answered, with a little shiver.

Mr. Cray withdrew the bottle from his companion's reach.

"Take my advice and leave the strong stuff alone," he said. "If it's as bad as it sounds, you'll want your head clear."

Donvers became no more communicative in the taxicab which drove them presently to a gloomy house in one of the southern squares. They were admitted by a soldier manservant, who ushered them into a sombrely-furnished library on the ground floor. A man who was seated at a desk—a grim, soldierly-looking person in the uniform of a Colonel—glanced up at their entrance and nodded curtly. Seated in an arm-chair was a pale-faced young woman in widow's weeds, who turned her head away at their entrance.

"You have brought a friend?" the Colonel inquired.

Donvers nodded in spiritless fashion.

"Mr. Joseph Cray—Colonel Haughton. Mr. Cray is an American and has not been in England for two years."

Colonel Haughton touched a bell by his side.

"Show the young lady in," he directed the soldier servant who answered it. "How much of this affair do you know, Mr. Cray?" he inquired coldly.

"Not a diddle," was the emphatic reply. "I wanted Mr. Donvers to put me wise on the way down, but he said he'd rather leave it to you."

Colonel Haughton made no reply. There was a knock at the door and a young woman was ushered in. She was fashionably dressed, and her face was familiar enough to any one studying the weekly papers. Mr. Cray recognised a compatriot at once. The woman in the chair glanced up at the girl and then away. Every now and then her shoulders shook. The Colonel pointed to a chair.

"Will you be seated, Miss Clare?" he said. "You gentlemen, please yourselves. I propose to recapitulate this unfortunate case for your benefit, Mr. Cray. I have my own ideas as to the course which Donvers should adopt."

"Go right ahead," Mr. Cray invited genially. "I'm kind of cramped in the legs with travelling to-day, so I'll take an easy-chair if there's no objection."

"A year ago," Colonel Haughton said, speaking in sentences of sharp, military brevity, "Donvers here held an appointment in a certain British Ministry. It was his duty frequently to bring dispatches of great importance to a certain branch of the War Office over which I presided. On one occasion, Donvers appears most improperly to have broken his journey at Miss Clare's flat in Clarges Street."

"There was no breaking the journey," Donvers interrupted. "My instructions were to deliver the dispatches into your own hands, and when I got to the War Office you were out for an hour. I came up to have tea with Miss Clare instead of waiting in the Office."

"Mr. Donvers left his wallet of dispatches hanging in Miss Clare's hall," Colonel Haughton continued, "a disgracefully careless proceeding. When he found me at the War Office that evening, he handed me two envelopes instead of three. He said nothing to me about the third, but, realising the loss, returned to Miss Clare's and searched his own rooms. Miss Clare knew nothing about the possibly missing dispatch, Donvers could discover nothing in his rooms. In the meantime, a prisoner in the Tower was shot at midnight that night. The contents of the letter, which never reached me, would have saved him."

The woman in mourning began to sob. Donvers wiped the perspiration from his forehead.

"Say, that's bad," Mr. Cray admitted.

"Owing to information patriotically tendered by Miss Clare," Colonel Haughton continued, "a constant visitor to her flat was arrested soon afterwards and dealt with in the usual way. He admitted having opened the dispatches which he found in Donvers' wallet, and made use of their contents. The one which he could not open he took away, and finding it of no interest to his cause, destroyed it. The situation, therefore, amounts to this. Owing to the criminal carelessness of Donvers, a young American whose innocence was beyond doubt was shot for a spy."

The woman in mourning looked up. Her eyes flashed fiercely across the room.

"My husband!" she sobbed, "All that I had in the world!"

Donvers looked at Cray as though pleading for his intercession. Cray turned to the young woman.

"Madam," he said, "may I ask your name?"

"Ellen Saunderson," was the tearful reply. "My husband was Joe Saunderson. He was as innocent as you or I. The letter which never reached Colonel Haughton would have proved it."

Mr. Cray fingered his chin thoughtfully.

"Shot for a spy, eh," he ruminated, "and that letter contained reports which would have saved him. Say, that's hard! Has any official notice been taken of this matter?" he continued, turning to the Colonel.

"Mr. Donvers came to me a few days later," the Colonel said, "and confessed that he had not delivered to me one of the dispatches entrusted to him, and explained that he was not in a position to trace it. A few days later, the contents of that dispatch reached me officially. I advised Mr. Donvers to tender his resignation, which he did. Communications have passed in secrecy between a certain department of the American Secret Service and our own, concerning this unfortunate mistake. It has been decided, for obvious reasons, that it shall not be made a Press matter. The question we now have to discuss is the amount of compensation which shall be offered to Mrs. Saunderson."

The woman turned away wearily.

"Compensation!" she murmured bitterly. "That won't give me back Joe."

"I regret to say," Colonel Haughton continued, "that I am not able to procure for Mrs. Saunderson any official recompense. On the evidence presented, the shooting of Joseph Saunderson was amply justified, and it is the official view that, if recompense be tendered to the widow, a mistake is admitted which might later have serious consequences. Mr. Donvers has made an offer which Mrs. Saunderson rejected with scorn. I will be perfectly frank to all of you. My interest in this matter is to see Mrs. Saunderson receive adequate compensation, and further, in the interests of my Department, to see that this matter is forgotten. If Mrs. Saunderson is not satisfied, she will probably drag into light a matter which, not for Donvers's sake, but for the sake of the Department, it is my wish to conceal. Mr. Donvers has offered—what was the sum, Donvers?"

"Five thousand pounds," the young man replied. "It is half the spare money I have in the world."

The woman turned around with a sudden burst of passion.

"You and your spare money!" she exclaimed. "Do you think your spare money, as you call it, will bring back Joe—the husband I lost while you stayed flirting with this hussy here?"

Miss Clare frowned, and her fingers twitched nervously.

"No shadow of blame can be attached to Miss Clare in this matter," the Colonel intervened coldly.

"Or to any one, I suppose?" the woman scoffed. "Look here," she went on, facing Donvers, "I don't want your money—I'd rather work my fingers to the bone than touch a penny of it—but I want to punish you, and if you're a poor man, so much the better. Ten thousand pounds I want from you by mid-day to-morrow, and if I don't have it, my story goes to the newspapers for the world to read."

There was a silence. Donvers turned towards his companion.

"How are you fixed financially?" Cray asked him.

"That five thousand pounds is my limit," Donvers replied bitterly. "If I have to find the rest, it will break up the business I've just started and beggar me altogether."

"And why shouldn't you be beggared?" the woman demanded, her hands working convulsively and her eyes filled with hate. "That's what I want. That's why I say I'll have ten thousand pounds to-morrow if it means your last sixpence."

There was an uneasy silence. Mr. Cray gathered up the threads of the situation.

"It don't seem like there's any more to be said," he declared. "If you'll bring the lady along to my rooms at the Milan Court to-morrow at twelve o'clock, Colonel, I'll go into this young man's affairs in the meantime and give him the best advice I can."

The colonel glanced at his engagement book.

"I will come," he promised, "but it is the last minute I can promise to give to this unfortunate affair. It must be concluded then, one way or the other."

He touched the bell. His soldier servant opened the door. Cray and his companion hurried off. The latter groaned as they reached the street.

"Very kind of you to come along, Mr. Cray," he said, "but you can see for yourself how hopeless the whole affair is. Not only have I got to go about all my life with the memory of that poor young man's death on my conscience, but if I find that ten thousand pounds I shall be beggared. There's only one way out that I can think of."

Mr. Cray was leaning back in his corner of the taxicab which they had just picked up, his chin resting upon his folded arms. The young man watched him furtively. It was not until they neared the Milan, however, that Mr. Cray spoke.

"There may be another way," he ventured. "I promise nothing, but be at my rooms at twelve o'clock to-morrow to meet those people and in the meantime don't make a fool of yourself. You'd better bring me a statement of just how much you've got, five minutes before that time."

Mr. Cray retired early, thoroughly enjoyed his first night in his luxurious bedchamber, was up betimes, and spent a busy morning. At five minutes to twelve, Donvers looking ghastly ill, presented himself and handed over a folded slip of paper.

"I've put down everything I'm worth there," he said. "If I have to find a penny more than six thousand pounds, I'm done. I've come to the conclusion," he went on, "that the fairest way will be to divide all I've got between that woman and my wife, and—disappear."

"Sit down," Mr. Cray replied. "I'll make the bargain for you."

There was a ring at the bell, a moment or two later, and Mrs. Saunderson was ushered in. A single glance into her face robbed Donvers of any hope he might have had. She was still lachrymose, but her face was set in hard and almost vicious lines. Colonel Haughton arrived a few minutes later. He received Mr. Cray's welcome frigidly.

"I desire," he said, refusing a chair, "as speedy a conclusion to this affair as possible."

"Miss Clare not coming?" Mr. Cray inquired, with unabated geniality.

"There is no necessity for her presence that I am aware of," the Colonel replied. "The only question that remains to be decided is whether Mr. Donvers here is prepared to satisfy Mrs. Saunderson's claims."

Mr. Cray was suddenly a different man. The smile had left his broad, good-natured face. His tone was still brisk, but as cold as the Colonel's.

"Colonel Haughton," he said, "you want a show down. Here it is. The whole thing is a ramp. Joe Saunderson was never shot, and you know it. Neither was he ever married."

"What the devil——" the Colonel began.

"Chuck it!" Mr. Cray interrupted. "Miss Clare, as you call her, is married to one of the worst crooks in the States, although you, Colonel, seem to have ruined yourself trying to support her for the last few years. This woman was once her dresser, and a very fair actress still. Joe Saunderson was in charge of the coffee urn in one of my Y.M.C.A. huts for over six months, and I heard the story of his detention and release, a dozen times. Now what are you going to do about it, Donvers? It's up to you."

Donvers suddenly reeled and would have fallen but that Cray caught him and laid him upon the couch. He forced some brandy between his teeth. In a minute the young man opened his eyes, the colour came back to his cheeks. He looked around him. Save for their two selves the room was empty.

"Mr. Cray!" he gasped. "Is this true?"

"Bible truth," Mr. Cray declared cheerfully.

"But Colonel Haughton? He's a well-known man—a D.S.O.—head of his department."

"I guessed he was the goods," Mr. Cray acknowledged. "They do give us the knock sometimes, you know, these men whom no one would suspect."

Donvers was on his feet now, going through all the phases of a rapid recovery to sanity.

"And you actually knew this Joseph Saunderson?" he exclaimed wonderingly.

"One of my washers-up," Mr. Cray explained with unabated cheerfulness, "who was promoted to the coffee urn two months ago. I've heard the story of his arrest half-a-dozen times. . . . What about going and looking for your wife, eh? I gave the ladies a hint that there might be something doing in the way of a little luncheon."

Mr. Cray led the way to the lounge, where Sara and Mrs. Donvers were seated.

"You go and take your wife off somewhere, Mr. Donvers," he said, "and don't let us see you again for an hour or so. If you wish it, we'll all dine together."

"At eight o'clock, here," Donvers declared enthusiastically. "I'm host, and I promise you Jules shall do his best. I'll try and say the things I ought to say to you, then, Mr. Cray. I'm going to take Lydia right off home now."

Mr. Cray nodded sympathetically, and drew Sara away.

"It's a long yarn, my dear," he told her, "but things are fixed up all right for young Donvers. He hasn't a worry left in the world. You shall have the whole story over luncheon."

Sara grasped her father's hand.

"Dad," she exclaimed enthusiastically, "you're a marvel! And to think that we have three months together!"

That night, Colonel Haughton, D.S.O., shot himself in his study owing, it was stated, to financial troubles and general depression, and Miss Clare accepted a suddenly proffered engagement for the States. Gerald Donvers's dinner-party however, was not postponed.

GRAHAM SETON

THE REPUTATION OF Scottish author Graham Seton Hutchison (1890–1946), as a fascist sympathizer has outpaced his memory as an author of espionage and adventure fiction, written under the Graham Seton byline.

Hutchison joined the army in 1909 and served in Africa until the outbreak of World War I, in which he served valiantly but controversially. He propounded several theories about warfare that proved effective for the British army to implement, earning him a promotion to lieutenant-colonel. He opposed retreating from an enemy's attack and is reported to have boasted that he once shot all but two of forty of his own men when they attempted to retreat from an advancing German army.

After World War I, he came to believe that the Versailles Treaty was unfair to Germany and became attracted to fascism and Hitler, ultimately being paid by Joseph Goebbels to write positive articles about the Nuremberg Rallies. He belonged to, and founded, several fascist and socialist organizations, though the advent of World War II softened his positions and finally changed them altogether.

Hutchison wrote a series of military adventure/espionage novels featuring Colonel Grant, beginning with *The W Plan* (1929), which had been proofread by D. H. Lawrence, who thought little of it. Nonetheless, it was plot-driven enough to inspire a Victor Saville–directed 1930 motion picture of the same title that starred Brian Aherne, Madeleine Carroll, and Gordon Harker. The series concluded with *The V Plan* (1941). By the time his literary output ended with *The Red Colonel* (1946) when Hutchison died, he had turned against Nazism and his novel reflected that turn of the tide. The poet Ezra Pound, who had his own flirtation with fascism, was a fan of the books, which are all but forgotten today.

I have been unable to trace the original publication of this story. It was collected in *My Best Spy Story*, edited anonymously (London, Faber & Faber, 1938).

GEORGETTE—A SPY

GRAHAM SETON

I HAD BEEN inside the barrel for nearly seventeen hours. In my confined position I could do nothing to stimulate the blood circulation and shivered continuously. This evening of the 4th February 1918 was icy cold. My limbs were cramped; hunger gnawed at the pit of the stomach, causing a sense of nausea immensely aggravated by the stench of tallow of which the empty barrel reeked. To add to my discomfort, the railway truck, in which among some two dozen others the barrel of my incarceration stood, had been jolted interminably over sidings and against couplings, until I was dizzy with sound and bruised from head to foot by the buffeting I had received.

With a Dutch passport and identification papers showing that I was an employee of the Fabrik Venus—soap and tallow works—I was returning to the Rhineland industrial area to pursue what had almost become routine investigations into the output and destination of munitions and war material. So far as I knew no-one had ever regarded me with suspicion in Düsseldorf, where as an agent for tallow and fats imported via Rotterdam I had a room which served both as lodging and office. My agency was genuine enough; but I had not the slightest

desire to make known all my comings and goings across the German-Dutch frontier, which would certainly have led to my being watched, and my contacts among factory workers and various women coming under suspicion. Hence the strange arrival at the *Haupt Bahnhof* of Düsseldorf in a barrel, and my reappearance among my fellow-men, grimed and slimed and reeking like a chandlery.

I suppose I should tell you that at this date I was a British officer, employed in the Intelligence Service, though I believe this fact is now fairly well known. I had not the slightest desire to court suspicion and had planned to slip back into the routine life of the office and agency. My papers showed that I was a Dutch citizen, while the Fabrik Venus was held in high esteem by the industrialists of the Rhine, for the organization I represented was a reliable source of supply of raw materials of which Germany stood in urgent need. But my passport conferred no right to travel from Holland to Germany in a grease tub.

So far as I was aware no-one knew that I had left Germany on the previous day, and on this occasion had returned in so strange a manner with the sole object of obtaining access to certain warehouses on a siding and blowing their contents sky-high. If indeed the Fabrik Venus provided the raw material necessary to the manufacture of high explosive, there was no reason why the Düsseldorf agent should not blow up the finished article as early as possible, and thus grease the wheels of commerce! The fact that the agent was a British officer pointed clearly to the desirability of explosions in German territory, with additional possibilities of destruction, rather than that he should tacitly aid and abet the annihilation of his fellow-countrymen entrenched "Somewhere in France." At any rate, that was my quite unofficial way of regarding the matter.

As the railway wagons rumbled across the bridge over the Rhine about seven o'clock in the evening, I raised the lid of the barrel. The keen wind, frozen as it was, refreshed me, but the first movement was agonizing. I wriggled from my cramped position and in a moment had clambered over the barrels, and, crouching upon the step, made ready to jump to the ground as soon as I saw a convenient opportunity. The warehouses I sought were some three hundred yards away from the main station; and, leaping clear, I ran towards them.

By appalling ill-fortune, my appearance was at once detected by some soldiers. I heard an officer cry out: "There he is! Arrest him!" It seemed as if they were on the look-out for my arrival. I turned in the darkness and fled along the track back towards the bridge. As someone carrying a lamp appeared to be following in my wake, I slid down the embankment, and with some agility succeeded in scaling the fencing and dropped into the street, for the moment a free, if somewhat bewildered, man.

During all these months I had been conducting the Venus agency I had never aroused any suspicion that it served as the camouflage for acquiring information. The agency was, in fact, quite a masterpiece of the art of espionage. It is true, of course, that I took risks. A number of persons had from time to time received substantial sums from me in return for the provision of information. I had always hinted that I desired

such information for commercial purposes and that my bribes were no less corrupt than were those of current commercial usage. No-one had known of my departure from Germany, neither could the hour nor manner of my return have been anticipated. My landlady was well accustomed to my occasional absences on business in Krefeld, Essen, or Mainz. Nevertheless, I was alarmed. I crouched for several minutes beside the fencing; and, as no-one appeared to have followed so far, I determined to abandon the role of a fugitive and to behave as an ordinary citizen, in fact as a workman returning to his lodgings.

Apprehension that I had come under the watchful eye of counter-espionage did not easily escape me. I was carrying dynamite and fuses; and before I decided whether or not to return to my lodgings I hurried to the Hofgarten beside the Rhine and flung these incriminating souvenirs into the river. The dynamiting of warehouses was not my proper vocation; it was really just a whim, only an adventurous sideline, which had so nearly ended in my falling into the arms of a squad of soldiers.

By this time I was almost famished with hunger, and was desperately anxious to find a haven of safety. I feared to return to my lodgings, so, casting my mind over those whom I had used for my business I decided to visit a lady of my acquaintance, whose flat, in common with other men, I frequented. She was not virtuous, as the world considers these things, and it was because of her relations with all manner of men that I had found in her a valuable contact. I had then persuaded her to use her charms and talents—neither of which were to be underrated—in procuring information for me. She was known as Georgette.

The girl was witty, well-informed, of a gay disposition, and always made me feel quite at home. Indeed, it was a little difficult to think of her as belonging to a profession which is held in such disrepute. I had paid her well for her services and she had never ventured a question for what purpose I desired the information she obtained. There was no reason why she should not receive me now, though she might have an assignation, in which case I should be obliged to find a different haven of retreat until all signs of danger were passed.

I knocked at this lady's apartment; and after two or three minutes, as I thought from her manner, with some apprehension, she opened the door, retaining the bolt on its chain until she should have seen who the caller might be. She was obviously delighted, if surprised, to see me; and I was at once admitted. I apologized for the state of my clothes and was assured that I should be made comfortable in a dressing-gown; and, while I washed and put off my soiled clothes, the girl promised to prepare me a meal. I observed a soldier's helmet hanging in the little hall; but with a laugh the girl assured me that this was only a souvenir and that we were alone.

After so painful a journey, followed by a scare which had chilled me even more than the icy wind, it was comforting indeed to recline in a deep chair after an excellent supper, with a pretty girl administering the heady wine of her laughter served with a warm caress. I must have fallen into a deep sleep.

I was awakened somewhere about seven in the morning by loud knocking on the outer door of the flat. The alarm of the previous evening recaptured my senses. My own clothes, Dutch passport and identification papers had vanished. I could not attempt an escape in a woman's kimono. I sprang to my feet and ran towards the door in search of the woman. I feared that while I slept she had betrayed me. But she came hurrying from her room, in one arm carrying a suit of German uniform, a finger raised to command my silence. In swift, whispered sentences, the girl urged me to don the uniform and adopt its personality. Whoever the intruders might be, I wavered for a few seconds as to whether I should declare myself to them as a respectable Dutch citizen, the agent of the Fabrik Venus, known to a score of highly respectable German manufacturers, or whether I should do as I was now bidden.

I was in a terrible predicament. The suspense of the previous night, my relations with the girl,

my activities in espionage and my camouflage, hitherto so completely successful, together conspired to place me on the horns of a frightful dilemma. Yet, even as the seconds ticked by, I slipped into the trousers and put on the jacket, that of a soldier of the 14th Jäger Regiment. As the banging upon the door increased in its fury, the girl returned to the room carrying boots, a helmet and field equipment. With emphasis she whispered to me that at all costs I must pretend to be her lover, Bruno Peltzer, on leave from the front.

I felt for the soldier's pay-book in the breast pocket and a glance at its pages confirmed the girl's intention that I had donned the uniform of Bruno Peltzer, a native of Tölz in Upper Bavaria. I was sure that within a few minutes those who knocked on the door would intrude into the apartment, so I lay back, feigning sleep, while I collected my wits to meet the forthcoming ordeal.

The girl smiled her approval and then ran towards the door calling to the interrupters to cease their hammering and that she was already on her way to answer their enquiry. The door was opened on the chain.

"Is Soldier Bruno Peltzer here?" demanded a voice of authority.

The girl laughed, replying that she did not trouble always to enquire the names of her visitors.

"Yes, there is a soldier asleep in a chair. Poor fellow, he was so tired. . . ."

Her chatter was cut short by a quick command to admit the callers, and within a few seconds an under-officer, accompanied by two soldiers, burst into the room where I reclined. He shook me roughly by the shoulder, demanding if my name was Bruno Peltzer. I yawned, nodded and glanced up at him, as might one recovering from deep sleep. Then suddenly I sprang from my chair, and stood rigidly to attention.

"Soldier Bruno Peltzer of the 14th Jäger Regiment," exclaimed the *Feldwebel*, "I arrest you for desertion."

I was a good-looking young man; twenty-seven years of age, a slight fair moustache, bronzed, well set-up, six feet in height, a fine figure of a man; and as I looked the old soldier in the eye, he smiled good-naturedly.

"You've got yourself into a nice mess, young fellow. For the sake of a pretty girl's face you've risked the firing squad! If you behave yourself, I'll do my best for you"—he glanced at the girl and winked—"but you've led us a dance since last night. I thought we'd got you at the railway station. . . ."

"So did I!" laughed I, then bit my tongue. The fact is, I was so overwhelmed with delight that I had not been arrested as a spy, but had been accepted as a bona fide deserter with whom the military escort seemed ready to be friendly, that for the moment I was off my guard.

While the girl made coffee for the escort and myself, I pulled on my boots, washed, and shaved—she always had every male convenience handy—and re-presented myself, determined to go through with the role of Bruno Peltzer as a safer camouflage at the moment than that of an agent for Venus soap.

It appeared that I had overstayed my leave for three days, that my earlier visits to the girl's flat had been noted, and that since there were quite a number of desertions across the frontier into Holland the military authorities had concluded that this was my intention. I had been observed at the railway station the previous evening. I endeavoured to get a word with the girl but she would only keep on assuring me, as indeed she sought also to persuade my captors, that I would be quite all right. I had no idea what had become of the genuine Bruno Peltzer, but presumed he had escaped in my clothes with a Dutch passport, and was now well on his way towards Holland. What did it matter, anyway? I was marched to the Uhlan Barracks on the north side of the city; and, after particulars had been taken, was placed in a cell.

About noon I was taken from the cell and brought before the Commandant to answer a charge which had been reduced from that of desertion to one of absence without leave. I imagined that the real Bruno Peltzer was probably guilty up to the hilt; but the charge of desertion could scarcely be brought against a man discovered, not attempting to escape, but asleep in his uniform in the house of a woman to whose privacies apparently most men, not excepting the *Feldwebel* himself, had ready access.

The Commandant, an elderly officer of the Reserve, spoke to me sharply; but the *Feldwebel* discreetly reminded him that youth must be served and, moreover, that Germany had need of the best of her sons in the firing line. Upon my promising not to repeat the offence, I received a nominal sentence, a fine, and was ordered to rejoin my regiment forthwith. The *Feldwebel* was instructed to put me on the next train, and I was given a paper which explained my absence and that I had both been apprehended and punished by the Commandant in Düsseldorf.

I was conducted to the guard-room to await notification of the exact hour of departure of the return-leave train via Aachen and Brussels which would land me at my destination somewhere between Passchendaele and Lille, unless the regiment had been withdrawn or suddenly moved elsewhere. The men in the Uhlan Barracks consisted of the older *Landwehr* reservists employed in guarding railways, bridges, and factories against sabotage, a few youngsters in training, and wounded, not yet fit to return to the front. The *Feldwebel* who had made my arrest seemed to have complete charge of details and of discipline. I had several hours to wait before the scheduled time of my train; and, about an hour after my arrival in the guard-room, the *Feldwebel* entered and brusquely ordered me to form one of an escort searching for a spy. For my edification, he added that such expeditions were by no means uncommon and were spiced with danger. Spies were desperate fellows! I detected no hint of irony in his tones, though, by now, I was again on my guard against anything which might arouse suspicion. I had to remember that I was an ordinary soldier, of some intelligence but no more.

What report I was eventually going to give to my superiors in the British Intelligence Service I could not now begin to contemplate. But now that I was no longer under suspicion, the notion of a spy being sent out to trap a spy struck me as most amusing. A motor-tender was waiting, and within a few minutes we had arrived in the familiar Herzogstrasse and drew up before the house in which was situated my own lodgings. Such an authority as the *Feldwebel* had no difficulty in obtaining the key from my landlady, whose glances I studiously avoided, and we burst into my humble abode. It was a strange experience; and even as I stepped into the familiar little hall I felt that something uncanny had occurred during my absence. The office of the Fabrik Venus showed that some one had ransacked desk-drawers and cupboards.

Lying face down at full length on the floor of the bedroom which led out from the office was the body of a man. He was wearing the clothes which I had discarded on the previous evening. As I stooped to turn the body over, my eye caught sight of a tiny puncture on the back of the man's neck. That sign to me was unmistakable. It was the mark of Joseph Crozier, master spy, chief director of the Fabrik Venus in Rotterdam, the sign made by one of the death-dealing darts, which Crozier and two or three of us acting in concert with him used as life-preservers—poisoned darts, noiseless, quick, infallible.

I was completely bewildered. I had thought that the woman had betrayed me, but now, it seemed that she had sent another to meet my fate. I turned the fellow over. He had been dead for several hours; a man of peasant type, about my own age. As I turned out the man's pockets not by the flicker of an eyelid did I show to the *Feldwebel* that perhaps, but for the forethought of a pretty girl, here lay an officer of the British Intelligence Service.

"A damned Dutchman," fumed the under-officer, glancing at the passport and identification papers. "That must certainly be our man. A spy?" he reflected. "I wonder who killed him?" He shook his head sagely. "This is outside my duty. A dirty business. I'll leave a sentry in the building and inform the police."

So we returned to the barracks, the *Feldwebel* shaking his head over a distasteful matter with which he had no desire to be mixed up. I was simply staggered by the events of the day. I began to reflect upon this woman, of whom in reality I knew so little. I gave the riddle up. She remained a complete enigma. A little later, with some words of advice as to soldierly conduct from the *Feldwebel*—proof that he harboured no suspicions that I was any one other than Bruno Peltzer—I was despatched to the railway station in company with an old reservist, whose business it was to see me safely entrained. I awaited the arrival of the train among a large crowd of soldiers returning from leave, many of them accompanied by wives, children, and sweethearts.

Threading her way through the crowd came the girl of my acquaintance. Neatly attired, paint and powder conspicuous by their absence, no-one would have guessed the nature of her profession. She had eyes for no-one but myself; and she glanced at me timidly, shyly, and nestled close to me.

"Why did you do it?" I whispered.

There was no mistaking the look she gave me—one of absolute adoration. I shall never forget the conversation which followed.

"You're the only man who's ever been kind and courteous to me; the only one who ever appreciated. . . ." I drew her close to me. "You gave me credit for intelligence. . . . The rest used me. . . . Men . . . bah! I'd go to hell for you!"

"But why did you do it?" I repeated softly.

"It saved your skin, silly one," she replied, laughing. Then she lowered her voice. "You were under suspicion, watched. *Gott sei dank!* You came to me last night. How I prayed that you would. They would have caught and shot you. I took in a soldier each night until you came. Now I won't be happy till I see your train going out."

"And then?" I asked, realizing the selfless heroism of the woman, knowing that if I had been discredited, inevitably suspicion would then fix itself upon her. Within a short while, my true identity screened within the uniform of a Bavarian rifleman, I should be free from the impending inquisition, while the girl remained. . . . Well I knew what was in store for her.

"Who killed the soldier?" I asked.

She lowered her eyes. "It was necessary. We went to your lodgings while you were asleep in my flat. It was the Joseph Crozier method." The girl glanced at me with twinkling eyes. "I, too, serve my country—France." I felt her tremble as I clasped her to me. "And I love you."

There was a stir on the platform. My escort, who had maintained a discreet distance, touched me on the arm, and bade me take my seat. For one brief moment the girl clung to me passionately; I kissed her lips in one long farewell.

Once more the girl hurriedly whispered to me: "You are ingenious, clever. You will escape. Do not trust too long to the uniform. Goodbye." She raised her hands to my face, and then gently kissed me. There were tears in her eyes. In a moment she had gone. I took my seat in the crowded compartment. As the train moved away, the occupants of my carriage were sunk in their own reflections. I wondered at the courage of this girl, who placed personal honour, life itself, as trivialities compared with service to her country.

She had been my guardian angel throughout. When I had jeopardized my cause and imperilled my life in a reckless whim, it was she who had saved me. That was a debt I could never repay. I wondered. Perhaps I had given her full measure, for she had loved me; and, treating her always with chivalry, in parting I had kissed her just as she wished.

I began to consider how I could best evade identification as an impostor when I rejoined the 2nd Battalion of the 14th Jäger Regiment. At length my fellow-passengers broke into desultory conversation. There were many movements going on at Douai and Lille. Many divisions and a vast number of guns had been transferred from the Russian front and were relieving hard-tried troops who had spent the winter in the Ypres sector. Ludendorff was getting something ready for the English. Yes, that was certain. Every available man was being sent up from reserve and convalescent camps. . . . No more men were being shot for desertion, but were being sent back to the front with regimental nursemaids. . . . There was much laughter at this observation in which we joined heartily. This was to be the last blow. . . . The English had had terrible losses at Ypres; they had no reserves and the battalions were being filled with schoolboys. They would never be able to withstand the hammer blows which Ludendorff was forging. . . . It was said that the offensive would open in the early spring, possibly before the end of March. . . .

A clerk, employed at one of the Army Headquarters, no doubt anxious to show his knowledge to advantage, spoke mysteriously of grandiose plans known as "Michael," "George," "Mars," "Valkyrie," "Hare Drive," "Georgette," which would follow one another in quick succession as the English armies were rolled back and eventually driven into the sea.

I pricked up my ears. After the collapse of Russia in 1917 we naturally expected the development of a great German offensive in the spring of 1918. The extraordinary industrial pressure which I had witnessed in the Rhineland served to corroborate this view. Ludendorff was about to strike, but when and where?

A plan began to shape itself in my mind. Fate, relentless and ruthless, seemed to be using me to shape her ends. By a chain of circumstances beyond my control, I had been removed from a sphere of comparative usefulness, in which my life had suddenly been imperilled; a girl had been committed to almost certain death by an act of amazing self-immolation at the shrine of patriotism; and now I listened to hints and suggestions—secrets which might prove of untold value to the Allied cause.

I was convinced that I could remain in the masquerade of a soldier of the 14th Jäger Regiment for the shortest possible time. My landlady of the Herzogstrasse would be called to identify the dead body discovered in my office. There would be a hue and cry. Orders would be sent to apprehend soldier Bruno Peltzer, and I should again be arrested. It would not be difficult at Roubaix or Lille to change my identity; but at all costs I must discover what was meant by "Michael," "George," "Mars," and "Valkyrie," in short where and when Ludendorff would strike. Then by hook or by crook, I must reach the British lines.

In the guise of an ordinary soldier I could obtain no access to information. I must somehow contrive to change that role. The idea now obsessed me to the exclusion of all else.

I therefore led the conversation to speculate as to where *Obersie Heeresleitung*—the German Supreme Command—would elect to strike. I confess that some of my suggestions were most absurd: but they provided an opportunity for the Staff clerk—who had been contemptuously twitted as a non-combatant—to retort with a display of superior knowledge. He declared that a decision as to the "Michael" offensive—against the British Fifth Army on the Somme front—had been reached on 21st January, and that Crown Prince Rupprecht was preparing a gigantic attack through Armentières and Ypres, with Mont Kemmel as the chief prize.

I made myself amiable to the Staff clerk. My guardian angel of Düsseldorf had forgotten nothing in equipping me for my journey. I had money to jingle in my pocket and a wad of notes in my wallet. The clerk surmised that I was a wealthy *bauer*, a small farmer, and if he smiled at my simulated peasant naïvety, he obviously thought me intelligent. At the infrequent halts, during the tedious journey, I took him to the canteen for refreshment; and, finding me a ready listener, he gave me a well-informed outline of Ludendorff's intentions. This secret information was of vital importance to Sir Douglas Haig's staff. By a strange turn of the wheel of Fate it had come into my possession.

I was now obsessed with the single-minded idea of reaching the British lines as soon as possible. The train halted at Courtrai, some fifteen miles behind the front lines at Passchendaele. During the British attacks in the Third Battle of Ypres, I had been attached to the Second Army to assist in the interrogation of prisoners, and was therefore entirely familiar with the topography and lie of the land in the Passchendaele Salient. At the concentration camp in Courtrai, where all men from leave reported, I learned that the 14th Jäger Regiment had been shifted to the Armentières front, and I was instructed to proceed south to Roubaix and from there rejoin my regiment. I had no such intention; so took the road west towards Moorslede.

Those who remember the soldier's life in Flanders during the war will recollect the numbers of men from every kind of unit and formation whom one might meet in the course of a few hours behind the lines—men going on and returning from leave, as escorts for prisoners, lightly wounded rejoining their units, batmen, runners, orderlies. Their business was seldom questioned by anyone in authority; and certainly, if zealously plodding towards the battle zone, no such man would court suspicion. I marched on. At the wayside I fell in with a group of soldiers and discovered that the 229th Reserve Infantry Regiment was in the line at Passchendaele, the defence consisting of scattered outposts in shell-hole positions and machine-guns in concrete "pill-boxes."

I then made up my mind to attempt to penetrate the line and cross no-man's-land under cover of darkness.

As soon as dusk set in, I set out towards the lines. Should I be interrogated I had made up my mind to declare quite simply that I was returning from leave and before rejoining my battalion which was not in the line I wished to recover the field-glasses of my *Oberleutnant* who had been wounded and whom I had visited in hospital while on leave. I had a good idea exactly where to find them, that was to say about one hundred paces due east of the gasometers, in the pill-box destroyed by a shell when he was wounded. It seemed a sufficiently plausible tale to tell to inquisitive soldiers; but if an officer questioned me, then I would simply state that I had lost my way, returning from leave. I would probably be ordered to remain in a dug-out during the night and return the following morning.

My intention was, therefore, far less hazardous than it may seem to anyone unfamiliar with the conditions in the Ypres Salient during the winter of 1917–18. I followed in the wake of a ration party. After two hours I reached the forward zone and trudged uphill towards the ridge on which were the shattered ruins of Passchendaele village. It was about nine o'clock in the evening and I could now see the Very rockets fired from the British posts as they rose into the air and fell behind the skyline.

As with growing assurance I was going forward, a group of men suddenly loomed from the darkness in front of me. A voice ordered me to halt and declare myself. I gave the usual curt reply of "Friend," and turned slightly aside to proceed.

"Who are you?" asked the voice. True, indeed, is it that "the best laid plans of men and mice gang aft agley!" I had prepared myself to answer every conceivable question except the most obvious which I might be asked.

I could not hesitate and replied simply, "Rifleman Bruno Peltzer."

My interrogator drew aside a blanket curtaining what I observed to be the entrance to a dug-out and surmised to be the headquarters of a battalion or company in the line, and shouted to someone below.

"*Herr Leutnant*, Rifleman Bruno Peltzer."

"*Mein Gott!*" replied an excited voice. "There's a telegram for his arrest. I told you! Quick! . . ." There were sounds of someone rushing up the stairway, cursing.

So my escape and ruse had been discovered. Telegrams had obviously been transmitted through headquarters to command posts along the whole German line.

I took to my heels and ran towards the British lines, distant I reckoned certainly another five hundred yards. It was hard going: I floundered through mud and slime, pitched into shell-holes and could hear shouting in my wake. Lights began to soar into the air. They made it easier for me to avoid the shell-holes, but I was sometimes obliged to cower for shelter when a light fell too dangerously near me and spluttered on the ground. I was terrified that my pursuers would open fire; but hoped that fear of inflicting casualties among their own men in front would deter them.

I leaped, stumbled, staggered, dived, swayed, and reeled on, with heart and brain bursting with the excitement of the chase and filled with unknown terrors that I should be stricken down before I could reach the British line. The German officer shouted orders to someone in front, and a moment later rifle fire opened in my rear. I judged that I must by now be about two hundred yards in advance of my pursuers, and working my way rapidly on hands and toes to the right flank, taking cover among the shell-holes, I evaded them for the moment. Then, summoning all my strength I rushed forward again, and had covered a further hundred yards when I was again spotted, and a machine-gun began to beat the ground, in a cavity of which I sprawled.

The excitement in the German lines provoked uneasiness among the British and more lights began to soar into the air. My heart sank. My safety lay in quietness but I had stirred up a hornets' nest; and within a few seconds machine-guns were hammering away on both sides, the air crackling with bullets above my wretched body. However, as long as the duel continued I was safe, and could rest in the shelter of the shell-hole until the alarm of the night had passed. The nervousness soon passed and the firing on both sides ceased. I again crawled forward carefully keeping my ear cocked for the sound of British voices. Some minutes later, to my joy I heard the familiar brogue from across the Scottish border; and, well concealed in a hole, I called "*Kamerad*," and again repeated the familiar cry of surrender.

A voice ordered me to come in. This time I replied with a wealth of expletives dear to the ear of the Scot, concluding by begging the men not to shoot even if I should appear in German uniform.

Sound carries far on such a night; and a further burst of machine-gun fire from the German lines again turned the night into a hell around my body. I lay quietly until the fury had subsided, and then came in and gave myself up to a post of the Scottish Rifles.

The details of how I was hurried down the line, preceded by telegrams to Lord Plumer's headquarters at Cassell, do not matter. I was able to deliver myself of my tale. That the vital message which I had to deliver, as I judged from subsequent events, was not at once acted upon, concerns high politics. Having also committed the unforgivable offence of kicking over the traces of red-tape, in not remaining to be shot as a spy in Düsseldorf, thanks indeed to the love and heroism of a woman to whose honour I pay deathless tribute, I was reposted to the command of a battalion on the 26th February, 1918. Thank heavens! With some knowledge of Ludendorff's intention I was enabled to play my little part in destroying "Georgette," the deadly German thrust towards Hazebrouck between 12th and 18th April, and had my revenge for the death of a sweet lady. It is strange that she, too, was known as "Georgette."

FLOOD ON THE GOODWINS

A. D. DIVINE

ALTHOUGH Arthur Durham (David) Divine (1904–1987) wrote sixteen espionage, political, adventure, and crime thrillers between 1930 (*Sea Loot*) and 1942 (*Tunnel from Calais*), his most successful books were such nonfiction titles as *Dunkirk* (1948), *The Blunted Sword* (1964), and *The Broken Wing* (1966), the latter two being severely critical of the British government's military for its lack of modernization and preparedness at the height of the Cold War.

Dunkirk recounts the famous World War II evacuation of the trapped British Expeditionary Force from Dunkirk across the English Channel in small boats. Divine made the trip three times on a thirty-five-foot boat, being wounded on the third run and winning a Distinguished Service Medal for his heroic actions. He also wrote a novel about that action, *The Sun Shall Greet Them* (1941), as well as a factual account, *Nine Days at Dunkirk* (1945), which he expanded to *Dunkirk* three years later. Divine also wrote the screenplay for *Dunkirk* (1958), the first film on the mission.

Born in Cape Town, South Africa, he was hired as a journalist for the *Cape Times* in 1922, where he worked until 1926 and again from 1931 to 1935. After the end of World War II, he was hired by the *Sunday Times* foreign news service in London to be its correspondent on matters of defense, a position he held until 1975. His boss for several years was the former naval intelligence officer Ian Fleming.

The most resonant title among Divine's more than two dozen books is *Boy on a Dolphin* (1955), which became a big-budget motion picture starring Sophia Loren, Alan Ladd, and Clifton Webb. Released in 1957, it is the charming, romantic story of a poor diver in Greece who discovers a gold and brass statue of a boy riding a dolphin. Idealistically, she wants to turn it over to the Greek government but her boyfriend wants to sell it to an unscrupulous art dealer for a lot of money. Legend has it that the sculpture has the magical ability to grant wishes, which is soon tested.

I have been unable to trace the original publication of "Flood on the Goodwins." It was collected in *My Best Spy Story*, edited anonymously (London, Faber & Faber, 1938).

FLOOD ON THE GOODWINS

A. D. DIVINE

DUNDAS LOOKED OUT into the fog and blew reflectively on his finger-tips. The night was cold, raw with the steady drift of the westerly wind, and the fog poured over the dark bulk of the harbour wall as flood water pours over a breach in the dykes—as evenly, as endlessly, as ominously.

The last greyness was fading out of it now, and within twenty minutes at the outside the night would be down, and the sea as lost as the black earth in a snowdrift. Dundas blew again; not a night for fishing, he decided. Not even for wartime fishing, when food was scarce and prices high.

The complete darkness of the harbour was daunting. No lights showed even on a clear night now—save when the immediate necessities of shipping demanded it. Even to find one's way through the narrow entrance was a matter for caution and skill. Dundas knew that he could do it despite the fog—but whether he could find his way home again was another matter—and this fog might easily be a two-day affair.

It was not as if he were a regular local fisherman—though, heaven knew, even the "locals" had not gone out this night. Dundas was a

"deep sea" man, third mate he had been when the war began, third mate of the *Rosvean*, five thousand tons, flush decked, running regularly like a ferry in the Rio Plata maize trade.

In the May of 1917 he had watched the *Rosvean* sink off the Casquets. The incident had made a considerable impression on him, but had in no way affected his nerves. His principal reaction had been largely one of scorn at the poorness of the shooting of the submarine which had put them down.

In the July he went down with his next ship, the *Moresby*, because the torpedo gave them rather less warning than the gun of the previous sinking.

He was picked up after two hours by a destroyer, and her commander commended him on his swimming ability.

That left him with nothing worse than a cold in the head, and at the end of July he signed on again. By this time he had won promotion. He signed on as second mate.

His new office lasted precisely seven hours, allowing for three hours in dock before the ship sailed. Off Selsey Bill, he being then on the poop supervising the readjustment of a hatch tarpaulin, the ship was struck just for'ard of the engine-room by a mine.

The explosion cracked five ribs, dislocated his shoulder, and three parts drowned him.

After he was brought ashore the doctors told him to take it easy for at least a month. By way of taking it easy he went down to Ramsgate, where his uncle had one of the new motor fishing boats. After five days of his aunt's cooking he began to get restless for the sea again. After seven days he was skipper of his uncle's fishing boat, and his uncle was taking a holiday.

It was a small boat, eighteen feet long, open, with the engine under a little dog-kennel cover, and no particular virtues. To-night the engine had been sulky, diffident over starting, and secretive about its disabilities.

Dundas was inclined to thank it. If the engine had started easily, he would now be out in the very thick of the fog. When he came down to the dock there had been little sign that it would close down on them suddenly an hour later.

He bent down after a moment's rest, and began tinkering with it again. He had found the trouble—dirt in the magneto—and nothing remained now but to put the pieces together again.

The lantern he was working by made a pleasant pool of reddish light in the wide blackness about him. There was little more to do now. He felt curiously alone. Save for the steady lap and splash of the water against the sides of the boat and the stone of the wall, the night was empty of sound. Even the long low chorus of bellows and wails and grunts that normally accompanies a Channel fog was absent.

He finished piecing the engine together, replaced the cover, rolled the strap round the groove, and, giving a mighty heave, jerked it into sudden life.

After a moment he throttled down and listened contentedly to the steady purring.

Above him a voice spoke suddenly. It was an educated voice, pleasant, with a faint burr to it. "May I come aboard?" said the unknown.

"Who are you?" said Dundas, startled suddenly out of the calm emptiness that had enclosed him.

"Cutmore's my name," said the unknown. "I'm from the minesweeper down the wall. Taking a breather before turning in."

"Mind the weed on the ladder as you come down," said Dundas.

The unknown came slowly down, a pair of long legs coming first into the glow of the lamp, followed gradually by a long body. The unknown wore a heavy overcoat, which appeared to impede somewhat his freedom of action.

"Been having trouble with that?" he said, indicating the engine. "I heard you cursing when I passed a few minutes ago."

"Yes," said Dundas; "she's a bitch, she is, but I think I've fixed her."

"Going sweetly now?" said the unknown.

"Yes," said Dundas.

"What can you get out of her?"

"Seven knots or thereabouts," said Dundas.

"And what's her range with full tanks?"

"Eighty miles or so, I suppose," said Dundas. "I've never tried her out, really."

"Tanks full now?" said the stranger.

"Yes—er——" Dundas's tone suddenly changed. "May I ask why you are cross-examining me like this?"

"Forgive me," said the stranger, "but can you keep your mouth shut?"

"I—well, I suppose so; what is it?"

"As a matter of fact," said the stranger, "I'm a member of the Naval Intelligence service, and it is urgently necessary that I should be landed on the Belgian coast to-night. Almost anywhere along the coast will do, as long as it's clear of the German lines. I've an extraordinarily important job on hand, and it's got to be done in complete secrecy."

Dundas lifted his face away from the glow of the lamp.

"Question of getting close enough in. You know the Belgian coast, I suppose. You know how it shoals? Difficult to get a destroyer close enough in to land me with comfort. The size is against it, too, she might easily be seen by the shore posts. It's essential that I should go by a small boat. As a matter of fact, the sweeper up the wall was to have taken me along, but she's developed engine-room defects. . . . That's why I came along to see if there was any possibility up here. They told me there was a motor-boat here. I came along, missed you the first time, and then found you by the noise of your engine."

"You said you heard me the first time," said Dundas. "Heard me swearing."

"Oh, yes," said the stranger. "I heard some-body swearing, but I didn't know it was you. As a matter of fact I went along to another boat up there, and they told me you were farther back."

"And that," said Dundas, feeling in the dark for a screw wrench, "proves you to be a liar, for there was only Terris up the wall, and he called good night to me an hour ago. Your story's a lot of bull. You're coming along with me to the sweeper now."

"I was wondering how long you'd take to see through it," said the stranger coolly. "No, don't move, I've got my foot on the monkey wrench, and I've got you covered with a fairly large calibre revolver. Now listen to me. . . ."

"You swine . . ." said Dundas provocatively.

"No you don't," said the stranger. "Keep absolutely still, because I shall shoot if you make the slightest movement, and I can hardly miss. I use soft-nosed bullets, too. Listen, I'm going to make you a fair offer. I want to charter this boat; it's absolutely necessary that I should charter it, and if you want it back you'll have to come with me. I've got to get to Bruges before ten o'clock to-morrow, and that means I've got to be on the Belgian coast by dawn. This boat can do it, and this fog makes it possible. If you'll take me there I'll give you sixty pounds, in one-pound notes. It's all I've got. If you won't do it, I'm going to shoot you now, and make a run for it myself. I can find my way out of this tin-pot basin, and I guess I can find the Belgian coast by myself. It's a fine night for yachting."

The stranger used the same tone as he had used in the early stages of his conversation, but a faint over-tone of menace had crept into it. Dundas, thinking as swiftly as the other talked, decided that he meant what he said.

"You wouldn't dare," said he after a moment. "The shot would rouse the whole harbour, and the sentries on the wall would get you long before you could clear the entrance."

"In this fog?" said the stranger scornfully. "I'll take the chance."

"There's a boom across the mouth," said Dundas.

"That's an afterthought," said the stranger equably. "I don't blame you. I'd lie myself if I were in your position, but it isn't any use, you know. Are you going to accept my offer?"

"No," said Dundas. He thought rapidly for a moment. If he could edge back slowly he could perhaps slip the tiller out of its socket and, hitting blindly in the dark, knock the other out of the boat.

The stranger seemed to be able to read his mind. "No you don't," he said. "If you edge back another inch I'll shoot, and I don't mind telling you that I am a prizewinner at revolver shooting."

"Give me a minute to think it over," said Dundas.

"I will if you turn round with your back to me. Do it slowly now. If you move too quickly I'll shoot."

Dundas moved slowly round, shuffling cautiously on the floor boards. Immediately he felt something prod him in the back.

"This bullet will rip your spine clear out," said the stranger softly. "I warn you to make up your mind quickly. If this fog clears I'm done for, you see, and I'm not taking any risks."

Dundas trod his mind as a squirrel treads its mill, but no help came. It was clear that this man was desperate. Whatever he had done, whatever he wanted to do, it was sufficiently obvious that he was prepared to risk his own life. It was equally obvious that he would not allow the life of any other to obstruct his purpose.

"Come on," said the stranger again; "sixty pounds is sixty pounds to a fisherman—and the season's bad, I know. Heroics won't help you if you're a corpse. Better take my offer and keep your mouth shut about it. Nobody will know, you can say you got lost in the fog, and couldn't get home again—engine broke down or something. Any tale. . . . Come on!"

"Can you give me any help when we get near the Belgian coast?" said Dundas suddenly. "I don't know the marks."

"Good man," said the stranger; "then you'll do it. No, I shan't be able to help you much. I don't know much about it."

"Oh, well," said Dundas slowly. "Doesn't seem as if I've any choice, and I don't suppose it'll do much harm."

"That's right," said the stranger. "That's splendid. Shall we unloosen the ropes."

"Er—cast off—er, yes. Just a minute. Let me light the binnacle lamp. It'll be no joke working through in the fog, you know."

"I know," said the other, "but I've been waiting for a fog for a whole week now."

Dundas knelt down and, striking a match, lit the tiny lamp of the boat compass that he carried. The green card shone wanly in its glow. He could feel the muzzle of the stranger's revolver still pressed against his back.

"Sorry," said the other, "but I must safeguard myself till we're out of the harbour anyway."

Fumbling, Dundas cleared the mooring lines, and the boat drifted away from the wall. Immediately she was lost to the world.

Dundas jerked at the starting strap, and the engine came throatily to life. Foam swirled under the stern of the boat, and she surged forward through the unseen water. The fog dragged past them, faintly gold in the light of the lamp.

"We'll have that out," said Dundas after a moment; "the visibility's impossible as it is."

The stranger had squatted himself down next to the engine casing on the starboard side. He stretched out and grasped the lamp, found the wick lever, and turned it out.

They went on into the blackness with only the faint green eye of the binnacle making sign of life in it all.

After a minute or two Dundas put down the helm gently. "We ought to make the entrance now," he said.

The boat lifted to a little swell in immediate answer, and there was a momentary glance of a high black wall. From its top someone challenged, and Dundas answered, giving his name and the name of the boat.

The next instant they were outside in the live water, pitching a little to the lop that came up from the Downs.

"A-ah," said the stranger relaxing. "And that's that. Now you play me straight, young fellow, and you'll be sixty pounds the richer. How soon can we get across? It's about fifty-five miles, I should say—that's seven hours by this boat?"

Dundas shrugged in the darkness. "It's sixty-five miles as the crow flies. We'll have to reckon with the tides, though."

"When's high tide?" said the stranger.

"High tide—oh, you mean the flood? Well, I'm not exactly sure," said Dundas slowly. "I'll tell you what I'm going to do. I'll go south and a little east now, and round the heel of the Goodwins, and then stand out with the flood, and get right across. With luck we'll make it by two o'clock."

"That'll suit me," said the stranger, "but why not go straight?"

"Well, you see, this is an underpowered boat . . ." said Dundas slowly. "Don't you know anything about the sea?"

"Nothing," said the other airily. "I was in the cavalry."

"The Uhlans?" said Dundas swiftly.

"Don't ask questions, my little friend. You look after your steering." He settled himself more comfortably. "Remember," he added after a moment, "I still have my revolver in my hand. If you betray me, take me up to one of your patrol ships or anything, we will both die."

Dundas grunted and peered into the binnacle.

For a long hour there was silence. Only the

steady mutter of the engine, and the occasional lift and rattle of the screw in the stern glands, broke across the silence of the night. Water noises from the bow, and the lap-lap along the sides were somehow merged in the immense silence of the sea.

Only once, far away, they heard a bell buoy, and once the clatter of a ship's bell at anchor. At the end of the hour Dundas spoke again. "We will have cleared the Goodwins now," he said. "I'm going to stand out across the heel of them. Like to see the course we're making?"

"How?" said the other.

"Look at the compass," said Dundas.

"And bring my head in front of you with my back to you?" said the other. "No, no, my little friend. Remember only that I have my revolver and the soft-nosed bullets—and that if I die, you die too. The steering is your business—so long as you remember that."

Dundas grunted again, and shifted his helm very slightly.

For another hour they held on in silence, then Dundas heard a slight noise from for'ard. A faint, rasping noise. A moment later it came again, an unmistakable snore.

He nodded grimly to himself.

The snoring went on, grew louder, became more steady, more settled. It was plain that the stranger was fast asleep. For three hours it went on, varied occasionally by little grunts and slight pauses following a change of position.

Dundas occupied himself steadily with his helm, making tiny alterations of course from time to time, checking them carefully with a great silver watch that he held in the light of the binnacle lamp.

Quarter of an hour before midnight the stranger awoke. Dundas felt the jerk as he straightened up, hurriedly.

"You've been asleep," he said quietly, "for a long time."

The other muttered incoherently for a moment, and then said yes. Presently the implication seemed to strike him. "And you tried nothing, no, no funny business." He paused.

"That was good," he said. "You are being sensible, my young friend. Sixty pounds is sixty pounds. Ach—I was tired. Three days and three nights without sleep, most of them spent in the fields of the wretched country behind Ramsgate. *Lieber Goit*, I was tired."

"Three days and three nights. That's since Monday, then?"

"Yes," said the other.

"Monday was the day of the big explosion?"

"What of it?" said the other.

"You. . . ."

"Partly," said the other cynically. "Since you are being sensible it does not matter if you know."

"But you are English, aren't you? Your voice. . . ."

"Come, come," said the stranger. "I was at an English school, but you knew from the start. . . ."

"I suppose so," said Dundas grudgingly.

"And how near are we?"

"Not far now," said Dundas. "We should get there a little earlier than I thought, half-past one perhaps."

"Good," said the German.

With long spells of silence and occasional brief conversations they pressed on through the night. Once or twice the fog thinned slightly, so that they could see a boat's length from them over the darkling water. Twice Dundas tried to get the German to tell him why he had to be at Bruges in so painful a hurry, but the other avoided his questions adroitly.

Every now and then he seemed to be listening.

"Strange," he said once. "Strange, we should have heard the sound of the guns by now."

"Nothing strange in fog," said Dundas; "you can hear something that's miles away sometimes, and another time miss a fog gun when you're right on top of it."

The night was getting on now. When Dundas next looked at his watch it was a quarter past one. "We should be very nearly there," he said. "Can you take a sounding?"

"What do I do?" said the other.

"Feel in the locker to your right and see if you can find a fishing line with a lead," said Dundas. "I'll slow down, and you throw it ahead of you, feel when it touches the bottom, and then measure it with your arms outstretched."

The other fumbled for a bit, experimented once, and then after a second cast said, "Nine times."

"Call it eight fathoms," said Dundas. "We're closing in on the coast."

Five minutes later he slowed for another cast.

"Six times," said the German.

"Getting there; we're inside the five fathom line."

Five minutes later they heard the sound of little seas on sand, a soft rustle that was yet loud enough to come over the noise of the engine, and the rustle and rush of their progress. Somewhere in the darkness a sleepy gull called.

"We're there," said Dundas whispering; "get ready."

The other stood up, wrapping his coat about him. Even as he did so Dundas switched off the engine, and in absolute silence they glided in. Suddenly the boat grated, dragged forward, and grated again. The German lurched, steadied himself with a hand on the thwart and said: "Lieber Gott."

"The money," said Dundas.

"But yes," said the German, fumbling in his pocket. "You are sure this is Belgium?"

"By the distance we've run," said Dundas, "and the time, it must be."

"Ha," said the other, "take it!"

Dundas met the other's hand and took a rolled bundle of notes. "Thank you," he said.

"Get out over the bows; there'll be a little more than a foot of water, and give me a shove off before you go. I must get afloat again."

The other lumbered over the side, splashed for a moment, and then, bending down, heaved. The boat slid astern, Dundas pushing on the other side with the loom of an oar.

In a moment it floated free, surging back into deepish water. Dundas straightened himself, the starting strap in his hand.

"High tide's at three," he called out loudly.

He heard the other splash through the shallows, and then a scrunch as he reached the dry sand beyond. A voice came clear out of the fog to him: "What's that?"

He heard the feet run on, scrunching over the sand and then stop suddenly. The voice came out to him again. "There's water here. A strip of sand and then. . . ."

"High tide's at three," shouted Dundas again, "but the Goodwins are covered before the flood." He bent down and jerked at the starting strap and the engine woke to life. Sitting down he headed the boat round until her bows pointed a little west of north.

Swiftly he crossed the four-mile circle of water inside the Goodwin sands that he had thrashed round and round so many times during the long night. There was six miles between home and the neck of the South Goodwins, upon which a lone man stood watching the slow, relentless, upward movement of the tide.

"Thirty dead in the big explosion," said Dundas softly to himself. "Women, too. Well . . ." he fingered the roll of notes. "Dirty money's as good as clean to the Red Cross fund. And the Goodwins pays for all."

CAPTAIN A. O. POLLARD

ALMOST ENTIRELY forgotten today, except by collectors of crime and espionage fiction, Captain Alfred Oliver Pollard (1893–1960) was once an enormously prolific writer of spy and adventure novels, producing forty-six novels in those genres, published between 1930 and 1962, as well as short stories and non-fiction, notably books about military deeds and history, including *Fire-Eater: the Memoirs of a V.C.* (1932), an autobiography focused on his military career in which he makes it obvious that he enjoyed the fighting—especially the killing of the enemy.

Pollard volunteered for service in the British Army in 1914 and was commissioned as a second lieutenant in 1914 in the Honourable Artillery Company. He saw combat frequently, being wounded twice, but returned to battle almost immediately both times. His extraordinary bravery on the front lines earned Britain's highest honors, including the Victoria Cross, and he is reported to have been England's most decorated soldier of the Great War.

His first book, *Pirdale Island* (1930), and other of his earliest titles were crime stories. He soon turned to thrillers pitting British soldiers and agents against the Nazis and, when that war was settled, turned his heroic characters against those from the Soviet Union

Among his other fiction, Pollard wrote science fiction novels in which he introduced inventions created by the villains, designed to be used for evil purposes. In *The Murder Germ* (1937), for example, a mad scientist infects innocent people with a concoction that causes them to commit unspeakable acts that mirror his own.

Virtually all of his books carry the byline that includes his rank.

I have been unable to trace the original publication of this story. It was collected in *My Best Spy Story*, edited anonymously (London, Faber & Faber, 1938).

UNDER ENEMY COLOURS

A. O. POLLARD

THE NIGHT WAS pitch black, absolutely ideal for the job, reflected Second-Lieutenant Martin Westlake of the Royal Flying Corps. Provided he did not lose his bearings, which, in his youthful self-confidence, he did not think at all likely, his task would be completed and he would be on his way home again in less than an hour.

"Five kilometres north-east of the G in Veldeghem," the Colonel had said. "Shut off your engine and glide down to fifteen hundred feet before you give the signal to jump."

Martin glanced over the side of his cockpit. There was very little to be seen except a feathery layer of cloud but, through a gap, twenty thousand feet below him, he glimpsed the everlasting Very lights which marked the position of the opposing trenches.

They were over the lines, then, and from now on he would have to keep his eyes skinned for signs of enemy scouts. If he were spotted before he had dumped his cargo the whole show would have to be abandoned.

The "cargo," seated grim and silent in the rear cockpit, was a Belgian agent who was being dropped by parachute to glean some vital information for the Intelligence Corps. Beyond the fact that the green-tabbed major who brought him to the aerodrome had introduced him as Monsieur Jacques Poulière, Martin knew nothing whatever about him.

From various rumours that had been circulating for the past month, however, he guessed that the spy's mission was connected with an expected German push. Aerial photographs had revealed the presence of a number of new dumps behind the enemy lines and no doubt Intelligence were anxious to ascertain the approximate date when the assault would begin.

Martin kept steady on his course for another ten minutes. At the end of that time he calculated he ought to be in the vicinity of Roulers. It was a German rail head and he was well aware, from a reconnaissance made a few days earlier, that there was a big concentration of troops in the neighbourhood. Had the night been clearer the sky would have been alive with searchlight beams and he would have been lucky to get by without a challenge.

After Roulers it should be safe enough to drop down to ten thousand feet, or even less. If a Hun searchlight unit caught him in a beam so far into enemy territory, the black crosses pasted on the underside of his lower wings would convince them that he was one of their own pilots.

111

Better give it another five minutes to make sure. Veldeghem was only ten kilometres farther on. Even if the wind had veered a bit and he was off his estimated track he should have no difficulty in spotting the place where Poulière was to leave him, once he got below the clouds which had stood him in such good stead.

"You can't make any mistake," the Colonel had assured him. "There's a river with the railway crossing it at right-angles. If Poulière drops off when your leading edge cuts the point of intersection he should land just right."

The five minutes was up at last, and closing down his throttle Martin put the nose of his Bristol Fighter into a glide. At every two thousand feet fall in height, registered on the altimeter, he reopened his throttle and flew for half a minute to prevent his engine getting too cold; then throttled back again and continued his descent.

He was down to eight thousand feet and still the cloud was too dense for him to make out any landmarks from which to check his position. According to time reckoning he ought to be very close to his objective.

For the first time he wished that visibility was a trifle clearer. Should he risk going down a little lower, or would it be better to fly about until he found a rift which would give him a peep at the ground?

The problem was acute. If he flew around and failed to find a break, he might lose himself. On the other hand if he went lower and was spotted before he was ready to dump his passenger he might jeopardize Poulière's chances of an undetected landing.

No great imagination was needed to visualize Poulière's fate if he fell into enemy hands. There would be a drumhead court martial followed by a dawn parade for a firing squad. A Belgian spy was too sharp a thorn in the German plans for any expectation of leniency.

All the same, he would have to do something, and going lower appeared to be the lesser of two evils. But Martin made a mental reservation as he closed the throttle for a further descent. If

he had boobed badly and made altogether the wrong landfall he would climb back into the sky again and return to the aerodrome as fast as his engine would take him.

He might incur the severe displeasure of the Intelligence Corps and of his superior officers in general. He might have to endure the ribald jests of his light-hearted companions in the mess, but he was hanged if he was going to have Poulière's death on his conscience through his inability to locate the right spot for dropping him, even if the fellow was only a Gonzubree spy.

Peering ahead through the murk, with one eye on the falling needle of his altimeter, Martin wondered anxiously if the clouds would ever break. Six thousand feet, five thousand, four thousand, three thousand and still the ground was totally invisible.

This was the very devil! It was madness to go any lower. Unless by the one chance in a million he had struck the exact spot for Poulière to get off, his presence would inevitably be discovered.

Martin cursed softly under his breath. However much he disliked the change of plan there was only one thing to be done. He must reopen his engine and cruise around until he found the break in the clouds that had so far eluded him.

Savagely pushing his throttle fully open, he eased back his control column and began to climb. Three thousand feet was much too low; he ought to have had the sense to stick at five thousand.

The engine responded smoothly and for some thirty seconds ran with unfaltering note. Then, suddenly, it spat.

Pist! it spat again; an ominous warning that would not be ignored. Wise with the experience of two months' active service on the Western front, Martin instinctively retarded the throttle to two-thirds. Probably the carburettors were not filling fast enough to supply gas for full revolutions.

The remedy appeared to take effect and for a minute and a half the engine functioned normally. But before Martin had had time to recover from the scare the temporary failure had given him, the rhythmic roar died abruptly to nothingness.

Was it fuel, magnetos, a mechanical break? The queries chased one another through Martin's mind as he instinctively depressed the nose of the Bristol into a glide. If it was a fuel stoppage he might get away with it yet; if ignition or mechanical trouble he had not a chance.

Feeling for the petrol tap he switched over to the reserve tank. By diving steeply the rush of air would revolve the propeller sufficiently to make the cylinders fire. Pray God she would pick up.

A hand clutched his shoulder and shook him with the fury of desperation.

"Qu'y a-t-il?" asked Poulière fearfully. "What's the matter?"

His voice sounded unnaturally loud in the dead silence that had succeeded the engine failure.

"Engine's stopped," snapped Martin.

"Mon Dieu! Mon Dieu, what is going to happen to me?"

He might have included me, thought Martin cynically. With those black crosses on the wings a British pilot could expect short shrift. The Belgian, in civilian clothes, and in his own territory, stood at least an even chance.

"Hold tight, I'm going to dive!" announced Martin shortly.

He held forward his control column until the wind was screaming through the bracing wires. Ahead of him he could see the propeller flapping round in spasmodic jerks. But although he waggled the throttle backwards and forwards there was not so much as a cough from the defunct power unit.

The Bristol was down below one thousand feet before he gave it up. It was no blinking use trying any longer. He would have to face the unpleasant fact of a forced landing behind the enemy lines.

A nasty lump kept rising in his throat as he looked wildly about him. He was so young to die; it would be his twenty-first birthday in a month and he had hoped for special leave to celebrate it at home. It would not have been so bad to have gone out in a scrap but there was something terrifying in the prospect of facing a firing squad.

A blubbing sound behind him cut through his fears like a knife. Poulière was evidently in a blue funk too. Surely he had more spunk than a common Gonzubree spy, Martin told himself firmly.

Of course he had. He had been entrusted with this job and he would see it through. Whatever happened to him afterwards there was no reason why he should not drop Poulière according to plan. The Colonel had been insistent that Poulière's mission was of vital importance.

Exerting all his will-power he brought himself under control.

"Listen to me, Monsieur Poulière," he cried over his shoulder. "Pull yourself together, man. You're going to be all right, even if I'm not. Get ready to jump and I'll land as far away from you as I can."

He had to repeat himself twice before the terrified Belgian grasped his meaning. When at last he understood, his extravagant joy was as nauseating as his former despondency.

"It is that I shall be safe after all. Oh la la, Monsieur, this ees a beet of all right. I am so 'appy, yes!"

A sudden thought struck his happiness from him.

"But where shall I land. Will it be safe country? Cannot you take me to the place agreed?"

"No, I damned well can't." What a swine the fellow was. "As far as I can tell we're to the south-west of Veldeghem instead of the north-east. You'll have to make the best of it."

"What a peety. I am not sure——"

"Nor am I—not of anything. Now get your parachute ready and prepare to jump when I tell you."

Martin glared in furious concentration at the earth beneath. He would be thundering glad to get rid of this self-centred blighter. Facing the music in his company would be too humiliating.

Steadying the Bristol into the wind he directed his passenger in climbing over the side of the cockpit. When he was finally in position for the drop, with his finger in the ring attached to the rip-cord of his parachute, Martin gave him his final instructions.

"When I say 'Now!' just let go everything and count three slowly before you pull. The envelope will open immediately and you'll be as right as ninepence. Now!"

Poulière stared at him in wide-eyed terror. His mouth was working.

"Now?" he echoed weakly.

"Yes, now. Go on, man, jump!"

"Non, non, I can't, I can't."

"You can and you've got to."

Leaning back, Martin brought down his fist on the spy's gripping fingers. The unexpected pain made him release his hold, but realizing he was beginning to fall he made a wild clutch with the hand which was holding the rip-cord.

In doing so his thumb jerked the ring and the pilot parachute was drawn from the case. The wind whisked it aft and it fluttered over the top of the tail unit, dragging the main envelope after it.

"Jump, you fool!" yelled Martin fiercely. Appreciating the danger of the apparatus becoming entangled in the tail plane he struck again and again at Poulière's hands. "My God!"

The exclamation was forced from him as his worst fears were realized. Poulière, unable to maintain his hold against Martin's furious onslaught, had dropped off into space. At the same instant the flapping envelope, caught in a sudden gust of wind, had wrapped itself round tail plane and elevator, and the spy was now swinging helplessly twenty feet below the fuselage.

The Bristol was no higher than eight hundred feet. Unless by some miracle the tangled parachute freed itself in the next few seconds, Poulière must be dashed to death against the rapidly approaching earth.

Nor was this the sum total of the disaster. Poulière's weight, acting on the flimsily constructed elevator, was tending to drag the control downwards, thus accelerating the gliding angle into a steep dive. Martin braced himself against

the joy-stick to counteract the movement, but in doing so he rendered himself impotent to control his approach and subsequent landing.

The next few moments were a nightmare. Wild thoughts raced through Martin's mind as he tried to find a solution to his dilemma. If only there were some way he could release the envelope from its entanglement.

Had his engine been functioning he could have climbed higher and endeavoured to cast it loose in a stunt, but with his motor dead he was powerless. He dare not release the control column and attempt to scramble back along the fuselage at that low altitude. There was no time. Hell!

The aircraft sank lower and lower. Martin thought bitterly of the task he had set out so light-heartedly to accomplish. He had failed miserably. He had let down his squadron and the British Army. Green tabs would wait in vain for his information. In another few seconds, twenty at the most——

Crack! The control column went limp in his hand. Great Scott, what had happened? He turned swiftly. The parachute had disappeared.

The combination of Poulière's weight and the force of the wind had proved too much for the starboard elevator. It had broken away from its hinges, allowing the Belgian to fall clear.

Martin barely had time to notice the envelope fluttering earthwards. His attention was at once fully occupied in fighting to retain the mastery of his crippled machine. With half the elevator gone the Bristol was in imminent danger of crashing.

Five hundred feet to go. Despite the fact that he was holding her up almost to stalling point the speed of descent was increasing.

Kicking over his rudder he went into a side-slip with the remaining port elevator uppermost. That was better. Perhaps if he kept like that the shock of the under wing striking the ground would give him a sporting chance of escape from serious injury.

What about Poulière? The white upper surface of the parachute was just visible through the darkness. Although it appeared to be almost at ground level the envelope was fully open.

Martin experienced a surge of thankfulness. Even if he were killed, it looked as though his job was finished after all. However it had come about, the bally spy was landed.

He had a blurred impression of the ground below him. A patch of water, the dark outline of a wood, a house. There were no lights to be seen anywhere in the neighbourhood. Perhaps——

Zunk! The starboard wing hit an invisible tree, crumpled. Martin felt his aircraft shudder, check, then it plunged nose foremost to the ground.

Afterwards he was never quite sure what actually happened. The tree must have acted as a buffer, he decided. One instant he was facing death, the next he was picking himself out of a large hawthorn bush that made an extremely painful cushion.

Thoroughly shaken by his experience he stood for a minute or two trying to pull himself together. By all that was wonderful he was alive. Except for hawthorn scratches he was unhurt.

The sound of hurrying feet reminded him that he was in enemy territory. His mind adverted instantly to the black crosses on the wings. He was rejoicing a trifle too soon.

He braced himself to face discovery. There was nothing he could do. He had no weapon and even if he had possessed a brace of machine-guns he could not engage the entire might of Germany.

Half a minute, though. Surely that was only one pair of feet. Perhaps if he overpowered this first arrival he would have time to remove those tell-tale crosses before any more enemies appeared.

Without the evidence that revealed his secret mission he would, since he was in uniform, be treated as an ordinary prisoner-of-war. The crosses made all the difference between life and a summary execution.

Stepping cautiously behind the hawthorn bush he waited with muscles tense for the enemy to appear. The footsteps were growing rapidly louder; quick short paces that suggested a smallish man, or possibly a woman.

Great heaven, it was a woman, a girl rather, slim and upright, walking with the grace of youth and health. He could see her outline distinctly as she advanced. She was dressed in a blouse and skirt with a shawl draped about her shoulders.

Acting on the impulse of the moment, Martin moved to meet her. Assuming that she was a native of the district he decided to throw himself on her mercy. At least she could tell him where he was.

Seeing him emerge from his hiding-place Clotilde Moreau halted abruptly. One hand clutched her shawl at the neck in a gesture of alarm. But the voice with which she challenged him was perfectly steady.

"Qui va là?"

"Je suis un officier anglais, Mademoiselle."

Martin could speak French fluently.

"Anglais? You are English, Monsieur? But how——?"

Martin laughed softly at the surprise in her tone.

"My aeroplane has alighted itself into this tree here. I fear from now on I shall be obliged to walk."

Clotilde did not consider his jest at all humorous.

"Oh la la! But this is terrible. The Germans will kill you if they find you."

Once again Martin remembered the black crosses, and the inclination to joke faded away.

"Not if you will help me, Mademoiselle," he begged earnestly. "Will you?"

She looked at him uncertainly.

"I will do what I can, of course, but it isn't very much. What do you want me to do?"

Martin took her arm and led her to the wrecked aircraft.

"There are some black paper crosses pasted on the wings," he explained. "We must scrape them off immediately. Water from the radiator will soften them. If the Germans saw them——"

Clotilde wrenched herself free.

"Did you fly over here alone?" she demanded excitedly.

"Yes, of course, why?"

The existence of Poulière must remain a secret even from his new-found ally.

"You are sure you did not bring someone with you?"

"Perfectly sure."

Clotilde sadly shook her head.

"Perhaps you do not trust me, Monsieur, but I know."

"You know what?"

"That you did not come alone."

"How can you possibly know that?"

"You carried a Belgian agent who was to be dropped near here by parachute."

Martin did not immediately reply. Her assertion was too correct to be mere guesswork. But how did she come to be in possession of such vitally important information.

He decided to head her off with banter.

"You'll be telling me his name next," he remarked lightly.

"That, too, if you wish. It is Jacques Poulière."

"Sacré Nom! How can you know that?"

She shrugged her shoulders daintily.

"It is very simple; Jacques is my fiancé and I was expecting him."

Astounding though the revelation was, it filled Martin with relief. It assured him that he was amongst friends and when Poulière presently put in an appearance they might agree to hide him until he could be smuggled over the Dutch frontier.

"That certainly alters matters," he declared. "Yes, you're quite right, Mademoiselle, I did bring Monsieur Poulière with me."

He went on to explain how the failure of his engine had upset their plans.

"You're sure he got down all right?" asked Clotilde anxiously.

"I see no reason to suppose otherwise; his parachute was fully extended."

"In which direction was it falling?"

Martin pointed to the west.

"Over there, I think, about half a mile. Here, I say——"

But she had gone, running swiftly into the night.

Had it not been an urgent necessity to remove the paper crosses, Martin would have followed but he dare not risk the possibility of their being discovered in his absence.

Draining some water from the radiator, which was fortunately undamaged, he set to work. He found that the mechanics who had pasted them in position had made a thorough job of it, and, hampered by the position of the wreck the task of removal was painfully slow.

He had not quite removed one sign when he heard a sound that made his blood run cold. It was a sharp word of command and it was addressed to a line of shadowy forms, spread out at regular intervals, advancing directly towards him.

A detachment of German infantry methodically scouring the neighbourhood. There could be little doubt about their objective. Someone had reported the fall of an unknown aircraft and they were searching for its whereabouts.

Martin made up his mind in a flash. He might not be able to avoid capture but he was hanged if he would let them find those crosses.

Seizing the petrol feed pipe, he wrenched with all his might. The copper tube snapped short and a steady stream of fuel poured from the tank. He struck a match; it spluttered and went out. He struck another with a similar result. The wind was wicked.

The approaching Germans were no more than two hundred yards distant. Unless he were successful in the next few seconds his ruse would be too late.

Cupping his hands he tried again with trembling fingers. The light flared and he bent swiftly to apply it to the soaked fabric of the wreck. But for the third time the wind proved his enemy.

Wild thoughts crowded his mind. Dare he risk another? No. Even if it lit, the enemy would be on the spot before the flames could destroy the evidence against him.

What should he do? Give himself up or make

a dash for it? If he surrendered they were certain to shoot him. Very well, he would remain at liberty as long as he could.

Keeping the aircraft between himself and the searchers, he walked swiftly through the little wood. Once clear of the trees he broke into a run. In a few seconds they would be looking for the missing pilot, but it would take them hours to search the whole district and in the meantime anything might happen.

His one chance of escape was to find Poulière. The Belgian had friends in the neighbourhood as was evidenced by the arrival of the girl. If they would hide him for a day or two and give him some civilian clothes he might succeed in making his way into Holland.

The country he was traversing was partly ploughed stubble, and by avoiding the newly turned furrows he left no footprints to guide his pursuers. Reaching a road, he crossed it and slowed to a walk. If only he had the vaguest idea where he was.

Estimating his bearings as well as he could, he steered in the direction in which he judged Poulière to have landed. Hope and despair alternately buoyed him up and weighed him down. Nothing but the knowledge that those black crosses were equivalent to his death warrant kept him from abandoning the seemingly impossible task.

It was ridiculous to imagine that Poulière would have remained in the one place. Once on the ground he would have gone directly to his friends. That might be anywhere. At the same time there was always a possible chance of meeting him, Martin told himself desperately.

He had been walking for nearly ten minutes and his hopes were fading fast when he spotted a patch of white flapping against the trunk of a tree. It was the abandoned parachute and since it must have been blown to its present position, it suggested that Poulière had come down to windward of it.

As he stood debating what to do next, Martin sensed rather than saw a slight movement on his left. At once his pulses raced with the anticipa-

tion of capture; then he realized it was a single figure outstretched on the ground and he sighed with relief.

A moment later he was kneeling beside the prostrate form of the man he sought. The spy was conscious although he was in a very bad way. Both his legs were fractured and his clothes were battered and torn where he had been drawn along the ground at the end of his parachute harness.

With his heart torn with pity for the poor creature's plight, Martin raised his head and endeavoured to make him more comfortable.

Evidently Poulière recognized him for his features twisted into the semblance of a smile.

"It opened too late," he whispered. "I fell so hard—so hard. Then it dragged me right across the field. Oh——hh!"

He blubbered distressfully at the recollection.

"Poor old chap," said Martin softly. "What damnably hard luck. But try not to worry about it. Now I've found you, I'll see you're all right. I hate to leave you like this, but it's only to get help."

Poulière slowly shook his head.

"It's no good, Monsieur Anglais, I'm—I'm finished."

"Nonsense!" Martin tried to reassure him. "They'll have you in bed in no time."

He rose abruptly to his feet and looked about him. There was only one thing to do in the circumstances, he told himself firmly. He must surrender immediately and appeal to the humanitarian instincts of his captors to attend to Poulière's injuries.

The only thing that made him hesitate was the disagreeable fact of Poulière's calling. However much he tried to camouflage the accident, the Germans could not help but place the correct interpretation upon it.

Whilst he had no doubt that they would give all the attention necessary to his shattered limbs, Martin had an uneasy feeling that Poulière would inevitably be brought to trial once he was restored to health.

Was anyone ever in such a damnable predicament, wondered Martin. It seemed utterly futile to hand Poulière over to his future executioners for medical treatment, but he must in common decency do something. But what could he do? If only the girl would turn up she would know where to find a Belgian doctor.

The man at his feet shuddered convulsively and Martin bent over him once more. Poulière was trying to say something; his mouth was working, but no sound would come. His hand plucked feebly at his coat.

Endeavouring to elucidate the message the injured man was attempting to convey, Martin felt in the ragged garment and drew out a packet of papers. Poulière's expression told him he was on the right track.

"You wish me to destroy these?" he asked, and received a nod of affirmation.

"Very well, but——"

Martin got no further. Poulière's head had fallen limply to one side. Death had solved his problem for him, reflected Martin and, despite the pitiful tragedy of the spy's ending, could not help a feeling of relief.

A moment later the relief vanished from his mind to be replaced by an overwhelming dismay. As long as Poulière was alive he had been too preoccupied to consider his own position; now he realized that his last hope of succour had gone.

He had been counting so much on Poulière's helping him; without Poulière he might as well have stayed by the smashed Bristol. Some of the Belgians might be willing enough to shelter him, but how was he to discover their whereabouts? In a British uniform with every German in the district on the lookout for him he had as much chance of eluding capture as a mouse in a roomful of cats.

Almost at once he perceived a way out of his dilemma; why should he not change places with the dead man? He could speak French sufficiently well to pass as a Belgian and if he wore Poulière's clothes and adopted his identity there was a strong possibility that no German would succeed in penetrating his disguise.

The idea was utterly reckless, no doubt, and would be overwhelmingly difficult to carry through, but surely any hazard was worth attempting when death was the sole alternative.

No sooner had the thought formed in his mind than he set to work. Carrying the corpse deeper into the wood he began the grisly task of stripping it. It was a slow and arduous job in the darkness and it took over an hour before it was completed.

With Poulière's remains now attired in the uniform of a Royal Flying Corps pilot he reattached the harness of the parachute and arranged the body artistically to make it appear that death had resulted from a hard landing. Then, thrusting the Belgian's papers into the pocket of his own tattered garments, he prepared to run the enemy gauntlet.

His intention was to make for the house he had glimpsed from the air immediately before the Bristol crashed. It lay on the farther side of the wreck and he would have to be very careful how he approached it. The German search-party would treat any civilian caught out at that time of night with scant courtesy.

Retracing his steps from the wood, he was within a few hundred yards of the road when he became aware that a solitary figure was approaching diagonally across his path. At once he stepped out of sight behind a group of haystacks; he did not yet feel sufficient confidence in his disguise to risk a premature encounter.

The figure passed within a few feet of where he was standing and peering through the darkness he recognized the girl who had declared herself to be Poulière's fiancée.

"Hist!" he called softly. "Venez ici, Mademoiselle. C'est moi."

Clotilde halted abruptly at his cry and for a moment he thought she was going to bolt.

"Are you the Englishman?" she asked incredulously.

Martin emerged from his ambush.

"Yes, I——"

He broke off as she screamed in sudden panic; he had overlooked his changed appearance.

"Shush!" he warned. "Please don't be frightened. I——"

"Where is Jacques?" she broke in. "I've been searching for hours. There was a party of Germans and I was forced to hide."

Martin bit his lip; telling her was not going to be very easy.

"I'm afraid he's met with an accident," he said slowly.

She caught her breath and clutched at her shawl.

"Is he—dead?" she whispered.

"Yes, Mademoiselle."

He explained as briefly as he could, but when he revealed that he had stripped the dead man of his clothes Clotilde protested violently.

"How could you do such a thing; it was sacrilege. How can he be buried in his own name when they think he is an English officer?"

It had not occurred to Martin that Poulière's relatives might consider his strategy offensive.

"I'm most terribly sorry, but it was the only thing I could do. I——"

"Sorry," she cried contemptuously. "What do I care for your sorrow. What about my sorrow and the sorrow of Jacques's father and mother?"

For the life of him Martin could not think of a suitable reply. He had believed that the local Belgian inhabitants would be ready and willing to assist him, but if they regarded his action as desecration of the dead it looked very much as though he would be forced to fend for himself.

"I was only thinking of escaping my enemies," he confessed lamely. "I was hoping you would be willing to help me."

Clotilde shook her head furiously.

"I wouldn't help you if—— What was that?"

She clutched fearfully at his arm.

Listening intently, Martin could hear the faint clink of military accoutrements. The sound seemed to come from all around.

"Germans!" he said tersely.

"Then we must run. Quick, quick, this way."

She dragged him round the corner of the rick and would have dashed into the open had not Martin restrained her. There were more of the enemy on this side. He could see them advancing relentlessly in extended order.

His mouth went suddenly dry as he realized they were surrounded. Someone must have heard the girl scream, with the result that the haystacks had been encircled by a cordon.

This was the end. His little subterfuge could not avail him now. They might accept his story for the moment, but when they found Poulière's body so close to the site of his capture the inference would be obvious. Besides, there were those papers in his pocket.

He lugged them out and gave them to the girl.

"These must not be found whatever happens," he declared earnestly. "They were Poulière's and will prove he was a spy."

"But what can I do with them?"

"Destroy them when you get a chance."

He lifted her to the top of a partly built rick.

"Lie low until they've gone," he whispered.

Squaring his shoulders, he raised his hands above his head and walked boldly into the open.

"Kamerad!" he roared. "Kamerad!"

There was a sharp word of command and the nearest section broke into a double. Rough hands seized Martin and hustled him before the commander of the detachment.

The officer, an infantry Captain, regarded his prisoner sternly in the light of a torch. He was decidedly peevish from having been ordered out of a comfortable mess to conduct the search, and he had no room for sympathy in his heart.

"Who are you and where do you come from?" he demanded in raw French.

"Jacques Poulière of Veldeghem," answered Martin meekly, "if it please you, Monsieur."

"It doesn't please me at all. If you ask me, you're a spy."

He gave an abrupt order in German.

"Detail four men, sergeant-major, and take him directly to the Kommandant. That'll keep the old sheep's head quiet for a bit. The rest break up and carry on as before. There's no-one else amongst those stacks, I suppose."

Martin held his breath for the answer; despite her unreasonable anger against him he felt a strong liking for her.

"Nein, Herr Kapitan, all clear here."

"Very well then, march!"

The detachment moved off toward the wood whilst Martin and his escort proceeded stolidly along the road to Veldeghem.

There was ample time to think on the way which Martin utilized in an endeavour to estimate his chances. Try as he would he could not bring himself to believe that the old sheep's head would be taken in by his impersonation; those black crosses on the Bristol were too clear an indication of the real facts of the case.

By the time they reached the Kommandant's headquarters he had made up his mind to tell the truth. If he had to die, and there seemed very little doubt about his fate, he would much rather face his end as a British officer than as a Belgian spy. Besides, his confession would give the girl the satisfaction of burying her lover in his right name.

But he was not to be allowed to unburden himself that night. The Kommandant was in bed, and since no-one dare disturb him, Martin was thrown into a cold and draughty cell to await the great man's pleasure.

It was seven o'clock on the following morning when he was paraded for the Kommandant's inspection. Escorted by a section of infantry he was marched through the streets of Veldeghem to a large château which stood about a kilometre outside the town.

Martin felt utterly miserable and friendless as he stumbled along in the midst of his guards. In a way he was glad of the exercise after the bitter cold of the night, but he had had nothing to eat or drink since he left the British lines and his physical endurance was sapped almost to breaking point.

On all sides he was conscious of an unusual stir of activity. Companies of stolid troops in field-grey were mustering in their various units; horses were being harnessed, guns and wagons limbered, and it was clearly evident that the huge camp was preparing for a move.

As the detachment approached nearer to the château the long lines of tents gave way to a field aerodrome. In front of a row of canvas hangars mechanics were busily engaged in preparing a number of Fokker two-seater biplanes for flight. Some already had their engines running; others were in process of being started.

Martin estimated that the force represented two complete squadrons and the familiar sight of the air-screws slowly revolving, to bring the water in the radiators to the required temperature for flight, made him feel desperately homesick.

If only he could break away from his guards and gain a sufficient lead to enable him to swarm into the cockpit of one of those fighters. He would jam the throttle lever fully open and yank her bodily into the air.

The enemy could do what they liked after that. Let them fire every Archie between here and Ypres, send every aircraft they possessed to try to shoot him down. He would jolly well put up such a fight that he was bound to win whatever the odds.

Even if he failed and they scuppered him it would not be so bad a death as the one he was now facing. At least he would have the satisfaction of dying in action instead of being shot down like a mad dog without a chance of retaliating.

He groaned unhappily as he realized how hopeless the idea was. Could he succeed in breaking through the ranks on either side of him, he must inevitably be picked off before he could cover half the distance to the nearest machine.

The rebound from his wild dream of escape made him more wretched than before, and when the party turned into the gates of the château he was on the point of bursting into tears. The only thing that restrained him was the knowledge that any display of weakness on his part would be against the national tradition; at all costs he must show these Huns how well a British officer could face his end.

He was forcibly reminded that he was no

longer a British officer, however, but a Belgian civilian, when the detachment halted in front of the house. The Kommandant was standing on the steps, enjoying a breath of early morning air whilst his breakfast was being prepared.

At sight of the woebegone and miserable-looking figure before him he scowled disdainfully and fixed his eyeglass in his eye.

"Um Gottes Willen, Leutnant, what do you mean by bringing that scarecrow here?"

The lieutenant in command of the party clicked his heels and delivered a stiff salute. His Excellency General von Makenhofen was a ruthless disciplinarian.

"Orders, Herr General. He is the suspected spy brought in last night."

Von Makenhofen scowled angrily. He had already heard about the wrecked British aircraft with the black crosses on the wings and the dead pilot fastened to his parachute. It infuriated him to think that anyone should have dared to attempt to land a spy in the area under his command.

"Take him away and shoot him," he said callously and entered the house in search of his breakfast.

Martin did not understand German and the significance of the order was lost upon him. All he knew was that the detachment faced about and retired from the château grounds to the main road. Instead of returning to Veldeghem, however, as he had anticipated, the officer in charge led his men along the edge of the flying-field to a spot where the blank wall of a stone-built barn provided a convenient butt for the bullets of the firing-party.

It was not until a halt had been called and two men proceeded to tie his hands securely behind his back that it dawned on Martin that he had reached the site of his execution.

For a moment or two the shock of realization bereft him of speech. He had never dreamed he would not be given a chance to defend himself. At the very least he had expected the Kommandant to demand some proof of his identity.

This was terrible. It was neither right nor fair.

Someone must listen to him. There was no hope that they would relent, but surely he could claim the privilege of being shot as an Englishman.

Twisting his neck, he appealed to the young lieutenant who was directing operations.

"I've something important to tell you!" he cried desperately in French. "I——"

"Silence!" roared a burly non-commissioned officer. "Get done there, you men!"

"I'm a British officer!" shouted Martin in English. "I demand the right——"

The non-commissioned officer struck him brutally on the mouth with his fist and when the lieutenant made no attempt to reprove him Martin knew that it was useless to continue with his appeal.

His thoughts were chaotic as they stood him with his back to the wall. Abject nerve-shattering fear, resolution not to show the white feather, bitter humiliation that he had by his own act renounced his British nationality, warred in his mind for mastery.

"I must be brave," he muttered again and again. "I must be brave."

It was like a hideous dream to watch the mechanical actions of the half dozen men who had been told off to shoot him down. Under their cowled helmets he could see their different expressions, some grim, some indifferent, some anguished. The rattle of the rifle bolts sounded harshly in his ears.

"Ready!" bellowed the non-commissioned officer. "Present!——"

There came the pattering of hurrying feet, a shrill scream, and Clotilde appeared running swiftly towards them.

"At ease!" snapped the lieutenant. "Catch her, one of you, and take her away."

Although he was utterly indifferent to the fate of an enemy spy he drew the line at a woman witnessing the execution.

"Stop!" shrieked Clotilde. "Wait! He's not what you think!"

Evading the clutch of the soldier who tried to detain her she reached the lieutenant's side and held a paper in front of his eyes.

"You see?" she cried excitedly. "Am I not right?"

Martin saw the young officer's eyes open wide with astonishment. He seized the paper from the girl's hand and read it eagerly.

"Himmelkreuzsakrament!" he exclaimed. "Where did you get this?"

She indicated the bewildered Martin.

"He gave it me last night. He is Jacques Poulière."

"So he is. Verdammt!" he declared fervently. "If we had shot him the Herr Kommandant would have skinned us alive."

He gave an order and the non-commissioned officer ran forward and released Martin's bonds. Then the party fell in once again and marched back into the château grounds. Clotilde walked beside Martin, gripping his arm with every appearance of a loverlike embrace.

"Courage," she managed to whisper. "Follow my lead and be careful what you say."

As the troops halted for the second time in front of the house a casement was thrown open and General von Makenhofen's head appeared. He was livid with rage.

"Verdammt nochmal!" he cried, his voice high-pitched and querulous. "What is the meaning of this, Leutnant? When I give you an order I expect it to be obeyed. Why in God's name have you brought that loathsome creature back here?"

The lieutenant advanced hurriedly to the window and held up the paper for his superior officer's inspection.

"The girl brought it," he explained. "She is his lover."

Von Makenhofen whistled softly under his breath as he read.

"So!" he exclaimed at length, and Martin noticed that his tone was vibrant with relief. "If we had shot this Jacques Poulière, Leutnant, I should have made the biggest blunder of my career. You did well to bring him back, my friend, very well."

His voice changed, became charged with feverish excitement.

"Do you realize what this means?" he cried. "The English have lengthened their line by fifteen miles without sufficient men to man the trenches, and we attack to-morrow at dawn. Gott in Himmel! We shall be in Amiens in two days."

He shouted to someone behind him in the room.

"Get on to Operations and have von Kampendorf come over here at once. This is stupendous."

He turned to Martin and beckoned him to approach.

"I ask your pardon for this terrible mistake, Monsieur Poulière. My subordinates failed to inform me of your correct identity, but be sure they will be punished for their carelessness. Have you breakfasted? You have not?"

He was on the point of inviting "Monsieur Poulière" to join him, but the grime on the spy's tattered garments decided him against such magnanimity.

"Well, Monsieur," he substituted. "Suppose you go into the village, have your meal and return here in an hour's time. Yes? I have no doubt you have many things to discuss with this charming mademoiselle.

"See to it, Leutnant, that Monsieur Poulière has everything he needs."

He nodded dismissal and Martin suffered Clotilde to lead him towards the road. He could not yet understand the miracle that she had worked, changing him from a condemned prisoner to a free man, nor was he concerned to hear about it.

That could wait. For the moment his mind was concentrated on the Fokkers displayed so temptingly with engines running on the flying-field.

"Tell him to go ahead and we'll meet him in the town," he said to Clotilde in response to a question from the lieutenant.

Dawdling behind as his late escort marched steadily towards Veldeghem, he left the road and strayed on to the aerodrome.

"Where are you going?" asked Clotilde interestedly.

"Back to France," declared Martin grimly. "Will you come?"

She nodded resolutely.

"Si, si, Monsieur Anglais, if I stay behind they will certainly kill me."

No-one took any notice of them as they strolled across the grass. Martin halted alongside the outermost machine. Swinging the girl into the rear cockpit he swarmed on to the wing and settled himself at the controls.

There was a sudden shout of alarm, grey figures came running, but they were too late. Martin opened the throttle to its fullest extent. The Fokker began to move, gathered speed. He eased back the control column and lifted her cleanly in a climbing turn. Headed east.

Looking back at the feverish activity that followed his departure he laughed triumphantly. They would never catch him now. He was safe, thanks to the wit of a girl.

Clotilde told him all about it when they landed in the British lines. The papers he had given her to destroy revealed that Jacques Poulière had been acting for the Germans as well as the British.

"To think that I had ever loved a man like that," declared Clotilde disgustedly. "He was one grand cochon, that one. And I was so very very cross because you took his clothes."

"I've taken his place, too," announced Martin significantly.

Mischievously she pretended not to understand.

"Of course, you can tell your Colonel that the Germans attack at dawn. You have it on the authority of General von Makenhofen."

Martin shook his head.

"I'll leave you to tell him that. What I propose to tell him is that I want special leave to marry the bravest girl in Belgium."

THE ALDERSHOT AFFAIR

CLARENCE HERBERT NEW

DESCRIBED BY ITS PUBLISHER as "the longest unbroken series of stories ever published," *Free Lances of Diplomacy* by Clarence Herbert New (1862–1933) ran in *Blue Book Magazine* continually from 1909 to 1934. Based to some degree on his youthful travels and adventures, this long series of stories focused on international intrigue and diplomatic activities. In their magazine appearances, the stories were often accompanied by photographs, maps, and other illustrative material. His extensive devotion to the genre has been credited with popularizing espionage fiction in the United States.

After graduating from the Brooklyn Polytechnic Institute, New served as the editor of *Truth*, *The New York and London Literary Press*, and *Reel Life*. In addition to his series for *Blue Book Magazine*, he wrote for *Adventure Magazine*, *The Premier*, and other pulp magazines, both under his own name and using the pseudonyms Culpeper Zandtt, Stephen Hopkins Orcutt, Devon Ames, and Norman Blake.

Three of his stories were made into short silent films, all in 1914: *A Mohammedan Conspiracy*, *The Cat's Paw*, and *A Leak in the Foreign Office*.

Upon the publication of *The Unseen Hand* during World War I, New revealed that the United States had been duping Germany for the past nine years with "a band of diplomatic free-lances" who worked to foil many of the Kaiser's intrigues. The leader of this covert coterie was termed "the Unseen Hand" by Germany, and New claimed that the stories in his book were based on confidential information received from him.

New's life as a photographer and adventurer was hampered in 1916 when his right arm was amputated following a bear attack in New York.

"The Aldershot Affair" was originally published in the May 1916 issue of *Blue Book Magazine;* it was first collected in *The Unseen Hand* by Clarence Herbert New (Garden City, NY, Doubleday, 1918).

THE ALDERSHOT AFFAIR

CLARENCE HERBERT NEW

AT THREE in the afternoon, a smart landaulet upholstered in Venetian-red suède rolled noiselessly up to the ladies' entrance of the Carlton Hotel. From his glass-enclosed sentry-box the doorman telephoned the reception office that the Condesa de la Monteneta's car was at the door, and one of the clerks repeated the information over the wire to Madame's suite on the third floor, where her two Moorish maids were assisting her into a hat and wrap just over from Paris—the envy of every woman who saw them. When she had descended in the lift, her footman—who, with the chauffeur, had also the appearance of being a Moor—assisted her into the landaulet.

As the Condesa's goings and comings were of interest to every one in the hotel on account of her undeniable beauty, taste in clothes, wealth, and social prominence, it was quite in the natural order of things for the page and chambermaids in charge of the third floor to be standing at the end of the corridor watching her as she came along to the lift. It was also a matter of daily occurrence for one of the maids to enter the room presently with an armful of clean towels and—attaching the hose to a baseboard-plug—groom the carpets and furniture with a vacuum-cleaner during

Madame's absence. The two Moorish girls occupied a small room at the end of the suite and were usually more or less in evidence when any of the hotel employees came in—not that they appeared suspicious, but they were seldom out of sight long enough for outsiders to do any prying whatever. This time, however, the chambermaid heard them talking in one of the farther rooms as if they hadn't noticed her coming in—and she made the most of a long-awaited opportunity.

Leaning the nozzle of her cleaner against the door-casing, she went noiselessly over to the davenport where the Condesa's correspondence by the morning's post lay neatly piled. It seemed to be, however, the pigeonholes which particularly interested the girl. With practised rapidity, she ran through a number of papers and letters—opened the secret drawer which every one knows how to open in the usual desk of this sort—and then began going systematically through the pile of correspondence. After fifteen minutes or so, she became conscious of a pricking sensation through the left side of her corset. Turning, with a chill of apprehension, she saw a pair of gleaming black eyes over her left shoulder. The point of a slender Moorish knife, with a razor-like edge, was pressing gently yet painfully into her flesh—and she realized that one quick shove from the sinewy arm would send it through her heart.

"Thou hast the desire to read what is written to the great and beautiful one? *Aie!* Thou shalt tell her of thy desire when she returns. Until then shalt thou sit in that corner with folded arms—and one will sit by thee with this knife against thy side."

Perforce, the girl made the best of it. To her amazement, Madame la Condesa paid no attention to the tableau in the corner when she finally returned. The other maid removed her hat and wrap, followed her into the dressing-room, where she took off Madame's afternoon costume, and replaced it with a négligée. Then the Condesa walked leisurely out and sat down before the davenport. She spoke beautiful English, with here and there a pretty Spanish accent.

"Ah! You found her going through my papers, Ayesha? I see! I wonder what you discovered of interest among them, Meess? Let me see. You are the maid on thees floor, I believe? An' your name is Betty—the short for Elizabeth, of course—or—should I say Bettina—eh?"

To her utter amazement, the girl noticed a peculiar position of Madame's hand as she lightly touched a wisp of hair just above her ear. Half incredulously, the chambermaid closed her eyes for a second and let her teeth rest upon her lower lip. It was a natural facial expression of weariness or pain, and would have attracted no attention from anyone not particularly observant—but it was promptly answered by another imperceptible signal from Madame, who began to smile at the maid's confusion and amazement.

"If you could have assisted me, I should have made use of you before this, Betty. The Herr Chudleigh Sammis, who is Member of Parliament, told me there were two of you, and a man, in this hotel—but it is dangerous that more than a few of us should know one another. There are too many of the *Downing Street* people to watch each one and note with whom they appear to have a secret understanding. As to my papers

here, I am quite sure you found nothing to interest you. We of *Wilhelmstrasse* are not careless—as you know. But you will forget everything you have seen in this room—everything which concerns me in any way! You recognize this ring, do you not?" [She held out her left hand, upon one finger of which was a beautiful table-cut emerald which the maid knew at a glance was worn only by those high in authority among the *Wilhelmstrasse* secret agents.] "Very good! You will make no mistake in regard to me! If I find myself in danger and can make use of you, I will give the emergency signal. If I need your assistance with a secret communication, I will ring the bell of my suite three times—so! Meanwhile, you will hint to your two companions in the hotel that I am not to be interfered with or spied upon in any way. A hint should be enough—without giving them further information concerning me. If they do not take that hint, they are likely to hear from Berlin—unpleasantly. Now—you may go."

The girl knew that several women of the nobility were among the higher, inner circle of the German Secret Service, and had no doubts whatever that the Condesa was one of them. Dropping upon one knee, she kissed the hand extended to her—murmuring profuse apologies for her mistake, and then hurriedly left the suite.

A few moments later, Madame was about to dress for dinner when there was a knock at the outer door of the suite, and Ayesha admitted Lady Blanche Parker, who—with Colonel Sir Thomas Parker, K.C.B.—was occupying a suite upon the same floor of the hotel while her town house was being redecorated. She had been among the first to whom the Condesa had taken a personal fancy after her arrival in London, and a somewhat intimate friendship had sprung up between them. Just now she appeared nervous—ill at ease.

"You were about to dress for dinner, Condesa? Don't let me delay you! May I come in and chat while you change?"

"I've really nothing on hand for the evening before eleven, my dear—and one should not talk confidentially before one's maids, don't you know. (You see? I have adopt' the English idiom. Si!) Let us remain here where there is nobody to overhear. I theenk you are not quite yourself. No. Tell me!"

"Oh—it's quite stupid of me to care! Men *do* such things—I suppose they don't really mean anything by it, half the time! Before this horrible war started, I thought I was the happiest woman in England! I loved my husband so much that I was foolish over him—I really did! And I hadn't the least doubt in the world that he returned it. We'd lived within a few miles of each other, in Hants, ever since we were born—I used to be crazy over the way he sat a horse when he rode to hounds—practised, day after day, so I could keep up with him and take the same jumps that he did. Then we settled down in *Feathercote* together, living a perfectly ideal life. Finally the war came—and I'd the awful dread that Tom would be among the first killed. I knew, of course, that his regiment would be sent at once, because they were veteran troops. He was slightly wounded near Lille and sent home. After he recovered, his capacity for organization got him a billet at one of the training camps; then he was transferred to Aldershot because it was his home neighborhood and he knew practically everybody within a radius of twenty miles. He's been most successful in the recruiting, you know. Well, of course his duties gave him little time for me—but his business with the War Office made it advisable to spend at least half his nights in town, and I thought I should see a lot more of him, up here."

"And—don't you? I see you with el Señor Coronel in the beeg dining room almos' every evening."

"Yes—but his manner has been very much changed during the last few weeks. He is more preoccupied—gives me less of the old perfect companionship. To-day I found out *why*! I came into our suite rather quietly, and walked through to the room where he does his writing. He was sitting at his desk, as I expected. But—one of the hotel maids was standing by his side, leaning on his shoulder. His arm was around her, and he was—well—*hugging* her! She—she seemed to be enjoying it—the hussy!"

"Oh—as you say, my dear, men do those things without theenking twice about them. They consider it mere passing amusement. You may be sure you 'ave nothing serious to fear from a hotel servant—it would be quite too ridiculous! In the lifetime of my 'usband, El Conde de la Montaneta, he had that weakness—like other men. But I was la Doña Condesa—I never did notice such little occurrences when he was indiscreet. There was one—a mantilla-maker of Seville—who dance' mos' divinely. El Conde would take her for a ride in the country in hees grand motor-car—the poor theeng needed fresh air. But I could discover no difference in hees respec' an' affection for me—no—nevaire. Which of the maids did el Señor Coronel honor with hees embrace?"

"The—the—well, I suppose some people might call her quite good-looking, in a bold, provocative way! It was that—that Betty woman!"

"So? El Coronel showed mos' perfec' taste when he married you, my dear—an' he compliments you by selecting a different but mos' handsome type for hees passing amour. The little Betty, she ees really beautiful, I theenk if one dressed her *au grande dame*. She ees plump—full of fire. What man with blood in hees veins could help the little embrace—perhaps a kiss or two—from a ripe little baggage like that, if there was opportunity and she was not unwilling! Eh, my dear? Pouf! Ect is nothing. A moment's relaxation—to lighten the anxieties of hees professional work. Come! I will propose you a diversion. You trust me, do you not? You do not theenk I would deliberately rob you of your 'usband's love?"

"You—rob me—Condesa? I—I don't understand!"

"I will be more plain. I weesh to show the young wife that passing flirtation ees merely a game weeth mos' men—that it has nothing to do with the love they have for their wives. It ees merely the excitement of the chase—the capture—the collecting tribute. Look you, my dear! You shall throw me in the society of el Señor Coronel—arrange that we shall be tête-à-tête, with no one to observe an' listen. Me—I am handsome woman, no? I shall make your 'usband to flirt weeth me—and forget the little Betty entirely. When I get him ver' much work' up, I shall make him to laugh with me at the game we both play. I shall keess him good-bye and say the joke mus' not go further any more because you are my dear friend and would be annoy' if you should discover us when we were careless. Then will he be punish' for the little Betty, with her neat ankles an' pretty figure. He will remember that yours are much prettier—and—and belong to him. You see?"

"Yes—I see. But—suppose you should fall in love with Tom yourself? I—I'd be afraid of you, Condesa!"

"I would make el Coronel Tom *theenk* I loved him, my dear—an' you also would theenk so until we 'ave the final laugh. But, for me, there is one man in all the world. He is married man. I shall never have him—even if hees wife die, he might never marry me. But once, he save' my life an' nearly lost hees own. From then, I am loving him more than everything in the world! With other men, I flirt to pass the time. *Si!* Why not? But none of them shall have me—except that one. When Andalusians really love, eet ees forever!"

Lady Parker's eyes were star-like with admiration. "Oh! That is something perfectly ideal, Condesa! I—I could love Tom like that if—if I thought he cared for me the same way! I suppose I mustn't try to guess who it is?"

"It ees better not, my dear. If you desire, I shall flirt weeth your 'usband, an' distrac' hees mind. But I will not love heem—I promise you that. You shall stan' behind the scenes an' see the game. When you tire of it, I will stop playing."

About one o'clock in the morning, a clerk in the hotel office—very well liked by the guests, on account of his pleasant manner and ability for straightening out their various grievances—went quietly from his room in the employees'

quarters up to the roof over the Haymarket side. As one of those who conducted the business of the hotel, his presence in any part of it, at any hour, would have been accepted as being in the line of his duties. So also, to a lesser extent, the third-floor chambermaid, Betty—who appeared upon the roof a few moments later, gazing into the murky atmosphere overhead in a terrified search for bomb-dropping zeppelins.

The few detached areas of flat roof, above the curved and sloping mansards, had been protected in a way that made demolition of the building unlikely. Their surface had been covered to a depth of three feet with bags of sand—and above the mansards which sloped toward the inner courts had been stretched a canopy of steel wire netting. After the one rather disastrous raid of German dirigibles, two watchmen had been stationed on the roofs, each night, to warn guests upon the upper floors in case of another—but their services had been discontinued after a while because of their doubtful utility in such an emergency. So that—excepting some of the help whose fears or curiosity impelled them to go up at night for a look around—the roofs were deserted.

As Betty stepped cautiously over the sand bags toward one of the farther chimneys, she stopped to gaze upward as if looking for a dirigible. Her actions were so entirely natural that, had anyone been watching her, it is doubtful if he would have been suspicious. Eventually, she stepped around behind a massive chimney—where Mr. James Crofton, the office clerk, was imperturbably smoking an excellent cigar.

As he noticed the direction from which she had approached, he started, apprehensively.

"Gott! Bettina! You came over the middle of those bags—yess?"

"Why, of course I did! Suppose anyone had been watching? It would never do to give an impression of skulking about, up here!"

"So? Better that risk than get blown to the devil before you have accomplished your work! Look you, Bettina! At every yard distance, all over this roof, is a bag of sand in which there are one or more sticks of dynamite. Your weight upon the loosely packed sand is sufficient to explode a stick, if it happened to come just right! If *one* explodes, they'll *all* go off! When just one little bomb from a zeppelin happens to drop on this roof, it must surely set off all the dynamite! There's enough of it up here to destroy every building within a hundred yards! I've planted those sticks, one at a time, and if we hear an explosion in another part of the city, we must get out of this hotel as quickly as we can dress!"

"Ach, Gott! Johann—this is terrible! It is not as if we were killing the English soldiers! If your dynamite goes off, it will kill all these pretty little children in the hotel—the young girls, just coming to their marrying time. *They* have done Germany no harm!"

"Woman—such talk is foolishness! Those *kinder* will grow up to be Englander men and women—mothers of Englander soldiers! They must be taught to *fear* Germany! That fear must be foremost in the mothers' minds—so the children will be marked with it! They must know it iss not *safe* to defy the kaiser as they haf done!"

"But, look you, Johann—these English only swear to fight us the more when we do such things! There has been no trouble in recruiting since the zeppelins came! I have been here much longer than you, and our campaigns of 'frightfulness' have had just the opposite effect from what we expected!"

"Ach! You are a woman! You cannot understand these things like the officers of our General Staff! But enough! Tell me what you haf discovered among the papers of the Condesa."

"Suppose you tell *me*, Johann, why you thought there might be anything of interest to us among them?"

"I am told by Karl Berndorf that the Condesa's family were practically unknown before she married the Conde de la Montaneta, six years ago—which is suspicious. Spanish grandees do not marry that sort of women, except morganatically. She hass, with her, four servants who are supposed to be Moors. They talk with each other in Arabic—very true—but in much too pure

Arabic for the Moors of Tangier or Cadiz, where Madame came from. Since her arrival in London she hass become quite intimate with some of the most brominent men and women in the country—she could scarcely haf brought letters that would haf secured such an entrée for her in a space of seven or eight weeks. She spends money as if her wealth were almost unlimited—yet Berndorf was quite possitive that the old Conde's estates in Andalusia had become very much curtailed before his death. I don't know, exactly, what to make of her, myself. Her Castilian iss so perfect that she must be Spanish, and yet——"

"She is probably of the Austrian Court circle, my friend—with a family dating back to Charles Fifth, or earlier, which accounts for her Spanish blood and home. And she is of *Wilhelmstrasse*, like ourselves—only far higher in authority. By the ring she wears, I think she must be one of the Imperial Special Agents. One of her Moorish maids caught me going through the papers in her desk, and held a knife against my ribs for three long hours—until Madame returned. I thought I must be drugged or dreaming when she casually gave me the first recognition sign—it made me feel like a fool! Getting caught at her papers like a clumsy sneak-thief, when some of those Cabinet men are probably dropping Government secrets to her which neither you nor I could get if our lives depended upon it! Oh, they wouldn't know they were telling her anything dangerous for England! Trust her for that! But the woman is a hypnotist and a mind-reader. She said that the Herr Chudleigh Sammis had told her there were three of us in this hotel—and I'm beginning to think she must have been working with him in influencing the Cabinet Ministers."

"*Himmel!* And I never even dreamed! It explains those Moorish servants, too! They must be high-caste Hindu revolutionists—the sort who will stop at nothing so long as they smash the English *Raj*! Valuable tools, if one knows how to handle them! Look you, Bettina! The Condesa hass become most intimate with Lady Parker—the Herr Colonel iss fascinated with her; I saw him looking at her as she talked with her ladyship in the foyer, last night. Why wouldn't she haf a better chance than you to obtain the plans from him?"

"She might—if he were anywhere near her own rank. But—women of her position do not go as far as those in our station of life—to obtain what *Wilhelmstrasse* requires. They will risk and sacrifice life—yes, if necessary. But giving *themselves* is something they are not likely to do. I'll admit that they're often successful, without."

"Er—you would pay the price, if necessary—Bettina?"

"That's something you'll never know—it's none of your business! I think I can make the Colonel tell me anything I want to know—when the conditions are just right. But if I can't, I'll ask Madame's assistance; you need have no doubts upon that score! Katrina heard Her Ladyship accepting an invitation for charity bridge to-morrow afternoon—when the Colonel is likely to be at Aldershot—and he asked me if I would come to their suite about three, with the vacuum-cleaner. He's quite sure to be there."

On the following day Lady Parker motored away from the hotel at half-past two—Sir Thomas being presumably at Aldershot. It occurred to her that he might run up to the city earlier than usual and amuse himself with the pretty chambermaid if she happened to be on duty at that hour—but the Condesa had talked to such good purpose that she believed it merely a passing foolishness upon her husband's part which she would better ignore, and she was dwelling with mischievous anticipation upon his punishment for it when the Condesa herself should take a hand. So she was in no hurry to return before it was time to dress for dinner.

At a few moments after three, Betty—in her dainty apron and short black skirt—came to Sir Thomas's door with the reel of vacuum-hose and long nozzle, letting herself in with a pass-key but taking care to bolt the door on the inside. As on a previous occasion, the Colonel was at his desk in the sitting room. While pointing out what he wished done, he managed to get a half-reluctant kiss or two that made him hungry for more. Presently, he told her to let the cleaning go for a while—and drew her down upon the sofa by his side.

"Betty, you use a dev'lish sight better language than any hotel chambermaid I ever saw! I'd be quite int'rested, don't you know, if you'd tell me all about yourself an' how you happen to be in such a position as this. Might be able to help you on a bit, d'ye see—one never can say. I fancy your family are a cut above the ord'n'ry lot—what?"

"Oh, my people were really very decent, sir. My father was a younger son of Major Bundy, who served in the Crimea—one of the Dorset Bundys, you know. There wasn't money enough to purchase a commission for him after his eldest brother went into the Guards, so he took orders and was appointed curate of a small parish on the Shaftesbury estates. He was made rector when we girls were in our 'teens, but died a year afterward—and of course, left us practically nothing. The living was a small one. My mother died several years before, and my sister married a small tradesman in Southampton. So there was nothing left for me to do but go out in service. We'd been decently educated, of course—I could have obtained a position as governess, but the wages are not so high as I get here, and I have a few hours to myself, every day. These grand hotels require maids who have some education—enough taste to assist the guests with their clothes, if necessary—and present an attractive appearance. When my father was living, my social position was good enough to permit of my calling upon any family in the county—while now, I'm a servant, and must know my place. But I'm much more independent, here, and am putting by a good bit of money each month. In a few years I shall go to America and open a little millinery shop. Over there I'm as good as anybody."

"Faith, and so you are in London—if people only knew it! I suppose you make a bit in tips, as well?"

"Perhaps more than you'd think, Sir Thomas. To a girl who has scrimped and denied herself even necessities while trying to be a lady on nothing a year, it's quite too ridiculous to have a fat dowager give one half a sovereign merely for selecting her most becoming gown, and turning her out at her very best for some dinner party! And the men! Why, I've had an old duke give me three sovereigns for promising to forget all about it after I'd slapped his face for trying to kiss me!"

"Eh? What's that? Do you mean to say it's an ord'n'ry occurrence for men to—er—take advantage of your position—and—er—kiss you? My word!"

"No. There's a difference—between kissing one and—well—trying to do it."

"But what—eh? Dash it all, you know—I've—eh? And I believe I've never tipped you a penny—as yet! Leave all that sort of thing to Her Ladyship, don't you know! Of course, if I'd known about your family—inexcusable liberty, you know! Quite welcome to slap me if you wish! And—er——"

"I trust, Sir Thomas, that you've too much taste and good sense to offer me money, now that you know something of my private affairs. I permitted you to do what you did because you have always treated me kindly—never taken a low advantage of me. There's no great harm in your kissing me, I fancy—but if you were seen doing it, I should probably lose my position here. I should have to complain of you to the management. Rather than have any trouble with a wealthy guest, they'd give me the sack."

"Faith, you need have no fears upon that score! If they discharged you, I'd find something better at once—or see that you had a good start in some other place. I say, Betty—er—do you know, I—I think an awful lot of you! 'Pon honor, I do! I say! Would it be possible for me to see you outside, anywhere? When do you—er—get out of the hotel? Where do you go?"

"I have three evenings off each week. Sometimes I go to a cinema show with two of the other maids. Occasionally, Mr. Crofton takes me out to a burlesque—or to one of the Strand restaurants for dinner. Or we go to a dance hall, where he teaches me the latest steps."

"Crofton? You mean the clark in the hotel office? Decent young fellow, that! You're not engaged to him—what?"

"No fear! Why did you wish to know that?"

"Well—d'ye see—after all, y'know, Crofton's merely a middle-class chap—not *your* sort, really. And—er—I'd jolly well like to have you go about with *me*—if we can manage it. And—er——"

"You couldn't take me to a theatre, Sir Thomas, or any public place where Her Ladyship might see us. Of course, when I am dressed for the street or for an evening out, I fancy no one in the hotel would recognize me. But still, Her Ladyship must be very well known in London society."

"Er—quite so, my dear. But I've cousins and other women relatives, d'ye see, whom I freq'ntly show the sights when they're up for a day or so. If Her Ladyship happens to run across us—most unlikely, don't you know—I can introduce you as one of 'm—or—er—one of a brother officer's family, d'ye see?—up from Aldershot for the evenin.' Eh? Meet me to-morrow evenin' in the lounge at the Cecil—an' we'll go somewhere for dinner—make a night of it. Eh? You will? That's jolly! Now—eh? Just one more kiss to seal the bargain?"

For a second or two her lips clung to his with a warmth that made him dizzy; then she was gone. He sat down at his desk and foolishly tried to fix his attention upon the papers he had been examining.

Two weeks later she accompanied him to his town house in order that he might show her some books and pictures which he had recently purchased. The decorators had finished their work. His butler had been up from Hampshire, superintending the cleaning for a day or two, and had finally returned—leaving the house ready for occupancy at any time he should be ordered to bring up the requisite staff of servants. A watchman inspected the premises, outside, at intervals—but the Colonel had told him that he should be working late, that night, with his private secretary. They had the house to themselves.

She had met him, that evening, in a chiffon gown of dark green which amazed him by its perfect taste and the way it set off her blonde prettiness. How she had managed to dress in such a garment in the servants' quarters of a hotel he couldn't understand. [She had really gone, with her maid's uniform covered by a mackintosh, to the house of a very respectable widow in Soho—a place which had been a secret rendezvous of German spies since the third month of the war—and changed there.] They had dined at a quiet but famous restaurant just off Pall Mall, and the Colonel had taken rather more than his usual allowance of champagne. When he produced two cobwebby bottles of Burgundy from his own cellar she made no remonstrance—but, had he noticed it, there was a calculating look in her eyes. She had learned, before this, about how much stimulation was needed to loosen his tongue—but the exact point at which mind and memory became oblivious to what he did was still a little uncertain. How far to let him go in his drinking—where to stop him before he became drowsily speechless—was a matter of nice calculation.

Early that afternoon the Condesa had motored to the Trevor mansion in Park Lane. Had any of her acquaintances been in the drawing room when she was admitted—presumably to call upon Lady Trevor—they would have been much astonished by the liberties she took. Running upstairs to Her Ladyship's boudoir, she closed the door and called up the Foreign Office, asking the operator to "put her on" to the private office of Sir Edward Wray, *Secretary of State for Foreign Affairs.* In a moment his voice came over the wire, saying that he would motor out to Park Lane at once. She received him in the big library on the ground floor fifteen minutes later.

"What mare's nest have you been stirring up, Nan?"

"You've been looking up Colonel Sir Thomas Parker, as I asked?"

"Aye—but there's nothing fishy that we can discover—except his weakness for women. An' that's hereditary, you know."

"I had supposed it must be" (dryly). "Tell me all you know about the man, Ned. I've heard of his courtship and marriage—in fact, pretty much everything Lady Blanche could give me."

"Well—let me see. He was a son of General Sir Harrington Parker, who was on the staff of Engineers in the sixties and had a good deal to do with the permanent improvements at Aldershot in 1890. It's within ten miles of *Feathercote*—the Parker estate in Hampshire—you know. Sir Thomas was a lad of eighteen at the time the reconstruction was started—and, during his vacations, he rode all over the place with his father. Had a taste for engineering even then—and was permitted to superintend bits of the minor construction work occasionally. I fancy he must have preserved every plan his father drew—because the War Office is finding his knowledge of Aldershot and other military camps valuable even now, and he frequently runs over to *Feathercote* for the purpose of consulting old drawings on file there."

"Do you know whether duplicates of those drawings were preserved in the War Office?"

"Never had occasion to look up anything of the sort—but, unquestionably, there must have been."

"Do you suppose Kitchener has men in his department who would be able to put their hands on those Aldershot drawings within half an hour or so?"

"I fancy there'll be no doubt of that. I'll have them put me on to him, and ask to have the papers sent here at once, if you think they'll be of use to us." (The telephoning was a matter of but a few moments—War Office calls having right of way.)

"Well—go on with the Colonel's history. We've not finished with that, yet. When a man of forty-three has as young and pretty a wife as

Lady Blanche, quite devoted to him, why does he kiss pretty chambermaids in a hotel, if he's presumably sober?"

"Eh? My word! Been up to that sort of thing, has he? Er—just casually, as anyone might, or is he taking her on for a continuous performance?"

"Well—I fancy he's had her out to dinner and the theatre more than once."

"Humph! Must be a cut above the ord'n'ry hotel maid! Is she pretty? Good taste in clothes?"

"Quite! She's a *Wilhelmstrasse* woman, Ned. What I'm trying to get at is her chance of pumping him for anything he may know."

"Why—h-m-m-m! Might be a bit serious if there were anything in his head that *Wilhelmstrasse* desired to know! For at least five or six generations the men of his family have been unable to resist a pretty woman. His great-grandfather jilted an English lady to run off with the princess of a small German State. Their marriage was never recognized, and he was killed in a duel with her cousin. His grandfather married a baroness—lovely woman, four beautiful children—and lived openly with a well-known *prima donna* in Paris. His father had various *affaires* in different parts of the world—wherever the War Office sent him on engineering work. They've all been quite open about it, don't you know—never seem to realize that what they do is anything more than a peccadillo which anyone of taste should ignore. They've all been fond of their wives and families, too—but there's something in the blood which catches fire at the glimpse of a pretty face or ankle. The trait is not uncommon. There's many a prominent and respectable man in London who has it.

"The principal thing which int'rests me in this affair of Sir Thomas's is what the little baggage may get out of him—and from the information at our disposal, I can think of practically nothing! The Colonel has no knowledge of where troops are going when they leave Aldershot. His work deals with barrack-construction—seeing that the various units are quartered to advantage for prompt assembling and departure when the orders come—sanitary matters—that sort of thing. He's not in position to know anything about munition-supply, new guns, new aeroplanes, or anything like that. Of course, he must have some knowledge that Germany would like to obtain, but it's second-hand when it comes to him; he's not the man from whom they'd attempt to get it. (Ah, here comes Leftenant Graham, from the War Office, with a bundle of papers—the Aldershot drawings, no doubt.) I say, Nan—you'd best disappear until I've sent him off again, don't you know! The Condesa de la Montaneta isn't supposed to be int'rested in anything of this sort—and I fancy you've no intention of discarding your make-up at present."

When the lieutenant had delivered the Aldershot drawings to Sir Edward and had left the house, Lady Nan—still with the black hair, darker complexion, and fuller figure of the Condesa—returned to the library, and they sat down to a study of the various plans in detail. The earlier sketches appeared to have been submitted to the War Office for a reconstruction of Aldershot Camp prior to those adopted during the administration of Secretary Stanhope in 1890. These were followed by the tentative plans subsequently approved, in part—including the replacing of the old wooden huts of the Crimean period by substantial brick and stone barracks. Considerable attention appeared to have been given the question of water supply—a number of drawings illustrating plans for bringing pure drinking water from streams or ponds at considerable distance. The system eventually carried out was found in its proper place, and was shown as completed in a survey made of the district in 1898—evidently a tracing from General Parker's original. It was Lady Nan who presently discovered upon this old survey of the General's some dotted lines which represented a four-foot main of cast-iron piping—not connected with the system which had been adopted, but leading off north-westward from a point near Fleet Pond, and terminating in the woods of Bramshill Common eight miles away. An asterisk called her attention to a note upon the margin of the tracing, in writing so fine and faded with age that she used a magnifying glass to read it.

Dotted lines represent section of four-foot water main laid underground at time the work was abandoned. Part of Sir John Folkham's plan in 1884 for bringing water from River Kennet, six miles S. W. of Reading. Was to have been emergency supply—location of line known only to Engineer Corps, in whose charge pumping station was to have been maintained. Plan was approved by Her Majesty, the Queen—but after ten months' work it was decided by War Office that artesian wells could be sunk, if necessary, at far less expense.

For several moments Lady Nan studied the dotted lines on the tracing, noting the location of turnpikes and other roads which crossed them between Aldershot and the spot where they terminated. Then she took from one of the library files a section of Bartholomew's half-inch-to-the-mile topographic map covering Berkshire, with the borders of Hampshire and Surrey.

"Ned, this is what *Wilhelmstrasse* is after—the original of this tracing! They want to know the exact survey-line of that old, long-forgotten water main. It must be there, just as it was laid down over thirty years ago. Probably a good deal eaten with rust, and yet, with neither water nor fresh air in it for all that time, there wouldn't be so much oxidization, after all. Now, what possible use could any German spy in England make of that water main? The Aldershot end of it is at the extreme westerly edge of the camp. Even if they had men enough in Berkshire, they couldn't get them crawling through that pipe fast enough to surprise the troops now camped around Aldershot; we must have over two hundred thousand there at this moment. My word! That's a lot of men, isn't it—for one instruction camp!

"Do you suppose that's the idea working in the German mind—a force of nearly a quarter of a million picked troops bunched within a limited radius? Couldn't have anything to do with a zeppelin attack, could it, Ned? I say! We're getting warm, don't you think? And we've spent all the time we need to on these drawings. The location of that old water main is undoubtedly what they're trying to get out of Sir Thomas—and that pretty little devil Betty will somehow manage it before she's through with him. Hmph! I shall have to take a hand in this—there's not a moment to lose! Is Achmet out there with my car? Let me lock this tracing in George's safety vault, down underground, and you take the rest back to Kitchener with my best love and thanks for the loan of them. . . . Oh, wait a moment! Perhaps I'd better keep one of those other drawings with this one—I think I can use it to advantage. Any one of the final plans will do!"

The Condesa knew that Sir Thomas's duties would keep him at Aldershot most of the following afternoon. Starting at two o'clock, she motored the thirty-three miles in something over an hour—and was in the ladies' room at the Officers' Club, with the wife of a well-known general, when Sir Thomas came in for his tea before running up to town. As both were returning in time to dress for dinner at the Carlton, she invited him to accompany her—an opportunity which he accepted with every appearance of unexpected pleasure. The Colonel admired his wife's distinguished friend extremely, but hadn't dared, for obvious reason, to make any advances in the way of flirtation; so when she started in with him on a basis of friendly intimacy, he began to imagine himself a devil of a fellow with the women. By the time they reached town, the flirtation had progressed far enough for her to agree that she would accompany him, that evening, to a rather exclusive cabaret in the West End, patronized by well-known musicians and writers. She was the woman-of-the-world in every word and action—so brilliant in repartee that his duller wits found it difficult to keep pace with her. One of the handsomest women in London—alluring, provocative, and beginning to be a celebrity. He knew, the moment they entered the cabaret, that her presence with him added materially to his reputation. Under conditions of this sort his infatuation was a foregone conclusion.

Inside of a week it had reached a point where he scarcely looked up from his papers when Betty came into his suite at the Carlton—which provoked and alarmed that intriguing young person. Before the Condesa took a hand in the game, she had obtained a part of what she hoped to get from him, but it wasn't enough for her purpose. Furthermore, she was in doubt as to where she stood with the Condesa—who certainly appeared to be interfering as far as Sir Thomas Parker was concerned. Bettina, however, gave no indication of having noticed this—until she went into the Condesa's suite, one day, and was invited to sit down for a chat after the Moorish maids had been sent from the room.

"Betty—you remember the day you were interested in my papers, and spent a few uncomfortable hours being prodded by Ayesha's knife?"

"Oh, yes, madame. I think your maid would have enjoyed killing me!"

"Had you made any resistance she most certainly *would* have killed you! That girl is worth her weight in *kronen* to anyone in our position! Well, you learned something about me which surprised you—even as we were surprised to know that you also were of *Wilhelmstrasse*. Since then we have ignored your connection with Berlin—and of course you've paid no further attention to me in that respect. Still, one cannot help noticing things which are apparent for anyone to see. I was in a theatre-box, one evening, when you sat in the stalls with Colonel Sir Thomas Parker. I could only guess at your object in cultivating him—until he began paying *me* very marked attentions. Then I heard all about his father's connection with Aldershot, and knew that you must be working upon

the plan which was under consideration several months ago. My own work has been in a different quarter altogether—in fact, I know nothing of the details which have been worked out in your affair. But an opportunity presented itself, unexpectedly, to pick up something which I am quite sure you can use to advantage. I didn't dare keep it—so made a tracing upon strong parchment tissue, at a certain house where I was sure of being undisturbed, and put the original back where I found it."

She drew from a drawer in her davenport a tracing of the old Folkham Water System, just as it had been drawn by General Parker in 1884, showing the dotted lines of the four-foot main, which had been partly laid down and then abandoned. Betty picked up a large reading glass and eagerly examined the drawing—going over it with an attention to detail which indicated considerable knowledge of engineering.

"It will be useful, madame, because the original—which we stole from a library drawer at *Feathercote*—Sir Thomas's place in Hampshire—was accidentally destroyed. A draught blew it into a sea-coal fire at our rendezvous in Soho. I was hoping—really hoping—that you had managed by sheer luck to obtain a plan of the present tent-encampments on Laffan's Plain and Farnborough Common—including the new barracks in the North and South Camps. That is the only thing we need to complete our preparations. The attempt should be made within a fortnight, because the number of troops now drilling there is larger than any future concentration is likely to be. The time to strike is now—as soon as we possibly can! The weather predictions are for a week or more of fog and rain—ideal conditions for the attempt!"

"You had already located the line of that four-foot main?"

"Six months ago! Our spies near Aldershot had talked with some of the older villagers west of the camp who remembered when the pipe was laid down, but couldn't point out the exact line. It was that report which started the discussion in Berlin. We leased three old manor houses in different localities. Two are near Hartford Bridge, and the other is on the border of the woods north-east of Bramshill Park House. There are thirty-five acres belonging to this manor—almost entirely wooded. We made borings in several places, and had the luck to strike the main less than three hundred feet from the house. It was a simple matter to excavate a tunnel from the cellar to it, but it took us a month before we could locate the line as far as the woods of Blackbushes, and tap it for ventilation without being caught. Of course, the air in it would have killed anyone attempting to crawl through before that. By the end of the second month we had rigged a little track for a miniature car and cleaned out the entire length to the first section, north of Fleet Pond at Aldershot. Then we commenced tunnelling in two directions, one toward the North Camp and the other toward the South Camp, with provision for piping under the present tent-encampments on Laffan's Plain, Farnborough Common, and Long Valley. That work has been completed. Our tunnels are twenty feet underground; we don't dare go upward toward the surface until we know exactly where we can shove up the ends of two-inch pipes without detection."

"You have your materials all assembled for the work—when the time comes?"

"Oh, yes, madame. We excavated a large chamber, underground, and brought in the machinery piece by piece. We run the place as a stock farm—breeding horses. The stables are fifteen hundred feet from the manor house, so that army officers who come to purchase mounts very rarely stop there. With nearly two hundred horses, mares, and foals, we use a great deal of hay and straw. All of our lime and acid—the glazed tiling for the storage tank and the conduit through the big water main—has been fetched to us inside great loads of hay and straw for the stables. It has been slow work, getting the amount we needed for the attempt, but it is amazing how much can be accumulated in six months. For the past fortnight we have been running eight air-compressors by small paraffin motors and storing the liquid chlorine in an airtight, porcelain-lined reservoir adjoining that underground chamber. The manor house stands upon high ground, and the big water main was laid twenty-five feet below the surface at that point—so the liquid chlorine will run down into, and along it, by gravity. The end section of the main at Aldershot is a hundred feet lower than that at Bramshill Park, and we have laid a porcelain-lined conduit through it for the entire distance, to carry the stuff. From the end of that conduit we will connect two-inch cast-iron pipes and shove them a few inches above the ground in spots among the tents and barracks where they will not be noticed—admitting the chlorine to them through a heavy gate-valve at the proper moment."

"You speak as though you had seen all these preparations yourself, Bettina!"

"I have, madame. It was necessary for me to know exactly what papers and drawings we required. Of course, if we cannot obtain the plan of the tent-encampments, we must take our chances in coming up to the surface at spots determined by an underground survey—but that greatly increases the risk."

"Suppose I succeed in obtaining that plan for you? I wonder if it would be safe for me to fetch it down to that manor house? Do you raise thoroughbreds at that stock farm? I ride in the Park every morning. That would be a perfectly reasonable excuse for motoring down there."

"Oh, yes, Madame—and Franz Schufeldt would feel much honored if you would inspect his work. One never knows whether he will succeed or fail in an attempt like this, but it helps his standing in *Wilhelmstrasse* if it is known that he performed his part of the work faithfully. It would please us much, madame, if you would inspect the work and report it in Berlin."

"The only point to be considered is whether by any chance my visit to that manor house might be remembered afterward, and arouse suspicion? We couldn't afford that—because my work is even more important than yours."

"We have sold horses to several of the aristocracy, madame—besides the army. You would be safe enough at the stables. And Franz could offer you tea at the manor house."

Three days later the Condesa motored down to Hampshire and had little difficulty in locating the Bramshill Stock Farm owned by Mr. Frank Sheffield—a genial, fox-hunting county squire whom nobody would have thought of being other than a roast-beef Englishman. After purchasing a beautiful chestnut mare for saddle use she accepted his courteous suggestion of tea, and gave him a lift in her car to the manor house. When secure from observation in his study she handed him a flat parcel which she had been carrying in her muff. When he unfolded this upon his desk it proved to be a tracing of the plan, less than ten months old, upon which the tent-encampments and new permanent barracks had been laid out—in fact, a detailed survey of everything in the Aldershot district, with smaller sheets of each camp.

After going over it for half an hour he led her down into the cellar by a concealed stairway and, through a tunnel, into the large underground chamber where the air-compressors, vats, and great storage reservoir were. From one corner of this he took her through a descending tunnel which ended in the old four-foot water main. Here he showed her the porcelain-lined conduit which had been laid along the bottom of the piping—providing an inner sluiceway for the liquid chlorine, sixteen inches wide and six high. At either side of this had been laid small rails upon which ran a miniature flat-car about large enough to carry an average-sized man, lying at full length. At one end of it was an electric motor, fed from a storage battery—and through the line of piping there was a strong current of fresh air from an electrically driven fan. Madame was strongly tempted to explore the entire seven miles of piping and inspect the system of tunnelling under Aldershot—but it would have taken at least three hours, and her long stay at the manor house might have been remembered.

After she had left him, Mr. Sheffield (or Franz Schufeldt, as he was known in Berlin) motored over to Aldershot, with the details of the tracings fixed in his mind, and satisfied himself that they were correct in every particular.

Next evening proved rainy and foggy. At ten o'clock a company of sappers left the South Camp in two motor-vans and disappeared, around Fleet Pond, on the road which led through Blackbushes. In the heart of the woods they came upon a cavalry patrol sitting his horse where a little blind path left the road—which was a rough one, seldom used. Following him along this path, they came to a big oak—in the bark of which they could just make out the lines of what had once been engineering symbols cut many years before. Here, after lighting a dozen lanterns, they began digging a hole ten feet in diameter—using great care to work as noiselessly as possible. At a depth of four feet they came upon a big cylindrical something which they carefully avoided striking with their spades. After two hours' work they had dug down at each side of the great cylinder until they could stow a number of packages under it.

Twice, while digging, they had heard a rumbling sound inside which seemed to approach from the westward and then recede again. Each time this occurred they stood without making a sound until the noise had died away entirely. When their preparations were complete, several ends from a main wire were attached to the packages under the big cylinder and they walked back to the road, paying out the wire after them. Then one of the engineers turned a crank in a square box—and there was a stunning concussion which shook the ground for a radius of half a mile. Groping their way back to where they had been digging, they found a yawning pit twenty feet deep and a hundred feet in diameter. The mangled trunks of a dozen trees had fallen into it, and upon opposite sides were torn and twisted sections of four-foot iron piping—choked solid with débris. Leaving guards at the edge of the pit, the sappers climbed into their motor-vans and returned to Aldershot.

In the meanwhile, three troops of cavalry had ridden by another road to Bramshill Park, silently drawing a cordon about the stock farm and manor house—concealing themselves behind trees and shrubbery. There they waited until some men from the house came along in a car. These were quietly arrested and sent to Aldershot. In the next two hours several other men and one woman came from the house and stables, being arrested like their fellows. At ten in the morning the troopers closed in, but the house appeared to be deserted, and the underground chambers also. Dynamite was then placed in various places, and the entire plant blown out of existence, after the troopers had ridden to a sufficient distance to be safe from the liberated chlorine in the big reservoir.

Late that evening Madame la Condesa—beautifully gowned for the opera—was awaiting the arrival of her escort, a Cabinet Minister, when there was a faint tapping at the door of her suite, and Ayesha admitted the girl Betty. When they were alone, with the doors locked, Betty staggered to a chair—her teeth chattering. Pouring a glass of wine, the Condesa held it to her lips until she had swallowed it—then said, guardedly:

"Wait a few moments until your nerves are steadier, my dear. You increase the danger for all of us by going to pieces in this way!"

"I know that, madame—oh, I *know* it! But—every second, I seem to feel the hand upon my shoulder; I fear some man I never saw before will take me by the elbow and whisper in my ear that I must go with him—quietly, without any show of resistance—as they did to poor Johann in the hotel office half an hour ago! It was done just as quietly as that. Johann knew—but he spoke to the manager and asked if he could go out for an hour or two with the gentleman upon a matter of importance; then he put on his hat and coat and walked out with the man, smoking a cigarette. It was the same with Katrina, on the second floor! A gentleman spoke to her in the corridor—told her to get into the servants' lift and go up to her room for her wraps. He didn't

let her out of his sight a second—made her walk out of the servants' entrance ahead of him! She knew there was no escape—so she didn't try to run away in the street. Mr. Chudleigh Sammis had been spending half an hour with Colonel Parker in his suite on this floor. He saw me in the corridor when he came out—whispered that he was leaving by the night train for Liverpool, and sailing on one of the Lamport and Holt steamers for Buenos Ayres; said he would tell the reporters that he was going down to study labor conditions in Argentina."

"The worst move he could possibly make—dangerous for all of us! Looks suspicious! They'll never let him sail! We must try to catch him on the telephone! What is it all about, anyhow?"

"Haven't you seen the evening papers, madame? It is said that someone at Aldershot heard a faint noise underground which made him suspect our tunnelling. Some of the Engineer officers looked up the old reconstruction drawings, traced that line of water main, suspected our stock farm, and began watching it. Last night the sappers dynamited a section of the piping in the woods two miles west of Aldershot. This morning a cavalry detail arrested nine of us from the manor house—found your tracings and other papers in Franz's desk—and blew up the whole plant. It is thought that half a dozen men, including Franz himself, are buried alive in the tunnels under the camps. The others were all shot at sunset. Johann and Katrina will be shot in the morning—or hanged—in the Tower, where they were taken."

"Do you think that any of them betrayed you or the rest of us in London?"

"No, madame; they died without any admission of their *Wilhelmstrasse* connection, I am sure. But if Sir Thomas by any chance remembers what he told me in the library of his town house—the night he was drunk there, alone with me—or if the disappearance of those plans is traced to you, madame—well, that would settle it!"

"Bettina, in the game we play, nothing is more certain to arouse suspicion than the slightest evidence of apprehension. I have faced death more than once with a laugh of amazed denial upon my lips—when I could see no possible escape, and believed my life was measured only by seconds. Never admit being guilty even while you are dying! That is a principle in all underground diplomacy. Do not compromise others even if you must yourself die! The safest place in the world for Chudleigh Sammis is on the floor of the House of Commons—representing his constituency. The safest place for you and me, just now, is right here in this hotel—doing exactly what we've been doing every day! I doubt if the management knows anything whatsoever against you. Your duties here constitute an almost perfect alibi."

Considerably reassured, Betty left the Condesa's suite and tried to forget her haunting terror in the activities demanded by her position. But for a fortnight several of the guests who really liked the girl thought from her paleness and lassitude that she must be coming down with a serious illness. In the room she occupied with three other girls, up under the roof, the dread of a zeppelin raid and annihilation from the dynamite in the sand bags over her head was enough to prevent her sleeping for more than a few moments at a time. Upon the streets, the passing glance of any unknown man sent a chill down her back which made her feel faint. One night—at the house in Soho—she typed a warning to the hotel management concerning the dynamite. When no attention was paid to it, she sent another anonymous warning—and was immensely relieved when finally the explosive was removed. The constant strain she had been under for ten months in London had developed a functional weakness in her heart which nothing but rest and freedom from anxiety could relieve. Had she known that she was under constant espionage from *Downing Street* men, she would probably have died of heart failure. But with the idea of using the girl to obtain future information vital to the safety of England, Lady Nan insisted that she be left unmolested unless caught in some fresh plot against the Empire. As for madame herself, Betty felt a wonderful admiration for her *sang froid* and apparent indifference to deadly risk.

CUNNINGHAM

W. F. MORRIS

BORN IN NORWICH and educated at Cambridge University, Walter Frederick Morris (1892–1975) served as the commander of the 8th Battalion of the Norfolk Regiment during World War I, attaining the rank of major by the age of twenty-seven, and was awarded the Military Cross.

After writing *The British Empire* (1927), Morris turned to writing crime and espionage fiction, beginning with a minor masterpiece, *Bretherton: Khaki or Field Grey?* (1929; the American title is *G. B.: A Story of the Great War*), that Eric Ambler named as one of the five greatest spy thrillers of all time.

Like all great books, it transcends the genre with which it is identified. In addition to the mystery and spy elements, it is a powerful depiction of what it was like to participate in World War I. Having been on the scene, he could tell first-hand the terror and boredom of the trenches, the gallows humor of the soldiers, romantic episodes away from the front, an exciting escape from a prisoner-of-war camp, and other adventures. Unlike most British books about the war, Morris sympathetically portrayed some German soldiers as decent human beings, every bit as patriotic and courageous as their adversaries.

The novel opens with a baffling mystery. As a small British raiding party comes across an evidently ruined and uninhabitable château, the soft sounds of a piano are heard. When they enter the house, they see a beautiful young woman in an evening gown, lying dead on a sofa. At the piano, a man in a German uniform also is dead. A closer look reveals that it is surely Bretherton, a British officer who disappeared some time ago. Is he a British spy in a German uniform, or a German who had served as a spy while in the British army?

Morris wrote a half dozen additional thrillers, but none after 1939, and none with much success. *The Strange Case of Gunner Rawley* (1930) was issued by the American publisher of *G. B.: A Story of the Great War*, but it was not published in England, and the remaining five novels were published only in England.

I have been unable to trace the original publication of this story. It was collected in *My Best Spy Story*, edited anonymously (London, Faber & Faber, 1938).

CUNNINGHAM

W. F. MORRIS

I FIRST MET Cunningham in the spring of 1916. It was outside the Company Headquarters' dug-out one glorious day in June when the birds were singing as though there were no war within a hundred miles, and the familiar smell of chloride of lime and herded humanity was held temporarily in abeyance by the fresh early morning air. He had come up with the rations during the night to replace young Merton who had been knocked out during one of those raids our Divisional Headquarters were so fond of ordering.

I could see at a glance that he had been out before, and I liked the look of him as he stood there by the dug-out steps, hands in pockets, pipe in mouth and the old pattern respirator satchel slung over one shoulder. The appearance of a new member of the mess was always a matter of importance, for when half a dozen men are cooped up together for what someone aptly described as long periods of intense boredom punctuated by moments of intense fear, tempers wore thin occasionally, and one man of the wrong sort could create more mischief than the proverbial wagon-load of monkeys.

But it went deeper even than that. Most commanding officers, I fancy, divided their juniors into two categories: those who did merely what they were told, and those who could be relied upon in an emergency to carry on upon their own initiative. Unhealthy duties such as raids and patrols were supposed to be allotted in rotation from a roster, but whenever it came to sending a party on some highly dangerous and important job, ninety-nine commanding officers out of a hundred would let the roster go hang and put an officer from the second category in command. Now as the number of names in this category was usually considerably smaller than that in the other group, there was undeniably a good deal of what is known as working the willing horse, and it was therefore a matter of considerable interest to all of us to see how a new-comer shaped.

Cunningham shaped well. He quickly graduated to that select band of soldiers that is distinguished by no particular rank—and by no kaleidoscope of chest colours for that matter—but possesses simply that little extra something that the others have not got. The men, quick in such matters, noticed it at once. Even the fussiest and jumpiest of them were calm and happy if he were in charge of them, and the usual good-natured blasphemy which the detailing of a working or wiring party called forth became noticeably milder when it was known that he was to lead it.

From the Colonel downwards we were quickly satisfied that Cunningham would "do," and we were the more glad to have him because with the Somme battle approaching, we knew that officers of his stamp were worth their weight in gold.

Cunningham and I hit it off very well together. We shared a brick-floored cottage room when we were back in rest, and on two memorable occasions, when the loan of a car enabled us to run into Amiens, we did ourselves superlatively well amid the varied wartime attractions of that remarkable city. Friendships in those days were usually strong but of short duration. One or other would receive a Blighty wound, if nothing worse, and pass back down the lines never to be seen again. In our case, however, a slight mishap to one of us served only to strengthen the attachment.

For some days the battalion had been holding on to one of those graveyards of bare, blasted tree-trunks and fallen branches that had been leafy woods less than a month before; and one morning just before dawn, it was discovered that Cunningham was missing. He had been out with a patrol which had returned safely, and he had last been seen no more than a few yards from the edge of the wood. It was certain he could not be far away, so I took a man with me and set out to look for him.

For twenty minutes we searched without success, but as soon as the light grew strong enough to see at all clearly, I spotted him out by a shell-hole no more than a few yards from the margin of the wood. My runner, young Sanders, Cunningham's devoted servant, ran forward before I could stop him, but he went no more than a couple of paces. The light was still poor, but a man running upright makes a conspicuous target at under two hundred yards.

I crawled out to find young Sanders with a neat hole drilled in his forehead; death must have been instantaneous. I had begun to fear that Cunningham too was dead, but to my great relief as I wriggled up to him, he turned his head and assured me that a broken arm was the full extent of the damage. It appeared that in the darkness he had tripped into a shell-hole and broken his arm, and on trying to crawl out had become entangled in some low-pegged wire. With but one arm in commission, his struggles to free himself had resulted only in his becoming further entangled, and there he had remained fuming and helpless ever since.

I had with me a small but very efficient pair of wire-cutters which had proved their worth on more than one occasion, and it took me no more than a few minutes to cut him free. Then we wriggled back to the shelter of the wood.

There was nothing heroic about this episode; it was no more dangerous than the ordinary daily round and common task of those hectic days above the Somme, but Cunningham chose to consider that I had saved his life. As a matter of fact I suppose I had, but it was those very efficient little wire-cutters he had to thank and the good luck that brought them with me.

With his arm in a sling he was of little use as a fighting soldier for the two or three weeks it took the bone to set, but he refused to go farther back than the transport lines and insisted on coming up to occupy a listening post we had established on the outskirts of Guillemont. He spoke German fluently, and on more than one occasion we had enjoyed a good laugh at some tit-bit of Teutonic humour he had overheard while lying inside the German wire.

Corps Headquarters in due season heard of this accomplishment and inevitably they took him from us. The Colonel fought a gallant rearguard action to defend our rights and, nobly backed up by the Brigadier, put down a heavy barrage of indignant chits on headquarters. But it was all in vain. Cunningham received orders to report to Corps Intelligence for duty at the prisoners' cage in the interrogation of prisoners.

After two years of trench warfare most men would have jumped at the chance of the comparative safety and luxurious comfort of headquarters life; but not so Cunningham. But orders were orders; he had to go. We gave him a great send-off and besought him half-seriously not to forget us when he was a brass-hatted general with rows of decorations, for like most infanteers we were firmly convinced that the farther one went from the line, the greater became one's chances of promotion and honours.

And so he departed for the august portals of Corps H.Q., and as though to emphasize the gulf that had now come between us, a large green staff car came to fetch him away. We did see him again, however, for twice he visited us when we were back in rest, and occasionally one of us drawing money from the Field Cashier ran into him in the little market town behind our front. Then the Division was shifted northwards to another Corps and we lost sight of him for good.

The history of our battalion from that time onwards did not differ materially from that of any other. We went into the line for our tours of duty and we came back for our rests; we tramped out of Arras one day over seven hundred strong and returned three days later with a little over two hundred; we had one glorious fortnight in a sleepy village in the back area where we lay on our backs by a stream in the sunshine and had new-laid eggs and cream for breakfast; then new faces crowded in on us and we marched out again at full strength towards the old familiar rumble. Christmas 1917 came and went and with it rumours of a great German spring offensive.

It is unnecessary to repeat the story of that great attack: it is now a matter of history that all may read. My own part in it was short and ignominious. I remember days of anxious waiting—surely the most trying of all a soldier's jobs—and I remember being awakened in the small hours by a tremendous cannonade and muttering to myself: "Thank God it's come at last!" as I felt for my flashlight and scrambled off the wire-netting bunk.

Outside it was cold and dark and misty and very noisy. Most of our deeply buried telephone lines had gone already and it was difficult to get any trustworthy information. We stood to in our scattered posts and waited for the deluge.

Dawn came at last, grey and cold and misty, and presently we knew by the lengthening range of the German barrage and the distant clatter of machine-guns that their storm-troops had gone over. But none of us knew what was really happening, though conflicting reports and rumours were plentiful.

After a cup of hot tea I set off to visit some outlying posts and gather if possible some definite information. Some of the posts, I found, had already beaten off one or more attacks; others had not even seen a German. On the face of it, this seemed highly satisfactory, but the clatter of machine-guns, unmistakably German, sounding from two directions well behind our front, gave pause to any hasty optimism. As the newspapers have it, the situation was obscure.

The mist lifted somewhat as the morning advanced, and from a Lewis-gun post above a sunken road I had my first sight that day of the enemy. They were no more than three hundred yards off and streaming towards us, not in closely packed ranks as in earlier offensives, but in little blobs and files.

That particular attack lasted no more than a bare half-hour, and I know from personal observation it suffered heavily. The dozen odd men in the little post were jubilant, but I was not so happy myself. I caught glimpses now and again of those little blobs and files among the folds of the country to right and left. It was clear that several of our posts had been scuppered and that the enemy were steadily penetrating our front by way of the dead ground between those posts which still held out.

I held on for another hour and then decided to send the gun back about half a mile to a place I knew of that commanded a shallow valley where there seemed to be considerable enemy movement.

The post we held must be described, however. A sunken road crossed the side of a hill from the slope of which there was a very good field of fire. Some ten yards from the road a redoubt had been dug on the hill-side and wired all round. In this redoubt was a perpendicular shaft some twelve feet deep leading to a low tunnel which came out on the sunken road behind.

The men went off under the sergeant while I remained to have a last look round. I stayed no more than three minutes at the most; then I slipped my glasses into the case, went down the rough ladder and groped my way along the tunnel. As I came out into the sunken road, stooping to avoid the low lintel, I cannoned into a man standing by the entrance. My eyes were dazzled after the darkness of the tunnel, and thinking the man was Sergeant Rowland, I started cursing him for having left the men; but I stopped suddenly with dropped jaw when I saw that he was wearing a scuttle-shaped helmet and field-grey. An automatic pistol was pressing gently against my ribs, a hand pulled my revolver from the holster, and my share in the great offensive was at an end.

In due course and with many halts and questionings by the way I came at length to a prison camp in northern Bavaria. There life assumed once more an ordered monotony. We took exercise, read what books were to be had, groused about the food, had fierce arguments about trifling matters, found hilarious enjoyment in playing practical jokes on a pompous little German lieutenant of the reserve, took up hobbies with the enthusiasm of schoolboys and dropped them as quickly, separated into cliques, and were intensely bored; in fact it was the same old war—intense monotony but without the periods of excitement and danger.

I became friends with a gunner captain named Benson. He confided to me one day that he had made up his mind to escape; he needed a partner for the venture and thought that I might be the man. I was; and from that moment I ceased to be bored.

Benson had been collecting the necessary kit for some time, and by various subterfuges had amassed a treasure consisting of a complete civilian outfit, maps, compass, concentrated food, German money and a pair of home-made wire-cutters. He had been learning German and had made considerable progress; and he was delighted when he found that I too had a smattering of the language. Actually my knowledge was confined to a very limited number of useful phrases I had picked up from Cunningham, but on the other hand I have a good ear for copying sounds, and I had been told on more than one occasion that my accent was very nearly perfect. We proposed to travel by night and avoid all contact with the people of the country, but we hoped our German would be good enough to carry us through a chance encounter.

My first task was to make or acquire a civilian outfit. I succeeded in dyeing a pair of khaki slacks a nondescript colour in a fearsome mixture of ink and boot polish and set about converting a service tunic into a civilian jacket by removing the pockets and buttons.

Benson had already formed the rough outlines of a plan of escape, and the all-important details were gradually beginning to fall into place. It will suffice to say that the plan was based upon a very careful study of the routine of the camp and a diversion to be staged by some boisterous spirits at the critical moment. We were confident that helpers for this part of the plan would not be wanting when the time came.

Then just when everything was shaping well, disaster descended upon us. Benson was playing deck-tennis one afternoon on an asphalt pitch, when in jumping for a high ring he slipped and fell. A broken leg takes six weeks or more to mend, and for some time after that he would be in no condition to tackle a long and exhausting march across country.

It could not be helped; we should have to possess our souls in patience and wait till he was fit again. But he would have none of it. He urged me to take his kit and find another partner or carry on by myself. He pointed out that he would probably be sent to the military hospital more than thirty miles away and might never return to that particular camp. In any case it would be impossible for him to smuggle his escaping kit with him, and therefore it was only common sense for me to take it and carry on.

He left the camp that night for hospital. It

seemed to me as though the bottom had been knocked out of my world. My one absorbing interest was gone, and in spite of his arguments I had not the heart to carry on without him. For two days I mooned about the camp by myself completely at a loose end. I did not try to find another partner; I gave up all idea of attempting to escape. Then chance took a hand.

Half a dozen officers arrived one day to inspect the camp. Such inspections were not infrequent, and we derived considerable amusement from them by watching, and occasionally innocently retarding, the feverish efforts of the camp staff to impress the visitors. On this occasion, however, no untoward incident occurred, but in the course of my prowling round the camp later that afternoon I chanced to pass close by the Kommandantur and saw through the open door the caps and greatcoats of the inspecting officers hanging in a row on the pegs in the passage. Evidently the visitors had stayed on for a drink and possibly a meal.

I passed on slowly but with my heart beating like a hammer, for it had come to me suddenly that in one of those coats and caps I would have a sporting chance of marching unchallenged out of the camp.

After Benson's departure I had given up all idea of escape, and I acted now on the spur of the moment. I turned and came back slowly, whistling and with my hands in my pockets. I gave one quick glance round and shot up the steps. My luck was in: the passage was empty. It would have been madness to have attempted to carry the clothes across the open square in broad daylight, but there was a window in the passage giving on to a small waste piece of ground backed by a high wall. I opened the window quietly, took the coat and cap from the nearest peg, and threw them out. Then I closed the window and slipped back down the steps.

The whole operation had taken less than half a minute. I was jubilant; but I had yet to retrieve the coat and cap from the waste ground and convey them to some place where I could put them on after I had changed into civilian clothes. What had been done had been done on the spur of the moment, and I had no plan, but as I strolled along thinking matters over, chance came again to my aid.

Two British orderlies from the adjacent Tommies' camp were crossing the square carrying a large laundry basket between them. I knew one of the men to be a good fellow who would probably be willing to help, and I turned slightly to the right so that our courses converged. "If you want to do me a good turn," I said quietly as we came near, "follow me and say nothing." The good fellow gave me one intelligent look and followed without a word. I strolled round the angle of the main building and up the side, where I was out of sight of the square, to the door of the waste piece of ground. The two orderlies with the basket followed me through.

Under the frosted glass window lay the coat and cap. I picked them up and began to whisper a word of explanation to the two orderlies, but at the sight of the German uniform, Read, the fellow I knew, just grinned and lifted the cover of the basket without a word. I pushed the coat and cap inside.

"March across past the back of the latrine by the side gate," I whispered; "but give me a minute to get there first." The two men grinned again and nodded, and with a word of thanks I strolled off towards the latrine.

As luck would have it, no-one was there, though it hardly mattered, since none of my fellow prisoners would have given me away. I waited till I heard the orderlies' footsteps at the back, and then I went out. The little building screened the spot from the rest of the square, though one of the sentries on the wire fence was in sight. Fortunately he had his back turned, and in a moment I had whipped the cap and coat from the laundry basket and shot back into the latrines. The orderlies, admirable fellows, continued imperturbably on their way.

I hid my spoil behind a cistern and strolled back as casually as I could to the main building. Up in my room I retrieved poor old Benson's escaping kit from its various hiding-places, put on the civilian clothes and pulled on my uniform over the top, while Grey, the only one of my room-mates who happened to be present, looked on with interest.

"Heading for home?" he asked laconically at last. I nodded as I stuffed the maps in an inside pocket. "Want any help?" I told him I would be grateful if he could manage to cover my absence from the evening appel or roll-call so as to give me as big a start as possible. He promised to see to it.

I had decided that the best time to make the attempt was at dusk when the daylight was failing and the big arcs surrounding the camp were still unlighted. The German is a most orderly animal, as I have proved to my own satisfaction more than once during the course of the war; the camp lights were switched on every night three-quarters of an hour after sunset to the minute, and I knew that if I timed my attempt ten minutes earlier, I should run no danger of being caught by the lights.

Unfortunately there was still half an hour to go, and I was in a fever of impatience. That half-hour was the longest I ever spent. Every moment I expected to hear the uproar that would announce that the visiting officers had finished their tippling and had discovered the loss of the coat and cap. But the longest wait must have an end and at last it was time to go.

Grey went with me. Trying to look as unconcerned as possible, we strolled slowly across to the latrines. As luck would have it they were empty. I tore off my uniform and put on the German greatcoat and cap. I had the maps, food, compass and money bestowed in various pockets of my civilian clothes; a trilby hat was rolled up in my trouser pocket. Grey gave me a final look over to see that all was well, pulled the cap to a more rakish angle, and as a final touch stuck his watch-glass in my eye as a monocle. Then he went out to see if the coast was clear, for we were close to the side gate and it would never do for the sentry there to see a German officer issuing from the prisoners' latrines.

I stood in the shadow of the entrance and waited, trying hard to keep calm; waiting is always so much more difficult than action. Perhaps a minute went by, or maybe two, and then at last I heard him call that the sentry's back was turned. It was now or never.

I stepped out from my shelter, gave him a wink as I passed and headed for the gate.

My heart was beating like a hammer, but I strutted along with a lord-of-all-creation air and tried to look as Prussian as I could. The sentry did not see me till I was close on the gate, and then for a moment he did nothing. I thought that he had recognized me and that the game was up; but suddenly he came to life and began to fumble with the lock. I stared at him coldly through my monocle, which combined with my stony silence and haughty air seemed to fluster him so that he took a long time to open the gate. Meanwhile I was in a cold fear that the man would recognize me.

At last he had the gate open. I passed through; but there still remained the gate in the outer wire to be opened, and he fumbled badly with that too. It was really a comic situation, for the poor man was even more scared than I was. But the second gate also was open at last, and I passed through it with a lordly acknowledgement of the sentry's salute.

The camp was surrounded by woods, and my first impulse was to dive for the shelter of the undergrowth; but I realized that my only chance of avoiding recapture was to get beyond them before my escape was discovered, for once a cordon were thrown round the woods, escape from them would be difficult. Therefore I walked down the road at a moderate pace till I was out of sight of the camp; then I dived in among the undergrowth, tore off the German coat and cap with feverish haste, put on the trilby, and emerged as an inconspicuous civilian. The road would take me beyond the woods more quickly than a winding woodland path, and as time was the all-important factor, I set off along the road again at my best speed.

I did not breathe really freely till I came to the end of the trees and saw the open sky above me. I took a deep breath then, pulled out my map and compass and set a course by the stars. I kept going steadily all night, skirting the villages, and by dawn when I lay up in a copse to sleep, I had put many miles between myself and the camp.

There is no need to give the details of that nightmare march, for a nightmare it became after the first few days. I marched at night and slept in hiding during the day. Twice at dusk I bought food in village shops, and I tried to mask any imperfections of language and accent by tying a handkerchief round my face and feigning toothache.

I was heading for the Dutch frontier on the course Benson and I had worked out together, but by the ninth day I had begun to wonder if I would ever make it. The cold nights, exposure to bad weather, and the poor food had tried my strength severely, and the wire fence guarding the Dutch frontier, which we had so cheerfully decided could present no real obstacle to determined men, seemed to grow more formidable with every mile I travelled.

One morning just before dawn as I dropped exhausted in the shelter of a wood, I knew that I could never reach the frontier now on foot. But I told myself that I was not done yet. The Rhine was only a few miles off, and if I could reach the river and find a Dutch bargee, it might be possible to bribe the man to smuggle me across the frontier in his barge. I was happier after that decision and I slept like a log all day.

I reached the river the following night after a comparatively easy march and began my search for a Dutch barge. But I failed to find one. A few German barges were moored along the bank— the port of registration painted on each told their nationality—but no Dutch.

While I lay in hiding the next day I did some hard thinking. A short distance lower down the river lay Cologne with large docks and many barges, and among them surely at least one Dutch. It was unfortunate that the city and the docks were on the opposite bank of the river and to reach them I should have to cross a bridge,

but that was a risk I was prepared to face. If the bridge were guarded it would be foolish to attempt to cross it at night when few wayfarers were about, but during the day I hoped it might be possible to slip across unchallenged among the crowd.

On the following morning I walked boldly into that suburb of Cologne that stands on the east bank of the river. I walked with a stiff leg and very square shoulders, as I thought that the role of a discharged wounded soldier was the best to adopt; and with my worn face and clothes hanging loosely about my emaciated body I must have looked the part to perfection.

A little short of the bridge I came upon a group of people waiting on the pavement. A tramcar rattled up as I pushed my way among them and I was carried forward with the rush. Acting on the impulse of the moment, I climbed inside and took my seat with the rest. Several of the passengers read newspapers and paid their fares in silence, and when the conductress came to me, I held out a few pfennigs as the others had done and received my ticket without having to utter a word. The tram rumbled on over the great bridge, and a few minutes later I got down unmolested in the shadow of the great cathedral.

After my long solitude it was a strange and exciting experience to find myself walking the streets of a busy city, but no-one of that hurrying throng took any notice of me, and as time passed my confidence grew. I searched along the river bank and the docks for a Dutch barge and found three, but each had many men about her loading or unloading, and it would have been suicidal to have approached a skipper there in broad daylight and put him to the test. I therefore decided to return after dark and try to creep aboard unseen.

I went back into the town and wandered about the busy streets. The fine shops fascinated me; it was many months since I had seen anything bigger than a village store, and I lingered in front of the plate-glass windows like an urchin on Christmas Eve.

I was standing on the busy pavement of the

Hohestrasse outside a cigar shop wondering if it would be foolish to risk asking for a packet of cigarettes, when without apparent reason I became acutely aware of two men standing near me. One tall and the other short, both dressed in civilian clothes, they had stopped for a moment to look at the shop window. Something vaguely familiar in the bearing of one of them fixed my attention. The shorter of the two had already turned away, and as the other followed him, he looked in my direction and our eyes met.

Recognition is as swift as the fastest camera shutter and may be equally revealing. It was Cunningham. I was taken completely by surprise, but I flatter myself that I gave no more than a slight start. As for Cunningham, not an eyelid flickered, not a muscle of his face moved, nor did he arrest the turning of his head for the fraction of a second; only the momentary spark in his eye betrayed his recognition. He went off beside his companion, chatting in German as though he had seen nothing.

That sight of Cunningham heartened me. It was comforting to know that there was even one fellow-countryman of mine in this great city. If he could play so gallantly his dangerous game, of which the penalty of failure was death, it would be shameful for me to falter in a game for lower stakes. I congratulated myself that I had made no sudden exclamation, and I was glad that his companion's back had been turned at the moment of recognition, for even my slight start might have given us away. I realized then the self-control and courage needed by the successful spy. My own wandering as a fugitive had given me some inkling of the utter loneliness of the work and of the self-reliance needed for the part.

I wandered down to the river-side again, and as I stood in the dusk gazing out across the water, a man came and leant on the rail beside me. It was the one thing I had been afraid of— that some loiterer would try to get into conversation with me; but as I turned hastily to move away I caught a glimpse of his profile. It was Cunningham's.

"Oh, it's you," I said with relief.

He nodded.

"Is this safe?" I asked. "I don't want to get you in a mess."

He looked at me curiously. "How do you mean?" he asked.

"Well—I'm only an escaped prisoner," I said, "and if I'm caught it's the prisoners-of-war camp again; but for you. . . ." I laughed shortly. "I suppose it would be the traditional firing-squad at dawn."

He gave me an odd look that made me feel like an ingénue at a party who has said the wrong thing. I suppose Intelligence men have their own etiquette of what is good luck and what is bad luck, like airmen, and after all it was only natural that a reference to a firing-squad at dawn should be one of the things that was not "done." Anyway, I felt a fool.

"So you have escaped from a prison camp, have you! Stout fellow!" he said in the old friendly manner. "Tell me about it." I told him. "You've had a rough time," he commented at the end. "It must have taken a bit of guts."

"Guts!" I echoed. "*You* to talk of guts! Why, half an hour of your job would reduce me to a nervous wreck."

He let that pass without comment, nor did he volunteer any information about his job or his life since he left his comfortable Intelligence post behind the lines for the hazardous one there in Germany. And I did not question him. I had heard enough about Intelligence to know that agents worked so secretly that often they did not know one another even.

He asked me about my future plans. I told him of my original intention and of my change of plan. He thought I was wise to have abandoned the idea of footing it to Holland. The frontier was closely watched and guarded by live wire in places; without special knowledge of the district I would have hardly stood a chance. But he shook his head over the other plan also. Of course there *were* Dutch bargees who would be willing to smuggle an escaped prisoner across the frontier, but there must be many more who would not take the risk. My difficulty would be to find the right man; if I approached the wrong one first I should be in the cart.

I asked what he advised. He was silent for a few moments. "I think I can help you," he said at last. "You had better come to my rooms for the night while I arrange it. You will be all right there."

I said I had no intention of adding to the obvious risks he ran, but he laughed and assured me it would be all right. "I owe you something, anyway," he said. "If you wander about Cologne all night, someone will talk to you, and then the game will be up. And besides you are in no fit condition to do that; what you need is a square meal and a bed. But I must see that the coast is clear first. Meanwhile, I advise you to keep on the move; I'll be back in half an hour." And with that he turned and left me.

I kept on the move as he had advised, and returned to the spot on the river bank as soon as the half-hour was up. But there was no sign of Cunningham. He was, I knew, a man of his word, and as the minutes went by without his putting in an appearance, my anxiety can be imagined.

Exhaustion can play strange tricks with the most equable temperament. After my meeting with Cunningham and his offer of help I had soared from a state not far removed from despair to one of rosy optimism; now I was sliding rapidly back again. Something had gone amiss; not only did I see that promised square meal recede into the distance and the prison camp loom near, but I heard in imagination the very volley that would end Cunningham's career. All this because he had delayed ten minutes beyond the appointed time. It will be seen that I was pretty near the end of my tether.

He came at last, and gave some explanation of his delay which I failed to hear in my joy at seeing him. He told me the coast was clear; he would go ahead and I was to follow a few paces behind. In this way we went back into the town, up one of the main streets, down a side turning and in through an open door. He led me up a short flight of stairs and through a small hall to a comfortably furnished room. After locking the door he put food and wine before me and sat smoking his pipe while I ate. And how I ate.

Afterwards we talked of old times, of the old battalion and of days in France. Then I had a glorious hot bath and he put me into a little bedroom opening off the hall. It was a spare room, he said, and was never used. He would be out all night, but he would lock the door and I would be quite safe. A woman would come in to tidy up in the morning, but she would not trouble me. My room had always been kept locked, and if I kept quiet she would not know I was there. He could not say exactly when he could give me breakfast—as though that mattered—but he gave me a loaf and some meat in case I was hungry. Then with a cheery good night he closed and locked the door. I heard him go out some minutes later.

Contrary to expectations I did not sleep well; the bed was too soft and comfortable after my spell of hard lying but I dropped off before dawn and awoke to hear the woman bustling about the flat. After she had gone, I dressed and ate some of the meat and bread.

I found it dull sitting there in that little room and I wished that Cunningham had thought of locking the door on the inside instead of on the outside, so that I could have gone into the other room and amused myself with the German illustrated papers I had seen there the night before. Except for a floor rug, a chair, a cupboard, and a bed, the room was bare. It amused me, however, to think that an English Intelligence man should have his own flat in Cologne and even a spare room in which to entertain his fellow-countrymen. In the cupboard I found a bag with an old label for Berlin and the name H. von Goburg written on it in Cunningham's handwriting. That too was amusing—but a grim jest for him if it were seen through.

It was nearly midday when he returned. He apologized for keeping me shut up so long, but said he had not been idle. And indeed he had not.

It was, as he had said, almost impossible to

get across the Dutch frontier if one did not know the ropes, but on the other hand it was a fairly simple matter for those who did. Actually the frontier was crossed pretty frequently by smugglers and others, and to cut a long story short, he had arranged for one who was an expert at the game to take me over that night. I was to catch the evening train to Aachen where he would hand me over to the frontier expert. Before dawn I would be on Dutch soil.

He brushed aside my objections to his coming with me; the risk to himself, he said, was negligible, and with my limited knowledge of German I could not possibly risk the journey alone. And besides it was all arranged.

So I thanked him gratefully and sat down to the excellent cold meal he had prepared.

He had to be busy all that afternoon again, but before he went he handed me a suit from his wardrobe and put me back into my little room. "We can't have you looking too much like a tramp," he laughed. I suggested he might let me have the run of the flat, but he said that was too risky as the woman had a key. So back I went to the little room and was locked in.

It was good to feel well dressed again. Cunningham and I were much the same size and the suit was a tolerably good fit. His nom de guerre, H. von Goburg, was written on the tab of the jacket below the name of a Berlin tailor. Now at least the cut of my clothes could not give me away.

Somehow I whiled away that interminable time of waiting. I had brought with me the German illustrated papers and they helped. The captions were not easy to follow, but the rather low humour of the pictures was obvious enough.

It was nearly eight o'clock when he returned. I laughed aloud when he opened the door, for he was dressed in the uniform of a German officer and looked a typical Prussian. He said it would save us from being bothered by petty officials. I laughed again and reminded him that I had adopted the same plan at the prison camp and with satisfactory results.

He had a taxi waiting outside, so that we drove to the station in style, and all the way I was grinning to myself at the thought of what the people on the crowded pavements would have said if they had known who we really were. He carried the whole thing off magnificently: he paid the taximan with a lordly air and marched up the platform to a first-class carriage with just the right swagger. Two other people were in the compartment, but they did not worry us. I sat undisturbed in my corner and pretended to read the magazine he had bought me.

The journey to Aachen was short and passed off without incident. Cunningham's uniform brought him salutes and respect, and carried us through the barrier without question. We walked from the station through the lighted streets of the town and out along a country road. Away to the left a lighted tramcar moved slowly on its way; ahead the red and green signal lights of a railway glowed through the darkness.

I remember feeling strangely unreal; it seemed absurd that this commonplace road could lead to freedom.

A man lounging by a gateway gave us a good night as we passed. Cunningham halted suddenly and gripped my hand. "Follow him," he whispered with a nod towards the dark figure. "He will see you through. Good-bye." And before I had recovered from my surprise he was several yards away striding back down the road.

That was the last I ever saw of Cunningham. I dared not call out or run after him. I could only turn sadly towards the dark figure by the gate. All my elation at the nearness of success had left me; it seemed a shameful thing that I should go on towards safety and freedom while he who had arranged it all was striding through the darkness back to his lonely, dangerous work.

The man by the gate turned without a word as I approached. He led me by a large dark house and through a hedge at the end of a long garden. After that we went very cautiously, sometimes we crawled, and once we lay still while two men passed close to us. Then we halted beyond a ditch on the edge of a small field. I could distinguish a narrow footpath winding towards a low building with one dimly lighted window.

I was just wondering when we should reach the wire and how we would cross it, when my guide put his lips to my ear and spoke for the first time. "You are now in Holland," he said. "Go straight ahead to the house." And before I could ask a question or even thank him he had turned and disappeared back the way we had come.

I shall not try to describe my feeling at that moment or the many little kindnesses of the friendly Dutch guards at the little house when they had satisfied themselves that I was really an escaped prisoner of war. I had a great reception from many British residents in Holland and from the British authorities to whom I reported. Everyone treated me as though I were a hero, and I felt very mean in taking all the credit to myself, for I thought it would be most unwise to mention Cunningham to anyone except an accredited Intelligence Officer. Madison, the one man I gathered I could have spoken freely to, was on leave in London and I did not see any of the higher Embassy officials.

One of the juniors came to the station to see me off for England, and as we stood chatting by the carriage door he said: "Madison will want to see you when you get to Town. He will be interested to hear you have been in Cologne." Then with a quick glance round and lowered voice he went on: "His department have had a spot of bother in that region lately. Two of our people have gone silent—and have disappeared."

A sudden chill came over me as I realized the meaning of his words; I thought of Cunningham back there in the centre of the danger. "You mean . . . ?" I began.

He nodded. "I'm afraid so. You see, the Huns have got a new man on counter-espionage in that area. A pretty live wire from all accounts. They say he's played the game himself behind our lines and knows every move. . . ." Then he added brightly as the train began to move: "A dangerous bloke—von Goburg is his name, Captain von Goburg, blast him! Well, good-bye, and good luck."

LIVE BAIT

J. M. WALSH

THE BIBLIOGRAPHY OF THE prolific James Morgan Walsh (1897–1952) is impressive, with fifty-seven novels of crime, espionage, and detective fiction published between 1921 (*Tap-Tap Island*) and 1952 (*King of Tiger Bay*). Then there is a realization that he also wrote twenty-five similar novels as Stephen Maddock, plus additional books in the thriller category, as well as fantasy and science fiction, as George M. White, H. Haverstock Hill, and Jack Carew. And, of course, he also was a prolific short story writer, his first being published when he was only sixteen while he worked in his father's stationery store. He asserted that in 1929 alone he had thirty stories accepted by magazines.

Born in Australia, he became a full-time writer in 1923 and moved to London in 1925, shortly after his marriage. While his early books were set in Australia, the Far East, and the Pacific Islands, the demand of his English publishers (mostly Collins and Hamish Hamilton) was that they be set in England. Walsh complied, even rewriting three novels with Australian backgrounds to have them set in England: *The White Mask* (1925), *The League of Missing Men* (1927), and *The Man Behind the Curtain* (1927). His popularity was so great that he was often called the Australian Edgar Wallace and the Australian E. Phillips Oppenheim, the two most popular English thriller writers of the time.

One of Walsh's most successful series characters was the British Secret Service agent Oliver Keene, who appeared in at least twelve books. In *Spies' Vendetta* (1936), he imagines an invention that would allow airplanes to be powered by radio waves, and in *Secret Weapons* (1940), he anticipates guided missiles being used as weapons.

I have been unable to trace the original publication of this story. It was collected in *My Best Spy Story*, edited anonymously (London, Faber & Faber, 1938).

LIVE BAIT

J. M. WALSH

THERE ONCE WAS a man called Luss, who, on occasion, described himself as a collector. What he collected was not specified. It was a convenient, if designedly misleading label, one open to many misconstructions and interpretations, but its main virtue in his own eyes was that it was strictly accurate. For Mr. Luss preferred whenever possible to tell the truth about himself. It left nothing to deny later. That it was by no means the whole truth, or even a considerable portion of it, did not to his way of thinking affect the issue in the least.

For he was a collector—of a kind. Mostly it was information of naval or military value that he sought. A pedant would have called him a spy. Mr. Luss could have countered that by pointing out that he seldom, if ever, engaged in espionage himself. It was his business to co-ordinate the results, and in due course pass them on to the right people.

Most often plans were brought to him by those he believed he could trust. That their loss did no great harm is neither here nor there. The fact that Mr. Luss was able to acquire them at all meant that there had been carelessness or worse somewhere, and as a consequence—I have in mind one or two particular instances—there was a shuffling of personnel in one department, and a tightening up of procedure in another.

Luss was not the man's real name. Probably by this time even he himself could not have said offhand what that was. He changed his identity almost as often as he changed his clothes. Only in certain files of the Power that employed him was there any immutable record. There he was known by a letter, a number, and a code word that had been added to the end of his dossier. But all this was years ago. A red line has since been drawn beneath the entry, and in a foreign hand and a foreign tongue a sentence has been appended intimating that he has fallen by the wayside.

In other words Mr. Luss tried once too often, over-reached himself, and despite all his precautions was caught. That his own Power promptly disowned him goes without saying. Anyway, Luss would not have claimed its protection even had there been any hope of obtaining it. He had blundered with full knowledge of what would happen if he did, and had been left to pay the price of failure.

Through the years of his imprisonment—they were not so long as they felt—he nourished two ambitions. One was to do something to rehabilitate himself, and the other, which gradually grew to be an obsession, was to exact payment from the man who had trapped him.

One bright summer's day in the present year of grace Sir Reginald Vallery, Colonel Ormiston's departmental chief, sent for the Secret Service man, and the latter answered the summons with dismay in his heart. Such calls most often came at an inconvenient moment. For two years in succession the holiday season had been spoiled for him by the inconsiderateness of foreign powers or their agents. One was on the occasion of the outbreak of the Spanish trouble, and the other . . . But there are reasons why the telling of that story must be postponed to a later year.

Sir Reginald Vallery began with apologies, for he knew by the look in Ormiston's eye that he had to be handled tactfully. He was quite capable of passing in his resignation if he was rubbed the wrong way, and despite the cant about no man being irreplaceable he was far too valuable to lose because of a hasty word.

Ormiston brushed the apologies dourly aside. "Let's get to business, Reg," he said with the frankness of an old friend. "What do you want me for?"

Vallery told him with commendable brevity. As everyone knew there were things happening in the Mediterranean, repercussions of the Spanish trouble. A new supplementary naval code had been constructed and distributed to the Grand Fleet. Even though copies of it had been obtained by the wrong people it was not possible, for administrative reasons, to alter it immediately.

Ormiston seized on the operative word. "'Obtained'?" he repeated. "What do you mean by that? Were they stolen?"

Vallery shook his head. "No, photographed," he said tersely.

Ormiston chewed thoughtfully over that. "But how?" he queried. "Did someone have access to them or was there a leakage?"

He saw other possibilities that Vallery's explanation did not seem to have dealt with.

"Neither," Vallery returned. "The work was done from the outside. A man posing as a window-cleaner had a camera with a tele-photo lens hidden in his bucket. He took a series of snaps of the room into which he was looking, and it was just our bad luck that this code of ours happened to be out on a table within range. Someone was consulting it at the moment."

Ormiston rubbed his chin thoughtfully. This didn't look too good.

Abruptly Vallery reached into the drawer of his table, extracted something, then triumphantly fluttered a number of prints out fanwise in front of him.

"These," he said coolly, "are the photos that were taken, and here"—his hand went into the drawer again—"are the negatives themselves."

"All of them?" Ormiston said shrewdly.

The other nodded. "Every single one of them," he answered. "We're sure of that." From under lowered lids he watched the Secret Service man's reaction to the confession.

"Well," said Ormiston, after a barely perceptible pause, "if you've got them back, there's no need for my services."

Vallery pursed his lips. "I'm rather afraid there is," he said deliberately.

Ormiston started slightly, then swiftly an idea came to him. "You haven't made an arrest, by any chance?" he asked.

"Yes." Vallery spoke as though he had been waiting for that question. "A man named Kioski."

"Never heard of him," said Ormiston curtly.

"I'm not surprised. He's new to us, too. His arrest came about quite by accident. He was going to the station in a taxi—to catch a boat-train to the Continent, as we know now—and the machine he was in collided with a private car. The inevitable policeman appeared while the two drivers were trying to sort things out. The delay annoyed Kioski. He kept crying that he must catch the train, refused to answer any questions, and wanted to stalk off and get another taxi. When the policeman—quite politely—tried to stop him Kioski lost his head and lashed out. He missed his train all right. People can't be allowed to assault policemen who are merely doing their duty."

"Naturally." Ormiston smiled understandingly. "I fancy I can guess the rest," he said. "He was searched at the police-station, and these"—he nodded towards the prints and negatives—"were found on him then?"

"Exactly. But there's a little more to it still." Vallery went on to relate what that was.

In some way not specified Kioski was induced to talk. Then it came out that he wasn't the principal by any means. He was merely acting under orders, those of Luss, to be precise. Luss had a copy of the code, it appeared. The arrangement he had made with Kioski was that if the man failed to notify him within forty-eight hours that he had effected delivery, Luss was to start off himself with his own copy.

The notification was to be made by means of an advertisement to appear in the personal columns of three Parisian dailies. All Luss had to do was to buy whichever of the journals he preferred, which he could at practically any large bookstall in the Home Counties within a few hours of the paper being issued.

"He's made it as nearly fool-proof as he possibly could," Ormiston grunted.

"He has. But we know that Luss is still in the country, and that he is hardly likely to be leaving for another thirty hours or so. You've got that time then to run him down, and retrieve that copy of the code."

Ormiston smiled wryly. "Isn't that more a job for the police?" he said gently.

"I'm afraid not. Of course you will have all the co-operation from them that you need, but, as you know, you can do things that the uniformed man dare not. Also you're one of the few people who should be able to recognize Luss, no matter how he is disguised. You had enough to do with him the last time we got our hands on him."

He had another reason, he might have added, though it was one he was reluctant to press on Ormiston. Luss was reputed to cherish an undying hatred for the one man who had ever trapped

him. Vallery fancied that something of value might yet emerge from that single fact.

II

Colonel Ormiston bent down to knock the ashes from his pipe against the side of the empty grate. In the very act of straightening up he paused, then swiftly ducked his head again. That action in all probability saved his life. For something swished through the air not a foot above the top of his skull, hit the side of the fireplace, and dropped with a faint thud on the tiles.

Ormiston's reaction was characteristic of the man. He twisted abruptly sideways out of his chair, so that he was no longer in a direct line between the open window and the fireless grate. At the same instant a revolver appeared as if by magic in his hand. Three quick strides took him across the room. Reaching gingerly from behind the shelter of the curtains on one side of the window he drew the sash swiftly down. Then he peered out.

As he had expected the prospect was deserted. There was no sign of any intruder in the garden now. But the topmost twigs of the laurel bush against the fence still moved perceptibly, and at the sight he smiled grimly.

The hidden marksman had gone that way, as quickly and as silently as he must have come. His haste had been such that he had not even remained to see the effect of his shot. Perhaps he was egotistical enough to assume that there would be no need for a second one. More probably he had been disturbed at his work, and had managed to make himself scarce just in time.

Ormiston felt that there was little to be gained by attempting to pursue his assailant. Since he had not caught even so much as a glimpse of the man, identification of him in his present incarnation was not going to be easy. As a strict matter of fact he abandoned the idea of pursuit before it had begun to take tangible form. Instead he turned back to the more hopefully interesting business of examining the missile that had just failed to put a period to his existence.

All the same it was with a view to what he called "improbable possibilities" that he moved so that he was able to keep one eye on the window, while the other was occupied in another direction. The unknown—and unseen—might or might not return. That was something on which Ormiston preferred to keep a deliberately open mind. But should the fellow reappear by any chance the Secret Service man meant to be so placed that the next shot would be fired by, not at, him.

The object that had just missed him was a tiny silvered dart with a feather of fluffed-out, red-coloured, silk-like material at one end. The other was pointed, and at first glance looked as though it had been dipped in glue.

Ormiston picked it up gingerly between two match stalks which he manipulated like a pair of pincers, stared hard at the dirty brown blob on the point, and whistled soundlessly. Next he placed the dart carefully on a sheet of paper, one of several on the table-top, and the red fluff seemed to glow up at him like a malignant eye.

Then and not till then did he open the door, thrust his head out into the hall, and call for his companion.

"Terry," he cried, "I want you."

Though his voice was decidedly low-pitched he somehow contrived to fling into it a note of urgency that he believed was bound to reach the other's ears. He was not wrong in this. Almost immediately he was answered from above.

"Coming," said a crisp voice, and the soft, swift clatter of feet on the stairs advertised that for once Terry was speaking the literal truth.

He burst into the room like a young whirlwind, then stopped dead, and his jaw sagged at the sight of the revolver in his brother-in-law's hand.

"What's up now?" he demanded jerkily. "Don't tell me you've called me down to witness you committing suicide? This Luss business isn't quite so hopeless as all that."

"I know it isn't," Ormiston said steadily, nevertheless the corners of his mouth twitched

slightly. For so understanding a man it was odd that this was the nearest he ever got to a smile. In a different voice he went on: "Terry, what were you doing upstairs?"

Terry's eyes widened, but: "Snoozing," he said promptly. "It seemed such a delightfully drowsy afternoon that I thought it was a pity to waste it. Why?"

Ormiston brushed the question aside with a gesture of impatience. He had some others of his own to ask before he answered Terry's.

"You didn't happen to be looking out of the window of your room, say, within the last five minutes or so?" he queried.

Terry, immensely serious now, his shrewd dark eyes raking the other's lean, sun-tanned face, slowly shook his head.

"No, I didn't," he declared. "Would I have seen anything had I been?"

Ormiston gave a curt little nod. "I should imagine so," he said. "As a matter of fact I've had a visitor. This is the kind of card he left me."

He pointed to the shining dart on the table. Terry started forward, put out his hand, and went to touch it.

"Don't! Leave it alone!" Ormiston snarled. His voice was so startlingly harsh that Terry froze abruptly in his tracks. Then curiously he turned his head to look at the other.

"What's wrong with it?" he demanded. "It looks like an airgun dart to me."

"So it does to me," said Ormiston with feeling, "but its real name is Death. You see, it was intended for me." Quickly he explained the circumstances of its arrival.

"Luss," said Terry laconically at the end.

"You think so?"

"There's little room for doubt. Anyway, he hasn't lost much time getting to work. It can't be much over an hour since you left Vallery."

"He could hardly have known that I'd been there," Ormiston said thoughtfully. "Still one always has to allow for the possibility of coincidence. He might have seen me in the neighbourhood, and deduced the rest. The one thing about which I can feel certain is that he doesn't yet know that Kioski has been pulled in. He would have been on the run before this if that was the case."

"With descriptions of him circulating all over the place it shouldn't be long before his turn comes," Terry opined.

"It's not so easy as all that," Ormiston protested. "Luss is a past master at disguise. That's why he has been able to keep going with impunity for so long. All the same he has one or two little peculiarities that I fancy may give him away if ever I clap eyes on him again."

Terry nodded. That, he surmised, was one of the two reasons why an attack had been made on Ormiston. Luss could never feel altogether safe anywhere as long as the Secret Service man remained alive.

Terry was turning away with some idea of scouting through the garden—perhaps the laurel bush or its vicinity might offer him something in the nature of a clue—when his eye fell on one of the sheets of paper on the table, and he pulled up short.

"What the deuce have you been doing there?" he asked in a voice suddenly gone husky. "Isn't it a breach of the Official Secrets Act, or whatever you call it, for you to have documents of that nature in your possession?"

"This?" Ormiston picked up one of the sheets in question. It was a neat little blueprint, apparently, of the very latest thing in anti-aircraft guns. "Rather nicely done, isn't it? Vallery has quite a few more like it. I may tell you something about them some day."

Terry stared at him. "You'd better be careful with it," he said warningly, and there was something oddly pinched about his face now. "Suppose Luss had killed you and got away with this, what then?"

"It would have been awkward," Ormiston said gravely. "That struck me at the time. Anyway, I have a rooted objection to being killed wantonly," he added with seeming inconsequence.

Terry's brows furrowed. There was a puzzle here whose depths he could not quite fathom.

He did not press the matter further, however. It was fairly obvious from Ormiston's manner that he was in no mood to answer questions about procedure. All the same:

"How do you propose to get on to Luss's track?" Terry asked anxiously.

Ormiston's glance did not waver in the least. "I don't propose," he said surprisingly.

"Then . . . ?" But Terry left the sentence unfinished.

"There is a popular superstition, Terry," Ormiston said meaningly, "to the effect that lightning doesn't strike twice in the same spot. I am hoping that Luss has never heard of it, or if he has, has common sense enough not to believe it."

For one long second he held the other's eyes with his own. Then Terry gasped audibly. All at once understanding had come to him.

III

There was no moon. It would not have mattered much had there been one. The clouds that had gathered earlier in the evening now completely blacked out the stars. Truly the gods were being good to him, thought the man who slipped like a gaunt shadow from behind the masking growth of the laurel bush. He could hardly have had a night more suited for his purpose had he ordered it specially well in advance.

There was no sign of life in the house. The last light had gone out more than an hour before. No servants slept on the premises, that he knew. There were only two men with whom he would have to deal, for the womenfolk were away for the week. All this he had ascertained by careful painstaking research. The final item of information that he needed had come to his hands only that very evening and with its receipt the last piece of his plan had clicked neatly into place.

His procedure was peculiar. He made a cautious circuit of the house. He stopped at every door, found the keyhole, or, if it was a lock of the Yale type, fumbled for a clear space beneath the door. But into whatever opening it was that he located he inserted a length of rubber piping. The other end clamped over a weapon curiously like a Lüger pistol except that its muzzle was inclined to be bell-shaped. On each occasion when he pressed the trigger there was no more than a faint hissing sound that died away as he plugged the keyhole or the space beneath the door with a handful of earth.

At last he finished. Then he turned his attention to effecting an entry. This he did through a window at the rear of the house, which he found conveniently unfastened. Had he stopped to think he might have felt inclined to regard this as suspicious, but he took it in his stride. If he thought about it at all it was to accept it as a piece of carelessness that played right into his hands.

But before he climbed through the window he slipped on his face a gas-mask that he had taken from under his coat.

The interior of the house was dark and silent. The light from his torch jetted round as he attempted to recall the geography of the place. Once he stopped as he passed the foot of the stairs, and he hesitated for a second. Then he raised the pistol, and fired twice into the gloom above him. Two faint tinkles followed on each other's heels as the little glass bombs the pistol had ejected struck the floor of the landing overhead.

Beneath the mask the man chuckled softly. He himself walked in an invisible sea of death, safe for the time being. Anyone aroused by his movements who came out on to the landing above would almost certainly sway and choke, then topple to the floor. But even if that failed no-one could come down the stairs without risking dissolution.

With some little difficulty he located the room in which Ormiston had been sitting at the moment of the attack on the afternoon of that very day. His preparations were quick and thorough. He made sure that the curtains were drawn across the window, and that the catch was fast. Then just to make assurance doubly sure he tilted the back of a chair under the handle of the door. No matter how he had miscalculated he could hardly be taken unawares now.

He worked for close on to an hour in a darkness punctuated only by the stabbing gleam of his pocket torch. At the end he had the little wall-safe open, and he thrust his hand in. There was only one thing there, two sections of cardboard clamped together by elastic bands. He slipped off the latter, and his eyes twinkled. The little blue-prints he had glimpsed through the window that afternoon lay there for the taking. The cardboard that had protected them he threw into the empty grate, the plans themselves he thrust deep into an inside pocket.

It had been easier even than he had dared hope. From first to last luck had been with him. He had come that afternoon in order to kill, and chance had shown him how he could do that and at the same time turn a moment's carelessness to advantage.

It remained only for him to get out of the house now.

He had no intention of departing by the way he had come. There was no need for that. Cautiously he drew the curtains aside just enough to allow him to peer out. The garden was empty, deserted, not even a shadow stirred.

Very, very gently, with a facile ease born of long experience in the art he began to raise the window inch by inch. To his immense relief it moved soundlessly. When the aperture was large enough to allow him to crawl through it he stopped, flung one leg over the sill, followed with the other, and gave a sigh of heartfelt gratitude as he felt the soft soil of the garden beneath his feet.

Meticulous always he turned, and closed the window before moving from the spot. He took half a dozen paces forward, then thought of the gas-mask still clamped to his nose. He tore it off, and gulped in the sweet fresh air of night. It struck him, however, that he had better get rid of it at once. It was a useless encumbrance now, and he might yet have to move with haste.

He was looking round for some convenient bush into which to fling it when he fancied he heard a faint sound behind him. Then he felt a touch on his shoulder.

"Hands up, Luss!" snapped a voice with a parade-ground rasp in it.

He whirled with an inarticulate cry, and the brilliant beam of a large hand torch struck him full in the face. For the moment he was blinded, then as his vision cleared he recognized Colonel Ormiston and saw the ugly-looking automatic he held in a rock-steady hand. Behind the Colonel were other shadowy figures.

Luss groaned. The game was up. He had walked into a trap.

IV

A room in the house was cleared, and when the gas had been dissipated the little party entered. Luss, handcuffed now, glared round at Ormiston, Terry, and the couple of men from the Special Branch who had helped to rope him in. The senior of the latter was speaking to Ormiston in a low voice.

"I've phoned," he said. "Our men will go through his house with a fine tooth-comb. If there's a copy of that code hidden there they'll find it."

Ormiston nodded approval. "And they'll let us know the result promptly?" he said with a shade of anxiety in his voice.

"They'll telephone through to here the moment they find anything," the man assured Ormiston. "You can trust them on a job of this sort, Colonel, you know that. They don't miss much, and they work with an amazing celerity. They have to."

Once again Ormiston nodded. He turned to the table where the things they had taken from Luss's pockets made a neat little pile. On the top was an envelope addressed to a Mr. Bula. The letter it had contained, innocuous in itself, was ample evidence that this was Luss's latest alias. More. The superscription had told them where the man had been lodging.

The proper course, so Terry thought, would have been to take Luss off to the police-station, and there charge him. Ormiston thought differ-

ently, and since he had been given a free hand in the matter it was his word that counted. Had he been asked to state the reasons why he hesitated he would have found some difficulty in marshalling them. All he could say was that something—instinct, if you like—warned him that the incident had not yet reached a climax. There was more to come, but what, or in what way he could not say.

Luss must have caught something of what had passed between Ormiston and the man from the Special Branch. The glum look cleared from his face, was replaced by something curiously like triumph.

"What do you think you're going to find at my place, Ormiston?" he demanded, twisting round.

"You know as well as I do," Ormiston retorted.

Luss grinned openly. "Perhaps I do. But I'm not telling."

"Listen." Ormiston took a step nearer to him. "It's a copy of that supplementary code."

Luss's face went blank. "What the devil are you talking about?" he said.

"Don't pretend you're innocent," Ormiston snapped back. "The gaff's been blown, Luss. Kioski's told us all he knew."

"Kioski!" Luss's face was a study in amazement. "Why, I've never even heard of the man!"

"No?" Ormiston's tone had suddenly become dangerously quiet. "That's queer. We roped him in this morning." Briefly, pungently, he outlined what had happened.

Luss took the blow without winking. Even now he was prepared to brazen it out, though his object was not very apparent.

"I repeat," he said at the end, "that I don't know anyone of that name, and if he says I do he's a liar."

"Perhaps." But there was not so much certainty in Ormiston's voice this time. He quite realized that it might not be so easy to prove to the satisfaction of a jury.

"Listen." Ormiston's voice tensed. "I set a trap for you . . . with live bait in it. Myself. You walked right into it. I guessed that before you left England for good you'd try to even up old scores with me."

"I'm damn well sorry I didn't succeed," Luss snarled.

"I can believe that. But you bungled both times. This afternoon you missed me as near as don't matter with that poisoned dart of yours. If your aim had only equalled your daring there might have been a different tale to tell. But I imagine that something distracted your attention at the crucial moment. What was it?"

"Never mind. I'm not telling."

"Perhaps I can guess. But we'll come to that later. Again to-night you made the mistake of assuming that we were in the house. We weren't. In anticipation of a visit from you we got outside, and kept ourselves concealed until it was time to pounce on you. So despite that remarkably efficient little gas pistol of yours we're still alive."

"But only just," Luss spat at him. "And talking of people assuming things, I'm not the only one who has made a mistake that way."

Ormiston jerked to attention. "What do you mean?" he demanded in a hard voice.

Luss laughed in his face. "Find out," he said.

"I'll make you talk," Ormiston threatened.

"You can't, not in England. You're not allowed to grill a man here."

Ormiston's face went an ugly red. At that exact moment a bell rang somewhere in the house.

"The telephone," Terry said startlingly.

The Special Branch man jumped to his feet. "That will be the boys," he said. "I'll answer it."

Ormiston hesitated. "All right," he said the next instant. "Be careful, though. That gas should be all cleared away by now, still you never know."

The man nodded, went out.

Two minutes later he returned. His face now wore a crestfallen look.

"They've searched everywhere," he announced, "practically pulled the place to pieces, and they've found just nothing."

Ormiston sat down heavily. Luss grinned in open triumph. "I told you," he said.

Terry watched him curiously. He had the feeling now that Luss meant to use the missing copy of the code as something with which to strike a bargain. Perhaps in the last resort he would barter it for his liberty.

Through Ormiston's heart a dreadful feeling stabbed. They had caught Luss, but all their work would count for nothing if the code got out of the country. Unless he could make the man speak they would be worse off than ever. He wished now that he had not invoked the help of the Special Branch. He and Terry should have handled the whole affair on their own. Had there been no outsiders present the two Secret Service men between them would have found some way of opening Luss's lips. But he dared not propose anything now that savoured in the least of third degree methods.

"How big," said Terry suddenly, "would the paper be on which the code would be copied?"

It was something that he had never thought of asking until this very moment. Despite the mixed way in which he put the question Ormiston guessed what was in his mind.

"It wouldn't take up so very much room, Terry, if that's what you're thinking about," he said. "It's not a complete code, by any means. That sort fills a small volume, you know. But this is only a number of supplementary alterations and additions dictated by exigencies that have only recently arisen. I should have made that plain to you at the start."

"So it wouldn't take up much room at all," Terry said thoughtfully. "It could be comfortably inscribed on both sides of a couple of sheets of writing-paper?"

"Less than that," said Ormiston unhappily.

Out of the corner of his eye he had been watching Luss, and saw the man's mouth open, then close abruptly again as though the fellow had been on the point of interrupting, and had immediately thought better of it. He wondered irritably what it was that had been said to catch the man's attention.

He swung round, and raked him with a withering glance. But Luss merely grinned evilly, with a show of white and perfect teeth, the significance of which did not at once strike Ormiston. Then suddenly he jerked upright. The Luss he had handled on that historic occasion in the past had been in rather more need of dental treatment.

"Luss," he said in the easy tone of one who is merely bent on satisfying an idle curiosity, "you've had your teeth out since I last saw you, haven't you? Those you've got now look to be false. Aren't they?"

Some queer apprehensive spark seemed to flicker in the other's eyes for an instant, and as quickly died away.

"Well, what of it?" he said defensively. "There's nothing wrong in that, is there?"

"I should hope not," Ormiston said virtuously, and would have added more had not Terry gasped suddenly.

All eyes flashed to him as he flung himself across the room on to Luss. What followed was never quite clear as far as details were concerned. The one fact that emerged was that somehow Terry had managed to get his hand into Luss's mouth, and the two of them were struggling violently.

"Hold him, you fellows!" Ormiston's voice cut into the chaos.

Terry lurched back abruptly. His fingers were clutching an upper case denture. Luss, with a dark malignant look on his face, was plunging in the hands of his captors like a maddened steer.

"Let me at him," he said thickly.

"The so-and-so swine's bitten me," Terry said ruefully. "It will be rotten luck if I've got the wrong lot, and have to give him the chance of another bite. Even a dog isn't legally entitled to more than one."

"Terry, what the hell . . . ! Here, talk sense!"

"I am." Terry was prodding over the denture now, seemed to be trying to take it to pieces. Suddenly some of the teeth parted from the vulcanite, swung sideways as though on a pivot.

"Has any one got a pin, please?" Terry asked in a mild self-satisfied voice. "This set seems to be hollow. I wondered why it felt so thick."

Some one produced the pin, and Terry set to work. In next to no time with its help he had extracted something from the hollow between the two plates of vulcanite with the dexterity with which the devotee harpoons a winkle. It was a tightly rolled wad, of paper apparently.

Ormiston took the exhibit from him, and unrolled it. It was extremely thin, yet quite strong paper, of a sort that could be compressed into a surprisingly small space, and yet remain of reasonable length and width. Back and front it was covered with writing in a microscopically small hand.

Ormiston dived on his desk, snatched open a drawer, seized a reading-glass and examined the paper in detail. Luss plunged like a frightened horse.

His mouth worked oddly. He looked as though he were going to have a fit.

Ormiston dropped the reading-glass back in the drawer.

"This is it!" he cried excitedly. "There's no longer any doubt whatsoever about it."

Had any still lingered in his mind Luss's behaviour would have been sufficient to banish it. Now that it had become evident that the game was up the man showed signs of going to pieces. Perhaps he realized at last the position in which he stood. There was no longer any hope for him.

Ormiston folded the paper carefully, put it into his wallet, and slid that into an inside pocket.

The chief of the Special Branch men looked up expectantly, but failed to catch Ormiston's eye. Luss had that temporarily.

"You win, Colonel," he said huskily. "Or rather it was that infernal brother-in-law of yours."

He looked balefully at Terry. Terry met the glance with a cheerful grin.

"I think," said Ormiston carefully, "that I

know what it was that distracted your attention when you fired at me this afternoon."

He crossed to the table and took up the little blue-prints Luss had found in the safe.

"These?" he said questioningly.

Luss nodded. He could not trust himself to speak now.

Ormiston looked at the prints a moment, then very slowly and methodically tore them across and tossed the pieces into the empty fireplace.

Terry gave a smothered exclamation of protest.

"It's all right," said Ormiston calmly. "They're only fakes. They, too, were bait of a kind."

The prisoner parted his lips in a sickly grin. He had lost all along the line.

UNCLE HYACINTH

ALFRED NOYES

ALTHOUGH BEST KNOWN as a poet, Alfred Noyes (1880–1958) also wrote fiction and nonfiction, frequently espousing pacifism.

After attending Oxford University, he published his first book of poems when he was only twenty-three, and followed it with many more collections during a prolific writing career. In 1906, he published his most famous work, "The Highwayman," a narrative poem based on the life and adventures of Dick Turpin, the notorious bandit, presenting him romantically as a swashbuckling knight of the road, though he was actually no more than a horse-stealer, burglar, murderer, and torturer. When the BBC polled the British public about its favorite poem, "The Highwayman" came in fifteenth. It has the rare distinction as a poem to have inspired two motion pictures, along with "Dick Turpin's Ride" (a ride actually made by a different highwayman). *The Highwayman* (1951) credits the poem as the basis for the screenplay by Henry Blankfort, with the adaptation of Noyes's work to the screen by Jack DeWitt and Duncan Renaldo; it starred Philip Friend, Charles Coburn, Wanda Hendrix, Cecil Kellaway, and Victor Jory. Oddly, it appears to have been remade in the same year under the title *The Lady and the Bandit*, with the same credits for the story (DeWitt and Renaldo) and inspiration ("The Highwayman"), but with a screenplay by Robert Libott and Frank Burt; it starred Louis Hayward, Patricia Medina, Suzanne Dalbert, and Tom Tully.

Noyes wrote numerous antiwar articles and poems but, when faced with the conflicts of World War I and World War II, he wrote patriotic stories about Great Britain's military history and the morality of its position. His short stories are largely forgotten today with the exception of two that may turn up in collections of vintage ghost stories, "The Lusitania Waits" (1916) and "The Log of the Evening Star" (1918). The stories have not been popular with current readers because, unfortunately, his dedication to the brevity and clarity of his poetry did not extend to his fiction.

"Uncle Hyacinth" was originally published in the February 2, 1918, issue of *The Saturday Evening Post;* it was first collected in *Walking Shadows* (London, Cassell, 1918).

UNCLE HYACINTH

ALFRED NOYES

ONE OF THE BEST code stories of the first World War centers in the ignominious exploit of the German light cruiser *Magdeburg* which, with other ships of the Kaiser's navy, had been roaming the Baltic, clashing with the British blockade and raiding as far as the Russian coast. On one of these missions, as Fletcher Pratt tells the story in his *Secret and Urgent*, the *Magdeburg* went hard aground in a fog and came under the naval guns of the Russians. As the cruiser was being pounded to pieces, the captain apparently ordered the code books taken by a small boat some distance from the ship and heaved overboard. This order for some reason was not completely carried out and the code officer instead plunged from the deck of the cruiser itself with the secret volumes in his arms.

At the close of the battle, the victorious Russians, with a gesture of chivalry, determined to give the German sailors a formal burial and hauled up those who were lying in the comparatively shallow water surrounding the *Magdeburg*. One of the officers thus retrieved still bore in his arms the weighted lead covers of the German naval code. Some very serious and determined diving followed and the code itself was found, damaged by water but still legible. A British

destroyer rushed the prize to London where the British Admiralty and its Room 40, famous in both fact and fiction, began to work on it.

The code was a multiple dictionary type, each German word being represented by not one but several code words or letter groups. It was soon evident, moreover, that although there were several code variants for each German word, these variations were always composed of the same letter groups, although in a different sequence for each variation. For example, the letter groups for German words beginning with B were used, in an alternate column, to represent words beginning with F, and again for words beginning with S, but the same sequence relationship was always maintained among these letter groups, thus making the decoding of any of these variations much easier. This permitted the Germans to change their code at intervals and the discovery of the system gave the Allies the same facility in decoding, so that the Germans were disastrously surprised in several naval engagements thereafter.

The badly scared Teuton in the following story was obviously not using a top naval code but the principles of his secret dispatches were much the same. There is also a significant similarity between the German psychology here and in the second World War; the story, moreover, is one of the few sinister accounts of unrestricted warfare which still manages to include a broad streak of humor.

1

On a bright morning, early in the year 1917, Herr Sigismund Krauss, secret agent for the German Government, stopped at the entrance of Harrods' Stores, looked at himself in one of the big mirrors, thought that he really did look a little like Bismarck, and adjusted his tie. To relieve the tension, let it be added that this scene was not enacted in London, but in the big branch of Harrods' that had recently been opened in Buenos Aires.

Nevertheless, it was because it looked so very much like the London branch that it had rasped the nerves of Herr Krauss. He was in a very nervous condition, owing to the state of his digestive system, and he was easily irritated. He had been annoyed in the first place because the German houses in Buenos Aires were unable to sell him several things which he thought necessary for the voyage he was about to take across the Atlantic. He had been almost angry when the bald-headed Englishman who had waited on him in Harrods' advised him to buy a safety waistcoat. All that he needed for his safety was the fraudulent Swedish passport, made out in the name of Erik Neilsen, which he carried in his breast pocket.

"I am an American citizen," he said, complicating matters still further. "I am sailing to Barcelona on an Argentine ship, vich the Germans are pledged nod to sink."

"This is the exact model of the waistcoat that saved the life of Lord Winchelsea," said the Englishman. "I advise you to procure one. You never know what those damned Germans will do."

Here was a chance of raising a little feeling against the United States, and Herr Krauss never lost an opportunity. He pretended to be even more angry than he really was.

"That is a most ungalled-for suggestion to a citizen of a neutral guntry," he snorted. "I shall report id to the authorities."

These mixed emotions had disarranged his tie. But he had obtained all that he wanted, and when he emerged into the street the magic of the blue sky and the brilliance of the sunlight on the stream of motor cars and gay dresses cheered him greatly. After all, it was not at all like London; and there were still places where a good German might speak his mind, if he did not insist too much on his allegiance.

He was in a great hurry, for his ship, the *Hispaniola*, sailed that afternoon. When he reached his hotel he had only just time enough to pack his hand luggage and drive down to the docks. His trunk had gone down in advance. It was very important, indeed, that he should not miss the boat. There was trouble pending, which might lead to his arrest if he remained in Argentina for another week; and there was urgent—and profitable—work for him to do in Europe.

In his cab on the way to the docks he examined the three letters which had been waiting for him at the hotel. Two of them were requests for a settlement of certain bills. "They can wait," he murmured to himself euphemistically, "till after the war."

The third letter ran thus:

Dear Erik: Bon voyage! Most amusing news. Operation successful. Uncle Hyacinth's appetite splendid. Six meals daily. Yours affectionately,

Bolo.

This was the most annoying thing of all. Herr Krauss knew nothing about any operation. He knew even less about Uncle Hyacinth; and in order to interpret the message he would require the code—Number Six, as indicated by the last word but two, and the code was locked up in his big brass-bound steamer trunk. It was not likely to be anything that required immediate attention. He had received a number of code messages lately which did not even call for a reply. It was merely irritating.

When he reached the docks he found that his trunk was buried under a mountain of other baggage on the lower deck of the *Hispaniola*, and that he would not be able to get at it before they sailed. He had just ten minutes to dash ashore and ring up the German legation on the telephone. He wasted nearly all of them in getting the right change to slip into the machine. A most exasperating conversation followed.

"I wish to speak to the German minister."

"He is away for the week-end. This is his secretary."

"This is Sigismund Krauss speaking."

"Oh, yes."

"I have received a message about Uncle Hyacinth."

"I can't hear."

"Uncle Hyacinth's appetite!" This was bellowed.

"Oh, yes." The voice was very cautious and polite.

"I want to know if it's important."

"Whose appetite did you say?"

"Uncle Hyacinth's!" This was like Hindenburg himself thundering.

There seemed to be some sort of consultation at the other end of the wire. Then the reply came very clearly:

"I'm sorry, but we cannot talk over the telephone. I can't hear anything you say. Please put your question in writing."

It was an obvious lie for anyone to say he could not hear the tremendous voice in which Herr Krauss had made his touching inquiry; but he fully understood the need for caution. He had tapped too many wires himself to blame his colleagues for timidity. He had only a minute to burst out of the telephone booth and regain the deck, before the gangplanks were hoisted in and the ship began to slide away to the open sea.

He was more than annoyed, he was disgusted, to find that half the people on board were talking English. Two or three of them, including the captain, were actually British subjects; while the purser, a few of the stewards, and several passengers were citizens of the United States.

It was late that evening and the shore lights had all died away over the pitch-black water when the brass-bound trunk belonging to Mr. Neilsen, as we must call him henceforward, was carried into his stateroom by two grunting stewards. The mysterious letter could be of no use to the Fatherland now, and he certainly did not expect it to be important from a selfish point of view. Also, he was hungry, and he did not hurry over his dinner in order to decode it. It was only his curiosity that impelled him to do so before he turned in; but a kind of petrifaction overspread his well-fed countenance as the significance of the message dawned upon him. He sat on a suitcase in his somewhat cramped quarters and translated it methodically, looking up the meaning of each word in the code, like a very unpleasant schoolboy with a dictionary. He was nothing if not efficient, and he wrote it all down in pencil on a sheet of note-paper, in two parallel columns, thus:

Bon voyage	U-boats
Most	Instructed
Amusing	Sink
News	Argentine
Operation	Ships
Successful	Destruction
Uncle Hyacinth's	Hispaniola
Appetite	Essential
Splendid	Cancel
Six	Code Number
Meals	Passage
Daily	Immediately

Perhaps to make sure that his eyes did not deceive him Mr. Neilsen wrote the translation out again mechanically, in its proper form, at the foot of the page, thus:

U-boats instructed sink Argentine ships. Destruction *Hispaniola* essential. Cancel passage immediately.

It seemed to have exactly the same meaning. It was ghastly. He knew exactly what that word "destruction" meant as applied to the *Hispaniola*. He had been present at a secret meeting only a month ago, at which it was definitely decided that it would be inadvisable to carry out a certain amiable plan of sinking the Argentine ships without leaving any traces, while an appearance of friendship was maintained with the Argentine Government. Evidently this policy had suddenly been reversed. There would be a concentration of half a dozen U-boats, a swarm of them probably, for the express purpose of sinking the *Hispaniola*, just as they had concentrated on the *Lusitania*; but in this case there would be no survivors at all. The ship's boats would be destroyed by gunfire, with all their occupants, because it was necessary that there should be no evidence of what had happened; and necessity knows no law. There was no chance of their failing. They would not dare to fail; and he himself had organized the system by which the most precise information with regard to sailings was conveyed to the German Admiralty.

He crushed all the papers into his breast pocket and hurried up on deck. It was horribly dark. At the smoking-room door he met one of the ship's officers.

"Tell me," said Mr. Neilsen, "is there any possibility of our—of our meeting a ship—er—bound the other way?"

The officer stared at him, wondering whether Mr. Neilsen was drunk or seasick.

"Certainly," he said; "but it's not likely for some days on this course."

"Will it be possible for me to be taken off and return? I have found among my mail an important letter. A friend is very ill."

"I'm afraid it's quite impossible. In the first place we are not likely to meet anything but cattle ships till we are in European waters."

"Oh, but in this case, even a cattle ship—" said Mr. Neilsen with great feeling.

"It is impossible, I am afraid, in any case. It is absolutely against the rules; and in wartime, of course, they are more strict than ever."

"Even if I were to pay?"

"Time is not for sale in this war, unfortu-nately. It's *verboten*," said the officer with a smile; and that of course Mr. Neilsen understood at once.

He was naturally an excitable man, and his inability to obtain his wish made him feel that he would give all his worldly possessions at this moment for a berth in the dirtiest cattle boat that ever tramped the seas, if only it were going in the opposite direction.

He returned to his stateroom almost panic-stricken. He sat down on the suitcase and held his head between his hands while he tried to think. He was a slippery creature and his fellow countrymen had often admired his "slimness" in former crises; but it was difficult to discover a cranny big enough for a cockroach here, unless he made a clean breast of it to the captain. In that case he would be incriminated with all the belligerents and most of the neutrals. There would be no place in the world where he could hide his head, except perhaps Mexico. He would probably be penniless as well.

At this point in his cogitations there was a knock on the door, which startled him like a pistol shot. He opened it a cautious inch or two—for his papers were all over his berth—and a steward handed him a telegram.

"This was waiting for you at the purser's office, sir," he said. "The mail has only just been sorted. If you wish to reply by wireless you can do so up to midnight." The man was smiling as if he knew the contents. There had been some jesting, in fact, about this telegram at the office.

A gleam of hope shot through Mr. Neilsen's chaotic brain as he opened the envelope with trembling fingers. Perhaps it contained reassuring news. His face fell. It simply repeated the former sickening message about Uncle Hyacinth. But the steward had reminded him of one last resource.

"Yes," he said, trying hard to be calm; "I shall want to send a reply."

"Here is a form, sir. You'll find the regulations printed on the back."

Mr. Neilsen closed the door and sank, gasping, on to the suitcase to examine the form. The regulations stated that no message would be accepted in code. This did not worry him at first, as he thought he could concoct an apparently straightforward and harmless message with the elaborate vocabulary of his Number Six. But the code had not been intended for agonizing moments like these. It abounded in commercial phrases, medical terms, and domestic greetings; and though there were a number of alternative words and synonyms it was not so easy as he had expected to make a coherent message which should be apparently a reply to the telegram he had received. After half an hour of seeking for the *mot juste* which would have melted the heart of a Flaubert, he arrived at the purser's office with wild eyes and handed in the yellow form.

"I wish to send this by Marconi wireless," he said.

The purser tapped each word with his pencil as he read it over:

> Splendid. Most—amusing. Use—
> heaps—butter. Congratulate—Uncle
> Hyacinth. Love. Erik.

"I beg your pardon, sir," said the purser, "but we can only accept messages *en clair*."

"It is as clear as I can make it," said Mr. Neilsen; and he was telling the truth. "It is the answer to the telegram which was handed to me on board."

"It looks a little unusual, sir."

"It is gonnected with an unusual operation," said Mr. Neilsen, who was getting thoroughly rattled, "and goncerns the diet of the batient."

The steward departed on his errand. Captain Abbey took another sheet of paper and laboriously, with tongue outthrust, constructed a sentence, consulting the purser's two columns from time to time, and occasionally chuckling as he altered or added a word.

The purser slapped his thighs with delight as he followed the work over the captain's shoulder; and when the form arrived he wrote out the captain's composition in a very large, clear hand, with the fervor of a man announcing good news. Then he licked the flap of the yellow envelope, closed it, addressed it and handed it to the steward.

"Give this wireless message to Mr. Neilsen in half an hour. Tell him it has just arrived. If there is any reply tonight he must send it before twelve o'clock."

"I 'ope that will make 'im sit up and think," said Captain Abbey. "I'll consider what steps I'd better take to save the ship; and then I shall probably 'ave a wireless or two of my own to send elsewhere."

Mr. Neilsen was greatly excited when the steward knocked at his door and handed him the second wireless message. He opened it with trembling fingers and read:

> Still more successful. Uncle Hyacinth's
> tonsils removed. Appetite now colossal.
> Bless him. Taking large quantities frozen
> meat.

He could hardly wait to translate it. He sat down on his suitcase again, and spelled it out with the help of his Number Six, word by word, refusing to believe his eyes, refusing even to read it as a consecutive sentence till the bottom of the two parallel columns had been reached, thus:

Still	Impossible
More	Total
Successful	Destruction
Uncle Hyacinth's	Hispaniola
Tonsils	Von Tirpitz
Removed	Advises
Appetite	Essential
Now	Squadron
Colossal	Twenty
Bless him	Submarines
Taking	Waiting
Large	Appropriate
Quantities	Death
Frozen	Good
Meat	German
Best	Enviable
Greetings	Position

This was hideous. He remembered all that he had done all over the world in the interests of the Fatherland. He remembered the skilful way in which long before the war he had stirred up feeling in America against Japan, and in Japan against both America and England. He remembered the way in which he had manipulated the peace societies in the interest of militarism. He had spent several years in London before the war, and he believed he had helped to make the very name of England a reproach in literary coteries; so that current English literature, unless it went far beyond honest criticism of English life, unless indeed it manifested a complete contempt for that pharisaical country and painted it as rotten from head to foot, lost caste among the self-enthroned British intellectuals.

It was very easy to do this, because, though English editors paid considerable attention to their leading articles, some of them did not care very much what kind of stuff was printed in their literary columns; and they would allow the best of our literature; old and new, and the most representative part of it, to be misrepresented by an anonymous Sinn Feiner in half a dozen journals simultaneously. The editors were patriotic enough, but they didn't think current literature of much importance. He had been able, therefore, to quote extracts from important London journals in the foreign press.

He had been helped, too, by lecturers who drew pensions from the British Government for their literary merits, and told American audiences that the one flag they loathed was the flag of the land that pensioned them. He had reprinted these utterances, together with the innocent bleatings of the intellectuals, and scattered them all over the world in pamphlet form. He had marked passages in their books and sent them to friends. Thousands of columns were devoted to them in the newspapers of foreign countries, while the English press occasionally referred to them in brief paragraphs, announcing to a drugged public at home that the vagaries of these writers were of no importance. He had carried out the program of his country to

the letter, and poisoned the intellectual wellsprings.

No grain of poison was too small. He had even written letters to the newspapers in Scotland, which had stimulated the belief of certain zealous Scots that whenever the name of England was used it was intended as a deliberate onslaught upon the Union. There was hardly any destructive force or thought or feeling, good, bad or merely trivial, which he had not turned to the advantage of Germany and the disadvantage of other nations. Then when the war broke out he had redoubled his activities. He was amazed when he thought of the successful lies he had fostered all over the world. He had plotted with Hindus on the coast of California, and provided them with the literature of freedom in the interests of autocracy. He worked for dissension abroad and union in Germany. He was hand-in-glove with the I. W. W. He was idealist, socialist, pacifist, anarchist, futurist, suffragist, nationalist, internationalist, and always publicist, all at once, and for one cause only—the cause of Germany.

And this was the gratitude of the—of the—swine! Well, he would teach them a lesson. God in heaven! There was only one thing he could do to save his skin. He would send them an ultimatum! It was their last chance. He shivered to think that it might be his own!

But it was not so easy as he thought it would be to burn all his boats. It cost him two days and two nights of tortuous thinking before he could bring himself to the point. At eleven o'clock on the third night the purser brought the captain a new message, which Mr. Neilsen had just handed in to be despatched by wireless. It ran as follows:

Continue treatment. Vastly amusing.
Uncle Hyacinth's magnificent
constitution stand anything. Apply
mustard. Try red pepper.

The group that met to consider this new development included three passengers, whom the captain had invited to share what he called the fun. They were a Miss Depew, an American girl who was going to Europe to do Red Cross work; and a Mr. and Mrs. Pennyfeather, English residents of Buenos Aires, with whom she was traveling. The message, as they interpreted it, ran as follows:

Unless instructions to sink *Hispaniola* countermanded, shall inform captain. No alternative. Most important papers my possession.

"Good!" said Captain Abbey. "'E's beginning to show symptoms of blackmail. I'd send this message on, only we're likely to make a bigger bag by keeping quiet. We'll let 'im 'ave the reply tomorrow morning. What shall we do to 'im next?"

"Shoot him," said Miss Depew with complete calm.

"Oh, I want to 'ave a little fun with 'im first," said Captain Abbey. "I'm afraid you 'aven't got much sense of humor, Miss Depew."

"Do you think so?" she said. She was of the purest Gibson type, and never flickered an innocent eyelash or twisted a corner of her red Cupid's bow of a mouth as she drawled: "I think it would be very humorous indeed to shoot him, now that we know he is a German."

"Well, after 'is trying to leave us without warning 'e deserves to be skinned and stuffed. But we're likely to make much more of it if we keep 'im alive for our entertainment. Besides, 'e's going to be useful on the other side. Now, what do you think of this for a scheme?"

The heads of the conspirators drew closer round the table; and Mr. Neilsen, wandering on deck like a lost spirit, pondered on the tragic ironies of life. The thoughtless laughter that rippled up to him from the captain's cabin filled him with no compassion toward any one but himself. It was merely one more proof that only the Germans took life seriously. All the same, if he could possibly help it, he was not going to let them take his own life.

2

There was no radiogram for Mr. Neilsen on the following day; and he was perplexed by a new problem as he walked feverishly up and down the promenade deck.

Even if he received an assurance that the *Hispaniola* would be spared, how could he know that he was being told the truth? Necessity, as he knew quite well, was the mother of murder. It was very necessary, indeed, that his mouth should be sealed. Besides, he had more than a suspicion that his use was fulfilled in the eyes of the German Government, and that they would not be sorry if they could conveniently get rid of him. He possessed a lot of perilous knowledge; and he wished heartily that he didn't. He was tasting, in fact, the inevitable hell of the criminal, which is not that other people distrust him, but that he can trust nobody else.

He leaned over the side of the ship and watched the white foam veining the black water.

"Curious, isn't it?" said dapper little Mr. Pennyfeather, who stood near him. "Exactly like liquid marble. Makes you think of that philosophic Johnny—What's-his-name—fellow that said 'everything flows,' don't you know. And it does, too, by Jove! Everything! Including one's income! It's curious, Mr. Neilsen, how quickly we've changed all our ideas about the value of human life, isn't it? By Jove, that's flowing too! The other morning I caught myself saying that there was no news in the paper; and then I realized that I'd overlooked the sudden death of about ten thousand men on the Western Front. Well, we've all got to die some day, and perhaps it's best to do it before we deteriorate too far. Don't you think so?"

Mr. Neilsen grunted morosely. He hated to be pestered by these gadflies of the steamer. He particularly disliked this little Englishman with the neat gray beard, not only because he was the head of an obnoxious bank in Buenos Aires, but because he would persist in talking to him with a ghoulish geniality about submarine operations and the subject of death. Also, he was one of those hopeless people who had been led by the wholesale slaughter of the war to thoughts of the possibility of a future life. Apparently Mr. Pennyfeather had no philosophy, and his spiritual being was groping for light through those materialistic fogs which brood over the borderlands of science. His wife was even more irritating; for she, too, was groping, chiefly because of the fashion; and they both insisted on talking to Mr. Neilsen about it. They had quite spoiled his breakfast this morning. He did not resent it on spiritual grounds, for he had none; but he did resent it because it reminded him of his mortality, and also because a professional quack does not like to be bothered by amateurs.

Mrs. Pennyfeather approached him now on the other side. She was a faded lady with hair dyed yellow, and tortoise-shell spectacles.

"Have you ever had your halo read, Mr. Neilsen?" she asked with a sickly smile.

"No. I don't believe in id," he said gruffly.

"But surely you believe in the spectrum," she continued with a ghastly inconsequence that almost curdled the logic in his German brain.

"Certainly," he replied, trying hard to be polite.

"And therefore in specters," she cooed ingratiatingly, as if she were talking to a very small child.

"Nod at all! Nod at all!" he exploded somewhat violently, while Mr. Pennyfeather, on the other side, came to his rescue, sagely repudiating the methods of his wife.

"No, no, my dear! I don't think your train of thought is quite correct there. My wife and I are very much interested in recent occult experiments, Mr. Nielsen. We've been wondering whether you wouldn't join us one night, round the ouija board."

"Id is all nonsense to me," said Mr. Neilsen, gesticulating with both arms.

"Quite so; very natural. But we got some very curious results last night," continued Mr. Pennyfeather. "Most extraordinary. The purser was with us, and he thought it would interest you. I wish you would join us."

"I should regard id as gomplete waste of time," said Mr. Nielsen.

"Surely, nothing can be waste of time that increases our knowledge of the bourne from which no traveler returns," replied the lyric lips of Mrs. Pennyfeather.

"To me the methods are ridiculous," said Mr. Neilsen. "All this furniture removal! Ach!"

"Ah," said Mr. Pennyfeather, "you should read What's-his-name. You know the chap, Susan. Fellow that said it's like a shipwrecked man waving a shirt on a stick to attract attention. Of course it's ridiculous! But what else can you do if you haven't any other way of signaling? Why, man alive! You'd use your trousers, wouldn't you, if you hadn't anything else? And the alternative—drowning—remember—drowning beneath what Thingumbob calls 'the unplumbed salt, estranging sea.'"

"Eggscuse me," said Mr. Neilsen; "I have some important business with the captain. I must go."

Mr. Neilsen had been trying hard to make up his mind, despite these irrelevant interruptions. He had received no assurance by wireless, and he had convinced himself that even if he did receive one it would be wiser to inform the captain. But there were many difficulties in the way. He had taken great care never to do anything that might lead to the death penalty—that is to say, among nations less civilized than his own. But there was that affair of the code. It might make things very unpleasant. A dozen other suspicious circumstances would have to be explained away. A dozen times he had hesitated, as he did this morning. He met the captain at the foot of the bridge.

"Ah, Mr. Neilsen," said Captain Abbey with great cordiality, "you're the very man I want to see. We're 'aving a little concert tonight in the first-class dining room on behalf of the wives and children of the British mine sweepers and the auxiliary patrols. You see, though this is a neutral ship, we depend upon them more or less for our safety. I thought it would be pleasant if you—as a neutral—would say just a few words. I understand that they've rescued a good many Swedish crews from torpedoed ships; and whatever view we may take of the war we 'ave to admit that these little boats are doing the work of civilization."

Mr. Neilsen thought he saw an opportunity of ingratiating himself, and he seized it. He could broach the other matter later on. "I vill do my best, captain."

"'Ere is a London newspaper that will tell you all about their work."

Mr. Neilsen retired to his stateroom and studied the newspaper fervently.

The captain took the chair that evening, and he did it very well. He introduced Mr. Neilsen in a few appropriate words; and Mr. Neilsen spoke for nearly five minutes, in English, with impassioned eloquence and a rapidly deteriorating accent.

"Dese liddle batrol boads," he said in his peroration, "how touching to the heart is der vork! Some of us forget ven ve are safe on land how much ve owe to them. But no matter vot your nationality, ven you are on the high sees, surrounded with darkness and dangers, not knowing ven you shall be torpedoed, vot a grade affection you feel then to dese liddle batrol boads! As a citizen of Sweden I speak vot I *know*. The ships of my guntry have suffered much in dis war. The sailors of my guntry have been thrown into the water by thousands through der submarines. But dese liddle batrol boads, they save them from drowning. They give them blankets and hot goffee. They restore them to their veeping mothers."

Mr. Neilsen closed amid tumultuous applause, and when the collection was taken up by Miss Depew his contribution was the largest of the evening.

The rest of the entertainment consisted chiefly of music and recitation. Mr. Pennyfeather contributed a song, composed by himself. Typewritten copies of the words were issued to the audience; and a very fat and solemn Spaniard accompanied him with thunderous chords on the piano. Every one joined in the chorus; but Mr. Neilsen did not like the song

at all. It was concerned with Mr. Pennyfeather's usual gruesome subject; and he rolled it out in a surprisingly rich barytone with the gusto of a schoolboy:

If they sink us we shall be
All the nearer to the sea!
That's no hardship to deplore!
We've all been in the sea before.

Chorus:
And then we'll go a-rambling,
A-rambling, a-rambling,
With all the little lobsters
From Frisco to the Nore.

If we swim it's one more tale,
Round the hearth and over the ale;
When your lass is on your knee,
And love comes laughing from the sea.

Chorus:
And then we'll go a-rambling,
A-rambling, a-rambling,
A-rambling through the roses
That ramble round the door.

If we drown, our bones and blood
Mingle with the eternal flood.
That's no hardship to deplore!
We've all been in the sea before.

Chorus:
And then we'll go a-rambling,
A-rambling, a-rambling,
The road that Jonah rambled
And twenty thousand more.

"Now," said Mr. Pennyfeather, holding out his hands like the conductor of a revival meeting, "all the ladies, very softly, please."

The solemn Spaniard rolled his great black eyes at the audience, and repeated the refrain *pianissimo*, while the silvery voices caroled:

With all the little lobsters
From Frisco to the Nore.

"Now, all the gentlemen, please," said Mr. Pennyfeather. The Spaniard's eyes flashed. He rolled thunder from the piano, and Mr. Neilsen found himself bellowing with the rest of the audience:

The road that Jonah rambled
From Hull to Singapore,
And twenty thousand, thirty thousand,
Forty thousand, fifty thousand,
Sixty thousand, seventy thousand,
Eighty thousand more!

It was an elaborate conclusion, accompanied by elephantine stampings of Captain Abbey's feet; but Mr. Neilsen retired to his room in a state of great depression. The frivolity of these people, in the face of his countrymen, appalled him.

On the next morning he decided to act, and sent a message to the captain asking for an interview. The captain responded at once, and received him with great cordiality. But the innocence of his countenance almost paralyzed Mr. Neilsen's intellect at the outset, and it was very difficult to approach the subject.

"Do you see this, Mr. Neilsen?" said the captain, holding up a large champagne bottle. "Do you know what I've got in this?"

"Champagne," said Mr. Neilsen with the weary pathos of a logician among idiots.

"No, sir! Guess again."

"Pilsener!"

"No, sir! It's plain sea water. I've just filled it. I'm taking it 'ome to my wife. She takes it for the good of 'er stommick, a small wineglass at a time. She always likes me to fill it for her in mid-Atlantic. She's come to depend on it now, and I wouldn't dare to go 'ome without it. I forgot to fill it once till we were off the coast of Spain. And, would you believe it, Mr. Neilsen, that woman knew! The moment she tasted it she knew it wasn't the right vintage. Well, sir, we shall soon be in the war zone now. But you are not looking very well, Mr. Neilsen. I 'ope you've got a comfortable room."

"I have reason to believe, captain, that there will be an attempt made by the submarines to sink the *Hispaniola*," said Mr. Neilsen abruptly.

"Nonsense, my dear sir! This is a neutral ship and we're sailing to a neutral country, under explicit guarantees from the German Government. They won't sink the *Hispaniola* for the pleasure of killing her superannuated English captain."

"I have reason to believe they intend to—er—change their bolicy. I was not sure of id till I opened my mail on the boad; but—er—I have a friend in Buenos Aires who vas in glose touch—er—business gonnections—with members of the German legation; he—er—advised me, too late, I had better gancel my bassage. I fear there is no doubt they vill change their bolicy."

"But they couldn't. There ain't any policy! The Argentine Republic is a neutral country. You can't make me believe they'd do a thing like that. It wouldn't be honest, Mr. Neilsen. Of course, it's war-time; but the German Government wants to be honorable, don't it—like any other government?"

"I don'd understand the reasons; but I fear there is no doubt aboud the facts," said Mr. Neilsen.

"Have you got the letter?"

"No; I thought as you do, ad first, and I tore id up."

"Was that why you wanted to get off and go back?" the captain inquired mercilessly.

"I gonfess I vas a liddle alarmed; but I thought perhaps I vas unduly alarmed at the time. I gouldn't trust my own judgment, and I had no ride to make other bassengers nervous."

"That was very thoughtful of you. I trust you will continue to keep this matter to yourself, for I assure you—though I consider the German Government 'opelessly wrong in this war—they wouldn't do a dirty thing like that. They're very anxious to be on good terms with the South American republics, and they'd ruin themselves for ever."

"But my information is they vill sink the ships vithoud leaving any draces."

"What do you mean? Pretend to be friendly, and then—Come, now! That's an awful suggestion to make!"

At these words Mr. Neilsen had a vivid mental picture of his conversation with the bald-headed Englishman in Harrods'.

"Do you mean," the captain continued, waxing eloquent, "do you mean they'd sink the ships and massacre every blessed soul aboard, regardless of their nationality? Of course I'm an Englishman, and I don't love 'em, but that ain't even murder. That's plain beastliness. It couldn't be done by anything that walks on two legs. I tell you what, Mr. Neilsen, you're a bit overwrought and nervous. You want a little recreation. You'd better join the party tonight in my cabin. Mr. and Mrs. Pennyfeather are coming, and a very nice American girl—Miss Depew. We're going to get a wireless message or two from the next world. Ever played with the ouija board? Nor had I till this voyage; but I must say it's interesting. You ought to see it, as a scientific man. I understand you're interested in science, and you know there's no end of scientists—big men too—taking this thing up. You'd better come. Half past eight. Right you are!"

And so Mr. Neilsen was ushered out into despair for the rest of the day, and booked for an unpleasant evening. He had accepted the captain's invitation as a matter of policy; for he thought he might be able to talk further with him, and it was not always easy to secure an opportunity. In fact, when he thought things over he was inclined to feel more amiably toward the Pennyfeathers, who had put the idea of psychical research into the captain's head.

Promptly at half past eight, therefore, he joined the little party in the captain's cabin. Miss Depew looked more Gibsonish than ever, and she smiled at him bewitchingly; with a smile as hard and brilliant as diamonds. Mrs. Pennyfeather looked like a large artificial chrysanthemum; and she examined his black tie and dinner jacket with the wickedly observant eye of

a cockatoo. Three times in the first five minutes she made his hand travel over his shirt front to find out which stud had broken loose. They had driven him nearly mad in his stateroom that evening, and he had turned his trunk inside out in the process of dressing, to find some socks.

Moreover, he had left his door unlocked. He was growing reckless. Perhaps the high sentiments of every one on board had made him trustful. If he had seen the purser exploring the room and poking under his berth he might have felt uneasy, for that was what the purser was doing at this moment. Mr. Neilsen might have been even more mystified if he had seen the strange objects which the purser had laid for the moment, on his pillow. One of them looked singularly like a rocket, of the kind which ships use for signaling purposes. But Mr. Neilsen could not see; and so he was only worried by the people round him.

Captain Abbey seemed to have washed his face in the sunset. He was larger and more like a marine Weller than ever in his best blue and gilt. And Mr. Pennyfeather was just dapper little Mr. Pennyfeather, with his beard freshly brushed.

"You've never been in London, Miss Depew?" said Captain Abbey reproachfully, while the Pennyfeathers prepared the ouija board. "Ah, but you ought to see the Thames at Westminster Bridge! No doubt the Amazon and the Mississippi, considered as rivers, are all right in their way. They're ten times bigger than our smoky old river at 'ome. But the Thames is more than a river, Miss Depew. The Thames is liquid 'istory!"

As soon as the ouija board was ready they began their experiment. Mr. Neilsen thought he had never known anything more sickeningly illustrative of the inferiority of all intellects to the German. He tried the ouija board with Mrs. Pennyfeather, and the accursed thing scrawled one insane syllable.

It looked like "cows," but Miss Depew decided that it was "crows." Then Mrs. Pennyfeather tried it with Captain Abbey; and they got nothing at all, except an occasional giggle from the lady to the effect that she didn't think the captain could be making his mind a blank. Then Mr. Pennyfeather tried it with Miss Depew—with no result but the obvious delight of that sprightly middle-aged gentleman at touching her polished finger tips, and the long uneven line that was driven across the paper by the ardor of his pressure. Finally Miss Depew—subduing the glint of her smile slightly, a change as from diamonds to rubies, but hard and clear-cut as ever—declared, on the strength of Mr. Neilsen's first attempt, that he seemed to be the most sensitive of the party, and she would like to try it with him.

Strangely enough Mr. Neilsen felt a little mollified, even a little flattered, by the suggestion. He was quite ready to touch the finger tips of Miss Depew, and try again. She had a small hand. He could not help remembering the legend that after the Creator had made the rosy fingers of the first woman the devil had added those tiny, gemlike nails; but he thought the devil had done his work, in this case, like an expert jeweler. Mr. Neilsen was always ready to bow before efficiency, even if its weapons were no more imposing than a manicure set.

The ouija board was quiet for a moment or two. Then the pencil began to move across the paper. Mr. Neilsen did not understand why. Miss Depew certainly looked quite blank; and the movement seemed to be independent of their own consciousness. It was making marks on the paper, and that was all he expected it to do.

At last Miss Depew withdrew her hand and exclaimed: "It's too exhausting. Read it, somebody!"

Mr. Pennyfeather picked it up, and laughed.

"Looks to me as if the spirits are a bit erratic tonight. But the writing's clear enough, in a scrawly kind of way. I'm afraid it's utter nonsense."

He began to read it aloud:

"Exquisitely amusing! Uncle Hyacinth's little appendix—"

At this moment he was interrupted. Mr. Neilsen had risen to his feet as if he were being hauled up by an invisible rope attached to his neck. His movement was so startling that Mrs. Pennyfeather emitted a faint, mouselike screech. They all stared at him, waiting to see what he would do next.

But Mr. Neilsen recovered himself with great presence of mind. He drew a handkerchief from his trousers pocket, as if he had risen only for that purpose. Then he sat down again.

"Bardon me," he said; "I thought I vas aboud to sneeze. Vat is the rest of id?"

He sat very still now, but his mouth opened and shut dumbly, like the mouth of a fish, while Mr. Pennyfeather read the message through to the end:

"Exquisitely amusing! Uncle Hyacinth's little appendix cut out. Throat enlarged. Consuming immense quantities pork sausages; also onions wholesale. Best greetings. Fond love. Kisses."

"I'm afraid they're playing tricks on us tonight," said Mr. Pennyfeather. "They do sometimes, you know. Or it may be fragments of two or three messages which have got mixed."

"Hold on, though!" said the captain. "Didn't you send a wireless the other day, Mr. Neilsen, to somebody by the name of Hyacinth?"

"Well—ha! ha! ha! It was aboud somebody by that name. I suppose I must have moved my hand ungonsciously. I've been thinking aboud him a great deal. He's ill, you see."

"How very interestin'," cooed Mrs. Pennyfeather, drawing her chair closer. "Have you really an uncle named Hyacinth? Such a pretty name for an elderly gentleman, isn't it? Doesn't the rest of the message mean anything to you, then, Mr. Neilsen?"

He stared at her, and then he stared at the message, licking his lips. Then he stared at Captain Abbey and Miss Depew. He could read nothing in their faces but the most childlike amusement. The thing that chilled his heart was the phrase about onions. He could not remember the meaning, but it looked like one of those innocent commercial phrases that had been embodied in the code. Was it possible that in his agitation he had unconsciously written this thing down?

He crumpled up the paper and thrust it into his side pocket. Then he sniggered mirthlessly. Greatly to his relief the captain began talking to Miss Depew, as if nothing had happened, about the Tower of London; and he was able to slip away before they brought the subject down to modern times.

3

Mr. Neilsen may have been a very skeptical person. Perhaps his intellect was really paralyzed by panic, for the first thing he did on reaching his stateroom that night was to get out the code and translate the message of the ouija board. It was impossible that it should mean anything; but he was impelled by something stronger than his reason. He broke into a cold sweat when he discovered that it had as definite a meaning as any of the preceding messages; and though it was not the kind of thing that would have been sent by wireless he recognized that it was probably far nearer the truth than any of them. This is how he translated it:

> Imperative sink *Hispaniola* after
> treacherous threat. Wiser sacrifice life.
> Otherwise death penalty inevitable.
> Flight abroad futile. Enviable position.
> Fine opportunity hero.

He could not understand how this thing had happened. Was it possible that in great crises an agitated mind two thousand miles away might create a corresponding disturbance in another mind which was concentrated on the same problem? Had he evolved these phrases of the code out of some subconscious memory and formed them into an intelligible sentence? Trickery was the only other alternative, and that was out of the question. All these people were of inferior intellect. Besides, they were in the same peril themselves; and obviously ignorant of it. His code had never been out of his possession. Yet he felt as if he had been under the micro-scope. What did it mean? He felt as if he were going mad.

He crept into his berth in a dazed and blundering way, like a fly that just crawled out of a honey pot. After an hour of feverish tossing from side to side he sank into a doze, only to dream of the bald-headed man in Harrods' who wanted to sell him a safety waistcoat, the exact model of the one that saved Lord Winchelsea. The most hideous series of nightmares followed. He dreamed that the sides of the ship were transparent, and that he saw the periscopes of innumerable submarines foaming alongside through the black water. He could not cry out, though he was the only soul aboard that saw them, for his mouth seemed to be fastened with official sealing wax—black sealing wax—stamped with the German eagle. Then to his horror he saw the quick phosphorescent lines of a dozen torpedoes darting toward the *Hispaniola* from all points of the compass. A moment later there was an explosion that made him leap, gasping and fighting for breath, out of his berth. But this was not a dream. It was the most awful explosion he had ever heard, and his room stank of sulphur. He seized the cork jacket that hung on his wall, pulled his door open and rushed out, trying to fasten it round him as he went.

When the steward arrived, with the purser, they had the stateroom to themselves; and after the former had thrown the remains of the rocket through the porthole, together with the ingenious contrivance that had prevented it from doing any real damage under Mr. Neilsen's berth, the purser helped him with his own hands to carry the brass-bound trunk down to his office.

"We'll tell him that his room was on fire and we had to throw the contents overboard. We'll give him another room and a suit of old clothes for tomorrow. Then we can examine his possessions at leisure. We've got the code now; but there may be lots of other things in his pockets. That's right. I hope he doesn't jump overboard in his fright. It's lucky that we warned these other staterooms. It made a hellish row. You'd better go and look for him as soon as we get this thing out of the way."

But it was easier to look for Mr. Neilsen than to find him. The steward ransacked the ship for three-quarters of an hour, and he began to fear that the worst had happened. He was peering round anxiously on the boat deck when he heard an explosive cough somewhere over his head. He looked up into the rigging as if he expected to find Mr. Neilsen in the cross-trees; but nobody was to be seen, except the watch in the crow's nest, dark against the stars.

"Mr. Neilsen!" he called. "Mr. Neilsen!"

"Are you galling me?" a hoarse voice replied. It seemed to come out of the air, above and behind the steward. He turned with a start, and a moment later he beheld the head of Mr. Neilsen bristling above the thwarts of Number Six boat. He had been sitting in the bottom of the boat to shelter himself from the wind, and some symbolistic Puck had made him fasten his cork jacket round his pyjamas very firmly, but upside down, so that he certainly would have been drowned if he had been thrown into the water.

"It's all right, Mr. Neilsen," said the steward. "The danger's over."

"Are ve torpedoed?" The round-eyed visage with the bristling hair was looking more and more like Bismarck after a debauch of blood and iron, and it did not seem inclined to budge.

"No, sir! The shock damaged your room a little, but we must have left the enemy behind. You had a lucky escape, sir."

"My Gott! I should think so, indeed! The ship is not damaged in any vay?"

"No, sir. There was a blaze in your room, and I'm afraid they had to throw all your things overboard. But the purser says he can rig you out in the morning; and we have another room ready for you."

"Then I vill gum down," said Mr. Neilsen. And he did so. His bare feet paddled after the steward on the cold wet deck. At the companionway they met the shadowy figure of the captain.

"I'm afraid you've 'ad an unpleasant upset, Mr. Neilsen," he said.

"Onbleasant! It was derrible! Derrible! But you see, Captain, I vas correct. And this is only the beginning, aggording to my information. I hope now you vill take every brecaution."

"They must have mistaken us for a British ship, Mr. Neilsen, I'm afraid. I'm having the ship lighted up so that they can't mistake us again. You see? I've got a searchlight playing on the Argentine flag aloft; and we've got the name of the ship in illuminated letters three feet high, all along the hull. They could read it ten miles away. Come and look!"

Mr. Neilsen looked with deepening horror.

"But dis is madness!" he gurgled. "The *Hispaniola* is marked, I tell you, marked, for gomplete destruction!"

The captain shook his head with a smile of skepticism that withered Mr. Neilsen's last hope.

"Very vell, then I should brefer an inside cabin this time."

"Yes. You don't get so much fresh air, of course; but I think it's better on the 'ole. If we're torpedoed we shall all go down together. But you're safer from gunfire in an inside room."

The unhappy figure in pyjamas followed the steward without another word. The captain watched him with a curious expression on his broad red face. He was not an unkindly man; and if this German in the cork jacket had not been so ready to let everybody else aboard drown he might have felt the sympathy for him that most people feel toward the fat cowardice of Falstaff. But he thought of the women and children, and his heart hardened.

As soon as Mr. Neilsen had gone below, the lights were turned off, and the ship went on her way like a shadow. The captain proceeded to send out some wireless messages of his own. In less than an hour he received an answer, and almost immediately the ship's course was changed.

It was a strange accident that nobody on board seemed to have any clothes that would fit Mr. Neilsen on the following day. He appeared at lunch in a very old suit, which the dapper little Mr. Pennyfeather had worn out in the bank.

Mr. Neilsen was now a perfect illustration of the schooldays of Prince Blood and Iron, at some period when that awful effigy had outgrown his father's pocket and burst most of his buttons. But his face was so haggard and gray that even the women pitied him. At four o'clock in the afternoon the captain asked him to come up to the bridge, and began to put him out of his misery.

"Mr. Neilsen," he said, "I'm afraid you've had a very anxious voyage; and, though it's very unusual, I think in the circumstances it's only fair to put you on another ship if you prefer it. You'll 'ave your chance this evening. Do you see those little smudges of smoke out yonder? Those are some British patrol boats; and if you wish I'm sure I can get them to take you off and land you in Plymouth. There's a statue of Sir Francis Drake on Plymouth 'Oe. You ought to see it. What d'you think?"

Mr. Neilsen stared at him. Two big tears of gratitude rolled down his cheeks.

"I shall be most grateful," he murmured.

"They're wonderful little beggars, those patrol boats," the captain continued. "Always on the side of the angels, as you said so feelingly at the concert. They're the police of the seas. They guide and guard us all, neutrals as well. They sweep up the mines. They warn us. They pilot us. They pick us up when we're drowning; and, as you said, they give us 'ot coffee; in fact, these little patrol boats are doing the work of civilization. Probably you don't like the British very much in Sweden, but—"

"I have no national brejudices," Mr. Neilsen said hastily. "I shall indeed be most grateful."

"Very well, then," said the captain; "we'll let 'em know."

At half past six, two of the patrol boats were alongside. They were the *Auld Robin Gray* and the *Ruth*, and they seemed to be in high feather over some recent success.

Mr. Neilsen was mystified again when he came on deck, for he could have sworn that he saw something uncommonly like his brass-bound trunk disappearing into the hold of the *Auld Robin Gray*. He was puzzled also by the tail end of the lively conversation that was taking place between Miss Depew and the absurdly young naval officer, with the lisp, who was in command of the patrols.

"Oh, no! I'm afraid we don't uth the dungeonth in the Tower," said that slender youth, while Miss Depew, entirely feminine and smiling like a morning glory now, noted all the details of his peaked cap and the gold stripes on his sleeve. "We put them in country houtheth and feed them like fighting cockth, and give them flower gardenth to walk in."

He turned to Captain Abbey joyously, and lisped over Mr. Neilsen's head:

"That wath a corking metthage of yourth, Captain. I believe we got three of them right in the courth you would have been taking today. You'll hear from the Admiralty about thith, you know. It wath magnifithent! Good-by!"

He saluted smartly, and taking Mr. Neilsen tightly by the arm helped him down to the deck of the *Ruth*.

"Good-by and good luck!" called Captain Abbey.

He beamed over the bulwarks of the *Hispaniola* like a large red harvest moon through the thin mist that began to drift between them.

"Good-by, Mr. Neilsen!" called Mr. and Mrs. Pennyfeather, waving frantically.

"Good-by, Herr Krauss!" said Miss Depew; and the dainty malice in her voice pierced Mr. Neilsen like a Röntgen ray.

But he recovered quickly, for he was of an elastic disposition. He was already looking forward to the home comforts which he now would be supplied by these idiotic British for the duration of the war.

The young officer smiled and saluted Miss Depew again. He was a very ladylike young man, Mr. Neilsen had thought, and an obvious example of the degeneracy of England. But Mr. Neilsen's plump arm was still bruised by the steely grip with which that lean young hand had helped him aboard, so his conclusions were mixed.

The engines of the *Ruth* were thumping now, and the *Hispaniola* was melting away over the smooth gray swell. They watched her for a minute or two, till she became spectral in the distance. Then the youthful representative of the British Admiralty turned, like a thoughtful host, to his prisoner.

"Would you like thum tea?" he lisped sympathetically. "Your Uncle Hyacinth mutht have given you an awfully anxiouth time."

Herr Krauss grunted inarticulately. He was looking like a very happy little Bismarck.

EDGAR WALLACE

WIDELY REPORTED to be the most popular writer in the world in the 1920s and 1930s, Richard Horatio Edgar Wallace (1875–1932) earned a fortune—reportedly more than a quarter of a million dollars a year during the last decade of his life, but his extravagant lifestyle left his estate deeply in debt when he died. The enormous success that he enjoyed in the 1920s and 1930s was unprecedented, with reports (perhaps exaggerated by his publishers) that one in every four books sold in Great Britain during those years had been from his pen.

The prolific Wallace reputedly wrote one hundred seventy novels, eighteen stage plays, and nine hundred fifty-seven short stories; precise numbers are impossible to pin down as many works attributed to him were "revised" after his death and offered as originals, while short story collections had contents shuffled in and out. He also wrote elements of numerous screenplays and scenarios, including the first British sound version of *The Hound of the Baskervilles* (1931); more than one hundred sixty films, both silent and sound, have been based on his books and stories, most famously *King Kong* (1933), for which he wrote the original story and film treatment.

Wallace created any number of recurring characters, the longest-running series being about Commissioner Sanders, representative of the Foreign Office of Great Britain, whose job was to keep the king's peace in Africa's River territories; he appeared in about a dozen books, beginning with *Sanders of the River* (1911). Wallace's most popular series featured the coterie who first appeared in *The Four Just Men* (1905); there were actually three, as one died before the story begins. They were wealthy dilettantes who set out to administer justice when the law is unable or unwilling to do the job; there were five sequels. Most of his other series characters appeared in short stories published in various newspapers and magazines and then collected in book form.

Atypically, the patriotic Wallace also wrote a short story collection devoted to the exploits of Heine, a German secret agent, told in first person. Not surprisingly, Heine constantly disparages the intelligence of the British—indeed, of everyone who isn't German—and regards the British Secret Service as a joke. Also not surprisingly, Heine is thwarted in adventure after adventure, almost humorously finding someone else to blame for his failures.

"Alexander and the Lady" was originally published in the October 1918 issue of *Short Stories;* it was first collected in *The Adventures of Heine* (London, Ward, Lock & Co., 1919).

ALEXANDER AND THE LADY

EDGAR WALLACE

SECRET SERVICE WORK is a joke in peace time and it is paid on joke rates. People talk of the fabulous sums of money which our Government spend on this kind of work, and I have no doubt a very large sum was spent every year, but it had to go a long way. Even Herr Kressler, of the Bremen-America Line, who gave me my monthly cheque, used to nod and wink when he handed over my two hundred marks.

"Ah, my good Heine," he would say, stroking his stubbly beard, "they make a fool of me, the Government, but I suppose I mustn't ask who is your other paymaster?"

"Herr Kessler," said I earnestly, "I assure you that this is the whole sum I receive from the Government."

"So!" he would say and shake his head: "Ah, you are close fellows, and I mustn't ask questions!"

There was little to do save now and again to keep track of some of the bad men, the extreme Socialists, and the fellows who ran away from Germany to avoid military service. I often wished there were more, because it would have been possible to have made a little on one's expenses. Fortunately, two or three of the very big men in New York and Chicago knew the work I was doing,

and credited me with a much larger income than I possessed. The reputation of being well off is a very useful one, and in my case brought me all sorts of commissions and little tips which I could profitably exploit on Wall Street, and in one way or another I lived comfortably, had a nice apartment on Riverside Drive, backed horses, and enjoyed an occasional trip to Washington, at my Government's expense.

I first knew that war was likely to break out in July. I think we Germans understood the European situation much better than the English and certainly much better than the Americans, and we knew that the event at Sarajevo—by the way, poor Klein of our service and an old colleague of mine, was killed by the bomb which was intended for the Archduke, though nobody seems to have noticed the fact—would produce the war which Austria had been expecting or seeking an excuse to wage for two years.

If I remember aright, the assassination was committed on the Sunday morning. The New York papers published the story on that day, and on the Monday afternoon I was summoned to Washington, and saw the Secretary, who was in charge of our Department on the Tuesday evening after dinner.

The Secretary was very grave and told me that war was almost certain, and that Austria was determined to settle with Serbia for good, but that it was feared that Russia would come in and that the war could not be localised because, if Russia made war, Germany and France would also be involved.

Personally, I have never liked the French, and my French is not particularly good. I was hoping that he was going to tell us that England was concerned and I asked him if this was not the case. To my disappointment, he told me that England would certainly not fight, that she would remain neutral, and that strict orders had been issued that nothing was to be done which would in any way annoy the English.

"Their army," he said, "is beneath contempt, but their navy is the most powerful in the world and its employment might have very serious consequences."

It seemed very early to talk about war with the newspapers still full of long descriptions of the Sarajevo murder and the removal of the Archduke's body and I remembered after with what astounding assurance our Secretary had spoken.

I must confess I was disappointed, because I had spent a very long time in England, Scotland, Ireland, and Wales, establishing touch with good friends who, I felt, would work with advantage for me in the event of war. I had prepared my way by founding The Chinese News Bureau, a little concern that had an office in Fleet Street and was ostensibly engaged in collecting items of news concerning China and distributing them to the London and provincial press, and in forwarding a London letter to certain journals in Pekin, Tientsien, and Shanghai.

Of course, the money was found by the Department, and it was not a financial success, but it was a good start in case one ever had to operate in London, since I was registered as a naturalised Chilean and it was extremely unlikely that Chile would be at war with any European Power.

On the 3rd August, 1914, I received a message from Washington in the Department code, telling me that war with England was inevitable and that I was to sail on the first boat and take up my duties in London in full control of the British Department.

I was overjoyed with the news and I know that men like Stohwasser, Wesser, and other men of my Department, looked at me with envy. They did not think they had an easy task because the American Secret Service is a very competent one; but they thought I was a lucky pig—as indeed I was—to be operating in a country containing a population of forty millions, most of whom, as one of their writers said, were fools.

I landed at Liverpool on August 11th. My passport was in order and I immediately went forward to London. There was no trace of any excitement. I saw a lot of soldiers on their way to their depots; and arriving in London, I immediately received the reports of our innumerable agents.

With what pride did I contemplate the splendid smoothness of our system! When the Emperor pressed the button marked "Mobilise," he called, in addition to his soldiers, a thousand gallant hearts and brilliant minds in a score of countries all eager and happy to work for the aggrandisement of our beloved Fatherland.

Six of us met at a fashionable restaurant near Trafalgar Square. There were Emil Stein who called himself Robinson, Karl Besser—I need not give all their aliases—Heine von Wetzl, Fritz von Kahn, and Alexander Koos.

Stein had arrived from Holland the night before and Fritz von Kahn had come down from Glasgow where he had been acting as a hotel porter. These men were, as I say, known to me, and to one another, but there were thousands of unknowns who had their secret instructions, which were only to be opened in case of war and with whom we had to get in touch.

I briefly explained the procedure and the method by which our agents would be identified. Every German agent would prove his bona fides by producing three used postage stamps of Nicaragua. It is a simple method of identification, for there is nothing treasonable or suspicious in a man carrying about in his pocket-book, a ten, twenty, or a fifty centime stamp of a neutral country.

I sent Emil Stein away to Portsmouth and instructed him to make contact with sailors of the Fleet especially with officers. Besser was dispatched to a West Coast shipping centre to report on all the boats which left and entered. I sent Kahn and his family on a motor-car tour to the East Coast with instructions to find out what new coast defences were being instituted.

"You must exercise the greatest care," I said; "even though these English are very stupid, they may easily blunder into a discovery. Make the briefest notes on all you see and hear and only use the Number 3 code in case of urgent necessity." We finished our dinner and we drank to "The Day" and sang under our breath "Deutschland uber Alles" and separated, Koos coming with me.

Koos was a staff officer of the Imperial Service, and though he was not noble he was held in the greatest respect. He was a fine, handsome fellow, very popular with the girls, and typically British in appearance. His English was as good as mine, and that is saying a great deal. I sent him to Woolwich because in his character as an American Inventor—he had spent four years in the States—he was admirably fitted to pick up such facts as were of the greatest interest to the Government.

I did not see Koos for a few days and in the meantime I was very busy arranging with my couriers who were to carry the result of our discoveries through a neutral country to Germany. The system I adopted was a very simple one. My notes, written in Indian ink, were separately photographed by means of a camera. When I had finished the twelve exposures, I opened the camera in a dark room, carefully re-rolled the spool and sealed it, so that it had the appearance of being an unexposed pellicle. I argued that whilst the English military authorities would confiscate photographs which had obviously been taken, they might pass films which were apparently unused.

I had arranged to meet Koos on the night of August 17th, and made my way to the rendezvous, engaging a table for two. I had hardly seated myself when, to my surprise, Koos came in accompanied by a very pretty English girl. He walked past me, merely giving me the slightest side-glance, and seated himself at the next table. I was amused. I knew the weakness of our good Koos for the ladies, but I knew also that he was an excellent investigator and that he was probably combining business with pleasure. In this I was right. The meal finished—and the innocent laughter of the girl made me smile again—and Koos walked out with the girl on his arm.

As he passed my table he dropped a slip of paper which I covered with my table-napkin. When I was sure I was not observed, I read the note.

"Making excellent progress. Meet me at a quarter to eleven outside Piccadilly Tube."

I met him at the appointed time and we strolled into Jermyn Street.

"What do you think of her?" was Koos's first question.

"Very pretty, my friend," said I. "You have excellent taste."

He chuckled.

"I have also excellent luck, my dear Heine. That lady is the daughter of one of the chief gun-constructors at Woolwich."

He looked at me to note the effect of his words, and I must confess I was startled.

"Splendid, my dear fellow!" said I, warmly. "How did you come to meet her?"

"A little act of gallantry," he said airily; "a lady walking on Blackheath twists her ankle, what more natural than that I should offer her assistance to the nearest seat? Quite a babbling little person—typically English. She is a mine of information. An only daughter and a little spoilt, I am afraid, she knows no doubt secrets of construction of which the technical experts of the Government are ignorant. Can you imagine a German talking over military affairs with his daughter?"

"What have you learnt from her?" I asked.

Koos did not reply for a moment, then he said: "So far, very little I am naturally anxious not to alarm her or arouse her suspicions. She is willing to talk and she has access to her father's study and, from what I gather, she practically keeps all the keys of the house. At present I am educating her to the necessity of preserving secrecy about our friendship and to do her justice, she is just as anxious that our clandestine meetings should not come to the ears of her father as I am."

We walked along in silence.

"This may be a very big thing," I said.

"Bigger than you imagine," replied Alexander; "there is certain to be an exchange of confidential views about artillery between the Allies, and though we have nothing to learn from the English it is possible that the French may send orders to Woolwich for armament. In that case our little friend may be a mine of information. I am working with my eyes a few months ahead," he said, "and for that reason I am allowing our friendship to develop slowly."

I did not see Koos again for a week, except that I caught a glimpse of him in the Cafe Riche with his fair companion. He did not see me, however, and as it was desirable that I should not intrude, I made no attempt to make my presence apparent.

At the end of the week we met by appointment, which we arranged through the agony column of a certain London newspaper. I was feeling very cheerful, for Stein, Besser, and Kahn had sent in most excellent reports, and it only needed Alexander's encouraging news to complete my sum of happiness.

"You remember the gun-lathe I spoke to you about," he said. "My friend—you may regard the blue prints as in your hands."

"How has this come about?"

"I just casually mentioned to my little girl that I was interested in inventions and that I had just put a new lathe upon the market in America and she was quite excited about it. She asked me if I heard about the lathe at Woolwich, and I said that I had heard rumours that there was such a lathe. She was quite overjoyed at the opportunity of giving me information and asked me whether in the event of her showing me the prints I would keep the fact a great secret because," he laughed softly, "she did not think her father would like the print to leave his office!"

"You must be careful of this girl," I said, "she may be detected."

"There is no danger, my dear fellow," said Alexander. "She is the shrewdest little woman in the world. I am getting quite to like her if one can like these abominable people—she is such a child!"

I told him to keep in communication with me and sent him off feeling what the English call in "good form," I dispatched a courier by the morning train to the Continent, giving details of the British Expeditionary Force. Only two brigades were in France—and that after three weeks of preparation! In Germany every man was mobilized and at his corps or army headquarters weeks ago—every regiment had moved up to its order of battle position. Two brigades! It would be amusing if it were not pathetic!

Besser came to me soon after lunch in a very excited state.

"The whole of the British Expeditionary Force of three Divisions is in France," he said, "and, what is more it is in line."

I smiled at him.

"My poor dear fellow, who has been pulling your foot?" I asked.

"It is confidentially communicated to the Press, and will be public to-morrow," he said.

"Lies," said I calmly, "you are too credulous. The English are the most stupid liars in the world."

I was not so calm that night when I ran down in my car to Gorselton, where our very good friend, the Baron von Hertz-Missenger, had a nice little estate.

"Heine," he said, after he had taken me to his study and shut the door. "I have received a radio through my wireless from Kreigsministerium [The Prussian Ministry of War] to the effect that the whole of the British Expeditionary Force has landed and is in line."

"Impossible, Herr Baron," I said, but he shook his head.

"It is true—our intelligence in Belgium is infallible. Now, I do not want to interfere with you, for I am but a humble volunteer in this great work, but I advise you to give a little more attention to the army. We may have underrated the military assistance which Britain can offer."

"The English Army, Herr Baron," said I firmly, "is almost as insignificant a factor as—as well—the American army, which only exists on paper! Nevertheless, I will take your advice."

I went back to town and dispatched another courier, for as yet the Torpington Varnish Factory (about which I will tell you later) had not been equipped with radio.

That night I again saw Alexander. It was at supper at the Fritz, and he looked a fine figure of a man. I felt proud of the country which could produce such a type. Where, I ask you, amongst the paunchy English and the scraggy Scotch, with their hairy knees and their sheepshank legs, could you find a counterpart of that beau sabreur? Cower treacherous Albion, shiver in your kilt, hateful Scotch (it is not generally known that the Royal and High-Born Prince Rupprecht of Bavaria is rightful King of Scotland), tremble, wild Wales, and unreliable Ireland, when you come in arms against a land which can produce such men as Alexander Koos!

I never saw a girl look more radiantly happy than did the young woman who was sitting vis-a-vis my friend. There was a light in her eye and a colour in her cheeks which were eloquent of her joy.

I saw Alexander afterwards. He came secretly to my room.

"Have you brought the blue print?" I asked. He shook his head smilingly. "Tomorrow, my friend, not only the blue print of the lathe, not only the new gun-mounting model, but the lady herself will come to me. I want your permission to leave the day after to-morrow for home. I cannot afford to wait for what the future may bring."

"Can you smuggle the plans past the English police?" I asked, a little relieved that he had volunteered to act as courier on so dangerous a mission.

"Nothing easier."

"And the girl—have you her passport?"

He nodded.

"How far shall you take her?"

"To Rotterdam," he said promptly.

In a way I was sorry. Yes, I am sentimental, I fear, and "sentiment does not live in an agent's pocket," as the saying goes. I wish it could have been done without. I shrugged my shoulders and steeled my soul with the thought that she was English and that it was all for the Fatherland.

"You must come to the Cafe Riche tonight and witness our going," said Alexander; "you will observe that she will carry a leather case such as schoolgirls use for their books and exercises. In that case, my friend, will be enough material to keep our friends in Berlin busy for a month."

I took leave of him giving him certain instructions as to the course he was to take after reporting at Headquarters, and spent the rest of the night coding a message for our Alexander to carry with him. The hour at which Alexander was to meet the girl was eight o'clock in the evening.

His table (already booked) was No. 47, which is near the window facing Piccadilly. I telephoned through to the cafe and booked No. 46, for I was anxious to witness the comedy.

All was now moving like clockwork—and let me say that the smoothness of the arrangements was due largely to the very thorough and painstaking organisation-work which I had carried out in the piping days of peace. We Germans have a passion for detail and for thoroughness and for this reason (apart from the inherent qualities of simplicity and honesty, apart from the superiority of our kultur and our lofty idealism) we have been unconquerable throughout the ages.

You must remember that I was in London as the representative of a Chinese News Bureau. I was also an agent for a firm of importers in Shanghai. It was therefore only natural that

I should be called up all hours of the day and night with offers of goods.

"I can let you have a hundred and twenty bales of Manchester goods at 125."

Now 120 and 125 added together make 245, and turning to my "simple code," to paragraph 245, I find the following:

"2nd Battalion of the Graniteshire Regiment entrained to-day for embarkation."

The minor agents carried this code (containing 1,400 simple sentences to covet all naval or military movements) in a small volume. The code is printed on one side of very thin paper leaves, and the leaves are as porous and absorbent as blotting paper.

One blot of ink dropped upon a sheet will obliterate a dozen—a fact which our careless agents have discovered. Clipped in the centre of the book (as a pencil is clipped in an ordinary book) is a tiny tube of the thinnest glass containing a quantity of black dye-stuff. The agent fearing detection has only to press the cover of the book sharply and the contents of the book are reduced to black sodden pulp. Need I say that this ingenious invention was German in its origin.

[As a matter of fact, it was invented by the American Secret Service—E. W.]

My days were therefore very full. There came reports from all quarters and some the most unlikely. How, you may ask, did our agents make these discoveries?

There are many ways by which information is conveyed. The relations of soldiers are always willing to talk about their men and will tell you, if they know, when they are leaving the ships they are leaving by, and will sometimes give you other important facts, but particularly about ports and dates of embarkations are they useful.

Also officers will occasionally talk at lunch and dinner and will tell their women folk military secrets which a waiter can mentally note and convey to the proper quarters. Our best agents, however, were barbers, tailors, chiropodists, and dentists. English people will always discuss matters with a barber or with the man who is fitting them with their clothes, and as almost every tailor was making military uniforms and a very large number of the tailors in London were either German or Austrian, I had quite a wealth of news.

Tailors are useful because they work to time. Clothes have to be delivered by a certain date and generally the man who has the suit made will tell the fitter the date he expects to leave England. Other useful investigators are Turkish-bath attendants and dentists. A man in a dentist's chair is always nervous and will try to make friends with the surgeon who is operating on him.

Of all agencies the waiter is in reality the least useful, because writers have been pointing out for so many years the fact that most waiters were German. But the truth is that most restaurant waiters are Italian, and it is amongst the bedroom waiters that you can find a preponderance of my fellow countrymen.

Prompt at eight o'clock, I took my place at the table and ordered an excellent dinner (my waiter was naturally a good German) and a bottle of Rhenish wine. A few minutes after I had given my order Alexander and the girl arrived. She was dressed in a long travelling coat of tussore silk, and carried—as I was careful to note—a shiny brown leather portfolio. This she placed carefully on be lap when she sat down and raised her veil.

She looked a little pale, but smiled readily enough at Alexander's jests. I watched her as she slowly peeled off her gloves and unbuttoned her coat. Her eyes were fixed on vacancy. Doubtless her conscience was pricking her.

Is it the thought of thy home, little maid from whence thou hast fled never to return? Is it the anguished picture of thy broken-hearted and ruined father bemoaning his daughter and his honour? Have no fear, little one, thy treason shall enrich the chosen of the German God, those World Encirclers, Foreordained and Destined to Imperial Grandeur!

So I thought, watching her and listening.

"Are you sure that everything will be all right?" she asked anxiously.

"Please trust me," smiled Alexander. (Oh, the deceiving rogue—how I admired his sang-froid!)

"You are ready to go—you have packed?" she asked.

"As ready as you, my dear Elsie. Come—let me question you," he bantered, "have you all those wonderful plans which are going to make our fortunes after we are married?"

So he had promised that—what would the gracious Frau Koos-Mettleheim have said to this perfidy on the part of her husband?

"I have all the plans," she began, but he hushed her with a warning glance.

I watched the dinner proceed but heard very little more. All the time she seemed to be plying him with anxious questions to which he returned reassuring answers. They had reached the sweets when she began to fumble at her pocket. I guessed (rightly) that she was seeking a handkerchief and (wrongly) that she was crying.

Her search was fruitless and she beckoned the waiter.

"I left a little bag in the ladies' room—it has my handkerchief; will you ask the attendant to send the bag?"

The waiter departed and presently returned with two men in the livery of the hotel. I was sitting side by side and could see the faces both of the girl and Alexander and I noticed the amusement in his face that two attendants must come to carry one small bag.

Then I heard the girl speak.

"Put your hands, palms upward, on the table," she said. I was still looking at Alexander's face. First amazement and then anger showed—then I saw his face go grey and into his eyes crept the fear of death. The girl was holding an automatic pistol and the barrel was pointing at Alexander's breast. She half turned her head to the attendants.

"Here is your man, sergeant," she said briskly. "Alexander Koos, alias Ralph Burton-Smith. I charge him with espionage."

They snapped the steel handcuffs upon Alexander's wrists and led him out, the girl following. I rose unsteadily and followed. In the vestibule was quite a small crowd which had gathered at the first rumour of so remarkable a sensation. Here, for the first time, Alexander spoke, and it was curious how in his agitation his perfect English became broken and hoarse.

"Who are you? You have a mistake maken, my frient."

"I am an officer of the British Intelligence Department," said the girl.

"Himmel! Secret Service!" gasped Alexander, "I thought it was not!"

I saw them take him away and stole home.

They had trapped him. The girl with the sprained ankle had been waiting for him that day on Blackheath. She led him on by talking of the plans she could get until he had told her of the rough plans he already had. Whilst (as he thought) he was tightening the net about her, she was drawing the meshes tighter about him . . . Phew! It makes me hot to think of it!

Was there a secret service in England after all? For myself, my tracks were too well covered; for Alexander I could do nothing. He would not betray me. I was sure of that. Yet to be perfectly certain I left the next night for Dundee, and I was in Dundee when the news came that Alexander had been shot in the Tower of London.

THE POPINJAY KNIGHT

VALENTINE WILLIAMS

THE SON OF G. Douglas Williams, the chief editor of Reuters, George Valentine Williams (1883–1946) followed in his father's footsteps and began his career as a journalist, returning to it frequently, even after he found success as the author of twenty-five novels of crime, mystery, and espionage.

In 1905, at twenty-one, he became the Berlin correspondent for Reuters but left in 1908 to work for the *Daily Mail*, becoming one of the first accredited war correspondents in World War I in 1915. Later that year, he enlisted in the Irish Guards, advanced to the rank of captain, and was awarded a Military Cross. While convalescing from shell shock, he began to write thrillers on the advice of his friend John Buchan.

He had written several memoirs of his war experiences, *With Our Army in Flanders* (1915) as by G. Valentine Williams, and *Adventures of an Ensign* (1917), but then produced his first work of fiction, *The Man with the Clubfoot* (1918), as by Douglas Valentine, introducing Dr. Adolph Grundt, known as "Clubfoot," one of the first great master criminals of fiction who appeared in a half dozen books. Other series characters created by Williams include Trevor Dene, a bespectacled genius English policeman (though most of his cases take place in the United States), and Mr. Treadgold, a Savile Row tailor and amateur detective.

Dividing his time between England, the French Riviera, and the United States, Williams went on to write thirty books while also acting, lecturing, and writing screenplays. When World War II began, he was recruited to the British Secret Service and was assigned to the British Embassy in Washington, DC, but resigned before the end of the war to move to Hollywood to work as a screenwriter, though none of his scripts were ever produced.

The Crouching Beast (1935), based on the 1928 Williams novel of the same title, was produced by the British studio Stafford. Set in the Dardanelles, it is the story of a mysterious British spy aided by an American girl in the theft of fortification plans. Williams's story "Fog" was the basis for the 1933 Columbia Pictures film of the same title. Directed by Albert S. Rogell, it starred Mary Brian, Donald Cook, and Reginald Denny.

"The Popinjay Knight" was originally published in *The Knife Behind the Curtain* (London, Hodder & Stoughton, 1930).

THE POPINJAY KNIGHT

VALENTINE WILLIAMS

I

I DON'T SUPPOSE you would have found anywhere on the British front in France a handsomer or better turned-out officer than my friend Lucius. Tall, blond, and blue-eyed, with a fair wisp of moustache, so beautifully trained that we used to call it the Flappers' Dream, he was always, in all circumstances, faultlessly dressed from head to foot. He used his captain's prerogative of wearing field-boots and spurs, and his boots, well fitting his shapely leg and as bright as a mirror, were a perpetual testimonial to the taste of their wearer and the excellence of his servant. His uniform was always spotless: his buttons were never dull; and never did I see him dirty or jaded or discomposed. For his temperament was as sprightly as the rest of him. Every time I saw him I used to think of that popinjay knight who excited the wrath of Harry Hotspur in *Henry IV.*

Lucius was my friend, but when one had paid this tribute to his outer man, I sometimes thought there was really nothing more to be said for him. For of all the decorative shirkers in khaki at the front, from the extra A.D.C.s down to the O.C.s God knows what at remote bases,

we used to think him the most glaring example. And the worst of it was that he was so shamelessly and blatantly frank about it. He had some vague job (carrying with it the sole disposition of a magnificent Vauxhall car) in the Corps Intelligence, and when my battalion was in rest he would often motor over from Corps Headquarters and look me up.

I shall never forget the occasion on which he openly proclaimed at our mess his satisfaction at not being a combatant. Now at the front, fellows were very broad-minded. A man kept himself to himself, as the saying is, and seldom inquired about any one else as long as the fellow did his job all right. This is by way of showing you that old Lucius was asking for it when he started bucking in our mess about being a shirker.

We were having tea in some filthy estaminet or other when Lucius blew in, impeccably attired as usual. He started in right away.

"Hullo, my brave foot-slogger," he said to me, "I've been meaning to come and look you up for ages, but I wasn't keen on coming as long as you were near the line. There's a damn sight too much shell-fire about this sector for my liking."

You could kind of feel a frost stealing over our fellows round the tea-table, but nobody said anything. I sat him down beside me, and got him a mugful of tea, pushed the condensed milk over, and the loaf and the butter and jam. I didn't have to introduce him round, for he had been over to our mess often enough before.

"Well, what kind of a time have you been having?" he asked me as he helped himself.

"Pretty thin," I replied. "We had a lot of shelling during our tour in the trenches and a lot more when we went into support."

"How perfectly horrible!" said Lucius, with his mouth full of bread and jam. "And to think that if I hadn't had a lively imagination I might have gone into the infantry too. I should be terrified if a shell came near me; I'm sure I should run away. I'm devilish glad I had the sense to pick a nice, safe job like mine, with decent quarters, and . . . why, damn it, I don't suppose you've slept in a bed for days, some of you fellows . . . have you?"

Now Blinkers, our second-in-command, a regular officer, out since Mons and all the rest, was having tea with us that afternoon, and I knew that to him this kind of talk was as a red rag to a bull. Out of the corner of my eye I could see him bristling up. I kicked Lucius under the table, but he took no notice and went babbling on.

"I've always been able to imagine exactly what being shelled is like," he continued, "and I was resolved that I should have a jolly good try to get a job that would keep me clear of it. So I reserved the infantry as my last string . . . to go into if all else failed."

Blinkers had been swelling and swelling and clearing his throat in a way that we all knew portended trouble.

". . . I knew I could always have come to you," Lucius went on, "you'd have got me a commission in your lot, wouldn't you, Billie?"

He turned to me with that winning smile of his, so that he did not see that Blinkers was on the point of bursting. So he positively jumped when Blinkers slapped the table with his hand and cried:

"And do you really suppose that this regiment that was complimented by the great Duke for the part it played at Waterloo, that fought alongside the Guards at Inkerman, that . . . that . . . that was one of the last to come off Spion Kop, that . . . that . . . has gained two V.C.s and four D.S.O.s in this war, would give a commission to a cowardly jackanapes like you? Do you really imagine that a . . . a . . . that an officer who glories in a soft job is a fit companion for gentlemen of England who have answered their country's call and are doing their bit? Allow me to tell you, sir, that it would be more becoming in you to hide your satisfaction at your immunity from . . . er . . . discomfort and . . . er . . . er . . . danger, and not discredit yourself as well as the officer who has seen fit to introduce you here!"

And old Blinkers got up and stalked out of the place.

Lucius turned to me with a blank face.

"Sorry, old boy, I seem to have bracketed you with myself in the Major's bad books. I really think the most graceful thing I can now do is to withdraw with humble apologies for having been the innocent instrument of this disagreeable scene . . ."

He rose to his feet and looked round the table.

". . . especially as I've finished my tea!" he added.

Nobody moved to stop him, and I went out with him to see him off. When we were clear of the estaminet he said, chuckling:

"My dear Billie, what a priceless type! He talked exactly like a recruiting poster! Did you see him wag his finger at me? 'Are you doing your bit?' Oh dear, I do so enjoy the army!"

"Lucius," I said, "I've always defended you when you've put people's backs up by the way you buck about your soft job. But I'm hanged if I'll stand for you doing it in my own mess."

"Damn it, old boy, I was only ragging. . . ."

"I don't know so much about that," I replied—I was pretty annoyed with him for drawing old Blinkers like that: Blinkers, for all his old-womanish ways, was a devilish good officer and as brave as a lion. "If you've got a cushy billet, that's your affair. But if you really are a funk you might keep your opinions to yourself instead of airing them in front of fellows who've just come out of the line. I can tell you this: next time they start crabbing you I'm damned if I stick up for you any more!"

It was pretty straight talk, wasn't it? And I meant it to wither him. But he never turned a hair.

"Poor old Billie," he said, smiling at me. "You know you'd always stick up for Mary's brother."

"The fact that I'm engaged to your sister has nothing to do with it. It certainly won't prevent me from going straight off to Blinkers and apologizing for having brought you in. . . ."

"Dear old chap!" He patted me on the back. "So you think I'm a funk, too, do you?"

"Didn't you say yourself you were afraid of shells?"

"Well, aren't you?"

"Yes. But, dash it all, one doesn't glory in it!"

"Why pretend to be something you're not?"

He was exasperatingly calm, and I felt a wave of anger surge over me again.

"It's all very well to pretend to misunderstand me. I know, we all know, there are lots of fellows in jobs behind the line because they have special qualifications. But what special qualifications have you got, apart from the fact that you're good at languages, to spend the whole of your time mucking about at the back in a car, a job that any old buffer like a modern languages master or a college don could do every bit as well? Listen, Lucius, you needn't worry to come and see me any more. I'm fed up!"

He grinned quite cheerfully. "All right, old boy. Sorry I made things awkward for you with the Major, but I simply can't resist pulling people's legs. As for my job . . ."

"Suppose you tell me just what your job is?"

He laughed. "Mucking about in a car at the back. But we all have our uses, old son. Ta-ta, William, try and cultivate a sense of humour— it's no end of a help in life!"

Then he got into his Vauxhall. But I turned my back on him and walked into the mess.

II

Now that the War is history, we fellows who were in it are a lot of blinking heroes. We bore the young generation a good deal, I always suspect, with our reminiscences of the battles we took part in. But to us at the time those battles, whose names are now gloriously inscribed on regimental colours and war memorials throughout the Empire, were just shows, as we used to call them, and we went into them and out the other side— some of us—without ever realizing that we were making history. The weather, the weight of one's equipment, the difficulty of keeping direction in the waste of shell-holes, the heavy going—in a word, the petty discomforts of the business, not heroics, were what engrossed us. That's war.

And so the first time I went over the bags in the Battle of the Somme my principal concern was a really agonizing corn. It was in an interval between pushes, and our battalion was in the front line. Opposite us the German front bulged in a small salient protected by a strong point known as the Rhomboid on the right. Before the advance was resumed, it was considered necessary to pinch out the salient and mop up the strong point. The first of these tasks was entrusted to our Division, while the Division on our right was to deal with the Rhomboid. Our battalion and the battalion on our left were to send over a company apiece after a short preliminary bombardment. In our case the job was entrusted to "D" company, of which I was second-in-command.

The staff had the bright idea of arranging for this jolly picnic to take place in broad daylight. We went over at four o'clock of a summer afternoon. My corn was hurting me so much that actually the physical pain of walking rendered me almost oblivious of the mixed lot of stuff that promptly came down on us. I know we caught it pretty hot in the open, and I was not surprised to find myself in command of the company as the only surviving officer by the time we reached our objective. Jerry hadn't stopped to argue, and the trench was empty.

Our orders were to consolidate and hold on until night, when we were to be relieved. Accordingly I lost no time in setting the men to dig themselves in. A lot of machine-gun stuff kept coming over from the Rhomboid, suggesting to me that the attack on the right had been held up. We had a good many casualties. I sent out patrols to link up with our left and right. Then the German barrage started.

Those gunners had the range to a T. Up and down in salvoes whizzbangs and five-nines came plumping, while a screen of shells shut us off from the trench from which we had started out. My corn was giving me gyp, and I had sat down on the fire-step to nurse my aching foot when the company sergeant-major, usually the most imperturbable of men, breezed up quivering with excitement.

"Our people on the left have fallen back, sir," he reported. "I've just been that far along the trench, and barrin' a lot of dead and two or three wounded there's nobody left."

"What about the right?" I asked. "The Rhomboid seems to be popping off as merrily as before."

"Don't know, sir, but I'll soon find out."

"I'll come with you, Sergeant-Major," I said. Fifty yards along the trench the sergeant of No. 16 platoon met us.

"They're away on the right, sir," he said. "Every man jack of them has hooked it."

"Best retire to conform, sir," suggested the sergeant-major.

"Ay, that we had," murmured the platoon sergeant.

"We can't without orders," I objected, feeling very wavy about the stomach.

Then a man appeared struggling along the press of men in the trench. It was a runner from Battalion Headquarters. He had come through the barrage and was badly scared. I had just taken the message from his hand when, without warning, two men loomed up on what had been the parados of the German trench. They wore hideous coal-scuttle helmets and leather equipment over grey uniform.

One of them was a big, fat man with a purple face running with moisture. He was wheezing like a grampus. The instant he saw me he yelled with a strong German accent: "Ach, bloody Englishman!"

I cried out a warning, and snatching up my revolver, which dangled from a lanyard about my neck, fired point-blank at him. He threw up his hands and crashed backwards with a curiously shrill exclamation of surprise. Then everybody seemed to shout together, there were two or three loud detonations, a louder explosion, and something hit me hard on the back of the head. I saw a shower of stars, then the ground slipped away. . . .

III

Of all the sensations of war, I herewith coldly and with deliberation proclaim, that of being made a prisoner is infinitely the worst. A German had got round behind me, and, using a stick-bomb like a club, had put me down for the count. When I came to, the trench was full of grey-green uniforms, and a party of us was being rounded up to go down to the rear.

What with my aching head and raging corn and the utter sense of humiliation that overcame me, I have very little recollection of our march. I know that we traversed a perfectly diabolical barrage of British shells, and I am still amazed to think that we all, prisoners and escort, came through alive.

They ran us into a barbed-wire compound, putting me in a corner wired off from the men. There were no other British officers there. A German captain, who was pretty civil, asked me my name and regiment, and started to cross-examine me in very fair English about our next attack. When he found that I would not talk he left me to my own devices.

A little later all my fellow-prisoners were marched away. The sergeant-major, who had got a flesh wound in the thigh from a German bayonet, waved his hand as he hobbled by and cried: "Good luck, sir!" I felt pretty forlorn as I saw them go.

Gosh, I shall never forget that afternoon. The sun blazed down hotly, and there was no cover. My head was splitting from the clout I had received; I was faint with hunger, for I had had nothing since a very early lunch; and my corn was throbbing abominably. But the thirst was the worst. Some kind of a main road ran close to the edge of the compound. All through the late afternoon the road was choked with traffic going in a dense stream towards the firing-line, sending up choking clouds of red dust that were simply stifling. And all the time the very air seemed to quiver to the throb of the guns.

I felt broken in spirit, absolutely abased to the ground. The hopelessness of the position was the awful thing—to count for nothing any more, to be just a captured piece tossed to the side of the chessboard until the game was done! It was not until a deep-throated hum in the sky and the angry barking of the archies made me look aloft that I got the whiphand of myself again. For there, very high in the bright blue sky and all ringed round with shrapnel bursts, was a covey of British planes, swift and proud and indomitable, soaring over the enemy lines. I could have stood up and cheered at the sight. It was the stimulus I required, of all others, in my sorry pass.

After that, nothing more happened. It was almost dark when an N.C.O. brought me a couple of pieces of rather nasty-looking black bread and a mess-tin of weak coffee. I ate and drank and then laid me down to sleep on the grass of the compound.

I awoke to the freshness of a pellucid, dewy morning. The officer I had seen before was standing at the gate of the cage talking to a slim young German officer with a white-and-black sash slung across his tunic. When they saw me on my feet they pushed open the gate and came in.

The young officer bowed stiffly. "Von Scheidemann of the Staff of the 161st Infantry Regiment," he introduced himself. "My Colonel has seen the bravery of your attack and invites you to breakfast with him. I have an automobile here." His English was stiff but reasonably fluent.

"So I am to be pumped," was my first thought. But I accepted the invitation. The prospect of a hot meal attracted me; besides, I reflected, a peep at a German Headquarters would be distinctly interesting. "If I might have a wash?" I suggested.

"You shall have that at Headquarters," von Scheidemann answered, and led the way to where, on the road outside the compound, a grey motor-car was throbbing gently. An orderly with a rifle, standing by the door, stiffened to attention as we approached.

My escort held the door open for me.

"You forgive that I mention it," he said pleasantly enough, "but both of us are armed," and he jerked his head towards the orderly, "just to prevent misunderstandings, yes?" The next minute we were off along that road at a good forty miles an hour.

In truth, we wanted all the speed the very skilful driver could whack out of that car. The first thing I had heard on waking had been the whirl and crash of bursting shells. As soon as we had turned off the main road—in a north-westerly direction, as far as I could make out by the position of the sun, for I had entirely lost my bearings—we seemed to come now into a zone swept by the British artillery. We had a hundred hairbreadth escapes. Again and again coal-boxes pitched with vast spouts of brown earth in the fields alongside us as we sped along, and twice crashed on to the road itself behind us. The road was all torn and pocketed by shell-craters, and the going was terribly rough.

We had travelled for barely ten minutes when the car slowed down and stopped at the entrance to a village. Here the road was screened with sacking against observation from the higher ground to the west where I knew the British trenches lay. Von Scheidemann jumped out and beckoned me to follow him. Hardly had my foot touched the ground than the car was in motion again, backing to turn, and in a second it was off once more, speeding back the way it had come. A great pall of smoke and dust hung over the village and from the tangle of red roofs and white walls in the centre where the houses clustered thick about a wrecked fragment of church tower, the iron slamming of bursting shells re-echoed deafeningly.

"Your compatriots are hard at it again!" said my companion; "this is a bad spot. Quick!" He gripped my arm and ran me to where, above the entrance of a dug-out, a black-and-white flag flapped from a blasted tree-trunk. He raised a blanket curtain, and there I saw a very steep flight of stairs lit by electric light, leading as it seemed into the very bowels of the earth. We went down together.

The entrance led into a very maze of subterranean chambers cut in past centuries out of the solid chalk and extended and modernized by the invader. The place was a veritable underground fortress, nay, a camp. Here were barrack-rooms and dormitories and baths and stores, a guard-room, offices . . . accommodation, apparently, for a whole Brigade.

Von Scheidemann led me swiftly along a main corridor, down one side-turning after another, until we came to a corridor bearing a notice-board inscribed: STAB 161 INF. REG. Here we ran into a burly Prussian officer who had a pair of tortoise-shell spectacles on his nose. He seemed irritable and rather excited. Von Scheidemann said to him in German:

"Things look lively again this morning!"

"*Herr Gott!*" replied the other, "it'll be bad for us again to-day!"

"I've got the Englishman along!" said my escort.

"Good!" answered the other, and continued on his way.

My companion entered the corridor and pushed open a wooden door with his name painted on it. He bowed me into a small, rather stuffy room, plainly furnished, where an orderly was making the bed.

Von Scheidemann sent the man for hot water. "Perhaps you'd like a shave too?" he asked.

I nodded gratefully, rubbing my chin.

"Franz is the man for you, then," he said. "He used to work at a barber's in Portsmouth. Franz, you rascal," he went on, addressing the orderly who had come in with a big can of hot water, "tell the gentleman about the time you used to shave the naval officers at Portsmouth!"

The orderly grinned sheepishly as he tucked a towel about my neck.

"T'ree year haf I vork at Portsmouse," he chuckled. "Dere ain't many Bridish admirals wot ain't got shafed by Vranz som taime or anoder. Gut monney I haf made there, *jawohl* . . . a naice down, Portsmouse, and loafly girls!"

Von Scheidemann roared with laughter.

But I sat in silence and let Franz shave me: I was thinking how far away it seemed to the Hard.

IV

War is a series of surprises, but I never anticipated sitting down to breakfast with a German Colonel and his regimental staff. Yet here I was, in a long, low-roofed room, lit with electric light, ventilated by long, slanting air-shafts driven up through the tons of chalk and earth above us, eating cold tongue and drinking coffee cheek by jowl with the O.C. 161st Prussian Infantry. The Colonel was a small, thick-set man with beady eyes, a red neck, and a grizzled moustache. Beside him was the bespectacled officer I had already seen, who turned out to be the First Adjutant: there was also a black-bearded *Stabsarzt*, wearing the velvet collar and badges of the German Army Medical Corps, and a young Captain whom I took to be the Signalling Officer.

They were all excessively polite. The Colonel, addressing me in very bad French, expressed his regret at having no English, but I told him

I could manage to get along with French. I saw no necessity for telling him that, while I was no German scholar, I could understand the general drift of a conversation in German.

I could not help noticing the general air of restlessness hanging over the company. All the officers at that breakfast-table looked absolutely worn out, oppressed by the shadow of some threatening danger. Messages kept on coming in by orderly to the Adjutant, and with each fresh arrival the Colonel cocked his eye in that officer's direction, while not interrupting his conversation with me.

The Colonel congratulated me on coming through the previous day's fighting alive.

"It was a good attack," he said. "I watched it from my observation station. The creeping barrage was excellently handled: a remarkable man, your General Horne . . . I should like to meet him!"

I bowed, but said nothing.

"But you hadn't a chance once you came up against our incomparable infantry," the Colonel went on. "Your troops are brave . . . they sacrifice themselves willingly . . . but they avail nothing against our years of training!"

Still I remained silent. This "artillery preparation" for a direct pumping attack was too childish for words.

And how they did try to pump me! The Colonel, the Adjutant, von Scheidemann, even the Doctor, they all took a hand and started discussions about infantry tactics, artillery preparation, Stokes mortars, Lewis guns, and heaven knows what else, flattering me, contradicting me, agreeing with me, praising and condemning British generalship, British initiative, even British pluck. I dodged and slithered and scraped through it all, never committing myself to a direct answer if possible, and keeping a tight hand on my temper lest I should be tempted to say a word more than I intended. For I realized that at the bottom of all this desultory discussion lay the desire to obtain from me some light on the big push which I knew to be impending in this sector of the Somme front.

All the time I kept my ears open for any asides I might be able to pick up. Once the Adjutant silently laid a message brought in by an orderly beside the Colonel's plate. The Colonel read it, then crashed his fist down on the table.

"And high time too!" he cried. "Scheidemann is my Staff Captain—he's not an interpreter. I told the Major-General himself that if prisoners were to be interrogated on the spot, the Corps would have to detail special officers. . . . What's the fellow's name?"

"It's not in the message, Herr Oberst . . . but the Corps telephoned just now. Rittmeister von dem Holzweg is the name!"

"Well, he'll be welcome whoever he is!" grunted the Colonel, and started talking to me about the tanks. He was particularly anxious to know whether our people were satisfied with their results.

"If you are willing to admit, *mon Colonel*," I answered, "that you are dissatisfied with our tanks, I should be better able to judge."

An orderly came in and spoke to the Adjutant, who, muttering an apology, got up and went out.

"Well answered!" cried the Colonel. "I must tell the Doctor that." And he translated question and answer for the benefit of the *Stabsarzt*, who, it appeared, was inordinately interested in the tanks. The Doctor burst into a hurricane of laughter (as, doubtless, he was expected to do), and the Colonel roared with him until the room fairly shook with noise.

In the middle of the din the door opened suddenly. Lucius stood there looking into the room.

V

He was dressed in the service uniform of a captain of Uhlans, grey-green tunic buttoned across the chest, grey-green breeches with the broad crimson stripe of the Great General Staff down the leg, *chapka* (the Uhlan helmet), strings and all. An eyeglass was firmly screwed in his left eye, and through it he calmly surveyed the room, whilst bowing stiffly, his right hand raised in salute to his helmet.

He was the Prussian officer to the life, impassive of feature, angular of movement. By some trick of the actor's art he actually seemed to have added that touch of woodenness to the face which is the hallmark of the Prussian officer.

His eye rested on me for the fraction of a second as his gaze travelled round the room. But his face remained immobile. As for me, I felt the blood rush to my head and I literally felt my heart thumping in jerks. The room seemed to swim and I grasped with twitching hand at my empty coffee cup and took a long draught of nothing . . . anything, anything, I felt, to cover my bewilderment. The nerve of the man! The cheek of it all!

A voice that seemed a long way off was speaking German in clipped nasal tones.

"Captain von dem Holzweg, 23rd Uhlan Regiment, sent by the Corps, Herr Oberst . . . they telephoned. . . ."

It was Lucius who was speaking in German. Behind him I saw the rotund form of the Adjutant.

Pushing back his chair, the Colonel rose and gave the Uhlan his hand.

"Delighted, Herr Rittmeister," he said. "Have you breakfasted?"

Lucius held up a white-gloved hand in assent.

"Then," the Colonel went on, looking at the Adjutant, "it's high time that you and I, Gelbhammer, went up to the headquarters of the 390th. If they are coming out to-night, I must see Colonel Krome. In the meantime," he added, waving his hand towards me, "since you are here, we have an excellent specimen for you to practice your arts on. You speak English, of course?"

"A-oh yes, sir," said Lucius in English, with a nicely graduated shade of German accent.

On that, after many deep bows and much saluting, the Colonel picked up his steel helmet and riding-crop from a chair and stumped out, the Adjutant at his heels. The rest of the party, with the exception of von Scheidemann and Lucius, followed suit. These two last were conferring in an undertone in a corner.

"We can use the Colonel's room," von Scheidemann said presently, "he won't be back before two or three o'clock this afternoon . . . it's the second door on the left . . . perhaps you'll take our friend in there. I'll just go along to the office and get the forms; I shan't be a minute."

He led the way out into the corridor, and pushing a door open, showed us a small room with the usual long, slanting air-shaft, with plain deal walls covered with maps, and plain, roughly carpentered deal table and chairs. On the wall was a telephone. As we went into the room I noticed a sentry just turning a bend in the corridor. I wondered if he was always on duty outside the C.O.'s room or whether he was posted for my benefit.

Von Scheidemann clanked off down the corridor, leaving us alone. I observed that he left the door open and that Lucius made no attempt to shut it.

"Cigarette?" said Lucius, handing me his case.

As I stretched across to take it, he whispered swiftly:

"Don't ask questions: don't be surprised at anything. Just sit down at the table there and listen to me. When I stop talking answer . . . anything . . . anything banal and unsuspicious."

He walked back to the door and, with his back to me and his face towards the door, began studying a map hanging on the wall. Then he spoke in a rapid undertone:

"Billie, old man, I'm right plumb up against it this time. It's eight o'clock now and I've got just one hour and a quarter before the man I am impersonating can turn up. I bagged his car and he can't possibly get here before 9:15, I think. If he turns up before that time, then I'm dished. Look out!"

A step sounded on the echoing timbers of the corridor.

". . . it entirely depends on the visibility prevailing at the time," I said quite irrelevantly, as the sentry hove into view in the opening of the door.

"*Himmel Sakrament!*" swore Lucius in German, "did one ever hear such lies?" Then he went into English and his voice was loud and clear:

"You *must* know that weather conditions have nothing to do with the use of tanks! *Esel!*" he added in German.

On that he switched back into English in the same rapid undertone as before:

"I should have got clear of the German lines last night, only I was held up. By a miraculous chance I stumbled upon this man Holzweg's special mission to these headquarters, so I made for this point. It's my only chance to get clear away, but a slender one at that. Billie, do you know where you are?"

I shook my head. Then, hearing the sentry again, I took up the thread of my imaginary interrogation until the man had passed the door once more.

"In front of this village," Lucius went on, "is the Stettiner Redoubt. I dare say you know it!"

Know it? I should say I did. The toughest nut to crack on the whole of this part of the enemy line, a fortress bristling with machine-guns that had hitherto defied all attempts at capture.

"Our fellows are attacking it at eight . . . no preliminary bombardment but full orchestra when they pop. Hark! They're off!"

I listened for the roar of guns, but heard nothing. Only I suddenly noticed that the atmosphere was vibrating and that the timber of the air-shafts, of floors and walls and ceilings, was oscillating as leaves shaken by the wind.

"The village where we are now is the final objective: our lads are due to be here about five minutes after nine. If they take the Stettiner Redoubt, they should get here all right: if they're held up, well, I shall be properly for it, for no power on earth can prevent my being unmasked!

"That's the whole bag of tricks," Lucius concluded, "and you and I must make it our business to prolong our sitting with Scheidemann here until 9:05 at all costs. After that, it doesn't matter much what happens!"

"But Holzweg?" I queried in a whisper; "won't he wire through and have you laid by the heels?"

"I left him tied up in a barn in a fairly desolate region at least three miles from the nearest unit. There is always the chance that he might be able to attract the notice of a passing car, but I'm risking that: one must hazard something in this game!"

Then there was a step in the corridor, and Scheidemann came in. He looked very harassed. As he entered, Lucius very swiftly and almost imperceptibly got between him and the door.

"Can we start the examination of this officer?" Lucius said in an annoyed kind of voice. "I seem to have been kept waiting for a very long time."

"You will not be able to examine this officer, Herr Rittmeister," Scheidemann answered coldly; "there has been a telephone message about you."

"About me?" said Lucius, who was standing, legs apart, hands behind his back, in front of the door.

"Yes. If you will come with me to the office, I will show you the message."

The Staff Captain stepped towards the door and Lucius stood aside to let him pass. As von Scheidemann drew level with him, however, Lucius raised his right arm like a flag; something descended heavily on the Prussian's head, and he crashed backwards into me.

"Catch him!" cried Lucius in a hoarse whisper. But I had forestalled him. The Staff Captain was prostrate in my arms.

We laid him down on the floor. I looked inquiringly at Lucius. He appeared to be listening intently. From within now reverberated distinctly the rumble and thud of artillery but blended with it the trample of feet echoing along the subterranean passages, hoarse cries and commands. Then flying footsteps came along the corridor.

Lucius sprang forward and put his weight against the door. Some one rattled the handle.

"Herr Hauptmann! Herr Hauptmann!" a voice cried, raucous with excitement, "they're all retreating. *Zurück, zurück!*"

The door-handle was twisted vainly for a second or two. We could hear the unseen messenger breathing heavily at the other side of the door. Peering over Lucius's shoulder I looked at his watch. It pointed to eight o'clock.

I shook Lucius by the arm, pointing.

He stared at the watch, then grinned cheerfully up in my face.

"Stopped, by God!" he said.

Hardly had he uttered the words when a loud detonation rang out quite close at hand, followed by another and another.

"Bombs!" I whispered, "they're here, they're here!"

The heavy breathing at the keyhole stopped. I heard a sharp cry of astonishment, a shout, a loud report, a heavy thud. And then the whole of that vast rabbit-warren seemed to break out into long reverberations of noise. Bombs crashed, shots pinged through the echoing spaces, voices shouted in a medley of languages, and there was a great blowing of whistles . . . then I heard a voice say at the very door of our room—and the voice was the voice of Lancashire:

"'Ere be another of 'em, laads!" and a rifle-butt smashed through the panels of the door.

Lucius turned to me with a smile. "You see I have my uses, Billie Boy!" he said.

I motioned to him to stand behind me, then plucked the door wide.

The next moment the little tomb-like place was full with a jostling, steel-helmeted, blood-stained, begrimed mass of British soldiers. . . .

VI

Lucius wanted a lot of explaining. I met a fellow I knew in the little crowd that had squeezed out this nest and he went bail for me. But nothing I could say availed to get permission for old Lucius to accompany me down to the rear. So I left him in charge of a corporal's guard, waiting for some Divisional Brass Hat to come and interrogate him. In the midst of all that khaki, I must say old Lucius looked his part.

"Not a word to any one!" was his parting injunction to me.

I was sorely tempted to disobey him when, six weeks later, he came to see me. Our Division was again in rest, and one afternoon Lucius turned up in his Vauxhall, spruce and immaculate as ever. I ran into him at the door of the mess, where he was inquiring for me.

Whilst we stood and chatted, old Blinkers passed along the village street. He recognized Lucius at once, and there was the unspoken reproach of "Shirker" in every line of the cold scrutiny of his glance. I was about to speak when Lucius squeezed my arm.

"Don't spoil my joke!" he pleaded.

So I held my peace and we both went in to lunch.

THE LINK

MICHAEL ANNESLEY

UNDER THE PSEUDONYM Michael Annesley, the prolific author Frederick Annesley Michael Webster (1886–1949) wrote sixteen espionage thrillers, while under his real name, bylined F. A. M. Webster, he wrote mysteries, fantasy novels for adults, works about sports, and science fiction aimed at young readers.

In a biographical sketch, Webster was described as "one of the most important names in the history of athletics in the twentieth century in Britain" and, with no evidence to suggest otherwise, it seems a reasonable statement, even if written by his grandson, Michael Webster.

F. A. M. Webster wrote more than thirty books on sports, was active in creating and leading several important sports organizations, and was the British National Champion in the javelin throw both in 1911 and 1923. As a journalist, he was a special correspondent at five Olympic Games and other major events, and had an international reputation as an authority on the history and technique of sports. In spite of his terrific skill on the field at school and on army teams, he was unable to serve in battle because of a knee damaged on the soccer field.

Among his fictional works as Michael Annesley were a series of espionage novels about Lawrie Fenton that appeared from 1935 (*Room 14;* published in the United States as *Fenton of the Foreign Office*) to 1950 (*Spy Island*, which was set on Cyprus). Other books in the series were set in Paris, Lithuania, Germany, Poland, and other international locations.

As F. A. M. Webster, his best-known mysteries featured Old Ebbie Entwhistle, who appeared in scores of short stories in such collections as *Old Ebbie: Detective Up-to-Date* (1923), *Old Ebbie Returns* (1925), and *The Crime Scientist* (1930).

Webster's nonseries crime and adventure stories were often set in exotic locales, such as Nairobi (*The Hill of Riches*, 1923), Africa (*Beyond All Fear*, 1934), and India (*East of Kashgar*, 1940).

I have been unable to trace the original publication of this story. It was collected in *My Best Spy Story*, edited anonymously (London, Faber & Faber, 1938).

THE LINK

MICHAEL ANNESLEY

STOUT MYNHEER LEIPSCHITZ came and went, much at his own sweet will, between his home at Zutfen and the towns of Western Germany which lie reasonably close to the frontier of the Netherlands. His unfailing kindliness endeared him to his fellow Dutchmen. He was well liked in Germany for a certain quiet, concentrated hatred of the British, which he had harboured since receiving, in the Boer War, a bullet wound which still caused him to walk with a pronounced limp.

In the spring of 1914 an accident had laid him abed for some weeks and then, despite his hatred of the British, he had gone to London for treatment. Certain high officials at the Marinamt smiled knowingly when they heard that story, for there had been occasions when Paul Leipschitz had rendered valuable service to the German Intelligence Department. Some weeks prior to the outbreak of the Great War he returned to the house in which he lived alone at Zutfen and resumed his journeys into Germany; but, even after the outbreak of hostilities, the frontier guards, Dutch and German alike—paid but the most perfunctory attention to his comings and goings.

Quite a number of people took to visiting him at outrageous hours of the night, but he showed no signs of annoyance at being thus disturbed and more often than not after his mysterious visitors had departed took a stroll to the loft where lived the carrier pigeons which had provided him with a hobby for quite a number of years.

His business seemed to be conducted mainly in Dortmund, Essen, and Düsseldorf; but sometimes he went as far as Cologne, and very occasionally to Berlin. In the German capital he ceased to be the provincial business man and became the intimate of important people in Government circles.

For the first few months of the war the luck was with him, although the character he bore was entirely different on opposite sides of the frontier. In Germany he was regarded as a valuable Secret Service agent, for news that came from him regarding the plans of the Allies was always reliable, although not so invariably useful. But, as he explained, it was not always possible to send information as promptly as he would wish to do.

In Holland he had not yet attracted the attention of the Dutch Government for he continued to play to perfection the part of an industrious business man. Early in 1915 he left Zutfen, presumably because the frequent visits paid by women to his lonely house at night had scandalized his fellow townsmen. The real cause of his removal to a small office in Rotterdam may have been a hint dropped by one of his furtive visitors that certain people in Berlin were growing suspicious and might take steps to interrogate him the next time he should cross the frontier.

Once he was in Rotterdam it did not take Paul Leipschitz long to find out who were the heads of the various Counter-Espionage Services located in the city. As a Dutch neutral he had no difficulty in making friends with most of them and having taken up his residence at the Maas Hotel, which was overrun with German agents, he re-established himself with the Berlin authorities by keeping up a regular supply of accurate information, which would have been invaluable had it arrived in time, or had not the British authorities changed their plans at the last moment, or taken steps to forestall any possible source of leakage.

Up to that time it had been surprisingly easy for the British, Belgian, and French Secret Services to get information out of Belgium, on account of the hundreds of Belgian refugees who had settled in Holland. But, shortly after the arrival of Paul Leipschitz in Rotterdam, Germany created a singularly effective barrier against the passage of information by erecting a deadly high-voltage wire fence along the Dutch-Belgian frontier. This fence was guarded by a cordon of sentries each within sight of the other and, further, was constantly patrolled by German Secret Police in plain clothes.

The erection of this barrier put a period to the activities of both Dutch and Belgian freelance agents, but from some mysterious British headquarters in Rotterdam lines radiated to courier centres for frontier agents at Terneuzen, Tilburg, and Eindhoven in Holland and were carried on to Maastricht in Belgium. People were established as "letter-boxes" in Belgium at Wachtebeke, Brussels, Antwerp, and Liège; there were a dozen frontier passages; boatmen bore messages along the Rivers Scheldt and Meuse;

the habitual smugglers below Sittard brought information out of Germany and but few of the *promeneurs, passeurs*, and train-watchers sent into Belgium to gather information regarding German activities were apprehended—for a time.

The success of the British organization puzzled not only the hostile, but also the Allied Counter-Espionage Services in Holland. The Hauptmann von Eberfeldt invited Paul Leipschitz to dine with him.

"Mynheer," said the Head of the German Counter-Espionage Service in Holland, "you have, in the past, rendered valuable services to my country——"

"For which I have been paid most generously," smiled the Dutchman.

Von Eberfeldt acknowledged the interruption with a stiff little bow.

"There are greater rewards to be earned," he said, with a hint of sarcasm. "This Herr Walford, now, whom we all know to be acting in the interests of England—you might become more intimate with him!"

"It would be difficult," Leipschitz faltered. "I have not troubled to hide my hatred of the British."

"But you have not quarrelled with him?"

"No."

"Then cultivate him. We will pay well for information leading to the destruction of his organization."

Tom Walford received a call from Paul Leipschitz upon the following morning and the men remained closeted together for a long time. Thereafter the same sort of people, and particularly women, who had come to his house at Zutfen by night, began frequenting the office of Paul Leipschitz in Rotterdam and, incidentally, several bargees who, besides conveying food to the Dutch and American relief organizations in Belgium and France along the many canals, had been in the habit of conveying valuable information collected by *promeneurs*, were caught red-handed and promptly executed.

Von Eberfeldt was proud of the inspiration which had led him to enlist the help of the limping Leipschitz. "Letter-boxes," too, were identified, *passeurs* were caught and further executions followed. Nevertheless the efficiency of the British Counter-Espionage organization remained unimpaired.

Among the women agents who visited Leipschitz was a certain Clothilde Bruun, of whom, at first, he was suspicious, because of a vague sense of familiarity which her personality aroused. It was a sensation so indefinite that he could not for the life of him remember whether he had seen her before in London or Berlin, although he was virtually certain that they had met previously in one or other of those cities.

Clothilde, for her part, proved reticent, or gave evasive answers to his guarded questions. Apart from the excellent work she did for him, he could not make the girl out. There was something of mystery and a certain haunting sadness about her. Many of the best female agents in the various secret services were no better than prostitutes, but Clothilde Bruun, quite definitely, did not come into that category. She had a quaint air of virginal sanctity, which seemed to be strangely at variance with the profession she had adopted. She did not appear to have become a spy through motives of patriotism, for she would confess to no nationality, and had, upon occasion, asserted laughingly that she owed allegiance to no particular country.

For a time Leipschitz suspected her of being of that most dangerous type, the international spy, who has no loyalty and is always ready to sell information to the highest bidder.

Nevertheless the girl served him well, often obtained the most valuable information and thus gradually gained both his confidence and his liking. Despite these circumstances, Clothilde herself could not make up her mind which side her employer was serving, for Paul Leipschitz was exceedingly clever and although he demanded information from her of troop movements in Belgium he gave her messages, just as frequently, to pass on to the German High Command. The playing of this double game on his part enabled her to come and go between Holland and Germany and Belgium by the frontier passages which her employer no longer used.

It was the capture of another of his agents, a sixteen-year-old Belgian girl named Marie, which finally revealed to Clothilde the true nature of her employer's allegiance.

Marie had proved the best type of agent since she was fourteen, for she was fired by a veritable Jeanne d'Arc spirit of patriotism and, moreover, her rosy, peasant cheeks and innocent blue eyes had endeared her to the old family men of the German Landsturm troops who guarded the deadly high-voltage fence delimiting the frontier.

By making particular friends with one of these old German soldiers, to whom she often took little dainties from her mother's kitchen, Marie had been able to get messages to a man in Wachtebeke who subsequently furnished valuable information as to a big concentration of German troops in the Wachtebeke-Moerbeke-Lokeren sector. The divisions making the concentration were from the Polish marshes and it was vitally important to find out for what purpose they were to be used on the Western Front. Marie was carrying the required report from the man at Wachtebeke, cleverly concealed on her person, when she was caught in the Selzaete sector by a German plain-clothes Secret Service man. The evidence against the child was damningly complete.

Leipschitz was appalled when he heard of the capture. He had often spoken to the child, without letting her have a notion of who he was, and, apart from that, had felt an abounding admiration for her resourcefulness and courage.

His first generous instinct was to slip across the frontier and to contrive her escape at any cost. Cool consideration brought wiser councils, for Leipschitz was, in reality, Chief of the British Counter-Espionage Service in Holland. As such, his life was worth the lives of many agents; for upon his genius the success of that organization depended. Remove him suddenly and the whole edifice he had so carefully erected would collapse like a house of cards.

To make matters worse, he was far from being

unaware of how closely he had been watched of late by recognized German agents in Rotterdam. He had a habit of limping about the streets, markets and harbours of the city, stopping here to gaze into a shop window that was being redressed, halting there to finger, and perhaps rearrange, the wares displayed upon some open stall, or he would sit drinking in dockside taverns with sailors and stevedores sometimes for hours on end. After such excursions he would work patiently behind the locked door of his room far into the night with a thin code book open at his elbow.

Lately all his actions had been carefully observed and once the door of his room had been tried stealthily while he was hard at work, but the passage beyond had been empty by the time he got the door open.

No, it certainly would not do for him to enter any territory that was in German occupation and so he sent for Clothilde Bruun.

"Clothilde," he said quietly, "a catastrophe has befallen. Marie has been captured; she is but a child and yet was one of our best *passeurs.*"

Clothilde dropped her eyes, lest the man should see the gleam of excited interest which must have shone in them.

"Marie—a Belgian, eh?" she queried.

"A Belgian refugee," he agreed.

"Then you really are working against Germany?"

"Does it matter for whom we work," he countered, "so long as both of us are well paid?"

"Not in the least," she shrugged. "What do you want me to do?"

Paul Leipschitz leaned eagerly across the table.

"Will you slip through the frontier passage at Selzaete and go to Wachtebeke?" he said. "Go to the last house but one in the village and if you see a flower-pot in the window it will be safe for you to approach M.29. He will tell you where Marie is imprisoned. Contrive her escape if you can; if that is not possible use every means in your power to get her sentence commuted to imprisonment. They are pretty well certain to sentence her to death in the first place, for she was caught red-handed."

"Very good," said Clothilde Bruun, and left her employer abruptly.

A fortnight later Paul Leipschitz received a message from M.29 to the effect that the death sentence passed on Marie had been commuted to one of imprisonment for the duration of the war, but of Clothilde he received no word.

That Clothilde Bruun had been able to arrange matters thus satisfactorily was not in the least surprising. After taking the precaution of satisfying herself as to the identity of M.29—the unfortunate man was shot in the cold of a grey dawn a fortnight later—she had stayed only for a short interview with the Officer Commanding the German troops before going straight through to Berlin.

Old Count von Reichofen, Chief of the Intelligence Department, received her in friendly fashion, for he knew that she would not have risked making the journey unless she had urgent information of the most important character to convey.

"Well, Count," she said, "I've got what you wanted. The Head of the British Secret Service in Holland is our pseudo-spy—Mynheer Paul Leipschitz."

"Paul Leipschitz! Impossible!" cried the Count. "Why, he risked his life by going to London to get the most valuable information about the British Navy. Besides, he has sent us much accurate information since then."

Clothilde crossed her silk-clad legs and lit a cigarette with slow deliberation.

"Information that *would* have been valuable *if* it had reached you in time, or *if* the British had not altered their plans so opportunely for themselves," she corrected. "I think Leipschitz has changed a great deal since he returned from London."

"You mean——?"

"A change of heart. He's the same man right enough, if one may go by the various portraits with which you provided me."

"But, Fräulein——" protested Reichofen.

Clothilde crushed out her cigarette and tapping out each point upon the edge of the great man's desk with the tip of a slender forefinger she set out, detail by detail, the evidence she had collected against Paul Leipschitz, right down to the damning corroboration of his own inferred admissions, supported by the orders he had given her concerning the child-spy named Marie.

After an hour or more had passed, the Count sat back, convinced at last.

"So!" His breath escaped in a gusty sigh and his fists clenched savagely. "So! He must be enticed into Belgium, or Germany, and dealt with. Will you be the pretty bait, *mein liebchen*?"

"Gladly, Count," replied Clothilde, "but can things be arranged just so simply?"

"You mean——?"

"Mynheer Leipschitz is a Dutch subject, whose hatred of the British is well-known in his own country. Also, there may be evidence in existence that he has served the Fatherland. To merely deal with him in our own land, or for trespassing in occupied territory, would cause bad feeling in Holland, *unless it could be proved that he was caught red-handed*."

"Then you suggest—what?"

Clothilde uncrossed her legs and folded her arms upon the desk as she leaned forward. Her great eyes blazed into the brooding ones of Karl von Reichofen.

"He has a fondness for me," she murmured. "If he believed I was in danger he might come."

"But that would not supply such evidence as would convict him to the satisfaction of his own people."

"Give me leave to finish, my Commandant."

"A thousand pardons, Fräulein. You were saying——?"

"I was about to tell you that Paul Leipschitz is moving heaven and earth to discover for what purpose the divisions are to be used that have come from the Russian front to the Wachtebeke-Moerbeke-Lokeren area. If he could be persuaded that I am in danger *because* I have obtained, and am prepared to hand over to him,

a copy of the orders for the disposition of those newly arrived divisions, then I think he would come to me in any place I care to name."

"Splendid!" cried the Count, thumping the desk. "A special set of plausible, but entirely false, orders shall be prepared at once."

The beautiful spy smiled a slow, contemptuous smile.

"You underrate the intelligence and the extensive knowledge of this man, my Commandant. He is himself an expert in supplying nearly true, or too-late authentic information. If I am to go through with this business you must entrust me with the real orders—or none at all."

"But suppose he snatches them from you and makes off at once?" protested von Reichofen.

"He is too chivalrous. I shall meet him at a house I know of in Wachtebeke—M.29, the agent who occupies it, can be removed just before Leipschitz is due to arrive and a certain flower-pot will be standing in the window. There I shall play the love-sick maiden who, to induce him to stay the night, will not give up the orders until her passion for him is satiated."

"But——" broke in the Chief of Intelligence.

"Oh, I know all about my enviable reputation for chastity," smiled Clothilde. "Do not worry about me, I can look after myself. Have the house surrounded and let your men enter when I remove the flower-pot from the window. I want time to find out as much as possible about the organization he has created."

Thus were matters arranged and hence when Paul Leipschitz was becoming really anxious over the prolonged absence of Clothilde Bruun a message was passed on to him, in all innocence, by M.29.

The message was remarkably cryptic, but cleverly conveyed its meaning to the man who held the main clue and was, moreover, not unused to the deepest kind of cogitation.

Once he understood the situation and realized that Clothilde was being hunted for her life, the effect upon Paul Leipschitz was remarkable, although in the case of a younger man, with the hot blood of youth flowing fast in his veins, it might have been easily understandable. In the first shock of receiving such news the fact that the girl was in possession of the all important Move, or Operation, Orders for the German divisions which had been released from the Russian front made no appreciable impression upon his mind. All he thought of was the fragrant sweetness of Clothilde as he had known, and not, he feared, appreciated her. Even that vague familiarity, that feeling of having known her elsewhere, which had caused him to distrust her slightly was forgotten.

By reason of his Secret Service training, however, the subsidiary, but, from considerations of duty, far more important, information contained in the message at last claimed his attention.

He would have liked to get in touch again with M.29 before moving, but that was impossible, because the message fixed a rendezvous for the next night at the last house but one in the main street of Wachtebeke.

Wherefore Paul Leipschitz laid his plans as carefully as possible and after dusk upon the following evening slipped across the Dutch border by the frontier passage at Selzaete, hard by the place where little Marie had been apprehended.

The night was intensely dark and a blinding rainstorm lashed pitilessly across the flat fields over which the man, disguised as a peasant whom no-one would have recognized as Paul Leipschitz, trudged doggedly. Surprisingly enough his habitual limp had disappeared. That limp, in fact, lay buried in the grave of the real Paul Leipschitz, who had faced a firing squad one morning in that tragic little rifle range at the grim old Tower of London.

The British Agent who had taken the dead Dutchman's place arrived at the rendezvous in Wachtebeke a full hour before the time appointed. The expected shadow of the flower-pot showed against the lamplit blind of the living-room and the door was unlatched; but to the British Agent's no small annoyance M.29 was absent.

"H'm," said the man who had been known as Leipschitz, "whether he's here or not doesn't much matter. I've an hour in which to make myself both comfortable and presentable before Clothilde arrives."

After locking the front door of the cottage he rummaged through the scullery for some time before unearthing an ancient wash tub. He had already set two kettles and four saucepans full of water upon the fire he had made up.

Then he went back to the living-room for the rush basket in which he had carried, wrapped in a ground-sheet, a suit of clothes suitable for the portly figure of Mynheer Leipschitz, together with sundry parcels of padding.

As he stooped to take up the basket he noticed for the first time a dull stain which was soaking brownly into the floor-boards. That stain was wet to the touch and the mark it left upon his questing finger was sticky and red, not brown.

A low whistle of surprise escaped from the man's lips. Then, quickly, he hid the rush basket and its contents in the grate of an unlighted copper. It is noteworthy that he laid close to hand, while he took his bath, a heavy revolver which was fitted with a silencer. It may appear strange that in the circumstances he showed no signs of panic; but, as he saw things, if M.29 had been caught and killed that night in the living-room adjoining, the man's murderers would by this time have taken their departure, well satisfied with their night's work. In which case Clothilde would find the coast well clear.

If, on the other hand, his own advent had been anticipated, the house, most certainly, would be surrounded already, so that there would be no possible harm in comforting his cold body by means of a hot bath.

The one eventuality for which he did not legislate was the arrival of Clothilde some time in advance of the hour of their assignation. And Clothilde, anxious to make sure that the removal of M.29 had been carried out without too much disturbance, came to the cottage within a few minutes of the man she had known as Leipschitz completing his bath.

Turning the well-oiled lock with a skeleton-key, she entered the dark living-room without making a sound. At once she became aware of a light in the scullery, where someone was singing softly. One glimpse she had of the back view of a lean, hard body, and then saw reflected in a mirror hung upon the scullery wall, the features of a face that she had never forgotten. Slowly the blood drained from her cheeks, leaving her pale and swaying slightly, for she was half stifled by the tumultuous beating of her heart, which, at first, had seemed to stand still for an age-long while. Very quietly she crept out again into the howling gale to wait patiently, despite the driving rain and tearing wind, until a light sprang up in the cottage living-room. Then she advanced and knocked four times on the door in a manner which would be recognized by M.29—or his master.

The man who opened to her was Mynheer Leipschitz to the very life; so wonderful, indeed, was the make-up that Clothilde was almost tempted to rub her eyes. No-one, however, knew better than she what a marvellous alteration can be made in the appearance of a person by the use of rubber pads held in the cheeks, plasticine to alter the shape of the nose, and padding to increase the girth of an otherwise good figure.

"Ah, my dear Clothilde, I am glad to see you," she was welcomed, and the voice had the slight thick oleaginousness that one associates with the voices of fat men who will never again see fifty. "I have come to meet you, of course, but the long tramp across those infernally heavy fields between here and Selzaete has made me more lame than ever."

Clothilde was watching him closely, trying to detect in the Mynheer Leipschitz who stood before her some trace of that Jim Lockton whom she had known long years ago in London and whose face she had seen again for one fleeting instant reflected in a mirror that very night. But neither in features, form, nor voice could she detect one single resemblance to the man she had known—and loved—in the long ago. For one wild moment she almost believed that both Leipschitz and Lockton had been in the cottage together and that Jim had departed by the back door while the other had remained. She had almost believed, that is, until she remembered that the small dwelling was entirely surrounded by soldiers of those troops from the Russian front, the orders for whose operations the British Agent had crossed the frontier to secure.

"Well," queried Leipschitz, "why do you look at me so strangely, Clothilde?"

"Oh," she murmured brokenly, "why did you come?" and before he could answer her she pushed him into the room and, turning, locked the door. Not satisfied with that she shot home the bolts at top and bottom, and would have closed the shutters also, but dared not remove the flower-pot from the window-ledge.

"There, there, my dear," he soothed and placed his hand affectionately upon her shoulder. At his touch she trembled like a frightened filly and, again, a low, distressful moan broke from her lips. "Why, Clothilde," he continued, "this is not like you. We're perfectly safe, my dear; of what are you afraid? I've brought food with me. Let us eat it while we wait for the storm to blow itself out and then we'll slip back home to Holland. I'm beginning to think that you've just about played your part in this game of ours."

"Too well," she answered bitterly. "I've played my part too well."

His eyes clouded suddenly, for he remembered that sinister stain upon the floor and wondered if she had betrayed M.29. But the question he put concerned the plans he had been led to believe that she would bring to their rendezvous.

"The Operation Orders for the divisions from the Russian front are safe," she answered. "It is you who are in danger. Before we talk of that, however, tell me one thing truly, Paul. Are you the international spy you have tried to make me believe you to be, or do you honestly serve England."

"Why, whatever difference does it make?" he smiled.

"Just all the difference in the world, Paul," she answered. "For a time I mistook you for a double agent, fancied that you were pretending to serve the Allies, but in reality were working for Germany. The fact that the information you sent to Berlin was accurate, but as a rule useless, first made me suspicious of you. The affair of Marie opened my eyes a good deal wider."

"And so——?" questioned Jim Lockton.

"And so I went to Berlin and told my story to the Chief of the Intelligence Department."

Jim Lockton's glittering eyes looked hard as agate and his hand closed upon the butt of the revolver in his pocket.

"Then you have been working for Germany all the time," he asserted.

"As you have been working for England," she countered. "But I have this justification, that my mother was a German by birth."

Slowly the hand that held the revolver emerged from Jim Lockton's pocket, but the sight of the weapon, which would make no sound that might be heard above the raging of the storm, did not alarm Clothilde.

"There's no need for that, Paul," she said wearily. "The house is surrounded and there can be no escape, unless——"

The girl faltered and the man cut in harshly.

"Unless what? You know the penalty for betrayal in the game we play."

"That doesn't matter either. But I've been thinking, remembering things perhaps, and so I've changed my mind."

"Too late perhaps." The words were charged with sarcasm, but there was infinite sweetness in the woman's answering smile.

"Listen, Paul," she said, "for I want you to understand my motives. I have hated England because my father was cashiered—unjustly, as I think—and shot himself. The shock killed my mother and, as I was left almost destitute I went to London. I could get no work, for I had no qualifications and so the easy road for a penniless girl lay open. I used to frequent a place in Glasshouse Street, but before the fatal first step was taken a strange thing happened. One night I went to the 'Folkestone' with three or four foreigners who had pestered me before and were very set upon making me drunk so that my downfall could be accomplished. It would not have been difficult, anyway, for the last of my small store of money was finished."

She paused for a moment, brooding eyes looking back into the past. The man stirred restlessly, for now he was able to interpret that vague feeling of familiarity he had always experienced in her presence.

"I was saved," she went on, "by a certain Jim Lockton whom I knew very slightly. He was in the 'Folkestone' that night and called me over to him. When he would have left the place the foreigners interfered and there was a fight. Oh, but he was splendid!" she cried, clasping her hands.

"Well, what happened afterwards? Did he keep you?" queried the man.

"Ah, no," she answered, "he wasn't that sort. He would have helped me with money perhaps, but the very next day I obtained a post as nursery governess in the family of a German officer who was returning to Berlin. From that I drifted easily into the German Secret Service—you see I am such a good linguist and something of an actress. Now I've made up my mind to repay the debt I owe to the memory of Jim Lockton."

"How?" The question came harshly, but there was a certain tenderness lurking somewhere at the back of the man's eyes.

"Listen, Paul," she answered eagerly, "the plan was to trap you here, with the Operation Orders for the divisions from the Russian front in your possession——"

"The *real* orders?" he demanded urgently.

"Yes, yes, you shall have them, Paul, but don't interrupt. I—I was to drug you, and the soldiers, who are waiting, were to enter when I removed the flower-pot from the window-ledge. They cannot know who is here, although they have your description, for they were not posted when I arrived. You must change your appearance as much as possible, Paul, and leave quite openly. If you are questioned you can tell them that I have sent you away because I am waiting for someone else, but you must conceal your lameness."

"That can be managed," Jim Lockton answered thoughtfully, and added: "But what will happen to you?"

For a barely perceptible fraction of a second she hesitated.

"Why, how dull you are, Paul," she laughed. "I shall tell them, of course, that you never came, and presently I shall join you in Rotterdam."

"Good," said he, "and perhaps there will be a surprise prepared against your arrival. I think that you and this Jim Lockton ought to meet again."

At last Clothilde saw the light in his eyes and knew that happiness, such as she had never experienced, was very near, but the rest of the road was yet to tread. Well she knew that her every movement had been watched that night, that the arrival of the man believed to be Leipschitz had, in all human probability, been observed. On the other hand, she argued, the troops would be likely to let any other person pass, who might leave the cottage, since they had been given definite orders neither to act, nor to interfere, until the flowerpot was removed from the window. Wherefore she lied bravely, looking him straight in the eyes and so, presently, persuaded him to go into the scullery and make ready for his return journey.

The slim young peasant who emerged in due course was like neither Leipschitz nor Jim Lockton and he did not limp. The complete metamorphosis was incredible and Clothilde eyed the stranger with almost professional approval. Jim's eyes, however, were fixed eagerly upon the thin sheets of typewritten orders she had laid on the table.

The girl would have hastened him away at once, but he would not take the orders with him, so sat down to commit them to memory before burning the document. This was fortunate, for subsequently, he was most thoroughly searched before being allowed to pass through the cordon of troops that encircled the cottage.

At last, when he bade good-bye to Clothilde, it seemed for a moment that he would take her into his arms, but that moment passed unused. Perhaps there lingered in his mind some doubt of her sincerity; perhaps he imagined fondly, not knowing what she knew, that any present revelation of his true personality would make parting too hard. In any case, he went his way, leaving unspoken the words which had trembled on his tongue.

Through the rest of that night Clothilde sat staring into the glowing embers of a dying fire, nothing heeding and nothing needing, living only in her memories.

At dawn the officer commanding the troops knocked heavily upon the door. Clothilde made one brave attempt to bluff her way out of the desperate situation, but the Count von Reichofen, never quite trusting her, had told the officer a great deal more than she suspected. The arrival overnight of the man who called himself Leipschitz had been observed and that circumstance, combined with her inability to produce the all-important Operation Orders, sealed her fate.

In Rotterdam Jim Lockton waited with what patience he could summon, but hope waned as the weeks went by. M.29 was dead, the frontier passage at Selzaete closed and so the war was ended before he learnt, for certain, of the execution of the woman who had taken the name of Clothilde Bruun.

WORLD WAR II

THE ARMY OF THE SHADOWS

ERIC AMBLER

ALONG WITH W. SOMERSET MAUGHAM, Eric Ambler (1909–1998) is one of the two most significant creators of the modern spy story. Unlike the earlier patriotic heroes of espionage fiction (as well as Ian Fleming's later James Bond thrillers and their imitators) who fearlessly battle enemy agents, Ambler's major characters are generally victims of circumstance who perform no willing acts of bravery but extricate themselves as best they can in order to survive. His goal, admirably achieved, was to add realism to the cloak-and-dagger stereotypes.

Born in London, Ambler studied engineering but soon quit to write songs and sketches for vaudeville acts, followed by writing advertising copy. His first book, *The Dark Frontier* (1936), anticipated something similar to the atom bomb but had little success. His next five, however, are generally regarded as among the greatest classics in the genre: *Uncommon Danger* (1937; US title, *Background to Danger*), *Epitaph for a Spy* (1938); *Cause for Alarm* (1938), *The Mask of Dimitrios* (1939; US title, *A Coffin for Dimitrios*), and *Journey into Fear* (1940).

Joining the army as a private in 1940, he was quickly commissioned and served with a combat film unit in Italy and then was named assistant director of army cinemaphotography in the War Office, in charge of all training, educational, and morale films for the British Army; he was discharged in 1946 as a lieutenant colonel.

After the war, Ambler wrote and produced several films for the J. Arthur Rank Organization, being nominated for an Academy Award for his screenplay of the 1953 film *The Cruel Sea*, based on a novel by Nicholas Monsarrat.

Perhaps Ambler's most famous novel is *The Mask of Dimitrios*, which was selected for the Haycraft-Queen Definitive Library of Detective-Crime-Mystery Fiction. It was released on film with the same title in 1944, starring Zachary Scott, Sydney Greenstreet, Peter Lorre, and Faye Emerson.

Numerous other films were based on Ambler's novels, the most successful being *Topkapi* (1964), based on his Edgar-winning novel *The Light of Day* (1962), an exciting caper-comedy starring Melina Mercouri, Peter Ustinov, Maximilian Schell, and Robert Morley.

"The Army of the Shadows" was originally published in *The Queen's Book of the Red Cross* (London, Hodder & Stoughton, 1939); it was first collected in *Waiting for Orders* (New York, The Mysterious Press, 1991).

THE ARMY OF THE SHADOWS

ERIC AMBLER

IT IS THREE YEARS since Llewellyn removed my appendix; but we still meet occasionally. I am dimly related to his wife: that, at least, is the pretext for the acquaintanceship. The truth is that, during my convalescence, we happened to discover that we both like the same musicians. Before the war we usually met when there was some Sibelius being played and went to hear it together. I was a little puzzled when, about three weeks ago, he telephoned with the suggestion that I should dine at his house that night. There was not, I knew, a concert of any sort in London. I agreed, however, to grope my way round to Upper Wimpole Street shortly before eight o'clock.

It was not until he had presented me with a brandy that I found out why I had been invited to dinner.

"Do you remember," he said suddenly, "that I spent a week or so in Belgrade last year? I missed Beecham doing the Second through it. There was one of those international medical bun fights being held there, and I went to represent the Association. My German is fairly good, you know. I motored. Can't stick trains. Anyway, on the way back a very funny thing happened to me. Did I ever tell you about it?"

"I don't think so."

"I thought not. Well"—he laughed self-consciously—"it was so funny now there's a war on that I've been amusing myself by writing the whole thing down. I wondered whether you'd be good enough to cast a professional eye over it for me. I've tried"—he laughed again—"to make a really literary job of it. Like a story, you know."

His hand had been out of sight behind the arm of his chair, but now it emerged from hiding holding a wad of typewritten sheets.

"It's typed," he said, planking it down on my knees. And then, with a theatrical glance at his watch, "Good Lord, it's ten. There's a telephone call I must make. Excuse me for a minute or two, will you?"

He was out of the room before I could open my mouth to reply. I was left alone with the manuscript.

I picked it up. It was entitled "A Strange Encounter." With a sigh, I turned over the title-page and began, rather irritably, to read:

The Stelvio Pass is snowed up in winter, and towards the end of November most sensible men driving to Paris from Belgrade or beyond take the long way round via Milan rather than risk being stopped by an early fall of snow. But I was in a hurry and took a chance. By the time I reached Bolzano I was sorry I had done so. It was bitterly cold, and the sky ahead was leaden. At Merano I seriously considered turning back. Instead, I pushed on as hard as I could go. If I had had any sense I should have stopped for petrol before I started the really serious part of the climb. I had six gallons by the gauge then. I knew that it wasn't accurate, but I had filled up early that morning and calculated that I had enough to get me to Sargans. In my anxiety to beat the snow I overlooked the fact that I had miles of low-gear driving to do. On the Swiss side and on the Sargans road where it runs within a mile or two of the Rhätikon part of the German frontier, the car spluttered to a standstill.

For a minute or two I sat there swearing at and to myself and wondering what on earth I was going to do. I was, I knew, the only thing on the road that night for miles.

It was about eight o'clock, very dark and very cold. Except for the faint creaking of the cooling engine and the rustle of the breeze in some nearby trees, there wasn't a sound to be heard. Ahead, the road in the headlights curved away to the right. I got out the map and tried to find out where I was.

I had passed through one village since I left Klosters, and I knew that it was about ten kilometres back. I must, therefore, either walk back ten kilometres to that village, or forward to the next village, whichever was the nearer. I looked at the map. It was of that useless kind that they sell to motorists. There was nothing marked between Klosters and Sargans. For all I knew, the next village might be fifteen or twenty kilometres away.

An Alpine road on a late November night is not the place to choose if you want to sleep in your car. I decided to walk back the way I had come.

I had a box of those small Italian waxed matches with me when I started out. There were, I thought, about a hundred in the box,

and I calculated that, if I struck one every hundred metres, they would last until I reached the village.

That was when I was near the lights of the car. When I got out of sight of them, things were different. The darkness seemed to press against the backs of my eyes. It was almost painful. I could not even see the shape of the road along which I was walking. It was only by the rustling and the smell of resin that I knew that I was walking between fir trees. By the time I had covered a mile I had six matches left. Then it began to snow.

I say "snow." It had been snow; but the Sargans road was still below the snow-line, and the stuff came down as a sort of half-dozen mush that slid down my face into the gap between my coat collar and my neck.

I must have done about another mile and a half when the real trouble began. I still had the six matches, but my hands were too numb to get them out of the box without wetting them, and I had been going forward blindly, sometimes on the road and sometimes off it. I was wondering whether I would get along better if I sang, when I walked into a telegraph post.

It was of pre-cast concrete and the edge was as sharp as a razor. My face was as numb as my hands and I didn't feel much except a sickening jar; but I could taste blood trickling between my teeth and found that my nose was bleeding. It was as I held my head back to stop it that I saw the light, looking for all the world as if it were suspended in mid-air above me.

It wasn't suspended in mid-air, and it wasn't above me. Darkness does strange things to perspective. After a few seconds I saw that it was showing through the trees on the hillside, up to the right of the road.

Anyone who has been in the sort of mess that I was in will know exactly how my mind worked at that moment. I did not speculate as to the origin of that God-forsaken light or as to whether or not the owner of it would be pleased to see me. I was cold and wet, my nose was bleeding, and I would not have cared if someone had told me that behind the light was a maniac with a machine-gun. I knew only that the light meant there was some sort of human habitation near me and that I was going to spend the night in it.

I moved over to the other side of the road and began to feel my way along the wire fence I found there. Twenty yards or so further on, my hands touched a wooden gate. The light was no longer visible, but I pushed the gate open and walked on into the blackness.

The ground rose steeply under my feet. It was a path of sorts, and soon I stumbled over the beginnings of a flight of log steps. There must have been well over a hundred of them. Then there was another stretch of path, not quite so steep. When I again saw the light, I was only about twenty yards from it.

It came from an oil reading-lamp standing near a window. From the shape of the window and the reflected light of the lamp, I could see that the place was a small chalet of the kind usually let to families for the summer season or for the winter sports. That it should be occupied at the end of November was curious. But I didn't ponder over the curiosity: I had seen something else through the window besides the lamp. The light from a fire was flickering in the room.

I went forward up the path to the door. There was no knocker. I hammered on the wet, varnished wood with my fist and waited. There was no sound from inside. After a moment or two I knocked again. Still there was no sign of life within. I knocked and waited for several minutes. Then I began to shiver. In desperation I grabbed the latch of the door and rattled it violently. The next moment I felt it give and the door creaked open a few inches.

I think that I have a normal, healthy respect for the property and privacy of my fellow-creatures; but at that moment I was feeling neither normal nor healthy. Obviously, the owner of the chalet could not be far away. I stood there for a moment or two, hesitating. I could smell the wood smoke from the fire, and mingled with it a bitter, oily smell which seemed faintly familiar.

But all I cared about was the fire. I hesitated no longer and walked in.

As soon as I was inside I saw that there was something more than curious about the place, and that I should have waited.

The room itself was ordinary enough. It was rather larger than I had expected, but there were the usual pinewood walls, the usual pinewood floor, the usual pinewood staircase up to the bedrooms, and the usual tiled fireplace. There were the usual tables and chairs, too: turned and painted nonsense of the kind that sometimes finds its way into English tea shops. There were red gingham curtains over the windows. You felt that the owner probably had lots of other places just like it, and that he made a good thing out of letting them.

No, it was what had been added to the room that was curious. All the furniture had been crowded into one half of the space. In the other half, standing on linoleum and looking as if it were used a good deal, was a printing press.

The machine was a small treadle platten of the kind used by jobbing printers for running off tradesmen's circulars. It looked very old and decrepit. Alongside it on a trestle table were a case of type and a small proofing press with a locked-up forme in it. On a second table stood a pile of interleaved sheets, beside which was a stack of what appeared to be some of the same sheets folded. The folding was obviously being done by hand. I picked up one of the folded sheets.

It looked like one of those long, narrow business-promotion folders issued by travel agencies. The front page was devoted to the reproduction, in watery blue ink, of a lino-cut of a clump of pines on the shore of a lake, and the display of the name "TITISEE." Page two and the page folded in to face it carried a rhapsodical account in German of the beauties of Baden in general and Lake Titisee in particular.

I put the folder down. An inaccessible Swiss chalet was an odd place to choose for printing German travel advertisements; but I was not disposed to dwell on its oddity. I was cold.

I was moving towards the fire when my eye was caught by five words printed in bold capitals on one of the unfolded sheets on the table: "DEUTSCHE MÄNNER UND FRAUEN, KAMERADEN!"

I stood still. I remember that my heart thudded against my ribs as suddenly and violently as it had earlier that day on the Stelvio when some crazy fool in a Hispano had nearly crowded me off the road.

I leaned forward, picked the folder up again, and opened it right out. The Message began on the second of the three inside pages.

GERMAN MEN AND WOMEN, COMRADES! We speak to you with the voice of German Democracy, bringing you news. Neither Nazi propaganda nor the Gestapo can silence us, for we have an ally which is proof against floggings, an ally which no man in the history of the world has been able to defeat. That ally is Truth. Hear then, people of Germany, the Truth which is concealed from you. Hear it, remember it, and repeat it. The sooner the Truth is known, the sooner will Germany again hold up its head among the free nations of the world.

Then followed a sort of news bulletin consisting of facts and figures (especially figures) about the economic condition of Germany. There was also news of a strike in the Krupp works at Essen and a short description of a riot outside a shipyard in Hamburg.

I put it down again. Now I knew why these "travel advertisements" were being printed in an inaccessible Swiss chalet instead of in Germany itself. No German railway official would distribute these folders. That business would be left to more desperate men. These folders would not collect dust on the counters of travel agencies. They would be found in trains and in trams, in buses and in parked cars, in waiting rooms and in bars under restaurant plates and inside table napkins. Some of the men that put them there would be caught and tortured to betray their fellows; but the distribution would go on. The folders would be read, perhaps furtively discussed. A little more truth would seep through Goebbels' dam of lies to rot still further the creaking foundation of Nazidom.

Then, as I stood there with the smell of wood smoke and printing in my nostrils, as I stood staring at that decrepit little machine as if were the very voice of freedom, I heard footsteps outside.

I suppose that I should have stood my ground. I had, after all, a perfectly good explanation of my presence there. My car and the blood from my nose would confirm my story. But I didn't reason that way. I had stumbled on a secret, and my first impulse was to try to hide the fact from the owner of the secret. I obeyed that impulse.

I looked around quickly and saw the stairs. Before I had even begun to wonder if I might not be doing something excessively stupid, I was up the stairs and opening the first door I came to on the landing. In the half-light I caught a glimpse of a bed; then I was inside the room with the door slightly ajar. I could see across the landing and through the wooden palings along it to the top of the window at the far side of the room below.

I knew that someone had come in: I could hear him moving about. He lit another lamp. There was a sound from the door and a second person entered.

A woman's voice said in German, "Thank God, Johann has left a good fire."

There was an answering grunt. It came from the man. I could almost feel them warming their hands.

"Get the coffee, Freda," said the man suddenly. "I must go back soon."

"But Bruno is there. You should take a little rest first."

"Bruno is a Berliner. He is not as used to the

cold as I am. If Kurt should come now he would be tired. Bruno could only look after himself."

There was silence for a moment. Then the woman spoke again.

"Do you really think he will come now, Stephan? It is so late." She paused. Her voice had sounded casual, elaborately casual; but now, as she went on, there was an edge to it that touched the nerves. "I can keep quite calm about it, you see, Stephan. I wish to believe, but it is so late, isn't it? You don't think he will come now, do you? Admit it."

He laughed, but too heartily. "You are too nervous, Freda. Kurt can take care of himself. He knows all the tricks now. He may have been waiting for the first snow. The frontier guards would not be so alert on a night like this."

"He should have been back a week ago. You know that as well as I do, Stephan. He has never been delayed so long before. They have got him. That is all. You see, I can be calm about it even though he is my dear husband." And then her voice broke. "I knew it would happen sooner or later. I knew it. First Hans, then Karl, and now Kurt. Those swine, those—"

She sobbed and broke suddenly into passionate weeping. He tried helplessly to comfort her.

I had heard enough. I was shaking from head to foot; but whether it was the cold or not, I don't know. I stood back from the door. Then, as I did so, I heard a sound from behind me.

I had noticed the bed as I had slipped into the room, but the idea that there might be someone in it had not entered my head. Now, as I whipped around, I saw that I had made a serious mistake.

Sitting on the edge of the bed in which he had been lying was a very thin, middle-aged man in a nightshirt. By the faint light from the landing I could see his eyes, bleary from sleep, and his grizzled hair standing ludicrously on end. But for one thing I should have laughed. That one thing was the large automatic pistol which he held pointed at me. His hand was as steady as a rock.

"Don't move," he said. He raised his voice. "Stephan! Come quickly!"

"I must apologize . . ." I began in German.

"You will be allowed to speak later."

I heard Stephan dash up the stairs.

"What is it, Johann?"

"Come here."

The door was pushed open behind me. I heard him draw in his breath sharply.

"Who is it?"

"I do not know. I was awakened by a noise. I was about to get up when this man came into the room. He did not see me. He has been listening to your conversation. He must have been examining the plant when he heard you returning."

"If you will allow me to explain . . ." I began.

"You may explain downstairs," said the man called Stephan. "Give me the pistol, Johann."

The pistol changed hands and I could see Stephan, a lean, raw-boned fellow with broad, sharp shoulders and dangerous eyes. He wore black oilskins and gum boots. I saw the muscles in his cheeks tighten.

"Raise your hands and walk downstairs. Slowly. If you run, I shall shoot immediately. March."

I went downstairs.

The woman, Freda, was standing by the door, staring blankly up at me as I descended. She must have been about thirty and had that soft rather matronly look about her that is characteristic of so many young German women. She was short and plump, and as if to accentuate the fact, her straw-coloured hair was plaited across her head. Wisps of the hair had become detached and clung wetly to the sides of her neck. She too wore a black oilskin coat and gum boots.

The grey eyes, red and swollen with crying, looked beyond me.

"Who is it, Stephan?"

"He was hiding upstairs."

We had reached the foot of the stairs. He motioned me away from the door and towards the fire. "Now, we will hear your explanation."

I gave it with profuse apologies. I admitted that I had examined the folders and read one. "It seemed to me," I concluded, "that my presence might be embarrassing to you. I was about to leave when you returned. Then, I am afraid, I lost my head and attempted to hide."

Not one of them was believing a word that I was saying: I could see that from their faces. "I assure you," I went on in exasperation, "that what I am telling . . ."

"What nationality are you?"

"British. I . . ."

"Then speak English. What were you doing on this road?"

"I am on my way home from Belgrade. I crossed the Yugoslav frontier yesterday and the Italian frontier at Stelvio this afternoon. My passport was stamped at both places if you wish to . . ."

"Why were you in Belgrade?"

"I am a surgeon. I have been attending an international medical convention there."

"Let me see your passport, please."

"Certainly. I have . . ." And then with my hand in my inside pocket, I stopped. My heart felt as if it had come right into my throat. In my haste to be away after the Italian Customs had finished with me, I had thrust my passport with the Customs carnet for the car into the pocket beside me on the door of the car.

They were watching me with expressionless faces. Now, as my hand reappeared empty, I saw Stephan raise his pistol.

"Well?"

"I am sorry." Like a fool I had begun to speak in German again. "I find that I have left my passport in my car. It is several kilometres along the road. If . . ."

And then the woman burst out as if she couldn't stand listening to me any longer.

"Don't you see? Don't you see?" she cried. "It is quite clear. They have found out that we are here. Perhaps after all these months Hans or Karl has been tortured by them into speaking. And so they have taken Kurt and sent this man to spy upon us. It is clear. Don't you see?"

She turned suddenly, and I thought she was going to attack me. Then Stephan put his hand on her arm.

"Gently, Freda." He turned to me again, and

his expression hardened. "You see my friend, what is in our minds? We know our danger, you see. The fact that we are in Swiss territory will not protect us if the Gestapo should trace us. The Nazis, we know, have little respect for frontiers. The Gestapo have none. They would murder us here as confidently as they would if we were in the Third Reich. We do not underrate their cunning. The fact that you are not a German is not conclusive. You may be what you say you are: you may not. If you are, so much the better. If not, then, I give you fair warning, you will be shot. You say your passport is in your car several kilometres along the road. Unfortunately, it is not possible for us to spare time tonight to see if that is true. Nor is it possible for one of us to stand guard over you all night. You have already disturbed the first sleep Johann has had in twenty-four hours. There is only one thing for it, I'm afraid. It is undignified and barbaric; but I see no other way. We shall be forced to tie you up so that you cannot leave."

"But this is absurd," I cried angrily. "Good heavens, man, I realize that I've only myself to blame for being here; but surely you could have the common decency to . . ."

"The question," he said sternly, "is not of decency, but of necessity. We have no time tonight for six-kilometre walks. One of our comrades has been delivering a consignment of these folders to our friends in Germany. We hope and believe that he will return to us across the frontier tonight. He may need our help. Mountaineering in such weather is exhausting. Freda, get me some of the cord we use for tying the packages."

I wanted to say something, but the words would not come. I was too angry. I don't think that I've ever been so angry in my life before.

She brought the cord. It was thick grey stuff. He took it and gave the pistol to Johann. Then he came towards me.

I don't think they liked the business any more than I did. He had gone a bit white and he wouldn't look me in the eyes. I think that I must have been white myself; but it was anger with me. He put the cord under one of my elbows. I snatched it away.

"You had better submit," he said harshly.

"To spare your feelings? Certainly not. You'll have to use force, my friend. But don't worry. You'll get used to it. You'll be a good Nazi yet. You should knock me down. That'll make it easier."

What colour there was left in his face went. A good deal of my anger evaporated at that moment. I felt sorry for the poor devil. I really believe that I should have let him tie me up. But I never knew for certain; for at that moment there was an interruption.

It was the woman who heard it first—the sound of someone running up the path outside. The next moment a man burst wildly into the room.

Stephan had turned. "Bruno! What is it? Why aren't you at the hut?"

The man was striving to get his breath, and for a moment he could hardly speak. His face above the streaming oilskins was blue with cold. Then he gasped out.

"Kurt! He is at the hut! He is wounded—badly!"

The woman gave a little whimpering cry and her hands went to her face. Stephan gripped the newcomer's shoulder.

"What has happened? Quickly!"

"It was dark. The Swiss did not see him. It was one of our patrols. They shot him when he was actually on the Swiss side. He was wounded in the thigh. He crawled on to the hut, but he can go no further. He . . ."

But Stephan had ceased to listen. He turned sharply. "Johann, you must dress yourself at once. Bruno, take the pistol and guard this man. He broke in here. He may be dangerous. Freda, get the cognac and the iodine. We shall need them for Kurt."

He himself went to a cupboard and got out some handkerchiefs, which he began tearing feverishly into strips, which he knotted together. Still gasping for breath, the man had taken the pistol and was staring at me with a puzzled frown. Then the woman reappeared from the kitchen carrying a bottle of cognac and a small tube of iodine of the sort that is sold for dabbing at cut fingers. Stephan stuffed them in his pockets with the knotted handkerchiefs. Then he called up the stairs, "Hurry, Johann. We are ready to leave."

It was more than I could bear. Professional fussiness, I suppose.

"Has any one of you," I asked loudly, "ever dealt with a bullet wound before?"

They stared at me. Then Stephan glanced at Bruno.

"If he moves," he said, "shoot." He raised his voice again. "Johann!"

There was an answering cry of reassurance.

"Has it occurred to you," I persisted, "that even if you get him here alive, which I doubt, as you obviously don't know what you're doing, he will need immediate medical attention? Don't you think that one of you had better go for a doctor? Ah, but of course; the doctor would ask questions about a bullet wound, wouldn't he? The matter would be reported to the police."

"We can look after him," Stephan grunted. "Johann! Hurry!"

"It seems a pity," I said reflectively, "that one brave man should have to die because of his friends' stupidity." And then my calm deserted me. "You fool," I shouted. "Listen to me. Do you want to kill this man? You're going about it the right way. I'm a surgeon, and this is a surgeon's business. Take that cognac out of your pocket. We shan't need it. The iodine too. And those pieces of rag. Have you got two or three clean towels?"

The woman nodded stupidly.

"Then get them, please, and be quick. And you said something about some coffee. Have you a flask for it? Good. Then we shall take that. Put plenty of sugar in it. I want blankets, too. Three will be enough, but they must be kept dry. We shall need a stretcher. Get two poles or broomsticks and two old coats. We can make a stretcher of sorts by putting the pole through the sleeves of them. Take this cord of yours too. It will be useful to make slings for the stretcher, and hurry! The man may be bleeding to death. Is he far away?"

The man was glowering at me. "Four kilometres. In a climbing hut in the hills this side of the frontier." He stepped forward and gripped my arm. "If you are tricking us . . ." he began.

"I'm not thinking about you," I snapped. "I'm thinking about a man who's been crawling along with a bullet in his thigh and a touching faith in his friends. Now get those poles, and hurry."

They hurried. In three minutes they had the things collected. The exhausted Bruno's oilskins and gum boots had, at my suggestion, been transferred to me. Then I tied one of the blankets round my waist under my coat, and told Stephan and Johann to do the same.

"I," said the woman, "will take the other things."

"You," I said, "will stay here, please."

She straightened up at that. "No," she said firmly, "I will come with you. I shall be quite calm. You will see."

"Nevertheless," I said rather brutally, "you will be more useful here. A bed must be ready by the fire here. There must also be hot bricks and plenty of blankets. I shall need, besides, both boiled and boiling water. You have plenty of ordinary salt, I suppose?"

"Yes, *Herr Doktor*. But . . ."

"We are wasting time."

Two minutes later we left.

I shall never forget that climb. It began about half a mile along the road below the chalet. The first part was mostly up narrow paths between trees. They were covered with pine needles and, in the rain, as slippery as the devil. We had been climbing steadily for about half an hour when Stephan, who had been leading the way with a storm lantern, paused.

"I must put out the light here," he said. "The frontier is only three kilometres from here, and the guards patrol to a depth of two kilometres. They must not see us." He blew out the lamp. "Turn round," he said then. "You will see another light."

I saw it, far away below us, a pinpoint.

"That is our light. When we are returning from Germany, we can see it from across the frontier and know that we are nearly home and that our friends are waiting. Hold on to my coat now. You need not worry about Johann behind you. He knows the path well. This way, *Herr Doktor*."

It was the only sign he gave that he had decided to accept me for what I said I was.

I cannot conceive of how anyone could know that path well. The surface soon changed from pine needles to a sort of rocky rubble, and it twisted and turned like a wounded snake. The wind had dropped, but it was colder than ever, and I found myself crunching through sugary patches of half-frozen slush. I wondered how on earth we were going to bring down a wounded man on an improvised stretcher.

We had been creeping along without the light for about twenty minutes when Stephan stopped and, shielding the lamp with his coat, relit it. I saw that we had arrived.

The climbing hut was built against the side of an overhanging rock face. It was about six feet square inside, and the man was lying diagonally across it on his face. There was a large blood-stain on the floor beneath him. He was semi-conscious. His eyes were closed, but he mumbled something as I felt for his pulse.

"Will he live?" whispered Stephan.

I didn't know. The pulse was there, but it was feeble and rapid. His breathing was shallow. I looked at the wound. The bullet had entered on the inner side of the left thigh just below the groin. There was a little bleeding, but it obviously hadn't touched the femoral artery and, as far as I could see, the bone was all right. I made a dressing with one of the towels and tied it in place with another. The bullet could wait. The immediate danger was from shock aggravated by exposure. I got to work with the blankets and the flask of coffee. Soon the pulse strengthened a little, and after about half an hour I told them how to prepare the stretcher.

I don't know how they got him down that

path in the darkness. It was all I could do to get down by myself. It was snowing hard now in great fleecy chunks that blinded you when you moved forward. I was prepared for them to slip and drop the stretcher, but they didn't. It was slow work, however, and it was a good forty minutes before we got to the point where it was safe to light the lamp.

After that I was able to help with the stretcher. At the foot of the path up to the chalet, I went ahead with the lantern. The woman heard my footsteps and came to the door. I realized that we must have been gone for the best part of three hours.

"They're bringing him up," I said. "He'll be all right. I shall need your help now."

She said, "The bed is ready." And then, "Is it serious, *Herr Doktor*?"

"No." I didn't tell her then that there was a bullet to be taken out.

It was a nasty job. The wound itself wasn't so bad. The bullet must have been pretty well spent, for it had lodged up against the bone without doing any real damage. It was the instruments that made it difficult. They came from the kitchen. He didn't stand up to it very well, and I wasn't surprised. I didn't feel so good myself when I'd finished. The cognac came in useful after all.

We finally got him to sleep about five.

"He'll be all right now," I said.

The woman looked at me and I saw the tears begin to trickle down her cheeks. It was only then that I remembered that she wasn't a nurse, but his wife.

It was Johann who comforted her. Stephan came over to me.

"We owe you a great debt, *Herr Doktor*," he said. "I must apologize for our behaviour earlier this evening. We have not always been savages, you know. Kurt was a professor of zoology. Johann was a master printer. I was an architect. Now we are those who crawl across frontiers at night and plot like criminals. We have been treated like savages, and so we live like them. We forget sometimes that we were civilized. We ask

your pardon. I do not know how we can repay you for what you have done. We . . ."

But I was too tired for speeches. I smiled quickly at him.

"All that I need by way of a fee is another glass of cognac and a bed to sleep in for a few hours. I suggest, by the way, that you get a doctor in to look at the patient later today. There will be a little fever to treat. Tell the doctor he fell on his climbing axe. He won't believe you, but there'll be no bullet for him to be inquisitive about. Oh, and if you could find me a little petrol for my car . . ."

It was five in the afternoon and almost dark again when Stephan woke me. The local doctor, he reported, as he set an enormous tray of food down beside the bed, had been, dressed the wound, prescribed, and gone. My car was filled up with petrol and awaited me below if I wished to drive to Zurich that night. Kurt was awake and could not be prevailed upon to sleep until he had thanked me.

They were all there, grouped about the bed, when I went downstairs Bruno was the only one who looked as if he had had any sleep.

He sprang to his feet. "Here, Kurt," he said facetiously, "is the *Herr Doktor*. He is going to cut your leg off."

Only the woman did not laugh at the jest. Kurt himself was smiling when I bent over to look at him.

He was a youngish-looking man of about forty with intelligent brown eyes and a high, wide forehead. The smile faded from his face as he looked at me.

"You know what I wish to say, *Herr Doktor*?"

I took refuge in professional brusqueness. "The less you say, the better," I said, and felt for his pulse. But as I did so his fingers moved and gripped my hand.

"One day soon," he said, "England and the Third Reich will be at war. But you will not be at war with Germany. Remember that, please, *Herr Doktor*. Not with Germany. It is people like us who are Germany, and in our way we shall fight with England. You will see."

I left soon after.

At nine that night I was in Zurich.

Llewellyn was back in the room. I put the manuscript down. He looked across at me.

"Very interesting," I said.

"I'd considered sending it up to one of these magazines that publish short stories," he said apologetically. "I thought I'd like your opinion first, though. What do you think?"

I cleared my throat. "Well, of course, it's difficult to say. Very interesting, as I said. But there's no real point to it, is there? It needs something to tie it all together."

"Yes, I see what you mean. It sort of leaves off, doesn't it? But that's how it actually happened." He looked disappointed. "I don't think I could invent an ending. It would be rather a pity, wouldn't it? You see, it's all true."

"Yes, it would be a pity."

"Well, anyway, thanks for reading it. Funny thing to happen. I really only put it down on paper for fun." He got up. "Oh, by the way. I was forgetting. I heard from those people about a week after war broke out. A letter. Let's see now, where did I put it? Ah, yes."

He rummaged in a drawer for a bit, and then tossed a letter over to me.

The envelope bore a Swiss stamp and the postmark was Klosters, 4 September 1939. The contents felt bulky. I drew them out.

The cause of the bulkiness was what looked like a travel agent's folder doubled up to fit the envelope. I straightened it. On the front page was a lino-cut of a clump of pines on the shore of a lake and the name "TITISEE." I opened out the folder.

"GERMAN MEN AND WOMEN, COMRADES!" The type was worn and battered. "Hitler has led you into war. He fed you with lies about the friendly Polish people. In your name he has now committed a wanton act of aggression against them. As a consequence, the free democracies of England and France have declared war against Germany. Comrades, right and justice are on their side. It is Hitler and National Socialism who are the enemies of peace in Europe. Our place as true Germans is at the side of the democracies against Hitler, against National Socialism. Hitler cannot win this war. But the people of Germany must act. All Germans, Catholics, Protestants, and Jews, must act now. Our Czech and Slovak friends are already refusing to make guns for Hitler. Let us stand by their sides. Remember . . ."

I was about to read on when I saw that the letter which accompanied the folder had fluttered to the carpet. I picked it up. It consisted of a few typewritten lines on an otherwise blank sheet of paper.

Greetings, *Herr Doktor.* We secured your address from the Customs carnet in your car and write now to wish you good luck. Kurt, Stephan, and Bruno have made many journeys since we saw you and returned safely each time. Today, Kurt leaves again. We pray for him as always. With this letter we send you Johann's newest work so that you shall see that Kurt spoke the truth to you. We are the army of the shadows. We do not fight for you against our countrymen; but we fight with you against National Socialism, our common enemy.

Auf Wiedersehen.
Freda, Kurt, Stephan,
Johann, and Bruno.

Llewellyn put my glass down on the table beside me. "Help yourself to a cigarette. What do you think of that? Nice of them, wasn't it?" he added. "Sentimental lot, these Germans."

THE TRAITRESS

SYDNEY HORLER

"HORLER FOR EXCITEMENT" appeared in advertisements and on the dust jacket of scores of books when the popular and prolific Sydney (Harry) Horler (1888–1954) was at his peak in the second quarter of the twentieth century.

His parents wanted him to be a schoolteacher but he refused and left school to become a copywriter for the *Bristol Evening News*, where he later became a reporter and went on to the same position in Manchester, Birmingham, and London. Horler had just started to write fiction when World War I broke out, so he stopped to enlist and was commissioned a second lieutenant to write propaganda for Air Force Intelligence. His poor eyesight prevented him from seeing combat. After the war, he began to write sports fiction but found his calling when he wrote his first mystery, *The Mystery of No. 1* (1925).

He wrote about a hundred fifty mystery novels, many serialized in the British periodical *News of the World*. His most famous series character is Timothy Overbury "Tiger" Standish, son of the Earl of Quorn—a hearty, two-fisted, soccer-playing superhero similar to H. C. McNeile's Hugh "Bulldog" Drummond. Standish makes his debut in *Tiger Standish* (1932) and the virile patriot was published regularly up to World War II.

Other characters featured in Horler's work include Ian Heath, a British secret agent, who first appeared in *The Curse of Doone* (1928), and Gerald Frost, known as "Nighthawk," an outraged burglar who steals jewelry from society ladies of questionable virtue, using their own lipstick to scrawl the word "wanton" on their pillowcases as they sleep.

Horler is seldom read today for several reasons, including unbelievable plots, a dreadful writing style, and overtly negative remarks about pretty much anyone who isn't British, an attitude reflected in his private life as well as his fiction, but he was enormously popular in his day and one of England's bestselling writers.

"The Traitress" was originally published in the November 1930 issue of *Hush* magazine; it was first collected in *The Screaming Skull and Other Stories* (London, Hodder & Stoughton, 1930).

THE TRAITRESS

SYDNEY HORLER

THAT DULL RED STAIN was blood.

The realization came swiftly to Chertsey as he stood, uncomfortable and bewildered, in the centre of the room.

At his feet was a murdered man.

Baintree, clad in evening dress, lay perfectly still; his arms were outflung, and his legs were supine. Their limpness was so horribly grotesque, they might have belonged to a giant doll. In Baintree's breast was the wound which the assassin had made. The stiff white shirt was ugly with it. With a shudder, Chertsey remembered that some of that life-blood was on his hand.

He looked round. He did not deny that he was nervous—very nervous. One had to live through an ordeal like this to know how deeply one could be stirred.

The sight of the telephone on its stand in the far corner reminded him of things outside—of the Police. . . . In such a case one always telephoned for the Police. He was suddenly filled with dread. . . . With that blood on his hand. . . .

Thirty yards away, in Piccadilly, a taxi-cab passed with hooting of horn. Inside this room there was a deep, immovable stillness—the uncanny silence of death. It began to frighten him. He felt he could not stand it any longer.

Whatever discomfiture the action might bring, he must ring up the Police.

And then, as he took the first step across the carpet, the door opened and a man walked into the room.

The suddenness of this man's appearance, following upon the tremendous shock he had just received, made him pull up with a start. And instantly the thought came as he looked into the stranger's face that he must appear a guilty person. He certainly felt one.

The stranger was calm and clear-headed; in the circumstances amazingly so. Keeping a steady gaze upon Chertsey, he quietly closed the door. After he had done this, his hand went into a pocket. It was withdrawn holding a revolver.

"Who are you?"

It was a voice with a vibrant note—like the sound of steel cutting the air. It matched the speaker. Mesmerized by the behaviour of the other, Chertsey continued to stare. He saw a thinnish man of perhaps forty-eight, dressed in a dinner-jacket suit beneath a light overcoat. Used to forming impressions, he swiftly summarized the man's face. The colour of the flesh was grey, and every feature was grim; the thin, tight-locked lips, the challenging jut of the jaw, the angry blaze of the eyes—a granite man, this.

"Who are you?" The demand was more peremptory this time.

"My name is Gilbert Chertsey."

"Profession?"

"I'm a novelist."

It seemed that the merest flicker of a smile passed over the other's stern mouth.

"A novelist—well, what are you doing here?"—and then, as Chertsey moved aside—"put your hands over your head! No nonsense!"

When Chertsey hesitated, the other crossed to him with startling speed. The novelist had the incredible sensation of feeling a revolver thrust against his heart. He obeyed the bizarre command, conscious that the other had noticed the bloodstain on his hand. The man said nothing, but his expression was significant.

"Sit in that chair and tell me everything you know about this"—he pointed with his left hand to the figure on the floor. "One moment!" Kneeling, the speaker examined the body of Baintree.

"Dead," he said.

"Yes."

The other showed his teeth.

"Who killed him?"

"I haven't the least idea—I can assure you I didn't. Possibly——"

"Possibly—what?" The inquisitor had his deeply-lined face out-thrust.

Chertsey felt himself hating the man almost as much as he feared him.

"Perhaps you will be good enough to tell me who you are," he said.

The thin lips parted in a mirthless smile.

"That can wait," was the reply; "in the meantime, let me assure you, Mr. Chertsey, that I occupy a position which entitles me to take up my present attitude. Unless the explanation of your presence in this flat is thoroughly satisfying, I shall have you immediately arrested. . . . What is that on your hands? I must hear all your movements to-night."

Chertsey pulled himself together. It was absurd to be afraid.

"I dined at the Club——"

"What Club?"

"The Mayflower."

A nod.

"After dinner a party of us played billiards and then went back to the smoking-room to talk. Someone—Ringwood I think—wanted to know if I was doing another novel. I said yes, but that I wasn't getting on very fast."

"Where does this lead?"

Chertsey kept his temper.

"If you will excuse me," he replied, "I am coming to the point."

The other growled: "Quickly, then!"

"I can fully understand that my work has no possible interest for you," commented the novelist, "but as it was my present book which brought me here to-night I had to mention the fact. Mr. Robert Baintree was, I understand, a great traveller."

"Possibly."

Chertsey endeavoured to remain unruffled.

"It was Ringwood—a friend of his—who sent me along to see Mr. Baintree to-night. Ringwood——"

"What Ringwood?"

"The Harley Street nerve specialist. He told me he was at Repington with Baintree."

"Did he tell you anything else?" There was a snapped eagerness about the question.

"He said that Baintree knew Europe from one end to the other and that if I wanted local colour for the Constantinople scenes in my new novel he was the man to see. Ringwood was good enough to ring up Baintree and fix an appointment. I was to drop in here at 10:30 to-night."

"And you kept this appointment?"

"I did. . . . But, I say, it's very disconcerting not to know to whom I am talking. . . ."

"Don't let that affect you—please continue your story. I find it very interesting." It was impossible to decide if the man was being grimly facetious.

"All right, I have already told you I kept the appointment. As a matter of fact, I was five minutes too early; when I entered the lift on the ground-floor I looked at my watch and saw that it was exactly twenty-two minutes past ten."

"There was no-one else in the lift?"

"No. I came up alone. Then——"

"Well?" growled the listener.

Chertsey winced. He was now reaching the crucial point of his narrative, and he realized that his conduct did not reflect the greatest credit on himself.

"There is a small brass plate outside this flat door with 'Baintree' on it. I rang the bell and waited. But no-one came and so I rang again. It was then that it happened——"

"What happened?" The listener was bending forward.

"The door suddenly opened and a man rushed out."

A sharp intake of breath came from the direction of the other chair.

"Describe him."

"I am afraid I can't. You see, he was past me in a flash."

"Didn't you notice anything about him?" The inquiry was rasped.

"Nothing—except that he had his overcoat collar turned up and that the upper part of his face was hidden by a soft felt hat turned down."

"You didn't follow him?—— Good God, man, why *didn't* you follow him? He had just committed a murder!"

"Look here," complained Chertsey, "I'm not going on any longer unless I can put my hands down. For one thing I want a smoke." He lowered his hands without waiting for the permission and thrust them into his overcoat pockets. From these he drew out a pipe and tobacco pouch. The stain on the fingers was a horrible reminder, but he filled his pipe, regardless of the revolver by which he was still menaced.

"How was I to know the man was a murderer?" He had filled his pipe somewhat unsteadily, had got it going by this time, and still kept his hands down. "Baintree was a stranger to me; it was no concern of mine if he entertained men who were eccentric enough to leave his flat as though the place was on fire. As a matter of

fact, however ridiculous it may sound now, that was the thought which came to me—the flat was on fire and this man was rushing out to get assistance."

"What about the telephone?"

Chertsey shrugged.

"Of course; I have already said that it sounds ridiculous. But this is the first time I have actually come into contact with . . . murder."

Lifting his hand, he found that his forehead was wet. The strain was beginning to tell. Who was this questioner, and why did he not give some hint of his identity? He was tempted to make a rush for the door in spite of the revolver. After all, he was innocent. Why should he tolerate such treatment?

"You did not disturb anything here?"

"Nothing. Let me finish. The fleeing man had left the flat door open. I walked inside—you understand I was vaguely suspicious; that was why I entered without ringing again. As I stepped into the hall I called out: 'Mr. Baintree'; but no answer came. Then I stepped into the first room I came to—this one."

"Was the light on?"

"No. The room was in darkness. That strengthened the feeling I had that something was wrong—very wrong. I found the switch after a little while and then I saw—*that!* I knew it to be the body of the man I had come to see because Ringwood had described Baintree.

"At first," continued the novelist, "I was bewildered, especially when, after stooping to examine how badly Baintree was injured, I found this"—he held up his right hand—"on my fingers. I realized that possibly I might be suspected of the crime myself, but I was just going to the telephone to ring up the Police when you entered. What I have told you is the truth," he concluded.

The other rose.

"You have withheld nothing?"

"Nothing."

"Then," said the other, placing the revolver back into his pocket, "you may go after giving me your address. Where do you live?"

"128B, Hertford Street, Mayfair. Practically round the corner."

With the receipt of this information the other appeared to lose all interest in him.

"Good night, Mr. Chertsey."

The novelist hesitated. He did not know if he were justified in leaving this man who refused to give any account of himself in the flat.

The other spoke sharply.

"There is one fact I must impress upon you before you go, Mr. Chertsey. It is that this affair to-night must not be discussed with anyone. It will be necessary for you to give me your promise on that point."

Chertsey bridled.

"You take a great deal for granted. I know absolutely nothing about you. Suppose I refuse?"

"Then, believe me, you will find yourself in a somewhat uncomfortable position."

"Oh—go to the devil!" His patience was exhausted. The interest which he had formerly experienced about this stranger had been replaced by annoyance. So exasperated that he felt he could not trust himself to say anything further, he opened the door. A minute later he was in the street, walking rapidly towards his own rooms.

It wasn't until the following morning that he found the thing. Going through the pockets of his evening kit, his fingers touched something soft. It proved to be a thin, black leather pocket-case. As it did not belong to him, Chertsey was puzzled. Although he had no clear recollection on the point, the only conclusion to which he could come was that he must have found the case on the floor of the murder-room the previous night and inadvertently placed it in his pocket.

It had a clear connection with the crime, no doubt, and his first inclination was to open the case, but he overcame the desire. Directly after breakfast he got into the taxi which had been ordered and gave an address: "New Scotland Yard."

The official to whose room he was conducted listened attentively to everything he said, before picking up the case. He asked only one question:

"Do you know what this contains, Mr. Chertsey?"

"I do not. You see it does not belong to me."

"Quite so. Well—thank you, Mr. Chertsey." The speaker rose, intimating that the interview might be considered over.

"I hope I did right in bringing it here?"

"Certainly. You did quite right. Thank you once again."

"If I had only known where to find the mysterious gentleman who cross-examined me last night in Mr. Baintree's flat I would have gone to him."

"Quite so."

"Am I committing a breach of official etiquette in asking where that gentleman can be found?"

The Scotland Yard official walked to the door and held it open.

"I'd forget all about this affair if I were you," was his reply.

Chertsey stalked out.

He would have been only too pleased to forget, but he could not dismiss the affair. He dealt professionally in mystery—his novels were of the "shocker" class—and the death of Robert Baintree contained all the elements to enchain a writer's attention. The escape of the supposed murderer, the finding of the body in that hushed room, the appearance of the unyielding, grim-visaged inquisitor, the peculiar reticence of the fellow at Scotland Yard—these were the circumstances which kept the tragedy fixed in his mind.

It was the secrecy of the whole thing which was so baffling. Much as he hated the idea, he expected to be besieged by reporters, but none of the newspapers even printed the story of Robert Baintree's death. So far as any publicity was concerned, the tragedy might not have happened. More and more strange!

That night he sought out Ringwood. The latter looked worried. Naturally enough, Chertsey commenced to talk about his experience. Long before he had finished his story, the Harley Street specialist, after glancing uneasily over his shoulder—and this was in the ultra-respectable atmosphere of the Mayflower Club—caught his arm.

"If I were you, old man, I'd forget everything about that business—try to persuade yourself it never happened."

"What the devil are you talking about? Wasn't it through you that I went to see Baintree?"

"Yes, yes. But—well, the truth is, old man, I can't tell you what I know—and you'll have to be satisfied with that."

Chertsey looked at him squarely.

"Do you know who that man—Grim-face—was?"

"Yes, I know."

"And you won't tell me?"

"I can't . . . have another drink?"

"To hell with you and your drinks!"

Reaching home disgruntled and annoyed, his servant told him a gentleman was waiting.

"What's his name?"

"He didn't give any name, sir. I said you were certain to be home by eleven, and he decided to wait."

"I don't exactly care for people who are afraid to give their names being allowed to wait in my rooms, Dixon."

"There's nothing suspicious about this gentleman, sir. But a very masterful type. He just brushed past me."

"Short, thin man?"

"Yes, sir—very grey."

Grim-face!

So it proved.

"I called, Mr. Chertsey, to thank you for handing over that case to Scotland Yard. You did not look inside it, you say?"

"I made that statement to the official at Scotland Yard, and, in the ordinary way, I usually endeavour to speak the truth."

Grim-face looked as though he contemplated a rebuke.

"Why did you not tell me about this case in the flat last night?" he went on.

"I say, excuse me not asking you before—but won't you have a drink?"

"I do not want a drink, thank you."

Chertsey continued to smile.

"I do wish you would have a drink. I'll tell you why; before I insult a man I always like to give him a drink."

"Do you intend to insult me?"

"I most certainly do. I'm going to answer one more question—the one you have just asked—and then I'm going to tell you to go to the devil. Do you imagine that I intend to spend the rest of my life being cross-examined by you?—a man whose name I do not even know? Now for the answer: I have no clear recollection of having picked up the black leather case which I took to Scotland Yard but the strong probability is that I found it on the floor of the room in Baintree's flat and that I inadvertently placed it in my pocket. Now—do you mind going? You irritate me."

For the first time since he had known him, the other smiled.

"I can quite understand you being irritated, Mr. Chertsey. My name," he added, "is Sir Harker Bellamy, and I am a Departmental Chief of the British Intelligence Department."

Chertsey became penitent.

"I say," he stammered, "forgive me for being such a fool. . . . I might have known. . . ."

"There is sufficient reason why Robert Baintree's death and everything connected with it should not be talked about. The essential quality about our work is its secrecy. I should not have said as much, Mr. Chertsey, if circumstances had not brought you into this business. And now I'll wish you good night."

Chertsey motioned to an easy-chair by the side of the glowing fire.

"Can't you stay a few more minutes, sir? . . . just long enough to smoke a cigarette? I—I rather wanted to ask you a favour."

The expression of Sir Harker Bellamy was

non-committal as he tapped the cigarette he had taken from the cedarwood box.

Chertsey was nervous.

"What I am going to say may sound very ridiculous," he started, "but I should like to be allowed to take a hand, if it is at all possible, in trying to solve the mystery of Robert Baintree's death. A man cannot have such an experience as I had two nights ago without feeling it. As you have said yourself, circumstances brought me into the affair. They brought me into it against my will, it's true, but, once in, I should like to stay in."

The only sign the other made was to flick the ash off his cigarette. It was not encouraging, but Chertsey went on:

"I don't mind confessing that my motive is not an entirely unselfish one. For months I have been fed up with the commonplace—ordinary existence, ordinary travel—but there was something so dastardly about Baintree's death that I should welcome the chance, for its own sake as it were, to get a hand on that beastly murderer. I'm expressing myself damned badly, I know, but——"

Bellamy rose and flung his cigarette-stub into the fire.

"Better stick to your novel-writing, Chertsey," he said.

"Does that mean——?"

"It means that novel-writing is considerably safer."

"I speak four languages. I am very fit——"

"Good night—sorry."

Grim-face was gone.

To every man at times comes a dangerous mood. One is inclined then to break with the settled order of ordinary existence. Life becomes stale and pallid; whatever tang it may once have held is gone. It is this chafing which sends some men into the Divorce Court, others into Africa to shoot lions.

A week before Chertsey had entered the open door of Robert Baintree's flat in Half Moon Street, he had crossed from New York in the *Berengaria*. The sea had upset him; made him restless. He had bought a number of novels at Brentano's in Fifth Avenue the last afternoon, but he had found it impossible to read one of them. Concentration of any sort was out of the question; he just loafed and he found even this fretting to the nerves.

He could have flirted, of course, but none of the would-be *amourettes*, whether married, single or widows, appealed. Even intense boredom—or whatever it was which was making him irritable—was preferable to an insipid love affair.

His mood of discontent became intensified during the first week in London. Usually he returned from a cross-Atlantic trip with a sense of renewed vigour and fresh interest. "Now," he would say to himself as he stepped back into his comfortable study, "for some work. . . ."

But, although the story he was on had been promised for an early date, he could not bring himself to write more than a few paragraphs a day. The fatal inability to concentrate still dogged him. Writing novels suddenly seemed a ridiculous and absurd occupation.

Then he had stepped across the threshold of a door and found himself face to face with something real, vital, dynamic. Life with the lid off.

But Grim-face had turned him down cold.

His mood had not improved by the experience.

There was the usual pile of letters on the breakfast-table, but he pushed them aside whilst he had his meal. Then, gathering them up, he crossed to the wide fireplace, lowered himself into a worn morocco chair, and filled and lit a pipe.

The mood of irritability was rather worse that morning—the memory of the talk with Grim-face the night before was very vivid—and Chertsey's perusal of his mail was marked by a series of short explosions. He was not a mean or selfish man—but he wished these charity-mongers would leave him alone for a bit. Then there were the immaculately typed envelopes which, upon being opened, proved to contain the compliments of Samuel MacJacob and his tribe, who, upon note of hand alone, were prepared to advance any sum up to twenty-five thousand pounds. . . .

Another. This from the editor of a monthly magazine:

Dear Chertsey,
I want to start that serial.
Where the deuce is it?
Yours sincerely,
JOHN BEZZANT.

The reader groaned. He was sick of work.

The last envelope of the batch was small and azure-coloured. A faint fragrance drifted to him as he picked it up. He viewed it curiously for a minute. The writing was not familiar, and it had been addressed to him c/o his English publishers. He tore the flap.

Dear Mr. Chertsey,
I hope you won't think me too much of an abandoned female if I write to say how much I enjoyed your last book? I have read them all—they are my favourite bed-time literature, as a matter of fact!—but "The Lure" beats all the rest.

I hope you are not too hopelessly conventional! Judging from the kind of stuff you write I should not imagine you were. If you feel capable of such a rash act, let me offer you some tea one afternoon. This is not an entirely disinterested invitation, I warn you—I want your autograph in some of my favourite novels.

You might ring me up if you think anything about it.
Sincerely yours,
SOPHIE LAURENT.

His worst enemy could not have said that Chertsey had many illusions about himself. He was fast advancing towards the unromantic forties, he was only moderately good-looking, and he regarded his novels mainly as a means of livelihood. It was necessary that he should make money somehow, and writing appealed to him as the easiest way he knew. Contrary to the average experience he had sold his stuff from the start and as time went on he got better and better prices for it. He was fond of change and he could work whilst he travelled.

He might have become conceited. His novels contained nothing of sex, and yet all classes appeared to read them. In the *Berengaria* library list there was a long row of them, and the library steward said they were always "out."

In the ordinary way he would probably have ignored the letter and concentrated on the business-like epistle of the editor of the *Centurion Magazine*. That meant something practical: English magazines paid badly compared to American ones, but he had got Bezzant up to one thousand pounds for the serial rights of "The Midnight Club"—and what was even more important, directly he delivered the manuscript he could receive his money.

But when he looked through the open door into his study which adjoined and saw the typewriter waiting . . . he reached out for the telephone. Holding the letter signed "Sophie Laurent," he asked for a number.

"So you have been bored? We must see to that."

Chertsey watched through the cigarette-smoke her eyes quizzing him.

"I am no longer bored," he said.

She reached out for a fresh cigarette from the jade box, and he sprang up—rather awkwardly, for the Chesterfield was deep—to strike a match. As he held the flame cupped, the girl's fingers touched the back of his hand. A gleam of amusement was in her eyes, which held a deeper challenge.

"It was very good of you to come."

"I hope you are not too disappointed?"

"On the contrary." She smiled again. "It would, I confess, have been a terrible blow if you had proved to be a fat, bearded person with a large family."

"Many of my tribe are just like that."

"Really? Then the beautiful emotions they express are nothing more than their secret longings and desires?"

"Probably. But what would you have done had I turned up with a beard and a family portrait album?"

"Given you tea, of course, got your signature to my books—and then discovered an acute headache. As it is——" She gestured with her free hand.

"I am flattered—and grateful."

"Thank you. This *is* rather jolly, don't you think?"

She motioned again with a white, ringless hand, exceptionally groomed. The movement was comprehensive. It embraced the glowing fire, the corner of the room in which they were entrenched, the Chesterfield on which they were both seated—and her visitor.

It was evidently intended as a compliment. Chertsey, soothed by his surroundings, accepted it as such. For the speaker was by no means ordinary; on the contrary, she was distinctly unusual.

Sophie Laurent was not beautiful in the orthodox, stereotyped fashion—her mouth was too large and her features too irregular for that—but she was a striking type, nevertheless. Her body had an attractive suppleness, and its grace was shown off to advantage by the afternoon gown she wore.

She had a personality, and it was compelling. Chertsey found himself becoming more and more interested—almost fascinated. This woman—he put her age down at twenty-six or so—was intensely alive. The movements of her body, the animation of her voice and glance, the play of her hands showed it. He liked people to be alive.

They drifted into more or less intimate talk: the girl had let the barriers down, and Chertsey, never a slave to convention, willingly stepped over the threshold. She told him that she was alone in London, that, although possessed of sufficient private means, she was herself oftentimes bored and——

"You don't think me too dreadful for writing you, I hope, old chap?" she asked. Her outstretched hand picked a speck of dust off his shoulder. "I've never done such a thing before, but there's something in your work which thrills me. Is it the way you make your heroines behave, or what?"

"My dear—you overwhelm me!" he replied.

"Not at all. I mean it. Tell me, have you had many adventures yourself?"

He looked at her; she was extremely attractive with the firelight playing on her white, opulent skin.

"Amorous or otherwise?"

"'Otherwise,' of course. You don't think I've lured you here in order to get details of your dreadful past? No, what I mean is, you describe action so well in your books that I always feel you must have actually taken part in something of the sort yourself. I should like you to have met a great—a very great—friend of mine. He's dead now. But Bob Baintree——"

"You knew Baintree?" His surprise made him interrupt.

She regarded him with astonishment. "Do you mean to say you were a friend of his, too? But, how extraordinary!"

"I saw him once—that's all." Some intuitive feeling—he could not tell what instinct it was which guided him—made him temporize.

She nodded.

"He died a couple of days ago—quite suddenly, and rather mysteriously. When I say 'mysteriously,' I mean that it seems strange to think of a man in the prime of life, and as strong as he was, dying at all. And no one seems to know what it was that struck him down."

Into the listener's mind flashed a picture. Chertsey saw that still form with the grotesquely limp limbs lying on the blue-patterned carpet with the blood staining the shirt-front. Should he tell this girl what he knew? He decided not—evidently she was ignorant of the truth—and it might cruelly distress her.

"My feelings for poor Bob were never more than those of a friend—a very dear friend—but he—he always said he was very much in love with me. He wrote me the most wonderful letters. The night before his death he called here. It was rather a painful scene we had. You see, he asked me once again to marry him and I refused. He was a dear, and I liked him awfully—but it's absolutely suicidal to marry anyone you do not love—don't you think?"

"I should imagine so."

"It was then I gave him back his letters. I felt I no longer had the right to them. I fancy I can see his face now"—she shivered slightly, although the room was very hot—"as he put them away in a black leather case. It's hateful to think that prying eyes may read the words which must have been sacred to him."

Chertsey leaned forward.

"You would like to have those letters back?" he asked.

"Only to destroy them. Now that Bob is dead . . . perhaps you can understand?"

"Of course. But if the letters are addressed to you, they are your property. Mr. Baintree's executors would deliver them up to you if you made application."

"Oh, but I have written—and received no reply. Do you know what I think?"

"What?"

"I have the idea—although Bob never told me, great friends as we were—that he was engaged on some private work for the Government. That would explain the secrecy which has so surrounded his death. It might also explain why I cannot get my letters returned. Being a woman, I feel so helpless——" She paused, biting her lower lip. "Then there is another possibility. They may have been stolen. There is the chance of blackmail."

It was obviously up to Chertsey.

"If I can do anything——" he started.

She turned to him so impulsively that one rounded arm encircled his neck.

"Oh, will you? Thank you! I know where the letters were put—if only you could find that black leather case. . . ."

The red lips were parted; her eyes sent forth

an invitation, but, strangely enough, when Chertsey found himself five minutes later out on the Earls Court pavement, it was not of the woman he had just left that he thought. His mind dwelt on the still form of a man lying on the floor of his flat—brutally murdered.

A month passed. It was during this month that Gilbert Chertsey's friends went round inquiring of each other what the deuce had happened to him. On the principle of going to the fountainhead, Ringwood, who was really anxious, rang up the novelist's literary agent.

"Don't ask me," replied that harassed individual; "all I know is that he won't work and that he spends all his time with some woman. . . . No, I don't know anything more than that. . . . I can't tell you her name, but she's got him all right; they're inseparable. I saw them lunching at the Savoy yesterday, and when I reminded Chertsey that he was already two months behind with his new novel he nearly bit my head off. . . . Yes, he's either mad, or is going to get married . . . 'bye."

Chertsey adjusted the gold-rimmed spectacles of plain glass, fingered the small moustache glued to his upper lip by spirit-gum, and walked on.

It was difficult to believe that he was in London—even in the noisome East End: this dark, fetid alley was more in keeping with the underworld of some foreign capital. It was so dark that he could scarcely see his hand in front of him.

Dread struck him: he might not be able to find the place again; he had been there only once before. And he had to find it.

He stumbled on until he reached the end of this unsavoury alley. A turn to the right brought him more light and a clearer knowledge of his surroundings. He was in a street now—a street lined with grimy-looking houses that frowned evilly upon the few persons walking furtively upon the pavement below.

Into one of these houses he turned, watched by many curious eyes. Up the rickety staircase he climbed until he reached a door on the third floor. He thrust this open without the preliminary of knocking.

For such a house it was a surprisingly comfortable room. At a big desk placed against the farther wall, a girl sat writing. As the door opened, she swung round in her chair.

"Yes?" she demanded. Her right hand was in a pocket of her skirt.

"Don't trouble to shoot, Sophie," said Chertsey.

The girl stared incredulously and then tilted back her head. There was relief—and something else—in her laugh.

"You're wonderful, old thing," she declared—"but why the disguise?"

Chertsey turned to lock the door.

"Yes, I should have done that; it was very careless of me. I don't know what Philip would say." Her tone changed. "By the way, he should be here—it's not like him to be late. You haven't seen him?"

"No—but I've heard about him."

Her expression changed as she saw the look in his eyes.

"What do you mean? Has anything happened to him?"

"He's been taken."

She opened her mouth to scream, but self-control asserted itself.

"How do you know? When did it happen? Philip! . . . Oh, God, they'll hang him!"

"Undoubtedly," Chertsey confirmed, "but then he always knew they would."

She passed over the singular remark in her urgent desire for further information.

"When did it happen?"

"He was arrested an hour ago in the *California Hotel* in Leicester Square."

She came closer.

"Gilbert, how do you know this?"

"Ever since the night of Baintree's death I have been shadowed—under suspicion——"

She caught his arm.

"That has been through me. Oh, my dear, they will not touch you . . . is that why you came here disguised?"

He disregarded her question, and continued: "I thought two could play at that game and so I did a bit of spying back. That is how I knew of your brother's arrest." He freed his arm from her hand.

"I came straight here to warn you. They know that your brother had a woman working with him. Although they have the murderer of Baintree"—he wondered she did not notice the hardening of his voice—"they will not be satisfied. I have heard of this man Bellamy: he's a tiger; and he will not rest until he has got you as well. He must know all about you by this time."

It seemed incredible that she did not suspect him. But the girl remained calm, almost impassive. Was she stunned by grief?

He went on hurriedly.

"They may be here any moment. This place can be traced now that they have O'Donnell."

She just smiled. It was pathetic.

"I do not care," she said; "let them come."

Chertsey caught her by the shoulders.

"You don't realize what you are saying, Sophie. Through O'Donnell there may be the clearest evidence against you. Although England is not at war, the country cannot afford to be sentimental against agents working for a foreign power which is known to be hostile. Don't you realize the risk?"

"I have taken a greater risk than that—and lost."

"A greater risk?" He was puzzled.

"When I endeavoured to make you love me, Gilbert." She sat down again at the big desk at which she had plotted so brilliantly against the country which was giving her hospitality.

"I, who had sworn to steel my heart against all emotion, have lamentably failed; that is why I do not care what the future may hold. . . ."

Chertsey kept silent because he did not know what to say. He had played the traitor to this girl who had trusted him, and the reflection was not pleasant. He had encouraged her to love him—

and now this love, unless she got away, might mean her death.

"This is the end—and I do not care," con tinued Sophie Laurent. "You know part of my story; I will be very brief with the rest. I am Irish. My father was killed—butchered is the better word—by those licensed murderers known as the Black and Tans in 1920. I had just left the Convent then. Philip, my half-brother, had sworn vengeance against England, the employer of my father's murderers, and he persuaded me to join him in his work. He soon found a way. . . ."

"Russia?" There was contempt in Chertsey's inquiry.

She shrugged her beautiful shoulders.

"What did it matter for whom we worked?" she said wearily. "Germany, France, Italy—it would all have been the same. We were out for vengeance, not money; neither Philip nor I ever received a penny."

Chertsey shifted in his chair. She paid no attention.

"Philip had no special personal animosity against Robert Baintree, but Baintree was the most dangerous member of the special branch of the Secret Service working against us. He had collected certain information——"

"Which was in the black leather case?"

"Yes. It was just a forlorn hope asking you to try to get it back."

"It was already in the hands of Scotland Yard; I took it to them on the morning after the murder."

She showed no surprise.

"I guessed it all along—but I would not allow myself to believe it true. Then it was you who betrayed Philip?"

Chertsey nodded.

"It was I. When I saw the dead body of Baintree, I swore I would bring his murderer to justice. I asked Sir Harker Bellamy to let me join his staff. He curtly refused and so I worked on my own. We have been on different sides, Sophie— the luck of the game, I happen to have won."

"Yes, Gilbert, you've won. You have been true to your principles, but I have been false—a traitress. If Philip knew, he would curse me with his dying breath." She stopped to bite her lip. "I have no desire to escape because I realize that you do not care sufficiently to go with me. So I will stay until—until Sir Harker Bellamy and your other friends come. You can hand me over to them yourself: it will be a further triumph for you."

He passed her gibe by.

"To the best of my knowledge they do not know of this address. They have not learned it through me. But Philip may have papers on him. . . ."

"By rights I should kill you, but, God help me, I love you! I started out to make a fool of you, but it is I who am the fool. . . . Gilbert, have you no pity for me! See to what depths I have sunk!"

A maddening desire to crush her to him, to take all that she was prepared out of her love to offer almost overwhelmed him. But between him and the temptation rose the never-to-be-forgotten picture—the image of a murdered man.

"We are on different sides, my dear," he replied.

"But, listen to me—God! how shameless I am!—I will throw up the work——"

There was a peremptory knock on the door.

He rushed to her.

"Quickly! Isn't there another way out? a secret exit? You must go!"

"No! Let them take me! Nothing matters now! You have won!"

"Open this door!" called a strident voice.

"I love you," lied Chertsey. "I will join you in Paris!"

"You swear that?"

"I swear it."

She pressed a hidden spring beneath the big desk and the wall fell apart. Into this opening, after snatching up hat and coat, she stepped.

"Gilbert!"

"Go!" he ordered.

The panel had scarcely swung to before the door of the room crashed open. A number of men rushed in. At their head was Sir Harker Bellamy.

"Arrest that man!" he ordered.

Chertsey tore off the false moustache and removed the plain-glass spectacles.

"Chertsey! What in the devil are you doing here?"

"Clearing up. I understand you have arrested a man named Philip O'Donnell for the murder of Robert Baintree. You did so on the strength of an anonymous typewritten communication—supplied by me."

"By *you*?"

"It's rather a long story, but when you turned me down I resolved to find Baintree's murderer on my own. Luck was on my side."

"How?"

"The circumstances are personal and I do not propose to explain them."

Bellamy came back to the essentials.

"O'Donnell worked with a woman named Sophie Laurent. She was his half-sister. She was the brains of this outfit—and we want her. Where is she?"

"How should I know?"

"Know! Of course, you know! You've been constantly in her company for weeks. I'm serious, Chertsey, and you had better understand it. Even now I'm not certain that you're not mixed up in this poisonous business yourself. We know this to be the hiding-place of O'Donnell—the woman can't be far away."

Chertsey shrugged with as much ostentation as he could contrive.

"Since you are so well-informed, find her."

"I know this much; the woman, Sophie Laurent, fooled you to the top of her bent, and perhaps made a traitor out of an honest man. Stand back! . . . Stevenson, see that crack in the wall by the side of the desk? . . . If you don't stand aside, Chertsey, I swear I'll shoot!"

"Don't be a fool, Bellamy!"

"Stand aside!"

From the other side of the wall came a voice, clear if unsteady:

"Gilbert—Good-bye!"

Then a revolver shot filled the room with sinister sound.

THIEF IS AN UGLY WORD

PAUL GALLICO

ONE OF AMERICA'S most famous sportswriters in his day, Paul William Gallico (1897–1976) nevertheless had always wanted to write fiction and eventually quit his job as sports editor and columnist at the New York *Daily News* to devote himself to producing novels and short stories, selling the latter for substantial fees to such popular magazines as *The Saturday Evening Post, Cosmopolitan, Liberty*, and *McCall's*, among many others in his prolific storytelling career.

Noted for the romanticism and sentimentality of his stories (which even extended to his nonfiction work), Gallico is not widely read today, though a great many of his books and stories inspired successful and much-loved motion pictures and television series.

Lou Gehrig: Pride of the Yankees (1942) became a movie tearjerker in the same year, titled *Pride of the Yankees*, with Gary Cooper playing the doomed young New York Yankees superstar, who retired at thirty-six and died less than two years later of ALS, the disease that now carries his name. Cooper and Theresa Wright, who played Gehrig's wife, received two of the film's eleven Oscar nominations.

The Clock (1945), based on Gallico's short story, is the charming romantic tale of a soldier (played by Robert Walker) on leave who meets a girl (Judy Garland) by the clock in Pennsylvania Station and falls in love with her.

Perhaps Gallico's most famous book (though not a successful one) was *The Poseidon Adventure* (1969), which became one of the biggest box office "disaster" films of all time when it was released in 1972. Produced by Irwin Allen and directed by Ronald Neame, it is the story of passengers on a giant steamship that has capsized and their challenges in attempting to escape before it sinks. Its huge all-star cast included Gene Hackman, Ernest Borgnine, Red Buttons, Carol Lynley, Shelley Winters, Roddy McDowall, Stella Stevens, and Leslie Nielsen.

The Love of Seven Dolls (1954) is an expansion of his 1950 short story "The Man Who Hated People," which was filmed as the Oscar-winning *Lili* (1953) with Leslie Caron and Mel Ferrer. The unapologetically sentimental *The Snow Goose* (1941), the author's first successful book, finally reached the screen in 1971 as a British made-for-television movie starring Richard Harris and Jenny Agutter.

"*Thief* Is an Ugly Word" was originally published in the May 1944 issue of *Cosmopolitan;* it was first collected in *Confessions of a Story Writer* (New York, Alfred A. Knopf, 1946).

THIEF IS AN UGLY WORD

PAUL GALLICO

IF ONE WERE TO take a pencil and upon a stereographic projection of a world map execute a series of straight lines connecting New York, Munich, and Buenos Aires, one would find oneself looking at a large isosceles triangle, the points of which are at such a distance from one another that they might seem to preclude the coincidences of a certain day early in January of 1944. However, since this is not a mathematical treatise, beyond the simple arithmetic of Mr. Augustus A. Swinney, an American refrigeration engineer whose life's philosophy could be summed up in the inescapable verity that two and two add up to four, we are less concerned with a geometric shape than the shape and pattern of the events that took place at those widely separated points.

For instance, take the functioning of two gentlemen of similar general titles, one in Munich and the other in New York, Herr Professor Hildebrand Bressar and Mr. Curtis Henry. Mr. Curtis Henry was active on the American Commission for Salvage and Protection of Art and Historic Monuments in Europe. His opposite number, Professor Bressar, operated under the beautiful title of *Kunstverwaltungsrat für arisch-europäische Altertumskultur*, which, liter-

ally translated, means "Art-Custodian-Adviser for Aryan-European Ancient Culture."

Boiling their work down to the very essence of its nature, Curtis Henry might be termed an art detective engaged in ferreting out the hundreds of thousands of objects of art pilfered throughout Europe by the Germans, with the eventual objective of returning them to their original owners. Professor Bressar, for all of his wing-collar dignity and high position as curator of the Pinakothek in Munich, was nothing more than a kind of superfence, engaged in the disposal of same. Being merely a good, Third-Reich German, and lacking, like most such good Germans, the moral and ethical probity of a cherrystone clam, it would have been difficult to make the professor understand that what he was doing was wrong.

But we are interested in Herr Bressar only because of his ill-concealed satisfaction at the dawning of that certain day in January, illuminated as any particular day of international villainy always is to a German by being thought of as *"Der Tag."*

In fact, that is what Herr Professor Bressar's assistant called it when he greeted him with

"Good morning, Herr Kunstverwaltungsrat. This is the day, is it not?"

"*Jawohl*, Herr Reinecke, today. I have had a cable from Buenos Aires."

"Ah. Then it—they arrived. Everything goes well."

Professor Bressar consulted a cablegram on his desk and then shifted his gaze to certain lists of items before he smiled and replied, "There is nothing that can go wrong. A member of the Argentine Government is the sponsor. The Americans remain stupid and asleep and besides they dare not interfere in Argentina. And human greed remains what it has always been. Think what it means, Reinecke: millions of dollar-credits for the *Partei*," and he rubbed his hands. Herr Reinecke licked his lips.

Mr. Curtis Henry's brief connection with this story is that some three thousand miles away in his office at the Metropolitan Museum of Art he was taking the deposition and claim of a Dutch refugee, a chubby, shabby-looking little man with the face of a careworn child by the name of Jan van Schouven.

He gave his address, one on the lower West Side, which confirmed the tale of penury and reduced circumstances hinted at by his clothes.

"And the art object to which you wish to lay claim—" said Curtis Henry, his pen posed over the blank he was filling in.

"Se *Old Woman uff Haarlem*, py Rembrandt van Rijn," said Van Schouven simply.

Henry put down his pen and whistled. "Great heavens! You are *that* Van Schouven?"

"I wass," replied Van Schouven with such simple dignity that all the questions Henry had been forming were stifled and he confined himself to the questions on the information blank.

"Family?"

"My wife iss with me. She iss ill. . . ." Some memory of misery and hatred flared in the Dutchman's placid eyes for a moment, a somber flash of indignities suffered. "My son iss in the English flying. My daughter iss a nurse. Also in England."

"Value of the picture?"

"It would bring between t'ree hundert and t'ree hundert fifty t'ousand dollars today."

Henry had a sudden insight into what such a sum would mean to a once wealthy merchant who had obviously suffered complete ruin at the hands of the Germans. He read the next line, "Proof of ownership—" and then checked himself, but Van Schouven chose to reply.

"Se picture hass been in our family for generations. I belief your expert, Mr. Chester Allen Buskirk, knows—"

Curtis Henry made a nose at the mention of one of America's foremost art critics and experts. "Ah—Mr. Buskirk is a little too internationally art-conscious for us. The world recognizes the picture as your property." He completed the form and then turned to the little refugee again.

"Ah—look here, Herr van Schouven. I'm sorry, but you realize of course that at present we can do no more than list these properties and the whereabouts of their rightful claimants. There is very little chance of their being recovered for a considerable period. Even after the Germans have been defeated, we—"

Van Schouven rose and bowed. "Sank you. I realize that. As a refugee honored with a home in your great country, I only felt it my duty to assist you in your work. Some day se time will come. . . ."

The thing was happening in his eyes again. Then it faded. He bowed again, put on his shabby hat, and went out.

It was on that same day at the end of the third leg of the triangle, five thousand three hundred airline miles from New York, that Mr. Augustus Swinney was attending a cocktail party in Buenos Aires.

From the first, Mr. Swinney had found himself fascinated by the intricacies of the diplomatic niceties, the frozen faces and the delicately balanced situations of a gathering under the sponsorship of a neutral nation.

Representatives of belligerent, semibelligerent, and neutral countries were collected uncomfortably under the same roof, munched at the same buffet table, from carefully studied positions, in which well-tailored but chilly backs formed impregnable circles, or gathered in tight, unassailable little groups in various corners of the two brilliantly lighted and ornate salons given over to the guests, opening the ranks only to admit one whose nationality or politics fitted them into the particular group.

Thus the Germans remained a hard core, hard-headed, hard-shirted, dark-suited, immediately beneath the splendid crystal chandelier suspended over the center of the inner room where the buffet table was located. Bright feminine bits of silk drifted toward the dark core, swirled, floated away. Small dark Argentines, distinguished by their dark eyes and English clothes, revolved around the rim; the solid Prussian center never changed or moved.

The British contingent, semiofficial and obviously on hand to see what was in the wind, managed to achieve a bland unawareness of the enemy by rallying beneath an excellent Romney hanging in the outer room, a gloomy portrait of the Duchess of Colchester gazing down dispassionately at her countrymen forming their own tight little isle in the swirl of humanity brought out by the exhibition of a new art treasure acquired by Alfonso de Paraná, Argentine millionaire and collector, and sponsored officially by the gray, frosty, super-correct person of Dr. José Calderriega, Sub-Minister of Culture of the Argentine Republic.

The British were bounded on the north by the Russians, who, looking as though they had slept in their clothes, held together a kind of lumpy and disheveled front, and on the south by a small satellite island of correct and careful Swiss. A small group of Americans, thoroughly ill at ease, remained close to the door for immediate escape in the event of any total loss of social composure. Italians and French drifted disconsolate and homeless, unable to create any nucleus that satisfied them. In spite of strong rocks of nationalism, the party was kept fluid by the circulating movement of lovely women of indeterminate allegiance and the many glowing-eyed men whose allegiance was plainly and simply to the lovely women.

Mr. Swinney, free American citizen, cosmopolite, due to his world wanderings as refrigeration engineer and expert for Swift & Co., the meat packers, unhindered by the social quavers that gripped other members of the American colony, drifted, moved, searched, came and went as he pleased, shouldering his tall, lean figure through the crush of uneasy celebrants.

He went everywhere, talking, chatting, listening with his skin as well as with his ears, and avoiding only the existence and perimeter of the dark, ugly core of Nazis, whose presence stank in his nostrils.

That two and two added up to four he was still quite certain, but of the real purpose behind this curious yet brilliant gathering he was not at all sure, beyond that it was for the ostensible occasion of viewing a painting, a canvas of sufficient importance to cause the Argentine Sub-Minister of Culture to spread the gray mantle of his sponsorship over the affair. It was only because of this semiofficial diplomatic mantle that such an extraordinarily mixed group was able to attend.

It was also, Mr. Swinney knew quite well, because of the quasi-Government sponsorship that social barriers were down, to him as well as three quarters of those in the rooms. Most of those present would otherwise never have been permitted to set foot in so much as the anteroom of the home of Señor Alfonso de Paraná, one of the wealthiest men in the Argentine and a social figure of importance in Buenos Aires and Paris.

The guest list apparently represented a cross-section of the wealth, diplomacy, industry, and international society of Buenos Aires. Mr. Swinney was not unaware why *he* in particular had been invited, since, holding the important position of chief refrigeration engineer for Swift & Co., the meat packers, he did belong to the upper stratum of industry.

He was also able to reason that since art is

generally accepted as an international commodity, this might well account for the international nature of the gathering. But since Mr. Swinney was also well aware, as was everyone else present, that their host, De Paraná, was an ardent Argentine fascist, a supporter of fascist Government policy and an enemy of the United Nations, he was alive with curiosity as to the real reasons underlying the gathering.

Where Allies and fascists met across the front lines, they shot at one another. Here they mingled and circulated, sipping champagne and nibbling delicacies.

It was Mr. Swinney's first experience of the grand diplomatic and social lie that covered human behavior under such circumstances, a lie that was acted out daily in Turkey before it swung to the side of the Allies, in Portugal, in Switzerland, in Buenos Aires. Mortal enemies met, rubbed shoulders, passed, pretended they were not there.

As a cultured American businessman in his early forties, a man at home in five languages and most of the European capitals, this curiously childish kind of pretending amused rather than outraged Mr. Swinney. It was the presence of a second lie that aroused his curiosity and vaguely disturbed him. He wondered whether the canvas hanging behind the closed doors of De Paraná's fabulous library, not yet thrown open to the guests, was actually, as rumored, Rembrandt's famous *Old Woman of Haarlem*. He doubted it. And yet—

That was just it. No one had said that this was the picture they had been invited to see, and yet everyone seemed to know. No one said anything, and everyone knew everything—how the Germans were bringing goods into the Argentine, how quinine was being diverted from Bolivia and sent into Germany via Franco Spain, how secret information about a British meat convoy found its way into the hands of the commander of a Nazi submarine wolf pack, how even perhaps a Dutch art treasure might conceivably turn up in Buenos Aires, the Paris of South America.

Once one was careful to maintain the fiction of Argentine neutrality, one seemed to pick up information and knowledge by osmosis, through the pores of the skin. Someone might say casually, "I understand that . . ." and the vague rumor understood would be closer to the truth than the news printed in the controlled press.

Mr. Swinney's sane, precise mathematical mind explored and sifted rumor and personalities in an attempt to reduce them to simple denominators such as two and two, which could then be added up to four—the gray, icily proper Dr. Calderriega conversing with the British commercial attaché fat De Paraná, his small nostrils twitching, his dark eyes gleaming sensually above the gray pouches that underlined them, fingering a small, priceless Cellini group and discussing it with a famous French sculptor now resident in Buenos Aires; the tawny, monocled, correct Baron von Schleuder of the German Embassy staff holding a thin-stemmed, gold-speckled Venetian champagne glass between his stubby fingers and exchanging polite small talk with the wife of an Argentine cattle king. . . .

Dammit, it was all so official and correct.

Mathematics and the consequences of the addition of simple sums were driven from the mind of Mr. Swinney when he again caught sight of the magnificent woman with the upswept Titian-bronze hair and cat-eyes. She was standing in the inner salon not far from the buffet table conversing with the paunchy little fussbudget of a man with the rimless eyeglasses, the gay-nineties stiff collar, and the obvious toupee.

God, she's good-looking, Mr. Swinney said to himself. *I wonder who she is.* He had seen her twice before, once during the noon *corso* on the Avenida Florida, and again in the American Bar of the Hotel Continental at cocktail time. Mr. Swinney was a bachelor by choice, but this did not prevent him from becoming profoundly stirred by certain types of women. Women with cat-eyes and the mysterious, introspective feline expression of countenance that went with them he found irresistible.

He edged through the throng and, entering the second salon, moved closer. He busied himself at the buffet table and watched her out of the corner of his eye. No doubt that her clothes had originally come from Paris. Only the French knew how to reveal a classic figure in daytime dress. The daring of the purple hat perched atop the thick, bronze-colored hair fascinated him. By Jove, she had the skin to carry it. The set of her head on her neck was a challenge to every man in the room. Mr. Swinney noticed other eyes upon her. He determined to meet the challenge in his own way.

She and Fuss-budget appeared to know each other well. If he could become acquainted with the fat little man with the toupee—

De Paraná suddenly appeared and joined the two, claiming the girl. Swinney hoped that he would name Fuss-budget, but he didn't. He said, "Forgive me for robbing you, my dear friend. It is only for an instant. I swear I will return the Countess to you in a few moments."

Fuss-budget's head waggled archly at the top of his stiff collar and he bowed and turned to the buffet table, loaded with the delicacies of five continents. Mr. Swinney contrived to be next to him.

Mr. Swinney was surprised to note that Fuss-budget did not smell of mothballs as he had expected. For he was a small, self-sufficient left-over from another era, the professional gentleman of the old school, and obviously an epicure.

He tasted the gray Malossol caviar and nibbled at Hungarian pâté, savoring texture and flavor. But the full expression of his ecstasy he reserved for the paper-thin, near-transparent slices of smoked, fuchsia-colored ham. He tasted. He chewed. He swallowed. He closed his eyes with reminiscent delight. When he opened them it was to find a tall, spare gentleman with a craggy, hawklike face, long, strong nose, and dark hair, sprinkled with gray at the side, eating of the same ham and smiling at him sympathetically.

"By Jove!" said Fuss-budget. "Genuine Westphalian ham. Perfectly cured."

"Delicious," said Mr. Swinney.

The little man polished his glasses with a scented silk handkerchief, replaced them, examined the old, dark-red ham from which the slices came, and helped himself to another portion. "Haven't tasted a real one for years. Don't know why they can get it here and we can't up in New York."

Mr. Swinney could have told him. It was one of the things that one knew—by osmosis again—when one lived in Buenos Aires. It was small in bulk like so many other of the German products that one could always find in Buenos Aires stores—the Leica cameras, the fine lenses and optical goods, the rare drugs and medicines labeled "I. G. Farben, Berlin."

But he was not of the mind to alarm or astonish the little man, but rather to make friends with him.

"The secret lies in the process of smoking. But have you ever tried one of our old Argentine hams? We have our own process of aging and curing. The hams are first soaked in wine for weeks."

The little man's ears cocked like a terrier's and his nostrils flared.

"Really? You mean better than—?"

"Tenderer. The flavor is unique. They are never exported."

Fuss-budget licked his lips, then glanced at Mr. Swinney. "But, ah—you are an American, are you not?"

"I am with Swift & Company. I should be delighted some time if you would care to sample—"

The man sighed regretfully. "Unfortunately, I am flying back in the morning." Then he added importantly, "I flew down only yesterday at the invitation of Dr. Calderriega. Hm—it would really be a new taste experience. Of course, there is no question as to the superiority of Argentine beef. . . ."

Mr. Swinney was thinking to himself, *Now, who the devil could you be? Flew down from New York at the invitation of the Argentine Sub-Minister of Culture. I suppose I ought to know you, but I don't.*

De Paraná returned with the cat-eyed girl

on his arm and returned her to Fuss-budget. "*Voilà, mon ami!* As I promised." The little man bowed in the manner of one careful not to disturb the set of a toupee. For an instant they made a little group of which Swinney was the outsider. Fuss-budget hastened to perform the politeness. He said to Mr. Swinney, "Ah, I did not catch your name, sir."

"Swinney. Augustus Swinney."

"Of course—Countess Amalie, may I present Mr. Augustus Swinney? The Countess Amalie Czernok. You know De Paraná of course."

The Countess Amalie gave Mr. Swinney her wide cat-smile and accepted him with her eyes. He was startled to find them violet-colored, the shade of her hat.

Later, when they were alone, he said, "I schemed to meet you. Are you angry?"

She spoke with an accent that might have been French. "Not at all. I saw you scheming. That is why I came back. It is always flattering to a woman when she sees an attractive man make up his mind to meet her."

Mr. Swinney made a mental note: *Aha, then she was watching. I wonder whether she noticed me in the Continental.* He said, "I intruded myself shamelessly upon the little man. By the way, who is he?"

"That is Mr. Buskirk, the art critic. Surely you know Mr. Chester Allen Buskirk. I met him many years ago in Paris. He is so sweet and old-fashioned."

Buskirk . . . Buskirk, the art critic, greatest living expert on the old masters. Flown down from New York to Buenos Aires at the invitation of Dr. José Calderriega. Now, what did that add up to if one was still convinced that in spite of the superimpeccability of congealed diplomatic face, two and two made four?

"You are French, Countess?"

"Part French, part Polish."

"A combination that inevitably results in a beautiful woman."

"You look like an American, but you do not talk like one. You have been to Paris too?"

Before he could reply, there was a sudden stir in the room, a kind of mass awareness of a change in the routine and the beginning of a movement through the second salon toward the massive carved-oak doors leading to the library.

The doors which previously had been shut were now swung back. The Countess Amalie drew in her breath and sighed, "Ah, the picture. Now we are permitted to see the picture. Are you not excited?"

"You mean Rembrandt's *Old Woman of Haarlem*?"

"Then you heard too?"

"One hears a great many things. I don't believe it."

"You do not believe it?" In the light from the crystal chandelier overhead, her eyes were wide and luminous. "But why should it not be possible?"

"Because," said Mr. Swinney, flatly, "they wouldn't dare."

But he found out when he came into the library and saw what hung on the wall of Brazilian teak-wood paneling that they did dare, after all, that two and two still added up to four, and four made a very ugly number.

In Munich, Kunstverwaltungsrat Bressar was burning the lights late in his office in the Pinakothek, poring over lists marked: *Final shipment following liquidation Cracow Museum, Cracow, occupied Poland*, and occasionally earmarking items for the Argentine.

In New York, Jan van Schouven, the little Dutchman with the tired-child expression and the desperate eyes, stood in the dingy hall outside the dingy furnished room and listened to the doctor say: "Madam van Schouven is a little better tonight. However, if it were at all possible I would say it was almost imperative that she be moved to a warmer climate, at least for a time."

And in a tiny cove just outside Avellaneda, some twenty-five miles south of Buenos Aires on the Río de la Plata, an impatient U-boat captain sat in the steel cell of his quarters reading over a three-weeks-old copy of the *Völkische*

Beobachter, digesting for the tenth time the accounts of the Wehrmacht's glorious advances to the rear in Russia and wondering how long it would be before the orders came through from the Embassy in Buenos Aires to unload his cargo, pick up the return load of tungsten, molybdenum, platinum, and quinine, and put to sea. He was tired, anyway, of being a damned freighter. There was no light's Cross with oak leaves for that kind of work.

Mr. Augustus Swinney looked up at Rembrandt's magnificent and touching masterpiece, the *Old Woman of Haarlem*, beautifully hung on the paneled wall of De Paraná's fabulous library near the fifteen-century Spanish fireplace, softly and glowingly lit to bring out all the deep warmth of the tones of gold and brown. He thought of the first time that he had gazed on its breath-taking perfection.

It had been in Amsterdam, he remembered in 1938. He had dined at the home of a business acquaintance, Mynheer Jan van Schouven, a wealthy tobacco merchant with plantations in Sumatra. They had been discussing the possibility of the use of refrigeration for the preservation of tobacco in transit over long distances.

Van Schouven lived in a timber house in Amsterdam that was four hundred years old. After the evening repast Vrouw van Schouven and her young son and daughter excused themselves and retired. The tobacco-grower had led Mr. Swinney to the library to drink Javanese coffee, smoke the strong black cigars of twisted Sumatran tobacco, and inhale the fragrance of a brandy that was laid down the year Wellington cornered Napoleon at Waterloo, not far to the south.

The ceiling timbers of the room were of blackened oak, the deep chairs of oak and leather. Candlelight shone on soft pewter and the glistening leather backs of old books. Many candles illuminated the glowing, lifelike portrait of a wrinkled old woman in a heavy carved gold frame that hung casually on the wall opposite the beamed fireplace where its surface would catch the reflection from the curling colored tongues of driftwood flame.

Mr. Swinney had not been able to take his eyes from it. Not only the portrait fascinated him, but the concept of its hanging. It was displayed not as an art treasure, but as a part of the warm, richly somber decoration of the old room, as an object, Mr. Swinney felt, that had occupied its place for a long, long time.

To Van Schouven he said finally, indicating the portrait, "How that lives, how warm and kindly it makes this room!"

Van Schouven nodded, drawing on his black cigar until the end glowed. "It iss called se *Old Woman uff Haarlem*. My ancestor Piet van Schouven received it from Rembrandt in payment of a debt. Piet made for Rembrandt a pair of Leiden boots of Spanish leather. It iss so rechistered in his account book." Van Schouven smiled his placid Dutch smile. "Se story iss told that my ancestor considered himself ill used in se exchange. Se leather cost him eleven florins. . . ."

That evening had always remained in Mr. Swinney's memory as a kind of island of deep peace and the ancient culture of living, standing out brightly in the turbulent streams of his travels.

The Germans had brought fire and flame and their new order to Amsterdam. Now the *Old Woman of Haarlem* gazed down at him with her wise, aged eyes peering out from beneath the white wimple from the paneled wall of another library, in Buenos Aires. The heavy, two-foot-square gold frame was a different one, but there was no mistaking the picture. To have seen it once was to know and recognize it forever.

The spell of Swinney's memories was broken when the Countess Amalie spoke softly at his side. Curiously she used almost the same words that had come to Swinney at his first sight of the masterpiece: "How it lives!" and then she added, "What would one not give to possess such beauty!"

A kind of bitter wave shook Mr. Swinney at

the sound of the word "possess" . . . "possess." To possess, the Germans had charred, blackened, and defiled the neighbor nations of Europe.

The guests had been filing into the massive library. They formed into their careful patterns, the Germans grouped in the far corner beneath the fifteenth-century Flemish tapestry whose warm reds and blues set off the pasty white of their faces, which were beginning to show signs of strain. The correct, tawny Baron von Schleuder was pale too. He kept licking his lips, affixing and removing his monocle, and staring at the picture.

The British shifted their island close to the massive carved Spanish table and whispered amongst themselves; the French and Italians gesticulated and made approving noises. The Argentines formed a group close to the picture itself, with the suave, gray, icily cold Dr. Calderriega, De Paraná flushed and excited, and Chester Allen Buskirk polishing his glasses briskly as a nucleus.

Mr. Swinney felt the tension that lay beneath the exclamations and the high-pitched conversations in the room and understood it. His own mathematics were complete. The sum of two and two still made four. The trial balloon was about to go up.

He said to himself, *Clever Calderriega. He'll help them get rid of their loot, but he doesn't trust his dear Nazi friends any farther than he can see them.*

Mr. Chester Allen Buskirk, having wiped the last speck off the windows of his lenses, adjusted his pince-nez, cleared his throat, and stepped toward the painting, which hung just above eye-level. An uneasy hush broken only by whisperings fell over the room.

Buskirk took full advantage of the center of the stage. He cocked his head gingerly, he stepped away, he stepped closer to examine the texture of the paint, he stepped away again. . . .

God, thought Swinney, *you've got it in your hands, little man. Tell 'em it's a fake and you'll spike them. Surely you know who owns that picture.*

Buskirk cleared his throat again, removed his pince-nez, and turned to De Paraná and Calderriega. "Unquestionably authentic! Unquestionably Rembrandt's *Old Woman of Haarlem!*"

The German group stirred first, shifting and turning. Several of them used their handkerchiefs. Baron von Schleuder gazed sternly and fixedly at the picture and said, "Colossal!" French and Italian shoulders were lifted higher, the Argentines broke into a torrent of excited Spanish, and the cynical whisperings of the British increased; the Russians glowered. There were no other Americans in the room besides Mr. Swinney and Buskirk.

The fussy, self-important little art expert was perfectly conscious of the figure he was cutting. He drifted over toward Mr. Swinney, attracted by the light from the tower of the Countess Amalie's bronze-colored hair.

The Countess turned her wide-set huntress's eyes on the little man and said, "What learning was embodied in that simple statement!"

Buskirk preened himself. "Learning? No. It is an emotion. Learning may be prey to error; the emotions aroused by the perfect blending of intellect with light and color, never."

"Damn your emotion," said Mr. Augustus A. Swinney, sharply.

Buskirk started so that his pince-nez fell into his hand. "I beg your pardon, sir!"

Mr. Swinney's voice was cold and cutting. "There is also such a thing as ethics."

Buskirk was confused, but with the slyly feline eyes of the girl moving from him to Swinney and back again, he retreated behind an epigram:

"Art is not concerned with ethics, but with truth."

"Bunk!" said Mr. Swinney, his voice made harsh by his rising anger. "You know to whom that picture belongs—and God knows where he is or what the Germans did to him. And yet, knowing it, you identified the picture for a pack of Nazi thieves in cutaway coats."

Buskirk became thoroughly flustered under the attack. Heat rising to his face fogged his glasses and he fell to polishing them furiously. "I am acquainted with Van Schouven. He is now in New York. He may have sold the picture."

"Did you inquire?"

Buskirk felt that he was being interrogated like a little boy and was being humiliated before the stunning and dramatic-looking Countess, who was now watching only Mr. Swinney with a curious expression at the corners of her full mouth. He drew himself up and attempted extrication.

"That is none of my concern, sir. There is an American branch of the International Art Salvage Commission to which Van Schouven can turn to press a claim. I do not deal with property rights, ha hum, but with the limitless horizons of eternal art." He stole a quick look at the Countess Amalie and thought he detected a flicker of approval in her face and felt encouraged to continue.

"Truth in art is not a matter of a bill of sale, sir. The fruits—"

"Hush!" said Mr. Swinney, curtly, the way one might have spoken to a child, but there was distaste on his lips. He looked down at Buskirk from his lean, clean height. "You are a living, walking, talking anachronism. You are as bad as they. You condone. It is time the world learned a better truth than yours—that nothing matters but the difference between right and wrong."

The Countess Amalie drew in a deep breath and veiled her eyes with her kohl-darkened lids.

Buskirk blustered, "You are insulting, sir. I am here as the guest of a Government official."

"That's just it," said Mr. Swinney, but he said it to the retreating, outraged back of the little art expert.

"You have hurt his feelings," said the Countess.

"Damn and hell," said Mr. Swinney from the depths of his growing anger. "It is sickening."

He stopped speaking and the Countess turned her enveloping gaze on him interrogatively to see whether he would continue and tell what was sickening.

Mr. Swinney did not do so. His thin lips closed and his indignant eyes roved over the room and the restless groups of people. But he knew—quite everything. The pattern was clear, unmistakable, and mathematically logical, but it was the perverted, graceless mathematics of the most evil men the world had ever known.

For three years the Germans had been looting captured Europe of its art treasures. Over and beyond what the Görings and Von Ribbentrops had pilfered for themselves and their estates, millions upon millions of dollars' worth of world-famous and historic paintings, sculptures, and antiquities had been pouring into Munich from gutted museums of Poland, Holland, France, Belgium, Italy, Czechoslovakia, Russia, and Norway, from galleries and private collections stripped bare, from ransacked homes.

Mr. Swinney knew that in every occupied city Quislings had waited with lists prepared of every art object of value in the vicinity. Like locusts the Gestapo and party boys had descended upon the communities with vans and trucks and carted it away. Germany might be losing the war in the military sense, but her thieves had cornered the art market of the world. Now the discredited and bankrupt party heelers were preparing to fence the swag for the dollar credits needed to bolster their collapsing financial bastions.

The German mind was no mystery to Mr. Swinney, who had traveled among them and done business with them. Crude and brash though their methods were, they knew they needed a sponsor for their transactions at least once removed from their persons, some group to act at once as window dressing, front, and buffer and raise some slight incense smoke screen of legitimacy to offset the stench of intrinsic German crookedness.

What was more logical than to turn to the strongest and wealthiest and most powerful South American nation, the only one whose Government was openly friendly and helpful to the Nazis and secretly hostile to the United States and the Allies?

Even Mr. Swinney had to admit that the use of the name of Dr. José Calderriega as sponsor of the exhibition had been brilliantly conceived.

For if this show was not exactly a Government affair, yet Dr. Calderriega was *of* the Government, as Sub-Minister of Culture. The Germans had calculated well that his name and position would stifle criticism and opposition from the outset.

The use of Alfonso de Paraná had been clever too. Known as one of the wealthiest men in the country, and connoisseur of art in his own right, with a notable private collection, the turning up of a famous picture in his possession was just the right touch.

But Mr. Swinney had no illusions about De Paraná. He was an out-and-out fascist and Germanophile. Enough of the booty would stick to his fingers to make it worth his while, but his role was strictly that of middleman. Mr. Swinney thought with disgust of the greed that would bring art dealers through these salons in the days to come, perhaps some of his own countrymen among them.

Nor did Mr. Swinney need the rumors, or pickups, or snatches of conversation caught on the fly to tell him how the stuff was to get there. Light, small, compact, a rolled-up canvas by Raphael would fit into any cranny in an undersea boat; a twelfth-century triptych, a medallion by Benvenuto Cellini, a tapestry by Gobelin, ancient jeweled candlesticks from Polish churches, encrusted chalices of the early popes, would take up little more space. One U-boat could load enough boodle to pay for a day of war. Mr. Swinney had no doubt that a Nazi submarine was lurking somewhere near by, waiting to unload the rest of its cargo if it had not already done so.

Once they had got away with the transfer and sale of the Rembrandt as a trial, the Nazis would flood the market for all the traffic would bear. It all dovetailed, even to that pompous ass Buskirk.

Fascists or no fascists, Calderriega and De Paraná were no fools. *They* knew their Germans and had cleverly protected themselves against having a fake put over on them. But in addition Buskirk's presence had served to set a further seal upon the affair.

A kind of silence fell over the room again, and Mr. Swinney saw that the icily gray Dr. Calderriega was about to say a few words. They came out in Spanish, as neat and clipped as his gray mustache, as tight and spare and reserved as his figure:

"Presence of this great painting . . . under the roof of Señor de Paraná . . . milestone in and monument to Latin-American culture . . . congratulations due this great art patron of Buenos Aires. . . ."

The Germans nudged one another, smirked, raised their champagne glasses as in a military drill, and said, *"Hoch!"*

A few desultory "Hear, hear"s came from the British contingent; a Frenchman cried, *"Epatant!"* the Russians glowered silently and shifted their feet uncomfortably. People in the room milled about a little.

Mr. Swinney's gorge rose. *Fire and damnation,* he thought to himself. *Not only I know; they all know! Every one of them! Everyone here knows, and the Germans and that gray Argentine and the fat one with the pouches know they know, and are ramming it down their throats.*

This, then, was the second lie that was being circulated there that afternoon, as lightly as the canapés and the Venetian cocktail glasses, as hushed and hidden as that other diplomatic fiction of the nonpresence of diplomats of countries engaged in war.

The British knew—it was in their tight lips and frigid bearing. The Russians knew, and showed it in their scowls and uneasily moving feet. The Swiss, the Slavs, the French, the Italians knew it. The Spaniards were laughing up their sleeves. The fashionably gowned women knew it, and showed it in the sly casting of their eyes and the heads bent forward to whisper. The men from the embassies had known it for weeks and merely moved a little more stiffly from the hips.

Everyone was privy to the same logic, the same reasoning, the same rumors, the same information as Mr. Augustus A. Swinney, simple loyal American citizen, refrigeration engineer, and fascist-hater.

But no one said anything.

Over them all, like an unseen, viscous garment, constricting and attenuating thought and movement and behavior, lay the cloak of diplomatic conduct. The soft net of protocol was tougher than steel. They might know what they knew, or whisper behind their hands what they pleased, but until something was said or done, the truth that they knew was not a truth at all, but a lie sealed in their bosoms.

Cleverly the net spun in the musty office of the Pinakothek had been cast the long way from Munich and ensnared them all.

That is, with one notable and fatal exception, that exception being the curious mathematical mind of Mr. Swinney, who lived by the addition of two and two.

Alfonso de Paraná was replying to the speech of the Sub-Minister of Culture, his voice oily with success and content:

"Let us not say that I am to be congratulated, but rather Argentina. The country that is permitted to be the host to such a peerless work of art is fortunate indeed. I am proud . . ."

Between the end of the speech, the polite murmurs of applause, the reiterated *"Hoch!"* of the Nazis, and what Mr. Swinney said and did, no more than a second or two elapsed. But in that brief interim in which his limbs were chill with rage, his mind leaped back to a tale he remembered reading as a boy, the story of the King's new suit of clothes, in which the three rascally tailors clad the King with imaginary thread and fabric, and none in the sycophant court dared contradict that the nonexistent garment was not as beautiful as they claimed it to be.

He remembered even, as sharply as though it had been thrown up on a screen before him, the illustration of the King walking through the streets mother-naked, past the cheering throngs lined up to view his fine new suit, the train-bearer behind, holding up the ends of the nonexistent cloak. And he remembered the little child in the throng at the curb who looked up and cried, "But the King hasn't any clothes on!"

Mr. Swinney took a sudden step forward, quite unaware of the gentle, detaining touch of the hand of the Countess Amalie upon his arm. His voice, clear, incisive, and steady, cut through the room and sheared a gaping rent in the binding fabric that ensnared them all.

"That picture has been stolen!"

In the awful silence someone dropped a glass and it shivered daintily with the sound of a Balinese cymbal.

Dr. José Calderriega, stiff, motionless, frosty as an icicle, sucked in his breath like a Japanese. Only his eyes were alive. No one moved. De Paraná blinked heavily. A slow purple crept into the pouches beneath his heavy eyes.

Mr. Swinney spoke again, and because there was now no sound but the tinkle and rustle and chatter from the outer salon, his voice had the terrible quality of a sledge hammer shattering heavy glass:

"That picture was stolen by the Germans in Amsterdam from a private house. It is the property of Mynheer Jan van Schouven, a Dutch refugee now living in New York."

A voice hissed in German, *"Was hat er gesagt?"* and was immediately stifled. The monocle of Baron von Schleuder dropped into his hand with a little meaty sound. Still no one moved. They were all in the grip of the horror that comes when a terrible truth is held aloft by the hair like a Gorgon's head to stare them to stone.

But Dr. José Calderriega, Sub-Minister of Culture, was in the grip of a worse horror than that. For the first time in his gray, icy, correct diplomatic life he was face to face with an insoluble situation. His breath kept hissing in and out between his gray lips and a kind of film like a lizard's lid had come over his eyes.

Mr. Swinney moved forward slowly with a kind of measured pace, a careful rhythm. It brought him to where the picture hung upon the paneled wall. It was as though he himself was the captive of a dream as he faced them once more. He said, quietly this time, to hold the static mood:

"I am removing this picture, which is the property of no one present, and taking it into custody until it can be returned to its rightful owner."

He lifted the picture from the wall, tucked the heavy frame under his arm, and began his fantastic march from the room.

He should have been pinioned, leaped upon, held, stopped a thousand times, but he was not. They were hypnotized by the shocking audacity of what he had said and what he was doing. For, that first dangerous moment, they did not even believe what they were seeing.

Three steps, four steps. . . . The cat-eyes of the Countess Amalie were round and staring and deep violet, and her small white teeth were showing like seeds through the red fruit of her lips.

Five—six—seven . . . through the open lane. The British were grinning. A big Russian had his head thrown back and mouth open in silent laughter. The Germans were blocked off in the far corner of the room. Mr. Swinney could no longer see them. When—? When would someone leap upon his back and carry him to the floor?

Nine, ten. . . . He was through the door and into the buffet room. He saw the back of Buskirk's toupee at the buffet table. The little man was helping himself to some more ham and did not turn around. Another moment and Mr. Swinney was in the outer salon.

No one there paid any attention to a tall gentleman carrying a gold picture frame under his arm, though several made room politely to permit him to pass.

How long? How long? Mr. Swinney thought to himself. *How long have I? They are none of them men of action except Von Schleuder, and he has none of his Nazi thugs with him. They are all gentlemen and not used to direct action. But sooner or later they must—*

He was on the broad, carved staircase of ancient Spanish oak that curved to the marble foyer below.

Now at last from above he was conscious of confused sounds at higher pitch than normal cocktail-party babel, a cry and a muffled thumping.

Through the greatest effort of his life, Mr. Swinney did not quicken his step, but kept his even, measured tread, nodded pleasantly to the footman who opened the heavy, grilled wrought-iron door for him, and went out into the balmy January summer twilight.

The lights were just beginning to come on bordering the broad, tree-lined Avenida Alvear. Slick, shiny cars with liveried chauffeurs and footmen waited in a long, elegant line for their masters outside the white mansion of Señor de Paraná. A green-and-black-checkered taxicab drifted by. Mr. Swinney hailed it and climbed in. *"Vamos al ciudad—subito!"*

"Sí, señor."

The cab moved away down the broad residential avenue in the direction of the city.

When the first of the pursuit led by the tawny-headed Baron von Schleuder and Señor de Paraná poured into the street, there was nothing to be seen of either Mr. Augustus Swinney or the *Old Woman of Haarlem*, or, for that matter, to indicate where they had gone.

The driver leaned back and inquired, "Where to, señor?" and when he received no reply, knocked on the window separating him from his passenger and inquired again, but received only a vague wave to proceed. Mr. Augustus A. Swinney was suffering from reaction. He was quite incapable for the moment of telling where he wanted to go or what he wanted to do.

He thought to himself, *Great and little gods, what have I done, and why did I do it? What ever possessed me? And what will I do next? And furthermore what will* they *do?*

Mr. Swinney needed time to think, to collect himself, to prepare for the unquestionably unpleasant consequences that were certain to follow upon the heels of his rash act.

He wrapped on the window. "Eighteen, Calle Garibaldi. Swift & Company."

"Sí, señor!"

When Mr. Swinney was in trouble or needed to reflect, somehow he gravitated to his office over the giant refrigerating plant near the waterfront docks. He could think there.

It was a little after six o'clock when he arrived and paid off the driver. Still bearing the heavy gold frame of the portrait carefully under his arm, he let himself in with his night key and went up the stairs.

Later, in the library of Alfonso de Paraná, Dr. Calderriega was addressing a group of the guests. The doors to the library were shut. Beyond in the other two salons the party still continued.

He said with icy self-containment, "Only you who were present in this room and who are here now were witness to—what occurred here. It is of the utmost importance to the Government that no hint, no word of this is permitted to leak out. If there is such a leak, we shall know where and how to trace it and the consequences will be of the utmost seriousness. We have to deal obviously with a man who is either drunk or insane. The picture will be recovered shortly. Until that time I must insist upon your silence."

But still later, closeted in another room with De Paraná and Baron von Schleuder, Dr. Calderriega was not quite so certain, though his doubts were never permitted to penetrate the smooth, chill correctness of his exterior.

The Baron adjusted his monocle and stared coldly at Dr. Calderriega.

"Na, my friend. You are in a pretty fix."

Dr. Calderriega elevated his gray eyebrows an eighth of an inch, the most violent display of emotion permitted himself. "If you will permit me, Herr Baron, so are you."

"Pah! Let me handle it my way and we will have the picture back in an hour. Who is this maniac?"

De Paraná consulted a small slip of paper. "His name is Augustus A. Swinney. He is an American engineer employed by Swift & Company. He lives alone in an apartment at No. 17 Avenida Manuel Quintana."

Dr. Calderriega made a note of the address.

"I will pay a visit to this gentleman and persuade him to return it."

The Baron said significantly: "If you do not succeed—we shall take steps. If this man escapes—"

"My dear Baron," said Dr. Calderriega patiently, "consider the utter impossibility of a man, the employee of a large American firm, leaving Buenos Aires accompanied by one of the most valuable pictures in the world. But in the meantime I strongly suggest that you hold the further development of this transaction in abeyance. I will be in touch with you and with Señor de Paraná later in the evening."

In New York City, where it was an hour earlier, Curtis Henry said to his wife over cocktails, "I can't get that little Dutchman, Van Schouven, out of my mind. He's got such dignity. There's a fellow who once had the best of everything, probably living on nothing now. I doubt whether even his own countrymen here know how hard up he must be. I wonder what one could do for a chap like that. Probably nothing."

In the damp, bare, dingy room that looked out over the dirty, noisy, winter-bound slum street, Jan van Schouven pondered over what the doctor had told him of the dire necessity of moving the woman with whom he had lived for all his life in faith and harmony to a warmer climate and wondered what he should do, for there was nothing more left to sell. And because he did not know, he did something he and many of his people had learned to do since the coming of the war. He turned to prayer and asked for help.

In South America, too, darkness had fallen over the little cove outside of Avellaneda where the captain of the U-boat was playing skat with the first officer. He said, "What the devil is the matter with that fellow Von Schleuder that we did not hear from him? Why can't we get that damned bric-a-bràc ashore and get out of here?"

The first officer took a trick. "We will probably hear from him tomorrow."

The captain spat. "Tomorrow—tomorrow. Always tomorrow. Some day tomorrow will be too late for Germany."

It was shortly after seven o'clock when Mr. Swinney emerged from the warehouse on the Calle Garibaldi, still tenderly lugging a square bundle under his arm. But now the two sides of the heavy carved and gilded frame peered out from heavy swathings of burlap that Mr. Swinney had wrapped around it to keep it from harm or damage.

He had to walk a block or two before he found a taxicab. He gave the driver the address of his apartment, No. 17 Avenida Manuel Quintana, and was more than a little impatient of the heavy traffic in the central part of the town because he was expecting visitors. He was rather anxious to arrive before his callers.

At that, he just did. Gabino, his houseman, let him in.

"Anyone call, Gabino?"

"No, señor."

"Very well. I am expecting some visitors. I will answer the door myself. If I should need anything I will call you."

Mr. Swinney lived in a modern three-room apartment on the sixth floor. The large multi-paned windows of the living-room looked out on the quiet, tree-lined avenue. A small vestibule led from the outer door to this room. Beyond was a small dining-room and a bedroom.

Mr. Swinney placed his package on the chrome mantel over the modern, decorative, but nonfunctional fireplace facing the entrance hallway, but he did not remove the protective burlap wrapping. The bright gilt of the frame showed up like pirate gold against the severe stainless steel of the mantel paneling.

Thereafter he had only time to light a cigarette and go to his bookshelf and briefly examine a small volume before the door buzzer rang. Mr. Swinney replaced the book and opened the door. It was, as he had expected, Dr. José Calderriega, Sub-Minister of Culture of the Argentine.

Dr. Calderriega came through the vestibule and into the living-room with a quick, nervous step, but he paused on the threshold for an instant as his gaze fell upon the mantel. He said, "Ah."

"Yes," said Mr. Swinney. "Won't you sit down?"

Dr. Calderriega sat on the edge of a chrome fauteuil, a perfection of a man in every small, icy detail, from his polished shoes to his faultless head. Age had not altered his appearance or the smoothness of his skin; it had merely frosted him. There was also frost in his voice as he inquired:

"You are Mr. Augustus Swinney?"

"I am."

"May I inquire before going any further, Mr. Swinney, whether this was a practical joke?"

"No," said Mr. Swinney softly, but definitely. "It was not a practical joke."

Dr. Calderriega's lips relaxed and he nodded slightly. Mr. Swinney thought, *Now that he has ascertained that I am neither drunk nor a maniac, he has had to back off and begin all over again. I must be careful to keep this conversation on a high diplomatic plane or he will be shocked and disappointed. Well, we shall see.*

"Mr. Swinney, we will overlook your indefensible behavior if you will permit me to leave with the picture and restore it to Señor de Paraná."

"That is generous, Dr. Calderriega. I regret I cannot permit it."

"I see. And what do you intend to do with it?"

"Secure it until I am able to restore it to its owner."

"The owner is Señor Alfonso de Paraná."

Mr. Swinney rose with a small sigh. "Under those circumstances I can no longer discuss the matter with you, Dr. Calderriega. Stealing is a matter for the police. I suggest that you call them. I will notify the American Embassy that I am ready to submit to arrest."

Dr. Calderriega sighed also, but like a dried leaf blown on ice. "Sit down, Mr. Swinney. There is—ah—no question of the police—at the moment. What is it you want?"

"To return the picture to its actual owner, Mynheer van Schouven."

Dr. Calderriega coughed. "You are certain of your ground? Supposing no proof of previous ownership exists?"

Mr. Swinney nodded. "I understand the Germans have shown their usual thoroughness in destroying all records, indexes, and proofs of ownership in connection with their national thieving expeditions. Well—" He paused, but he was not looking at the Sub-Minister. His eyes had wandered to his bookshelves across the room. He then tried very hard to suppress a grin, but was unable to and let it happen. He went over to the shelf and plucked out a small red volume, the one he had examined previously.

"The Germans, Dr. Calderriega, should have liquidated one of their most prolific cataloguers before they undertook their tour of looting. The evidence of their own uncle Karl Baedeker will yet brand them as the most shameless nation of thieves the world has ever known."

He thumbed through the little book. "Do you remember these little guidebooks clutched to the breasts of Americans rushing about Europe? Baedeker's *Belgium and Holland*, 1930, page 257, Amsterdam—the Rijks Museum. I quote: 'First floor . . . third room . . . on the right is hung Rembrandt's masterpiece *Old Woman of Haarlem*, parenthesis, on loan for five years by its owner, J. van Schouven, close parenthesis. This magnificent head, in the warmest tones of the master, depicts—' Well, the canvas is quite well described. Any court of law would recognize this as evidence."

Dr. Calderriega exhaled slowly and correctly. A single glistening bead of water no bigger than a seed pearl appeared beside the close-clipped gray mustache. Finally he said softly, "Do you really believe, Mr. Swinney, that you will be able to remove this picture from Buenos Aires?"

Mr. Swinney considered the question for a moment before he replied, "Yes, I believe I will."

"Permit me to say that you are playing a dangerous game, sir."

"Permit me to say that you are too, doctor. Your name appears upon the invitation as sponsor to the exhibition of Señor de Paraná."

A second bead, in perfect balance, appeared on the other side of the Sub-Minister's lip. Mr. Swinney wondered whether they were both congealed there.

For the first time Dr. Calderriega's voice took on an edge, like a figure skater grating a blade on a turn: "You understand, sir, that the Government is not officially involved."

"Naturally," said Mr. Swinney with a slight bow. "It is obviously beneath the dignity of the government of Argentina to assist in—ah—the disposal of purloined articles. Still, publicity would be regrettable. The Argentine people might not understand."

The shudder that Dr. Calderriega gave at the word "publicity" was almost human.

"However," continued Mr. Swinney, "it seems to me that no publicity is necessary, if—"

Dr. Calderriega leaned forward slightly. "If—?"

"If the art market in Buenos Aires were closed to—foreign export, the subject would never come up, I feel certain."

"Ah. It is perhaps fortunate that the Ministry of Culture has the final say in—such matters."

"As you say, it is most fortunate."

Dr. Calderriega rose and gazed for a moment at the object on the mantel. Something approaching a groan burst from him. "It is impossible! Impossible! Do you realize that there will be other—forces interested in the repossession of that picture, forces that will stop at nothing—absolutely nothing?"

"That," said Mr. Swinney succinctly, "is your worry as much as mine, Dr. Calderriega. I wish you luck. Good evening."

Shortly after the Sub-Minister had left, Mr. Swinney went to the window and looked down into the street. He saw two policemen in their dark-blue uniforms with black leather puttees, Sam Browne belts, and peaked caps with red bands. They strolled fifty yards up the street, then stopped and strolled back again.

Mr. Swinney smiled. He thought, *I'd give a*

lot to know whether they're there to keep me in or to keep others out.

He did not trust Dr. Calderriega. When a man walks the thin crust of such scandal, disgrace, and disaster as the Sub-Minister trod, he might also be tempted to join those forces that would stop at nothing.

He wondered when those would begin to arrive.

It was nearly nine o'clock before Baron von Schleuder let himself out of the self-operating lift at the sixth floor of Number 17 Avenida Manuel Quintana and pressed the button outside Mr. Swinney's door.

Upon being admitted, the Baron entered briskly and with an air of busy determination. He was a large man with one of those large-featured faces which look as though they had been fashioned roughly in putty. His tawny, leonine hair was slicked back from his forehead and he wore his monocle. He, too, paused at the living-room threshold, stared stonily at the exhibit on the mantel, and said, "So."

Mr. Swinney made no comment, nor did he invite the Baron to sit down. Instead he remained silent, waiting for the conversation to open. The Baron permitted his monocle to drop into his left hand and said, "Mr. Svinney?"

"Yes?"

"Von Schleuder! Cherman Embassy!" His sentences came out curt and harsh, like military commands. "We will speak about this picture."

Mr. Swinney replied, "Very well. Whom are you representing? Señor de Paraná?"

"Certainly not!"

"I see. The German Government, then?"

Baron von Schleuder opened his large lips to reply and then closed them firmly and glared at Mr. Swinney.

"It is not a question of whom I represent. The picture must be returned immediately."

"I don't recognize your authority."

"By what right you presume to keep this picture?"

"Well," said Mr. Swinney reflectively, glancing at the gilt-edged bundle on the mantel, "let us say the right of immediate possession. You had it. Dr. Paraná had it. Now I have it. I might add that I got it the way your Government did. I took it."

Von Schleuder's thoughts playing over his heavy face were as transparent as a newly washed window.

Mr. Swinney said quietly, "Are you thinking of trying to take it from me physically? It would raise the most awful row. People would come. . . ."

"Ach!" said the Baron, "don't be ridiculous. That kind of extravagances is for romances." He suddenly made an elephantine gesture that was supposed to indicate change of attitude, good-fellowship, and a new-found understanding. "Let us play all the cards on the table, Mr. Svinney. We wish the picture returned of your own will. What is your price?"

Mr. Swinney looked as innocent as a newborn child. "I would have to get in touch with the owner, Mynheer van Schouven, from whom the picture was originally stolen by the Germans. I doubt whether he would wish to sell it to you."

The Baron was not amused. He abandoned his jovial air as quickly as he assumed it. "Ah so! Well, you have ask for trouble. You will have only yourself to blame."

"That's better," said Mr. Swinney. "That's how we love you."

The Baron gave Mr. Swinney a measuring and even slightly quizzical look in which he raised his brows a full inch, like a tenor on a high note.

"Well," he said at last in the conversational tone of one who is about to take his departure, having concluded his business, "at least we understand one another. I hope you do not get hurt, Mr. Svinney. If you attempt to remove this picture from this room, much less from Buenos Aires, you will do so at your own risk, is that not so?"

"Thanks," said Mr. Swinney. "I'll let you know when it gets to New York. Then you and Calderriega both will be able to relax. And, ah—I usually shoot at burglars."

The Baron smiled a quiet, lemony smile, replaced his monocle, glanced once more at the object on the mantel, and departed. Mr. Swinney went to the window and saw the Baron emerge into the street. Three men climbed out of a car parked at the curb. The Baron spoke to them briefly, entered the car, and drove away. The three remained standing in the shadows. Mr. Swinney was under no illusions as to what *their* presence meant.

Mr. Swinney was also under no illusions as to his position. He was in a fix and he knew it. If because of circumstances Calderriega and Von Schleuder were unable for the moment to avail themselves of normal procedures to recover the painting, neither was Mr. Swinney in any position to ask for protection. Once he succeeded in getting the picture out of the country, the game would be won. But Mr. Swinney gave a kind of rueful snort. He would have given much at the moment for an idea as to how that was to be accomplished.

Augustus Swinney was a businessman with a strong sense of justice, and not an adventurer, even though his quixotic impulses and deep-seated hatred of his country's enemies sometimes landed him in strange situations. Nevertheless he took natural precautions.

From a drawer he secured a small .32 automatic, tested its action, saw that it was loaded and a shell in the chamber, and slipped it into his pocket. He then wrote out a list of groceries and canned goods and summoned Gabino.

"*Vaya al bodega.* The one on the corner of Vincente Lopez is open until ten. When you return, knock and call out. It will be locked."

From the window he watched the houseman emerge from the service entrance down the street. The three Nazis in the shadows did not budge, but one of the two uniformed policemen detached himself from his post on the other side of the street and strolled after him.

"Damn!" said Mr. Swinney.

When an hour passed and the houseman had not returned, he knew. He reflected that they would not hurt him. The servant had probably been arrested on some trumped-up pretext, thoroughly searched, and held.

Then it was to be a siege. Mr. Swinney locked and bolted the rear service door, fastened the short chain to the front door leading to the lift and stairway, and inspected his larder. With careful rationing there was enough food—cereals and a few items of canned goods—to last him for quite a while. He was glad to note a plentiful supply of coffee. He would need that to keep awake. He set about brewing himself a potful at once.

In the living-room Mr. Swinney sipped the thick, strong drink, considered his situation and his chances, and tried to figure from whence the attack would come. The procession of polite diplomatic visitors he knew was over. The next parties to ring his doorbell would mean business. And if they came in force—well, even a dead American refrigeration engineer in a burgled apartment could be hushed up in a dictatorship.

Shortly before midnight Mr. Swinney heard the humming of the automatic lift and the click and thump as it stopped at his floor. After a moment's pause the buzzer sounded.

Polite of them! he said to himself. *Well, it's about time. As the Baron put it, I asked for it.*

He slipped the safety catch of the gun in his pocket and went to the door. "Who is it?"

No reply. Mr. Swinney wondered whether he was being a fool and whether the next move would not be a fusillade through the door. Nevertheless, leaving the short chain on, he opened the door to the width it permitted.

He smelled, not gunpowder, but the sweet, exciting fragrance of perfume, caught a glimpse of white skin and bronze hair and a drape of fur.

"Amalie!" said Mr. Swinney, and took the chain off the door.

The Countess Amalie was framed magnificently by the doorway. She wore an evening sheath of black satin without a single ornament to distract from the immediate form beneath it. The fur drape of chinchilla made a background for the wide cat-eyes slanting into the high cheekbones.

She said, "Am I terrible? If you misunderstand, I shall hate you to the day I die."

"My dear Countess," said Mr. Swinney, "won't you come in?" He understood very well, and her presence thrilled him to the core. He had met many women of the genre of the Countess Amalie in Europe and had invariably found the experience stimulating and enchanting. They made practically no demands.

He had recognized the type immediately the first time he had seen her. The meeting in the salon of Señor de Paraná had confirmed it to him. He had read the answer in the first glance they had exchanged. In a masculine and quite unrefined manner, Mr. Swinney had entertained great hopes for the development of a beautiful friendship with the Countess Amalie Czernok. Mr. Swinney had not traveled extensively for nothing. Then the somewhat florid events he had precipitated had quite driven thoughts of her out of his head.

Misunderstand indeed! That was how the game began.

She crossed the threshold and faced the steel and chrome mantel and the gilt-edged, burlap-wrapped object that reposed thereon. Her gaze never left it as Mr. Swinney removed the downy, feather-light, exquisite fur from her shoulders.

"That is why I had to come," she said—"to tell you what I felt. For no other reason." The sensual mysteries of centuries lay behind her cat-smile.

"I have thought of nothing else since it happened—your courage to do this thing for our people. I thought that I had seen and known brave men. I am European. I have seen what our people have suffered and I have met courage, but until today I have never known the meaning of pure . . ."

Mr. Swinney's nerves were badly jangled by what he had been through. He felt suddenly like a soldier who knows that on the morrow he returns to the firing line and, because time as well as desire is of the essence, is impatient of delay.

He faced her, put his hands to her shoulders, and said, "Amalie—for God's sake—stop talking."

"Oh God," said the Countess. "I can't help myself. What is it you have done to me?"

Mr. Swinney held her in his arms and sought for the key to the barrier that was between them, the resolution of the mood that made her suddenly shake with sobs.

She said, "I do not know what has happened to me. I cannot help myself. And now I am afraid."

"Afraid?"

"For you, my dear—what they will do. A moment ago what you had done seemed the bravest, noblest deed in the world. And now—"

She escaped him and he let her go. She went to the mantel and with her fingers touched the gilt frame, the burlap wrapping.

Mr. Swinney said, "I love you, Amalie."

She turned to him. "Oh, I hate it—I hate it," she burst out. "It will come between us. Can I help being a woman? There are too many of them—they are too strong. What can one man do against them? Don't you understand? If they—"

Mr. Swinney went to her, but not precipitately, because he did not wish to frighten her further. Not until she was in his arms again did he say, "My dear, what can we do—now?"

"Give it up. We can't fight them alone. I could not bear to lose you—now."

Mr. Swinney heaved a deep sigh. "Maybe I'm a fool, Amalie. It was different until you came here. Perhaps you are right."

"My dear—my dear. . . ."

There were no more barriers—so much so that at first Mr. Swinney had some little difficulty in extricating himself. Rage and cold distaste aided him. The Countess was facing him, her cat-eyes as wide open and mouse-wary as they would go. He took the feather-light chinchilla and dropped it around her shoulders.

"All right," said Mr. Swinney. "Get out." He said, "Go back to the company you came from, the spying sluts of Stieber and Bismarck and all the rest of the master race, whose dirty work you do."

He said further, "Go back to the Middle Ages, where you belong. You are old-fashioned, outmoded. We are tired of you and we are tired of your Germans. The whole world is tired to death of you all. You smell of blood and money and the dead. When we finish with this world we are making today, there will be no room left in it for you or any other of their filthy works."

The Countess Amalie, who could recognize a closed book when she saw one, went quietly, without a word, and with only a hint of genuine regret in her wide, violet eyes.

Mr. Swinney locked and chained the door and went out into the kitchen and heated himself some coffee. It was while he was drinking it that he remembered the look in her eyes. He said to himself, *Swinney, you're an idiot. Couldn't you have been so damned noble a little later?*

Then he set himself to the task of remaining awake. But there were no further incidents of any kind that night.

In the morning, while he was shaving, Mr. Swinney reviewed the debit and credit sides of his performance, and for the first time since he had insulted him he thought of Chester Allen Buskirk, the stuffy little Old World gentleman and art critic, and his conscience hurt him a little.

The man was a product of a dead and bygone era. He had meant no harm; he had even been honest, according to his own lights. Mr. Swinney wished there were some way in which he might convey to him that he regretted his behavior toward him.

The idea of how this might be done came to him with such suddenness that he cut himself shaving, which was hardly worth the salvaging of social amenities with a man he would never see again. But Mr. Swinney stanched the blood without regrets or rancor and went out to see that the time was after nine o'clock, which meant that his office would be available.

He picked up the telephone and dialed his office number. There was a clicking on the line, which told him no more than he expected. The phone was tapped. He didn't care; he got his secretary on the line and said, "I may not be in for a while—might be a week. If anything turns up, you can reach me at home."

Then he gave some business directions and concluded with: "Is Miguel there? Put him on."

Miguel was the refrigerator foreman. When he came on the line, Swinney said, "Hello, Miguel. Swinney speaking. Have we any of those special hams left? You know, the old ones?"

"I am not sure, señor. Shall I look?"

"I'll wait. Take a look. Try locker nine. There were some there last month."

After a five-minute wait the foreman came back on the line. "*Si, señor.* I have found one."

"Good. Do it up. Attach one of my cards. Miss Diega will give you one. Have her write on it: 'My compliments and apologies.' Right? Jump into your car and take it out to the airport and deliver it to Mr. Chester Allen Buskirk. He is leaving on the eleven-o'clock plane. Let me know if he received it. That's all."

Mr. Swinney looked out the window to see whether the new shift had come on yet. It had. Both the local police and the Nazi honor guard had been changed.

He thought what he would do if he were in the enemy's place, and the logic of what must be their reasoning struck him as simple as the adding of two and two. They were prepared to wait him out. Mr. Swinney's problem was equally simple. It was to stay awake. He wondered just how long a man could go without sleep and still function.

At one o'clock Miguel telephoned. "The señor received the ham, sir. He say to you thank you."

Now, that was nice of him, Mr. Swinney thought to himself.

The second night without sleep was bad, but the third was plain hell, and Mr. Swinney did not know how he could go on.

He had thought to devise a way to steal catnaps by setting his alarm clock to ring after a half hour of sleep. But the second time he tried it, he woke up at the last faint tinkle of the bell to find the mechanism quite run down. Another moment and he would have slept on through.

Twice there had been action on both nights, once at the front door and once at the back. He had gone there and called through the door, "Skip it, boys." He heard them departing, and the last time he heard them laughing.

Also, the second day his telephone was cut off. Mail and papers were no longer delivered. He lost track of time and dates, even though he marked the calendar, but his exhausted brain was playing him tricks. He learned all there was to know about the deadly and exquisite torture of sleeplessness, and several times he was on the verge of giving up.

Then he would down more coffee, prod himself, force himself to pace the apartment, show himself at the window. He would become confused and look at the calendar to see the time instead of his watch.

He had marked off the days—Tuesday, January 11—Wednesday, January 12. Thursday, January 13, took on the terrible aspects of a mountain peak he might never achieve. They, on the other hand, were fresh and strong. If he fell asleep . . . they would force the door. . . . He fought on desperately. . . .

On Thursday, January 13, Mr. Augustus Swinney, having somehow survived the night, took an icy shower, shaved, put on clean linen and a fresh white suit, plucked a geranium from his window box and stuck it in his buttonhole, put on his Panama hat, and went out.

As he closed the front door of his apartment he did not so much as throw a glance at the thing still resting on the chrome mantel, where it had been ever since he had put it there so long ago.

The Baron von Schleuder answered his telephone. "He has gone out? *Donnervetter!* Kurt is following him? He is breakfasting at the Continental? Yes! At once. No—wait! I will come immediately."

Dr. José Calderriega also answered an insistent ringing of his private line.

"What? Left? At the Continental? An officer is still there? No one else has come or gone? No, no! Do not enter until I arrive."

They made quite a party in the foyer of No. 17 Avenida Manuel Quintana, too many of them to crowd into the automatic elevator all at once, so Dr. José Calderriega and Baron von Schleuder, eyeing each other warily, went up ahead, leaving the others to follow and taking only the police department expert with the skeleton keys.

The keys, however, proved to be quite unnecessary, because, upon their trying the handle of the outer apartment door, it proved to be unlocked.

Outside of hundreds of cigarette stubs and some empty coffee cups, the apartment was unchanged as the two men remembered it. There was even the burlap-wrapped affair on the mantel. Dr. Calderriega, in spite of his age, was the first to reach it, but the Baron helped him unwrap the protective sacking and reveal the empty frame and the note in the middle of it, which was brief and to the point.

Dear Dr. Calderriega—or Von Schleuder:

Will you oblige me by returning this frame to Señor de Paraná or whoever owns it, as it does not belong either to me or to Mynheer van Schouven.

The Old Woman of Haarlem *is now in New York City.*

I beg that you will believe me and refrain from ransacking my property. I shall be forced to present a bill for whatever damage is done to my premises.

> *Very truly yours,*
> *Augustus A. Swinney.*

They did not believe him and tore the apartment to shreds, and later on Dr. Calderriega paid a large bill without a murmur. But they did not find the *Old Woman of Haarlem*, for a very simple reason. Mr. Swinney had told the truth.

In New York City, Mr. Curtis Henry pounded on the door of the third-floor room of Jan van Schouven, shouting:

"Van Schouven! Van Schouven! Open at once! I must see you!"

The little Dutchman emerged looking pale and worn and more childlike than ever.

Curtis Henry said, "Van Schouven! You must come at once. I—I am so excited I can hardly speak. I have not yet got it straight. It is about the *Old Woman of Haarlem*. That ass Buskirk telephoned me. He was in a state himself. Something about a ham from South America and the Rembrandt painting. He has just returned from Buenos Aires and discovered the canvas wrapped around a ham that was given him. He is frightened to death of scandal, realizes the picture was stolen from you, and insists you come at once. If it is true—"

"If it is true," said Mynheer Jan van Schouven, "God is merciful in answering the prayers of those who love Him."

Off Avellaneda, a score or so of miles south of Buenos Aires on the Rio de la Plata, the muddy brown waters of the river gurgled and stirred some two days later and finally healed the breach that had been made in its viscous surface by the disappearance of a steel conning tower.

The U-Boat commander was in a wretched temper for reasons beyond the discomfort of already cramped quarters, further narrowed by carefully wrapped and buttressed packages, packages that if divested of their straw and canvas coverings might reveal a carved Gothic eleventh-century saint, a Botticelli Madonna, or a Florentine chalice.

The second-in-command looked in. "At least we are going home, no? Cleared at 13:05."

The U-boat commander regarded his junior with distaste and delivered himself quietly of the German equivalent of "That's a hell of a way to run a war."

In Munich, Professor Kunstverwaltungsrat Bressar entered his littered office in the Pina-kothek at nine o'clock in the morning in an irritable mood, which was not improved by the spectacle of his assistant, Herr Reinecke, standing at his desk pale and greasy and licking his lips.

"Good morning, Reinecke."

"G-Good morning, Herr Kunstverwaltungs-rat."

"Na! What are you standing there like that for? What is the matter with you?"

"Herr Professor—a—a cable has come. It is not good. Buenos Aires has refused to permit the—shipment to land. It is being returned."

And in Buenos Aires, at the far other end of the hypotenuse of the triangle with Munich and New York, Mr. Augustus A. Swinney was having a cocktail.

But this time he was having it all by himself in the fashionable Boston Bar in the Calle Florida.

He was feeling considerably refreshed after twenty-nine hours of solid sleep. He was also further refreshed by a brief item in *La Prensa*. He had the paper folded to it and could not refrain from reading it over and over again.

It was a New York Associated Press dateline, headed: *Negotiations for Old Master*, and read: *Negotiations were completed today for the acquisition by the Metropolitan Museum of Art of Rembrandt's famous canvas*, Old Woman of Haarlem, *from its owner, Jan van Schouven, Dutch refugee and former wealthy tobacco merchant, for a price reputed to be between $350,000 and $400,000.*

Mr. Swinney would have given much to have seen Buskirk's expression when he cut away the outer wrappings of his special ham and found himself looking into the wonderful, warm old face of the *Old Woman of Haarlem*.

Mr. Swinney knew it had been sheer panic that had caused him to cut the portrait from the frame that evening when he had fled with the picture to his office, and wrap it around an old smoked ham to hide it. The idea had come to him when he had noticed how much the back of the canvas resembled the age and smoke-stained wrappings of these delicacies. Cellophane inside to protect the surface of the canvas, and a few "Swift & Co., Buenos Aires, S.A." packer's rubber stamps had completed the job.

But Mr. Swinney would have been quite as willing to admit that the idea of palming it off on Chester Allen Buskirk and letting him take it to New York was nothing less than sheer inspiration.

Mr. Swinney was conscious of a troublesome, stimulating perfume and the feeling that someone was looking over his shoulder. He turned and looked up into the cat-face of the Countess Amalie Czernok, who had just finished reading the A.P. item.

She tapped him gently on the shoulder and said, "You are a devil!"

Mr. Swinney rose to his feet. He said, "Amalie! You ought to be pretty angry with me."

"I—I am not sure that I am not."

Mr. Swinney had had much time to rest and think. He said, "As to a woman, I want to apologize to you for the things I said to you."

The Countess reflected for a moment and her tongue showed for an instant, red like a kitten's at the gates of her teeth. She replied, "As a woman, there is no need to apologize. At no time did you say—that I was unattractive."

She smiled her slow cat-smile and went on, but her look remained with Mr. Swinney for quite some time and kept his thoughts from dwelling too much and exclusively on the *Old Woman of Haarlem*. After all, *she* had been dead several hundred years, while Amalie was very much alive. He reflected that only a fool bore a grudge against a beautiful woman.

FRAULEIN JUDAS

C. P. DONNEL JR.

CORNELIUS PETER DONNEL JR. (1906–1977) was a professional writer who began his career as a police reporter for various publications. As was commonplace for working writers in an earlier era, he had a wide range of skills that ranged from light verse, published in *The Saturday Evening Post*, to pulp crime fiction for the top magazines in the field, including *Black Mask*, *Dime Detective Magazine*, and *Argosy*. He also wrote for such slick magazines as *Esquire*.

As was true for most pulp writers, Donnel created several series characters. For *Black Mask*, he wrote sixteen stories about Walter "Doc" Rennie, beginning with "The Man Who Knew Fear" in the January 1941 issue. Rennie had been a brain surgeon but switched to psychiatry; his small-town friends were convinced that he could read minds. With World War II looming, Rennie joined the United States Army Medical Corps as a colonel and frequently found himself involved in counterespionage adventures.

Even more dedicated to spying was Colonel Stephen Kaspir, who appeared in fifteen stories in *Dime Detective Magazine*, beginning with "Fraulein Judas" in the August 1941 issue. Although his name appears in large type at the top of the story (*Colonel Kaspir on Pressure Island* or some such heading), he is not always the major character in a story, being called upon when other agents are unable to satisfactorily complete an assignment. Apart from his enormous girth, he has few distinguishing characteristics and is less colorful than many other pulp heroes.

Donnel's writing career does not appear to have been a long one, as nearly all the pulp stories were published in the 1940s, and his only book, *Murder-Go-Round*, was issued in 1945. It is a World War II espionage thriller featuring a Swedish industrialist and an obscure haberdasher in a little shop in Stockholm who displays ties in his show window according to certain patterns that can indicate secret messages. Donnel's short story "Recipe for Murder," published in the January 1947 issue of *The American Legion Magazine*, was selected for *The 50 Greatest Mysteries of All Time* (1998).

"Fraulein Judas" was originally published in the August 1941 issue of *Dime Detective Magazine*.

FRAULEIN JUDAS

C. P. DONNEL JR.

CAMP GREENWOOD is for people who like to rough it in log cabins with French windows and tiled baths. It occupies a lush clearing halfway up Apple Orchard Mountain in the soft, purple Blue Ridge range northwest of Lynchburg, and the fried chicken served in its pine-paneled dining-hall is not a dish, but an experience, like love at first sight.

Over a platter of this unrivaled chicken, Martin Rice scowled at me. Not a personal scowl. Simply an expression of his attitude toward the human race, of which I happened to be the nearest unit.

I countered with a smile. Rice and I had every reason to be gay. The Rhys-Eccles Report, offspring of Martin Rice's peculiar brain and my own crudely efficient typing—born paragraph by paragraph over three days and nights of paralyzing mental labor—reposed in my inside pocket and crackled reassuringly as I speared another chicken breast.

Tomorrow—Monday—we would leave Camp Greenwood for Washington. There I would deliver Martin Rice and the Rhys-Eccles Report into the hands of Colonel Stephen Kaspir, chief of Section Five, who would start them on their way to Great Britain. In Britain the Rhys-Eccles Report would undoubtedly start something.

My smile broadened as the chicken breast parted obediently under the affectionate stroke of my knife. Martin Rice was alive, the Rhys-Eccles Report was completed, and Colonel Kaspir was a false prophet. He had predicted trouble. It had failed to materialize. No shots from ambush, not even a hellish attempt to sabotage my typewriter ribbon.

I would prick him with that one tomorrow. "No," I would say sweetly, "not even an attempt to sabotage my typewriter ribbon." And he would squirm.

Kaspir had hinted, through chocolate-stained teeth, of possible action by one Maria Hencken, who, I had gathered, was a sort of Gestapo superwoman. Description of Maria Hencken? "None available," Kaspir had muttered, twiddling pudgy fingers and wagging his fat head dramatically.

Maria Hencken indeed! My lip curled as I surveyed the dining-hall for perhaps the fiftieth time in three days.

————

259

Take Professor Davis and his little girl, for instance, who had been on our train and ridden up in the station wagon with Rice and me Friday afternoon. A hawk-nosed man in his late thirties, Davis was a widower, and his fortified black eyes softened only when he addressed his daughter. His eyes were soft now as he cut up a piece of chicken for the child, and his mid-Western voice was a caressing murmur as he said something to her across their table. The child, a pallid little thing of ten or eleven small for her age and shy almost to mutism, watched her father with large, luminous eyes. Her right arm, recently fractured in some playground mishap, was in sling, and the triangle of black silk that narrowed to her chin intensified her pallor.

Then there were the Misses Alicia and Alethea Ogilvie, gaunt, gray-haired twins nearing sixty, addicted to long khaki skirts, mannish coats, and floppy straw hats. They came up from Norfolk each year at this time (it was May) to paint the laurel blossoms which lay like snow over the spur hills about the camp. Of forbidding aspect in the mornings, the Misses Ogilvie, I had noted, mellowed amazingly by dinner time. Annie, the raw-boned mountain woman who cleaned the rooms, ascribed this mellowness to bottles of gin which, she informed me resentfully, the Misses Ogilvie kept locked in their trunks.

And, finally, there were the Hinkles, John and Martha, as thoroughly anesthetized by love as any bride and groom I have ever seen. Their assault on the chicken was punctuated by long ineffable looks. John Hinkle, big, blond, serious, was a telephone company official from somewhere in Delaware. Martha was dark, sleepy-eyed, exotic. Her figure, as outlined by a sweater suit, was something a man might die for, and Hinkle was obviously ready to make the supreme sacrifice at a moment's notice.

And that was all our company, aside from the servants and Oliver Sparklet, the owner, manager, desk-clerk, social secretary of Camp Greenwood, pink of cheek and oppressive with innkeeper's charm.

My eyes returned to Martin Rice, now scowling at his plate. A tiny gamecock of a man, white hair rising from his narrow skull like an angry crest. A face ever ridden by the memory of that night in London when a stray bomb, whistling down through the clouds like a satanic judgment, had taken his wife, his daughter, and his left arm.

A shadow at my shoulder, a whiff of eau-de-cologne introduced Oliver Sparklet. He treated Rice and me to a heavenly smile. Rice grunted in pure, unadulterated ill-humor. I raised an eyebrow.

"You'll join the picnic, of course," Sparklet beamed.

"Not interested." This from Rice in clipped accents of disapproval.

I said, "Picnic?"

"We go each Sunday afternoon to Lichened Rock," explained Sparklet alluringly. "I cook the steaks myself."

"Who's going?" I made it offhand.

"Everyone." Sparklet included the whole dining-hall in a womanish wave of his plump hands.

"You go," snapped Rice at me. "I have work—"

"In that case," I cut in, disappointed, "I'd better—"

"I said you were to go, Potts." It was a command. I flushed. But I was—for Camp Greenwood's benefit—Rice's secretary, so what could I say? I nodded to Sparklet. He passed on to the Ogilvies, who accepted with old-maidenish squeals of delight.

Rice stuck out his single, blue-veined hand. "Give me the report." He had sense enough to keep his voice down.

I shook my head. His eyes flamed.

"Give me that report." His voice rose. I glanced quickly around the dining-hall. No one was watching. I whipped out the master copy as surreptitiously as possible, thrust it at him under the table. He got up, stuffing the dozen typewritten sheets into his coat pocket. I jumped up and followed him outside, boiling.

On the flagstoned veranda he faced me, peppering me with short, hot words before I could tell him what I thought of his idiotic action in the dining-room. He made it very clear that he looked upon Kaspir and me as imbeciles—that our fears concerning the Gestapo were childish—that he, Mortimer Rhys-Eccles, resented this three-day seclusion under the name of Martin Rice, and that his opinion of our Government Intelligence and Counter-Espionage services was—

I interrupted angrily, reminding him that future British policy would be vitally affected by the report—that any Axis agent would give his ears for a five-minute perusal of it. "Furthermore," I threw at him, "that report may eventually affect my country as well as yours. I can't permit you to take chances."

He subsided to a tone of quiet contempt. With exaggerated deference he told me that he simply intended to sit in his room and review it in detail—that my presence would only distract him—that if there were any last-minute changes we could make them together that night.

I agreed to join the picnic on two conditions. The first: that everyone else in camp went. The second: that he would promise to lock both the hall door of our two-room suite and the French window giving on our private porch.

He exploded into an exasperated affirmative and stalked off to the big guest cabin.

I rejoined the others in the lounge of the main lodge, and at three thirty we all went down to the guest cabin for blankets and wraps. Rhys-Eccles had been as good as his word. The door was locked. He unlocked it peevishly, returned to his big chair and lost himself immediately in the report. On my way out I closed the door and rattled the knob suggestively until I heard him stamp across the floor and turn the key.

We straggled lazily up to Lichened Rock, only half a mile from camp. From the rock the forest dropped away beneath us to Wheat's Valley, and the valley stretched like a toy panorama into the warm afternoon haze.

We loafed in the ripe sunlight. Little Effie Davis climbed around the rock, followed by her father's anxious eyes. The Ogilvies sketched. The Hinkles disappeared hand-in-hand up a leafy side trail, returning while Sparklet and I were laying a fire under a grill set into a cleft of the rock. In the dying rays of the sun we ate our excellent meal.

Two incidents marred the party.

Little Effie Davis complained, in her semi-audible whisper, of a tummy pain. Miss Alethea Ogilvie solicitously insisted upon accompanying the child back to camp, ordering Professor Davis to stay and enjoy himself. Overwhelmed, Professor Davis gave in.

The other incident came about three-quarters of an hour later, just as a golden moon-rim showed in Gunstock Gorge. Heavy feet crashed along the trail. Someone was running, gasping. The raw-boned Annie burst into the circle of firelight, an apparition of disheveled hair and wild eyes. Her first dozen words sent Davis and me streaking back to camp, plunging recklessly ahead by the wavering beam of a flashlight I had snatched from Sparklet.

Annie's words sent us first to Davis's suite on the second floor of the guest cabin. Miss Alethea Ogilvie hovered distractedly over the bed. On the bed lay little Effie Davis, cheeks like skimmed milk, a great purple bruise down one side of her small face.

Davis bent over the child. Miss Ogilvie, almost incoherent from terror and gin, blurted out her tale.

She had brought Effie back, laid her on the bed. The child, already better, had sipped water, declined medicine, quickly dozed off. Miss Ogilvie had gone to her own room, next to the Davis suite, and sat there with the door open, in case Effie should awake and call out. Downstairs she could hear "Mr. Rice" moving about.

Some fifteen minutes later Effie had appeared

at Miss Ogilvie's door, a handkerchief tied peasant-fashion around her head, a doll in her good arm. She said she was all right and was going downstairs and play on the front veranda. Miss Ogilvie heard her go down the steps. Almost immediately there was a cry, a rustling noise, another cry, then the sound of running feet. Rushing down, Miss Ogilvie had found Effie lying unconscious near the foot of the stairs, the handkerchief torn from her head and exposing the great bruise. Her assailant was nowhere to be seen, nor could Miss Ogilvie tell which way he ran out.

Miss Ogilvie had run down the hall to our suite to seek help from "Mr. Rice." The door was open. "Mr. Rice" was in the big chair, apparently asleep. She had shaken him by the shoulder several times, until she realized . . .

Then she had screamed until Annie ran down from the main lodge. Together they got Effie, now mumbling something about a "big man" who had struck her, upstairs again, and Annie had run for Lichened Rock.

I left Miss Ogilvie, dived downstairs to our suite. Rhys-Eccles was quite dead, his scrawny throat rasped reddish-brown by whatever had strangled him. Three minutes of frantic searching convinced me that the Rhys-Eccles Report was gone. Not that I didn't have a carbon copy in the money-belt around my waist, but what good, now?

I left Rhys-Eccles to his calm contemplation of the ceiling and tore for the main lodge and its telephone. It took me five dancing, cursing minutes to get through to Kaspir in Washington. He mumbled something about a military plane and said he'd be at the Lynchburg airport in less than three hours. I ran to the servants' quarters and snatched Joe, the Negro handyman-chauffeur away from his supper with the rotund black cook, ordering him to get out the station wagon at once. Fortunately he knew the airport. As I hurried back to the guest cabin the station wagon whizzed past me and its tail light sank away down the mountain-side like a falling star.

Circling Rhys-Eccles's still figure in a second and more thorough search of our rooms,

I found nothing of importance. In his steamer trunk, insolently undisturbed, were the three-hundred-odd typewritten reports which his fine machine of a mind had condensed, in three days and nights, into the Rhys-Eccles Report, for which His Majesty's Government was waiting impatiently.

I dropped helplessly into a chair and lit a cigarette. It seemed impossible that I had known Rhys-Eccles—and Colonel Kaspir, too—for only four days. It seemed more like years.

My West Coast assignment had ended in a blaze of glory the previous Tuesday when Weber had walked into my arms in the lobby of a San Francisco movie theater, a stroke of dumb luck. That afternoon I was ordered back to Washington. I boarded the plane determined to ask for a transfer to Propaganda the minute I hit the capital. I'd done enough in Frisco to convince me that Counter-Espionage was not my racket.

Captain Ed Bell, my immediate superior, met the plane at the Washington airport Thursday morning. He stuck out his hand. "Nice going, Kettle. Thought you told me you'd never make an Intelligence man?"

"Pure dumb luck." I said it wearily, knowing he wouldn't believe me.

"Horsefeathers!" He clapped me on the shoulder. He looked around. The other passengers were almost to the gate.

"Kaspir wants you," he said, half under his breath. "I've got your orders here." He shook his head as I extended my hand. "Verbal orders."

"Who's Kaspir?" I'd never heard the name before. "What does he want me for?"

"I don't know." Bell was embarrassed. "As near as I can find out, it's a new department, hush-hush as hell—kind of a bastard by Treasury out of State. Some sort of liaison tie-up with the British. Overlaps into C.E. work now and then. I know one thing though."

"Go on," I said grimly.

"Kaspir's the white-haired boy around Washington just now," said Bell, with interdepartmental jealousy. "What he asks for, he gets. Took Williams and McCreary off us last week."

"What are they doing now?" I was startled. They were top men in our line.

Bell blushed. "I don't know." He looked around again. "At least, I'm not supposed to."

He bent even closer to me. "I did think I saw Williams this morning," he said darkly. "Driving a cab. What do you think of that?"

"How're my chances of getting into Propaganda?" I said hastily.

Bell stiffened officially. "Here are your orders, Kettle."

When he finished his spiel I just looked at him. His mouth twitched. "No kidding," he said, and walked off.

So I took a cab downtown and caught a bus. When I reached a certain corner I got off and ambled along a row of old, tall, brownstone houses until I found the number Bell had given me. A colored houseboy in a white coat answered my ring. It seemed to be a boarding house. But as the boy led me up to the second floor I noticed a bulge on his right hip. At the foot of the dark wood stairway leading to the third floor he stopped, jerked his thumb upward.

"Last door down, boss." His accent was that of an uneducated Virginia Negro, but—

"New York University," I said on impulse.

His puzzled look made me feel like a fool. Then he smiled and shook his head. The puzzled look had been an act.

"Columbia Law School," he said, smiling, and turned away.

Still following Bell's instructions, I mounted to the third floor, entered the door at the end without knocking, to find myself in a crudely equipped office that obviously had once been a bedroom. There was an inner door. It was shut. I was reaching for its knob when a man's voice, high, neighing, gusty with passion, cut through its flimsy panels.

"Where did you put 'em?" demanded this neighing voice. I stopped dead.

A woman's voice, low, angry, answered: "Where you won't find 'em. And you know why."

Brief silence, during which I could visualize the antagonists glaring at one another.

The man's voice went up a quarter-octave. "I order you to tell me—"

"Fiddlesticks!" High heels clicked across the inner room. I jumped back and to one side. The door flew open and a tall woman flounced out. A second glance showed her to be a superb blonde, beautifully turned out, probably thirty. Under her plentiful but skillfully-applied make-up her face was scarlet with anger. To my amazement she flung herself down at a typewriter desk and began to pound the keys of an old Underwood. I coughed introductively. She looked around quickly.

"Who're you?" she demanded pettishly.

This was too much. "I'm beginning to wonder," I barked.

"Then you must be Mike Kettle," she retorted. "What're you waiting for? He's in there." She shrugged a shapely shoulder toward the half-open door. Whereupon she ignored me and the Underwood began to chatter like a mad thing.

The doorway filled slowly with a man. From a small, precise mouth set in a great moon face the same neighing voice, now controlled and courteous as a politician's, said: "Welcome to Section Five, Lieutenant."

Momentarily speechless, I bowed.

"Come in." The figure turned on its heel, showing a back broad as a barn door.

I paused irresolutely in the doorway, hand on the knob. A swivel chair squealed in agony as the owner of the neighing voice dropped into it.

"Don't bother to close the door," said Colonel Kaspir, with some bitterness. "She'll only listen at the keyhole."

The typewriter had stopped. Behind me the blond woman snorted contemptuously.

Kaspir waved a fat hand toward a straight wooden chair, and, as I sat down, lost himself in thought, eyes closed. I seized the opportunity to take stock of my new boss.

Weight about two-eighty, but the fat hands and round face make him look tubbier than he really is, I decided. Suit of good tweeds, expensive shirt, grotesque tie. But untidy. Looks as if he'd been held down and clothes put on him by force.

"Nursemaid job," said Kaspir suddenly, eyes opening full on mine. "You can typewrite, can't you?"

"I was an editorial writer on the *Sun*," I replied with dignity. Then a forlorn hope. "That is why Propaganda is really my—"

"Lot o' reports," said Kaspir. "Took 'em months. Their men, our men, working together." This meant nothing. I noticed his teeth were stained, as though with tobacco juice.

"This feller Rhys-Eccles'll do it, though," continued Kaspir, nodding solemnly in admiration of Rhys-Eccles. "All brain, no brawn." He smacked his lips. "Put 'em all together. That's where you come in."

His voice trailed off. I realized incredulously that he believed he had told me everything, that my instructions were now complete, and that the interview was over.

"Oh!" Kaspir's face lighted up, his middle finger snapped against his pulpy palm like a small firecracker. He had remembered something. "Hencken."

"Hencken?" I don't know why I bothered to ask. I suspected that the answer would mean nothing, and it did.

"Yep, Hencken." Kaspir was impatient now. He jiggled in the swivel chair which cursed him. "People over there"—he waved in the direction of the rising sun—"give a good deal for Rhys-Eccles's results, o' course. We've heard some woman named Hencken is due to try for 'em— you'll have to watch out—"

His train of thought was obviously miles past me, but I leaped figuratively for the caboose. "May I have a description of this Hencken woman?"

He leaned forward, highly pleased at my grasp on the matter in hand. "None available," he said, staging a pantomime with fingers and head to emphasize the utter unavailability of a description of the woman Hencken. "Just have to do the best . . ."

"Where do I—" I began desperately. If whitecoated attendants had rushed in and thrown Kaspir into a straitjacket at that moment it would not have raised a single pulsebeat of surprise in me.

Kaspir rose, all six and a half feet of him. "Rhys-Eccles demands quiet—no distractions. Camp Greenwood. Got tickets here." He rummaged in his pants pockets. "He'll be Martin Rice, author. You'll be Potts, his secretary"— still digging deep—"Get it? Your name's Kettle. You'll use Potts. Easy to remember?" A laugh rumbled up from his ample belly. Both hands came up clutching wads of what looked like waste paper, and a roll of greenbacks tumbled to the floor. Kaspir frowned down at it. "Maude!" he bawled.

Neither of us had seen the blond woman poised statuesquely in the doorway. Now she stepped forward with a purposeful swing of her rangy hips. She retrieved the money, slapped it down on the desk. From Kaspir's hands she snatched the crumpled papers. She sorted them swiftly, efficiently, and handed me two railroad tickets. She faced Kaspir. "May I put in my dime's worth now?" she inquired, plucked eyebrows arched.

"Why, of course!" Kaspir was genuinely hurt at the implication that he was a petty tyrant.

Maude turned fine brown eyes on me.

"A joint British and American commission has just completed a survey of our war industries," she said. "Potential production, potential aid-to-Britain—that sort of thing. Dull but extremely important."

I sighed with relief as the room's atmosphere became tinged with sanity.

"It adds up to three hundred-odd separate reports," went on Maude. "They need a digest of this material in London at once. Rhys-Eccles is a political economist and a bit of a mental freak. They brought him along just for the job. He's to go off to some quiet place with these reports. They say that in three days he'll be able to come up with a four or five-thousand word summation which will give the British government a basis for immediate formulation of policy.

"Section Five has been assigned to look after Rhys-Eccles. We're sending him up to Camp Greenwood in the Blue Ridge. You'll go along to do his typing, give him whatever assistance you can, and see that he lives to finish the job."

Kaspir was pacing up and down inspecting his fingernails. "I told him all that," he put in, bored.

"Keep him alive?" I said.

"Just this," said Maude. "The Gestapo people most certainly know of the commission's work. We have reason to believe they're keeping an eye on Rhys-Eccles. We even have information that an agent named Maria Hencken has been assigned to obtain his summary. About Maria Hencken we know nothing."

"Nothing," neighed Kaspir from the window, with gloomy pleasure.

"Rhys-Eccles is at the Tuart Hotel under the name of Martin Rice. You'll be George Potts, his secretary. Pick him up tonight at eight. Your train leaves at eight thirty. Take a portable typewriter, of course. You'll find Rhys-Eccles difficult. Put up with him as best you can. And if anything should happen—"

"Call me," said Kaspir over his shoulder. I scribbled down the private number Maude gave me.

"Now run along and be a good boy," ordered this surprising woman, bestowing a motherly kiss on my forehead as she pushed me gently toward the door. The kiss sent a tingle down to my heels. Outside, in the hall, I paused to stuff the tickets into my wallet.

"Now," I heard Kaspir say menacingly, "where did you put 'em?"

Maude's voice was full of shrewish satisfaction. "I threw 'em every one out of the window."

Kaspir's shrill moan rattled the door. "The whole box?" he screamed.

"If you think, with your figure," said Maude acidly, "that you're going to sit in that office and stuff down those nauseating chocolate cherries all day . . ."

I hurried away to preserve what remained of my reason. The Negro houseboy–Columbia law graduate let me out. His intelligent mouth broadened at my dazed expression, but his "Good-day, suh," was strictly in character.

That was how I met Colonel Stephen Kaspir, the strange head of Section Five. Now I sat beside Rhys-Eccles's cooling corpse. Voices in the night told of the return of the rest of the picnic party. I went out to take charge of things until Kaspir arrived.

I relayed Miss Ogilvie's account of the attack on Effie Davis and the finding of Rhys-Eccles's body to Colonel Kaspir as soon as we had laid him on the bed in Rhys-Eccles's room. It was two A.M. and he had just arrived, wobbling into the guest cabin supported by Maude, resplendent in mink over a dazzling dinner gown, and Joe, the chauffeur. Kaspir was in full evening dress, very rumpled, and there were spots on his shirtfront.

Maude said crisply to Joe: "Bicarbonate of soda. Plenty of it."

She turned to me. "Plane-sick all the way from Washington. When he got out at Lynchburg he got ground-sick. In the station wagon he was car-sick."

She wheeled on Kaspir, who lay with his eyes shut, his broad face the color of a mud beach at low tide. "Have a chocolate cherry?" she cooed cruelly, throwing off the mink wrap and filling the room with the glitter of sequins. "Well, what happened, Kettle?"

So I told everything. Kaspir struggled up on an elbow. His eyes were on the sheeted figure in the big chair, but I could feel him listening. When I got through he rolled himself to the edge of the bed.

Maude smoothed the sequins over her hips. "Well," she said to Kaspir, "what about it, Steve?

Do we form a posse and beat the woods for the masked intruder?"

Kaspir pursed his lips contemptuously. When he spoke, it was to me, an unintelligible mumbling accompanied by a village-idiot waving of the hands.

"In English," said Maude resignedly, "that means 'where is everybody now?'"

"Professor Davis and Effie are in the room overhead, of course," I replied. "The others are all in their rooms. The Ogilvies are next to the Davises. The Hinkles—that's the bride and groom—are in the suite next to this one. The servants are in their own quarters. Sparklet, the owner, has rooms at the main lodge. I told him to stay there."

Kaspir spoke clearly now. "What else did you do?"

"Not a thing, except call you," I returned defensively. "Murder's not in my line. My specialty is propaganda."

Kaspir chuckled delightedly. "We'll make something of Kettle yet." He was on his feet now, a monolith of black broadcloth and smudged line. The weakness seemed to have passed.

"I hope so," I said sourly. "Something in Propaganda preferred."

"Balderdash," said Kaspir goodnaturedly. "You haven't seen a lady bareback rider in camp, have you?"

"Not a spangle of one." What could you do but humor the big maniac? "Unless its Mrs. Hinkle. Why?"

"Hinkle?" said Kaspir. "First name?"

"Martha."

"Hmmm!" He addressed the silent Maude. "Heard today that the Hencken female used to be a circus performer—"

His bulk became suddenly animated, so unexpectedly that Maude and I both jumped. He minced over to the big chair and twitched the sheet from Rhys-Eccles with a magician's flourish. Bending with a grunt, he peered into the dead man's face. Then he drew a forefinger down the stiff left cheek, like a man sampling wet paint, and stared myopically at the fingertip,

clucking softly to himself. I glanced sardonically at Maude. To my surprise, her expression was no longer scornful. She was watching Kaspir intently.

Kaspir flung the sheet carelessly over Rhys-Eccles's peaked face and turned to the paneled wall beside the chair, his back to us. The next instant he walked with short steps over to the French windows and flung them open, sticking his head into the night, still clucking. He withdrew his head after a minute and slammed the French window. A pane of glass fell in gleaming shards at his feet.

"Clumsy, eh?" He was beaming. He looked at the big chair. "Poor little guy. Not much to live for now, except his job. Done that."

He addressed me directly. "Keep Maude amused. Gotta see some people." And he left the room, apparently under the impression that because he was tip-toeing he was making no noise. The door banged behind him like a studio sound effect.

Maude looked pityingly at me. "You're bearing up better than most," she said. "He gave one man Cheyne-Stokes breathing." She passed me slowly in an aura of gardenia perfume and once more brushed my forehead with her lips. Again I tingled. She sat down on Rhys-Eccles's bed, crossing her admirable legs. "Listen," she said.

So we listened, and my muddled brain conceived the notion that Rhys-Eccles was listening, too. I had a feeling that if I removed that sheet I would find a mocking smile on his thin lips.

Colonel Kaspir was very busy. We needed no television set to follow his progress through the guest cabin.

He clumped up the steps and went to the Davises's suite, directly overhead first. His chat with Professor Davis was mild and brief. Next we heard him knocking at the Ogilvies's door, and for a few minutes high, harsh, undistinguishable words caromed about the whole cabin. The door slammed.

Then the stairway shook again and he pounded on the Hinkles's door down the hall from us. He involved himself in a neighing altercation with John Hinkle that gradually simmered into whispers.

Next he poked his head in our door and Maude, after a long look at the grimace on his face, got up.

"Come on," he neighed gaily. "We're all going up to Effie's room."

I'll never forget that brief quarter-hour in "Effie's room," which was really her father's.

In the first place, it was strangely like a courtroom, with the child herself, propped up in bed, chalk-white except for the bruised area on her face, as the judge. A little red wrapper around her shoulders hid most of the long-sleeved, old-fashioned nightgown she wore. The white edge of the plaster cast around her right wrist framed the wrist like a cuff inside the black silk sling.

Kaspir sat mountainously on the bed beside her, fingering a heavy oak walking stick belonging to Professor Davis. As the company straggled in, the Ogilvies heavy-eyed but apparently sober, the Hinkles oddly apprehensive, I noticed that Professor Davis shifted, too casually, to a position beside John Hinkle, and that Hinkle was breathing hard.

Kaspir drew a bead on John Hinkle with the walking stick.

"Left the picnic awhile, didn't you?" he asked unpleasantly. His blue eyes glinted. "Effie," he said very gently, his other hand touching the child's thin shoulder, "Mr. Hinkle was the man you saw leaving Mr. Rice's room—the man who knocked you down—wasn't he?"

Effie's eyes were riveted on Hinkle. We could barely hear her "Yes."

Hinkle's laugh was a feeble effort.

"I want," said Kaspir with flute-like clarity, "that report."

But Hinkle was gone, tearing himself from Professor Davis's frantic grasp, upending an Ogilvie sister as he dived for the hall. Davis was after him like a fighting hound. Kaspir, clutching the oak stick, materialized beside me and

shot after them, screaming "Close the door!" I ran after Kaspir, jerking the door shut.

Davis and Hinkle were struggling on the floor at the head of the stairs as Kaspir and I reached them, a tangle of thrashing fists and feet. Kaspir took what I instantly saw to be very bad aim with the walking stick. Before I could catch his arm it hissed downward. A dull sound of wood on scalp and bone.

"Ah!" said Kaspir, straightening himself and looking down at the unconscious figure of Professor Davis. He stretched out a long arm, helped Hinkle up. "Stay with him," he said to Hinkle, indicating the prone Davis. "Also," he added, turning away, "thanks."

We re-entered the bedroom. I was quite resigned now. Somebody was crazy. I only hoped it was Kaspir, not me.

Kaspir lumbered over to the bed. "Your father's quite safe, Effie." His ironical tone was like a slap at the child's face. An Ogilvie sister stepped forward angrily. Maude held her back.

"Let me see that arm of yours, Effie," demanded Kaspir, stretching out his left hand. His right still gripped the stick.

Then I went sick inside.

For Kaspir snatched the plaster cast-enclosed arm from its black silk sling and was battering the plaster to pieces with the handle of the walking stick—

I can't remember the rest in detail, but I do remember something flashing in Effie's free hand and Kaspir screaming, "Little devil!" and his great hand shaking out and closing around her little throat.

Then there was turmoil among the spectators as Kaspir and the child flopped across the bed in an absurd, squirming battle that was awkward but deadly.

It ended with Kaspir flinging Effie heavily against the headboard. The impact dazed her. We crowded around the bed as Kaspir rolled off and got to his feet. I heard Maude gasp. The Ogilvie sisters clung to each other, whimpering.

The struggle had ripped away the upper portion of Effie's nightgown. A single glance explained many things to me: why Effie always wore long-sleeved dresses and little cape-like coats, why she spoke in a whisper, why woolen stockings always encased her spindly legs.

For Effie Davis was a woman. Her torso, bare, made that very plain. And her thin arms were weirdly muscular.

A midget, if you like, but a woman.

Kaspir paid no attention to her, even when she stirred, sat up, and cursed him shamelessly in a shrill, evil voice.

He was plucking bits of plaster from the Rhys-Eccles Report, newly freed from the plaster cast that had encircled Effie's "broken" arm. He said quietly: "I suppose that thing out in the hall is your husband, eh, Maria?"

Effie's reply, describing her relationship to Davis, was unprintable.

"Handkerchief business, you see o' course," mumbled Kaspir thickly through a ham sandwich. He gulped two mouthfuls of scalding coffee. "Powder on the old boy's cheek. That gin-swizzling female don't use it. Clean plaster on cast, too. And porch. Got that?"

Maude's sequins rattled venomously as she tossed pad and pencil to the bed, lit a cigarette, and fixed Kaspir with a grim, uncompromising eye, "Tell it straight and I'll take it down," was her ruthless ultimatum.

The relaxed hulk of Kaspir filled the big chair lately vacated by Mortimer Rhys-Eccles, who had been removed and deposited on the bed in my room. The Hinkles were present by invitation. Upstairs the Ogilvies slumbered alcoholically. Behind the main lodge, we knew, Annie and Joe sat with shotguns before the strong door of the vegetable dugout, serving as a detention cell for Maria Effie Davis Hencken and her "father."

Kaspir looked diffidently at Maude.

"Oh, all right," he said mildly. He put the sandwich down, leaned forward. Maude reached for the pad, poised the pencil above it in her slender crimson-nailed fingers.

"Little she-Judas strangled Rhys-Eccles, o' course," began Kaspir. "See a lot o' midgets doing bareback stuff—acrobatics—in circuses around Germany, Poland, Hungary.

"Old Miss Gin-Swizzler lays Fraulein Judas on bed after coming back from picnic. Miss Gin-Swizzler goes to own room. Little she-Judas eases outa bed, slips off plaster cast, slides down porch support to Rhys-Eccles's porch—" He nodded toward the French windows. "Taps on window," he said.

"Who'd Rhys-Eccles open French window for but child? Lost his own in London. Likes children. They probably knew that—reason they used little Judas-devil. He opens window, lets her in, sits down in chair. She, affectionate, goes coyly around back of chair, slips arm around his neck. About time Rhys-Eccles begins to wonder where plaster cast on arm is, little she-Judas tightens arm around his neck—braces herself against back of chair.

"You saw that arm. Like wire rope."

Maude's pencil flew across her pad. The Hinkles were hunched forward in their chairs.

"Garroted, Rhys-Eccles was, by that little arm. But he fought. Banged Fraulein Judas's head against wall. But he caved in. She took report, shinnied back up to own room, unlocking hall door of this room before she left.

"Face badly bruised, though. Must be explained somehow. Ties handkerchief around head to hide bruise, replaces cast on arm, goes to old Miss Gin, tells her she's going out to play. Goes downstairs. Stamps feet, cries out, tears handkerchief off, lies down, swears she's been struck down by mysterious man. Bruise visible now. Ha! Simple!

"Rest's easy. Davis and little she-Judas get rid of old cast, make new one around Rhys-Eccles Report.

"Powder was give-away. Fraulein Judas had to powder up to look pale and frail. Left some on Rhys-Eccles's cheek when she"—here Kaspir was human enough to shudder—"cuddled her cheek against his. Also some on wall when face banged against it. And how could child with broken arm tie handkerchief around head, unless she used 'broken' arm?"

"But why that scene with Mr. Hinkle here?" I protested.

"Davis armed," growled Kaspir. "Wary, too. So told him Hinkle was man—get ready to help. Very pleased to, Davis was. Wonder what Davis's real name is. Maybe Washington knows."

He yawned cavernously. The Hinkles got up, silent.

"Siddown," ordered Kaspir hospitably. They sat. "Chat with Maude and friend Kettle-Potts here." He glanced at his watch. "We leave at daylight, and that's only an hour."

He yawned again. "Little nap," he murmured apologetically and ambled into the next room.

"There's only one bed in there," I called hastily, cringing at the thought of what reposed on that bed.

Kaspir turned benignly in the doorway. "Won't disturb him," he said, drawing the door to behind him.

Through the closed door we heard the bed creak. "Move over, old boy," said Colonel Kaspir. Then all was serene.

THE COURIER

DAN FESPERMAN

THE AUTHORS OF BOOKS about secret agents often have started their careers as agents too, and their assignments, taking them to distant lands, have provided background color for their novels. Dan Fesperman (1955–) has traveled to thirty countries, including three war zones, but not as a spy. He has worked as a foreign correspondent for several newspapers, including the *Miami Herald* and *The Sun* and *Evening Sun of Baltimore*, leading to several adventures, one of which was assisting in the capture of ten Iraqi soldiers in Kuwait in 1991 and narrowly surviving an ambush of a convoy of journalists in Afghanistan in 2001.

Fesperman's work has received numerous accolades, including winning the 1999 (British) Crime Writers' Association John Creasey Memorial Dagger for best first novel for *Lie in the Dark* (1999), which features Vlado Petric, a homicide detective in Sarajevo who is confronted with the assassination of the chief of the Interior Ministry's special police.

The CWA's Ian Fleming Steel Dagger for best thriller was given to *The Small Boat of Great Sorrows* (2003), which again featured Vlado Petric, the now-retired homicide investigator who has been exiled to Berlin, where an American working for the International War Crimes Tribunal recruits him to return to Sarajevo to bring an old Nazi collaborator to justice.

The 2006 Hammett Prize, awarded by the International Association of Crime Writers, was given to *The Prisoner of Guantánamo* (which, incidentally, Fesperman visited); *USA Today* selected it as the best mystery/thriller of the year. An Arabic-speaking former FBI agent is brought to Gitmo to work on a Yemeni holdout, a prisoner who is believed to have valuable information about al-Qaeda, but the focus changes when the body of an American soldier washes up in Cuban territory, raising fears of Cold War antagonisms.

In 2016, *The New York Times* named *The Letter Writer* one of the ten best crime novels of the year. Set in New York in February 1942, it concerns a shabby, gnarled old man named Danziger who writes letters for illiterate immigrants. When one of them is found floating in the Hudson River, NYPD detective Woodrow Cain enlists the multilingual Danziger to find the murderer, but the death is merely the tip of a wide-reaching conspiracy.

"The Courier" was originally published in *Agents of Treachery*, edited by Otto Penzler (New York, Vintage, 2010).

THE COURIER

DAN FESPERMAN

IN THIS BONEYARD of Nazi memory where I make my living, we daily come across everything from death lists to the trifling queries of petty bureaucrats. Our place of business is known simply as the Federal Records Center, and it is housed on the first floor of an old torpedo factory down by a rotting wharf on the Potomac.

I am told that elsewhere in this cavernous building there is a Smithsonian trove of dinosaur bones and an archive of German propaganda films. But on our floor there is only paper, box after box of captured documents, with swastikas poking like shark fins from gray oceans of text. The more papers we move, the dustier it gets, and by late afternoon of each day the air is thick with motes of decomposing history. Sunbeams angling through the high windows shimmer like the gilded rays of a pharaonic tomb.

Seeing as how the war ended thirteen years ago, you might figure we'd have this mess sorted out by now. But, as I've discovered lately, lots of things about the war aren't so easily categorized, much less set aside.

My name is Bill Tobin, and it is my job to decide which papers get tossed, declassified, or locked away. The government hired me because I am fluent in German and know how to keep a secret. I've worked here for a year, and up to now the contents have been pretty much what I expected—memos from various Nazi ministries, asking one nagging question after another. Have Herr Muller's new ration coupons arrived? Must we initial every page of every armaments contract? How many Poles should we execute this Saturday?

What I didn't expect to find—here or anywhere—was the name of Lieutenant Seymour Parker, a navigator from the 306th Bomb Group, U.S. Army Air Force. Yet there it was just the other day on the bent tab of a brown folder, our latest retrieval from a mishmash we have begun calling the Total Confusion File, mostly because we never know which ministry letterhead will turn up next.

At first, seeing Parker's name was a pleasant surprise, like having an old pal visit from out of the blue. After reading what was inside, I was wishing he hadn't dropped by.

It's been fourteen years since we handed Parker over to the Germans in the spring of 1944, along with three other American flyboys. It was part of a prisoner exchange. The Germans had agreed to ship our boys home via occupied France. We gladly would have done it ourselves, of course, but at the time I was working for the OSS in Switzerland, a neutral country surrounded by Axis armies. To put it bluntly, we had no way out, and neither did the U.S. airmen who regularly parachuted into Swiss meadows and pastures after their bombers got shot up over Germany.

So we escorted Parker and the others up to the French border at Basel and then watched as a haughty SS officer in black ushered them onto a train bound for Paris. From there they would make their way to Spain, to be turned over to American custody for the voyage home.

I had helped Parker pack for the trip. His duffel was filled with cartons of cigarettes, and his head was stuffed with secrets. The former were for handing out to Germans along the way. As for the latter, well, that was more complicated.

It was the last time I saw him, and from then on our crew in Bern rarely mentioned his name, because surely everything had gone according to plan. Kevin Butchart had volunteered as much a year later, on the same afternoon the radio broke in with the happy news that Hitler had blown out his brains in Berlin. Someone else—I think it was Wesley Flagg—happened to ask if anyone knew what had ever become of Parker.

"Didn't you hear?" Butchart said. "He's back home in Kansas. Down on the farm with Dorothy and Toto, and didn't even have to click his heels. Whole thing went off without a hitch."

Since then, I had thought of Parker only once—last summer, while watching my son play Little League baseball on a leisurely Saturday. It was a key moment in the game. The best player on his team, one of those natural athletes who you can tell right away has a college scholarship in his future, was rounding third as the opponent's shortstop threw home. Runner, ball, and catcher arrived at the plate simultaneously, and there was a jarring collision.

The catcher, a pudgy kid with glasses who had been flinching on every swing, took the impact square in the gut and went facedown in the dirt. As he righted himself and pulled off his mask you could see the conflict of emotions on his face—a rising storm of tears that might burst loose at any moment, yet also a fierce determination to tough it out without a whimper.

To everyone's surprise he held aloft the ball, which had never left his mitt. The umpire called the runner out. The catcher then nodded for play to resume even as tears rolled down his dusty cheeks.

Something about the kid brought Parker to mind. He, too, had that contradictory bearing— flinching in one moment, stoic in the next— and for the remainder of the afternoon I was weighted by an inexplicable gloom. I wrote it off as yet another flashback, one of those anxious moments in which you realize yet again that the war still hasn't left you behind. Then I mixed a crystal pitcher of gimlets for my wife and me, and by the following morning I'd forgotten all about it.

Not long afterward, I was offered my current job at the Records Center. The pay wasn't great, but it sounded a hell of a lot more interesting than signing invoices at my father-in-law's shoe factory in Wilmington, Delaware. So we packed up and moved to a rented town house in Alexandria, Virginia.

When I came across Parker's file, I was standing in one of those golden beams of late sunlight as I pulled the last batch of documents from Box #214. My plan was to knock off early and take my son to the movies. Then I began to read, and within a few paragraphs I was transported back to the afternoon in early 1944 when I first met Parker aboard a Swiss passenger train.

Switzerland was the strangest of places then. Hemmed in by the Axis, its studious neutrality had turned it into an island of intrigue. On the surface it was Europe's eye of the storm, an orderly refuge from gunfire and ruin, a place where weary émigrés could catch their breath and tend their wounds. Bankers still moved money. Industrialists kept cutting deals.

But playing out beneath this facade was a gentleman's war of espionage among the snoops of all nations, and at times it seemed as if everyone was involved—émigrés, bankers, washed-up aristocrats, deal-hunting factory barons, and, of course, the Swiss themselves, who were trying to curry favor with the Americans even as they sweet-talked Hitler into not sending in tanks from the north. Everyone had information to offer—some of it dubious, some of it spectacular—and, as I discovered first-hand, the competing intelligence agencies were all too happy to vie for them by every means at their disposal.

On the day in late March that I met Parker, I was accompanied by the aforementioned Kevin Butchart. We were lurching down the aisle of a swaying train car, bound for Adelboden from Zurich via Bern.

The view out the windows was of an alpine meadow—cows and early spring wildflowers—but our attention was focused on the passengers. Several freshly arrived American airmen were on board, looking tired and dispirited. They had dropped from the skies after their B-17 had limped into Swiss airspace, following a bombing run over Bavaria. Butchart and I had come to scout them out as they made their way to an internment camp. We were hoping to find just the right one for use in an upcoming operation.

We knew we had to tread lightly. Even though the country was filled with spies, espionage was illegal. Swiss gumshoes regularly kept an eye on us, and we would be recruiting an operative right beneath their noses.

The flyboys had to mind their manners as well. The Swiss had already interned more than five hundred up in Adelboden, a resort town in the Alps, where they played Ping-Pong, read paperbacks, hiked around the town, and ate cheese three meals a day. The restless ones who tried to make their way back to the war by escaping into occupied France risked detention at a harsh little camp called Wauwilermoos. It was run by a supposedly neutral little martinet who would have done Hitler proud. Strange people, the Swiss.

I tugged at Butchart's sleeve.

"How 'bout him?"

I pointed at a stout fellow in a leather flight jacket who was munching on a chocolate bar from his escape kit.

"No way," Butchart answered. "Look how worn the jacket is. He's been at it for ages. And stop pointing. I saw your minder in the next car back."

I glanced behind me for the bearded Swiss gumshoe whom I called Alp Uncle, mostly because I didn't know his real name. Nowhere to be seen, thank goodness.

Butchart herded me along.

"Keep moving. We've only got an hour."

He was pushy that way, one of those short, muscular fellows whose aggressive movements can quickly get on your nerves. But as an employee of the U.S. legation's military attaché, this was his show, so I nodded and kept moving.

When Butchart wanted to engage you in conversation he came at you like a boxer, cutting and weaving, as if looking for an opening. Any suggestion that his point of view was flawed prompted an immediate counterpunch. He jabbed at your weak spots until your opinions were on the mat. I had learned not to pick these fights unless I could deck him with the first sentence, or unless we were in the presence of a superior officer, when he tended to pull his punches. For the moment I was inclined to defer to his judgment.

He tugged at my sleeve.

"There's our boy. Next compartment on the right. Skinny guy with red hair. See him?"

About then the train lurched into a long descending curve, wheels squealing, and there was a sudden improvement in the scenery out to the right. A tall blonde milkmaid with braided hair was carrying buckets toward a barn. Wolf whistles and applause erupted in the railcar. One of the flyboys slid open a window and yelled, "Hey, good lookin'!"

Then he was shouted down.

"Close the fucking window!"

"It's freezing in here. You outta your mind?"

"But it was Heidi!" the offending airman protested. "Only she's all grown up!"

Heidi, indeed. My own experience with local women had already provided ample proof that the natives were friendly, even though in this neck of the woods most of them spoke German. But it could be dangerous to let the hospitality fool you.

"Any sign of Alp Uncle?" Butchart asked.

I turned, scanning the car.

"Still out of sight."

Lately our minders seemed to be losing interest. We first noticed it after the German defeat at Stalingrad. The worse things went for the Wehrmacht, the more lenient the Swiss got with the Allies.

I eased closer to our target, but Butchart grabbed my sleeve.

"Never mind. Scratch him."

"Why?"

"Scar, back of his neck. Saw it when he turned to look at Heidi."

"So?"

"So it was probably a major wound, but he went back up anyway. Not our man. We're looking for Clark Kent, not Superman."

Butchart and I had been chosen for this assignment because we knew exactly what these fellows had been through. We, too, had come to Switzerland on crippled bombers that couldn't make it back to England.

I am not ashamed to admit that for me it was a welcome development. It had occurred the previous fall during my seventeenth mission. Seventeen doesn't sound like much until you've tried your first one—a terrifying ride through flak bursts and the raking fire of Messerschmitts and Focke-Wulfs. As a starboard waist gunner in a B-17, it was my job to shoot down these tormentors, a strategy roughly as effective as pumping a Flit gun at a sky full of locusts. If you're lucky you get one or two. The rest eat their fill.

On my sixth run I was sprayed by the entrails of the port gunner when a 20-millimeter shell exploded in his midsection. On the eighth my gun jammed, and I spent the next two hours watching helplessly as bandits blew holes in the skin of our plane. On the fourteenth we ditched in the Channel but were rescued from rafts. Three of our crewmen drowned. After each trip it took me hours to warm up, and all too soon the mission day routine became unbearable: Rise at two a.m. for the briefing. Swallow a queasy breakfast. Inhale gas fumes and the sweet scent of pasture grass while you loaded up in the dark. Then eight hours or more in cramped quarters, freezing most of the way while people tried to kill you from every angle. After a while the throb of the engines was the only thing you could still feel in your hands and feet. Staticky voices shouted their panic and pain in your headset. Out the gun port you saw carnage everywhere—your colleagues' bombers smoking and then spiraling, spewing black dots as crewmen ejected. That could be me, I always thought, falling toward a field in Germany.

Until finally one day it was me. Three of our four engines were out, and Harmon, our pilot, was nursing us south toward the Swiss border. When he gave the order to bail, we weren't yet sure we had made it. The rest of us jumped while Harmon fought the controls. Fighters were still in the neighborhood, so I didn't pull the rip cord until I was below a thousand feet. Even then, as soon as the canopy opened I heard a Messerschmitt buzzing toward me from behind. I turned awkwardly in my harness and waited for the flash of guns. None came. The plane roared by, close enough for the prop wash to rock my chute. Only then did I notice the large white cross on its side—the Swiss air force, welcoming us with their German planes.

That left me feeling pretty good until I watched our plane hit the ground in a ball of flame and black smoke. Someone else said Harmon jumped just before impact, but his chute never opened.

Swiss soldiers rounded us up. They boarded us overnight at a nearby school, and the next morning they put us on a train for Adelboden, where we were supposed to be billeted in an old hotel. But that's when I lucked out. The man who would soon be my new boss came across me napping in a rear compartment. Apparently what caught his eye was a dog-eared copy of Arthur Koestler's *Darkness at Noon* splayed across my chest. I awoke when I felt someone picking it up, and looked into the blue eyes of an older gentleman with a pipe between his teeth. The pockets of his overcoat were stuffed with newspapers. He took a seat opposite me and began speaking American English.

"Any good?" he said, holding up the book.

"Not bad."

"I'm Allen Dulles, from the American legation."

We chatted long enough for him to find out I was fluent in German and had spent two years in graduate school. He then surprised me by suggesting I come to work for him. I was flattered, but I needn't have been. I learned later that Dulles had made it into Switzerland only hours before the country's last open border was closed, cutting him off from reinforcements.

That meant he had to be creative about finding new employees. Stranded American bankers and socialites were already on his payroll, so it was hardly surprising he would take an interest in me once a bunch of American airmen literally began dropping to him from the skies. I told him I liked the idea, and he said he would see what he could do. Two weeks later I was summoned to his office in Bern.

Only then did I learn I would be working for the OSS. It was the closest thing we had to a CIA, but I had never heard of it. I decided it must be a little out of the ordinary when the job application included an "Agent's Checklist" that asked me for a countersign "by which agent may identify himself to collaborators." They also gave me a code name, an ID number for use in all official correspondence, and a desk in a windowless office in an old brick town house on Dufourstrasse.

Most of my duties involved translation, but I suppose that officially I was a spy, unless there is some other name you'd give a job in which the boss sends memos on tradecraft and insists that you call him no, or Burns, or whatever the

hell you wanted as long as you never used his real name. That first meeting on the train was the only time I felt comfortable calling him Mr. Dulles.

So there I was, then, with Butchart on the train, trying to recruit someone else the same way that Dulles had recruited me, except we were seeking an altogether different sort of prospect.

"What about him?" I said, pointing even though Butchart had asked me not to.

"Where?"

"Last compartment on the left, by the window. The guy with glasses."

The fellow in question looked like one of the younger crewmen, but it was his wariness that caught my eye. While most of the others wore a weary look of relief, this one still had his guard up. There was also a softness to his features, and a little boy wonderment as he stared out the window. You could tell he had never seen mountains like these.

"He's got potential," Butchart said. "Navigator, I'll bet."

"How you figure?"

"The glasses. Must have a special talent or they'd have never let him in the air corps, and they're always short on navigators. Keep an eye on him while I check the next car."

I did just that. A few seconds later Butchart returned, shaking his head.

"I'm liking your navigator more and more."

"Want me to take him aside?"

"Wait 'til we're almost into the station. In the meantime I'll let his CO know. I'll also grab the Swiss officer in charge and start greasing the skids."

"What will you tell him?"

"Same thing Colonel Gill told them when he hired me. That I'm from the military attaché and we're short on staff and looking for volunteers."

By now you may be thinking this isn't exactly the most glamorous spy mission you've ever heard of, but it definitely beat what I had been doing up to then. Dulles had confined me to office duty, and I was going stir-crazy. It wasn't so much that I craved excitement as that I needed distraction. At least twice a week I was still dreaming about being back in the bomber—the bed rocking as if shaken by a flak burst, a high-altitude chill creeping beneath the sheets. I'd wake up exhausted, hands numb, as if I'd just returned from an all-night mission. Frankly, I was worried about going 'round the bend if something didn't come along soon to occupy my mind.

Butchart had heard I was eager for action, and he had suggested I meet his boss, Colonel Gill, who kept track of intelligence matters for the military attaché. He said they might have a special job for me.

I told him to give it a try, and it must have worked, because the next evening Dulles summoned me to his place on Herrengasse. I went after dark, which was the drill for just about everybody who went to his house. He had the ground-floor apartment in a grand old building that dated back to medieval times. It was in the heart of all those arcaded streets in the old part of Bern. Gumshoes kept an eye on his front door, so visitors like me entered through the back, after approaching uphill through terraced gardens overlooking the river Aare.

It was always a treat visiting Dulles. He had a maid, a French cook, some mighty fine port, and plenty of logs for the fire. He also had a couple of mistresses, a Boston debutante married to a Swiss banker and an Italian countess who was the daughter of the conductor Toscanini. Dulles was probably the only warrior in the European Theater of Operations who suffered from gout.

Not that he looked much like a Lothario. He was very much the old-school gentleman, all tweeds and pipe smoke, with an understated grace that immediately put you at ease. He was a hell of a good listener—which is probably what the ladies liked—and on any topic he zeroed in right away on the stuff that mattered. Glancing into his lively blue eyes when his mind was fully engaged was like peering into the works of some gleaming piece of sophisticated machinery, an information mill that never stopped running.

Those newspapers in his pockets were no mere props. He devoured all knowledge within reach and chewed it over even as he engaged you in small talk about, say, the virtues of your university, or the quirks of some mutual acquaintance. Try to slip some half-baked thought past his field of vision and he'd seize upon it like a zealous customs inspector, and you'd end up wishing you had kept prattling on about your alma mater.

When the maid showed me in, there was a fire on the hearth. Dulles was knocking at the logs with a poker.

"Help yourself," he said, gesturing to a decanter of port on a side table.

Someone had left a bowler hat next to it, and I figured there must be another guest waiting elsewhere in the house. Dulles confirmed this suspicion when he dispensed with the usual pleasantries and got right down to business.

"I hear your services are in demand by Colonel Gill."

"Yes, sir. A little something to get me out of the office."

Dulles smiled and nodded.

"I know you're restless, but I do plan to get you out on the beat before long. Still, maybe this will offer some useful practice. Stretch your legs a bit. So you have my blessing if you're so inclined, even if they do think of themselves as our competition. That's not my view, mind you, but some of those Pentagon fellows seem to have a chip on their shoulders as far as we're concerned. So mind your step, Bill. And don't let them try anything fast and loose with you."

"Any reason to think they might?"

"Not really, other than Gill himself. He's bucking for promotion, which always makes a man a little dangerous. Sometimes in a good way, I'll allow, but you never know."

"Yes, sir."

"And Bill."

"Yes?"

"Even if you say yes, if the first step is squishy, don't feel as if you have to take the second one. Don't let pride shame you into doing something foolish. Perfectly fine by me if you bow out. Just don't tell them I said so."

Early the next morning, Butchart ushered me into Gill's office. Gill had set up shop in the back of a legation town house on Dufourstrasse, with a view onto a lush narrow garden. He stood behind a big varnished desk, a tall, trim fellow going gray at the temples. He offered a big handshake and spoke in a smoky baritone, which made for a powerful first impression. The starched uniform and all the ribbons didn't hurt, either.

Butchart stayed in the room after introductions, which was a little annoying although I wasn't about to say so. Gill referred to him by name instead of rank. Maybe that was his way of signaling that the meeting was off the books.

"Kevin here tells me you're a little unhappy over in Allen's shop. All cloak and no dagger, I hear."

"Maybe I'm just impatient."

"A man is entitled to impatience when there's a war on. It's no time to be sitting behind a typewriter. Not that I can promise you much dagger, either, I'm afraid. But at least you'll be out in the field."

"Yes, sir. Sergeant Bu . . . uh, Kevin said you had an assignment in mind?"

"I do. You'd be working it together. Are you familiar with the prisoner exchange that occurred a few weeks ago, those six American airmen we sent up into France?"

"Yes, sir. Did something go wrong?"

"Quite the opposite. Worked like a charm. All six are currently back in the States awaiting reassignment. Apparently the Germans were happy to get their six men back as well. From all accounts they're amenable to doing it again. But were you aware that your boss, Mr. Dulles, arranged the whole show?"

I wasn't, and it must have shown in my face.

"I didn't think so. Well, he did. And he was quite clever about it. Secretive, too. Even my bosses didn't know what he was up to until a few days ago, and that didn't go down so well in Washington. When some civilian wants to put

their soldiers at risk, they prefer to be told in advance. Of course, now that it has turned out so well, they're wisely keeping complaints to a minimum. And, frankly, it has opened up an opportunity for a similar effort by us. Which is where you and Kevin come in."

"So it was some sort of operation?"

"Oh, yes. Unbeknownst to us, two of the airmen were functioning as OSS couriers. Apparently Dulles had gathered a lot of information on German troop movements up along the Atlantic Wall. He figured it was too hot to send out by wireless, even by code, so he drilled it into these two fellows instead. Strict memorization. Gave the lessons himself."

In those days it was no secret to anyone that the invasion of France was coming soon, and that's why information on German troop strength along the French coast was at a premium.

"Sounds like a smart idea," I said.

"It was. The only problem is that he left the job half-finished."

"How so?"

"Well, think of it for a minute. In the intelligence business, the only thing better than passing along a lot of good information is convincing the enemy that you actually have a lot of bad information. That way, they're more likely to miscalculate when they try to guess where you're going to come ashore."

"So you'd like to load up a couple of prisoners, too, except with a lot of bad information?"

"Exactly. One is all you need, in my opinion. Then, of course, you find some way to make the Germans suspicious enough to haul in your fellow for questioning. Of course, that means you have to choose just the right man for the job. One who will tell them what they want to hear, but in a convincing enough fashion."

"A good enough liar, you mean."

"Exactly. And what do you suppose would be the best way to make our fellow a good enough liar?"

"Training?"

"Only if you have months or even years at your disposal. We don't have that luxury. We've only got weeks, if that. So I've come up with an alternative. Send in a novice. Just don't tell him he's carrying bad information. That way, he believes in the material enough to make it convincing."

"If he talks."

"Exactly. Which is why you have to pick just the right fellow. Not a hero, or someone who will keep his secret to the bitter end. Someone a little more, well, malleable. A weaker vessel, if you will."

"Someone who will break under pressure?"

"And preferably not too much pressure. Which is why Kevin and you are perfect for the job. You've experienced firsthand what these airmen go through, and you know their state of mind when they arrive. More to the point, you've seen firsthand the ones who can't cut it, the ones who break under pressure."

Like me, I almost said. I could have told him all about my latest nightmare, but I doubt he would have understood.

"So what do you think?" he asked. He seemed quite pleased with himself.

I thought the idea was dubious, and I recalled Dulles's advice. Maybe it was time for me to bail. Or maybe Dulles had offered an easy escape merely to test me. Bow out now, and he might keep me deskbound for the rest of the war. You never knew for sure what was going on in a mind like his.

So, despite my reservations, I decided to say yes. But first I had some questions.

"How will we make sure the Germans pick him up?"

"I'm afraid that aspect of the operation is above your pay grade, Bill."

It rankled, but it was the right thing to say, even though Dulles would have just winked and said nothing at all. But Colonel Gill, as I would soon discover, could never pass up an opportunity to impress you, even when he should have kept his mouth shut. And just as I was about to reply, he began elaborating on his statement in a way that obviously was intended to show the genius of his grand design.

"Surely a smart fellow like you shouldn't have too much trouble figuring out how we'll do it," he said. "Let's face it, the Germans are all over town. You can't even have a drink at the Bellevue without bumping into half the local Gestapo. So maybe we will have to arrange for a few well-placed leaks. A slipup here and there. Just enough to let them know that our man might be of interest to them as he makes his way through their territory. That's the beauty of it, you see? No need to run too tight of a ship in the run-up to zero hour. The only real need for precision is in picking the right man for the job."

"But then what?"

"What do you mean?"

"Well, let's say they take our man in for questioning. Pressure him. He talks, tells them everything, just like we want. Then what? Is he still exchanged as a prisoner?"

"Oh, we'll make it all work out, one way or another. If worse comes to worst, he'll end up back where he started, as a captive."

"Except in German hands, not Swiss."

"Your concern is admirable, Bill. But have you been over to Wauwilermoos lately? Pretty brutal, I'm told. I'm sure there are some German stalags that would be an improvement over that rat hole. It's wartime, Bill. Besides, anyone who volunteers will know the risks. If he were the hard type, the type to fight to the bitter end, then I'd say okay, you have a point. But this is the beauty of our operation. With the right man, the right temperament, the risk is minimal. So it really is all up to you. Or to you and Kevin, of course."

Translation: Failure would be on our heads, and mostly on mine. By recruiting an OSS man, Gill had arranged for a fall guy who could be laid at the feet of Dulles, his rival. If it succeeded, he could claim he knew better how to use OSS personnel.

I said yes anyway. I can be stubborn that way, especially when I sense that an opportunity, no matter how chancy, might be the only one to come along. And a few days later there I was, entering a train compartment to talk to the young man who we had decided was our hottest prospect.

"Morning, Lieutenant. I'm from the American legation in Bern and I have some questions for you. The first thing I need to know is your name."

The young airman looked suitably intimidated and clutched his escape kit to his chest. But he answered without first asking for my name, which I took as a good sign. Easily cowed by authority, I surmised, even though he carried a decent rank of his own.

"Lieutenant Seymour Parker. Emporia, Kansas."

"Navigator, right?"

"How'd you know?"

"I know a lot of things. Come with me, please. We've got some more questions for you."

"Are you an officer?"

"Like I said. I'm with the legation."

"But the Swiss officers said . . ."

"They've been notified. So has your CO. Let's go."

He looked around at his seatmates, who shrugged. I got the impression they hadn't known one another long, or else they would have risen to his defense.

Parker rose awkwardly. A long flight in a Fortress stiffened you up, especially when followed by an uneasy night of sleep on a Swiss cot in an empty schoolhouse. He followed me meekly up the aisle to where Butchart was waiting, just as the train was pulling into Adelboden. We had arranged for the legation to send down a car and driver, which seemed to impress him. Butchart and I sat on either side of him on the backseat of a big Ford.

If I had been in Parker's shoes, I would have been asking a million questions. He tried one or two, then stopped altogether when Butchart told him brusquely to shut up. If we had been Germans posing as Americans we could have hijacked him every bit as easily. Butchart looked over at me and nodded, as if he was thinking the same thing.

The roads were clear of snow, and we made it to Bern in about an hour. We said little along the way, letting the pressure build, and when we reached the city we took him to an empty back room in one of the legation offices. Seeing the American flag out front and hearing other people speaking English seemed to put him at ease. We shut the door and settled Parker into a stiff-backed chair. The first thing Butchart asked was how many missions he'd flown.

"This, uh, this was my first."

Perfect, and we both knew it. Enough to get a taste of terror without growing accustomed to it.

"Some of your crewmates looked pretty experienced," I said.

"They are. I was a replacement."

"So what happened to you guys up there?" Butchart asked. "You fuck up the charts or something, get everybody lost?"

Parker reddened, and for the first time defiance crept into his voice.

"No, it wasn't like that at all. We were in the middle of the formation and took some hits. Didn't even reach the target. We came out below Regensburg with only two engines, and one of those was smoking. Lieutenant Braden, he's our pilot, asked me to plot a course toward Lake Constance."

"Well, you did that part okay, I guess."

Butchart then eased up a bit by asking a few personal questions. He companionably pulled up a chair next to Parker's and started nodding sympathetically as the kid answered. I say "kid," but Parker was twenty, the son of a wheat farmer. He was a third-year engineering student at the University of Kansas, which explained how he had qualified for navigator training.

As he spoke it became clear that he was a man of simple, innocent tastes. He liked to read, didn't smoke, preferred soda over beer, and didn't have a serious girlfriend. Up to the time of his arrival in England he seemed to have believed that his hometown of Emporia was the center of the universe, and his college town of Lawrence was a veritable Athens. The most important bit of intelligence to come out of this part of our chat was that he had spent the previous summer as a lifeguard at a local pool.

"A lifeguard, huh?" Butchart sounded worried. "You volunteered?"

"Sure."

"And went through all the training?"

"Well . . ."

"Well what?"

"I was kinda filling in. All the regulars had enlisted, so there really wasn't time for me to take the courses."

"Sorta like with your bombing mission?"

"I guess."

Parker went meek and quiet again, as if we'd just exposed him as a fraud.

"Can I ask you guys something?"

"Sure." Butchart said.

"What's this all about? I mean. I know you mentioned something about a job. But what kind of job?"

"A onetime deal. A mission, provided you qualify. You'd be sent home on a prisoner exchange. But you'd have to memorize some information for us to pass along to the generals once you got back to the States. Facts and figures, maybe a lot of them."

"I'm good at that."

"I'll bet. And in return you'd get a free trip home. Not bad, huh?"

He smiled at that, then frowned, as if realizing it sounded too good to be true.

"But why me? There are plenty of other guys who've earned it more."

"Do you always look a gift horse in the mouth? Did you turn down the lifeguard job?"

"No, but . . ."

"But what?"

"I dunno. Something seems kinda funny about the whole thing."

I tried to put him at ease.

"Look, you're a navigator, which means you probably have a head for numbers and memorization. So there you go. You said it yourself, you'd be good at it."

He nodded, but didn't say anything more.

Butchart spent the next few minutes going over the preparation that would be required. He also described the likely route home—up through occupied France in the company of German escorts from the SS. Parker's eyes got a little wide during that part, and Butchart nodded at me in approval.

"So let's say you get caught, Parker. Let's say that halfway through this nice little train ride to Paris, one of those Krauts gets suspicious and takes you off at the next stop for a little questioning. What do you do then?"

"You mean if I'm captured?"

"No, dumb ass. You're already captured. That's why you're part of an exchange. But let's say they decide to check you out, grill you a little. What you gonna tell 'em?"

"Name, rank, and serial number?"

"Yeah, sure. But what else?"

"Well, nothing, I hope."

Butchart got in his face like a drill sergeant.

"You *hope*?"

"Okay, I *know*. Or know I'll try."

"C'mon, Parker, you can level with us. You really think you could handle some Gestapo thug getting all over you? What would you tell him?"

"I like to think I wouldn't say a damn thing."

"You mean like if they try this?"

Butchart slid a knife from his belt. Then he grabbed Parker by a shank of hair and pulled back his head. Before the kid even realized what was happening, Butchart had put the flat of the blade against the white of Parker's neck—steel on skin, as if he were about to peel him like a piece of fruit.

Parker swallowed hard, his Adam's apple rising and falling. For a moment I thought he was going to cry.

"Whadda you doin'?"

"Checkin' you out."

Butchart yanked Parker's head lower while holding the blade steady. Sweat beaded at Parker's temples, and his eyes bulged. When he next spoke his voice was an octave higher.

"I'm not the enemy, okay?"

"Oh, yeah? How do we know that for sure?"

Another tug on his hair, this time eliciting a sharp squeal of pain.

"You coulda been a plant, put on that train to fool us. Or to infiltrate all our other boys and steal their secrets. Air routes, evasion tendencies, stuff about the new bombsight. How come nobody in your compartment acted like they knew you?"

"I'm new!" he said shrilly. "Nobody talks to replacements!"

Butchart abruptly released him and put away the knife. Parker sat up and tried to collect himself, but it was no good. His skin was pale gooseflesh, and he was swallowing so fast that his throat was working like a piston. He touched the spot where Butchart had held the blade. There were still red marks from Butchart's knuckles. A little cruel, no doubt, but I guess it was necessary.

Butchart turned toward me and nodded, and I knew without a word that it was his confirmation signal.

"I'll tell Colonel Gill," he said, rising from his chair.

"You mean I'm out?"

It wasn't clear if Parker was relieved or disappointed, which for us only enhanced his suitability.

"No," I said, avoiding his eyes. "You're in. You passed with flying colors."

"You'll start your training tomorrow," Butchart said. "Tobin here will go over the timetable."

We had two weeks to bring him up to speed on all the garbage information Colonel Gill wanted drilled into his head. Figuring that his taskmaster needed to be just as committed to the "facts" as his clueless student, the colonel assigned a sergeant from his staff named Wesley Flagg to handle the learning sessions.

Flagg was the perfect choice—pleasant, goodhearted, and as sincere as they come. Flagg's earnestness drove Butchart crazy, enough that he assigned me to keep tabs on the lessons. But as far as Colonel Gill was concerned, Flagg's greatest attribute was that he never questioned orders.

Even if Flagg were to suspect that the information was flawed, there was virtually no chance he would have raised a fuss. He would simply assume that his superiors knew best.

Parker was a fast learner. Every time I asked Flagg for an update, he gushed about his pupil's ability to handle a heavy workload. But for all his boasting I sensed an unspoken uneasiness about Parker's fitness for the job. Flagg dared to bring it up only once, asking, "Are you sure Colonel Gill has signed off on this guy? I mean, Parker's great with the material, but, well . . ."

"Well what? He's the colonel's top choice."

"Nothing, then."

He never brought it up again.

The night before the exchange was to take place, Butchart asked me to take Parker his consignment of cigarettes. All four of the airmen were getting several cartons to help them spread goodwill along the way. They also might need to bribe some petty bureaucrat, even though the SS would be their official escorts.

Parker was billeted at a small hotel in the center of Bern. Conveniently—as far as we were concerned—it was just down the block from an apartment rented by a pair of Gestapo officers. Presumably they had passed him in the streets by now. He still wore his uniform from time to time, and they would have wondered right away what he was up to.

OSS operatives who worked for Dulles were taught that when meeting contacts it was best to disguise their comings and goings and to rendezvous on neutral ground. In Parker's case I was instructed not to bother, even though it put a knot in my stomach simply to walk into the hotel's small lobby and ask for him by name. A man was seated in the lobby on a couch. I didn't know his name or nationality, and I didn't ask.

Parker was restless, as anyone might have been on the eve of such an undertaking. But somehow he was not quite the same as the fellow I remembered from a few weeks earlier. Was my imagination playing tricks on me, or had he lost some of his callowness as he settled into his new role?

He finished packing in almost no time, so I asked if I could treat him to a beer.

"No, thanks," he said. "I probably won't be able to sleep much either way, so I might as well try to do it with a clear head. But there is one favor you can do me."

"Sure."

"Tell me, is there something funny about this operation? Something that, well, maybe no one has mentioned?"

I made it a point to look him straight in the eye, as much for myself as for him.

"There are always aspects of operations that aren't disclosed to the operatives. It's for their own protection."

"That's all you're allowed to say?"

As he asked it, his face was like that of the catcher in my son's Little League game—vulnerable yet determined, timid yet willing to go forward, come what may. For a moment I was tempted to tell him everything.

But I didn't, if only because the advice I had just imparted was true. It *was* in his best interests not to know. For one thing, the truth would have devastated him. For another, the Germans would have read his intentions immediately. And while it's one thing to have the enemy catch you functioning as a secret courier, it's quite another to be caught operating as an agent of deception. Setting Parker up for that fate would have been tantamount to marching him before a firing squad.

So I tried offering an oblique word of advice, hoping that when the right time came he would recall my words and put them to good use.

"Look, if for some unforeseen reason push does come to shove, just keep in mind that it's *you* who will be out there taking the blows, not us. So go with your own instincts."

It only seemed to puzzle him. Finally, he smiled.

"Maybe I should take you up on that beer, after all."

"Good enough."

He drank three, as it turned out, the first time in his life he had downed more than one at a sit-

ting, and it showed in his wobble as I escorted him back to the room. He turned out his light just as I was leaving.

The actual exchange at the border was almost anticlimactic.

Oh, the SS man showed up, all right, just as he had for the previous swap engineered by Dulles. I suppose he was appropriately sinister with his swagger stick and stiff Prussian walk, and certainly for the way he snapped his heels and offered a crisp Nazi salute along with the obligatory "Heil Hitler."

It definitely got Parker's attention, but I don't recall it striking much fear into me. Or maybe I've rewritten the scene in my memory, having watched countless Hollywood versions that have turned the officer's dark gestures into costumed parody, complete with cheesy accent. I suppose I've always wanted to regard him as a harmless stereotype, not some genuine menace who still had a war to fight and enemies to kill.

Whatever the case, Parker offered me a wan smile over his shoulder as he lined up with his three fellow airmen and stepped aboard the train. They were all a bit nervous, but to a man they were also excited about the prospect of returning home.

I got back to Bern late that night. A taxi dropped me at the legation so I could report that all had gone well. But Butchart and Colonel Gill weren't there, and neither had left word on where to reach them. Only Flagg was waiting, eager to hear how his pupil had fared.

He smiled after I described the scene at the train station.

"I'll admit that for a while I had my doubts," he said. "But you know, by the end I was feeling pretty good about it. Parker's the type who can fool you. Hidden reserves and all that."

"You really think so?"

"Oh, yes. And he was such a fast learner with the material that I even had time to teach him a few escape and evade tactics. Just in case."

"Good thinking," I said weakly.

We said good night, and I walked across the lonely bridge to my apartment. I was exhausted and it was well past midnight, but I don't remember getting a moment of sleep.

Two days later a French rail worker, one of our contacts with the maquis, reported through the usual channels that Parker had been removed from the train at the third stop, well before Paris. No one in our shop said much about it, especially when there was no further word in the following days.

Soon enough I was busy with new assignments. If Dulles had been testing me through Colonel Gill, then I must have passed, because he began making good right away on his promise to get me out and about.

The extra distractions were welcome, and within a few weeks I was no longer dreaming of Messerschmitts and butchered comrades, although Parker's guileless face did swim before me from time to time. Then came the day when Hitler shot himself. Flagg popped his question, Butchart supplied the reassuring answer, and from then on I had no more dreams of Parker. I was content to let him reside in my memory as a quirky sidelight of the war years. At least, I was until coming across his folder at the Records Center.

It was a thin file, with only four typewritten pages inside. But what really caught my attention was the Gestapo markings across the sleeve. As I steeled myself to read it in the sunlight of 1958, it occurred to me that soon there would be little need for fellows like Parker. Only months earlier, Sputnik had fallen to earth after its successful voyage. Bigger and better replacements were already on the launchpad, and, if you believed the newspapers, the chatter in intelligence circles was that half the work of spies would soon be obsolete. Both sides would soon be able simply to look down at enemy positions from high in the sky. But in 1944 we had people like Parker, good soldiers who did as they were told, even when they were told very little.

By the second paragraph I learned that Parker had been considered a probable spy almost from the moment he had boarded the train. By the fourth paragraph I learned they had grilled him

for twelve hours, off and on. The details were scanty—they always were in these reports when the Gestapo was pulling out all the stops—but I was familiar with enough eyewitness accounts of their usual tactics to fill in the blanks: Force them to stand for hours on end. Let them pee in their pants while they waited. Beat them, perhaps, and, if that didn't work, beat them harder, or threaten them with a firing squad.

Spy was the word the report kept using, over and over. Twelve hours of this, yet Parker, the veteran of only a single combat mission over Germany, held out. Flagg's judgment proved correct. He had hidden reserves. In fact, he had done us all one better. Lieutenant Parker had tried to escape.

It happened early on the following morning, the report said, right after the sentry left the room for a smoke. The officer in charge okayed the break because the subject had been at his lowest ebb. And at this point in the report, perhaps to cover his ass, the officer allowed himself the luxury of a detailed description of the subject's physical state: one eye swollen shut, bruises about the face and chest, shins bleeding, apparent exhaustion due to sleep deprivation. Yet no sooner had the sentry made himself scarce than Parker had somehow managed to overcome the interrogating officer and throw open the door.

He made it about twenty yards before the gunshots caught him. He then survived another two hours before dying of his wounds. The reporting officer seemed resigned to the idea of being reprimanded for his lapse in judgment, which had led to the loss of a potentially valuable prisoner before any useful information had been extracted.

By then my hands were cold, my feet as well. I sighed deeply, shut the folder, and looked up at the clock. It was an hour past our usual closing time, and my assistant was eyeing me curiously from his desk. He was anxious to leave. What I needed was a stiff drink, although this time a pitcher of gimlets wasn't going to be enough. But first I had one more bit of business here to take care of.

I carried the folder to a table next to my assistant's desk. For a moment I hovered over the burn box. As I prepared to drop in the report for destruction, I like to believe that I was not guided chiefly by an instinct of self-preservation. I was thinking as well of Parker's parents, perhaps still on their farm near Emporia. Having a son of my own now. I wondered what it would be like to hear that your only child had died while protecting secrets that he wasn't supposed to protect, that he had failed in his mission by being too brave and too strong.

But I couldn't bring myself to let go of the folder.

"Sir?" my assistant asked. "Is something wrong?"

"This one belongs with the OSS stuff."

"Classified?"

I paused, still hovering.

"No. In fact, I'd like it to get some circulation. You go on. I'll prepare the translation and a distribution list and have it ready for you to send out copies in the morning."

He was gone within seconds, and I settled back at my desk with the folder still in hand. The list came immediately to mind. Colonel Gill and Butchart, wherever they might be, would receive copies. Dulles, too, down at his big desk in the director's office of the agency we now called the CIA. Or perhaps each of them already knew, and always had. In that case, they needed to know that others had also found out.

But what about Parker's parents? I would spare them the gory details, of course, but they at least deserved the gist of the story, beginning with that first meeting aboard the train. The most important part, however, would be the summation, and I already had one in mind: Your son didn't tell the Germans a word. Not one. In fact, he did exactly as we asked, even if not at all as we had planned. The ball never left his mitt.

CITADEL

STEPHEN HUNTER

ALTHOUGH HE IS BEST KNOWN as a national bestseller for his contemporary thrillers, Stephen Hunter (1946–   ) has also written some works of outstanding historical fiction that have been fully researched and bring the authentic sound of someone who has always been comfortable in another era. His novel *I, Ripper* (2015) was a bestseller that was told in alternating chapters between a newspaperman and the diary of Jack the Ripper. *G-Man* (2017) featured a Zelig-like federal agent who was at the center of the final days of John Dillinger, Bonnie and Clyde, Baby Face Nelson, and other major gangsters who met their ends in the 1930s.

Hunter also forged a highly successful career as a journalist and author of nonfiction, working as the film critic for *The Baltimore Sun* and *The Washington Post*, winning a Pulitzer Prize for criticism in 2003.

Hunter has enjoyed enormous success with his hard-boiled, often violent thrillers, beginning with *The Master Sniper* (1980) and continuing for more than twenty novels. Several of his most popular books feature Bob "the Nailer" Swagger, a Marine sniper given the sobriquet for his extraordinary skill with a rifle. There are eleven books in the Bob Lee Swagger series, beginning with *Point of Impact* (1993), on which the 2007 film titled *Shooter* was based, with Mark Wahlberg in the starring role.

Shooter became a national television series that lasted for three seasons (2016–2018) after a rocky beginning. Scheduled to be broadcast in the beginning of July 2016, its premiere was sensitively postponed after several shootings—a mass killing of five police officers in Dallas, followed by the murder of a Louisiana policeman—until it finally aired in November. It starred Ryan Phillippe as Bob Lee Swagger, a former Marine marksman forced into action when a plot to assassinate the president is uncovered; he is set up, unjustly accused, and targeted by the military of his own country.

"Citadel" was originally published as a volume in the *Bibliomystery* series (New York, The Mysterious Bookshop, 2015).

CITADEL

STEPHEN HUNTER

FIRST DAY

THE LYSANDER TOOK OFF in the pitch dark of 0400 British Standard War Time, Pilot Officer Murphy using the prevailing south-southwest wind to gain atmospheric traction, even though the craft had a reputation for short takeoffs. He nudged it airborne, felt it surpass its amazingly low stall speed, held the stick gently back until he reached 150 meters, then commenced a wide left-hand bank to aim himself and his passenger toward Occupied France.

Murphy was a pro and had done many missions for his outfit, No. 138 (Special Duties Squadron), inserting and removing agents in coordination with the Resistance. But that didn't mean he was blasé, or without fear. No matter how many times you flew into Nazi territory, it was a first time. There was no predicting what might happen, and he could just as easily end up in a POW camp or against the executioner's wall as back in his quarters at RAF Newmarket.

The high-winged, single-engine plane hummed along just over the 150-meter notch on the altimeter to stay under both British and, twenty minutes on, German radar. It was a moonless night, as preferred, a bit chilly and

damp, with ground temperature at about four degrees centigrade. It was early April 1943; the destination, still two hours ahead, was a meadow outside Sur-la-Gane, a village forty-eight kilometers east of Paris. There, God and the Luftwaffe willing, he would deviate from the track of a railroad, find four lights on the ground, and lay the plane down between them, knowing that they signified enough flatness and tree clearance for the airplane. He'd drop his passenger, the peasants of whichever Maquis group was receiving that night (he never knew) would turn the plane around, and in another forty seconds he'd be airborne, now headed west toward tea and jam. That was the ideal, at any rate.

He checked the compass at the apex of the Lysander's primitive instrument panel and double-checked his heading (148° ENE), his fuel (full), and his airspeed (175 mph), and saw through the Perspex windscreen, as expected, nothing. Nothing was good. He knew it was a rare off-night in the war and that no fleets of Lancasters filled the air and radio waves to and from targets deep in Germany, which meant that the Luftwaffe's night fighters, Me110s, wouldn't be up and about. No 110 had ever shot down a Lysander because they operated at such different altitudes and speeds, but there had to be a first time for everything.

Hunched behind him was an agent named Basil St. Florian, a captain in the army by official designation, commissioned in 1932 into the Horse Guards—not that he'd been on horseback in over a decade. Actually Basil, a ruddy-faced, ginger-haired brute who'd once sported a giant moustache, didn't know or care much about horses. Or the fabulous traditions of the Horse Guards, the cavalry, even the army. He'd only ended up there after a youth notorious for spectacular crack-ups, usually involving trysts with American actresses and fights with Argentine polo players. His father arranged the commission, as he had arranged so much else for Basil, who tended to leave debris wherever he went, but once in khaki Basil veered again toward glamorous self-extinction until a dour little chap from Intelligence invited him for a drink at Boodle's. When Basil learned he could do unusual things and get both paid and praised for it, he signed up. That was 1934, and Basil had never looked back.

As it turned out, he had a gift for languages and spoke French, German, and Spanish without a trace of accent. He could pass for any European nationality except Irish, though the latter was more on principle, because he despised the Irish in general terms. They were so loud.

He liked danger and wasn't particularly nonplussed by fear. He never panicked. He took pride in his considerable wit, and his bons mots were famous in his organization. He didn't mind fighting, with fist or knife, but much preferred shooting, because he was a superb pistol and rifle shot. He'd been on safari at fifteen, again at twenty-two, and a third time at twenty-seven; he was quite used to seeing large mammals die by gunshot, so it didn't particularly perturb him. He knew enough about trophy hunting to hope that he'd never end up on another man's wall.

He'd been in the agent trade a long time and had the nightmares to show for it, plus a drawerful of ribbons that someone must organize sooner or later, plus three bullet holes, a raggedy zigzag of scar tissue from a knife (don't ask,

please, don't *ever* ask), as well as piebald burn smears on back and hips from a long session with a torturer. He finally talked, and the lies he told the man were among his finest memories. His other favorite memory: watching his torturer's eyes go eightball as Basil strangled him three days later. Jolly fun!

Basil was cold, shivering under an RAF sheepskin over an RAF aircrew jumpsuit over a black wool suit of shabby prewar French manufacture. He sat uncomfortably squashed on a parachute, which he hadn't bothered to put on. The wind beat against him, because on some adventure or another the Lysander's left window had been shot out and nobody had got around to replacing it. He felt vibrations as the unspectacular Bristol Mercury XII engine beat away against the cold air, its energy shuddering through all the spars, struts, and tightened canvas of the aircraft.

"Over Channel now, sir," came the crackle of a voice from the earphones he wore, since there was entirely too much noise for pilot and passenger to communicate without it. "Ten minutes to France."

"Got it, Murphy, thanks."

Inclining toward the intact window to his starboard, Basil could see the black surface of the Channel at high chop, the water seething and shifting under the powerful blast of cold early-spring winds. It somehow caught enough illumination from the stars to gleam a bit, though without romance or beauty. It simply reminded him of unpleasant things and his aversion to large bodies of the stuff, which to him had but three effects: it made you wet, it made you cold, or it made you dead. All three were to be avoided.

In time a dark mass protruded upon the scene, sliding in from beyond to meet the sea.

"I say, Murphy, is that France?"

"It is indeed, sir."

"You know, I didn't have a chance to look at the flight plan. What part of France?"

"Normandy, sir. Jerry's building forts there, to stop an invasion."

"If I recall, there's a peninsula to the west, and the city of Cherbourg at the tip?"

"Yes, sir."

"Tell me, if you veered toward the west, you'd cross the peninsula, correct? With no deviation then, you'd come across coastline?"

"Yes, sir."

"And from that coastline, knowing you were to the western lee of the Cherbourg peninsula, you could easily return home on dead reckoning, that is, without a compass, am I right?"

"Indeed, sir. But I have a compass. So why would—"

Basil leaned forward, holding his Browning .380 automatic pistol. He fired once, the pistol jumping, the flash filling the cockpit with a flare of illumination, the spent casing flying away, the noise terrific.

"Good Christ!" yelped Murphy. "What the bloody hell! Are you mad?"

"Quite the opposite, old man," said Basil. "Now do as I suggested—veer westerly, cross the peninsula, and find me coastline."

Murphy noted that the bullet had hit the compass bang on, shattered its glass, and blown its dial askew and its needle arm into the vapors.

A FEW DAYS EARLIER

"Basil, how's the drinking?" the general asked.

"Excellent, sir," Basil replied. "I'm up to seven, sometimes eight whiskies a night."

"Splendid, Basil," said the general. "I knew you wouldn't let us down."

"See here," said another general. "I know this man has a reputation for wit, as it's called, but we are engaged in serious business, and the levity, perhaps appropriate to the officers' mess, is most assuredly inappropriate here. There should be no laughing here, gentlemen. This is the War Room."

Basil sat in a square, dull space far underground. A few dim bulbs illuminated it but showed little except a map of Europe pinned to the wall. Otherwise it was featureless. The table was large enough for at least a dozen generals, but there were only three of them—well, one was an admiral—and a civilian, all sitting across from Basil. It was rather like orals at Magdalen, had he bothered to attend them.

The room was buried beneath the Treasury in Whitehall, the most secret of secret installations in wartime Britain. Part of a warren of other rooms—some offices for administrative or logistical activities, a communications room, some sleeping or eating quarters—it was the only construction in England that might legitimately be called a lair. It belonged under a volcano, not a large office building. The prime minister would sit in this very place with his staff and make the decisions that would send thousands to their death in order to save tens of thousands. That was the theory, anyway. And that also is why it stank so brazenly of stale cigar.

"My dear sir," said the general with whom Basil had been discussing his drinking habits to the general who disapproved, "when one has been shot at for the benefit of crown and country as many times as Captain St. Florian, one has the right to set the tone of the meeting that will most certainly end up getting him shot at quite a bit more. Unless you survived the first day on the Somme, you cannot compete with him in that regard."

The other general muttered something grumpily, but Basil hardly noticed. It really did not matter, and since he believed himself doomed no matter what, he now no longer listened to those who did not matter.

The general who championed him turned to him, his opposition defeated. His name was Sir Colin Gubbins and he was head of the outfit to which Basil belonged, called by the rather dreary title Special Operations Executive. Its mandate was to Set Europe Ablaze, as the prime minister had said when he invented it and appointed General Gubbins as its leader. It was the sort of organization that would have welcomed Jack the Ripper to its ranks, possibly even promoted, certainly decorated him. It existed primarily to destroy—people, places, things, anything that could be destroyed. Whether all this was just mischief for the otherwise unemployable or long-term strategic wisdom was as yet undetermined. It was up for considerable debate among the other intelligence agencies, one of which was represented by the army general and the other by the naval admiral.

As for the civilian, he looked like a question on a quiz: Which one does not belong? He was a good thirty years younger than the two generals and the admiral, and hadn't, as they did, one of those heavy-jowled authoritarian faces. He was rather handsome in a weak sort of way, like the fellow who always plays Freddy in any production of *Pygmalion*, and he didn't radiate, as did the men of power. Yet here he was, a lad among the Neanderthals, and the others seemed in small ways to defer to him. Basil wondered who the devil he could be. But he realized he would find out sooner or later.

"You've all seen Captain St. Florian's record, highly classified as it is. He's one of our most capable men. If this thing can be done, he's the one who can do it. I'm sure before we proceed, the captain would entertain any questions of a general nature."

"I seem to remember your name from the cricket fields, St. Florian," said the admiral. "Were you not a batsman of some renown in the late twenties?"

"I have warm recollections of good innings at both Eton and Magdalen," said Basil.

"Indeed," said the admiral. "I've always said that sportsmen make the best agents. The playing field accustoms them to arduous action, quick, clever thinking, and decisiveness."

"I hope, however," said the general, "you've left your sense of sporting fair play far behind. Jerry will use it against you, any chance he gets."

"I killed a Chinese gangster with a cricket bat, sir. Would that speak to the issue?"

"Eloquently," said the general.

"What did your people do, Captain?" asked the admiral.

"He manufactured something," said Basil. "It had to do with automobiles, as I recall."

"A bit hazy, are we?"

"It's all rather vague. I believe that I worked for him for a few months after coming down. My performance was rather disappointing. We parted on bad terms. He died before I righted myself."

"To what do you ascribe your failure to succeed in business and please your poor father?"

"I am too twitchy to sit behind a desk, sir. My bum, pardon the French, gets all buzzy if I am in one spot too long. Then I drink to kill the buzz and end up in the cheap papers."

"I seem to recall," the admiral said. "Something about an actress—'31, '32, was that it?"

"Lovely young lady," Basil said, "A pity I treated her so abominably. I always plucked the melons out of her fruit salad and she could not abide that."

"Hong Kong, Malaysia, Germany before and during Hitler, battle in Spain—shot at a bit there, eh, watching our Communists fight the generalissimo's Germans, eh?" asked the army chap. "Czecho, France again, Dieppe, you were there? So was I."

"Odd I didn't see you, sir," said Basil.

"I suppose you were way out front then. Point taken, Captain. All right, professionally, he seems capable. Let's get on with it, Sir Colin."

"Yes," said Sir Colin. "Where to begin, where to begin? It's rather complex, you see, and someone important has demanded that you be apprised of all the nuances before you decide to go."

"Sir, I could save us all a lot of time. I've decided to go. I hereby officially volunteer."

"See, there's a chap with spirit," said the admiral. "I like that."

"It's merely that his bum is twitchy," said the general.

"Not so fast, Basil. I insist that you hear us out," said Sir Colin, "and so does the young man at the end of the table. Is that not right, Professor?"

"It is," said the young fellow.

"All right, sir," said Basil.

"It's a rather complex, even arduous story.

Please ignore the twitchy bum and any need you may have for whisky. Give us your best effort."

"I shall endeavor, sir."

"Excellent. Now, hmm, let me see . . . oh, yes, I think this is how to start. Do you know the path to Jesus?"

THE FIRST DAY (CONT'D.)

Another half hour flew by, lost to the rattle of the plane, the howl of the wind, and the darkness of Occupied France below. At last Murphy said over the intercom, "Sir, the west coast of the Cherbourg Peninsula is just ahead. I can see it now."

"Excellent," said Basil. "Find someplace to put me down."

"Ah . . ."

"Yes, what is it, Pilot Officer?"

"Sir, I can't just land, you see. The plane is too fragile—there may be wires, potholes, tree stumps, ditches, mud, God knows what. All of which could snarl or even wreck the plane. It's not so much me. I'm not that important. It's actually the plane. Jerry's been trying to get hold of a Lysander for some time now, to use against us. I can't give him one."

"Yes, I can see that. All right then, perhaps drop me in a river from a low altitude?"

"Sir, you'd hit the water at over 100 miles per hour and bounce like a billiard ball off the bumper. Every bone would shatter."

"On top of that, I'd lose my shoes. This is annoying. I suppose then it's the parachute for me?"

"Yes, sir. Have you had training?"

"Scheduled several times, but I always managed to come up with an excuse. I could see no sane reason for abandoning a perfectly fine airplane in flight. That was then, however, and now, alas, is now."

Basil shed himself of the RAF fleece, a heavy leather jacket lined with sheep's wool, and felt the coldness of the wind bite him hard. He shivered. He hated the cold. He struggled with the straps of the parachute upon which he was sitting. He found the going rather rough. It seemed he couldn't quite get the left shoulder strap buckled into what appeared to be the strap nexus, a circular lock-like device that was affixed to the right shoulder strap in the center of his chest. He passed on that and went right to the thigh straps, which seemed to click in admirably, but then noticed he had the two straps in the wrong slots, and he couldn't get the left one undone. He applied extra effort and was able to make the correction.

"I say, how long has this parachute been here? It's all rusty and stiff."

"Well, sir, these planes aren't designed for parachuting. Their brilliance is in the short takeoff and landing drills. Perfect for agent inserts and fetches. So, no, I'm afraid nobody has paid much attention to the parachute."

"Damned thing. I'd have thought you RAF buckos would have done better. Battle of Britain, the few, all that sort of thing."

"I'm sure the 'chutes on Spits and Hurricanes were better maintained, sir. Allow me to make a formal apology to the intelligence services on behalf of the Royal Air Force."

"Well, I suppose it'll have to do," sniffed Basil. Somehow, at last, he managed to get the left strap snapped in approximately where it belonged, but he had no idea if the thing was too tight or too loose or even right side up. Oh, well, one did what one must. Up, up, and play the game, that sort of thing.

"Now, I'm not telling you your job, Murphy, but I think you should go lower so I won't have so far to go."

"Quite the opposite, sir. I must go higher. The 'chute won't open fully at 150 meters. It's a 240-meter minimum, a thousand far safer. At 150 or lower it's like dropping a pumpkin on a sidewalk. Very unpleasant sound, lots of splash, splatter, puddle, and stain. Wouldn't advise a bit of it, sir."

"This is not turning out at all as I had expected."

"I'll buzz up to a thousand. Sir, the trick here is that when you come out of the plane, you must keep hunched up in a ball. If you open up, your arms and legs and torso will catch wind and stall your fall and the tail wing will cut you in half or at least break your spine."

"Egad," said Basil. "How disturbing."

"I'll bank hard left to add gravity to your speed of descent, which puts you in good shape, at least theoretically, to avoid the tail."

"Not sure I care for 'theoretically.'"

"There's no automatic deployment on that device, also. You must, once free of the plane, pull the ripcord to open the 'chute."

"I shall try to remember," said Basil.

"If you forget, it's the pumpkin phenomenon, without doubt."

"All right, Murphy, you've done a fine job briefing me. I shall have a letter inserted in your file. Now, shall we get this nonsense over with?"

"Yes, sir. You'll feel the plane bank, you should have no difficulty with the door, remember to take off earphones and throat mike, and I'll signal go. Just tumble out. Rip cord, and down you go. Don't brace hard in landing—you could break or sprain something. Try to relax. It's a piece of cake."

"Very well done, Murphy."

"Sir, what should I tell them?"

"Tell them what happened. That's all. I'll happily be the villain. Once I potted the compass, it was either do as I say or head home. On top of that, I outrank you. They'll figure it out, and if they don't, then they're too damned stupid to worry about!"

"Yes, sir."

Basil felt the subtle, then stronger pull of gravity as Murphy pulled the stick back and the plane mounted toward heaven. He had to give more throttle, so the sound of the revs and the consequent vibrations through the plane's skeleton increased. Basil unhitched the door, pushed it out a bit, but then the prop wash caught it and slammed it back. He opened it a bit again, squirmed his way to the opening, scrunched to fit through, brought himself to the last point where he could be said to be inside the airplane, and waited.

Below, the blackness roared by, lit here and there by a light. It really made no difference where he jumped. It would be completely random. He might come down in a town square, a haystack, a cemetery, a barn roof, or an SS firing range. God would decide, not Basil.

Murphy raised his hand, and probably screamed "Tally-ho!"

Basil slipped off the earphones and mike and tumbled into the roaring darkness.

A FEW DAYS EARLIER (CONT'D)

"Certainly," said Basil, "though I doubt I'll be allowed to make the trip. The path to Jesus would include sobriety, a clean mind, obedience to all commandments, a positive outlook, respect for elders, regular worship, and a high level of hygiene. I am happily guilty of none of those."

"The damned insouciance," said the army general. "Is everything an opportunity for irony, Captain?"

"I shall endeavor to control my ironic impulses, sir," said Basil.

"Actually, he's quite amusing," said the young civilian. "A heroic chap as imagined by Noël Coward."

"Coward's a poof, Professor."

"But a titanic wit."

"Gentlemen, gentlemen," said Sir Colin. "Please, let's stay with the objective here, no matter how Captain St. Florian's insouciance annoys or enchants us."

"Then, sir," said Basil, "the irony-free answer is no, I do not know the path to Jesus."

"I don't mean in general terms. I mean specifically *The Path to Jesus*, a pamphlet published in 1767 by a Scottish ecclesiastic named Thomas MacBurney. Actually he listed twelve steps on the way, and I believe you scored high on your account, Basil. You only left out thrift, daily prayer, cold baths, and regular enemas."

"What about wanking, sir? Is that allowed by the Reverend MacBurney?"

"I doubt he'd heard of it. Anyway, it is not

the content of the reverend's pamphlet that here concerns us but the manuscript itself. That is the thing, the paper on which he wrote in ink, the actual physical object." He paused, taking a breath. "The piece began as a sermon, delivered to his congregation in that same year. It was quite successful—people talked much about it and requested that he deliver it over and over. He did, and became, one might say, an ecclesiastical celebrity. Then it occurred to him that he could spread the Word more effectively, and make a quid or two on the side—he was a Scot, after all—if he committed it to print and offered it for a shilling a throw. Thus he made a fair copy, which he delivered to a jobbing printer in Glasgow, and took copies around to all the churches and bookstores. Again, it was quite successful. It grew and grew and in the end he became rather prosperous, so much so that— this is my favorite part of the tale—he gave up the pulpit and retired to the country for a life of debauchery and gout, while continuing to turn out religious tracts when not abed with a local tart or two."

"I commend him," said Basil.

"As do we all," said the admiral.

"The fair copy, in his own hand, somehow came to rest in the rare books collection at the Cambridge Library. That is the one he copied himself from his own notes on the sermon, and which he hand-delivered to Carmichael and Sons, printers, of 14 Middlesex Lane, Glasgow, for careful reproduction on September 1, 1767. Mr. Carmichael's signature in receipt, plus instructions to his son, the actual printer, are inscribed in pencil across the title page. As it is the original, it is of course absurdly rare, which makes it absurdly valuable. Its homilies and simple faith have nothing to do with it, only its rarity, which is why the librarian at Cambridge treasures it so raptly. Are you with me, Basil?"

"With you, sir, but not with you. I cannot begin to fathom why this should interest the intelligence service, much less the tiny cog of it known as Basil St. Florian. Do you think exposure to it would improve my moral character?

My character definitely needs moral improvement, but I should think any book of the New Testament would do the job as well as the Reverend MacBurney."

"Well, it happens to be the key to locating a traitor, Basil. Have you ever heard of the book code?"

THE SECOND DAY

There was a fallacy prevalent in England that Occupied France was a morose, death-haunted place. It was gray, gray as the German uniforms, and the conquerors goose-stepped about like Mongols, arbitrarily designating French citizens for execution by firing squad as it occurred to them for no reason save whimsy and boredom and Hun depravity. The screams of the tortured pierced the quiet, howling out of the many Gestapo torture cellars. The Horst Wessel song was piped everywhere; swastikas emblazoned on vast red banners fluttered brazenly everywhere. Meanwhile the peasants shuffled about all hangdog, the bourgeoisie were rigid with terror, the civic institutions were in paralysis, and even the streetwalkers had disappeared.

Basil knew this to be untrue. In fact, Occupied France was quite gay. The French barely noted their own conquest before returning to bustling business as usual, or not as usual, for the Germans were a vast new market. Fruit, vegetables, slabs of beef, and other provisions gleamed in every shop window, the wine was ample, even abundant (if overpriced), and the streetwalkers were quite active. Perhaps it would change later in the war, but for now it was rather a swell time. The Resistance, such as it was—and it wasn't much—was confined to marginal groups: students, Communists, bohemians, professors— people who would have been at odds with society in any event; they just got more credit for it now, all in exchange for blowing up a piddling bridge or dynamiting a rail line which would be repaired in a few hours. Happiness was general all over France.

The source of this gaiety was twofold. The first was the French insistence on being French, no matter how many panzers patrolled the streets and crossroads. Protected by their intensely high self-esteem, they thought naught of the Germans, regarding the *feldgrau* as a new class of tourist, to be fleeced, condescended to ("Red wine as an aperitif! *Mon Dieu!*"), and otherwise ignored. And there weren't nearly as many Nazi swastikas fluttering on silk banners as one might imagine.

The second reason was the immense happiness of the occupiers themselves. The Germans loved the cheese, the meals, the whores, the sights, and all the pleasures of France, it is true, but they enjoyed one thing more: that it was Not Russia.

This sense of Not-Russia made each day a joy. The fact that at any moment they could be sent to Is-Russia haunted them and drove them to new heights of sybaritic release. Each pleasure had a melancholy poignancy in that he who experienced it might shortly be slamming 8.8 cm shells into the breach of an antitank gun as fleets of T-34s poured torrentially out of the snow at them, this drama occurring at minus thirty-one degrees centigrade on the outskirts of a town with an unpronounceable name that they had never heard of and that offered no running water, pretty women, or decent alcohol.

So nobody in all of France in any of the German branches worked very hard, except perhaps the extremists of the SS. But most of the SS was somewhere else, happily murdering farmers in the hundreds of thousands, letting their fury, their rage, their misanthropy, their sense of racial superiority play out in real time.

Thus Basil didn't fear random interception as he walked the streets of downtown Bricquebec, a small city forty kilometers east of Cherbourg in the heart of the Contentin Peninsula. The occupiers of this obscure spot would not be of the highest quality, and had adapted rather too quickly to the torpor of garrison life. They lounged this way and that, lazy as dogs in the spring sun, in the cafés, at their very occasional roadblocks, around city hall, where civil administrators now gave orders to the French bureaucrats, who had not made a single adjustment to their presence, and at an airfield where a flock of Me110 night fighters were housed, to intercept the nightly RAF bomber stream when it meandered toward targets in southern Germany. Though American bombers filled the sky by day, the two-engine 110s were not nimble enough to close with them and left that dangerous task to younger men in faster planes. The 110 pilots were content to maneuver close to the Lancasters, but not too close, to hosepipe their cannon shells all over the sky, then to return to schnapps and buns, claiming extravagant kill scores which nobody took seriously. So all in all, the atmosphere was one of snooze and snore.

Basil had landed without incident about eight kilometers outside of town. He was lucky, as he usually was, in that he didn't crash into a farmer's henhouse and awaken the rooster or the man but landed in one of the fields, among potato stubs just barely emerging from the ground. He had gathered up his 'chute, stripped off his RAF jumpsuit to reveal himself to be a rather shabby French businessman, and stuffed all that kit into some bushes (he could not bury it, because a) he did not feel like it and b) he had no shovel, but c) if he had had a shovel, he still would not have felt like it). He made it to a main road and walked into town, where he immediately treated himself to a breakfast of eggs and potatoes and tomatoes at a railway station café.

He nodded politely at each German he saw and so far had not excited any attention. His only concession to his trade was his Browning pistol, wedged into the small of his back and so flat it would not print under suit and overcoat. He also had his Riga Minox camera taped to his left ankle. His most profound piece of equipment, however, was his confidence. Going undercover is fraught with tension, but Basil had done it so often that its rigors didn't drive him to the edge of despair, eating his energy with teeth of dread. He'd simply shut down his imagination and considered himself the cock of the walk, presenting a smile, a nod, a wink to all.

But he was not without goal. Paris lay a half day's rail ride ahead; the next train left at four, and he had to be on it. But just as he didn't trust the partisans who still awaited his arrival 320 kilometers to the east, he didn't trust the documents the forgery geniuses at SOE had provided him with. Instead he preferred to pick up his own—that is, actual authentic docs, including travel permissions—and he now searched for a man who, in the terrible imagery of document photography, might be considered to look enough like him.

It was a pleasant day and he wandered this way and that, more or less sightseeing. At last he encountered a fellow who would pass for him, a well-dressed burgher in a black homburg and overcoat, dour and official-looking. But the bone structure was similar, given to prominent cheekbones and a nose that looked like a Norman axe. In fact the fellow could have been a long-lost cousin. (Had he cared to, Basil could have traced the St. Florian line back to a castle not 100 kilometers from where he stood now, whence came his Norman forebears in 1044—but of course it meant nothing to him.)

Among Basil's skills was pickpocketing, very useful for a spy or agent. He had mastered its intricacies during his period among Malaysian gunrunners in 1934, when a kindly old rogue with one eye and fast hands named Malong had taken a liking to him and shown him the basics of the trade. Malong could pick the fuzz off a peach, so educated were his fingers, and Basil proved an apt pupil. He'd never graduated to the peach-fuzz class, but the gentleman's wallet and document envelopes should prove easy enough.

He used the classic concealed hand dip and distraction technique, child's play but clearly effective out here in the French hinterlands. Shielding his left hand from view behind a copy of that day's *Le Monde*, he engineered an accidental street-corner bump, apologized, and

then said, "I was looking at the air power of *les amis* today." He pointed upward, where a wave of B-17s painted a swath in the blue sky with their fuzzy white contrails as they sped toward Munich or some other Bavarian destination for an afternoon of destruction. "It seems they'll never stop building up their fleet. But when they win, what will they do with all those airplanes?"

The gentleman, unaware that the jostle and rhetoric concealed a deft snatch from inside not merely his overcoat but also his suit coat, followed his interrupter's pointed arm to the aerial array.

"The Americans are so rich, I believe our German visitors are doomed," said the man. "I only hope when it is time for them to leave they don't grow bitter and decide to blow things up."

"That is why it is up to us to ingratiate ourselves with them," said Basil, reading the eyes of an appeaser in his victim, "so that when they do abandon their vacation, they depart with a gentleman's deportment. *Vive la France.*"

"Indeed," said the mark, issuing a dry little smile of approval, then turning away to his far more important business.

Basil headed two blocks in the opposite direction, two more in another, then rotated around to the train station. There, in the men's loo, he examined his trove: 175 francs, identity papers for one Jacques Piens, and a German travel authority "for official business only," both of which wore a smeary black-and-white photo of M. Piens, moustachioed and august and clearly annoyed at the indignity of posing for German photography.

He had a coffee. He waited, smiling at all, and a few minutes before four approached the ticket seller's window and, after establishing his bona fides as M. Piens, paid for and was issued a first-class ticket on the four p.m. Cherbourg–Paris run.

He went out on the platform, the only Frenchman among a small group of Luftwaffe enlisted personnel clearly headed to Paris for a weekend pass's worth of fun and frolic. The train arrived, as the Germans had been sensible enough not to interfere with the workings of the French railway system, the continent's best. Spewing smoke, the engine lugged its seven cars to the platform and, with great drama of steam, brakes, and steel, reluctantly halted. Basil knew where first class would be and parted company with the privates and corporals of the German air force, who squeezed into the other carriages.

His car half empty and comfortable, he put himself into a seat. The train sat . . . and sat . . . and sat. Finally a German policeman entered the car and examined the papers of all, including Basil, without incident. Yet still the train did not leave.

Hmm, this was troubling.

A lesser man might have fumbled into panic. The mark had noticed his papers missing, called the police, who had called the German police. Quickly enough they had put a hold on the train, fearing that the miscreant would attempt to flee that way, and now it was just a matter of waiting for an SS squad to lock up the last of the Jews before it came for him.

However, Basil had a sound operational principle which now served him well. *Most bad things don't happen.* What happens is that in its banal, boring way, reality bumbles along. The worst thing one can do is panic. Panic betrays more agents than traitors. Panic is the true enemy.

At last the train began to move.

Ah-ha! Right again.

But at that moment the door flew open and a late-arriving Luftwaffe colonel came in. He looked straight at Basil.

"There he is! There's the spy!" he said.

A FEW DAYS EARLIER (CONT'D)

"A book code," said Basil. "I thought that was for Boy Scouts. Lord Baden-Powell would be so pleased."

"Actually," said Sir Colin, "it's a sturdy and almost impenetrable device, very useful under certain circumstances, if artfully employed. But Professor Turing is our expert on codes. Perhaps, Professor, you'd be able to enlighten Captain St. Florian."

"Indeed," said the young man in the tweeds, revealing himself by name. "Nowadays we think we're all scienced up. We even have machines to do some of the backbreaking mathematics to it, speeding the process. Sometimes it works, sometimes it doesn't. But the book code is ancient, even biblical, and that it has lasted so long is good proof of its applicability in certain instances."

"I understand, Professor. I am not a child."

"Not at all, certainly not given your record. But the basics must be known before we can advance to the sort of sophisticated mischief upon which the war may turn."

"Please proceed, Professor. Pay no attention to Captain St. Florian's abominable manners. We interrupted him at play in a bawdy house for this meeting and he is cranky."

"Yes, then. The book code stems from the presumption that both sender and receiver have access to the same book. It is therefore usually a common volume, shall we say Lamb's *Tales from Shakespeare.* I want to send you a message, say 'Meet me at two p.m. at the square.' I page through the book until I find the word 'meet.' It is on page 17, paragraph 4, line 2, fifth word. So the first line in my code is 17-4-2-5. Unless you know the book, it is meaningless. But you, knowing the book, having the book, quickly find 17-4-2-5 and encounter the word 'meet.' And on and on. Of course variations can be worked—we can agree ahead of time, say, that for the last designation we will always be value minus two, that is, two integers less. So in that case the word 'meet' would actually be found at 17-4-2-3. Moreover, in picking a book as decoder, one would certainly be prone to pick a common book, one that should excite no excitement, that one might normally have about."

"I grasp it, Professor," said Basil. "But what, then, if I take your inference, is the point of choosing as a key book the Right Reverend Mac-

Burney's *The Path to Jesus*, of which only one copy exists, and it is held under lock and key at Cambridge? And since last I heard, we still control Cambridge. Why don't we just go to Cambridge and look at the damned thing? You don't need an action-this-day chap like me for that. You could use a lance corporal."

"Indeed, you have tumbled to it," said Sir Colin. "Yes, we could obtain the book that way. However, in doing so we would inform both the sender and the receiver that we knew they were up to something, that they were control and agent and had an operation under way, when our goal is to break the code without them knowing. That is why, alas, a simple trip to the library by a lance corporal is not feasible."

"I hope I'm smart enough to stay up with all these wrinkles, gentlemen. I already have a headache."

"Welcome to the world of espionage," said Sir Colin. "We all have headaches. Professor, please continue."

"The volume in the library is indeed controlled by only one man," Turing said. "And he is the senior librarian of the institution. Alas, his loyalties are such that they are not, as one might hope and expect, for his own country. He is instead one of those of high caste taken by fascination for another creed, and it is to that creed he pays his deepest allegiance. He has made himself useful to his masters for many years as a 'talent spotter,' that is, a man who looks at promising undergraduates, picks those with keen policy minds and good connections, forecasts their rise, and woos them to his side as secret agents with all kinds of babble of the sort that appeals to the mushy romantic brain of the typical English high-class idiot. He thus plants the seeds of our destruction, sure to bloom a few decades down the line. He does other minor tasks too, running as a cutout, providing a safe house, disbursing a secret fund, and so forth. He is committed maximally and he will die before he betrays his creed, and some here have suggested a bullet in the brain as opposite, but actually, by the tortured rules of the game, a live spy in place is worth more than a dead spy in the ground. Thus he must not be disturbed, bothered, breathed heavily upon—he must be left entirely alone."

"And as a consequence you cannot under any circumstances access the book. You do not even know what it looks like?" Basil asked.

"We have a description from a volume published in 1932, called *Treasures of the Cambridge Library*."

"I can guess who wrote it," said Basil.

"Your guess would be correct," said Sir Colin. "It tells us little other than that it comprises thirty-four pages of foolscap written in tightly controlled nib by an accomplished freehand scrivener. Its eccentricity is that occasionally apostolic bliss came over the author and he decorated the odd margin with constellations of floating crosses, proclaiming his love of all things Christian. The Reverend MacBurney was clearly given to religious swoons."

"And the librarian is given to impenetrable security," said the admiral. "There will come a time when I will quite happily murder him with your cricket bat, Captain."

"Alas, I couldn't get the bloodstains out and left it in Malay. So let me sum up what I think I know so far. For some reason the Germans have a fellow in the Cambridge library controlling access to a certain 1767 volume. Presumably they have sent an agent to London with a coded message he himself does not know the answer to, possibly for security reasons. Once safely here, he will approach the bad-apple librarian and present him with the code. The bad apple will go to the manuscript, decipher it, and give a response to the Nazi spy. I suppose it's operationally sound. It neatly avoids radio, as you say it cannot be breached without giving notice that the ring itself is under high suspicion, and once armed with the message, the operational spy can proceed with his mission. Is that about it?"

"Almost," said Sir Colin. "In principle, yes, you have the gist of it—manfully done. However, you haven't got the players quite right."

"Are we then at war with someone I don't know about?" said Basil.

"Indeed and unfortunately. Yes. The Soviet Union. This whole thing is Russian, not German."

THE SECOND DAY (CONT'D.)

If panic flashed through Basil's mind, he did not yield to it, although his heart hammered against his chest as if a spike of hard German steel had been pounded into it. He thought of his L-pill, but it was buried in his breast pocket. He thought next of his pistol: Could he get it out in time to bring a few of them down before turning it on himself? Could he at least kill this leering German idiot who . . . but then he noted that the characterization had been delivered almost merrily.

"You must be a spy," said the colonel, laughing heartily, sitting next to him. "Why else would you shave your moustache but to go on some glamorous underground mission?"

Basil laughed, perhaps too loudly, but in his chest his heart still ran wild. He hid his blast of fear in the heartiness of the fraudulent laugh and came back with an equally jocular, "Oh, that? It seems in winter my wife's skin turns dry and very sensitive, so I always shave it off for a few months to give the beauty a rest from the bristles."

"It makes you look younger."

"Why, thank you."

"Actually, I'm so glad to have discovered you. At first I thought it was not you, but then I thought, Gunther, Gunther, who would kidnap the owner of the town's only hotel and replace him with a double? The English are not so clever."

"The only thing they're any good at," said Basil, "is weaving tweed. English tweed is the finest in the world."

"I agree, I agree," said the colonel. "Before all this, I traveled there quite frequently. Business, you know."

It developed that the colonel, a Great War aviator, had represented a Berlin-based hair tonic firm whose directors had visions, at least until 1933, of entering the English market. The colonel had made trips to London in hopes of interesting some of the big department stores in carrying a line of lanolin-based hair creams for men, but was horrified to learn that the market was controlled by the British company that manufactured Brylcreem and would use its considerable clout to keep the Germans out.

"Can you imagine," said the colonel, "that in the twenties there was a great battle between Germany and Great Britain for the market advantage of lubricating the hair of the British gentleman? I believe our product was much finer than that English goop, as it had no alcohol and alcohol dries the hair stalk, robbing it of luster, but I have to say that the British packaging carried the day, no matter. We could never find the packaging to catch the imagination of the British gentleman, to say nothing of a slogan. German as a language does not lend itself to slogans. Our attempts at slogans were ludicrous. We are too serious, and our language is like potatoes in gravy. It has no lightness in it at all. The best we could come up with was, 'Our tonic is very good.' Thus we give the world Nietzsche and not Wodehouse. In any event, when Hitler came to power and the air forces were reinvigorated, it was out of the hair oil business and back to the cockpit."

It turned out that the colonel was a born talker. He was on his way to Paris on a three-day leave to meet his wife for a "well-deserved, if I do say so myself" holiday. He had reservations at the Ritz and at several four star restaurants.

Basil put it together quickly: the man he'd stolen his papers from was some sort of collaborationist big shot and had made it his business to suck up to all the higher German officers, presumably seeing the financial opportunities of being in league with the occupiers. It turned out further that this German fool was soft and supple when it came to sycophancy and he'd mistaken the Frenchman's oleaginous demeanor with actual affection, and he thought it quite keen to have made a real friend among the well-born French. So Basil committed himself to six hours of chitchat with the idiot, telling himself to keep autobiographical details at a minimum in case the real chap had already spilled some and he should contradict something previously established.

That turned out to be no difficulty at all, for the German colonel revealed himself to have an awesomely enlarged ego, which he expressed through an autobiographical impulse, so he virtually told his life story to Basil over the long drag, gossiping about the greed of Göring and the reluctance of the night fighters to close with the Lancasters, Hitler's insanity in attacking Russia, how much he, the colonel, missed his wife, how he worried about his son, a Stuka pilot, and how sad he was that it had come to pass that civilized Europeans were at each other's throats again, and on and on and on and on, but at least the Jews would be dealt with once and for all, no matter who won in the end. He titillated Basil with inside information on his base and the wing he commanded, Nachtjagdgeschwader-9, and the constant levies for Russia that had stripped it of logistics, communications, and security people, until nothing was left but a skeleton staff of air crew and mechanics, yet still they were under pressure from Luftwaffe command to bring down yet more Tommies to relieve the night bombing of Berlin. Damn the Tommies and their brutal methods of war! The man considered himself fascinating, and his presence seemed to ward off the attention of the other German officers who came and went on the trip to the Great City. It seemed so damned civilized that you almost forgot there was a war on.

It turned out that one of the few buildings in Paris with an actual Nazi banner hanging in front of it was a former insurance company's headquarters at 14 rue Guy de Maupassant in the sixth arrondissement. However, the banner wasn't much, really just an elongated flag that hung limply off a pole on the fifth floor. None of the new occupants of the building paid much attention to it. It was the official headquarters of the Paris district of the Abwehr, German military intelligence, ably run from Berlin by Admiral Canaris and beginning to acquire a reputation for not being all that crazy about Herr Hitler.

They were mostly just cops. And they brought cop attributes to their new headquarters: dyspepsia, too much smoking, cheap suits, fallen arches, and a deep cynicism about everything, but particularly about human nature and even more particularly about notions of honor, justice, and duty. They did believe passionately in one cause, however: staying out of Russia.

"Now let us see if we have anything," said Hauptmann Dieter Macht, chief of Section III-B (counterintelligence), Paris office, at his daily staff meeting at three p.m., as he gently spread butter on a croissant. He loved croissants. There was something so exquisite about the balance of elements—the delicacy of the crust, which gave way to a kind of chewy substrata as you peeled it away, the flakiness, the sweetness of the inner bread, the whole thing a majestic creation that no German baker, ham-thumbed and frosting-crazed, could ever match.

"Hmmm," he said, sifting through the various reports that had come in from across the country. About fifteen men, all ex-detectives like himself, all in droopy plain clothes like himself, all with uncleaned Walthers holstered sloppily on their hips, awaited his verdict. He'd been a Great War aviator, an actual ace in fact, then the star of Hamburg Homicide before this war, and had a reputation for sharpness when it came to seeing patterns in seemingly unrelated events. Most of III-B's arrests came from clever deductions made by Hauptmann Macht.

"Now this is interesting. What do you fellows make of this one? It seems in Sur-la-Gane, about forty kilometers east of here, a certain man known to be connected to inner circles of the Maquis was spotted returning home early in the morning by himself. Yet there has been no Maquis activity in that area since we arrested Pierre Doumaine last fall and sent him off to Dachau."

"Perhaps," said Leutnant Abel, his second-in-command, "he was at a meeting and they are becoming active again. Netting a big fish only tears them down for a bit of time, you know."

"They'd hold such a meeting earlier. The French like their sleep. They almost slept through 1940, after all. What one mission gets a Maquis up at night? Anyone?"

No one.

"British agent insertion. They love to cooperate with the Brits because the Brits give them so much equipment, which can either be sold on the black market or be used against their domestic enemies after the war. So they will always jump lively for the SOE, because the loot is too good to turn down. And such insertions will be late-night or early-morning jobs."

"But," said Leutnant Abel, "I have gone through the reports too, and there are no accounts of aviation activities in that area that night. When the British land men in Lysanders, some farmer always calls the nearby police station to complain about low-flying aviators in the dark of night, frightening the cows. You never want to frighten a peasant's cows; he'll be your enemy for life. Believe me, Hauptmann Macht, had a Lysander landed, we'd know from the complaints."

"Exactly," said Macht. "So perhaps our British visitor didn't arrive for some reason or other and disappointed the Sur-la-Gane Resistance cell, who got no loot that night. But if I'm not mistaken, that same night complaints did come in from peasants near Bricquebec, outside Cherbourg."

"We have a night fighter base there," said Abel. "Airplanes come and go all night—it's meaningless."

"There were no raids that night," said Macht. "The bomber stream went north, to Prussia, not to Bavaria."

"What do you see as significant about that?"

"Suppose for some reason our fellow didn't trust the Sur-la-Gane bunch, or the Resistance either. It's pretty well penetrated, after all. So he directs his pilot to put him somewhere else."

"They can't put Lysanders down just anywhere," said another man. "It has to be set up, planned, torches lit. That's why it's so vulnerable to our investigations. So many people—someone always talks, maybe not to us, but to someone, and it always gets to us."

"The Bricquebec incident described a roar, not a put-put or a dying fart. The roar would be a Lysander climbing to parachute altitude. They normally fly at 500, and any agent who made an exit that low would surely scramble his brains and his bones. So the plane climbs, this fellow bails out, and now he's here."

"Why would he take the chance on a night drop into enemy territory? He could come down in the Gestapo's front yard. Hauptsturmführer Boch would enjoy that very much."

Actually the Abwehr detectives hated Boch more than the French and English combined. He could send them to Russia.

"I throw it back to you, Walter. Stretch that brain of yours beyond the lazy parameters it now sleepily occupies and come up with a theory."

"All right, sir, I'll pretend to be insane, like you. I'll postulate that this phantom Brit agent is very crafty, very old school, clever as they come. He doesn't trust the Maquis, nor should he. He knows we eventually hear everything. Thus he improvises. It's just his bad luck that his airplane awakened some cows near Bricquebec, the peasants complained, and so exactly what he did not want us to know is exactly what we do know. Is that insane enough for you, sir?"

Macht and Abel were continually taking shots at each other, and in fact they didn't like each other very much. Macht was always worried about Is-Russia as opposed to Not-Russia, while the younger Abel had family connections that would keep him far from Stalin's millions of tanks and Mongols and all that horrible snow.

"Very good," said Macht. "That's how I read it. You know when these boys arrive they stir up a lot of trouble. If we don't stop them, maybe we end up on an antitank gun in Russia. Is anyone here interested in that sort of a job change?"

That certainly shut everyone up fast. It frightened Macht even to say such a thing.

"I will make some phone calls," Abel said. "See if there's anything unusual going on."

It didn't take him long. At the Bricquebec prefecture, a policeman read him the day's incident report, from which he learned that a prominent collaborationist businessman had claimed that his papers were stolen from him. He had been arrested selling black-market petrol and couldn't identify himself. He was roughly treated until his identity was proven, and he swore he would complain to Berlin, as he was a supporter of the Reich and demanded more respect from the occupiers.

His name, Abel learned, was Piens.

"Hmmm," said Macht, a logical sort. "If the agent was originally going to Sur-la-Gane, it seems clear that his ultimate destination would be Paris. There's really not much for him to do in Bricquebec or Sur-la-Gane, for that matter. Now, how would he get here?"

"Clearly, the railway is the only way."

"Exactly," said Hauptmann Macht. "What time does the train from Cherbourg get in? We should meet it and see if anyone is traveling under papers belonging to M. Piens. I'm sure he'd want them returned."

A FEW DAYS EARLIER (CONT'D.)

"Have I been misinformed?" asked Basil. "Are we at war with the Russians? I thought they were our friends."

"I wish it were as easy as that," said Sir Colin. "But it never is. Yes, in one sense we are at war with Germany and at peace with Russia. On the other hand, this fellow Stalin is a cunning old brute, stinking of bloody murder to high heaven, and thus he presumes that all are replicas of himself, equally cynical and vicious. So while we are friends with him at a certain level, he still spies on us at another level. And because we know him to be a monster, we still spy on him. It's all different compartments. Sometimes it's damned hard to keep straight, but there's one thing all the people in this room agree on: the moment

the rope snaps hard about Herr Hitler's chicken neck, the next war begins, and it is between we of the West and they of the East."

"Rather dispiriting," said Basil. "One would have thought one had accomplished something other than clearing the stage for the next war."

"So it goes, alas and alack, in our sad world. But Basil, I think you will be satisfied to know that the end game of this little adventure we are preparing for you is actually to help the Russians, not to hurt them. It benefits ourselves, of course, no doubt about it. But we need to help them see a certain truth that they are reluctant, based on Stalin's various neuroses and paranoias, to believe."

"You see," said the general, "he would trust us a great deal more if we opened a second front. He doesn't think much of our business in North Africa, where our losses are about one-fiftieth of his. He wants our boys slaughtered on the French beaches in numbers that approach the slaughter of his boys. Then he'll know we're serious about this Allies business. But a second front in Europe is a long way off, perhaps two years. A lot of American men and matériel have to land here before then. In the meantime we grope and shuffle and misunderstand and misinterpret. That's where you'll fit in, we hope. Your job, as you will learn at the conclusion of this dreadful meeting about two days from now, is to shine light and dismiss groping and shuffling and misinterpretation."

"I hope I can be of help," said Basil. "However, my specialty is blowing things up."

"You have nothing to blow up this time out," said Sir Colin. "You are merely helping us explain something."

"But I must ask, since you're permitting me unlimited questions, how do you know all this?" said Basil. "You say Stalin is so paranoid and unstable he does not trust us and even spies upon us, you know this spy exists and is well placed, and that his identity, I presume, has been sent by this absurd book-code method, yet that is exactly where your knowledge stops. I am baffled beyond any telling of it. You know so much, and then it stops cold. It seems to me that you would be more likely to know all or nothing. My head aches profoundly. This business is damned confounding."

"All right, then, we'll tell you. I think you have a right to know, since you are the one we are proposing to send out. Admiral, as it was your service triumph, I leave it to you."

"Thank you, Sir Colin," said the admiral. "In your very busy year of 1940, you probably did not even notice one of the world's lesser wars. I mean there was our war with the Germans in Europe and all that blitzkrieg business, the Japanese war with the Chinese, Mussolini in Ethiopia, and I am probably leaving several out. 1940 was a very good year for war. However, if you check the back pages of the *Times*, you'll discover that in November of 1939, the Soviet Union invaded Finland. The border between them has been in dispute since 1917. The Russians expected an easy time of it, mustering ten times the number of soldiers as did the Finns, but the Finns taught them some extremely hard lessons about winter warfare, and by early 1940 the piles of frozen dead had gotten immense. The war raged for four long months, killing thousands over a few miles of frozen tundra, and ultimately, because lives mean nothing to Communists, the Russians prevailed, at least to the extent of forcing a peace on favorable terms."

"I believe I heard a bit of it."

"Excellent. What you did not hear, as nobody did, was that in a Red Army bunker taken at high cost by the Finns, a half-burned codebook was found. Now since we in the West abandoned the Finns, they were sponsored and supplied in the war by the Third Reich. If you see any photos from the war, you'll think they came out of Stalingrad, because the Finns bought their helmets from the Germans. Thus one would expect that such a high-value intelligence treasure as a codebook, even half burned, would shortly end up in German hands.

"However, we had a very good man in Finland, and he managed somehow to take possession of it. The Russians thought it was burned.

The Germans never knew it existed. Half a code is actually not merely better than nothing, it is *far* better than nothing, and is in fact almost a whole codebook, because a clever boots like young Professor Turing here can tease most messages into comprehension."

"I had nothing to do with it," said the professor. "There were very able men at Bletchley Park before I came aboard."

What, wondered Basil, *would Bletchley Park be?*

"Thus we have been able to read and mostly understand Soviet low- to midlevel codes since 1940. That's how we knew about the librarian at Cambridge and several other sticky lads who, though they speak high Anglican and know where their pinkie goes on the teacup, want to see our Blighty go all red and men like us stood up to the wall and shot for crimes against the working class."

"That would certainly ruin my crease. Anyhow, before we go much further, may I sum up?" said Basil.

"If you can."

"By breaking the Russian crypto, you know that a highly secure, carefully guarded book code has been given to a forthcoming Russian spy. It contains the name of a highly important British traitor somewhere in government service. When he gets here, he will take the code to the Cambridge librarian, present his bona fides, and the librarian will retrieve the Reverend Thomas MacBurney's *Path to Jesus*—wait. How would the Russians themselves have . . . Oh, now I see, it all hangs together. It would be easy for the librarian, not like us, to make a photographed copy of the book and have it sent to the Russian service."

"NKVD, it is called."

"I think I knew that. Thus the librarian quickly unbuttons the name and gives it to the new agent, and the agent contacts him at perhaps this mysterious Bletchley Park that the professor wasn't supposed to let slip—"

"That was a mistake, Professor," said Sir Colin. "No milk and cookies for you tonight."

"So somehow I'm supposed to, I don't know what, do something somewhere, a nasty surprise indeed, but it will enable you to identify the spy at Bletchley Park."

"Indeed, you have the gist of it."

"And you will then arrest him."

"No, of course not. In fact, we shall promote him."

THE SECOND DAY/THE THIRD DAY

It was a pity the trip to Paris lasted only six hours with all the local stops, as the colonel had just reached the year 1914 in his life. It was incredibly fascinating. Mutter did not want him to attend flying school, but he was transfixed by the image of those tiny machines in their looping and spinning and diving that he had seen—and described in detail to Basil—in Mühlenberg in 1912, and he was insistent upon becoming an aviator.

This was more torture than Basil could have imagined in the cellars of the Gestapo, but at last the conductor came through, shouting, "Paris, Montparnasse station, five minutes, end of the line."

"Oh, this has been such a delight," said the colonel. "Monsieur Piens, you are a fascinating conversationalist—"

Basil had said perhaps five words in six hours.

"—and it makes me happy to have a Frenchman as an actual friend, beyond all this messy stuff of politics and invasions and war and all that. If only more Germans and French could meet as we did, as friends, just think how much better off the world would be."

Basil came up with words six and seven: "Yes, indeed."

"But, as they say, all good things must come to an end."

"They must. Do you mind, Colonel, if I excuse myself for a bit? I need to use the loo and prefer the first class here to the *pissoirs* of the station."

"Understandable. In fact, I shall accompany you, *monsieur*, and—oh, perhaps not. I'll check my documents to make sure all is in order."

Thus, besides a blast of blessed silence, Basil earned himself some freedom to operate. During the colonel's recitation—it had come around to the years 1911 and 1912, vacation to Cap d'Antibes—it had occurred to him that the authentic M. Piens, being a clear collaborationist and seeking not to offend the Germans, might well have reported his documents lost and that word might, given the German expertise at counterintelligence, have reached Paris. Thus the Piens documents were suddenly explosive and would land him either in Dachau or before the wall.

He wobbled wretchedly up the length of the car—thank God here in first class the seats were not contained as in the cramped little compartments of second class!—and made his way to the loo. As he went he examined the prospective marks: mostly German officers off for a weekend of debauchery far from their garrison posts, but at least three French businessmen of proper decorum sat among them, stiff, frightened of the Germans and yet obligated by something or other to be there. Only one was anywhere near Basil's age, but he had to deal with things as they were.

He reached the loo, locked himself inside, and quickly removed his M. Piens documents and buried them in the wastebasket among repugnant wads of tissue. A more cautious course would have been to tear them up and dispose of them via the toilet, but he didn't have time for caution. Then he wet his face, ran his fingers through his hair, wiped his face off, and left the loo.

Fourth on the right. Man in suit, rather blasé face, impatient. Otherwise, the car was stirring to activity as the occupants set about readying for whatever security ordeal lay ahead. The war—it was such an inconvenience.

As he worked his way down the aisle, Basil pretended to find the footing awkward against the sway of the train on the tracks, twice almost stumbling. Then he reached the fourth seat on the right, willed his knees to buckle, and, with a squeal of panic, let himself tumble awkwardly, catching himself with his left hand upon the shoulder of the man beneath, yet still tumbling further, awkwardly, the whole thing seemingly an accident as one out-of-control body crashed into the other, in-control body.

"Oh, excuse me," he said, "excuse, excuse, I am so sorry!"

The other man was so annoyed that he didn't notice the deft stab by which Basil penetrated his jacket and plucked his documents free, especially since the pressure on his left shoulder was so aggressive that it precluded notice of the far subtler stratagem of the pick reaching the brain.

Basil righted himself.

"So sorry, so sorry!"

"Bah, you should be more careful," said the mark.

"I will try, sir," said Basil, turning to see the colonel three feet from him in the aisle, having witnessed the whole drama from an advantageous position.

Macht requested a squad of *feldpolizei* as backup, set up a choke point at the gate from the platform into the station's vast, domed central space, and waited for the train to rumble into sight. Instead, alas, what rumbled into sight was his nemesis, SS Hauptsturmführer Boch, a toadlike Nazi true believer of preening ambition who went everywhere in his black dress uniform.

"Dammit again, Macht," he exploded, spewing his excited saliva everywhere. "You know by protocol you must inform me of any arrest activities."

"Herr Hauptsturmführer, if you check your orderly's message basket, you will learn that at ten-thirty p.m. I called and left notification of possible arrest. I cannot be responsible for your orderly's efficiency in relaying that information to you."

"Calculated to miss me, because of course I was doing my duty supervising an *aktion* against Jews and not sitting around my office drinking coffee and smoking."

"Again, I cannot be responsible for your schedule, Herr Hauptsturmführer." Of course Macht had an informer in Boch's office, so he knew exactly where the SS man was at all times. He knew that Boch was on one of his Jew-hunting trips; his only miscalculation was that Boch, who was generally unsuccessful at such enterprises, had gotten back earlier than anticipated. And of course Boch was always unsuccessful because Macht always informed the Jews of the coming raid.

"Whatever, it is of no consequence," said Boch. Though both men were technically of the same rank, captains, the SS clearly enjoyed Der Führer's confidence while the Abwehr did not, and so its members presumed authority in any encounter. "Brief me, please, and I will take charge of the situation."

"My men are in place, and disturbing my setup would not be efficient. If an arrest is made, I will certainly give the SS credit for its participation."

"What are we doing here?"

"There was aviation activity near Bricquebec, outside Cherbourg. Single-engine monoplane suddenly veering to parachute altitude. It suggested a British agent visit. Then the documents of a man in Bricquebec, including travel authorization, were stolen. If a British agent were in Bricquebec, his obvious goal would be Paris, and the most direct method would be by rail, so we are intercepting the Cherbourg–Paris night train in hopes of arresting a man bearing the papers of one Auguste M. Piens, restaurateur, hotel owner, and well-known ally of the Reich, here in Paris."

"An English agent!" Boch's eyes lit up. This was treasure. This was a medal. This was a promotion. He saw himself now as Obersturmbannführer Boch. The little fatty all the muscular boys had called Gretel and whose underdrawers they tied in knots, an Obersturmbannführer! That would show them!

"If an apprehension is made, the prisoner is to be turned over to the SS for interrogation. I will go to Berlin if I have to on this one, Macht. If you stand in the way of SS imperatives, you know the consequences."

The consequence: *"Russian tanks at 300! Load shells. Prepare to fire." "Sir, I can't see them. The snow is blinding, my fingers are numb from the cold, and the sight is frozen!"*

Even though he had witnessed the brazen theft, the colonel said nothing and responded in no way. His mind was evidently so locked in the beautiful year 1912 and the enchantment of his eventual first solo flight that he was incapable of processing new information. The crime he had just seen had nothing whatsoever to do with the wonderful French friend who had been so fascinated by his tale and whose eyes radiated such utter respect, even hero worship; it could not be fitted into any pattern and was thus temporarily disregarded for other pleasures, such as, still ahead, a narration of the colonel's adventures in the Great War, the time he had actually shaken hands with the great Richthofen, and his own flight-ending crash—left arm permanently disabled. Luckily, his tail in tatters, he had made it back to his own lines before going down hard early in '18. It was one of his favorite stories.

He simply nodded politely at the Frenchman, who nodded back as if he hadn't a care in the world.

In time the train pulled into the station, issuing groans and hisses of steam, vibrating heavily as it rolled to a stop.

"Ah, Paris," said the colonel. "Between you and me, M. Piens, I so prefer it to Berlin. And so especially does my wife. She is looking forward to this little weekend jaunt."

They disembarked in orderly fashion, Germans and Frenchmen combined, but discovered on the platform that some kind of security problem lay ahead, at the gate into the station, as soldiers and SS men with machine pistols stood along the platform, smoking but eyeing the passengers carefully. Then the security people screamed out that Germans would go to the left, French to the right, and on the right a few dour-looking men in fedoras and lumpy raincoats examined identification papers and travel authorizations. The Germans merely had to flash leave papers, so that line moved much more quickly.

"Well, M. Piens, I leave you here. Good luck with your sister's health in Paris. I hope she recovers."

"I'm sure she will, Colonel."

"Adieu."

He sped ahead and disappeared through the doors into the vast space. Basil's line inched its way ahead, and though the line was shorter, each arrival at the security point was treated with thorough Germanic ceremony, the papers examined carefully, the comparisons to the photographs made slowly, any bags or luggage searched. It seemed to take forever.

What could he do? At this point it would be impossible to slip away, disappear down the tracks, and get to the city over a fence; the Germans had thrown too many security troops around for that. Nor could he hope to roll under the train; the platform was too close to it, and there was no room to squeeze through.

Basil saw an evil finish: they'd see by the document that his face did not resemble the photograph, ask him a question or two, and learn that he had not even seen the document and had no idea whose papers he carried. The body search would come next, the pistol and the camera would give him away, and it was off to the torture cellar. The L-pill was his only alternative, but could he get to it fast enough?

At the same time, the narrowing of prospects was in some way a relief. No decisions needed to be made. All he had to do was brazen it out with a haughty attitude, beaming confidence, and it would be all right.

———

Macht watched the line while Abel examined papers and checked faces. Boch meanwhile provided theatrical atmosphere by posing heroically in his black leather trench coat, the SS skull on his black cap catching the light and reflecting impulses of power and control from above his chubby little face.

Eight. Seven. Six. Five.

Finally before them was a well-built chap of light complexion who seemed like some sort of athlete. He could not be a secret agent because he was too charismatic. All eyes would always turn to him, and he seemed accustomed to attention. He could be English, indeed, because he was a sort called "ginger." But the French had a considerable amount of genetic material for the hue as well, so the hair and the piercing eyes communicated less than the Aryan stereotypes seemed to proclaim.

"Good evening, M. Vercois," said Abel in French as he looked at the papers and then at the face, "and what brings you to Paris?"

"A woman, Herr Leutnant. An old story. No surprises."

"May I ask why you are not in a prisoner-of-war camp? You seem military."

"Sir, I am a contractor. My firm, M. Vercois et Fils—I am the son, by the way—has contracted to do much cement work on the coastline. We are building an impregnable wall for the Reich."

"Yes, yes," said Abel in a policeman's tired voice, indicating that he had heard all the French collaborationist sucking-up he needed to for the day. "Now do you mind, please, turning to the left so that I can get a good profile view. I must say, this is a terrible photograph of you."

"I take a bad photograph, sir. I have this trouble frequently, but if you hold the light above the photo, it will resolve itself. The photographer made too much of my nose."

Abel checked.

It still did not quite make sense.

He turned to Macht.

"See if this photo matches, Herr Hauptmann. Maybe it's the light, but—"

At that moment, from the line two places behind M. Vercois, a man suddenly broke and ran crazily down the platform.

"That's him!" screamed Boch. "Stop that man, goddammit, stop that man!"

The drama played out quickly. The man ran and the Germans were disciplined enough not to shoot him, but instead, like football athletes, moved to block him. He tried to break this way, then that, but soon a younger, stronger, faster Untersharführer had him, another reached the melee and tangled him up from behind, and then two more, and the whole scrum went down in a blizzard of arms and legs.

"Someone stole my papers!" the man cried. "My papers are missing, I am innocent. Heil Hitler. I am innocent. Someone stole my papers."

"Got him," screamed Boch. "Got him!" and ran quickly to the melee to take command of the British agent.

"Go on," said Abel to M. Vercois as he and Macht went themselves to the incident.

His face blank, Basil entered the main station as whistles sounded and security troops from everywhere ran to Gate No. 4, from which he had just emerged. No one paid him any attention as he turned sideways to let the heavily armed Germans swarm past him. In the distance German sirens sounded, that strange two-note *caw-CAW* that sounded like a crippled crow, as yet more troops poured to the site.

Basil knew he didn't have much time. Someone smart among the Germans would understand quickly enough what had happened and would order a quick search of the train, where the M. Piens documents would be found in the first-class loo, and they'd know what had transpired. Then they'd throw a cordon around the station, call in more troops, and do a very careful examination of the horde, person by person, looking for a man with the papers of poor M. Vercois, currently undergoing interrogation by SS boot.

He walked swiftly to the front door, though the going was tough. Too late. Already the *feldpolizei* had commanded the cabs to leave and had halted buses. More German troops poured from trucks to seal off the area; more German staff cars arrived. The stairs to the Métro were all blocked by armed men.

He turned as if to walk back, meanwhile hunting for other ways out.

"Monsieur Piens, Monsieur Piens," came a call. He turned and saw the Luftwaffe colonel waving at him.

"Come along, I'll drop you. No need to get hung up in this unfortunate incident."

He ran to and entered the cab, knowing full well that his price of survival would be a trip back to the years 1912 through 1918. It almost wasn't worth it.

A FEW DAYS EARLIER (CONT'D.)

"Promote him!" said Basil. "The games you play. I swear I cannot keep up with them. The man's a traitor. He should be arrested and shot."

But his anguish moved no one on the panel that sat before him in the prime minister's murky staff room.

"Basil, so it should be with men of action, but you posit a world where things are clear and simple," said Sir Colin. "Such a planet does not exist. On this one, the real one, direct action is almost always impossible. Thus one must move on the oblique, making concessions and allowances all the way, never giving up too much for too little, tracking reverberations and rebounds, keeping the upper lip as stiff as if embalmed in concrete. Thus we leave small creatures such as our wretch of a Cambridge librarian alone in hopes of influencing someone vastly more powerful. Professor, perhaps you could put Basil in the picture so he understands what it is we are trying to do, and why it is so bloody important."

"It's called Operation Citadel," said Professor Turing. "The German staff has been working on it for some time now. Even though we would like to think that the mess they engineered on themselves at Stalingrad ended it for them, that is mere wishful dreaming. They are wounded but still immensely powerful."

"Professor, you speak as if you had a seat in the OKW general officers' mess."

"In a sense he does. The professor mentioned the little machines he builds, how they are able to try millions of possibilities and come up with solutions to the German code combinations and produce reasonable decryptions. Thus we have indeed been able to read Jerry's mail. Frankly, I know far more about German plans than about what is happening two doors down in my own agency, what the Americans are doing, or who the Russians have sent to Cambridge. But it's a gift that must be used sagely. If it's used sloppily, it will give up the game and Jerry will change everything. So we just use a bit of it now and then. This is one of those nows or thens. Go on, Professor."

"I defer to a strategic authority."

"General Cavendish?"

Cavendish, the army general, had a face that showed emotions from A all the way to A–. It was a mask of meat shaped in an oval and built bluntly around two ball bearings, empty of light, wisdom, empathy, or kindness, registering only force. He had about a pound of nose in the center of it and a pound of medals on his tunic.

"Operation Citadel," he delivered as rote fact, not interpretation, "is envisioned as the Götterdämmarung of the war in the East, the last titanic breakthrough that will destroy the Russian warmaking effort and bring the Soviets to the German table, hats in hand. At the very least, if it's successful, as most think it will be, it'll prolong the war by another year or two. We had hoped to see the fighting stop in 1945; now it may last well into 1947, and many more millions of men may die, and I should point out that a good number of those additional millions will be German. So we are trying to win—yes, indeed—but we are trying to do so swiftly, so that the dying can stop. That is what is at stake, you see."

"And that is why you cannot crush this little Cambridge rat's ass under a lorry. All right, I see that, I suppose, annoyed at it though I remain."

"Citadel, slated for May, probably cannot

happen until July or August, given the logistics. It is to take place in southwest Russia, several hundred miles to the west of Stalingrad. At that point, around a city called Kursk, the Russians find themselves with a bulge in their lines—a salient, if you will. Secretly the Germans have begun massing matériel both above and beneath the bulge. When they believe they have over-whelming superiority, they will strike. They will drive north from below and south from above, behind walls of Tigers, flocks of Stukas, and thousands of artillery pieces. The infantry will advance behind the tanks. When the encircle-ment is complete, they will turn and kill the 300,000 men in the center and destroy the 50,000 tanks. The morale of the Red Army will be shat-tered, the losses so overwhelming that all the American aid in the world cannot keep up with it, and the Russians will fall back, back, back to the Urals. Leningrad will fall, then Moscow. The war will go on and on and on."

"I'm no genius," said Basil, "but even I can figure it out. You must tell Stalin. Tell him to fortify and resupply that bulge. Then when the Germans attack, they will fail, and it is they who will be on the run, the war will end in 1945, and those millions of lives will have been saved. Plus I can then drink myself to death uninterrupted, as I desire."

"Again, sir," said the admiral, who was turn-ing out to be Basil's most ardent admirer, "he has seen the gist of it straight through."

"There is only one thing, Basil," said Sir Colin. "We have told Stalin. He doesn't be-lieve us."

THE THIRD DAY

"Jasta 3 at Vraignes. Late 1916," said Macht. "Albatros, a barge to fly."

"He was an ace," said Abel. "Drop a hat and he'll tell you about it."

"Old comrade," said Oberst Gunther Scholl, "yes. I was Jasta 7 at Roulers. That was in 1917. God, so long ago."

"Old chaps," said Abel, "now the nostalgia is finished, so perhaps we can get on with our real task, which is staying out of Russia."

"Walter will never go to Russia," said Macht. "Family connections. He'll stay in Paris, and when the Americans come, he'll join up with them. He'll finish the war a lieutenant-colonel in the American army. But he does have a point."

"Didi, that's the first compliment you ever gave me. If only you meant it, but one can't have everything."

"So let's go through this again, Herr Oberst," said Macht to Colonel Scholl. "Walter reminds us that there's a very annoyed SS officer stomp-ing around out there and he would like to send you to the Russian front. He would also like to send all of us to the Russian front, except Walter. So it is now imperative that we catch the fellow you sat next to for six hours, and you must do better at remembering."

The hour was late, or early, depending. Oberst Scholl had imagined himself dancing the night away at Maxim's with Hilda, then retiring to a dawn of love at the Ritz. Instead he was in a dingy room on the rue Guy de Maupassant, being grilled by gumshoes from the slums of Germany in an atmosphere seething with des-peration, sour smoke, and cold coffee.

"Hauptmann Macht, believe me, I wish to avoid the Russian front at all costs. Bricque-bec is no prize, and command of a night fighter squadron does not suggest, I realize, that I am expected to do big things in the Luftwaffe. But I am happy to fight my war there and surren-der when the Americans arrive. I have told you everything."

"This I do not understand," said Leutenant Abel. "You had previously met Monsieur Piens and you thought this fellow was he. Yet the pho-tography shows a face quite different from the one I saw at the Montparnasse station."

"Still, they are close," explained the colonel somewhat testily. "I had met Piens at a reception put together by the Vichy mayor of Bricquebec, between senior German officers and prominent, sympathetic businessmen. This fellow owned two restaurants and a hotel, was a power behind the throne, so to speak, and we had a brief but pleasant conversation. I cannot say I memorized his face, as why would I? When I got to the station, I glanced at the registration of French travelers and saw Piens's name and thus looked for him. I suppose I could say it was my duty to amuse our French sympathizers, but the truth is, I thought I could charm my way into a significant discount at his restaurants or pick up a bottle of wine as a gift. That is why I looked for him. He did seem different, but I ascribed that to the fact that he now had no moustache. I teased him about it and he gave me a story about his wife's dry skin."

The two policemen waited for more, but there wasn't any "more."

"I tell you, he spoke French perfectly, no trace of an accent, and was utterly calm and collected. In fact, that probably was a giveaway I missed. Most French are nervous in German presence, but this fellow was quite wonderful."

"What did you talk about for six hours?"

"I run on about myself, I know. And so, with a captive audience, that is what I did. My wife kicks me when I do so inappropriately, but unfortunately she was not there."

"So he knows all about you but we know nothing about him."

"That is so," said the Oberst. "Unfortunately."

"I hope you speak Russian as well as French," said Abel. "Because I have to write a report, and I'm certainly not going to put the blame on myself."

"All right," said Scholl. "Here is one little present. Small, I know, but perhaps just enough to keep me out of a Stuka cockpit."

"We're all ears."

"As I have told you, many times, he rode in the cab to the Ritz, and when we arrived I left and he stayed in the cab. I don't know where he took it. But I do remember the cabbie's name. They must display their licenses on the dashboard. It was Philippe Armoire. Does that help?"

It did.

That afternoon Macht stood before a squad room filled with about fifty men, a third his own, a third from Feldpolizei Battalion 11, and a third from Boch's SS detachment, all in plain clothes. Along with Abel, the *feldpolizei* sergeant, and Hauptsturmführer Boch, he sat at the front of the room. Behind was a large map of Paris. Even Boch had dressed down for the occasion, though to him "down" was a bespoke pin-striped, double-breasted black suit.

"All right," he said. "Long night ahead, boys, best get used to it now. We think we have a British agent hiding somewhere here," and he pointed at the fifth arrondissement, the Left Bank, the absolute heart of cultural and intellectual Paris. "That is the area where a cabdriver left him early this morning, and I believe Hauptsturmführer Boch's interrogators can speak to the truthfulness of the cabdriver."

Boch nodded, knowing that his interrogation techniques were not widely approved of. "The Louvre and Notre Dame are right across the river, the Institut de France dominates the skyline on this side, and on the hundreds of streets are small hotels and restaurants, cafés, various retail outlets, apartment buildings, and so forth and so on. It is a catacomb of possibilities, entirely too immense for a dragnet or a mass cordon and search effort.

"Instead, each of you will patrol a block or so. You are on the lookout for a man of medium height, reddish to brownish hair, squarish face. More recognizably, he is a man of what one might call charisma. Not beauty per se, but a kind of inner glow that attracts people to him, allowing him to manipulate them. He speaks French perfectly, possibly German as well. He may be in any wardrobe, from shabby French clerk to priest, even to a woman's dress. If confronted he will offer well-thought-out words, be charming, agreeable, and slippery. His papers don't mean much. He seems to have a sneak thief's skills at picking pockets, so he may have traded off several identities by the time you get to him. The best tip I can give you is, if you see a man and think what a great friend he'd be, he's probably the spy. His charm is his armor and his principle weapon. He is very clever, very dedicated, very intent on his mission. Probably armed and dangerous as well, but please be forewarned. Taken alive, he will be a treasure trove. Dead, he's just another Brit body."

"Sir, are we to check hotels for new registrations?"

"No. Uniformed officers have that task. This fellow, however, is way too clever for that. He'll go to ground in some anonymous way, and we'll never find him by knocking on hotel room doors. Our best chance is when he is out on the street. Tomorrow will be better, as a courier is bringing the real Monsieur Piens's photo up from Bricquebec and our artist will remove the moustache and thin the face, so we should have a fair likeness. At the same time, I and all my detectives will work our phone contacts and listen for any gossip, rumors, and reports of minor incidents that might reveal the fellow's presence. We will have radio cars stationed every few blocks, so you can run to them and reach us if necessary and thus we can get reinforcements to you quickly if that need develops. We can do no more. We are the cat, he is the mouse. He must come out for his cheese."

"If I may speak," said Hauptsturmführer Boch.

Who could stop him?

And thus he delivered a thirty-minute tirade that seemed modeled after Hitler's speech at Nuremberg, full of threats and exotic metaphors and fueled by pulsing anger at the world for its injustices, perhaps mainly in not recognizing the genius of Boch, all of it well punctuated by the regrettable fact that those who gave him evidence of shirking or laziness could easily end up on that cold antitank gun in Russia, facing the Mongol hordes.

It was not well received.

————

Of course Basil was too foxy to bumble into a hotel. Instead, his first act on being deposited on the Left Bank well after midnight was to retreat to the alleyways of more prosperous blocks and look for padlocked doors to the garages. It was his belief that if a garage was padlocked, it meant the owners of the house had fled for more hospitable climes and he could safely use such a place for his hideout. He did this rather easily, picking the padlock and slipping into a large vault of a room occupied by a Rolls-Royce Phantom on blocks, clear evidence that its wealthy owners were now rusticating safely in Beverly Hills in the United States. His first order of the day was rest: he had, after all, been going full steam for forty-eight hours now, including his parachute arrival in France, his exhausting ordeal by Luftwaffe Oberst on the long train ride, and his miraculous escape from Montparnasse station, also courtesy of the Luftwaffe Oberst, whose name he did not even know.

The limousine was open; he crawled into a back seat that had once sustained the arses of a prominent industrialist, a department store magnate, the owner of a chain of jewelry stores, a famous whore, whatever, and quickly went to sleep.

He awoke at three in the afternoon and had a moment of confusion. Where was he? In a car? Why? Oh, yes, on a mission. What was that mission? Funny, it seemed so important at one time; now he could not remember it. Oh, yes, *The Path to Jesus.*

There seemed no point in going out by day, so he examined the house from the garage, determined that it was deserted, and slipped into it, entering easily enough. It was a ghostly museum of the aristocratic du Clercs, who'd left their furniture under sheets and their larder empty, and by now dust had accumulated everywhere. He amused himself with a little prowl, not bothering to go through drawers, for he was a thief only in the name of duty. He did borrow a book from the library and spent the evening in the cellar, reading it by candlelight. It was Tolstoy's great *War and Peace*, and he got more than three hundred pages into it.

He awakened before dawn. He tried his best to make himself presentable and slipped out, locking the padlock behind himself. The early-morning streets were surprisingly well populated, as workingmen hastened to a first meal and then a day at the job. He melded easily, another anonymous French clerk with a day-old scrub of beard and a somewhat dowdy dark suit under a dark overcoat. He found a café and had a *café au lait* and a large piece of buttered toast, sitting in the rear as the place filled up.

He listened to the gossip and quickly picked up that *les boches* were everywhere today; no one had seen them out in such force before. It seemed that most were plainclothesmen, simply standing around or walking a small patrol beat. They performed no services other than looking at people, so it was clear that they were on some sort of stakeout duty. Perhaps a prominent Resistance figure—this brought a laugh always, as most regarded the Resistance as a joke—had come in for a meet-up with Sartre at Les Deux Magots, or a British agent was here to assassinate Dietrich von Choltitz, the garrison commander of Paris and a man as objectionable as a summer moth. But everyone knew the British weren't big on killing, as it was the Czechs who'd bumped off Heydrich.

After a few hours Basil went for his reconnaissance. He saw them almost immediately, chalk-faced men wearing either the tight faces of hunters or the slack faces of time-servers. Of the two, he chose the latter, since a loafer was less apt to pay attention and wouldn't notice things and furthermore would go off duty exactly when his shift was over.

The man stood, shifting weight from one foot to the other, blowing into his hands to keep them warm, occasionally rubbing the small of his back, where strain accumulated when he who does not stand or move much suddenly has to stand and move.

It was time to hunt the hunters.

A FEW DAYS AGO (CONT'D.)

"It's the trust issue again," said General Cavendish, in a tone suggesting he was addressing the scullery mice. "In his rat-infested brain, the fellow still believes the war might be a trap, meant to destroy Russia and Communism. He thinks that we may be feeding him information on Operation Citadel, about this attack on the Kursk salient, as a way of manipulating him into overcommitting to defending against that attack. He wastes men, equipment, and treasure building up the Kursk bulge on our say-so, then, come July, Hitler's panzer troops make a feint in that direction but drive en masse into some area of the line that has been weakened because all the troops have been moved down to the Kursk bulge. Hitler breaks through, envelops, takes, and razes Moscow, then pivots, heavy with triumph, to deal with the moribund Kursk salient. Why, he needn't even attack. He can do to those men what was done to Paulus's Sixth Army at Stalingrad, simply shell and starve them into submission. At that point the war in the East is over and Communism is destroyed."

"I see what where you're going with this, gentlemen," said Basil. "We must convince Stalin that we are telling the truth. We must verify the authenticity of Operation Citadel, so that he believes in it and acts accordingly. If he doesn't, Operation Citadel will succeed, those 300,000 men will die, and the war will continue for another year or two. The soldiers now say 'Home alive in '45,' but the bloody reality will be 'Dead in heaven in '47.' Yet more millions will die. We cannot allow that to happen."

"Do you see it yet, Basil?" asked Sir Colin. "It would be so helpful if you saw it for yourself, if you realized what has to be done, that no matter how long the shot, we have to play it. Because yours is the part that depends on faith. Only faith will get you through the ordeal that lies ahead."

"Yes, I do see it," said Basil. "The only way of verifying the Operation Citadel intercepts is to have them discovered and transmitted quite innocent of any other influence by Stalin's most secret and trusted spy. That fellow has to come across them and get them to Moscow. And the route by which he encounters them must be unimpeachable, as it will be vigorously counterchecked by the NKVD. That is why the traitorous librarian at Cambridge cannot be arrested, and that is why no tricky subterfuge of cracking into the Cambridge rare books vault can be employed. The sanctity of the Cambridge copy of *The Path to Jesus* must be protected at all costs."

"Exactly, Basil. Very good."

"You have to get these intercepts to this spy. However—here's the rub—you have no idea who or where he is."

"We know where he is," said the admiral. "The trouble is, it's not a small place. It's a good-sized village, in fact, or an industrial complex."

"This Bletchley, whose name I was not supposed to hear—is that it?"

"Professor, perhaps you could explain it to Captain St. Florian."

"Of course. Captain, as I spilled the beans before, I'll now spill some more. We have Jerry solved to a remarkable degree, via higher mathematical concepts as guidelines for the construction of electronic 'thinking machines,' if you will . . ."

"Turing engines, they're called," said Sir Colin. "Basil, you are honored by hearing this from the prime mover himself. It's like a chat with God."

"Please continue, your Supreme Beingness," said Basil.

Embarrassed, the professor seemed to lose his place, then came back to it. ". . . thinking machines that are able to function at high speed, test possibilities, and locate patterns which cut down on the possible combinations. I'll spare you details, but it's quite remarkable. However, one result of this breakthrough is that our location—Bletchley Park, about fifty kilometers out of London, an old Victorian estate in perfectly abominable taste—has grown from a small team operation into a huge bureaucracy. It now employs over eight hundred people, gathered from all over the empire for their specific skills in extremely arcane subject matters.

"As a consequence, we have many streams of communication, many units, many subunits, many sub-subunits, many huts, temporary quarters, recreational facilities, kitchens, bathrooms, a complex social life complete with gossip, romance, scandal, treachery, and remorse, our own slang, our own customs. Of course the inhabitants are all very smart, and when they're not working they get bored and to amuse themselves conspire, plot, criticize, repeat, twist, engineer coups and countercoups, all of which further muddies the water and makes any sort of objective 'truth' impossible to verify. One of the people in this monstrous human beehive, we know for sure from the Finland code, reports to Joseph Stalin. We have no idea who it is—it could be an Oxbridge genius, a lance corporal with Enfield standing guard, a lady mathematician from Australia, a telegraph operator, a translator from the old country, an American liaison, a Polish consultant, and on and on. I suppose it could even be me. All, of course, were vetted beforehand by our intelligence service, but he or she slipped by.

"So now it is important that we find him. It is in fact mandatory that we find him. A big security shakeout is no answer at all. Time-consuming, clumsy, prone to error, gossip, and resentment, as well as colossally interruptive and destructive to our actual task, but worst of all a clear indicator to the NKVD that we know they've placed a bug in our rug. If that is the conclusion they reach, then Stalin will not trust us, will not fortify Kursk, et cetera, et cetera."

"So breaking the book code is the key."

"It is. I will leave it to historians to ponder the irony that in the most successful and sophisticated cryptoanalytic operation in history, a simple book code stands between us and a desperately important goal. We are too busy for irony."

Basil responded, "The problem then refines itself more acutely: it is that you have no practical access to the book upon which the code that contains the name for this chap's new handler is based."

"That is it, in a nutshell," said Professor Turing.

"A sticky wicket, I must say. But where on Earth do I fit in? I don't see that there's any room for a boy of my most peculiar expertise. Am I supposed to—well, I cannot even conjure an end to that sentence. You have me . . ."

He paused.

"I think he's got it," said the admiral.

"Of course I have," said Basil. "There has to be another book."

THE FOURTH DAY

It had to happen sooner or later, and it happened sooner. The first man caught up in the Abwehr observe-and-apprehend operation was Maurice Chevalier.

The French star was in transit between mistresses on the Left Bank, and who could possibly blame Unterscharführer Ganz for blowing the whistle on him? He was tall and gloriously handsome, he was exquisitely dressed, and he radiated such warmth, grace, confidence, and glamour that to see him was to love him. The sergeant was merely acting on the guidance given the squad by Macht: if you want him to be your best friend, that's probably the spy. The sergeant had no idea who Chevalier was; he thought he was doing his duty.

Naturally, the star was not amused. He threatened to call his good friend Herr General von Choltitz and have them *all* sent to the Russian front, and it's a good thing Macht still had some diplomatic skills left, for he managed to talk the elegant man out of that course of action by supplying endless amounts of unction and flattery. His dignity ruffled, the star left huffily and went on his way, at least secure in the knowledge that in twenty minutes he would be making love to a beautiful woman and these German peasants would still be standing around out in the cold, waiting for something to happen. By

eight p.m. he had forgotten entirely about it, and on his account no German boy serving in Paris would find himself on that frozen antitank gun.

As for SS Hauptsturmführer Otto Boch, that was another story. He was a man of action. He was not one for the patience, the persistence, the professionalism of police work. He preferred more direct approaches, such as hanging around the Left Bank hotel where Macht had set up his headquarters and threatening in a loud voice to send them all to Russia if they didn't produce the enemy agent quickly. Thus the Abwehr men took to calling him the Black Pigeon behind his back, for the name took into account his pigeon-like strut, breast puffed, dignity formidable, self-importance manifest, while accomplishing nothing tangible whatsoever except to leave small piles of shit wherever he went.

His SS staff got with the drill, as they were, fanatics or not, at least security professionals, and it seemed that even after a bit they were calling him the Black Pigeon as well. But on the whole, they, the Abwehr fellows, and the 11th Battalion *feldpolizei* people meshed well and produced such results as could be produced. The possibles they netted were not so spectacular as a regal movie star, but the theory behind each apprehension was sound. There were a number of handsome men, some gangsters, some actors, one poet, and a homosexual hairdresser. Macht and Abel raised their eyebrows at the homosexual hairdresser, for it occurred to them that the officer who had whistled him down had perhaps revealed more about himself than he meant to.

Eventually the first shift went off and the second came on. These actually were the sharper fellows, as Macht assumed that the British agent would be more likely to conduct his business during the evening, whatever that business might be. And indeed the results were, if not better, more responsible. In fact one man brought in revealed himself to be not who he claimed he was, and that he was a wanted jewel thief who still plied his trade, Occupation or no. It took a shrewd eye to detect the vitality and fearlessness this fellow wore behind shoddy clothes and darkened teeth and an old man's hobble, but the SS man who made the catch turned out to be highly regarded in his own unit. Macht made a note to get him close to any potential arrest situations, as he wanted his best people near the action. He also threatened to turn the jewel thief over to the French police but instead recruited him as an informant for future use. He was not one for wasting much.

Another arrestee was clearly a Jew, even if his papers said otherwise, even if he had no possible connection to British Intelligence. Macht examined the papers carefully, showed them to a bunco expert on the team, and confirmed that they were fraudulent. He took the fellow aside and said, "Look, friend, if I were you I'd get myself and my family out of Paris as quickly as possible. If I can see through your charade in five seconds, sooner or later the SS will too, and it's off to the East for all of you. These bastards have the upper hand for now, so my best advice to you is, no matter what it costs, get the hell out of Paris. Get out of France. No matter what you think, you cannot wait them out, because the one thing they absolutely will do before they're either chased out of town or put against a wall and shot is get all the Jews. That's what they live for. That's what they'll die for, if it comes to that. Consider this fair warning and probably the only one you'll get."

Maybe the man would believe him, maybe not. There was nothing he could do about it. He got back to the telephone, as, along with his other detectives, he spent most of the time monitoring his various snitches, informants, sympathizers, and sycophants, of course turning up nothing. If the agent was on the Left Bank, he hadn't moved an inch.

And he hadn't. Basil sat on the park bench the entire day, obliquely watching the German across the street. He got so he knew the man well: his gait (bad left hip, Great War wound?); his policeman's patience at standing in one place for an hour, then moving two meters and standing in that place for an hour; his stubbornness at never, ever abandoning his post, except once, at three p.m., for a brief trip to the *pissoir*, during which he kept his eyes open and examined each passerby through the gap at the *pissoir*'s eye level. He didn't miss a thing—that is, except for the dowdy Frenchman observing him from ninety meters away, over an array of daily newspapers.

Twice, unmarked Citroëns came by and the officer gave a report to two other men, also in civilian clothes, on the previous few hours. They nodded, took careful records, and then hastened off. It was a long day until seven p.m., a twelve-hour shift, when his replacement moseyed up. There was no ceremony of changing the guard, just a cursory nod between them, and then the first policeman began to wander off.

Basil stayed with him, maintaining the same ninety-meter interval, noting that he stopped in a café for a cup of coffee and a sandwich, read the papers, and smoked, unaware that Basil had followed him in, placed himself at the bar, and also had a sandwich and a coffee.

Eventually the German got up, walked another six blocks down Boulevard Saint-Germain, turned down a narrower street called rue de Valor, and disappeared halfway down the first block into a rummy-looking hotel called Le Duval. Basil looked about, found a café, had a second coffee, smoked a Gauloise to blend in, joked with the bartender, was examined by a uniformed German policeman on a random check, showed papers identifying himself as Robert Fortier (picked freshly that morning), was checked off against a list (he was not on it, as perhaps M. Fortier had not yet noted his missing papers), and was then abandoned by the policeman for other possibilities.

At last he left and went back to rue de Valor, slipped down it, and very carefully approached the Hotel Duval. From outside it revealed nothing—a typical Baedeker two-star for commercial travelers, with no pretensions of gentility or class. It would be stark, clean, well run, and banal. Such places housed half the population every night in Europe, except for the past few years, when that half-the-population had slept in bunkers, foxholes, or ruins. Nothing marked this place, which was exactly why whoever was running this show had chosen it. Another pro like himself, he guessed. It takes a professional to catch a professional, the saying goes.

He meekly entered as if confused, noting a few sour-looking individuals sitting in the lobby reading *Deutsche Allgemeine Zeitung* and smoking, and went to the desk, where he asked for directions to a hotel called Les Deux Gentilhommes and got them. It wasn't much, but it enabled him to make a quick check on the place, and he learned what he needed to know.

Behind the desk was a hallway, and down it Basil could see a larger room, a banquet hall or something, full of drowsy-looking men sitting around listlessly, while a few further back slept on sofas pushed in for just that purpose. It looked police.

That settled it. This was the German headquarters.

He moseyed out and knew he had one more stop before tomorrow.

He had to examine his objective.

A FEW DAYS PREVIOUSLY (CONT'D.)

"Another book? Exactly yes and exactly no," said Sir Colin.

"How could there be a second original? By definition there can be only one original, or so it was taught when I was at university."

"It does seem like a conundrum, does it not?" said Sir Colin. "But indeed, we are dealing with a very rare case of a second original. Well, of sorts."

"Not sure I like the sound of that," said Basil.

"Nor should you. It takes us to a certain awkwardness that, again, an ironist would find heartily amusing."

"You see," said Basil, "I am fond of irony, but only when applied to other chaps."

"Yes, it can sting, can it not?" said General Cavendish. "And I must say, this one stings quite exhaustively. It will cause historians many a chuckle when they write the secret history of the war in the twenty-first century after all the files are finally opened."

"But we get ahead of ourselves," said Sir Colin. "There's more tale to tell. And the sooner we tell it, the sooner the cocktail hour."

"Tell on, then, Sir Colin."

"It all turns on the fulcrum of folly and vanity known as the human heart, especially when basted in ambition, guilt, remorse, and greed. What a marvelous stew, all of it simmering within the head of the Reverend MacBurney. When last we left him, our God-fearing Mac-Burney had become a millionaire because his pamphlet *The Path to Jesus* had sold endlessly, bringing him a shilling a tot. As I said, he retired to a country estate and spent some years happily wenching and drinking in happy debauchery."

"As who would not?" asked Basil, though he doubted this lot would.

"Of course. But then in the year 1789, twenty-two years later, he was approached by a representative of the bishop of Gladney and asked to make a presentation to the Church. To commemorate his achievement, the thousands of souls he had shepherded safely upon the aforenamed path, the bishop wanted him appointed deacon at St. Blazefield's in Glasgow, the highest church rank a fellow like him could achieve. And Thomas wanted it badly. But the bishop wanted him to donate the original manuscript to the church, for eternal display in its ambulatory. Except Thomas had no idea where the original was and hadn't thought about it in years. So he sat down, practical Scot that he was, and from the pamphlet itself he back-engineered, so to speak, another 'original' manuscript in his own hand, a perfect facsimile, or as perfect as he could make it, even, one must assume, to the little crucifix doodles that so amused the Cambridge librarian. That was shipped to Glasgow, and that is why to this day Thomas MacBurney lounges in heaven, surrounded by seraphim and cherubim who sing his praises and throw petals where he walks."

"It was kind of God to provide us with the second copy," said Basil.

"Proof," said the admiral, "that He is on our side."

"Yes. The provenance of the first manuscript is well established; as I say, it has pencil marks to guide the printer in the print shop owner's hand. That is why it is so prized at Cambridge. The second was displayed for a century in Glasgow, but then the original St. Blazefield's was torn down for a newer, more imposing one in 1857, and the manuscript somehow disappeared. However, it was discovered in 1913 in Paris. Who knows by what mischief it ended up there? But to prevent action by the French police, the owner anonymously donated it to a cultural institution, in whose vaults it to this day resides."

"So I am to go and fetch it. Under the Nazis' noses?"

"Well, not exactly," said Sir Colin. "The manuscript itself must not be removed, as someone might notice and word might reach the Russians. What you must do is photograph certain pages using a Riga Minox. Those are what must be fetched."

"And when I fetch them, they can be relied upon to provide the key for the code and thus give up the name of the Russian spy at Bletchley Park, and thus you will be able to slip into his hands the German plans for Operation Citadel, and thus Stalin will fortify the Kursk salient, and thus the massive German summer offensive will have its back broken, and thus the boys will be home alive in '45 instead of dead in heaven in '47. Our boys, their boys, all boys."

"In theory," said Sir Colin Gubbins.

"Hmm, not sure I like 'in theory,'" said Basil.

"You will be flown in by Lysander, dispatched in the care of Resistance Group Philippe, which will handle logistics. They have not been alerted to the nature of the mission as yet, as the fewer who know, of course, the better. You will explain it to them, they will get you to Paris for recon and supply equipment, manpower, distraction, and other kinds of support, then get you back out for Lysander pickup, if everything goes well."

"And if it does not?"

"That is where your expertise will come in handy. In that case, it will be a maximum hugger-mugger sort of effort. I am sure you will prevail."

"I am not," said Basil. "It sounds awfully dodgy."

"And you know, of course, that you will be given an L-pill so that headful of secrets of yours will never fall in German hands."

"I will be certain to throw it away at the first chance," said Basil.

"There's the spirit, old man," said Sir Colin.

"And where am I headed?"

"Ah, yes. An address on the Quai de Conti, the Left Bank, near the Seine."

"Excellent," said Basil. "Only the Institut de France, the most profound and colossal assemblage of French cultural icons in the world, and the most heavily guarded."

"Known for its excellent library," said Sir Colin.

"It sounds like quite a pickle," said Basil.

"And you haven't even heard the bad part."

THE FOURTH DAY, NEAR MIDNIGHT

In the old days, and perhaps again after the war if von Choltitz didn't blow the place up, the Institut de France was one of the glories of the nation, emblazoned in the night under a rippling tricolor to express the high moral purpose of French culture. But in the war it, too, had to fall into line.

Thus the blazing lights no longer blazed and the cupola ruling over the many stately branches of the singularly complex building overlooking the Seine on the Quai de Conti, right at the toe of the Île de la Cité and directly across from the Louvre, in the sixth arrondissement, no longer ruled. One had to squint, as did Basil, to make it out, though helpfully a searchlight from some far-distant German antiaircraft battery would backlight it and at least accentuate its bulk and shape. The Germans had not painted it *feldgrau*, thank God, and so its white stone seemed to gleam in the night, at least in contrast to other French buildings in the environs. A slight rain fell; the cobblestones glistened; the whole thing had a cinematic look that Basil paid no attention to, as it did him no good at all and he was by no means a romantic.

Instead he saw the architectural tropes of the place, the brilliant façade of colonnades, the precision of the intersecting angles, the dramatically arrayed approaches to the broad steps of the grand entrance under the cupola, from which nexus one proceeded to its many divisions, housed each in a separate wing. The whole expressed the complexity, the difficulty, the arrogance, the insolence, the ego, the whole *je ne sais quoi* of the French: their smug, prosperous country, their easy treachery, their utter lack of conscience, their powerful sense of entitlement.

From his briefing, he knew that his particular goal was the Bibliothèque Mazarine, housed in the great marble edifice but a few hundred meters from the center. He slid that way, while close at hand the Seine lapped against its stone banks, the odd taxi or bicycle taxi hurtled down Quai de Conti, the searchlights crisscrossed the sky. Soon midnight, and curfew. But he had to see.

On its own the Mazarine was an imposing building, though without the columns. Instead it affected the French country palace look, with a cobblestone yard which in an earlier age had allowed for carriages but now was merely a car park. Two giant oak doors, guarding French propriety, kept interlopers out. At this moment it was locked up like a vault; tomorrow the doors would open and he would somehow make his penetration.

But how?

With Resistance help he could have mounted an elaborate ruse, spring himself to the upper floors while the guards tried to deal with the unruliness beneath. But he had chosen not to go that way. In the networks somebody always talked, somebody always whispered, and nothing was really a secret. The Resistance could get him close, but it could also earn him an appetizer of strychnine L-pill.

The other, safer possibility was to develop contacts in the French underworld and hire a professional thief to come in from below or above, via a back entrance, and somehow steal the booklet, then replace it the next day. But that took time, and there was no time.

In the end, he only confirmed what he already knew: there was but one way. It was as fragile as a Fabergé egg, at any time given to yield its counterfeit nature to anyone paying the slightest attention. Particularly with the Germans knowing something was up and at high alert, ready to flood the place with cops and thugs at any second. It would take nerve, a talent for the dramatic, and, most important, the right credentials.

A FEW DAYS PREVIOUSLY (FINI)

"Are you willing?" said Sir Colin. "Knowing all this, are you willing?"

"Sir, you send men to their death every day with less fastidiousness. You consign battalions to their slaughter without blinking an eye. The stricken gray ships turn to coffins and slide beneath the ocean with their hundreds; *c'est la guerre.* The airplanes explode into falling pyres and nobody sheds a tear. Everyone must do his bit, you say. And yet now, for me, on this, you're suddenly squeamish to an odd degree, telling me every danger and improbability and how low the odds of success are. I have to know why. It has a doomed feel to it. If I must die, so be it, but somebody wants nothing on his conscience."

"That is very true."

"Is this a secret you will not divulge?"

"I will divulge, and what's more, now is the time to divulge, before we all die of starvation or alcohol withdrawal symptoms."

"How very interesting."

"A man on this panel has the ear of the prime minister. He holds great power. It is he who insisted on this highly unusual approach, it is he who forces us to overbrief you and send you off with far too much classified information. Let him speak, then."

"General Sir Colin means me," said the professor. "Because of my code-breaking success, I find myself uniquely powerful. Mr. Churchill likes me, and wants me to have my way. That is why I sit on a panel with the barons of war, myself a humble professor, not even at Oxford or Cambridge but at Manchester."

"Professor, is this a moral quest? Do you seek forgiveness beforehand, should I die? It's really not necessary. I owe God a death, and he will take it when he sees fit. Many times over the years he has seen fit not to do so. Perhaps he's bored with me and wants me off the board. Perhaps he tires of my completely overblown legendary wit and sangfroid and realizes I'm just as scared as the next fellow, am a bully to boot, and that it ended on a rather beastly note with my father, a regret I shall always carry. So, Professor, you who have saved millions, if I go, it's on the chap upstairs, not you."

"Well spoken, Captain St. Florian, like the hero I already knew you to be. But that's not quite it. Another horror lies ahead and I must burden you with it, so I will be let alone enough by all those noisy screamers between my ears to do my work if the time comes."

"Please enlighten."

"You see, everyone thinks I'm a genius. Of course I am really a frail man of many weaknesses. I needn't elucidate. But I am terrified of one possibility. You should know it's there before you undertake."

"Go ahead."

"Let us say you prevail. At great cost, by great ordeal, blood, psychic energy, morale, whatever it takes from you. And perhaps other people die as well—a pilot, a Resistance worker, someone caught by a stray bullet, any of the routine whimsies of war."

"Yes."

"Suppose all that is true, you bring it back, you sit before me exhausted, spent, having been burned in the fire, you put it to me, the product of your hard labors, and *I cannot decode the damned thing.*"

"Sir, I—"

"*They* think I can, these barons of war. Put the tag 'genius' on a fellow and it solves all problems. However, there are no, and I do mean no, assurances that the pages you bring back will accord closely enough with the original to yield a meaningful answer."

"We've been through this a thousand times, Professor Turing," said the general. "You will be able, we believe, to handle this. We are quite confident in your ability and attribute your reluctance to a high-strung personality and a bit of stage fright, that's all. The variations cannot be that great, and your Turing engine or one of those things you call a bombe ought to be able to run down other possible solutions quickly and we will get what we need."

"I'm so happy the men who know nothing of this sort of work are so confident. But I had to face you, Captain St. Florian, with this truth. It may be for naught. It may be undoable, even by the great Turing. If that is the case, then I humbly request your forgiveness."

"Oh, bosh," said Basil. "If it turns out that the smartest man in England can't do it, it wasn't meant to be done. Don't give it a thought, Professor. I'll simply go off and have an inning, as best I know how, and if I get back, then you have your inning. What happens, then that's what happens. Now, please, gentleman, can we hasten? My arse feels as if Queen Victoria used it for needlepoint!"

ACTION THIS DAY

Of course one normally never went about in anything but bespoke. Just wasn't done. Basil's tailor was Steed-Aspell, of Davies & Son, 15 Jermyn Street, and Steed-Aspell ("Steedy" to his clients) was a student of Frederick Scholte, the Duke of Windsor's genius tailor, which meant he was a master of the English drape.

His clothes hung with an almost scary brilliance, perfect. They never just crumpled. As gravity took them, they formed extraordinary shapes, presented new faces to the world, gave the sun a canvas for compositions playing light against dark, with gray working an uneasy region between, rather like the Sudetenland. Basil had at least three jackets for which he had been offered immense sums (Steed-Aspell was taking no new clients, though the war might eventually open up some room on his waiting list, if it hadn't already), and of course Basil merely smiled drily at the evocations of want, issued a brief but sincere look of commiseration, and moved onward, a lord in tweed, perhaps *the* lord of the tweeds.

Thus the suit he now wore was a severe disappointment. He had bought it in a secondhand shop, and *monsieur* had expressed great confidence that it was of premium quality, and yet its drape was all wrong, because of course the wool was all wrong. One didn't simply use *any* wool, as its provincial tailor believed. Thus it got itself into twists and rumples and couldn't get out, its creases blunted themselves in moments, and it had already popped a button. Its rise bagged, sagged, and gave up. It rather glowed in the sunlight. Buttoned, its two breasts encased him like a girdle; unbuttoned, it looked like he wore several flags of blue pinstripe about himself, ready to unfurl in the wind. He was certain his clubman would not let him enter if he tried.

And he wanted very much to look his best this morning. He was, after all, going to blow up something big with Germans inside.

"I tell you, we should be more severe," argued SS Hauptsturmführer Otto Boch. "These Paris bastards, they take us too lightly. In Poland we enacted laws and enforced them with blood and steel and incidents quickly trickled away to nothing. Every Pole knew that disobedience meant a polka at the end of a rope in the main square."

"Perhaps they were too enervated on lack of food to rebel," said Macht. "You see, you have a different objective. You are interested in public order and the thrill of public obedience. These seem to you necessary goals, which must be enforced for our quest to succeed. My goal is far more limited. I merely want to catch the British agent. To do so, I must isolate him against a calm background, almost a still life, and that way locate him. It's the system that will catch him, not a single guns-blazing raid. If you stir things up, Herr Hauptsturmführer, I guarantee you it will come to nothing. Please trust me on this. I have run manhunts, many times successfully."

Boch had no remonstrance, of course. He was not a professional like Macht and in fact before the war had been a salesman of vacuums, and not a very good one.

"We have observers everywhere," Macht continued. "We have a photograph of M. Piens, delicately altered so that it closely resembles the man that idiot Scholl sat next to, which should help our people enormously. We have good weather. The sun is shining, so our watchers won't hide themselves under shades or awnings to get out of the rain and thus cut down their visibility. The lack of rain also means our roving autos won't be searching through the slosh and squeal of wiper blades, again reducing what they see. We continue to monitor sources we have carefully been nurturing since we arrived. Our system will work. We will get a break today, I guarantee it."

The two sat at a table in the banquet room of the Hotel Duval, amid a batch of snoozing agents who were off shift. The stench of cigarette butts, squashed cigars, and tapped-out pipe tobacco shreds hung heavy in the room, as did the smell of cold coffee and unwashed bodies. But that was what happened on manhunts, as Macht knew and Boch did not. Now nothing could be done except wait for a break, then play that break carefully and . . .

"Hauptmann Macht?" It was his assistant, Abel.

"Yes?"

"Paris headquarters. Von Choltitz's people. They want a briefing. They've sent a car."

"Oh, Christ," said Macht. But he knew this was what happened. Big politicos got involved, got worried, wanted credit, wanted to escape blame. No one anywhere in the world understood the principle that sometimes it was better not to be energetic and to leave things alone instead of wasting energy in a lot of showy ceremonial nonsense.

"I'll go," said Boch, who would never miss a chance to preen before superiors.

"Sorry, sir. They specified Hauptmann Macht."

"Christ," said Macht again, trying to remember where he'd left his trench coat.

A street up from the Hotel Duval, Basil found the exact thing he was looking for. It was a Citroën Traction Avant, black, and it had a large aerial projecting from it. It was clearly a radio car, one of those that the German man-hunter had placed strategically around the sixth arrondissement so that no watcher was far from being able to notify headquarters and get the troops out.

Helpfully, a café was available across the street, and so he sat at a table and ordered a coffee. He watched as, quite regularly, a new German watcher ambled by, leaned in, and reported that he had seen nothing. Well organized. They arrived every thirty minutes. Each man came once every two hours, so the walk over was a break from standing around. It enabled the commander to get new information to the troops in an orderly fashion, and it changed the vantage point of the watchers. At the same time, at the end of four hours, the car itself fired up and its two occupants made a quick tour of their men on the street corners. The point was to keep communications clear, keep the men engaged so they didn't go logy on duty, yet sacrifice nothing in the way of observation. Whoever was running this had done it before.

He also noted a new element. Somehow they had what appeared to be a photograph. They would look it over, pass it around, consult it frequently in all meetings. It couldn't be of him, so possibly it was a drawing. It meant he had to act today. As the photo or drawing circulated, more and more would learn his features and the chance of his being spotted would become greater by degrees. Today the image was a novelty and would not stick in the mind without constant refreshment, but by tomorrow all who had to know it would know it. The time was now. Action this day.

When he felt he had mastered the schedule and saw a clear break coming up in which nobody would report to the car for at least thirty minutes, he decided it was time to move. It was about three p.m. on a sunny, if chilly, Paris spring afternoon. The ancient city's so-familiar features were everywhere as he meandered across Boulevard Saint-Germain under blue sky. There was a music in the traffic and in the rhythm of the pedestrians, the window shoppers, the pastry munchers, the café sitters, the endless parade of bicyclists, some pulling passengers in carts, some simply solo. The great city went about its business, Occupation or no, action this day or no.

He walked into an alley and reached over to fetch a wine bottle that he had placed there early this morning, while it was dark. It was, however, filled with kerosene drained from a ten-liter tin jug in the garage. Instead of a cork it had a plug of wadded cotton jammed into its throat, and fifteen centimeters of strip hung from the plug. It was a gasoline bomb, constructed exactly to SOE specification. He had never done it before, since he usually worked with Explosive 808, but there was no 808 to be found, so the kerosene, however many years old it was, would have to do. He wrapped the bottle in newspaper, tilted it to soak the wad with the fuel, and then set off jauntily.

This was the delicate part. It all turned on how observant the Germans were at close quarters, whether or not Parisians on the street noticed him, and if so, if they took some kind of action. He guessed they wouldn't; actually, he gambled that they wouldn't. The Parisians are a prudent species.

Fortunately the Citroën was parked in an isolated space, open at both ends. He made no eye contact with its bored occupants, his last glance telling him that one leaned back, stretching, to keep from dozing, while the other was talking on a telephone unit wired into the radio console that occupied the small back seat. He felt that if he looked at them they might feel the pressure of his eyes, as those of predatory nature sometimes do, being weirdly sensitive to signs of aggression.

He approached on the oblique, keeping out of view of the rear window of the low-slung sedan, all the rage in 1935 but now ubiquitous in Paris. Its fuel tank was in the rear, which again made things convenient. In the last moment as he approached, he ducked down, wedged the bottle under the rear tire, pulled the paper away, lit his lighter, and lit the end of the strip of cloth. The whole thing took one second, and he moved away as if he'd done nothing.

It didn't explode. Instead, with a kind of air-sucking gush, the bottle erupted and shattered, smearing a billow of orange-black flame into the atmosphere from beneath the car, and in the next second the gasoline tank also went, again without explosion as much as flare of incandescence a hundred meters high, bleaching the color from the beautiful old town and sending a cascade of heat radiating outward.

Neither German policeman was injured, except by means of stolen dignity, but each spilled crazily from his door, driven by the primal fear of flame encoded in the human race, one tripping, going to hands and knees and locomoting desperately from the conflagration on all fours like some sort of beast. Civilians panicked as well, and screaming became general as they scrambled away from the bonfire that had been an automobile several seconds earlier.

Basil never looked back, and walked swiftly down the street until he reached rue de Valor and headed down it.

Boch was lecturing Abel on the necessity of severity in dealing with these French cream puffs when a man roared into the banquet room, screaming, "They've blown up one of our radio cars. It's an attack! The Resistance is here!"

Instantly men leaped to action. Three ran to a gun rack in a closet where the MP 40s were stored and grabbed those powerful weapons up. Abel raced to the telephone and called Paris command with a report and a request for immediate troop dispatch. Still others pulled Walthers, Lugers, and P38s from holsters, grabbed overcoats, and readied themselves to move to the scene and take command.

Hauptsturmführer Boch did nothing. He sat rooted in terror. He was not a coward, but he also, for all his worship of severity and aggressive interrogation methods, was particularly inept at confronting the unexpected, which generally caused his mind to dump its contents in a steaming pile on the floor while he sat in stupefaction, waiting for it to refill.

In this case, when he found himself alone in the room, he reached a refill level, stood up, and ran after his more agile colleagues.

He stepped on the sidewalk, which was full of fleeing Parisians, and fought against the tide, being bumped and jostled in the process by those who had no idea who he was. A particularly hard thump from a hurtling heavyweight all but knocked him flat, and the fellow had to grab him to keep him upright before hurrying along. Thus, making little progress, the Hauptsturmführer pulled out his Luger, trying to remember if there was a shell in the chamber, and started to shout in his bad French, "Make way! German officer, make way!" waving the Luger about as if it were some kind of magic wand that would dissipate the crowd.

It did not, so taken in panic were the French, so he diverted to the street itself and found the going easier. He made it to Boulevard Saint-Germain, turned right, and there beheld the atrocity. Radio Car Five still blazed brightly. German plainclothesmen had set up a cordon around it, menacing the citizens with their MP 40s, but of course no citizens were that interested in a German car, and so the street had largely emptied. Traffic on the busy thoroughfare had stopped, making the approach of the fire truck more laggard—the sound of klaxons arrived from far away, and it was clear that by the time the firemen arrived the car would be largely burned to a charred hulk. Two plainclothesmen, Esterlitz, from his SS unit, and an Abwehr agent, sat on the curb looking completely unglued while Abel tried to talk to them.

Boch ran to them.

"Report," he snapped as he arrived, but nobody paid any attention to him.

"Report!" he screamed.

Abel looked over at him.

"I'm trying to get a description from these two fellows, so we know who we're looking for."

"We should arrest hostages at once and execute them if no information is forthcoming."

"Sir, he has to be in the area still. We have to put people out in all directions with a solid description."

"Esterlitz, what did you see?"

Esterlitz looked at him with empty eyes. The nearness of his escape, the heat of the flames, the suddenness of it all, had disassembled his brain completely. Thus it was the Abwehr agent who answered.

"As I've been telling the lieutenant, it happened so quickly. My last impression in the split second before the bomb exploded was of a man walking north on Saint-Germain in a blue pinstripe that was not well cut at all, a surprise to see in a city so fashion-conscious, and then *whoosh*, a wall of flame behind us."

"The bastards," said Boch. "Attempting murder in broad daylight."

"Sir," said Abel, "with all due respect, this was not an assassination operation. Had he wanted them dead, he would have hurled the Molotov through the open window, soaking them with burning gasoline, burning them to death. Instead he merely ignited the petrol tank, which enabled them to escape. He didn't care about them. That wasn't the point, don't you see?"

Boch looked at him, embarrassed to be contradicted by an underling in front of the troops. It was not the SS way! But he controlled his temper, as it made no sense to vent at an ignorant police rube.

"What are you saying?"

"This was some sort of distraction. He wanted to get us all out here, concentrating on this essentially meaningless event, because it somehow advanced his higher purpose."

"I—I—" stuttered Boch.

"Let me finish the interview, then get the description out to all other cars, ordering them to stay in place. Having our men here, tied up in this jam, watching the car burn to embers, accomplishes nothing."

"Do it! Do it!" screamed Boch, as if he had thought of it himself.

Basil reached the Bibliothèque Mazarine within ten minutes and could still hear fire klaxons sounding in the distance. The disturbance would clog up the sixth arrondissement for hours before it was finally untangled, and it would mess up the German response for those same hours. He knew he had a window of time—not much, but perhaps enough.

He walked through the cobbled yard and approached the doors, where two French policemen stood guard.

"Official business only, *monsieur*. German orders," said one.

He took out his identification papers and said frostily, "I do not care to chat with French policemen in the sunlight. I am here on business."

"Yes, sir."

He entered a vast, sacred space. It was composed of an indefinite number of hexagonal galleries, with vast air shafts between, surrounded by very low railings. From any of the hexagons one could see, interminably, the upper and lower floors. The distribution of the galleries was invariable. Twenty shelves, five long shelves per side, covered all the sides except two; their height, which was the distance from floor to ceiling, scarcely exceeded that of a normal bookcase. The books seemed to absorb and calm all extraneous sounds, so that as his heels clicked on the marble of the floor on the approach to a central desk, a woman behind it hardly seemed to notice him. However, his papers got her attention and her courtesy right away.

"I am here on important business. I need to speak to *le directeur* immediately."

She left. She returned. She bade him follow. They went to an elevator where a decrepit Great War veteran, shoulders stooped, medals tarnished, eyes vacant, opened the gate to a cage-like car. They were hoisted mechanically up two flights, followed another path through corridors of books, and reached a door.

She knocked, then entered. He followed, to discover an old Frenchie in some kind of frock coat and goatee, standing nervously.

"I am Claude De Marque, the director," he said in French. "How may I help you?"

"Do you speak German?"

"Yes, but I am more fluent in my own tongue."

"French, then."

"Please sit down."

Basil took a chair.

"Now—"

"First, understand the courtesy I have paid you. Had I so chosen, I could have come with a contingent of armed troops. We could have shaken down your institution, examined the papers of all your employees, made impolite inquiries as we looked for leverage and threw books every which way. That is the German technique. Perhaps you shield a Jew, as is the wont of your kind of prissy French intellectual. Too bad for those Jews, too bad for those who shield him. Are you getting my meaning?"

"Yes, sir, I—"

"Instead I come on my own. As men of letters, I think it more appropriate that our relationship be based on trust and respect. I am a professor of literature at Leipzig, and I hope to return to that after the war. I cherish the library, this library, any library. Libraries are the font of civilization, do you not agree?"

"I do."

"Therefore, one of my goals is to protect the integrity of the library. You must know that first of all."

"I am pleased."

"Then let us proceed. I represent a very high science office of the Third Reich. This office has an interest in certain kinds of rare books. I have been assigned by its commanding officer to assemble a catalog of such volumes in the great libraries of Europe. I expect you to help me."

"What kinds of books?"

"Ah, this is delicate. I expect discretion on your part."

"Of course."

"This office has an interest in volumes that deal with erotic connections between human beings. Our interest is not limited to those merely between male and female but extends to other combinations as well. The names de Sade and Ovid have been mentioned. There are more, I am sure. There is also artistic representation. The ancients were more forthright in their descriptions of such activities. Perhaps you have photos of paintings, sculptures, friezes?"

"Sir, this is a respectable—"

"It is not a matter of respect. It is a matter of science, which must go where it leads. We are undertaking a study of human sexuality, and it must be done forthrightly, professionally, and quickly. We are interested in harnessing the power of eugenics and seek to find ways to improve the fertility of our finest minds. Clearly the answer lies in sexual behaviors. Thus we must fearlessly master such matters as we chart our way to the future. We must ensure the future."

"But we have no salacious materials."

"And do you believe, knowing of the Germans' attributes of thoroughness, fairness, calm and deliberate examination, that a single assurance alone would suffice?"

"I invite you to—"

"Exactly. This is what I expect. An hour, certainly no more, undisturbed in your rare book vault. I will wear white gloves if you prefer. I must be free to make a precise search and assure my commander that either you do not have such materials, as you claim, or you do, and these are the ones you have. Do you understand?"

"I confess a first edition of Sade's *Justine*, dated 1791, is among our treasures."

"Are the books arranged by year?"

"They are."

"Then that is where I shall begin."

"Please, you can't—"

"Nothing will be disturbed, only examined. When I am finished, have a document prepared for me in which I testify to other German officers that you have cooperated to the maximum degree. I will sign it, and believe me, it will save you much trouble in the future."

"That would be very kind, sir."

At last he and the Reverend MacBurney were alone. *I have come a long way to meet you, you Scots bastard*, he thought. *Let's see what secrets I can tease out of you.*

MacBurney was signified by a manuscript on foolscap, beribboned in a decaying folder upon which *The Path to Jesus* had been scrawled in an ornate hand. It had been easy to find, in a drawer marked *1789*; he had delicately moved it to the tabletop, where, opened, it yielded its treasure, page after page in the round hand of the man of God himself, laden with swoops and curls of faded brown ink. In the fashion of the eighteenth century, he had made each letter a construction of grace and agility, each line a part of the composition, by turning the feather quill to get the fat or the thin, these arranged in an artistic cascade. His punctuation was precise, deft, studied, just this much twist and pressure for a comma, that much for a (more plentiful) semicolon. It was if the penmanship itself communicated the glory of his love for God. All the nouns were capitalized, and the *S*'s and the *F*'s were so close it would take an expert to tell which was which; superscript showed up everywhere, as the man tried to shrink his burden of labor; frequently the word "the" appeared as "ye," as the penultimate letter often stood in for *th* in that era. It seemed the words on the page wore powdered periwigs and silk stockings and buckled, heeled shoes as they danced and pirouetted across the page.

Yet there was a creepy quality to it, too. Splats or droplets marked the creamy luster of the page—some of wine perhaps, some of tea, some of whatever else one might have at the board in the eighteenth century. Some of the lines were crooked, and the page itself felt off-kilter, as though a taint of madness had attended, or perhaps drunkenness, for in his dotage old MacBurney was no teetotaler, it was said.

More psychotic still were the drawings. As the librarian had noticed in his published account of the volume in *Treasures of the Cambridge Library*, the reverend occasionally yielded to artistic impulse. No, they weren't vulvas or naked boys or fornicators in pushed-up petticoats or farmers too in love with their cows. MacBurney's lusts weren't so visible or so nakedly expressed. But the fellow was a doodler after Jesus. He could not compel himself to be still, and so each page wore a garland of crosses scattered across its bottom, a Milky Way of holiness setting off the page number, or in the margins, and at the top silhouetted crucifixions, sketches of angels, clumsy reiterations of God's hand touching Adam's as the great Italian had captured upon that ceiling in Rome. Sometimes the devil himself appeared, horned and ambivalent, just a few angry lines not so much depicting as suggesting Lucifer's cunning and malice. It seemed the reverend was in anguish as he tried desperately to finish this last devotion to the Lord.

Basil got to work quickly. Here of all places was no place to tarry. He untaped the Riga Minox from his left shin, checked that the overhead light seemed adequate. He didn't need flash, as Technical Branch had come up with extremely fast 21.5 mm film, but it was at the same time completely necessary to hold still. The lens had been prefocused for 15 cm, so Basil did not need to play with it or any other knobs, buttons, controls. He took on faith that he had been given the best equipment in the world with which to do the job.

He had seven pages to photograph—2, 5, 6, 9, 10, 13, and 15—for the codebreaker had assured him that those would be the pages on which the index words would have to be located, based on the intercepted code.

In fact, Sade's *Justine* proved very helpful, along with a first edition of Voltaire's *Pensées* and an extra-illustrated edition of *Le Decameron de Jean Boccace*, published in five volumes in Paris in 1757, Ah, the uses of literature! Stacked, they gave him a brace against which he could sustain the long fuselage of the Minox. Beneath it he displayed the page. Click, wind, click again, on to the next one. It took so little time. It was too sodding easy. He thought he might find an SS firing squad just waiting for him, enjoying the little trick they'd played on him.

But when he replaced all the documents in their proper spots, retaped the camera to his leg, and emerged close to an hour later, there was no firing squad, just the nervous Marque, *le directeur*, waiting with the tremulous smile of the recently violated.

"I am finished, *monsieur le directeur*. Please examine, make certain all is appropriate to the condition it was in when I first entered an hour ago. Nothing missing, nothing misfiled, nothing where it should not be. I will not take offense."

The director entered the vault and emerged in a few minutes.

"Perfect," he said.

"I noted the Sade. Nothing else seemed necessary to our study. I am sure copies of it in not so rare an edition are commonly available if one knows where to look."

"I could recommend a bookseller," said *le directeur*. "He specializes in, er, the kind of thing you're looking for."

"Not necessary now, but possible in the future."

"I had my secretary prepare a document, in both German and French."

Basil looked at it, saw that it was exactly as he had ordered, and signed his false name with a flourish.

"You see how easy it is if you cooperate, *mon-sieur*? I wish I could teach all your countrymen the same."

By the time Macht returned at four, having had to walk the last three blocks because of the traffic snarl, things were more or less functioning correctly at his banquet hall headquarters.

"We now believe him to be in a pinstripe suit. I have put all our watchers back in place in a state of high alert. I have placed cars outside this tangled-up area so that we can, if need be, get to the site of an incident quickly," Abel briefed him.

"Excellent, excellent," he replied. "What's happening with the idiot?"

That meant Boch, of course.

"He wanted to take hostages and shoot one every hour until the man is found. I told him that was probably not a wise move, since this fellow is clearly operating entirely on his own and is thus immune to social pressures such as that. He's now in private communication with SS headquarters in Paris, no doubt telling them what a wonderful job he has been doing. His men are all right, he's just a buffoon. But a dangerous one. He could have us all sent to Russia. Well, not me, ha-ha, but the rest of you."

"I'm sure your honor would compel you to accompany us, Walter."

"Don't bet on it, Didi."

"I agree with you that this is a diversion, that our quarry is completing his mission somewhere very near. I agree also that it is not a murder, a sabotage, a theft, or anything spectacular. In fact, I have no idea what it could be. I would advise that all train stations be double-covered and that the next few hours are our best for catching him."

"I will see to it."

In time Boch appeared. He beckoned to Macht, and the two stepped into the hallway for privacy.

"Herr Hauptmann, I want this considered as fair warning. This agent must be captured, no matter what. It is on record that you chose to disregard my advice and instead go about your duties at a more sedate pace. SS is not satisfied and has filed a formal protest with Abwehr and others in the government. SS Reichsführer Himmler himself is paying close attention. If this does not come to the appropriate conclusion, all counterintelligence activities in Paris may well come under SS auspices, and you yourself may find your next duty station rather more frosty and rather more hectic than this one. I tell you this to clarify your thinking. It's not a threat, Herr Hauptmann, it's simply a clarification of the situation."

"Thank you for the update, Herr Hauptsturmführer. I will take it under advisement and—"

But at that moment Abel appeared, concern on his usually slack, doughy face. "Hate to interrupt, Herr Hauptmann, but something interesting."

"Yes?"

"One of Unterscharführer Ganz's sources is a French policeman on duty at the Bibliothèque Mazarine, on Quai de Conti, not far from here. An easy walk, in fact."

"Yes, the large complex overlooking the river. The cupola—no, that is the main building, the Institut de France, I believe."

"Yes, sir. At any rate, the report is that at about three p.m., less than twenty minutes after the bomb blast—"

"Flare is more like it, I hear," said Macht.

"Yes, Captain. In any event, a German official strode into the library and demanded to see the director. He demanded access to the rare book vault and was in there alone for an hour. Everybody over there is buzzing because he was such a commanding gentleman, so sure and smooth and charismatic."

"Did he steal anything?"

"No, but he was alone in the vault. In the end, it makes very little sense. It's just that the timing works out correctly, the description is accurate, and the personality seems to match. What British intelligence could—"

"Let's get over there, fast," said Macht.

This was far more than *monsieur le directeur* had ever encountered. He now found himself alone in his office with three German policemen, and none were in a good mood.

"So, if you will, please explain to me the nature of this man's request."

"It's highly confidential, Captain Macht. I had the impression that discretion was one of the aspects of the visit. I feel I betray a trust if I—"

"*Monsieur le directeur,*" said Macht evenly, "I assure you that while I appreciate your intentions, I nevertheless must insist on an answer. There is some evidence that this man may not be who you think he was."

"His credentials were perfect," said the director. "I examined them very carefully. They were entirely authentic. I am not easy to fool."

"I accuse you of nothing," said Macht. "I merely want the story."

And *le directeur* laid it out, rather embarrassed.

"Dirty pictures," said Macht at the conclusion. "You say a German officer came in and demanded to check your vault for dirty pictures, dirty stories, dirty jokes, dirty limericks, and so forth in books of antiquarian value?"

"I told you the reason he gave me."

The two dumpy policemen exchanged glances; the third, clearly from another department, fixed him with beady, furious eyes behind pince-nez glasses and somehow seemed to project both aggression and fury at him without saying a word.

"Why would I make up such a story?" inquired *le directeur*. "It's too absurd."

"I'll tell you what we'll do," said the third officer, a plumper man with pomaded if thinning hair showing much pate between its few strands and a little blot of moustache clearly modeled on either Himmler's or Hitler's. "We'll take ten of your employees to the street. If we are not satisfied with your answers, we'll shoot one of them. Then we'll ask again and see if—"

"Please," the Frenchman implored, "I tell the truth. I am unaccustomed to such treatment. My heart is about to explode. I tell the truth, it is not in me to lie, it is not my character."

"Description, please," said Macht. "Try hard. Try very hard."

"Mid-forties, well-built, though in a terrible-fitting suit. I must say I thought the suit far beneath him, for his carriage and confidence were of a higher order. Reddish-blond hair, blue eyes, rather a beautiful chin—rather a beautiful man, completely at home with himself and—"

"Look, please," said the assistant to the less ominous of the policemen. He handed over a photograph.

"Ahhhh—well, no, this is not him. Still, a close likeness. Same square shape. His eyes are not as strong as my visitor's, and his posture is something rather less. I must say, the suit fits much better."

Macht sat back. Yes, a British agent had been here. What on Earth could it have been for? What in the Mazarine Library was of such interest to the British that they had sent a man on such a dangerous mission, so fragile, so easily discovered? They must have been quite desperate.

"And what name did he give you?" Abel asked.

"He said his name was . . . Here, look, here's the document he signed. It was exactly the name on his papers, I checked very closely so there would be no mistake. I was trying my hardest to cooperate. I know there is no future in rebellion."

He opened his drawer, with trembling fingers took out a piece of paper, typed and signed.

"I should have shown it to you earlier. I was nonplussed, I apologize, it's not often that I have three policemen in my office."

He yammered on, but they paid no attention, as all bent forward to examine the signature at the bottom of the page.

It said, "Otto Boch, SS Hauptsturmführer, SS-RHSA, 13 rue Madeleine, Paris."

ACTION THIS DAY (CONT'D.)

The train left Montparnasse at exactly five minutes after five p.m. As SS Hauptsturmführer Boch, Gestapo, 13 rue Madeleine, Paris, Basil did not require anything save his identification papers, since Gestapo membership conferred on him an elite status that no rail clerk in the Wehrmacht monitoring the trains would dare challenge. Thus he flew by the ticket process and the security checkpoints and the flash inspection at the first-class carriage steps.

The train eased into motion and picked up speed as it left the marshaling yards resolving themselves toward blur as the darkness increased. He sat alone amid a smattering of German officers returning to duty after a few stolen nights in Paris. Outside, in the twilight, the little toy train depots of France fled by, and inside, the vibration rattled and the grumpy men tried to squeeze in a last bit of relaxation before once again taking up their vexing duties, which largely consisted of waiting until the Allied armies came to blow them up. Some of them thought of glorious death and sacrifice for the fatherland; some remembered the whores in whose embraces they had passed the time; some thought of ways to surrender to the Americans without getting themselves killed, but also of not being reported, for one never knew who was keeping records and who would see them.

But most seemed to realize that Basil was an undercover SS officer, and no one wanted to brook any trouble at all with the SS. Again, a wrong word, a misinterpreted joke, a comment too politically frank, and it was off to that dreaded 8.8 cm antitank gun facing the T-34s and the Russians. All of them preferred their luck with the Americans and the British than with the goddamn Bolsheviks.

So Basil sat alone, ramrod straight, looking neither forward nor back. His stern carriage conveyed seriousness of purpose, relentless attention to detail, and a devotion to duty so hard and true it positively radiated heat. He permitted no mirth to show, no human weakness. Most of all, and hardest for him, he allowed himself to show no irony, for irony was the one attribute that would never be found in the SS or in any Hitlerite true believer. In fact, in one sense the

Third Reich and its adventure in mass death was a conspiracy against irony. Perhaps that is why Basil hated it so much and fought it so hard.

Boch said nothing. There was nothing to say. Instead it was Macht who did all the talking. They leaned on the hood of a Citroën radio car in the courtyard of the Bibliothèque Mazarine.

"Whatever it was he wanted, he got it. Now he has to get out of town and fast. He knows that sooner or later we may tumble to his acquisition of Herr Boch's identity papers, and at that point their usefulness comes to an abrupt end and they become absolutely a danger. So he will use them now, as soon as possible, and get as far away as possible."

"But he has purposefully refused any Resistance aid on this trip," said Abel.

"True."

"That would mean that he has no radio contact. That would mean that he has no way to set up a Lysander pickup."

"Excellent point, Walter. Yes, and that narrows his options considerably. One way out would be to head to the Spanish border. However, that's days away, involves much travel and the danger of constant security checks, and he would worry that his Boch identity would have been penetrated."

They spoke of Boch as if he were not there. In a sense, he wasn't. *"Sir, the breech is frozen." "Kick it! They're almost on us!" "I can't, sir. My foot fell off because of frostbite."*

"He could, I suppose, get to Calais and swim to Dover. It's only thirty-two kilometers. It's been done before."

"Even by a woman."

"Still, although he's a gifted professional, I doubt they have anyone quite that gifted. And even if it's spring, the water is four or five degrees centigrade."

"Yes," said Macht. "But he will definitely go by water. He will head to the most accessible seaport. Given his talents for subversion,

he will find some sly fisherman who knows our patrol boat patterns and pay the fellow to haul him across. He can make it in a few hours, swim the last hundred yards to a British beach, and be home with his treasure, whatever that is."

"If he escapes, we should shoot the entire staff of the Bibliothèque Mazarine," said Boch suddenly. "This is on them. He stole my papers, yes, he pickpocketed me, but he could have stolen anyone's papers, so to single me out is rather senseless. I will make that point in my report."

"An excellent point," said Macht. "Alas, I will have to add that while he *could* have stolen anyone's papers, he *did* steal yours. And they were immensely valuable to him. He is now sitting happily on the train, thinking of the jam and buns he will enjoy tomorrow morning with his tea and whether it will be a DSC or a DSO that follows his name from now on. I would assume that as an honorable German officer you will take full responsibility. I really don't think we need to go shooting up any library staffs at this point. Why don't we concentrate on catching him, and that will be that."

Boch meant to argue but saw that it was useless. He settled back into his bleakness and said nothing.

"The first thing: which train?" Macht inquired of the air. The air had no answer and so he answered it himself. "Assuming that he left, as *le directeur* said, at exactly three forty-five p.m. by cab, he got to the Montparnasse station by four-fifteen. Using his SS papers, he would not need to stand in line for tickets or checkpoints, so he could leave almost immediately. My question thus has to be, what trains leaving for coastal destinations were available between four-fifteen and four forty-five? He will be on one of those trains. Walter, please call the detectives."

Abel spoke into the microphone by radio to his headquarters and waited. A minute later an answer came. He conveyed it to the two officers.

"A train for Cherbourg left at four-thirty, due to arrive in that city at eleven-thirty p.m. Then another at—"

"That's fine. He'd take the first. He doesn't want to be standing around, not knowing where we are in our investigations and thus assuming the worst. Now, Walter, please call Abwehr headquarters and get our people at Montparnasse to check the gate of that train for late-arriving German officers. I believe they have to sign a travel manifest. At least, I always do. See if Hauptsturmführer—ah, what's the first name, Boch?"

"Otto."

"SS Hauptsturmführer *Otto* Boch, Gestapo, came aboard at the last moment."

"Yes, sir."

Macht looked over at Boch. "Well, Hauptsturmführer, if this pans out, we may save you from your 8.8 in Russia."

"I serve where I help the Führer best. My life is of no consequence," said Boch darkly.

"You may feel somewhat differently when you see the tanks on the horizon," said Macht.

"It hardly matters. We can never catch him. He has too much head start. We can order the train met at Cherbourg, I suppose, and perhaps they will catch him."

"Unlikely. This eel is too slippery."

"Please tell me you have a plan."

"Of course I have a plan," said Macht.

"All right, yes," said Abel, turning from the phone. "Hauptsturmführer Boch did indeed come aboard at the last moment."

He sat, he sat, he sat. The train shook, rattled, and clacked. Twilight passed into lightless night. The vibrations played across everything. Men smoked, men drank from flasks, men tried to write letters home or read. It was not an express, so every half hour or so the train would lurch to a stop and one or two officers would leave, one or two would join. The lights flickered, cool air blasted into the compartment, the French conductor yelled the meaningless name of the town, and on and on they went, into the night.

At last the conductor yelled, "Bricquebec, twenty minutes," first in French, then in German.

He stood up, leaving his overcoat, and went to the loo. In it, he looked at his face in the mirror, sallow in the light. He soaked a towel, rubbed his face, meaning to find energy somehow. Action this day. Much of it. A last trick, a last wiggle.

The fleeing agent's enemy is paranoia. Basil had no immunity from it, merely discipline against it. He was also not particularly immune to fear. He felt both of these emotions strongly now, knowing that this nothingness of waiting for the train to get him where it had to was absolutely the worst.

But then he got his war face back on, forcing the armor of his charm and charisma to the surface, willing his eyes to sparkle, his smile to flash, his brow to furl romantically. He was back in character. He was Basil again.

"Excellent," said Macht. "Now, Boch, your turn to contribute. Use that SS power of yours we all so fear and call von Choltitz's adjutant. It is important that I be given temporary command authority over a unit called Nachtjagdgeschwader-9. Luftwaffe, of course. It's a wing headquartered at a small airfield near the town of Bricquebec, less than an hour outside Cherbourg. Perhaps you remember our chat with its commandant, Oberst Gunther Scholl, a few days ago. Well, you had better hope that Oberst Scholl is on his game, because he is the one who will nab Johnny England for us."

Quite expectedly, Boch didn't understand. Puzzlement flashed in his eyes and fuddled his face. He began to stutter, but Abel cut him off.

"Please, Herr Hauptsturmführer. Time is fleeing."

Boch did what he was told, telling his Uber-Hauptsturmführer that Hauptmann Dieter Macht, of Abwehr III-B, needed to give orders to Oberst Scholl of NJG-9 at Bricquebec. Then the three got into the Citroën and drove the six blocks back to the Hotel Duval, where they went quickly to the phone operator at the board. Though the Abwehr men were sloppy by SS standards, they were efficient by German standards.

The operator handed a phone to Macht, who didn't bother to shed his trench coat and fedora.

"Hullo, hullo," he said, "Hauptmann Macht here, call for Oberst Scholl. Yes, I'll wait."

A few seconds later Scholl came on the phone.

"Scholl here."

"Yes, Oberst Scholl, it's Hauptmann Macht, Paris Abwehr. Have things been explained to you?"

"Hello, Macht. I know only that by emergency directive from Luftwaffe Command I am to obey your orders."

"Do you have planes up tonight?"

"No, the bomber streams are heading north tonight. We have the night off."

"Sorry to make the boys work, Herr Oberst. It seems your seatmate is returning to your area. I need manpower. I need you to meet and cordon off the Cherbourg train at the Bricquebec stop. It's due in at eleven-thirty p.m. Maximum effort. Get your pilots out of bed or out of the bars or brothels, and your mechanics, your ground crews, your fuelers. Leave only a skeleton crew in the tower. I'll tell you why in a bit."

"I must say, Macht, this is unprecedented."

"Oberst, I'm trying to keep you from the Russian front. Please comply enthusiastically so that you can go back to your three mistresses and your wine cellar."

"How did—"

"We have records, Herr Oberst. Anyhow, I would conceal the men in the bushes and inside the depot house until the train has all but arrived. Then, on command, they are to take up positions surrounding the train, making certain that no one leaves. At that point I want you to lead a search party from one end to the other, though of course start in first class. You know who you are looking for. He is now, however, in a dark blue pin-striped suit, double-breasted. He has a dark overcoat. He may look older, more abused, harder, somehow different from when last you saw him. You must be alert, do you understand?"

"Is he armed?"

"We don't know. Assume he is. Listen here, there's a tricky part. When you see him, you must not react immediately. Do you understand? Don't make eye contact, don't move fast or do anything stupid. He has an L-pill. It will probably be in his mouth. If he sees you coming for him, he will bite it. Strychnine—instant. It would mean so much more if we could take him alive. He may have many secrets, do you understand?"

"I do."

"When you take him, order your officers to go first for his mouth. They have to get fingers or a plug or something deep into his throat to keep him from biting or swallowing, then turn him facedown and pound hard on his back. He has to cough out that pill."

"My people will be advised. I will obviously be there to supervise."

"Oberst, this chap is very efficient, very practiced. He's an old dog with miles of travel on him. For years he's lasted in a profession where most perish in a week. Be very careful, be very astute, be very sure. I know you can do this."

"I will catch your spy for you, Macht."

"Excellent. One more thing. I will arrive within two hours in my own Storch, with my assistant, Abel."

"That's right, you fly."

"I do, yes. I have over a thousand hours, and you know how forgiving a Storch is."

"I do."

"So alert your tower people. I'll buzz them so they can light a runway for the thirty seconds it takes me to land, then go back to blackout. And leave a car and driver to take me to the station."

"I will."

"Good hunting."

"Good flying."

He put the phone down, turned to Abel, and said, "Call the airport, get the plane flight-checked and fueled so that we can take off upon arrival."

"Yes, sir."

"One moment," said Boch.

"Yes, Herr Hauptsturmführer?"

"As this is a joint SS-Abwehr operation, I demand to be a part of it. I will go along with you."

"The plane holds only two. It loses its agility when a third is added. It's not a fighter, it's a kite with a tiny motor."

"Then I will go instead of Abel. Macht, do not fight me on this. I will go to SS and higher if I need to. SS must be represented all through this operation."

"You trust my flying?"

"Of course."

"Good, because Abel does not. Now, let's go."

"Not quite yet. I have to change into my uniform."

Refreshed, Basil left the loo. But instead of turning back into the carriage and returning to his seat, he turned the other way, as if it were the natural thing to do, opened the door at the end of the carriage, and stepped out onto the rattling, trembling running board over the coupling between carriages. He waited for the door behind him to seal, tested for speed. Was the train slowing? He felt it was, as maybe the vibrations were further apart, signifying that the wheels churned slightly less aggressively, against an incline, on the downhill, perhaps negotiating a turn. Then, without a thought, he leaped sideways into the darkness.

Will I be lucky? Will the famous St. Florian charm continue? Will I float to a soft landing and roll through the dirt, only my dignity and my hair mussed? Or will this be the night it all runs out and I hit a bridge abutment, a tree trunk, a barbed-wire fence, and kill myself?

He felt himself elongate as he flew through the air, and as his leap carried him out of the gap between the two cars the slipstream hit him hard, sending his arms and legs flying wildly.

He seemed to hang in the darkness for an eternity, feeling the air beat him, hearing the roar of both the wind and the train, seeing nothing.

Then he hit. Stars exploded, suns collapsed, the universe split atomically, releasing a tidal wave of energy. He tasted dust, felt pain and a searing jab in his back, then high-speed abrasion of his whole body, a piercing blow to his left hand, had the illusion of rolling, sliding, falling, hurting all at once, and then he lay quiet.

Am I dead?

He seemed not to be.

The train was gone now. He was alone in the track bed, amid a miasma of dust and blood. At that point the pain clamped him like a vise and he felt himself wounded, though how badly was yet unknown. Could he move? Was he paralyzed? Had he broken any bones?

He sucked in oxygen, hoping for restoration. It came, marginally.

He checked his hip pocket to see if his Browning .380 was still there, and there indeed it was. He reached next for his shin, hoping and praying that the Minox had survived the descent and landfall.

It wasn't there! The prospect of losing it was so tragically immense that he could not face it and exiled the possibility from his brain as he found the tape, still tight, followed it around, and in one second touched the aluminum skin of the instrument. Somehow the impact of the fall had moved it around his leg but had not sundered, only loosened, the tape. He pried it out, slipped it into his hip pocket. He slipped the Browning into his belt in the small of his back, then counted to three and stood.

His clothes were badly tattered, and his left arm so severely ripped he could not straighten it. His right knee had punched through the cheap pin-striped serge, and it too had been shredded by abrasions. But the real damage was done to his back, where he'd evidently encountered a rock or a branch as he decelerated in the dust, and it hurt immensely. He could almost feel it bruising, and he knew it would pain him for weeks. When he twisted he felt shards of glass in his side and assumed he'd broken or cracked several ribs. All in all, he was a mess.

But he was not dead, and he was more or less ambulatory.

He recalled the idiot Luftwaffe colonel on the ride down.

"Yes, our squadron is about a mile east of the tracks, just out of town. It's amazing how the boys have dressed it up. You should come and visit us soon, *monsieur*. I'll take you on a tour. Why, they've turned a rude military installation in the middle of nothing into a comfortable small German town, with sewers and sidewalks and streets, even a gazebo for summertime concerts. My boys are the best, and our wing does more than its share against the Tommy bombers."

That put the airfield a mile or so ahead, given that the tracks had to run north–south. He walked, sliding between trees and gentle undergrowth, through a rather civilized little forest, actually, and his night vision soon arrived through his headache and the pain in his back, which turned his walk into Frankenstein's lumber, but he was confident he was headed in the right direction. And very shortly he heard the approaching buzz of a small plane and knew absolutely that he was on track.

The Storch glided through the air, its tiny engine buzzing away smoothly like a hummingbird's heart. Spindly from its overengineered landing gear and graceless on the ground, it was a princess in the air. Macht held it at 450 meters, compass heading almost due south. He'd already landed at the big Luftwaffe base at Caen for a refueling, just in case Bricquebec proved outside the Storch's 300-kilometer range. He'd follow the same route back, taking the same fuel precautions. He knew: in the air, take nothing for granted. The western heading would bring him to the home of NJG-9 very soon, as he was flying throttle open, close to 175 km per hour. It was a beautiful little thing, light and reliable; you could feel that it wanted to fly, unlike the planes of the Great War, which had mostly been underpowered and overengineered, so close to the maximum they seemed to want to crash. You had to fight them to keep them in the air, while the Storch would fly all night if it could.

A little cool air rushed in, as the Perspex window was cranked half down. It kept the men cool; it also kept them from chatting, which was fine with Macht. It let him concentrate and enjoy, and he still loved the joy of being airborne.

Below, rural France slipped by, far from absolutely dark but too dark to make out details. That was fine. Macht, a good flier, trusted his compass and his watch and knew that neither would let him down, and when he checked the time, he saw that he was entering NJG-9's airspace. He picked up his radio phone, clicked it a few times, and said, "Anton, Anton, this is Bertha 9-9, do you read?"

The headset crackled and snapped, and he thought perhaps he was on the wrong frequency, but then he heard, "Bertha 9-9, this is Anton—I have you; I can hear you. You're bearing a little to the southwest. I'd bear a few degrees to the north."

"Excellent, and thanks, Anton."

"When I have you overhead, I'll light a runway."

"Excellent, excellent. Thanks again, Anton."

Macht made the slight correction and was rewarded a minute later with the sudden flash to illumination of a long horizontal *V*. It took seconds to find the line into the darkness between the arms of the *V* which signified the landing strip. He eased back on the throttle, hearing the engine rpm's drop, watched his airspeed indicator fall to seventy-five, then sixty-five, eased the stick forward into a gentle incline, came into the cone of lights, and saw grass on either side of a wide tarmac built for the much larger twin-engine Me110 night fighters, throttled down some more, and alit with just the slightest of bumps.

When the plane's weight overcame its decreasing power, it almost came to a halt, but he revved back to taxi speed, saw the curved roofs of hangers ahead, and taxied toward them. A broad staging area before the four arched buildings, where the fighters paused and made a last check before deploying, was before him. He took the plane to it, pivoted it to face outward-bound down the same runway, and hit the kill switch. He could hear the vibrations stop, and the plane went silent.

Basil watched the little plane taxi to the hangers, pause, then helpfully turn itself back to the runway. Perfect. Whoever was flying was counting on a quick trip back and didn't want to waste time on the ground.

He crouched well inside the wire, about 300 meters from the airplane, which put him 350 meters from the four hangars. He knew, because Oberst Scholl had told him, that recent manpower levies had stripped the place of guards and security people, all of whom were now in transit to Russia, where their bodies were needed urgently to feed into the fire. As for the patrol dogs, one had died of food poisoning and the other was so old he could hardly move, again information provided by Scholl. The security of NJG-9's night fighter base was purely an illusion; all nonessential personnel had been stripped away for something big in Russia.

In each hangar Basil could see the prominent outlines of the big night fighters, each cockpit slid open, resting at the nose-up, tail-down, fifteen-degree angle on the buttress of the two sturdy landing gears that descended from the huge bulge of engine on the broad wings. They were not small airplanes, and these birds wore complex nests of prongs on the nose, radar antennae meant to guide them to the bomber stream 7,600 meters above. The planes were all marked by the stark black Luftwaffe cross insignia, and their metallic snouts gleamed slightly in the lights, until the tower turned them off when the Storch had come to a safe stop.

He watched carefully. Two men. One wore a pilot's leather helmet but not a uniform, just a tent of a trench coat that hadn't seen cleaning or pressing in years. He was the pilot, and he tossed the helmet into the plane, along with an unplugged set of headphones. At the same time he pulled out a battered fedora, which looked like it had been crushed in the pocket of the coat for all the years it hadn't been pressed or cleaned.

No. 2 was more interesting. He was SS, totally, completely, avatar of dark style and darker menace. The uniform—jodhpurs and boots under a smart tunic, tight at the neck, black cap with death's head rampant in silver above the bill at a rakish angle—was more dramatic than the man, who appeared porky and graceless. He was shakier than the pilot, taking a few awkward steps to get his land legs back and drive the dizziness from his mind.

In time a Mercedes staff car emerged from somewhere in the darkness, driven by a Luftwaffer, who leaped out and offered a snappy salute. He did not shake hands with either, signifying his enlisted status as against their commissions, but obsequiously retreated to the car, where he opened the rear door.

The two officers slid in. The driver resumed his place behind the wheel, and the car sped away into the night.

"Yes, that's very good, Sergeant," said Macht as the car drove in darkness between the tower and administration complex on the left and the officers' mess on the right. The gate was a few hundred meters ahead. "Now, very quickly, let us out and continue on your way, outside the gate, along the road, and back to the station at Bricquebec, where your commanding officer waits."

"Ah, sir, my instructions are—"

"Do as I say, Sergeant, unless you care to join the other bad boys of the Wehrmacht on an infantry salient on some frozen hill of dog shit in Russia."

"Obviously, sir, I will obey."

"I thought you might."

The car slipped between two buildings, slowed, and Macht eased out, followed by Boch. Then the car rolled away, speeded up, and loudly issued the pretense that it was headed to town with two important passengers.

"Macht," hissed Boch, "what in the devil's name are you up to?"

"Use your head, Herr Hauptsturmführer. Our friend is not going to be caught like a fish in a bucket. He's too clever. He presumes the shortest possible time between his escape from Paris and our ability to figure it out and know what name he travels under. He knows he cannot make it all the way to Cherbourg and steal or hire a boat. No indeed, and since that idiot Scholl has conveniently plied him with information about the layout and operational protocols of NJG-9, as well as, I'm certain, a precise location, he has identified it as his best opportunity for an escape. He means, I suppose, to fly to England in a 110 like the madman Hess, but we have provided him with a much more tempting conveyance—the low, slow, gentle Storch. He cannot turn it down, do you see? It is absolutely his best—his only—chance to bring off his crazed mission, whatever it is. But we will stop him. Is that pistol loaded?"

Boch slapped the Luger under the flap of his holster on his ceremonial belt.

"Of course. One never knows."

"Well, then, we shall get as close as possible and wait for him to make his move. I doubt he's a quarter kilometer from us now. He'll wait until he's certain the car is gone and the lazy Luftwaffe tower personnel are paying no attention, and then he'll dash to the airplane, and off he goes."

"We will be there," said Boch, pulling his Luger.

"Put that thing away, please, Herr Hauptsturmführer. It makes me nervous."

Basil began his crawl. The grass wasn't high enough to cover him, but without lights, no tower observer could possibly pick him out flat against the ground. His plan was to approach on the oblique, locating himself on such a line that the plane was between himself and the watchers in the tower. It wouldn't obscure him, but it would be more data in a crowded binocular view into an already dark zone, and he hoped that the lazy officer up there was not really paying that much attention, instead simply nodding off on a meaningless night of duty far from any war zone and happy that he wasn't out in the godforsaken French night on some kind of insane catch-the-spy mission two kilometers away at the train station.

It hurt, of course. His back throbbed, a bruise on his hip ached, a pain between his eyes would not go away, and the burns on knee and arm from his abrasions seemed to mount in intensity. He pulled himself through the grass like a swimmer, his fear giving him energy that he should not have had, the roughness of his breath drowning out the night noise. He seemed to crawl for a century, but he didn't look up, because, as if he were swimming the English Channel, if he saw how far he had to go, the blow to his morale would be stunning.

Odd filaments of his life came up from nowhere, viewed from strange angles so that they made only a bit of sense and maybe not even that. He hardly knew his mother, he had hated his father, his brothers were all older than he was and had formed their friendships and allegiances already. Women that he had been intimate with arrived to mind, but they did not bring pride and triumph, only memories of human fallibility and disappointment, theirs and his; and his congenital inability to remain faithful to any of them, love or not, always revealed its ugliness. Really, he had had a useless life until he signed with the crown and went on his adventures—it was a perfect match for his adventurer's temperament, his casual cruelty, his cleverness, his ruthlessness. He had no problem with any of it: the deceit, the swindles, the extortion, the cruel manipulation of the innocent, even the murder. He had killed his first man, a corrupt Malaysian police inspector, in 1935, and he remembered the jump of the big Webley, the smell of cordite, the man's odd deflation as he surrendered to gravity. He thought it would have been so much more; it was, really, nothing, nothing at all, and he supposed that his own death, in a few minutes, a few hours, a few days, a few weeks, or next year or the year after, would mean as little to the man who killed him, probably some Hanoverian conscript with a machine pistol firing blindly into the trees that held him.

So it would go. That is the way of the wickedness called war. It eats us all. In the end, it and it alone is the victor, no matter what the lie called history says. The god of war, Mars the Magnificent and Tragic, always wins.

And then he was there.

He was out of grass. He had come to the hard-packed earth of the runway. He allowed himself to look up. The little plane was less than fifty meters away, tilted skyward on its absurdly high landing-gear struts. He had but to jump to the cockpit, turn it on, let the rpm's mount, then take off the brakes, and it would pull itself forward and up, due north, straight on till morning.

Fifty meters, he thought. *All that's between myself and Blighty.*

He gathered himself for the crouched run to it. He checked: *Pistol still with me, camera in my pocket, all nice and tidy.* He had one last thing to do. He reached into his breast pocket and shoved his fingers down, probing, touching, searching. Then he had it. He pulled the L-pill out, fifty ccs of pure strychnine under a candy shell, and slid it into his mouth, back behind his teeth, far in the crevice between lip and jawbone. One crunch and he got to Neverland instantly.

"There," whispered Boch. "It's him, there, do you see, crouching just off the runway." They knelt in the darkness of the hangar closest to the Storch.

Macht saw him. The Englishman seemed to be gathering himself. *The poor bastard is probably exhausted. He's been on the run in occupied territory over four days, bluffed or brazened his way out of a dozen near misses.* Macht could see a dark double-breasted suit that even from this distance looked disheveled.

"Let him get to the plane," said Macht. "He will be consumed by it, and under that frenzy we approach, keeping the tail and fuselage between ourselves and him."

"Yes, I see."

"You stand off and hold him with the Luger. I will jump him and get this"—he reached into his pocket and retrieved a pipe—"into his mouth, to keep him from swallowing his suicide capsule. Then I will handcuff him and we'll be done."

They watched as the man broke from the edge of the grass, running like an athlete, with surprising power to his strides, bent double as if to evade tacklers, and in a very little time got himself to the door of the Storch's cockpit, pulled it open, and hoisted himself into the seat.

"Now," said Macht, and the two of them emerged from their hiding place and walked swiftly to the airplane.

His Luger out, Boch circled to the left to face the cockpit squarely from the left side while Macht slid along the right side of the tail boom, reached the landing struts, and slipped under them.

"Halt!" yelled Boch, and at precisely that moment Macht rose, grabbed the astonished Englishman by the lapels of his suit, and yanked him free of the plane. They crashed together, Macht pivoting cleverly so that his quarry bounced off his hip and went into space. He landed hard, far harder than Macht, who simply rode him down, got a knee on his chest, bent, and stuffed his pipe in the man's throat. The agent coughed and heaved, searching for leverage, but Macht had wrestled many a criminal into captivity and knew exactly how to apply leverage.

"Spit it out!" he cried in English. "Damn you, spit it out!" He rolled the man as he shook him, then slapped him with a hard palm between the shoulder blades, and in a second the pill was ejected like a piece of half-chewed, throat-obstructing meat, riding a propulsive if involuntary spurt of breath, and arched to earth, where Macht quickly put a heavy shoe on it, crushing it.

"Hands up, Englishman, goddamn you," he yelled as Boch neared, pointing the Luger directly into the face of the captive to make the argument more persuasively.

There was no fight left in him, or so it seemed. He put up his hands.

"Search him, Macht," said Boch.

Macht swooped back onto the man, ran his hands around his waist, under his armpits, down his legs.

"Only this," he said, holding aloft a small camera. "This'll tell us some things."

"I think you'll be disappointed, old man," said the Englishman. "I am thinking of spiritual enlightenment, and my photographs merely propose a path."

"Shut up," bellowed Boch.

"Now," said Macht, "we'll—"

"Not so fast," said Boch.

The pistol covered both of them.

It happened so fast. He knew it would happen fast, but not this fast. *Halt!* came the cry, utterly stunning him with its loudness and closeness, and then this demon rose from nowhere, pulled him—the strength was enormous—from the plane, and slammed him to the ground. In seconds the L-pill had been beaten from him. Whoever this chap was, he knew a thing or two.

Now Basil stood next to him. Breathing hard, quite fluttery from exhaustion, and trying not to face the enormity of what had just happened, he tried to make sense, even as one thing, his capture, turned into another—some weird German command drama.

The SS officer had the Luger on both of them.

"Boch, what do you think you are doing?" said the German in the trench coat.

"Taking care of a certain problem," said the SS man. "Do you think I care to have an Abwehr bastard file a report that will end my career and get me shipped to Russia? Did you think I could permit *that*?"

"My friends," said Basil in German, "can't we sit down over a nice bottle of schnapps and talk it out? I'm sure you two can settle your differences amicably."

The SS officer struck him across the jaw with his Luger, driving him to the ground. He felt blood run down his face as the cheek began to puff grotesquely.

"Shut your mouth, you bastard," the officer said. Then he turned back to the police officer in the trench coat.

"You see how perfectly you have set it up for me, Macht? No witnesses, total privacy, your own master plan to capture this spy. Now I kill the two of you. But the story is, he shot you, I shot him. I'm the hero. Moreover, whatever treasure of intelligence that little camera holds, it comes to me. I will weep pious tears at your funeral, which I'm sure will be held under the highest honors, and I will express my profound regrets to your unit as it ships out to Russia."

"You lunatic," said Macht. "You disgrace."

"Sieg Heil," said the SS officer as he fired.

He missed.

This was because his left ventricle was interrupted mid-beat by a .380 bullet fired a split second earlier by Basil's .380 Browning in the Abwehr agent's right hand. Thus Boch jerked and his shot plunged off into the darkness.

The SS officer seemed to melt. His knees hit first—not that it mattered, because he was already quite dead, and he toppled to the left, smashing his nose, teeth, and pince-nez.

"Excellent shot, old man," said Basil. "I didn't even feel you remove my pistol."

"I knew he would be up to something. He was too cooperative. Now, sir, tell me what I should do with you. Should I arrest you and earn the Iron Cross, or should I give you back your pistol and camera and watch you fly away?"

"Even as a philosophic exercise, I doubt I could argue the first proposition with much force," said Basil.

"Give me an argument, then. You saved my life, or rather your pistol did, and you saved the lives of the men in my unit. But I need a justification. I'm German, you know, with that heavy, irony-free, ploddingly logical mind."

"All right, then. I did not come here to kill Germans. I have killed no Germans. Actually the only one who has killed Germans, may I point out, sir, is *you*. Germans will die, more and more, and Englishmen and Russians and even the odd Frog or two. Possibly an American. That can't be stopped. But I am told that the message on the film, which is completely without military value, by the way, has a possibility of ending the war by as much as two years sooner than expected. I don't know about you, sir, but I am sick to death of war."

"Fair enough. I am, too. Here, take this, and your camera, and get out of here. There's the plane."

"Ah, one question, if I may?"

"Yes?"

"How do you turn it on?"

"You don't fly, do you?"

"Not really, no. At least, not *technically.* I mean I've watched it, I've flown in them, I know from the cinema that one pulls the stick up to climb, down to descend, right and left, with pedals—"

"God, you are something, I must say."

And so the German told him where the ignition was, where the brakes were, what groundspeed he had to achieve to go airborne, and where the compass was for his due north heading.

"Don't go over 150 meters. Don't go over 150 kilometers per hour. Don't try anything fancy. When you get to England, find a nice soft meadow, put her down, and just before you touch down, switch off the magnetos and let the plane land itself."

"I will."

"And remember one thing, Englishman. You were good—you were the best I ever went after. But in the end I caught you."

THE WAR ROOM

"Gentlemen," said Sir Colin Gubbins, "I do hope you'll forgive Captain St. Florian his appearance. He is just back from abroad, and he parked his airplane in a tree."

"Sir, I am assured the tree will survive," said Basil. "I cannot have *that* on my conscience, along with so many other items."

Basil's right arm was encased in plaster of Paris; it had been broken by his fall from the tree. His torso, under his shirt, was encased in strong elastic tape, several miles of it, in fact, to help his four broken ribs mend. The swelling on his face, from the blow delivered by the late SS Hauptsturmführer Boch, had gone down somewhat, but it was still yellowish, corpulent, and quite repulsive, as was the blue-purple wreath that surrounded his bloodshot eye. He needed a cane to walk, and of all his nicks, it was the abraded knee that turned out to hurt the most, other than the headache, constant and throbbing, from the concussion. In the manly British officer way, however, he still managed to wear his uniform, even if his jacket was thrown about his shoulders over his shirt and tie.

"It looks like you had a jolly trip," said the admiral.

"It had its ups and downs, sir," said Basil.

"I think we know why we are here," said General Cavendish, ever irony-free, "and I would like to see us get on with it."

It was the same as it always was: the darkish War Room under the Treasury, the prime minister's lair. That great man's cigar odor filled the air, and too bad if you couldn't abide it. A few posters, a few maps, a few cheery exhortations to duty, and that was it. There were still four men across from Basil, a general, an admiral, Gubbins, and the man of tweed, Professor Turing.

"Professor," said Sir Colin, "as you're just in from the country and new to the information, I think it best for you to acquire the particulars of Captain St. Florian's adventures from his report. But you know his results. He succeeded, though he got quite a thrashing in the process. I understand it was a close-run thing. Now you have had the results of his mission on hand at Bletchley for over a week, and it is time to see whether or not St. Florian's blood, sweat, and tears were worth it."

"Of course," said Turing. He opened his briefcase, took out the seven Minox photos of the pages from *The Path to Jesus*, reached in again, and pulled out around three hundred pages of paper, whose leaves he flipped to show the barons of war. Every page was filled with either numerical computation, handwriting on charts, or lengthy analysis in typescript.

"We have not been lazy," he said. "Gentleman, we have tested everything. Using our decryptions from the Soviet diplomatic code as our index, we have reduced the words and letters to numerical values and run them through every electronic bombe we have. We have given them to our best intuitive code breakers—it seems to be a gift, a certain kind of mind that can solve these problems quickly, without much apparent effort. We have analyzed them up, down, sideways, and backwards. We have tested the message against every classical code known to man. We have compared it over and over, word by word, with the printed words of the Reverend MacBurney. We have measured it to the thousandth of an inch, even tried to project it as a geometric problem. Two PhDs from Oxford even tried to find a pattern in the seemingly random arrangement of the odd crosslike formations doodled across all the pages. Their conclusion was that the *seemingly* random pattern was *actually* random."

He went silent.

"Yes?" said Sir Colin.

"There is no secret code within it," the professor finally said. "As any possible key to a book code, it solves nothing. It unlocks nothing. There is no secret code at all within it."

The moment was ghastly.

Finally Basil spoke.

"Sir, it's not what I went through to obtain those pages that matters. I've had worse drubbings in football matches. But a brave and decent man has put himself at great risk to get them to you. His identity would surprise you, but it seems there are some of them left on the other side. Thus I find it devastating to write the whole thing off and resign him to his fate for nothing. It weighs heavily."

"I understand," said Professor Turing. "But you must understand as well. Book codes work with books, don't they? Because the book is a closed, locked universe—that is the *point*, after all. What makes the book code work, as simple a device as it is, is, after all, that it's a *book*. It's mass-produced on Linotype machines, carefully knitted up in a bindery, festooned with some amusing imagery for a cover, and whether you read it in Manchester or Paris or Berlin or Kathmandu, the same words will be found on the same places on the same page, and thus everything makes sense. This, however, is not a book but a manuscript, in a human hand. Who knows how age, drinking, debauchery, tricks of memory, lack of stamina, advanced syphilis or gonorrhea may have corrupted the author's effort? It will almost certainly get messier and messier as it goes along, and it may in the end not resemble the original at all. Our whole assumption was that it would be a close enough replica to what MacBurney had produced twenty years earlier for us to locate the right letters and unlock the code. Everything about it is facsimile, after all, even to those frequent religious doodles on the pages. If it were a good facsimile, the growth or shrinkage would be consistent and we could alter our calculations by measurable quantities and unlock it. But it was not to be. Look at the pages, please, Captain. You will see that even among themselves, they vary greatly. Sometimes the letters are large, sometimes small. Sometimes a page contains twelve hundred letters, sometimes six hundred, sometimes twenty-three hundred. In certain of them, it seems clear that he was drunk, pen in hand, and the lines are all atumble, and he is just barely in control. His damnable lack of consistency dooms any effort to use this as a key to a code contained in the original. I told you it was a long shot."

Again a long and ghastly silence.

"Well, then, Professor," said Gubbins, "that being the case, I think we've taken you from your work at Bletchley long enough. And we have been absent from our duties as well. Captain St. Florian needs rest and rehabilitation. Basil, I think all present will enthusiastically endorse you for decoration, if it matters, for an astonishing and insanely courageous effort. Perhaps a nice promotion, Basil. Would you like to be a major? Think of the trouble you could cause. But please don't be bitter. To win a war you throw out a million seeds and hope that some of them produce, in the end, fruit. I'll alert the staff to call—"

"Excuse me," said Professor Turing. "What exactly is going on here?"

"Ah, Professor, there seems to be no reason for us to continue."

"I daresay you chaps have got to learn to listen," he said.

Basil was slightly shocked by the sudden tartness in his voice.

"I am not like Captain St. Florian, a witty ironist, and I am not like you three high mandarins with your protocols and all that elaborate and counterfeit bowing and scraping. I am a scientist. I speak in exact truth. What I say is true and nothing else is."

"I'm rather afraid I don't grasp your meaning, sir," said Gubbins stiffly. It was clear that neither he nor the other two mandarins enjoyed being addressed so dismissively by a forty-year-old professor in baggy tweeds and wire-frame glasses.

"I said listen. *Listen!*" repeated the professor, rather rudely, but with such intensity it became instantly clear that he regarded them as intellectual inferiors and was highly frustrated by their rash conclusion.

"Sir," said General Cavendish, rather icily, "if you have more to add, please add it. As General Sir Colin has said, we have other duties—"

"*Secret* code!" interrupted the professor.

All were stupefied.

"Don't you see? It's rather brilliant!" He laughed, amused by the code maker's wit. "Look here," he said. "I shall try to explain. What is the most impenetrable code of all to unlock? You cannot do it with machines that work a thousand times faster than men's brains."

Nobody could possibly answer.

"It is the code that pretends to be a code but isn't at all."

More consternation, impatience, yet fear of being mocked.

"Put another way," said the professor, "the code is the absence of code."

No one was going to deal with that one.

"Whoever dreamed this up, our Cambridge librarian or an NKVD spymaster, he was a smart fellow. Only two people on earth could know the meaning of this communication, though I'm glad to say they've been joined by a third one. Me. It came to me while running. Great for clearing the mind, I must say."

"You have the advantage, Professor," said Sir Colin. "Please, continue."

"A code is a disguise. Suppose something is disguised as itself?"

The silence was thunderous.

"All right, then. Look at the pages. *Look at them!*"

Like chastened schoolboys, the class complied.

"You, St. Florian, you're a man of hard experience in the world. Tell me what you see."

"Ah . . ." said Basil. He was completely out of irony. "Well, ah, a messy scrawl of typical eighteenth-century handwriting, capitalized nouns, that sort of thing. A splotch of something, perhaps wine, perhaps something more dubious."

"Yes?"

"Well, I suppose, all these little religious symbols."

"Look at them carefully."

Basil alone did not need to unlimber reading spectacles. He saw what they were quickly enough.

"They appear to be crosses," he said.

"Just crosses?"

"Well, each of them is mounted on a little hill. Like Calvary, one supposes."

"Not like Calvary. There were three on Calvary. This is only one. Singular."

"Yes, well, now that I look harder, I see the hill isn't exactly a hill. It's segmented into round, irregular shapes, very precisely drawn in the finest line his nib would permit. I would say it's a pile of stones."

"At last we are getting somewhere."

"I think I've solved your little game, Professor," said General Cavendish. "That pile of stones, that would be some kind of road marker, eh? Yes, and a cross has been inserted into it. Road marker, that is, marking the path, is that what it is? It would be a representation of the title of the pamphlet, *The Path to Jesus*. It is an expression of the central meaning of his argument."

"Not what it *means*. Didn't you hear me? Are you deaf?"

The general was taken aback by the ferocity with which Professor Turing spoke.

"I am not interested in what it means. If it means something, that meaning is different from the thing itself. I am interested in what it *is*. Is, not means."

"I believe," said the admiral, "a roadside marker is called a cairn. So that is exactly what it is, Professor. Is that what you—"

"Please take it the last step. There's only one more. Look at it and tell me what it is."

"Cairn . . . cross," said Basil. "It can only be called a cairncross. But that means nothing unless . . ."

"Unless what?" commanded Turing.

"A name," said Sir Colin.

Hello, hello, said Basil to himself. He saw where the path to Jesus led.

"The Soviet spymaster was telling the Cambridge librarian the name of the agent at Bletchley Park so that he could tell the agent's new handler. The device of communication was a 154-year-old doodle. The book-code indicators were false, part of the disguise."

"So there is a man at Bletchley named Cairncross?" asked Sir Colin.

"John Cairncross, yes," said Professor Turing. "Hut 6. Scotsman. Don't know the chap myself, but I've heard his name mentioned—supposed to be first-class."

"John Cairncross," said Sir Colin.

"He's your Red spy. Gentlemen, if you need to feed information to Stalin on Operation Citadel, you have to do it through Comrade Cairncross. When it comes from him, Stalin and the Red generals will believe it. They will fortify the Kursk salient. The Germans will be smashed. The retreat from the East will begin. The end will begin. What was it again? 'Home alive in '45,' not 'Dead in heaven in '47.'"

"Bravo," said Sir Colin.

"Don't *bravo* me, Sir Colin. I just work at sums, like Bob Cratchit. Save your bravos for that human fragment of the Kipling imagination sitting over there."

"I say," said Basil, "instead of a *bravo*, could I have a nice whisky?"

OTHER TERRORS, OTHER BATTLES

CHARLIE'S SHELL GAME

BRIAN GARFIELD

THE AUTHOR OF seventy novels and scores of short stories, Brian Francis Wynne Garfield (1939–2018) was not only prolific but also versatile and accomplished. He wrote numerous westerns, beginning with *Range Justice* (1960), written when he was eighteen. He eventually was chosen to be the president of the Western Writers of America. He also wrote adventure, war, sea, and historical novels, as well as nonfiction.

It is for his mystery, crime, and espionage fiction, however, that Garfield is best known. His first great success was *Hopscotch* (1975), which won the Edgar as the best novel of the year and was made into a very successful motion picture in 1980 with Walter Matthau and Glenda Jackson. The book was a tense suspense film set in the Cold War era and seemed a natural for the movies. Several attempts with various screenwriters failed until Garfield became involved and helped turn the story into a comedy.

As popular as the movie was, Garfield was even better known for the 1974 motion picture made from his novel *Death Wish* (1972). It stars Charles Bronson as a New York man whose wife and child are brutalized and who turns into a vigilante, putting himself in dangerous positions and exacting vengeance when attacked. Set in a time of seemingly relentless street violence, the film divided liberals, who loathed the notion of a citizen taking the law into his own hands, and conservatives, who applauded what they regarded as street justice. The tremendous success of the film spawned four sequels. A decade after the first film was released, Bernie Goetz, a mugging victim, also became a vigilante in events reminiscent of Garfield's novel and the film adaptation. Though largely vilified by the media and New York's politicians, "Bernie for Mayor" buttons sprouted all over the city.

Nineteen films were inspired by Garfield's work, though none had the impact of *Death Wish* or the critical acclaim of *Hopscotch*. Perhaps the best was *The Stepfather* (1987), a low-budget suspense film for which he and his longtime friend Donald E. Westlake had created a story that was remade in 2009 with more money but less suspense.

His short story collection *Checkpoint Charlie* (1981) was a sequel to *Hopscotch* that featured Charlie Dark, an inept CIA agent whose main fear was losing his job.

"Charlie's Shell Game" was originally published in the February 1978 issue of *Ellery Queen's Mystery Magazine;* it was first collected in *Checkpoint Charlie* (New York, Mysterious Press, 1981).

CHARLIE'S SHELL GAME

BRIAN GARFIELD

BY THE END of the afternoon I had seen three of them check in at the reception desk and I knew one of them had come to kill me but I didn't know which one.

Small crowds had arrived in the course of the afternoon and I'd had plenty of time to study them while they stood in queues to check in at the reception desk. One lot of sixteen had come in together from an airport bus—middle-aged couples, a few children, two or three solitary businessmen; tourists, most of them, and sitting in the lobby with a magazine for a prop I wrote them off. My man would be young—late twenties, I knew that much.

I knew his name too but he wouldn't be traveling under it.

Actually the dossier was quite thick; we knew a good deal about him, including the probability that he would come to Caracas to kill me. We knew something of his habits and patterns; we'd seen the corpses that marked his backtrail; we knew his name, age, nationality; we had several physical descriptions—they varied but there was agreement on certain points: medium height, muscularly trim, youthful. We knew he spoke at least four languages. But he hadn't been photo-

graphed and we had no fingerprints; he was too clever for that.

Of the check-ins I'd espied at the Tamanaco desk three were possibles—any of them could be my intended assassin.

My job was to take him before he could take me.

Myerson had summoned me back from Helsinki and I had arrived in Langley at midnight grumpy and rumpled after the long flight but the cypher had indicated red priority so I'd delivered myself directly to the office without pause to bathe or sleep, let alone eat. I was famished. Myerson had taken a look at my stubble and plunged right in: "You're flying to Caracas in the morning. The eight o'clock plane."

"You may have to carry me on board."

"Me and how many weightlifters?" He glanced at the clock above the official photograph of the President. "You've got eight hours. The briefings won't take that long. Anyhow you can sleep on the plane."

"Maybe. I never have," I said, "but then I've

344

never been this exhausted. Have you got anything to eat around here?"

"No. This should perk you up, though—it's Gregorius."

"Is it now."

"I knew you'd wag your tail."

"All right, you have my attention." Then I had to fight the urge to look straight up over my head in alarm: Myerson's smile always provokes the premonition that a Mosler safe is falling toward one's head.

"You've gained it back. Gone off the diet?" Now that he had me hooked in his claws he was happy to postpone the final pounce: like a cat with a chipmunk. I really hate him.

I said, "Crawfish."

"What?"

"It's what you eat in Finland. You take them fresh out of a lake, just scoop them up off the bottom in a wooden box with a chickenwire bottom. You throw them straight into the pot and watch them turn color. I can eat a hundred at a sitting. Now what's this about Caracas and Gregorius?"

"You're getting disgustingly fat, Charlie."

"I've always been fat. As for disgusting, I could diet it off, given the inclination. You, on the other hand, would need to undergo brain surgery. I'd prescribe a prefrontal lobotomy."

"Then you'd have no one left to spice your life."

"Spice? I thought it was hemlock."

"In this case more likely a few ounces of plastique. That seems to be Gregorius's preference. And you do make a splendid target, Charlie. I can picture two hundred and umpty pounds of blubber in flabby pieces along the ceiling. Gregorius would be most gratified."

He'd mentioned Gregorius now; it meant he was ready to get down to it and I slumped, relieved; I no longer enjoy volleying insults with him—they cut too close and it's been a long while since either of us believed they were jokes. Our mutual hatred is not frivolous. But we need each other. I'm the only one he can trust to do these jobs without a screw-up and he's the only one who'll give me the jobs. The slick militaristic kids who run the organization don't offer their plums to fat old men. In any section but Myerson's I'd have been fired years ago—overage, overweight, overeager to stay in the game by the old rules rather than the new. I'm the last of the generation that puts ingenuity ahead of computer print-outs.

They meet once a month on the fifth floor to discuss key personnel reassignments and it's a rare month that goes by without an attempt being made by one of the computer kids to tie a can to my tail; I know for a fact Myerson has saved me by threatening to resign: "If he goes, I go." The ultimatim has worked up to now but as we both get older and I get fatter the kids become more strident and I'm dubious how long Myerson can continue the holding action. It's not loyalty to me, God knows; it's purely his own self-interest—he knows if he loses me he'll get the sack himself: he hasn't got anybody else in the section who knows how to produce. Nobody worthwhile will work for him. I wouldn't either but I've got no choice. I'm old, fat, stubborn, arrogant, and conceited. I'm also the best.

He said, "Venezuela is an OPEC country, of course," and waited to see if I would attend his wisdom—as if the fact were some sort of esoterica. I waited, yawned, looked at my watch. Myerson can drive you to idiocy belaboring the obvious. Finally he went on:

"The oil-country finance ministers are meeting in Caracas this time. Starting Thursday."

"I haven't been on Mars, you know. They have newspapers even in Helsinki."

"Redundancies are preferable to ignorance, Charlie." It is his litany. I doubt he passes an hour, even in his sleep, when that sentence doesn't run through his mind: he's got it on tape up there.

"Will you come to the point?"

"They'll be discussing the next round of oil-price hikes," he said. "There's some disagreement among them. The Saudis and the Venezuelans want to keep the increase down below five percent. Some of the others want a big boost—perhaps twenty-five or thirty percent."

"I plead. Tell me about Gregorius."

"This is getting us there. Trust me."

"Let's see if I can't speed it up," I said. "Of course it's the Mahdis——"

"Of course."

"They want Israel for themselves, they don't want a Palestinian peace agreement, they want to warn the Arab countries that they won't be ignored. What is it, then? They've arranged to have Gregorius explode a room full of Arab leaders in Caracas? Sure. After that the Arab countries won't be so quick to negotiate a Middle East settlement without Mahdi participation. Am I warm?"

"Scalding. Now I know you're awake."

"Barely."

The Mahdi gang began as an extremist splinter arm of the Black Septemberists. The gang is small but serious. It operates out of floating headquarters in the Libyan desert. There's a long and tedious record of hijackings, terror bombings, assassinations. Nothing unique about that. What makes the gang unusual is its habit of using mercenaries. The Mahdis—they named themselves after the mystic who wiped out Gordon at Khartoum—are Palestinians but they're Bedouins, not Arabs; they're few in number and they're advanced in age compared with the teenage terrorists of the PLO. The Mahdi staff cadre consists of men who were adults at the time of the 1947 expulsion from Palestine. Some of the sheikhs are in their seventies by now.

Rather than recruit impassioned young fools the gang prefers to hire seasoned professional mercenaries; they get better results that way and they don't need to be concerned about generation-gap factionalism. They are financed by cold-blooded groups of various persuasions and motivations, most of them in Iraq and Germany.

They had used Gregorius at least twice in the past, to my knowledge: the Hamburg Bahnhof murders and the assassination of an Israeli agent in Cairo. The Hamburg bomb had demolished not only a crowd of Israeli trade officials but also the main staircase of the railroad station. The Cairo setup had been simpler, just one victim, blown up when he stepped onto the third stair of his entrance porch.

Gregorius was a killer for hire and he was well paid; apparently his fees were second only to those of Carlos the Jackal, who had coordinated the Munich athlete murders and the Entebbe hijack; but Gregorius always chose his employment on ideological grounds—he had worked for the PLO, the Baader-Meinhof Group, the Rhodesian rebels, the Cuban secret service, but he'd never taken a job for the West. Evidently he enjoyed fighting his own private war of liberation. Of course he was a psychotic but there was no point dwelling on his lunacy because it might encourage one to underestimate him; he was brilliant.

Myerson said, "We've got it on authority— fairly good authority—that the Mahdis have hired Gregorius for two targets in Caracas. Ministers. The Saudi and the Venezuelan. And of course whatever bonus prizes he may collect— bombs usually aren't too selective."

"How good is 'fairly good'?"

"Good enough to justify my pulling you off the Helsinki station and posting you to Venezuela."

"All right." If he didn't want to reveal the source he didn't have to; it wasn't really my affair. Need-to-know and all that.

Myerson got down to nuts and bolts and that pleased me because he always hurries right through them; they bore him. He has a grand image of himself as the sort of master strategist who leaves tactical detail to junior staff. Unhappily our section's budget doesn't permit any chain of command and Myerson has to do his own staff work and that's why I usually have to go into the field with a dearth of hard information; that's one reason why nobody else will work for him—Myerson never does much homework.

"It could happen anywhere," he concluded. "The airport, a hotel lobby, a state banquet, any of the official ministerial meetings, a limousine. Anywhere."

"Have you alerted Venezuelan security?"

"I didn't have to. But I've established your liaison out of courtesy."

In other words the tip had come from Venezuelan security. And they didn't feel confident of their own ability to contain Gregorius. Very astute of them; most small-nation security chiefs lack the humility to admit it when a job is too big for them.

Myerson continued, in the manner of an afterthought, "Since we don't know where he plans to make the strike we've taken it upon ourselves to—"

"Is that a royal 'we'?"

"No. The fifth floor. As I was saying, it's been decided that our best chance at him is to lure him into the open before the ministers begin the conference. Of course he doesn't tempt easily."

Then he smiled. My flesh crawled.

"You're the bait, Charlie. He'll come out for you."

"In other words it's an open secret that I'll be in Caracas and you've spread the word where you know he'll hear it." I brooded at him, hating him afresh. "Maybe you've neglected something."

"Oh?"

"Gregorius is like me in one respect. He's——"

"Young, fast, up-to-date and sexy. Yes indeed, Charlie, you could be twins."

I cut across his chuckle. "He's a professional and so am I. Business comes first. He'd love to nail me. All right. But first he'll do the job he's being paid for."

"Not this time. We've leaked the news that you're being sent down there to terminate him regardless of cost. He thinks you're being set up to nail him *after* he exposes himself by blowing up a few oil ministers. He can't risk that—you got closer to nailing him than anybody else ever has. He knows if you're set on him again you won't turn loose until you've done the job. And he knows if he sets off a bomb while you're in earshot of it you'll reach him. He needs more lead time than that if he means to get away."

And he smiled again: "He's got to put you out of the way before he goes after the ministers. Once the bombs go off he can't hang around afterwards to take you on. He's got to do it first."

I said, "I've heard stronger reasoning. He's confident of his skills. Suppose he just ignores me and goes ahead with the job as if I weren't there?"

"He hates you too much. He couldn't walk away, could he? Not after Beirut. Why, I believe he hates you even more than I do."

Two years earlier we'd known Gregorius was in Beirut to blast the Lebanese coalition prime minister. I'd devised one of the cleverer stunts of my long career. In those days Gregorius worked in tandem with his brother, who was six years older and nearly as bright as Gregorius. Our plan was good and Gregorius walked into it but I'd had to make use of Syrian back-up personnel on the alternate entrances to that verminous maze of alleys and one of the Syrians had been too nervous or too eager for glory. He'd started the shooting too early by about seven-tenths of a second and that was all the time Gregorius needed to get away.

Gregorius left his brother behind in ribbons in the alley; still alive today but a vegetable. Naturally Gregorius made efforts afterward to find out who was responsible for the ambush. Within a few weeks he knew my name. And of course Gregorius—that's his code name, not the one he was born with—was Corsican by birth and personal revenge is a religion with those people. I knew one day he'd have to come for me; I'd lost very little sleep over it—people have been trying to kill me for thirty-five years.

Just before Myerson sent me to the airport he said, "We want him alive, Charlie."

"You're joking."

"Absolutely not. It's imperative. The information in his head can keep the software boys busy for eight months. Alive—it's an order from the fifth floor."

"You've already blindfolded me and sent me into the cage with him and now you want to handcuff me too?"

"Why, Charlie, that's the way you like it best, you old masochist."

He knows me too well.

I'd watched them check in at the hotel desk and I'd narrowed the possibilities to three; I'd seen which pigeonholes the room clerk had taken the keys from so I knew which rooms they were in. I didn't need to look at the register because it wouldn't help me to know what names or passports they were using.

It was like the Mexican Shell Game: three shells, one pea. Under which shell is the pea?

He had to strike at me today because Myerson's computer said so. And it probably had to be the Tamanaco Hotel because I had studied everything in the Gregorius dossier and I knew he had a preference—so strong it was almost a compulsion—for the biggest and best old hotel in a city. Big because it was easy to be anonymous there; best because Gregorius had been born dirt-poor in Corsica and was rich now; old because he had good taste but also because old walls tend to be soundproof. The Tamanaco, in Caracas, was it.

I was making it easy for him, sitting in plain sight in the lobby.

Earlier in the day I'd toured the city with Cartlidge. He looks like his name: all gaunt sinews and knobby joints. We'd traced the route in from the airport through the long mountain tunnel and we'd had a look at the hotel where the Saudi minister was booked in; on my advice the Venezuelans made a last-minute switch and when the Saudi arrived tomorrow morning he'd be informed of the move to another hotel. We had a look at the palace where the conference would take place and I inquired about the choice

of halls: to forestall Gregorius the Venezuelans had not announced any selection—there were four suitable conference rooms in the building—and indeed the final choice wouldn't actually be made until about fifteen minutes before the session began. They were doing a good job. I made a few minor suggestions and left them to it.

After lunch we'd set up a few things and then I'd staked myself in the Tamanaco lobby and four hours later I was still there.

Between five and six I saw each of the three again.

The first one spent the entire hour at the pool outside the glass doors at the rear of the lobby. He was a good swimmer with the build and grace of a field-and-track contender; he had a round Mediterranean face, more Italian than French in appearance. He had fair hair cut very short—crew cut—but the color and cut didn't mean anything; you could buy the former in bottles. For the convenience of my own classification I dubbed him The Blond.

The second one appeared shortly after five, crossing the lobby in a flared slim white tropical suit. The heels of his beige shoes clicked on the tiles like dice. He stopped at the side counter to make a phone call—he could have been telephoning or he could have been using it as an excuse to study my abundant profile—and then he went along to the bell captain's desk and I heard him ask the captain to summon him a taxi, as there weren't any at the curb in front. His voice was deep; he spoke Spanish with a slight accent that could have been French. He had a very full head of brown hair teased into an Afro and he had a strong actorish face like those of Italians who play Roman gigolos in Technicolor films. He went right outside again, presumably to wait for his taxi. I dubbed him The Afro. If he'd actually looked at me I hadn't detected it— he had the air of a man who only looked at pretty girls or mirrors.

The third one was a bit more thickly muscled and his baldness was striking. He had a squarish face and a high pink dome above it. Brynner and Savalas shave their heads; why not Gregorius?

This one walked with an athlete's bounce—he came down about half past five in khaki Bermudas and a casual Hawaiian tourist shirt; he went into the bar and when I glanced in on my way past to the gents' he was drinking something tall and chatting up a buxom dark-haired woman whose bored pout was beginning to give way to loose fourth-drink smiles. From that angle and in that light the bald man looked very American but I didn't cross him off the list; I'd need more to go on.

I was characterizing each of them by hair style but it was useless for anything but shorthand identification. Gregorius, when last seen by witnesses, had been wearing his hair long and black, shoulder-length hippie style. None of these three had hair remotely like that but the sightings had been five weeks ago and he might have changed it ten times in the interval.

The Blond was on a poolside chaise toweling himself dry when I returned from the loo to the lobby. I saw him shake his head back with that gesture used more often by women than by men to get the hair back out of their eyes. He was watching a girl dive off the board; he was smiling.

I had both room keys in my pocket and didn't need to stop at the desk. It was time for the first countermove. I went up in the elevator and walked past the door of my own room and entered the connecting room with the key Cartlidge had obtained for me. It was a bit elaborate but Gregorius had been known to hook a detonator to a doorknob and it would have been easy enough for him to stop a chambermaid in the hall: "My friend, the very fat American, I've forgotten the number of his room."

So I entered my room through the connecting door rather than from the hall. The precaution was sensible; I didn't really expect to find anything amiss but I didn't want to risk giving Myerson the satisfaction of hearing how they'd scraped sections of blubber off the ceiling.

Admittedly I am fat but nevertheless you could have knocked me over with a feather at that moment.

Because the bomb was wired to the doorknob.

I looked at it from across the room. I didn't go any closer; I returned to the adjoining room, got the Do Not Disturb placard and went out into the hall and hung the placard on the booby-trapped doorknob. One of the many differences between a professional like Gregorius and a professional like Charlie Dark is that Charlie Dark tends to worry about the possibility that an innocent hotel maid might open the door.

Then I made the call from the phone in the adjoining room. Within ninety seconds Cartlidge was there with his four-man bomb squad. They'd been posted in the basement beside the hotel's wine cellar.

The crew went to work in flak vests and armored masks. Next door I sat with Cartlidge and he looked gloomy. "When it doesn't explode he'll know we defused it." But then he always looks gloomy.

I said, "He didn't expect this one to get me. It's a signal flag, that's all. He wants me to sweat first."

"And are you? Sweating?"

"At this altitude? Heavens no."

"I guess it's true. The shoptalk. You've got no nerves."

"No nerves," I agreed, "but plenty of nerve. Cheer up, you may get his fingerprints off the device."

"Gregorius? No chance."

Any of the three could have planted it. We could ask the Venezuelans to interrogate every employee in the hotel to find out who might have expressed an interest in my room but it probably would be fruitless and in any case Gregorius would know as soon as the interrogations started and it would only drive him to ground. No; at least now I knew he was in the hotel.

Scruples can be crippling. If our positions had been reversed—if I'd been Gregorius with one of three men after me—I'd simply kill all three of them. That's how Gregorius would solve the problem.

Sometimes honor is an awful burden. I feel such an anachronism.

The bomb squad lads carried the device out

in a heavy armored canister. They wouldn't find clues, not the kind that would help. We already knew the culprit's identity.

Cartlidge said, "What next?"

"Here," I said, and tapped the mound of my belly, "I know which one he is. But I don't know it here yet." Finger to temple. "It needs to rise to the surface."

"You *know*?"

"In the gut. The gut knows. I have a fact somewhere in there. It's there; I just don't know what it is."

I ordered up two steak dinners from room service and when the tray-table arrived I had Cartlidge's men make sure there were no bombs under the domed metal covers. Then Cartlidge sat and watched with a kind of awed disgust while I ate everything. He rolled back his cuff and looked at his watch. "We've only got about fourteen hours."

"I know."

"If you spend the rest of the night in this room he can't get at you. I've got men in the hall and men outside watching the windows. You'll be safe."

"I don't get paid to be safe." I put away the cheesecake—both portions—and felt better.

Of course it might prove to be a bullet, a blade, a drop of poison, a garrote, a bludgeon—it could but it wouldn't. It would be a bomb. He'd challenged me and he'd play it through by his own perverse rules.

Cartlidge complained, "There's just too many places he could hide a satchel bomb. That's the genius of plastique—it's so damn portable."

"And malleable. You can shape it to anything." I looked under the bed, then tried it. Too soft: it sagged near collapse when I lay back. "I'm going to sleep on it."

And so I did until shortly after midnight when someone knocked and I came awake with the reverberating memory of a muffled slam of sound. Cartlidge came into the room carrying a portable radio transceiver—a walkie-talkie. "Bomb went off in one of the elevators."

"Anybody hurt?"

"No. It was empty. Probably it was a grenade—the boys are examining the damage. Here, I meant to give you this thing before. I know you're not much for gizmos and gadgets but it helps us all keep in touch with one another. Even cavemen had smoke signals, right?"

"All right." I thought about the grenade in the elevator and then went back to bed.

In the morning I ordered up two breakfasts; while they were en route I abluted and clothed the physique that Myerson detests so vilely. One reason why I don't diet seriously is that I don't wish to cease offending him. For a few minutes then I toyed with Cartlidge's walkie-talkie. It even had my name on it, printed onto a plastic strip.

When Cartlidge arrived under the little dark cloud he always carries above him I was putting on my best tie and a jaunty face.

"What's got you so cheerful?"

"I lost Gregorius once. Today I'm setting it right."

"You're sure? I hope you're right."

I went down the hall. Cartlidge hurried to catch up; he tugged my sleeve as I reached for the elevator button. "Let's use the fire stairs, all right?" Then he pressed the walkie-talkie into my hand; I'd forgotten it. "He blew up one elevator last night."

"With nobody in it," I pointed out. "Doesn't it strike you as strange? Look, he only grenaded the elevator to stampede me in to using the stairs. I suggest you send your bomb squad lads to check out the stairs. Somewhere between here and the ground floor they'll doubtless find a plastique device wired to a pressure-plate under one of the treads, probably set to detonate under a weight of not less than two hundred and fifty pounds."

He gaped at me, then ran back down the hall to phone. I waited for him to return and then we entered the elevator. His eyes had gone opaque. I pressed the lobby-floor button and we rode down; I could hear his breathing. The doors slid open and we stepped out into the lobby and

Cartlidge wiped the sweat off his face. He gave me a wry inquiring look. "I take it you found your fact."

"I think so."

"Want to share it?"

"Not just yet. Not until I'm sure. Let's get to the conference building."

We used the side exit. The car was waiting, engine running, driver armed.

I could have told Cartlidge which one was Gregorius but there was a remote chance I was wrong and I didn't like making a fool of myself.

Caracas is a curiously Scandinavian city—the downtown architecture is modern and sterile; even the hillside slums are colorful and appear clean. The wealth of 20th century oil has shaped the city and there isn't much about its superficial appearance, other than the Spanish-language neon signs, to suggest it's a Latin town. Traffic is clotted with big expensive cars and the boulevards are self-consciously elegant. Most of the establishments in the central shopping district are branches of American and European companies: banks, appliances, couturiers, Cadillac showrooms. It doesn't look the sort of place where bombs could go off: Terrorism doesn't suit it. One pictures Gregorius and his kind in the shabby crumbling wretched rancid passageways of Cairo or Beirut. Caracas? No; too hygienic.

As we parked the car the walkie-talkies crackled with static. It was one of Cartlidge's lads—they'd found the armed device on the hotel's fire stairs. Any heavy man could have set it off. But by then I was no longer surprised by how indiscriminate Gregorius could be, his chilly indifference to the risk to innocents.

We had twenty minutes before the scheduled arrivals of the ministers. I said, "It'll be here somewhere. The bomb."

"Why?"

"It's the only place he can be sure they'll turn up on schedule. Are the three suspects still under surveillance? Check them out."

He hunched over the walkie-talkie while I turned the volume knob of mine down to get rid of the distracting noise and climbed out of the car and had my look around; I bounced the walkie-talkie in my palm absently while I considered the possibilities. The broad steps of the *palacio* where the conference of OPEC ministers would transpire were roped off and guarded by dark-faced cops in Sam Brownes. On the wide landing that separated the two massive flights of steps was a circular fountain that sprayed gaily; normally people sat on the tile ring that contained it but today the security people had cleared the place. There wasn't much of a crowd; it wasn't going to be the kind of spectacle that would draw any public interest. There was no television equipment; a few reporters clustered off to one side with microphones and tape recorders. Routine traffic, both vehicular and pedestrian. That was useful because it meant Gregorius wouldn't be able to get in close; there would be no crowd to screen him.

Still, it wasn't too helpful. All it meant was that he would use a remote-control device to trigger the bomb.

Cartlidge lowered the walkie-talkie from his face. "Did you hear?"

"No." I had difficulty hearing him now as well: the fountain made white noise, the constant gnashing of water, and I moved closer to him while he scowled at my own walkie-talkie. His eyes accused me forlornly. "Would it kill you to use it? All three accounted for. One in his room, one at the hotel pool, one in the dining room having his breakfast."

I looked up past the rooftops. I could see the upper floors of the Hotel Tamanaco—it sits on high ground on the outskirts—and beyond it the tiny swaying shape of a cable car ascending the lofty mountain. Cotton ball clouds over the peaks. Caracas is cupped in the palm of the mountains; its setting is fabulous. I said to Cartlidge, "He has a thing about stairs, doesn't he."

"What?"

"The Hamburg Bahnhof—the bomb was on the platform stairway. The Cairo job, again stairs. This morning, the hotel fire stairs. That's the thing about stairways—they're funnels." I pointed at the flight of stone steps that led up to the portals of the *palacio*. "The ministers have to climb them to get inside."

"Stone stairs. How could he hide a bomb there? You can't get underneath them. Everything's in plain sight."

I brooded upon it. He was right. But it had to be: suddenly I realized it had to be—because I was here and the Saudi's limousine was drawing up at the curb and it meant Gregorius could get both of us with one shot and then I saw the Venezuelan minister walk out of the building and start down the stairs to meet the limousine and it was even more perfect for Gregorius: all three with one explosion. It *had* to be: right here, right now.

Where was the damned thing? Where?

I had the feeling I needed to find the answer within about seven seconds because it was going to take the Venezuelan minister that long to come this far down the steps while the Saudi was getting out of the limousine; already the Venezuelan was nearly down to the fountain and the Saudi was ducking his berobed head and poking a foot out of the car toward the pavement. The entourage of Arab dignitaries had hurried out of the second limousine and they were forming a double column on the steps for the Saudi to walk through; a police captain drew himself to attention, saluting; coming down the stairs the Venezuelan minister had a wide welcoming smile across his austere handsome face.

They'd picked the limousine at random from a motor pool of six. So it couldn't be in the car.

It couldn't be on the steps because the *palacio* had been guarded inside and out for nearly a week and it had been searched half an hour ago by electronic devices, dogs and human eyes.

It couldn't be in the fountain either. That had been too obvious. We'd exercised special care in searching the fountain; it had only been switched on ten minutes earlier. In any case you can't plant a bomb under water because the water absorbs the force of the explosion and all you get is a big bubble and a waterspout.

In other words there was no way for Grego-

rius to have planted a bomb here. And yet I knew he had done so. I knew where Gregorius was; I knew he had field glasses to his eyes and his finger on the remote-control button that would trigger the bomb by radio signal. When the Saudi met the Venezuelan and they shook hands on the steps not a dozen feet from me Gregorius would set it off.

Six seconds now. The Venezuelan came past the fountain.

The walkie-talkie in my hand crackled with static but I didn't turn it up. The mind raced at Grand Prix speed. If he didn't plant the bomb beforehand—and I knew he hadn't—then there had to be a delivery system.

Five seconds. Gregorius: cold, brutal, neat, ingenious. Then I knew—*I* was the bomb.

Four seconds and my arm swung back. It has been a long time since I threw a football and I had to pray the instinct was still in the arm and then I was watching the walkie-talkie soar over the Venezuelan's head and I could only stand and watch while it lofted and descended. It struck the near lip of the fountain and for a moment it looked ready to fall back onto the stairs but then it tipped over the rim and went into the water.

His reaction time would be slowed by distance and the awkwardness of handling binoculars and the unexpectedness of my move. Instinctively he reached for the trigger button but by the time he pressed it the walkie-talkie had gone into the water. The explosion wasn't loud. Water blistered at the surface and a crack appeared in the surrounding rim; little spouts began to break through the shattered concrete; a great frothy mushroom of water bubbled up over the surface and cascaded down the steps.

Nobody was hurt.

We went into the hotel fast. I was talking to Cartlidge: "I assume the one who's still upstairs in his room is the blond one with the crew cut."

"How the hell did you know that?"

"He's Gregorius. He had to have a vantage point."

Gregorius was still there in the room because he'd had no reason to believe we'd tumbled to his identity. He was as conceited as I; he was sure he hadn't made any mistake to give himself away. He was wrong, of course. He'd made only one but it was enough.

Cartlidge's bomb squad lads were our flying wedge. They kicked the door in and we walked right in on him and he looked at all the guns and decided to sit still.

His window overlooked the *palacio* and the binoculars were on the sill. I said to Cartlidge, "Have a look for the transmitter. He hasn't had time to hide it too far away."

The Blond said, "What is this about?" All injured innocence.

I said, "It's finished, Gregorius."

He wasn't going to admit a thing but I did see the brief flash of rage in his eyes; it was all the confirmation I needed. I gave him my best smile. "You'll be pleased to talk in time."

They searched him, handcuffed him, gave the room a toss and didn't find anything; later that day the transmitter turned up in a cleaning-supplies cupboard down the hall.

To this day Cartlidge still isn't sure we got the right man because nobody ever told him what happened after we got Gregorius back to the States. Myerson and I know the truth. The computer kids in Debriefing sweated Gregorius for weeks and finally he broke and they're still analyzing the wealth of information he has supplied. I'd lost interest by that time; my part of it

was finished and I knew from the start that I'd got the right man. I don't make that kind of mistake; it didn't need confirmation from the shabby hypodermics of Debriefing. As I'd said to Myerson, "The binoculars on the windowsill clinched it, of course. When the Venezuelan and the Saudi shook hands he planned to trigger it—it was the best way to hit all three of us. But I knew it had to be The Blond much earlier. I suppose I might have arrested him first before we went looking for the bomb but I wasn't absolutely certain."

"Don't lie," Myerson said. "You wanted him to be watching you in his binoculars—you wanted him to know you were the one who defused him. One of these days your brain's going to slow down a notch or two. Next time maybe it'll blow up before you throw it in the pond. But all right, since you're waiting for me to ask—how did you pick the blond one?"

"We knew until recently he'd worn his hair hippie length."

"So?"

"I saw him at the pool toweling himself dry. I saw him shake his head back the way you do when you want to get the hair back out of your eyes. He had a crew cut. He wouldn't have made that gesture unless he'd cut his hair so recently that he still had the old habit."

Myerson said, "It took you twelve hours to figure that out? You *are* getting old, Charlie."

"And hungry. Have you got anything to eat around here?"

"No."

ERLE STANLEY GARDNER

WHEN THINKING ABOUT Erle Stanley Gardner (1889–1970), numbers pop out that would impress even the most blasé. He created the most famous criminal defense attorney in literature, Perry Mason, when he published *The Case of the Velvet Claws* on March 1, 1933, and went on to produce eighty Mason novels which, in all editions, have sold more than three hundred million copies.

Gardner began his lengthy writing career in the pulps in *Breezy Stories* in 1921, eventually producing hundreds of short stories, countless articles, more than a hundred novels, and numerous nonfiction books on the law and, as a noted outdoorsman, on travel and environmental issues. At the time of his death, he was the bestselling writer in the history of American literature.

The Perry Mason novels were the ultimate in formulaic genre fiction, with the lawyer taking on the role of detective to prove his client innocent at trial, turning at the end to point a finger at the real culprit, who generally broke down and confessed. The television series based on the character, starring Raymond Burr, was enormously successful for nine years, running from September 21, 1957, to May 22, 1966, and showing in reruns pretty much ever since.

The relentless popularity of the Burr TV series suggested it should be tried again, resulting in the 1973 debut of *The New Perry Mason*, a series of hour-long programs starring Monte Markham in the title role and Sharon Acker as Della. Generally criticized as lacking the power of the original series, it was short-lived.

During the 1940s and early 1950s, Mason had a successful career on several radio programs, most notably a Monday-through-Friday afternoon serial with John Larkin as the lawyer and Joan Alexander as a cool Della.

The novels had quickly become so popular that, inevitably, Hollywood wasn't far behind. A half dozen Perry Mason films were made between 1934 and 1937, with Warren William in the first four with different female stars in each, including Mary Astor in the first, *The Case of the Howling Dog* (1934), Margaret Lindsay in the second, *The Case of the Curious Bride* (1935), followed by Genevieve Tobin in *The Case of the Lucky Legs* (1935), and Winifred Shaw in *The Case of the Velvet Claws* (1936). Ricardo Cortez and June Travis starred in *The Case of the Black Cat* (1936), then Donald Woods and Ann Dvorak ended the Warner Brothers series with *The Case of the Stuttering Bishop* (1937).

"Flight into Disaster" was originally published in the May 11, 1952, issue of *This Week Magazine*.

FLIGHT INTO DISASTER

ERLE STANLEY GARDNER

ONLY ONCE BEFORE had the woman in the club car ever known panic—not merely fear but the real panic which paralyzes the senses.

That had been in the mountains when she had tried to take a short cut to camp. When she realized she was lost there was a sudden overpowering desire to run. What was left of her sanity warned her, but panic made her feel that only by flight could she escape the menace of the unknown. The silent mountains, the somber woods, had suddenly become enemies, leering in hostility. Only by running did she feel she could escape—by running—the very worst thing she could have done.

Now, surrounded by the luxury of a crack transcontinental train, she again experienced that same panic. Once more there was that overpowering desire to run.

Someone had searched her compartment while she had been at dinner. She knew it was a man. He had tried to leave things just as he had found them, but there were little things that a woman would have noticed that the man didn't even see. Her plaid coat, which had been hung in the little steel closet so that the back was to the door, had been turned so the buttons were toward the door. A little thing, but a signifi-

cant thing which had been the first to catch her attention, leaving her, for the moment, cold and numb. Now, seated in the club car, she strove to maintain an attitude of outward calm by critically inspecting her hands. Actually she was taking stock of the men who were in the car.

Her problem was complicated by the fact that she was a compactly formed young woman, with smooth lines, clear eyes, a complete quota of curves, and under ordinary circumstances, a latent smile always quivering at the corners of her mouth. It was, therefore, only natural that every male animal in the club car sat up and took notice.

The fat man across the aisle who held a magazine in his pudgy hands was not reading. He sat like a Buddha, motionless, his half-closed, lazy-lidded eyes fixed upon some imaginary horizon far beyond the confines of the car—yet she felt those eyes were taking a surreptitious interest in everything she did. There was something sinister about him, from the big diamond on the middle finger of his right hand to the rather ornate twenty-five-dollar cravat which begged for attention above the bulging expanse of his vest.

Then there was the man in the chair on her right. He hadn't spoken to her but she knew that he was going to, waiting only for an opportunity to make his remark sound like the casual comment of a fellow passenger.

He was in his late twenties, bronzed by exposure, steely-blue of eye. His mouth held the firmness of a man who has learned to command first himself and then others. The train lurched. The man's hand reached for the glass on the little stand between them. He glanced apprehensively at her skirt.

"Sorry," he said.

"It didn't spill," she replied almost automatically.

"I'll lower the danger point," he said, raising the glass to his lips. "Going all the way through? I'm getting off at six o'clock in a cold Wyoming morning."

For a moment her panic-numbed brain failed to appreciate the full significance of his remark, then she experienced a sudden surge of relief. Here, then, was one man whom she could trust. She knew that the man who had searched her baggage hadn't found what he wanted because she had it with her, neatly folded, fastened to the bottom of her left foot by strong adhesive tape. Therefore the enemy would stay on the train as long as she was on it, waiting, watching, growing more and more desperate, until at last, perhaps in the dead of night, he would . . . She knew only too well that he would stop at nothing. One murder had already been committed.

But now she had found one person whom she could trust, a man who had no interest in the thing she was hiding, a man who might well be a possible protector.

He seemed mildly surprised at her sudden friendliness.

"I didn't know this train stopped anywhere at that ungodly hour," she ventured, smiling.

"A flag stop," he explained.

Across the aisle the fat man had not moved a muscle, yet she felt absolutely certain that those glittering eyes were concentrating on her and that he was listening as well as watching.

"You live in Wyoming?" she asked.

"I did as a boy. Now I'm going back. I lived and worked on my uncle's cattle ranch. He died and left it to me. At first I thought I'd sell it. It would bring a small fortune. But now I'm tired of the big cities, I'm going back to live on the ranch."

"Won't it be frightfully lonely?"

"At times."

She wanted to cling to him now, dreading the time when she would have to go back to her compartment.

She felt the trainmen must have a master key which could open even a bolted door—in the event of sickness, or if a passenger rang for help. There *must* be a master key which would manipulate even a bolted door. And if trainmen had such a key, the man who had searched her compartment would have one.

Frank Hardwick, before he died, had warned her. "Remember," he had said, "they're everywhere. They're watching you when you don't know you're being watched. When you think you're running away and into safety, you'll simply be rushing into a carefully laid trap."

She hoped there was no trace of the inner tension within her as she smiled at the man on her right. "Do tell me about the cattle business," she said . . .

All night she had crouched in her compartment, watching the door, waiting for that first flicker of telltale motion which would show the doorknob was being turned. Then she would scream, pound on the walls of the compartment, make sufficient commotion to spread an alarm.

Nothing had happened. Probably that was the way "they" had planned it. They'd let her spend one sleepless night, then when fatigue had numbed her senses . . .

The train abruptly slowed. She glanced at her wristwatch, saw that it was 5:55, and knew the train was stopping for the man who had inherited the cattle ranch. Howard Kane was the name he had given her after she had encouraged him to tell her all about himself. Howard Kane, twenty-eight, unmarried, presumably wealthy, his mind scarred by battle experiences, seeking the healing quality of the big, silent places, the one man on the train whom she knew she could trust.

There was a quiet competency about him, one felt he could handle any situation—and now he was getting off the train.

Suddenly a thought gripped her—"They" would hardly be expecting her to take the initiative. "They" always kept the initiative—that was why they always seemed so damnably efficient, so utterly invincible.

They chose the time, the place and the manner—give them that advantage, and . . .

There wasn't time to reason the thing out. She jerked open the door of the little closet, whipped out her plaid coat, turned the fur collar up around her neck, and, as the train eased to a creaking stop, opened the door of her compartment and thrust out a cautious head.

The corridor was deserted.

She could hear the vestibule door being opened at the far end of the Pullman.

She ran to the opposite end of the car, fumbled for a moment with the fastenings of the vestibule door on the side next to the double track, then got it open and raised the platform.

Cold morning air, tanged with high elevation, rushed in to meet her, dispelling the train atmosphere, stealing the warmth from her garments.

The train started to move. She scrambled down the stairs, jumped for the graveled roadbed by the side of the track.

The train gathered speed. Dark, silent cars whizzed past her with continuing acceleration until the noise of the wheels became a mere hum. The steel rails readjusted themselves to the cold morning air, giving cracking sounds of protest. Overhead, stars blazed in steady brilliance. To the east was the first trace of daylight.

She looked for a town. There was none.

She could make out the faint outlines of a loading corral and cattle chute. Somewhere behind her was a road. An automobile was standing on this road, the motor running. Headlight sent twin

cones of illumination knifing the darkness, etching into brilliance the stunted sagebrush shivering nervously under the impact of a cold north wind.

Two men were talking. A door slammed. She started running frantically.

"Wait!" she called. "Wait for me!"

Back on the train the fat man, fully dressed and shaved, contemplated the open vestibule door, then padded back to the recently vacated compartment and walked in.

He didn't even bother to search the baggage that had been left behind. Instead he sat down in the chair, held a telegraph blank against a magazine, and wrote out his message:

THE BUNGLING SEARCH TRICK DID THE JOB. SHE'S LEFT THE TRAIN. IT ONLY REMAINS TO CLOSE THE TRAP. I'LL GET OFF AT THE FIRST PLACE WHERE I CAN RENT A PLANE AND CONTACT THE SHERIFF.

Ten minutes later the fat man found the porter. "I find the elevation bothering me," he said. "I'm going to have to leave the train. Get the conductor."

"You won't get no lower by gettin' off," the porter said.

"No, but I'll get bracing fresh air and a doctor who'll give me a heart stimulant. I've been this way before. Get the conductor."

This time the porter saw the twenty-dollar bill in the fat man's fingers.

Seated between the two men in the warm interior of the car, she sought to concoct a convincing story.

Howard Kane said, by way of introduction, "This is Buck Doxey. I'm afraid I didn't catch your name last night."

"Nell Lindsay," she said quickly.

Buck Doxey, granite-faced, kept one hand on the steering wheel while he doffed a five-gallon hat. "Pleased to meet yuh, ma'am."

She sensed his cold hostility, his tight-lipped disapproval.

Howard Kane gently prodded for an explanation.

"It was a simple case of cause and effect," she said, laughing nervously. "It was so stuffy in the car I didn't sleep at all.

"So," she went on quickly, "I decided that I'd get out for a breath of fresh air. When the train slowed and I looked at my wristwatch I knew it was your stop and . . . Well, I expected the train would be there for at least a few minutes. I couldn't find a porter to get the vestibule open, so I did it myself, and jumped down to the ground. That was where I made my mistake."

"Go on," he said.

"At a station you step down to a platform that's level with the tracks. But here I jumped onto a slanting shoulder of gravel, and sprawled flat. When I got up, the step of the car was so far above me . . . Well, you have to wear skirts to understand what I mean."

Kane nodded gravely. Buck turned his head and gave Kane a quartering glance.

She said, "I guess I could have made it at that if I'd had sense enough to pull my skirt all the way up to the hips, but I couldn't make it on that first try and there wasn't time for a second one. The train started to move. Good heavens, they must have just *thrown* you off!"

"I'm traveling light," Kane said.

"Well," she told him, "that's the story. Now just what do I do?"

"Why, you accept our hospitality, of course."

"I couldn't . . . couldn't wait here for the next train?"

"Nothing stops here except to discharge passengers coming from a division point," he said.

"But there's a . . . station there. Isn't there someone on duty?"

"Only when cattle are being shipped," Buck Doxey explained. "This is a loading point."

"Oh."

She settled back against the seat, and was conscious of a reassuring masculine friendship on her right side, a cold detachment on her left side.

"I suppose it's horribly ravenous of me, but do we get to the ranch for breakfast?"

"I'm afraid not," Kane said. "It's slow going. Only sixty feet of the road is paved."

"Sixty feet?"

"That's right. We cross the main transcontinental highway about five miles north of here."

"What *do* we do about breakfast?"

"Well," Kane said, "in the trunk of the car there's a coffee pot and a canteen of water. I'm quite certain Buck brought along a few eggs and some ham . . ."

"You mean you stop right out here in the open and cook?"

"When yuh stop here, you're in the open, ma'am," Buck said and somehow made it seem his words were in answer to some unjustified criticism.

She gave him her best smile. "Would it be impertinent to ask when?"

"In this next coulee . . . right here . . . right now."

The road slanted down to a dry wash that ran east and west. The perpendicular north bank broke the force of the north wind. Buck attested to the lack of traffic on the road by stopping the car squarely in the ruts.

They watched the sun rise over the plateau country, and ate breakfast. She hoped that Buck Doxey's cold disapproval wouldn't communicate itself to Howard Kane.

When Buck produced a battered dishpan, she said, "As the only woman present I claim the right to do the dishes."

"Women," Buck said, "are . . ." and abruptly checked himself.

She laughingly pushed him aside and rolled up her sleeves. "Where's the soap?"

As she was finishing the last dish she heard the motor of the low-flying plane.

All three looked up.

The plane, which had been following the badly rutted road, banked into a sharp turn.

"Sure givin' us the once-over," Buck said, his eyes steady on Kane's face. "One of 'em has binoculars and he's as watchful as a cattle buyer at a loading chute. Don't yuh think it's about time we find out what we've got into, Boss?"

"I suppose it is," Kane said. Before her startled mind could counter his action, Buck Doxey picked up the purse which she had left lying on the running-board of the car.

She flew toward him.

Doxey's bronzed, steel fingers wrapped around her wet wrist. "Take it easy, ma'am," he said. "Take it easy."

He pushed her back, found her driving license. "The real name," he drawled, "seems to be Jane Marlow."

"Anything else?" Kane asked.

"Gobs of money, lipstick, keys and . . . Gosh, what a bankroll."

She went for him blindly.

Doxey said, "Now, ma'am, I'm goin' to have to spank yuh if yuh keep on like this."

The plane circled, its occupants obviously interested in the scene on the ground below.

"Now—here's something else," Doxey said, taking out a folded newspaper clipping.

She suddenly went limp. There was no use in further pretense.

Doxey read aloud, "'Following the report of an autopsy surgeon, police, who had never been entirely satisfied that the unexplained death of Frank Hardwick was actually a suicide, are searching for his attractive secretary, Jane Marlow. The young woman reportedly had dinner with Hardwick in a downtown restaurant the night of his death.

"'Hardwick, after leaving Miss Marlow, according to her story, went directly to the apartment of Eva Ingram, a strikingly beautiful model who has however convinced police that she was dining out. Within a matter of minutes after entering the Ingram apartment, Hardwick either jumped or fell from the eighth story window.

"'With the finding of a witness who says Frank Hardwick was accompanied at least as far as the apartment door by a young woman whose

description answers that of Jane Marlow, and evidence indicating several thousand dollars was removed from a concealed floor safe in Hardwick's office, police are anxious once more to question Miss Marlow. So far their efforts have definitely not been crowned with success.'

"And here's a picture of this young lady," Buck said, "with some more stuff under it.

"'Jane Marlow, secretary of scientist who jumped from apartment window to his death, is now sought by police after witness claims to have seen her arguing angrily with Frank Hardwick when latter was ringing bell at front door of apartment house from which Hardwick fell or jumped to sidewalk.'"

Overhead, the plane suddenly ceased its circling and took off in a straight line to the north.

As the car proceeded northward, Buck put on speed, deftly avoiding the bad places in the road.

Jane Marlow, who had lapsed into hopeless silence, tried one more last desperate attempt when they crossed the paved road. "Please," she said, "let me out here. I'll catch a ride back to Los Angeles and report to the police."

Kane's eyes asked a silent question of the driver.

"Nope," Buck said decisively. "That plane was the sheriff's scout plane. He'll expect us to hold you. I don't crave to have no more trouble over women."

"All right," Jane said in a last burst of desperation, "I'll tell you the whole story. Then I'll leave it to your patriotism. I was secretary to Frank Hardwick. He was working on something that had to do with cosmic rays."

"I know," Doxey interrupted sarcastically. "And he dictated his secret formula to you."

"Don't be silly," she said, "but he *did* know that he was in danger. He told me that if anything happened to him, to take something, which he gave me, to a certain individual."

"Just keep on talking," Buck said. "Tell us about the money."

Her eyes were desperate. "Mr. Hardwick had a concealed floor safe in the office. He left reserve cash there for emergencies. He gave me the combination, told me that if anything happened to him, I was to go to that safe, take the money and deliver it and a certain paper to a certain scientist in Boston."

Buck's smile of skepticism was certain to influence Kane even more than words.

"Frank Hardwick never jumped out of any window," she went on. "They were waiting for him, and they threw him out."

"Or," Buck said, "a certain young lady became jealous, followed him, got him near an open window and then gave a sudden, unexpected shove. It *has* been done, you know."

"And people *have* told the truth," she blazed, "*I* don't enjoy what I'm doing. I consider it a duty to my country—and I'll probably be murdered, just as Frank Hardwick was."

"Now listen," Kane said. "Nice little girls don't jump off trains before daylight in the morning and tell the kind of stories you're telling. You got off that train because you were running away from someone."

She turned to Kane. "I was hoping that *you* would understand."

"He understands," Buck said, and laughed.

After that she was silent . . .

Overhead, from time to time, the plane came circling back. Once it was gone for nearly forty-five minutes and she dared to hope they had thrown it off the track, but later she realized it had only gone to refuel and then it was back above them once more.

It was nearly nine when Buck turned off the rutted road and headed toward a group of unpainted, squat, log cabins which seemed to be bracing themselves against the cold wind while waiting for the winter snow. Back of the buildings were timbered mountains.

The pilot of the plane had evidently spotted the ranch long ago. Hardly had Buck turned off the road than the plane came circling in for a landing.

Jane Marlow had to lean against the cold wind as she walked from the car to the porch of the cabin. Howard Kane held the door open for her, and she found herself inside a cold room which fairly reeked of masculine tenancy, with a paper-littered desk, guns, deer and elk horns.

Within a matter of seconds she heard the pound of steps on the porch, the door was flung open, and the fat man and a companion stood on the threshold.

"Well, Jane," the fat man said, "you gave us quite a chase, didn't you?" He turned to the others.

"Reckon I'd better introduce myself, boys." He reached in his pocket, then took out a wallet and tossed it carelessly on the desk.

"I'm John Findlay of the FBI," he said.

"That's a lie," she said. "Can't you understand? This man is an enemy. Those credentials are forged."

"Well, ma'am," the other newcomer said, stepping forward, "there ain't nothing wrong with my credentials. I'm the sheriff here, and I'm taking you into custody."

He took her purse, said, "You just might have a gun in here."

He opened the purse. Findlay leaned over to look, said, "It's all there."

"Come on, Miss Marlow," the sheriff said, "You're going back in that plane."

"That plane of yours holds three people?" Findlay asked.

The sheriff looked appraisingly at the fat man. "Not us three."

"I can fly the crate," Findlay said. "I'll take the prisoner in, lock her up and then fly back for you and . . ."

"No, no, no!" Jane Marlow screamed. "Don't you see, can't you realize, this man isn't an officer. I'd never get there. He . . ."

"Shut up," the sheriff said.

"Sheriff, please! You're being victimized. Call up the FBI and you'll find out that . . ."

"I've already called up the Los Angeles office of the FBI," the sheriff said.

Kane's brows leveled. "Was that because you were suspicious, Sheriff?"

"Findlay himself suggested it."

Jane was incredulous. "You mean they told you that . . . ?"

"They vouched for him in every way," the sheriff said. "They told me he'd been sent after Jane Marlow, and to give him every assistance. Now I've got to lock you up and . . ."

"She's my responsibility, Sheriff," Findlay said.

The sheriff frowned, then said. "Okay, I'll fly back and send a deputy out with a car."

"Very well," Findlay agreed. "I'll see that she stays put."

Jane Marlow said desperately, "I presume that when Mr. Findlay told you to call the FBI office in Los Angeles, he gave you the number so you wouldn't have to waste time getting it through an operator, didn't he?"

"Why not?" the sheriff said, smiling good-humoredly. "He'd be a hell of an FBI man if he didn't know his own telephone number."

The fat man fished a cigar from his pocket. Biting off the end and scraping a match into flame, he winked at the sheriff.

Howard Kane said to Findlay, "Mind if I ask a question?"

"Hell no. Go right ahead."

"I'd like to know something of the facts in this case. If you've been working on the case you'd know . . ."

"Sure thing," Findlay agreed, getting his cigar burning evenly. "She worked for Hardwick, who was having an affair with a model. We followed him to the model's apartment. They had a quarrel. Hardwick's supposed to have jumped out of the window. She went to his office and took five thousand dollars out of the safe. The money's in her purse."

"So she was jealous?"

"Jealous and greedy. Don't forget she got five grand out of the safe."

"I was following my employer's specific instructions in everything I did," Jane said.

Findlay grinned.

"What's more," she blazed, "Frank Hardwick wasn't having any affair with that model.

He was lured to her apartment. It was a trap and he walked right in."

Findlay said, "Yeah. The key we found in his vest pocket fitted the apartment door. He must have found it on the street and was returning it to the owner as an act of gallantry."

The sheriff laughed.

Howard Kane glanced speculatively at the very young woman. "She doesn't look like a criminal."

"Oh, thank you!" she blazed.

Findlay's glance was patronizing. "How many criminals have you seen, buddy?"

Doxey rolled a cigarette. His eyes narrowed against the smoke as he squatted down cowboy fashion on the backs of his highheeled riding boots. "Ain't no question but what she's the one who jimmied the safe, is there?"

"The money's in her purse," Findlay said.

"Any accomplices?" Buck asked.

"No. It was a combination of jealousy and greed." Findlay glanced inquiringly at the sheriff.

"I'll fly in and send that car out," the sheriff said.

"Mind if I fly in with yuh and ride back with the deputy, Sheriff?" Buck asked eagerly. "I'd like to see this country from the air once. There's a paved road other side of that big mountain where the ranger has his station. I'd like to look down on it. Some day they'll connect us up. Now it's an hour's ride by horse . . ."

"Sure," the sheriff agreed. "Glad to have you."

"Just give me time enough to throw a saddle on a horse," Doxey said. "Kane might want to ride out and look the ranch over. Yuh won't mind, Sheriff?"

"Make it snappy," the sheriff said.

Buck Doxey went to the barn and after a few minutes returned leading a dilapidated-looking range pony saddled and bridled. He casually dropped the reins in front of the ranch "office," and called inside:

"Ready any time you are, Sheriff."

They started for the airplane. Buck stopped at the car to get a map from the glove compartment, then hurried to join the sheriff. The propeller of the plane gave a half-turn, stopped, gave another half-turn, the motor sputtered, then roared into action. A moment later the plane became the focal point of a trailing dust cloud, then raised and swept over the squat log buildings in a climbing turn and headed south.

Jane Marlow and Kane watched it through the window until it became but a speck.

Howard Kane said, "Now, Mr. Findlay, I'd like to ask you a few questions."

"Sure, go right ahead."

"You impressed the sheriff very cleverly," Kane said, "but I'd like to have you explain . . ."

"Now that it's too late," Jane Marlow blazed indignantly. "You've let him . . ."

Kane motioned her to silence. "Don't you see, Miss Marlow, I had to get rid of the sheriff. He represents the law, right or wrong. But if this man is an impostor, I can protect you against him."

Findlay's hand moved with such rapidity that the big diamond made a streak of glittering light.

"Okay, wise guy," he said. "Try protecting her against this."

Kane rushed the gun.

Sheer surprise slowed Findlay's reaction time. Kane's fist flashed out in a swift arc, just before the gun roared.

The fat man moved with amazing speed. He rolled with the punch, spun completely around on his heel and jumped back, the automatic held to his body, his eyes glittering with rage.

"Get 'em up," he said.

The cold animosity of his tone showed that this time there would be no hesitancy.

Slowly Kane's hands came up.

"Turn around," Findlay said. "Move over by that window. Press your face against the wall. Give me your right hand, Kane . . . Now the left hand."

A smooth leather thong, which had been defty knotted into a slipknot, was jerked tight, then knotted into a quick half hitch.

The girl, taking advantage of Findlay's preoccupation, flung herself on him.

The bulk of Findlay's big shoulders absorbed the onslaught without making him even shift the position of his feet. He jerked the leather thong into a last knot, turned and struck the girl in the pit of the stomach.

She wobbled about for a moment on rubbery legs, then fell to the floor.

"Now, young lady," Findlay said, "you've caused me a hell of a lot of trouble. I'll just take the thing you're carrying in your left shoe. I could tell from the way you were limping there was something . . ."

He jerked off the shoe, looked inside, seemed puzzled, then suddenly grabbed the girl's stockinged foot.

She kicked and tried to scream, but the wind had been knocked out of her.

Findlay reached casual hands up to the top of her stocking, jerked it loose without bothering to unfasten the garters, pulled the adhesive tape off the bottom of the girl's foot, ran out to the car, and jumped in.

"Well, what do you know!" he exclaimed. "The damn yokel took the keys with him . . . So there's a paved road on the other side of the mountains, is there?"

"Come on, horse, I guess there's a trail we can find. If we can't they'll never locate us in all that timber."

Moving swiftly, the fat man ran over to where the horse was standing on three legs, drowsing in the sunlight.

Findlay gathered up the reins, thrust one foot in the stirrup, grabbed the saddle, front and rear, and swung himself awkwardly into position.

Jane heard a shrill animal squeal of rage. The sleepy-looking horse, transformed into a bundle of dynamite, heaved himself into the air, ears laid back along his neck.

The fat man, grabbing the horn of the saddle, clung with frenzied desperation.

"Well," Kane asked, "are you going to untie me, or just stand there gawking?"

She ran to him then, frantically tugging at the knot.

The second his hands were freed Kane went into action.

Findlay, half out of the saddle, clung drunkenly to the pitching horse for a moment, then went into the air, turned half over and came down with a jar that shook the earth.

Kane emerged from the cabin holding a rifle.

"All right, Findlay, it's my turn now," Kane said. "Don't make a move for that gun."

The shaken Findlay seemed to have trouble orienting himself. He turned dazedly toward the sound of the voice, clawed for his gun.

Kane, aiming the rifle carefully, shot it out of his hand.

"Now, ma'am," Kane said, "if you want to get that paper out of his pocket . . ."

She ran to Findlay, her feet fairly flying over the ground despite the fact that she was wearing only one shoe and the other foot had neither shoe nor stocking . . .

Shortly before noon Jane Marlow decided to invade the sacred precincts of Buck Doxey's thoroughly masculine kitchen to prepare lunch. Howard Kane showed his respect for Findlay's resourcefulness by keeping him covered despite the man's bound wrists.

"Buck is going to hate me for this," she said. "Not that he doesn't hate me enough already—and I don't know why."

"Buck's soured on women," Kane explained. "I tried to tip you off. He was engaged to a girl in Cheyenne. No one knows exactly what happened, but they split up. I think she's as miserable as he is, but neither one will make the first move. But for heaven's sake don't try to rearrange his kitchen according to ideas of feminine efficiency. Just open a can of something and make coffee."

Findlay said, "I don't suppose there's any use trying to make a deal with you two."

Kane scornfully sighted along the gun by way of answer.

Jane, opening drawers in the kitchen, trying to locate the utensils, inadvertently stumbled on Buck Doxey's private heartache. A drawer containing letters, and the photograph of a girl.

The photograph had been torn into several pieces, and then laboriously pasted together and covered with Cellophane.

The front of the picture was inscribed "To Buck with all my heart, Pearl."

Jane felt a surge of guilt at even having opened the drawer, but feminine curiosity caused her to hesitate long enough before closing it to notice Pearl's return address in the upper left-hand corner of one of the envelopes addressed to Buck Doxey . . .

It was as they were finishing lunch that they heard the roar of the plane.

They went to the door to watch it turn into the teeth of the cold north wind, settle to a landing, then taxi up to the low log buildings.

The sheriff and Buck Doxey started running toward the cabins, and it was solace to Jane Marlow's pride to see the look of almost comic relief on the face of the sheriff as he saw Kane with the rifle and Findlay with bound wrists.

Jane heard the last part of Doxey's hurried explanation to Kane.

"Wouldn't trust a woman that far but her story held together and his didn't. I thought you'd understand what I was doing. I flew in with the sheriff just so I could call the FBI in Los Angeles. What do you know? Findlay is a badly wanted enemy spy. They want him bad as . . . How did *you* make out?"

Kane grinned. "I decided to give Findlay a private third-degree. He answered my questions with a gun. If it hadn't been for that horse . . ."

Buck's face broke into a grin. "He fell for that one?"

"Fell for it, and off it," Kane said.

"If he hadn't been a fool tenderfoot he'd have noticed that I led the horse out from the corral instead of riding him over. Old Fox is a rodeo horse, one of the best bucking broncs in Wyoming. Perfectly gentle until he feels it's time to do his stuff, and then he gives everything he has until he hears the ten-second whistle. I sort of figured Findlay might try something before I could sell the sheriff a bill of goods and get back."

It had been sheer impulse which caused Jane Marlow to leave the train early in the morning.

It was also sheer impulse which caused her to violate the law by forging Pearl's name to a telegram as she went through Cheyenne.

The telegram was addressed to Buck Doxey, care of the Forest Ranger Station and read:

BUCK I AM SO PROUD OF YOU. PEARL.

Having started the message on its way, Jane looked up Pearl and casually told her of the torn picture which had been so laboriously pasted together.

Half an hour later Jane was once more speeding East aboard the sleek streamliner, wondering whether her efforts on behalf of Cupid had

earned her the undying enmity of two people, or had perhaps been successful.

When she reached Omaha two telegrams were delivered. One was from Howard Kane and read simply:

YOU WERE SO RIGHT. IT GETS TERRIBLY LONELY AT TIMES. HOLD A DINNER DATE OPEN FOR TONIGHT. YOU NEED A BODYGUARD ON YOUR MISSION AND I AM FLYING TO CHICAGO TO MEET YOU AT TRAIN AND DISCUSS THE WYOMING CLIMATE AS A PERMANENT PLACE OF RESIDENCE. LOVE, HOWARD

The second telegram was the big surprise. It read:

I GUESS I HAD IT COMING. PEARL AND I BOTH SEND LOVE. I GUESS I JUST NEVER REALIZED WOMEN ARE LIKE THAT. YOURS HUMBLY, BUCK DOXEY.

OLEN STEINHAUER

THE INTERNATIONALLY BESTSELLING Olen Steinhauer (1970–   ) has carved out several niches in the demanding literary category of espionage fiction. One way in which he has made the subject his own has been for the peripatetic author to live in numerous Eastern European countries to engage in deep research. When he writes about Hungary or Romania or the Czech Republic, he knows what he's writing about, giving his novels an extraordinary authenticity.

He took on the challenging goal of writing about the Cold War in historical breadth, with each of the five novels in what he termed his "Yalta Boulevard Sequence" set in a different decade. *The Bridge of Sighs* (2003), his first published book, was set in 1948; *The Confession* (2004) in 1956; *36 Yalta Boulevard* (2005) in 1966–1967; *Liberation Movements* (2006) from 1968 to 1975; and *Victory Square* (2007) in 1989.

Steinhauer followed this quintet of award-winning novels with a trilogy of espionage adventures that was focused on the post-9/11 world, beginning with *The Tourist* (2009), which has been translated into twenty-five languages. This was followed by *The Nearest Exit* (2010), which won the Hammett Prize, awarded to the best literary crime novel of the year by the International Crime Writers Association. The third book in the sequence was *An American Spy* (2012) which, like its predecessors, was a critical and commercial success.

His more recent books continue to have an international flavor. *The Cairo Affair* (2014) is set in Budapest, then moves to Cairo and Libya during the Arab Spring. *All the Old Knives* (2015) moves between Vienna another foreign country—California. *The Middleman* (2018) deals with domestic American terrorism.

The highly cinematic books have often been optioned for films. *All the Old Knives* is in production by Chockstone Pictures, directed by James Marsh and starring Michelle Williams and Chris Pine, featuring Steinhauer's own screenplay. Sony Pictures acquired *The Tourist* some years ago for Doug Liman to direct but it has not yet been made. Steinhauer has also been hired to write the screenplay for *The Nearest Exit*. He also created the television series *Berlin Station* (2016–2019), which lasted for twenty-nine episodes, and for which he wrote several scripts and served as executive producer for ten episodes.

"You Know What's Going On" was originally published in *Agents of Treachery* edited by Otto Penzler (New York, Vintage, 2010).

YOU KNOW WHAT'S GOING ON

OLEN STEINHAUER

PAUL

WHAT TROUBLED HIM MOST was that he was afraid to die. Paul believed, though he had no evidence of it, that other spies did not suffer from this. But evidence holds little sway over belief, and so it was for him.

He thought of Sam. The last time they'd spoken had been in Geneva, in the international lounge before Sam's flight back here to Kenya. Years before, they had trained together, and while Paul had done better than Sam on the written tests, it was on the course that Sam had shown himself superior. Later, when he heard rumors that Sam was plagued by suicidal tendencies, he understood. Those unafraid of death usually were better on the course.

But the visit was a surprise. After Rome, the only way he'd expected to hear from Sam was via a disciplinary cable or at the head of a Langley tribunal. But Sam's unexpected invitation to the Aéroport International de Genève had included no threats or reprimands.

"You're just following," Sam told him in the airport. "You're the money, a banker; I'm the deal maker. I'll use my Wallis papers—remember that. You won't have to say a thing,

and they'll want to keep you well so you can take care of the transfer. It's a walk in the park." When Paul, wondering if any operation in Africa could legitimately be called a walk in the park, didn't answer, Sam raised his right index finger and added, "Besides, I'll be right there beside you. Nothing works without this fingerprint."

The target was Aslim Taslam, a six-month-old Somali splinter group formed after an ideological dispute within Al-Shabaab. Over the last month Aslim Taslam had begun an intense drive to raise cash and extend its contacts in preparation for some large-scale action—details unknown. "We're going to nip them in the bud," was the way Sam put it.

Sam had come across them in Rome, just after things had gone to hell—perhaps *because* things had gone to hell. Aslim Taslam was in Italy to establish an alliance with Ansar al-Islam, the very group that he, Paul, Lorenzo, Saïd, and Natalia had been performing surveillance on.

Now, their cover was information. Sam—energetic, perpetual-motion-machine Sam—had contacted Aslim Taslam's Italian envoy with an offer of two million euros for information on the Somali pirates who had been plaguing the Gulf of Aden shipping lanes. Which was why he'd called this rushed meeting in the airport. In three days—on Thursday—Paul would show up in Nairobi as a bank employee. He would carry a small black briefcase, empty. His contact at the hotel would have an identical case containing the special computer. "Once we make the transfer, you board the plane back to Geneva. Simple."

But everything sounded simple from Sam's lips. Rome had sounded simple, too.

"You're still pissed off, aren't you?"

Sam shook his head but avoided Paul's eyes, peering past him at the pretty cashier they'd bought the coffee from. He'd just returned from a working vacation in Kenya, a cross-country race that had left a permanent burn on his cheeks. "It's a damned shame, but these things do happen. I've gotten over it, and you should, too. Keep your head in this job."

"But you can't let it go," Paul said, because he could feel the truth of this. Only three weeks had passed since Rome. "Lorenzo and Saïd—they're dead because of me. It's not a small thing. You deserve to hate me."

Sam's smile was tight-lipped. "Consider this a chance to redeem yourself."

It was a tempting thing to be offered a way to wash such dirt off the surface of his soul. "I'm still surprised."

"We're not all cut out for this kind of work, Paul. You never were. But with those losses I've got no choice but to use you. I can't send Natalia down there—a woman wouldn't do. Don't worry. I'll be right there with you."

That was the first and last time Sam had let it be known that he could see Paul's secret soul. After Rome, the evidence of Paul's cowardice had become too glaring for even an old classmate to ignore. Drinking tall caffe lattes in the too-cold terminal, they had smiled at each other the way they had been trained to smile, and Paul had decided that, even if his old friend didn't feel the same way, he certainly hated Sam.

This radical shift in emotions wasn't new. Paul had always been repelled by those who saw him for what he was. In high school, a girlfriend had told him that he was the most desperate person

she'd ever known. He would do anything to keep breathing. She'd said this after sex, when they both lay half-naked on her parents' couch, and in her adolescent logic she'd meant it as a compliment. To her, it meant that he was more alive than anyone she'd known. It was why she loved him. Yet once she had said it, Paul's love—authentic and all-encompassing—had begun to fade.

In a way, Paul felt more affection for the two very dark strangers questioning him now than he did for Sam, because they didn't know him at all. It was twisted, but that was just the way it was.

"Listen to this guy," said the lanky one in the T-shirt and blue jacket, who had introduced himself as Nabil. He spoke as if he'd learned English from Hollywood, which was probably what he'd done. He was speaking to his friend. "He wants us to believe he doesn't even know Sam Wallis."

"I do not believe it," the friend—one of the two men who'd abducted him at gunpoint—said glumly. His English was closer to the formal yet quaintly awkward English of the rest of Kenya, though neither man was Kenyan.

"I might believe it if I was an idiot," Nabil said. "But I'm not."

Though they were probably still within the Nairobi city limits, both these men, as well as the gunman in the hall, were Somali. He suspected that simply being outside their wild fortress of a country, stuck in a largely Christian nation, made these jihadis nervous. From his low wooden chair, Paul raised his head to meet their gazes, then lowered his eyes again because there was no point. The windowless room was hot, a wet hot, and he found himself dreaming of Swiss air-conditioning. He said, "I work for Banque Salève. I don't know Mr. Wallis personally, but I came here at his request. Where is Mr. Wallis?"

"He wants to know where Sam is," said the unnamed one.

"Hmm," Nabil hummed.

Paul had followed Sam to Nairobi that very morning. It was on the long taxi ride down

Mombasa Road that he'd received the call from Geneva station that Sam had gone missing. Yesterday, a Kenyan witness had spotted him in the neighborhood of Mathare with his Aslim Taslam contact. A van pulled up beside them, and some men wrestled Sam inside and roared off, leaving the contact behind. That hadn't helped his upset stomach, nor had the black Mercedes following him from the airport all the way to the hotel.

There were rumors that Aslim Taslam, in an effort to collect money as quickly as possible, had entered the black-market organ trade. Occasional victims appeared with slices in their lower backs or opened chest cavities, missing vital parts.

But not even in his secret soul did Paul fear this. He could live with fewer hands, with half his kidneys or one less lung. He would never wander willingly into that world of pain, but he didn't fear it with the intensity that he feared the actual end point.

For most people it was the reverse: They feared pain but not death. Paul could not understand this. When a film ends, the viewer can replay it in his head for the rest of his life. But each person is the sole witness to his own life, and when that witness dies, no memory of the viewing remains. Death works backward; it eats up the past, so that even that sweat-stained couch on which he'd stopped loving his girlfriend would cease to exist.

Paul said, "I'm not going to pretend I'm not scared. You've locked that door, and I saw the gun the man outside is wearing. I can only tell you what I know. I work for Banque Salève, and Mr. Wallis asked me to fly here to perform an account transfer."

The unnamed one, who had earlier used his fists on Paul's back, spoke quickly in Arabic, and Nabil said, "All right, then. Let's do the transfer."

"I'll need Mr. Wallis's authorization. Where is he?"

"I don't think you need Sam."

"You don't understand," Paul said patiently. "The transfer is done with a computer. It's in my hotel room. It has a fingerprint scanner, and we calibrated it to Mr. Wallis's index finger."

"Which hand?"

"Excuse me?"

"The left or the right index finger?"

"The right."

Nabil pursed his lips. He had a young, pretty face made barely masculine by a short beard that reached up to his cheekbones. Paul imagined that he would have had to work particularly hard to be taken seriously in an industry full of battle-scarred compatriots. He wondered if, in a final need to prove himself, Nabil would someday end up driving a car full of explosives through a roadblock, or sitting in the pilot's chair of a passenger airplane, praising his god and then holding his breath. Men like Nabil were careless about the only important thing. They were as foolish as Sam.

There had been a Kenyan contact waiting in his stuffy hotel room. Benjamin Muoki, from the National Security Intelligence Service, was sitting on Paul's bed when he entered, sucking on a brown cigarette that streamed heavily from both ends. After they had exchanged introductory codes, Benjamin said, "This is what happens when you run an operation without proper help."

"Sam got your help, didn't he?"

"This isn't help. I'm giving you a machine, that's all. This is what happens when your people are not completely open with us."

"I don't think we're the only ones keeping secrets," Paul said as he began to unpack his clothes.

"Is that what Washington tells you?"

"Washington doesn't have to tell us anything."

"We get no points for giving you a president?"

"If another Kenyan tells me that I'm going to have a fit."

Benjamin sucked on his cigarette and stared at the floor, where a heavy black briefcase lay.

His color was lighter than that of most of his countrymen, his nose long, and Paul found himself wondering about the man's parentage.

"That's the computer?"

Benjamin nodded. "You know the codes?"

Paul tapped his temple. "Right here. As long as the machine works, it should be a cinch. You've tested it?"

The question seemed to make the Kenyan uncomfortable. "Don't worry, it works." He lifted the case onto the bed and opened it up to reveal an inlaid keyboard and screen. "Turn it on here and press this to connect to the bank. Type in the codes, and there you are."

"Where's the fingerprint scanner?"

"The what?"

"For Sam's authorization."

"You'll have to ask him."

Paul wasn't sure if that was supposed to be a joke. "Does it really connect to the bank?"

"How should I know? I'm just the courier." Benjamin closed the briefcase and set it on the floor again. He squinted as if the light were too strong, though the blinds were down. "They picked up Sam yesterday. They suspect him, and so they suspect you. They will be after you."

"They already are," Paul told him. "They followed me from the airport."

That seemed to surprise the Kenyan. "You are very cold about this."

Paul slipped a shirt onto a wooden hotel hanger. "Am I?"

"Were I you, I would be planning my escape from Africa."

Paul didn't bother mentioning that he was here to clean his soul, or that the idea of running had already occurred to him a hundred times; instead, he said, "Leaving's not as easy as it sounds."

"All you must do is ask."

Paul reached for another shirt, waiting for more.

"Listen to me," said Benjamin. "I keep secrets, and so do you. But no matter what Washington tells you or Nairobi tells me, we are in this together. Your friend Sam, he's been captured. He was stupid; he should have asked for my help. There's no need for you to follow in his footsteps. If you show up dead, missing your liver or your heart, then that is a tragedy. The operation is already blown. If you stay, you will die."

Benjamin Muoki made plenty of sense. More than Sam, who placed abstract principles above life itself. Only a man with such a twisted value system could have been able to forgive Paul his failure in Rome. So he agreed. Benjamin whispered a prayer of thanks for Paul's sudden wisdom. They settled on an eight o'clock extraction, and Benjamin insisted that Paul remain in the hotel until then.

Paul didn't contact Geneva, or Sam's case officer in Rome. They would either agree to eighty-sixing the operation, or they wouldn't, and in that case, he didn't want to be forced to refuse a direct order. There were far better places to die when the time came. Places with air-conditioning. He repacked his bag, left it beside the briefcase computer, and went down to the ground-floor bar. It was there, during his third gin and tonic, that they arrived.

He hadn't been able to see the faces that had followed him from the airport, but he knew that these were the same men. Tall, hard-looking, pitch black. They asked him to come quietly, pressing into his back so that he could feel their small pistols. He began to do as they asked, but then remembered the simple equation Benjamin had drawn for him: *If you stay, you will die.*

He swung his arms above his head. They wanted quiet, so he screamed. Hysterically. "I'm being kidnapped! Help!" The bartender froze in the midst of cleaning glasses. Two Chinese businessmen stopped their conversation and stared. The other few customers, all Kenyans, ducked instinctively even before they saw the guns his kidnappers began to wave around as they shouted in Arabic and pulled him out onto the street, into the waiting Mercedes.

They were infuriated by Paul's lack of cooperation. While one drove, the other pushed him down in the backseat and kept punching his kidneys to keep him still. It made Paul think that, if nothing else, they had no plans to take that organ. But all hierarchies are riddled with fools and bad communication, and there was no reason to think that later, in the operating room, the Aslim Taslam surgeon wouldn't recoil at the sight of his bruised and bloody kidneys.

It was cooler when Nabil finally returned. No one had turned off the blaring white ceiling light during the hours he'd been gone, but Paul suspected it was night. Nabil looked pleased with himself. He said, "You can do what you came here to do."

"And then I can leave?"

"Of course."

"Then let's get to it."

Nabil tugged a black hood from his pants pocket. "We'll take a trip first."

During his long wait, Paul had begun to believe that things were going too easily for him. Though he was still sore from his rough abduction, once he'd arrived in that bare room, no one had laid a finger on him. They had talked tough and hadn't offered him anything to eat or drink, but other than his hunger he was feeling fine.

Nabil walked him hooded through corridors, down a narrow staircase, and outside into the backseat of a car. An unknown voice asked him to lie on his side. He did so. They drove for a long time, taking many turns, and Paul believed they were turning back on themselves in order to confuse his sense of direction. If so, they were successful. Before they finally stopped, they drove up a steep incline noisy with gravel they later crunched over as Nabil walked him into a building.

When the hood was removed, Paul stood facing three men in a long, wood-paneled room that seemed built solely to hold the long dining table that filled it. Two small, barred windows looked out on darkness and the bases of palm trees; this room was half in the earth. Two of them he recognized from the kidnapping; they smoked in the corner, and the one who had earlier helped

Nabil with the interrogation even gave him a nod of recognition. The third one, a heavy man, wore a business suit. His name, Paul knew, was Daniel Kwambai.

Sam was the one with the long Kenyan background, not Paul, and so before leaving Switzerland Paul had browsed the Kenya files for background. Daniel Kwambai, the one Kenyan in the room, was a former National Security Intelligence Service officer who, after a falling-out with the Kibaki administration, was suspected to have allied himself with the Somali jihadis just over the border. The reason was simple: money. He was a gambling addict with expensive tastes that he couldn't give up even after washing out of political life. Here, then, was the evidence. Whatever good that did him.

Kwambai held out a hand. "Mr. Fisher, thank you for coming."

Unsure, Paul took it, and Kwambai's shake was so brief that he got the feeling the man was afraid to hold his hand too long. Then he noticed that the computer briefcase wasn't anywhere in the room; there was only a crystal ashtray on the far end of the table, which the kidnappers used. Paul said, "Well, I didn't have much choice. Can we get this over with?"

"First, some questions," said Kwambai. He waved at a chair. "Please."

Paul sat at the head of the table. Behind him, Nabil had withdrawn to the door; the kidnappers remained in their corner, smoking. Daniel Kwambai sat a couple chairs down and wove his fingers together, as if in prayer. He said, "We would like to know some more about Mr. Matheson, the man you know as Wallis. You see, we discovered that he was working for the Central Intelligence Agency. He wanted to purchase something from us, and we think that by this transaction he was going to try and destroy us."

"By giving you two million euros?"

"Yes, it seems unbelievable. But there it is. Nabil here fears trackers."

Paul shook his head. "It's my bank's computer, and it hasn't been out of my sight."

"Except when you left it in your room and went to the hotel bar."

"Well, yes. Except for then."

Kwambai smiled sadly. "Nabil puts his faith in trackers and things he can hold in his hands. I put my faith in the ephemeral. Data, information. No, I don't think there's a tracker on your computer. I think the act of transferring the money is part of the plan."

Uncomfortably, Paul realized that Daniel Kwambai was nearly there. As Sam had explained it, the virtual euros sent to their account were flagged, leaving traces in each account they touched. As Aslim Taslam moved the money among accounts, it left a trail. Tracking it to a final account was unimportant, because within that data flag was a time bomb, a virus that would in two weeks clear the entire contents of that final account, then backtrack, emptying whatever accounts it had passed through. The more accounts it moved through, the more damage it caused.

In the Geneva airport, Sam had said, "I know, I don't understand it either, but it works. Langley tested it out last month on some shell accounts—wiped the fuckers out."

Now, on the outskirts of Nairobi, Paul said, "I wouldn't call myself an expert in these matters—I've only been at the bank two months—but I don't see how that could be done. If the money moves through enough accounts, tracking it becomes impossible." He shook his head convincingly, because that part was the truth—even having Sam explain it to him had made it no easier to understand. "I don't think it could be done."

Kwambai considered that. He rapped his knuckles on the table before standing up. "Yes, I don't see it either. But something else has ruined our transaction. Which is a shame."

"Is it?"

"For you, yes."

The man's tone was all too final. "What about the transfer? I just need Mr. Wallis's—Matheson's—fingerprint."

Behind him, Nabil moved, and Paul heard a thump on the tabletop. A hand. A roughly chopped hand, the severed end black with old, stiff blood. Paul's stomach went bad again.

"As you see," said Kwambai, "we were prepared to do the transfer. But there's one problem. Your computer. It's not in your hotel room."

That cut through his sickness. He stared at the politician, mouth dry. "It has to be."

"Your suitcase, yes, full of clothes—you hadn't even unpacked. But no magical computer."

Despite the old fear slipping up through his guts, Paul went through possibilities. Benjamin had taken it. He had either secured it because he didn't think it would be needed, or he had stolen it for his own reasons.

The hotel staff—but what use would they have for it?

Or Daniel Kwambai was lying. They had the case somewhere and were sweating him. That, or . . .

Or they had found the case, then checked it for one of Nabil's trackers. And found one. Sam had sworn that there would be none, because they were too easy to detect. But . . . Lorenzo and Saïd. Perhaps this was some act of posthumous revenge. Perhaps Sam had cared about life after all.

"I don't believe you," Paul said, because it was the only role left to him. He heard the door behind him open and glanced back full of nerves. Nabil was leaving; the hand was gone. "Where's he going?"

"I'm going, too," said Kwambai. "It hurts me, it really does. Know that." He spoke with the fluid false compassion of a politician.

"Wait!" Paul said as Kwambai began to walk away. The kidnappers, still in their corner, looked up at his outburst. "Tell me what's going on."

Kwambai paused in mid-step. "You know what's going on."

"But, why?"

"Because we all do the best we can do, and this is the best thing for us to do."

The undertow pulled at his feet; the fear in his intestines felt like concrete. Everything seemed to be slowing down, even his desperate reply: "But you don't understand! I don't *work* for the bank. I never did! I work with Sam. I'm CIA, too!"

Kwambai tilted his head and licked his lips, interested. "Sam said you were, but we weren't sure we believed him."

"Sam said what?" Paul blurted, confused. What was going on?

"Thank you for clearing it up," said Kwambai. "And?"

Kwambai's hand settled on his shoulder. It was heavy and damp. He patted a few times. "And I must go."

"But the money's real," Paul told him. "It's *real*. And I know the codes."

"But there's no computer. The codes are useless."

"Someone has it. As soon as you find it, I can use the codes."

Kwambai stepped back, frowning. He wasn't a man used to doubt. "But who has the computer?"

"Benjamin Muoki. From the NSIS. He's got to have it."

"Benjamin?" Kwambai grinned. "Well, well. Benjamin."

"You go get it. Or I'll get it myself. Then I—"

"Tell me the codes."

"They're," Paul began, then stopped. "I'll type them in."

"We can't risk you typing some emergency signal. Tell me the codes now," said Kwambai. "Please."

Paul looked up at his fleshy face. "If I told you, I'd need some assurance that I'd be safe."

Kwambai blinked at him then, and suddenly began to laugh. It was a deep, room-filling laugh. "Of course, of course." He shook his head. "You didn't think we were going to kill you?"

Paul tried to remember the man's words. No, he hadn't said that Paul was going to die. He'd never said that. Just hint, nuance. Threat. He exhaled loudly, then, closing his eyes, recited the key combination to connect to the bank, the ten-digit number that accessed the accounts section, and then the holding account number.

"There's nothing else?" asked Kwambai, a smile still on his face.

"No. That's all."

"Good." Again, the politician patted his shoulder. "You've been very cooperative. Aslim Taslam will be sure to let your family know."

And he was gone. The logic of that last sentence didn't arrange itself in his head until Daniel Kwambai was closing the door behind himself and the two men were putting out their cigarettes in the crystal ashtray.

Paul began to say more things, but no one was listening. He couldn't see the men's expressions as they approached; fresh tears made details impossible to make out. He remembered Sam saying, *We're not all cut out for this kind of work. You never were.* Then, as the two men neared— one had already taken out his pistol—he realized they hadn't tied him down. He was just sitting there, waiting for death. They hadn't tied him down!

He stood, knocking the chair over, feeling a burst of hope that remained even as he felt the hammer of the first bullet in his chest. He stumbled, tripping backward over the chair. The breath went out of him; he couldn't get it back. His wet arms floundered on the floor as he tried to find a handhold, and even when the two men appeared, looking down on him, his wet hands didn't stop trying to hold on to something, anything. They kept slipping. The two men spoke briefly to their god.

"Don't," Paul managed, thinking of a damp couch and a beautiful girl who could see his secret soul. Then they all disappeared—the couch, the girl, the soul—as if they had never been.

NABIL

The Imam reminded him of those unnaturally serene Afghans who first taught him the Truth behind the truth. The hairs of his long beard were thick, black wires that paled to white as they traveled down his robe. Around his lips they were stained yellow by hours spent around the communal water pipe.

His Arabic was fattened by his Kurdish accent, but his grammar was beautifully precise. It almost seemed out of place in this tenement building on the outskirts of Rome. "You have brought your offerings to me, young Nabil, and for this I thank the Prophet (praise be upon him). Though few in number, your people seem to me to be a worthy addition to our holy fight. It is not your heart we question here, but your abilities."

Nabil, sitting cross-legged on the rug before him, kept his head low. "We are gathering weapons, Imam. We have communications abilities and the support of three major tribes in Puntland."

"That is good," said the old man. "But what I refer to is the ability of the mind." He smiled and tapped his weathered skull. "How does one discern truth from deception? How does one know the right path from the wrong, or the easy, one? Even the heart softened with love for Allah must be like stone when facing the infidels. The eyes must be clear."

Nabil wanted to have an answer ready but didn't. He was a fisherman's son. He had no special qualifications beyond the fact that he loved his faith and had learned to speak English like a native. So he waited.

After a moment of silence, the Imam said, "Young Nabil knows when to hold his tongue, which is not only a virtue but a sign of wisdom." He looked at the other men in the room, the young Kurds who now lived as his Roman bodyguards. By this look he seemed to be requesting their input, but they gave none. "And I believe you came to us via our mutual friend, Mr. Daniel Kwambai?"

"We've known him for some time. He is sometimes of use."

"Yes," the Imam said, pausing significantly. "But do not confuse use with friendship."

"We endeavor to know the difference, Imam."

"Those who can help are welcome, but those whose help takes too much from us, those should be dealt with harshly."

Again Nabil nodded but could find no words.

The Imam leaned back and patted his knees. "Let us agree first of all that one does not give one's hand without first knowing the other hand intimately. So it shall be here. We will come to you, young Nabil. You may or may not recognize us—that is of no concern. You should act as you believe correct. That is all we ask. Once we have observed your sense of right, we will come to our decision. Does that strike you as satisfactory?"

"It strikes me as a blessing, Imam," Nabil said, though his chest tightened. How much longer would this go on? He'd brought the money Ansar al-Islam had demanded, had given them a layout of the entire organization, and had even let them keep one of his men. Yet here he was, still feeling very much like the darkest man in the room.

"You are very patient for a man of your age," the Imam told him, as if he could read his thoughts. "This does not go unnoticed." He folded his hands together in his lap. "There is something you can do for us today, in fact. Something that would move things along more quickly."

"However I may be of service," said Nabil.

A smile. A nod. "Downstairs, in the basement of this very building, are two men. They became our guests only yesterday. Through questioning we have learned that they work for the Americans. One is an Italian, while the other is more despicable because he is not even European. He is Moroccan. A foul, homosexual Moroccan, in fact. What they attempted to do to Ansar al-Islam is not important; it is only important that they failed. I would consider it a great kindness if you would kill them for us."

One of the guards, sensing his cue, stepped forward. He held a long cardboard box, the kind used for long-stemmed flowers, and opened it on the floor in front of Nabil. Inside was a rather beautiful sword.

Four days later, on Sunday, after he'd finished his Dhuhr prayer and was packing to return to the continent he understood, where when you left you could say exactly what you had accomplished, the American knocked on his hotel room door. He found a light-haired but dark-eyed man in the spy hole who said, "Signore Nabil Abdullah Bahdoon?"

"Sí?"

The man peered up and down the corridor, then lowered his voice and spoke in English. "My name is Sam Wallis. I'm here with a business offer. May I come in?"

Though his impulse was to send the man away, he remembered, *We will come to you, young Nabil*, and opened the door.

Once inside, Sam Wallis was surprisingly—perhaps even refreshingly—straightforward. He wanted information on the pirates. He represented some companies interested in securing their shipping lanes through the Gulf of Aden. "I don't know what your rank is," Sam told him, "but I'll lay odds that the money I can give you will move you upward."

"Upward?"

"In your organization."

Nabil frowned. "What do you think my organization is?"

"Does it matter?" Sam said, flopping his hands in an expression of nonchalance. "There's always some position above our heads that we'd prefer to fill."

"You think like an American."

"I think like a human being."

Despite his pretty face. Nabil was a man of broad experience. He'd trained for three months in the mountains of Afghanistan, then spent a harrowing six months in Iraq on the front lines; then, once his worth was proven, he helped plan pinpoint strikes. Despite what Paul Fisher would later think, Nabil had not had to prove himself to his fellow fighters for years, and it was because of this respect that he would never find himself driving a truck or a speedboat laden with high explosives. He was too valuable to be wasted like that.

It was why he had been chosen to be Aslim Taslam's envoy to Ansar al-Islam's Roman cell. His comrades knew that he would think through each detail and come to the correct conclusions.

So when Sam Wallis offered a half million euros for intelligence on the pirates—a sum that Aslim Taslam needed desperately to further its plans—he did not answer immediately. He stepped back from the immediate situation and tried to see it from the outside.

You may or may not recognize us—that is of no concern. You should act as you believe correct.

Could this relaxed American be a messenger—witting or unwitting—from the Imam? Might this be the initial stage of the test? He pulled the blinds in the room, turned on the overhead lamp, and examined the American's dark eyes. Refusing money from an infidel was a morally unambiguous way of dealing with the situation. But perhaps too simple for the Imam. Too simple to assist the jihad.

If the money was real, then it could buy weapons. Using the infidels' technology and finances against them was a historically proven method of jihad. As for the information on the pirates, it could easily be manufactured, though there was no love lost between Aslim Taslam and those drunken thugs of the high seas.

"If you're serious," Nabil told him, "come to Africa and we'll discuss it further. Mogadishu."

Sam Wallis shook his head. "I'm not going anywhere near Mogadishu. I'm paid well, but not that well. Next week I'll be in Kenya for the Kajiado Cross-Country Rally. Can we meet in Nairobi?"

Nabil was careful not to keep this a secret. He was thinking in layers now. If he kept the American a secret from his comrades, it would look to Ansar al-Islam's observers—who he had to assume were everywhere—that he was either planning to keep the American's money himself or hiding him because he was going to sell real information. Neither of these were true, and in a small house east of Botiala he sat with his five most trusted men and talked them through it.

All five of these tall, dark men were from his village, and in another world they would have remained fishermen like their fathers. But in this world the fish started to disappear from the gulf, their sleek bodies absorbed by the big trawlers from Yemen and Saudi Arabia and Egypt. They watched as the other young fishermen, many of them friends, learned that taking to the seas with speedboats and weapons, full of liquor and marijuana, could bring in more money than fishing ever had. They blew their money on satellite televisions and four-by-fours they sped up and down the coastline, sometimes running over children on the way. Nabil and his friends watched, remembering what the visitors from Afghanistan had taught them.

There were no fish left, and piracy was despicable to them. But there was a third way. A better way.

When he told them of the American, they pulled back visibly, so he took them through his line of reasoning. While the pirates were not their friends, giving them up was not an option. So they would fabricate the information. Transit routes, bank accounts, hierarchies. "And if it looks as if the American is going to cheat us, we will kill him."

"But what of the Imam?" asked Ghedi, looking for unambiguously good news.

That he suspected the American had been sent by the Imam was too much for them to absorb, so he only said, "He wants to teach us patience."

He returned to Kenya by one of the softer land routes, and on Saturday, before the start of the cross-country rally, he entered Sam Wallis's InterContinental room with a look of pain on his face. "I'm sorry, I cannot risk it. It's an impressive amount of money, but in my region of Somalia if you become an enemy of the pirates, your life is no longer worth anything."

Sam settled on the end of his bed and considered the problem. "It's one reason I came to you, you know. Your group separated from Al-Shabaab because of their cooperation with the pirates. I thought you'd have the balls to stand up to them."

"You think you know a lot about me, Mr. Wallis."

"My employers think they do."

"We may not like the pirates, but we still have to live in their country."

"You needn't stay in Somalia."

"It's our home."

Clearly, this argument carried no weight with the American, but he accepted it as the logic of primitive peoples. "I shouldn't tell you this," he said after some thought, "but my bosses say I can go up to two million euros. So I'll do that. The offer is now two million."

It was as Nabil had suspected. No opening offer is a final one, and now he had quadrupled Aslim Taslam's income. "How will you pay it?"

"Account transfer. I can get one of the bank employees to come to Nairobi to take care of it."

"We would prefer diamonds."

"We'd all prefer diamonds, but I'm limited by what my employers are willing to do."

"How quickly can it be prepared?"

Sam considered this. "The race ends next Sunday, then I'll go to Switzerland to set everything up. I can be back the following Wednesday. I'd guess that the banker could make it by Thursday. Will that work?"

Before returning home, Nabil set up a meeting with Daniel Kwambai, the man who had originally connected him to Ansar al-Islam. For the appropriate fees, Kwambai had been useful to Aslim Taslam, as well as to Al-Shabaab before Nabil and his comrades left.

They had met face-to-face a few times before, but this was Nabil's first visit to one of Kwambai's houses, a four-bedroom in the low hills north of the Karura Forest. In the comfort of his own house, fat Kwambai chain-smoked and sipped whiskey as if it were water. His house was full of representational art that made a mockery of Creation. It was an unnerving place to be.

While he gave Kwambai the layout of the

situation, he was careful to avoid actual names, which didn't trouble the politician. "You'll need a secure place for a transaction," Kwambai told him. "And the money—you can't just send it directly to your account. I'll have to move it around some."

"Through your accounts?"

Kwambai shrugged, pulling at his fat lower lip. "I do have some accounts already set up. They've served the purpose before. I can put them at your disposal."

Nabil had the feeling that Kwambai had been waiting for him, the accounts ready. He reminded himself that Kwambai was a politician, and as such had been thinking in layers since childhood. He was a man to watch carefully.

Kwambai was also nearly bankrupt. With his fall from political grace he'd lost the bribes that had kept his lifestyle and three large houses in operation. Debt was a wonderful motivator. "I suppose you'll ask for a commission," Nabil said.

"What's this attitude?" Kwambai said, waving his empty glass. "I've helped your people for a long time now. Of course I'll need some money— there are bank charges, after all—but without my help you'd have nothing. Remember that."

Nabil acceded that this was true enough. "How about this place?" he asked, looking around at all the decadence.

"What?"

"This house, for the transfer. I see there's a basement. We can bring the banker here blindfolded and take him away likewise."

Kwambai seemed troubled by the idea, which Nabil had expected. Though he had an attic apartment over in Ngara West he could use initially, he wanted to give the politician a reason beyond money to keep security tight.

"We would of course pay you for the trouble," Nabil insisted.

He returned to Somalia and filled in his comrades on the developments. He asked Ghedi and Dalmar to come back with him for the final stage, and after a week, as they settled on their path back through the border, Kwambai called in a panic. "It's off, Nabil. We're not doing this."

"Explain yourself."

"Sam Wallis? One of my friends in the NSIS knows him. It's the work name of Sam Matheson. Of the CIA."

The question posed itself again: Was this a test? It didn't look like one, but the Imam, he knew, plotted in the labyrinthine way he interpreted the Koran. His reach was long, and his thoughts were deep. Might he have knowingly sent an American agent to perform the examination?

But this was what happened when you began thinking in layers: It was addictive. There was always another layer to be discovered, another truth to be found. He said, "I never told you his name."

"Don't be petty, Nabil. You should be pleased I caught this early."

With a smoothness that surprised even himself, Nabil said, "I was already aware of this."

Stunned silence. "You were?"

"Of course. It wasn't important for you to know."

"Not important? Are you mad? Of course it's important! I'm not bringing a CIA agent into my house."

"He's not going anywhere near your house," Nabil said, not knowing if this was true or not. "Only the banker."

It seemed to calm him some. "But still. This isn't what I was expecting."

"If that's how you feel, Mr. Kwambai, then we can double your fee."

Silence again, but there was nothing stunned about it. It was the silence of mental calculations.

"That's my offer," Nabil said, feeling very sure of himself, more sure than he had in a long time. "If you're not interested I'll take my business elsewhere. We'll know not to approach you again."

"Let's not be rash," said Kwambai.

On Wednesday he again found Sam Matheson in his room at the InterContinental. There were heavy rings beneath his eyes, sunburn across his forehead and cheeks, and Nabil wondered if the cross-country race had taken a serious toll on him. He'd verified that a man named Sam Wallis had registered, and that his car had come in eleventh among thirty-eight participants. According to the records, he'd originally signed on with a partner, one Saïd Mourit, but Mourit had been dropped before the race began.

He gave no sign that he knew Matheson's real name, only suggested that they continue their conversation in the street.

"Too claustrophobic?" asked Sam.

"Exactly."

In the nearby city market, they walked on packed earth among the crowds and vendors hiding under umbrellas. Nabil quietly said, "Mr. Matheson, I know who you work for."

To his credit, the American didn't slow his step. Above, the blazing sun made his sunburn look all the worse. A nonchalant grin remained plastered to his face, and he shrugged. "Who do I work for?"

"The CIA."

"My assumption was that if I'd told you, you wouldn't have accepted the deal."

"You were right."

Beside a table piled high with overpriced fabrics, he turned to face Nabil. He was a few inches shorter, but the confidence in his movements made him seem taller than he was. "The offer's the same, Nabil. Those pirates are a public menace. They're screwing with business. We're getting pressured from all sides to get any kind of intel we can."

"Even from people like us?"

Sam waved that off. "Your group's new. No one knows about you. In a few years, maybe we'll pay the pirates for intel on you. It all depends on what our masters ask for."

"This is something we have in common," Nabil said as he gazed at the intelligence agent who had suddenly opened himself up in a way that he would never have done. It was almost suicidal. What he'd expected was a denial, and

then a quick withdrawal. Perhaps even this had been calculated by Rome.

Or perhaps, he thought suddenly, Ansar al-Islam had nothing to do with this, and it was precisely how the American presented it. The CIA just wanted some information.

It was time to make a decision.

"And this man from the bank who's coming tomorrow?" he asked. "What is he?"

The smile faded from the American's lips before returning. It was a momentary lapse—less than a second—but Nabil didn't forget it. Sam said, "His name's Paul Fisher. Yes, he's an agent, too. But the money is real. After he's finished the transfer you can do what you like to him."

"You want us to kill your colleague?"

"I didn't say that," Sam corrected. "It's up to you. Consider it a gift. If you like, you can claim responsibility, and he'll be your first public execution."

"A videotaped beheading. Is that what you imagine?"

"It's not like you haven't done it before."

That was unexpected. "Have I?"

Sam Matheson licked his lips—nervousness . . . or appetite? "As I say, it's up to you."

It was only then that Nabil knew what to do. This man, whether or not he was from the CIA, had been sent by the Imam. Like the blinding sunlight pouring down on them, the realization fell upon him, and he knew. He was to kill a man named Paul Fisher. That was the Imam's desire. Why? Matheson was little help on this; perhaps he didn't know.

"He's become a liability. We don't need him anymore."

Nabil turned toward Koinange Street, began walking, and reached into his pocket. He took out a pair of mirrored sunglasses and slipped them on, signaling Ghedi and Dalmar. "It's a remarkable gift. First, money, and then one of your own. I just wonder why the CIA would give him to us. It's not as if you couldn't get rid of him yourself."

"Despite what people say, the CIA prefers not to kill its own employees."

"You're very wicked, Sam."

Sam Matheson didn't answer. He seemed to consider the statement as they reached the street, and the van drew up, its large door sliding open. Ghedi and Dalmar jumped out and grabbed Matheson by the biceps and flung him inside. Nabil watched the door close again and the van jerk forward and swerve away. He watched it disappear into the afternoon traffic.

As he walked back to his car, he rummaged through his pocket and came up with a pack of Winstons. He lit one and inhaled deeply. It was the first one he'd had in three days; he was doing well.

When you're being watched, all your actions, however small, take on a presence of their own—each has its own significance and its own variety of interpretations. You light a cigarette, and that might mean that you're nervous, you're relaxed, you've been co-opted by Western forms of decadence, or that you're desperately stopping time in order to invent your next lie.

He had to stop thinking this way. If Ansar al-Islam was watching, the only important detail was the taking of Sam Matheson. They would know that Aslim Taslam left hesitation to those with less faith.

Nabil took Sam Matheson's dry, surprisingly heavy hand from the table and dropped it back into the crumpled plastic bag, then slipped the bag into the pocket of his jacket as Kwambai fed Paul Fisher the lie: "Your suitcase, yes, full of clothes—you hadn't even unpacked. But no magical computer."

Nabil disagreed with this tactic, but Kwambai had been living with the doublespeak of politics for too long. He no longer knew how to be straight, and now he'd gone over the deep end. Yesterday's evidence had been irrefutable. Nabil had returned from the market, having stopped at a mosque along the way to offer his Asr prayer. After Sam Matheson, he'd felt the need for some community. He'd driven up the hill to find Ghedi in the driveway, looking distraught. "He killed him," Ghedi said. "Kwambai killed the American."

Kwambai explained himself as they stood over Sam Matheson's corpse in the basement. "He saw me. Your men brought him through the living room without a hood and he *saw* me. I couldn't let him live."

Kwambai had put two bullets in Sam's chest and one through his neck; sticky blood covered the floor, and the flies had already begun to swarm. Standing over him, the politician began to tremble all over. It was probably the first man he'd ever killed with his own hand. Kwambai said, "His fingerprints. He said we'll need them for the computer."

"Why did he say that?"

"He thought it would save his life."

"So you had a conversation first?"

The politician seemed to have run out of words, so Nabil asked Ghedi and Dalmar to remove the American's hands while he took Kwambai outside and they looked for a spot to bury him among the low, dry trees in his backyard. Together, they dug a deep hole. Nabil stopped once, asked where east was, and kneeled in the dirt to offer his Maghrib prayer, while Kwambai ran into the house for more drink. By the time they finished, it was dark. All four men carried the body to the hole, and then Ghedi and Dalmar were given the unenviable task of cleaning the basement room.

Over those later hours, as they filled the hole and stumbled back to the house, Kwambai's drunkenness faded and was replaced by a strange giddiness. He talked about the act he'd committed, the feel of the pistol, the kick of the bullet as it left the chamber, the American's stunned eyes that slowly lost their sheen. He described these things as a man describes his first time with a woman, with the pleasure of a wonderful thing newly discovered.

The old politician had become a murderer, and he had enjoyed it.

Afterward, the dynamic changed. Kwambai wanted nothing more than to be at the forefront of their operation. He quit mentioning money, only asked endless questions and offered suggestions for improvement, and when they brought in Paul Fisher, he was waiting in the basement to stare directly into his eyes. He no longer cared who saw him, because he wanted to kill this one, too. Nabil had lost control of the operation.

And now Kwambai was twisting the interrogation with his doublespeak and lies. The computer was sitting upstairs on the long oak table, awaiting the codes and the fingerprint. All he had to do was ask Fisher to type in the code, and they would all be two million euros richer. But Kwambai wanted to stretch this out, wanted to torture the American, and Nabil had no interest in watching it.

So when Paul Fisher said, "I don't believe you," Nabil gave a quick but crucial signal to Dalmar and Ghedi, walked out, and climbed the stairs to the living room.

During the weeks since that bloody basement in Rome, he'd grown so tired of it all. He wondered when the light would begin to shine. People were not dying for the jihad; they were dying for the preparation for the jihad. For the bank accounts and the arms and the escapes from capture. One spent so much time dealing with the moment that the original dream, the one that made him cast away his fishing nets, seemed more distant than ever. How long could this go on?

Even the Imam had asked him afterward if he still had the heart for the fight. For fighting, yes, always. But when you descend into a tenement basement in Rome and find two bruised, broken men tied up, facing a camera on a tripod, and then use a beautiful ceremonial sword to remove their heads, there is no battle rush, no visible battle won. Just a flooded floor, your body soaked in blood and sweat, and the ache in your arms from hacking with a blade better suited to adorning a wall.

Daniel Kwambai's woody house was full of European furniture mixed with Kenyan folk kitsch. It was as uncomfortable as Kwambai himself. Nabil settled at the long table beneath an iron chandelier and opened the briefcase, running his fingers lightly over the keyboard and the flat screen, the things that offered entrance to a Swiss bank's deepest secrets.

It was all still so strange to him. For a fisherman's son, none of this could ever feel comfortable. The computer. The narrow, Vespa-buzzing streets of Rome and the cacophony of Nairobi's taxi horns. The wily, now quite mad, political animal that was Daniel Kwambai. He felt more comfortable with those drunk ex-fishermen the world called pirates.

He heard Kwambai climbing the steps slowly as the muted gunshots filled the house. The fat man paused, looked back, then continued. By the time he reached the end of the table Ghedi and Dalmar had finished. It could happen so quickly.

"I thought they would wait," Kwambai said.

"I told them to do it as soon as you'd left the room. He'd been tortured enough."

"Torture?" Kwambai shook his head. "Perhaps you would have given him all the facts up front, Nabil? We now know that Benjamin Muoki is working with them, but that's all we're going to get because you don't want the poor American feeling distraught."

Nabil shrugged.

"And what if the codes are fake?"

"I've considered that," Nabil said, because he had. If they lost two million euros, then so be it. He wasn't going to give this monster another happy murder.

Kwambai turned the computer around, closer to himself, and sat down. "Well, it's reckless, and with this much money you can't afford to be reckless. You know what's going on here; you have to *think*. That's what Rome expects of you. It's what I expect of you."

It was remarkable, really, how Kwambai was acting as if Aslim Taslam were his own fiefdom. But the politician was wrong. Nabil had been thinking for weeks. He'd been noting Kwambai's own reckless moves and raising each one to the light to see it better, pairing them up randomly to find connections. But only now, hearing his command to *think*, did a single thread of logic form to connect all the disparate clues. It was so perfectly simple that his hands became warm from embarrassment. He'd been thinking in the wrong direction.

Do not confuse use with friendship.

"The hand?" said Kwambai. A pause. "What is it, Nabil?"

Nabil blinked but still couldn't see the old man well. He rooted around his jacket pocket and came up with the hand. He dropped it on the table.

Those who can help are welcome, but those whose help takes too much from us, those should be dealt with harshly.

He heard the crackle of plastic as Kwambai took it out. "This had better work," he heard the Kenyan say. "This thing is foul. You smell it?"

"Disgusting," Nabil muttered as Kwambai powered up the computer.

"Where the hell am I supposed to scan the fingerprint?"

"Perhaps the Americans lied to you, Daniel."

An awkward pause. "Perhaps."

From downstairs came the sound of Ghedi and Dalmar grunting, moving Paul Fisher's body around. Bodies everywhere. Yet here Nabil was, planning on one more, as soon as the money had been transferred.

SAM

"They're inside," Natalia chirped through the radio in his ear.

Sam leaned toward the apartment's high window, careful not to touch the tripod and shotgun mike, and gazed across Via del Corso at the mosque, the sound of car horns and buzzing Vespas rising through the heat to him. Ticklish sweat rolled down his back. From her position at an outdoor café, Natalia had a clear view of the entrance, while Sam could see only the upper window to the room where Saïd and Lorenzo would be taken once they'd introduced themselves to the Imam.

It was a tricky operation, enough so that a week ago, sweating in his temporary Repubblica apartment near the station, he'd suggested that Saïd leave town. The Moroccan had gotten up on his elbow, the light playing over his long olive body, and stared, a flash of anger in his thick brows. "You think I can't do this?"

"Of course you can."

"I've built up all the contacts. It's taken months. You know that."

"I know. I'm just . . ."

"We shouldn't have gotten involved."

It was true, perhaps. But by now Sam couldn't quite imagine what life would look like without Saïd in it. "Too late," he said, watching his lover's fleshy lips. "You want me to hide what I'm feeling?"

The Moroccan smiled. "It's what we do. We should be good at it." Seeing that the joke hadn't played well, Saïd kissed him and said officiously, "Plenty of time, young man. We're still on for the rally?"

"Absolutely."

"You and me under the Kenyan stars again. We'll have plenty of time to figure out our future."

Which, Sam noted with satisfaction, was the first time Saïd had used that blessed word, *future.*

So he'd gone over the operation a hundred times more, adjusting details here and there and even bringing in an extra agent to provide coverage inside. Paul Fisher, from Geneva.

"Paul," he said from his window perch. "You're there?"

"Sì," came the whisper.

"Everything's smooth. Just keep doing what you're doing."

Though they'd known each other in the academy, it was a surprise to see Paul again. He was the most visibly nervous agent he'd ever dealt with. Sam even called Geneva to make sure that this was a man he could depend on. "Fisher's top-notch for his age," was the reply, which told him nothing.

While briefing Paul in his apartment, though, Sam had discovered a small P-83, a Polish gun, in Paul's jacket. "Where'd this come from?"

"A Milanese I know."

"Why?"

Paul shrugged. "I like backup."

"Not on this job," he said and put the gun in his desk drawer. "I'm not having you get them killed."

Paul had been sitting at the foot of the bed where Sam had last made love to Saïd. He hated this fidgety man touching those sheets. Paul said, "I wasn't planning on using it."

"Then you don't need to carry it."

Paul nodded unsurely.

While it had taken weeks to set up and could go wrong easily, the operation itself was simple. Lorenzo and Saïd were to visit the mosque and sit down with the Imam in his study to discuss a Camorra arms shipment they had intercepted and wished to sell to like-minded people. From his post across the street, Sam would record the conversation. Natalia would watch the street for activity or reinforcements. Paul was to wait in the prayer hall to help facilitate any emergency escape.

It took them a while to reach the Imam's study. A body search would be de rigueur, as would an electronics sweep. In the far window, a light came on. A young man in a white skullcap pulled the thin curtains shut. Sam held one side of the headphones to his free ear, checked the levels against some language, perhaps Kurdish, being spoken in the room, and began to record.

A total of seventeen minutes passed before their arrival in the Imam's chamber. During that time Sam talked briefly with Natalia and listened to Paul mouthing the late-afternoon Asr prayer with the congregation. Then a door opened in the room, and the Imam greeted Saïd and Lorenzo in Arabic. For the benefit of Lorenzo, they switched to Italian. The proposal was on.

In his other ear, Paul whispered, "There's some activity."

"Problem?"

"Three guys breaking off prayer. Talking."

"It's nothing."

"They're going to the stairs."

"How do they look?"

"Not happy."

Sam felt the old tension rising in his chest. The conversation with the Imam was going well. They had moved on to the makes of the weapons.

Paul said, "They're gone."

"Stay there," Sam ordered.

"Shit."

"What?"

"Another one. He's looking at me."

"Because you're not praying. Now pray."

"That's not it."

"Ignore him and pray."

Silence, just the throb of voices speaking to their god.

"Natalia?"

"All clear."

In his right ear, the Imam mentioned a price. As planned, Lorenzo was trying to raise it. A knock on the Imam's door stopped him. Someone came in. Arabic was spoken. Sam's grasp of the language was sketchy, but he knew enough to understand that they were discussing a suspicious worshipper in the prayer hall. According to the visitor, it was clear from the bulge in his pocket that he was carrying a pistol.

"You fucker," Sam said. "You brought your gun."

No reply.

"Stand up and walk out of there before you get them killed."

No reply.

"You better be walking."

No reply, just the sound of movement, a grunt, and then a single gunshot that thumped into Sam's eardrum. A pause, then Paul's wavering voice through the whine of his damaged left ear: "Shit." On the right, the Imam's room had gone silent. Lorenzo said, "What was that?" Movement.

Saïd: "What're you doing?"

The Imam, in Arabic: "Get them out."

More movement. Struggling.

Natalia: "Paul's out. He's running. Should I chase?"

A door in the Imam's quarters slammed shut.

"Sam? What do I do?"

It wasn't until Thursday afternoon, two days later and a couple hours after he'd gotten the news, that he tracked Paul Fisher to a bar near the Colosseum, hunched in the back with a nearly empty bottle of red wine. Sam waited near the front, observing the shivering wreck of a man who was too drunk to see him. Behind Sam, two Italian men slapped on a poker machine, shouting at it, and he reconsidered the one thing he'd felt sure he would do once he found Paul Fisher.

Though both had made a game of hiding their true feelings, he and Saïd had known from the start, when they were going about their various embassy duties in Nairobi, that they had found something unprecedented. Both had a broad enough sexual history—Sam in the Bay Area meat markets, where you could be as open as you were moved to be, Saïd in the underground discos of Casablanca—but from their second night together they'd opened up more than they had with anyone else before. Perhaps, Saïd had suggested, they were like this because they knew that Sam was leaving for Rome in a month. Perhaps. But six months later, in Rome, Sam's phone rang. Saïd had wrangled a transfer and convinced his superiors that he should offer help to the Americans.

"This is a bed of liars," Saïd liked to say during their secret liaisons in what they started to call their Roman summer. But then he used that fantastical word, *future*, and Sam pounced on him with joyous descriptions of the Castro. Saïd was entranced, though he offered a countersuggestion: Rio de Janeiro.

"Too hot," Sam told him.

"Northern California is too cold."

Now, listening to the angry Italians and *blip-bleep* of the poker machine, Sam wondered what would have happened. Might they have bought a place in some high-rise along the Rio beaches? Or had their optimism been a symptom of the Roman summer, and in the end things would have gone the way of all his previ-

ous relationships—nowhere? There was no way to know. Not anymore.

Because of this drunk man in the corner.

Kill Paul Fisher? Sam wasn't that kind of agent—he'd never actually committed murder, and until now he'd never wanted to. Yet as he approached the table he thought how easy it would be, how satisfying. Revenge, sure, but he began to think that Paul Fisher's death would be something good for the environment, the subtraction of an unwholesome element from the surface of the planet.

Terrified—that was how Paul looked when he finally recognized him. Drunk and terrified. Sam sat down and said, "We heard from the carabinieri. Two bodies, minus their heads, were found in the Malagrotta landfill."

Paul's wet mouth worked the air for nearly half a minute. "Do they know?"

"Yes, it's them. They'll turn up the heads eventually."

"Jesus." His forehead sank to the dirty table, and he muttered something indecipherable into his lap.

"Tell me what happened," said Sam.

Paul raised his head, confused, as if the answer were obvious. "I *panicked*."

"Where'd you get the gun?"

"I always have a spare."

"This one?" Sam said as he reached into his jacket and took out the Beretta Natalia had given him. He placed it on the table in front of himself so that no one behind them could see it.

"Jesus," Paul repeated. "Are you going to use that?"

"You dropped it when you ran off. Natalia found it."

"Right . . ."

"Take it back and get rid of it."

Paul hesitated, then reached out, knocking the wine bottle into a totter. He yanked the pistol into his stomach and held it under the table.

"I unloaded it," Sam told him, "so don't bother trying to shoot yourself."

The sweat on Paul's forehead collected and

drained down his temple. "What's going to happen?"

"To you?"

"Sure. But all of it. The operation."

"The operation's dead, Paul. I haven't decided about you yet."

"I should get back to Geneva."

"Yeah. You should probably do that," Sam said, and stood. No, he wasn't going to kill Paul Fisher. At least not here, not now.

He left the bar and took a taxi to the Porta Pinciana and walked down narrow Via Sardegna past storefronts and cafés to the embassy. As he unloaded his change and keys and phone for the doormen, Randall Kirscher came marching up the corridor. "Where the hell have you been, Sam?" Though there was panic in his case officer's voice, nothing was explained as they took the stairs up to his third-floor office. Inside, two unknown men, one wearing rubber gloves, stood around a cardboard box lined with plastic that folded out of the top. Though he knew better, Sam stepped forward and looked inside.

"Sent with a fucking *courier* service," muttered Randall.

Sam's feet, his stomach, and then his eyes grew warm and bloated. Though the men in the room continued talking, all he could hear was the hum in his left ear, the residue of complete failure.

No one saw him for three days. Randall Kirscher was inundated by calls demanding Sam's whereabouts—in particular from the Italians, who wanted an explanation for shots fired in a mosque. But he knew nothing. All he knew was that, after seeing Saïd's severed head on Thursday, Sam had walked out of the embassy, leaving even his keys and cell phone with the embassy guards.

The next day the video appeared on the Internet, routed through various servers around the globe. Lorenzo and Saïd on their knees. Behind them hung a black sheet with a bit of white Ara-

bic, and then a hooded man with a ceremonial sword. And so on. Kirscher didn't bother watching the entire thing, only asked Langley to please have their analysts do their magic on it. In reply, they asked for the report Sam hadn't filed. He told them it was on its way.

On Saturday, two days after his disappearance, Kirscher sent two men over to Sant'Onofrio, where Sam's debit card had been used on two cash machines to take out about a thousand dollars' worth of euros. They, however, found no sign of him.

Then on Monday morning, as if the entire embassy hadn't been on alert to find him, he appeared at the gate a little after eight-thirty, dressed in an immaculate suit, and politely asked the guards if they still had the cell phone and keys he'd forgotten last week. Randall called him up to his office and waited for an explanation. All Sam gave him at first were oblique references to "groundwork" he'd been doing on a deal to provide inside intelligence on Somali pirates.

"What?" Randall demanded, hardly believing this.

"I got in touch with one of my Ansar sources. A member of Aslim Taslam was in town, and I approached him about selling us intel. I wasn't about to blow my cover by contacting the embassy before we'd met."

"What was your cover?"

"Representing some businesses."

"Sounds like the Company to me."

Sam didn't seem to get the joke. "I talked with him yesterday. He's loaded with information."

"How'd you verify this?"

Sam blinked in reply.

"And how much did you offer him?"

"A half mil. Euros."

Randall began to laugh. He wasn't being cruel; he just couldn't control himself. "Five hundred grand for a *storyteller*?"

Sam finally settled into a chair and wiped at his nose. What followed was so quiet that Randall had to lean close to hear: "He's the one who cut their heads off."

The clouds parted, and Randall could see it all now. "Absolutely not, Sam. You're taking a vacation."

"His name is Nabil Abdullah Bahdoon. Somali. Not a foot soldier, but one of the heads of Aslim Taslam. They're desperate for cash, and we can use it against him."

"Against them."

Sam frowned.

"Them, not him. We're not into vengeance here. We're not Mossad."

"Then think of it this way," said Sam. "We have a chance to decapitate the group before it gains momentum."

"Decapitate?"

Sam shrugged.

Randall stifled a sigh. "Step back. Once again from the top."

"A bomb," Sam said without hesitation. "In the bank computer. Nabil will want to be on hand to witness the transfer."

"Here in Rome?"

Sam hesitated. "Not settled. Probably not here."

"Somalia?"

"Maybe."

"You're going to take a bomb through customs?"

"I can have it made locally. I have the contacts."

Randall considered the loose outline, flicking over details one after the other. Then he ran into a wall. "Wait a minute. How does this bomb go off?"

"With the transfer code."

"So who's going to perform the transfer?"

Sam coughed into his hand. "Me."

"Again?"

"I'll type in the code."

"You're going to commit suicide."

Sam didn't answer.

"May I ask why?"

"It's personal."

"Personal?" Randall said, shouting despite himself. "I really should advise you to see the counselor."

"You probably should."

Silence followed, and Randall found a pen on his desk to twirl. "It's ridiculous, Sam, and you know it. I know you're upset about what happened to Lorenzo and Saïd, but it wasn't your fault. Hell, it probably wasn't even that idiot Paul Fisher's fault. It just happened, and I'm not going to lose one of our best agents over this. You can see that, can't you?"

Sam's face gave no sign either way.

"Post-traumatic stress disorder. That's what's going on here, you know. It's a sickness."

Sam blinked slowly at him.

"I won't insist on the therapist—not *yet*—but I am insisting on the vacation. Aren't you supposed to go car racing next week?"

"Cross-country rally."

"Good. Write up a report on the fiasco and then take three weeks."

Sam was already on his feet, nodding.

"Keep safe," Randall told him, "and do consider the therapist. Voluntarily. I'll not lose you."

But Sam was already out the door.

There had been an unexpected storm along the south side of snowcapped Mount Kenya that morning, and so by noon he was soaked with mud, and by late afternoon it had dried to a crust, turning his clothes into a lizard skin of hard scales. But he went on. His empty passenger seat set him apart from most of the Europeans and Americans taking part in the rally, and when asked, he told them his partner had dropped out because of business obligations, an excuse they all understood.

At the end of each day, they drank together in tents set up by their Kenyan hosts. The Italians were loud, the French condescending, the Brits sneering, the Americans annoyingly boisterous. A hive of multinational caricatures bound together by speed and beer, business and tall tales about women they'd had. These things were, he reflected, the lifeblood of Western masculinity.

It was Friday, two days before the end of the race, when through his exhausted eyes and muddy goggles he saw Benjamin Muoki standing among the T-shirted organizers wearing a suit, one hand on his hip, and no expression on his face. In his other hand was a bottle of Tusker lager. Sam pulled up amid the other drivers' shouts and hoots, flipped up his goggles, and nodded at Benjamin, who took the cue and wandered away from the camp. Sam checked his time, rinsed off, and changed into shorts, a blue cotton button-up, and leather sandals from his waterproof bag. By then, Benjamin was a silhouette against a backdrop of fading mountains. Sam had to run to catch up with him.

"Here," Benjamin said, holding out his beer. "You need it more than I do."

They shared the bottle in silence, walking slowly, until Benjamin remembered and said, "You're nearly the last one in."

"The rain does it to me."

"I'll pray for clear skies."

"The sun is even worse."

Having known each other for three years, the men used the exchange of pass phrases not to recognize each other, but to signal if one or the other was compromised. "But really," said Benjamin, "are you driving well?"

"I'm surviving."

"It's a difficult course."

They paused and looked back at the bustling activity of the camp. Lights flickered on to hold back the encroaching dark. A dusty wind came at them, raising little tornadoes, then died down. "Did you receive the instructions?" Sam asked.

"I'm here, aren't I?"

"I mean the rest of it."

"Yes."

"And?"

"What would you like me to say? That I think it's dangerous? I've said that about too many of your plans to keep on with it."

"But do you see any obvious flaws?"

"Just that you'll end up dead."

Sam didn't answer; he was too tired to lie convincingly.

Benjamin looked into his face. "A life for a life? It's a lot to pay."

"More than one life, we hope."

"We," Benjamin said quietly. "I had a talk with your fat attaché. I don't think he knows the first thing about this."

Sam felt his expression betraying too much. "You told him?"

"No, Sam. I felt around some. I'm good at that."

"Good."

"It's not on the books, is it?"

"It's above his clearance," Sam lied, but it was an easy lie. "The computer finished?"

"By Monday."

"I'll be back next Wednesday."

"So I'll give it to you then."

"Not me. You'll give it to someone else."

A light seemed to go on in Benjamin's always-astute eyes. "Someone even more foolish than you?"

"I'll let you know. You'll give it to him, but you won't say a thing about it. You're a good enough liar for that, aren't you?"

Benjamin's expression faltered. "This is a very stupid man?"

"A nervous man. Just give him the case. He knows what to do with it."

"He knows he'll die?"

"You're full of questions, Benjamin. We're paying you well enough, aren't we?"

"You have always paid well, Sam."

On Monday, as he sat across from Paul Fisher in the Aéroport International de Genève, he wondered why he was pushing it so far. Was he pushing it *too* far? He hadn't seen Paul since that bar in Rome, and now that they were face-to-face again the prospect of killing him here, now, seemed much more inviting. Easier. More wholesome.

But he'd begun to fall in love with the balance of his plan. One bomb would take out not only the man indirectly responsible for Saïd's gruesome murder, but also the man who had worked the blade through the muscles and bone. Now it was just a matter of persuasion. So after the invention of the technology that would wash bank accounts clean, he assured Paul that he wouldn't be alone—Sam would be there, right by his side, to authorize the transfer with his index finger. That seemed to calm him. Then he told Paul what they both knew, that he wasn't cut out for this kind of work and never had been. "Consider this a chance to redeem yourself," Sam said, and it felt as if, through lies, he had cut to a deeper truth than he ever could have come upon honestly.

His love of the plan kept him moving forward even when, on Wednesday, Saïd's murderer told him his real name and the name of his employer. Sam had put too much work into the plan to let it fall apart now, so he improvised. He absorbed this discovery into his tale, and even encouraged Nabil to murder Paul. He admitted the issue was personal. It was reckless, yes, but his sense of the rightness and beauty of his plan had made him delirious.

Yet it was too late. He realized his mistake only when they plucked him off the street and drove him out of town to that finely appointed house. Even then, however, he clung to hope. They still wanted the money, and if necessary he would type in the code himself. He would prefer if Paul were beside him to accept the blast as well, but he would make do with what was possible.

What he never expected was the politician sitting with a scotch in the living room, the fat one with the round eyes that stared in horror as he was dragged in. Their eyes met, but neither said a thing. Surprise kept them both mute. His captors dragged him to the basement and locked the door, and Sam settled at the table, thinking through the implications of Daniel Kwambai working with Aslim Taslam.

As if he'd read Sam's mind, some ten minutes later Kwambai opened the door and stepped inside wearing a wrinkled linen jacket stretched on one side by something heavy in the pocket. He closed the door and stared at Sam. "What are you *doing* here?" came his falsetto whisper.

"You're playing both sides, Daniel. Aren't you?"

Kwambai shook his head and took a seat across from him. "Don't judge me, Sam. You're not in a position."

"We don't pay you enough?"

"No one pays enough. You know that. But maybe after this money you're bringing I'll be able to quit playing any sides at all. If the money's legitimate. Is it?"

"Sure it is. Is the information going to be legitimate?"

"They don't tell me much, but no, I don't think so."

Sam feigned disappointment. "You going to help me get out of here, then?"

"Not before the money's transferred."

"And then?"

Kwambai didn't answer. He seemed to be thinking of something, while Sam was thinking about the bulge in Kwambai's pocket.

"Well?"

"I'm considering a lot of things," said Kwambai. "For instance, how you would stand up to Nabil's interrogation."

"No better or worse than most men, probably."

"And I'm wondering what you'd say."

"About you?" Sam shook his head. "I don't think you have to worry about that. If he doesn't follow that line of questioning, there'll be no reason to answer."

A sad smile crossed Kwambai's face. "And if he just asks for a reason to end the pain?"

Sam knew what he was getting at, but things had become confused enough by this point that he couldn't be sure how he wanted to answer. The obvious thing to say was that he'd protect Kwambai's relationship with the Company to his dying breath, but no one would believe that, least of all him. The truth was that he recognized that sad look on the politician's face. It was the same expression Kwambai had given just before accepting that initial deal, a year ago, to make contact with the Somali extremists who'd been doing business in Kenya. The look signified that, while he could hardly admit it to himself, Kwambai had already made up his mind.

So he repeated the lie he had used to encourage the coward Paul Fisher: "You still need me. For the transfer." He raised his hands and tickled the air with his fingers. "My prints."

But nothing changed in Kwambai's face.

"Take it out, then," said Sam.

"What?"

"The gun. Take it out and do what you have to do. I personally don't think you can. Not here in your own house. Not with your own hands. And how would you explain it to Nabil? He wants me. Like you, he wants the money. He—" Sam stopped himself because he recognized that he was rambling. Panic was starting to overcome him.

Dutifully, though, Kwambai removed a revolver from his pocket and placed it on the table, pointing it at Sam much the way Sam had pointed the Beretta at Paul Fisher. Unlike the Beretta, this was an old gun, a World War II model Colt .45. Kwambai's eyes were red around the edges. "I like you, Sam. I really do."

"But not that much."

"No," Kwambai said as he lifted the pistol and shot three times before he could think through what he was doing.

BENJAMIN

Benjamin had lived most of his life making snap decisions and only afterward deciding whether or not they'd been correct. Intuition had been his primary guide. Even the occasional services he performed for the Americans and the Brits had begun that way. So all afternoon, as he tracked

down a friend who would be willing to drive Paul Fisher to the border, he had wrestled with it, weighing Fisher's life against the comforts of his family. If the Americans cut him off, George would probably not get to football camp this year; Elinah's confirmation party would be more modest than planned; and Murugi, his long-suffering yet intractable wife, would start questioning the shift in the monthly budget. Was one stranger's life worth it?

It wasn't until the trip back to the hotel in his friend's Toyota pickup that he really convinced himself that he'd done right. We're all employed by someone, he told himself philosophically, but in the end it's self-employment that motivates us. The sentence charmed him, provoking a mysterious, proud smile on his lips, and that only made it more disappointing when he arrived at the hotel and learned that it had all been for nothing.

His first clue was Chief Japhet Obure in the lobby, talking with the hotel manager and the bartender. The local police chief rolled his eyes at the sight of Benjamin. "Kidnapped American, and then you appear, Ben. Why am I not surprised?"

"You know me, Japhi. I can smell scandal a mile away."

Benjamin's disappointment was breathtakingly vast, bigger than he would have imagined. He hadn't known Paul Fisher. Had he liked him? Not really. He had liked Sam, but not the feeble man who affected coldness to overcome an obvious cowardice. And it wasn't as if Paul Fisher had been an innocent; none of the connected Americans who wandered into his country were. But his disappearance hurt just the same.

"Looks like he hadn't even unpacked," Japhet said once they were both in his room.

Benjamin, by the door, watched the chief touch the wrinkled bedspread and the dusty bedside table. But what the chief didn't notice was the empty space, just beside the luggage stand, where the briefcase had been. As Japhet opened closets and drawers, Benjamin watched over his shoulder, but the all-important case wasn't there. Why hadn't Benjamin taken it with him when he'd left?

He knew the answer, but it was so banal as to be embarrassing. He, like anyone, didn't want to run around town carrying a bomb.

Once everything had been brushed for prints, a long line of witnesses interviewed, and darkness had fallen, Chief Obure invited him out for a drink. Benjamin called Murugi and told her he'd be late. "Because of the kidnapped American?" It was already making the news.

By nine he and Japhet were sitting at a sidewalk café, drinking cold bottles of Tusker and eyeing a trio of twelve-year-old boys across the road sucking on plastic bags of glue.

"Breaks my heart to see that," said Japhet.

"Then you should be dead sixty times over by now," Benjamin answered as his cell phone rang a monotone sound. Simultaneously, Japhet's played a recent disco hit.

A house northeast of the city, not so far from the United Nations compound in Runda Estate, had been demolished by an explosion. Benjamin knew the house, and back when Daniel Kwambai had still been in the government's favor he'd even visited it. Still, the fact that the bomb had ended up in one of Kwambai's houses was a surprise.

"Time for a field trip," Japhet said when they'd both hung up.

It took them forty minutes to reach Runda Estate and head farther north, where they followed the tower of smoke down to the inferno on the hill. The firefighters had left to collect more water, and Pili, one of Benjamin's assistants, was standing in the long front yard, staring at the flames. He was soaked through with sweat.

"The explosion came from inside. That's what the fire chief says."

"What else would they expect?" asked Japhet. Since his boss didn't reply, Pili said, "Car bomb."

"Right, right."

Both Pili and Japhet watched as Benjamin approached the burning house on his own. He stopped where the temperature rose dramatically, then began to perspire visibly, his shirt blackening down the center and spreading outward.

From behind, he heard Japhet's voice: "What're you thinking, Ben?"

"Just that it's beautiful," he answered, because that was true. Flames did not sit still. They buckled and wove and snapped and rose so that you could never hold their true form. Perhaps they had no true form. Wood popped and something deep inside the inferno exploded.

"Do you know what's going on here, Ben?"

The wailing fire truck was returning, full of water. Farther out, headlights moved down the long road toward them. That would be absolutely everyone—government representatives, religious leaders, the Americans, the United Nations, the press.

He took Japhet's arm and walked him toward his car. "Come on. I'll buy you a drink wherever you like."

"A rare and wonderful offer," Japhet said. "You steal something?"

"I've earned every cent I have," he answered, twirling keys around his finger. "I just feel like forgetting."

"This?"

"If I forget it, maybe it'll just go away," Benjamin said, smiling pleasantly as he got in and started the car. In no time at all, they had passed the incoming traffic and made it over the hills and back into the city. It was as if the burning house had never been. Despite the sweltering heat, Benjamin had even stopped sweating.

THE LADY OF THE GREAT NORTH ROAD

WILLIAM LE QUEUX

THE AUTHOR OF more than a hundred novels and countless short stories, William Tufnell Le Queux (1864–1927) wrote detective and romance fiction but is remembered today for his espionage stories. As a correspondent for London's *Daily Mail* during the Balkan War that preceded the outbreak of World War I, he is reputed to also have been a member of the British Secret Service. He was a pioneer expert in wireless transmission, mainly as it related to espionage activity. He appears to have spent the major portion of his life in behind-the-scenes patriotic activities for England and began writing stories about secret agents largely to finance his work for British Intelligence, which required extensive travel and personal contact with royalty and other high-ranking people.

While *The Bond of Black* (1899), an early detective novel by Le Queux, was compared to Wilkie Collins, especially *The Moonstone* (1868), it was due more to his plagiarism than his style, which rarely achieved heights of a three on a scale of one to ten. He borrowed from the romantic melodramas that were so popular in the Victorian era to include a lovely and pure young woman, a handsome, fearless, heroic protagonist, and enemies of pure vileness.

Largely because of his efforts at being an undercover agent, and certainly because of his ability to contrive so many plots, Le Queux anticipated most of the tropes of spy fiction, however inadvertently he may have stumbled upon them. His fiction was aimed at the lower middle classes as literacy became more common in the latter part of the nineteenth century and lending libraries made rented books affordable. Shopkeepers and clerks suddenly had the opportunity to read about the rich and powerful, as well as the luxurious lives they led—lives that they would never taste themselves.

His early dedication to the importance of espionage in real life, combined with the success of the inventiveness of his fiction, convinced the British government to develop a strong Secret Service. Le Queux's significance in the history of espionage is acknowledged in Graham Greene's *The Ministry of Fear* (1943) when Arthur Rowe, its beleaguered protagonist, has a nightmare and screams, "The world has been remade by William Le Queux."

In the present story, a young Italian aristocrat, Count Bindo di Ferraris, like so many of the landed gentry of his time, owns a grand touring car and employs a chauffeur to take him where he wants to go, or to assist in other ways. Being well-paid enables the solid English chauffeur to turn an unquestioning blind eye to some of his chores because the count is little more than a rogue, though his chicanery is often employed to help others.

"The Lady of the Great North Road" was originally published in the December 1904 issue of *Cassell's Magazine;* it was first collected in *The Count's Chauffeur Being the Confessions of George Ewart, Chauffeur to Count Bindo di Ferraris* (London, Eveleigh Nash, 1907).

THE LADY OF THE GREAT NORTH ROAD

WILLIAM LE QUEUX

IT OCCURRED about a month after my return from Germany. A strange affair, assuredly; and stranger still that my life should have been spared to relate it.

After luncheon at the Trocadero I stepped into the car, a new Bentley that we had purchased only a week before, to drive to Barnack, an old-world Northamptonshire village near Stamford, where I had to meet the audacious rascal Count Bindo. From Piccadilly Circus I started forth upon my hundred-mile run with a light heart, in keen anticipation of a merry time. The Houghs, with whom Bindo was staying, always had gay house-parties, for the Major, his wife, and Marigold, his daughter, were keen on hunting, and we usually went to the meets of the Fitzwilliam, and got good runs across the park, Castor Hanglands, and the neighbourhood.

Through the grey, damp afternoon I drove on up the Great North Road. Simmons, Bindo's new valet, was suffering from neuralgia; therefore I had left him in London, and, sitting alone, had ample time for reflection.

The road surface was good, the car running like a clock, and on the level, open highway out of Biggleswade through Tempsford and Eaton Socon along to Buckden the speedometer was registering fifty and even sixty miles an hour. I was anxious to get to Barnack before dark, therefore I "let her rip."

The cheerless afternoon had drawn to a close, and rain had begun to fall. In a week or ten days we should be on the Riviera again, amid the sunshine and the flowers; and I pitied those compelled to bear the unequal rigour of the English winter. I was rushing up Alconbury Hill, having done seventy miles without stopping, when of a sudden I felt that drag on the steering-wheel that every motorist knows and dreads. The car refused to answer to the wheel—there was a puncture in the near hind tyre.

It took me some time to put things right, but at last I recommenced to climb the hill and drop down into Sawtry.

About two miles beyond Sawtry, when, by reason of the winding of the road, I had slackened down, I came to cross-roads and a signpost, against which something white shone in the darkness. At first I believed it to be a white dog, but next moment I heard a woman's voice hailing me, and turning, saw in the lamplight as I flashed past, a tall, handsome figure, with a long dark cloak over a light dress. She raised her arms frantically, calling to me. Therefore I put down the brakes hard, stopped, and then reversed the car, until I came back to where she stood in the muddy road.

The moment she opened her mouth I recognized that she was a lady.

"Excuse me," she exclaimed breathlessly, "but would you do me a great favour—and take us on to Wansford—to the railway?" And looking, I made out that she held by the hand a fair-haired little lad of about seven years of age, well dressed in a thick overcoat and knitted woollen cap and gloves. "You will not refuse, will you?" she implored. "The life of a person very dear to me depends upon it." And in her voice I detected an accent by which I knew she was not English.

Seeing how deeply in earnest she was, and that she was no mere wayfarer desirous of a "lift," I expressed my readiness to do her a favour, and, getting down, opened the door and assisted the little lad and herself to get in.

"Ah, sir, this kindness is one for which I can never sufficiently thank you. Others may be able to render you some service in return," she said, "but for myself I can only give you the heartfelt thanks of a distressed woman."

In her refined voice there was a ring of deep earnestness. Who could she be?

The hood of her heavy, fur-lined coat was drawn over her head, and in the darkness I could not distinguish her features. The little boy huddled close to her as we tore on towards Wansford station, her destination, fifteen miles distant. As we entered the long, old-world village of Stilton, my tyre again gave out, and I pulled up at the "Bell."

"You are not surely going to make a stop here, are you? No one must see us. Let us go on!" she urged in apprehension.

"I must attend to the tyre," I said. "No one shall see you. There is a little sitting-room at the side where you will be quite secluded." And then, with apparent reluctance, she allowed me to lead her and the boy through the old stone hall and into the little, low, old-fashioned room, the window of which, with its red blind, looked out upon the village street.

As she seated herself in the high-backed arm-chair beside the fire, her dark, refined face was turned towards me, while the little lad stood huddled up against her, as though half afraid of me. That she was a lady was at once apparent. Her age was about twenty-two, and her countenance one of the most beautiful that I had ever gazed upon. Her dark, luminous eyes met mine with an expression half of innate modesty, half of fear. The white hand lying in her lap trembled, and with the other she stroked the child's head caressingly.

She had unhooked her dripping cloak, and I saw that beneath she wore a well-cut travelling-gown of pale-grey cloth. Her dress betrayed her foreign birth, but the accent when she spoke was only very slight, a rolling of the "r"s, by which I knew that she was French.

"I'm so afraid that someone may see me here," she said, after a slight pause.

"Then I take it, mademoiselle, that you are leaving the neighbourhood in secret?" I remarked in French, with some suspicion, still wondering who she might be. The boy was certainly not her child, yet he seemed to regard her as his guardian.

"Yes, m'sieur," was her brief reply; and then in French she said, after a pause: "I am wondering whether I can trust you further."

"Trust me?" I echoed. "Certainly you can, mademoiselle." And taking out a card, I handed it to her, declaring my readiness to serve her in any way in my power.

She was silent for some moments.

"To-morrow, or the next day, there will be a sensation in the neighbourhood where I joined you," she said at last.

"A mystery, you mean?" I exclaimed, looking straight into her handsome face.

"Yes," she answered in a deep, hoarse voice. "A mystery. But," she added quickly, "you will not prejudge me until you know—will you? Recollect me merely as an unhappy woman whom you have assisted, not as——" She sighed deeply, without concluding the sentence.

I saw that her splendid eyes were filled with tears—tears of regret, it seemed.

"Not as what?" I inquired softly. "May I not at least know your name?"

"Ah!" she said bitterly. "Call me Clotilde, if you like. The name will be as good as any other—until you know the truth."

"But, mademoiselle, you are in distress, I see. Cannot I do anything else for you now than merely dropping you at the roadside station? I am on my way to Stamford."

"No," she sighed; "you can do nothing more at present. Only deny that you have ever met me."

Her words puzzled me. At one moment I wondered if she were not some clever woman who was abducting the lad, and by whose plausible tale I was being led into rendering her assistance. And yet, gazing at her as she sat, I recognized a something about her that told me she was no mere adventuress.

Upon her finger was a magnificent ring—a coronet of fine diamonds that flashed and sparkled beneath the lamplight, and when she smiled at me her face assumed a sweet expression that held me in fascination.

"Cannot you tell me what has occurred?" I asked at last, in a quiet, earnest voice. "What is the nature of the sensation that is imminent?"

"Ah no!" she answered hoarsely. "You will know soon enough."

"But, mademoiselle, I confess I should like to meet you again in London, and offer you my services. In half an hour we shall part."

"Yes, we shall part; and if we do not meet again I shall always remember you as one who performed one of the greatest services a man can perform. To-night, m'sieur, you have saved my life—and *his*," she added, pointing to the little lad at her side.

"Saved your lives? How?"

"You will know one day," was her evasive reply.

"And who is he?"

"I regret that I am not permitted to tell you," she answered.

At that instant heavy footsteps sounded in the hall, and gruff voices exchanged greetings.

"Hark!" she gasped, starting to her feet in alarm. "Is the door locked?"

I sprang to it, and, as the waiting-maid had left it slightly ajar, I could see the new-comers. I closed it, and slid the bolt into its socket.

"Who are they?" she inquired.

"Two men in dark overcoats and soft felt hats. They look like foreigners."

"Ah! I know!" she gasped, terrified, her face blanched in an instant. "Let us go! They must not see me! You will help me to escape, won't you? Can I get out without them recognizing me?"

Was it possible that she had committed some crime, and they were detectives? Surely this adventure was a strange and mysterious one.

"Remain here," I exclaimed quickly. "I'll go out and see to the car. When all is ready, I will keep watch while you and the boy slip out."

I attended to the tyre, this time a light job, and returning, and finding no one in the passage—the two men having evidently passed on into the tap-room—I beckoned to her, and she and the lad stole softly along and out into the roadway.

In a moment they were both in the car, and a few seconds later we were tearing along the broad road out of Stilton village.

What was the forthcoming "sensation"? Why was she flying from the two strangers?

She feared we might be followed, therefore I decided to drive her to Peterborough. We tore on, past Water Newton and Orton, until we drew up at the Great Northern Station at Peterborough, where she descended, and for a moment held my hand in a warm grasp of heartfelt thankfulness.

"You must thank this gentleman," she said to the lad. "Recollect that to-night he has saved your life. They meant to kill you."

"Thank you, sir," said the little lad simply, holding out his hand.

When they had gone I drove away to Barnack, utterly dumbfounded. The fair stranger, who-ever she was, held me in fascination. Never in all my life had I met a woman possessed of such perfect grace and such exquisite charm. She had fled from her enemies. What startling event had occurred that evening to cause her and the lad to take to the road so ill-prepared?

What was the "sensation" which she had prophesied on the morrow? I longed for day to dawn, when I might learn the truth.

Yet though I chatted with the grooms and other outdoor servants at Barnack during the next day, I heard nothing.

Over the dinner-table that evening, however, old Colonel Cooper, who had driven over from Polebrook, near Oundle, related to the guests a strange story that he had heard earlier in the day.

"A mysterious affair has happened over at Buckworth, near the Great North Road, they say," he exclaimed, adjusting his monocle and addressing his hostess and Bindo, who sat on her right. "It seems that a house called 'The Cedars,' about a mile out of the village, has been rented furnished by some foreigners, a man named Latour and his wife and son, whose movements were rather suspicious. Yesterday they received three visitors, who came to spend a week; but just before dinner one of the servants, on enter-ing the drawing-room, was horrified to find both her master and mistress lying upon the floor dead, strangled by the silken cords used to loop up the curtains, while the visitors and the little boy were missing. So swiftly and quietly was it all done," he added, "that the servants heard nothing. The three visitors are described as very gentlemanly-looking men, evidently Frenchmen, who appeared to be on most intimate terms of friendship with their hostess. One of them, how-ever, is declared by the groom to be a man he had met in the neighbourhood two days before; therefore it would seem as though the affair had been very carefully planned."

"Most extraordinary!" declared Bindo, while a chorus of surprise and horror went around the table. "And the boy is missing with the assassins?"

"Yes; they have apparently taken him away with them. They say that there's some woman at the bottom of it all—and most probably," sniffed the old Colonel. "The foreigners who live here in England are mostly a queer lot, who've broken the laws of their own country and efface their identity here."

I listened at the open door with breathless interest as the old fellow discussed the affair with young Lady Casterton, who sat next him, while around the table various theories were advanced.

"I met the man Latour once—one day in the summer," exclaimed Mr. Molesworth, a tall, thin-faced man, rector of a neighbouring parish. "He was introduced to me at the village flower-show at Alconbury, when I was doing duty there. He struck me as a very pleasant, well-bred man, who spoke English perfectly."

I stood in the corridor like a man in a dream. Had I actually assisted the mysterious woman to abduct the child? Every detail of my adventure on the previous night arose vividly before me. That she had been aware of the terrible trag-edy was apparent, for without doubt she was in league with the assassins. She had made me promise to deny having seen her, and I ground my teeth at having been so cleverly tricked by a pretty woman.

Yet ought I to prejudge her when still igno-rant of the truth, which she had promised to reveal to me? Was it just?

Next day, making the excuse that I wished to test the car, I ran over to the sleepy little vil-lage of Buckworth, which lay in a hollow about two miles from the sign-post where I had been stopped by Clotilde. "The Cedars" was a large, old-fashioned house, standing away from the village in its own grounds, and at the village inn, where I called, I learned from the landlord many additional details of how the three mysterious visitors had arrived in a taxi from Huntingdon, how eagerly Mr. Latour had welcomed them, and how they had disappeared at nightfall, after accomplishing their object.

"I hear it said that a woman is at the bottom of it all," I remarked.

"Of course we can't say, sir," he replied; "but a little while ago Mr. Latour was seen several times by men working in the fields to meet, down at Alconbury Brook, a rather handsome, dark young lady, and walk with her."

Was that lady Clotilde? I wondered.

The inquest, held two days later, revealed nothing concerning the antecedents of the Latours, except that they had taken "The Cedars" furnished a year before, and very rarely received visitors. Mr. Latour was believed to be French, but even of that nobody was certain.

A week afterwards, after taking Bindo up to Nottingham, I returned to London, and watched daily for some communication, as Clotilde had promised. Weeks passed, but none came, and I gradually became more and more convinced that I had been the victim of an adventuress.

One afternoon, however, I received at my rooms in Bloomsbury a brief note in a woman's handwriting, unsigned, asking me to call at an address in Eccleston Street, Pimlico, that evening, at half-past nine. "I desire to thank you for your kindness to me," was the concluding sentence of the letter.

Naturally, I kept the appointment, and on ringing at the door was shown up by a manservant to a sitting-room on the first floor, where I stood prepared again to meet the woman who held me entranced by her beauty.

But instead of a woman there appeared two dark-faced, sinister-looking foreigners, who entered without a word and closed the door behind them. I instantly recognized them as those I had seen in the passage of the "Bell" at Stilton.

"Well? So you have come?" laughed the elder of the two. "We have asked you here because we wish to know something." And I saw that in his hand he held some object which glistened as it caught my eye. It was a plated revolver. I had been trapped!

"What do you want to know?" I inquired, quickly on the alert against the pair of desperate ruffians.

"Answer me, Mr. Ewart," said the elder of the two, a man with a grey beard and a foreign accent. "You were driving a car near Alconbury on a certain evening, and a woman stopped you. She had a boy with her, and she gave you something—a packet of papers—to keep in safety for her. Where are they? We want them."

"I know nothing of what you are saying," I declared, recollecting Clotilde's injunction. "I think you must be mistaken."

The men smiled grimly, and the elder made a signal, as though to someone behind me, and next instant I felt a silken cord slipped over my head and pulled tight by an unseen hand. A third man had stepped noiselessly from the long cupboard beside the fireplace, to which my back had been turned.

I felt the cord cutting into my throat, and tried to struggle and shout, but a cloth was clapped upon my mouth, and my hands secured by a second cord.

"Now," said the elder man, "tell us the truth, or, if not, you die. You understand? Where is that packet?"

"I know nothing of any packet," I gasped with great difficulty.

"It's a lie! She gave it to you! Where did you take her to?"

I was silent. I had given my promise of secrecy, and yet I was entirely helpless in their unscrupulous hands. Again and again they demanded the papers, which they said she had given me to keep for her, and my denial only brought upon me the increased torture of the cord, until I was almost black in the face, and my veins stood out knotted and hard.

I realized, to my horror, that they intended to murder me, just as they had assassinated Latour and his wife. I fought for life, but my struggles only tightened the cord, and thus increased my agony.

"Tell us where you have put those papers," demanded the younger of the villainous, black-eyed pair, while the third man held me helpless with hands of steel. "Where is the boy?"

"I have no idea," I replied.

"Then die," laughed the man with the grey

beard. "We have given you a chance of life, and you refuse to take it. You assisted her to escape, and you will share the fate of the others."

I saw that to save myself was impossible, but with a superhuman effort I succeeded in slipping the noose from my hands and hooking my fingers in the cord around my throat. The fellow behind placed his knee in my back, and drew the cord with all his might to strangle me; but I cried hoarsely for help, and clung to the fatal cord.

In an instant the two others, joined by a fourth, fell upon me, but by doing so the cord became loosened, and I ducked my head. For a second my right hand was freed, and I drew from my belt the long Italian knife which I often carry as a better weapon in a scrimmage than a revolver, and struck upward at the fellow who had sentenced me to death. The blade entered his stomach, and he fell forward with an agonized cry. Then slashing indiscriminately right and left, I quickly cleared myself of them. A revolver flashed close to me, but the bullet whizzed past, and making a sudden dash for the door I rushed headlong down the stairs and out into the Buckingham Palace Road, still holding my knife, my hands smeared with the blood of my enemies, and the cord still around my neck.

I went direct to the police-station, and within five minutes half a dozen constables were on their way round to the house. But on arrival they found that the men, notwithstanding their severe wounds, had fled, fearing the information I should give. The owner of the house knew nothing, save that he had let it furnished a fortnight before to the grey-bearded man, who had given the name of Burton, although he was a foreigner.

The shock had upset my nerves considerably, but, accompanied by Blythe and Bindo, I drove the car down to Dover, took her across to Calais, and then drove across France to Marseilles, and along the Riviera to Genoa and Pisa, and on to Florence—a delightful journey, which I had accomplished on three previous occasions, for we preferred the car to the stuffy *wagon-lit* of the Rome express.

Times without number I wondered what was the nature of those documents, and why the gang desired to obtain possession of them. But it was all a mystery, inscrutable and complete. And I told the Count nothing.

Our season at Florence was a gay one, and there were many pleasant gatherings at Bindo's villa. The season was, however, an empty one as far as *coups* were concerned. The various *festas* had succeeded one another, and the month of May, the brightest and merriest in Italy, was nearly at an end when one afternoon I was walking in the Cascine, the Hyde Park of the Florentines. Of a sudden there passed a smart car, in which lolled the figure of a well-dressed woman.

Our eyes met. In an instant the recognition was mutual, and she gave an order to stop. It was the sweet-faced wayfarer of the Great North Road—the woman who had enchanted me!

I stood in the roadway, hat in hand, as Italian etiquette requires.

"Ah! I am so pleased to meet you again," she said in French. "I have much to tell you. Can you call on me—to-night at seven, if you have no prior engagement? We have the Villa Simoncini, in the Viale. Anyone will direct you to it. We cannot talk here."

"I shall be delighted. I know the villa quite well," was my answer; and then, with a smile, she drove on, and somehow I thought that the idlers watching us looked at me strangely.

At seven o'clock I was conducted through the great marble hall of the villa, one of the finest residences on the outskirts of Florence, and into the beautiful *salon*, upholstered in pale-green silk, where my pretty companion of that exciting run on the Great North Road rose to greet me with eager, outstretched hand; while behind her stood a tall, white-headed, military-looking man, whom she introduced as her father, General Stefanovitch.

"I asked you here for seven," she said, with a sweet smile, "but we do not dine until eight, therefore we may talk. How fortunate we should meet to-day! I intended to write to you."

I gathered from her subsequent conversation that we might speak frankly before her father, therefore I described to her the exciting adventure that had happened to me in Eccleston Street, whereupon she said:

"Ah! it is only to-day that I am able to reveal to you the truth, relying upon you not to make it public. The secret of the Latours must still be strictly kept, at all hazards."

"What was their secret?" I inquired breathlessly.

"Listen, and I will tell you," she said, motioning me to a seat and sinking into a low lounge-chair herself, while the General stood astride upon the bear-skin stretched before the English fire-grate. "Those men sought the life of one person only—the boy. They went to England to kill him."

"And would have done so, Clotilde, had you not saved him," declared her father.

"It was not I," she said quickly. "It was Mr. Ewart, who snatched us from them. They were following, and we both should have shared the fate of the Latours had he not taken us up and driven us away. The thanks of the State are due to Mr. Ewart." And at that moment the little lad entered shyly, and, walking towards her, took her hand.

"The State—what do you mean?" I asked, puzzled.

"The truth is this," she said, smiling. "Little Paul, here, lived in England incognito as Paul Latour, but he is really His Royal Highness the Crown Prince Paul of Bosnia, heir to the throne. Because there was a conspiracy in the capital to kill him, he was sent to England in secret in the care of his tutor and his wife, who took the name of Latour, while he passed as their son. The revolutionists had sworn to kill the King's son, and by some means discovered his whereabouts in England; whereupon four of them were chosen to go there and assassinate him. By good fortune I learnt the truth, and as maid-of-honour to the Queen resolved to say nothing, but to go alone to England in secret and rescue the Crown Prince. The four conspirators had already left our capital; therefore I went in hot pursuit, travelling

across Europe, and reaching London on the day before we met. I managed to overtake them, and, watching their movements, I travelled by the same train down to Huntingdon. On arrival there I hurried from the station, got into a taxi, and drove with all speed out to Buckworth. I had been there before, and knew the place well. I crossed the lawn, entered the drawing-room by the French window, and found little Paul alone. The Latours were out, he said; so I induced him to leave the place with me without the knowledge of the servants. I desired to see the Latours, and also to watch the movements of the assassins; therefore we hid in the wood close to the house at a spot where I had once met Latour secretly with a message from Her Majesty, who somehow mistrusted Latour's wife. In half an hour three of the men arrived, and were met by Latour, who had returned almost at the same moment. They entered, carrying some hand-baggage with them, and I was compelled to remain in hiding, awaiting an opportunity to speak with him. At half-past seven, however, to my great surprise I saw them slip out one by one, and disappear into the wood close to where little Paul and I were hiding in the undergrowth. Then, suspecting something was wrong by the stealthiness of their movements, I crept across the grounds and re-entered the drawing-room from the lawn, where, to my horror, I found Latour and his wife lying dead. I saw that a tragedy had been enacted, and, regaining the wood, hastened on with little Paul in the opposite direction, until I came to the Great North Road, and there met you driving your car. They had heard from Latour that the child had wandered out somewhere, and were, I knew, scouring the country for him. Only by your aid the Crown Prince was saved, and we came here into hiding, the King sending my father to meet me and to live here as his son's protector."

"But why did they kill the Latours?"

"It was part of the conspiracy. Latour, who had recently been back in Bosnia, had, they discovered, given information to the Chief of Police regarding a plot against the Queen, and they, the revolutionists, had condemned both him and his wife to death."

"And the packet which they demanded of me?"

"It contains certain papers concerning the royal family of Bosnia, secrets which the revolutionists desire to obtain and publish," she explained. "The King, distrustful of those about him, gave the packet into the hands of his faithful subject Latour, in England, and he, in preference to putting it into a safe, which might attract the spies of the conspirators, kept it in a small cavity behind the wainscoting in the drawing-room at Buckworth—a spot which he showed me, so that if any untoward event occurred I should at least know where the documents were secreted. When I realized the terrible fate of the unfortunate Latour and noticed the disordered state of the room and study beyond, I suspected that a search had been made for them, and going to the spot I pressed the spring, and, finding them still safe, secured them. The revolutionists undoubtedly saw us leaving the inn at Stilton together, and believed that I had secured the documents as well as the boy, and that I had probably, in my flight, handed them to you for safe keeping."

"And the assassins? What has become of them?"

"They returned to Bosnia when they had recovered from the wounds you inflicted, but were at once arrested on information supplied by me, and have all four been condemned to solitary confinement for life—a punishment which is worse than death."

Since that evening I have been a frequent visitor at the Stefanovitchs', who still live in Florence under the name of Darfour, and more than once has the little Crown Prince thanked me. The pretty, dark-eyed Clotilde and her father are quite popular in society, but no one dreams that little Paul, who is so carefully guarded by the old General and his trusty soldier-servant, is heir to a European throne, or that his life was saved in curious circumstances by "the Count's chauffeur."

CALLOWAY'S CODE

O. HENRY

THERE HAS NEVER BEEN a more beloved short story writer in America than William Sydney Porter (1862–1910), more commonly known as O. Henry. He never wrote a novel, but his miniature masterpieces encapsulated whole lives of ordinary people—his favorite subjects.

After being convicted of embezzling money from the bank in which he worked, he spent time in prison, reputedly taking the name of a kindly guard for his pseudonym.

O. Henry wrote more than six hundred short stories that once were as critically acclaimed as they were popular. Often undervalued today because of their sentimentality, many nonetheless remain iconic and familiar, notably such classics as "The Gift of the Magi," "The Furnished Room," "The Ransom of Red Chief," and "A Retrieved Reformation" (better known for its several stage and film versions as *Alias Jimmy Valentine*). More than two hundred motion pictures and television programs were based on O. Henry's work, including the eponymous *O. Henry Playhouse*.

The O. Henry Prize Stories, a prestigious annual anthology of the year's best short stories, has been published since 1919. His book *The Gentle Grafter* (1908) was regarded so highly that Ellery Queen selected it for *Queen's Quorum*, the list of the one hundred and six greatest mystery short story collections of all time.

In "Calloway's Code," a newspaper staff takes on the responsibility of deciphering a coded message sent by a reporter on the front of the Russo–Japanese War. This is a remarkable departure for O. Henry, most of his works being set close to home in familiar settings and featuring everyday people living ordinary lives.

"Calloway's Code" was originally published in the September 1906 issue of *Munsey's Magazine;* it was first collected in *Whirligigs* by O. Henry (New York, Doubleday, Page, 1910).

CALLOWAY'S CODE

O. Henry

THE NEW YORK ENTERPRISE sent H. B. Calloway as special correspondent to the Russo–Japanese–Portsmouth war.

For two months Calloway hung about Yokohama and Tokio, shaking dice with the other correspondents for drinks of 'rickshaws—oh, no, that's something to ride in; anyhow, he wasn't earning the salary that his paper was paying him. But that was not Calloway's fault. The little brown men who held the strings of Fate between their fingers were not ready for the readers of the *Enterprise* to season their breakfast bacon and eggs with the battles of the descendants of the gods.

But soon the column of correspondents that were to go out with the First Army tightened their field-glass belts and went down to the Yalu with Kuroki. Calloway was one of these.

Now, this is no history of the battle of the Yalu River. That has been told in detail by the correspondents who gazed at the shrapnel smoke rings from a distance of three miles. But, for justice's sake, let it be understood that the Japanese commander prohibited a nearer view.

Calloway's feat was accomplished before the battle. What he did was to furnish the *Enterprise* with the biggest beat of the war. That paper published exclusively and in detail the news of the attack on the lines of the Russian General on the same day that it was made. No other paper printed a word about it for two days afterward, except a London paper, whose account was absolutely incorrect and untrue.

Calloway did this in face of the fact that General Kuroki was making his moves and living his plans with the profoundest secrecy, as far as the world outside his camps was concerned. The correspondents were forbidden to send out any news whatever of his plans; and every message that was allowed on the wires was censored—with rigid severity.

The correspondent for the London paper handed in a cablegram describing Kuroki's plans; but as it was wrong from beginning to end the censor grinned and let it go through.

So, there they were—Kuroki on one side of the Yalu with forty-two thousand infantry, five thousand cavalry, and one hundred and twenty-four guns. On the other side, Zassulitch waited for him with only twenty-three thousand men, and with a long stretch of river to guard. And Calloway had got hold of some important inside information that he knew would bring the *Enterprise* staff around a cablegram as thick as flies around a Park Row lemonade stand. If he could only get that message past the censor—the new censor who had arrived and taken his post that day!

Calloway did the obviously proper thing. He lit his pipe and sat down on a gun carriage to think it over. And there we must leave him; for the rest of the story belongs to Vesey, a sixteen-dollar-a-week reporter on the *Enterprise*.

Calloway's cablegram was handed to the managing editor at four o'clock in the afternoon. He read it three times; and then drew a pocket mirror from a pigeon-hole in his desk, and looked at his reflection carefully. Then he went over to the desk of Boyd, his assistant (he usually called Boyd when he wanted him), and laid the cablegram before him.

"It's from Calloway," he said. "See what you make of it."

The message was dated at Wi-ju, and these were the words of it:

Foregone preconcerted rash witching
goes muffled rumour mine dark silent
unfortunate richmond existing great hotly
brute select mooted parlous beggars ye
angel incontrovertible.

Boyd read it twice.

"It's either a cipher or a sunstroke," said he.

"Ever hear of anything like a code in the office a secret code?" asked the m.c., who had held his desk for only two years. Managing editors come and go.

"None except the vernacular that the lady specials write in," said Boyd. "Couldn't be an acrostic, could it?"

"I thought of that," said the m.e., "but the beginning letters contain only four vowels. It must be a code of some sort."

"Try 'em in groups," suggested Boyd. "Let's see—'Rash witching goes'—not with me it doesn't. 'Muffled rumour mine'—must have

an underground wire. 'Dark silent unfortunate richmond'—no reason why he should knock that town so hard. 'Existing great hotly'—no it doesn't pan out. I'll call Scott."

The city editor came in a hurry, and tried his luck. A city editor must know something about everything; so Scott knew a little about cipher-writing.

"It may be what is called an inverted alphabet cipher," said he. "I'll try that. 'R' seems to be the oftenest used initial letter, with the exception of 'm.' Assuming 'r' to mean 'e,' the most frequently used vowel, we transpose the letters—so."

Scott worked rapidly with his pencil for two minutes; and then showed the first word according to his reading—the word "Scejtzez."

"Great!" cried Boyd. "It's a charade. My first is a Russian general. Go on, Scott."

"No, that won't work," said the city editor. "It's undoubtedly a code. It's impossible to read it without the key. Has the office ever used a cipher code?"

"Just what I was asking," said the m.e. "Hustle everybody up that ought to know. We must get at it some way. Calloway has evidently got hold of something big, and the censor has put the screws on, or he wouldn't have cabled in a lot of chop suey like this."

Throughout the office of the *Enterprise* a dragnet was sent, hauling in such members of the staff as would be likely to know of a code, past or present, by reason of their wisdom, information, natural intelligence, or length of servitude. They got together in a group in the city room, with the m.e. in the centre. No one had heard of a code. All began to explain to the head investigator that newspapers never use a code, anyhow—that is, a cipher code. Of course the Associated Press stuff is a sort of code—an abbreviation, rather—but—

The m.e. knew all that, and said so. He asked each man how long he had worked on the paper. Not one of them had drawn pay from an *Enterprise* envelope for longer than six years. Calloway had been on the paper twelve years. "Try old Heffelbauer," said the m.e. "He was here when Park Row was a potato patch."

Heffelbauer was an institution. He was half janitor, half handy-man about the office, and half watchman—thus becoming the peer of thirteen and one-half tailors.

Sent for, he came, radiating his nationality. "Heffelbauer," said the m.e., "did you ever hear of a code belonging to the office a long time ago—a private code? You know what a code is, don't you?"

"Yah," said Heffelbauer. "Sure I know vat a code is. Yah, apout dwelf or fifteen year ago der office had a code. Der reborters in der city-room haf it here."

"Ah!" said the m.e. "We're getting on the trail now. Where was it kept, Heffelbauer? What do you know about it?"

"Sometimes," said the retainer, "dey keep it in der little room behind der library room."

"Can you find it?" asked the m.e. eagerly. "Do you know where it is?"

"Mein Gott!" said Heffelbauer. "How long you dink a code live? Der reborters call him a masket. But von day he butt mit his head der editor, und—"

"Oh, he's talking about a goat," said Boyd. "Get out, Heffelbauer."

Again discomfited, the concerted wit and resource of the *Enterprise* huddled around Calloway's puzzle, considering its mysterious words in vain.

Then Vesey came in.

Vesey was the youngest reporter. He had a thirty-two-inch chest and wore a number fourteen collar; but his bright Scotch plaid suit gave him presence and conferred no obscurity upon his whereabouts. He wore his hat in such a position that people followed him about to see him take it off, convinced that it must be hung upon a peg driven into the back of his head. He was never without an immense, knotted, hard-wood cane with a German-silver tip on its crooked handle. Vesey was the best photograph hustler in the office. Scott said it was because no living

human being could resist the personal triumph it was to hand his picture over to Vesey. Vesey always wrote his own news stories, except the big ones, which were sent to the rewrite men. Add to this fact that among all the inhabitants, temples, and groves of the earth nothing existed that could abash Vesey, and his dim sketch is concluded.

Vesey butted into the circle of cipher readers very much as Heffelbauer's "code" would have done, and asked what was up. Some one explained, with the touch of half-familiar condescension that they always used toward him. Vesey reached out and took the cablegram from the m.e.'s hand. Under the protection of some special Providence, he was always doing appalling things like that, and coming off unscathed.

"It's a code," said Vesey. "Anybody got the key?"

"The office has no code," said Boyd, reaching for the message. Vesey held to it.

"Then old Calloway expects us to read it, anyhow," said he. "He's up a tree, or something, and he's made this up so as to get it by the censor. It's up to us. Gee! I wish they had sent me, too. Say—we can't afford to fall down on our end of it. 'Foregone, preconcerted rash, witching'—h'm."

Vesey sat down on a table corner and began to whistle softly, frowning at the cablegram.

"Let's have it, please," said the m.e. "We've got to get to work on it."

"I believe I've got a line on it," said Vesey. "Give me ten minutes."

He walked to his desk, threw his hat into a waste-basket, spread out flat on his chest like a gorgeous lizard, and started his pencil going. The wit and wisdom of the *Enterprise* remained in a loose group, and smiled at one another, nodding their heads toward Vesey. Then they began to exchange their theories about the cipher.

It took Vesey exactly fifteen minutes. He brought to the m.e. a pad with the code-key written on it.

"I felt the swing of it as soon as I saw it," said Vesey. "Hurrah for old Calloway! He's done the

Japs and every paper in town that prints literature instead of news. Take a look at that."

Thus had Vesey set forth the reading of the code:

Foregone—conclusion
Preconcerted—arrangement
Rash—act
Witching—hour of midnight
Goes—without saying
Muffled—report
Rumour—hath it
Mine—host
Dark—horse
Silent—majority
Unfortunate—pedestrians*
Richmond—in the field
Existing—conditions
Great-White Way
Hotly—contested
Brute—force
Select—few
Mooted—question
Parlous—times
Beggars—description
Ye—correspondent
Angel—unawares
Incontrovertible—fact

"It's simply newspaper English," explained Vesey. "I've been reporting on the *Enterprise* long enough to know it by heart. Old Calloway gives us the cue word, and we use the word that naturally follows it just as we 'em in the paper. Read it over, and you'll see how pat they drop into their places. Now, here's the message he intended us to get."

Vesey handed out another sheet of paper.

Concluded arrangement to act at hour of

---

* Mr. Vesey afterward explained that the logical journalistic complement of the word "unfortunate" was once the word "victim." But, since the automobile became so popular, the correct following word is now pedestrians. Of course, in Calloway's code it meant infantry.

midnight without saying. Report hath it that a large body of cavalry and an overwhelming force of infantry will be thrown into the field. Conditions white. Way contested by only a small force. Question the *Times* description. Its correspondent is unaware of the facts.

"Great stuff!" cried Boyd excitedly. "Kuroki crosses the Yalu to-night and attacks. Oh, we won't do a thing to the sheets that make up with Addison's essays, real estate transfers, and bowling scores!"

"Mr. Vesey," said the m.e., with his jollying—which—you—should—regard—as—a—favour manner, "you have cast a serious reflection upon the literary standards of the paper that employs you. You have also assisted materially in giving us the biggest 'beat' of the year. I will let you know in a day or two whether you are to be discharged or retained at a larger salary. Somebody send Ames to me."

Ames was the king-pin, the snowy-petalled Marguerite, the star-bright looloo of the rewrite men. He saw attempted murder in the pains of green-apple colic, cyclones in the summer zephyr, lost children in every top-spinning urchin, an uprising of the down-trodden masses in every hurling of a derelict potato at a passing automobile. When not rewriting, Ames sat on the porch of his Brooklyn villa playing checkers with his ten-year-old son.

Ames and the "war editor" shut themselves in a room. There was a map in there stuck full of little pins that represented armies and divisions. Their fingers had been itching for days to move those pins along the crooked line of the Yalu. They did so now; and in words of fire Ames translated Calloway's brief message into a front page masterpiece that set the world talking. He told of the secret councils of the Japanese officers; gave Kuroki's flaming speeches in full; counted the cavalry and infantry to a man and a horse; described the quick and silent building of the bridge at Stuikauchen, across which the Mikado's legions were hurled upon the surprised Zassulitch, whose troops were widely scattered along the river. And the battle!—well, you know what Ames can do with a battle if you give him just one smell of smoke for a foundation. And in the same story, with seemingly supernatural knowledge, he gleefully scored the most profound and ponderous paper in England for the false and misleading account of the intended movements of the Japanese First Army printed in its issue of the same date.

Only one error was made; and that was the fault of the cable operator at Wi-ju. Calloway pointed it out after he came back. The word "great" in his code should have been "gage," and its complemental words "of battle." But it went to Ames "conditions white," and of course he took that to mean snow. His description of the Japanese army strum, struggling through the snowstorm, blinded by the whirling flakes, was thrillingly vivid. The artists turned out some effective illustrations that made a hit as pictures of the artillery dragging their guns through the drifts. But, as the attack was made on the first day of May, "conditions white" excited some

amusement. But it made no difference to the *Enterprise*, anyway.

It was wonderful. And Calloway was wonderful in having made the new censor believe that his jargon of words meant no more than a complaint of the dearth of news and a petition for more expense money. And Vesey was wonderful. And most wonderful of all are words, and how they make friends one with another, being oft associated, until not even obituary notices them do part.

On the second day following, the city editor halted at Vesey's desk where the reporter was writing the story of a man who had broken his leg by falling into a coal-hole—Ames having failed to find a murder motive in it.

"The old man says your salary is to be raised to twenty a week," said Scott.

"All right," said Vesey. "Every little helps. Say—Mr. Scott, which would you say—'We can state without fear of successful contradiction,' or, 'On the whole it can be safely asserted'?"

THE STORY OF A CONSCIENCE

AMBROSE BIERCE

IT SEEMS THAT THE entire life of Ambrose Gwinnett Bierce (1842–1914?), and every word he wrote, was dark and cynical, earning him the sobriquet "Bitter Bierce." It is not surprising that his greatest success came in the dark world of supernatural fiction, where he has been described as America's greatest writer of horror fiction between Edgar Allan Poe and H. P. Lovecraft.

Born in Meigs County, Ohio, he grew up in Indiana with his mother and eccentric father as the tenth of thirteen of children, all of whose names began with the letter *A*. When the Civil War broke out, he volunteered and was soon commissioned a first lieutenant in the Union Army, seeing action in the Battle of Shiloh.

He became one of the most important and influential journalists in America, writing columns for William Randolph Hearst's *San Francisco Examiner*. His darkest book may be the devastating *The Devil's Dictionary* (1911), in which he defined a saint as "a dead sinner revised and edited," befriend as "to make an ingrate," and birth as "the first and direst of all tragedies." His most famous story is probably "An Occurrence at Owls Creek Bridge," in which a condemned prisoner believes he has been reprieved—just before the rope snaps his neck. It was filmed three times and was twice made for television, by Rod Serling for *The Twilight Zone* and by Alfred Hitchcock for *Alfred Hitchcock Presents*.

In 1913, he accompanied Pancho Villa's army as an observer. He wrote a letter to a friend dated December 26, 1913. He then vanished—one of the most famous disappearances in history, once as famous as those of Judge Crater and Amelia Earhart.

"The Story of a Conscience" was first published in the June 1, 1890, issue of the *San Francisco Examiner*; it was first published in book form in *In the Midst of Life: Tales of Soldiers and Civilians* (New York, G. P. Putnam's Sons, 1898); with three more stories, this is an enlarged edition of *Tales of Soldiers and Civilians* (San Francisco, E. L. G. Steele, 1891).

THE STORY OF A CONSCIENCE

AMBROSE BIERCE

I

CAPTAIN PARROL HARTROY stood at the advanced post of his picket-guard, talking in low tones with the sentinel. This post was on a turnpike which bisected the captain's camp, a half-mile in rear, though the camp was not in sight from that point. The officer was apparently giving the soldier certain instructions—was perhaps merely inquiring if all were quiet in front. As the two stood talking a man approached them from the direction of the camp, carelessly whistling, and was promptly halted by the soldier. He was evidently a civilian—a tall person, coarsely clad in the home-made stuff of yellow gray, called "butternut," which was men's only wear in the latter days of the Confederacy. On his head was a slouch felt hat, once white, from beneath which hung masses of uneven hair, seemingly unacquainted with either scissors or comb. The man's face was rather striking; a broad forehead, high nose, and thin cheeks, the mouth invisible in the full dark beard, which seemed as neglected as the hair. The eyes were large and had that steadiness and fixity of attention which so frequently mark a considering intelligence and a will not easily turned from its purpose—so say those physiognomists who

have that kind of eyes. On the whole, this was a man whom one would be likely to observe and be observed by. He carried a walking-stick freshly cut from the forest and his ailing cowskin boots were white with dust.

"Show your pass," said the Federal soldier, a trifle more imperiously perhaps than he would have thought necessary if he had not been under the eye of his commander, who with folded arms looked on from the roadside.

"'Lowed you'd rec'lect me, Gineral," said the wayfarer tranquilly, while producing the paper from the pocket of his coat. There was something in his tone—perhaps a faint suggestion of irony—which made his elevation of his obstructor to exalted rank less agreeable to that worthy warrior than promotion is commonly found to be. "You-all have to be purty pertickler, I reckon," he added, in a more conciliatory tone, as if in half-apology for being halted.

Having read the pass, with his rifle resting on the ground, the soldier handed the document back without a word, shouldered his weapon, and returned to his commander. The civilian passed on in the middle of the road, and when he had penetrated the circumjacent Confederacy a few yards resumed his whistling and was soon out of sight beyond an angle in the road, which at that point entered a thin forest. Suddenly the officer undid his arms from his breast, drew a revolver from his belt and sprang forward at a run in the same direction, leaving his sentinel in gaping astonishment at his post. After making to the various visible forms of nature a solemn promise to be damned, that gentleman resumed the air of stolidity which is supposed to be appropriate to a state of alert military attention.

II

Captain Hartroy held an independent command. His force consisted of a company of infantry, a squadron of cavalry, and a section of artillery, detached from the army to which they belonged, to defend an important defile in the Cumberland Mountains in Tennessee. It was a field officer's command held by a line officer promoted from the ranks, where he had quietly served until "discovered." His post was one of exceptional peril; its defense entailed a heavy responsibility and he had wisely been given corresponding discretionary powers, all the more necessary because of his distance from the main army, the precarious nature of his communications and the lawless character of the enemy's irregular troops infesting that region. He had strongly fortified his little camp, which embraced a village of a half-dozen dwellings and a country store, and had collected a considerable quantity of supplies. To a few resident civilians of known loyalty, with whom it was desirable to trade, and of whose services in various ways he sometimes availed himself, he had given written passes admitting them within his lines. It is easy to understand that an abuse of this privilege in the interest of the enemy might entail serious consequences. Captain Hartroy had made an order to the effect that any one so abusing it would be summarily shot.

While the sentinel had been examining the civilian's pass the captain had eyed the latter narrowly. He thought his appearance familiar and

had at first no doubt of having given him the pass which had satisfied the sentinel. It was not until the man had got out of sight and hearing that his identity was disclosed by a revealing light from memory. With soldierly promptness of decision the officer had acted on the revelation.

III

To any but a singularly self-possessed man the apparition of an officer of the military forces, formidably clad, bearing in one hand a sheathed sword and in the other a cocked revolver, and rushing in furious pursuit, is no doubt disquieting to a high degree; upon the man to whom the pursuit was in this instance directed it appeared to have no other effect than somewhat to intensify his tranquillity. He might easily enough have escaped into the forest to the right or the left, but chose another course of action—turned and quietly faced the captain, saying as he came up: "I reckon ye must have something to say to me, which ye disremembered. What mout it be, neighbor?"

But the "neighbor" did not answer, being engaged in the unneighborly act of covering him with a cocked pistol.

"Surrender," said the captain as calmly as a slight breathlessness from exertion would permit, "or you die."

There was no menace in the manner of this demand: that was all in the matter and in the means of enforcing it. There was, too, something not altogether reassuring in the cold gray eyes that glanced along the barrel of the weapon. For a moment the two men stood looking at each other in silence; then the civilian, with no appearance of fear—with as great apparent unconcern as when complying with the less austere demand of the sentinel—slowly pulled from his pocket the paper which had satisfied that humble functionary and held it out, saying:

"I reckon this 'ere parss from Mister Hartroy is——"

"The pass is a forgery," the officer said, interrupting. "I am Captain Hartroy—and you are Dramer Brune."

It would have required a sharp eye to observe the slight pallor of the civilian's face at these words, and the only other manifestation attesting their significance was a voluntary relaxation of the thumb and fingers holding the dishonored paper, which, falling to the road, unheeded, was rolled by a gentle wind and then lay still, with a coating of dust, as in humiliation for the lie that it bore. A moment later the civilian, still looking unmoved into the barrel of the pistol, said:

"Yes, I am Dramer Brune, a Confederate spy, and your prisoner. I have on my person, as you will soon discover, a plan of your fort and its armament, a statement of the distribution of your men and their number, a map of the approaches, showing the positions of all your outposts. My life is fairly yours, but if you wish it taken in a more formal way than by your own hand, and if you are willing to spare me the indignity of marching into camp at the muzzle of your pistol, I promise you that I will neither resist, escape, nor remonstrate, but will submit to whatever penalty may be imposed."

The officer lowered his pistol, uncocked it, and thrust it into its place in his belt. Brune advanced a step, extending his right hand.

"It is the hand of a traitor and a spy," said the officer coldly, and did not take it. The other bowed.

"Come," said the captain, "let us go to camp; you shall not die until to-morrow morning."

He turned his back upon his prisoner, and these two enigmatical men retraced their steps and soon passed the sentinel, who expressed his general sense of things by a needless and exaggerated salute to his commander.

IV

Early on the morning after these events the two men, captor and captive, sat in the tent of the former. A table was between them on which lay, among a number of letters, official and private,

which the captain had written during the night, the incriminating papers found upon the spy. That gentleman had slept through the night in an adjoining tent, unguarded. Both, having breakfasted, were now smoking.

"Mr. Brune," said Captain Hartroy, "you probably do not understand why I recognized you in your disguise, nor how I was aware of your name."

"I have not sought to learn, Captain," the prisoner said with quiet dignity.

"Nevertheless I should like you to know—if the story will not offend. You will perceive that my knowledge of you goes back to the autumn of 1861. At that time you were a private in an Ohio regiment—a brave and trusted soldier. To the surprise and grief of your officers and comrades you deserted and went over to the enemy. Soon afterward you were captured in a skirmish, recognized, tried by court-martial and sentenced to be shot. Awaiting the execution of the sentence you were confined, unfettered, in a freight car standing on a side track of a railway."

"At Grafton, Virginia," said Brune, pushing the ashes from his cigar with the little finger of the hand holding it, and without looking up.

"At Grafton, Virginia," the captain repeated. "One dark and stormy night a soldier who had just returned from a long, fatiguing march was put on guard over you. He sat on a cracker box inside the car, near the door, his rifle loaded and the bayonet fixed. You sat in a corner and his orders were to kill you if you attempted to rise."

"But if I *asked* to rise he might call the corporal of the guard."

"Yes. As the long silent hours wore away the soldier yielded to the demands of nature: he himself incurred the death penalty by sleeping at his post of duty."

"You did."

"What! you recognize me? you have known me all along?"

The captain had risen and was walking the floor of his tent, visibly excited. His face was flushed, the gray eyes had lost the cold, pitiless look which they had shown when Brune had seen them over the pistol barrel; they had softened wonderfully.

"I knew you," said the spy, with his customary tranquillity, "the moment you faced me, demanding my surrender. In the circumstances it would have been hardly becoming in me to recall these matters. I am perhaps a traitor, certainly a spy; but I should not wish to seem a suppliant."

The captain had paused in his walk and was facing his prisoner. There was a singular huskiness in his voice as he spoke again.

"Mr. Brune, whatever your conscience may permit you to be, you saved my life at what you must have believed the cost of your own. Until I saw you yesterday when halted by my sentinel I believed you dead—thought that you had suffered the fate which through my own crime you might easily have escaped. You had only to step from the car and leave me to take your place before the firing-squad. You had a divine compassion. You pitied my fatigue. You let me sleep, watched over me, and as the time drew near for the relief-guard to come and detect me in my crime, you gently waked me. Ah, Brune, Brune, that was well done—that was great—that——"

The captain's voice failed him; the tears were running down his face and sparkled upon his beard and his breast. Resuming his seat at the table, he buried his face in his arms and sobbed. All else was silence.

Suddenly the clear warble of a bugle was heard sounding the "assembly." The captain started and raised his wet face from his arms; it had turned ghastly pale. Outside, in the sunlight, were heard the stir of the men falling into line; the voices of the sergeants calling the roll; the tapping of the drummers as they braced their drums. The captain spoke again:

"I ought to have confessed my fault in order to relate the story of your magnanimity; it might have procured you a pardon. A hundred times I resolved to do so, but shame prevented. Besides, your sentence was just and righteous. Well, Heaven forgive me! I said nothing, and my regiment was soon afterward ordered to Tennessee and I never heard about you."

"It was all right, sir," said Brune, without visible emotion; "I escaped and returned to my colors—the Confederate colors. I should like to add that before deserting from the Federal service I had earnestly asked a discharge, on the ground of altered convictions. I was answered by punishment."

"Ah, but if I had suffered the penalty of my crime—if you had not generously given me the life that I accepted without gratitude you would not be again in the shadow and imminence of death."

The prisoner started slightly and a look of anxiety came into his face. One would have said, too, that he was surprised. At that moment a lieutenant, the adjutant, appeared at the opening of the tent and saluted. "Captain," he said, "the battalion is formed."

Captain Hartroy had recovered his composure. He turned to the officer and said: "Lieutenant, go to Captain Graham and say that I direct him to assume command of the battalion and parade it outside the parapet. This gentleman is a deserter and a spy; he is to be shot to death in the presence of the troops. He will accompany you, unbound and unguarded."

While the adjutant waited at the door the two men inside the tent rose and exchanged ceremonious bows, Brune immediately retiring.

Half an hour later an old negro cook, the only person left in camp except the commander, was so startled by the sound of a volley of musketry that he dropped the kettle that he was lifting from a fire. But for his consternation and the hissing which the contents of the kettle made among the embers, he might also have heard, nearer at hand, the single pistol shot with which Captain Hartroy renounced the life which in conscience he could no longer keep.

In compliance with the terms of a note that he left for the officer who succeeded him in command, he was buried, like the deserter and spy, without military honors; and in the solemn shadow of the mountain which knows no more of war the two sleep well in long-forgotten graves.

JOHN P. MARQUAND

ONCE DESCRIBED BY *Life* magazine as "the most successful novelist in the United States," John Phillips Marquand (1893–1960) was a prolific short story writer, mostly for *The Saturday Evening Post*, one of the most popular and highest-paying magazines in the country.

After graduating from Harvard, he began his literary career as a reporter for the *Boston Evening Transcript*, followed by a time in the magazine department of the *New York Tribune*. He took a job as copywriter for the J. Walter Thompson advertising agency, replacing Richard Connell, the outstanding author of numerous stories, including the relentlessly anthologized "The Most Dangerous Game."

Marquand turned to the longer form with serialized novels (again in *The Saturday Evening Post*) and novels, many of which were social satires largely set in the somewhat claustrophobic atmosphere of upper-class Boston society. He had delivered a manuscript to his literary agent, which she called a "humorless fantasy," advising him to put it in a desk drawer and forget it. After being serialized in *The Saturday Evening Post* in 1936–1937, *The Late George Apley* was published in book form in 1937 and won the 1938 Pulitzer Prize as the best novel of the year. He soon followed that success with *H. M. Pulham, Esquire* in 1941, which was nearly identical in structure and tone to *The Late George Apley*.

His earliest commercial success had come from his series about Mr. Moto, a Japanese spy. The first book in the series was *No Hero* (serialized in *The Saturday Evening Post* in 1935 and published in book form the same year; it was later retitled *Your Turn, Mr. Moto* to capitalize on the famous name of the recurring character). Four more Moto novels followed in the next eight years but, after the Japanese attack on Pearl Harbor on December 6, 1941, the publication of *Last Laugh, Mr. Moto* early in 1942 put a halt to the series. Marquand did publish one more Mr. Moto novel, *Stopover: Tokyo*, in 1957.

The books inspired a popular series of eight motion pictures starring Peter Lorre, beginning with *Thank You, Mr. Moto* (1937), though they bore small resemblance to the novels. An often cold, ruthless spy in the books, he was morphed into a mild-spoken Charlie Chan–like detective for the films. A late addition to the series, *The Return of Mr. Moto* (1965), starring Henry Silva, was not successful. The last Moto novel was filmed as *Stopover Tokyo* (1957), but eliminated the character.

"High Tide" was first published in the October 8, 1932, issue of *The Saturday Evening Post*; it was first collected in *Thirty Years* (Boston, Little, Brown, 1954).

HIGH TIDE

JOHN P. MARQUAND

SOMETIMES, in the sultry warmth of summer at Deer Bottom, Scott Mattaye could remember the high tide; and sometimes, when he was feeling in the mood, he might even tell of how he went through a hostile country to find an army which was lost, and how the Battle of Gettysburg might have been wholly different if his horse had not gone lame. At such an hour, after his second glass, the old man would sit straighter at the table, and his voice, slightly cracked, but soft and gently drawling, would rise above the whirring of the moths which kept fluttering around the guttering candles like incarnations of the quiet sounds from the warm, dark night outside.

"You follow me, gentlemen?" he would say. "I'm referrin', of co'se, to the lack of cavalry in the opening phases of that engagement— cavalry, the eyes and ears. And I'm referring, above all, to the temp'rary absence—an' I maintain the just and unavoidable absence—of our cavalry general, on whose staff I had the honour of servin'. I'm referrin' to that immortal hero, gentlemen, Major-General J. E. B. Stuart— Beauty Stuart—in the Army of Northern Virginia of the Confederate States of America—the ve'y greatest cavalry commander in that army,

gentlemen, which, of co'se, is the same as sayin' the greatest cavalry leader in the history of the world."

He meant no exaggeration when he said it. Some impression had been left upon him which transcended time. He would smile beneath his drooping white mustache as though he had a secret, and he had the secret of his days. Strange, unrelated moments were flitting before him like the shadows of the moths upon the wall—plumed hats, boots of yellow leather that came above the knee, girls snipping buttons off grey coats, eggnogs, Virginia hams, black boys dancing the buck and wing beneath the lantern light, a kiss, a lock of hair, the Bower, Frederick, Winchester, high tide.

"High tide," he said: "it was all accident and time."

It was clear what he was thinking, although his words had a way of wandering when his mind was groping in the mazes of his vanished world. He was going back to the hours when the tide of the Confederacy lapped over the Potomac to reach its high-water mark of the war. He was thinking of Rowser's Ford and the captured wagon train at Cooksville—twisted iron rails, staggering horses, men reeling in the saddle, drunk with sleep. He was thinking of a spy, and of Stuart's last great raid. The Army of Northern Virginia was pouring into Pennsylvania. Lee and Longstreet were arguing over plans.

"Sammy," he said to the cook's small boy, "bring refreshment to the gentleman. . . . Now, Gettysburg—of co'se, we should have whipped 'em if Stuart had been there. I should have fetched him—yes, indeed. If that horse had not gone lame near East Berlin, why, sholy I'd have fetched him. If I had not stopped by the stone house near the road. A matter of a spy, you understand—a foul, ugly matter. . . . I share in the responsibility, gentlemen. It all was accident and time."

He did not add that he had nearly died in cold blood in that square stone house.

He could see the beginning, and he knew that the hand of fate was in it, though it happened more than sixty years ago. Stuart had been stroking his fine brown beard, as he did when he was troubled. It was in the cool of an early summer morning, the first day of July. The horses' heads were drooping, and faces were blank from lack of sleep.

"Mattaye," Stuart was saying, "I'm lost. Early's gone. Everybody's gone. I've sent off three officers already. You go out, too, and find the army. You see this map? We're here. Ride out towards that place Gettysburg yonder. Keep riding till you find it."

It was a fine day, he could remember. The fields were green and fresh from early summer, and the land was richer than the land at home. It was a country of fine, rolling fields of pasture and wheat and corn, of neat hedges, neat houses and compact, ungenerous trees. It was a land uncompromising in its plenty, without warmth of welcome. But the dead weight of weariness was what he remembered best. After two days of steady march, men were lying exhausted with bridles in hands, watching horses that stood too tired to eat. There was food in the Yankee wagons they had taken. He could see the white tops

of the wagons down the road, but there were many too tired for food.

Scott Mattaye was made of iron and rawhide then, but he was very tired.

"The army, sir?" he said. "Which army, sir?"

His question made Stuart laugh, and the sound of it came back across the years. He was in a hostile country with his column too tired to move. He was lost and he was worried, and he had not slept an hour in the last three days. Yet the general seemed to feel none of the lethargy of exhaustion. The way he wore his sash, the tilt of the plume in his hat, the angle of his cloak about one shoulder made his equipment look as fresh as when he had started. Nothing ever wilted in the general.

"Which army?" he said. "Well, I'm not aiming to encounter Federal troops in force this minute. I'd prefer to meet the Army of Northern Virginia, General Robert E. Lee commanding, now engaged in invasion of Pennsylvania, and due to end this war. I'm out of touch, and I don't like it—not right now. They're somewhere over there—somewhere."

He waved his arm towards the south-west, but there was no dust or smoke or sound; nothing but open rolling fields, stretching to the horizon in the tranquil light of early morning. The very peace was like a disturbing suspicion that something had gone wrong. It could only have been anxiety that made Stuart speak so frankly.

"The corps should be coming together," he said, "and we should be in front. There should be word, you understand? . . . Your horse all right?"

Scott's horse was a light sorrel caked with sweat and dust.

"He's worn down, sir," said Scott. "But he's as good as any in the column, I reckon, sir."

"Take your blankets and saddle off," Stuart said. "Kill him if you have to, but report to General Lee, you understand? Ask for orders and a new horse to take you back."

"Yes, sir," said Scott. "Where will I find you, sir?"

"We're resting here two hours," said Stuart. "Then we're moving on to Carlisle. Watch out for cavalry, and don't get caught. We've lost too many on the staff. Good-bye."

Only the impression of small things was left to Scott Mattaye, and the touch of all the great sights meant much less, until all his memory of camp and bivouac came down to little things. Bodies of men, the sound of marching troops and firing were a part of his life, and were blurred into the monotony of days, but the smell of bacon grease in smoke, a voice or the squeal of a horse would be like yesterday. He remembered how his blankets sprawled over the tailboard of the headquarters wagon, inertly, like a dead man's limbs. As they did so, he had a glimpse of fine grey cloth among them. It was his new uniform coat, which he had planned to wear in Washington City, certain they would take Washington.

An impulse made him put it on which was composed of various thoughts—the idea that he might never wear it, through accident or theft, the desire to appear in an enemy country like a gentleman, and the conviction that a staff officer should look his best. The coat had the buff facings of the staff. Though it was wrinkled and still damp from a wetting in the Potomac, it was very well cut. He strapped his belt over it, with his sabre and his pistol—a fine, ivory-handled weapon which he had taken from a Yankee colonel in Centerville. His saddle was a Yankee saddle; even his horse had a U.S. brand, but his coat was Richmond, bought with two hundred and fifty dollars of his country's notes.

"You, Jerry," he said to the horse, "step on. We're bound to go." Then he remembered that the animal sighed almost exactly like a man.

He went down the road past the picket at a trot, and half a mile farther on he met a patrol, riding back. He knew the officer. He was Travis Greene, from Maryland, and Scott had always liked him. He liked the way he handled horses; there was something in him which Scott had always trusted—a candour, a vein of sympathy.

"Trav," he said, "seen anything out there?"

Trav shook his head and grinned. The corners of his thin mouth wrinkled.

"No," he answered. "Where yo' headin'?"

"Message," said Scott.

"Seems like the general's getting nervous," Trav said. "Nothing but the staff with messages. Yo' won't get far on that old crock of yours. He's powerful near through."

"Why, boy," said Scott, "this animal can go a week and never drop. Why, he just craves to run. Why, boy, you've never seen a raid. This is only triflin' up to now."

"Where we headin'?" the other asked. "I reckon you don't know."

Scott felt the importance of his knowledge and smiled. "Don't you wish you knew?" he said. "Where Beauty Stuart wants. That's where. Come to think of it, seems to me you're always asking questions."

"Saucy, aren't you?" said Trav. "I reckon you're out calling in that new coat of yours. I'd take you for a damn Yank if it wasn't for that coat."

"Would you?" said Scott. "Well, you ask Beauty Stuart where I'm going. No doubt he'd just delight to tell you, and call for your advice. I'll be seeing you. Good-bye."

Then, almost without thinking, he pulled his watch from his breeches pocket. It was a fine, heavy repeater.

"You, Trav," he called, "keep this, and if I don't get back, send it on to Deer Bottom, and I'll be much obliged."

He could still hear their voices, low and pleasant, and could recall the way Trav started as he reached and caught the watch.

"To Deer Bottom? Certain sure! I'm proud of your confidence," he said. "Good-bye!"

Scott Mattaye loosened his revolver in its holster and put his horse to a trot again, not fast, for he had to save the animal's strength, and the horse was tired.

"You, Jerry," he said, "take your time."

Then, as he spoke the word, he knew that he had made a blunder. He had three hundred dollars in Confederate bills in his pocket, which would have been more useful at Deer Bottom than a watch; and now, because of a sentimental impulse, he had no way of judging the distance he was travelling, except by instinct and the sun. He knew that one could conceivably ride all day through an opposing army with a good horse and a knowledge of the road. He had seen enough in the raids around McClellan and Pope to have gained a contempt for Yankee horsemanship. He could get safe away from a regiment of Yankee cavalry.

But now he could detect a difference. He had been in a friendly country on other rides alone, where there had been a careless tangle of woods and grown-over fields. Friendly people had waved to him; girls had brought him milk. His horse beneath him had been like a reservoir of untapped strength, but now his horse was tired. There was no spring in the trot, nor a trace of willingness to increase the pace, and the country itself was foreign. There was a plenty in the Pennsylvania fields, like the rolling land along the Shenandoah, but there was no generosity in that plenty. There was the same sinister threat in the meticulous furrows and the abundance of that earth which he had seen in the armies that sprang from it.

There was a menace in that hostile land, for everything was watching him. He could feel a hatred in that country rising against him like a wave. The sun, glinting on the windows of small farmhouses, made those windows look like eyes, reflecting the hatred of unseen faces, staring towards the road. And the uncertainty of time was weighing on him, because he did not know the time. The uncertainty made him remember Stuart's own uncertainty. "Time," the hoofbeats of his horse were saying, and the humming of the insects and the rustling of the corn were speaking of that flowing, unseen principle which connected life and death.

A sound made him draw his reins, and his horse stopped, obedient and still. It came, a swift, metallic click, from behind a clump of small trees near a bend which shut out his vision to the right. His revolver was cocked in his hand,

while he sat staring, listening. He did not know that he was speaking until he heard his voice.

"Pshaw," he heard himself mutter.

A man in overalls was hoeing a potato patch just around the bend. He turned and stared at Scott.

"Morning, friend," said Scott. "It looks like a right fine morning."

The man spat on a potato hill. "I ain't no friend of yourn," he said, "nor any of your kind."

Scott laughed. "Why, mister," he said, "I mean you no harm, and that's why I say 'friend.' I only aim to ask you if you can let me know the time."

"Would it give you comfort," the other asked, "if you was to know the time?"

"Why, sholy," Scott said, still smiling. "I'd like right well to know."

The man's voice became louder.

"Then I'll die before I tell yer, ye n———tradin' thief! Two of my sons has died, and I can die before I raise a hand to give one mite of comfort to your lot! I only hope your time is short, and I may see your carcass rotting! Now git on!"

Scott Mattaye put his horse to the trot and hurried down the road, amazed. He saw other men pause to gaze at him from the roadside. Women stared from doorways. Children, when they saw him, ran screaming. He did not stop again to ask the time.

He did not stop again until his horse went lame. By then a high forenoon sun was beating on his plumed felt hat, and the farming country lay before him as beautiful as a picture, incongruously far from war. The horse went lame so suddenly you might have thought he had been shot—a stumble, a sharp snort of pain, and he was limping. After Scott Mattaye was off the saddle, it did not take half a minute to convince him that his horse was through, and, though he had grown callous to the suffering of animals, he had a pang of sorrow.

The road, he remembered, was sloping down to a ford across a brook. Beyond the ford it wound up again past a rutted lane, which led to a square house of deep-grey limestone, set back perhaps a hundred yards from the roadway.

That house on its little rise of ground always came back to his memory as aloofly pleasant—heavy chimneys, small-paned windows, a fine, arched doorway of an earlier time. It always seemed to him to speak of kindliness and of sober, decent lives, and to be without a taint of anything sinister or bizarre. A long cattle barn stood behind the house, flanked by young apple trees set in even rows. He looked for half a minute, then hooked the bridle through his arm, walking slowly with his limping horse.

"Jerry," he said, "I'm going to leave you yonder."

The windows were blank and impassive as he walked up the lane, and everything was silent—too silent.

"Hello," he called. "Is anybody home?"

The sound of his voice was like the breaking of a spell. Two shepherd dogs rushed at him, snarling. A door had slammed and an old man ran towards them with a stick, a picture of towering strength, half worn away by age. A white shirt, bare, scrawny arms and a fine white beard half-way down his chest, but his height was what Scott remembered best. He was very tall.

"Grandpa!" he heard a child's voice calling from the house. "Don't take on so, grandpa! You'll have another bad turn if you do!"

The noise of the dogs seemed to ebb away. All his memory of the barnyard seemed to ebb away, leaving only that figure of age—something never to forget. The old man was breathing much too heavily. His shirt and knit suspenders and baggy trousers took nothing from his dignity. Something in his face made his beard like ashes over glowing coals—a mobile, powerful face. His forehead was high. His eyes were serene and steely blue. Scott Mattaye took off his hat and bowed, though the man was plain and not a gentleman.

"I'm intrudin', sir," he said. "My horse—he's broken down. I reckon that—"

"Mary Breen!" the old man shouted. "You, Mary Breen!"

A girl—she could not have been above thirteen—came rushing from the house. Her gingham dress, her face and eyes, had a washed-out look; her bleached yellow pigtails were slapping on her shoulders.

"Mary Breen," the old man said, "put up that hoss. . . . I made haste, as I always will, to serve the Lord. . . . Young man, you come with me. This is a day of glory."

Scott Mattaye stared at him, bewildered for a moment.

"Put up that horse," the old man said, "and put the saddle on the bay that's waiting. . . . You'll need another horse for sure. Now, please to follow me."

"Sholy, sir," said Scott. "With great pleasure. I'll be pleased to settle for another animal, of co'se. Excuse me. Could you let me know the time?"

He had no premonition on entering the house. He had seen enough peculiar people and places in that war. The tide of war had pushed him into mean kitchens and stables for a night, or just as strangely it had whirled him into dining-rooms of plantation houses, where he had touched on lives which he would never touch again. He did not bother to put an implication on the old man's words, except that they were friendly. The friendliness brought back Scott's confidence in inevitable fortune, and he straightened his sash and dusted off his coat.

"Yes," the old man said again, "this is a day of glory. I'm glad I've lived to see it, because I'm gettin' old."

The kitchen was very neat. A kettle was humming on the stove, so that the steam made the air humidly pleasant. There were two strong wooden chairs and a deal table, but what he noticed first was the asthmatic, hurried ticking of a clock above the humming of the boiling water. He turned to glance at it where it stood on a shelf between two windows. A dingy clock in a veneered mahogany case—he could shut his eyes and see it still. The hour was just eleven.

"No," the old man said, "not here. The parlour's just this way."

He had opened a door to the front entry, and Scott began to smile, amused by the formality which led him to the parlour. He had a glimpse of himself in the entry mirror; his face was thin and brown; and his coat, he was pleased to notice, fitted very well.

"Here you be," the old man said, "and we give thanks you're here."

He opened the parlour door as he spoke, and Scott had a whiff of fresh cigar smoke and a blurred vision of a horsehair sofa and of faded floral wallpaper, but he only half saw the room. For a second—the time could not have been long—he stood on the threshold stonily.

A sabre and a revolver were lying on the parlour table, and behind the table, smoking a cigar, his coat half unbuttoned and his black hat slouched over his eyes, a Federal major was sitting. In that instant of surprise Scott could think of nothing. A sharp nose and deep-brown eyes, florid cheeks, a drooping black mustache half covering a lantern jaw, clean linen, dark blue broadcloth, gold on the shoulders—Scott Mattaye saw it all in an instant, and then, before speech or motion could touch him, the major began to smile.

"Howdy, Captain James," the major said. "I saw you from the window. I'm from—you know where. Let's get down to business. I've got a way to ride. Do you want to see my papers?"

"No," said Scott; his voice was hoarse. "No, Major."

"No doubt about you," the major said. "New coat, Yankee saddle, Yankee boots. You've got your nerve to go among 'em so, and, by gad, you're young to be in a game like this."

The major was watching him curiously, but not suspiciously, beneath the brim of his black hat, and Scott Mattaye had learned to read the capabilities of an individual. Something told him that this officer was an accurate and dangerous man. The major's hand, with thick, blunt fingers, was resting on the table just six inches away from his pistol butt. Scott could see it from the cor-

ner of his eye, and he could notice four notches cut in the black walnut of the butt, telling him in silent voices that the chances were the major would shoot him dead if he made a sudden move. Scott was standing in the doorway, with the old man just behind him. If he should make a move to draw his weapon, before his pistol was out of the holster he knew he would be dead.

"A dirty game," the major said with his cigar between his teeth, "a thankless game. You should be more careful, Captain. Your uniform's too new."

Scott Mattaye was not a fool. He knew, if he had not known before, what he was supposed to be and why the major was waiting.

"Thank you, sir," said Scott, and he contrived to smile. A little talk, a word, a gesture, and he might have a chance to snatch that pistol from the table. "I agree, sir, it's a right dirty business, and I detest a—scout. . . . But, excuse me, we'd better be alone."

It would help to get the old man out. He turned slowly, until their eyes met—the old man's eyes were as blue as a china plate at home—and he heard the major laughing.

"Don't worry about Pa Breen," he said. "He's as straight as string. . . . Father, you go out and close the door."

"Young man," old Mr. Breen said, "don't fret about me none. I can die for a cause as good as you, I guess. Amen."

When he closed the door, there was no sound outside in the entry, but the farmer must have had the tread of an Indian, because, five seconds later, Scott heard the kitchen door slam shut.

"The old man's cracked," the major said. "You know, one of those fanatic abolitionists—agent in the underground, friend of Garrison and Whittier, leader of the party hereabouts. Why, he'd kill a man in grey as easily as he'd stick a pig, and he's in the butcher business. They had to hide his pants so he wouldn't go to Harpers Ferry with Brown."

"Yes, sir," said Scott. "It's been my observation that he's a right smart old man."

The major tapped his fingers on the table, but

some perversity kept them close to the revolver butt.

"Mad," said the major. "Ideas drive men mad, when ideas and religion mix. . . . What's your notion of their strength, James? . . . Sit down. There's a chair."

Scott Mattaye drew his chair carefully to the opposite side of the table. Being an officer of the staff, he had heard enough rumours and secrets to enable him to twist them plausibly into lies. It surprised him how quickly his mind was working, and as smoothly as his voice.

"Major," said Scott, "Marse Bob, he has a heap of men. Reserves have been drawn from the state garrisons. I'm safe saying General Lee's across the river with a hundred and ten thousand. It's high tide."

He tossed out the number glibly, though he knew he was naming twice the strength. He did so from his knowledge of the Yankee obsession of superior numbers, and he saw that his guess was right. The major whistled softly.

"You're high," he said, "I hope. Can you name the strength of corps?"

He had never thought of the meaning of information until he sat there, waiting for the Yankee major to move his hand. As he spoke, he could think of armies moving like blind monsters, each groping towards the other to the tune of lies like this. He paused and leaned a trifle across the table.

"Major," he said, "have you another of those cigars? I'm perishin' for a smoke."

He gathered his feet under him noiselessly. He could not sit there talking. If he could make the major move his hand, he could push the table over.

"Beg pardon," the major said, and reached with his left hand inside his coat and tossed a leather case across the table. "A light?" The major pushed across a silver match safe, still with his left hand. "Believe me, your information's worth a box of those cigars."

A tap on the door made him stop. It was the little girl with the bleached pigtails; she was carrying two glasses and a small stone jug.

"Why," said Scott Mattaye, "hello, honey-bee!"

"Grandpop," said the little girl, "he said to fetch you this."

"Set it on the floor," the major said, "and close the door behind you. We're not thirsty, sister."

"Grandpop," said the little girl, "he don't touch it since he was took with spells. Somethin' 'pears to git aholt of him, like a rope across the chest. First a pain under his arm, like, and then acrost the chest."

"You tell your grandpop to take a pill," the major said, "and go out and close the door."

The major leaned back in his chair. His deliberation set Scott's nerves on edge, but the major did not move his hand.

"Well," he said. "It's a quaint, strange world. Here you and I are sitting, smoking good Havanas. There an old man is 'took with spells.' And somewhere else two armies are jockeying for position. Suppose they ran into each other blind, neither of them ready. War's like walking in the dark."

"Believe me, sir," Scott said, and he half forgot what he was supposed to be, "Robert E. Lee is never in the dark. He's the greatest man alive."

"You've got the cant," said the major. "But you don't believe that, do you? Where's his cavalry? Off with Stuart, when it should be in front of his army. Either Lee or Stuart's a plain fool."

Scott Mattaye half rose from his chair, and sat down again. Just in time he remembered where he was.

"Yes, sir," the major was saying, as though he were reading from a textbook. "Cavalry should form a screen in front of any army of invasion, as any plebe knows at the Point, instead of being detached on a needless mission, moving northwest when the main body's thirty miles south."

Then Scott Mattaye forgot, and spoke before he thought. "Here," he asked sharply. "How did you know that?"

The major's head went forward; his eyes were suddenly sharp: "Why, you sent us word from Hanover yourself."

"Hanover?" said Scott, but the major was not listening. At last he had raised his right hand from the table.

"Hush!" the major said. "Hush! Listen!"

For a second Scott forgot the hand. The major had good ears. Through the closed windows Scott became conscious of what the major heard, though it was not a sound exactly. It was rather a very faint concussion, a stirring in the air, which might have been summer thunder if the sun were not shining. Even in the parlour Scott could feel its strength.

"I hear 'em. Guns," he said.

Though the major was looking at him, his eyes were blank from listening.

"Yes," he said, "a scad of guns. We've struck into something heavy. . . . There. You hear?"

Scott could hear, and he could see. In that same instant the officer turned his head towards the direction of the sound, and then Scott moved. He was very quick in those days, when a sudden motion might make the difference between life and death. That Yankee moved also, but he was not fast enough. Scott had snatched the pistol up, and he was stepping backward.

"Here, you!" the Major shouted. "Set that down!"

"Mister major," Scott told him, "yo' step backward from that table and keep down yo' voice, if yo' want to save yo' skin. . . . That's better, Major. . . . You've told me somethin' right valuable. General Stuart will be pleased to know he's got a spy out with him. I'll be surprised if that spy keeps livin' long."

The major was a cool man. He leaned against the wall, twisting an end of his mustache and speaking in a careful nasal drawl.

"All right for now," the major said, "but you listen to me, staff officer. A spy's more valuable than you or me. I hope you realize I'll do my best to stop you if I can."

Scott smiled back at him. "I realize," he said. "That's why I beg of you to stand right still. If there's a battle yonder, I'm goin' to it, mister major, and yo' horse is goin' with me."

"You've got a most consoling voice," the major said.

"Put your hands above your head," said Scott.

Then he knew that there was something wrong. The major's eyes had narrowed and he was looking across Scott's shoulder towards the little parlour door.

"Certainly," the major said. "Don't get excited, Johnny."

There was a creak of a floorboard behind him. He remembered the impulse to turn and the certainty that something was just behind him, but almost with the impulse a weight landed on his back and he was pitching forward.

Scott fired just as he was falling, so that the crash of the shot and the smell of black powder blended with a taste of sulphur in his mouth. Someone had him by the throat. He kicked to free himself, but someone held his legs.

"Tie his hands," he heard the major say. "Steady. He's all right."

He was choking; flashes of searing light were darting across his eyes.

"Breen"—another voice was speaking—a soft Southern voice—"take yo' hands off him. We've got him all right now."

Then he was struggling to his feet. His hands were tied behind him, and he noticed that a cloud of powder smoke was rising softly towards the ceiling. There was a haze before his eyes and a drumming in his ears.

"Scott," someone was saying, "I'm right sorry it is you."

The haze was lifting like a curtain, until he could see the room again. The major was perhaps four feet away, lighting another of his cigars. Old Breen, with one of his braces snapped, leaned against the table. Scott could hear the old man's breath.

"Hush, hush," it seemed to say. "Hush, hush."

There was a fourth man in the room, in Confederate uniform. Scott felt a wave of nausea as he saw him. The man was Travis Greene, whom he had met that very morning.

"Johnny," the major said, "you stand still."

"So it's you, Trav, is it?" Scott Mattaye was saying.

The other cleared his throat, looked at Scott and then away.

"Scott," he said, "I reported to the general your horse looked mighty bad. He sent me on to follow you. I was looking for a chance to get away. Scott, I'm sorry it should be you."

Scott Mattaye answered dully. "Trav," he said, "I won't say what I think."

"I reckon I don't mind," said Greene. "That's part of it."

Scott drew in his breath. The old man's breathing, with its wheezing haste, was all that disturbed him.

"Trav," he said, "you better keep out of our lines, if once I get away."

"Scott," said Greene again, "it makes me sick it's you."

Then the major was speaking impersonally, almost kindly: "Listen, Johnny. I'd take you back as prisoner if I dared to run the risk, but we're too close to rebel cavalry for anything like that. This officer"—he waved his cigar slowly and was careful with his words—"this officer is going back where he's useful, son. You see my point. There's no hard feeling in it; you and I don't amount to shucks. This officer is going back, and there must be no—er—chance of your going. See my point?"

Scott moistened his lips.

"I understand," he said. "Well, I'd be pleased if you get it over with. Perhaps we'd all be pleased."

There was a silence. He heard Greene start to speak, and stop. The old man's breathing was easier. He became aware that the old man was watching him with his steady light-blue eyes.

"Gentlemen," said Grandpa Breen, "you leave this yere to me. There's been enough goin's on to attract attention. I'll gladly mind this yere."

There was no doubt of his meaning or any doubts that the major took his meaning. The major was buttoning his coat with steady, rapid fingers.

"There's a time," the old man said, "and a place for everything under the sun. Take him to the kitchen and tie him to the hick'ry chair. I'll fetch rope."

"Major," said Greene, "you take him."

"Oh," the major said, "let's get out of this! Come on!"

The major was a good hand with the ropes. He lashed Scott to the kitchen chair so efficiently that there was no chance of moving. Just above his head, where he could not see it, the clock was ticking, and the kettle was bubbling on the stove. Once he was alone, he found himself searching the pine floor for a speck of dust. They were in the parlour, talking. He could hear the murmur of their voices.

". . . soon's it's dark," he heard the old man say.

"Major!" he shouted. "Here, you, Major!"

The door from the entry opened, he remembered, and the major stood there pulling on his gloves.

"Johnny," he said, "you keep your nerve."

"Yes, sir," said Scott, "I've got my nerve. I simply wish to ask you, are you leaving me alone?"

"Yes," the major said. "Johnny, keep your nerve."

Their glances met, but only for a fraction of a second, as though they saw something indecent in each other's eyes.

"I'm not letting your friend come in," the major said.

"You tell him good-bye," said Scott.

"Good-bye," the major said. "I should have shot you, Johnny, when you were rolling on the floor."

Then the kitchen door opened, letting in warm air that was sweet with the scent of hay. Old Mr. Breen, still in his shirt sleeves, was standing in the doorway with a shovel in his hand. The homeliness of the kitchen and the peaceful warmth from outdoors made everything grotesque.

"Brother," said Mr. Breen to the major, "the hosses are ready. You'd best be gittin' on. . . . And you, young man, I wish you no pain, but I know what you are figurin'. It won't do no good to holler. No one'll hear who cares. It won't do no good to tip over in the chair. I made it. It won't break. But I'll be near if you should call."

Scott Mattaye did not speak again, and the door slammed shut. He tried to move, but he was as helpless as a hog tied by the legs. First the dogs were yelping, and then there was a sound of hoofs outside the door, and then the place was still except for the humming of the kettle and the ticking of the clock, and in back of everything was that almost soundless vibration of cannon a long way off. He closed his eyes, but even when he closed them he could see Mr. Breen.

He had no proper sense of sequence, for his mind was like a sick man's; but there was one thing in his thoughts, Scott Mattaye remembered. He could not divide an hour from the next when his mind was carrying him to a hundred places. Bits of his life would whirl about him. He was shooting wild turkey at Deer Bottom; he was with the cavalry again; but there was one thing on his mind. He must not let the old man know that he was in deathly fear.

The light was growing softer outside the kitchen windows when the kitchen door opened again and Mr. Breen came in. Clay was smeared on his hands and over his gaunt, bare arms. He walked past the chair and began washing at the kitchen sink.

"Young man," said Mr. Breen, "do you need water?"

"No," said Scott. . . . "So you're going to kill me, mister?"

The old man walked in front of him with a clean towel in his hands.

"Yes," he said, "I'm the Lord's poor instrument. Young man, are you afraid?"

"No," said Scott, "but if I were you, I reckon I'd be afraid."

Old Mr. Breen stared down at him and began to wipe his hands.

"Did your people fear," he asked, "when they sent an anointed saint to heaven?"

"Mister," said Scott—and he kept his voice even—"I'd be pleased to know, for the comfort of my mind, when you propose to kill me."

"After dark," said Mr. Breen. "I don't aim to lug you out for burial in daylight. I'm pleased you ain't afraid. I ain't afraid, and I'll die presently. There's somethin' gits me—here."

Suddenly his eyes were childlike, Scott remembered. He was drawing his hand across his chest.

"Mister," said Scott quickly, "I've seen a heap of illness. Step here and show me where."

"Young man," said Mr. Breen, "I can read your mind, I guess. You want to tip your chair and yourself atop me. No, young man. I'll be goin', but I'll be ready in case you call."

The light outside the kitchen windows was growing soft and mellow, and he could hear the cannon. The time was going past him like a flood again, leaving him motionless like a rock against that flow. For a long while he was entirely alone. As the dusk came down he heard the lowing of cows and the clatter of the milk pails which had stood beside the barn. It must have been when the old man had started milking that the little girl came in through the doorway from the entry. The door squeaked and opened just a crack at first.

"Why, hello, honeybee," said Scott. "Come in. Don' go away. Sholy I can't hurt you, honeybee."

She came tiptoeing towards him. He did not blame her for being frightened.

"Honeybee," he said—the child was not attractive, but he could see she liked the name—"I'm powerful thirsty. Could you fetch a cup of water from the sink?"

"I'm scared," the little girl whispered.

"Why, shucks!" said Scott. "You scared—a saucy girl like you? You fetch that cup now, honeybee. Isn't your grandpop milking? How'll he know? . . . There . . . And I've got something for you in my coat. Just ease this rope off my hand so I can reach—"

"No," she whispered, "I'm too scared."

He could hear his own voice still, not like his own, with its undercurrent of appeal beneath its ridiculous pretence at playfulness, as he pleaded for life. He was ashamed of that moment always—his begging from a child so that one hand could be free.

"I dassent," she whispered, but he knew better. She would dare, because there was something inside his coat. All the repression of her life gleamed in her pale blue eyes in little points of light.

"Honeybee," said Scott, "it's something mighty fine—something you won't guess."

There was no sound which made him look up, but he had the sense that there was something different in the gathering of the dusk. The dusk seemed to settle over him like a blanket thrown about his head. He looked up to see the old man, standing in the doorway, watching. There was something in the way he stood that made Scott sure that he had planned that scene for his own pleasure. He must have been there for several minutes, as inevitable as the figure with the hourglass and the scythe.

"Mary Breen," the old man said, "you step away. Now, Mary Breen, you fetch the papers by the wood box. . . . So. Now lay 'em on the floor around the chair—under it. . . . You'd best lay on some more. And now go up to your chamber and close your door tight shut."

They were silent for a while. Old Mr. Breen seemed taller in the dark—more like an immense abstraction than a man.

"It's gittin' dark," he said. "Young man, I'll leave you five minutes to say your prayers."

He turned on his heel silently, walked out and closed the door.

"Time," the clock was whispering, "time!"

Inside the stove a piece of wood snapped sharply. He could see the glow of coals through the lids on top. The homely smells of the kitchen came round him in a rush. He strained sideways at his ropes, and the heaviness of his breathing drowned every other sound.

"Help!" he shouted.

The dogs in the yard began to bark, so that his shout mingled with the wave of barking.

"Help!" he shouted. "Murder!"

He hitched forward, and the chair fell forward, throwing him headfirst into the dusk whiteness of the paper on the floor. The blow on his head must have stunned him, but he could not have been out long. There was still a little daylight when he found himself, lying sideways, still lashed to the kitchen chair.

"Mister soldier!" someone was calling. "You hear me, mister soldier?" It was the little girl in the gingham dress again.

"Yes," he said, "I hear you, honeybee."

"It's grandpop," she was sobbing. "He's took again. He's flopped flat down right on the parlour floor. When you hollered, he flopped down."

"Yo' get a knife and cut me loose," said Scott. "I reckon I can help your grandpop then."

"Mister," she sobbed, "please, you won't hurt him?"

"No," he answered, "I won't hurt him."

Once he was loose, his arms and legs were useless for a while. They burned and ached, once the blood came back, until tears stood in his eyes.

"Strike a candle light," he said, "and help me up. I'm very pressed for time."

He hobbled through the entry. Old Mr. Breen was lying on the parlour floor, face up, flat out. The candle which the girl was holding made a frame about the high head and the flowing beard. He was conscious, in great pain, staring up at Scott Mattaye. Scott's own ivory-handled revolver was lying on the floor, where it must have fallen from old Breen's hand. He stooped painfully and picked it up, but for half a minute no one spoke.

"Your heart, sir?" said Scott. He was incomprehensibly courteous and polite, but the old man did not speak.

"Something gits him right across the chest," said Mary Breen. "It pulls him down."

"Set that candle on the table," Scott was speaking gently. He saw his belt and sabre in the corner. He walked over and strapped on his belt.

"Sir," he said, still gently, "I'm sorry to leave you in distress, but you and I don't matter. You've a horse in the barn, I recall yo' saying. I'm leaving you a hundred dollars on this table for the horse. I'll call at a neighbour's to send you help. . . . And now good night."

He was in the barnyard among the snarling dogs, holding a stable lantern. There was a heavy smell from hay and from the soft, warm breath of cattle. There was a drumming in his ears like the hurry of the clock.

"Time," it was saying, "time."

He heard himself speaking to Mary Breen, and then he was mounted and in the yard again. The horse was coarse and wild.

"Scuse me," Mary Breen was calling. "Ain't you forgot—somethin' in your pocket?"

He pulled out the rest of his bills. "There," he said, "take 'em, honeybee."

He saw the house like a sharp, ungainly blot against the sky where a deep-red gash of something burning in the west made the outline clear. As he moved down the lane towards that distant glow, he did not know what he felt or thought, except that he must hurry, but suddenly he leaned forward on the neck of the farm horse. He felt sick—deathly sick.

There he was, sitting at his table at Deer Bottom, too old by any right to feel the force of memory. The wings of death were hovering near him, but no such death as that. He had the consolation from the knowledge he had gained that life was all dirt cheap.

"Only two things," he said, "matter—accident and time. Now, Gettysburg—all that mattered were accident and time."

His mind was back on the night again. It always seemed to him that most of the Gettysburg affair was night—mistaken roads and Union pickets, and other roads choked by ammunition trains and infantry, and wounded moving back—two crawling, passing lines. Though the discipline was good, roads were always confused in the rear of a line of battle. There was the vagueness of a dream when one rode at such a time. There was no hope in haste or wishing.

"You come from Stuart?" someone said. "Well, it's too late for cavalry until we drive 'em. Where've you been? We've been fighting here since yesterday."

The night was never clear, but when he saw the leader of the army that was clear enough. He reported to General Lee at a quarter before ten in the morning, outside a half-demolished house on the outskirts of the town of Gettysburg.

Couriers were holding horses, and staff officers were standing a few paces back, so that he always thought of the general as entirely alone. He could remember a tall, solitary man with a greying beard and deep, dark eyes whose face was passionless. He was looking, Scott remembered, across a valley of green fields to a long, gentle slope, which was held by the Union lines about half a mile away.

He was speaking to a dusty, worried officer, Scott remembered, unhurriedly, except for one short gesture, and Scott could hear the words:

"Is he ready to attack, sir?"

"No, sir."

"Very well," the general said. "Hurry back; tell him he's very late already."

He stared back across the valley as Scott stood waiting. The stones of a cemetery were visible upon the ridge opposite, and an ugly building, which would be some sort of school. The ridge was heavy with troops, throwing up lines of earthworks. Beyond were the dust clouds of more troops moving up, and more. That ridge was a fine position, which was growing stronger every hour. Now and then there would be a burst of rifle fire, but there was no forward movement.

He stood waiting while the general looked, forgetting his fatigue as he watched. Then Scott saw him strike his hands together in a sudden, swift motion, and he heard him say:

"It's too bad—too bad."

Scott had a wish to be somewhere else. He felt

like an eavesdropper who had heard a dangerous secret, but the general was turning towards him slowly.

"Well," he said, "what is it, Captain?"

"Captain Mattaye, sir," began Scott, "from General Stuart's staff—"

"Yes," the general stopped him. "When did you leave the general, Captain? How far is he along?"

"Six o'clock yesterday morning, sir," said Scott. "General Stuart was at Dover then."

For a moment the general looked at him, and it seemed to Scott that the general was very tired, though his expression did not change.

"Captain," the general said, "you're very late."

Scott felt his face grow red. "Sir—" he began, but the general stopped him.

"Never mind," he said. "Of course, you were delayed."

"Sir," said Scott, "will the general send me back with orders?"

"No"—the voice was tranquil and very courteous—"General Stuart has his orders. It's too late to make it better. . . . It would have been too late unless he had come yesterday." He raised his voice, and Scott knew again that he was thinking of time: "Colonel, send another officer to General Longstreet to find out his delay. And give this officer food and rest. He's too tired to go on."

A BATTLE OF WITS

EMMUSKA ORCZY

IT IS EXTRAORDINARY TO NOTE, in view of the fact that she became one of the world's most successful authors in her time, that Baroness Emmuska Orczy (1865–1947) was born in Hungary and spoke no English until she was fifteen years old. Her family moved to England, she learned the language, and wrote all her novels, plays, and short stories in English.

To detective fiction aficionados, she is best known as the creator of The Old Man in the Corner, an armchair detective who relied entirely on his cerebral faculties to solve crimes. The character who brought her worldwide popularity, although without critical acclaim, was Sir Percy Blakeney, an effete English gentleman who secretly was a courageous espionage agent during the days of the French Revolution, daringly saving the lives of countless French aristocrats who had been condemned to the guillotine.

Emmuska Orczy was unsuccessful in selling her novel about Sir Percy, so she and her husband converted it into a stage play in 1905; although reviewers were unenthusiastic, audiences loved it. *The Scarlet Pimpernel* was published as a novel of the same title in the same year, the first of numerous adventures about the thorn in the side of the bloodthirsty citizens of the Committee of Public Safety and the Committee of General Security and the *gendarmerie*. His success inspired the doggerel:

We seek him here . . .   *Is he in heaven?*
We seek him there . . .   *Is he in h–ll?*
Those Frenchies seek him . . .   *That demmed elusive*
Everywhere.   *Pimpernel?*

Other novels featuring Blakeney include *I Will Repay* (1906), *The Elusive Pimpernel* (1908), *Eldorado* (1913), and *The Triumph of the Scarlet Pimpernel* (1922). There have also been numerous screen versions of the Pimpernel saga, beginning with the 1917 silent film, *The Scarlet Pimpernel*, and the classic motion picture of the same title, released in 1934 and starring Leslie Howard in the title role. The Scarlet Pimpernel took his name from a wildflower that blooms and dies in a single night.

"A Battle of Wits" was originally published in the March 1919 issue of *The Story-Teller*; it was first collected in *The League of the Scarlet Pimpernel* by Emmuska Orczy (London, Cassell, 1919).

A BATTLE OF WITS

EMMUSKA ORCZY

I

WHAT HAD HAPPENED was this:

Tournefort, one of the ablest of the many sleuth-hounds employed by the Committee of Public Safety, was out during that awful storm on the night of the twenty-fifth. The rain came down as if it had been poured out of buckets, and Tournefort took shelter under the portico of a tall, dilapidated-looking house somewhere at the back of St. Lazare. The night was, of course, pitch dark, and the howling of the wind and beating of the rain effectually drowned every other sound.

Tournefort, chilled to the marrow, had at first cowered in the angle of the door, as far away from the draught as he could. But presently he spied the glimmer of a tiny light some little way up on his left, and taking this to come from the *concierge*'s lodge, he went cautiously along the passage, intending to ask for better shelter against the fury of the elements than the rickety front door afforded.

Tournefort, you must remember, was always on the best terms with every *concierge* in Paris. They were, as it were, his subordinates; without their help he never could have carried on his unavowable profession quite so successfully.

And they, in their turn, found it to their advantage to earn the goodwill of that army of spies, which the Revolutionary Government kept in its service, for the tracking down of all those unfortunates who had not given complete adhesion to their tyrannical and murderous policy.

Therefore, in this instance, Tournefort felt no hesitation in claiming the hospitality of the *concierge* of the squalid house wherein he found himself. He went boldly up to the lodge. His hand was already on the latch, when certain sounds which proceeded from the interior of the lodge caused him to pause and to bend his ear in order to listen. It was Tournefort's *métier* to listen. What had arrested his attention was the sound of a man's voice, saying in a tone of deep respect:

"*Bien*, Madame la Comtesse, we'll do our best."

No wonder that the servant of the Committee of Public Safety remained at attention, no longer thought of the storm, or felt the cold blast chilling him to the marrow. Here was a wholly unexpected piece of good luck. "Madame la Comtesse!" *Peste!* There were not many such left in Paris these days. Unfortunately, the tempest of the wind and the rain made such a din that it was difficult to catch every sound which came from the interior of the lodge. All that Tournefort caught definitely were a few fragments of conversation.

"My good M. Bertin . . ." came at one time from a woman's voice. "Truly I do not know why you should do all this for me."

And then again:

"All I possess in the world now are my diamonds. They alone stand between my children and utter destitution."

The man's voice seemed all the time to be saying something that sounded cheerful and encouraging. But his voice came only as a vague murmur to the listener's ears.

Presently, however, there came a word which set his pulses tingling. Madame said something about "Gentilly," and directly afterwards: "You will have to be very careful, my dear M. Bertin. The château, I feel sure is being watched."

Tournefort could scarce repress a cry of joy. "Gentilly? Madame la Comtesse? The château?" Why, of course, he held all the necessary threads already. The *ci-devant* Comte de Sucy—a pestilential aristo if ever there was one!—had been sent to the guillotine less than a fortnight ago. His château, situated just outside Gentilly, stood empty, it having been given out that the widow Sucy and her two children had escaped to England. Well! she had not gone apparently, for here she was, in the lodge of the *concierge* of a mean house in one of the desolate quarters of Paris, begging some traitor to find her diamonds for her, which she had obviously left concealed inside the château.

What a haul for Tournefort! What commendation from his superiors! The chances of a speedy promotion were indeed glorious now! He blessed the storm and the rain which had driven him for shelter to this house where a poisonous plot was being hatched to rob the people of valuable property, and to aid a few more of those abominable aristos in cheating the guillotine of their traitorous heads.

He listened for a while longer, in order to get all the information that he could on the subject of the diamonds, because he knew by experience that those perfidious aristos, once they were under arrest, would sooner bite out their tongues than reveal anything that might be of service to the Government of the people. But he learned little else. Nothing was revealed of where Madame la Comtesse was in hiding, or how the diamonds were to be disposed of once they were found.

Tournefort would have given much to have at least one of his colleagues with him. As it was, he would be forced to act single-handed and on his own initiative. In his own mind he had already decided that he would wait until Madame la Comtesse came out of the *concierge*'s lodge, and that he would follow her and apprehend her somewhere out in the open streets, rather than here where her friend Bertin might prove to be a stalwart as well as a desperate man, ready with a pistol, whilst he—Tournefort—was unarmed.

Bertin, who had, it seemed, been entrusted with the task of finding the diamonds, could then be shadowed and arrested in the very act of filching property which by decree of the State belonged to the people.

So he waited patiently for a while. No doubt the aristo would remain here under shelter until the storm had abated. Soon the sound of voices died down, and an extraordinary silence descended on this miserable, abandoned corner of old Paris. The silence became all the more marked after a while, because the rain ceased its monotonous pattering and the soughing of the wind was stilled.

It was, in fact, this amazing stillness which set citizen Tournefort thinking. Evidently the aristo did not intend to come out of the lodge to-night. Well! Tournefort had not meant to make himself unpleasant inside the house, or to have a quarrel just yet with the traitor Bertin, whoever he was; but his hand was forced and he had no option.

The door of the lodge was locked. He tugged vigorously at the bell again and again, for at first he got no answer. A few minutes later the sound of shuffling footsteps upon creaking boards. The door was opened, and a man in night attire, with bare, thin legs and tattered carpet slippers on his feet, confronted an exceedingly astonished ser-vant of the Committee of Public Safety.

Indeed, Tournefort thought that he must have been dreaming, or that he was dreaming now. For the man who opened the door to him was well known to every agent of the Commit-tee. He was an ex-soldier who had been crippled years ago by the loss of one arm, and had held the post of *concierge* in a house in the Ruelle du Paradis ever since. His name was Grosjean. He was very old, and nearly doubled up with rheu-matism, had scarcely any hair on his head or flesh on his bones. At this moment he appeared to be suffering from a cold in the head, for his eyes were streaming and his narrow, hooked nose was adorned by a drop of moisture at its tip. In fact, poor old Grosjean looked more like a dilap-idated scarecrow than a dangerous conspirator. Tournefort literally gasped at sight of him, and Grosjean uttered a kind of croak, intended, no doubt, for complete surprise.

"Citizen Tournefort!" he exclaimed. "Name of a dog! What are you doing here at this hour and in this abominable weather? Come in! Come in!" he added, and, turning on his heel, he shuf-fled back into the inner room, and then returned carrying a lighted lamp, which he set upon the table. "Amélie left some hot coffee on the hob in the kitchen before she went to bed. You must have a drop of that."

He was about to shuffle off again when Tournefort broke in roughly:

"None of that nonsense, Grosjean! Where are the aristos?"

"The aristos, citizen?" queried Grosjean, and nothing could have looked more utterly, more ludicrously bewildered than did the old *concierge* at this moment. "What aristos?"

"Bertin and Madame la Comtesse," retorted Tournefort gruffly. "I heard them talking."

"You have been dreaming, citizen Tourne-fort," the old man said, with a husky little laugh. "Sit down, and let me get you some coffee——"

"Don't try and hoodwink me, Grosjean!" Tournefort cried now in a sudden access of rage. "I tell you that I saw the light. I heard the aris-

tos talking. There was a man named Bertin, and a woman he called 'Madame la Comtesse,' and I say that some devilish royalist plot is being hatched here, and that you, Grosjean, will suffer for it if you try and shield those aristos."

"But, citizen Tournefort," replied the *con-cierge* meekly, "I assure you that I have seen no aristos. The door of my bedroom was open, and the lamp was by my bedside. Amélie, too, has only been in bed a few minutes. You ask her. There has been no one, I tell you—no one! I should have seen and heard them—the door was open," he reiterated pathetically.

"We'll soon see about that!" was Tournefort's curt comment.

But it was his turn indeed to be utterly bewil-dered. He searched—none too gently—the squalid little lodge through and through, turned the paltry sticks of furniture over, hauled little Amélie, Grosjean's grand-daughter, out of bed, searched under the mattress, and even poked his head up the chimney.

Grosjean watched him wholly unperturbed. These were strange times, and friend Tourne-fort had obviously gone a little off his head. The worthy old *concierge* calmly went on getting the coffee ready. Only when presently Tournefort, worn out with anger and futile exertion, threw himself, with many an oath, into the one arm-chair, Grosjean remarked cooly:

"I tell you what I think it is, citizen. If you were standing just by the door of the lodge you had the back staircase of the house immediately behind you. The partition wall is very thin, and there is a disused door just there also. No doubt, the voices came from there. You see, if there had been any aristos here," he added naively, "they could not have flown up the chimney, could they?"

That argument was certainly unanswerable. But Tournefort was out of temper. He roughly ordered Grosjean to bring the lamp and show him the back staircase and the disused door. The *concierge* obeyed without a murmur. He was not in the least disturbed or frightened by all this blustering. He was only afraid that getting out of bed had made his cold worse. But he knew Tournefort of old. A good fellow, but inclined to be noisy and arrogant since he was in the employ of the Government.

Grosjean took the precaution of putting on his trousers and wrapping an old shawl round his shoulders. Then he had a final sip of hot coffee; after which he picked up the lamp and guided Tournefort out of the lodge.

The wind had quite gone down by now. The lamp scarcely flickered as Grosjean held it above his head.

"Just here, citizen Tournefort," he said, and turned sharply to his left. But the next sound which he uttered was a loud croak of astonishment.

"That door has been out of use ever since I've been here," he muttered.

"And it certainly was closed when I stood up against it," rejoined Tournefort, with a savage oath, "or, of course, I should have noticed it."

Close to the lodge, at right angles to it, a door stood partially open. Tournefort went through it, closely followed by Grosjean. He found himself in a passage which ended in a *cul de sac* on his right; on the left was the foot of the stairs. The whole place was pitch dark save for the feeble light of the lamp. The *cul de sac* itself reeked of dirt and fustiness, as if it had not been cleaned or ventilated for years.

"When did you last notice that this door was closed?" queried Tournefort, furious with the sense of discomfiture, which he would have liked to vent on the unfortunate *concierge*.

"I have not noticed it for some days, citizen," replied Grosjean meekly. "I have had a severe cold, and have not been outside my lodge since Monday last. But we'll ask Amélie!" he added more hopefully.

Amélie, however, could throw no light upon the subject. She certainly kept the back stairs cleaned and swept, but it was not part of her duties to extend her sweeping operations as far as the *cul de sac*. She had quite enough to do as it was, with grandfather now practically helpless. This morning, when she went out to do her

shopping, she had not noticed whether the disused door did or did not look the same as usual.

Grosjean was very sorry for his friend Tournefort, who appeared vastly upset, but still more sorry for himself, for he knew what endless trouble this would entail upon him.

Nor was the trouble slow in coming, not only on Grosjean, but on every lodger inside the house; for before half an hour had gone by Tournefort had gone and come back, this time with the local commissary of police and a couple of agents, who had every man, woman and child in that house out of bed and examined at great length, their identity books searchingly overhauled, their rooms turned topsy-turvy and their furniture knocked about.

It was past midnight before all these perquisitions were completed. No one dared to complain at these indignities put upon peaceable citizens on the mere denunciation of an obscure police agent. These were times when every regulation, every command, had to be accepted without a murmur. At one o'clock in the morning, Grosjean himself was thankful to get back to bed, having satisfied the commissary that he was not a dangerous conspirator.

But of anyone even remotely approaching the description of the *ci-devant* Comtesse de Sucy, or of any man called Bertin, there was not the faintest trace.

II

But no feeling of discomfort ever lasted very long with citizen Tournefort. He was a person of vast resource and great buoyancy of temperament.

True, he had not apprehended two exceedingly noxious aristos, as he had hoped to do; but he held the threads of an abominable conspiracy in his hands, and the question of catching both Bertin and Madame la Comtesse red-handed was only a question of time. But little time had been lost. There was always someone to be found at the offices of the Committee of Public Safety, which were open all night. It was possible that citizen Chauvelin would be still there, for he often took on the night shift, or else citizen Gourdon.

It was Gourdon who greeted his subordinate, somewhat ill-humouredly, for he was indulging in a little sleep, with his toes turned to the fire, as the night was so damp and cold. But when he heard Tournefort's story, he was all eagerness and zeal.

"It is, of course, too late to do anything now," he said finally, after he had mastered every detail of the man's adventures in the Ruelle du Paradis; "but get together half a dozen men upon whom you can rely, and by six o'clock in the morning, or even five, we'll be on our way to Gentilly. Citizen Chauvelin was only saying to-day that he strongly suspected the *ci-devant* Comtesse de Sucy of having left the bulk of her valuable jewellery at the château, and that she would make some effort to get possession of it. It would be rather fine, citizen Tournefort," he added with a chuckle, "if you and I could steal a march on citizen Chauvelin over this affair, what? He has been extraordinarily arrogant of late and marvellously in favour not only with the Committee, but with citizen Robespierre himself."

"They say," commented Tournefort, "that he succeeded in getting hold of some papers which were of great value to the members of the Committee."

"He never succeeded in getting hold of that meddlesome Englishman whom they call the Scarlet Pimpernel," was Gourdon's final dry comment.

Thus was the matter decided on. And the following morning at daybreak, Gourdon, who was only a subordinate officer on the Committee of Public Safety, took it upon himself to institute a perquisition in the château of Gentilly, which is situated close to the commune of that name. He was accompanied by his friend Tournefort and a gang of half a dozen ruffians recruited from the most disreputable *cabarets* of Paris.

The intention had been to steal a march on citizen Chauvelin, who had been over-arrogant of late; but the result did not come up to expec-

tations. By midday the château had been ransacked from attic to cellar; every kind of valuable property had been destroyed, priceless works of art irretrievably damaged. But priceless works of art had no market in Paris these days; and the property of real value—the Sucy diamonds, namely—which had excited the cupidity or the patriotic wrath of citizens Gourdon and Tournefort could nowhere be found.

To make the situation more deplorable still, the Committee of Public Safety had in some inexplicable way got wind of the affair, and the two worthies had the mortification of seeing citizen Chauvelin presently appear upon the scene.

It was then two o'clock in the afternoon. Gourdon, after he had snatched a hasty dinner at a neighbouring *cabaret*, had returned to the task of pulling the château of Gentilly about his own ears if need be, with a view to finding the concealed treasure.

For the nonce he was standing in the centre of the finely proportioned hall. The rich ormolu and crystal chandelier lay in a broken, tangled heap of scraps at his feet, and all around there was a confused medley of pictures, statuettes, silver ornaments, tapestry and brocade hangings, all piled up in disorder, smashed, tattered, kicked at now and again by Gourdon, to the accompaniment of a savage oath.

The house itself was full of noises: heavy footsteps tramping up and down the stairs, furniture turned over, curtains torn from their poles, doors and windows battered in. And through it all the ceaseless hammering of pick and axe, attacking these stately walls which had withstood the wars and sieges of centuries.

Every now and then Tournefort, his face perspiring and crimson with exertion, would present himself at the door of the hall. Gourdon would query gruffly:

"Well?"

And the answer was invariably the same:

"Nothing!"

Then Gourdon would swear again and send curt orders to continue the search relentlessly, ceaselessly.

"Leave no stone upon stone," he commanded. "Those diamonds must be found. We know they are here, and, name of a dog! I mean to have them."

When Chauvelin arrived at the château he made no attempt at first to interfere with Gourdon's commands. Only on one occasion he remarked curtly:

"I suppose, citizen Gourdon, that you can trust your search party?"

"Absolutely," retorted Gourdon. "A finer patriot than Tournefort does not exist."

"Probably," rejoined the other dryly. "But what about the men?"

"Oh, they are only a set of barefooted, ignorant louts. They do as they are told, and Tournefort has his eye on them. I dare say they'll contrive to steal a few things, but they would never dare lay hands on valuable jewellery. To begin with, they could never dispose of it. Imagine a *va-nu-pieds* peddling a diamond tiara!"

"There are always receivers prepared to take risks."

"Very few," Gourdon assured him, "since we decreed that trafficking with aristo property was a crime punishable by death."

Chauvelin said nothing for the moment. He appeared wrapped in his own thoughts, listened for a while to the confused hubbub about the house, then he resumed abruptly:

"Who are these men whom you are employing, citizen Gourdon?"

"A well-known gang," replied the other. "I can give you their names."

"If you please."

Gourdon searched his pockets for a paper which he found presently and handed to his colleague. The latter perused it thoughtfully.

"Where did Tournefort find these men?" he asked.

"For the most part at the Cabaret de la Liberté—a place of very evil repute down in the Rue Christine."

"I know it," rejoined the other. He was still studying the list of names which Gourdon had given him. "And," he added, "I know most

of these men. As thorough a set of ruffians as we need for some of our work. Merri, Guidal, Rateau, Desmonds. *Tiens!*" he exclaimed; "Rateau! Is Rateau here now?"

"Why, of course! He was recruited, like the rest of them, for the day. He won't leave till he has been paid, you may be sure of that. Why do you ask?"

"I will tell you presently. But I would wish to speak with citizen Rateau first."

Just at this moment Tournefort paid his periodical visit to the hall. The usual words, "Still nothing," were on his lips, when Gourdon curtly ordered him to go and fetch the citizen Rateau.

A minute or two later Tournefort returned with the news that Rateau could nowhere be found. Chauvelin received the news without any comment; he only ordered Tournefort, somewhat roughly, back to his work. Then, as soon as the latter had gone, Gourdon turned upon his colleague.

"Will you explain——" he began with a show of bluster.

"With pleasure," replied Chauvelin blandly. "On my way hither, less than an hour ago, I met your man Rateau, a league or so from here."

"You met Rateau!" exclaimed Gourdon impatiently. "Impossible! He was here then, I feel sure. You must have been mistaken."

"I think not. I have only seen the man once, when I, too, went to recruit a band of ruffians at the Cabaret de la Liberté, in connexion with some work I wanted doing. I did not employ him then, for he appeared to me both drink-sodden and nothing but a miserable, consumptive creature, with a churchyard cough you can hear half a league away. But I would know him anywhere. Besides which, he stopped and wished me good morning. Now I come to think of it," added Chauvelin thoughtfully, "he was carrying what looked like a heavy bundle under his arm."

"A heavy bundle!" cried Gourdon, with a forceful oath. "And you did not stop him!"

"I had no reason for suspecting him. I did not know until I arrived here what the whole affair was about, or whom you were employing.

All that the Committee knew for certain was that you and Tournefort and a number of men had arrived at Gentilly before daybreak, and I was then instructed to follow you hither to see what mischief you were up to. You acted in complete secrecy, remember, citizen Gourdon, and without first ascertaining the wishes of the Committee of Public Safety, whose servant you are. If the Sucy diamonds are not found, you alone will be held responsible for their loss to the Government of the People."

Chauvelin's voice had now assumed a threatening tone, and Gourdon felt all his audacity and self-assurance fall away from him, leaving him a prey to nameless terror.

"We must round up Rateau," he murmured hastily. "He cannot have gone far."

"No, he cannot," rejoined Chauvelin dryly; "though I was not thinking specially of Rateau or of diamonds when I started to come hither. I did send a general order forbidding any person on foot or horseback to enter or leave Paris by any of the southern gates. That order will serve us well now. Are you riding?"

"Yes; I left my horse at the tavern just outside Gentilly. I can get to horse within ten minutes."

"To horse, then, as quickly as you can. Pay off your men and dismiss them—all but Tournefort, who had best accompany us. Do not lose a single moment. I'll be ahead of you and may come up with Rateau before you overtake me. And if I were you, citizen Gourdon," he concluded, with ominous emphasis, "I would burn one or two candles to your compeer the devil. You'll have need of his help if Rateau gives us the slip."

III

The first part of the road from Gentilly to Paris runs through the valley of the Bière, and is densely wooded on either side. It winds in and out for the most part, ribbon-like, through thick coppice of chestnut and birch. Thus it was impossible for Chauvelin to spy his quarry from afar; nor did he expect to do so this side

of the Hôpital de la Santé. Once past that point, he would find the road quite open and running almost straight, in the midst of arid and only partially cultivated land.

He rode at a sharp trot, with his caped coat wrapped tightly round his shoulders, for it was raining fast. At intervals, when he met an occasional wayfarer, he would ask questions about a tall man who had a consumptive cough, and who was carrying a cumbersome burden under his arm.

Almost everyone whom he thus asked remembered seeing a personage who vaguely answered to the description: tall and with a decided stoop—yes, and carrying a cumbersome-looking bundle under his arm. Chauvelin was undoubtedly on the track of the thief.

Just beyond Meuves he was overtaken by Gourdon and Tournefort. Here, too, the man Rateau's track became more and more certain. At one place he had stopped and had a glass of wine and a rest; at another he had asked how close he was to the gates of Paris.

The road was now quite open and level; the irregular buildings of the hospital appeared vague in the rain-sodden distance. Twenty minutes later Tournefort, who was riding ahead of his companions, spied a tall, stooping figure at the spot where the Chemin de Gentilly forks, and where stands a group of isolated houses and bits of garden, which belong to la Santé. Here, before the days when the glorious Revolution swept aside all such outward signs of superstition, there had stood a Calvary. It was now used as a sign-post. The man stood before it, scanning the half-obliterated indications.

At the moment that Tournefort first caught sight of him he appeared uncertain of his way. Then for a while he watched Tournefort, who was coming at a sharp trot towards him. Finally, he seemed to make up his mind very suddenly and, giving a last, quick look round, he walked rapidly along the upper road. Tournefort drew rein, waited for his colleagues to come up with him. Then he told them what he had seen.

"It is Rateau, sure enough," he said. "I saw

his face quite distinctly and heard his abominable cough. He is trying to get into Paris. That road leads nowhere but to the barrier. There, of course, he will be stopped, and——"

The other two had also brought their horses to a halt. The situation had become tense, and a plan for future action had at once to be decided on. Already Chauvelin, masterful and sure of himself, had assumed command of the little party. Now he broke in abruptly on Tournefort's vapid reflections.

"We don't want him stopped at the barrier," he said in his usual curt, authoritative manner. "You, citizen Tournefort," he continued, "will ride as fast as you can to the gate, making a detour by the lower road. You will immediately demand to speak with the sergeant who is in command, and you will give him a detailed description of the man Rateau. Then you will tell him in my name that, should such a man present himself at the gate, he must be allowed to enter the city unmolested."

Gourdon gave a quick cry of protest.

"Let the man go unmolested? Citizen Chauvelin, think what you are doing!"

"I always think of what I am doing," retorted Chauvelin curtly, "and have no need of outside guidance in the process." Then he turned once more to Tournefort. "You yourself, citizen," he continued, in sharp, decisive tones which admitted of no argument, "will dismount as soon as you are inside the city. You will keep the gate under observation. The moment you see the man Rateau, you will shadow him, and on no account lose sight of him. Understand?"

"You may trust me, citizen Chauvelin," Tournefort replied, elated at the prospect of work which was so entirely congenial to him. "But will you tell me——"

"I will tell you this much, citizen Tournefort," broke in Chauvelin with some acerbity, "that though we have traced the diamonds and the thief so far, we have, through your folly last night, lost complete track of the *ci-devant* Comtesse de Sucy and of the man Bertin. We want Rateau to show us where they are."

"I understand," murmured the other meekly.

"That's a mercy!" riposted Chauvelin dryly. "Then quickly, man. Lose no time! Try to get a few minutes' advance on Rateau; then slip into the guard-room to change into less conspicuous clothes. Citizen Gourdon and I will continue on the upper road and keep the man in sight in case he should think of altering his course. In any event, we'll meet you just inside the barrier. But if, in the meanwhile, you have contrived to get on Rateau's track before we have arrived on the scene, leave the usual indications as to the direction which you have taken."

Having given his orders and satisfied himself that they were fully understood, he gave a curt command, *"En avant,"* and once more the three of them rode at a sharp trot down the road towards the city.

IV

Citizen Rateau, if he thought about the matter at all, must indeed have been vastly surprised at the unwonted amiability or indifference of Sergeant Ribot, who was in command at the gate of Gentilly. Ribot only threw a very perfunctory glance at the greasy permit which Rateau presented to him, and when he put the usual query: "What's in that parcel?" and Rateau gave the reply: "Two heads of cabbage and a bunch of carrots," Ribot merely poked one of his fingers into the bundle, felt that a cabbage leaf did effectually lie on the top, and thereupon gave the formal order: "Pass on, citizen, in the name of the Republic!" without any hesitation.

Tournefort, who had watched the brief little incident from behind the window of a neighbouring *cabaret*, could not help but chuckle to himself. Never had he seen game walk more readily into a trap. Rateau, after he had passed the barrier, appeared undecided which way he would go. He looked with obvious longing towards the *cabaret*, behind which the keenest agent on the staff of the Committee of Public Safety was even now ensconced. But seemingly a halt within those hospitable doors did not form part of his programme, and a moment or two later he turned sharply on his heel and strode rapidly down the Rue de l'Oursine.

Tournefort allowed him a fair start, and then made ready to follow.

Just as he was stepping out of the *cabaret* he spied Chauvelin and Gourdon coming through the gates. They, too, had apparently made a brief halt inside the guard-room, where—as at most of the gates, a store of various disguises was always kept ready for the use of the numerous sleuth-hounds employed by the Committee of Public Safety. Here the two men had exchanged their official garments for suits of sombre cloth, which gave them the appearance of a couple of humble bourgeois going quietly about their business. Tournefort had donned an old blouse, tattered stockings, and shoes down at heel. With his hands buried in his breeches pockets, he, too, turned into the long narrow Rue de l'Oursine, which after a sharp curve abuts on the Rue Mouffetard.

Rateau was walking rapidly, taking big strides with his long legs. Tournefort, now sauntering in the gutter in the middle of the road, now darting in and out of open doorways, kept his quarry well in sight. Chauvelin and Gourdon lagged some little way behind. It was still raining, but not heavily—a thin drizzle, which penetrated almost to the marrow. Not many passers-by haunted this forlorn quarter of old Paris. To right and left tall houses almost obscured the last quickly fading light of the grey September day.

At the bottom of the Rue Mouffetard, Rateau came once more to a halt. A network of narrow streets radiated from this centre. He looked all round him and also behind. It was difficult to know whether he had a sudden suspicion that he was being followed; certain it is that, after a very brief moment of hesitation, he plunged suddenly into the narrow Rue Contrescarpe and disappeared from view.

Tournefort was after him in a trice. When he reached the corner of the street he saw Rateau, at the farther end of it, take a sudden sharp turn to the right. But not before he had very obviously spied his pursuer, for at that moment his entire demeanour changed. An air of furtive anxiety was expressed in his whole attitude. Even at that distance Tournefort could see him clutching his bulky parcel close to his chest.

After that the pursuit became closer and hotter. Rateau was in and out of that tight network of streets which cluster around the Place de Fourci, intent, apparently, on throwing his pursuers off the scent, for after a while he was running round and round in a circle. Now up the Rue des Poules, then to the right and to the right again; back in the Place de Fourci. Then straight across it once more to the Rue Contrescarpe, where he presently disappeared so completely from view that Tournefort thought that the earth must have swallowed him up.

Tournefort was a man capable of great physical exertion. His calling often made heavy demands upon his powers of endurance; but never before had he grappled with so strenuous a task. Puffing and panting, now running at top speed, anon brought to a halt by the doubling-up tactics of his quarry, his great difficulty was the fact that citizen Chauvelin did not wish the man Rateau to be apprehended; did not wish him to know that he was being pursued. And Tournefort had need of all his wits to keep well under the shadow of any projecting wall or under cover of open doorways which were conveniently in the way, and all the while not to lose sight of that consumptive giant, who seemed to be playing some intricate game which well-nigh exhausted the strength of citizen Tournefort.

What he could not make out was what had happened to Chauvelin and to Gourdon. They had been less than three hundred metres behind him when first this wild chase in and out of the Rue Contrescarpe had begun. Now, when their presence was most needed, they seemed to have lost track both of him—Tournefort—and of the very elusive quarry. To make matters more complicated, the shades of evening were drawing in very fast, and these narrow streets of the faubourg were very sparsely lighted.

Just at this moment Tournefort had once more caught sight of Rateau, striding leisurely this time up the street. The worthy agent quickly took refuge under a doorway and was mopping his streaming forehead, glad of this brief respite in the mad chase, when that awful churchyard cough suddenly sounded so close to him that he gave a great jump and well-nigh betrayed his presence then and there. He had only just time to withdraw farther still into the angle of the doorway, when Rateau passed by.

Tournefort peeped out of his hiding-place, and for the space of a dozen heart-beats or so remained there quite still, watching that broad back and those long limbs slowly moving through the gathering gloom. The next instant he perceived Chauvelin standing at the end of the street.

Rateau saw him too—came face to face with him, in fact, and must have known who he was, for, without an instant's hesitation and just like a hunted creature at bay, he turned sharply on his heel and then ran back down the street as hard as he could tear. He passed close to within half a metre of Tournefort, and as he flew past he hit out with his left fist so vigorously that the worthy agent of the Committee of Public Safety, caught on the nose by the blow, staggered and measured his length upon the flagged floor below.

The next moment Chauvelin had come by. Tournefort, struggling to his feet, called to him, panting:

"Did you see him? Which way did he go?"

"Up the Rue Bordet. After him, citizen!" replied Chauvelin grimly, between his teeth.

Together the two men continued the chase, guided through the intricate mazes of the streets by their fleeing quarry. They had Rateau well in sight, and the latter could no longer continue his former tactics with success now that experienced sleuth-hounds were on his track.

At a given moment he was caught between the two of them. Tournefort was advancing cautiously up the Rue Bordet; Chauvelin, equally stealthily, was coming down the same street, and Rateau, once more walking quite leisurely, was at equal distance between the two.

V

There are no turnings out of the Rue Bordet, the total length of which is less than fifty metres; so Tournefort, feeling more at his ease, ensconced himself at one end of the street, behind a doorway, whilst Chauvelin did the same at the other. Rateau, standing in the gutter, appeared once more in a state of hesitation. Immediately in front of him the door of a small *cabaret* stood invitingly open; its signboard "Le Bon Copain" promised rest and refreshment. He peered up and down the road, satisfied himself presumably that, for the moment, his pursuers were out of sight, hugged his parcel to his chest, and then suddenly made a dart for the *cabaret* and disappeared within its doors.

Nothing could have been better. The quarry, for the moment, was safe, and if the sleuth-hounds could not get refreshment, they could at least get a rest. Tournefort and Chauvelin crept out of their hiding-places. They met in the middle of the road, at the spot where Rateau had stood a while ago. It was then growing dark and the street was innocent of lanterns, but the lights inside the *cabaret* gave a full view of the interior. The lower half of the wide shop-window was curtained off, but above the curtain the heads of the customers of "Le Bon Copain," and the general comings and goings, could clearly be seen.

Tournefort, never at a loss, had already climbed up on a low projection in the wall of one of the houses opposite. From this point of vantage he could more easily observe what went on inside the *cabaret*, and in short, jerky sentences he gave a description of what he saw to his chief.

"Rateau is sitting down . . . he has his back to the window . . . he has put his bundle down close beside him on the bench . . . he can't speak for a minute, for he is coughing and spluttering like an old walrus. . . . A wench is bringing him a bottle of wine and a hunk of bread and cheese. . . . He has started talking . . . is talking volubly . . . the people are laughing . . . some are applauding. . . . And here comes Jean Victor, the landlord . . . you know him, citizen . . . a big, hulking fellow, and as good a patriot as I ever wish to see. . . . He, too, is laughing and talking to Rateau, who is doubled up with another fit of coughing."

Chauvelin uttered an exclamation of impatience:

"Enough of this, citizen Tournefort. Keep your eye on the man and hold your tongue. I am spent with fatigue."

"No wonder," murmured Tournefort. Then he added insinuatingly: "Why not let me go in there and apprehend Rateau now? We should have the diamonds and——"

"And lose the *ci-devant* Comtesse de Sucy and the man Bertin," retorted Chauvelin with sudden fierceness. "Bertin, who can be none other than that cursed Englishman, the——"

He checked himself, seeing Tournefort was gazing down on him, with awe and astonishment expressed in his lean, hatchet face.

"You are losing sight of Rateau, citizen," Chauvelin continued calmly. "What is he doing now?"

But Tournefort felt that this calmness was only on the surface; something strange had stirred the depths of his chief's keen, masterful mind. He would have liked to ask a question or two, but knew from experience that it was neither wise nor profitable to try and probe citizen Chauvelin's thoughts. So after a moment or two he turned back obediently to his task.

"I can't see Rateau for the moment," he said, "but there is much talking and merriment in there. Ah! there he is, I think. Yes, I see him! . . . He is behind the counter, talking to Jean Victor . . . and he has just thrown some money down upon the counter . . . gold, too! name of a dog! . . ."

Then suddenly, without any warning, Tournefort jumped down from his post of observation. Chauvelin uttered a brief:

"What the——are you doing, citizen?"

"Rateau is going," replied Tournefort excitedly. "He drank a mug of wine at a draught and has picked up his bundle, ready to go."

Once more cowering in the dark angle of a doorway, the two men waited, their nerves on edge, for the reappearance of their quarry.

"I wish citizen Gourdon were here," whispered Tournefort. "In the darkness it is better to be three than two."

"I sent him back to the Station in the Rue Mouffetard," was Chauvelin's curt retort; "there to give notice that I might require a few armed men presently. But he should be somewhere about here by now, looking for us. Anyway, I have my whistle, and if——"

He said no more, for at that moment the door of the *cabaret* was opened from within and Rateau stepped out into the street, to the accompaniment of loud laughter and clapping of hands which came from the customers of the "Bon Copain."

This time he appeared neither in a hurry nor yet anxious. He did not pause in order to glance to right or left, but started to walk quite leisurely up the street. The two sleuth-hounds quietly followed him. Through the darkness they could only vaguely see his silhouette, with the great bundle under his arm. Whatever may have been Rateau's fears of being shadowed a while ago, he certainly seemed free of them now. He sauntered along whistling a tune, down the Montague Ste. Geneviève to the Place Maubert, and thence straight towards the river.

Having reached the bank he turned off to his left, sauntered past the Ecole de Médecine and went across the Petit Pont, then through the New Market, along the Quai des Orfèvres. Here he made a halt, and for a while looked over the embankment at the river and then round about him, as if in search of something. But presently he appeared to make up his mind, and continued his leisurely walk as far as the Pont Neuf, where he turned sharply off to his right, still whistling, Tournefort and Chauvelin hard upon his heels.

"That whistling is getting on my nerves," muttered Tournefort irritably; "and I haven't heard the ruffian's churchyard cough since he walked out of the 'Bon Copain.'"

Strangely enough, it was this remark of Tournefort's which gave Chauvelin the first inkling of something strange and, to him, positively awesome. Tournefort, who walked close beside him, heard him suddenly mutter a fierce exclamation:

"Name of a dog!"

"What is it, citizen?" queried Tournefort, awed by this sudden outburst on the part of a man whose icy calmness had become proverbial throughout the Committee.

"Sound the alarm, citizen!" cried Chauvelin in response. "Or, by satan, he'll escape us again!"

"But——" stammered Tournefort in utter bewilderment, while, with fingers that trembled somewhat, he fumbled for his whistle.

"We shall want all the help we can get," retorted Chauvelin roughly. "For, unless I am much mistaken, there's more noble quarry here than even I could dare to hope for!"

Rateau in the meanwhile had quietly lolled up to the parapet on the right-hand side of the bridge, and Tournefort, who was watching him with intense keenness, still marvelled why citizen Chauvelin had suddenly become so strangely excited. Rateau was merely lolling against the parapet, like a man who has not a care in the world. He had placed his bundle on the stone ledge beside him. Here he waited a moment or two, until one of the small craft upon the river loomed out of the darkness immediately below the bridge. Then he picked up the bundle and threw it straight into the boat. At that same moment Tournefort had the whistle to his lips. A shrill, sharp sound rang out through the gloom.

"The boat, citizen Tournefort, the boat!" cried Chauvelin. "There are plenty of us here to deal with the man."

Immediately, from the quays, the streets, the bridges, dark figures emerged out of the dark-

ness and hurried to the spot. Some reached the bridgehead even as Rateau made a dart forward, and two men were upon him before he succeeded in running very far. Others had scrambled down the embankment and were shouting to some unseen boatmen to "halt, in the name of the people!"

But Rateau gave in without a struggle. He appeared more dazed than frightened, and quietly allowed the agents of the Committee to lead him back to the bridge, where Chauvelin had paused, waiting for him.

VI

A minute or two later Tournefort was once more beside his chief. He was carrying the precious bundle, which, he explained, the boatman had given up without question.

"The man knew nothing about it," the agent said. "No one, he says, could have been more surprised than he was when this bundle was suddenly flung at him over the parapet of the bridge."

Just then the small group, composed of two or three agents of the Committee, holding their prisoner by the arms came into view. One man was walking ahead and was the first to approach Chauvelin. He had a small screw of paper in his hand, which he gave to his chief.

"Found inside the lining of the prisoner's hat, citizen," he reported curtly, and opened the shutter of a small dark lantern which he wore at his belt.

Chauvelin took the paper from his subordinate. A weird, inexplicable foreknowledge of what was to come caused his hand to shake and beads of perspiration to moisten his forehead. He looked up and saw the prisoner standing before him. Crushing the paper in his hand he snatched the lantern from the agent's belt and flashed it in the face of the quarry who, at the last, had been so easily captured.

Immediately a hoarse cry of disappointment and of rage escaped his throat.

"Who is this man?" he cried.

One of the agents gave reply:

"It is old Victor, the landlord of the 'Bon Copain.' He is just a fool, who has been playing a practical joke."

Tournefort, too, at sight of the prisoner had uttered a cry of dismay and of astonishment.

"Victor!" he exclaimed. "Name of a dog, citizen, what are you doing here?"

But Chauvelin had gripped the man by the arm so fiercely that the latter swore with the pain.

"What is the meaning of this?" he queried roughly.

"Only a bet, citizen," retorted Victor reproachfully. "No reason to fall on an honest patriot for a bet, just as if he were a mad dog."

"A joke? A bet?" murmured Chauvelin hoarsely, for his throat now felt hot and parched. "What do you mean? Who are you, man? Speak, or I'll——"

"My name is Jean Victor," replied the other. "I am the landlord of the 'Bon Copain.' An hour ago a man came into my *cabaret*. He was a queer, consumptive creature, with a churchyard cough that made you shiver. Some of my customers knew him by sight, told me that the man's name was Rateau, and that he was an *habitué* of the 'Liberté' in the Rue Christine. Well! he soon fell into conversation, first with me, then with some of my customers—talked all sorts of silly nonsense, made absurd bets with everybody. Some of these he won, others he lost; but I must say that when he lost he always paid up most liberally. Then we all got excited, and soon bets flew all over the place. I don't rightly know how it happened at the last, but all at once he bet me that I would not dare to walk out then and there in the dark, as far as the Pont Neuf, wearing his blouse and hat and carrying a bundle the same as his under my arm. I not dare? . . . I, Jean Victor, who was a fine fighter in my day!

"I bet him a gold piece that I would, and he said that he would make it five if I came back without my bundle, having thrown it over the parapet into any passing boat. Well, citizen!"

continued Jean Victor with a laugh, "I ask you, what would you have done? Five gold pieces means a fortune these hard times, and I tell you the man was quite honest and always paid liberally when he lost. He slipped behind the counter and took off his blouse and hat, which I put on. Then we made up a bundle with some cabbage heads and a few carrots, and out I came. I didn't think there could be anything wrong in the whole affair—just the tomfoolery of a man who has got the betting mania and in whose pocket money is just burning a hole. And I have won my bet," concluded Jean Victor, still unabashed, "and I want to go back and get my money. If you don't believe me, come with me to my *cabaret*. You will find the citizen Rateau there, for sure; and I know that I shall find my five gold pieces."

Chauvelin had listened to the man as he would to some weird dream-story, wherein ghouls and devils had played a part. Tournefort, who was watching him, was awed by the look of fierce rage and grim hopelessness which shone from his chief's pale eyes. The other agents laughed. They were highly amused at the tale, but they would not let the prisoner go.

"If Jean Victor's story is true, citizen," their sergeant said, speaking to Chauvelin, "there will be witnesses to it over at 'Le Bon Copain.' Shall we take the prisoner straightway there and await further orders?"

Chauvelin gave a curt acquiescence, nodding his head like some insentient wooden automaton. The screw of paper was still in his hand; it seemed to sear his palm. Tournefort even now broke into a grim laugh: He had just undone the bundle which Jean Victor had thrown over the parapet of the bridge. It contained two heads of cabbage and a bunch of carrots. Then he ordered the agents to march on with their prisoner, and they, laughing and joking with Jean Victor, gave a quick turn, and soon their heavy footsteps were echoing down the flagstones of the bridge.

Chauvelin waited, motionless and silent, the dark lantern still held in his shaking hand, until he was quite sure that he was alone. Then only did he unfold the screw of paper.

It contained a few lines scribbled in pencil—just that foolish rhyme which to his fevered nerves was like a strong irritant, a poison which gave him an unendurable sensation of humiliation and impotence:

"We seek him here, we seek him there!
Chauvelin seeks him everywhere!
Is he in heaven? Is he in hell?
That dammed, elusive Pimpernel!"

He crushed the paper in his hand and, with a loud groan of misery, fled over the bridge like one possessed.

VII

Madame la Comtesse de Sucy never went to England. She was one of those French women who would sooner endure misery in their own beloved country than comfort anywhere else. She outlived the horrors of the Revolution and speaks in her memoirs of the man Bertin. She never knew who he was nor whence he came. All that she knew was that he came to her like some mysterious agent of God, bringing help, counsel, a resemblance of happiness, at the moment when she was at the end of all her resources and saw grim starvation staring her and her children in the face. He appointed all sorts of strange places in out-of-the-way Paris where she was wont to meet him, and one night she confided to him the history of her diamonds, and hardly dared to trust his promise that he would get them for her.

Less than twenty-four hours later he brought them to her, at the poor lodgings in the Rue Blanche which she occupied with her children under an assumed name. That same night she begged him to dispose of them. This also he did, bringing her the money the next day.

She never saw him again after that.

But citizen Tournefort never quite got over his disappointment of that night. Had he dared, he would have blamed citizen Chauvelin for the discomfiture. It would have been better to have apprehended the man Rateau while there was a chance of doing so with success.

As it was, the impudent ruffian slipped clean away, and was never heard of again either at the "Bon Copain" or at the "Liberté." The customers at the *cabaret* certainly corroborated the story of Jean Victor. The man Rateau, they said, had been honest to the last. When time went on and Jean Victor did not return, he said that he could no longer wait, had work to do for the Government over the other side of the water and was afraid he would get punished if he dallied. But, before leaving, he laid the five gold pieces on the table. Everyone wondered that so humble a workman had so much money in his pocket, and was withal so lavish with it. But these were not the times when one inquired too closely into the presence of money in the pocket of a good patriot.

And citizen Rateau was a good patriot, for sure. And a good fellow to boot!

They all drank his health in Jean Victor's sour wine; then each went his way.

ADVENTURE OF THE SCRAP OF PAPER

GEORGE BARTON

THE PROLIFIC AUTHOR and journalist George Barton (1866–1940) was born in Philadelphia, where he lived for most of his life, and in 1887 became a journalist at the *Philadelphia Enquirer* before being hired as an editorial writer for the *Philadelphia Evening Bulletin* and later for the *Philadelphia Enquirer*. He was also a composer and instrumentalist.

Working in numerous writing fields, Barton produced books and magazine articles in such diverse areas as history, biography, juvenile works, criticism, illustrated books, novels, true crime, and mystery fiction.

Among the books for which he is best known are *Adventures of the World's Greatest Detectives* (1909), which provides largely romanticized and even fictionalized profiles of members of official police forces, including such historic figures as Vidocq and the Pinkertons; *The World's Greatest Military Spies and Secret Service Agents* (1917), the first comprehensive history of spies throughout history; *Celebrated Spies and Famous Mysteries of the Great War* (1919), a companion volume to the previous book, which focused on the espionage agents of all sides in World War I while also examining numerous adventures and mysteries of the battles on the front and behind the lines; and *Famous Detective Mysteries* (1926), a collection of true crime stories in fictionalized form.

Barton's mystery fiction was less successful than his true crime, resulting in just three novels—*The Mystery of the Red Flame* (1918), *The Ambassador's Trunk* (1919), and *The Pembroke Mason Affair* (1920)—and a single short story collection, *The Strange Adventures of Bromley Barnes* (1918).

Barnes was a bachelor who lived in Washington, DC, where he worked as an investigator with a career of thirty years in the employ of the United States government, first as an agent in the Secret Service, then as Chief of the Special Agents of the Treasury Department.

"Adventure of the Scrap of Paper" was originally published in *The Strange Adventures of Bromley Barnes* (Boston, The Page Company, 1918).

ADVENTURE OF THE SCRAP OF PAPER

GEORGE BARTON

BROMLEY BARNES and Admiral Hawksby sat on either side of a flat-topped desk in the Navy Department, talking in low, earnest tones. The grizzled face of the old sea fighter looked sterner than usual, while the attentive, earnest countenance of the veteran investigator indicated that he fully appreciated the importance of the communication which was being made to him. The purport of it was simple enough, and sufficiently alarming to call for prompt action. The secrets of the Department were being peddled to the enemy. Orders, that were presumably known to only three persons in Washington, were finding their way to hostile quarters with a rapidity and a certainty that was almost uncanny.

"We've got to locate the leak, Barnes," said the admiral, emphasizing the remark with a resounding blow on the desk with his closed fist, "or I'll feel like handing in my resignation."

An incredulous laugh came from the bald-headed man with the fringe of iron-gray hair which encircled his head with a halo–like effect.

"Resign," he retorted; "that sounds like retreat, and I didn't think that word had any place in the vocabulary of the man who ran the blockade—"

"Never mind that," hastily interrupted Hawksby, who feared the usual eulogy for the gallant action which had won him a gold medal and the thanks of Congress: "you know what I mean. I feel so impotent in this underhand business that I scarcely know what to do. If it was an out-and-out, face-to-face fight, I'd know just how to act. I'm depending on you to get to the bottom of the thing. Will you help me?"

"Yes," was the prompt reply, "but you've got to help me first. Now, you say the last message that was intercepted related to the movements of the Asiatic fleet. Please let me see a copy of the order."

The admiral pressed a button on the desk, and in a few moments a young man, with coal black hair and brown skin, entered the room.

"Lee," said the sailor, "get me the order book. I think you will find it in the copying press."

As the Admiral sat stroking his mustache and imperial, Barnes looked at him curiously.

"Who is that man?" he asked.

"That chap—oh, that's a West Indian who acts as a sort of personal servant to me."

"Do you mean to say that he has access to the copy book and is given the run of the place?"

Hawksby drew himself up stiffly.

"I don't know what you mean by the 'run of

the place'—and, besides, the orders are in code and would be Greek to him or any other man except to myself and the Secretary of the Navy."

Presently the messenger returned, and for the next ten minutes the two men were deeply engrossed in the intricacies of the naval code and the details of how the orders had been transmitted. Barnes asked a hundred and one questions and finally departed with the intimation that he might return and ask some more before he started in on his difficult task.

"It all depends upon circumstances," he said, "and, in the meantime, I'm going to take a long walk to get the cobwebs out of my head."

He went to his apartments near the Capitol first, and gave some general orders to his assistant and general factotum. He consulted a number of maps and then he started out on one of the long strolls which had made him as familiar with the streets of the National Capital as the famous Caliph was with the equally celebrated city of Bagdad.

No member of the Cabinet, and not one of the foreign diplomats at Washington could have been more fastidious in his dress than this investigator who had come from his retirement to assist his Government during a critical stage in its history. The frock coat, the carefully creased trousers, the gray spats, the opal in his green tie, and the tightly rolled silk umbrella which took the place of a walking stick, were all just as they should be—or at least, just as Barnes felt they should be. He walked up one street and down another, thinking all the while of the problem that had been given into his care. A stranger, noting the cold gray eyes and the quizzical smile, would have thought him a man without a care in the world. He must have been walking for an hour when his steps led him into that section of the city known as Farragut Circle. He noticed, in a casual way, that an automobile was standing in front of one of the houses. And then an incident, seemingly insignificant in itself, roused all of his thinking faculties.

The driver of the car had taken the cover from a sandwich. Instead of tossing it aside he care-

fully rolled the oiled paper into a little ball and threw it on the sidewalk. At the same moment a nattily dressed man with a waxed mustache and a pink carnation in the buttonhole of his stylish coat came down the steps of the house and picked up the discarded bit of paper. He looked up and down the street in a nervous manner, as if to make sure that he was not observed, and then turning briskly, reëntered the house. The incident did not take a minute, but to the watching Barnes it was like a drama itself. Instantly the driver of the car put his foot on the lever of the machine and it whizzed away. But in that brief time the detective had obtained the number of the machine and a mental picture of the chauffeur. He noted the number and location of the house, and then, with his quizzical smile broadening, hastened to his own apartment.

On the morning after the incident of the oiled paper, a new janitor appeared at the apartment house on Farragut Circle. He wore a blouse and overalls and seemed to fit into the scheme of the place much better than the house itself did with the richer and more pretentious dwellings with which it was surrounded. The new tyrant of the place was most industrious and showed a desire to please that was truly amazing upon the part of a modern janitor. His round face and bald head were smudged with soot and dirt, and his features were all but recognizable. But even the evidence of praiseworthy toil could not change the cold, gray eyes and the quizzical smile which were a part of the personality of Bromley Barnes. He made friends with everybody—especially the women and children—and he had the run of the house, which was to be expected in one who was presumably charged with its destinies.

In twenty-four hours the new janitor was familiar with the place and its occupants. No matter how unkempt he might seem himself, he showed a real desire to keep the house tidy. Residents were delighted to find a man who was willing to carry off the contents of their waste paper baskets and trash cans, and they were united in designating him as "a jewel" of a janitor. On the evening of the second day the new man sat in his quarters in the basement of the house smoking a corn-cob pipe and looking the picture of contentment. But later that night, when most of the guests were sleeping the sleep of the just, the janitor had pulled down the blinds of his own modest apartment and was restlessly pawing over scraps of paper that had been found in the waste baskets.

For more than an hour he worked there, with a patience and a persistence beyond all praise. At the end of that time he began to show signs of weariness. But just when he seemed ready to quit, he gave a cry of delight. He had found a little scrap of oiled paper, twisted and rolled into a tiny ball. Slowly and carefully he unrolled it and spread it out on the little wooden table. It contained several typewritten lines which the old man found some difficulty in deciphering. But the hardest task has its end and finally he was able to read these significant words:

"Gunboats *Philadelphia* and *Newark* have been ordered to join the Asiatic fleet. 200 jackies have been assigned to special duty in this connection. Ammunition in large quantities is to be shipped. More details in the next twenty-four hours."

Bromley Barnes gave a sigh of relief. He picked up the little scrap of paper reverently and placed it in his wallet. Then, with that quizzical smile hovering about his lips, he undressed and went to bed to enjoy a well-earned night's rest.

Things in the apartment house moved along in their accustomed grooves for some days. The man with the waxed mustache and pink carnation did not appear to have any occupation, yet for a man without regular employment he seemed to be amazingly busy. Percival Roberts, for by that name he was addressed, had a room near the top of the house—an attic room that by no means corresponded with his careful dress and fastidious manners. He suggested a person who spends much time at the barber's, and regarded the manicuring of his nails as a sort of religious rite. Such a one was not likely to bestow much attention on a mere janitor, and when the bald-headed man with the cold gray eyes and the quizzical smile passed him on the stairs, Roberts did not even deign to throw a glance in his direction. There were many things that the wax-mustached person was not, but there was one thing he was—or thought he was—and that was a lady killer.

One morning he was coming out of the house when he passed a young woman with a singularly attractive face. She had taken an apartment on the third floor back and Mr. Percival Roberts made it his business to find out all about her. Gossip flows quite as freely in the modern apartment house as it formerly did in the less pretentious boarding house, and by putting this and that together, the young man learned a number of things. First, she was Miss Marie Johnson, and she had come from the far West for the purpose of attending an art school in Washington. Secondly, she had been quite as much taken with Mr. Percival Roberts as he had been with her. That was a hopeful beginning, and before long he had managed to make her acquaintance, and even offered to escort her to the institution where she proposed to take up the study of art. But she smilingly declined this on the ground that it was not wise to mix business with pleasure.

In less than a week, however, the acquaintance had prospered to such an extent that Miss Johnson accepted an invitation to accompany Mr. Roberts to the theater, and after that he pressed his suit with much ardor. She did not precisely repulse him, but she tried to make him understand that she had a serious purpose in life, and that she did not propose to be diverted from the plan which had brought her to the National Capital. She let him know that she admired men with a purpose in life, and gently intimated that his indolent existence did not promise well for the woman who would consent to be his wife. The bald-headed man with the fringe of gray hair, and the cold gray eyes and the quizzical smile noticed the growing intimacy between the pair, and he merely shrugged his shoulders as much as to say that in the matter of love he could not be regarded as a competent authority. But Percival Roberts felt that when it came to the tender passion he was in his element, and he plainly was flattered at the evident impression he had made upon the studious young woman.

It was on the evening of the fifth day that Percival found himself in the cozy sitting room of Marie Johnson, making his first formal call. He found it very pleasant there. The apartment, furnished with exquisite taste, made an appropriate setting for the girl. She was not "beautiful" in the usually accepted sense of that much-abused word. But she was undeniably fascinating. He took in every detail of the picture—and it satisfied him. Her coal black hair, parted in the middle, and glowing with life and vitality, her dark, gray eyes, full of spirit and intelligence, and the masterful manner—always feminine—in which she carried herself, convinced Percival that here at last was the one girl in the world for him. They talked of indifferent topics for some time, and finally the young man, taking her shapely hand in his, began to declare his passion. She did not withdraw her hand, neither did she show any inclination to encourage his words. There was just the right degree of modesty mixed with friendliness.

"My dear," he began, "you have my happiness in your keeping. Marie, I want to ask—"

But at this point there was a terrific hooting of an automobile horn just outside the apartment house. To the surprise of Marie, the ardent wooer dropped her hand, and rising, walked over to the window. One look was sufficient, for turning to her, he exclaimed:

"Pardon me, I'll be back in a moment."

Before Marie realized what was going on, he had grabbed his hat and hurried from the room. She did not betray any emotion, disappointment or otherwise, but she evidently possessed the curiosity of her sex, because she went to the window and, raising the sash, looked below. It was worth while, for a curious performance was being enacted. An automobile had halted in front of the house. The driver had just finished taking the covering from a sandwich. Instead of tossing the oiled paper to one side, he rolled it into a small ball and then threw it, with great deliberation, over on the sidewalk. At the same moment, Mr. Percival Roberts, descending the steps of the house, reached over and picked up the discarded paper. The automobile, with a farewell honk-honk, dashed away, while Roberts, with simulated indifference, reëntered the house.

Marie closed the window and sat down and awaited the return of the young man. Five minutes and then ten passed, and still he did not come back. Presently, with a look of determination on her face, she left the room and ascended the staircase in the direction of his apartment. It did not take long to reach the entrance to his attic room. The door, fortunately, was slightly ajar, and without the slightest compunction Marie pushed it open and entered.

Roberts was not there. The room was empty. She glanced about hastily and noted the bareness of its furnishings. There was a small cot in a corner of the attic, but it seemed out of place because the room was fitted up more like an office than a place of habitation. A roll-top desk was against the wall and it was open, showing a mass of papers in much confusion as though the owner had left in a hurry. What did it all mean? Where had Percival Roberts gone? What was his occupation, and what was the meaning of his sudden agitation? Presently Marie noticed a light screen that shut off one corner of the attic. She had gone too far to retreat, and walking over, she moved the obstruction. She gave a gasp because she saw revealed a flight of steps, leading to a trap door that looked out on the roof. Slowly and cautiously she began to climb the ladder and continued until her head emerged into the outside air.

"Zip-zip-zip" came from nearby, followed by a spluttering sound. She looked in that direction, and saw Roberts, his face white and concentrated, working at an instrument. Like a flash, the truth dawned on her. It was a wireless telegraph outfit and he was the operator. Summoning all her strength, she climbed on to the roof and stood there, supporting herself by holding on to the edge of the trap door. At that moment he looked up and saw her standing there like an accusing spirit. His face went white and his voice trembled:

"What are you doing here?"

The color had vanished from her countenance too, and her eyes danced with excitement. Nevertheless, she managed to speak composedly:

"That is the very question I was going to ask you. What are you doing up here like a thief in the night?"

He had evidently finished with his telegraphing, because he threw a cover over the outfit and advanced toward her in a threatening way. Her words had cut him like a whip, and he approached her shakily. Bewildered rage and childish fright seemed to be struggling for the mastery. He grabbed her by the wrist, and when he spoke again, it was in a thick, husky voice:

"What do you mean by spying on me—what do you mean by creeping up that ladder—what are you doing here, anyhow?"

She gave a long-drawn breath before she replied. Her hand, holding the edge of the trap door, trembled in spite of her effort to be composed, but presently she spoke in a voice that had a note of pathos in it.

"Don't—don't you think that you are the one to explain? You leave me without a word of warning, and when I come to find you, I find you out on the roof, acting—acting like a criminal."

He pulled himself together. The look of half-dazed fury left his face. He loosened his hold on her wrist and spoke in low, tender tones:

"Forgive me, Marie. I—I lost control of myself. You scared me for a moment. I'm sorry. Say that you'll forgive me for my nasty outbreak."

She looked up at him with humid eyes. She seemed to be seeing him through a mist. But this passed quickly and she said:

"That's very well, but it doesn't explain anything."

He placed his arm about her waist, and began to assist her gently down the rude ladder. He closed the trap door, and presently they stood facing one another in that attic room. The seconds seemed like minutes, and when he spoke it was in a slow voice, as though the words were being dragged from his reluctant lips:

"Marie, I'm going to tell you what I would not tell another living soul. But—but you are entitled to know it. You have often asked me to tell you my occupation. You wondered what I did for—for a living. I'll tell you. I'm engaged in secret service work."

He had locked the door before he began to speak, and she stood there now with her delicate fingers nervously handling the knob. She seemed to be quivering with terror. Then she raised a white hand and pointed it at him in a shaky manner.

"You—you mean to say that you are a spy?"

His face reddened. That look of bewildered rage returned for a second, and then he said doggedly:

"You can put it that way if you want to do so."

She stood for a moment, swaying with fright. Her voice was very low, and it quivered:

"And in the face of this, you have dared to make love to me—you pretended to care for me."

He rushed over to where she stood and threw his arms about her in frantic fashion.

"Oh, Marie, can't you see that I have been doing it for you—can't you see that I have been trying to earn the reward that will make us independent? I care for you more than anything in the world. If you care for me, nothing else matters. Say that I am forgiven. Say that you will be my wife."

Her face hardened at that, and she spoke with determination, with that air of decisiveness which he had admired in her so much.

"If you care for me as much as you say, you will tell me everything. Tell me the truth. You must keep nothing from me. You were working against the United States, against your own country. Isn't that a fact?"

"Don't put it that way. I'll tell you everything. I have been representing another nation.

You speak of my country. What does that mean? I owe nothing to the country. It has not even given me the chance of making a decent living. And patriotism! What is that? Merely a word. The work I have been doing will give me the means to keep you in comfort. We can go away and live in comfort for the rest of our lives."

"But a traitor," she murmured, "to be married to a traitor!"

"Please don't talk like that," he implored, "and think only that I am doing it for you. The thing we do for love cannot be wrong. And, Marie, I love you so much."

She melted at that and looked at him in a way that seemed to say that she might forgive the offense for the sake of the love. He grasped at his opportunity as a drowning man grasps at a straw. He led her to a chair and then began to fumble among the papers on his desk. Presently he secured a number of them in a package and he waved them in front of her dark gray eyes.

"Look!" he exclaimed, "these few pieces of paper carry with them the power to give us wealth and happiness for the rest of our lives. Promise me that you will say nothing of what you have seen. In a few days all will be well, and then we may go away and be happy with each other. You want to be happy, don't you?"

"Yes," she said softly, "I want to be happy."

"Ah," he shouted gayly, "I was sure that you were a sensible woman; I realized that from the start!"

She looked very tired standing there. There were dark circles under her lustrous eyes, and her chin seemed to quiver from weariness and excitement. She looked at him appealingly.

"Now," she said in a half whisper, "if you will unlock the door, I will go to my own room. I need rest."

He moved as if to comply with her request, but at that instant there came a sharp, peremptory knock on the panel of the door. He opened it quickly, and a smallish man, with coal black hair and brown skin, confronted him. The visitor was agitated and he spoke hurriedly:

"We have been discovered. They know about the wireless. The police are likely to be here at any moment. Get away!"

As he uttered the last word, the black-haired, brown-skinned man turned and ran down the stairway. Marie had heard all, and she looked the picture of fright and terror. Roberts's eyes had narrowed as he received the message, but when he noted the fear in her eyes he put his arms around her in a comforting way.

"It's all right, little girl. We have reached the end of the chapter, but we won't go away empty handed."

He hastened to the desk and picked up a small packet of papers. He fondled them as one might a favorite child. He looked up with cupidity and triumph in his face.

"They've discovered the wireless, but it's too late to prevent the damage. I've got enough here to shake the whole Department of State, not to speak of the Navy. And there's a fortune in it for us. And don't be frightened. I'll take care of you."

He moved toward her, and with a smothered cry she clung to his shoulders. He saw that she was white about the lips, and he could feel that she was trembling. As they stood thus a gust of wind swept beneath the closed door and rustled a bit of paper on the floor. She gave a cry of terror and he let out an oath.

"I'm like a skittish horse," he said, half apologetically, "but it will be all right. We'll have to make a quick get-away. I'll call a taxicab and we'll shoot off to the Union Station." He looked at his watch. "We've just got time to catch the southern train. Before they know it, we'll be at El Paso, and then, once across the border and on Mexican soil, I'll defy the whole bunch to get me."

He was tossing articles of clothing into a grip by this time, and then he paused for a moment to say to Marie:

"You'd better go to your room and get a few things together. We'll only have a few minutes. Hurry. I'll have the cab by the time you're ready."

The girl seemed to be more composed by this time. She looked at him with a glance of endearment.

"Percival," she said softly—and the first mention of his given name from her lips thrilled him—"I'll try to be useful. I'll call the cab."

He was delighted beyond measure by her acceptance of the situation. He stooped down and kissed her on the lips. That one act seemed to change the whole character of the enterprise. Instead of a fugitive from justice, he felt like a man about to enter on his honeymoon.

"Do so," he murmured in return, "and by the time it is here I will be all ready for you."

During the next few minutes there were scenes of feverish activity in that apartment house on Farragut Circle. Percival Roberts lived in a Heaven of his own creating. He pictured himself and his beloved in a far-away land enjoying the fruits of his "hard work." But in the midst of his day dreaming he roused himself to the actualities. If the police were on the way he did not have much time to spare. He finished his preparations in record time, and started down stairs to meet Marie. To his satisfaction, the door of her room was open and he saw her standing there, attired for a journey, and looking as neat and as pretty as anything he had seen in a long while. He gave a sigh of joy. His cup of happiness was full indeed.

She was fastening her gloves as he entered the room, and she gave him a smile that thrilled him. Quite evidently her scruples had vanished and she was going to imitate him by making the most of her life. He felt flattered, and as he tried to put his thought into words she interrupted him to say prettily, and with just a shade of deference:

"Percival, the cab is at the door now—and we'd better not lose any time."

"Very well, my dear," he replied, "we'll make tracks." But in spite of his hurry he paused to admire her costume. She was dressed like a bride—that is to say, in the traveling costume usually affected by the newly wedded. And added to this was a stylish coat that came almost to her shoe tops. As he gazed at this garment it seemed to give him an inspiration.

"Marie," he said, "have you a pocket on the inside of that coat?"

She had and she displayed it with the pride with which members of the gentler sex usually exhibit their articles of clothing. Percival looked the satisfaction he felt. He drew the package of papers from his own pocket and handed them to her.

"I want you to put them in your inside pocket," he suggested, "and then I'll know they are in no danger of being lost."

She complied with this request, smilingly, and as she buttoned her coat carefully he surveyed her for the fifth time with intense pride and an undisguised sense of ownership.

"Before you took those papers," he cried, banteringly, "I thought you were the loveliest girl in the world. Now, you're that and more. You are the most valuable. You're worth your weight in gold. Those papers are worth millions to the enemy and they mean wealth and comfort for us. I'm sure you'll guard them—especially if anything should happen to me."

She gently boxed his ears.

"Don't talk like a pessimist," she cried; "it's not a bit like you—and, besides, there's a machine out there tooting away for dear life."

Two minutes later they were seated in the taxicab to the relief of the driver who grumbled something about having to wait all day for people that didn't know the value of time. That seemed to amuse Percival, who grimaced at the fellow behind his back and whispered to Marie that time at that moment was the most important thing in his life. He looked at his watch and said to the girl:

"We've got twenty minutes, and I think it would be wise to make a circuit instead of going directly to the station. Then, if by chance we should be followed, we can throw them off the scent."

She laughed gayly.

"You're the most cautious man I ever met. They'll never catch you napping. But do just as you please, my dear."

Accordingly he gave direction to the greengoggled chauffeur, who resolutely kept his back to his passengers as if still resenting the indignity of having to wait. But he nodded that he understood his orders, especially the one which directed him to let his two passengers off about a square from the Union Station.

"That may keep them from knowing that we actually went to the station," he whispered with a sagacious look at the girl.

The drive took them beyond the White House, and then past the Army and Navy Building and the Treasury Department. The driver kept mumbling to himself as though he were questioning the sanity of any one driving about the city at random while the automatic clock was registering a fare that might appal any one except a bride and groom. As they passed the Navy Building a little man was seen entering a conveyance.

"That's Admiral Hawksby," explained Roberts to his companion; "he's going home now after what he calls a 'hard day's work.' He'll be the sorest man in Washington when he hears of my escape. But it serves him right, the arrogant old ass. He thinks he knows it all, and he doesn't know anything."

For five minutes after that the man and the girl simply sat and admired each other. It was a real mutual admiration society, with only two members. Marie Johnson certainly looked attractive. Her coal black hair, parted in the middle, contrasted with the coquettishness of her face, and her dark gray eyes sparkled in the half gloom of the cab. Percival complacently stroked his mustache and leaning toward her, said tenderly:

"I'll mark this day down as the luckiest day of my life—the day you insured my happiness. And if I only thought you fully reciprocated my feelings—"

"I do," she interrupted, "I do—and as soon as I can get one I'm going to put a red mark around the date on the calendar."

They both laughed at this conceit, and after that there was a blissful silence. It was broken by the voice of the girl, speaking seriously and with a certain pathos:

"You've been very frank with me, Percival. There is something I should tell you."

He interrupted her with a loyalty that astonished even himself. He had not thought he was capable of such high flights.

"Never mind about your past, Marie—I don't want to hear a word."

"Oh, it isn't anything terrible," she retorted with feminine inconsistency; "I simply wanted you to know that before I came to this city I was an actress. Do you mind?"

Roberts laughed heartily.

"Mind? Well, I should say not. I should say it was a sort of distinction. And I'll bet my bottom dollar you were a mighty clever actress."

"Well," she said reflectively, "I know I wasn't dismissed for incompetence."

By this time the outlines of the Union Station began to loom in sight. Percival looked ahead and prepared to alight as soon as the cab drove up to the curb. On and on they went until they were within a block of their destination. The spy uttered an exclamation of impatience and called to the driver:

"Hey, out there—didn't I tell you to stop before we got to the station?"

But the taxi went right ahead as though nothing had been said. The young man half arose in his seat. Marie turned to him with a look of alarm.

"What's the trouble? You mustn't do that while the machine is in motion."

Roberts fell back into his seat with a muttered oath.

"It's that infernal driver. He's so stupid that he doesn't know enough to do as I tell him. Well, I guess we'll have to go into the station after all."

But, strangely enough, the taxicab did not go into the regular driveway of the station. Instead, it circled around the building and paused in front of the entrance to a small room. The driver jumped from his seat and opened the door. Percival Roberts alighted first, and then assisted Marie to the ground. He turned to give the driver a piece of his mind for his stupidity, but that personage, with unlooked for insolence, gave him a push and sent him into the little room. Percival was furious and he doubled up his fist menacingly. As he did so he noticed a figure in the half-darkened room. It gave him a start—and no wonder, for it was Admiral Hawksby, stroking his mustache and imperial, and with deep satisfaction depicted on his grizzled face.

Roberts was scared, but he kept his self-possession. The presence of the old sea fighter might be merely a coincidence. He turned around to the driver of the taxicab, and as he did so the stupid one tossed away his glazed cap and took off his green goggles. The spy looked at the other man with half-dazed fury.

He was staring into the face of Bromley Barnes—special investigator of the United States Government.

Bewilderment filled his mind. Then gradually he rallied. He looked around the room. The Admiral and the detective were looking at him curiously. Presently his eyes fell upon Marie Johnson. She stood by a table in the center of the room, and she seemed to be trembling like a leaf. Her head was buried in the folds of her coat and her breast heaved convulsively. He remembered that the incriminating papers were in the inside pocket of her coat. In that instant his resolution was formed.

"Well, gentlemen," he said, fingering the pink carnation in his coat, and with that nonchalant smile which he could assume so quickly, "what is the meaning of this?"

Barnes grinned at him amiably.

"We wanted to be sociable—we couldn't bear to see you go off without saying good-by. We've already got Lee Hallman and the code man."

Roberts smiled in return, but his brain was working furiously. He looked again in the direction of Marie. She seemed to be trying to control her emotions. At any moment she might break down. He must anticipate anything she might say. In those seconds of thought any affection he might have felt for her vanished into thin air. He felt a new emotion—and yet it was not new. It was as old as the everlasting hills. It was the

impulse of self-preservation. He was willing to sacrifice anything and any one to save himself. He moistened his lips with the tip of his tongue, and steadying himself, said slowly:

"Well, gentlemen, you've anticipated me a little bit, but still I think I can claim credit for helping my country."

The detective looked at him in a puzzled way. When he spoke it was brusquely:

"What in thunder are you talking about?"

In reply to this question, Percival pointed an accusing finger in the direction of Marie.

"Simply this. I have arrested that woman as a spy and I now desire to transfer her to your custody. I still have some evidence to get, but I will appear against her in the morning."

The woman, who had been standing, sank into a chair, as if in total collapse. She buried her face in her hands and refused to look up.

Bromley Barnes gazed at the man with a curious smile hovering about his lips. He spoke in a voice of authority:

"Young man, it is one thing to accuse and another to prove. Where is the proof of what you say?"

Percival Roberts took a turn up and down the room before replying. He was considering the dramatic effect of what he was about to say. Then he pointed his hand at the girl for the second time and exclaimed loudly:

"Search her and you will find a number of messages that have been intercepted from the Navy Department. They are in the inside pocket of her coat. I saw her put them there, and I am willing to so testify in a court of law!"

Something like a sob was heard to come from the woman with the bowed head and then the murmur in a muffled voice:

"Oh, Percival, how could you?"

Several speechless seconds passed. A dramatic tableau was being enacted in the little room. Admiral Hawksby broke the silence with one brusque sentence:

"Well, Barnes, why don't you search the woman?"

The cold gray eyes of the investigator softened just a little bit, and the quizzical smile became more pronounced, but he went over to Marie and commanded her to arise. She did so and he unbuttoned her coat, and took out the packet of letters from the inside pocket. As he read them his eyes widened and he emitted a low, significant whistle.

"Are these all of the papers?" he asked the girl.

"Yes," was the reply with downcast eyes, "all that I know anything about."

Percival Roberts had been watching her intently, and her manner seemed to reassure him, for turning to Barnes, he exclaimed:

"You see, I've told the truth, and now if you'll excuse me for the present, I'll appear at your office the first thing in the morning."

Barnes looked at him with a sort of contempt, and then producing a whistle, blew it softly. Two officers rushed into the room, and the next thing Roberts knew he was on the floor of the patrol wagon. He managed to regain his feet just as the Admiral, the Detective, and the Girl came out of the railroad station. He turned to one of the officers and pointed in the direction of the trio.

"Who—" he spluttered, "who is that woman going down the street?"

The policeman shaded his eyes with one hand in order to get a better view of the girl, and then replied, in the most matter-of-fact way:

"That? That's Miss Johnson—the smartest little woman in the United States Secret Service."

THE NAVAL TREATY

ARTHUR CONAN DOYLE

SHERLOCK HOLMES did not become the most famous fictional character in the world because the stories by Arthur Conan Doyle (1859–1930) were classroom assignments, as is the case with so many other distinguished authors of the Victorian and Edwardian eras in which he worked. It is astonishing to realize that, although mostly written more than a century ago, they remain as readable and fresh as anything produced in recent times, lacking the overwrought verbosity so prevalent in the prose of that more leisurely time.

Equally astonishing is that Doyle believed that his most important works were such historical novels and short story collections as *Micah Clarke* (1889), *The White Company* (1891), *The Exploits of Brigadier Gerard* (1896), and *Sir Nigel* (1906). He believed his most significant nonfiction work was in the spiritualism field, to which he devoted the last twenty years of his life, a considerable portion of his fortune, and prodigious energy, producing many major and not-so-major works on the subject.

He was deluded, of course, as Holmes was his supreme achievement. The great detective's first appearance was in the novel *A Study in Scarlet* (1887), followed by *The Sign of Four* (1890), neither of which immediately changed the course of the detective story. This occurred when the first short story, "A Scandal in Bohemia," was published in *The Strand Magazine* (July 1891), bringing the world's first private detective to a huge readership. Monthly publication of new Holmes stories became so widely anticipated that eager readers queued up at news stalls awaiting each new issue. Remarkably, the Holmes opera lasted a half century (1887–1927).

It was Sherlock Holmes's older brother Mycroft who worked for the British government while Sherlock worked as a private eye, but they occasionally called on each other for help and advice. While Mycroft does not appear in this story, the first one in which his younger brother becomes involved with government secrets and affairs of state, we can be assured that he would have been called on if the detective had not found the solution to be so simple.

"The Naval Treaty" was first published in the October and November 1893 issues of *The Strand Magazine*, although the claim could be made that it first appeared in its entirety in the United States in the October 14 and October 21, 1893, issues of *Harper's Weekly*; it was first collected in book form in *The Memoirs of Sherlock Holmes* (London, George Newnes, 1893).

THE NAVAL TREATY

ARTHUR CONAN DOYLE

THE JULY which immediately succeeded my marriage was made memorable by three cases of interest, in which I had the privilege of being associated with Sherlock Holmes and of studying his methods. I find them recorded in my notes under the headings of "The Adventure of the Second Stain," "The Adventure of the Naval Treaty," and "The Adventure of the Tired Captain." The first of these, however, deals with interest of such importance and implicates so many of the first families in the kingdom that for many years it will be impossible to make it public. No case, however, in which Holmes was engaged has ever illustrated the value of his analytical methods so clearly or has impressed those who were associated with him so deeply. I still retain an almost *verbatim* report of the interview in which he demonstrated the true facts of the case to Monsieur Dubugue of the Paris police, and Fritz von Waldbaum, the well-known specialist of Dantzig, both of whom had wasted their energies upon what proved to be side-issues. The new century will have come, however, before the story can be safely told. Meanwhile I pass on to the second on my list, which promised also at one time to be of national importance, and was marked by several incidents which give it a quite unique character.

During my school-days I had been intimately associated with a lad named Percy Phelps, who was of much the same age as myself, though he was two classes ahead of me. He was a very brilliant boy, and carried away every prize which the school had to offer, finishing his exploits by winning a scholarship which sent him on to continue his triumphant career at Cambridge. He was, I remember, extremely well connected, and even when we were all little boys together we knew that his mother's brother was Lord Holdhurst, the great conservative politician. This gaudy relationship did him little good at school. On the contrary, it seemed rather a piquant thing to us to chevy him about the playground and hit him over the shins with a wicket. But it was another thing when he came out into the world. I heard vaguely that his abilities and the influences which he commanded had won him a good position at the Foreign Office, and then he passed completely out of my mind until the following letter recalled his existence:

Briarbrae, Woking.

My dear Watson:

I have no doubt that you can remember "Tadpole" Phelps, who was in the fifth form when you were in the third. It is possible even that you may have heard that through my uncle's influence I obtained a good appointment at the Foreign Office, and that I was in a situation of trust and honor until a horrible misfortune came suddenly to blast my career.

There is no use writing of the details of that dreadful event. In the event of your acceding to my request it is probable that I shall have to narrate them to you. I have only just recovered from nine weeks of brain-fever, and am still exceedingly weak. Do you think that you could bring your friend Mr. Holmes down to see me? I should like to have his opinion of the case, though the authorities assure me that nothing more can be done. Do try to bring him down, and as soon as possible. Every minute seems an hour while I live in this state of horrible suspense. Assure him that if I have not asked his advice sooner it was not because I did not appreciate his talents, but because I have been off my head ever since the blow fell. Now I am clear again, though I dare not think of it too much for fear of a relapse. I am still so weak that I have to write, as you see, by dictating. Do try to bring him.

—Your old school–fellow,
PERCY PHELPS.

There was something that touched me as I read this letter, something pitiable in the reiterated appeals to bring Holmes. So moved was I that even had it been a difficult matter I should have tried it, but of course I knew well that Holmes loved his art, so that he was ever as ready to bring his aid as his client could be to receive it. My wife agreed with me that not a moment should be lost in laying the matter before him, and so within an hour of breakfast-time I found myself back once more in the old rooms in Baker Street.

Holmes was seated at his side-table clad in his dressing-gown, and working hard over a chemical investigation. A large curved retort was boiling furiously in the bluish flame of a Bunsen burner, and the distilled drops were condensing into a two-litre measure. My friend hardly glanced up as I entered, and I, seeing that his investigation must be of importance, seated myself in an arm-chair and waited. He dipped into this bottle or that, drawing out a few drops of each with his glass pipette, and finally brought a test-tube containing a solution over to the table. In his right hand he held a slip of litmus-paper.

"You come at a crisis, Watson," said he. "If this paper remains blue, all is well. If it turns red, it means a man's life." He dipped it into the test-tube and it flushed at once into a dull, dirty crimson. "Hum! I thought as much!" he cried. "I will be at your service in an instant, Watson. You will find tobacco in the Persian slipper." He turned to his desk and scribbled off several telegrams, which were handed over to the page-boy. Then he threw himself down into the chair opposite, and drew up his knees until his fingers clasped round his long, thin shins.

"A very commonplace little murder," said he. "You've got something better, I fancy. You are the stormy petrel of crime, Watson. What is it?"

I handed him the letter, which he read with the most concentrated attention.

"It does not tell us very much, does it?" he remarked, as he handed it back to me.

"Hardly anything."

"And yet the writing is of interest."

"But the writing is not his own."

"Precisely. It is a woman's."

"A man's surely," I cried.

"No, a woman's, and a woman of rare character. You see, at the commencement of an investigation it is something to know that your client is in close contact with some one who, for good or evil, has an exceptional nature. My interest is already awakened in the case. If you are ready we will start at once for Woking, and see this diplomatist who is in such evil case, and the lady to whom he dictates his letters."

We were fortunate enough to catch an early train at Waterloo, and in a little under an hour we found ourselves among the fir-woods and the heather of Woking. Briarbrae proved to be a large detached house standing in extensive grounds within a few minutes' walk of the station. On sending in our cards we were shown into an elegantly appointed drawing-room, where we were joined in a few minutes by a rather stout man who received us with much hospitality. His age may have been nearer forty than thirty, but his cheeks were so ruddy and his eyes so merry that he still conveyed the impression of a plump and mischievous boy.

"I am so glad that you have come," said he, shaking our hands with effusion. "Percy has been inquiring for you all morning. Ah, poor old chap, he clings to any straw! His father and his mother asked me to see you, for the mere mention of the subject is very painful to them."

"We have had no details yet," observed Holmes. "I perceive that you are not yourself a member of the family."

Our acquaintance looked surprised, and then, glancing down, he began to laugh.

"Of course you saw the J H monogram on my locket," said he. "For a moment I thought you had done something clever. Joseph Harrison is my name, and as Percy is to marry my sister Annie I shall at least be a relation by marriage. You will find my sister in his room, for she has nursed him hand-and-foot this two months back. Perhaps we'd better go in at once, for I know how impatient he is."

The chamber in which we were shown was on the same floor as the drawing-room. It was furnished partly as a sitting and partly as a bedroom, with flowers arranged daintily in every nook and corner. A young man, very pale and worn, was lying upon a sofa near the open window, through which came the rich scent of the garden and the balmy summer air. A woman was sitting beside him, who rose as we entered.

"Shall I leave, Percy?" she asked.

He clutched her hand to detain her. "How are you, Watson?" said he, cordially. "I should never have known you under that moustache, and I dare say you would not be prepared to swear to me. This I presume is your celebrated friend, Mr. Sherlock Holmes?"

I introduced him in a few words, and we both sat down. The stout young man had left us, but his sister still remained with her hand in that of the invalid. She was a striking-looking woman, a little short and thick for symmetry, but with a beautiful olive complexion, large, dark, Italian eyes, and a wealth of deep black hair. Her rich tints made the white face of her companion the more worn and haggard by the contrast.

"I won't waste your time," said he, raising himself upon the sofa. "I'll plunge into the matter without further preamble. I was a happy and successful man, Mr. Holmes, and on the eve of being married, when a sudden and dreadful misfortune wrecked all my prospects in life.

"I was, as Watson may have told you, in the Foreign Office, and through the influences of my uncle, Lord Holdhurst, I rose rapidly to a responsible position. When my uncle became foreign minister in this administration he gave me several missions of trust, and as I always brought them to a successful conclusion, he came at last to have the utmost confidence in my ability and tact.

"Nearly ten weeks ago—to be more accurate, on the twenty-third of May—he called me into his private room, and, after complimenting me on the good work which I had done, he informed me that he had a new commission of trust for me to execute.

"'This,' said he, taking a gray roll of paper from his bureau, 'is the original of that secret treaty between England and Italy of which, I regret to say, some rumors have already got into the public press. It is of enormous importance that nothing further should leak out. The French or the Russian embassy would pay an immense sum to learn the contents of these papers. They should not leave my bureau were it not that it is absolutely necessary to have them copied. You have a desk in your office?'

"'Yes, sir.'

"'Then take the treaty and lock it up there. I shall give directions that you may remain behind when the others go, so that you may copy it at your leisure without fear of being overlooked. When you have finished, relock both the original and the draft in the desk, and hand them over to me personally to-morrow morning.'

"I took the papers and—"

"Excuse me an instant," said Holmes. "Were you alone during this conversation?"

"Absolutely."

"In a large room?"

"Thirty feet each way."

"In the centre?"

"Yes, about it."

"And speaking low?"

"My uncle's voice is always remarkably low. I hardly spoke at all."

"Thank you," said Holmes, shutting his eyes; "pray go on."

"I did exactly what he indicated, and waited until the other clerks had departed. One of them in my room, Charles Gorot, had some arrears of work to make up, so I left him there and went out to dine. When I returned he was gone. I was anxious to hurry my work, for I knew that Joseph— the Mr. Harrison whom you saw just now—was in town, and that he would travel down to Woking by the eleven-o'clock train, and I wanted if possible to catch it.

"When I came to examine the treaty I saw at once that it was of such importance that my uncle had been guilty of no exaggeration in what he had said. Without going into details, I may say that it defined the position of Great Britain towards the Triple Alliance, and fore-shadowed the policy which this country would pursue in the event of the French fleet gaining a complete ascendancy over that of Italy in the Mediterranean. The questions treated in it were purely naval. At the end were the signatures of the high dignitaries who had signed it. I glanced my eyes over it, and then settled down to my task of copying.

"It was a long document, written in the French language, and containing twenty-six separate articles. I copied as quickly as I could, but at nine o'clock I had only done nine articles, and it seemed hopeless for me to attempt to catch my train. I was feeling drowsy and stupid, partly from my dinner and also from the effects of a long day's work. A cup of coffee would clear my brain. A commissionaire remains all night in a little lodge at the foot of the stairs, and is in the habit of making coffee at his spirit-lamp for any of the officials who may be working over time. I rang the bell, therefore, to summon him.

"To my surprise, it was a woman who answered the summons, a large, coarse-faced, elderly woman, in an apron. She explained that she was the commissionaire's wife, who did the charing, and I gave her the order for the coffee.

"I wrote two more articles and then, feeling more drowsy than ever, I rose and walked up and down the room to stretch my legs. My coffee had not yet come, and I wondered what the cause of the delay could be. Opening the door, I started down the corridor to find out. There was a straight passage, dimly lighted, which led from the room in which I had been working, and was the only exit from it. It ended in a curving staircase, with the commissionaire's lodge in the passage at the bottom. Half way down this staircase is a small landing, with another passage running into it at right angles. This second one leads by means of a second small stair to a side door, used by servants, and also as a short cut by clerks when coming from Charles Street. Here is a rough chart of the place."

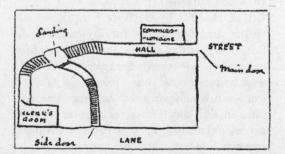

454

"Thank you. I think that I quite follow you," said Sherlock Holmes.

"It is of the utmost importance that you should notice this point. I went down the stairs and into the hall, where I found the commissionaire fast asleep in his box, with the kettle boiling furiously upon the spirit-lamp. I took off the kettle and blew out the lamp, for the water was spurting over the floor. Then I put out my hand and was about to shake the man, who was still sleeping soundly, when a bell over his head rang loudly, and he woke with a start.

"'Mr. Phelps, sir!' said he, looking at me in bewilderment.

"'I came down to see if my coffee was ready.'

"'I was boiling the kettle when I fell asleep, sir.' He looked at me and then up at the still quivering bell with an ever-growing astonishment upon his face.

"'If you was here, sir, then who rang the bell?' he asked.

"'The bell!' I cried. 'What bell is it?'

"'It's the bell of the room you were working in.'

"A cold hand seemed to close round my heart. Some one, then, was in that room where my precious treaty lay upon the table. I ran frantically up the stair and along the passage. There was no one in the corridors, Mr. Holmes. There was no one in the room. All was exactly as I left it, save only that the papers which had been committed to my care had been taken from the desk on which they lay. The copy was there, and the original was gone."

Holmes sat up in his chair and rubbed his hands. I could see that the problem was entirely to his heart. "Pray, what did you do then?" he murmured.

"I recognized in an instant that the thief must have come up the stairs from the side door. Of course I must have met him if he had come the other way."

"You were satisfied that he could not have been concealed in the room all the time, or in the corridor which you have just described as dimly lighted?"

"It is absolutely impossible. A rat could not conceal himself either in the room or the corridor. There is no cover at all."

"Thank you. Pray proceed."

"The commissionaire, seeing by my pale face that something was to be feared, had followed me upstairs. Now we both rushed along the corridor and down the steep steps which led to Charles Street. The door at the bottom was closed, but unlocked. We flung it open and rushed out. I can distinctly remember that as we did so there came three chimes from a neighboring clock. It was quarter to ten."

"That is of enormous importance," said Holmes, making a note upon his shirt-cuff.

"The night was very dark, and a thin, warm rain was falling. There was no one in Charles Street, but a great traffic was going on, as usual, in Whitehall, at the extremity. We rushed along the pavement, bare-headed as we were, and at the far corner we found a policeman standing.

"'A robbery has been committed,' I gasped. 'A document of immense value has been stolen from the Foreign Office. Has any one passed this way?'

"'I have been standing here for a quarter of an hour, sir,' said he; 'only one person has passed during that time—a woman, tall and elderly, with a Paisley shawl.'

"'Ah, that is only my wife,' cried the commissionaire; 'has no one else passed?'

"'No one.'

"'Then it must be the other way that the thief took,' cried the fellow, tugging at my sleeve.

"But I was not satisfied, and the attempts which he made to draw me away increased my suspicions.

"'Which way did the woman go?' I cried.

"'I don't know, sir. I noticed her pass, but I had no special reason for watching her. She seemed to be in a hurry.'

"'How long ago was it?'

"'Oh, not very many minutes.'

"'Within the last five?'

"'Well, it could not be more than five.'

"'You're only wasting your time, sir, and

every minute now is of importance,' cried the commissionaire; 'take my word for it that my old woman has nothing to do with it, and come down to the other end of the street. Well, if you won't, I will.' And with that he rushed off in the other direction.

"But I was after him in an instant and caught him by the sleeve.

"'Where do you live?' said I.

"'16 Ivy Lane, Brixton,' he answered. 'But don't let yourself be drawn away upon a false scent, Mr. Phelps. Come to the other end of the street and let us see if we can hear of anything.'

"Nothing was to be lost by following his advice. With the policeman we both hurried down, but only to find the street full of traffic, many people coming and going, but all only too eager to get to a place of safety upon so wet a night. There was no lounger who could tell us who had passed.

"Then we returned to the office, and searched the stairs and the passage without result. The corridor which led to the room was laid down with a kind of creamy linoleum which shows an impression very easily. We examined it very carefully, but found no outline of any footmark."

"Had it been raining all evening?"

"Since about seven."

"How is it, then, that the woman who came into the room about nine left no traces with her muddy boots?"

"I am glad you raised the point. It occurred to me at the time. The charwomen are in the habit of taking off their boots at the commissionaire's office, and putting on list slippers."

"That is very clear. There were no marks, then, though the night was a wet one? The chain of events is certainly one of extraordinary interest. What did you do next?"

"We examined the room also. There is no possibility of a secret door, and the windows are quite thirty feet from the ground. Both of them were fastened on the inside. The carpet prevents any possibility of a trap-door, and the ceiling is of the ordinary whitewashed kind. I will pledge my life that whoever stole my papers could only have come through the door."

"How about the fireplace?"

"They use none. There is a stove. The bell-rope hangs from the wire just to the right of my desk. Whoever rang it must have come right up to the desk to do it. But why should any criminal wish to ring the bell? It is a most insoluble mystery."

"Certainly the incident was unusual. What were your next steps? You examined the room, I presume, to see if the intruder had left any traces—any cigar-end or dropped glove or hairpin or other trifle?"

"There was nothing of the sort."

"No smell?"

"Well, we never thought of that."

"Ah, a scent of tobacco would have been worth a great deal to us in such an investigation."

"I never smoke myself, so I think I should have observed it if there had been any smell of tobacco. There was absolutely no clue of any kind. The only tangible fact was that the commissionaire's wife—Mrs. Tangey was the name—had hurried out of the place. He could give no explanation save that it was about the time when the woman always went home. The policeman and I agreed that our best plan would be to seize the woman before she could get rid of the papers, presuming that she had them.

"The alarm had reached Scotland Yard by this time, and Mr. Forbes, the detective, came round at once and took up the case with a great deal of energy. We hired a hansom, and in half an hour we were at the address which had been given to us. A young woman opened the door, who proved to be Mrs. Tangey's eldest daughter. Her mother had not come back yet, and we were shown into the front room to wait.

"About ten minutes later a knock came at the door, and here we made the one serious mistake for which I blame myself. Instead of opening the door ourselves, we allowed the girl to do so. We heard her say, 'Mother, there are two men in the house waiting to see you,' and an instant afterwards we heard the patter of feet rushing down the passage. Forbes flung open the door, and we both ran into the back room or kitchen, but the woman had got there before us. She stared at us with defiant eyes, and then, suddenly recognizing me, an expression of absolute astonishment came over her face.

"'Why, if it isn't Mr. Phelps, of the office!' she cried.

"'Come, come, who did you think we were when you ran away from us?' asked my companion.

"'I thought you were the brokers,' said she, 'we have had some trouble with a tradesman.'

"'That's not quite good enough,' answered Forbes. 'We have reason to believe that you have taken a paper of importance from the Foreign Office, and that you ran in here to dispose of it. You must come back with us to Scotland Yard to be searched.'

"It was in vain that she protested and resisted. A four-wheeler was brought, and we all three drove back in it. We had first made an examination of the kitchen, and especially of the kitchen fire, to see whether she might have made away with the papers during the instant that she was alone. There were no signs, however, of any ashes or scraps. When we reached Scotland Yard she was handed over at once to the female searcher. I waited in an agony of suspense until she came back with her report. There were no signs of the papers.

"Then for the first time the horror of my situation came in its full force. Hitherto I had been acting, and action had numbed thought. I had been so confident of regaining the treaty at once that I had not dared to think of what would be the consequence if I failed to do so. But now there was nothing more to be done, and I had leisure to realize my position. It was horrible. Watson there would tell you that I was a nervous, sensitive boy at school. It is my nature. I thought of my uncle and of his colleagues in the Cabinet, of the shame which I had brought upon him, upon myself, upon every one connected with me. What though I was the victim of an extraordinary accident? No allowance is made for accidents where diplomatic interests are at stake. I was ruined, shamefully, hopelessly ruined. I don't know what I did. I fancy I must have made a scene. I have a dim recollection of a group of officials who crowded round me, endeavoring to soothe me. One of them drove down with me to Waterloo, and saw me into the Woking train. I believe that he would have come all the way had it not been that Dr. Ferrier, who lives near me, was going down by that very train. The doctor most kindly took charge of me, and it was well he did so, for I had a fit in the station, and before we reached home I was practically a raving maniac.

"You can imagine the state of things here when they were roused from their beds by the doctor's ringing and found me in this condition. Poor Annie here and my mother were brokenhearted. Dr. Ferrier had just heard enough from the detective at the station to be able to give an idea of what had happened, and his story did not mend matters. It was evident to all that I was in for a long illness, so Joseph was bundled out of this cheery bedroom, and it was turned into a sick-room for me. Here I have lain, Mr. Holmes, for over nine weeks, unconscious, and raving with brain-fever. If it had not been for Miss Harrison here and for the doctor's care I should not be speaking to you now. She has nursed me by day and a hired nurse has looked after me by night, for in my mad fits I was capable of anything. Slowly my reason has cleared, but it is only during the last three days that my memory has quite returned. Sometimes I wish that it never had. The first thing that I did was to wire to Mr. Forbes, who had the case in hand. He came out, and assures me that, though everything has been done, no trace of a clue has been discovered. The commissionaire and his wife have been examined in every way without any light being thrown upon the matter. The suspicions of the police then rested upon young Gorot, who, as you may remember, stayed over time in the office that night. His remaining behind and his French name were really the only two points which could suggest suspicion; but, as a matter of fact, I did not begin work until he had gone, and his people are of Huguenot extraction, but as English in sympathy and tradition as you and I are. Nothing was found to implicate him in any way, and there the matter dropped. I turn to you, Mr. Holmes, as absolutely my last hope. If you fail me, then my honor as well as my position are forever forfeited."

The invalid sank back upon his cushions, tired out by this long recital, while his nurse poured him out a glass of some stimulating medicine. Holmes sat silently, with his head thrown back and his eyes closed, in an attitude which might seem listless to a stranger, but which I knew betokened the most intense self-absorption.

"Your statement has been so explicit," said he at last, "that you have really left me very few questions to ask. There is one of the very utmost importance, however. Did you tell any one that you had this special task to perform?"

"No one."

"Not Miss Harrison here, for example?"

"No. I had not been back to Woking between getting the order and executing the commission."

"And none of your people had by chance been to see you?"

"None."

"Did any of them know their way about in the office?"

"Oh, yes, all of them had been shown over it."

"Still, of course, if you said nothing to any one about the treaty these inquiries are irrelevant."

"I said nothing."

"Do you know anything of the commissionaire?"

"Nothing except that he is an old soldier."

"What regiment?"

"Oh, I have heard—Coldstream Guards."

"Thank you. I have no doubt I can get details from Forbes. The authorities are excellent at amassing facts, though they do not always use them to advantage. What a lovely thing a rose is!"

He walked past the couch to the open window, and held up the drooping stalk of a moss-rose, looking down at the dainty blend of crimson and green. It was a new phase of his character to me, for I had never before seen him show any keen interest in natural objects.

"There is nothing in which deduction is so necessary as in religion," said he, leaning with his back against the shutters. "It can be built up as an exact science by the reasoner. Our highest assurance of the goodness of Providence seems to me to rest in the flowers. All other things, our powers, our desires, our food, are all really necessary for our existence in the first instance. But this rose is an extra. Its smell and its color are an embellishment of life, not a condition of it. It is only goodness which gives extras, and so I say again that we have much to hope from the flowers."

Percy Phelps and his nurse looked at Holmes during this demonstration with surprise and a good deal of disappointment written upon their faces. He had fallen into a reverie, with the mossrose between his fingers. It had lasted some minutes before the young lady broke in upon it.

"Do you see any prospect of solving this mystery, Mr. Holmes?" she asked, with a touch of asperity in her voice.

"Oh, the mystery!" he answered, coming back with a start to the realities of life. "Well, it would be absurd to deny that the case is a very abstruse and complicated one, but I can promise you that I will look into the matter and let you know any points which may strike me."

"Do you see any clue?"

"You have furnished me with seven, but, of course, I must test them before I can pronounce upon their value."

"You suspect some one?"

"I suspect myself."

"What!"

"Of coming to conclusions too rapidly."

"Then go to London and test your conclusions."

"Your advice is very excellent, Miss Harrison," said Holmes, rising. "I think, Watson, we cannot do better. Do not allow yourself to indulge in false hopes, Mr. Phelps. The affair is a very tangled one."

"I shall be in a fever until I see you again," cried the diplomatist.

"Well, I'll come out by the same train to-morrow, though it's more than likely that my report will be a negative one."

"God bless you for promising to come," cried our client. "It gives me fresh life to know that something is being done. By the way, I have had a letter from Lord Holdhurst."

"Ha! What did he say?"

"He was cold, but not harsh. I dare say my severe illness prevented him from being that. He repeated that the matter was of the utmost importance, and added that no steps would be taken about my future—by which he means, of course, my dismissal—until my health was restored and I had an opportunity of repairing my misfortune."

"Well, that was reasonable and considerate," said Holmes. "Come, Watson, for we have a good day's work before us in town."

Mr. Joseph Harrison drove us down to the station, and we were soon whirling up in a Portsmouth train. Holmes was sunk in profound thought, and hardly opened his mouth until we had passed Clapham Junction.

"It's a very cheery thing to come into London by any of these lines which run high, and allow you to look down upon the houses like this."

I thought he was joking, for the view was sordid enough, but he soon explained himself.

"Look at those big, isolated clumps of building rising up above the slates, like brick islands in a lead-colored sea."

"The board-schools."

"Light-houses, my boy! Beacons of the future! Capsules with hundreds of bright little seeds in each, out of which will spring the wise, better England of the future. I suppose that man Phelps does not drink?"

"I should not think so."

"Nor should I, but we are bound to take every possibility into account. The poor devil has certainly got himself into very deep water, and it's a question whether we shall ever be able to get him ashore. What did you think of Miss Harrison?"

"A girl of strong character."

"Yes, but she is a good sort, or I am mistaken. She and her brother are the only children of an iron-master somewhere up Northumberland way. He got engaged to her when traveling last winter, and she came down to be introduced to his people, with her brother as escort. Then came the smash, and she stayed on to nurse her lover, while brother Joseph, finding himself pretty snug, stayed on too. I've been making a few independent inquiries, you see. But to-day must be a day of inquiries."

"My practice—" I began.

"Oh, if you find your own cases more interesting than mine—" said Holmes, with some asperity.

"I was going to say that my practice could get along very well for a day or two, since it is the slackest time in the year."

"Excellent," said he, recovering his good-humor. "Then we'll look into this matter together. I think that we should begin by seeing Forbes. He can probably tell us all the details we want until we know from what side the case is to be approached."

"You said you had a clue?"

"Well, we have several, but we can only test their value by further inquiry. The most difficult crime to track is the one which is purposeless. Now this is not purposeless. Who is it who profits by it? There is the French ambassador, there is the Russian, there is who-ever might sell it to either of these, and there is Lord Holdhurst."

"Lord Holdhurst!"

"Well, it is just conceivable that a statesman might find himself in a position where he was not sorry to have such a document accidentally destroyed."

"Not a statesman with the honorable record of Lord Holdhurst?"

"It is a possibility and we cannot afford to disregard it. We shall see the noble lord to-day and find out if he can tell us anything. Meanwhile I have already set inquiries on foot."

"Already?"

"Yes, I sent wires from Woking station to every evening paper in London. This advertisement will appear in each of them."

He handed over a sheet torn from a notebook. On it was scribbled in pencil:

"£10 reward. The number of the cab which dropped a fare at or about the door of the Foreign Office in Charles Street at quarter to ten in the evening of May 23d. Apply 221B, Baker Street."

"You are confident that the thief came in a cab?"

"If not, there is no harm done. But if Mr. Phelps is correct in stating that there is no hiding-place either in the room or the corridors, then the person must have come from outside. If he came from outside on so wet a night, and yet left no trace of damp upon the linoleum, which was examined within a few minutes of his passing, then it is exceeding probable that he came in a cab. Yes, I think that we may safely deduce a cab."

"It sounds plausible."

"That is one of the clues of which I spoke. It may lead us to something. And then, of course, there is the bell—which is the most distinctive feature of the case. Why should the bell ring? Was it the thief who did it out of bravado? Or was it some one who was with the thief who did it in order to prevent the crime? Or was it an accident? Or was it—?" He sank back into the state of intense and silent thought from which he had emerged; but it seemed to me, accustomed as I was to his every mood, that some new possibility had dawned suddenly upon him.

It was twenty past three when we reached our terminus, and after a hasty luncheon at the buffet we pushed on at once to Scotland Yard. Holmes had already wired to Forbes, and we found him waiting to receive us—a small, foxy man with a sharp but by no means amiable expression. He was decidedly frigid in his manner to us, especially when he heard the errand upon which we had come.

"I've heard of your methods before now, Mr. Holmes," said he, tartly. "You are ready enough to use all the information that the police can lay at your disposal, and then you try to finish the case yourself and bring discredit on them."

"On the contrary," said Holmes, "out of my last fifty-three cases my name has only appeared in four, and the police have had all the credit in forty-nine. I don't blame you for not knowing this, for you are young and inexperienced, but if you wish to get on in your new duties you will work with me and not against me."

"I'd be very glad of a hint or two," said the detective, changing his manner. "I've certainly had no credit from the case so far."

"What steps have you taken?"

"Tangey, the commissionaire, has been shadowed. He left the Guards with a good character and we can find nothing against him. His wife is a bad lot, though. I fancy she knows more about this than appears."

"Have you shadowed her?"

"We have set one of our women on to her. Mrs. Tangey drinks, and our woman has been with her twice when she was well on, but she could get nothing out of her."

"I understand that they have had brokers in the house?"

"Yes, but they were paid off."

"Where did the money come from?"

"That was all right. His pension was due. They have not shown any sign of being in funds."

"What explanation did she give of having answered the bell when Mr. Phelps rang for the coffee?"

"She said that he husband was very tired and she wished to relieve him."

"Well, certainly that would agree with his being found a little later asleep in his chair. There is nothing against them then but the woman's character. Did you ask her why she hurried away that night? Her haste attracted the attention of the police constable."

"She was later than usual and wanted to get home."

"Did you point out to her that you and Mr. Phelps, who started at least twenty minutes after her, got home before her?"

"She explains that by the difference between a 'bus and a hansom."

"Did she make it clear why, on reaching her house, she ran into the back kitchen?"

"Because she had the money there with which to pay off the brokers."

"She has at least an answer for everything. Did you ask her whether in leaving she met any one or saw any one loitering about Charles Street?"

"She saw no one but the constable."

"Well, you seem to have cross-examined her pretty thoroughly. What else have you done?"

"The clerk Gorot has been shadowed all these nine weeks, but without result. We can show nothing against him."

"Anything else?"

"Well, we have nothing else to go upon—no evidence of any kind."

"Have you formed a theory about how that bell rang?"

"Well, I must confess that it beats me. It was a cool hand, whoever it was, to go and give the alarm like that."

"Yes, it was a queer thing to do. Many thanks to you for what you have told me. If I can put the man into your hands you shall hear from me. Come along, Watson."

"Where are we going to now?" I asked, as we left the office.

"We are now going to interview Lord Holdhurst, the cabinet minister and future premier of England."

We were fortunate in finding that Lord Holdhurst was still in his chambers in Downing Street, and on Holmes sending in his card we were instantly shown up. The statesman received us with that old-fashioned courtesy for which he is remarkable, and seated us on the two luxuriant lounges on either side of the fireplace. Standing on the rug between us, with his slight, tall figure, his sharp features, thoughtful face, and curling hair prematurely tinged with gray, he seemed to represent that not too common type, a nobleman who is in truth noble.

"Your name is very familiar to me, Mr. Holmes," said he, smiling. "And, of course, I cannot pretend to be ignorant of the object of your visit. There has only been one occurrence in these offices which could call for your attention. In whose interest are you acting, may I ask?"

"In that of Mr. Percy Phelps," answered Holmes.

"Ah, my unfortunate nephew! You can understand that our kinship makes it the more impossible for me to screen him in any way. I fear that the incident must have a very prejudicial effect upon his career."

"But if the document is found?"

"Ah, that, of course, would be different."

"I had one or two questions which I wished to ask you, Lord Holdhurst."

"I shall be happy to give you any information in my power."

"Was it in this room that you gave your instructions as to the copying of the document?"

"It was."

"Then you could hardly have been overheard?"

"It is out of the question."

"Did you ever mention to any one that it was your intention to give any one the treaty to be copied?"

"Never."

"You are certain of that?"

"Absolutely."

"Well, since you never said so, and Mr. Phelps never said so, and nobody else knew anything of the matter, then the thief's presence in the room was purely accidental. He saw his chance and he took it."

The statesman smiled. "You take me out of my province there," said he.

Holmes considered for a moment. "There is another very important point which I wish to discuss with you," said he. "You feared, as I understand, that very grave results might follow from the details of this treaty becoming known."

A shadow passed over the expressive face of the statesman. "Very grave results indeed."

"And have they occurred?"

"Not yet."

"If the treaty had reached, let us say, the French or Russian Foreign Office, you would expect to hear of it?"

"I should," said Lord Holdhurst, with a wry face.

"Since nearly ten weeks have elapsed, then, and nothing has been heard, it is not unfair to suppose that for some reason the treaty has not reached them."

Lord Holdhurst shrugged his shoulders.

"We can hardly suppose, Mr. Holmes, that the thief took the treaty in order to frame it and hang it up."

"Perhaps he is waiting for a better price."

"If he waits a little longer he will get no price at all. The treaty will cease to be secret in a few months."

"That is most important," said Holmes. "Of course, it is a possible supposition that the thief has had a sudden illness—"

"An attack of brain-fever, for example?" asked the statesman, flashing a swift glance at him.

"I did not say so," said Holmes, imperturbably. "And now, Lord Holdhurst, we have already taken up too much of your valuable time, and we shall wish you good-day."

"Every success to your investigation, be the criminal who it may," answered the nobleman, as he bowed us out the door.

"He's a fine fellow," said Holmes, as we came out into Whitehall. "But he has a struggle to keep up his position. He is far from rich and has many calls. You noticed, of course, that his boots had been re-soled? Now, Watson, I won't detain you from your legitimate work any longer. I shall do nothing more to-day, unless I have an answer to my cab advertisement. But I should be extremely obliged to you if you would come down with me to Woking to-morrow, by the same train which we took yesterday."

I met him accordingly next morning and we traveled down to Woking together. He had had no answer to his advertisement, he said, and no fresh light had been thrown upon the case. He had, when he so willed it, the utter immobility of countenance of a red Indian, and I could not gather from his appearance whether he was satisfied or not with the position of the case. His conversation, I remember, was about the Bertillon system of measurements, and he expressed his enthusiastic admiration of the French savant.

We found our client still under the charge of his devoted nurse, but looking considerably better than before. He rose from the sofa and greeted us without difficulty when we entered.

"Any news?" he asked, eagerly.

"My report, as I expected, is a negative one," said Holmes. "I have seen Forbes, and I have seen your uncle, and I have set one or two trains of inquiry upon foot which may lead to something."

"You have not lost heart, then?"

"By no means."

"God bless you for saying that!" cried Miss Harrison. "If we keep our courage and our patience the truth must come out."

"We have more to tell you than you have for us," said Phelps, reseating himself upon the couch.

"I hoped you might have something."

"Yes, we have had an adventure during the night, and one which might have proved to be a serious one." His expression grew very grave as he spoke, and a look of something akin to fear sprang up in his eyes. "Do you know," said he, "that I begin to believe that I am the unconscious centre of some monstrous conspiracy, and that my life is aimed at as well as my honor?"

"Ah!" cried Holmes.

"It sounds incredible, for I have not, as far as I know, an enemy in the world. Yet from last night's experience I can come to no other conclusion."

"Pray let me hear it."

"You must know that last night was the very first night that I have ever slept without a nurse in the room. I was so much better that I thought I could dispense with one. I had a night-light burning, however. Well, about two in the morning I had sunk into a light sleep when I was suddenly aroused by a slight noise. It was like the sound which a mouse makes when it is gnawing a plank, and I lay listening to it for some time under the impression that it must come from that cause. Then it grew louder, and suddenly there came from the window a sharp metallic snick. I sat up in amazement. There could be no doubt what the sounds were now. The first ones had been caused by some one forcing an instrument through the slit between the sashes, and the second by the catch being pressed back.

"There was a pause then for about ten minutes, as if the person were waiting to see whether the noise had awakened me. Then I heard a gentle creaking as the window was very slowly opened. I could stand it no longer, for my nerves are not what they used to be. I sprang out of bed and flung open the shutters. A man was crouching at the window. I could see little of him, for he was gone like a flash. He was wrapped in some sort of cloak which came across the lower part of his face. One thing only I am sure of, and that is that he had some weapon in his hand. It looked to me like a long knife. I distinctly saw the gleam of it as he turned to run."

"This is most interesting," said Holmes. "Pray what did you do then?"

"I should have followed him through the open window if I had been stronger. As it was, I rang the bell and roused the house. It took me some little time, for the bell rings in the kitchen and the servants all sleep upstairs. I shouted, however, and that brought Joseph down, and he roused the others. Joseph and the groom found marks on the bed outside the window, but the weather has been so dry lately that they found it hopeless to follow the trail across the grass. There's a place, however, on the wooden fence which skirts the road which shows signs, they tell me, as if some one had got over, and had snapped the top of the rail in doing so. I have said nothing to the local police yet, for I thought I had best have your opinion first."

This tale of our client's appeared to have an extraordinary effect upon Sherlock Holmes. He rose from his chair and paced about the room in uncontrollable excitement.

"Misfortunes never come single," said Phelps, smiling, though it was evident that his adventure had somewhat shaken him.

"You have certainly had your share," said Holmes. "Do you think you could walk round the house with me?"

"Oh, yes, I should like a little sunshine. Joseph will come, too."

"And I also," said Miss Harrison.

"I am afraid not," said Holmes, shaking his head. "I think I must ask you to remain sitting exactly where you are."

The young lady resumed her seat with an air of displeasure. Her brother, however, had joined us and we set off all four together. We passed round the lawn to the outside of the young diplomatist's window. There were, as he had said, marks upon the bed, but they were hopelessly blurred and vague. Holmes stopped over them for an instant, and then rose shrugging his shoulders.

"I don't think any one could make much of this," said he. "Let us go round the house and see why this particular room was chosen by the burglar. I should have thought those larger windows of the drawing-room and dining-room would have had more attractions for him."

"They are more visible from the road," suggested Mr. Joseph Harrison.

"Ah, yes, of course. There is a door here which he might have attempted. What is it for?"

"It is the side entrance for trades-people. Of course it is locked at night."

"Have you ever had an alarm like this before?"

"Never," said our client.

"Do you keep plate in the house, or anything to attract burglars?"

"Nothing of value."

Holmes strolled round the house with his hands in his pockets and a negligent air which was unusual with him.

"By the way," said he to Joseph Harrison,

"you found some place, I understand, where the fellow scaled the fence. Let us have a look at that!"

The plump young man led us to a spot where the top of one of the wooden rails had been cracked. A small fragment of the wood was hanging down. Holmes pulled it off and examined it critically.

"Do you think that was done last night? It looks rather old, does it not?"

"Well, possibly so."

"There are no marks of any one jumping down upon the other side. No, I fancy we shall get no help here. Let us go back to the bedroom and talk the matter over."

Percy Phelps was walking very slowly, leaning upon the arm of his future brother-in-law. Holmes walked swiftly across the lawn, and we were at the open window of the bedroom long before the others came up.

"Miss Harrison," said Holmes, speaking with the utmost intensity of manner, "you must stay where you are all day. Let nothing prevent you from staying where you are all day. It is of the utmost importance."

"Certainly, if you wish it, Mr. Holmes," said the girl in astonishment.

"When you go to bed lock the door of this room on the outside and keep the key. Promise to do this."

"But Percy?"

"He will come to London with us."

"And am I to remain here?"

"It is for his sake. You can serve him. Quick! Promise!"

She gave a quick nod of assent just as the other two came up.

"Why do you sit moping there, Annie?" cried her brother. "Come out into the sunshine!"

"No, thank you, Joseph. I have a slight headache and this room is deliciously cool and soothing."

"What do you propose now, Mr. Holmes?" asked our client.

"Well, in investigating this minor affair we must not lose sight of our main inquiry. It would be a very great help to me if you would come up to London with us."

"At once?"

"Well, as soon as you conveniently can. Say in an hour."

"I feel quite strong enough, if I can really be of any help."

"The greatest possible."

"Perhaps you would like me to stay there to-night?"

"I was just going to propose it."

"Then, if my friend of the night comes to revisit me, he will find the bird flown. We are all in your hands, Mr. Holmes, and you must tell us exactly what you would like done. Perhaps you would prefer that Joseph came with us so as to look after me?"

"Oh, no; my friend Watson is a medical man, you know, and he'll look after you. We'll have our lunch here, if you will permit us, and then we shall all three set off for town together."

It was arranged as he suggested, though Miss Harrison excused herself from leaving the bedroom, in accordance with Holmes's suggestion. What the object of my friend's manoeuvres was I could not conceive, unless it were to keep the lady away from Phelps, who, rejoiced by his returning health and by the prospect of action, lunched with us in the dining-room. Holmes had a still more startling surprise for us, however, for, after accompanying us down to the station and seeing us into our carriage, he calmly announced that he had no intention of leaving Woking.

"There are one or two small points which I should desire to clear up before I go," said he. "Your absence, Mr. Phelps, will in some ways rather assist me. Watson, when you reach London you would oblige me by driving at once to Baker Street with our friend here, and remaining with him until I see you again. It is fortunate that you are old school-fellows, as you must have much to talk over. Mr. Phelps can have the spare bedroom to-night, and I will be with you in time for breakfast, for there is a train which will take me into Waterloo at eight."

"But how about our investigation in London?" asked Phelps, ruefully.

"We can do that to-morrow. I think that just at present I can be of more immediate use here."

"You might tell them at Briarbrae that I hope to be back to-morrow night," cried Phelps, as we began to move from the platform.

"I hardly expect to go back to Briarbrae," answered Holmes, and waved his hand to us cheerily as we shot out from the station.

Phelps and I talked it over on our journey, but neither of us could devise a satisfactory reason for this new development.

"I suppose he wants to find out some clue as to the burglary last night, if a burglar it was. For myself, I don't believe it was an ordinary thief."

"What is your own idea, then?"

"Upon my word, you may put it down to my weak nerves or not, but I believe there is some deep political intrigue going on around me, and that for some reason that passes my understanding my life is aimed at by the conspirators. It sounds high-flown and absurd, but consider the facts! Why should a thief try to break in at a bedroom window, where there could be no hope of any plunder, and why should he come with a long knife in his hand?"

"You are sure it was not a house-breaker's jimmy?"

"Oh, no, it was a knife. I saw the flash of the blade quite distinctly."

"But why on earth should you be pursued with such animosity?"

"Ah, that is the question."

"Well, if Holmes takes the same view, that would account for his action, would it not? Presuming that your theory is correct, if he can lay his hands upon the man who threatened you last night he will have gone a long way towards finding who took the naval treaty. It is absurd to suppose that you have two enemies, one of whom robs you, while the other threatens your life."

"But Holmes said that he was not going to Briarbrae."

"I have known him for some time," said I, "but I never knew him do anything yet without a very good reason," and with that our conversation drifted off on to other topics.

But it was a weary day for me. Phelps was still weak after his long illness, and his misfortune made him querulous and nervous. In vain I endeavored to interest him in Afghanistan, in India, in social questions, in anything which might take his mind out of the groove. He would always come back to his lost treaty, wondering, guessing, speculating, as to what Holmes was doing, what steps Lord Holdhurst was taking, what news we should have in the morning. As the evening wore on his excitement became quite painful.

"You have implicit faith in Holmes?" he asked.

"I have seen him do some remarkable things."

"But he never brought light into anything quite so dark as this?"

"Oh, yes, I have known him solve questions which presented fewer clues than yours."

"But not where such large interests are at stake?"

"I don't know that. To my certain knowledge he has acted on behalf of three of the reigning houses of Europe in very vital matters."

"But you know him well, Watson. He is such an inscrutable fellow that I never quite know what to make of him. Do you think he is hopeful? Do you think he expects to make a success of it?"

"He has said nothing."

"That is a bad sign."

"On the contrary, I have noticed that when he is off the trail he generally says so. It is when he is on a scent and is not quite absolutely sure yet that it is the right one that he is most taciturn. Now, my dear fellow, we can't help matters by making ourselves nervous about them, so let me implore you to go to bed and so be fresh for whatever may await us to-morrow."

I was able at last to persuade my companion to take my advice, though I knew from his excited manner that there was not much hope of sleep for him. Indeed, his mood was infectious, for I lay tossing half the night myself, brooding over this strange problem, and inventing a hundred theories, each of which was more impossible than the last. Why had Holmes remained at Woking? Why had he asked Miss Harrison to remain in the sick-room all day? Why had he been so careful not to inform the people at Briarbrae that he intended to remain near them? I cudgelled my brains until I fell asleep in the endeavor to find some explanation which would cover all these facts.

It was seven o'clock when I awoke, and I set off at once for Phelps's room, to find him haggard and spent after a sleepless night. His first question was whether Holmes had arrived yet.

"He'll be here when he promised," said I, "and not an instant sooner or later."

And my words were true, for shortly after eight a hansom dashed up to the door and our friend got out of it. Standing in the window we saw that his left hand was swathed in a bandage and that his face was very grim and pale. He entered the house, but it was some little time before he came upstairs.

"He looks like a beaten man," cried Phelps.

I was forced to confess that he was right. "After all," said I, "the clue of the matter lies probably here in town."

Phelps gave a groan.

"I don't know how it is," said he, "but I had hoped for so much from his return. But surely his hand was not tied up like that yesterday. What can be the matter?"

"You are not wounded, Holmes?" I asked, as my friend entered the room.

"Tut, it is only a scratch through my own clumsiness," he answered, nodding his good-mornings to us. "This case of yours, Mr. Phelps, is certainly one of the darkest which I have ever investigated."

"I feared that you would find it beyond you."

"It has been a most remarkable experience."

"That bandage tells of adventures," said I. "Won't you tell us what has happened?"

"After breakfast, my dear Watson. Remember that I have breathed thirty miles of Surrey air this morning. I suppose that there has been no answer from my cabman advertisement? Well, well, we cannot expect to score every time."

The table was all laid, and just as I was about to ring Mrs. Hudson entered with the tea and coffee. A few minutes later she brought in three covers, and we all drew up to the table, Holmes ravenous, I curious, and Phelps in the gloomiest state of depression.

"Mrs. Hudson has risen to the occasion," said Holmes, uncovering a dish of curried chicken. "Her cuisine is a little limited, but she has as good an idea of breakfast as a Scotch-woman. What have you here, Watson?"

"Ham and eggs," I answered.

"Good! What are you going to take, Mr. Phelps—curried fowl or eggs, or will you help yourself?"

"Thank you. I can eat nothing," said Phelps.

"Oh, come! Try the dish before you."

"Thank you, I would really rather not."

"Well, then," said Holmes, with a mischievous twinkle, "I suppose that you have no objection to helping me?"

Phelps raised the cover, and as he did so he uttered a scream, and sat there staring with a face as white as the plate upon which he looked. Across the centre of it was lying a little cylinder of blue-gray paper. He caught it up, devoured it with his eyes, and then danced madly about the room, passing it to his bosom and shrieking out in his delight. Then he fell back into an armchair so limp and exhausted with his own emotions that we had to pour brandy down his throat to keep him from fainting.

"There! there!" said Holmes, soothing, patting him upon the shoulder. "It was too bad to spring it on you like this, but Watson here will tell you that I never can resist a touch of the dramatic."

Phelps seized his hand and kissed it. "God bless you!" he cried. "You have saved my honor."

"Well, my own was at stake, you know," said Holmes. "I assure you it is just as hateful to me to fail in a case as it can be to you to blunder over a commission."

Phelps thrust away the precious document into the innermost pocket of his coat.

"I have not the heart to interrupt your breakfast any further, and yet I am dying to know how you got it and where it was."

Sherlock Holmes swallowed a cup of coffee, and turned his attention to the ham and eggs. Then he rose, lit his pipe, and settled himself down into his chair.

"I'll tell you what I did first, and how I came to do it afterwards," said he. "After leaving you at the station I went for a charming walk through some admirable Surrey scenery to a pretty little village called Ripley, where I had my tea at an inn, and took the precaution of filling my flask and of putting a paper of sandwiches in my pocket. There I remained until evening, when I set off for Woking again, and found myself in the high-road outside Briarbrae just after sunset.

"Well, I waited until the road was clear—it is never a very frequented one at any time, I fancy—and then I clambered over the fence into the grounds."

"Surely the gate was open!" ejaculated Phelps.

"Yes, but I have a peculiar taste in these matters. I chose the place where the three fir-trees stand, and behind their screen I got over without the least chance of any one in the house being able to see me. I crouched down among the bushes on the other side, and crawled from one to the other—witness the disreputable state of my trouser knees—until I had reached the clump of rhododendrons just opposite to your bedroom window. There I squatted down and awaited developments.

"The blind was not down in your room, and I could see Miss Harrison sitting there reading by the table. It was quarter-past ten when she closed her book, fastened the shutters, and retired.

"I heard her shut the door, and felt quite sure that she had turned the key in the lock."

"The key!" ejaculated Phelps.

"Yes, I had given Miss Harrison instructions to lock the door on the outside and take the key with her when she went to bed. She carried out every one of my injunctions to the letter, and certainly without her cooperation you would not have that paper in your coat-pocket. She departed then and the lights went out, and I was left squatting in the rhododendron-bush.

"The night was fine, but still it was a very weary vigil. Of course it has the sort of excitement about it that the sportsman feels when he lies beside the water-course and waits for the big game. It was very long, though—almost as long, Watson, as when you and I waited in that deadly room when we looked into the little problem of the Speckled Band. There was a church-clock down at Woking which struck the quarters, and I thought more than once that it had stopped. At last however about two in the morning, I suddenly heard the gentle sound of a bolt being pushed back and the creaking of a key. A moment later the servant's door was opened, and Mr. Joseph Harrison stepped out into the moonlight."

"Joseph!" ejaculated Phelps.

"He was bare-headed, but he had a black coat thrown over his shoulder so that he could conceal his face in an instant if there were any alarm. He walked on tiptoe under the shadow of the wall, and when he reached the window he worked a long-bladed knife through the sash and pushed back the catch. Then he flung open the window, and putting his knife through the crack in the shutters, he thrust the bar up and swung them open.

"From where I lay I had a perfect view of the inside of the room and of every one of his movements. He lit the two candles which stood upon the mantelpiece, and then he proceeded to turn back the corner of the carpet in the neighborhood of the door. Presently he stopped and picked out a square piece of board, such as is usually left to enable plumbers to get at the joints of the gas-pipes. This one covered, as a matter of fact, the T joint which gives off the pipe which supplies the kitchen underneath. Out of this hiding-place he drew that little cylinder of paper, pushed down the board, rearranged the carpet, blew out the candles, and walked straight into my arms as I stood waiting for him outside the window.

"Well, he has rather more viciousness than I gave him credit for, has Master Joseph. He flew at me with his knife, and I had to grasp him twice, and got a cut over the knuckles, before I had the upper hand of him. He looked murder out of the only eye he could see with when we had finished, but he listened to reason and gave up the papers. Having got them I let my man go, but I wired full particulars to Forbes this morning. If he is quick enough to catch his bird, well and good. But if, as I shrewdly suspect, he finds the nest empty before he gets there, why, all the better for the government. I fancy that Lord Holdhurst for one, and Mr. Percy Phelps for another, would very much rather that the affair never got as far as a police-court.

"My God!" gasped our client. "Do you tell me that during these long ten weeks of agony the stolen papers were within the very room with me all the time?"

"So it was."

"And Joseph! Joseph a villain and a thief!"

"Hum! I am afraid Joseph's character is a rather deeper and more dangerous one than one might judge from his appearance. From what I have heard from him this morning, I gather that he has lost heavily in dabbling with stocks, and that he is ready to do anything on earth to better his fortunes. Being an absolutely selfish man, when a chance presented itself he did not allow either his sister's happiness or your reputation to hold his hand."

Percy Phelps sank back in his chair. "My head whirls," said he. "Your words have dazed me."

"The principal difficulty in your case," remarked Holmes, in his didactic fashion, "lay in the fact of there being too much evidence. What was vital was overlaid and hidden by what was irrelevant. Of all the facts which were presented to us we had to pick just those which we deemed to be essential, and then piece them together in their order, so as to reconstruct this very remarkable chain of events. I had already begun to suspect Joseph, from the fact that you had intended to travel home with him that night, and that therefore it was a likely enough thing that he should call for you, knowing the Foreign Office well, upon his way. When I heard that some one had been so anxious to get into the bedroom, in which no one but Joseph could have concealed anything—you told us in your narrative how you had turned Joseph out when you arrived with the doctor—my suspicions all changed to certainties, especially as the attempt was made on the first night upon which the nurse was absent, showing that the intruder was well acquainted with the ways of the house."

"How blind I have been!"

"The facts of the case, as far as I have worked them out, are these: this Joseph Harrison entered the office through the Charles Street door, and knowing his way he walked straight into your room the instant after you left it. Finding no one there he promptly rang the bell, and at the instant that he did so his eyes caught the paper upon the table. A glance showed him that chance had put in his way a State document of immense value, and in an instant he had thrust it into his pocket and was gone. A few minutes elapsed, as you remember, before the sleepy commissionaire drew your attention to the bell, and those were just enough to give the thief time to make his escape.

"He made his way to Woking by the first train, and having examined his booty and assured himself that it really was of immense value, he had concealed it in what he thought was a very safe place, with the intention of taking it out again in a day or two, and carrying it to the French embassy, or wherever he thought that a long price was to be had. Then came your sudden return. He, without a moment's warning, was bundled out of his room, and from that time onward there were always at least two of you there to prevent him from regaining his treasure. The situation to him must have been a maddening one. But at last he thought he saw his chance. He tried to steal in, but was baffled by your wakefulness. You remember that you did not take your usual draught that night."

"I remember."

"I fancy that he had taken steps to make that draught efficacious, and that he quite relied upon your being unconscious. Of course, I understood that he would repeat the attempt whenever it could be done with safety. Your leaving the room gave him the chance he wanted. I kept Miss Harrison in it all day so that he might not anticipate us. Then, having given him the idea that the coast was clear, I kept guard as I have described. I already knew that the papers were probably in the room, but I had no desire to rip up all the planking and skirting in search of them. I let him take them, therefore, from the hiding-place, and so saved myself an infinity of trouble. Is there any other point which I can make clear?"

"Why did he try the window on the first occasion," I asked, "when he might have entered by the door?"

"In reaching the door he would have to pass seven bedrooms. On the other hand, he could get out on to the lawn with ease. Anything else?"

"You do not think," asked Phelps, "that he had any murderous intention? The knife was only meant as a tool."

"It may be so," answered Holmes, shrugging his shoulders. "I can only say for certain that Mr. Joseph Harrison is a gentleman to whose mercy I should be extremely unwilling to trust."

THE BLACK DOCTOR

T. T. FLYNN

A PROLIFIC AUTHOR OF mystery fiction, producing a story, "The Pullman Murder," for the very first issue of *Dime Detective Magazine* in November 1931, Thomas Theodore Flynn (1902–1979) was even more famous as a writer of western fiction for the pulps, the prestigious *Saturday Evening Post*, and in book form.

He led the type of macho life that many male writers thought helpful in learning about the world, spending time as a hobo and working as a carpenter, door-to-door salesman, clerk, and traveling salesman, as well as in a shipyard, steel mills, on ships in the engine and fire rooms, and in a railroad shop, inspecting locomotives.

One of Flynn's five western novels published with Dell between 1954 and 1961, *The Man from Laramie* (1954), was released on film in 1955, starring James Stewart and directed by Anthony Mann.

Flynn's only two mystery novels were paperback originals published in Great Britain by Hector Kelly, *It's Murder* (1950) and *Murder Caravan* (1950).

His mystery pulp stories tended to be humorous and cheerful, as exemplified by the series featuring Mike Harris and Trixie Meehan, both of whom work for the Blaine International Agency. Mike is tough, redheaded, and wisecracking; Trixie is cute and pert and, while depending upon her partner if a fight breaks out, is also smart and inventive when necessary.

There is less humor in Flynn's series of spy stories about Val Easton, the crack Secret Service operative, in which his foe is "the Black Doctor," a genuine doctor who did not fully understand the Hippocratic oath about first doing no harm; he uses his medical training and surgical tools to inflict maximum pain on his torture victims. The Black Doctor is a spy without any national affiliation who will sell secrets to the highest bidder.

"The Black Doctor" was originally published in the December 1932 issue of *Dime Detective Magazine*.

THE BLACK DOCTOR

T. T. FLYNN

CHAPTER ONE

S13

IT WAS THE LAST EVENING on the *Laurentic*, the last dinner before quarantine, and the slow progress up the bay past the Statue of Liberty and into the river where snorting tugs would skilfully guide the big liner into her berth. Six days out from Southampton, the *Laurentic* had found five days of bad weather, of plunging seas and gale-swept decks. Four days in which fully half the passengers had remained below, shunning decks, games, amusements—and food.

But all that had passed magically. The skies had cleared. The sweeping seas had smoothed in the sunny calm that followed. And now the big dining saloon was crowded. Val Easton ate with only half an ear on the table conversation.

His mind was on other things. The mission that had taken him to London and Rome, by way of Paris, and then back to London again. The weeks of piecing together tiny bits of information to make the pattern which took shape in his final report. It had been good work too. The cable from his chief, calling him back to Washington, had said so.

A fragment of the conversation jerked his attention back to the table, without sign of it showing on his lean features.

The full-bosomed woman at the head of the table—a Mrs. Beamish—had said aggressively: "The whole thing was bosh! In wartime, perhaps. But not now. Spies are as old-fashioned as the dodo bird." And Mrs. Beamish glared around the table as if daring anyone to take issue with her over the matter.

They were, Val realized, talking about the picture that had been shown the evening before. One of the latest thrillers built around the adventures of a famous woman spy during the War.

Most of them had seen it. The discussion at once became heated. The most outspoken was the blond young Mr. Miller at Mrs. Beamish's left, who looked like a poet just out of college, and who stood by his convictions heatedly.

"Of course there are spies," he protested. "They're always working. You read about them all the time."

"And see silly pictures about them," Mrs. Beamish declared sarcastically.

"That picture was based on historical facts," he said with the positive assurance of youth. "Whether you liked it or not, it happened.

Why—why, any of us here at the table might be a spy! I might be one working for a foreign government." And visibly set up by the thought, he looked gallantly across the table at the pretty girl on Val's right.

Val smiled inwardly. It seemed funny, this talk about spies. Almost like a fiction story. Something sinister and diabolical about it. He wondered if he looked the part. Wondered too, what would happen if this tableful of peaceful travelers were apprized of his identity, and could look for a moment into the roiling currents of international intrigue.

But Mrs. Beamish leaned forward with a glitter in her eye. "Young man," she asked sharply, "did you ever see a spy?"

"Er—well, no."

"Ahhh!" said Mrs. Beamish with a cutting smile, and leaned back in her chair as if that settled everything. And young Miller's weak retort of "How would I know one if I saw him? They don't go labeled," made no impression in her self-satisfied armor.

There was a chuckle from the slender, middle-aged Englishman who had sat at the end of the table every meal, beaming through rimless eyeglasses and talking books and authors to whomsoever would listen. Carmody was his name, a book salesman on a business trip to the States. Now he smiled and bobbed his head as he leaned forward and spoke.

"I fancy Mrs. Beamish is more than a little bit right. This is not wartime, nor is there the wide interest in such things that we had in the days of the old worldwide Imperial German spy service. My firm, by the way, has published two books on such things and I can—er—modestly claim to know something about it. Spies are practically as dead as the dodo. We have about as much chance of finding one here at the table as we have of missing our dinner in New York tomorrow evening." And Carmody beamed at them all.

The young man retorted sulkily: "Just the same, I'm still betting on spies. You might be one yourself."

"Ha ha, so I might," Carmody chortled. "And if you'll drop around to the nearest bookstore as soon as you land, at least I'll guarantee you a corking good book on the subject. Make your hair stand up on end if you believe everything that's in it."

"I don't have to read a book to have my mind made up," young Miller said darkly, and applied himself to his dessert with irritated jabs of his spoon.

Val said to Carmody good naturedly as he left the table: "I may get that book myself. I've always been curious about such things."

"Do," Carmody beamed. "At least it's jolly good reading. Almost made me wish I had been one myself back in the days when they were taken seriously."

A trim, blue-uniformed young man from the Marconi room came in, paging, "Mr. Easton. Mr. Easton."

Val lifted a finger; the blue uniform met him and an envelope was placed in his hands. "Radiogram, sir."

Val tore it open and deciphered the coded message with the ease of long practice.

V EASTON
ON BOARD SS LAURENTIC
CONTACT S13 BEAMISH ASSIST
IF NEEDED
SIGNED GREGG

Sheer amazement almost made Val wheel around and glance back at the table. The signature "Gregg" was the code word for the chief, housed at the right elbow of the State Department in Washington. Its sense was plain. Its information stunning. And for the thousandth time Val was swept with admiration for the perfection of the intricate and farflung web of which he was only one strand.

S13—Beamish.

Only one meaning to that. That full-bosomed, majestic woman, who had sat at the head of the table day after day on this crossing, was a part of the same web. That woman who looked like the stodgy, opinionated wife of some equally stodgy business man; that severe matron whose tall, slender daughter had appeared once briefly on deck with her, was—*must* be—a clever Intelligence operative.

Val smiled wryly at the thought of how he himself had swallowed her aggressive declaration that no longer did such people exist.

Why had she done it?

And Val paid her the compliment of believing that there had been a purpose behind it. He tucked the radiogram in his inside coat pocket and strolled out on deck.

Half an hour later Val found Mrs. Beamish standing by the rail, peering pensively down at the endless ribbon of foam-flecked water that rushed astern. A blue coat was wrapped around her ample figure, a chiffon veil held her hair in place against the rush of the night breeze. Even now his critical scrutiny found it hard to believe she was the one Gregg referred to. He leaned against the rail beside her, said casually: "S13."

"What?" Mrs. Beamish demanded in a startled voice.

Val repeated it. She frowned at him. "Young man," she asked tartly, "is this a new way of flirting with an old woman like me?"

"Gregg suggested it," Val said idly.

"*Hmmmmp!*" said Mrs. Beamish shortly. She drew her coat closely around her shoulders, adjusted her veil slowly, turned and eyed him deliberately. A smile slowly broke over her angular face.

"So you're the one?" she said. "My, my—and to think we've been eating at the same table. Gregg radioed that one of his men would see us this evening. Come down and meet Nancy. She's been feeling bad the whole trip."

"Your daughter?"

Mrs. Beamish sniffed. "Bosh! It makes good

atmosphere. Whoever would suspect an old fogy like me? I wish Nancy Fraser was my daughter. She's a girl in a million."

"Nancy Fraser? I've heard of her."

Val had indeed. Nancy Fraser, tales of whose daring ingenuity were already becoming classics of the Intelligence Service. An adept at disguise, a quick thinker, a beautiful girl, fearless, resourceful, and blessed with uncanny luck was this Nancy Fraser.

Mrs. Beamish, preceding him into the cabin on B Deck, said: "This is our man, Nance. Mr. Easton, Miss Fraser."

The girl who slid effortlessly to her feet from the bed almost took Val's breath away. She was softly feminine at first glance, a beauty with fine cleancut features, slightly sun-tanned. Her chin was firm and her mouth fairly wide, with a humorous quirk at the corners. She was a platinum blonde, and her silky hair, cut short, was waved close to her head in a style almost mannish.

He was to learn later that there was a reason for that. But at the moment he was conscious only of the calm, boring gaze of a pair of the bluest and deepest eyes he had ever seen. They took him apart in one swift look, examined the pieces—and approved. For she smiled and gave him a firm hand.

"I'm glad to see you, Mr. Easton. Sit down. This has been a rocky passage for me. I'm still a little wobbly."

"I was surprised to get Gregg's radiogram," Val told her as he seated himself. "I suppose something is up?"

Nancy Fraser's smile faded as she sank on the edge of the bed. She nodded. "Something is up. I coded Gregg a resumé of it, and he radioed back that he would have one of his men who was on the ship get in touch with me. I've been waiting for you."

"I would have guessed every other man on the ship," said Mrs. Beamish with a critical look at Val. "You're such a nice, harmless-looking young man. I thought you might be a college professor or a bond salesman."

The front of Nancy Fraser's silk negligée trembled as she laughed softly at Val's wry smile. "Don't mind Norah, Mr. Easton. She's apt to break out with some startling remarks."

"Hmmmp!" said Mrs. Beamish. "I say what I think, when it suits me."

Nancy Fraser became serious once more.

"Here's what we're up against, Mr. Easton. I'm working on a delicate matter. As near as I understand it, the stage is all set for some world-shaking moves that haven't even been hinted at in the newspapers. Anything may come out of it. The Shanghai business was only a move in a bigger game. Japan, Russia, England, France, and Italy are all holding different hands in the Far East. Our government is vitally concerned. Treaties, agreements, protestations by statesmen are all for public consumption. Behind that the real moves are being made. The different foreign offices are the only ones who really know."

"And some of them don't know as much as they'd like to," Val commented.

"Exactly. None of them do. Each one is afraid of what the others may be doing. I doubt if the Intelligence Services have been half as busy since the War as they are now. Wires, cables, and radio services are being tapped. Confidential codes being broken down and deciphered. Mails are being watched. Intelligence operators planted where they can get at the contents of diplomatic pouches, and scores of men in high position are being watched day and night for some clue as to what their governments are driving at. It's a mess. World peace, or another war that will make the last look like a kindergarten exercise, are in the balance."

Val knew all that. But he liked the crisp way this Nancy Fraser went to the heart of the matter. He was seeing another side of the beautiful girl who had cordially greeted him. A woman, this, who was steely hard beneath her femininity; who thought straight and to the point.

"Where do you come in?" he questioned bluntly.

"At the moment I'm following a man who stands high in the British diplomatic service. A man who is coming to the States on a secret mission. He is traveling incognito as a Mr. Galbraith. I am confident he is carrying secret papers or instructions that can't be entrusted to the mails or cables."

"Who is he?"

"Sir Edward Lyne. A tall, thin man with a close-clipped black mustache."

"Haven't noticed him."

"Probably not. He has kept to his cabin most of the trip."

"That seems simple enough," Val said, offering his cigarettes to the two women, and holding a light for them.

Nancy Fraser leaned back on one arm and nodded. "It is simple enough. Only—we're being followed too."

Those last sharp, vibrant words brought a sudden tang of danger into the atmosphere of the cabin. Val snapped alert, eyed her keenly.

"Who is following you?"

Nancy Fraser shook her head. "That's the trouble," she confessed. "Neither Norah nor I have been able to find out. But someone knows who we are, or suspects us. Our cabin was entered one of the few times we both were out of it. Entered, searched cleverly, and left exactly as it had been."

"How did you discover it?"

Norah Beamish smiled proudly. "That girl is a wonder, Mr. Easton. She never leaves her room without fixing it so she knows at once whether it has been disturbed."

"A few little ends of silk thread that are never noticed when they are displaced," Nancy Fraser explained. "To make certain this time, I questioned the stewardess closely. She had not been in here."

She didn't have to say anything more. Too well Val understood why she was disturbed. It was bad enough to match wits with dangers one was aware of. But there was nothing more unnerving than to find that one's disguise had been penetrated, that unknown danger lurked close, and to be unable to discover it and take precautions. Until Nancy Fraser found out who had searched her cabin, she must suspect every one on the boat, must look for anything to happen at any hour of the day or night.

"Suspect anyone?" he prompted.

"No. We're up in the air."

The room had a narrow window opening on the promenade deck. A window halfway up, with the drawn curtains inside swaying slightly in the wind. And just as Nancy Fraser answered him, a harder gust than usual blew the right curtain aside. Val's eye caught a fleeting glimpse of a shoulder shifting hastily back to one side.

Someone was out there listening!

CHAPTER TWO

DEATH ON B DECK

Val made a catlike lunge to his feet, reached the window in a silent stride, and grabbed through it. As he expected, the shoulder was just outside. His fingers dug hard into the rough woolen cloth, and he jerked hard to bring the lurking figure over where he could see the face.

The other made no sound. But the hard edge of a taut palm struck the bone just above his wrist a terrific blow. It was *jiu-jitsu* skilfully, savagely, and instantly applied. His hand went numb and useless, and the blinding pain shot above his elbow.

With a twist the shoulder tore away and was gone.

Val jerked his arm in, biting his lower lip against the gasp of agony that rushed to his teeth. Nancy Fraser had come to her feet alertly and was staring wide-eyed as Val whirled toward the door.

"Someone listening out there!" he threw

at her, and jerked the door open with his good hand and rushed out on deck.

The promenade was brightly lighted. At least a score of people were visible from the back of the long sweep of deck. But most of them were leaning over the rail; the others were strolling astern. No one at the moment had his eyes fixed on the spot. And the deck was empty!

A deck bay was a few yards away. His man must have gone there. But when Val reached it he found the bay empty and none of the chairs occupied. The companion door at the back was closed. He opened it, looked into the passage beyond, and swore under his breath. His man had moved fast and surely. Had gotten away. Val was forced to admit that fact after a few moments' search.

He met a steward in the passage, asked the man sharply: "Did you see a man come through here a few moments ago?"

His tense manner drew a curious look from the white-jacketed little Cockney.

"Ayn't seen a soul, sir."

"Sure?"

"H'I don't myke mistakes, sir. A man carn't afford to w'en 'e's holdin' down a nick on a top'oler like the *Laurentic*, sir. Is there something wrong?"

"Nothing," said Val, turning back. "Thank you."

Nancy Fraser had put on pumps and a coat that covered her negligée. She was standing near her door when Val returned. She met him with a questioning look.

"He got away," Val admitted unwillingly. "I was a fool to grab at him through the window like that. But I wanted a quick look at his face. He gave my wrist a crack that paralyzed it, and was gone."

"You didn't see him at all!"

"No."

"Let's take a turn around the deck," she said abruptly. "We've made a mess of things. Whoever it is knows you're with us now. I wish we had thought of that."

"I shouldn't have gone to your cabin," Val admitted. "Wouldn't have if I'd known what was up. But I didn't suspect it was this bad."

"Norah knew. She should have stopped you. And I should have closed that window. But we all make mistakes. I wonder how much he overheard."

"We weren't talking loud."

"Loud enough, I'm afraid," she said gloomily. "Darn it, the cat's out of the bag now. I'm much worse off than I was when I radioed Gregg. It's terrible! We've got to find out who it was."

"Line up a few hundred first-class passengers and look them in the eye, I suppose?" Val suggested.

"Your ideas are about as good as mine."

"This is the last night. On shore we may be able to do something about it."

"And maybe not. Don't you see we're both practically useless now until we get at the truth of this?"

They made the circuit of the deck twice, and finally Val suggested: "You might as well turn in. I'll stay up later and keep my eyes open. I'll let you know if I see anything."

Her handclasp was cool and firm, her "good night" brief, but her smile warm. Val walked away thinking about her.

At midnight the deck lights were dimmed. The strollers began to thin out. Val stayed out, for he was not sleepy. For hours he had been thinking about Nancy Fraser and this new bit of business. Who was so interested in her? What did it mean?

In other professions one might have shrugged the whole matter aside until something else happened. But not in his and Nancy Fraser's. If they didn't think at least two jumps ahead of the other party the results might be disastrous.

A steward passed with a tray holding a pot of coffee.

"Bring me a pot of coffee," Val told him.

And the steward touched his cap. "Yes, sir. Soon as I get back, sir."

Val leaned on the rail and stared out at the vast expanse of sea heaving slowly under the moonlight. Light steps came to his side. It was Nancy Fraser.

"I couldn't sleep," she said under her breath. "I wondered if I would find you out here."

"I'm having coffee in a few minutes. Care for some?"

"Sounds good. It might help my memory. I've been lying in bed trying to think of any suspicious move I've seen since I came aboard. I'm stymied."

"Ditto," Val admitted.

They waited there at the rail, talking low. Nancy said finally: "I thought you had ordered coffee."

Val looked at his wrist watch and saw that twenty-five minutes had passed as they lingered at the rail. "That steward must have forgotten it," he said irritably. "Let's look him up."

They walked slowly back along the deck. And suddenly, without warning, a woman screamed with shrill hysterical fear!

Nancy Fraser stopped short, her hand gripping Val's arm convulsively. "What's wrong?" she gasped.

The scream had come from ahead of them. Near the rear of the dimly lighted promenade Val saw two feminine figures backing toward the rail.

"I'll see," he jerked out under his breath, and leaving Nancy Fraser to follow, he ran toward the spot. He met the two women hurrying toward him. Two middle-aged spinsters. He had noticed them before during the trip. And now they were badly frightened. One was near hysteria as she turned and pointed back to the spot where Val had first seen them.

"There's something wrong there!" she cried shrilly. "I s-stumbled over an arm sticking out of the doorway! I—I think someone is d-dead!"

"Wait here!" Val ordered sharply. "If anyone's dead you can't be hurt!"

He found the door a moment later, and as he

came up to it saw an arm thrust out at the bottom. A white-clad arm, sticking straight and motionless into the dim light of the deck. An arm that lay on the floor, its rigid fingers grasping talonlike at the empty air.

Val swore softly under his breath. It was a ghastly sight. For that arm seemed to be reaching, groping with desperate futility for something that had withdrawn beyond reach.

He stooped and lifted the hand. The flesh was clammy and cooling already. It was flaccid, limp, with that slackness which comes only from one thing. Whatever the arm had been reaching for, it had found only—death.

The door was ajar. The cabin inside was dark, silent.

Doors were opening along the deck; passengers were looking out. Nancy Fraser joined him.

"What is it?" she asked breathlessly.

Val reached inside for the light switch. "You'd better not look," he advised. "This won't be nice."

"I've probably seen worse sights," she retorted coolly, and looked in past his shoulder as the light flashed on inside.

Whatever sights Nancy had witnessed before, they had not hardened her enough to stop the gasp of horror which burst from her. Even Val himself could not take it coolly. The steward whom he had accosted half an hour before was lying there on the floor before them. Lying, twisted on his side, knees pulled half up, one hand clutching the front of his white jacket and the other reaching out through the door in that frantic, gruesome gesture. And on the doorsill his face was turned up to them drawn and crimsoned with congested blood, mouth open, tongue protruding, and bulging eyes set in a horrible sightless stare.

"He's dead!" Nancy said huskily.

Val nodded. "Yes. Dead all right. This is the man I ordered coffee from. No wonder he didn't bring it!"

Looking beyond the body, he saw on the floor the tray the steward had been carrying. It had been dropped. Cup and saucer were shattered into bits. The pot lay on its side, the dark brown contents making a long stain on the rug, surrounded by a snowy sprinkling of sugar.

"He died almost as soon as he entered," Val muttered. "Didn't even have a chance to put his tray down. Dropped it cold."

His eyes ran over the body as he said that. There was no sign of blood. And no marks of a struggle either. Except for the spot in front where the starched white cloth was caught in convulsive fingers, the coat was neat and trim. Even the man's carefully combed black hair was in place. It had been smoothed down with hair dressing, and was as sleek as it had been when he had walked along the deck.

Nancy noticed all that too, for she said: "It must have been heart failure."

"Looks that way," Val agreed.

A deck officer came running up in the van of half a dozen passengers closing in on the spot. "What is it?" he panted.

"One of your stewards must have had a heart attack," Val said, standing aside so that the officer could get a good look.

The bronze-cheeked, broad-shouldered young man pushed the door open all the way and stepped inside.

"Here's what's this?" he uttered in a startled voice. "Wake up, sir!" And over his shoulder: "The man must be a sound sleeper!"

Stepping in too, Val saw what he had missed with the door partly closed and his attention centered around the doorway. The bed was occupied by a man clad in blue silk pajamas.

"That man's not sleeping!" Val said sharply.

The young deck officer swore softly. "He—he's dead too!" he said shakily.

In fact, it was hard to see how the officer had been mistaken in the first place. No man would be sleeping that way. For the occupant of the bed lay in a twisted, contorted position also. One hand clutched his throat. The other had hooked around a pillow drawing it tightly against his side as if he had grabbed wildly at the nearest thing. The covers had been kicked down. One more roll would have taken the body off on the floor. And the mouth was open, the tongue protruding, the features congested with blood exactly as the steward's were.

Both men had died the same way.

All that Val got in a glance. And in the same moment he recognized the man on the bed with dumbfounded surprise. It was Carmody, the cheerful British book salesman!

Carmody's body bore no marks of violence either. No wounds. No blood. The death that had come to him as he lay in bed was the more ghastly and mysterious because of it.

"I'll get the captain and the ship's doctor here!" said the deck officer hoarsely. "Watch the cabin will you, please? Keep these people out." And as he stepped out, the young man closed the door as far as he could and said appealingly to the passengers gathering outside: "Please return to your cabins."

But by the excited remarks that drifted in, none of them paid any attention to the request. Val bent over the bed and touched the arm clutching the pillow. It was rigid. Frowning, he tested one of the legs. *Rigor mortis* had already set in. The flesh was cold.

It was not logical. He turned to the steward. That body was still flaccid, and the flesh was warm in comparison with the body on the bed.

Val fumbled for a cigarette, and then thought better of it and stood staring from one to the other. Both men had died in the same manner. One body was cold and set with *rigor mortis* and the other was warm and limp. It did not make sense.

There were cases, Val knew, where *rigor mortis* set in quickly. But this death that had come in the same manner to both men would not react so differently. There was only one conclusion to draw. The steward had been dead for half an hour—Carmody had been dead for hours.

And yet both had died in the same manner! Both had died horribly, yet without marks of violence! The door opened and Nancy slipped in and closed it behind her. "They're gabbling out there like a flock of excited chickens and roosters," she whispered. "What's the explanation of all this?"

Val shrugged helplessly. "I'm wondering." He told her what he had discovered. "D'you know this man?" he asked, jerking a thumb toward Carmody.

"No."

Carmody's coat and trousers were neatly hung up; his shoes were together on the floor, his shirt and tie and underwear on a chair as he had taken them off and arranged them. Under the bed was a gladstone bag, apparently undisturbed. Everything else in the cabin was in order.

The window was closed. A fragment of memory sent Val to the door. In the outside of the lock was a key with a small wooden handle to it—the steward's master key which he had apparently used to open the locked door.

Val shook his head in answer to the questions that were thrown at him by the people outside, and closed the door again.

"It's got me stumped," he confessed to Nancy. "There's a gruesome mystery here."

And when, a few moments later, the captain and the ship's surgeon entered, Val explained how he and Nancy happened to be in there, and pointed out what he had found.

Captain MacCreagh was a burly, weather-beaten man who still carried the dogged gruff manner of old sailing days. Doctor Simms, the ship's doctor, was short and slender, with a neat Vandyke and shell-rimmed glasses. He made a swift examination of the bodies, and then pulled the steward's outstretched arm in enough to let the door close tightly.

Captain MacCreagh had been watching impatiently. Now he demanded: "What do you think of it, doctor?"

The doctor polished his glasses with the middle of a handkerchief. "Mr. Easton is right," he said slowly. "These men did not die at the same time. That one on the bed has been dead for hours. And this steward died very recently."

"What killed them?"

The doctor fitted his glasses precisely on his nose, glanced at the bodies, and then at the captain. "I would suggest an autopsy, captain. Neither of them has been wounded in any manner, as far as I can see. They have all the appearance of dying from suffocation, yet there are no marks about their throats to indicate any violence which would cause that."

"In other words," the captain snorted, "you don't know anything about it."

The doctor was unruffled. "Precisely," he answered calmly. "I have never seen anything quite like it. The window is closed. The door was apparently locked, or the steward would not have used his key from the outside."

"That means," Val pointed out quickly, "that the steward was delivering an order to a man who had been dead in his locked cabin for hours."

The captain glared at him. "Then who ordered it?" he snapped.

"Perhaps the autopsy will show that," Val smiled.

"*Hmmmmph!*"

The captain stepped to the door, opened it, beckoned the deck officer, and growled: "Check up on the order that was brought here by this steward. Find what time it was given and who ordered it." And when he closed the door again, the captain said: "I wonder who this chap is."

Val mentioned what he knew of Carmody, which was little enough.

"We'll search his effects and see if there's anything more," the captain decided. "He ought to have his passport and some papers. His people will have to be notified by radio, and asked what to do with the body. Blast it, I hate a business like this! It's bad for a ship's reputation."

Val suggested: "Right now it's more to the point to find out what killed them."

"You talk like a detective."

"I'm not," said Val calmly, and let the matter rest there. But he and Nancy Fraser stayed as the captain and the doctor hurriedly searched the cabin.

They found a billfold and some small change, a pocketknife, a fountain-pen flashlight clipped inside the coat, passport book and several letters, a key that opened the locked gladstone.

The captain's thick fingers fumbled through the clothes inside. With a grunt he drew out an English army–model automatic pistol and two extra clips filled with cartridges.

"*Hmmmph,*" he said, tossing them on the bed. "What does he want to carry these for? Army model too. I guess that's all. No—what's this?"

The captain drew out a small thin black leather wallet. As he opened it a little silver badge dropped to the floor. He let it lie as he looked inside. The wallet was empty and he tossed it and the silver badge on the bed also.

"That's all," he said. "And not much. His address is on the passport. That will be enough for my purpose, I guess."

Val hardly heard him. His glance had riveted in startled surprise on the badge the captain had picked up. And Nancy Fraser's had done the same thing. Their eyes met for a moment and it would have taken many words to interpret the meaning that flashed between them.

For Carmody, the smiling book salesman, had been proved by that badge to be a Secret Service agent of the British government!

CHAPTER THREE

COLD STEEL—WELL DONE

There are times when terror can be quiet, insidious, hidden. So it was now. Murder had been done. Cold-blooded murder, unbelievably clever in its execution. How it had been done Val Easton did not pretend to know at the moment. Why, he might never know. But from the instant he was aware of Carmody's real mission, he knew it hooked up with Nancy Fraser. The man who had been lurking outside her cabin window was the one to explain this.

And if Carmody had been removed so skilfully and ruthlessly, why not Nancy Fraser and her companion? Why not himself, now that he was identified with them?

The deck officer returned.

"The coffee's easy to explain, sir," he told Captain MacCreagh. "This chap Carmody left an order with the steward to bring him coffee around midnight every night. Seems he was troubled with insomnia, or something like that. Couldn't sleep if he didn't have his coffee in the middle of the night."

"He'll have no trouble sleeping now," the captain remarked grimly. Doctor Simms fingered his Vandyke thoughtfully. "Queer. Mighty queer," he murmured, glancing at the bodies.

"What?" the captain rasped.

"This steward's death. Carmody had been dead for hours when the man arrived with the tray. The cabin was dark and the door was locked. It isn't reasonable to suppose that the killer remained in here all that time."

"No," admitted the captain testily. "He'd be a fool to do it."

"Exactly. The steward arrived, unlocked the door, stepped in—and died almost instantly. There was no struggle. There could not have been any noise, or someone out on the deck would have heard it. He simply died on the spot as Carmody had done. From the position of the body I would say he died as he was trying to back out the door."

"Dammit, man, something happened to him!" the captain snorted impatiently.

"I can't suggest what it was," Doctor Simms remarked coolly.

And there the matter rested.

While preparations were being made to put the bodies in the morgue, Val casually glanced at the papers which had been taken from Carmody's coat. He found nothing that might help him, and left the cabin a few moments later with Nancy Fraser.

They walked half the length of the deck before either spoke. Then Val said soberly: "It looks pretty bad."

"I think I'll stay up tonight," Nancy said calmly. "I don't want to be found that way in the morning."

Val shot her a quick look. "You think it touches you?"

"Don't you?" she countered.

"Perhaps. . . ."

Nancy said with conviction: "I'm not timid, but I have a hunch this is far worse than anything I've been up against before. This isn't wartime. Murder isn't on the cards now. An ordinary espionage agent wouldn't try a thing like that. It's creepy, ghastly."

"American and British agents are out," Val said soberly. "Carmody didn't seem especially dangerous to me. I think you're right. You've walked into something bigger than you think."

"Big enough for—murder," said Nancy slowly. She chuckled softly in a way that showed her nerve was unshaken, and laid a steady hand on Val's arm. "At least, my friend, we should be thankful we know as much as we do. We might have gone ahead blindly—and drawn the same thing. Tomorrow is another day. We'll see. . . ."

Tomorrow was another day, of bright sunshine over the fantastic, serrated skyline of New York, as the big liner plowed slowly up the bay.

During the night the ship had been in the grip of suppressed excitement. The bodies had been removed to the ship's morgue. The room had been locked and sealed. Wireless messages had crackled forth to shore. Passengers had been questioned, scrutinized. And at quarantine detectives hastily summoned from shore had come over the side with the ship reporters. Flashlight pictures of the cabin were taken: thumbprints were photographed. Passengers were diplomatically interrupted at their packing and last-minute preparations for going ashore, and questioned suavely. The newspapermen probed like hawks.

Val and Nancy were questioned by newspapermen and detectives. Their stories were brief and of little help. Of their business, or the man who had been lurking outside Nancy Fraser's cabin window nothing was said.

Carmody, it appeared, was a man who had little to do with anyone, outside of those he met at his meals. He had had no trouble with anyone, had no intimates.

Val himself had radioed Washington in code before daylight, giving such details as he knew. And Washington had replied in code. Val took the message to Nancy Fraser.

V EASTON
ON BOARD SS LAURENTIC
LONDON DISCLAIMS
KNOWLEDGE OF CARMODY OR
INTEREST IN HIM SAVE AS BRITISH
SUBJECT YOUR IDENTIFICATION
AS INTELLIGENCE AGENT
ERRONEOUS ON NO ACCOUNT
LET IT INTERFERE WITH MATTER
IN HAND WORK TOGETHER
UNTIL FURTHER INSTRUCTIONS
SIGNED GREGG

When Nancy had read the decoded words, Val tore the message into bits and dribbled them over the rail.

"Chalk up another puzzle on your list," he said drily. "If Carmody isn't a British agent, what is he? What was he doing with that badge? And why was he killed? It's more tangled than ever if we take that honor away from him."

"Could it be possible," Nancy suggested, "that London is pulling Gregg's leg? Won't admit Carmody's their man, for fear it might tip their hand on something they're anxious to keep hidden?"

"Quite possible. It's been done plenty of times before. Carmody's dead. They can't help him now. And again, they may have told the truth."

"The badge?"

"He might have found it."

Nancy tossed her head. "Badges like that aren't left lying around for people to find. What about his gun?"

"People carry guns."

"It's an official issue."

"Might have found it too," Val grinned.

"Your suggestions grow worse," Nancy told him.

Val lit a cigarette. "We're cleared on it, anyhow. Gregg seems a trifle annoyed. Suppose I pick your man up when he leaves the Customs and get in touch with you at your hotel? Give you a little leisure that way. I don't think we'll be held on board. They won't detain a shipload of people without evidence."

"That would be nice," Nancy nodded. "We'll go to the Blockman."

No one had shown any interest in them that morning. And yet Val could not shake off the feeling that he was being watched. He tried every trick he knew to prove it, and got nowhere. The feeling persisted, irritating him finally. Nerves, he told himself. And yet he knew it wasn't. They were both under silent, insidious scratiny, and there was nothing worse.

And the thought of Carmody horribly dead behind a locked door made things no better.

Val had been right about the ship's passengers. Among them were many influential people who could not even be considered as suspects. The men from shore were as baffled as the ship's company had been. They had no clues, no concrete suspicions. Names and addresses were taken, and other data, but nothing else was done. The debarkation was under way in full force shortly after the ship was moored in her berth.

Val had looked up Galbraith, studied the man from a distance. He was typically British in a quiet, unassuming way. A sparse, medium-built man in tweeds, with a long, pale, unsmiling face, a neatly trimmed mustache, an indifference to his surroundings that bespoke much travel. He conversed with no one, kept to himself. Carmody's death, of which Galbraith evidently knew, aroused no visible interest in the man. Val, following him that morning on a stroll around the deck, noticed that Galbraith did not even glance at the door of Carmody's cabin.

And Galbraith's manner when he left the ship was leisurely and indifferent. He went to the "G" section in the Customs line-up, stood by indifferently while his kit bags were examined, and then followed a porter and the bags to a taxi.

Val had managed to have a few words with the man in charge of his own luggage. His bags were mysteriously passed and whisked out of line. Val caught a taxi ahead of Galbraith. Outside the pier shed he ordered the driver to wait. A few moments later they were following Galbraith's cab.

Galbraith did not look back, seemed not to suspect he might be followed.

Val kept watch behind to see if any cab was noticeably following him. But in the crowded traffic it was almost a hopeless gesture.

Galbraith went directly to the Rosecrans, one of the big hotels overlooking Central Park from Fifty-ninth Street.

He entered the lobby behind his luggage in time to see Galbraith step into an elevator. The card registration system was in use at this hotel. There was no way of telling what room Galbraith had been given. Val smiled disarmingly at the clerk, and tried a random shot.

"My friend, Mr. Galbraith from London, told me on the boat he was going to register here. I'd like a room near him, if possible."

"Mr. Galbraith has just registered," the clerk replied. "Let's see—I can give you Room 717. That's just across the corridor from him. Mr. Galbraith is in 716."

"Excellent," Val nodded.

As soon as he was settled in his room he telephoned Nancy.

"Norah and I will come over there and register," Nancy said. "If he goes out, follow him. We must know whom he sees."

But Galbraith did not go out at first. He had a caller. Through his door, which had been left ajar an inch or so, Val saw a gray-clad back as the visitor was admitted to Galbraith's room. Just

a glimpse, and then the door closed on them as Galbraith said formally: "How do you do, Mr. Ramey?"

The two were closeted in Galbraith's room for half an hour. In that time Nancy Fraser and her companion registered and Nancy telephoned from their room on the third floor. Val told her of Galbraith's visitor, suggested she be ready to tail him when he left.

Val was sitting inside his door when Galbraith's visitor stepped out into the hall once more. He heard the man say unctuously: "Tomorrow night at Oakridge then. Follow those directions after you reach Washington and you can't miss it."

And the fleeting glimpse, through the cracked door showed a stocky, pasty-faced fellow, whose downsnapped hat brim shaded features that were as unctuous and oily as his voice had sounded. Before he was a dozen paces down the hall Val had closed the door and was at the telephone, calling Nancy's room. "All right—catch the next elevator," he rapped to her. "Blue suit, pudgy, pasty face, brim of gray hat snapped down."

"Right," said Nancy briefly and her receiver clicked.

Val was smiling thinly with satisfaction as he lighted a cigarette and resumed his watch at the door again. Galbraith's visitor would have a hard time shaking her. But as he conned over his one hasty glimpse of the fellow his smile faded to a thoughtful scowl. Ramey was a queer person to be calling on Sir Edward Lyne, to give Galbraith his right name. If long experience in judging people at a glance held good, Ramey was a shyster, tricky, smooth, untrustworthy.

Tomorrow night at Oakridge—near Washington.

What was behind that rendezvous which had been arranged?

Galbraith left his room shortly. He walked down Fifth Avenue and over to Times Square, slowly window shopping. He went to two of the Times Square newsreel theaters, window-shopped some more, dined leisurely and walked back to the hotel, with a leg weary Val Easton still within sight of him.

Val called Nancy Fraser's room when he got in. Norah Beamish answered instantly, and her voice was sharp with worry.

"You haven't seen Nancy?" she queried anxiously.

"No. Isn't she in?"

"I haven't heard from her since she went out this afternoon," Norah informed him. "Do you think something could have happened?"

"I doubt it," Val reassured her. "She'll show up in a little while. Have you eaten?"

"I had some food sent up," Norah told him. "I won't leave the room until I hear from her. She may telephone."

"If she does, let me know. And if she comes back have her telephone my room at once. I'll leave word at the desk if I go out."

Galbraith seemed set for the time being. Val hastily stripped, took a hot shower and dressed again. He found himself wondering about Nancy Fraser. Had something happened to her? She was the kind of girl who would take chances. Val found it impossible to forget those two still forms on the *Laurentic*, grim warning of the price of carelessness.

He had barely finished dressing when knuckles rapped sharply on the door. Val answered it with a feeling of relief. It must be Nancy, returned finally and come up for a word with him. He opened the door with a grin on his face.

And . . .

The grin faded to astonishment. A black-coated waiter confronted him, bearing a cloth-covered tray.

"You've made a mistake," Val told him. "I didn't order anything."

The waiter looked doubtful. "Mr. Easton, isn't it?"

"Yes."

"This is right then. A young lady telephoned down and said to bring this order to your room. It's for two. I believe she is supposed to share it also."

"Oh," said Val blankly. "All right, bring it in."

His reaction was pleasure. This was such a thing as Nancy Fraser would do. Thoughtful of her. Eat while they talked. She was back then, and everything was all right. And he wondered what news she was bringing.

The waiter had a small folding rack under his arm. Opening it, he set the tray carefully down. He was a swarthy, poker-faced man with powerful shoulders bulging inside his black jacket and wrists which protruded out of sleeves that were too short.

"The young lady said to cook the steak well done," he declared. "Will you see it now, sir?"

From the moment the fellow had entered the room, closing the door behind him, Val had been struggling with a feeling of bafflement. Something was out of place in this picture. Wouldn't Nancy have telephoned him, after all, as soon as she got in? And he hadn't been under the shower more than a few minutes. Hardly long enough to have a steak well cooked and a full meal sent up to the room after she returned.

And there was something else. . . .

Suddenly he got it. How the devil did the waiter know that the woman who ordered the dinner over the telephone was a young woman? He couldn't know.

And the man's coat was too small, his face was tanned where a man used to working indoors would be pale. And a degree of insolence had come into his manner. He leered at Val across the tray as he whisked the cloth away.

One look was enough to tell Val that his suspicions had been right. For the dishes that had obviously contained food a short while before were empty now, and in the midst of them lay a large flat automatic.

Val jumped for that gun instantly.

It was a long chance—and it failed. A muscular hand closed over the gun and its muzzle jerked up and met him.

Val stopped short, arms tensed at his sides. For a moment silence held the room, while Val's eyes locked with a pair of dead slate eyes which stared at him with a cold unwinking gaze. Politeness, mockery, pretense were gone now.

"Lift your hands!" the other ordered across the littered tray.

"What's the idea?" Val countered.

"Shut up! Don't argue! Put your hands up!" As he spoke the other stepped around to Val's side. The gun was steady in his hand and his manner was venomous. A slight foreign accent tinged his words.

Slowly Val raised his arms.

"Turn around!"

Val did that too. And a second later steel crashed against the side of his head brutally. Everything went blank, black. He pitched forward to the floor.

CHAPTER FOUR

THE HOLLOW NEEDLE

The light overhead was still burning brightly when Val's eyes opened again. He was stupid for a moment, senses whirling, pain roiling in his head. He couldn't think what it was all about.

And then he remembered. The waiter—the cloth-covered tray—the gun—the stunning blow against his head. . . .

The tray was still sitting on the rack in the center of the floor before him, the white cloth tossed on the floor and the soiled dishes mocking him.

The waiter and his gun were gone. The room was silent, deserted.

And there by the side of the bed Val sat in the straight-backed chair, tied hand and foot with lengths of fine silk cord.

His ankles were fastened to the legs of the chair and his arms were tied behind it. Silk cord was lashed about his wrists so tightly the circulation had been cut off. His hands were numb. Cloth had been stuffed into his mouth and tied in place by a towel, making an extremely uncomfortable but highly efficient gag.

He was helpless, miserable and impotent.

As his predicament burst over him, Val's first reaction was a struggle to free himself. He quickly saw it was impossible. He couldn't rub the gag out of his mouth and call for help. Over his shoulder he saw that the window had been closed and the shade pulled down.

The phone was on the other side of the bed. By the side of the door was the bell button that would quickly bring help. Only a few feet away—and yet it might have been as many miles.

Val raged at himself for a moment. He had been a fool to be caught off guard that way. And yet it had been smooth work, well planned and executed. Whoever had done it had known about his connection with Nancy Fraser; had known that Nancy was out and might be back any time.

Only one man could have known that—the one who had been watching them on the *Laurentic*.

What was the reason for it? Not Nancy. She was out of the hotel. Hardly Norah Beamish, on a lower floor. Galbraith then! Galbraith across the hall, where Val's door commanded his, where no move could have been made without danger of interruption.

He didn't know how long he had been tied here in the chair before regaining consciousness. It might have been minutes, or an hour or more.

In that time what had happened to Galbraith?

Val eyed the telephone narrowly. If he could inch the chair around to it he might tip the phone over. Using his toes and throwing the weight of his body at the same time he managed to shift the chair inch by inch. But it was slow, hard work. Perspiration broke out on his forehead.

And in the midst of that the telephone suddenly buzzed.

Val cursed behind his gag. That was Nancy or Norah. And he couldn't answer. It was maddening to know help was so near and be unable to summon it.

The telephone buzzed again and again and then stopped. He hadn't covered a quarter of the distance to the instrument. Stubbornly Val kept on.

And then a few minutes later a key grated suddenly in the door. A bare-headed, broad-shouldered stranger stepped into the room, took one look and uttered in a startled voice: "Hey—what's this?"

From behind his back Nancy Fraser darted into the room. Relief broke over her face as she saw Val staring mutely at her. With a swift little rush she reached his side, snatched the towel down and pulled the wadded cloth out of his mouth.

"Thanks," Val mumbled through cramped lips.

"Who did this?" Nancy asked tensely.

"Fellow disguised as a waiter. Get across hall and see if Galbraith's all right. I think they got me out of the way because of him."

"This looks mighty funny to me," the broad-shouldered stranger said ponderously. "You hurt, buddy?"

Val had him placed by now. A hotel detective, already muddled, and uncertain about everything.

"I telephoned as soon as I got in," Nancy said swiftly. "When you didn't answer I queried the desk and they said you hadn't left any word there. I suspected something was wrong, so I got the hotel detective to come up here with me and unlock your door."

Nancy whirled around on the detective. "Cut him loose from there!" she snapped. "Where's your master key?"

The master key was produced with a puzzled frown. Nancy snatched it and made for the door. "Hey, where you going with that?" the detective protested.

But Nancy whirled out of the room without answering either of them. The detective turned after her in indecision. "Is that dame gone nutty?" he uttered plaintively.

"Cut these damn ropes!" Val snarled. "Don't stand there like a lunkhead! Get me out of this chair!"

The fierce command in his voice brought the desired result. The detective's thick fingers fumbled open a small pocketknife, and he hacked at the cords. Val was chafing his wrists and wringing circulation back in them as the detective stooped over and slashed at the cords around his ankles.

Val staggered to his feet.

From across the hall keened a cry of distress that broke off sharply in a choked gasp. Nancy's voice!

Val plunged for the doorway without stopping for the gun in his bag. Galbraith's door was standing ajar. He crashed it open with his shoulder and plunged into the room—into a scene of confusion and violence.

The place had been looted hurriedly. Bureau drawers were out and their contents tossed heedlessly on the floor. Bags had been slit open with a sharp knife and searched hastily. The closet door was open, the bed turned down. And Galbraith's body lay huddled in the center of the floor.

All that went unheeded. For before him Nancy was fighting off a tall, stooped, black-caped figure which clutched her throat with one long talonlike hand as it tried to wrench its other hand from Nancy's desperate grip.

They staggered around as Val entered the room.

A pale, ghastly, cadaverous face turned toward Val. He was aware of a parted, writhing mouth, of blazing, green-flecked eyes, of teeth that showed momentarily like fangs.

It was the face of a monster, a fiend, lashed by murderous fury, indescribably venomous, vicious, dangerous. Some horrible fate had been in store for Nancy. The hand she clutched so desperately held no gun, no knife, no club. Its talonlike fingers were tensed about the small, gleaming barrel of a doctor's hypodermic. And the long sharp needle was bending in toward her wrist with all the shuddery menace of a deadly serpent's fang.

As the door slammed shut behind Val he threw himself at that sinister black-caped figure. A swift turn brought Nancy between them. She was hurled violently back, her grip tearing away.

Val's arm saved her from a bad fall.

Behind him the house detective hammered violently on the door, bawling: "Open up, inside there!"

"Look out!" Nancy gasped warningly. "He'll kill you!"

Her words were too late. A hand plunged under the black cape as its wearer backed toward the open window. It came out with something that looked like a small, shiny metal fountain pen. But the instant he saw it leveling at them Val knew better.

He tried to shove Nancy behind him, and was too late. There was a dull *pop*. A whitish ball of vapor leaped at them, expanded rapidly, enveloped them. . . .

And suddenly they were blinded with tears, coughing, choking, sneezing and fighting for breath. Helpless, Val backed toward the door, sweeping Nancy with him when his arm touched hers. He was thinking of that vicious hypodermic needle and the man who wielded it. They were at his mercy now.

It had been long since Val Easton had known such fear. And it was for Nancy Fraser, not himself. When the tear gas cleared out of the room, would she be stretched out there on the floor also?

The door was shaking before the assault of the house detective. The commands to open up were growing loud and furious. The tumult guided Val to the door. That dick had a gun. His hand found the knob. And still nothing had happened to him as he turned that knob. For some reason the black-caped attacker was holding back.

The door was shoved in violently against him, knocking him off balance.

"By God, what's the idea of all—" the house man bawled as he charged in, breaking off into a fit of sneezing and choking before he could finish the question.

———

Val was mopping at his streaming eyes with his handkerchief, trying to see. The dick blundered into him. The hard muzzle of a gun poked roughly into his ribs.

"Watch that gun, you big ox!" Val yelled. "You'll shoot the wrong person!"

The gun was pulled away. "Come out in the hall!" Nancy choked. Val stumbled out after her. And there, away from the insidious gas, they gained a measure of control and sight.

The house dick was standing in the doorway, mopping at his eyes and swearing under his breath. Peering blearily at Val, he raved: "Did you shoot that stuff off?"

"Do I look like it?" Val retorted. "Is that fellow in the room yet?"

"What fellow?"

"Tall chap with a black cape."

Peering through the doorway, the dick said angrily: "There ain't no one in there! Hell—is that him on the floor?"

But it was Galbraith's body he spoke of. It had not moved since Val first saw it. Air was pouring through the doorway, driving the last of the gas out the window. Wiping his eyes and peering as best he could, Val edged into the room. The tall, black-caped figure had vanished!

From nearby rooms other guests had poured out into the corridor, gathering around the door now. A woman caught sight of Galbraith's body on the floor and gave a stifled cry.

"Get back, you folks!" the house man ordered through his teeth.

Val looked out at them. "Did anyone escape from this room?" he demanded.

One of the men said flatly: "I was looking when the door was opened. You two men and the young lady were the only ones who came out. What happened?"

Val hurried over to the window without answering. It was open, and when he looked out he saw four stories below the dark roof of an adjoining building.

It was to this window that Nancy Fraser's assailant had been backing when Val last saw him. He hadn't gone out into the hall. He wasn't here in the room. He must have gone out of the window.

But the sheer side of the tall building offered no refuge. There was no ledge by which he could have gained an adjoining window. No fire escape near. No ladder of any kind, up or down. And yet it was the only way he could have left the room. Val whirled on the house man, jerking a thumb at Galbraith's body as he did so.

"The man who did that went out the window!" he rapped out. "He may have fallen. I can't see the roof down there very well. Better search it and the building underneath. And the hotel here. He was tall, thin, wore a black cape and dark suit."

So fast and furious had everything happened that this was the first chance for more than a fleeting look at Galbraith. Val dropped to his knees beside the motionless body as he spoke.

Galbraith lay on his face, one arm under his head, the other thrown out awkwardly. He was dreadfully still and limp. Had no pulse in neck or wrist. And as Val lowered the lifeless wrist, his gaze was caught by a tiny smear of blood just below the coat sleeve.

Taking care not to disarrange the body before the medical examiner viewed it, he bent over and scrutinized the spot closely. Skin and flesh had been punctured by a needlelike instrument. A drop or two of blood had welled out before the wound closed. An area of flesh around the spot, no larger than a dime, was discolored slightly. That was all. And yet Val shivered as he rose to his feet, rubbing his hands slowly together. He was thinking of that glistening hypodermic needle in those talonlike hands . . .

The hotel dick was staring at him with wide eyes. "Is he dead?" he queried, nodding at the body.

"Very," Val answered drily. "Better call the police. And then get down after that man!"

The detective had closed the door against the curious in the hall. He stepped to the telephone, called headquarters, and reported the matter. And then swung around and glowered at Val and Nancy.

"I didn't see anyone else in here," he said deliberately. "I'll just wait here with you two until the coppers come."

CHAPTER FIVE

THE BLACK DOCTOR

It took Val a moment to realize that he and Nancy Fraser were under suspicion. And when he did a wave of anger rushed through him.

"You fool!" he said crisply. "Can't you see we didn't have anything to do with this? I was tied up in the other room, and Miss Fraser was only in here a few seconds. You heard her cry out, didn't you? And you got a dose of the gas that chap left!"

"No one could have got out of here," was the stubborn answer. "If there was a guy, he jumped, and he's down there on the roof dead. And if there wasn't, you two can explain it to the cops. Better sit down there on the bed an' make yourselves comfortable."

Nancy Fraser met Val's angry glance with a philosophical shrug. "He's gone by now, anyway," she said. "We might as well make the best of it. I've got something to tell you."

While talking with the detective, Val had been conning over something else in the back of his mind. That pale, furious face with the blazing, green-flecked eyes had been strangely familiar. He was certain he had not seen the man before, and equally certain he knew something about him.

Nancy's face was pale from the shock she had just experienced, but her voice was steady. "That man," she said under her breath. "Did you ever see him before?"

"No. But I've a feeling that I should have," Val confessed.

"I saw him once in Switzerland," Nancy declared. "He was pointed out to me in Geneva. That was Carl Zaken, better known as the Black Doctor."

"Good God—the Black Doctor?"

"Yes!"

And neither of them needed to say any more.

Through the shady, secret channels of international espionage, tales of Carl Zaken, the Black Doctor, seeped like fantastic nightmares. He was in the way of becoming a legend to those who dealt in such matters. There were men willing to swear that no such person existed, but they did not know the facts.

No country claimed the Black Doctor, and he served none more than momentarily. Master spy, incredibly clever, cold-blooded, ruthless, a wizard at disguise, the Black Doctor gave orders to a wide-flung web of desperate characters. That much was definitely known. How many people received those sinister orders, only the Black Doctor himself knew.

At times he worked alone, and at others as many as a score had helped him. His influence was like an evil miasma. When murder suited his ends, he killed with technical skill. If torture would help, he used torture with all the fiendishness of expert medical training. He was an adept at languages and disguise. And his favorite role was that of a doctor, friend of man and trusted by everyone. For, so rumor had it, Carl Zaken had once been a doctor.

He dealt in information for the most part, stopping at nothing to get what he wanted, and selling the results to the highest bidder if he could not use them better himself.

"Are you certain he was the Black Doctor?" Val urged in amazement.

"The man who pointed him out had been caught by the Black Doctor once. He'd never forget him, and warned me never to. We only caught a glimpse of him, but I marked that face for good. This was the man." Nancy smiled wryly. "And I had to meet him without a gun."

"What happened?"

Nancy gave a little shudder. "He jumped at me just as soon as I slipped through the door. I caught one glimpse of his face and that hypodermic in his hand, and knew what I was up against. I tried to scream for you, and he caught me by the throat. All I could do was try and keep that needle away. There was murder in his face. It—it was ghastly."

"And a good thing you dodged it," Val said soberly. "Galbraith evidently didn't."

"Was that what killed him?"

"Needle puncture in the wrist. If he'd had time, he'd probably have cleaned the smear of blood away, and there would have been another mystery for the police to solve."

"You think he was on the ship?"

"Who else?"

"But why kill that poor devil, Carmody?" Nancy asked.

"Ask the Black Doctor. He must have a good reason. He's after something."

"What?"

"God knows. Galbraith here knew—and he's dead."

"Do you think he got it?"

"He tried hard enough," Val said, looking around the looted room. "I don't know. Evidently he was still busy when you walked in on him." Val's jaw set. "He killed that chap on the boat and Galbraith here in cold blood. It wasn't a question of putting him out of the way while he searched the room. He simply slaughtered him and then went about his business. Evidently came all ready to kill."

"Was he the man who tied you up?"

"No. Must have been one of his men. And clever work it was. The fellow came to the door disguised as a waiter, saying he had brought a meal you had ordered for us. I let him in without thinking, and when I did tumble that something was wrong it was too late. He had a gun on me then. Knocked me out and trussed me up."

"I can't understand why they didn't kill you," Nancy said. "It would have been easy enough."

Val rubbed his forehead and shook his head. "Lord knows," he admitted. "It would have been easy enough all right."

They were silent for a moment.

"That pseudo waiter must have left a trail around the hotel here some place," Nancy muttered.

"I'm not worrying about him," Val shrugged. "I'm wondering what this is all about. Why kill Galbraith and search his room here? He could have done it just as easily on the boat. Even the Black Doctor doesn't go around killing people for the fun of it. He could have left Galbraith alive just as well as he did me, if he had only wanted to look through his things. What about that chap you followed? He had evidently made a date to see Galbraith somewhere near Washington tomorrow. He was an oily-looking bird."

"Wasn't he?" Nancy agreed. "And a suspicious one, too. I think he was afraid someone might be following him. He tried all the tricks to shake anyone off."

"D'you think he saw you?"

Nancy rubbed the side of her nose carelessly and shrugged. "I've cut my teeth at that sort of thing. I'm pretty sure he didn't see me. After riding around town, taking the subway, ducking into a movie and out a side exit right away, he finally went into a telegraph office and sent a wire."

"Who to?"

"I didn't have a chance to find out. I wanted to see what else he did."

"The little bloodhound." Val grinned. "Did you?"

"I did. He popped into a telephone booth in a cigar store, and then took the elevated to Battery Park and went through the Aquarium."

"What?"

"'Pon honor. He looked at all the little fishes like he was going into his second childhood. And then met a man and woman back in one of the dark corners and talked at least fifteen minutes with them."

"What did they look like?"

"It was shadowy where they were standing," Nancy said. "I couldn't see them well. And my man left first. I had to tag him. He chivvied back uptown on the 'El' again, got off at Forty-second Street, hailed a taxi—and I lost him there. I couldn't get another cab quick enough. Any other time there would have been a dozen on hand."

"It doesn't matter. He's going to Washington."

Nancy arched a delicate eyebrow. "How do you know?"

Before Val could reply the door burst open and admitted the hotel manager, patrolmen, and detectives. The law took charge of the situation; and the ponderous house detective stated his case flatly.

"That lady there," waving his hand at Nancy, "comes down and says will I come up and open a door for her. She thinks maybe there's trouble. And when I do that gentleman is tied up in a chair. While I'm cuttin' him loose she takes my key an' runs into this room. He follows her an' they slam the door in my face. I don't know what happened in here, but when they opened the door the room was full of tear gas an' that body was on the floor. They tried to tell me there was another guy in here who knocked him off, but I didn't see no one. There wasn't no way he could have gotten out. So when they tried to run me off the scene after this guy they claim was in here, I call headquarters an' sit on the lid."

Though no direct charge was made, the house detective's story was damning as he told it.

A brusk, lantern-jawed detective seemed to be in charge of things. He had examined the body and made a quick survey of the room while the house man talked. Now he stepped to the window, looked out, and turned on Val and Nancy.

"No one could have gotten out that window!" he rasped at them. "What's the straight of this?"

"What's your name?" Val asked coolly.

"I'm Lieutenant Ives of the homicide squad. And since this is murder I warn you to make your statements correct."

"Step into the bathroom with me, Lieutenant Ives," Val requested curtly.

Ives hesitated, fingered his lantern jaw, and then said gruffly: "All right, if it'll make you feel any better."

Val closed the door behind them and met Ives's scowl with an icy stare.

"I didn't bother to reason with that addle-pated fool who suspected us," he said icily. "I'm going to tell you what happened; and then I want to get away as quickly as possible. You can check us at Washington, of course."

Val palmed a small badge for Ives to see. The detective took one look at it and whistled softly. His manner changed abruptly to fraternal courtesy.

"I couldn't know," he apologized. "What's the lowdown on all this?"

Val told him what had happened.

"What's your interest in this fellow who got bumped off?" Ives asked when he finished.

"That doesn't matter," Val refused him. "A lot of things don't matter right now. The man who killed him went out the window. May have gone up a rope ladder to a window above, or slid down a rope to that roof below."

"Where's the rope then?" Ives demanded skeptically.

"A hard flip from below on the rope would have loosened the hook over the window. You may find marks on the sill made by a hook. I'd suggest you try and trace him, and look over this hotel for a check on the pseudo waiter who took me in."

"I don't need to," Ives commented. "Coming up in the elevator the manager told me they had just found a waiter who had taken a meal up to Room 701 and hadn't returned. They found him tied up and minus his coat. The tray and dishes he had brought up were gone also. The fellow who had occupied the room had checked out ten minutes before. All the waiter could say was that as soon as he brought the tray into the room he was knocked out, and when he came to, stuffed under the bed, two men were eating the meal as if he wasn't there. He didn't get a look at them."

Val thought with unwilling admiration that the Black Doctor would have the nerve to stop and eat part of the meal, which had evidently been ordered to get the waiter and tray where they could be used. But he said nothing of that. Too much information might throw obstructions in their way. For there was small doubt in Val's mind now that this murder of Galbraith was only a move in another, bigger game that the Black Doctor was playing. And it was that game in which he was most concerned. Time enough when it was uncovered to think about bringing the Black Doctor to book for murder.

Ives took out a little black book and wrote down the description of the Black Doctor and the man who had impersonated the waiter. He asked for more information. Val referred him to Washington. Ives gave up with a shrug.

"I don't know what it's all about," he confessed. "You evidently know what you're doing. I'll call headquarters and they can let the commissioner decide what to do."

"Tell him to get in touch with Washington at once," Val ordered. "We've got work to do. Later on we can return for testimony."

"It's unusual," Ives warned.

"Washington will settle it."

And Washington did settle it in a bit less than an hour, such was the power of that secret arm of the government which Nancy Fraser and Val Easton represented.

Neither of them knew exactly what had flashed back and forth over the wires; but Ives himself, still at the hotel, answered a telephone call, and told Val with a wry grin: "I guess you two have got something on the ball all right. Orders from the commissioner himself are to let you go and forget about you for the time being. So long—and luck to you."

"We'll probably need it," Val said.

Val regarded the penciled message which he had obtained from the manager of the telegraph office. It had taken pressure to get a look at it against all rules of the company. But it told him what he wanted to know.

J. B. Tillson,
Oakridge Manor,
Hartsville, Virginia.
Party arriving tomorrow.
Signed, Ramey.

So Galbraith had intended to meet Ramey at Oakridge. Hartsville, Virginia, was close to Washington. The answer to everything must center there.

He returned to the hotel and looked in at Nancy Fraser's room on the way to his own.

"Pack up," he said with a grin. "There's just time to catch the next plane to Washington."

Norah Beamish shifted her ample form on the edge of the bed and said tartly: "Nancy needs a good night's rest. She's been through an ordeal, young man."

"That's right," Val said contritely. "Get your rest then and I'll run along."

Nancy had just been powdering her nose when Val stepped in, and a nice nose it was too, he noted. She tossed the powder puff on the dresser and stretched slender arms over her head, yawning luxuriously like a lazy cat.

"Nonsense," she said cheerfully. "I'm just getting warmed up. You must stay here and get the rest and we'll run on."

Norah Beamish charged to her feet like a formidable battle cruiser getting under way.

"Leave me here?" she snorted. "My great aunt's transformation you will! Do I look like an old grandma who needs to be parked in the corner? The idea! I won't have it! Where're those bags, Nancy? Get packed, young man! We'll be ready!"

Though Nancy had disavowed fatigue, when the wide-winged monoplane swept off the lighted landing field with a roaring rush, climbed high, and swiftly dropped the blazing panorama of lights that were New York back over the horizon, she promptly closed her eyes.

Norah Beamish sat behind her with a defiant tilt to her chin. When Val looked at her he received a visible sniff. Plainly Norah held him responsible for the suggestion that she be left behind to take her case.

Val grinned, and then glanced across the aisle at the smooth curve of Nancy's throat. Her eyelids lifted and she smiled lazily at him, and then they closed and she seemed to doze.

What a girl, Val thought. Nerves like steel, inexhaustible energy, ready to tackle anything. She had come through an ordeal that would have reduced most women to nervous hysteria. And now, knowing that they were pitting their wits against Carl Zaken, the dreaded Black Doctor, she was dozing as peacefully as an untroubled child.

He felt a slight tightening of his throat as he remembered again that heart-stopping moment when death had grazed her wrist. And hard on the heels of that Val felt a cold chill as he wondered what lay ahead for her before this business was done.

The Black Doctor had not earned his reputation without cause; and somewhere at this very moment he was moving craftily through the mystifying web he was spinning about them.

CHAPTER SIX

MYSTERY AT OAKRIDGE MANOR

By fast passenger plane the service from New York to Washington is a matter of less than two hours air time. Considerably less. And if a long-distance telephone call has been made from the New York airport, resulting in a speedy automobile waiting at the Washington airport, the time elapsed from Central Park to upper Pennsylvania Avenue is phenomenally low.

It lacked five minutes to midnight when Val, Nancy Fraser, and Nora Beamish stepped into that sedan and were gruffly greeted by the heavy-set, saturine man behind the wheel. It was Gregg himself, as unknown and overlooked by the world as were the actions of that subtle force which he controlled.

"You people are playing hob with my sleep!" Gregg snarled as he sent the car through the gears with a rush and they whirled off the air field. "One would think I had nothing to do but stay up nights and nurse a lot of agents joyriding around the world. Let's have the straight of all this. I couldn't make heads or tails of your gabble over long distance a while ago, Easton."

That was Gregg's way, and no one who took his orders paid any attention to it for very long. Behind it Gregg was fanatically on the job, as witness his presence here tonight, when he could have remained in bed and sent any of a score of men in his place. His presence too, was testimony of the importance he placed on the curt reference to the Black Doctor that Val had made over long distance.

Val sketched what had happened as they rolled swiftly toward the heart of the city, with the slim white-lighted shaft of the Washington Monument spearing the heavens to their left, and the flood-lighted dome of the Capitol ballooning toward the sky off to their right.

Gregg sucked a cigar and listened closely, grunting to himself now and then. At the end he blew his horn viciously at another car that seemed about to pass in front of them, flicked cigar ash out the car window, and spoke.

"Carl Zaken, eh? I'd give my liver to get him. He's caused me trouble before. Get this—there'll be hell and furies over this business. Two English citizens murdered, one on a ship flying the United States flag, and the other in New York. We can't pretend to know much about it or the fact that we've been watching one of their men will be known. Can't have that. If they catch on we're suspicions of this chap who called himself Galbraith, they'll start hunting for the source of our information. It'll be embarrassing. Blast it!"

"What was Galbraith after?" Val asked bluntly.

"Don't know," Gregg said equally bluntly. "We got a tip that something unusual was in the air, and a man was being sent over here *sub rosa* empowered to spend as high as a million pounds for something. That's a hell of a lot of money, if you'll excuse my English, ladies."

"Hmmmph!" Norah snapped from the back seat beside Nancy. "I can do better than that, Jim Gregg, as you well know. Go right ahead."

Val grinned in the darkness, remembering that Nancy had said Norah Beamish had once been Gregg's private secretary.

"Huh? Er—all right," said Gregg, thrown off his stride for a moment. "As I was saying, I cabled Miss Fraser to pick this man up and see what he did. And all this other has broken out of a clear sky. It's hard to tell what to make of it."

"I'd do a lot for a million pounds," Norah observed acidly. "Doubtless this Zaken would do the same. Has that occurred to you?"

"Galbraith didn't have a million pounds on him!" Gregg snapped. "He was only empowered to offer it."

"If you were to offer me a million pounds—" Norah said, undaunted.

"I wouldn't," Gregg growled. "But I'll offer you a suggestion. Let Easton give me his views on the matter."

"Well, I like that!" Norah commented indignantly. "Ouch, Nancy, stop poking me with your elbow."

The silence was thick for a moment as Gregg restrained himself with an effort. "Norah Beamish," he said ominously, "pipe down."

"Oh, all, right," Norah said sulkily.

A match flare lighted Val's red face as he held the flame to a cigarette. "Zaken is after that money," he stated, tossing the match out the window. "If it's worth that to someone else, it's worth it to him. He can cash in on it."

"If he gets it you're all fired," Gregg said calmly. "This thing is getting out of hand. I want Zaken in custody before he gets a chance to do any more harm, and I want to know what Galbraith was after over here. Those two murders will go unsolved until we have all that. There'll be complications. You say you haven't the slightest idea what happened to Zaken?"

"He vanished out of the room," Val said slowly. "His man had the room directly above that. By the time I could do anything it was too late. Both were gone."

Val paused and looked out of the window.

"Yes?" Gregg urged.

"I don't know what Zaken was after in Galbraith's room," Val admitted, looking at him. "Or why he killed Galbraith. But I've got a good hunch that wherever Galbraith was heading for, we can expect Zaken to appear, sooner or later. He gained no money immediately by killing Galbraith. And, from everything I've ever heard about the fellow, he never kills unless there's a good reason for it."

"Where does that get you?" Gregg countered impatiently.

"I know where Galbraith was going."

"Ahhhh—you do?" Gregg suddenly chuckled and laid an approving hand on Val's arm. "I knew you wouldn't let them run you out on the end of a limb and saw it off. Now, let's have the rest of it."

Val remembered Norah Beamish sitting quietly in the back seat and letting him talk. "This isn't really my case," he reminded. "Miss Fraser may like to handle it her own way."

"Ridiculous!" Nancy jeered. "The thing had gotten out of my hands. Where would I be if you hadn't barged into Galbraith's room just in time? I'm helping you now, and bother all the modesty."

"She's right. Let's have it," Gregg agreed.

"I don't know where this Ramey comes in, with his dodging around New York, or what to think of the couple he talked to," Val admitted. "But the next move seems to be at Oakridge Manor. I came down here tonight as quick as possible to do that. If Zaken shows up there we'll collar him and get the truth."

"Why all the rush, if you're going out there tomorrow?" Gregg queried irritably. "You could have let me sleep."

"Going out tonight," Val told him. "It's only about an hour's drive. We'll stage an auto breakdown and go up to the house in search of a telephone. Or I'll say that Galbraith was found dead in New York with that address in his pocket, and pass as a newspaperman asking for information. And in the morning you can post men around the place, working with the information I get tonight."

Gregg considered. "Good enough," he decided. "But don't mention Galbraith. Let them expect him. Just look around the place and play dumb. It ought to work. They'll know nothing about what happened in New York tonight, of course."

They had traversed the long length of Pennsylvania Avenue as they talked. Gregg turned in to the curb at Fourteenth and the Avenue, opened the door and stepped out.

"You might as well take this car," he said. "I'll taxi home and get some sleep. I'll take you with me, Norah. You're probably tired out."

"You will not, Jim Gregg," Norah said defiantly. "Don't think because you O.K. my pay check you can order me around all the time. I'm going out there with Nancy. If there're any car breakdowns and shenanigans I'll fit right into the picture as the helpless mother—what are you laughing at?"

"At the idea of anyone thinking of you as helpless!" Gregg choked. "God, help the people at the Manor! They don't know what's landing on their doorstep. And I warn you, Norah, if you bungle anything you'll come back in the office and take dictation. Good night." And Gregg departed hastily, still shaking with laughter.

"The old hyena!" Norah said heatedly, glaring out the window. "I'll make him sweat for that."

Hartsville was a small suburban town south of Washington, some thirty minutes of fast driving. Houses were dark and wanly lighted streets deserted. But a gas station and a drugstore were still open for business. In the drugstore Val asked casually as he bought a package of cigarettes: "Know of a place around here called Oakridge Manor?"

"Sure," was the prompt reply. "That's the old Mason place out on the river road. Fellow by the name of Long bought it a few years back and tacked that name on it."

"What's he like?"

"Don't see much of him," said the druggist as he rang up the sale. "Queer sort of man, I hear. Don't welcome visitors. And when people want to be let alone around here, folks most generally let 'em alone."

"How do you get there?"

"Six miles out on the highway, and you turn to the left. It's about three miles down the river road, I reckon. Kind of lonesome country back in there, although the road is used a heap. Long's land backs up clear to the Potomac. You'll see a sign over his gate."

Val thanked the man and went back to the car. As soon as they got away from the little village it became apparent that the druggist had not been wrong when he had described the country as lonesome.

Mist was rising off the river, swirling across the stabbing headlight beams in ghostly streamers. The damp smell of the river bottoms off to the left of the road poured in through the car windows. Great oaks and poplars grew alongside the road, and they passed many stretches of scrub-pine woodland. Now and then a small house was visible behind a whitewashed picket fence, but for the most part the country seemed deserted.

Norah Beamish said flatly: "I don't like this country. It gives me the creeps. I didn't know you could get this wild so close to Washington."

"You should have stayed in the city and gone to sleep," said Val.

It was the wrong thing to say. "Young man, I know my business!" Norah crushed him. "I may have the creeps, but I'm as good as any man we'll find in this section. Nancy, give me a cigarette."

A match flared; and Norah Beamish had taken perhaps half a dozen puffs from her cigarette when a stout wire fence on the left of the road suddenly gave way to massive stone gate posts with a wooden arch between them. A lettered sign hanging from the arch said: OAKRIDGE MANOR.

Val cut the ignition and brought the car to a stop at the side of the road.

"Here we are," he said. In the sudden silence which wrapped them his voice sounded with startling clarity.

Nancy chuckled softly. "Broken down and everything. And where is the house?"

The fog was thicker, if anything, rolling its damp breath through the open car window at Val's side, swirling through the yellow glare of the headlights like endless tenuous tentacles. The distant boom of frogs pulsed dismally on the night. It was a lonely, deserted spot.

Norah Beamish said with conviction: "Anyone who would park himself out in a place like this for very long must be a trifle addled. If anybody had told me this morning on the ship that I'd be here tonight, I'd have hooted them down."

Nevertheless she followed Nancy with alacrity when Val stepped out and opened the rear door.

"You can wait in the car," Val told her.

"Young man," Norah answered majestically, "if Jim Gregg can't tell me what to do, it's useless for you to try. I came here to play a helpless old mother and I'm going to hobble up to that house and play her. Save your breath."

"Hobble on," Val surrendered. "Let's go. I can't see the house, but it must be back there somewhere."

"Are you taking a gun?" Nancy questioned.

"Hardly need one," Val assured her. "After all, we can't possibly be suspected. And with—er—a helpless mother along, we'll fit the part perfectly."

"Nancy shan't stir one step from this car without a gun in the party," Norah said firmly. "She's a helpless girl—and I don't like the looks of this place. It gives me the creeps."

"A gun it'll be then," Val agreed cheerfully. He leaned in the car, pulled his bag out from their luggage, and slipped his automatic in his pocket. On second thought he added the flashlight he always carried somewhere in his effects.

They walked back to the gate and headed along the driveway into the fog. The hoarse booming of the frogs gradually grew louder, and by that Val knew they were approaching the river. Huge old trees lined the driveway, stretching heavy branches out over their heads. Once the fog parted briefly and he caught sight of a gibbous moon hanging high in the sky. But for the most part they walked blindly in the mist, which blotted and enfeebled the beam of his flashlight.

And the walk seemed endless.

"I don't believe there's a house around here," Norah panted finally. And then said something not entirely ladylike as her heel turned on a stone and she lurched against Val. "Drat it!" she grumbled. "I should have put on hunting boots!"

Val himself was beginning to wonder how much farther they would have to walk. This estate of Oakridge Manor seemed to be endless. The drive made several turns, seeming to run almost in the shape of a sprawling "S." He judged the house was invisible from the road. And then without warning a dark automobile appeared before them; and beyond it the lighted windows of a large house emitted a sickly glow through the mist.

"Thank heavens we won't have to wake them up," Norah remarked with relief.

Val turned the flash into the machine. It was empty; and bore D.C. license plates. Oakridge Manor, he judged, was having visitors this night. All the better.

The drive widened into a big circle in front of the house, with a flower bed in the center, and they could make out dimly the looming bulk of a large Colonial mansion, with a wing at each end. They started around the flower bed; and suddenly Norah stumbled again, and gasped sharply as she jumped quickly aside.

"What is this?"

Val's light was on it a moment later—a huge Great Dane dog lying dead on the driveway with a trickle of blood staining the ground in front of its chest. It had been shot, and had not been dead long as Val discovered when he touched it with his foot.

The sight shocked them out of their calm. "I don't like this!" Nancy whispered sharply.

"I'd like to get my hands on the man who killed that beautiful animal!" Norah exclaimed indignantly under her breath. "Look at him—poor thing!"

Val looked at the house instead. Looked warily. Of a sudden the drear silence had taken on an ominous quality. He couldn't say why. After all, there were a score of reasons why the dog might have been killed. It might have been a strange dog, for instance, trespassing in some way. But nevertheless the feeling persisted.

"Perhaps you two had better go back to the car," he suggested under his breath.

"We'll stick together," Nancy told him quietly.

"I'm not afraid!" Norah Beamish insisted defiantly. "It takes more than a dead dog to upset me. Go on."

Val hesitated, and then against his better judgment led the way to the front door. It was made of heavy planks, with small diamond-shaped panes of leaded glass at the top. Curtains inside cut off the view beyond. He found a big wrought-iron knocker breast high, and used it. The clanging sounds seemed to echo back through the house, which despite the lights was strangely silent.

The knocking was not answered. He repeated it. And while he waited, he roved the beam of the flash around the big dark front porch. Not ten feet away the bottoms of a pair of shoes caught his eye.

It was a man, lying there on his face, with the bone handle of a knife sticking up grotesquely from under one shoulder blade!

CHAPTER SEVEN

THE WOMAN UPSTAIRS

Nancy Fraser saw that sight past Val's shoulder an instant later. Her fingers bit into his arm as she pressed close to him. "Is—is he dead?" she asked unsteadily.

"Looks that way," Val muttered, stepping forward to the side of the motionless body.

He stooped, caught a shoulder and turned the face up. The flashlight showed a dapper, well-dressed young man with a sharp face, prominent nose and tousled black hair. It was no one he had ever seen before.

Norah had moved to the spot also. She did not cry out. She was calm as usual. "Nancy—I think we had better go back to the machine."

"What do you think is happening here?" Nancy asked Val swiftly.

"Haven't the slightest idea," he confessed. "But it looks bad."

Just then the front door opened, letting a bright swath of light out across the front porch.

Val whirled around, sliding his hand into his pocket.

A broad-shouldered, heavy-set man stepped out into the light and peered at them. He had a gun in his hand, and as he stared at them the weapon slowly lowered to his side and he asked gruffly: "What's this?"

"I think you're the one to do the explaining," Val countered, walking toward him. "Who killed that man?"

"You aren't the sheriff?" the stranger mumbled, looking at the two women.

"No. I'm not the sheriff."

"Then who the devil are you?"

Norah Beamish ranged alongside Val, and there was not the slightest trace of a quaver in her voice as she said firmly: "Our car ran out of gasoline down there on the road, and we came in here looking for a telephone or enough gasoline to take us on."

The man who stood there in the light had a wide flat face, with lumpy, muscular jowls, blue-black with a close-shaven beard. His eyes were narrowed, his mouth was a tight line and his manner suspicious as Norah Beamish spoke to him. But the suspicion gradually left.

"Out of gasoline, eh?" he said.

"Yes," Norah answered clamly. "Have you any to spare? And while we're asking questions, what is that dead man doing there? It's—it's horrible."

Val kept his hand on the automatic in his pocket. He was aware of the narrowed eyes resting on the pocket for a moment, and suspected that the fellow knew what was in it. But the fact seemed to make no difference. They couldn't look very suspicious with Norah Beamish standing there very much the *grande dame*, asking imperious questions.

"I guess it does look pretty funny to find a thing like that on a front porch, doesn't it, madam?" the man chuckled. "The fact is, I'm waiting for the sheriff now. I thought when you knocked it was he. You see, this fellow, whoever he is," with a jerk of his head at the body, "was prowling around here tonight with at least one other man. The dog ran out barking at them, and they shot him."

"They should have been shot themselves for that!" Norah sniffed.

"My sentiments exactly, madam," she was assured. "I heard the disturbance and ran out to see what was the matter. One of them took a shot at me in the dark. I made a good target against the light, I imagine. The bullet just missed me. See where it hit the side of the door?"

He turned and pointed to a small round hole in the wood at the side of the door which Val had not noticed when he knocked.

"And so you stabbed him?" Norah queried, wide-eyed.

That drew another chuckle. "No, madam, I did not stab him. I had stepped out without my gun, and I ran back inside and slammed the door. It was 'Big Buck,' the n——— yard man, who

496

threw that knife. He's quite handy with one, and he had dodged out at the side of the house when he heard the noise. Standing there, he saw one of the men run up on the porch and take a stand at the side of the door with a gun in his hand. Evidently waiting for me to show myself again, madam. Buck didn't know what it was all about. But he knew I was in danger, and when I started to open the door again, having gotten my gun, Buck threw his knife. Unfortunately with fatal effect. The man fell. And his companions must have gone one way while Buck went the other. When I stepped out on the porch with this revolver, I found the fellow breathing his last, and it took me ten minutes or so to get the straight of the matter. I've telephoned the sheriff, and he said he would get out here as soon as he could.

"And that," said the man drily, "explains the gory scene, madam. If you people will step inside you may use the telephone, and save yourselves the unpleasantness of being out here with him."

With a polite inclination of his head he indicated the doorway hospitably.

"Thank you. We will do that," said Norah firmly, and she sailed inside before Val could say anything to her. Nancy looked at him inquiringly.

Val swiftly conned the facts. "You say there were two of them?" he asked.

"At least that many."

"And the others ran?"

"I haven't seen anything more of them. I guess they didn't know how many men were out there in the darkness throwing knives, so they left while the leaving was good," the man chuckled again.

Galbraith had been intending to come here. He had been killed. Now violence had appeared at this house a few hours later. Was it the work of the Black Doctor, Val wondered. Was this house unaware of the danger threatening it? Had the Black Doctor, or some of his men, been closing in on it and been checked by an unexpected knife thrown out of the darkness?

It looked that way.

The mystery was growing thicker at every move, but this was the chance he had wanted to get inside the house. Val nodded slightly at Nancy and followed her into a wide, spacious hall.

"My name is Easton," he said calmly as their host joined them, closing the door behind him.

"Tillson is my name, sir," the other answered promptly.

This was the man, then, to whom Ramey's wire had been sent. But what about Long, the city man who had bought the place several years before, according to the owner of the drugstore back in Hartsville? Val had been wondering about that all the way out. Long owned Oakridge Manor, yet Ramey had wired a J. B. Tillson. Did they live here together? Were they partners, friends? Those were questions he wanted to ask, but didn't dare to, under the circumstances.

"You are the owner, I presume?" he suggested.

And received a negative shake of the head.

"No. Mr. Long is the owner here. He's upstairs in bed with a broken leg."

Norah Beamish had been looking around as they talked. "You have a nice place here," she complimented.

"Thank you, madam," Tillson bowed. "I think it is myself."

He was a curious combination of hard-boiled sophistication and ultra-polite civility. The fact that a man lay dead on the front porch did not seem to disturb him in the slightest. In fact he seemed amused, if anything. Val surprised a quirk at the corner of his mouth that was suppressed almost instantly. And since the telephone was not pressed on them at once, he talked casually.

"Do you have a farm here?"

Tillson shook his head. "Only a vegetable garden. I guess there isn't enough money in farming these days to tempt John. And since he has enough money to live on he lets the place lie as it is."

"I imagine the women folks are upset by this

business tonight," Norah Beamish observed shrewdly.

"There are no women in the house," Tillson told her. "John is a bachelor, and my wife is in California."

"Where all wives should be," said Norah.

Tillson was the perfect host as he smiled at her sadly. "There are different opinions about that, of course, madam. I miss Mrs. Tillson a great deal. Won't you ladies sit down? Mr. Easton, the telephone is in the back of the house. I'll take you there. Better get the call in before the sheriff gets here."

Talking to this man, looking about the spacious hall, listening to the peaceful quiet of the old house, Val had felt increasingly that something was wrong.

All this did not hook up with Galbraith's errand to this country; with Gregg's declaration that the man had been empowered to spend a million pounds; with the British agent that had evidently been tagging Galbraith; and the cold-blooded way both men had died. What could one of the great powers find interesting in this spot? In this man Tillson or his friend who lay upstairs with a broken leg? What did New York have to do with this peaceful lonely spot on the banks of the Potomac?

And while those thoughts had flashed through Val's mind, he was wondering about Tillson also. For despite the ultra politeness, the soft, almost genial manner of the man, the effect fell flat. He didn't look like a country gentleman, or a man who would be satisfied to hibernate in a quiet spot like this. He looked hard, cold, clever. And every once in a while there was a glint in his eyes, a catlike scrutiny of his surroundings, a cold, quickly caught inflection of his voice, that bore out that impression.

No, the man didn't ring true. The situation didn't ring true. There was peace in the air. But it was a taut, quivering peace, a quiet that seemed charged with electric tension.

Instead of quieting the nerves it put them on edge. Val had a very definite feeling that all this pleasantry might change instantly to tragedy.

And against all the facts he had marshaled there was the evidence of the dead dog and the lifeless corpse out there on the front porch. That dead man belonged to the cities. He wasn't a casual country prowler. He didn't belong out here in the mist-filled night, far from houses or people—unless the facts were right. Unless there were more to all this than appeared on the surface. Unless Galbraith had been intending to come here, and the Black Doctor was also interested in the place.

That was evidence that could not be disputed. Val wished the women were back in the machine, heading toward Washington. He was, he told himself, a fool for bringing them out there. He could have done the job just as well himself.

"I'll use your telephone," he agreed briskly. "And then we'll go out to our car and cause you no further trouble."

"It is a pleasure," Tillson assured him. "It does this house good to have women in it once in a while."

And the words were barely out of the man's mouth as he turned to the door on his right when the quiet of the house was rudely shattered by a rush of feet upstairs. And following that came the high, shrill, terror-stricken cry of a woman . . .

They all froze in their tracks, staring toward the top of the wide sweeping stairs that led up to the second floor, whence that scream had come.

Val's eyes dropped to Tillson, whose head had hunched forward and whose face had darkened with an ugly scowl.

That was all the proof Val needed of his suspicions. Tillson had lied flatly when he said there were no women in the house. And that woman who had screamed was in mortal terror or great pain. It drove a shiver down his back.

"What's wrong up there?" Norah Beamish uttered explosively, swinging around on Tillson.

It all happened in seconds. Later on Val was to wonder why he hadn't moved fast enough.

But he didn't have a chance, couldn't guess what was going to happen.

After the scream cut off sharp, the running feet still pounded upstairs. They reached the head of the stairs and started down.

The four of them standing below in the hall saw the feet, the legs, the whole figure of a man dashing down the stairs. He was hatless, coatless, shirtless—a sleek, pudgy form half running, half falling down the stairs in his mad haste.

His hair was rumpled wildly; blood was streaming from the corner of his mouth, spattering the white front of his under shirt and his arms. And one hand brandished a gleaming revolver.

With a shock Val recognized Galbraith's New York visitor—Ramey!

Only now the sleek unctuousness of the man had given away to wild, uncontrollable fright and desperation. His face was twisted in a mask of terror as he catapulted to the turn of the stairs.

"Get back!" Val cried at Nancy Fraser. His arm swept her roughly back against the wall.

And an instant later, as Ramey reached the turn in the stairs, their ears were deafened by the report of a gun. It was Tillson shooting. Standing there calmly, jaws clenched until the bunching muscles ridged out. His gun spat once—twice—three times. . . .

Ramey's legs gave way under him. The terror-stricken mask of his face suddenly looked horrible as it was struck by a bullet. His body raced forward, the gun flying from his fingers.

And as Norah Beamish lost her poise and screamed aloud, Ramey's limp body tumbled and bounced and slid to the floor of the hall at their feet.

CHAPTER EIGHT

THE £1,000,000 SECRET

The odor of burnt powder was strong on the air. Their ears were ringing from the shattering explosions in the confined space of the hall. And ghastly death there before them was stark evidence that they were not dreaming.

Val turned on Tillson, tugging at the automatic in his pocket—and met the steady muzzle of Tillson's revolver. Behind it he saw a new Tillson. A man no longer smiling, polite. The narrowed eyes were cold and hard. The flat face was a mask that was not good to see.

"Put your arms up!" Tillson ordered through his teeth.

Val hesitated only a fraction of a second. Proof of what might happen if he did not was too close at hand. He jerked his hands from his coat pocket and lifted his arms in the air.

"You—you cold-blooded killer!" Norah Beamish gasped.

"Shut up!" Tillson ordered her roughly. "You talk too much, old lady!"

"Old?" Norah choked. "Why—why—"

"Do I have to shut your mouth for you?" Tillson asked coldly.

"Norah, be quiet," Nancy ordered clearly. She stepped to Norah's side and laid slender fingers on Norah's arm.

Tillson gave her a cold grin. "You have some sense, young lady," he remarked.

"You haven't acted as if you had," Nancy told him in the same cool voice. Her deep blue eyes were boring at the man as if she were trying to look behind his face and see things that had not become visible heretofore.

Tillson sneered at them. "Gas!" he said. "Ran out of it right by the front gate. It was convenient, wasn't it? And too bad."

"Your name isn't Tillson," Nancy said coolly.

"No? What is it?"

That was what Val was wondering. The whole picture had changed. He was trying to get his bearings again, linking up the facts to make a new picture. And while he was doing that someone else came to the top of the stairs and descended leisurely.

Val saw black-clad legs, a white shirt, with sleeves rolled up—and a tall, stooped figure descended into view. A pale, cadaverous face looked down at them as the newcomer halted at the turn of the stairs and surveyed the scene for a moment with an inscrutable smile on his lips. The bony arms below the rolled-up sleeves were covered thickly with dark matted hair. And the long talonlike fingers of the right hand held a keen, gleaming surgeon's scalpel.

Nancy uttered a choked cry. Val swore under his breath, and a chill crawled down his back. For that stooped figure holding the little gleaming knife was Carl Zaken, the Black Doctor.

"So?" said Zaken mildly, gesturing with the scalpel. "These are our visitors. This is a surprise."

And the very mildness of his voice made the words sound worse. For Val and Nancy had seen what the man could do, and had heard tales of what he was capable of. Standing there holding the surgeon's scalpel he looked like a smiling fiend.

Norah Beamish's harsh whisper to Nancy was audible to all of them. "Who—who is that man?"

Nancy's face was pale. Val saw the fingers of her free hand curling tightly into her pink palm, and guessed the terrific effort she was making to keep a grip on herself. But her voice was steady as she spoke.

"That is the man who attacked me in the hotel this evening. His name is Carl Zaken."

"Oh!" said Norah weakly, and for once she seemed at a loss for words as she stared up at Zaken.

Zaken leaned against the railing, toying with the scalpel. He betrayed no surprise at Nancy's knowledge of his identity. His greenish eyes seemed to blaze and glow as the light from the hall fixture struck into them.

"What were you doing to that fellow?" Val asked harshly, nodding at Ramey.

"We were having a little confidential talk," the Black Doctor said smoothly, and his lips parted in a ghastly grimace and he slowly tapped the back of the scalpel against a thumb.

"You mean," asked Val thickly, "you were torturing him?"

"Persuading," Zaken corrected. "Unfortu-nately he knocked my man down, seized his gun and tried to leave us, forgetting entirely his woman friend. But then, cheap criminals of his type think only of their own skins."

All the tales Val had ever heard about the Black Doctor flashed before him now. He understood the terrible fright and agony on Ramey's face as he had plunged down the stairs. This lonely house was being given over to things too horrible to contemplate. And Nancy was thinking the same, for he saw her smooth white throat flutter as she swallowed convulsively.

"He was in New York this afternoon," Val said mechanically.

"Yes. He and his friends should have stayed there instead of hurrying here as soon as he was through with Sir Edward Lyne," Zaken said contemptously.

"You came quick enough. How did you get out of that room and down here in Virginia so fast?"

Zaken grimaced again with amusement. "I have found that he who moves fastest moves safest, Mr. Easton. Leaving the room was a small matter. My man, who had tied you up so I would not be interrupted, had lowered a thin silk rope from his room just over Sir Edward's, to call our late friend by his right name. I left you via the rope, the fire escape from the roof below, and a taxicab that I hailed at the mouth of the alley. I picked my man up at the hotel entrance a few minutes later. We passed the police car as we turned into Fifth Avenue. A fast ride out to a chartered plane. A faster trip to Washington and out here. *Voila*—and the thing was done. I presume you came by plane also?"

Val nodded. "I didn't expect to find you here," he confessed bluntly.

"*Touché*—the surprise is mutual. I did not believe you had been able to find out where Galbraith was going. I killed him for that reason—so the matter would end there for you—and him. Had I suspected otherwise I would have used lethal gas."

"Like you used on those poor devils aboard ship," Val charged swiftly.

Zaken gestured delicately with the scalpel. "The steward was an accident. The gas lingered in that closed room longer than I thought it would. He walked into it. The wind must have blown in through the door he left open and aired the cabin thoroughly before he was discovered. You found no trace of it?"

"No," said Val shortly.

"Just as well," Zaken murmured. "It is very deadly. It had to be because of the small amount I was able to inject through the keyhole."

"Why do it?"

"He was a member of the British Secret Service, dispatched as an unofficial guard over Sir Edward Lyne. We bumped into each other on deck that evening, and I think he recognized me. I couldn't take chances. You understand how it is in delicate matters like this, Mr. Easton?"

"In a small way," Val agreed sarcastically. "I suppose you found out what Lyne was after when you searched his hotel room. And then put him out of the way because you needed him no longer."

"But I knew what he was after," Zaken declared humorously, showing his fanglike incisor teeth as he smiled. "But I did not know where it was. You are quite right about the rest. I simply—ah—eliminated competition which might have proved embarrassing. He would have come here at once, of course. You would have followed—and my plans might have been upset. I have only three men with me. The whole matter broke so suddenly I barely had time to get passage on the same boat with Lyne. No matter what I pay for information, my sources are not always infallible."

Zaken's casual manner changed abruptly. "Bring them upstairs," he commanded. "Shoot the first one who makes a wrong move. Are you sure they're alone?"

"Yes. I was waiting near the gate when they stopped their car."

Zaken nodded, waited until they were almost up to him and then preceded them. He turned to the left at the top of the stairs and led the way to the back of the house, to a long, high-ceilinged room with a great bay window, curtained now, opening out into the night.

Standing beside the door and furtively fingering a swelling eye was the man who had posed as a waiter only a few hours earlier. "Did you get him?" he asked Zaken uncertainly.

"Yes," returned Zaken coldly. "And the next time you grow careless, Stubbs, it will be the end. I stand for blundering no more than once."

"Yes, sir," Stubbs replied uneasily, his eyes dropping before the greenish glare that transfixed him. And pallor swept over his face as Zaken led the way into the room.

It was an upstairs library, with bookcases along the walls, comfortable chairs, and a large brick fireplace against the end wall. Over the fireplace hung a large copy of the Stuart painting of George Washington, and the inscrutable eyes of the stately figure seemed to look down and ponder this strange scene that was taking place.

Six people were seated in that room, as strange and heterogeneous a collection as Val had ever seen. Every one of them was marked with the sickly brand of fright and terror.

Sitting in the bay window were two; a pretty, slinky, tawdry young woman dressed in flashy clothes, who was slowly rubbing an angry red wrist; and a hard, sophisticated man of about thirty, wise, worldly, and at this moment pale and haggard as he wet his lips and stared at them.

On a bench beside the fireplace were a lanky negro in overalls and a fat negress, the whites of their eyes rolling.

Two chairs near the end of the library table held a stiff, severe, waspish woman of about forty-five, and a small, slight man with a bulging forehead and shrewd eyes, a strange mixture of intelligence and pomposity. He was haggard also, with sunken, feverish eyes and a limp appearance, as if worry and fear had crushed him.

———

Standing near the doorway, a gun in his hand, was a cool, self-possessed man in his early thirties, his face cast in a shrewd cold mold, with a cruel mouth under a small black mustache. He looked foreign—was foreign Val found out a moment later.

For Carl Zaken, continuing with the same mocking politeness, gestured at them with a scalpel. "The people you came to see, Mr. Easton. Study them at your leisure. In the window there we have Miss Dolly Mae Hall, as perfect a sample of your shopworn New York night-club siren as one could wish to find. Her specialty is understanding love, and she seems to be good at it."

Val saw the pompous little man with the bulging forehead wriggle uneasily in his chair, and glance fearfully at the severe woman at his strive, who pursed her mouth and glared at him.

Zaken flashed them a humorous glance and went on.

"With her is 'Badger Bill' Marcus, a sterling partner, I understand. Those two negroes work about the place. And in these chairs by the table we have Professor Henry Long and his gentle wife. This man guarding them is Vollonoff, who has been with me for some years, under one name and another. You recognize these three, Vollonoff? Easton, Miss Fraser, and a Mrs. Beamish, of the American Secret Service. They worked faster than we thought possible. Don't underestimate Easton and the girl, Fyodor. They are dangerous."

Vollonoff flashed a cold smile under his black mustache. Val judged him to be almost as dangerous as Carl Zaken himself.

"The man you saw on the front porch," continued Zaken, "is Sammy McGee, alias Tillson, a partner of Ramey and Marcus. The story, as I gather it to date, is that Professor Long, to celebrate the successful culmination of several years' work, and the undoubtedly trying company of his wife in this isolated spot, went to New York to taste the bright lights. Or, as I have heard your countrymen say, 'to throw a bust.' He drank not wisely but too well, talked indiscreetly about what he had been working on and had accom-

plished, and in that alcoholic daze found himself in the grip of an undying passion for Dolly Mae. They progressed to her apartment—control yourself, Mrs. Long—the flesh is weak at times.

"The play that was staged must have been masterly, Easton. When it was over Professor Long found himself apparently laboring under the onus of having shot his new love's husband, with Ramey, one of her men friends in the role of rescuer, who hustled him away from the police net to safety. It developed that the price of continued safety and silence was a share in the fortune that Professor Long stood to gain from his invention.

"Under duress Professor Long was constrained to turn the marketing of his invention over to the gang controlled by Ramey, which had him in its grip. They sent Sammy McGee down here under the name of Tillson to keep an eye on the professor and make certain he did not forget that at any moment he might be hauled back to New York for murder. And Ramey took up the marketing of the invention, not with his own country as any patriotic citizen would do, but with the British government, who could be counted on to pay almost any price for it. The upshot of the negotiations was the hurried dispatch of Sir Edward Lyne, with instructions to look into the matter and offer anything up to a million pounds on the spot if he considered the claims correct."

Carl Zaken shrugged.

"And that's where we came in, Easton. Ramey had evidently stipulated a secret rendezvous in New York with the man sent over, with more directions there. His intention was to bring Lyne down here, convince him, wait until the money was paid over, and probably decamp with all of it. After giving Lyne directions, he and his confederates hurried down here instantly. We found them here when we arrived. The dog barked as we came up and had to be put out of the way. McGee rushed out, and Vollonoff dispatched him with his usual skill. And so we came in and went to work. I had just finished a little session with Ramey in the other room, finding out that Professor Long has been canny enough to keep the final drawings of his invention hidden. And now I am ready to take that little matter up with him."

Zaken smiled without mirth as he stood there in his shirt sleeves, drawing the gleaming little knife through his fingers. Professor Long's face went grayish as he met the grimacing smile the Black Doctor gave him.

Mrs. Long sprang to her feet and cried shrilly: "You'd better leave Henry alone! You—you'll suffer for this outrage, whoever you are!"

Vollonoff stepped forward and shoved her roughly back in her chair.

Val hardly saw the play. His mind was on the astounding revelations Zaken had made apparently under the impression that he knew almost as much about it. What could that shrinking, pompous little man with the bulging forehead control that would be worth almost any price to a foreign government?

He said casually: "I doubt if Lyne would have offered much for it. And you probably won't get anything for your trouble, either."

"No?" Zaken mocked. "Not for the answer to the problem that every general staff in the world has been seeking for fifteen years? An infallible range finder that will locate and bring correctly to bear anti-aircraft guns by day or night, or in fog? Your own army engineers have been working on it for years. And according to Ramey, the professor here has solved the problem with a sensitive finder that picks up the spark emanations from the motor timer, calibrates their distance and height and speed by instant triangulation, and brings the guns hooked up to the system to bear instantly. With it a fleet of bombing planes can be located whether seen or not, and shot down at once. It will make the country that controls it safe from aerial invasion. Think what that will mean to England—to know that she is safe from attack by air! Millions saved in defensive air fleets, and probably the winning or losing of the next war.

"Japan, with her great cities near her island coasts, will pay any price for it. The general staffs of every great power will be bidding wildly for it, once the information gets out that Carl Zaken can turn that invention over to them."

And Val knew with a sickening feeling that the man was right. If this Professor Long had perfected an invention like that—and it looked as if he had—no price was too much to pay for it. And Carl Zaken, master spy, would offer it to the highest bidder. The chances were that some other country would get it, possibly a future enemy of the United States. In this lonely house tonight a world issue was being decided. And in the balance were only himself, Nancy Fraser, and Norah Beamish.

Zaken's mocking glance was on him. "You don't agree?" Zaken questioned.

Val shrugged. "Perhaps. D'you think Long will tell you? He doesn't look like the type of man who would give as important a secret as that into the wrong hands."

Professor Henry Long sat up and spoke for the first time. "I'm not!" he burst out passionately. "I didn't know what Ramey was going to do! He said he was dealing with our government! I won't turn it over to another country! I won't. . . ."

Zaken showed his fanglike incisors in another grimace. "Your sentiments do you credit, professor. We will see what a short consultation will do. I have been very successful in the past as a persuader. Kroner, bring him in. We won't embarrass the ladies by doing it in here."

The powerful fellow who had posed as Tillson pushed to the professor's chair without a word, seized his arm and hauled him up. When the little man tried to struggle, he received a blow in the face that knocked him limp and mumbling. And in that state, while his wife wailed shrilly and the others looked on with horrified helplessness, the professor was half dragged, half carried out of the room.

The Black Doctor slowly scraped the edge of his scalpel across the matted hairs of his left arm. The gesture was casual, but the effect was ghastly as he grimaced and turned to follow.

"I shall write Gregg tomorrow and compliment him on his agents," he said to Val and Nancy. "A pity I can't let you live to tell him about this. But a million pounds is too much to risk . . ."

CHAPTER NINE

GAS TRAP

Norah Beamish cast a venemous glance at Vollonoff and went over and tried to comfort the nearly hysterical Mrs. Long. Twin spots of color were vivid on Nancy's face as she looked at Val silently. Stubbs stood outside the door, fingering his gun. Vollonoff lounged inside, his eyes watching every move they made. The couple in the window seat huddled together miserably. And the fat negress began to mumble, "Oh, Lawd—Oh, Lawd—Oh, Lawd . . ."

A piercing shriek suddenly rang through the house, the cry of a man in torment and agony.

Professor Long's wife gasped and fainted, which was perhaps best, for more shrieks followed.

Norah Beamish whirled on Val, her eyes blazing. "Can't you do something about it?" she cried.

Vollonoff smirked expectantly.

And Val stood there with his shoulders slumped, the picture of dejection. "And get shot for trying?" he answered Norah helplessly. "You saw what happened to that chap downstairs."

Norah glared at him. "I thought you were a man!"

"Val—" said Nancy helplessly.

"It's no use," Val said wretchedly.

"We're going to die anyway," she reminded through stiff lips.

"Perhaps they'll let us go if we promise to let them get away. They could tie us up—"

"Oh!" Norah blazed contemptuously.

Even Vollonoff was affected by this show of helplessness. "Sit down," he advised, with a curl of contempt on his lips. "Not so dangerous, after all."

Val shrugged helplessly and turned toward the nearest chair. And as he passed slowly in front of Nancy, with his back to Vollonoff, words slid almost inaudibly from the corner of his mouth. He didn't even look at her to see what their effect was.

Nancy's face suddenly twisted in helpless grief. She fished for a handkerchief and dabbed at her eyes as she turned toward the other end of the room.

"He c-can't help us," she wept. "Come over here with me, Norah."

Norah stared at her in amazement and then swiftly followed her. "Don't you cry, honey," she begged bruskly "There's a way out of this."

"No, there's not!" Nancy wailed.

Val could see them as he pulled the chair around to sit down. But an instant later he heard Nancy gasp: "Catch me! I'm—I'm . . ."

And Val snapped the chair off the floor, whirled around and hurled it with every ounce of strength in his body. As he had planned, Nancy's gasp had drawn Vollonoff's attention for a second. Vollonoff sensed what was happening—too late. As he jerked his head back the edge of the chair seat caught him squarely in the face. The gun in his hand roared deafeningly, missing. And an instant later Val was on him, smashing his fist over the top of the falling chair.

The jar of the blow rocked Val's arm clear to the shoulder. And it drove Vollonoff reeling backward, knocked out cold, the gun falling from his hand.

Val ducked into the protection of his body, caught Vollonoff under the arms and heaved him at the doorway. Stubbs, leaping into the room in confused surprise, caught the full impact of Vollonoff's weight, and for an instant was tied up in confusion there in the doorway.

"Here!" Nancy cried at Val's side. She thrust Vollonoff's gun into his hand. She had seized it off the floor. Her eyes were shining, her voice thrilling in its disregard for danger.

"Get down on the floor!" Val rapped at her as his fingers closed over the revolver. A wave of confidence swept through him. No longer were his hands tied by futile helplessness. The very thought of the odds against them, and the consequences if he failed, brought strength.

The revolver leveled just as Stubbs hurled Vollonoff's falling body back into the room and raised the automatic in his hand. Both guns spat at once. A cold, searing sensation raked Val's side. He knew he had been shot there. But Stubbs reeled around, clasping a shattered elbow. And then dodged out of sight beside the door before Val could fire again.

A leap, a kick, and the door crashed shut. An instant later Stubbs poured a fusillade of shots through the door. But they all went wide, hitting no one.

Everyone had come to their feet. The negress began to shriek in terror.

"Shut up!" Val yelled at her, and when that had no effect he ignored her.

He heard Carl Zaken's voice shout in the hallway. "What happened in there?"

And Stubbs replying shakily: "He knocked Vollonoff out with a chair, got his gun, and shot me in the elbow! I'll bleed to death!"

"And good enough for you!" Zaken snarled. He broke off into French, cursing Vollonoff and Stubbs for ignorant fools. "Clumsy pig! Son of a goat!" Zaken shouted. "Watch that door! Don't let them get out! They can't get away! I'll fix them! With gas!"

Nancy and Val both understood the words. The rest did not. Marcus asked uncertainly: "What'll we do?"

"Gas!" Nancy whispered to Val. "It won't be tear gas this time!"

"No," Val agreed bruskly. "He's gambling high tonight. He'll slaughter the lot of us as quick as he can now."

Nancy looked at him desperately. "What will we do? We can't get out that door."

"Here! Watch the door! Don't waste the bullets! We'll need them!"

Val grabbed up a chair, stepped to the great bay window and began to swing the chair vigorously. Glass crashed and fell away before it. A few seconds of that and the windows were cleared away.

Wraiths of fog swirled in. The croaking of the riverside frogs sounded very close. He judged the house sat almost on the river bank. He turned around and snapped at the others:

"Get out on that roof! Quick! Your lives may depend on it!"

Professor Long's wife was still unconscious in her chair. Val picked her up and strode to the window. He had to wait a moment as Marcus and his girl friend and the two negroes scrambled through, ignoring the jagged edges of glass. None of them waited to help him. Val hadn't expected it. Their nerves were too shattered by terror. He heaved his burden through and lowered her roughly to the roof below. She would have a measure of safety out there.

Norah Beamish and Nancy were at his side, waiting for orders. Norah's eyes were shining too. "Young man," she cried, "I apologize!"

Outside the door Carl Zaken's voice snapped in French: "One side, pig!"

"Give me that gun!" Val husked to Nancy. He fired two shots at the door. Couldn't see whether he had hit anything or not.

Vollonoff stirred on the floor just before he fired. The sound of the shots seemed to bring him out of his daze. He sat up groggily. And an instant later Nancy caught Val's arm and pointed to the doorway.

"Look!"

Through one of the bullet holes in the door thrust the glistening point of a sharp needle. From its end a tiny spray of liquid spurted into the room. And that spray dissolved into a bluish vapor as they stared at it.

"Out that window quick!" Val urged. He whirled Nancy around himself, and started her with a shove.

And as he waited for them to get through to safety, Val saw a sight he never forgot. Vollonoff was staggering to his feet just in front of the door, his eyes on them with dazed surprise.

"Look out!" Val shouted at him. "Come over here, quick!"

Instead Vollonoff turned around to the door, obviously intending to escape. And the first dissolving wave of gas closed about him. Vollonoff's hand shot to his throat. He strangled. Too late he realized what was happening and turned toward the window.

The gas cloaked him like an evil halo now. He staggered, his face turning purple and his eyes starting from their sockets. His mouth opened to cry out—and only a horrible strangling issued from it. Vollonoff took one lurching step toward the window, and then tumbled forward on his face, kicked and lay still.

Val ducked out the window, white-faced and shaken.

"God!" he husked to Nancy. "No wonder that steward couldn't get out the door! Get down off this roof before it starts to drift out the window. One good whiff of it seems to be all that's needed."

He dragged Long's wife to the end of the roof. She recovered consciousness as he did that. The negro was down on the ground. The negress slid off, hung by her hands a moment, blubbering, and then dropped the short distance to the ground and was caught by her companion.

"Pass her down to me," Val ordered Nancy.

He dropped the same way. Nancy and Norah Beamish lowered the protesting woman and he caught her. Nancy and Norah followed. And while they did that Marcus and his girl companion made the drop successfully. They were all safe.

"Get back out of sight and stay there!" Val said to Nancy and Norah. "No more foolishness! I'll see what I can do."

He raced through the damp mist to the front of the house, gun in one hand and his flash in the other. The front porch was still and quiet.

A wink of the flash showed the dead body lying where he had left it. The front door was closed.

But as he looked, it was jerked open from inside and the man who had opened it once before stepped out. Val shot at him and missed. The man jumped back inside, slamming the door.

Val waited tensely, wondering what would happen next.

It came from behind; running feet poked out of the fog and closed in on him. Val faced them crouching, wondering with a sick feeling if Carl Zaken had lied, and had more men out here in the night.

But a voice shouted: "That you Easton?"

It was Gregg. And as Val relaxed and lowered the gun, Gregg came running up with half a dozen men. "We heard the shouts," he panted. "Having trouble?"

And all Val could think of at that instant was to say foolishly: "I thought you were going home to sleep."

"Got to thinking that this was too important to leave up in the air till morning," Gregg told him. "I called some of the men and started out here to get the lay of the land myself, and station them. We saw your car back there by the gate and had started to look the ground over when we heard something that sounded like shots. And then we heard you shoot here again. What happened?"

"Two of you go around and watch there!" Val ordered before he replied. "Shoot anyone you see trying to leave. Anyone outside is all right."

"Do that!" Gregg ordered hastily.

And as two of the men ran, Val hurriedly gave Gregg the highlights.

"Surround this house!" Gregg snapped to the rest of his men. "And shoot to kill. We've got one of the most dangerous men in the world cornered."

The words were hardly out of his mouth when three quick shots barked at the back of the house.

Val sprinted for the front door, and Gregg pounded after him, gun in hand also. Val opened the front door and peered in cautiously. The hall was empty. Ramey's body sprawled at the foot of the stairs. The interior of the house was still. Ominously still. Deathly still. But as he and Gregg stared in, the door at the back swung silently open. Carl Zaken leaped into the hall with a catlike movement, holding a gun in each hand.

He saw them at the same instant and jerked the two weapons up.

Val shot him first. Emptied the revolver in a tearing burst as fast as he could pull the trigger. Zaken went down, shooting wildly and futilely. He tried to rise on his two hands, dragging his guns with him. And slumped forward again. And then with a sudden movement he threw them weakly from him.

"*Touché*, Easton," he called weakly, turning a ghastly, pain-racked face toward the doorway. "I told Vollonoff you were a dangerous man."

And so it ended. Zaken's other two men had been trapped at the rear of the house, where they thought no one was watching, shot seriously and captured. They found Professor Long upstairs in one of the bedrooms, half dead from fear rather than pain. A few moments later, downstairs, he thrust a roll of drawings in Val's hand.

"Here," he said weakly. "Keep these. I—I never want to see them again. I'll take whatever the government offers for them."

Gregg's men, after performing hurried first aid, were already loading the wounded into their car, which they had brought up to the house and the body of Carl Zaken went with them.

Gregg was saying to Norah Beamish: "Want to ride back with us?"

"Nonsense!" Norah snapped. "I'll go with Nancy and Mr. Easton. Nancy needs me."

There was a slight inscrutable smile on Nancy's face as she said: "I think I'll be taken care of all right, if you want to go, Norah."

For a moment the older woman looked at Nancy shrewdly. And then she, too, smiled, and sighed. "I'll go with you, Jim Gregg," she said. "I think I'm getting old after all. Nancy doesn't need a mother tonight. Do you, Nancy?"

But Nancy was smiling at Val and didn't hear her.

H. BEDFORD-JONES

ONCE KNOWN AS the "King of the Pulps" for his prolificity and popularity, Henry James O'Brien Bedford-Jones (1887–1949) wrote about 1,400 short stories and approximately 80 books under his own name and at least seventeen pseudonyms, including Allan Hawkwood, Gordon Keyne, and Michael Gallister, as well as various house names for publishers of boys' books and pulps. He customarily wrote between five thousand and ten thousand words a day, but on occasion wrote a complete novella of twenty-five thousand words in a single day. He was the ultimate writer of historical adventure fiction and all its subgenres, including stories about pirates, the French Foreign Legion, big game hunting, sports, aviation, etc., while also producing an enormous body of work in the science fiction and fantasy fields. Although largely unremembered today except by historians and fans of the pulps, he was highly regarded in his day and sold to all the top magazines, including *Argosy*, *Adventure*, *Blue Book*, *Munsey's*, and *All-Story*.

Born in Ontario, Canada, Bedford-Jones became an American citizen in 1908 and lived mostly in New York and California. As one of the highest-paid writers in America, even during the Great Depression, he owned several homes and enjoyed a flamboyant lifestyle, hindered in no way by his good looks (he was compared to the dashing Errol Flynn). One of his novels, *Garden of the Moon*, cowritten with Barton Browne, was serialized in six parts in *The Saturday Evening Post* (August 28–October 2, 1937) and served as the basis for an unlikely musical comedy in 1938, directed by Busby Berkeley, who was noted for his elaborate dance numbers, and starring Pat O'Brien, Margaret Lindsay, and John Payne.

The hero of "Free-Lance Spy" is Barnes, who appears in a series of stories in which he and his colleagues battle the spies of various countries. He belongs to a loose affiliation of spies that has no official connection to the United States government. One of the many women who are attracted to him called him the Sphinx because of his reluctance to discuss his cases, and he liked the appellation.

"Free-Lance Spy" was originally published in the March 30, 1935, issue of *Argosy* magazine.

FREE-LANCE SPY

H. BEDFORD-JONES

CHAPTER I

A NEW GAME

IN THE DARKNESS of a room overlooking the courtyard of the old Hotel des Anglais, in Nice, a slight sound broke the early morning silence. A warning bell, so thin and silvery that it might have been imagination. Day after day, night after night, Marie Nicolas had been awaiting this sound.

She swiftly flung back the covers, threw herself out of bed, and over her nightgown drew a padded bathrobe. In her hand glowed a tiny flashlight. The faintly reflected radiance showed a glimpse of her dark and lovely features, her wide, hurried eyes ablaze with excitement. Then darkness closed down again.

A large Bible was on her dresser. She snapped it open; the book, made solid with glue and cut out in the center, was a box. From this she took a set of head-phones. The tiny finger of light touched a mark on the wall paper. She inserted a plug, pushing it into the paper; the round points, so different from those of American plugs, shoved neatly home. In her ears leaped a voice.

"They are fools, these Americans. Smart Yankees! I'll show you the truth, Truxon. I've taken care of them, all of them. I know everything about them."

Excitement set her pulses hammering. She could visualize the scene in that room, only two doors away from hers. The speaker was Rothstern; fat, jovial, with gold teeth and a shining bald spot. One of the cleverest secret agents of all Central Europe. Who employed Rothstern? No one knew, positively.

He was identified with Germany, but he might be working for the Nazi party, for Hitler personally, for Poland, now the close ally of Germany, or for any other cause.

Truxon? Yes, she knew this lean, dark, savage man, this renegade Englishman who had been kicked out of the British diplomatic ranks. It was Truxon's room yonder, his and Stacey's. Another of the same sort was Stacey, but weak and vicious, diabolically crafty.

Now she crouched closer, listening intently. The dictaphone worked perfectly. She had been two weeks getting it in place, since learning that Truxon always occupied this same room when in the city.

"They're not fools," cracked out Truxon's hard, smashing voice. "They're smart. The smartest of them is that fellow Barnes."

Marie Nicolas thrilled to the name, to the grudging admiration of this enemy.

"Barnes will be dead within the week," and Rothstern laughed softly. "Let me explain two things to you: this American activity, and the general situation."

"Damn the situation," growled Truxon. "I work for whomever pays me."

"I pay you." Rothstern spoke with abrupt authority. "Listen. Certain Americans like Barnes are working for their government. Idealistic fools, who place themselves and their brains and money at the service of their country; they have no standing, they have no acknowledged connection with Washington.

"They are free-lances who prate of bringing a new deal into diplomacy, of fighting us here in Europe with our own weapons."

The scorn in his voice was acid.

"Barnes is one. He pretends to be a fool, but is smart enough; however, he is in my hand. There's Hutton in Vienna, Morlake in Berlin, McGibbons in Warsaw, Pratt in Moscow, Williams in London, Reilly in Paris; also, there are half a dozen less important ones who have no steady position. Every one of these men is under the most strict watch. So is this girl, Marie Nicolas."

"What?" ejaculated Truxon. "But she's working for Italy!"

Rothstern laughed, and at his jovial laugh, Marie Nicolas trembled.

"So you think; so others think. She is really one of these American amateurs, my friends. She is here, in this same hotel; she has been here for two weeks, ill with influenza, or so she pretends. She leaves her room only twice a day, to sit in the sun in the courtyard. Well, she is attended to. Now, here's your pay for the next month."

A rustle of paper as banknotes were counted out.

"You don't care to go into the general situation?" Rothstern asked, with a note of mockery.

"No!" shot out Truxon. "Perhaps we know it as well as you do. We're only interested in earning our money."

"You shall earn it, I assure you. I have met this Barnes and know him well; he is open to bribery if rightly handled. But he's not the fool he looks, as you've found to your cost. On next Friday he will be in Ostend; you'll be there ahead of him, and so shall I. My work is to trap him; yours is to kill him. Understood?"

"Gladly," and Truxon's voice held a savage note of hatred. "But how?"

"How? Once and for all," and Rothstern's voice shook with laughter at his own jest. Then he sobered. "Now listen carefully. Next Friday evening, Ostend is to witness a gala performance of Beethoven's Solemn Mass, with chorus and artists from Paris. The king will attend. From Paris come a number of diplomats to attend, among them the American ambassador, and also Grimaldi, the Italian ambassador.

"Barnes is going to meet the American ambassador and obtain the signed draft of the tentative Abyssinian treaty."

"Abyssinian treaty!" echoed Truxon. "Are you insane? The States make a treaty with Abyssinia? That's nonsense."

Rothstern's jovial laugh boomed out. "Ah, you know so much, you care so little for information! Well, never mind. There is much more to the business than appears on the surface. The main thing is that this man Barnes must be killed."

"Leave it to me," said Truxon.

"I can't leave it entirely to you. I must obtain the treaty draft from him."

"Sounds like nonsense," growled the renegade. "Why doesn't the American ambassador put it on the cables?"

"He has done so. We do not desire to keep it from Washington; merely to know its terms; so we prefer to intercept the original draft which Barnes is to take to London for inclusion in the diplomatic pouch to Washington. You see, these people have learned that we have a friend planted in the Paris embassy. They have become cautious."

"Looks to me, Rothstern," Truxon stated coolly, "as though you're lying about the whole thing; or you're covering up the real truth. Well, no matter. It's none of our concern."

"You are right, it is not," said Rothstern with a touch of asperity. "Barnes is the most dangerous of these American fools. He must be removed for good and all—ah! Someone at the door."

Silence; incoherent sounds, a mutter of voices. The crouched girl strained against the dresser in the darkness, shivering, but not with cold. Fear was in her heart, and not for herself alone! Then the voice of Rothstern exploded violently.

"A message for me! Give it here. Ah, a telegram, eh! It is—it is—ten thousand devils!" His voice broke in a passionate oath. "Greetings to our pleasant conference; signed merely 'The Sphinx, U.S.A.' Is this a joke? Damn you, answer me!"

The Sphinx! A thrill ran through the crouching girl. Then she started violently and turned. Outside her door was a step. It paused there.

She moved like a flash. Snatching off the head-phones, she silently slapped them and the cord into their false Bible, and next instant was beside the bed. She poised there, holding her breath.

A low, soft rustle came from the door, then ceased. The step sounded again, moving away.

After a moment she threw the pencil-beam of her tiny flashlight on the door, then to the floor below it. A folded paper lay there; apparently a bluish French telegraph form. She went to it, picked it up, and opened it. It was no telegram, but on the form was typed in English:

THE FRENCH POLICE ARE ARRESTING YOU TOMORROW. CATCH THE PARIS EXPRESS AT 5 A.M. LEAVE TRAIN AT LYON, HIRE A BLUE RENAULT WHICH WILL BE WAITING ON EAST SIDE OF PLATFORM WITH A "FOR HIRE" SIGN ON THE RADIATOR. IT WILL TAKE YOU TO BRUSSELS.

The only signature at the bottom of this message was the red figure of a Sphinx, stamped there with a rubber stamp. Beneath the figure were the letters, "U.S.A."

The Sphinx! She, and she alone, knew whom that could be—whom it must be!

Suddenly she turned, darted to the dresser, seized her head-phones again, and listened. She caught Rothstern's voice. "I tell you, the French police are working with me! In this affair, France is with us—but not openly. Yes, come along to my room. I'll get the things you need, and there'll be no trouble at the frontier."

A door slammed. Silence. The girl swiftly put away her phones again. She flashed the tiny light on her wristwatch. Four A.M. It would still be dark at five. If she were to catch that express for Paris—

The French police working with Rothstern? What was it all about? She had no idea. But she had been ordered to wait here for some message from Barnes. On her own responsibility she had arranged this dictaphone, this communication with Truxon's room. This hotel was well known to her. For the past two years she had been on the go all over Europe. And now something had happened, something big was coming up. War? No telling. All Europe was a hotbed of intrigue, of rivalry; France and Italy stood out against each other.

The Sphinx! Her brain rocked with indecision. She remembered that day when she had called Barnes a Sphinx, and how his face had lighted up. Now he had sent an ironic message to Rothstern, another message to her. Barnes! Yes, it must be Barnes, it could be no one else. Why was he adopting this *nom-de-guerre*? Why were the police about to arrest her? They had nothing against her. Yet she could not doubt. Rothstern knew everything about this little band of gallant Americans who were pitting themselves against the secret agents of Europe. They would have no recourse if they failed. They had no connection with Washington.

A thousand questions rioted in her brain; she

sat with eyes closed, trying to evoke some order out of the mental chaos. Gradually it came. She must reach Barnes with what she had heard, yes! She had something definite now. Rothstern knew everything. Not one of the unofficial American agents, these free-lances who risked everything for their country, was safe. Rothstern knew of them all. He boasted that he had her in his hand. Yes, it was he who intended to have her arrested. How did Barnes know of it? Again the questions rioted. Again she beat them down, crushed them back. Nothing mattered now except to follow the orders of the Sphinx. Barnes? Ah—

She broke off abruptly, rose, switched on the lights in her room, after closing the window and drawing the blinds. She looked around. If there were danger from the police, she could not take away her belongings. She must abandon everything, her luggage, her clothes, and take only what she could carry in her handbag. No one must see her leave; well, that could be managed!

The holes in the wall paper she carefully patched; this room might again come in handy. The head-phones she must throw away in the street. Clothes, personal effects—she swiftly made her choice among them. Queer, that Barnes should know what the French police intended! It was two months since she had seen him; in this interval he had completely dropped from sight.

Now she was clear-headed, cool, alert. She left money for her hotel bill, with a note asking to have her effects held; she had gone to Menton for a few days. This might throw the police off the track. If only she did not have to buy a ticket and a place in the train! There was the danger-point, if the police were on the lookout. Room lights off, she slipped out into the deserted corridor.

In the street, the chill wind of coming dawn, the sparse lights, the emptiness and absence of life, appalled her. She came into the Boulevard Gambetta; a long way still to the station. A glance at her wrist-watch and she stepped out more briskly. Only twenty minutes left now.

With a hoot-hoot and a flicker of yellow lights, a taxicab rattled along behind, overtook her, and passed on. She paused, shivering. From the open cab window, floated a laughing voice; the hearty, jovial tones of Fat Rothstern, accompanied by the harsh, inhuman laugh of Truxon. She faltered. On their way to that same train? No help for it. She feared Rothstern more than the renegade Englishman, because his merry deviltry was abnormal. The same train? Well, she must go on. She had her orders.

Resolute, she hastened on with something very like a suppressed oath at her own heart-hurried fears. After all, she could take care of herself. She was the equal of any man of them, as she had proved ere this. What folly, to let the chill morning darkness oppress her! A laugh, and she flung off the weight. The thrill of it all seized upon her. Her pulses leaped to the fervor, the quick chances of the game.

She took the short-cut out of the Place Franklin. Two bicycle police rolled along, eyed her sharply, went their way. Ahead opened the width of the Avenue Thiers and the railroad, the glittering lights of the station beyond. The train was there; the engine was huff-huffing like all French engines. No time to lose if she were to make the express!

Suddenly a man appeared ahead, a dark, thin man, a stranger. He was aiming to intercept her. Hand flew to bag; her little pistol was jerked out. She went straight at him. Then, to her astonishment, she heard her own name.

"Mademoiselle Nicolas, is it not? Correct. Your *billet*—everything. Hurry!"

She took the envelope thrust at her. The man turned away and was gone, slouching off into the shadows. Hurriedly, she examined the envelope. Yes; a seat to Paris, a ticket to Paris. Also a ticket to Lyon. She understood in a flash. She must show the Paris ticket in case she were traced. At Lyon, where she would leave, she must give up her ticket before getting out of the station. No Frenchwoman would give up a Paris ticket before getting halfway there; hence, the Lyon ticket to avoid comment.

Who had done this? She caught her breath, as she turned over the envelope in her hand. Upon it was the rubberstamp of the Sphinx. Barnes? No, no, that was impossible. Barnes knew his way around Europe, but he was an innocent, a new hand at this game. She must be on some false scent after all.

The whistles of the guards were shrilling when she came on to the platform. She had one glimpse of Truxon standing there, tall, lean, savage, waving his hand. Rothstern was on this same train, then!

CHAPTER II

DISGUISE

Daylight crept down from the Alps, with Toulon still well ahead. It would be afternoon before they reached Lyon. Sunlight filled the morning. Marie Nicolas wakened from her nap, stretched, found her handbag and little toilet case at her side, and her brain leaped alert instantly. She forced herself to forget all the mystery of the night, even the dark stranger who had supplied her with tickets. She now had to face the danger of the day, with Rothstern on the same train.

Fortunately, she was no longer an apprentice at this business. She had brought with her all she needed.

She went into the dressing room between the compartments, glanced into the next compartment and found it empty, and went to work rapidly. She grimaced into the mirror at her neat, trim face and figure, her warm cape and the Rue Vignon dress. She was indeed very lovely, the essence of good taste; well, this must be altered!

Her masses of dark hair were rearranged in careless, sloppy fashion. Cheap, musky perfume was liberally splashed about her dress. She deliberately ripped her chic little hat and sewed it together again, a flimsy ruin; the lines of her dress, her figure, could not be spoiled, but the set of the dress could be spoiled with a reckless

tug here, a pull there. When she looked in the mirror again, it was with a sigh.

Now for her face. Gaudy, splashy earrings were nipped in place, dangling almost to her shoulders. Deft touches darkened her brows, changed their contours. Darker skin about her eyes, the lids darkened; a hideous, flashy lipstick completely out of harmony with her complexion changed and spoiled her mouth. Last of all, glasses; pince-nez that really pinched. Another grimace when she inspected the result.

"A woman in the worst possible taste—can it be you?" she observed cheerfully. "Yes, it really is little Marie; but who would know it? Especially a man. And the hair, the hair! That's the best of all. Marie Nicolas, you're a perfectly horrid person—and hungry!"

All this had taken time. The dining-car messenger appeared, reserved her a place, and went on. She left her cape behind, bunched her dress still more shapelessly, and ventured forth.

She was early; she wanted to be early. The train was wakening as it thundered along. Tourists of all kinds, many French, but few Americans; the rate of exchange kept Americans out of France, these days. Fortunately, the restaurant car was close at hand, and with relief she entered and found herself placed at table. The waiter addressed her significantly in English; she, who was invariably taken for Russian or French, was now an obvious tripper! She smiled brightly.

Then, for an instant, she shrank, and her pulse stopped. A presence behind her, a jovial, hearty voice—Rothstern. Coming in with another man.

"Yes, *garçon*, yes, a good breakfast," she exclaimed in an abominably harsh voice. Her English accent made the waiter wince. "Muffins and everything. And don't forget the marmalade, my man. Right!"

To her horror, Rothstern paused at the next table. Then he turned his back; he sat down with his back to her. She could see the shiny bald spot, the clipped hair, the roll of fat above his collar—but thank heavens, he could not look at her! For an instant she closed her eyes, then opened them.

They dilated. Incredulity came into her face and passed. For there, sitting opposite Rothstern and chatting gaily with him, was Franklin. Young Franklin, the laughing Baltimore boy who was the latest recruit to the free-lances; he was supposed to be in Rome, getting on to the ropes. And Rothstern had him in tow!

She watched them. Once or twice Franklin's gaze rested upon her and flicked away again. He looked tired, a bit drawn, but evidently he was charmed with Rothstern. Most men were, who did not know him well. Marie could hear Franklin's voice at times.

"Yes, a bit of business in Paris. Importing is pretty well wrecked these days . . . sightseeing in Italy. Wonderful place under the Facist régime! No, I didn't hear any talk of war . . . in the wine business, eh? You speak perfect English, really!"

From what snatches of talk she caught, the girl gathered that they occupied the same compartment. Was this by chance? She doubted it. Was it by chance that she was on this train with Franklin? The question startled her with its implications. How far ahead did this unknown Sphinx see and plan? Questions be hanged! She dared not let them engulf her, and resolutely put them aside.

Somehow she must warn the young fellow. That he did not recognize her was quite evident. It was unfair to pit him against the veteran Rothstern, who had already enmeshed the boy. As she lingered over her breakfast, more questions rushed upon her; what was going on, what game was being played out with its final scene reaching up to Ostend in Belgium? She could not guess. She struggled to keep her mind on the business in hand, on her own perilous strait.

Toulon was behind them; the train was creeping on westward to Marseilles, before it turned north to Avignon and Lyon. Suddenly the bulk of Rothstern heaved up. His voice came to her clearly.

"You will pardon me? I must prepare telegrams to go from Marseilles. We may meet again on the platform, eh?"

Telegrams, eh? The fat fox was up to something; yes, the boy must be warned. Rothstern brushed past the table of Marie Nicolas without a glance and went his way. Quickly, the girl seized pencil and a scrap of paper.

I am Marie Nicolas. Destroy this. The man with you is Rothstern. He knows every one of us. If you bear any messages look out. Keep away from me.

Presently Franklin rose, paid his bill, and started past Marie's table. Her handbag was knocked from the edge as he passed, though not by his doing. He halted, and with a word of apology stooped for it. As he rose and handed it to her, she slipped the note in his hand. He gave no sign of astonishment, but went on and was gone.

She breathed more easily. After a moment she, also, paid for her breakfast and departed. On the way back to her compartment she kept a sharp eye out, but saw nothing of either man; therefore, they must be beyond her car, toward the rear of the train.

They were flashing into Marseilles now. As by magic, the station appeared and the express slid to a smooth halt. Ten minutes here. Marie opened the door and stepped out to the platform. The news-wagon was almost opposite. She bought Paris editions of English papers, a couple of English magazines, and ducked back into her own compartment again. She had not seen a paper, except the French journals, for two weeks.

Minutes passed. Suddenly Franklin appeared, opening the compartment door that led into the passage. He came suddenly, his voice leaped at her.

"They've got me. Do your best—"

Something flashed in the air and fell at her feet. An envelope. She kicked it under the seat. Franklin was gone; at the same instant, the outer door was wrenched open and two Frenchmen entered, typical business men. Politely, with many apologies, they asked if they might share the apartment. She affected ignorance of French. One explained himself in halting English. Marie Nicolas shrugged, nodded, and opened up her newspapers. The two Frenchmen settled down, deep in talk.

Men moved rapidly past the passage door. After a moment, glancing out at the platform, she saw Franklin there with several suave gentlemen; he was being arrested, then. The engine whistled, the guards slammed the doors, the train moved out of the station. Arrested! Then Rothstern had done it. And her warning had come barely in time. That fat devil was checkmated for once, thank heaven!

The guard appeared, verified the first-class tickets of the two Frenchmen, and went on. Suddenly their words reached into her consciousness.

"Did you see the statement of Count de Prorok, the explorer? He has just left Abyssinia. He says the Italians have massed troops in their colony of Eritrea and are preparing to seize Abyssinia, that France and England have consented, that Italy has caused the frontier fighting. It means war!"

"Bah!" was the response. "No one knows or cares anything about Abyssinia. It is the Balkans that should worry us!"

"No worry," said the first. Marie abruptly realized that she was listening to a keen analyst who knew whereof he spoke. England, France, Germany, want no war. Russia allied with the French, wants no war. Mussolini will keep the peace, depend on it! He'll permit no Balkan conflict. All this is a mask; he intends to seize Abyssinia. Forty years ago, an entire Italian army was destroyed there, at Adowa, and Il Duce means to avenge the loss and seize the whole country. Just as Prorok says. Another Manchuria, my friend!"

"Well, you should know." And the other laughed. "You have a nose in the Quai d'Orsay. But what is it to us, to France? Let Italy rule the black savages. Her rule will be good for them."

"Shall we step out into the passage and smoke?" was the reply. "This Englishwoman will be sure to object if we smoke here—"

The two left the compartment. Marie Nicolas leaned over, picked up the fallen envelope, and glanced at it. Sealed, and addressed only to John Barnes. She thrust it away beneath her dress and pinned it there securely.

She returned to her papers. There, she found the key to the conversation she had just heard; conflict on the borders of Abyssinia and Eritrea, an appeal to the League of Nations by the former, a refusal of any arbitration by Mussolini. So Il Duce would keep the peace in Europe in order to have a free hand in Abyssinia? Very likely. She shrugged and dismissed the matter as of no interest.

Suddenly, with a leap of the pulse, she remembered what Rothstern had told his two mercenaries. A commercial treaty with Abyssinia? It was nonsense, on the face of it. The United States had no commerce, no interests, there. Then why was Rothstern so desperately set on learning the terms of this alleged treaty?

"More questions," she muttered angrily. "Plague take them all!"

Back to the newspapers. A short, sharp exclamation broke from her; she stared at the news items with distended eyes. Morlake in Berlin, Hutton in Vienna, had been arrested the previous evening. American business men, charged with espionage. And both were members of the freelances! Rothstern again, striking savagely. Why?

The two Frenchmen came back into the compartment, apologized politely, and went back to their rapid French conversation in supreme confidence that their fellow-traveler could not follow. The one who had his "nose in the Quai d'Orsay" explained a detail to his companion.

"I tell you, a month ago ships went out of Marseilles loaded with munitions for Abyssinia! There is only one railroad into that country; we control it. Are we letting arms reach the Ethiopian emperor? Then why this disregard of treaties? It looks singular. Watch. You will see things happen in that country."

A fat shape bulked against the glass of the

passage door, looking in. Rothstern. Then he went on. A sense of suffocation oppressed Marie Nicolas. The Frenchmen had switched to a discussion of business conditions. She listened no longer.

The express rolled on to the north. The Sphinx, the Sphinx! Incredible as it seemed, this might be Barnes. At least, he had given Rothstern and the two renegades a startling surprise with his telegram. He seemed to be aware of their secrets; no, he could not be Barnes, after all. A glow crept into the girl's eyes as she thought of him. A splendid fellow, Barnes, but new at this business. No, he could not be this mysterious Sphinx.

Avignon fell behind; a brief stop only. Crossing the river, she had a glimpse of the storied castle of the Popes, with its towering height and the broken bridge below. No stop now until Lyon.

The chief of the train, the "conductor" in America, made his appearance, heavy with gold braid and authority, as befitted a trusted employee of the government. He beckoned the two Frenchmen outside and there, in the passage, conferred with them; many shrugs, gestures, explosive sounds. Finally they appeared to agree. A guard arrived and came in, taking their luggage out. They all vanished up the corridor.

Another guard came in sight, carrying two suitcases, an umbrella, a portable typewriter. He lugged them in, disposed of them in the racks. The girl spoke quickly.

"Is someone else coming in here?"

"But yes, *ma'mselle*," he responded, touching his cap. "A rearrangement, you comprehend; many passengers came on at Avignon. A gentleman from the second class is moving in here. It will not inconvenience you."

She could not reply. The words died in her throat. For there at the door was the gentleman from the second class. It was Rothstern.

He entered, tipped the guard, and lowered himself upon the opposite seat. He did not glance at the girl. His heavy, jovial features were intent upon a number of telegrams which he must have received at Avignon. At length he stuffed them into his pocket, picked up a newspaper, and began to peruse it.

Marie Nicolas sat reading. She felt stifled; her thoughts were inchoate; terror was upon her. She, who was supposed to be so fearless, so well able to take care of herself, stood in absolute fear of this man. She could face the brutality of Truxon, but the gold-toothed smile of Rothstern unnerved her.

She became aware of furtive glances stealing at her. What to do? She could not leave without making a scene, if he were really suspicious of her. If not, her best bet was to keep quiet. Suddenly he chuckled slightly and laid aside his paper.

"Madame is, no doubt, a tourist?" he said in English. The girl gave him a cold look through her glasses, and returned to her magazine.

"The eye is a wonderful organ," he went on, with another chuckle. "When it follows lines of type, it moves back and forth, one sees it at work. But the eyes of madame are fastened upon one point, they do not move—"

"Sir, are you determined to be insulting?" demanded the girl icily.

"A thousand pardons!" said Rothstern humbly, and spread out his hands. "I merely pass the time with observations. I am a philosopher."

He paused to light a cigarette. Marie Nicolas felt a cold, chill thrill pass up her spine. She knew what was coming; and she was right.

"Elimination," murmured Rothstern, as though to himself, "can solve many things. A young lady disappeared from her hotel at Nice. I learn of it later on. I determine that she must be on a certain train. I search, I see nothing of her. I speak with my friend the conductor. Yes, a young lady bound for Paris did come aboard. She is not the one I seek, obviously; yet I think she must be the same. One thing she cannot change, and that is the little foot. The shoe made in America is so obvious in France! So is the shoe made in England—but she does not wear the English shoe."

————

Marie Nicolas shrank for a moment, conscious that the blood had drained from her face. Then she quietly laid down her magazine and looked at Rothstern. He met her gaze, a twinkle in his eye, his jovial laugh showing his gold teeth.

"So?" he asked. "You would not tell a lie to old Papa Rothstern, *hein?*"

She knew the grim, ruthless cruelty behind that laugh. "Not much use trying to fool you, is it?" she said quietly.

"Not a bit. Ah, now you are sensible!" Rothstern beamed upon her. "Why did you run away from the hotel at Nice, my dear?"

"To see where you went, if you must know."

Rothstern chuckled. "Good. We are in company; we go to Paris together. Now, my dear Marie, shall we be frank and abandon all fencing? Good. Perhaps you caught this train to meet Mr. Franklin, *hein?* And somehow, somewhere, he gave you what I want very much to have. Perhaps you warned him, even, about poor old Papa Rothstern."

The girl shrugged. "Yes, I did. But I didn't know he was on the train until I saw both of you together. After that, I had no chance to speak with him again."

"Evasion, eh?" Rothstern rubbed his pudgy hands—big hands, massive hands they were. The gesture chilled her. "Very good. No doubt you have read the paper there. No doubt you saw what happened to poor Franklin; an estimable young man whom I had no chance to warn. Very well. Now, suppose we are friends, eh? Suppose you tell me something I want to know. We lunch together, we reach Paris friends, and part. I will protect you against anything unpleasant, such as happened to poor Franklin. You will not do badly to have Papa Rothstern for a friend, Miss Nicolas. Yes or no?"

"What do you want to know?" she demanded. The threat was clear enough. She would be arrested if she refused. Probably she would be arrested anyway, later.

"Just who is the gentleman who calls himself The Sphinx, U.S.A.?"

She started, her eyes widened. "But I can't tell you that! I must not tell—at any price!"

Rothstern beamed. "The price? It is simple. You remain free, my dear, as you should remain. Come; I see you know. Tell Papa Rothstern."

Beneath his joviality the threat began to appear more pronounced.

"If I tell you—but no, no, I cannot!" she exclaimed in agitation. "No one—"

Rothstern's ponderous features came closer, as she shrank. He seemed fully aware of the terrifying effect he exerted upon her.

"The French police can be most unkind to a poor prisoner," he suggested. "It would pay you, really, to make a friend of me. And nobody would know, upon my honor!"

"I—could—I trust you?" she breathed, staring wide-eyed. "But wait! I must send a telegram from Lyon."

"We shall lunch together, then. If when we leave Lyon I feel that you won't betray me—I'll tell you."

Rothstern beamed, and nodded. "Good! We shall have a nice luncheon with champagne, my dear. Ah, if I were twenty years younger! But we shall see. Yes, you'll find that it pays to trust Papa Rothstern."

She shivered a little, thinking of the envelope pinned within her dress.

CHAPTER III

PURSUIT AND SUBTERFUGE

John Barnes stood on the station platform at Lyon and waited for the P.L.M. north-bound express.

Over one ear was cocked a disreputable chauffeur's cap. Over the other ear, in the approved chauffeur's custom, was tucked a spare cigarette. A dirty white chauffeur's dust-coat, the French survival of a prehistoric motoring age, cloaked most of his body. He had a sandwich in one hand, a bottle of *vin blanc* in the other, and excitement blazing in both eyes.

A thin, dark man drifted up to the lunch-counter, bought a sandwich, and began to eat it. He drifted away, paused for an instant beside Barnes to inspect his sandwich suspiciously, and spoke under his breath.

"M. Franklin was taken off the train at Avignon by agents of the Sûreté. I just got the wire."

"Cover the exit gate," muttered Barnes, and the dark man drifted on.

You must see Barnes as he stood there, munching ravenously, drinking from the bottle, dirty hands, face ingrained with dirt and beard-rubble. An impudent chauffeur type, a humorous glitter in his excited eyes, a strong, hard jaw, lean in the sunlight as he tipped his head back to drink. And those stabbing, dancing gray eyes of his covered everything in sight. A man playing the greatest game in the world, and playing it for life or death. His own included.

Let us suppose, to get the picture, that a Frenchman stands before the lunch-counter of the Pennsylvania station in Philadelphia. The Federal secret service is after him. The local police are watching for him. The railroad detectives have his description. And he stands there, eating, drinking, laughing, ready to pull off the biggest coup of his career! That was the situation of John Barnes as he waited.

The sandwich gone, he finished the bottle, handed it back over the counter, took the cigarette from behind his ear, and struck a match. At the other side of the platform a south-bound train had pulled up, and people were drifting everywhere. A French station platform is like a jail. To get in and out, one buys a ticket; to leave it from a train, one gives up the railroad ticket. Barnes took the ticket he had bought and held it ready in his hand. The north-bound express was coming in. He made his way toward the nearest exit, glanced at the guard there, then turned to watch.

There was the express now. Newswagons trundled out, wine and sandwich wagons; police strutted about importantly; porters rushed about, their straps aswing. Barnes puffed at his cigarette, motionless. The express came to its swift and silent stop. Bells clanged, whistles blew. Passengers began their frantic concourse, shrieking at porters. The carriages were emptied, everyone strolling up and down.

A girl appeared. Barnes threw away his cigarette, pulled down his cap over one eye, stood tensed. Marie Nicolas, holding a telegraph blank in her hand, hurrying. Behind her loomed up the fat figure of Rothstern, overtaking her with a jovial laugh. She swung around. Rothstern took her by the arm.

Like a flash, she slapped him across the face, hard. Her voice shrilled up in a torrent of rapid French: "Dirty pig! You would insult a woman of France—oh, to me, to me, *messieurs*! This *sale cochon* of a German would insult me—"

Instantly, the platform was in an uproar. From all sides, Frenchmen came on the jump. Rothstern, incapable of a word, was surrounded and drowned in a rushing hostile mass of figures.

Barnes turned to the exit, gave up his ticket, and strode swiftly out to the street. There, where a blue Renault stood with a "For Rent" sign on the radiator, was a dark, sad man. Barnes made him one quick gesture, and got into the car. The other turned and departed at a run and was gone around the next corner.

Out from the exit slipped the figure of Marie Nicolas. One swift look, and she came toward the car. Barnes swung open the door. Without hesitation, she ducked in and slammed the door behind her as she half fell on the rear cushions, the car already in motion.

With a swoop and a roar, the Renault went leaping away.

"*M'sieu*," came the girl's voice from behind, breathless, excited. "Are you sure that it is all right? You expected me?"

"Hold your breath, baby," said Barnes in English, and chuckled. "Change cars at the next transfer stop. This is fast work; no time to talk."

A startled gasp from behind, and he chuckled again. Then he settled down to business.

He drove fast and hard for five minutes, dodging traffic and rounding corners like a madman. Then he slowed. A garage appeared ahead, before it a large gray roadster, and beside the roadster, the same thin, sad, man who had departed so hurriedly from the station. Barnes came to a halt behind the roadster, which bore an English license.

"All out, Marie!" he exclaimed, and ducked from the front seat. With a swift movement he was out of his cap and white robe. "Ready, Eremian?"

"Quite, *monsieur*." The thin, sad man handed him a little packet. "Passports, touring permit, everything. Here is the driver's license in your new name."

"Good. In with you, Marie."

He settled under the wheel of the roadster, Marie Nicolas beside him. The car leaped away. Ten minutes later, they had passed the city tax-barrier without question. Then Barnes drew a long breath, and glanced at Marie, his gray eyes dancing merrily.

"Made it! By glory, that was a tight squeeze, young lady. Did you see Franklin?"

"Yes. He gave me a letter for you."

"Thank heaven! Keep it for the present. How are you?"

She gestured helplessly. "Bewildered. Utterly bewildered. John Barnes, you're not the same man I knew!"

A joyous, eager laugh escaped Barnes. "You bet I'm not! But I've got you safe away out of the smash."

"It looks crazy to me," she said. "I could have got across the border from Nice without heading north over the whole of France."

"Not a chance," Barnes said decisively. "Every road, every border station, on the south and east, was stopped this morning. This trip, we've got the whole of France against us. Germany as well. What I predicted to our ambassador in London, months ago, has happened. Every one of our men has either been clapped into jail or is under the closest sort of scrutiny; they've smashed our organization, Marie."

"And Rothstern did it. He said so," she cut in swiftly. Then she caught the arm of Barnes. "Tell me! Are you the Sphinx? Are you?"

Barnes gave her a quick, hard glance, then watched the road again.

"Yes. I thought you'd guess it. I heard of Rothstern's coup just one jump too late. He's tried to clear the slate at one crack, and he's darned near done it, too. Half Europe is behind him—just for this one occasion. Two weeks from now, the storm will be over; but right now we're sure in the soup all around."

"But why?" she demanded. "What is it about? Is there really an Abyssinia treaty?"

"Good Lord!" Barnes flung her a look of startled wonder. "How the devil did you catch on to that? You certainly are a marvel! Go on, talk. That was a lovely getaway you made on the platform. Tell me about it. About everything."

"For one thing, they plan to get you when you go to that musical thing at Ostend, to meet the ambassador from Paris. Truxon has that job."

Barnes started, then whistled softly. "Damn it! They have a spy in the Paris embassy; we can't locate him. All right, tell me how you know so much."

Laughing, she complied, delighted at having puzzled him, and still lost in wonder at finding him to be the Sphinx in sober earnest. And as she talked, Barnes kept the roadster roaring to the northward at high speed.

What a girl she was! Her vibrant personality, her keen ability fascinated him. She was the one person he had determined to save at all costs, from this sudden debacle which had burst upon the little company of free-lances. She was worth all the rest; not because she was a woman, or from any personal interest, but because her wits, her brain, was worth the others combined.

"There you have everything," she concluded. "Is it really something about Abyssinia? What we could have to do with that country, I've no idea."

Barnes nodded frowningly. "We have. Their envoy in Paris has arranged terms with our ambassador there; tentative terms, to be confirmed in Washington. The mutually signed draft is the crux of this situation. It must go by special messenger, and getting it out of Europe is the very devil. Why, I'm not sure. Why Rothstern must have the terms, I don't know. Abyssinia no doubt hopes that a special treaty throwing her borders open to our commerce will forestall Italy, for Mussolini is intent upon grabbing the country. Reilly is to meet us at Dijon, if he gets out of Paris safely.

"He'll know the answer, and why France is so suddenly backing Rothstern's hand."

"But, tell me about yourself, about the Sphinx!" exclaimed the girl eagerly. "How did you send those messages to Nice? How did you have those tickets awaiting me as by magic? Who was the dark, sad man in Lyon?"

"I almost hate to tell you," said Barnes slowly. "And yet, Marie, you're the one person whom I can trust, and who must know the truth. For weeks, I've been sitting in front of a café doing nothing, while Rothstern's agents watched me. In that time, I've built up an organization to take the place of our own. I saw the smash coming. Good as we are, we're nothing against these double-crossing rats who call themselves secret agents."

"Apparently you've done the impossible," she said dryly.

"I have. Everybody has overlooked a great bet. For fifteen years, France has been the haven of Armenians—not the low-class peddlers we know at home, but people of the highest class. That man in Lyon is a graduate of the Sorbonne, Oxford, and Geneva. His father was an intimate friend of the sultan before the war. The man who gave you the tickets in Nice was once a prince. These refugees have no country, no cause, no hope. I have given them all these things.

"One of them alone might betray me; banded together, they would never betray one another. They have a cohesion of blood, of race; America helped the Armenians, and they remember this. I am cashing in on by-products of past history."

She drew a quick breath; her eyes dilated as she watched his keen, alert profile.

"You? Who else?"

"No one else—except you. I figure on keeping the wrecks of our organization and using them, chiefly as a mask. Rothstern and the like will never look beyond to seek a second-degree organization."

"Then you—single-handed—you are doing this—"

Barnes smiled thinly. "The Sphinx, my dear; the Sphinx, U.S.A.!"

"Who supplies the money?"

"I furnish some of it. Other Americans have contributed. I have friends who trust me, remember, and who ask no questions."

"Either you are an absolute madman—or a genius!"

The gray eyes twinkled at her. "Which do you say?"

"Both. Oh, it's wonderful, it's splendid!" she broke out passionately. "If only you can depend on these people—"

"I can. They have relatives, friends, all over France. They are like the Jews, a race absolutely banded together in ruin; they have an infinite genius for detail. I give one of my key men certain instructions; he arranges everything. I can hand one a message today in Paris, and it will be delivered in the most spy-proof manner that same night in Vienna, Naples, Marseilles, Petrograd— and at the same identical moment. You see, the possibilities are vast, almost unlimited."

A sobering thought. "And you see why I've picked on you?" Barnes glanced at her, laughing. "Any other woman would have been mourning her clothes, her personal possessions, everything she'd lost. You don't. You're always a good campaigner."

"Oh, we can always buy more!" she exclaimed brightly. "But don't you want that letter?"

Barnes shook his head. "Wait until we reach Dijon. It'll be in code; it was given Franklin for delivery to me, by an Armenian in Rome."

"So you're using codes, which can always be broken down?"

Barnes chuckled. "I'm using the German code system, which has never been broken down, and never will be. With an Armenian complex, it's invulnerable. You'll see." She shrugged and relaxed on the cushions.

It was nearly dark when they came into Dijon; Barnes did not want to arrive in full daylight. They avoided the grand Hotel de la Cloche and in a side-street off the main Rue de la Liberté, halted before a small hostelry, the Hotel Burgundy.

"We become brother and sister; the name is Smith; passports are ready in that name," said Barnes. "I'll take that letter, if I may. Meet you downstairs in half an hour."

She produced the letter Franklin had turned over, and they entered the little hotel, which had for lobby only the usual small office.

Once in his own room, Barnes tore open the letter, which contained a single sheet of paper. On this were three lines of unbroken typing in capital letters.

In ten minutes he had reduced this to the "cable-ese" of newspaper correspondents, which he then amplified into familiar English. The result was very definite:

BALKAN TENSION HOLDING UP ABYSSINIAN CAMPAIGN BUT PREPARATIONS GOING STEADILY FORWARD. LEAGUE OF NATIONS WILL CONTROL JUGO-SLAVIA. AIRPLANE FLEET PREPARING HERE FOR LONG FLIGHT.

Mussolini had once sent a squadron of twenty-odd ships across the Atlantic to America. He would be able to send a fleet of fifty bombers to Eritrea to act against the Ethiopians. No particular news here; Franklin might have lost this message without any dire consequences, thought Barnes angrily. Then he started, at a sudden thought. He held the paper against the electric bulb in his room. Between the lines of typing, appeared writing as the paper grew warm. He copied it swiftly, decoded this second and more secret message, then whistled softly.

MY BROTHER AT MARSEILLES INFORMS ME THAT TWO BELGIAN SHIPS CLEARED FROM THERE FOR BOMBAY. REALLY FOR DJIBOUTI WITH IMMENSE QUANTITIES WAR SUPPLIES CONSIGNED ADIS ABEBA.

There, by glory, was something!

Djibouti was the French port of Somaliland, whence the railroad ran to Adis Abeba, capital of Abyssinia. The French, then, were permitting war supplies to go through, in defiance of all conventions. Why? Stumbling block. And Marie Nicolas had heard talk of those two ships. Belgian ships; and the Belgians had furnished drill-masters for the Abyssinian army. Something here, something big, if only the key could be obtained.

Hastily washing up, Barnes went downstairs and found Marie awaiting him in the lobby. They left the hotel; they were going to dine, he told her, at the Grande Taverne in the Rue de la Gare, near the railroad station. Reilly, if he got through alive from Paris, was to meet them there about eight.

"It is a risk meeting him, of course, but it must be done," said Barnes. "He has the key to all this business. Now, listen to what was in the letter," and he swiftly sketched the contents of the missive she had brought.

"What does it mean, then?" she asked.

"I don't know. That's what Reilly can tell us. Washington is involved somewhere; so is half Europe. Abyssinia is helpless, but has money to burn—an important point. Well, here we are."

They entered the café, took a corner table within view of the door, and settled down to satisfy hunger.

"Where did you leave the car?" asked the girl.

"In the street, handy for a quick getaway. Whether we'll stay the night, I can't say. Depends on Reilly and Rothstern. Our fat friend isn't so slow, you know," Barnes added thoughtfully. "We're taking chances stopping at hotels. By this time, our registration slip is at the police prefecture. Rothstern might figure you for Dijon, of course. We're bound to take chances any way you look at it," and he shrugged.

"Have you anyone here? Any of your friends?"

"No."

Dinner arrived. As the meal drew to its close and eight o'clock came and passed, Barnes grew more and more uneasy. Then the door opened; a gangling man with flaming red hair and clipped mustache entered and glanced around. He sighted Barnes, who rose.

"Hello, old chap," said Reilly. "Ah! And Marie as well, eh? Glad to see you enjoying life. You won't very long."

He dropped into a chair and fired a rapid order at the waiter, who vanished.

"Trouble getting here?" asked Barnes.

"Nothing else but. I've been driving that old Ford of mine over half the back roads in France. You know what's happened to the gang?" Barnes nodded. He liked this brisk, energetic Chicagoan.

"Sure. But we're not washed up yet. What have you for me? Spit it out."

"You're welcome to it," said Reilly, and grinned. From inside his hat he brought a small envelope. "And, by the way, you'd better be prepared to hustle. Ten miles out of town they caught me. I rammed their car into the ditch, but it'll mean that the net is spread here."

Barnes took the envelope and looked at Marie. "Sorry, comrade; you'll have to wait to get the news. Will you slip back to the hotel, get my suitcase put into the car, and drive the car here?

"Tell the hotel people we're going to join friends at the Hotel de la Cloche. The rooms are paid for."

With a quick nod, the girl rose and swung away. Reilly looked after her; his face was suddenly drawn and tired.

"A swell girl, there," he said. "I'm done for. I'll stop here and let 'em grab me."

"You will not," said Barnes quickly. "You'll go with us. What's this thing?"

He tapped the envelope as he put it out of sight.

"Photostat of an agreement between Rothstern and that chap Forville, in the French Foreign Office," Reilly said crisply. "Cost me a thousand bucks cash, but I got it a week ago. Forville will be made the goat if it should become public, of course; the French government is really back of it. Ever hear of Abyssinia?"

"Once or twice," Barnes replied. "Anything to do with war munitions?" Reilly chuckled. "You're not so slow, huh? Right. Here's the layout—hold on."

The waiter came with the ordered dishes. Reilly, saying he had not eaten since morning, pitched in ravenously. When the waiter was gone, he spoke between bites.

"For three months, Rothstern, on the basis of this secret agreement, has shipped munitions into Abyssinia. Made money hand over fist at it. That Italy's going to grab the country is no secret. France is bitterly jealous of her already; so is Germany. Mussolini is all burned up over the disaster of Adowa, forty years ago, and means to avenge it. Well, he's going to run into another Adowa, that's all. The Italian army will be smashed; his prestige will never recover. Rothstern is behind the whole thing. A gigantic trap in the mountains.

"Get the picture? France then becomes the dominant power in Europe, and so forth."

"Holy smoke!" exclaimed Barnes, as he comprehended the reality. "What's it got to do with Washington? We don't give a hang about Abyssinia?"

"Sure," grunted Reilly, "they've hung it on the Paris ambassador; he thinks it's swell. The Abyssinian envoy has let it be understood that America will guarantee the integrity of Abyssinia; which is all rot. But they've got Rothstern scared stiff about it. So the fat boy wants to find out about that treaty. He thinks we might stop Italy from grabbing; more rot. He wants Italy to grab, burn her fingers, and take a tumble."

"I get you. What good is this photostat to us?"

"Proof. Our diplomatic corps doesn't dare

touch it; the thing was swiped out of the French archives, you know. But any of us can handle it, with the fervent blessing of Washington. If Mussolini gets it, he has proof that France is double-crossing him. You knew I was bringing you orders to meet Grimaldi in Ostend, on neutral ground?"

"No! I was told to meet our ambassador there and take the treaty to London."

"All hooey, brother. You're to do it, sure, but the important thing is to meet Grimaldi. He's Mussolini's best friend. We didn't dare reach him in Paris; you can do it in Ostend. Give him the photostat—on condition Italy won't grab Abyssinia. If Grimaldi assents, Il Duce will probably stick to it."

Barnes saw the whole thing now. If Italy held off, that commercial treaty might or might not go through. All this was a job that no accredited diplomat could handle for a moment. Grimaldi, not the American ambassador, was the real work ahead of him.

"I get you. Grimaldi might not agree, though."

"He will if you tell him that Italy gets a fifty-fifty split in the treaty, and a concession to build a railroad into Adis Abeba. The black boys will probably repudiate the whole thing, even if Washington makes the treaty, but we should worry. Our game is to smash Rothstern—wheels within wheels, savvy?"

Barnes nodded. "What a whale of a scheme! It saves Abyssinia's independence and yet profits all concerned. Who thought it all up?"

"Those blacks aren't so dumb," and Reilly grinned. "Look here, you'd better skip out! Leave me here to act as decoy."

"Nothing doing. Come along. Marie must be outside by this time," and Barnes beckoned the waiter.

He paid his bill, and a moment later the two men left the restaurant together.

As they went out the door, a man rose from a table on the other side of the room, and made an abrupt signal. Two other men joined him, and all three hurriedly departed.

CHAPTER IV

PLAYING THE MOST DANGEROUS GAME

Reilly, crowded into the roadster seat with Barnes and Marie, continued his sketch of the situation as Barnes headed out of the city.

"You see, once the proof is in Grimaldi's hands, he's got Rothstern by the neck. And believe me, Mussolini would like to see that bird done for! France will have to sacrifice Rothstern, and so will Germany. They won't dare let him squawk. That's added incentive for us. We owe him something. Where you heading for now?"

"Troyes," said Barnes. "I'll have a man waiting there for me with news, food and anything else needed—including gas. We'll get there long before midnight. Then on to the Belgian border."

"I can't cross it," said Reilly. "You had better let me go."

"Be hanged to you!" Barnes snapped. "I'll manage it somehow."

They got out of town without incident and the powerful roadster began to eat up the miles of the highway, as the rolling hills of Burgundy fled past.

"Light's behind!" said Marie Nicolas, presently.

Although Barnes knew the road, it was strange to him at night; a hilly road with sharp curves and blind turns. Speed was impossible. Gradually the following car lights crept closer.

"Looks like a pinch," commented Reilly. "And those birds will shoot. They shot at me; that's why I rammed them off the road."

Barnes reached down with one hand, drew a pistol from the car pocket, and laid it in his lap. "This stuff has to get through," he said grimly. "If we're nabbed, you two step out and give up. You'll only get a week in jail at worst. Orders, understand?"

The minutes passed. That the other car was the faster now became all too apparent. Barnes reflected swiftly, and came to a decision. Alone, he might outrun or outfight the enemy, no matter which; they were not French police, who would use pistols only as a last resource. But with Marie in the car, he could not risk her life so freely.

"Be ready to pile out," he said curtly. The other car was close now, its lights holding them in full glare.

Barnes slowed gradually. He ran along the edge of the road, giving plain evidence of his intention to stop. There was still a chance, of course, that the other car held nothing but tourists or fast travelers who wanted to pass. A "honk-honk" from behind as the pursuing car closed in and began to pass. It came alongside, roaring along without slowing. Then—

The jets of fire, the crashing of the windshield, the barking explosions of pistols. A wild cry from Marie.

Sheer blind fury seized Barnes. The whole windshield in front of him was shattered out. Glass flinders stung his face.

Like a flash, he stepped full on the gas, snatched up his own pistol, and as the roadster spurted into a roar after the other car, he began to fire. Shot after shot, steadily, always in the one place. Suddenly a scream drifted back to him. Then a chorus of voices. The car ahead veered, skidded off the road, went slap-bang into a tree with a terrific crash. One of his bullets had found the driver.

The roadster shot past. Barnes looked back once, saw no flames, and grimly held his course. To hell with them! They could take the consequences, so long as their car had not caught afire.

"Marie! Hurt?"

"No, no," came her gasp. "But Reilly—you'll have to stop—"

Barnes slowed, and presently ran to a stop. Like all European cars, this one had a right-hand drive. Thus, the other two had acted as shields for him against those bullets. And one had found Reilly. The red-headed Chicagoan was dead—had died at once, for a bullet had gone through his head.

"What'll we do?" exclaimed Marie, careless of the gashes in her arms from the shattered glass. "We can't leave him here."

"No. You drive. I'll hold him. We're well on our way to Troyes. I'll leave him with my man there, who will take care of it. The body can't be shipped home in any case; anyone who dies from violence must remain buried in France. That can all be taken care of later. The main thing now is to get on." They went on.

It was a grim ride. Barnes sent his thoughts flitting ahead, groping with what might lie across the border. No such danger from the police as here. The whole French bureaucracy was riddled with graft and corruption and scandal; Belgium was another thing. He could understand why Reilly had held this photostat for days, no doubt in the hope of getting it to the Italian embassy, but in vain. Rothstern had paralyzed the little band of American volunteers.

For Rothstern knew of this photostat. What an incredible devil of mental agility, of information, of secret sources, that fat man must be! He had learned of this. He knew his own peril. He even knew—or guessed—that it was to reach Grimaldi on the Ostend musical expedition.

Barnes voiced his thoughts, as Marie sent the roadster roaring on. She had the whole story in her mind, now.

"If I'm stopped, you must carry on," he said. "The photostat is in my inside right coat pocket. You must put through the deal if I fail. Understand?"

"Yes," she said simply. The one word held volumes.

"Get the thing straight. Rothstern probably knows what I don't know—that I'm picked to meet the American ambassador in Ostend and carry that treaty over to London, where it can be sent in the diplomatic pouch without danger. That arrangement is of course a mask. I'm to meet Grimaldi, or someone is, with this photostat and make the deal. And Rothstern surely knows of the photostat."

"But you're to meet the American ambassador too?"

"Naturally. That can be done openly enough, without danger. There is probably going to be a whole diplomatic gathering at this musical affair next Friday. Which reminds me—I must arrange about tickets. It'll be held at the Kursaal, of course; that's the big concert place in Ostend. My man at Troyes will attend to it."

"Are you going to explain that code to me?"

"Yes. The minute we have an hour to ourselves. Over the border."

"Shall we get over?"

"We must."

Troyes was at last on the horizon, and the ghastly ride was presently at an end, and poor Reilly at peace. This was in a furtive little street behind the Hotel Terminus, where a plump, gray-bearded man and his two sons saw to everything. He put into the roadster a hamper of food and wine, and when Barnes introduced the girl to his unpronounceable name, he bowed to her like a courtier.

"*Mademoiselle*, I am honored. You behold but a damned dirty dog of an Armenian, as they called me at Eton in my youth; yet we Armenians may have our uses, eh? Here, Mr. Barnes, are telegrams. One, I fear, will cause you sadness."

They drove on, Marie taking the wheel while Barnes looked at the telegrams.

"I suppose," she asked, "that man was a prince or something?"

"Eh? Oh, not at all," said Barnes. "He was a multi-millionaire before the war. Look here! McGibbons was killed today, in Warsaw. An automobile accident."

"McGibbons?" she echoed in dismay. "Sandy McGibbons? Oh—"

"Exactly; one of our best men. Accident? Not a bit of it." The voice of Barnes was grim. "Now we've come down to murder. Poland, remember, is a close ally of Germany in the new alignment. Our other news isn't so good, either. Truxon left Nice today and landed in Paris this afternoon, by air; Stacey was with him. Rothstern went on

by the same train from Lyon to Paris. Gave you up as a bad job, evidently. Once we get out of town, I'll drive. Tired?"

"Not a bit," she lied bravely.

Troyes fell behind.

A meal as they drove, with hot coffee and a dash of cognac from the hamper, made the cold night look different. Spare gasoline was in the luggage compartment; later, they filled the tank. It was a mad, wild flight through the morning hours; dawn found them speeding forward, with Marie huddled up asleep. Sunrise at last, and in the golden morning they rolled up to the frontier station of the Douane, and Barnes adroitly conveyed a thousand-franc note to the customs inspector in a packet of cigarettes.

Ten minutes later they were in Belgium, unhindered; even the broken windshield had drawn no suspicion.

"Now what?" asked the girl.

"On to the city of Mons. Then hotel; sleep; rest; buy whatever we need. No hurry," and Barnes uttered a gay, joyous laugh. "To-day is Wednesday. We'll stop here till morning, get the windshield replaced, and drive on to Ostend tomorrow. Comrade, we've done it!"

"At a price," she murmured. Barnes lost his cheery air; his face darkened.

"Right. Let me tell you something; when I fight fire with fire, I don't use water. Rothstern murdered Reilly and McGibbons, and that signed his death-warrant. You can pull out of my game if you don't like it. Fair warning!"

She eyed his harsh, strong features with their hint of savage determination, and nodded. She made answer with quiet restraint.

"You're not the man you were; not the same. You're getting bigger, if not better. You're going far. And I'm trailing along, thanks."

"Good girl. You know. I've got something to fight for; we both have," broke out Barnes with sudden deep feeling. "Back home, these callow university pinks, these agitators, these damned communists who never heard of patriotism, say that Americans have no cause, nothing to fight for, no reason for loving country. Wait and see. By God, I'm going to carry things home to these murdering rats over here! This organization is now mine. I'm going to use it in my own way. And everyone else be hanged!"

"Good for you!" came her voice, low, vibrant, rich. "You're not afraid to do things; right or wrong, you do things. Most men don't, any more. They're afraid to make mistakes, afraid somebody will call them down. Ugh!"

"And let me tell you one thing," Barnes said, tapping her on the knee. "Your report on that conversation in the hotel in Nice—girl, that's big! It's going to change everything, all my plans. It shows me a lot. We'll not go into it now, for my brain's dead. By the way, take this photostat, won't you? Pin it under your dress and carry it; I'll feel safer."

"All right, Mr. Sphinx," she said, smiling, and the precious thing passed into her keeping.

Mons grew ahead of them at last, in mid-morning. Ten minutes after they arrived, Barnes was asleep. For the present, worries and cares were left behind.

That same evening, after Barnes had dispatched a sheaf of telegrams, they visited a movie together in delicious relaxation and safety. A good night's sleep followed. With morning, they were off, driving unhurried through the rich Belgian fields. The wild and frenzied flight north was like an evil dream over and done with.

Before reaching Ostend they halted for dinner, in order to delay their arrival until after dark. Marie Nicolas, getting a postcard, demanded a fountain pen.

"Haven't one," said Barnes. She stared at him blankly.

"But you have! What's that clipped to your waistcoat pocket?"

Barnes grunted, drew out the pen to which she referred, and replaced it.

"That," he said, "is a little improvement of my own on a parlor toy. Waiter! *De quoi écrire.* Well, Marie, this time tomorrow night either you

or I should be hearing the Beethoven Mass and talking business with Grimaldi. I've instructed all my agents, by the way, that you're second in command."

"Oh! But—do you know you haven't explained that cipher?"

Barnes whistled. "Right! Later on, then. It'll take time. Get your postcard off and we'll be on our way."

Ostend, the glittering Atlantic City of the Belgian coast, opened before them. Ostend, the cheap and flashy, shop-worn with years and British trippers. Barnes, as usual, avoided the big hotels and drew to a halt before a small and unostentatious hostelry half a block from the "board walk," as it would be termed in America.

"Behold the Belgian Lion!" he exclaimed gaily. "Warranted a cheap, inconspicuous, and small inn. As soon as we get rooms, will you chase out and find me a stenographer?"

"I'm one," she said.

"I must have one who can put English or French into Italian, which I don't know."

"I speak Italian perfectly."

Barnes broke into a laugh. "Good! We'll dispense with the stenographer."

They secured rooms on the same floor. Half an hour later, Barnes finished his dictation. He took the photostat, which he had requested from Marie.

"Doesn't it seem rather silly to have only one of those?" she asked.

"Precisely," and the gray eyes twinkled at her. "I'm going out now to find one of my men and have another made. Then we'll each have one. I've decided to let you conduct all negotiations with Grimaldi."

"What?" Her gaze widened on him. "But you—"

"Will be throwing Truxon off the trail. The performance begins at eight tomorrow evening. At seven, two tickets will be delivered here; the two seats next to Grimaldi, his wife, and secretary. You'll take them and go, presuming nothing happens to prevent you. If I don't show up, you'll have an empty seat beside you.

"Make an extra copy of that dictation and leave it for me, if you don't see me in the morning, at the hotel desk. Take your own copy with you. First, is the contents of the photostat; give that to Grimaldi and get his instant attention. Then give him the terms on which he may have the photostat—the second dictation. If he signs these, give him the photostat and the game's finished."

"But you—"

"What? Are you going around all your life repeating those two words?" demanded Barnes. "Me, I've got to see the American ambassador in the afternoon, let Truxon and possibly Rothstern follow me around, and maybe buy me off.

"Who knows? I'll shove the photostat under your door if you're asleep when I get back."

"I was trying to tell you," she retorted, "that you can't have a copy made at night."

Barnes regarded her with lifted brows.

"You might tell me, also," he rejoined, "that it is impossible to get, from the eye of a dead man, the picture of his murderer. In both cases, you would be wrong—quite contrary to general belief. I'll go into the matter scientifically with you the next time we find a murdered man and no clue to his killer. Meanwhile, my dear, enjoy yourself, keep off the streets, and don't talk with strange men. *Au revoir!*"

He departed, with a grin, leaving her half angry, half perplexed.

An hour later, after a long conversation with a lean, dark man whose curio shop-window bore the startling name of Djismardahossian, Barnes went to one of the largest hotels in Ostend. No other, in fact, than the singularly named Hotel Delicious. Here he displayed himself prominently about the lobby, registered, secured a room, went to his room and turned in for the night.

"She can handle Grimaldi better than I can anyhow," he reflected cheerfully, as he switched off his light. "And I'm the bird they're all out to catch. So, with luck and one stone, I'm lia-

ble to kill two birds and prove that the hand is quicker than the eye. Good hunting tomorrow, Rothstern—damn your black heart!"

When Marie Nicolas wakened next morning, she found an envelope shoved under her door. In the envelope was the photostat. On the envelope was the rubber stamp of The Sphinx, U.S.A. But she saw nothing of Barnes that day.

CHAPTER V

A STRANGE SUDDEN END

At three o'clock on Friday afternoon, Barnes was ushered into the presence of the American ambassador to France, who by some curious chance was also stopping at the Hotel Delicious. The diplomat looked worried, and he was worried.

"Barnes, this damned nonsense must stop," he exclaimed, in the undiplomatic language of big business. "Your wild-cat organization is busted. These European crooks have got the whole crowd by the tail. Reilly's dead. McGibbons is dead. Others are in jail. You must give up the whole show; it's come to an end."

"On the contrary," said Barnes coolly, "it's just begun. If you think two boys like Reilly and McGibbons are going to be bumped off, and nothing done about it, guess again. The crowd's busted, sure, just as I predicted it would be. I'm running the show with a crowd of my own, now."

The other gave him a keen, angry glance.

"You're in earnest?"

"Absolutely and entirely, sir." The level glance of Barnes was like gray steel.

"You're a fool. These secret agents are dirty, double-crossing, treacherous rats. Men like you can't hope to fight 'em."

"Terriers wipe out rats," said Barnes. "Me, I'm the damndest terrier you ever saw, right now. This time tomorrow I can walk down the boulevards in Paris and the police will tip their hats to me instead of trying to grab me. Wait and see."

"You're a blasted ass. Europe is in a ticklish condition. None of us in the service can be responsible for you. If you get in a jam, you're without appeal. You've no connection with Washington. Damn it, I admire you with all my heart, but—"

"You stick in the embassy and I'll play the small-time circuit," and Barnes grinned. "What you don't know, won't hurt you. With Marie Nicolas and a few of the old gang, I'm going ahead; you might tip off the other appointees from Washington to this effect. Now, I'm in a bit of a rush. Do you want me to take that treaty draft over to the London embassy?"

"Yes. It's blasted important too." The ambassador extended a sealed envelope.

"Wrong; it'll die a-borning," said Barnes. "I've learned something about it. This treaty is a blind to get Europe all het up over America's butting into the African game. Abyssinia would repudiate the treaty even if we bothered about it, which we won't."

And he departed, leaving the ambassador frowning after him, more worried than ever.

Barnes left the hotel. He strolled over toward the plage, the wide expanse of sands, villas, bathing huts, stretching up to the massive concrete harbor works. He paused at a café, seated himself with a sigh, and ordered a Rossi. It was just four o'clock. He squirted the glass full of seltzer water, pinched the slice of lemon peel into the blood-red mixture, then sipped at it contentedly and watched the passing throng.

Ten minutes later a large, beaming, jovial figure came swinging along, stopped short at sight of Barnes in well-simulated astonishment, then came to his table.

"My friend, Mr. Barnes, of all people!" exclaimed Rothstern, cordially. "May I sit down."

"Why not?" Barnes said. "Trailed me, have you? No use lying about it?"

Rothstern chuckled, as he seated himself and ordered a beer. "I suppose not. We need not lie to each other, *hein*?" He wiped his bald spot and beamed. "Well, like you Americans, I shall get down to business. Come, Mr. Barnes, we need not be unfriendly. You are going to England; would not a little English money come in useful over there?"

"A little? No," said Barnes curtly. "A whole lot might, though."

Rothstern heaved with laughter. "Ah, you Americans! Come, my friend. I will make you an offer," and his voice dropped until it was barely audible. "Two thousand English pounds if you will let me copy the document you received from the American ambassador. No one will ever know. It will take ten minutes."

"You think I'd sell out? To you?"

"Yes," said Rothstern blandly. "Remember we have met before; you were ready enough to take my money then. Why not now? The cash is ready. We need only step over to my hotel. Why should we not remain friends, to the advantage of both?"

The gaze of Barnes lowered. "Hm! Maybe you're right, Rothstern. If what I hear is true, the game is up for most of us Americans, anyhow."

"Ah, my boy! With Papa Rothstern your friend, who knows? Come. Finish your drink, step to the Grand Hotel with me, and in fifteen minutes—*pouf!* It is over."

Barnes kept his eyes veiled, to hide their hot agitation. So plausible was the man that he might have been fooled, had not Marie Nicolas overheard the actual intention of Rothstern, had he not known who was responsible for the deaths of Reilly and McGibbons. Abruptly, he tossed down his drink.

"All right," he said with decision. "But I'll not walk over with you, naturally."

"Oh, as you like!" Rothstern rose. "Come in five minutes. Take the elevator to the fourth floor; I'll be awaiting you in the corridor. So long!"

He swung away with a wave of his malacca stick. Barnes looked after him, eyes narrowed, cold, implacable.

Five minutes later, Barnes rose, paid for the drinks, and walked toward the Grand Hotel. The die was cast now; he was gambling everything on one turn of the cards, almost literally. As he had told the ambassador, it was make or break this same night.

He had no illusions whatever about Rothstern's intentions, or the trap laid for him.

The Grand Hotel, with its gardens and spacious lobby, opened before him.

He walked steadily to the elevators, took a car up, and left it at the floor designated. Rothstern was waiting.

"Ah! You are wise, my friend, very wise; I welcome you," said the fat man with hearty cordiality. "Come along. I have everything ready. Here is the room—" and he flung open the door of a corner room, with a laughing bow.

Barnes, with a slight shrug, walked in. The door closed behind him. At one side stood Truxon, at the other the rat-like Stacey, each with a pistol in hand.

"Hello," exclaimed Barnes. "Why not a machine gun? I thought this was a private affair, Rothstern."

"An excess of zeal, perhaps—merely to make sure you are not armed, my friend," purred Rothstern. "You do not object?"

"Not in the least." Barnes held up his arms. Truxon, he of the lean and savage features, stepped forward and frisked him—efficiently.

"So that is finished!" exclaimed Rothstern. "Now we shall all be friends, Stacey! Go and get the motor-car ready for us. Mr. Truxon, you will remain, if Mr. Barnes has no objection?"

"I have," said Barnes coolly. "Our talk is to be private."

"Very well." Rothstern turned, and winked significantly at Truxon. "Go into the adjoining room, and wait. But leave the door open, mind! Come, Mr. Barnes, we can settle matters comfortably at the table."

Stacey departed, with an air of disappointment. Truxon, scowling savagely, went into the next room of the suite. Rothstern showed his victim to a chair at the center table, himself taking a seat opposite.

"Now," he said, rubbing his hands, "first, the treaty draft. Here, I have paper ready."

"And the money?" asked Barnes in a cold voice.

"Ah, yes! The money, of course." Rothstern reached into his pocket and brought forth an envelope, which he handed over. His gaze was greedy, excited, nervous. Barnes produced the sealed envelope which the ambassador had given him, and Rothstern snatched at it, broke the seals, drew out the folded paper. "Ah, this is it!"

"Of course," said Barnes. "You want to copy it. Here's a pen."

He took the fountain pen from his pocket—then froze abruptly. Rothstern's hand jumped forward, covering him with a pistol. The fat, jovial features were suddenly cruel, tense, deadly.

"Hands there on the table—that's right!" cried Rothstern. "All right, Truxon."

The latter appeared, giving Barnes a quick, cold grin.

"So, my very good friend!" snarled Rothstern viciously. "You think to play with me, eh? You think to take my money and go? Not so quickly, young man. You have a lot to learn. You have other things I want to see; what about your meeting with the Italian ambassador, Grimaldi? Yes, I know about that. You're helpless. You're in my hands now; I have the treaty entrusted to you. Be careful, or I can ruin you!"

"Rothstern, you're a good actor," said Barnes coolly. "Trying to work me, are you? Trying to force me to cough up all I know—and then you'll kill me. Oh, don't deny it. What about your instructions to Truxon and Stacey, that night you met them in the hotel at Nice?"

Rothstern started. His eyes distended a trifle. "Ah! *Herr Gott!* How do you know that?" he muttered thickly.

"Never mind. No time to discuss it," Barnes rejoined. "I've only time to remind you of something, Rothstern. You're a damned murderer. You were behind the death of Reilly, of McGibbons, just as you expected to be behind my death."

"Well?" The gaze of Rothstern bored into

him, no longer jovial, but wicked and cold with hatred. "What of it?"

Barnes shrugged and looked down. "I'm just reminding you, that's all. Suppose you go ahead and copy the paper."

And, casually, he unscrewed the top of the fountain pen and laid it down. Then he leaned back in his chair, produced a cigarette, and lit it, with an air of perfect unconcern.

Rothstern stared at him for a moment, as though trying to figure out his attitude. Then, putting the pistol on the table at one side, Rothstern emitted a grunt.

"You damned American swine!" he said slowly. "Ah, if I could only have my way, all of you would go—would go—"

He swallowed hard, opened and shut his mouth spasmodically, then fell back in his chair. A little sigh escaped him, and his chin sank on his breast.

"Good God!" cried out Truxon. "A stroke—"

With the word, Truxon darted forward, caught at the pistol, shoved it into his pocket, then leaned over the crumpled figure of Rothstern. He glanced up suddenly at Barnes, who had not moved. What he read in the face of Barnes, brought him erect.

"You!" he cried out. "You devil—"

His hand went to his pocket. Like a flash, Barnes was out of his chair, flinging himself forward—too late! Truxon had no idea whatever of using a pistol here in the hotel. A supple "persuader" leaped out in his hand. As Barnes came into him, he struck, struck once and with the swiftness of light.

Barnes went down like a shot and lay on the floor beneath the table, face to the carpet, senseless.

With a scornful oath, Truxon straightened up, then once more leaned over and caught Rothstern by the shoulder and shook him. He looked down and saw the paper in the hand of Rothstern. His eyes dilated upon it. There upon the paper was a scarlet rubber stamp—the figure of a Sphinx.

"So that was it!" muttered Truxon. "That was what—what—"

He caught his breath suddenly, turned, started for the door; but he did not reach it. Barnes came to himself presently. His eyes opened, as he lay there with his face against the carpet. For a moment he lay quiet. His gaze swept the floor. He saw the feet of the dead Rothstern, and over near the door he saw Truxon outstretched, both hands gripping at the carpet.

Then, without rising, Barnes drew himself away from the table, little by little. There was a trickle of blood on his cheek, and his head was swollen. Truxon had not spared strength in that blow. Presently Barnes gathered himself, came to one knee, and rose. He went to the nearest window and opened it, not without difficulty, for his head was swimming. He turned and looked at the room again.

"So! He knocked me over—and put me in the safest place of all," he murmured, and a thin, hard smile touched his lips for an instant, and was gone.

He took from his pocket the envelope of Bank of England notes Rothstern had given him, and made a gesture of repugnance. He crossed to where Truxon lay, and felt the man's limp, dead hand. He took the notes from the envelope and pressed the dead fingers hard about them; he kept the envelope, which bore his finger-marks. Then he came back to the table, reached out gingerly, and took up his fountain pen. He screwed the cap in place and pocketed the thing.

"Executions by gas," he observed, his voice striking low and sharp upon the terrible silence of the room, "are still a novelty—in Europe."

"There's your warning, Europe!" he said grimly. "Tell 'em all your story, Rothstern; chancelleries, police, detectives, secret agents, cabinet members—tell the whole blasted crowd your story! They'll understand, right enough!"

A TILT WITH THE MUSCOVITE

GEORGE BRONSON-HOWARD

THE SHORT BUT OVERFULL LIFE of George Fitzalan Bronson-Howard (1884–1922) began with his birth in Howard County, Maryland, and included his acceptance to Johns Hopkins University at the precocious age of fourteen. When his mother died, his heartbroken father died by suicide two weeks later, so he was forced to go to work to take care of his four siblings. For the next seven years, he worked in several government departments and as a journalist in Baltimore, New York, San Francisco, and Manila.

It was during his time in the Philippines that he began to write fiction and had immediate success, selling work to the top pulps of the day, including *Argosy*, which published his first story, "The Making of Hazelton," in its July 1903 issue. Two years later, *Popular* published the first Yorke Norroy story, his most successful fictional creation. A Norroy story appeared in each of the next six issues and, when they were collected in book form as *Norroy, Diplomatic Agent* (1907), he reaped a financial bonanza.

With his new financial comfort, he turned to write for the theater and got married in 1907. The marriage fared badly as he and his bride separated on their honeymoon; she claimed he spent the nights churning out stories and articles; their divorce became official the following year.

He had produced twenty-two stories in 1907, but by 1910 he had only one published, generally attributed to his drug addiction as he is reputed to have prodigiously smoked opium with his major playwriting collaborator, Wilson Mizner, and the cultural critic Willard Huntington Wright, who went on to fame and fortune writing mystery novels about Philo Vance under the pseudonym S. S. Van Dine.

He married again, a Ziegfield Follies chorus girl, and worked in Hollywood as a writer and director of eight two-reel Norroy films. In 1918, he served in World War I, joining the British Ambulance Corps. He appears to have suffered injuries in the war and died by suicide by inhaling gas in 1922.

Yorke Norroy works as a secret agent for the United States government. He appears to be little more than a fun-loving fashionable fop but in fact he is a highly intelligent and dedicated man of action. His adventures appeared in three books after his debut: *Slaves of the Lamp* (1917), *The Black Book* (1920), and *The Devil's Chaplain* (1922).

Bronson-Howard's stories served as the basis for more than fifty films, mostly silent shorts, many featuring Norroy, including seven episodes of *Perils of the*

Secret Service (1917), *The Further Adventures of Yorke Norroy* (1922), *The Man from Headquarters* (1928, based on *The Black Book*), and *The Devil's Chaplain* (1929).

"A Tilt with the Muscovite" was originally published in the May 1905 issue of *Popular*; it was first collected in *Norroy, Diplomatic Agent* (New York, Saalfield Publishing Company, 1907).

A TILT WITH THE MUSCOVITE

GEORGE BRONSON-HOWARD

CHAPTER 1

THE LETTER FROM PARIS

NO MATTER WHERE Yorke Norroy might go, the messages sent by the secretary of state always followed him. They were commonplace enough in wording, were signed simply with an initial, and were sent through the usual channels of the Western Union office. The boy assigned with the delivering of this particular message had followed Norroy from the Metropolitan Club to the secret agent's apartment on Connecticut Avenue, and from there had perforce to transport his small person to the golf links at Chevy Chase.

Norroy never lost time in answering these summons, and that was his excuse for appearing in golf tweeds and tan shoes, with long loose coat and slouched hat. He removed the latter two articles of attire on entering the secretary's residence, and when shown into the private library, lighted one of his ever-present cigarettes with the gold crest and waited the new detail. He was quite ready for it, as two months spent in enforced idleness was quite enough for him at one time.

They shook hands on the secretary's entrance, but the head of the Department of State made no comment further than to request that Norroy read a letter, written in French, which he put into his hand.

"It's rather badly put together. Writer isn't a Frenchman," observed Norroy, when he had glanced over it.

"Translate it aloud," directed the secretary. "I have the gist of it, but I imagine your French is better than mine."

To the Chief of the Foreign Office,
Washington, United States of America.

Sir: If you would know what has become of M. Leo Gaylord, about whom your newspapers said so much two years ago, you can discover what you wish to know by sending someone to Paris, and have him write to M. Anton Dumercier, 16 Faubourg St. Gregoire. I cannot tell more by mail, as I am not authorized to do so. This is a most serious thing for Mr. Gaylord, as he is being held a prisoner by an European power for certain reasons unnecessary to explain to you.

When you receive this, please telegraph me immediately when your agent will be in Paris. With much respect,

Your obedient servant,

Paris, November 6th.   *A. D.*

"Translated out of idiomatic French into idiomatic English, that is about the size of the letter," remarked Norroy, as he returned the paper to the secretary.

"So I thought." The secretary took from the pocket of his coat a number of newspaper clippings. "You had better read these at some time. They will be useful to you."

"I am to go to Paris, then?" questioned the secret agent.

The secretary nodded. "You know about this man Gaylord, of course. Everyone does, thanks to the press. But there are two things that for two years you have not known, along with the general public. The first is: To where did he disappear——"

Norroy flicked some ashes from his cigarette. "Pardon me if I suggest that you also are in the dark concerning that, Mr. Secretary."

"That I grant you. I am. But on the second point I am fully informed. You are well aware of Gaylord's ability as an inventor, and of the many astoundingly clever devices he placed on the market, making a fortune for himself out of them. Now, for four years before his disappearance he had been at work on a gun—a rapid-firing gun—of tremendous power, which would carry the almost unbelievable distance of twenty-five miles—fired from a ship."

Norroy seemed on the point of whistling, so great was his surprise. He did not, however, but his slender fingers beat a rapid tattoo on the table.

"You can readily understand what such an invention would mean to naval warfare. Twenty-five miles! It would render practically useless the navies of other nations—"

"But was it practicable?" inquired Norroy.

"That we do not know. Gaylord went away from the United States to work on it—received a concession from the secretary of war to utilize one of the islands in the Samoan group for the purpose of testing his invention. He refused any assistance in the way of skilled helpers, and went there to work by himself. Two years ago he appeared in Tutuila and wired the secretary of war a message to this effect: 'Have completed model, tested it, found it practicable, destroyed it. Proceeding to United States via Europe. Need rest. Will confer with you in Washington three months' time, probably utilizing naval gun factory purposes of building.'" The secretary had been reading the quotation from a notebook in his hand. He closed the book and replaced it in his pocket.

"That sounds as though he had succeeded," remarked Yorke Norroy.

"We heard from him again from Hong-kong, from Cairo and from Vienna. His next place to stop at was St. Petersburg. He is supposed to have never arrived there. The clippings and the detectives' reports will tell you all you may not know, but which has been brought to light. Perhaps Anton Dumercier may be able to supply the missing links."

Norroy rose and the secretary also. "Remember, Norroy, the importance of this affair is without parallel. I do not think we have ever had any case on our hands which caused as many sleepless nights as has Leo Gaylord's. Imagine a gun that would destroy at twenty-five miles in the possession of any European power! It would mean the supremacy of the sea—the absolute supremacy. And what would be the result?"

There was no need for either man to answer the question. Both understood perfectly what the mission meant.

"I shall go to New York to-night and take the *Lucania* to-morrow. You will hear from me in six days from Paris."

"And remember," were the secretary's parting words, "spare no expense and no effort to glean every atom of the truth from Dumercier— or whoever wrote that letter."

The hard lines around Norroy's mouth were excellent reasons to believe that no such instructions were needed to exert him to his utmost in this case.

The large, fair-haired man with the military carriage hesitated at the entrance of the cafe of the Hotel Continental, and his eyes roamed about the low-ceilinged room as though he were in search of some one. Presently the vision of an elaborately attired *boulevardier* in frock coat and tall hat was mirrored in his orbs to the exclusion of the other patrons of the cafe. For the letter had said that the representative of the United States would wear a yellow chrysanthemum as a boutonniere. Such lapel decorations being rare in Paris, M. Dumercier hesitated no more.

He approached the table and stood before it, regarding the man with the chrysanthemum and the rimless monocle.

"Comment vous portez-vous, m'sieur?" he inquired, with respect.

"Tres bien, merci, m'sieur," was the calm reply.

"C'est M'sieur Lemaire?" asked the fair-haired man, tentatively.

"Oui, m'sieur," replied the monocled one, with brevity.

It was sufficient introduction, and the two men studied each other over the foaming bocks which the *garçon* brought at the command of the one addressed as Lemaire. The conversation was mainly on the weather and the recent turmoils in the Senate. By Dumercier's speech it was easily told he was not a Parisian—the average listener would have decided he was from one of the lost provinces. Lemaire, too, had a slight accent which proved him not of the Boulevards, but which might easily obtain with a native of Languedoc or perhaps Gascony.

They did not linger long in the cafe, but adjourned to Lemaire's apartments on the second floor of the hotel. No words were wasted between the two on the way. Lemaire threw open the door of his private reception room and bade Dumercier enter. The door was locked and both men went into the bedroom adjoining, Lemaire closing the second door as they passed in.

From his pocket Lemaire drew a letter which he handed to his companion.

"You wrote this?" he inquired.

The other replied in the affirmative.

"Well?" It was easily seen from Lemaire's manner that he expected to share little in the conversation and that he did not intend to draw it out to the extent of a personal chat.

"I am a Pole, M. Lemaire," began the other, apologetically almost, "and I was an officer in his imperial Russian majesty's army. I am not now. I was lucky to escape unharmed. That is all regarding myself that I need say, is it not?"

"Unless it concerns M. Gaylord—yes."

"Well, M. Gaylord is in a Russian prison. He has been there for two years. That was news to you until my letter came, was it not, m'sieur?"

The other nodded.

"I was a sergeant in the Paulowskis when he came. Afterward I became an officer—but no matter. How I came to discover what I know is also no matter. Briefly, I will tell you. M. Gaylord was arrested near Moscow, and he is now a prisoner but a few versts from that city—in the fort of St. Basil.

"They did not intend to keep M. Gaylord prisoner long. They thought to find on his person some sketch or plan which would tell them about the new cannon which he had invented. But there were no papers of any kind on him or in his bags and boxes. Therefore, he was taken to St. Basil.

"He might have been free the next day after his capture if he had given up his ideas to M. Mobrikoff. But he would not. M. Mobrikoff is chief of the Bureau of Engineers and Ordnance. It was he who knew that M. Gaylord had completed his new gun which he would make for the United States.

"When M. Gaylord refused to tell him how it was done, he told M. Gaylord that he should remain prisoner until he did so. A prisoner, then, he has been for two years, but nothing would he say.

"Three months ago, M. Mobrikoff, who is also a colonel and a noble of Russia—a count—made up his mind that M. Gaylord *should* tell what he knew. So M. Gaylord was ordered to be knouted if he would not tell."

The teeth of his listener came together with a savage snap, and he crumpled the letter in his hand into a shapeless mass. The man who called himself Dumercier looked up quickly. His auditor had begun to straighten out the paper and was now tearing it slowly to pieces.

"Proceed," he commanded.

"So M. Gaylord was knouted. You know the knout, m'sieur? It is long and has brass ends to it. With this M. Gaylord was scourged—fifty strokes he received.

"But he would not tell what they wished to know. The count then said that each week would the knout be given him. But he would not answer. He only closed his mouth as you did but a moment ago; closed his mouth and ground one tooth against another. And what he said was in your English tongue. The language I do not know, but so many times has M. Gaylord said this that I have learned it, too. 'Gotter 'ell!' he said—only that, no more—'Gotter 'ell!'

"Now, as for me, I was foolish. I was an officer. I was a noble, too, then, for one may not be an officer without he be noble. But Poland—they wish to be free there. And I—but that is concerning myself, m'sieur. It only serves for you to know that I determined to leave Russia before it was so arranged that I might never leave it.

"M. Gaylord I liked. I went to him. I told him that I was coming out of Russia. So then he told me this. I dared not write it down, for I knew I might be searched, but this I learned from him and repeated it again and again:

"'I have been beaten like a dog and caged like a criminal. I love my country, but if my country cannot aid me, or will not, I must aid myself. As yet Russia knows nothing of my new weapon. Three months from to-day, if I am not free, she will know all.'"

The paper in the hands of the other had been reduced to the tiniest fragments. He looked up.

"That was all?" he inquired.

"All except that if I succeeded in carrying the message the person to whom I gave it should pay me ten thousand rubles, and collect the same from his brother, Douglas Gaylord, of Birming-ham, Alabama. If he were freed, ten thousand more he would himself pay me."

"This man Mobrikoff—what of him?"

"I have told you. He is a noble and a colonel in the army. He is also the chief of the engineers and of the ordnance. He has Romanoff blood."

They talked more. The monocled one asked many questions—searching questions which went into the history of Mobrikoff's past career and all those connected with him; his likes and his dislikes; his habits and his manners.

There was a satisfied gleam on the questioner's face when the information was elicited that Mobrikoff's failings lay in the direction of women.

"Ah, yes!" the Pole said. "The *chanteuses* of the Palermo. They indeed are the favorites of M. Mobrikoff. To one he threw a thousand-ruble note. I was there, m'sieur, for a girl from my village danced. Afterward she told me. It is that, m'sieur. Stage women—I know not why—he seeks his feminine society among them——"

He was cut short by the other rising.

"There is a note for five hundred francs, M. Dumercier," he said, curtly. "I will see more of you again. I will write you. Meanwhile I must think——"

"But the ten thousand?"

"All in good time. I must see for myself. I go to Moscow to-night. But have no fear. It is but a trip of inspection. I will return before the week is out. *Au revoir, m'sieur.*"

He saw him to the door, and then sat down in the reception room. For some minutes he sat perfectly still. Then he lighted a cigarette, and after that many more, his slender fingers meanwhile drumming a devil's tattoo on the arm of the chair in which he sat.

That evening the six o'clock express for the north bore the person of M. Lemaire, described in his passport as a French-American; occupation, the management of theaters; residence, New York City, and object in visiting Moscow, business connected with the theaters. The passport was signed by the minister of the United States to France.

In Moscow M. Lemaire remained several days. He exhibited a tourist's curiosity with regard to the old city. M. Mikhaelovitch, the manager of the *cafe chantant*—the Palermo—gratified this curiosity personally. In his company M. Lemaire visited the Kremlin, the Cathedral of Ostankino, the Church of the Nativity, and that weird architectural monstrosity, the Church of St. Basil the Beatified, with its forest of bell towers, ornamented with heraldic designs, pots of flowers and many grotesque figures.

Naturally, from the Church of St. Basil, it was not strange that the mind wandered to the prison of the same saint. So thither they went, too. M. Lemaire seemed to take but little interest in the grim criminal institution, so they remained but a short while.

When M. Lemaire left Moscow and M. Mikhaelovitch, he promised the proprietor that his *chanteuses* would arrive within several weeks. Whereupon M. Mikhaelovitch smiled in a gratified manner, soon afterward conferring with the disreputable journalist who aided him in his work, when he was not overfull of vodka. The disreputable journalist wrote a sonnet which exalted the beauty and ravishing charms of certain English and American singers who would delight the inhabitants of the Kitai-Gorod with ballads sung in M. Mikhaelovitch's charming resort, the Palermo. This sonnet was published in the newspapers of Moscow and was read by noblemen and officers of the navy and marine who sojourned within the Kitai-Gorod. These exalted personages were frequenters of M. Mikhaelovitch's *cafe chantant*. Consequently they were interested.

Meanwhile two cablegrams had been despatched by M. Lemaire as soon as the train left the realm of the Great White Czar. Both were in code, and the German telegrapher who handled them scowled, for such messages were not liked in his Teutonic majesty's realm. But they were despatched nevertheless.

One was to the secretary of state, and requested that Miss Adelaide Hardesty be ordered to Paris immediately to join Theophile Lemaire

at the Hotel Continental. The other was to Miss Hardesty herself and is perhaps worth quoting:

> Secretary wired to-day request for your assistance. Select three prettiest show girls in Manhattan. Bring them with you. Consult secretary regarding reasons.

Thus Edna Follis, Mabel Dupree, and Nanette Edmonds forsook the Rialto and journeyed with Miss Adelaide Hardesty to Paris.

A letter fully explaining the reasons for the two cablegrams reached the secretary of state by the *Campania*. It bore the postmark of Paris. In part it read:

> The man who gives the information is a Polish nihilist, formerly an officer in the Russian army. If we were to take the matter up legally with Russia, his oath would not be worth the word of a Chinese diplomat. He is discredited and disgraced, and acknowledges the fact himself. To make a serious charge against another power on the strength of such a man's statement would be impossible and absurd. It would be denied, and if things came to the worst Gaylord would probably be sacrificed and his body put into some vault of the fort. My plan seems to be the only feasible one. If it fails, be assured that I am quite aware of the fact that I can expect no assistance from the United States—officially.

This screed was signed with the initials of Yorke Norroy.

CHAPTER II

THE GIRL FROM BROADWAY

For two weeks, the American *chanteuses* had sung and danced before the critical audience which nightly gathered in the *cafe chantant* of M. Mikhaelovitch. Incidentally, their twinkling feet, coquettish gestures, trim forms, and speaking orbs had caused the Odessa Jewesses and Georgian beauties, hitherto such favorites, to fill the position commonly denominated as "facing the wall." Even Yvette d'Alencon, Parisian and consequently charming, was not acclaimed as of yore. The American beauties had caused her star to wane and become dim.

The Americans brought rag-time with them. Moscow had heard rag-time before, but not sung as the Rialto girls sang it, nor accompanied with the complement of "goo-goo" eyes and buck and wing dances.

The receipts of M. Mikhaelovitch increased, and he one day, in an excess of jubilance, embraced M. Lemaire and kissed him affectionately on both cheeks; which was Russian sentiment and meant that he cherished M. Lemaire as a brother. M. Lemaire, being French, should have appreciated this, but evidently his residence in America had deprived him of the mental light which approved of osculation between those of the same sex. As it was, M. Mikhaelovitch narrowly missed being stunned into unconsciousness by a blow from M. Lemaire's fist. M. Lemaire, however, remembered his part and restrained himself.

Back in the dressing-rooms, the girls chatted among themselves.

"Talk about your New York Johnnies," sniffed Mabel Dupree. "Why, they're not in it for a minute with these fly Russian guys. Say, Edie, you remember that chap that sat in that second walled-off pen last night and threw me a pearl bracelet, eh? Well, he's here again to-night. I just peeped out behind the curtain and saw him."

Edna Follis adjusted her pompon. "You'd better leave the new ones alone and stick to the old," she said, warningly. "That Captain Wishtoff——"

"Wesshoff," corrected Mabel, indignantly.

"Well, anyhow, he's a good fellow. You won't find many will hand you out a diamond brooch like the one he gave you. He'll be angrier than the seven Satans if you throw any eyes at this other fellow. I know——"

"Victor?" suggested Mabel, pleasantly.

"Shut up! You don't know anything about Victor. Why don't you try to act as though you had some sense? Act like Adelaide. Adelaide hasn't mixed up with any smelling Russkis."

The third girl, who had been silent, now spoke. "Adelaide is a fool," she commented. "There's that fellow who comes here every night. Sends her candy and flowers and—everything. I know who he is. Lieutenant Ogareff told me. He's Count Mobrikoff, and he's related somehow to the czar's family. And Adelaide won't pay any attention to him."

"I believe Adelaide has a mash on Lemaire, and hasn't got any time for anybody else. Can't say I like him much. Do you?" observed Miss Follis.

"No, I don't. He's altogether too fond of browbeating people. Say, do you know I have my doubts about him being French? I heard him talking to Adelaide day before yesterday in the corridor, and he spoke as good English as you or I."

There was a rap on the door and the call for Miss Follis was made. Whereupon Miss Follis donned her light top-coat over her red skirts, and, taking her beribboned cane, departed to delight the souls of the children of the czar with the amatory strains of "I've Got a Feelin' for You."

There was no dearth of auditors for Miss Follis's coon song. The brass-railinged tiers of the pit had their tables crowded with men in the various uniforms of the army of the czar; the blue-black of the marine, the sky-blue of the infantry, the red of the telegraph, the orange of the light cavalry—all were represented there. The sight catching the singer's eye from the stage was reminiscent of a rainbow. The electric lights shone on patent leather boots, gold braiding, silver spurs and jingling swords. The spectators themselves were mostly of the same class—army officers, naval officers, employees of the government in some shape and form, all wearing uniforms, and all ready to cast upon the stage money extorted from the government, as evidence of their pleasure in the antics of those who appeared before them.

But there was one man in all this crowd who was immediately brought to the attention of any who entered. He sat on a raised platform, almost on a level with the stage, and it was known that this platform was one which was occupied by none save those of high rank. The man who occupied this place was attired in the uniform of colonel of engineers, and he wore on his breast the Order of St. Nicholas. He was a well-known patron of the Palermo, this nobleman—the Count Mobrikoff.

To Miss Follis, Mobrikoff paid little heed, only frowning when she was recalled for the fourth time to sing over the ballad regarding the "sneaking feeling." Miss Dupree, who followed her, likewise gave him no pleasure, to judge from the scowl with which he favored the inoffensive waiter on ordering his second bottle of Paul Roget. After Miss Dupree came Mlle. Yvette d'Alencon, who was received coldly and encored but once, and that only by a few of the faithful.

The entrance of the next *chanteuse* was preceded by loud applause and clapping of hands, for Miss Adelaide Moray, as the bills styled her, had made more than an ordinary hit with the patrons of the *cafe chantant*. At her appearance Mobrikoff leaned forward and watched closely, with the light of admiration in his eye. At the conclusion of her song he joined in the applause and tossed a tiny box upon the stage. Adelaide stooped down and secured it.

She was forced to repeat her song several times, but after the ordeal had been gone through with she made her way hastily to her dressing-room and opened the box. It contained a heart-shaped pin set with diamonds and rubies, around which was wrapped a note in French. A few moments later M. Lemaire and she were conversing over the note.

"H'm, h'm!" Lemaire was reading it. "'Scorned my advances, refused my gifts, beg interview'—h'm, h'm—'wear the pin as token of acceptance.'" He looked up and, speaking in English, said: "Johnnies are the same the world over, aren't they, Adelaide?"

She nodded. "Shall I accept? It seems to me I've held him off enough already."

He meditated. "You have the necessary liquors in your reception room to satisfy his lordship?"

"Considering that you sent them there, you should know. I haven't touched any of them. You know how I despise intoxicants."

"And you have—the other?"

She eyed him scornfully. "Kindly give me credit for having some foresightedness."

He examined his watch. Then he looked at her thoughtfully. "Do you know, Adelaide, you're rather a stunning-looking girl?" he said.

If healthy, rounded form, milk-white skin with the faintest ruddy tinge, and deep black eyes constitute "stunningness," then M. Lemaire was correct. Adelaide Hardesty—or Moray—was the type of a woman who appeals to the mind looking for outward charm. The finer workings of her mind were not apparent to many, for she chose not to reveal them, passing rather as a woman whose sole desire in life was to cling to the wheel of pleasure as long as life held forth within.

She looked out at Lemaire from under her long lashes. "That is part of the game," she returned, without the faintest show of emotion of any kind. "I suppose your examination of your watch is a question which I am to answer. I think if you enter my reception room at the hotel at twelve o'clock you will find the gentleman in a condition fit for our ends."

As he smiled and patted her shoulder paternally, her smile was very bitter. When he had gone, after giving a few further instructions, she became pensive. "A good tool for his ends, that is all," she told herself. The bitterness was gone, there was only sadness in the whisper.

When she went on for her second turn, she wore the pin which M. Mobrikoff had thrown to her. The eyes of the Russian nobleman lighted up, and he ordered more champagne. She watched him as she sang and threw him several looks which she strove to make unstudied.

At eleven o'clock the droshky of Count Mobrikoff was at the narrow door out of which the performers passed from the stage, while within the outer room the owner of the droshky sat, rubbing his booted legs together, toying with his sword, and watching the door to Miss Hardesty's dressing-room with ill-concealed anticipation.

When she emerged, clad in sealskins, her masses of heavy hair adorned with a toque of the same material, he sprang to his feet. Her dark eyes fell upon him rather shyly.

"I am your slave, mademoiselle," he said, in French, and with the customary extravagance of the Russian. He took one of her little gloved hands and pressed it to his lips.

"Almost every night for two weeks past I have watched you. I had thought that you were cold to me, and that you preferred another——"

"*Merci, m'sieur,*" she returned. "But I must hurry on now. Some other time, perhaps——"

"What! will you leave me so soon, now that I have found you? Ah, no, mademoiselle—ah, no! You must come with me to the Ulamen. There we will have a little supper and some wine—and I will feast my eyes upon you."

She blushed. The blush was real. Adelaide Hardesty had not yet hardened herself to playing the part which her chief had assigned her. The scraping Russian disgusted her. She knew what lay behind this flattery. She knew of the knouting of Gaylord and of other things. At the thought of the last, she braved herself to the ordeal.

"If you insist, m'sieur," she said, smiling faintly, "I will allow you to go with me to my hotel."

"Ah, yes! You have lifted me out of Hades into Heaven. My droshky awaits without."

He took her arm, and she allowed him to help her into the vehicle. A word to his driver, and they were whirling across the snow in the direction of the Hotel d'Angleterre, where Adelaide Hardesty maintained a suite of rooms. She strove to make it appear to the Russian that she was

interested in him, and, thanks to his egotism, her rather studied attempts passed for realities. And now the hotel loomed up before them. He stepped to the ground and helped her to alight.

"And now, *M. le Comte,*" she said, as she released his hand, "I will say good night and thank you."

"You will leave me now? Ah, no! Let us go within this hotel of yours. Let us have the supper of which I spoke——"

He talked on more in the same strain, and presently she assented reluctantly.

"I have a reception room, *M. le Comte,*" she told him. "In that you may stay for a while if you wish. I do not care for the public dining room, nor do I care for food."

Mobrikoff, delighted at his supposed victory, followed her, and after the servant had gone ahead to light the rooms, she motioned him to the elevator, which raised them to the third floor. Down the uncarpeted hall she led him to where the attendant stood, holding the door of her apartments open. The count bowed for her to pass in, and when she had done so followed her.

He did not waste time. The man was plainly attracted by the girl, and he brought all his previous knowledge of women to bear upon her. But he would have failed even had she not known of him what she did, for Adelaide Hardesty had her own ideas of mankind, and the use of flattery did not come in as part of the character of her ideal man. But she had been an actress too long to fail in any part once she entered into the spirit of it.

She had placed various liqueurs on the table soon after her entrance, and he had done full justice to all of them. She had waited to see him a trifle influenced by the intoxicants before bringing out the *chef-d'oeuvre.*

"You have heard of the American drink—the cocktail?" she asked, her deep eyes turned full upon him and her red lips curving in a smile which she intended to appear tender. "That is the drink which surpasses them all."

"Of that I have heard," he responded. "And I will never rest until I have drunk it, for is it not the national drink of Mlle. Adelaide's own land?"

She smiled at his lofty words, a natural smile this, for, now that she had hardened herself to what she was about to do, the Russian's extravagance was humorous to her American mind. "You need not wait long for the cocktail, *M. le Comte*," she said. "I myself will make one for you."

He was almost maudlin now and murmured something about Hebe and the nectar of Olympus. She took the vermuth, the whisky, the bitters and the lemon, making the drinks on a little tabouret with her back turned to him. Then she placed the ice within the frail-stemmed glasses and poured in the decoction. In one of them she dropped something which she had been holding in the palm of her hand, and quickly broke the tiny tablet to pieces with the spoon, stirring it vigorously. Then she placed both glasses on a tiny tray, with the one over which she had expended so much trouble on the Russian's side.

"Will you drink?" she asked, gayly.

He reached out his hand and took the glass. She raised hers and they clinked them together.

"To mademoiselle's eyes!" he cried.

He drank it down with every appearance of enjoyment and then threw the glass over his shoulder. It alighted on the hearth and broke into tiny fragments. "A fitting end for a glass which has served its purpose," she thought.

And now came the hardest part of all, for the drink mounting to the Russian's head aroused all his hitherto suppressed boldness, and in the manner of his race he made love to the American girl. At first a mere pressing of the hand to his lips, with the accompanying declarations of affection. She had purposely seated herself upon a tiny chair in order that he might not come nearer.

He was determined that he would take the girl into his arms. His feet were unsteady now and his head whirled. Out of the mist that enveloped him, he could see only her eyes shining in the light of the shaded lamp. He rose to his feet, trying to fight down his weakness.

"I love you," he muttered. "I love you."

He moved forward, still holding her hand.

She rose. The latent beast in his eyes terrified her. He stretched out his arms as though to envelop her within them. But at that moment a great desire for rest overmastered him. He forgot the shining eyes.

"I—I——" he began. Then his legs became weak at the knee, and he toppled forward, gripping the table. But his muscles were inert, and his head slipped along the polished surface, and, with a crash of bottles and glasses, the form of the chief of engineers flattened itself on the floor.

She stood erect, pale and afraid. Then her eyes turned to the senseless body of the man. There was no sound in the room save his heavy breathing.

She looked at her watch. It was rapidly nearing the hour of twelve. She sat down, supporting her head with her hands, among the broken remains of bottles and glassware, the trickling liqueurs dripping on her gown. She knew it, but she hardly cared.

Out of the distance the toll of the second Tsar Kolokol, the great bell of the Kremlin, rumbled out the strokes of midnight. Then came a gentle knock on the door. She arose and admitted Lemaire.

"Successful, of course?"

"Of course," she responded, wearily. "He lies there."

"Then I must ask you to go into your room, Adelaide," said Lemaire. The girl obeyed him, leaving him alone with the man. Lemaire lifted the frame of the senseless Russian in his arms and deposited him on the divan.

"It is lucky for me that I am the average height of a man," soliloquized Lemaire. "Quite lucky, indeed."

It was but a matter of a few moments before the gorgeous uniform had been stripped from the person of M. Mobrikoff. His despoiler opened a bag which he carried, and which contained a suit of coarse brown serge. In this he arrayed the drugged officer, gathering up Mobrikoff's uniform and placing it in the bag from which he had taken the brown clothes.

"Now, Adelaide," he called.

The girl re-entered. "Where is that long wardrobe trunk of yours?" he inquired.

The girl threw back the hangings at the end of the room and disclosed one of those monstrosities which are the trial of the baggage-smasher—a theatrical wardrobe trunk and property box. In length it approximated six feet and in height about three. She unlocked it. It was empty.

"The drug will hold good for about six hours. During that time he will be safe, but after that——We had better bind him now, Adelaide."

He took some stout manila rope from the same bag he had before utilized, and the feet and hands of Count Mobrikoff were securely bound. A gag was placed in the Russian's mouth and bound tightly about his head. Lemaire picked up the trussed body and placed it within the trunk.

"You have bored the air holes?" he inquired.

"There are four on each side and ten in the top. He isn't in any danger of asphyxiation," was her reply.

Lemaire straightened out the knees of the captive.

"All that is necessary now is to throw in enough clothes to keep him from bumping from side to side," he said. "I should advise you to lock the trunk to-night, for he will be sensible in the morning."

Then he turned to go, but she caught him by the arm.

"Haven't you a word of praise?" she asked, brokenly.

He regarded her with much intentness. "Too much praise, Adelaide, to put it into words. I know how distasteful it is to you. You are a brave little girl!" He patted her shoulder in his old way. "But remember what this man has done. He deserves more than a cramping of his limbs for several days."

She tried to be calm. "Will you be successful?" she asked tremulously.

"There is no reason why I should not be," he answered. "I rely on you to carry out your part, you know. And I know you will. Good night, little girl."

When she had closed the door she stared long and blankly at the entrance through which he had passed. Then she rocked herself to and fro, murmuring and whispering to herself: "A good tool for his ends—a good tool."

She threw the required clothes into the trunk, closed and locked it. "After all," she sighed, "it's better to be a tool for him than——" She did not finish her sentence.

CHAPTER III

WITHIN THE PRISON HOUSE

A little after twelve word had been taken to the driver of the droshky of Count Mobrikoff that the Count would remain at the hotel for the night, but that the droshky was to be waiting for him the next morning at nine o'clock, when he would visit the fort of St. Basil. This message was sent from the room of M. Theophile Lemaire.

Within that same apartment several changes took place between midnight and morning, and had there been an observer near by, he might have sworn that three men occupied the same room. For into the room and to bed went M. Theophile Lemaire, a Frenchman with a slightly bald pate, a small waxed mustache and heavy eyebrows. When the rays of morning sunlight disclosed the sleeper there was no sign of M. Theophile Lemaire. The snowy counterpane covered the form of a man with light brown hair, clean-shaven, and evidently of Anglo-Saxon origin. When he awoke and stood erect in his pajamas, it would not have been hard for anyone who knew him to recognize Mr. Yorke Norroy.

But Yorke Norroy existed only during the time that he took his bath and shaved. Nine o'clock saw him standing in the lobby of the Hotel d'Angleterre an officer of his imperial Russian majesty's army, whose hair was coal-black and whose mouth was shaded by an enormous military mustache turned upward in German style; his eyebrows were heavy and his military cap was pulled down to shade his eyes. Evidently, M. le Comte Mobrikoff had contracted a severe cold, for he spoke hoarsely and his neck was swathed with a white silk kerchief. The collar of his greatcoat was turned upward to protect his throat.

He lighted a cigarette and inquired in a husky tone if his droshky awaited him. On being informed it did, he went out of the hotel lobby and into the street where his driver assisted him into the vehicle. In the same hoarse tone, he directed him to drive to the fort of St. Basil.

Through the streets of the Kitai-Gorod and over the frozen snow the droshky sped, its owner smoking cigarette after cigarette and gazing out on the passing crowd. Many peasants and moujiks doffed their caps and he saluted them gravely, while occupants of other vehicles called to him as they sped by.

Through the Kitai-Gorod, into the Beloi-Gorod, and finally into the Zemlianai, the droshky of Mobrikoff went. The last, being the Chinese city, was naturally dirtier than either the European or the Tartar quarters, and the vehicle went more slowly on account of the slippery streets.

When the Iverskaya Chasnovnia was reached, the driver reined in his horses and doffed his hat to the sacred icon within the Iberian Chapel, and Norroy, sitting behind him, perforce did the same. After this act of devotion, the horses, started again by a swift cut from the driver's whip, dashed through the Resurrection Gate of the Chinese wall and out beyond the city, where, a few versts away, the fort of St. Basil frowned ominously on the waters of the Moskowa.

It required but little time to make the journey now, and they were soon halted by the Siberian sentinel who stood beside the first gate of St. Basil.

"It is the great colonel, Count Mobrikoff," the driver informed him, in the queer *argot* of the Baltic provinces—half Slav, half Teutonic.

Instantly the soldier's carbine was raised in salute. The iron gates swung open ponderously, and the droshky rolled over the stones of the courtyard of the outer fort, through an embrasure, and, after several more halts and salutes, stopped in the central courtyard.

The sergeant who was in charge of the guards of the inner court evidently recognized the occupant of the droshky to be the chief of engineers, for he clicked his heels together sharply and saluted.

The false Mobrikoff saluted the sergeant in return, alighted and walked past the line of guards, following the non-commissioned officer.

"You wish to see M. le Colonel Mebristiwsky, colonel?" the sergeant had asked.

"Yes," replied the supposed colonel, shortly. He still spoke in the hoarse tone which indicated that his cold affected his throat muscles to the extent of preventing him from speaking plainly.

He followed the sergeant through a succession of passages, and waited while he knocked on the door of the room which held the illustrious presence of M. le Colonel Mebristiwsky, governor of the fort of St. Basil.

The door was opened by an orderly and Norroy passed into the room.

The man with grizzled hair who sat at the desk in the middle of the room arose on Norroy's entrance and bade him the usual good-morning.

"I have a cold, M. Mebristiwsky," he replied, in answer to the request that he remove his cloak. "I fear it is getting close to my lungs."

Norroy's Russian was without a flaw, but he found little occasion to use it on this mission, for Mebristiwsky conversed with him in French, as is usual between gentlemen in Russia, their own language being reserved more for the purpose of speaking to inferiors. After several inquiries regarding some matters of which Norroy knew nothing, but which he managed to answer in a discreet manner which aroused no suspicion, the secret agent asked concerning the American prisoner.

"He is violent, as usual," answered the governor. "He swears at anyone who enters his cell, and curses the Little Father in terms which would shock even a hardened *roue* like yourself."

"I wish to see him again," said Norroy, cutting the governor's peroration short. The governor, frowning, rang for the orderly.

"Take the Colonel Mobrikoff to the cell of the American."

Norroy followed the orderly, seemingly into the bowels of the earth. A lantern was necessary to show the way, and they plunged into dank, evil-smelling corridors where the lanterns of other soldiers, keeping guard, bobbed up and down like will-o'-the-wisps in the darkness. Finally the orderly asked a question of one of the guards, and a huge key was fitted into a lock, a bolt shot and an iron door swung open.

"Here is the lantern, Colonel Mobrikoff," said the orderly, with respect. "Do you wish me to remain?"

Norroy replied in the negative, and then addressed the guard: "Close the door, fellow. I have something to say to the prisoner in private. Close the door and bolt it."

The guard saluted and murmured acquiescence. Whereupon the iron door clanged to again, and the bolt was shot. Norroy lifted the lantern, and its light fell upon a mass of straw and a man lying with his back to the door, who was apparently unconcerned at his entrance.

"M'sieur Gaylord," he said, in French.

The prisoner snarled: "Is that you, you frog-eyed coyote?" in English; then, remembering that Mobrikoff did not understand that tongue, translated it into French—"Frog-eyed son of a—a—a—loup-garou," he finished, desperately. The insult seemed ineffective in the tongue of the Gaul, and he racked his brain for a fitting addition.

Yorke Norroy wasted little time. He walked over to the recumbent man, who was now glaring at him, and said in very low tones, and in English: "Don't be surprised; don't cry out, and don't make any sort of a noise. I am not Mobrikoff."

The man stared at him in the light of the lantern, and Norroy had a chance to see the hollow eyes, the sunken cheeks and the wasted hands.

"Not Mobrikoff?" he gasped. "Not Mobrikoff? You are not——"

Norroy seated himself on the rude stool by the side of the straw. "I received your message, Mr. Gaylord. I have come to get you out of this. Now, please don't ask any questions, but do exactly as I tell you."

Omitting the preliminaries, Norroy told him of the capture of Mobrikoff, and the way in which he had gained entrance to St. Basil. The listener's eyes glowed in admiration, and the weary, haggard look faded from them.

"We must waste no time," said Norroy. "Take off those clothes of yours as I take off mine." He spoke in a whisper and immediately proceeded to disrobe. He continued to speak while in the process, and by the time they had exchanged garments the whole scheme was perfectly plain to Gaylord.

Norroy whisked off the false mustache and wig and placed them on Gaylord's face. Then from an inner pocket, he took out a make-up box, such as is carried by those of the theatrical profession, and by the dim light of the lantern proceeded to make Gaylord's face a passable imitation of the Russian's whose uniform he now wore.

"Speak hoarsely, as though you have a cold, and do not answer any questions unless forced to do so—your Russian is execrable and your French is worse. It will not be necessary for you to return to the governor's room. Simply follow the orderly out of this dungeon to the upper floors and then tell him to lead you to your droshky. Salute each soldier who salutes you. When you enter the droshky simply say Hotel d'Angleterre, and the driver will take you there. Dismiss him when you reach the hotel, and send up one of Mobrikoff's cards to Miss Moray. She knows who you are, and she will assist you and accompany you. The grand express leaves for Konigsberg at noon. She has reserved berths in the wagonlit for you and for herself. Here is your passport, which I secured from the United States minister before leaving Paris. It reads for Mr. John Moray, actor. You are supposed to be Miss Moray's brother. When you arrive in Konigsberg, you will both go to the Hotel Zu Hohenloe. There will be a third person in the party, but he is provided with a comfortable sleeping apartment in a trunk."

Gaylord suddenly burst into hysterical laughter as he thought of his arch-enemy cramped within the confines of a narrow box and forced to endure a railway journey in such quarters. Norroy placed his hand over Gaylord's mouth.

"Don't make an ass of yourself," he said, roughly. "The rest of the scheme Miss Moray will explain to you. See that you carry out her instructions, for my life may depend on it. You understand?"

"But how will you escape?" demanded the inventor. "I feel like a cad, leaving you in this hole. God! if you knew——"

"Rest easy," Norroy assured him. "I am no *Sidney Carton*. This is not a question of heroics. I have my orders to see that you are free, and this is part of the carrying out of them. I hope to see you in Washington within the month." He raised his voice and called out in the hoarse tones which he had assumed for the part of Mobrikoff. "I have finished with the prisoner. Open the door."

Again the bolt was released and the door creaked. "Now go," he whispered to Gaylord. "And be cautious—very cautious."

Gaylord pushed up the collar of the coat and as the door opened passed out. Norroy heard him tell the orderly to lead him to the courtyard.

As the door grated back to its former place, and Norroy knew that now he was a prisoner in a Russian dungeon, it would have seemed that a feeling of unquiet would have come over him. But Mr. Yorke Norroy only laughed softly, as was his wont, and twirled about on his finger the seal ring of the Count Mobrikoff.

CHAPTER IV

THE PLIGHT OF THE GOVERNOR

"You took great risks," said the secretary gravely, when Norroy had proceeded thus far with his narrative.

Norroy waved his cigarette airily. "Really, I think you overrate my modest endeavors, Mr. Secretary," he replied. "I took no risks at all, strictly speaking." He straightened the crescent of pearls in the crimson scarf which he wore, and crossed his legs, showing a pair of well-formed ankles in crimson hose, and shapely feet shod in tan shoes. He was attired for the tennis courts, carried a racquet in his hand and wore a suit of white flannels. He was seated in the place where his conversations with the secretary were generally held—in that gentleman's private library.

The sun streamed through the bay windows and revealed the trees in the grounds without just about ready to open their buds in the warm zephyr of a beautiful spring day. It was just a month since Norroy had taken Gaylord's place in the Moscow prison.

"However, to cut the story rather short—for I have an appointment at three and it only lacks twenty minutes of that at the present time—I remained in that cell for that day and night and well into the next day. By that time I was quite sure that Gaylord and Miss Hardesty were ensconced in the Zu Hohenloe, so I decided that it was about time to teach M. Mebristiwsky that there were other people capable of playing a high-handed game outside of his imperial Russian majesty's domains. Therefore I kicked up an infernal racket that brought the guard in with blood in his eye and a desire to murder me. I told him that I wished to see the governor immediately. You see, it was the day for the second knouting of Gaylord, and I had no desire to pose as a martyr for the cause, especially after having seen Gaylord's back. It appears that the governor had given instructions that if Gaylord thought better of being knouted he was to be brought into his worshipful presence, so into that presence I was taken.

"The guard, being a squat Siberian and as devoid of intelligence as a hedgehog, didn't notice any difference in my appearance and that of Gaylord's—all foreigners looking alike to him, I suppose. But when I was put before M. Mebristiwsky, that gentleman's face was a study. Finally he managed to call the soldier two or three things which I wouldn't care to translate into English, and told him he had brought the wrong man. I presumed it was about time for me to cut in then, consequently I did. I told him that I was the only M. Gaylord in the prison, and that if he would send away his soldiers I would explain. He was rather timorous, so he had my hands tied behind my back and then told the soldiers to leave the room.

"It didn't take me very long to explain to M. Mebristiwsky exactly how the trick had been turned, and his cheeks got flabby and his complexion an ashy-gray. I told him that if he would examine the index finger of my right hand, he would see M. Mobrikoff's seal ring. I further informed him that M. Mobrikoff was out of Russia, and that he was in the hands of my confederates, and closely guarded by M. Gaylord himself.

"Deponent further saith that M. Mobrikoff will be held for the space of one week. If, at the end of that time, I do not appear in a certain city outside the czar's domains, there will be one Russian nobleman the less in the Almanach de Gotha. Also, M. Gaylord would immediately file his complaint against the Russian Government with the United States minister at Berlin, telling the whole story, but omitting the death of Mobrikoff. Somehow, this method of reasoning seemed to appeal to M. Mebristiwsky."

The secretary laughed. "I should imagine that it would have influenced him."

"It did, and there were rare doings about the fort of St. Basil for some time after that. I assured the governor that I was a gentleman and would make no attempt to get away if my hands were untied. He untied them and gave me some vodka—he was not a bad sort, but the vodka was. Then he sent out messengers to Moscow, and before an hour had passed I became the center of an astounded group of Russkis. The governor of Moscow was there, and the czar's civil administrator; also the Grand Duke Vladimir and any number of high ranking army officers.

"They went into another room and held a consultation, leaving me to my cigarettes and vodka, and the perusal of some English magazines lying about. At the end of a little time the governor entered. It had evidently been decided that I had the whip hand.

"The governor said my story had been received with great surprise; that it was news to them that they were holding an American prisoner; that M. Mobrikoff had stated that Gaylord was a dangerous Finnish nihilist who had threatened the life of the Little Father of all the Russias; that if I had come to them and told them the story, they would have released Gaylord and disgraced Mobrikoff. It was a beautiful string of falsehoods; well-constructed lies, with the local color all correct and told in the most sincere manner.

"The governor emphasized the love which lay between the countries of Russia and the United States—sang me that old song about Russia having saved the Union during the Civil War by sending her fleet to protect us. Hold me prisoner? Why, certainly not. They admired my courage and devotion in rescuing my friend, and insinuated that I was in the service of the United States. I told them that I was not; that Gaylord was my cousin and that I was an actor by profession; that I had a Russian nurse and had learned the language from her; my name was Harold Mellin; in fact, I handed them just as intricate a tangle of untruths as they handed me.

"The governor finished by saying that if Mobrikoff were killed it would serve him right; and that if my companions did not harm him they had better warn him not to return to Russia, for if he did so he would be given a pleasant assignment in Omsk or thereabouts, with a coal pick as his means of sustenance. Of course I knew all this was not true, and that Mobrikoff would not be deprived of a single perquisite of his rank and station unless the United States wanted revenge and a scapegoat was needed.

"Of course it was perfectly plain to them that they lost everything and gained nothing by keeping me a prisoner, or by harming me in any way. They wanted Mobrikoff back, and they didn't want the United States to kick up any shindy. Now that they had lost the secret of the gun, they didn't care anything about me.

"To cut the story short"—Norroy looked at his watch and replaced it—"I dined that evening with the whole assortment of dignitaries, and they made a sweet attempt to get me drunk and let loose all I knew. But, boasting aside, it is a good Russian who can take more of the fiery liquor than I can, so that failed. After dinner we went to a ball at the Winter Palace, and I met many and various pretty women, who enticed me to drink more. However, that doesn't matter.

"The next morning, to the sorrow of M. Mikhaelovitch, I gathered up the three Broadway show girls and deposited them on the express for Paris. The next train was for Konigsberg, and that I took, promising the governor, who accompanied me to the station in state, that M. Mobrikoff would arrive in Moscow at an early date.

"Of course there were four or five of the governor's spies on the train, and they had the temerity to suppose that I didn't know them. They followed me to the hotel, but they learned nothing.

"Adelaide Hardesty and Gaylord were there, Gaylord under the name of Moray, and Adelaide also. Gaylord had two rooms, and in one of them he kept that big trunk. Adelaide said that it gave him great pleasure to go in there and talk to the repentant Mobrikoff. I am afraid Gaylord was a little cruel, for he kept Mobrikoff bound hand and foot all the time, feeding him with oats and black bread only—prison fare. When I arrived, I swear I think the beggar was sorry, for I fear he had set his mind on dispatching M. Mobrikoff.

"Of course I had given my word, and that ended his homicidal schemes. Mobrikoff was given a plentiful meal, and told to eat all of it possible, in order that it might last him for three. Then we packed him neatly into his box, put the clothes about him, gagged him, locked the trunk, and I stenciled on it in large letters: 'M. Mebristiwsky, governor of Fort St. Basil, Moscow, Russia,' and in red ink on the corner: 'Game. Perishable. Open at once.'"

The secretary burst into a hearty laugh, and Norroy arose, twirling his racquet. "I should like to have seen the governor's face," the secretary remarked; "and to have heard what Mobrikoff said when he was unbound and ungagged."

"Mr. Secretary," said Yorke Norroy, "you have never heard a Russian when he is extremely angry. I have. Therefore, as I do not like the profane and the vulgar, I cannot share in your wish."

The secretary stretched out his hand. "Well, play your tennis, Yorke," he said, paternally. "You've done a good piece of work. I thank you. Come in to-morrow at five."

Norroy's eyes had in them a glint of satisfaction. A great respect and friendship existed between these two men.

"Thank you, Mr. Secretary," said Norroy. "I rather think you're right. But you really owe me no thanks. I discovered a marvelous brand of cigarettes in a little place in Moscow, and the trip was worth while just for that."

He offered his Chinese case to the secretary, who shook his head. Norroy lighted one himself, drew on his gloves, caught the racquet in his left hand, and bade the secretary good-afternoon.

TROUBLE ON THE BORDER

JOHN FERGUSON

THE SCOTTISH-BORN clergyman, playwright, and mystery writer John Alexander Ferguson (1873–1952) was at one time ranked among the best writers of "sensational" mystery stories, along with Edgar Wallace, Gerald Fairlie, and a handful of others. H. Douglas Thomson, in his *Masters of Mystery* (1931), one of the tiny number of pre–World War II critical works devoted to mystery fiction, describes him as "one of the most delightful stylists in this genre," and forgives him for being more focused on thrills and excitement than pure detection. Having read two of the Reverend Ferguson's novels, it is clear that the bar for thrills and excitement was lower in the Golden Age between the world wars than it is today.

In *The Dark Geraldine* (1921), Ferguson introduces Francis MacNab, a likable policeman, but he is replaced by his son, also named Francis MacNab, a private detective, as a series character soon after with *The Man in the Dark* (1928).

In the nonmystery field, he wrote several plays, including a once-famous one-act play titled *Campbell of Kilmhor* (1921), which opened in Glasgow's Royalty Theatre, where a critic praised it as "a new and significant type of Scottish drama." It is set in 1745 at the time of the Jacobite uprising and features Mary Stuart, attempting to save her son. The BBC made a thirty-minute film version of it that aired on January 2, 1939.

Born in Callander, Perthshire, Ferguson's role as an Episcopal minister caused him to move frequently, including stays at Skye, the island of Guernsey, Dundee, Glasgow, and Fife (he lived in the oppresive Dunimarle Castle, where Macbeth murdered Macduff's wife and child).

I have been unable to trace the original publication of this story. It was collected in *My Best Spy Story*, edited anonymously (London, Faber & Faber, 1938).

TROUBLE ON THE BORDER

JOHN FERGUSON

JOHN PURCHAS, of the political staff, waited on the broad platform of Lahore railway station for the south-bound night express. He was like a keen young dog straining at the leash, for the mission on which he had been sent out was both delicate and dangerous. It was, besides, his first big job. He knew that out at the Anarkali headquarters some thought the business far too delicate for him to handle, while saying it was far too dangerous. He did not know that the Chief had insisted on sending him in spite of all protests. For Purchas considered he had earned this job. And for this reason:

All through that summer the political administration had been aware that there was bad, black trouble brewing in the Punjab. At first it was evident only to the sensitive and experienced heads of the political staff, but after certain news filtered through from the Tigris the symptoms could be read by the rawest subaltern out with the last draft from home. The bazaars seethed with disaffection, and the native police spies were for once at fault.

They all came in with reports of a mysterious and subtle propaganda working like leaven through the native quarters; but they never got hold of anything precise and specific. The mili-

tary administration when *they* began to feel the pressure of the rising temperature clamoured for something to be done. Beyond insolent looks, however, there was no overt act for a long time, and from this it was inferred that a very strong hand held the hidden strings of intrigue.

Then one afternoon, in broad daylight, on the Mall, a stone was flung at a deputy commissioner as he mounted the steps of the club. It laid his chin open, but for all the notice he took it might have been no more than a fly settling on his cheek. Purchas had chanced to see the incident, and he overheard the scant sympathy accorded the sufferer by the soldiers present when the commissioner came in mopping up the blood.

"Now," an old colonel growled, "perhaps you political swells will *do* something."

"Do no end of good, that stone; we all need waking up at times," another agreed.

"Sorry old Jenkins got it, though—good chap. Someone should go out and tell them they hit the wrong bird."

"Yes, I'd like to see some other civil blighter get it in the neck—hard."

"What *are* you proposing to do, Jenkins?" another asked the commissioner.

Jenkins looked over.

"Do?" he said innocently. "Oh, I don't know—apply some sticking plaster if the steward has any."

There was a chorus of indignant grunts over this wilful misunderstanding of the question. Jenkins relented when the steward left the room.

"As a matter of fact," he said, "we are hanging on to this thing with teeth and nails. You think it's bad. I tell you it's ten times worse than you think. The Punjab goes on fire usually like dry straw, and it's easily stamped out. This time there's someone holding them back for the moment, but it will be a bonfire when it comes."

"Meanwhile," the colonel persisted, "what are you chaps doing?"

"Looking for the man with the match," said Jenkins.

"I heard it said he is a Rajah of some native State," Blane interjected.

"Who told you that?" the commissioner asked sharply.

"I—I forget," said the other.

The colonel thumped the table.

"Then," he cried, "why not send out half a platoon to fetch him in?"

"There are thirty-four native States in the N.W. Provinces alone," said Jenkins; "to which would you send?"

They waited till the steward who had come in with the plaster had withdrawn.

Purchas had been amused at the blank look with which this information had been received. But he knew that to many of these native States men from his department had already gone, not in platoons, but singly and unobtrusively. First one, then another, went east, west, south, and—yes, even north, though *he* did not go by rail or travel as a Sahib.

"I heard," said Blane again, "it's some Rajah with a diamond who's piling up the trouble."

Jenkins laughed as he drained off his peg and got on his feet.

"*Now* we're getting warm," he said. "We've only to find out which of the thirty-four Rajahs owns a diamond."

They all laughed at Blane then, and in the midst of the merriment Jenkins left.

Young Blane got very red, and turning aside to Purchas, began to explain.

"But this was a very special diamond—something supernatural—a gift from some old god or other."

"Who told you about it?" Purchas asked, affecting interest.

"Oh, I don't mind telling *you* that," said Blane. "It came from one of my men. There was a native woman got soft on him. This jewel, it appears, is a sort of Aladdin's Lamp affair—Lord, isn't it all here rather like the Arabian Nights. The holder of the gem, it seems, can get *anything* he wishes. It's a regular rag with my men against Saunders—he's the man the woman warned, you know. The other fellows pretend he's got it in his pocket, and go up to him asking for the most impossible things. When they get nothing from him they say it's because he's a Scotchman and keeps it all to himself."

Purchas did not need to affect interest in the anecdote now. Knowing his India he recognized the possible value of the clue chance had put into his hand. It was just in this way a hint might percolate through—a hint utterly beyond the reach of their native police spies.

"I've a great wish to see this Saunders," he said at length.

"Easily gratified," said the youthful Blane; "he's my batman. But don't *mention* the diamond; it's like a red rag to a bull. He's been chaffed no end. They call him Bumali Bill now."

"Bumali!" said Purchas.

"That's where the girl came from. I say," he added in a changed tone, "you don't think there's anything in it?"

"Do you think we could get hold of the woman—on the quiet?"

"I'll find out tactfully," said Blane, sober enough now. "Come to tiffin to-morrow."

"No," said Purchas, "I'll come now."

They went straight out to the cantonments, and after a little judicious handling, Saunders first told his story, and then when it was dark took them round to the lady's quarters. They had some difficulty in getting in. When they did succeed they found her in bed—with her throat cut. Her tongue, looking like a little red snail, lay in a brass plate standing on her breast.

Blane held the lamp high, looking down with fascinated horror.

"Seems we are too late," he said stupidly.

But, nevertheless, if that gaping and tongueless mouth did not tell John Purchas all he had hoped to learn, if yet spoke eloquently enough, for it was a witness to the seriousness of what she had said. This was no idle babble of the bazaars. Inside twenty minutes he had laid the facts before his Chief.

"How many people know this?" the old man asked.

"About half a battalion perhaps."

"That's bad. Still, they don't know the story of the Bumali stone."

"I'm afraid they do, sir," said Purchas. "You see, they are a mixed lot, drawn, Blane says, from all sorts of occupations, and one of them, who was an assistant librarian in some municipal library, has hunted up the story of the diamond in order to rag this man Saunders."

"Do they know the stone was lost, centuries ago?"

"Yes, and they pretend Saunders has got it."

The Chief took a pace or two away, hands behind his back.

"This is a queer thing, Mr. Purchas. The tradition is that the Bumali jewel was given to the Sundra dynasty in the ninth century by the Serpent God, Nag, and that it brought with it the supernatural power which enabled the Sundras to drive the Mohammedan invaders out of Upper India. When it was lost the House of Sundra was said to have lost its power, and the British Raj became paramount. Now, Mr. Purchas, take this tradition in conjunction with the present unrest in the Punjab and let me hear your explanation."

The old man stopped before Purchas and eyed him under his grizzled brows.

"I should think, sir, they are about to find that stone."

The Chief extended a hand and patted his shoulder.

"You'll do," he nodded approvingly. "That is what is going to happen. That old fox, Duleep Sundra, will find it, or another, and when he does there will be another mutiny."

He sat down at his desk and gave himself up to thought.

"Somebody's got to go to Bumali," he said at length, half to himself.

"I'd like nothing better," Purchas promptly affirmed.

The Chief turned to look at him consideringly.

"You? Do you know the sort of place it is? There's Duleep Sundra, the rajah who can contrive *accidents* for unwelcome white men that look more natural than Nature can make them. And they'd know you were coming. You'd be expected, you see. No, *that* won't do."

Again he fell into profound meditation, while Purchas waited, watching his face. Occasionally a half whisper fell from his lips, but beyond a disconnected word here and there the young man overheard little. Bitterly disappointed at not getting the mission after his hopes had risen so high, Purchas had ceased to look at his Chief and, disheartened, let himself sink back in his chair to regard the toes of his boots.

How long he sat so with only the solemn ticking of the clock audible, he did not know, but anyhow he was suddenly startled when he did look up to find the Chief staring at his face, a new light in his eyes.

"I am going to send you to Bumali," he said quietly.

Purchas was thunderstruck, and jumped impulsively up to thank him. But the other put up a hand as if to ward off the gratitude.

"You can thank me when you come back," he said so brusquely, uncomfortably, that Purchas somehow felt he himself was but a pawn in some game about to open between players of ruthlessness and skill. Out there in Bumali sat the subtle rajah, Duleep Sundra; here in Lahore the wise old Chief; and Purchas knew that if the first had all the wisdom of the serpent from which his dynasty was said to descend, the Chief had on his side a good deal more than the harmlessness of the dove.

Within twenty-four hours he seemed to have decided his game, and John Purchas was moved up to the big platform of Lahore station. His instructions were to go to Bumali, stay there with Sam Burgoyne, the resident, and nose around. Purchas, being young, would have much preferred to go in disguise, but this the Chief absolutely prohibited. He was to be quite open in all his movements, as if on a friendly visit to the resident.

As he walked up and down the platform waiting for his train, Purchas wondered much as to what all this portended. That it was a move in the game he did not doubt. Then his eye lighted on two soldiers coming along the platform through the motley throng of natives, and he thought that they at least were in disguise, since anything less *martial* would have been hard to find. Both were undersized, but one had very bandy legs.

He wondered what their occupations in civil life had been. But when they squatted on their kits and began to exchange hilarious repartee with each other one soon gathered a variety of information about both. They were, it seemed, on leave, going down to Amritzar, to visit friends in another regiment quartered there, and their names were Alf and Fred. They had no reticence whatever. Even their past love affairs and present financial position they discussed aloud with complete frankness. Purchas was vastly amused by their boyish high spirits, and by a contrast to the pair which presented itself when a couple of majestic Sikhs came down the platform, silent men with dark inscrutable faces, their heads, as it were, towering among the stars. As they passed the jabbering pair who had come out to assist in holding the Punjab, Purchas was struck by the immense *cheek* of the thing. It was as if the guttersnipes of Bermondsey had taken over control of the London police. Even to allow men away on leave at such a critical moment— that also was pure cheek. It was an affectation

of strength on the part of the military who, as Purchas knew, were all the time most seriously alarmed.

Then the express came thundering in, and the noisy pair passed out of the young man's mind. He had two changes to make before he reached his destination. At Kurrapur he had to take the branch line which runs on to Attaka Finnegar. Some thirty miles short of that terminus, at a little place called Bagiah, he had to change into the Rajah's private, narrow-gauge railway, which ran up for some fifty miles to the capital. It was at Karrapur that Purchas again, much to his surprise, fell in with Alf and Fred.

He saw, or rather heard, them at three o'clock in the morning, tumbling out of the express after their heavy kit. Soon a mighty noisy altercation arose between the two soldiers and the railway officials. The stationmaster, a Babu who spoke English, was summoned. But as the Babu, who had probably been educated at Bombay University, and whom Alf addressed as Sambo, spoke a very bookish English, not in the least like the kind affected by Alf and Fred, his intervention only increased the dispute. In the end Purchas offered his help.

"You passed Amritzar two hours ago," he said.

Fred eyed him doubtfully, as if uncertain which side Purchas was taking.

"That's all right, old sport, we saw it."

"Oh, I thought you were going there," said Purchas.

Overhearing this, Alf turned from the gesticulating stationmaster.

"We only *said* that at Lahore to kid the red cap. We're out to see a bit of the *real* India— afore we go back 'ome."

The bandy-legged Fred slapped his friend on the back.

"That's right, old Eleven-three-four," he cried approvingly.

Then Purchas, observing that the stationmaster seemed to be entering the figures in his notebook, drew the two companions away towards the Attaka Finnegar train. He spoke to them like a father of the many dangers into which they might easily run their simple, careless heads. The view that they were simple-minded seemed new to them. But as an example of their simplicity Purchas instanced the mention of Alf's regimental number before a native official, who, merely out of self-importance, might report all sorts of crime against them.

Hearing this, a fit of merriment so overcame both that they gripped each other for support.

"Lor' bless you, *that* wasn't his regimental number," Fred cried, wiping his eyes. "That's only the name he goes by—eleven-three-four—him having been a draper before he joined up."

"A draper!" cried Purchas.

"Yes," Alf agreed. "Served me time at it in 'Ackney."

"And your friend?" Purchas asked.

"Me?" said Fred. "Oh, I was what you might call a furniture remover, though I *was* bred as a house decorator reely."

"And where exactly are you going?"

"To see a bit of India—native State for choice—jungle, ellerphunts, but no snakes, by request."

"Alf and me was always fond of the Zoo ever since we was little nippers, wasn't we, Alf?"

Fred took his friend's arm affectionately, shaking him so that he rocked on his bandy legs.

Now it might have been very awkward had the pair by some chance blundered into Bumali. Purchas saw he must head them off.

"What about Attaka Finnegar?" he suggested, well knowing that once the train reached that terminus they would be taken care of by the military police. Fred wiped his mouth.

"Don't mind," he said, "if the refreshment room is open."

"Lime juice for me," Alf put in; "them foreign drinks upset me stummick."

Purchas explained the situation to them very seriously, warning them, above all, to keep clear of native States. At first they seemed very much impressed, and had quite a number of questions to ask; but in the end they turned his warning, as they turned most things, into a jest, as is the way with soldiers out on a spree.

"Supposing we got into trouble and they caught us, what 'ud 'appen?"

"Fill you with red pepper, perhaps."

"Anything else?"

"I've known them to tie a man up, pull his head back, fix his jaws open, and let water dribble into him for days."

"D'ye think they'd make it beer for a London boy?" Fred asked with affected eagerness.

Purchas then lost patience with them and spoke sharply.

Still, the warning did not seem to have been in vain, for when Purchas left the Attaka Finnegar train at Bagiah, and transferred himself to the Rajah's little train, he saw nothing of the two wanderers; and he thought of them as peacefully sleeping, their heads on their kit, till the train ran into the terminus, where they would be roused up by the hated red cap on duty there.

At Bumali Purchas was met by Burgoyne.

"Bit run down, I hear," said the resident, gripping Purchas's hand very hard.

"So, so," he returned, taking the cue, as they passed through the line of Punjabi officials.

"Well," Burgoyne nodded, "Bumali will set you up all right. Pretty hot in Lahore, I'm told."

"That's it," Purchas assented. "And as there's nothing doing, the Chief gave me a holiday."

Burgoyne laughed heartily.

"Oh, Lahore is a dull place. There never *is* anything doing there."

"Well, as a matter of fact, most of the staff are away on leave," Purchas rejoined lightly.

But once they were alone and closeted in the study the careless gaiety dropped out of Burgoyne's manner.

"There's something afoot," he said. "The place is just too damn quiet. It frightens me."

Purchas related the recent developments in Lahore, and Burgoyne questioned him about his interview with the Chief, more particularly in regard to the instructions he had received.

"I have got to smell around, that's all," said Purchas.

"Well," said Burgoyne, "you won't light on much. The Rajah is away too, though that in itself is not a disadvantage."

For the first few days Purchas loafed about the house, playing the part of the semi-invalid, seeming to take an interest in nothing, but wondering all the while what eyes were upon him. Then he began to stroll about the place, in a languid fashion, but with much alertness behind his apparently lack-lustre eyes. He never lighted on a single hint of anything in the wind. Not a ripple showed on the surface. Bumali was as placid as a sleeping duck-pond. Purchas feared he would have to return with no more than that to report, while aware that there was ever so much more, if only he could put his hand on it. That would mark him out in the Chief's mind as a man who had failed. It gave him a sort of sensation as of nightmare, and he felt like a man who had only to crack an egg-shell to save his life, but whose hands were bound with cobwebs which he could not break.

Then one evening when he was returning in something like despair Burgoyne met him at the door and drew him into his study. His *sais*, Abdulla, had brought in the rumour of a great *tamasha* about to be held in the old temple out in the woods. Abdulla had been concealed in the stables to surprise some corn thieves, when three stableboys entered, and he had overheard their talk.

"A gathering!" Purchas cried, "but there's no room in a temple for many people."

"This old temple belongs to the primitive worship; it's not a mere shrine like a Hindu temple," Burgoyne explained.

"What do you make of it then?"

"What I think," said the other, "is that the secret underground work has now been done, and this meeting is being held to stir up fanaticism in the mob."

Purchas nodded agreement.

"You mean the fanaticism that sets a crowd on fire when it is moved by a common purpose?"

"Exactly," said Burgoyne. "You mark my words, the curtain is about to rise for the drama."

Next morning more news, which disquieted both men still further, came to the residency—a *faquir* of exceptional holiness had arrived in Bumali. The news made both sit up at once, for both knew these *faquirs* very well—experts every one of them at rousing the passions of the mob.

"I hear," said Burgoyne, "that he has been sitting for two days without speaking a single word, under the sacred peepul tree outside the city walls. What do you make of that?"

"Very clever—that silence. When he does speak his message will be listened to."

"Not a doubt of it," Burgoyne agreed. "Let's go out and have a look at him."

They found the holy man seated under the great spreading tree which sheltered the shrine of Gaupati. At a respectful distance a large crowd stood regarding him with awe-struck eyes, and Burgoyne heard that people were flocking in hourly from the outlying villages to see the holy man who had suddenly appeared, none knew whence or why.

From the outskirts of the crowd the two Englishmen for a while watched the man, who sat there cross-legged and motionless, like a tailor cut out of stone. Both wished for a closer sight of him, but the mob did not appear to be as willing as usual to make way for the Sahibs, and Burgoyne, as resident, would not risk a possible insult at that moment. Purchas, however, as a stranger, had more freedom to display curiosity, and accordingly he passed through the throng till he reached the inner fringe of the crowd.

Then, amazed by what he saw, he even advanced a few steps into the open space which the deference of the spectators kept between themselves and the *faquir* and his servant. Before him sat the holy man, as motionless as the image of the god above his head and as naked. But there wasn't an inch of him that wasn't bedaubed with paint. He was all a riot of colour.

His face was scarlet, and his eyes with circles round them looked like the centres of two targets. Hanging from his yellow neck by a blue ribbon was the representation of a quart pot, foaming. Startled beyond measure, Purchas cast a look at the servant who stood beside his master, and who was as freely bedecked with colour, though without the other's fancy decorative designs. He was bandy-legged! Again Purchas's stare went back to the master, and as he looked him full in the face he distinctly saw the holy man's left eyelid droop at him for an instant! A murmur ran like a wave through the crowd when they saw how deeply the Sahib was impressed.

Impressed? It is a feeble word. John Purchas was being torn by conflicting emotions, both anger and laughter struggling in him for expression. Of course he dared not give vent to either; and so, wheeling abruptly round, he pushed his way clear and rejoined his friend. Burgoyne had seen enough to be aware that something unusual had occurred, but he asked no questions till they were once more in his bungalow. Purchas had not mentioned his encounter with the two men at Karrapur; indeed, Alf and Fred had passed out of his mind. Burgoyne heard the tale with amazement.

"Do you think they are up to some game?" he asked.

"Just a lark," said Purchas; "a silly, rotten lark."

"It will be a costly one for them; they are sure to be found out, and then——" He made a gesture.

"Oh, deuce take them. Can't we get them cleared out before then?"

"They'll not be allowed to go. Don't you see, whether detected or not—and the chances are that the Rajah's people already know they are frauds—they are being mighty useful. See how excited that crowd was! To a certainty, the holy man will be taken into the temple on the night of the *tamasha*."

"On the night of the *tamasha*," Purchas cried. "If only I knew what night that was!"

Burgoyne stared at him.

"You don't mean to say——" he began.

"I mean to be there," the other said with finality. "Do help me if you can." And when the appeal met with no response he continued: "See here, Burgoyne, so far I've failed in this job. Am

I to go back and say so? I'd sooner be skinned alive."

Eagerly watching his friend's face, he saw he had made his point.

"Well," said Burgoyne, "the risk is awful, but of course you are right to take it. And if I can read the symptoms it will be soon over. The fact is, I think the gathering is for to-night. You saw that people were flocking in; well, they are not *all* drawn by the *faquir*, for they could not have heard of his presence here so quickly. In any event, the meeting will be summoned in the usual fashion—by the beating of a drum. We have only to listen for that."

But the drum was not heard that night, and Purchas, a prey to uncertainty, and chafing at the inaction forced on him, passed a feverish, sleepless night. The next evening, however, he had scarcely changed into old Abdulla's toggery to be ready for a possible summons from Burgoyne, who was out on the verandah listening, when he himself heard the faint, far-away throbbing of a drum.

In a few minutes he had done up his face to his friend's satisfaction, and very soon he was slipping along noiselessly in the direction of the temple. The old building stood well beyond the walls, a lonely place, encircled by peepuls and deodars. When he was close enough to discern in the darkness the glimmer of the white walls he diverged from the direct path, and hung about, watching many figures go stealing past him, like white moths among the dark tree trunks.

When the flow of men had ceased he ran forward, and, passing under the side arches of the portico, slipped into a place just inside the doorway of the great inner shrine. He found the building to be full of squatting figures, dimly lit by a few lanterns.

At the far end, high up the wall, he could just discern the niches occupied by the stone images of Gaupati, Lashni, and Nag. But in the centre of the floor, instead of the Pindi of orthodox Hinduism, there was that which showed John Purchas that something unusual was indeed afoot. Seeing the tall column with the square top which stood there, he wondered if he were about to witness an act of that serpent worship which was said to be the oldest worship in the world.

For a long time nothing happened. An old fat pujari, standing under the column, went on mumbling some sort of long ritual in a tongue not Punjabi. While this interminable and monotonous chant proceeded Purchas cautiously surveyed the audience for any trace of the two masqueraders, thinking that if present they must now be in a fine state of funk. He found it eerie enough himself.

But the low rumble of the old priest's voice ended at last, and a faint, thin, refined sound, as from some stringed instrument at a vast distance, became audible. All those squatting figures at once bowed forward, thrice, with machine-like precision, and Purchas, on the alert to copy the actions of those around him, was in time to do the trick twice, catching sight, as he did so, of two figures away on the left, and close to the column, who remained without motion.

Even in the obscurity he knew who they were. Then the lanterns were extinguished suddenly, and the darkness was complete. Prepared as Purchas was for any queer barbaric practice to follow, what actually did follow took him by surprise.

Through the open doorway behind him, from the direction of the kneeling sacred bull of Shiva on the portico, there came a long spear of brilliant light, for all the world so like the shaft of light that goes over the spectators' heads from an old type cinema lantern that Purchas smiled at the incongruity. Smiled, that is, till he saw what it illuminated. That narrow spear of light caught the top of the column only, and on the flat top of the column he saw the gleaming coils of a huge sleeping snake, green and yellow and black.

The music grew louder, a drum began, gently beaten, a queer sobbing note; and, roused either by the light or the music, the reptile slowly lifted its head and looked down, swaying from side to side. The beady eyes caught and reflected the light. Purchas saw them glittering, like little green jewels. Every soul in the building was prostrate on the floor, their heads reverently covered with some portion of their garments. Lying prone like the others around him, Purchas yet watched from beneath the fold of Abdulla's robe, which he had drawn over his head.

Then above the viper's head he saw such a dazzling point of light as a poet might have imagined for the Star of Bethlehem. In a moment he saw what it was. Around the serpent's neck was a ring of yellow metal from which, at the back, rose a slender rod some five inches long, and from this, by a thin wire or a hair—something at least invisible—the flashing jewel was suspended. John Purchas thrilled as he looked, for he knew he was gazing at the lost Bumali diamond, the stone with the fabled origin, the gift of Nag, which had been the secret of the Sundra's power over Northern India, and which had earned for that dynasty the title of Sons of the Serpent, a title which, even in their decline after its loss, the Sundra still lived up to.

As Purchas lay watching while the little point of light twisted and turned at the end of the suspending hair, he wondered what all this portended. Was it a trick? Was this the real jewel, or one substituted for a purpose? If so, what? Was he about to witness some *hocus pocus*, perhaps some pretended return of the gift to the present foxy Rajah from Nag—to empower *him*, like his far-off ancestor, to drive out the Sahibs from Nag's domains?

But suddenly his speculations were scattered by a sharp angry *hiss* from the viper on the pillar. In the death-like silence it sounded so horribly full of all malice and evil that the watcher's nerves jumped to the sound. His blood chilled and contracted, as if from a sudden injection of icy water.

He saw that others beside himself must have been taking a fearful peep at the ancient serpent and the sacred stone, for heads suddenly went down here and there around him. But Purchas did not suppose that venomous hiss to be a reproof of impiety, and so he continued watching, to see what had aroused the brute's anger.

He was almost sorry he did, for what followed startled him horribly. Above the heads of the prostrate natives, as high as the tall pillar itself, he saw a *hand*. It came out of the darkness slowly, and passed into the spear of light. It was impossible to tell what the hand was like, or to whom it belonged, whether to native or to European, whether to the dead or to the living, for a very simple reason—*it was covered with a white cotton glove*.

Indeed, all that Purchas actually saw of the hand was but the thumb and forefinger; yet these were so large and misshapen that they must have belonged to a giant or a beast.

But no beast or giant was visible behind them. The finger and thumb though attached to a hand and arm were certainly detached from any *body*. They crept slowly nearer and nearer to the viper, keeping just above its swaying head. Then Purchas saw them close on the jewel—saw them give a swift tug and jerk—and the next instant both jewel and hand had vanished.

But even before the diamond disappeared John Purchas thought he understood the kind of game he was witnessing. Though he couldn't imagine how the trick with the hand had been done, he knew well enough the astonishing feats a Hindu juggler could do, and he was quite sure it was a trick. Presently, he thought, that hand will approach the Rajah, and bestow the diamond on him as a gift from Nag, and as a symbol of a new divine authority committed to the Sundra.

But Purchas was very quickly undeceived.

There must have been some other impious person present—a priest perhaps, or Duleep Sundra himself. Anyhow, someone saw the diamond go, for a sudden cry of horror rang through the building. Heads must have been lifted; like an echo the cry was taken up by numberless voices, and dark forms leaped to their feet.

In a moment all was confusion, shouting and jostling. Purchas ran out by the door behind him, across the portico, leaped down the steps, and shot straight into the forest. Yet quick as he had been, he was not quite the first, for he saw at least *two* leaping figures in front. He heard many following, for the wrath of the Sundra was apt to be wholesale and undiscerning.

An hour later, when he was again in Burgoyne's study and had told his story, a little reflection threw some light on the mystery.

"The two masqueraders did it," said Burgoyne at length.

"It is incredible," Purchas affirmed. "Two private soldiers——"

"A draper and a furniture remover. Furniture remover is good, eh? Smash and grab raider, I'd guess."

"There was a lot of talk about this diamond among them at Lahore, of course."

"Oh, it was an admirably planned *coup*," said Burgoyne.

"Still, it is incredible that those two planned it. Think of the preparations—the intimate knowledge of native life needed."

"Ah, my boy, your new criminal is very different, I'm told."

"I see what you mean. Even so, how was it done?" Purchas asked.

"Ah, that I can't tell you—wish I knew. Anyhow the Duleep Sundra plot is at an end, you can bank on that. The Rajah won't have an ounce of credit in India once the story spreads. It will be said that Nag took back his gift."

On the following day Purchas returned to Lahore. Burgoyne, in seeing him off, begged that if ever he ran across his two friends in that city he should find out how the trick with the gloved hand was done and let him know. Purchas promised though with little hope that he would ever be able to keep that promise.

On arrival he hurried out to headquarters, knowing how much his news would serve to dispel his Chief's anxiety. Rather to his surprise, when he was ushered in, he found the old man in very cheerful spirits. He listened happily to Purchas's tale until the splendour of the diamond was mentioned.

"Poof," said the Chief; "there are many better stones in the windows of Bond Street."

"I assure you——" Purchas protested.

"A very ordinary stone," the old man interrupted. "Look at it for yourself."

He put his hand into his pocket and clapped the diamond down on the desk.

There was a long silence, during which a great respect for his Chief was born in John Purchas's mind. He remembered his first impression, on setting out, of being himself but a pawn in the game, and now he wondered who were the big pieces this consummately skilful player had manoeuvred—Alf and Fred? But who, then, were Alf and Fred?

He put the question. The Chief smiled and shrugged his shoulders.

"Didn't they tell you? They might be men from your friend Blane's regiment," he said. "They are a very mixed lot, didn't you say?"

Purchas saw he had been indiscreet. Still, one other question he risked. He would risk it though he now knew he had been sent to Bumali to draw suspicion on himself while the real experts did the job.

"I should like it, sir," he said humbly, "if you could suggest how the trick was actually done."

The Chief's eyes twinkled with approbation.

"Mr. Purchas," he said, "I'll tell you all about it. I once was waiting for my wife—we were newly married then—outside a draper's shop in Oxford Street. The window was full of trumpery knick-knacks, and some were hanging against the glass. While I stood there a lady and a little girl came up, and the little girl straightway fell in love with a string of coral beads which hung on a line in the very front of the window. They went inside and I waited, curious to see how on earth the coral beads could be reached, wondering how much stuff would have to be taken out to get even near those beads. Well, it was very simple. The shopman had a pair of pincers at the end of two long, thin bamboo poles.

"Had that instrument been enclosed in a long sleeve, and if only the pincers had had a glove— say a soldier's white cotton glove—on them, you might have thought it was two deft fingers at the end of a very long arm, so neatly were those coral beads removed. A very trivial thing to remember so long, you say to yourself, perhaps? Ah well, you never know, you never know."

THE CASE OF THE DIXON TORPEDO

ARTHUR MORRISON

ESPIONAGE AND COUNTERESPIONAGE stories were extremely uncommon in the Victorian era. Although spies existed from the beginning of nation-states and before, it was seldom openly acknowledged. It wasn't until William Le Queux pressed the British government to create a secret service soon after the turn of the nineteenth century that it became officially acceptable for a nation to engage in spying. Famously, one British government official was reluctant to enter this arena, stating that a gentleman doesn't read someone else's mail.

Most early spy stories were really detective stories in which governments' secrets were pilfered, rather than money or jewels. After the staggering success enjoyed by Arthur Conan Doyle with his Sherlock Holmes series, other authors, undoubtedly pressed by publishers who hoped to cash in on the new phenomenon of detective adventures, produced a deluge of novels and short stories whose protagonists followed in the footsteps of Holmes. The most successful was Arthur Morrison's (1863–1945) Martin Hewitt, who made his debut in *Martin Hewitt: Investigator* (1894), followed by two more short story collections and a novel, *The Red Triangle* (1903).

Like Doyle, Morrison had little interest in, or affection for, his detective, convinced that his atmospheric tales of the London slums were far more significant. He may have been right, as they sold well in their time, show greater vitality, and are said to have been instrumental in initiating many important social reforms, particularly with regard to housing.

In addition to his naturalistic novels of crime and poverty in London's East End and the exploits of Hewitt, Morrison wrote other books connected to the mystery genre, including *Cunning Murrell* (1900), a fictionalized account of a witch doctor's activities in early nineteenth-century rural Essex; *The Hole in the Wall* (1902), a story of murder in a London slum; and *The Dorrington Deed-Box* (1897), a collection of stories about the unscrupulous Horace Dorrington, a con man and thief who occasionally earns his money honestly—by working as a private detective!

The present story features Martin Hewitt, Morrison's most significant contribution to the mystery genre, in which the detective engages in counterespionage activity—functioning as a private detective, of course.

"The Case of the Dixon Torpedo" was originally published in *Martin Hewitt, Investigator* (London, Ward, Lock & Bowden, 1894).

THE CASE OF THE DIXON TORPEDO

ARTHUR MORRISON

HEWITT WAS VERY APT, in conversation, to dwell upon the many curious chances and coincidences that he had observed, not only in connection with his own cases, but also in matters dealt with by the official police, with whom he was on terms of pretty regular, and, indeed, friendly, acquaintanceship. He has told me many an anecdote of singular happenings to Scotland Yard officials with whom he has exchanged experiences. Of Inspector Nettings, for instance, who spent many weary months in a search for a man wanted by the American Government, and in the end found, by the merest accident (a misdirected call), that the man had been lodging next door to himself the whole of the time; just as ignorant, of course, as was the inspector himself as to the enemy at the other side of the party-wall. Also of another inspector, whose name I can not recall, who, having been given rather meager and insufficient details of a man whom he anticipated having great difficulty in finding, went straight down the stairs of the office where he had received instructions, and actually *fell over* the man near the door, where he had stooped down to tie his shoe-lace! There were cases, too, in which, when a great and notorious crime had been committed, and various

persons had been arrested on suspicion, some were found among them who had long been badly wanted for some other crime altogether. Many criminals had met their deserts by venturing out of their own particular line of crime into another; often a man who got into trouble over something comparatively small found himself in for a startlingly larger trouble, the result of some previous misdeed that otherwise would have gone unpunished. The ruble note-forger Mirsky might never have been handed over to the Russian authorities had he confined his genius to forgery alone. It was generally supposed at the time of his extradition that he had communicated with the Russian Embassy, with a view to giving himself up—a foolish proceeding on his part, it would seem, since his whereabouts, indeed even his identity as the forger, had not been suspected. He *had* communicated with the Russian Embassy, it is true, but for quite a different purpose, as Martin Hewitt well understood at the time. What that purpose was is now for the first time published.

The time was half-past one in the afternoon, and Hewitt sat in his inner office examining and comparing the handwriting of two letters by the aid of a large lens. He put down the lens and glanced at the clock on the mantel-piece with a premonition of lunch; and as he did so his clerk quietly entered the room with one of those printed slips which were kept for the announcement of unknown visitors. It was filled up in a hasty and almost illegible hand, thus:

Name of visitor: *F. Graham Dixon.*
Address: *Chancery Lane.*
Business: *Private and urgent.*

"Show Mr. Dixon in," said Martin Hewitt.

Mr. Dixon was a gaunt, worn-looking man of fifty or so, well, although rather carelessly, dressed, and carrying in his strong, though drawn, face and dullish eyes the look that characterizes the life-long strenuous brain-worker. He leaned forward anxiously in the chair which Hewitt offered him, and told his story with a great deal of very natural agitation.

"You may possibly have heard, Mr. Hewitt—I know there are rumors—of the new locomotive torpedo which the government is about adopting; it is, in fact, the Dixon torpedo, my own invention, and in every respect—not merely in my own opinion, but in that of the government experts—by far the most efficient and certain yet produced. It will travel at least four hundred yards farther than any torpedo now made, with perfect accuracy of aim (a very great desideratum, let me tell you), and will carry an unprecedentedly heavy charge. There are other advantages—speed, simple discharge, and so forth—that I needn't bother you about. The machine is the result of many years of work and disappointment, and its design has only been arrived at by a careful balancing of principles and means, which are expressed on the only four existing sets of drawings. The whole thing, I need hardly tell you, is a profound secret, and you may judge of my present state of mind when I tell you that one set of drawings has been stolen."

"From your house?"

"From my office, in Chancery Lane, this morning. The four sets of drawings were distributed thus: Two were at the Admiralty Office, one being a finished set on thick paper, and the other a set of tracings therefrom; and the other two were at my own office, one being a penciled set, uncolored—a sort of finished draft, you understand—and the other a set of tracings similar to those at the Admiralty. It is this last set that has gone. The two sets were kept together in one drawer in my room. Both were there at ten this morning; of that I am sure, for I had to go to that very drawer for something else when I first arrived. But at twelve the tracings had vanished."

"You suspect somebody, probably?"

"I can not. It is a most extraordinary thing. Nobody has left the office (except myself, and then only to come to you) since ten this morning, and there has been no visitor. And yet the drawings are gone!"

"But have you searched the place?"

"Of course I have! It was twelve o'clock when I first discovered my loss, and I have been turning the place upside down ever since—I and my assistants. Every drawer has been emptied, every desk and table turned over, the very carpet and linoleum have been taken up, but there is not a sign of the drawings. My men even insisted on turning all their pockets inside out, although I never for a moment suspected either of them, and it would take a pretty big pocket to hold the drawings, doubled up as small as they might be."

"You say your men—there are two, I understand—had neither left the office?"

"Neither; and they are both staying in now. Worsfold suggested that it would be more satisfactory if they did not leave till something was done toward clearing the mystery up, and, although, as I have said, I don't suspect either in the least, I acquiesced."

"Just so. Now—I am assuming that you wish me to undertake the recovery of these drawings?"

The engineer nodded hastily.

"Very good; I will go round to your office. But first perhaps you can tell me something about your assistants—something it might be awkward to tell me in their presence, you know. Mr. Worsfold, for instance?"

"He is my draughtsman—a very excellent and intelligent man, a very smart man, indeed, and, I feel sure, quite beyond suspicion. He has prepared many important drawings for me (he has been with me nearly ten years now), and I have always found him trustworthy. But, of course, the temptation in this case would be enormous. Still, I can not suspect Worsfold. Indeed, how can I suspect anybody in the circumstances?"

"The other, now?"

"His name's Ritter. He is merely a tracer, not a fully skilled draughtsman. He is quite a decent young fellow, and I have had him two years. I don't consider him particularly smart, or he would have learned a little more of his business by this time. But I don't see the least reason to suspect him. As I said before, I can't reasonably suspect anybody."

"Very well; we will get to Chancery Lane now, if you please, and you can tell me more as we go."

"I have a cab waiting. What else can I tell you?"

"I understand the position to be succinctly this: The drawings were in the office when you arrived. Nobody came out, and nobody went in; and *yet* they vanished. Is that so?"

"That is so. When I say that absolutely nobody came in, of course I except the postman. He brought a couple of letters during the morning. I mean that absolutely nobody came past the barrier in the outer office—the usual thing, you know, like a counter, with a frame of ground glass over it."

"I quite understand that. But I think you said that the drawings were in a drawer in your *own* room—not the outer office, where the draughtsmen are, I presume?"

"That is the case. It is an inner room, or, rather, a room parallel with the other, and communicating with it; just as your own room is, which we have just left."

"But, then, you say you never left your office, and yet the drawings vanished—apparently by some unseen agency—while you were there in the room?"

"Let me explain more clearly." The cab was bowling smoothly along the Strand, and the engineer took out a pocket-book and pencil. "I fear," he proceeded, "that I am a little confused in my explanation—I am naturally rather agitated. As you will see presently, my offices consist of three rooms, two at one side of a corridor, and the other opposite—thus." He made a rapid pencil sketch.

"In the outer office my men usually work. In the inner office I work myself. These rooms communicate, as you see, by a door. Our ordinary way in and out of the place is by the door of the outer office leading into the corridor, and we first pass through the usual lifting flap in the barrier. The door leading from the *inner* office to the corridor is always kept locked on the inside, and I don't suppose I unlock it once in three months. It has not been unlocked all the morning. The drawer in which the missing drawings were kept, and in which I saw them at ten o'clock this morning, is at the place marked D; it is a large chest of shallow drawers in which the plans lie flat."

"I quite understand. Then there is the private room opposite. What of that?"

"That is a sort of private sitting-room that I rarely use, except for business interviews of a very private nature. When I said I never left my office, I did not mean that I never stirred out of the inner office. I was about in one room and another, both the outer and the inner offices, and once I went into the private room for five minutes, but nobody came either in or out of any of the rooms at that time, for the door of the private room was wide open, and I was standing at the book-case (I had gone to consult a book), just inside the door, with a full view of the doors opposite. Indeed, Worsfold was at the door of the outer office most of the short time. He came to ask me a question."

"Well," Hewitt replied, "it all comes to the simple first statement. You know that nobody left the place or arrived, except the postman, who couldn't get near the drawings, and yet the drawings went. Is this your office?"

The cab had stopped before a large stone building. Mr. Dixon alighted and led the way to the first-floor. Hewitt took a casual glance round each of the three rooms. There was a sort of door in the frame of ground glass over the barrier to admit of speech with visitors. This door Hewitt pushed wide open, and left so.

He and the engineer went into the inner office. "Would you like to ask Worsfold and Ritter any questions?" Mr. Dixon inquired.

"Presently. Those are their coats, I take it, hanging just to the right of the outer office door, over the umbrella stand?"

"Yes, those are all their things—coats, hats, stick, and umbrella."

"And those coats were searched, you say?"

"Yes."

"And this is the drawer—thoroughly searched, of course?"

"Oh, certainly; every drawer was taken out and turned over."

"Well, of course I must assume you made no mistake in your hunt. Now tell me, did anybody know where these plans were, beyond yourself and your two men?"

"As far as I can tell, not a soul."

"You don't keep an office boy?"

"No. There would be nothing for him to do except to post a letter now and again, which Ritter does quite well for."

"As you are quite sure that the drawings were there at ten o'clock, perhaps the thing scarcely matters. But I may as well know if your men have keys of the office?"

"Neither. I have patent locks to each door and I keep all the keys myself. If Worsfold or Ritter arrive before me in the morning they have to wait to be let in; and I am always present myself when the rooms are cleaned. I have not neglected precautions, you see."

"No. I suppose the object of the theft—assuming it is a theft—is pretty plain: the thief would offer the drawings for sale to some foreign government?"

"Of course. They would probably command a great sum. I have been looking, as I need hardly tell you, to that invention to secure me a very large fortune, and I shall be ruined, indeed, if the design is taken abroad. I am under the strictest engagements to secrecy with the Admiralty, and not only should I lose all my labor, but I should lose all the confidence reposed in me at headquarters; should, in fact, be subject to penalties for breach of contract, and my career stopped forever. I can not tell you what a serious business this is for me. If you can not help me, the consequences will be terrible. Bad for the service of the country, too, of course."

"Of course. Now tell me this: It would, I take it, be necessary for the thief to *exhibit* these drawings to anybody anxious to buy the secret—I mean, he couldn't describe the invention by word of mouth."

"Oh, no, that would be impossible. The drawings are of the most complicated description, and full of figures upon which the whole thing depends. Indeed, one would have to be a skilled expert to properly appreciate the design at all. Various principles of hydrostatics, chemistry, electricity, and pneumatics are most delicately manipulated and adjusted, and the smallest error or omission in any part would upset the whole. No, the drawings are necessary to the thing, and they are gone."

At this moment the door of the outer office was heard to open and somebody entered. The door between the two offices was ajar, and Hewitt could see right through to the glass door left open over the barrier and into the space beyond. A well-dressed, dark, bushy-bearded man stood there carrying a hand-bag, which he placed on the ledge before him. Hewitt raised his hand to enjoin silence. The man spoke in a rather high-pitched voice and with a slight accent. "Is Mr. Dixon now within?" he asked.

"He is engaged," answered one of the draughtsmen; "very particularly engaged. I am afraid you won't be able to see him this afternoon. Can I give him any message?"

"This is two—the second time I have come

to-day. Not two hours ago Mr. Dixon himself tells me to call again. I have a very important— very excellent steam-packing to show him that is very cheap and the best of the market." The man tapped his bag. "I have just taken orders from the largest railway companies. Can not I see him, for one second only? I will not detain him."

"Really, I'm sure you can't this afternoon; he isn't seeing anybody. But if you'll leave your name——"

"My name is Hunter; but what the good of that? He ask me to call a little later, and I come, and now he is engaged. It is a very great pity." And the man snatched up his bag and walking-stick, and stalked off, indignantly.

Hewitt stood still, gazing through the small aperture in the doorway.

"You'd scarcely expect a man with such a name as Hunter to talk with that accent, would you?" he observed, musingly. "It isn't a French accent, nor a German; but it seems foreign. You don't happen to know him, I suppose?"

"No, I don't. He called here about half-past twelve, just while we were in the middle of our search and I was frantic over the loss of the drawings. I was in the outer office myself, and told him to call later. I have lots of such agents here, anxious to sell all sorts of engineering appliances. But what will you do now? Shall you see my men?"

"I think," said Hewitt, rising—"I think I'll get you to question them yourself."

"Myself?"

"Yes, I have a reason. Will you trust me with the 'key' of the private room opposite? I will go over there for a little, while you talk to your men in this room. Bring them in here and shut the door; I can look after the office from across the corridor, you know. Ask them each to detail his exact movements about the office this morning, and get them to recall each visitor who has been here from the beginning of the week. I'll let you know the reason of this later. Come across to me in a few minutes."

Hewitt took the key and passed through the outer office into the corridor.

Ten minutes later Mr. Dixon, having questioned his draughtsmen, followed him. He found Hewitt standing before the table in the private room, on which lay several drawings on tracing-paper.

"See here, Mr. Dixon," said Hewitt, "I think these are the drawings you are anxious about?"

The engineer sprang toward them with a cry of delight. "Why, yes, yes," he exclaimed, turning them over, "every one of them! But where— how—they must have been in the place after all, then? What a fool I have been!"

Hewitt shook his head. "I'm afraid you're not quite so lucky as you think, Mr. Dixon," he said. "These drawings have most certainly been out of the house for a little while. Never mind how—we'll talk of that after. There is no time to lose. Tell me—how long would it take a good draughtsman to copy them?"

"They couldn't possibly be traced over properly in less than two or two and a half long days of very hard work," Dixon replied with eagerness.

"Ah! then it is as I feared. These tracings have been photographed, Mr. Dixon, and our task is one of every possible difficulty. If they had been copied in the ordinary way, one might hope to get hold of the copy. But photography upsets everything. Copies can be multiplied with such amazing facility that, once the thief gets a decent start, it is almost hopeless to checkmate him. The only chance is to get at the negatives before copies are taken. I must act at once; and I fear, between ourselves, it may be necessary for me to step very distinctly over the line of the law in the matter. You see, to get at those negatives may involve something very like house-breaking. There must be no delay, no waiting for legal procedure, or the mischief is done. Indeed, I very much question whether you have any legal remedy, strictly speaking."

"Mr. Hewitt, I implore you, do what you can. I need not say that all I have is at your disposal. I will guarantee to hold you harmless for anything that may happen. But do, I entreat you, do everything possible. Think of what the consequences may be!"

"Well, yes, so I do," Hewitt remarked, with a smile. "The consequences to me, if I were charged with house-breaking, might be something that no amount of guarantee could mitigate. However, I will do what I can, if only from patriotic motives. Now, I must see your tracer, Ritter. He is the traitor in the camp."

"Ritter? But how?"

"Never mind that now. You are upset and agitated, and had better not know more than is necessary for a little while, in case you say or do something unguarded. With Ritter I must take a deep course; what I don't know I must appear to know, and that will seem more likely to him if I disclaim acquaintance with what I do know. But first put these tracings safely away out of sight."

Dixon slipped them behind his book-case.

"Now," Hewitt pursued, "call Mr. Worsfold and give him something to do that will keep him in the inner office across the way, and tell him to send Ritter here."

Mr. Dixon called his chief draughtsman and requested him to put in order the drawings in the drawers of the inner room that had been disarranged by the search, and to send Ritter, as Hewitt had suggested.

Ritter walked into the private room with an air of respectful attention. He was a puffy-faced, unhealthy-looking young man, with very small eyes and a loose, mobile mouth.

"Sit down, Mr. Ritter," Hewitt said, in a stern voice. "Your recent transactions with your friend Mr. Hunter are well known both to Mr. Dixon and myself."

Ritter, who had at first leaned easily back in his chair, started forward at this, and paled.

"You are surprised, I observe; but you should be more careful in your movements out of doors if you do not wish your acquaintances to be known. Mr. Hunter, I believe, has the drawings which Mr. Dixon has lost, and, if so, I am certain that you have given them to him. That, you know, is theft, for which the law provides a severe penalty."

Ritter broke down completely and turned appealingly to Mr. Dixon.

"Oh, sir," he pleaded, "it isn't so bad, I assure you. I was tempted, I confess, and hid the drawings; but they are still in the office, and I can give them to you—really, I can."

"Indeed?" Hewitt went on. "Then, in that case, perhaps you'd better get them at once. Just go and fetch them in; we won't trouble to observe your hiding-place. I'll only keep this door open, to be sure you don't lose your way, you know—down the stairs, for instance."

The wretched Ritter, with hanging head, slunk into the office opposite. Presently he reappeared, looking, if possible, ghastlier than before. He looked irresolutely down the corridor, as if meditating a run for it, but Hewitt stepped toward him and motioned him back to the private room.

"You mustn't try any more of that sort of humbug," Hewitt said with increased severity. "The drawings are gone, and you have stolen them; you know that well enough. Now attend to me. If you received your deserts, Mr. Dixon would send for a policeman this moment, and have you hauled off to the jail that is your proper place. But, unfortunately, your accomplice, who calls himself Hunter—but who has other names besides that—as I happen to know—has the drawings, and it is absolutely necessary that these should be recovered. I am afraid that it will be necessary, therefore, to come to some arrangement with this scoundrel—to square him, in fact. Now, just take that pen and paper, and write to your confederate as I dictate. You know the alternative if you cause any difficulty."

Ritter reached tremblingly for the pen.

"Address him in your usual way," Hewitt proceeded. "Say this: 'There has been an alteration in the plans.' Have you got that? 'There has been an alteration in the plans. I shall be alone here at six o'clock. Please come, without fail.' Have you got it? Very well; sign it, and address the envelope. He must come here, and then we may arrange matters. In the meantime, you will remain in the inner office opposite."

The note was written, and Martin Hewitt, without glancing at the address, thrust it into his pocket. When Ritter was safely in the inner office, however, he drew it out and read the address. "I see," he observed, "he uses the same name, Hunter; 27 Little Carton Street, Westminster, is the address, and there I shall go at once with the note. If the man comes here, I think you had better lock him in with Ritter, and send for a policeman—it may at least frighten him. My object is, of course, to get the man away, and then, if possible, to invade his house, in some way or another, and steal or smash his negatives if they are there and to be found. Stay here, in any case, till I return. And don't forget to lock up those tracings."

It was about six o'clock when Hewitt returned, alone, but with a smiling face that told of good fortune at first sight.

"First, Mr. Dixon," he said, as he dropped into an easy chair in the private room, "let me ease your mind by the information that I have been most extraordinarily lucky; in fact, I think you have no further cause for anxiety. Here are the negatives. They were not all quite dry when I—well, what?—stole them, I suppose I must say; so that they have stuck together a bit, and probably the films are damaged. But you don't mind that, I suppose?"

He laid a small parcel, wrapped in a newspaper, on the table. The engineer hastily tore away the paper and took up five or six glass photographic negatives, of a half-plate size, which were damp, and stuck together by the gelatine films in couples. He held them, one after another, up to the light of the window, and glanced through them. Then, with a great sigh of relief, he placed them on the hearth and pounded them to dust and fragments with the poker.

For a few seconds neither spoke. Then Dixon, flinging himself into a chair, said:

"Mr. Hewitt, I can't express my obligation to you. What would have happened if you had failed, I prefer not to think of. But what shall we do with Ritter now? The other man hasn't been here yet, by the by."

"No; the fact is I didn't deliver the letter. The worthy gentleman saved me a world of trouble by taking himself out of the way." Hewitt laughed.

"I'm afraid he has rather got himself into a mess by trying two kinds of theft at once, and you may not be sorry to hear that his attempt on your torpedo plans is likely to bring him a dose of penal servitude for something else. I'll tell you what has happened.

"Little Carton Street, Westminster, I found to be a seedy sort of place—one of those old streets that have seen much better days. A good many people seem to live in each house—they are fairly large houses, by the way—and there is quite a company of bell-handles on each door-post, all down the side like organ-stops. A barber had possession of the ground floor front of No. 27 for trade purposes, so to him I went. 'Can you tell me,' I said, 'where in this house I can find Mr. Hunter?' He looked doubtful, so I went on: 'His friend will do, you know—I can't think of his name; foreign gentleman, dark, with a bushy beard.'

"The barber understood at once. 'Oh, that's Mirsky, I expect,' he said. 'Now, I come to think of it, he has had letters addressed to Hunter once or twice; I've took 'em in. Top floor back.'

"This was good so far. I had got at 'Mr. Hunter's' other alias. So, by way of possessing him with the idea that I knew all about him, I determined to ask for him as Mirsky before handing over the letter addressed to him as Hunter. A little bluff of that sort is invaluable at the right time. At the top floor back I stopped at the door and tried to open it at once, but it was locked. I could hear somebody scuttling about within, as though carrying things about, and I knocked again. In a little while the door opened about a foot, and there stood Mr. Hunter—or Mirsky, as you like—the man who, in the character of a traveler in steam-packing, came here twice today. He was in his shirt-sleeves, and cuddled something under his arm, hastily covered with a spotted pocket-handkerchief.

"'I have called to see M. Mirsky,' I said, 'with a confidential letter——'

"'Oh, yas, yas,' he answered hastily; 'I know—I know. Excuse me one minute.' And he rushed off down-stairs with his parcel.

"Here was a noble chance. For a moment I thought of following him, in case there might be something interesting in the parcel. But I had to decide in a moment, and I decided on trying the room. I slipped inside the door, and, finding the key on the inside, locked it. It was a confused sort of room, with a little iron bedstead in one corner and a sort of rough boarded inclosure in another. This I rightly conjectured to be the photographic dark-room, and made for it at once.

"There was plenty of light within when the door was left open, and I made at once for the drying-rack that was fastened over the sink. There were a number of negatives in it, and I began hastily examining them one after another. In the middle of this our friend Mirsky returned and tried the door. He rattled violently at the handle and pushed. Then he called.

"At this moment I had come upon the first of the negatives you have just smashed. The fixing and washing had evidently only lately been completed, and the negative was drying on the rack. I seized it, of course, and the others which stood by it.

"'Who are you, there, inside?' Mirsky shouted indignantly from the landing. 'Why for you go in my room like that? Open this door at once, or I call the police!'

"I took no notice. I had got the full number of negatives, one for each drawing, but I was not by any means sure that he had not taken an extra set; so I went on hunting down the rack. There were no more, so I set to work to turn out all the undeveloped plates. It was quite possible, you see, that the other set, if it existed, had not yet been developed.

"Mirsky changed his tune. After a little more banging and shouting I could hear him kneel down and try the key-hole. I had left the key there, so that he could see nothing. But he began talking softly and rapidly through the hole in a foreign language. I did not know it in the least, but I believe it was Russian. What had led him to believe I understood Russian I could not at the time imagine, though I have a notion now.

"I went on ruining his stock of plates. I found several boxes, apparently of new plates, but, as there was no means of telling whether they were really unused or were merely undeveloped, but with the chemical impress of your drawings on them, I dragged every one ruthlessly from its hiding-place and laid it out in the full glare of the sunlight—destroying it thereby, of course, whether it was unused or not.

"Mirsky left off talking, and I heard him quietly sneaking off. Perhaps his conscience was not sufficiently clear to warrant an appeal to the police, but it seemed to me rather probable at the time that that was what he was going for. So I hurried on with my work. I found three dark slides—the parts that carried the plates in the back of the camera, you know—one of them fixed in the camera itself. These I opened, and exposed the plates to ruination as before. I suppose nobody ever did so much devastation in a photographic studio in ten minutes as I managed.

"I had spoiled every plate I could find, and had the developed negatives safely in my pocket, when I happened to glance at a porcelain washing-well under the sink. There was one negative in that, and I took it up. It was *not* a negative of a drawing of yours, but of a Russian twenty-ruble note!

"This *was* a discovery. The only possible reason any man could have for photographing a bank-note was the manufacture of an etched plate for the production of forged copies. I was almost as pleased as I had been at the discovery of *your* negatives. He might bring the police now as soon as he liked; I could turn the tables on him completely. I began to hunt about for anything else relating to this negative.

"I found an inking-roller, some old pieces of blanket (used in printing from plates), and in a corner on the floor, heaped over with newspapers and rubbish, a small copying-press. There was also a dish of acid, but not an etched plate or a printed note to be seen. I was looking at the press, with the negative in one hand and the inking-roller in the other, when I became conscious of a shadow across the window. I looked up quickly, and there was Mirsky hanging over from some ledge or projection to the side of the window, and staring straight at me, with a look of unmistakable terror and apprehension.

"The face vanished immediately. I had to move a table to get at the window, and by the time I had opened it there was no sign or sound of the rightful tenant of the room. I had no doubt now of his reason for carrying a parcel down-stairs. He probably mistook me for another visitor he was expecting, and, knowing he must take this visitor into his room, threw the papers and rubbish over the press, and put up his plates and papers in a bundle and secreted them somewhere down-stairs, lest his occupation should be observed.

"Plainly, my duty now was to communicate with the police. So, by the help of my friend the barber down-stairs, a messenger was found and a note sent over to Scotland Yard. I awaited, of course, for the arrival of the police, and occupied the interval in another look round—finding nothing important, however. When the official detective arrived, he recognized at once the importance of the case. A large number of forged Russian notes have been put into circulation on the Continent lately, it seems, and it was suspected that they came from London. The Russian Government have been sending urgent messages to the police here on the subject.

"Of course I said nothing about your business; but, while I was talking with the Scotland Yard man, a letter was left by a messenger, addressed to Mirsky. The letter will be examined, of course, by the proper authorities, but I was not a little interested to perceive that the envelope bore the Russian imperial arms above the words 'Russian Embassy.' Now, why should Mirsky communicate with the Russian Embassy? Certainly not to let the officials know that he was carrying on a very extensive and lucrative business in the manufacture of spurious Russian notes. I think it is rather more than possible that he wrote—probably before he actually got your drawings—to say that he could sell information of the highest importance, and that this letter

was a reply. Further, I think it quite possible that, when I asked for him by his Russian name and spoke of 'a confidential letter,' he at once concluded that *I* had come from the embassy in answer to his letter. That would account for his addressing me in Russian through the key-hole; and, of course, an official from the Russian Embassy would be the very last person in the world whom he would like to observe any indications of his little etching experiments. But, anyhow, be that as it may," Hewitt concluded, "your drawings are safe now, and if once Mirsky is caught, and I think it likely, for a man in his shirt-sleeves, with scarcely any start, and, perhaps, no money about him, hasn't a great chance to get away—if he is caught, I say, he will probably get something handsome at St. Petersburg in the way of imprisonment, or Siberia, or what not; so that you will be amply avenged."

"Yes, but I don't at all understand this business of the drawings even now. How in the world were they taken out of the place, and how in the world did you find it out?"

"Nothing could be simpler; and yet the plan was rather ingenious. I'll tell you exactly how the thing revealed itself to me. From your original description of the case many people would consider that an impossibility had been performed. Nobody had gone out and nobody had come in, and yet the drawings had been taken away. But an impossibility is an impossibility, after all, and as drawings don't run away of themselves, plainly somebody had taken them, unaccountable as it might seem. Now, as they were in your inner office, the only people who could have got at them besides yourself were your assistants, so that it was pretty clear that one of them, at least, had something to do with the business. You told me that Worsfold was an excellent and intelligent draughtsman. Well, if such a man as that meditated treachery, he would probably be able to carry away the design in his head—at any rate, a little at a time—and would be under no necessity to run the risk of stealing a set of the drawings. But Ritter, you remarked, was an inferior sort of man. 'Not particularly smart,'

I think, were your words—only a mechanical sort of tracer. *He* would be unlikely to be able to carry in his head the complicated details of such designs as yours, and, being in a subordinate position, and continually overlooked, he would find it impossible to make copies of the plans in the office. So that, to begin with, I thought I saw the most probable path to start on.

"When I looked round the rooms, I pushed open the glass door of the barrier and left the door to the inner office ajar, in order to be able to see any thing that *might* happen in any part of the place, without actually expecting any definite development. While we were talking, as it happened, our friend Mirsky (or Hunter—as you please) came into the outer office, and my attention was instantly called to him by the first thing he did. Did you notice anything peculiar yourself?"

"No, really, I can't say I did. He seemed to behave much as any traveler or agent might."

"Well, what I noticed was the fact that as soon as he entered the place he put his walking-stick into the umbrella-stand over there by the door, close by where he stood, a most unusual thing for a casual caller to do, before even knowing whether you were in. This made me watch him closely. I perceived with increased interest that the stick was exactly of the same kind and pattern as one already standing there, also a curious thing. I kept my eyes carefully on those sticks, and was all the more interested and edified to see, when he left, that he took the *other* stick—not the one he came with—from the stand, and carried it away, leaving his own behind. I might have followed him, but I decided that more could be learned by staying, as, in fact, proved to be the case. This, by the by, is the stick he carried away with him. I took the liberty of fetching it back from Westminster, because I conceive it to be Ritter's property."

Hewitt produced the stick. It was an ordinary, thick Malacca cane, with a buck-horn handle and a silver band. Hewitt bent it across his knee and laid it on the table.

"Yes," Dixon answered, "that is Ritter's

stick. I think I have often seen it in the stand. But what in the world——"

"One moment; I'll just fetch the stick Mirsky left behind." And Hewitt stepped across the corridor.

He returned with another stick, apparently an exact fac-simile of the other, and placed it by the side of the other.

"When your assistants went into the inner room, I carried this stick off for a minute or two. I knew it was not Worsfold's, because there was an umbrella there with his initial on the handle. Look at this."

Martin Hewitt gave the handle a twist and rapidly unscrewed it from the top. Then it was seen that the stick was a mere tube of very thin metal, painted to appear like a Malacca cane.

"It was plain at once that this was no Malacca cane—it wouldn't bend. Inside it I found your tracings, rolled up tightly. You can get a marvelous quantity of thin tracing-paper into a small compass by tight rolling."

"And this—this was the way they were brought back!" the engineer exclaimed. "I see that clearly. But how did they get away? That's as mysterious as ever."

"Not a bit of it! See here. Mirsky gets hold of Ritter, and they agree to get your drawings and photograph them. Ritter is to let his confederate have the drawings, and Mirsky is to bring them back as soon as possible, so that they sha'n't be missed for a moment. Ritter habitually carries this Malacca cane, and the cunning of Mirsky at once suggests that this tube should be made in outward fac-simile. This morning Mirsky keeps the actual stick, and Ritter comes to the office with the tube. He seizes the first opportunity—probably when you were in this private room, and Worsfold was talking to you from the corridor—to get at the tracings, roll them up tightly, and put them in the tube, putting the tube back into the umbrella-stand. At half-past twelve, or whenever it was, Mirsky turns up for the first time with the actual stick and exchanges them, just as he afterward did when he brought the drawings back."

"Yes, but Mirsky came half an hour after they were—Oh, yes, I see. What a fool I was! I was forgetting. Of course, when I first missed the tracings, they were in this walking-stick, safe enough, and I was tearing my hair out within arm's reach of them!"

"Precisely. And Mirsky took them away before your very eyes. I expect Ritter was in a rare funk when he found that the drawings were missed. He calculated, no doubt, on your not wanting them for the hour or two they would be out of the office."

"How lucky that it struck me to jot a pencil-note on one of them! I might easily have made my note somewhere else, and then I should never have known that they had been away."

"Yes, they didn't give you any too much time to miss them. Well, I think the rest pretty clear. I brought the tracings in here, screwed up the sham stick and put it back. You identified the tracings and found none missing, and then my course was pretty clear, though it looked difficult. I knew you would be very naturally indignant with Ritter, so, as I wanted to manage him myself, I told you nothing of what he had actually done, for fear that, in your agitated state, you might burst out with something that would spoil my game. To Ritter I pretended to know nothing of the return of the drawings or *how* they had been stolen—the only things I did know with certainty. But I *did* pretend to know all about Mirsky—or Hunter—when, as a matter of fact, I knew nothing at all, except that he probably went under more than one name. That put Ritter into my hands completely. When he found the game was up, he began with a lying confession. Believing that the tracings were still in the stick and that we knew nothing of their return, he said that they had not been away, and that he would fetch them—as I had expected he would. I let him go for them alone, and, when he returned, utterly broken up by the discovery that they were not there, I had him altogether at my mercy. You see, if he had known that the drawings were all the time behind your book-case, he might have brazened it out, sworn that the drawings had been there all the time, and we could have done nothing with him. We couldn't have sufficiently frightened him by a threat of prosecution for theft, because there the things were in your possession, to his knowledge.

"As it was he answered the helm capitally: gave us Mirsky's address on the envelope, and wrote the letter that was to have got him out of the way while I committed burglary, if that disgraceful expedient had not been rendered unnecessary. On the whole, the case has gone very well."

"It has gone marvelously well, thanks to yourself. But what shall I do with Ritter?"

"Here's his stick—knock him down-stairs with it, if you like. I should keep the tube, if I were you, as a memento. I don't suppose the respectable Mirsky will ever call to ask for it. But I should certainly kick Ritter out of doors—or out of window, if you like—without delay."

Mirsky was caught, and, after two remands at the police-court, was extradited on the charge of forging Russian notes. It came out that he had written to the embassy, as Hewitt had surmised, stating that he had certain valuable information to offer, and the letter which Hewitt had seen delivered was an acknowledgment, and a request for more definite particulars. This was what gave rise to the impression that Mirsky had himself informed the Russian authorities of his forgeries. His real intent was very different, but was never guessed.

"I wonder," Hewitt has once or twice observed, "whether, after all, it would not have paid the Russian authorities better on the whole if I had never investigated Mirsky's little note factory. The Dixon torpedo was worth a good many twenty-ruble notes."

A CURIOUS EXPERIENCE

MARK TWAIN

OFTEN REGARDED AS America's greatest humorist, and possibly its greatest writer, Samuel Langhorne Clemens (1835–1910) took the pseudonym Mark Twain, a term used to describe water's depth that he heard while working as a pilot on the Mississippi River.

Although he described and commented on serious events of the day in his work, he generally employed humor to soften his often-controversial positions. It is seldom acknowledged, but Mark Twain played a major role in the development of detective fiction. His first published book, *The Celebrated Jumping Frog of Calaveras County and Other Sketches* (1867), tells the story of a slick stranger who filled Jim Smiley's frog with quail shot to win a bet—an early and outstanding tale of a confidence game.

More important is Twain's *Life on the Mississippi* (1883), in which chapter thirty-one is a complete, self-contained story, "A Thumb-print and What Came of It," which is the first time in fiction that fingerprints are used as a form of identification. Twain used the same device in *The Tragedy of Pudd'nhead Wilson* (1894), in which the entire plot revolves around Wilson's courtroom explanation of the uniqueness of a person's print.

Most of Twain's contributions to the mystery genre arc humorous. "The Stolen White Elephant" (1882) is an out-and-out parody, as is *A Double-Barrelled Detective Story* (1902), which has Sherlock Holmes in its cross-hairs. *Tom Sawyer, Detective* (1896) is a classic tale of the humorous consequences of leaping to conclusions. Less successful are *A Murder, a Mystery, and a Marriage* (1945), unpublished at the time of Twain's death and issued in an unauthorized sixteen-copy edition, and *Simon Wheeler, Detective* (1963), an unfinished novel published more than a half century after the author's death by the New York Public Library.

"A Curious Experience" was originally published in the November 1881 issue of *Century Magazine*; it was first collected in *The Stolen White Elephant, Etc.* (Boston, James R. Osgood and Company, 1882).

A CURIOUS EXPERIENCE

MARK TWAIN

THIS IS THE STORY which the Major told me, as nearly as I can recall it:—

In the winter of 1862–3, I was commandant of Fort Trumbull, at New London, Conn. Maybe our life there was not so brisk as life at "the front"; still it was brisk enough, in its way— one's brains didn't cake together there for lack of something to keep them stirring. For one thing, all the Northern atmosphere at that time was thick with mysterious rumors—rumors to the effect that rebel spies were flitting everywhere, and getting ready to blow up our Northern forts, burn our hotels, send infected clothing into our towns, and all that sort of thing. You remember it. All this had a tendency to keep us awake, and knock the traditional dullness out of garrison life. Besides, ours was a recruiting station—which is the same as saying we hadn't any time to waste in dozing, or dreaming, or fooling around. Why, with all our watchfulness, 50 percent of a day's recruits would leak out of our hands and give us the slip the same night. The bounties were so prodigious that a recruit could pay a sentinel three or four hundred dollars to let him escape, and still have enough of his bounty-money left to constitute a fortune for a poor man. Yes, as I said before, our life was not drowsy.

Well, one day I was in my quarters alone, doing some writing, when a pale and ragged lad of fourteen or fifteen entered, made a neat bow, and said—

"I believe recruits are received here?"

"Yes."

"Will you please enlist me, sir?"

"Dear me, no! You are too young, my boy, and too small."

A disappointed look came into his face, and quickly deepened into an expression of despondency. He turned slowly away, as if to go; hesitated, then faced me again, and said, in a tone which went to my heart—

"I have no home, and not a friend in the world. If you could only enlist me!"

But of course the thing was out of the question, and I said so as gently as I could. Then I told him to sit down by the stove and warm himself, and added—

"You shall have something to eat, presently. You are hungry?"

He did not answer; he did not need to; the gratitude in his big soft eyes was more eloquent than any words could have been. He sat down by the stove, and I went on writing. Occasionally I took a furtive glance at him. I noticed that his clothes and shoes, although soiled and damaged, were of good style and material. This fact was suggestive. To it I added the facts that his voice was low and musical; his eyes deep and melancholy; his carriage and address gentlemanly; evidently the poor chap was in trouble. As a result, I was interested.

However, I became absorbed in my work, by and by, and forgot all about the boy. I don't know how long this lasted; but, at length, I happened to look up. The boy's back was toward me, but his face was turned in such a way that I could see one of his cheeks—and down that cheek a rill of noiseless tears was flowing.

"God bless my soul!" I said to myself; "I forgot the poor rat was starving." Then I made amends for my brutality by saying to him, "Come along, my lad; you shall dine with me; I am alone to-day."

He gave me another of those grateful looks, and a happy light broke in his face. At the table he stood with his hand on his chair-back until I was seated, then seated himself. I took up my knife and fork and—well, I simply held them, and kept still; for the boy had inclined his head and was saying a silent grace. A thousand hallowed memories of home and my childhood poured in upon me, and I sighed to think how far I had drifted from religion and its balm for hurt minds, its comfort and solace and support.

As our meal progressed, I observed that young Wicklow—Robert Wicklow was his full name—knew what to do with his napkin; and—well, in a word, I observed that he was a boy of good breeding; never mind the details. He had a simple frankness, too, which won upon me. We talked mainly about himself, and I had no difficulty in getting his history out of him. When he spoke of his having been born and reared in Louisiana, I warmed to him decidedly, for I had spent some time down there. I knew all the "coast" region of the Mississippi, and loved it, and had not been long enough away from it for my interest in it to begin to pale. The very names that fell from his lips sounded good to me—so good that I steered the talk in directions that would

bring them out. Baton Rouge, Plaquemine, Donaldsonville, Sixty-mile Point, Bonnet-Carre, the Stock-Landing, Carrollton, the Steamship Landing, the Steamboat Landing, New Orleans, Tchoupitoulas Street, the Esplanade, the Rue des Bons Enfants, the St. Charles Hotel, the Tivoli Circle, the Shell Road, Lake Pontchartrain; and it was particularly delightful to me to hear once more of the *R. E. Lee*, the *Natchez*, the *Eclipse*, the *General Quitman*, the *Duncan F. Kenner*, and other old familiar steamboats. It was almost as good as being back there, these names so vividly reproduced in my mind the look of the things they stood for. Briefly, this was little Wicklow's history:—

When the war broke out, he and his invalid aunt and his father were living near Baton Rouge, on a great and rich plantation which had been in the family for fifty years. The father was a Union man. He was persecuted in all sorts of ways, but clung to his principles. At last, one night, masked men burned his mansion down, and the family had to fly for their lives. They were hunted from place to place, and learned all there was to know about poverty, hunger, and distress. The invalid aunt found relief at last: misery and exposure killed her; she died in an open field, like a tramp, the rain beating upon her and the thunder booming overhead. Not long afterward, the father was captured by an armed band; and while the son begged and pleaded, the victim was strung up before his face. [At this point a baleful light shone in the youth's eyes, and he said, with the manner of one who talks to himself: "If I cannot be enlisted, no matter—I shall find a way—I shall find a way."] As soon as the father was pronounced dead, the son was told that if he was not out of that region within twenty-four hours, it would go hard with him. That night he crept to the riverside and hid himself near a plantation landing. By and by the *Duncan F. Kenner* stopped there, and he swam out and concealed himself in the yawl that was dragging at her stern. Before daylight the boat reached the Stock-Landing, and he slipped ashore. He walked the three miles which lay between that point and the house of an uncle of his in Good-Children Street, in New Orleans, and then his troubles were over for the time being. But this uncle was a Union man, too, and before very long he concluded that he had better leave the South. So he and young Wicklow slipped out of the country on board a sailing vessel, and in due time reached New York. They put up at the Astor House. Young Wicklow had a good time of it for a while, strolling up and down Broadway, and observing the strange Northern sights; but in the end a change came—and not for the better. The uncle had been cheerful at first, but now he began to look troubled and despondent; moreover, he became moody and irritable; talked of money giving out, and no way to get more—"not enough left for one, let alone two." Then, one morning, he was missing—did not come to breakfast. The boy inquired at the office, and was told that the uncle had paid his bill the night before and gone away—to Boston, the clerk believed, but was not certain.

The lad was alone and friendless. He did not know what to do, but concluded he had better try to follow and find his uncle. He went down to the steamboat landing; learned that the trifle of money in his pocket would not carry him to Boston; however, it would carry him to New London; so he took passage for that port, resolving to trust to Providence to furnish him means to travel the rest of the way. He had now been wandering about the streets of New London three days and nights, getting a bite and a nap here and there for charity's sake. But he had given up at last; courage and hope were both gone. If he could enlist, nobody could be more thankful; if he could not get in as a soldier, couldn't he be a drummer-boy? Ah, he would work so hard to please, and would be so grateful!

Well, there's the history of young Wicklow, just as he told it to me, barring details. I said—

"My boy, you are among friends, now—don't you be troubled any more." How his eyes glistened! I called in Sergeant John Rayburn—he was from Hartford; lives in Hartford yet; maybe you know him—and said, "Rayburn, quarter

this boy with the musicians. I am going to enroll him as a drummer-boy, and I want you to look after him and see that he is well treated."

Well, of course, intercourse between the commandant of the post and the drummer-boy came to an end, now; but the poor little friendless chap lay heavy on my heart, just the same. I kept on the lookout, hoping to see him brighten up and begin to be cheery and gay; but no, the days went by, and there was no change. He associated with nobody; he was always absent-minded, always thinking; his face was always sad. One morning Rayburn asked leave to speak to me privately. Said he—

"I hope I don't offend, sir; but the truth is, the musicians are in such a sweat it seems as if somebody's got to speak."

"Why, what is the trouble?"

"It's the Wicklow boy, sir. The musicians are down on him to an extent you can't imagine."

"Well, go on, go on. What has he been doing?"

"Prayin', sir."

"Praying!"

"Yes, sir; the musicians haven't any peace of their life for that boy's prayin'. First thing in the morning he's at it; noons he's at it; and nights— well, nights he just lays into 'em like all possessed! Sleep? Bless you, they can't sleep: he's got the floor, as the sayin' is, and then when he once gets his supplication-mill agoin', there just simply ain't any let-up to him. He starts in with the band-master, and he prays for him; next he takes the head bugler, and he prays for him; next the bass drum, and he scoops him in; and so on, right straight through the band, givin' them all a show, and takin' that amount of interest in it which would make you think he thought he warn't but a little while for this world, and believed he couldn't be happy in heaven without he had a brass band along, and wanted to pick 'em out for himself, so he could depend on 'em to do up the national tunes in a style suitin' to the place. Well, sir, heavin' boots at him don't have no effect; it's dark in there; and, besides, he don't pray fair, anyway, but kneels down behind the big drum; so it don't make no difference if they rain boots at him, he don't give a dern—warbles right along, same as if it was applause. They sing out, 'Oh, dry up!' 'Give us a rest!' 'Shoot him!' 'Oh, take a walk!' and all sorts of such things. But what of it? It don't phaze him. He don't mind it." After a pause: "Kind of a good little fool, too; gits up in the mornin' and carts all that stock of boots back, and sorts 'em out and sets each man's pair where they belong. And they've been thronged at him so much now, that he knows every boot in the band—can sort 'em out with his eyes shut."

After another pause, which I forebore to interrupt—

"But the roughest thing about it is, that when he's done prayin'—when he ever does get done—he pipes up and begins to sing. Well, you know what a honey kind of a voice he's got when he talks; you know how it would persuade a cast-iron dog to come down off of a doorstep and lick his hand. Now if you'll take my word for it, sir, it ain't a circumstance to his singin'! Flute music is harsh to that boy's singin'. Oh, he just gurgles it out so soft and sweet and low, there in the dark, that it makes you think you are in heaven."

"What is there 'rough' about that?"

"Ah, that's just it, sir. You hear him sing

"*Just as I am—poor, wretched, blind*'

"—just you hear him sing that, once, and see if you don't melt all up and the water come into your eyes! I don't care what he sings, it goes plum straight home to you—it goes deep down to where you live—and it fetches you every time! Just you hear him sing:—

"*Child of sin and sorrow, filled with dismay,*
Wait not till to-morrow, yield thee to-day;
Grieve not that love
Which, from above'

"—and so on. It makes a body feel like the wickedest, ungratefulest brute that walks. And when he sings them songs of his about home, and mother, and childhood, and old memories, and things that's vanished, and old friends dead and gone, it fetches everything before your face that you've ever loved and lost in all your life—and it's just beautiful, it's just divine to listen to, sir—but, Lord, Lord, the heart-break of it! The band—well, they all cry—every rascal of them blubbers, and don't try to hide it, either; and first you know, that very gang that's been slammin' boots at that boy will skip out of their bunks all of a sudden, and rush over in the dark and hug him! Yes, they do—and slobber all over him, and call him pet names, and beg him to forgive them. And just at that time, if a regiment was to offer to hurt a hair of that cub's head, they'd go for that regiment, if it was a whole army corps!"

Another pause.

"Is that all?" said I.

"Yes, sir."

"Well, dear me, what is the complaint? What do they want done?"

"Done? Why, bless you, sir, they want you to stop him from singin'."

"What an idea! You said his music was divine."

"That's just it. It's too divine. Mortal man can't stand it. It stirs a body up so; it turns a body inside out; it racks his feelin's all to rags; it makes him feel bad and wicked, and not fit for any place but perdition. It keeps a body in such an everlastin' state of repentin', that nothin' don't taste good and there ain't no comfort in life. And then the cryin', you see—every mornin' they are ashamed to look one another in the face."

"Well, this is an odd case, and a singular complaint. So they really want the singing stopped?"

"Yes, sir, that is the idea. They don't wish to ask too much; they would like powerful well to have the prayin' shut down on, or leastways trimmed off around the edges; but the main thing's the singin'. If they can only get the singin' choked off, they think they can stand the prayin', rough as it is to be bully-ragged so much that way."

I told the sergeant I would take the matter under consideration. That night I crept into the musicians' quarters and listened. The sergeant had not overstated the case. I heard the praying voice pleading in the dark; I heard the execrations of the harassed men; I heard the rain of boots whiz through the air, and bang and thump around the big drum. The thing touched me, but it amused me, too. By and by, after an impressive silence, came the singing. Lord, the pathos of it, the enchantment of it! Nothing in the world was ever so sweet, so gracious, so tender, so holy, so moving. I made my stay very brief; I was beginning to experience emotions of a sort not proper to the commandant of a fortress.

Next day I issued orders which stopped the praying and singing. Then followed three or four days which were so full of bounty-jumping excitements and irritations that I never once thought of my drummer-boy. But now comes Sergeant Rayburn, one morning, and says—

"That new boy acts mighty strange, sir."

"How?"

"Well, sir, he's all the time writing."

"Writing? What does he write—letters?"

"I don't know, sir; but whenever he's off duty, he is always poking and nosing around the fort, all by himself—blest if I think there's a hole or corner in it he hasn't been into—and every little while he outs with pencil and paper and scribbles something down."

This gave me a most unpleasant sensation. I wanted to scoff at it, but it was not a time to scoff at anything that had the least suspicious tinge about it. Things were happening all around us, in the North, then, that warned us to be always on the alert, and always suspecting. I recalled to mind the suggestive fact that this boy was from the South—the extreme South, Louisiana—and the thought was not of a reassuring nature, under the circumstances. Nevertheless, it cost me a pang to give the orders which I now gave to Rayburn. I felt like a father who plots to expose his own child to shame and injury. I told Rayburn to keep quiet, bide his time, and get me some of those writings whenever he could manage it without the boy's finding it out. And I charged him not to do anything which might

let the boy discover that he was being watched. I also ordered that he allow the lad his usual liberties, but that he be followed at a distance when he went out into the town.

During the next two days, Rayburn reported to me several times. No success. The boy was still writing, but he always pocketed his paper with a careless air whenever Rayburn appeared in his vicinity. He had gone twice to an old deserted stable in the town, remained a minute or two, and come out again. One could not pooh-pooh these things—they had an evil look. I was obliged to confess to myself that I was getting uneasy. I went into my private quarters and sent for my second in command—an officer of intelligence and judgment, son of General James Watson Webb. He was surprised and troubled. We had a long talk over the matter, and came to the conclusion that it would be worth while to institute a secret search. I determined to take charge of that myself. So I had myself called at two in the morning; and, pretty soon after, I was in the musicians' quarters, crawling along the floor on my stomach among the snorers. I reached my slumbering waif's bunk at last, without disturbing anybody, captured his clothes and kit, and crawled stealthily back again. When I got to my own quarters, I found Webb there, waiting and eager to know the result. We made search immediately. The clothes were a disappointment. In the pockets we found blank paper and a pencil; nothing else, except a jackknife and such queer odds and ends and useless trifles as boys hoard and value. We turned to the kit hopefully. Nothing there but a rebuke for us!—a little Bible with this written on the fly-leaf: "Stranger, be kind to my boy, for his mother's sake."

I looked at Webb—he dropped his eyes; he looked at me—I dropped mine. Neither spoke. I put the book reverently back in its place. Presently Webb got up and went away, without remark. After a little I nerved myself up to my unpalatable job, and took the plunder back to where it belonged, crawling on my stomach as before. It seemed the peculiarly appropriate attitude for the business I was in.

I was most honestly glad when it was over and done with.

About noon next day Rayburn came, as usual, to report. I cut him short. I said—

"Let this nonsense be dropped. We are making a bugaboo out of a poor little cub who has got no more harm in him than a hymn-book."

The sergeant looked surprised, and said—

"Well, you know it was your orders, sir, and I've got some of the writing."

"And what does it amount to? How did you get it?"

"I peeped through the key-hole, and see him writing. So when I judged he was about done, I made a sort of a little cough, and I see him crumple it up and throw it in the fire, and look all around to see if anybody was coming. Then he settled back as comfortable and careless as anything. Then I comes in, and passes the time of day pleasantly, and sends him of an errand. He never looked uneasy, but went right along. It was a coal-fire and new-built; the writing had gone over behind a chunk, out of sight; but I got it out; there it is; it ain't hardly scorched, you see."

I glanced at the paper and took in a sentence or two. Then I dismissed the sergeant and told him to send Webb to me. Here is the paper in full:—

"FORT TRUMBULL, the 8th.

COLONEL—I was mistaken as to the calibre of the three guns I ended my list with. They are 18-pounders; all the rest of the armament is as I stated. The garrison remains as before reported, except that the two light infantry companies that were to be detached for service at the front are to stay here for the present—can't find out for how long, just now, but will soon. We are satisfied that, all things considered, matters had better be postponed un—"

There it broke off—there is where Rayburn coughed and interrupted the writer. All my affection for the boy, all my respect for him and charity for his forlorn condition, withered in a moment under the blight of this revelation of cold-blooded baseness.

But never mind about that. Here was business—business that required profound and immediate attention, too. Webb and I turned the subject over and over, and examined it all around. Webb said—

"What a pity he was interrupted! Something is going to be postponed until—when? And what is the something? Possibly he would have mentioned it, the pious little reptile!"

"Yes," I said, "we have missed a trick. And who is 'we,' in the letter? Is it conspirators inside the fort or outside?"

That "we" was uncomfortably suggestive. However, it was not worth while to be guessing around that, so we proceeded to matters more practical. In the first place, we decided to double the sentries and keep the strictest possible watch. Next, we thought of calling Wicklow in and making him divulge everything; but that did not seem wisest until other methods should fail. We must have some more of the writings; so we began to plan to that end. And now we had an idea: Wicklow never went to the post-office—perhaps the deserted stable was his post-office. We sent for my confidential clerk—a young German named Sterne, who was a sort of natural detective—and told him all about the case and ordered him to go to work on it. Within the hour we got word that Wicklow was writing again. Shortly afterward, word came that he had asked leave to go out into the town. He was detained awhile, and meantime Sterne hurried off and concealed himself in the stable. By and by he saw Wicklow saunter in, look about him, then hide something under some rubbish in a corner, and take leisurely leave again. Sterne pounced upon the hidden article—a letter—and brought it to us. It had no superscription and no signature. It repeated what we had already read, and then went on to say:—

"We think it best to postpone till the two companies are gone. I mean the four inside think so; have not communicated with the others—afraid of attracting attention. I say four because we have lost two; they had hardly enlisted and got inside when they were shipped off to the front. It will be absolutely necessary to have two in their places. The two that went were the brothers from Thirty-mile Point. I have something of the greatest importance to reveal, but must not trust it to this method of communication; will try the other."

"The little scoundrel!" said Webb; "who could have supposed he was a spy? However, never mind about that; let us add up our particulars, such as they are, and see how the case stands to date. First, we've got a rebel spy in our midst, whom we know; secondly, we've got three more in our midst whom we don't know; thirdly, these spies have been introduced among us through the simple and easy process of enlisting as soldiers in the Union army—and evidently two of them have got sold at it, and been shipped off to the front; fourthly, there are assistant spies 'outside'—number indefinite; fifthly, Wicklow has a very important matter which he is afraid to communicate by the 'present method'—will 'try the other.' That is the case, as it now stands. Shall we collar Wicklow and make him confess? Or shall we catch the person who removes the letters from the stable and make him tell? Or shall we keep still and find out more?"

We decided upon the last course. We judged that we did not need to proceed to summary measures now, since it was evident that the conspirators were likely to wait till those two light infantry companies were out of the way. We fortified Sterne with pretty ample powers, and told him to use his best endeavors to find out Wicklow's "other method" of communication. We meant to play a bold game; and to this end we proposed to keep the spies in an unsuspecting state as long as possible. So we ordered Sterne to return to the stable immediately, and, if he found the coast clear, to conceal Wicklow's letter where it was before, and leave it there for the conspirators to get.

The night closed down without further event. It was cold and dark and sleety, with a raw wind blowing; still I turned out of my warm bed several times during the night, and went the rounds in person, to see that all was right and that every sentry was on the alert. I always found them wide awake and watchful; evidently whispers of mysterious dangers had been floating about, and the doubling of the guards had been a kind of indorsement of those rumors. Once, toward morning, I encountered Webb, breasting his way against the bitter wind, and learned then that he, also, had been the rounds several times to see that all was going right.

Next day's events hurried things up somewhat. Wicklow wrote another letter; Sterne preceded him to the stable and saw him deposit it; captured it as soon as Wicklow was out of the way, then slipped out and followed the little spy at a distance, with a detective in plain clothes at his own heels, for we thought it judicious to have the law's assistance handy in case of need. Wicklow went to the railway station, and waited around till the train from New York came in, then stood scanning the faces of the crowd as they poured out of the cars. Presently an aged gentleman, with green goggles and a cane, came limping along, stopped in Wicklow's neighborhood, and began to look about him expectantly. In an instant Wicklow darted forward, thrust an envelope into his hand, then glided away and disappeared in the throng. The next instant Sterne had snatched the letter; and as he hurried past the detective, he said: "Follow the old gentleman—don't lose sight of him." Then Sterne skurried out with the crowd, and came straight to the fort.

We sat with closed doors, and instructed the guard outside to allow no interruption.

First we opened the letter captured at the stable. It read as follows:—

"HOLY ALLIANCE—Found, in the usual gun, commands from the Master, left there last night, which set aside the instructions heretofore received from the subordinate quarter. Have left in the gun the usual indication that the commands reached the proper hand—"

Webb, interrupting: "Isn't the boy under constant surveillance now?"

I said yes; he had been under strict surveillance ever since the capturing of his former letter.

"Then how could he put anything into a gun, or take anything out of it, and not get caught?"

"Well," I said, "I don't like the look of that very well."

"I don't, either," said Webb. "It simply means that there are conspirators among the very sentinels. Without their connivance in some way or other, the thing couldn't have been done."

I sent for Rayburn, and ordered him to examine the batteries and see what he could find. The reading of the letter was then resumed:—

"The new commands are peremptory, and require that the MMMM shall be FFFFF at 3 o'clock to-morrow morning. Two hundred will arrive, in small parties, by train and otherwise, from various directions, and will be at appointed place at right time. I will distribute the sign to-day. Success is apparently sure, though something must have got out, for the sentries have been doubled, and the chiefs went the rounds last night several times. W. W. comes from southerly to-day and will receive secret orders—by the other method. All six of you must be in 166 at sharp 2 A.M. You will find B. B. there, who will give you detailed instructions. Password same as last time, only reversed—put first syllable last and last syllable first. REMEMBER XXXX. Do not forget. Be of good heart; before the next sun rises you will be heroes; your fame will be permanent; you will have added a deathless page to history. Amen."

"Thunder and Mars," said Webb, "but we are getting into mighty hot quarters, as I look at it!"

I said there was no question but that things were beginning to wear a most serious aspect. Said I—

"A desperate enterprise is on foot, that is plain enough. To-night is the time set for it—that, also, is plain. The exact nature of the enterprise—I mean the manner of it—is hidden away under those blind bunches of M's and F's, but the end and aim, I judge, is the surprise and capture of the post. We must move quick and sharp now. I think nothing can be gained by continuing our clandestine policy as regards Wicklow. We must know, and as soon as possible, too, where '166' is located, so that we can make a descent upon the gang there at 2 A.M.; and doubtless the quickest way to get that information will be to force it out of that boy. But first of all, and before we make any important move, I must lay the facts before the War Department, and ask for plenary powers."

The despatch was prepared in cipher to go over the wires; I read it, approved it, and sent it along.

We presently finished discussing the letter which was under consideration, and then opened the one which had been snatched from the lame gentleman. It contained nothing but a couple of perfectly blank sheets of notepaper! It was a chilly check to our hot eagerness and expectancy. We felt as blank as the paper, for a moment, and twice as foolish. But it was for a moment only; for, of course, we immediately afterward thought of "sympathetic ink." We held the paper close to the fire and watched for the characters to come out, under the influence of the heat; but nothing appeared but some faint tracings, which we could make nothing of. We then called in the surgeon, and sent him off with orders to apply every test he was acquainted with till he got the right one, and report the contents of the letter to me the instant he brought them to the surface. This check was a confounded annoyance, and we naturally chafed under the delay; for we had fully expected to get out of that letter some of the most important secrets of the plot.

Now appeared Sergeant Rayburn, and drew from his pocket a piece of twine string about a foot long, with three knots tied in it, and held it up.

"I got it out of a gun on the water-front," said he. "I took the tompions out of all the guns and examined close; this string was the only thing that was in any gun."

So this bit of string was Wicklow's "sign" to signify that the "Master's" commands had not miscarried. I ordered that every sentinel who had served near that gun during the past twenty-four hours be put in confinement at once and separately, and not allowed to communicate with any one without my privity and consent.

A telegram now came from the Secretary of War. It read as follows:—

"Suspend habeas corpus. Put town under martial law. Make necessary arrests. Act with vigor and promptness. Keep the Department informed."

We were now in shape to go to work. I sent out and had the lame gentleman quietly arrested and as quietly brought into the fort; I placed him under guard, and forbade speech to him or from him. He was inclined to bluster at first, but he soon dropped that.

Next came word that Wicklow had been seen to give something to a couple of our new recruits; and that, as soon as his back was turned, these had been seized and confined. Upon each was found a small bit of paper, bearing these words and signs in pencil:—

EAGLE'S THIRD FLIGHT. REMEMBER XXXX. 166.

In accordance with instructions, I telegraphed to the Department, in cipher, the progress made, and also described the above ticket. We seemed to be in a strong enough position now to venture to throw off the mask as regarded Wicklow; so I sent for him. I also sent for and received back the letter written in sympathetic ink, the surgeon accompanying it with the information that thus far it had resisted his tests, but that there were others he could apply when I should be ready for him to do so.

Presently Wicklow entered. He had a somewhat worn and anxious look, but he was composed and easy, and if he suspected anything it did not appear in his face or manner. I allowed him to stand there a moment or two, then I said pleasantly—

"My boy, why do you go to that old stable so much?"

He answered, with simple demeanor and without embarrassment—

"Well, I hardly know, sir; there isn't any particular reason, except that I like to be alone, and I amuse myself there."

"You amuse yourself there, do you?"

"Yes, sir," he replied, as innocently and simply as before.

"Is that all you do there?"

"Yes, sir," he said, looking up with childlike wonderment in his big soft eyes.

"You are sure?"

"Yes, sir, sure."

After a pause, I said—

"Wicklow, why do you write so much?"

"I? I do not write much, sir."

"You don't?"

"No, sir. Oh, if you mean scribbling, I do scribble some, for amusement."

"What do you do with your scribblings?"

"Nothing, sir—throw them away."

"Never send them to anybody?"

"No, sir."

I suddenly thrust before him the letter to the "Colonel." He started slightly, but immediately composed himself. A slight tinge spread itself over his cheek.

"How came you to send this piece of scribbling, then?"

"I nev—never meant any harm, sir."

"Never meant any harm! You betray the armament and condition of the post, and mean no harm by it?"

He hung his head and was silent.

"Come, speak up, and stop lying. Whom was this letter intended for?"

He showed signs of distress, now; but quickly collected himself, and replied, in a tone of deep earnestness—

"I will tell you the truth, sir—the whole truth. The letter was never intended for anybody at all. I wrote it only to amuse myself. I see the error and foolishness of it, now—but it is the only offence, sir, upon my honor."

"Ah, I am glad of that. It is dangerous to be writing such letters. I hope you are sure this is the only one you wrote?"

"Yes, sir, perfectly sure."

His hardihood was stupefying. He told that lie with as sincere a countenance as any creature ever wore. I waited a moment to soothe down my rising temper, and then said—

"Wicklow, jog your memory now, and see if you can help me with two or three little matters which I wish to inquire about."

"I will do my very best, sir."

"Then, to begin with—who is 'the Master'?"

It betrayed him into darting a startled glance at our faces, but that was all. He was serene again in a moment, and tranquilly answered—

"I do not know, sir."

"You do not know?"

"I do not know."

"You are sure you do not know?"

He tried hard to keep his eyes on mine, but the strain was too great; his chin sunk slowly toward his breast and he was silent; he stood there nervously fumbling with a button, an object to command one's pity, in spite of his base acts. Presently I broke the stillness with the question—

"Who are the 'Holy Alliance'?"

His body shook visibly, and he made a slight random gesture with his hands, which to me was like the appeal of a despairing creature for compassion. But he made no sound. He continued to stand with his face bent toward the ground. As we sat gazing at him, waiting for him to speak, we saw the big tears begin to roll down his cheeks. But he remained silent. After a little, I said—

"You must answer me, my boy, and you must tell me the truth. Who are the Holy Alliance?"

He wept on in silence. Presently I said, somewhat sharply,

"Answer the question!"

He struggled to get command of his voice; and then, looking up appealingly, forced the words out between his sobs—

"Oh, have pity on me, sir! I cannot answer it, for I do not know."

"What!"

"Indeed, sir, I am telling the truth. I never have heard of the Holy Alliance till this moment. On my honor, sir, this is so."

"Good heavens! Look at this second letter of yours; there, do you see those words, 'Holy Alliance'? What do you say now?"

He gazed up into my face with the hurt look of one upon whom a great wrong had been wrought, then said, feelingly—

"This is some cruel joke, sir; and how could they play it upon me, who have tried all I could to do right, and have never done harm to anybody? Some one has counterfeited my hand; I never wrote a line of this; I have never seen this letter before!"

"Oh, you unspeakable liar! Here, what do you say to this?"—and I snatched the sympathetic-ink letter from my pocket and thrust it before his eyes.

His face turned white!—as white as a dead person's. He wavered slightly in his tracks, and put his hand against the wall to steady himself. After a moment he asked, in so faint a voice that it was hardly audible—

"Have you—read it?"

Our faces must have answered the truth before my lips could get out a false "yes," for I distinctly saw the courage come back into that boy's eyes. I waited for him to say something, but he kept silent. So at last I said—

"Well, what have you to say as to the revelations in this letter?"

He answered, with perfect composure—

"Nothing, except that they are entirely harmless and innocent; they can hurt nobody."

I was in something of a corner now, as I couldn't disprove his assertion. I did not know exactly how to proceed. However, an idea came to my relief, and I said—

"You are sure you know nothing about the Master and the Holy Alliance, and did not write the letter which you say is a forgery?"

"Yes, sir—sure."

I slowly drew out the knotted twine string and held it up without speaking. He gazed at it indifferently, then looked at me inquiringly. My patience was sorely taxed. However, I kept my temper down, and said in my usual voice—

"Wicklow, do you see this?"

"Yes, sir."

"What is it?"

"It seems to be a piece of string."

"Seems? It is a piece of string. Do you recognize it?"

"No, sir," he replied, as calmly as the words could be uttered.

His coolness was perfectly wonderful! I paused now for several seconds, in order that the silence might add impressiveness to what I was about to say; then I rose and laid my hand on his shoulder, and said gravely—

"It will do you no good, poor boy, none in the world. This sign to the 'Master,' this knotted string, found in one of the guns on the waterfront—"

"Found in the gun! Oh, no, no, no! do not say in the gun, but in a crack in the tompion!—it must have been in the crack!" and down he went on his knees and clasped his hands and lifted up a face that was pitiful to see, so ashy it was, and wild with terror.

"No, it was in the gun."

"Oh, something has gone wrong! My God, I am lost!" and he sprang up and darted this way and that, dodging the hands that were put out to catch him, and doing his best to escape from the place. But of course escape was impossible. Then he flung himself on his knees again, crying with all his might, and clasped me around the legs; and so he clung to me and begged and pleaded, saying, "Oh, have pity on me! Oh, be merciful to me! Do not betray me; they would not spare my life a moment! Protect me, save me. I will confess everything!"

It took us some time to quiet him down and modify his fright, and get him into something like a rational frame of mind. Then I began to question him, he answering humbly, with downcast eyes, and from time to time swabbing away his constantly flowing tears.

"So you are at heart a rebel?"

"Yes, sir."

"And a spy?"

"Yes, sir."

"And have been acting under distinct orders from outside?"

"Yes, sir."

"Willingly?"

"Yes, sir."

"Gladly, perhaps?"

"Yes, sir; it would do no good to deny it. The South is my country; my heart is Southern, and it is all in her cause."

"Then the tale you told me of your wrongs and the persecution of your family was made up for the occasion?"

"They—they told me to say it, sir."

"And you would betray and destroy those who pitied and sheltered you. Do you comprehend how base you are, you poor misguided thing?"

He replied with sobs only.

"Well, let that pass. To business. Who is the 'Colonel,' and where is he?"

He began to cry hard, and tried to beg off from answering. He said he would be killed if he told. I threatened to put him in the dark cell and lock him up if he did not come out with the information. At the same time I promised to protect him from all harm if he made a clean breast. For all answer, he closed his mouth firmly and put on a stubborn air which I could not bring him out of. At last I started with him; but a single glance into the dark cell converted him. He broke into a passion of weeping and supplicating, and declared he would tell everything.

So I brought him back, and he named the "Colonel," and described him particularly. Said he would be found at the principal hotel in the town, in citizen's dress. I had to threaten him again, before he would describe and name the "Master." Said the Master would be found at No. 15 Bond Street, New York, passing under the name of R. F. Gaylord. I telegraphed name and description to the chief of police of the metropolis, and asked that Gaylord be arrested and held till I could send for him.

"Now," said I, "it seems that there are several of the conspirators 'outside,' presumably in New London. Name and describe them."

He named and described three men and two women—all stopping at the principal hotel. I sent out quietly, and had them and the "Colonel" arrested and confined in the fort.

"Next, I want to know all about your three fellow-conspirators who are here in the fort."

He was about to dodge me with a falsehood, I thought; but I produced the mysterious bits of paper which had been found upon two of them, and this had a salutary effect upon him. I said we had possession of two of the men, and he must point out the third. This frightened him badly, and he cried out—

"Oh, please don't make me; he would kill me on the spot!"

I said that that was all nonsense; I would have somebody near by to protect him, and, besides, the men should be assembled without arms. I ordered all the raw recruits to be mustered, and then the poor trembling little wretch went out and stepped along down the line, trying to look as indifferent as possible. Finally he spoke a single word to one of the men, and before he had gone five steps the man was under arrest.

As soon as Wicklow was with us again, I had those three men brought in. I made one of them stand forward, and said—

"Now, Wicklow, mind, not a shade's divergence from the exact truth. Who is this man, and what do you know about him?"

Being "in for it," he cast consequences aside, fastened his eyes on the man's face, and spoke straight along without hesitation—to the following effect.

"His real name is George Bristow. He is from New Orleans; was second mate of the coast-packet *Capitol*, two years ago; is a desperate character, and has served two terms for manslaughter—one for killing a deck-hand named Hyde with a capstan-bar, and one for killing a roustabout for refusing to heave the lead, which is no part of a roustabout's business. He is a spy, and was sent here by the Colonel, to act in that capacity. He was third mate of the *St. Nicholas*, when she blew up in the neighborhood of Memphis, in '58, and came near being lynched for robbing the dead and wounded while they were being taken ashore in an empty wood-boat."

And so forth and so on—he gave the man's biography in full. When he had finished, I said to the man—

"What have you to say to this?"

"Barring your presence, sir, it is the infernalest lie that ever was spoke!"

I sent him back into confinement, and called the others forward in turn. Same result. The boy gave a detailed history of each, without ever hesitating for a word or a fact; but all I could get out of either rascal was the indignant assertion that it was all a lie. They would confess nothing. I returned them to captivity, and brought out the rest of my prisoners, one by one. Wicklow told all about them—what towns in the South they were from, and every detail of their connection with the conspiracy.

But they all denied his facts, and not one of them confessed a thing. The men raged, the women cried. According to their stories, they were all innocent people from out West, and loved the Union above all things in this world. I locked the gang up, in disgust, and fell to catechising Wicklow once more.

"Where is No. 166, and who is B. B.?"

But there he was determined to draw the line. Neither coaxing nor threats had any effect upon him. Time was flying—it was necessary to institute sharp measures. So I tied him up a-tiptoe by the thumbs. As the pain increased, it wrung screams from him which were almost more than

I could bear. But I held my ground, and pretty soon he shrieked out—

"Oh, please let me down, and I will tell!"

"No—you'll tell before I let you down."

Every instant was agony to him, now, so out it came—

"No. 166, Eagle Hotel!"—naming a wretched tavern down by the water, a resort of common laborers, longshoremen, and less reputable folk.

So I released him, and then demanded to know the object of the conspiracy.

"To take the fort to-night," said he, doggedly and sobbing.

"Have I got all the chiefs of the conspiracy?"

"No. You've got all except those that are to meet at 166."

"What does 'Remember XXXX' mean?"

No reply.

"What is the password to No. 166?"

No reply.

"What do those bunches of letters mean— 'FFFFF' and 'MMMM'? Answer! or you will catch it again."

"I never will answer! I will die first. Now do what you please."

"Think what you are saying, Wicklow. Is it final?"

He answered steadily, and without a quiver in his voice—

"It is final. As sure as I love my wronged country and hate everything this Northern sun shines on, I will die before I will reveal those things."

I triced him up by the thumbs again. When the agony was full upon him, it was heartbreaking to hear the poor thing's shrieks, but we got nothing else out of him. To every question he screamed the same reply: "I can die, and I will die; but I will never tell."

Well, we had to give it up. We were convinced that he certainly would die rather than confess. So we took him down and imprisoned him, under strict guard.

Then for some hours we busied ourselves with sending telegrams to the War Department, and with making preparations for a descent upon No. 166.

It was stirring times, that black and bitter night. Things had leaked out, and the whole garrison was on the alert. The sentinels were trebled, and nobody could move, outside or in, without being brought to a stand with a musket levelled at his head. However, Webb and I were less concerned now than we had previously been, because of the fact that the conspiracy must necessarily be in a pretty crippled condition, since so many of its principals were in our clutches.

I determined to be at No. 166 in good season, capture and gag B. B., and be on hand for the rest when they arrived. At about a quarter past one in the morning I crept out of the fortress with half a dozen stalwart and gamy U.S. regulars at my heels—and the boy Wicklow, with his hands tied behind him. I told him we were going to No. 166, and that if I found he had lied again and was misleading us, he would have to show us the right place or suffer the consequences.

We approached the tavern stealthily and reconnoitred. A light was burning in the small bar-room, the rest of the house was dark. I tried the front door; it yielded, and we softly entered, closing the door behind us. Then we removed our shoes, and I led the way to the bar-room. The German landlord sat there, asleep in his chair. I woke him gently, and told him to take off his boots and precede us; warning him at the same time to utter no sound. He obeyed without a murmur, but evidently he was badly frightened. I ordered him to lead the way to 166. We ascended two or three flights of stairs as softly as a file of cats; and then, having arrived near the farther end of a long hall, we came to a door through the glazed transom of which we could discern the glow of a dim light from within. The landlord felt for me in the dark and whispered to me that that was 166. I tried the door—it was locked on the inside. I whispered an order to one of my biggest soldiers; we set our ample shoulders to the door and with one heave we burst it from its hinges. I caught a half-glimpse of a figure in a bed—saw its head dart toward the candle; out went the light, and we were in pitch darkness. With one big bound I lit on that bed and pinned its occupant down with my knees. My prisoner struggled fiercely, but I got a grip on his throat with my left hand, and that was a good assistance to my knees in holding him down. Then straightway I snatched out my revolver, cocked it, and laid the cold barrel warningly against his cheek.

"Now somebody strike a light!" said I. "I've got him safe."

It was done. The flame of the match burst up. I looked at my captive, and, by George, it was a young woman!

I let go and got off the bed, feeling pretty sheepish. Everybody stared stupidly at his neighbor. Nobody had any wit or sense left, so sudden and overwhelming had been the surprise. The young woman began to cry, and covered her face with the sheet. The landlord said, meekly—

"My daughter, she has been doing something that is not right, nicht wahr?"

"Your daughter? Is she your daughter?"

"Oh, yes, she is my daughter. She is just to-night come home from Cincinnati a little bit sick."

"Confound it, that boy has lied again. This is not the right 166; this is not B. B. Now, Wicklow, you will find the correct 166 for us, or—hello! where is that boy?"

Gone, as sure as guns! And, what is more, we failed to find a trace of him. Here was an awkward predicament. I cursed my stupidity in not tying him to one of the men; but it was of no use to bother about that now. What should I do in the present circumstances?—that was the question. That girl might be B. B., after all. I did not believe it, but still it would not answer to take unbelief for proof. So I finally put my men in a vacant room across the hall from 166, and told them to capture anybody and everybody that approached the girl's room, and to keep the landlord with them, and under strict watch, until further orders. Then I hurried back to the fort to see if all was right there yet.

Yes, all was right. And all remained right. I stayed up all night to make sure of that. Nothing happened. I was unspeakably glad to see the dawn come again, and be able to telegraph the Department that the Stars and Stripes still floated over Fort Trumbull.

An immense pressure was lifted from my breast. Still I did not relax vigilance, of course, nor effort either; the case was too grave for that. I had up my prisoners, one by one, and harried them by the hour, trying to get them to confess, but it was a failure. They only gnashed their teeth and tore their hair, and revealed nothing.

About noon came tidings of my missing boy. He had been seen on the road, tramping westward, some eight miles out, at six in the morning. I started a cavalry lieutenant and a private on his track at once. They came in sight of him twenty miles out. He had climbed a fence and was wearily dragging himself across a slushy field toward a large old-fashioned mansion in the edge of a village. They rode through a bit of woods, made a detour, and closed up on the house from the opposite side; then dismounted and skurried into the kitchen. Nobody there. They slipped into the next room, which was also unoccupied; the door from that room into the front or sitting room was open. They were about to step through it when they heard a low voice; it was somebody praying. So they halted reverently, and the lieutenant put his head in and saw an old man and an old woman kneeling in a corner of that sitting-room. It was the old man that was praying, and just as he was finishing his prayer, the Wicklow boy opened the front door and stepped in. Both of those old people sprang at him and smothered him with embraces, shouting—

"Our boy! our darling! God be praised. The lost is found! He that was dead is alive again!"

Well, sir, what do you think! That young imp was born and reared on that homestead, and had never been five miles away from it in all his life, till the fortnight before he loafed into my quarters and gulfed me with that maudlin yarn of his! It's as true as gospel. That old man was his father—a learned old retired clergyman; and that old lady was his mother.

Let me throw in a word or two of explanation concerning that boy and his performances. It turned out that he was a ravenous devourer of dime novels and sensation-story papers—therefore, dark mysteries and gaudy heroisms were just in his line. Then he had read newspaper reports of the stealthy goings and comings of rebel spies in our midst, and of their lurid purposes and their two or three startling achievements, till his imagination was all aflame on that subject. His constant comrade for some months had been a Yankee youth of much tongue and lively fancy, who had served for a couple of years as "mud clerk" (that is, subordinate purser) on certain of the packet-boats plying between New Orleans and points two or three hundred miles up the Mississippi—hence his easy facility in handling the names and other details pertaining to that region. Now I had spent two or three months in that part of the country before the war; and I knew just enough about it to be easily taken in by that boy, whereas a born Louisianian would probably have caught him tripping before he had talked fifteen minutes. Do you know the reason he said he would rather die than explain certain of his treasonable enigmas? Simply because he couldn't explain them!—they had no meaning; he had fired them out of his imagination without forethought or afterthought; and so, upon sudden call, he wasn't able to invent an explanation of them. For instance, he couldn't reveal what was hidden in the "sympathetic ink" letter, for the ample reason that there wasn't anything hidden in it; it was blank paper only. He hadn't put anything into a gun, and had never intended to—for his letters were all written to imaginary persons, and when he hid one in the stable he always removed the one he had put there the day before; so he was not acquainted with that knotted string, since he was seeing it for the first time when I showed it to him; but as soon as I had let him find out where it came from, he straightway adopted it, in his romantic fashion, and got some fine effects out of it. He invented Mr. "Gaylord"; there wasn't any 15 Bond Street, just then—it had been pulled down three months before. He invented the "Colonel"; he invented the glib histories of those unfortunates whom I captured and confronted with him; he invented "B. B."; he even invented No. 166, one may say, for he didn't know there was such a number in the Eagle Hotel until we went there. He stood ready to invent anybody or anything whenever it was wanted. If I called for "outside" spies, he promptly described strangers whom he had seen at the hotel, and whose names he had happened to hear. Ah, he lived in a gorgeous, mysterious, romantic world during those few stirring days, and I think it was real to him, and that he enjoyed it clear down to the bottom of his heart.

But he made trouble enough for us, and just no end of humiliation. You see, on account of him we had fifteen or twenty people under arrest and confinement in the fort, with sentinels before their doors. A lot of the captives were soldiers and such, and to them I didn't have to apologize; but the rest were first-class citizens, from all over the country, and no amount of apologies was sufficient to satisfy them. They just fumed and raged and made no end of trouble! And those two ladies—one was an Ohio Congressman's wife, the other a Western bishop's sister—well, the scorn and ridicule and angry tears they poured out on me made up a keepsake that was likely to make me remember them for a considerable time—and I shall. That old lame gentleman with the goggles was a college president from Philadelphia, who had come up to attend his nephew's funeral. He had never seen young Wicklow before, of course. Well, he not only missed the funeral, and got jailed as a rebel spy, but Wicklow had stood up there in my quarters and coldly described him as a counterfeiter, rigger-trader, horse-thief, and fire-bug from the most notorious rascal-nest in Galveston; and this was a thing which that poor old gentleman couldn't seem to get over at all.

And the War Department! But, O my soul, let's draw the curtain over that part!

NOTE.—I showed my manuscript to the Major, and he said: "Your unfamiliarity with military matters has betrayed you into some little mistakes. Still, they are picturesque ones—let them go; military men will smile at them, the rest won't detect them. You have got the main facts of the history right, and have set them down just about as they occurred."—M. T.

AMBROSE BIERCE

AMBROSE GWINNETT BIERCE (1842–1914?) was a famously cynical, intolerant, and angry writer, but perhaps less well-known is that his life was much the same—and with good reason. With the exception of his brother Albert, he loathed his entire rather large family (he was one of thirteen children, all of whose names began with the letter *A*), but he was following in his family's footprints, as his father, Marcus Aurelius Bierce, had detested everyone in his family as well, barring his brother Lucius Verus.

Ambrose left his home at fifteen to become a printer's devil and joined the Union army as soon as the Civil War broke out, serving with bravery and honor, especially at the battle of Shiloh. His military trials and encounters served as the background for many of his best stories, notably *Tales of Soldiers and Civilians* (1891). After his discharge from the army he moved to San Francisco to join Albert and quickly became a newspaperman, becoming notorious for his cartoons and his satirical writings.

Soon after his marriage in 1871, he and his wife moved to England but his poor health, a combination of war wounds and asthma, drove him back to California five years later, where he resumed his journalistic career while also writing fiction. During most of his lifetime, he was more famous as a newspaperman than a fiction writer, deeply admired by William Randolph Hearst, who gave him his own influential column and promoted his work relentlessly until Bierce retired in 1909.

At the age of seventy-one, Bierce decided to tour the Civil War battlefields on which he fought as a young man. He later crossed the border into Mexico and joined Pancho Villa's army as an observer in the civil war between Villa and Carranza. It is in Mexico that he disappeared without trace. His last recorded word was a letter written to a friend on December 26, 1913. Rumors abound that he had been killed by a firing squad, that he had committed suicide, or that he had been killed by one side or the other in battle. Despite several investigations into his disappearance, no concrete evidence was ever discovered and his death remains a great mystery.

"Parker Adderson, Philosopher" was originally published in the February 22, 1891, issue of the *San Francisco Examiner*; it was first published in book form in *Tales of Soldiers and Civilians* (San Francisco, E. L. G. Steele, 1891).

PARKER ADDERSON, PHILOSOPHER

AMBROSE BIERCE

"PRISONER, what is your name?"

"As I am to lose it at daylight tomorrow morning, it is hardly worth concealing. Parker Adderson."

"Your rank?"

"A somewhat humble one; commissioned officers are too precious to be risked in the perilous business of a spy. I am a sergeant."

"Of what regiment?"

"You must excuse me; if I answered that it might, for anything I know, give you an idea of whose forces are in your front. Such knowledge as that is what I came into your lines to obtain, not to impart."

"You are not without wit."

"If you have the patience to wait, you will find me dull enough tomorrow."

"How do you know that you are to die tomorrow morning?"

"Among spies captured by night that is the custom. It is one of the nice observances of the profession."

The General so far laid aside the dignity appropriate to a Confederate officer of high rank and wide renown as to smile. But no one in his power and out of his favour would have drawn any happy augury from that outward and visible sign of approval. It was neither genial nor infectious; it did not communicate itself to the other persons exposed to it—the caught spy who had provoked it and the armed guard who had brought him into the tent and now stood a little apart, watching his prisoner in the yellow candle-light. It was no part of that warrior's duty to smile; he had been detailed for another purpose. The conversation was resumed; it was, in fact, a trial for a capital offence.

"You admit, then, that you are a spy—that you came into my camp disguised as you are, in the uniform of a Confederate soldier, to obtain information secretly regarding the numbers and disposition of my troops?"

"Regarding, particularly, their numbers. Their disposition I already knew. It is morose."

The General brightened again; the guard, with a severer sense of his responsibility, accentuated the austerity of his expression and stood a trifle more erect than before. Twirling his grey slouch hat round and round upon his forefinger, the spy took a leisurely survey of his surroundings. They were simple enough. The tent was a common "wall tent," about eight feet by ten in dimensions, lighted by a single tallow-candle stuck into the haft of a bayonet, which was itself stuck into a pine-table, at which the general sat, now busily writing and apparently forgetful of his unwilling guest. An old rag-carpet covered the earthen floor; an older hair-trunk, a second chair, and a roll of blankets were about all else that the tent contained; in General Clavering's command, Confederate simplicity and penury of "pomp and circumstance" had attained their highest development. On a large nail driven into the tent-pole at the entrance was suspended a sword-belt supporting a long sabre, a pistol in its holster and, absurdly enough, a bowie knife. Of that most unmilitary weapon it was the General's habit to explain that it was a cherished souvenir of the peaceful days when he was a civilian.

It was a stormy night. The rain cascaded upon the canvas in torrents, with the dull, drum-like sound familiar to dwellers in tents. As the whooping blasts charged upon it the frail structure shook and swayed and strained at its confining stakes and ropes.

The General finished writing, folded the half sheet of paper, and spoke to the soldier guarding Adderson: "Here, Tassman, take that to the adjutant-general; then return."

"And the prisoner, General?" said the soldier, saluting, with an inquiring glance in the direction of that unfortunate.

"Do as I said," replied the officer, curtly.

The soldier took the note and ducked himself out of the tent. General Clavering turned his handsome, clean-cut face toward the Federal spy, looked him in the eyes, not unkindly, and said: "It is a bad night, my man."

"For me, yes."

"Do you guess what I have written?"

"Something worth reading, I dare say. And—perhaps it is my vanity—I venture to suppose that I am mentioned in it."

"Yes; it is a memorandum for an order to be read to the troops at reveille concerning your execution. Also some notes for the guidance of the provost-marshal in arranging the details of that event."

"I hope, General, the spectacle will be intelligently arranged, for I shall attend it myself."

"Have you any arrangements of your own that you wish to make? Do you wish to see a chaplain, for example?"

"I could hardly secure a longer rest for myself by depriving him of some of his."

"Good God, man! do you mean to go to your death with nothing but jokes upon your lips? Do you not know that this is a serious matter?"

"How can I know that? I have never been dead in all my life. I have heard that death is a serious matter, but never from any of those who have experienced it."

The General was silent for a moment; the man interested, perhaps amused, him—a type not previously encountered.

"Death," he said, "is at least a loss—a loss of such happiness as we have, and of opportunities for more."

"A loss of which we will never be conscious can be borne with composure and therefore expected without apprehension. You must have observed, General, that of all the dead men with whom it is your soldierly pleasure to strew your path, none shows signs of regret."

"If the being dead is not a regrettable condition, yet the becoming so—the act of dying—appears to be distinctly disagreeable in one who has not lost the power to feel."

"Pain is disagreeable, no doubt. I never suffer it without more or less discomfort. But he who lives longest is most exposed to it. What you call dying is simply the last pain—there is really no such thing as dying. Suppose, for illustration, that I attempt to escape. You lift the revolver that you are courteously concealing in your lap, and——"

The General blushed like a girl, then laughed softly, disclosing his brilliant teeth, made a slight inclination of his handsome head, and said nothing. The spy continued: "You fire, and I have in my stomach what I did not swallow. I fall, but am not dead. After a half hour of agony I *am* dead. But at any given instant of that half hour I was either alive or dead. There is no transition period.

"When I am hanged tomorrow morning it will be quite the same; while conscious I shall be living; when dead, unconscious. Nature appears to have ordered the matter quite in my interest—the way that I should have ordered it myself. It is so simple," he added with a smile, "that it seems hardly worth while to be hanged at all."

At the finish of his remarks there was a long silence. The General sat impassive, looking into the man's face, but apparently not attentive to what had been said. It was as if his eyes had mounted guard over the prisoner, while his mind concerned itself with other matters. Presently he drew a long, deep breath, shuddered, as one awakened from a dreadful dream, and exclaimed almost inaudibly: "Death is horrible!"—this man of death.

"It was horrible to our savage ancestors," said the spy, gravely, "because they had not enough intelligence to dissociate the idea of consciousness from the idea of the physical forms in which it is manifested—as an even lower order of intelligence, that of the monkey, for example, may be unable to imagine a house without inhabitants, and seeing a ruined hut fancies a suffering occupant. To us it is horrible because we have inherited the tendency to think it so, accounting for the notion by wild and fanciful theories of another world—as names of places give rise to legends explaining them, and reasonless conduct to philosophies in justification. You can hang me, General, but there your power of evil ends; you cannot condemn me to heaven."

The General appeared not to have heard; the spy's talk had merely turned his thoughts into an unfamiliar channel, but there they pursued their will independently to conclusions of their own. The storm had ceased, and something of the solemn spirit of the night had imparted itself to his reflections, giving them the sombre tinge of a supernatural dread. Perhaps there was an element of prescience in it. "I should not like to die," he said—"not tonight."

He was interrupted—if, indeed, he had intended to speak further—by the entrance of an officer of his staff, Captain Hasterlick, the Provost-Marshal. This recalled him to himself; the absent look passed away from his face.

"Captain," he said, acknowledging the officer's salute, "this man is a Yankee spy captured inside our lines with incriminating papers on him. He has confessed. How is the weather?"

"The storm is over, sir, and the moon shining."

"Good; take a file of men, conduct him at once to the parade-ground, and shoot him."

A sharp cry broke from the spy's lips. He threw himself forward, thrust out his neck, expanded his eyes, clenched his hands.

"Good God!" he cried hoarsely, almost inarticulately; "you do not mean that! You forget—I am not to die until morning."

"I have said nothing of morning," replied the General, coldly; "that was an assumption of your own. You die now."

"But, General, I beg—I implore you to remember; I am to hang! It will take some time to erect the gallows—two hours—an hour. Spies are hanged; I have rights under military law. For Heaven's sake, General, consider how short——"

"Captain, observe my directions."

The officer drew his sword, and, fixing his eyes upon the prisoner, pointed silently to the opening of the tent. The prisoner, deathly pale, hesitated; the officer grasped him by the collar and pushed him gently forward. As he approached the tent-pole the frantic man sprang to it and, with cat-like agility, seized the handle of the bowie knife, plucked the weapon from the scabbard, and, thrusting the Captain aside, leaped upon the General with the fury of a madman, hurling him to the ground and falling headlong upon him as he lay. The table was overturned, the candle extinguished, and they fought blindly in the darkness. The Provost-Marshal sprang to the assistance of his superior officer, and was himself prostrated upon the struggling forms. Curses and inarticulate cries of rage and pain came from the welter of limbs and bodies; the tent came down upon them, and beneath its hampering and enveloping folds the struggle went on. Private Tassman, returning from his errand and dimly conjecturing the situation, threw down his rifle, and, laying hold of the flouncing canvas at random, vainly tried to drag it off the men under it; and the sentinel who paced up and down in front, not daring to leave his beat though the skies should fall, discharged his piece. The report alarmed the camp; drums beat the long roll and bugles sounded the assembly bringing swarms of half-clad men into the moonlight, dressing as they ran, and falling into line at the sharp commands of their officers. This was well; being in line the men were under control; they stood at arms while the General's staff and the men of his escort brought order out of confusion by lifting off the fallen tent and pulling apart the breathless and bleeding actors in that strange contention.

Breathless, indeed, was one; the Captain was dead, the handle of the bowie knife protruding from his throat and pressed back beneath his chin until the end had caught in the angle of the jaw, and the hand that delivered the blow had been unable to remove the weapon. In the dead man's hand was his sword, clenched with a grip that defied the strength of the living. Its blade was streaked with red to the hilt.

Lifted to his feet, the General sank back to the earth with a moan and fainted. Besides his bruises he had two sword-thrusts—one through the thigh, the other through the shoulder.

The spy had suffered the least damage. Apart from a broken right arm, his wounds were such only as might have been incurred in an ordinary combat with nature's weapons. But he was dazed, and seemed hardly to know what had occurred. He shrank away from those attending him, cowered upon the ground, and uttered unintelligible remonstrances. His face, swollen by blows and stained with gouts of blood, nevertheless showed white beneath his dishevelled hair—as white as that of a corpse.

"The man is not insane," said the surgeon in reply to a question; "he is suffering from fright. Who and what is he?"

Private Tassman began to explain. It was the opportunity of his life; he omitted nothing that could in any way accentuate the importance of his own relation to the night's events. When he had finished his story and was ready to begin it again, nobody gave him any attention.

The General had now recovered consciousness. He raised himself upon his elbow, looked about him, and, seeing the spy crouching by a camp-fire, guarded, said simply:

"Take that man to the parade-ground and shoot him."

"The General's mind wanders," said an officer standing near.

"His mind does *not* wander," the Adjutant-General said. "I have a memorandum from him about this business; he had given that same order to Hasterlick"—with a motion of the hand toward the dead Provost-Marshal—"and, by God! it shall be executed."

Ten minutes later Sergeant Parker Adderson, of the Federal army, philosopher and wit, kneeling in the moonlight and begging incoherently for his life, was shot to death by twenty men. As the volley rang out upon the keen air of the winter midnight, General Clavering, lying white and still in the red glow of the camp-fire, opened his big blue eyes, looked pleasantly upon those about him, and said, "How silent it all is!"

The surgeon looked at the Adjutant-General, gravely and significantly. The patient's eyes slowly closed, and thus he lay for a few moments; then, his face suffused with a smile of ineffable sweetness, he said faintly, "I suppose this must be death," and so passed away.

THE HAND OF CARLOS

CHARLES McCARRY

IT CAN BE NO SURPRISE that there is a long history of real-life espionage agents employing the secrets of their surreptitious trade, embellishing and fictionalizing them for the printed page. W. Somerset Maugham, Ian Fleming, John le Carré, and Graham Greene had worked for the Secret Service, and so did Charles McCarry (1930–2019), who spent eleven years as a deep cover agent for the Central Intelligence Agency in Europe, Asia, and Africa. He left the agency in 1967 so was bemused when reviewers mentioned his service, ascribing inside knowledge to him, thirty or forty years later.

Although he told absolutely no one, including his family, about his exploits, he clearly used some background material in his spy stories—not the actual incidents, of course, but the general sense of spycraft and the life of a solitary person in an often-hostile environment.

McCarry's greatest novels feature Paul Christopher, an American agent who works for the Outfit (the CIA) modeled, inevitably, to some degree on himself; both, for example, wrote first-rate poetry. Christopher made his debut in *The Miernik Dossier* (1973), which is told entirely in letters, dossiers, and other documents. It was followed by his bestselling fictional theory of the assassination of President Kennedy, *The Tears of Autumn* (1974), in which he lays the murder at the feet of the South Vietnamese, with assistance by the Cubans and the Mafia, for what was perceived as the president's role in the death of President Ngo Dinh Diem and the Bay of Pigs episode. Other Paul Christopher novels include *The Secret Lovers* (1977) and several in which he is a presence but the primary protagonists are members of his family: cousins in *The Better Angels* (1979) and again in *Shelley's Heart* (1995), his parents in *The Last Supper* (1983), a daughter in *Second Sight* (1991), and a son in *Christopher's Ghosts* (2007). *The Bride of the Wilderness* (1988) features seventeenth-century ancestors. Christopher Hyde, a widely read author, has written his espionage novels under the pseudonym Paul Christopher.

Countless film options of McCarry's work have been tendered, especially for *The Tears of Autumn*, but only a very loosely adapted version of *The Better Angels* ever made it to the screen when *Wrong Is Right* (1982), starring Sean Connery, was released.

"The Hand of Carlos" was originally published in the Fall 1992 issue of *The Armchair Detective* magazine.

THE HAND OF CARLOS

CHARLES McCARRY

THE TERRORIST'S ARABIC was poor and his Farsi was nonexistent, but he had a quick ear for hidden meanings. That was why he was still alive. That was why he was alone with this mad old man, speaking French, waiting to hear the name of his target.

He inclined his head and waited for the holy man to speak again. They were seated on the floor of a plain small room in a simple house in the holy city of Qum. The holy man, squatting on the coarse wool blanket that was his bed by night and his throne by day, smelled of dust. Beside him lay the bowl from which he had eaten his lunch of rice and yoghurt; the terrorist, whose taste ran to steak *au poivre*, had been unable to eat the food. Now, smelling it on the old man's sour breath, he wished that he had.

The holy man was the most successful revolutionary in the world. The richest and most ancient kingdom in the Near East lay at his feet. He imagined that he had conquered Iran by the power of his faith and the strength of his voice. But the terrorist knew that he had had help; the militant youth who were the cutting edge of the holy man's revolution had been trained and armed in the camps of the Palestinian terror front. The terrorist himself had learned to use his workmanlike Soviet weapons—the 9-mm Makarov pistol, the Skorpion machine pistol, the AK47 assault rifle—in those camps.

In the name of the Palestinian struggle, which was the personal cause of every progressive revolutionary in the world, the terrorist had shot an old Jew in London. He had bombed innocent people in Paris, kidnapped the head of the Iranian secret police, killed two French counterintelligence men and a traitor, shot an Arab by mistake. He was not even an Arab: he had spilled all that blood out of idealism.

The holy man understood. It meant little to him. He was the spiritual leader of the Shi'a Moslems. To him, there was no blood except the blood spilled on the 19th of Ramadan, A.H. 40 (655 A.D.), when Ali, the son-in-law, cousin, and chosen heir of the Prophet Mohammed, was assassinated as he prayed in Mosque of Kufa.

The Shi'a believed that Islam had been led ever since by usurpers, for none but a descendant of Ali and of Mohammed's daughter Fatima could be the true successor to the Prophet. The holy man wore the black turban of a descendant of Mohammed: he slept always on his right side, as Ali had commanded the imams to do.

The terrorist was in the presence of the holy

man because he was a famous assassin. But the Shi'a had given the world the very word "assassin." From the ranks of this sect, 800 years ago, came the Order of Assassins, the hashikin, takers of hashish, who set out systematically to murder the usurpers.

The enemies of Ali's younger son, Hussein, had refused him water when they slew him in the desert. The Shi'a had never forgotten or forgiven this bitter act of cruelty. It was a rite of remembrance to Hussein, and to the justice of the Shi'a cause, that no pious Shi'a ever put any creature to death—not a sheep on a feast day, not a chicken bought in the bazaar, not the most hated human enemy—without first offering it a drink of water.

The holy man, at last, opened his dry lips. The terrorist leaned closer.

"The shah," said the holy man, "must be offered a cup of water."

The terrorist handed him a slip of paper on which a dollar sign followed by six digits had been written. The holy man nodded, wearily, in agreement.

"Shah mat," the terrorist said. It was the only Persian he knew. It meant "the king is dead."

For this operation, the terrorist took the name Paco, and he traveled out of Tehran like any ordinary person in a first-class airline seat. In his attache case, in addition to the bottle of gasoline that he could sprinkle over a stewardess in an emergency, he carried an excellent Mexican passport, forged by East German experts working with the Libyan intelligence service.

Paco was enjoying himself thoroughly. The stewardesses had that wonderful silken skin that only German girls had, and those slender long legs that bourgeois German girls were so willing to spread for the revolution. He put his hand on the waist of one of the stewardesses and smiled at her and asked for another Martell brandy.

"Only Martell," he said. "No substitutes."

The stewardess smiled at him and he thought that he saw the beginning of something in her eyes. Even before his plastic surgery he had always had all the girls he wanted. Now he had even more. The East German doctors had given him a better face, thinning the lips that once had looked like blue slugs, taking the flab out of the cheeks and the chin.

Paco turned back to the American professor who was his seat mate. It pleased Paco, who loved to talk and loved to lie, to tell this man that he, Paco, was an important figure in the Popular Front for the liberation of Palestine.

"The PFLP is the terrorist arm of the PLO, isn't it?" the American asked. There was respect in his voice. Not for a moment did he doubt that Paco, who spoke English with a heavy latinate accent and drank enough cognac to kill a horse, was an Arab and a devout Moslem.

"You disapprove of terror?" Paco asked.

The professor lifted a soft bourgeois hand—who could imagine a gun or a woman's breast in such a hand?—to protest. "I sympathize," he said, "but . . ."

"There can be no 'buts,'" said Paco, scowling, making this sympathizer squirm. "Did you sympathize before the terror started? We were invisible to you. We are doctors of philosophy. George Habash, our chief terrorist, is a children's doctor. But you forced us to kill before you would see our suffering, before you would sympathize. That shows how sick you and your capitalist society are!"

The American professor gave him a look filled with shame. "I hate it as much as you do," he said. "More, because all the heroes are on your side."

Paco felt a rush of pleasure. How these pretenders, these toy store revolutionaries, loved to be insulted, whipped, blamed! They hated their country, their parents, their species, because they hated themselves. They were doomed.

The stewardess came back with the Martell brandy, a whole bottle, and Paco put a forefinger on the back of her hand as she poured, pressing down so that she had to fill the glass to the rim. If she knew who he really was, he could have her in the lavatory. Watching her legs as she walked away, he was tempted to follow and tell her. Showing them a gun made them hot, he knew that from experience.

"It is not possible," said the sweating major. "It is not possible to go out to the camps without the personal permission of Colonel Kaddafi."

Paco stared through his sunglasses at the sweating German. How was it that a country which produced such perfect women as the stewardess on the Lufthansa flight could also produce such pigs for men? The major was past his youth, the desert sun had reddened his skin, and there was a great wrinkle of fat on the back of his thick neck. Also, like all the East Germans who sat in every office of Libyan intelligence, he was a racist, filled with contempt for Arabs. Paco himself was exasperated by Arabs. They were undependable, inefficient, maddening in their bloody-mindedness. But they were, to Paco, the symbol of the cause. To this German, they were a subject race: beaky and circumcised.

"Kaddafi refuses me nothing," Paco said.

"That's your story," the German major said. But he lifted the telephone and ordered the transport that Paco had requested.

For a rarity, it was quite true, what Paco had said: Colonel Muammar Kaddafi, dictator of Libya, financier and keeper of the weapons warehouse of international terrorism, refused this peacock of a Latin-American nothing. It was even said, and the major believed it, that Kaddafi had given Paco ten million dollars in payment for kidnapping the oil minister of Saudi Arabia and the head of Savak, the shah's secret police. It was also said that the Saudis and the shah had put $50 million in ransom into Paco's Swiss bank account. Anyway, he had let his prisoners go without harming a hair of their heads.

The major didn't like him. He didn't care if the KGB had recruited and trained him. He didn't care about his exploits. He was a romantic, a weakling who liked women and food and liquor—and, above all, money—too much. Paco was a show-off. If he couldn't be bought, he could be out-witted. Paco was smoking a stinking Gauloise; he chain-smoked the things.

The Bedouin band moved across the desert floor—black figures trudging along beside a file of camels and a horse or two. A few miles ahead of the main body, a Land Rover bucked through the rough country, stirring up a plume of dust that could be seen for miles.

Through the Perspex window of the small plane. Paco could see the weapons in the hands of the three men who rode with the headman in the Land Rover. He focused the plane's binoculars on the vehicle. Two of the men were equipped with Czech VZ-58s, a version of the AK47 that had a nasty tendency to climb when fired on full automatic. The other carried a Dragunov sniper's rifle, a heavy, clumsy Soviet weapon that could put a heavy slug through a vest button at 900 meters. These desert tramps were coming up in the world.

On the horizon, an hour's drive for the Land Rover and four hours' march for the camels, Paco could see the Bedouins' objective, a well among the scrub. He had the Palestinian pilot make a long circle to the south, then come in low, below the crest of the hills and out of sight of the Bedouins, and land. "Fly out low, circle, and pass over the column again," Paco said. "Don't let them know you've landed."

The plane, an American Bonanza (Paco didn't trust Russian aircraft engines over the desert), churned away, creating a stinging sandstorm. Paco found a hiding place on a knoll overlooking the camp ground and settled down in the shade of a rubbery anemic bush that probably had roots 50 meters deep. If you cut it down, it would reach into the soil and find moisture and grow again. Like the revolution.

In the distance Paco could see the column of dust raised by the Land Rover. He opened his pack and checked its contents. First, he checked the two 9-mm Makarov pistols, oiled and loaded and stored in Ziploc plastic bags, another marvelous contribution to civilization by the Americans. He worked the bolt on his Skorpion, only 10.6 inches long with the butt folded, but capable of spewing 7.65-mm rounds at a rate of 14 rounds a second. Four RGD-5 anti-personnel grenades, painted cheap Russian green, nestled like eggs at the bottom of the sack. They weighed only a little over half a pound, about half as much as the far more powerful U.S. Army M52 fragmentation grenades stolen from a U.S. base in West Germany by the Baader-Meinhoff Gang. Paco waited, watching the dust of the Land Rover. When he could hear its gearbox howling he took off his sunglasses so that the mirrors would not flash in the sun and give away his position.

It was dusk before Paco moved again. The crew of the Land Rover had searched the perimeter of the camp, studying the tracks of the light plane on the floor of the wadi. At last the camels came, the tents sprang up, and the cooking fires were lighted. Paco, crawling over the flinty ground, took up a position near the latrine, some 50 meters from the black tents.

The leader had been haranguing his men. Now he slung his assault rifle across his back and headed for the latrine. Paco, who knew his habits, waited. The leader hiked up his robes, swirling the layers of cloth around his body, holding up the robes with both hands and both elbows. Straddling the ditch, he was absolutely helpless. Paco smiled at the man's buttocks, fish-white, and fired all eight rounds from the Makarov between his legs. The slugs, traveling at the tremendous velocity of 1,023 feet per second, zipped into the earth. Paco had known there was no chance of a ricochet with this weapon.

The leader fell over sideways, more afraid of the filth in the ditch than of death, clawing for his slung weapon, swaddled and tripped by his robes. Paco put another clip into his Makarov, just in case, and began to laugh uproariously. The fallen man, tearing at his VZ-58, now looked up at Paco. Paco put on his mirror sunglasses.

"It's you," said the Bedouin leader, "you turd conceived by a jackal on a syphilitic whore rutting on a dung heap."

The other members of the band were running toward them, assault rifles and machine pistols at the ready. Paco pulled the leader to his feet.

"You'd better tell them who I am," said Paco. The leader gave a hand signal and the advancing tribesmen halted.

The leader introduced Paco, never mentioning the name by which the world knew him. He spoke first in Arabic, for he was a Palestinian from Jerusalem, and then in English, German, and French, for the tribesmen were men and women, all in their early twenties, who had come from the cities of Europe to learn how to do all the things that Paco already did so well. They knew perfectly well who their visitor was: Paco could see it in their eyes.

Paco ate the spartan dinner, almost as bad as the rice and yoghurt he had been given in Qum, and kept an aloof silence. The young terrorists, apprentices, watched his every move. It was hard to tell what the girls looked like under these robes, but he sat next to the one with the prettiest face. When she put down her plate, he tossed his dirty Makarov into her lap. "Clean this," he said.

Of the dozen bands of terrorists, disguised as Bedouins, that were now training in the Libyan desert, Paco had chosen this one because he knew that his old friend would have trained its members well in the use of weapons and in the making of bombs, and trained them even better in the most indispensable weapon of all, blind obedience. Paco, speaking to them, a legend speaking in the desert with the firelight flickering in the mirrors of his sunglasses, did not tell them that.

"Some of you have been chosen for a historic job," Paco told them. "I am leading. I expect we will all die, but before we do, we will accomplish our objective. I need two Germans, four Italians, two Spanish-speakers, two explosives experts from the IRA Provos, one American. Amir will tell you which of you is chosen. That's all."

Later, lying beside the girl who had cleaned

his pistol, Paco advised her, as a sign of his satisfaction with her, never to carry any pistol other than the Makarov. "I shot a Jew in London with a Browning," he said, "and the bullet was stopped by his teeth. Not enough muzzle velocity. In Paris, a round from the Makarov went through a French DST man, through the floor, through a table in the room below, and then into the floor boards under the table. Or so the newspapers said."

Paco placed the cold gun on the girl's flat stomach. She put her hand over the gun. That was all the invitation he needed. While he had her, she shuddered and said wonderful things in Spanish.

"I thought you were the prize American," he said to her afterward. "How do you speak such . . . learned Spanish?"

The girl explained. She had gone to Cuba to work with the Venceremos Brigades, cutting sugar cane for Castro. The DGI, the Cuban Intelligence service, had picked her up. She'd been trained in one of the camps outside Havana before she was chosen for Libya.

"What's your name?"

"Layal."

"Not your gamename. Your name."

"My name is Rosemary Kadowaki."

"Rosemary?"

"I was born in Los Angeles. Are you really who the others say you are? They said you were dead, that you had disappeared, that you had left the movement."

"They say what they like. I act," said Paco.

Paco loved to talk; he had always loved to talk. He lifted the girl's hair, it was damp with sweat, and whispered into her ear. "Shah mat," he whispered. "Do you know what that means?"

The girl looked up at him with adoring eyes. He had only been in bed with her for an hour—less—and she was willing to die for him. Paco knew from experience that this was so.

The Israeli whose workname was Eleazar closed the file and looked across the desk at his control.

"Carlos is going to kill the shah?" he said.

"Someone who is perhaps Carlos has been hired to kill the shah," said the control. "There is a report that the holy man personally gave him the contract."

"Do we have a description of this Carlos?"

"He's using the name Paco. The story is that his appearance has been altered by plastic surgery. He has all of Carlos's behavior patterns—ego, lust, recklessness, loquacity, contempt for women and the opposition."

"Fingerprints? Did they blood-type him when he entered Libya?"

Each terrorist who entered Libya for training gave up a smear of blood; other smears were taken at every subsequent meeting and the DNA was compared. It was an ingenious, foolproof method of identification: the East German touch.

"What good are fingerprints?" asked the control. "The fingerprints Carlos left in Paris and the fingerprints he left on the plane after the OPEC kidnapping were not the same."

"Do you think he was bought on that plane?" asked Eleazar. "Did the Saudis and the shah buy him with $50 million in a Swiss account?"

"Anything is possible. Hans Joachim Klein, the German terrorist who was wounded with Carlos in Vienna, swears that he was bought."

"So," said Eleazar, "maybe it's Carlos and maybe it isn't, but they are going to kill the shah."

"They are going to try. Do you think we should let fools murder a friend of Israel?"

"What about the Americans?"

A droplet of contemptuous silence formed in the stale air of the windowless room. "The Americans," said the control. "Impotent."

Then he said, "Eleazar, I want you to get your team together again."

Eleazar's Wrath of God team, Israelis trained as commandos, had reached into the rat holes of Europe—Germany, Scandinavia, even Poland—to liquidate, in a cold fury of revenge, the Palestinians who had murdered the Israeli athletes at the Munich Olympics, and all who had helped them.

Eleazar picked up his medical bag. "I'll contact the team," he said.

With Paco at his side, Colonel Muammar al-Kaddafi watched impassively as Amir's team carried out an exercise. They handled all the weapons of the Soviet arsenal, up to the RPG-7 portable rocket launcher and the shoulder-fired SAM 7 Strela anti-aircraft missile, with consummate skill. Paco did not like these heavy weapons; he had tried to rocket an Israeli airliner at Orly Airport in Paris, and later had attempted to bring down a passenger jet with the Strela. Neither operation had gone right. These clumsy battlefield devices were not for terrorists. They gave too much warning.

Kaddafi wore his usual outfit: starched safari suit, British-style officer's cap, burnished buckled shoes without socks. He was always ready to dart, barefoot, into the mosque to pray. He carried a swagger stick.

Revolution makes strange bedfellows, thought Paco. Here he was, an atheist whose millionaire father, a cafe Communist from Venezuela, had named his three sons Vladimir, Ilich, and Lenin, after the first Soviet saint, standing on a dune with a fanatical Moslem who had gone to Sandhurst, watching a crowd of children from good bourgeois Christian homes shoot up the landscape with guns made in Russia and Czechoslovakia.

Paco followed Kaddafi down the ranks of terrorists. The colonel asked each where he, or she, had come from. "Red Brigades, Milano!" they replied. Or "Red Army Faction, Hamburg!" Or "Euskadi to Askatunsa, Bilbao!" Or "Provisional IRA, Belfast!"

To Layal, standing at attention with her assault rifle across her chest, Kaddafi said, in English, "And you are from the heroic Japanese Red Army."

"No, Brother Colonel," said Layal. "I was born in California. In 1942, because we were Japanese, my family was robbed of its little farm and put into a concentration camp by the two-faced U.S. liberal imperialists. I have come here to help build the people's prisons where the American oppressors will pay for their crimes against humanity."

"Good," said Kaddafi. "Very good."

Kaddafi led Paco to his helicopter. The interior, like every interior belonging to Kaddafi, was decorated in shades of Islamic green: green bulkheads, green upholstery, green Perspex; the Brother Colonel drank tea from a green glass. He had left the machine guns blue-black. Kaddafi was in the middle of one of his long philosophical soliloquies. Paco sipped his tea, sickly sweet and minted. He liked the sweetness but hated the tea itself. It was hard enough following Kaddafi's ravings when you hadn't drunk a liter of tea. With your bladder bursting, it was next to impossible.

"You can do this?" Kaddafi asked.

"Yes. The plan is good. We have the people. Now we have your blessing, Brother Colonel, so we have everything."

"One thing only I demand," said Kaddafi.

Merde, thought Paco.

"The shah has one friend in the world, this swine Sadat," Kaddafi said. "In the end, he must run to Sadat, in Egypt. Kill him there. Kill him before Sadat's eyes. Humiliate Sadat. Let him see how long my arm is, that it can reach into his very house and kill a king."

"At your orders, Brother Colonel," said Paco. And again he thought, *merde*. How am I going to get around this piece of madness?

After fleeing from Iran on January 16, 1979, the shah had gone to Egypt, then to Morocco, then to the Bahamas. Now word came to Paco that the shah had rented a villa in the Mexican city of Cuernavaca, Mexico.

The word came at night. It was June, and cold in the desert. Layal woke and listened in her silent way as Paco talked to the courier. He and the courier, an officer of the Cuban Directorate General of Intelligence, spoke in Spanish. It did not matter if she understood, here in the middle of nowhere.

"It's a tough target," said the Cuban. "We have a man inside the shah's household, a survivor of the Communist League 23rd of September movement."

"Training?"

"He took our course in Havana, then the GRU picked him up and shipped him to Doupov."

Trained in Czechoslovakia by Soviet military intelligence, and smart enough to survive the brutal Mexican search for the Communist League 23rd of September after it had massacred 40 Mexican policemen, kidnapped the daughter of the Belgian ambassador, and killed the son of the Mexican ambassador to the United States. A light came into Paco's eyes. He could use such a man.

"No," said the Cuban, who had been reading Paco's eyes since Paris days. "He's our last operative in Mexico who isn't scared shitless. You can't have him."

The Cuban told Paco about "La Villa," the shah's rented house in Cuernavaca. It was located at 100 del Rio Street, on a steep hill near the river, screened by trees. "No chance of using rockets, of course, because of the trees," said the Cuban. "There is a watchtower, ramproof steel gates, the usual electronic stuff—infra-red intruder detectors, temblor alarms to pick up footsteps."

"How many guards?"

"Twenty Americans, thirty-four Mexicans, six Iranians. Very well armed, very well paid. Oil company thugs."

"You're telling me nothing cheerful."

The Cuban grinned. "I saved the best for last. There is a tunnel, dug just before the shah arrived, that leads from La Villa to another house."

"Good. We can mine it."

"That's not all. The shah's men buy books about Trotsky at the local bookstores. He's fascinated with the details of how Stalin had Trotsky killed in Mexico. Second, a green station wagon brings in supplies twice a week and is not challenged at the gates. Third, the shah has been talking about going out to dinner."

"Going out to dinner?"

"To show he's got balls. He hears that Las Manitas is a good restaurant. Peacocks stroll in the grounds. He'll like that—the Peacock Throne."

Paco was in command now. He had separated the team into national groups, forbidding them to associate with each other or to speak each other's languages. The kids, thirsty for their chance to be a symbol of the revolution like Paco, gladly put up with this pointless bullying.

He routed out the two Germans. Klaus (Paco had stripped the band, except for Layal, of their Arab gamenames) was a typical Baader-Meinhoff type: sullen, fanatical, intellectual, the son of a man who manufactured cars that he sold to Americans for $50,000 apiece, dressed his wife in sable and his teenage mistresses in Wehrmacht uniforms (black lace underneath), and was now as good a democrat as he had once been a Nazi. Which was to say, in both cases, not awfully good, because money was what he was interested in and there was very little money in ideals unless, like Paco, you provided certain unique services idealists could not do without.

His son Klaus wanted to believe in something, he wanted to live like a soldier, sleeping rough and eating frugally, he wanted to die for a cause. His friend, Bernhild, was just as sullen, but simpler: she just wanted to kill. Anyone would do. Gabriele Krocher-Tiedemann, Paco's teammate in Vienna, had been like that. "Are you a policeman?" she had asked an old man during their raid on OPEC headquarters. "Yes," the old man replied. She shot him in the back of the neck and sent him down an elevator. Later, she shot another security guard, and wanted to shoot more.

In Paco's experience, Germans were useful people. So operatic in their love of themselves and in their love of death. They'd kill themselves if there was no one else around to murder.

Klaus and Bernhild, trying not to shiver in the frigid desert air, awaited their orders. Paco, as he spoke to them, faced the dawn, and they saw the big yellow Saharan sun come up in his sunglasses.

"I have a very important job for you," Paco said. "Everything, I mean everything, depends on your success."

"We will die for the revolution," said Klaus.

"Probably. But first you will help others to do so," said Paco.

Two weeks later, a man and a woman, posing as German tourists, were arrested in Cuernavaca. They had been observed loitering near La Villa. When the Mexican police followed them home, they found grenades and automatic weapons.

There were rumors that the Germans had in their possession a list of prominent Mexican citizens who were going to be assassinated if the shah was not thrown out of the country. It was said that under questioning by Mexico Federal Security the Germans had told everything about a plot to murder the shah.

No one asked the Germans, because they disappeared.

Miguel Nazar Haro, director of Mexico Federal Security, would not confirm that the Germans had ever existed. "We do not deal lightly with terrorists in Mexico," said Nazar. "That is why we have none." He added that the shah would always be safe in Mexico, and that his agency was on the lookout for German and Japanese terrorists especially. He smiled a confident smile.

When the green station wagon came through the gates of La Villa, after the Germans had disappeared, it carried, among the groceries, a copy of a book about Trotsky. One of the security men picked it up.

"I thought we had a copy of this one," he said.

The book exploded, taking off both his hands and most of his face.

This was Paco's way of saying, "Time to move."

Paco, lunching in Las Manitas, watched the man beside the shah taste his master's food before it was chewed by the royal teeth and swallowed by the royal esophagus. The shah drank vodka on the rocks and ate a steak.

There were thugs with walkie-talkies all over the place. "Someone could kill him," said the woman with Carlos. She trembled at being so close to a king, never knowing how close she was to the Makarov strapped to Paco's right leg.

Paco could have killed him then and there—and died romantically a moment afterward. At home, the shah was always accompanied by two Dobermans and a huge wolfhound. No man trained, like Paco, in the KGB technique (press the gun against the flesh before firing, no cowboy stuff) could have got close enough to shoot him. Here there were no dogs.

I am the dog, thought Paco, the wolf, in sheepdog's clothing, herding this royal sheep to Egypt.

He giggled. The woman gave him a puzzled look. Had he no regard for royalty?

Paco looked down on the snarled, braying traffic on Sixth Avenue. The big cars and the yellow taxis glittered in the unswept street—New York was having one of its garbagemen's strikes—like gems in the feces of a capitalist trying to escape from a revolution. Carlos drank what was left of the Lafite-Rothschild 1962 he had had with lunch, and padded in his bare feet across the living room of his suite at the Hilton. He loved Hiltons: the shrimp cocktails, the steaks you didn't have to chew, the jolly bars, filled with girls.

He slapped the sleeping girl in the bed on the buttocks. She woke with a snarl. Carlos undid the belt of his Sulka dressing gown and started to turn her over. The girl put a cold hand on his hairless chest.

"This is New York, killer," she said. "It's a hundred dollars a pop."

Paco threw her clothes at her. He got a handful of hundreds out of his shoulder bag and waved them at her, to show she wasn't worth it to him. "Out," he said, "before I flush your nose down the toilet."

When Flaherty came into the room a half-hour later, he stopped dead in his tracks and stared long and hard at Paco.

"It can't be you," said Flaherty. "No, it's a prank the lads are playing on me."

"It's the plastic surgery," said Paco.

"You mean to say you let the Arabs go at you with a scalpel and this handsome matinee idol is the result?"

Paco lifted his chin, turned his head.

"Even your voice is different," said Flaherty. "Less of a whinny, more of a baritone."

"They fixed my vocal chords too."

"Did they now? And what else? Can you fuck the way you used to?" The KGB had castrated more than one great agent, the better to control him. The odd thing was, it made men more loyal to their mutilators, even grateful.

These were friendly insults. Paco and Flaherty, who was one of the truly great bombers of the Provisional IRA, the Provos, went back a long way. They had met in the KGB school for terrorists at Karlovy Vary, in Czechoslovakia, and had ever since done each other favors. Paco had bought some dynamite in Zurich for Flaherty, who had used it to blow up a British politician in a London street. Flaherty had drilled a hole in the kneecap of a Swede Paco had suspected of being an informer; he'd used an electric drill, Provo style. Paco hadn't been quite suspicious enough to kill the man, who was a world-class sniper and might, if he proved to be innocent, turn out useful.

"So what is it this time?" asked Flaherty.

Paco told him. The shah was in a New York hospital, the Cornell Medical Center.

"If it's the shah you're after, it's no more trouble to blow up the hospital where he's recuperating from his dreadful surgical ordeal," said Flaherty. "There must be a good reliable lad who drives an ambulance or something, or a lonely nurse, or one of the oppressed who needs a few quid to put the kiddies through college. We'd wheel in, say 20 kilos of plastic, nicely molded to the underside of one of them rolling stretchers they use. It would go off in the room below the shah's bed and blow his majesty and most of the bloody hospital into the East River. Or is that too gruesome for a squeamish lad like you?"

"Can you use a time fuse?"

"Sure. I can do much fancier stuff than that book in Mexico."

"Call me here and give me the exact time it's set to go. I need at least an hour's notice," said Paco.

"What're you going to do, warn 'em?" asked Flaherty, and they both laughed and had more of the Old Bushmill out of Paco's bottle.

When Paco called, from a pay phone outside the men's room on the hotel mezzanine, to warn the shah's security about Flaherty's bomb, a voice said, "We have already taken care of that. Who's calling, please?"

Later, Flaherty came by for some more whiskey. "How could they have known?" asked Paco.

"My lad inside says the Israelis called up. They're still very thick with the shah; it was them that trained the Savak, you know, not the silly bloody CIA like everyone says."

"The Israelis?" Paco said. He didn't like their being after him, so close, so early in the game.

Captain Shariar Mustapha Chafik of the Royal Iranian Navy was walking down the Rue Villa Dupont, in the 16th arrondissement of Paris on the afternoon of December 7, 1979. He was on his way to a nearby apartment owned by his mother, Princess Ashraf, twin sister to the shah.

A young man in a plastic motorcyclist's helmet walked up behind Captain Chafik and, placing the muzzle of a Makarov pistol within an inch of his skull, fired two shots. The killer escaped.

Next day, in the windowless room in Jerusalem, Eleazar and his control discussed this event.

"Carlos wanted to kill Chafik himself," said the control. "Kaddafi's East Germans told him he had to let the Iranians do something. It's obvious from the close-in technique, pure KGB-Palestinian, who trained the assassin."

"But why? Why Chafik? Why Paris? It's a sideshow."

"It's all a sideshow. The Germans in Mexico, the bomb in New York. Carlos, if he is Carlos, could have killed the shah in either place."

"Then what is he waiting for?"

"To kill him in a particular place, for a particular reason."

A silence fell. It was stifling in the room despite the air conditioning, and notwithstanding thick sealed walls the peculiar noise of the Near East, a surf of voices breaking on the bleak shore of the jumbled city, came to their ears.

"Your team is ready?" asked the control, knowing that it was. Each member could speak Arabic and at least one other language, each could kill—kill with an Uzi machine pistol, kill with a knife, kill in ingenious ways. ("Is this really you?" one member had asked over a telephone. "Yes," replied his target, a Palestinian terrorist who happened to be in bed with a woman at the other end. The phone exploded in the terrorist's hand. They found the girl, quite mad, with her lover's severed head in her lap.)

"I'd like you to take your team to Cairo," said Eleazar's control. He handed him six British passports, six driver's licenses, six sets of credit cards, a few letters, stamped, postmarked, and opened, addressed to the fictitious names on the forged documents.

Their weapons would be waiting in Egypt.

In Havana, Paco woke up to find Layal's black eyes fixed on his face. They were strange eyes, all one glassy dark color, lacking pupils, absent light. It was disconcerting to wake up every day to find this flat, utterly expressionless, but beautiful face staring into his own.

"Why don't you learn to sleep?" Paco asked.

"I already know how to sleep," Layal said. "I need to learn how to stay awake."

"We have pills for that."

Something happened behind Layal's unrippled face that might have been a smile. She had no physical shame; clothed or unclothed, her behavior was the same. Her body, smooth as a court kimono, was as lithe and hard as the body of a gymnast. She had amazing muscular control.

Just before dark, the telephone rang—the first time since they had arrived in Cuba. Paco spoke a code phrase and listened to another. Then he got out his leather bag, unlocked it, and removed one of his Makarovs. He took five extra clips.

"Stay with the bag. Don't let anyone touch it," he said to Layal. "Not even your Cuban friends, not even Kotchergine if he stops by."

Colonel Vadim Kotchergine of the KGB had established the camps in Cuba that had trained the first pioneering terrorists from the Americas and Europe. Not many people knew that. Paco liked to show his women that the revolution kept no secrets from him.

Night fell. Paco departed. "I know you want to come with me," he said to Layal, "but this is not the operation for you, I'm saving you for the real work."

It was always a relief to Paco to speak Spanish. But Spanish is not a good language to speak in a boat, because voices carry over the water, and Latin Americans only speak softly when they are in a brothel or in a church. Paco made his joke not to calm the men he was sending to attack Contadora Island off the coast of Panama, the shah's last refuge, but because he was, in some ways, weak. He wanted men he was sending to their deaths to think he was a good fellow.

There were two men from the desert band, a pair of Basques who had been sent to Libya by ETA to learn how to kill Spanish policemen. One of them was very good with explosives; it was the ETA that had tunneled under a Madrid street and planted a hundred kilos of dynamite in the hole and blown a Dodge Dart carrying Admiral Luis Carrero Blanco, the premier of Spain, over a five-story building. Paco had given them the dynamite.

The two Basques laughed at Paco's joke. The third man did not. He was a Montonero, which is like saying that he was a tyrannosaur—terrifying, but thought to be extinct. The Montoneros, originally the secret bullies of the Peronist movement in Argentina, had turned sharply left and been crushed, 9,000 of them killed by the police and the army in a single year. Some had escaped and taken refuge with cells of the Red Brigades in Italy. They were rich fugitives: in just one operation, the Montoneros had extorted $60 million in kidnap ransom from one of Argentina's richest families.

Like all Montoneros, this one, Raul by game-name, thought that he was an aristocrat. Paco had wanted to use M-19 people for this operation—a nifty outfit of doctors, lawyers, architects from Colombia—but they had just had a disaster when they released, rather than killed, the 14 foreign ambassadors they had seized as hostages in the Dominican Embassy at Bogota. The media could only cover one embassy full of hostages at a time, and they had a big investment in the Americans in Iran. Now M-19, to redeem itself, was planning to liquidate Anastasio Somoza Debayle, the former dictator of Nicaragua. Their best men were in Paraguay, stalking Somoza.

Raul stepped into the boat. It was the best money could buy, but old—one of the many inflatable Zodiacs with powerful engines that the Cubans had captured from CIA teams 20 years before during the Kennedys' secret war against Castro.

"Come back," said Paco. Raul got out of the boat, wetting his shoes and trousers in the surf. "Remember, follow the plan of the mission," Paco said. "You're not shooting to kill. We just want two rounds from the bazooka to land near the house, not hit it." Raul looked with contempt at the RPG-7 rocket launcher lying in the bottom of the boat. It had a range of 500 meters and its projectile could, in theory, pierce 12 inches of armor. "If we hit the fucking island of Contadora from a moving boat, we'll be lucky," he said. "And why two rounds? So they'll see the flame from the backblast and have time to blow us out of the water?" Paco smiled. "After

you fire, dive. The Basques will show you how," he said. All three men wore wet suits. Tanks and respirators lay beside the Russian bazookas in the bottom of the Zodiac.

This operation meant nothing. It was just a little something extra to let the shah and the Americans know it was time to move again, that there was danger that the sick monarch might yet be killed before he died of cancer. The Americans around President Carter were terrified that this might happen. Then they would lose their hostages, lose the election. Somebody from the White House was talking at this very moment to Ghotbzadeh, the Iranian foreign minister, about ways to betray the shah. The man from the White House was wearing a false beard.

Paco didn't bother to wait on the beach for Raul and the Basques to come back from Contadora. He just left an observer with a good pair of binoculars looking out over the Pacific. The observer saw, reflected from the low cloud over the choppy sea, two small red flashes, as from the backblast of a bazooka. Moments later he saw a helicopter hovering with tracer rounds falling lazily into the sea from its guns, and then the much larger flash, as from a boat loaded with gasoline going up.

He sent Paco the prearranged message: "The sheep is running."

At last the shah was on his way to Egypt. Outside Cairo, in a house directly under the glide path to the airport, Eleazar watched through the big glasses as the two men came out on the roof in Heliopolis. An American M-1 rifle, fitted with a telescope and certain other refinements, lay on the rug in which he had carried it through the streets. The men were wearing caftans, long roughspun gowns that reached to their ankles. Jets, approaching Cairo Airport, screamed overhead. The airport was almost two miles away. The men on the rooftop, though their faces were young in the bright circle of the powerful optic, moved stiffly, as if they had some crippling disease of the spine. Such things were not unusual in Egyptians, but the faces Eleazar saw were not Egyptians, but European. Italian? Yes, Italian.

The Italians lay down on the rooftop. From beneath their caftans one man drew a long tube, the other a missile with fins. The chartered jet carrying the shah was due in half an hour. The Italians were fitting the missile, a Strela SAM 7 infra-red projectile that could nose into the hot orifice of a jet engine at an altitude of 2,000 meters. There was no time to call the Egyptians; 30 minutes was not enough for them. Eleazar sighed. He picked up the rifle and gazed through the scope. He shot the first Italian in the spine and the second through the head. Then he put two rounds through the launcher, in case there was a backup team, abandoned his equipment, and went out into the teeming street.

"What was that noise?" asked an old fruit peddler.

"The world is nothing but noise," Eleazar said in his flawless Arabic. "What great price are you asking a thirsty man for one of those oranges?"

Paco closed his eyes and listened to the sound of the straight razor on his cheek. What a sensuous thing it was to be shaved by a woman. No female had taken such care of him before Layal. She massaged his body with oils, she gave him baths, scrubbing him down with a rough sponge, she even cleaned the wax from his ears. Without opening his eyes, Paco put his hand between Layal's thighs. He knew how much she enjoyed that, but she gave no sign: the razor kept moving in small, precise strokes over his face and throat. It was the sharpest instrument Paco had ever seen; Layal stropped it every day. She carried it always, in a little chamois sheath at the small of her back.

"Now we know for sure that the Israelis are after us," said Paco. "It's probably one of their Wrath of God teams. The Mossad wouldn't risk blowing their own people."

"But you lost two men. They were found with a Strela missile and launcher beside them. They were identified as Italians."

The speaker was an emissary from George Habash's PFLP Headquarters in Aden. Because Habash's people had trained a lot of European terrorists, they thought they were in charge of every operation. But they were just Palestinians. Everything they had, someone had given them: money from Kaddafi, arms from the GRU and the KGB, terrorists from the romantic upper middle class of the Free World. Even Paco himself was a gift. He controlled this operation.

"I have four Italians left," said Paco. "That should be enough."

"You have also the two Iranians," said the emissary. "They must be used."

"They're so good."

"Your employer insists. A Shi'a must offer the shah water before he is killed."

"I know more about the requirements than you do," Paco said. Layal took the hot towel off his face and rubbed his skin with an astringent. Paco opened his eyes for the first time and stared at the emissary. A television set flickered behind him, the sound turned up loud to muffle their conversation.

"We all wonder what private understanding you might have with the holy man," said the emissary.

There it was again: the suggestion that he, Paco, was stealing from the revolution, that he was risking everything for pay, that he was a mercenary and worse than a mercenary.

"Get out!" Paco shouted. "I don't like your manners!"

The emissary gave a sardonic smile. Layal whipped the barber's sheet off Paco, snapping it in the air. The emissary saw the Makarov, fitted with a long silencer, lying on Paco's lap, and stopped smiling.

"We would like to have the details of your plan," the emissary said.

"I'm sure you would," said Paco. "Now get out."

Layal was incredibly useful. Among the band in the desert, she had been the best shot with every kind of weapon. She spoke perfect Arabic in several regional variations. She even wrote Arabic: her only pastime was practicing Arabic script and Japanese calligraphy. She was strong: in the desert, in a training exercise at night, she had taken a loaded Skorpion—a loaded hair-trigger Skorpion!—away from one of the Germans who had come up behind her, and broken the man's arm. She was adept at Akihido, a kind of martial art Paco had not encountered before. She had the calm fearlessness of the true professional killer.

Also, she had type B-negative blood. This was going to get her into Maadi Military Hospital, where a team of American surgeons was preparing to remove the shah's cancerous spleen. The shah had B-negative blood, a rare type. So rare that donors would be let into the hospital through the crowd of Elite Guards and police who had kept out even the wailing relatives of other patients.

"Get dressed and go," Paco said.

Layal did as she was told. She did not nod, she did not say yes, nothing happened in her eyes. Unless Paco had her on the bed, she was a stone.

In the garage in Helwan, a village south of Cairo, Paco inspected the van while the Italians from the Red Brigades and the Iranians from the Islamic Revolutionary Youth, or whatever they called themselves, watched nervously. The team leader, gamename Bruno, showed Paco how it would work. It was one of those camper vans, the roof could be cranked open, to give headroom and air. Open, it looked like a lean-to, with mosquito netting over the opening. They had sanded the paint off the van, which was new and in perfect mechanical condition, in order to make it look old; the Italians were proud of the dents they had put in the van, using an old truck, not hammers.

"Very realistic," said Paco.

Inside the roof the Italians had fitted a device called "Stalin's organ." It was a rack holding 12 RPG-7 rocket launchers. Bruno cranked up the roof. The muzzles of the launchers were hidden by the mosquito netting.

"The weight won't be too much for the roof?" asked Paco. "You'll have to drive to the hospital with it open."

"No, we strengthened it," said Bruno. "The circuits are wired together, so all the rockets fire at the same instant. When they hit the hospital, they'll tear a hole the size of the van right through the side. We'll go in shooting."

"Good," said Paco. "Remember one thing; the timing. You fire your rockets from the corniche road at exactly 0852. You must be inside the building, shooting and throwing grenades, at 0857. I want noise, noise, noise."

Paco turned to the two Iranians. They actually came to attention when he looked in their direction, like Gungha Din in his rags, ready to die for the regiment.

"I will be in the operating room in the basement," Paco said. He pointed to the plan of the hospital taped to the side of the van. "What's your name?" he said to the less intelligent of the Iranians.

"Espendiar."

"Okay. Espendiar. You come straight to the operating room. You'll have a Skorpion. Use it. Kill everyone in your way. I want you rolling grenades into every room as you go by. By the time you get to the operating room, I will have killed all the doctors, all the nurses. Espendiar, you will give the shah his drink of water. Then I will kill him."

"But if he is being operated on, he'll be unconscious when I offer him the cup of water," Espendiar said.

"The noise will wake him up," said Paco.

Since the day of his arrival in Cairo, Paco had been wearing a black beret. He took it off and put it on the head of Expendiar. "Wear this at all times," he said. "I want you to be recognizable."

Paco could hear his own breathing inside the mask. It was terribly hot inside the wet suit, inside the drain that led into the Nile. He had swum two miles under the brown tumbling water and found this tiny opening by luck as much as anything else. He had had good frog-man training under the Cubans at the Raz Hilal camp near Tokra, in Libya, but he had never liked being underwater.

He used his light to find the fluorescent marks on the wall. Sewage—who knew what unimaginable foul sewage laden with disease—flowed around him. He was under the hospital. He found the mark. The advance diving team had done a good job. They had been the back-up team for the frogman who had blown up Lord Mountbatten's yacht, using one of Flaherty's splendid waterproof bombs. Carlos got out his tools, unscrewed the bolts, and pulled off the hatch the ETA bombers had made.

He slithered feet first into the basement room, clumsy in his fins and wet suit. His mask was fouled and he could hardly see. He knew what he was going to smell like when he took off the mask and respirator. Sewage was pouring out of the drain into the room. He ripped off the mask.

On the stairs, above the flooding floor, stood a small figure wearing a black chadar, the all-enveloping Islamic costume for women in purda.

Paco stripped off his wet suit and waded, naked, toward her. She held something in her hand. He saw what it was—a fire hose—and grinned. Layal turned the hose on him, wash-ing the filth from his body. Under the chadar, Layal carried a change of clothes for Paco and the other things they would need: two Makarov pistols, two Skorpions, all with silencers, plastic explosive and detonators. She kept one Makarov and handed the other to Paco. Hers was marked with a tiny strip of tape on the butt.

"Did you load these yourself?" Paco asked.

Layal nodded. She dropped the chadar again, to conceal the weapons. With Layal leading, they went up the stairs, then through a maze of cel-lars with pipes overhead and dust everywhere, arriving at last in a small, windowless room. There was no electric light. Layal shone a torch and Paco saw the holes in the wall, drilled by the ETA frogmen after they came out of the drain.

Layal stripped off her chadar and handed Paco a pair of earphones. He put them on. She had wired the wall, drilling through the mor-tar and threading a pencil microphone into the outside world. He could hear as well as if he were standing on the beaten dust in the hospital courtyard. He heard the soldiers outside talking in slurred Upper Nile Arabic.

Through another pair of earphones he could hear the American doctors as they worked on the shah in the operating room beyond the wall in which the holes were drilled.

Layal began, methodically, to fill the holes in the wall with plastic explosive. She inserted the detonators and strung the wire. When the plastic blew, it would open a hole three feet in diameter. Paco would duck through, shooting as he went. He smiled in pleasure. In his mind's eye he could see the profile of the shah, like the head of a dead chicken, lying on the table. And, already, he could hear the shrieks of panic—he had heard the shrieks so often before.

Eleazar and his team were waiting on the cor-niche, dressed as Elite Guards. They wore big, inefficient Tokagypt automatics, relics of Egypt's arms deal with the U.S.S.R., in holsters on their belts, and concealed small 9-mm auto-matics in the palms of their hands. Inside their truck were more useful weapons.

They stopped the Volkswagen van. Eleazar had not shaved, and he had washed out his mouth with raki. Bruno, at the wheel of the van, noticed these signs of corruption. His papers were per-fectly in order. In the back of the van, dressed as Arabs, were the other Italians and the two Irani-ans. Eleazar saw the beret on Espendiar's head, as Paco had meant him to do.

At this moment, one of Eleazar's team, dressed as a sergeant in the Elite Guard, said something to Eleazar. Eleazar flew into a rage. He screamed at the sergeant in Arabic, he stood him at atten-tion. Finally, in a gesture of discipline that has all but disappeared from the Egyptian army, he com-manded the sergeant to open his mouth. Eleazar spit into the sergeant's mouth, to show him that he could do anything he liked to him.

Eleazar waved the Volkswagen van by. In the mirror, Bruno could see this mad Egyptian, still shouting at his sergeant. It was the last thing he saw. Just as the island that splits the Nile opposite Maadi Military Hospital came into sight, the magnetic radio-controlled bomb that another of Eleazar's men had fastened to the gas tank of the van exploded. The Volkswagen vanished as the combined force of the Israeli bomb, the gas in the tank, the ammunition in the interior, and 12 RPG-7 rocket grenades produced an explosion that looked, just for an instant, like the sun reddened by a sandstorm, only brighter. The air over the Nile was filled with the smoky trails of exploding rounds.

Paco heard the racket through his earphones, strangely muffled. He heard the soldiers shouting, the beat of their running feet, and a burst or two of small arms fire. He ripped off the headset. It was only 0846.

"They're early, the fools," he said to Layal "Blow it now!"

Layal ran backward—he had to admire her physical capabilities even in such a moment—playing out the detonator wire from a spool. Paco followed her, a Makarov in his right hand.

Outside the door, they met a man. He held an Uzi submachine gun, an Israeli weapon, in his hands, and he had the look of a Jew; something about the mouth and eyes, the contempt, the intelligence: Paco could always tell.

Paco lifted the Makarov, clumsy as it was with the long silencer attached to the end of the barrel, and squeezed the trigger. The pistol exploded in his hand. In the same microsecond, Paco looked at his mangled hand, and also saw Layal shoot the intruder in the exact center of the forehead with her own Makarov. The intruder was Espendiar, without the black beret Paco had given him. Fool.

Paco was whimpering. He had no right hand. He couldn't look at it. Blood spurted from the shredded crimson thing at the end of his arm.

"Layal," he said, in a voice that sounded to him as thin as a thread. "What happened?"

"Special ammunition," she replied. Then, for the first time ever, she smiled. "Special for you, comrade."

Layal held her razor in her square small hand. Ah, Paco thought, she is going to save me, she is probably a surgeon too. Then he remembered! "Special ammunition."

Layal had loaded his Makarov. She had booby-trapped it. He tried to seize her weapon with the hand he had left. She stepped easily out of his reach.

He could feel, actually feel, his heart emptying through his wrist. "Not me," he said, in a strong voice, his last words.

Layal watched him die. Then she picked up his left hand and bent it backward at the wrist. As if she were disjointing a chicken, she cut off the hand with the razor.

She pinned a note, written in her beautiful Arabic script, to Paco's shirt. It read: "Islamic justice has cut off the hand of a thief who stole from the revolution."

The woman Paco had known as Layal drank an ice-cold Coca-Cola straight from the can while her American case officer, working cheerfully, fingerprinted the severed hand.

"Was he Carlos or was he not?" asked the case officer.

"He never actually claimed to be," Layal said. "He had all the mannerisms, all the skills, all the ego. All the vices, too. I can't get the taste of Martell brandy out of my mouth or the smell of Gauloise Disques Bleus out of my hair."

The case officer examined the card smudged with the fingerprints. "If these don't belong to the Carlos of Paris or the Carlos of Vienna, we may have to believe that the KGB or George Habash are outwitting us," he said. "Or somebody."

"Outwitting us was his thing. Paco thought it was easy."

"Is that what he said about us?"

"That's what they all say about us."

"What good news."

The case officer had a charming smile. "I can hardly believe the things they will believe."

He shook his head. The Japanese girl who was such a perfect American type smiled back at him, her eyes alive with humor and affection and a touch of mockery. She liked this outrageous Wasp with his St. Grottlesex accent and his sense of fun. The worst part of being out in the desert with crazed louts like the Bedouin band was their solemnity. The case officer dropped Paco's hand into a Ziploc plastic bag.

"But then again," he said, dropping the hand into his out basket, "where would we be, love, if strangers, men we'll never know, didn't give us a hand now and then?"

NEIGHBORS

JOSEPH FINDER

ALTHOUGH RECRUITED by the Central Intelligence Agency, Joseph Finder (1958–   ) decided he would rather write about spies than work as one. His university credentials, first at Yale, where he majored in Russian Studies, then at Harvard, where he got his master's degree from its Russian Research Center, provided a solid foundation for his first book, *Red Carpet: The Connection Between the Kremlin and America's Most Powerful Businessmen* (1983), which famously revealed Dr. Armand Hammer's connection to the KGB, making headlines.

Perhaps more significantly, when considering the direction of Finder's career, his deep understanding of Russia and its intelligence agencies informed *The Moscow Club* (1991), which accurately predicted a planned coup d'état that would doom the Soviet Union. *Publishers Weekly* ranked it as one of the ten best espionage novels of all time.

Finder's second novel was *Extraordinary Powers* (1994), a thriller in which the head of the CIA dies in an apparent car accident, though there are questions about who might have wanted him dead as rumors swirl about the possibility of his being a double agent.

High Crimes (1998) is the story of a powerful attorney who is forced to defend her husband when he is arrested by government agents for having been responsible for the massacre of a village when he was in the marines. It served as the basis for a 2002 film of the same title that was directed by Carl Franklin and starred Ashley Judd, Morgan Freeman, Jim Caviezel, Adam Scott, and Amanda Peet.

Another film based on a book by Finder is *Paranoia* (2004), released on the big screen in 2013, which illustrates that industrial espionage can be as fearsome as international undercover work. Directed by Robert Luketic, it starred Liam Hemsworth, Gary Oldman, and Harrison Ford.

Finder is a founding member of the International Thriller Writers Association.

"Neighbors" was originally published in *Agents of Treachery* (New York, Vintage, 2010).

NEIGHBORS

JOSEPH FINDER

"I CAN'T SHAKE the feeling that they're up to something," Matt Parker said. He didn't need to say: the new neighbors. He was peering out their bedroom window through a gap between the slats of the venetian blinds.

Kate Parker looked up from her book, groaned. "Not this again. Come to bed. It's after eleven."

"I'm serious," Matt said.

"So am I. Plus, they can probably see you staring at them."

"Not from this angle." But just to be safe he dropped the slat. He turned around, arms folded. "I don't like them," he said.

"You haven't even met them."

"I saw you talking to them yesterday. I don't think they're a real couple. She's, like, twenty years younger than him."

"Laura's eight years younger than Jimmy."

"He's got to be an Arab."

"I think Laura said his parents are Persian."

"Persian," Matt scoffed. "That's just a fancy word for Iranian. Like an Iraqi saying he's *Mesopotamian* or something."

Kate shook her head and went back to her book. Some girl novel: an Oprah Book Club selection with a cover that looked like an Amish quilt. At the foot of their bed, the big flat-screen TV flickered a blue light across her delicate features. She had the sound muted: Matt didn't get how she could concentrate on a book with the TV on.

"Also, does he look like a Norwood to you?" Matt said when he came back from brushing his teeth, a few stray white flecks of Colgate on his chin. "Jimmy *Norwood*? What kind of name is *Norwood* for an Arab guy? That can't be his real name."

Kate gave a small, tight sigh, folded down the corner of a page and closed her book. "It's Nourwood, actually." She spelled it.

"That's not a real name." He climbed into bed. "And where's their furniture? They didn't even have a moving van. They just showed up one day with all their stuff in that stupid little Toyota hybrid sardine can."

"Boy, you really have been stalking them."

Matt jutted his jaw. "I notice stuff. Like foreign-made cars."

"Yeah, well, I hate to burst your bubble, but they're renting the house furnished from the Gormans. Ruth and Chuck didn't want to sell their house, given the market these days, and there's no room in their condo in Boca for—"

"What kind of people would rent a furnished house?"

"Look at us," Kate pointed out. "We move, like, every two years."

"You knew when you married me that was how it would be. That's just part of the life. I'm telling you, there's something not quite right about them. Remember the Olsens in Pittsburgh?"

"Don't start."

"Did I or did I not tell you their marriage was in trouble? You insisted Daphne had postpartum depression. Then they got divorced."

"Yeah, like five years after we moved," Kate said. "Half of all marriages end in divorce. Anyway, the Nourwoods are a perfectly nice couple."

Something on TV caught Matt's eye. He fumbled for the remote, found it under the down comforter next to Kate's pillow, touched a button to bring up the sound.

"—officials tell WXBS *NightCast* that FBI intelligence reports indicate an increased level of terrorist chatter—"

"I love that word, *chatter*," Kate said. "Makes it sound like they bugged Perez Hilton's tea set or something."

"Shh." Matt raised the volume.

The anchorman of the local news, who wore a cheap pin-striped suit and looked as if he was about sixteen, went on, ". . . heightened concerns about a possible terrorist strike in downtown Boston just two days from now." The chyron next to him was a crude rendering of a crosshair and the words "Boston Terror Target?"

Now the picture cut to a reporter standing in the dark outside one of the big new skyscrapers in the financial district, the wind whipping his hair. "Ken, a spokesman for the Boston police told me just a few minutes ago that the mayor has ordered heightened security for all Boston landmarks, including the State House, Government Center, and all major office buildings."

"Isn't it a little loud?" Kate said.

But Matt continued to stare at the screen.

"—speculates that the terrorists might be locally based. The police spokesman told me that their pattern seems to be to establish residence in or near a major city and assimilate themselves into the fabric of a neighborhood while they make their long-range plans, just as law enforcement authorities believe happened in the bombing in Chicago last year, also on April nineteenth, which, though never solved, is believed to be—"

"Yeah, yeah, yeah," Kate said.

"Shh!"

"—FBI undercover operatives throughout the Boston area in an attempt to infiltrate this suspected terrorist ring," the reporter said.

"I love that," Kate said. "It's always a 'ring.' Why not a terrorist *bracelet*? Or a necklace."

"This isn't funny," Matt said.

Matt couldn't sleep.

After tossing and turning for half an hour, he slipped quietly out of bed and padded down the hall to the tiny guest room that served as their home office. It was furnished with little more than a couple of filing cabinets, for household bills and owner's manuals and the like, and an old Dell PC atop an Ikea desk.

He opened a browser on the computer and entered "James Nourwood" in Google. It came back:

Did you mean: James *Norwood*

No, dammit, he thought. I meant what I typed.

All Google pulled up was a scattering of useless citations that happened to contain "James" and "wood" and words that ended in "-nour." Useless. He tried typing just "Nourwood."

Nothing. Some import-export firm based in Syria called Nour Wood, a high-pressure-laminate company founded by a man named Nour. But if Google was right, and it usually was, there was nobody named Nourwood in the entire world.

Which meant that either their new neighbor was really flying under the radar, or that wasn't his real name.

So Matt tried a powerful search engine called ZabaSearch, which could give you the home addresses of just about everybody, even celebrities. He entered "Nourwood" and then selected "Massachusetts" in the pull-down menu of states.

The answer came back instantly in big, red, mocking letters:

No Results Match NOURWOOD
Check Your Spelling and
Try Your Search Again

Well, he thought, they've just moved here. Probably too recent to show up yet. Anyway, they were renters, not owners, so maybe that explained why they didn't show up on the database yet in Massachusetts. He went back to the ZabaSearch home page and this time left the default "All 50 States" selected.

Same thing.

No Results Match NOURWOOD

What did that mean, they didn't show up *anywhere* in the country? That was impossible.

No, he told himself. Maybe not. If Nourwood, as he'd suspected, wasn't a real name.

This strange couple was living right next door under an assumed name. Matt's Spidey Sense was starting to tingle.

He remembered how once, as a kid, he'd entered the toolshed in back of the house in Bellingham and suddenly the hairs on the back of his neck stood up, thick as cleats. He had no idea why. A few seconds later, he realized that the coil of rope in the corner of the dimly lit shed was actually a snake. He stood frozen in place, fascinated and terrified by its shiny skin, its bold orange and white and black stripes. True, it was only a king snake, but what if it had been one of the venomous pit vipers sometimes found in western Washington State, like a prairie rattlesnake? Since that day he'd learned to trust his instincts. The unconscious often senses danger long before the conscious mind.

"What are you doing?"

He started at Kate's voice. The wall-to-wall carpet had muffled her approach.

"Why are you awake, babe?" he said.

"Matt, it's like two in the morning," Kate said, her voice sleep-husky. "What the hell are you doing?"

He quickly closed the browser, but she'd already seen it.

"You're Googling the neighbors now?"

"They don't even exist, Kate. I told you, there's something wrong with them."

"Believe me, they exist," Kate said. "They're very real. She even teaches Pilates."

"You sure you have the right spelling?"

"It's on their mailbox," she said. "Look for yourself."

"Oh, right, that's real hard proof," he said, a little too heavy on the sarcasm. "Did they give you a phone number? A cell phone, maybe?"

"Jesus Christ. Look, you have any questions for them, why don't you ask them yourself, tomorrow night? Or I guess it's tonight by now."

"Tonight?"

"The Kramers' cocktail party. I told you about it like five times. They're having the neighbors over to show off their new renovation."

Matt groaned.

"We've turned down their last two invitations. We have to go." She rubbed her eyes. "You know, you're really being ridiculous."

"Better safe than sorry. When I think about my brother, Donny—I mean he was a great soldier. A true patriot. And look what happened to him."

"Don't think about your brother," she said softly.

"I can't stop thinking about him. You know that."

"Come back to bed," Kate said.

For the rest of the night, Matt found himself listening to Kate's soft breathing and watching the numbers change on the digital clock. At 4:58 A.M. he finally gave up trying to sleep.

Slipping quietly out of bed, he threw on yesterday's clothes and went downstairs to pee, so he wouldn't wake Kate. As he stood at the toilet, he found himself looking idly out the window, over the café curtains, at the side of the Gormans' house, not twenty feet away. The windows were dark: the Nourwoods were asleep. He saw their car parked in the driveway, which gave him an idea.

Grabbing a pen from the kitchen counter and the only scrap of paper he could find quickly—a supermarket register receipt—he opened the back door and stepped out into the darkness, catching the screen door before it could slam, pushing it gently closed until the pneumatic hiss stopped and the latch clicked.

The night—really, the morning—was moonless and starless, with just the faintest pale glow on the horizon. He could barely see five feet in front of him. He crossed the narrow grassy rectangle that separated the two houses, and stood at the verge of Nourwood's driveway, the little car a hulking silhouette. But gradually his eyes adjusted to the dark, and there was a little ambient light from a distant streetlamp. Nourwood's car, a Toyota Yaris, was one of those ridiculous foreign-made econobox hybrids. It looked as if you could lift it up with one hand. The license plate was completely in shadow, so he came closer for a better look.

Suddenly his eyes were dazzled by the harsh light from a set of halogen floods mounted above the garage. For a sickening moment he thought that maybe Nourwood had seen someone prowling around and flicked a switch. But no: Matt had apparently tripped a motion sensor.

What if they kept their bedroom curtains open and one of them wasn't a sound sleeper? He'd have to move quickly now, just to be safe.

Now, at least, he could make out the license plate clearly. He wrote the numbers on the register receipt, then turned to go back, when he collided with someone.

Startled, Matt gave an involuntary shout, a sort of *uhhh!* sound at exactly the same time as someone said, "Jesus!"

James Nourwood.

He was a good six inches taller than Matt, with a broad, athletic build, and wore a striped bathrobe, unruly tufts of black chest hair sprouting over the top. "Can I help you?" Nourwood said with an imperious scowl.

"Oh—I'm sorry," Matt said. "I'm Matt Parker. Your, uh, next-door neighbor." His mind was spinning like a hamster on a wheel, trying to devise a plausible explanation for why he'd been hunched over his neighbor's car at five in the morning. What could he possibly say? I was curious about your hybrid? Given the Cadillac Escalade in Matt's garage, whose mileage was measured in gallons per mile, not exactly.

"Ah," Nourwood said. "Nice to meet you." He sounded almost arch. He had a neatly trimmed goatee and a dark complexion that made him look as if he had a deep suntan. Nourwood extended a hand and they shook. His hand was large and dry, his clasp limp. "You scared the living daylights out of me. I came out to see if the paper was here yet. . . . I thought someone was trying to steal my car." He had the faintest accent, though hardly anyone else would have picked up on the telltale traces. Something slightly off about the cadence, the intonation, the vowel formation. Like someone born and raised in this country of parents who weren't native speakers. Who perhaps spoke Arabic since infancy and was probably bilingual.

"Yeah, sorry about that, I—my wife lost an earring, and she's all upset about it, and I figured it might have dropped when she came over to visit you guys yesterday."

"Oh?" Nourwood said. "Did she visit us yesterday? I'm sorry I missed her."

"Yep," Matt said. Did Kate say she'd gone over to their house yesterday, or was he remembering that wrong? "Pretty sure it was yesterday. Anyway, it's not like it's fancy or anything, but it sort of has sentimental value."

"I see."

"Yeah, it was the first gift I ever gave her when we started going out, and I'm not much of a gift-giver, so I guess that makes it a collector's item."

Nourwood chuckled politely. "Well, I'll let you know if I see anything." He cocked a brow. "Though it might be a bit easier to look after the sun comes up."

"I know, I know," Matt said hastily, "but I wanted to surprise her when she woke up."

"I see," Nourwood said dubiously. "Of course."

"I notice you have Mass plates—you from in-state?"

"Those plates are brand-new."

"Uh-huh." Matt noticed he didn't say whether he was or wasn't from Massachusetts. Just that the license plates were new. He was being evasive. "So you're not from around here, I take it."

Nourwood shook his head slowly.

"Yeah? Where're you from?"

"Good Lord, where *aren't* I from? I've lived just about everywhere, it seems."

"Oh yeah?"

"Well, I hate to be rude, but I have some work to do, and it's my turn to make breakfast. Will we see you tonight at the Kramers' party?"

"I thought I heard voices outside," Kate said, scraping the last spoonful of yogurt and Bran Buds from her bowl. She looked tired and grumpy.

Matt shrugged, shook his head. He was embarrassed about what had happened and didn't feel like getting into it. "Oh yeah?"

"Maybe I dreamed it. Mind if I finish this off?" She pointed her spoon at the round tub of overpriced yogurt she'd bought at Trader Joe's.

"Go ahead," he said, sliding the yogurt toward her. He hated the stuff. It tasted like old gym socks. "More coffee?"

"I'm good. You were up early."

"Couldn't sleep." He picked up the quart of whole milk and was about to pour some into his coffee when he noticed the date stamped on the top of the carton. "Past the sell-by date," he said. "Any more in the fridge?"

"That's the last," she said. "But it's fine."

"It's expired."

"It's perfectly good."

"*Perfectly good*," he repeated. "Ever notice how you always say something's 'perfectly good' when something's actually not-quite-right about it?" He sniffed the carton but couldn't detect any sour smell. That didn't mean it hadn't begun to turn, of course. You couldn't always tell from the smell alone. He poured the milk slowly, suspiciously, into his coffee, alert for the tiniest curds, but he didn't see any. Maybe it was okay after all. "Just like the Nourwoods. You said they were 'perfectly nice.' Which means you *know* something's off about them."

"I think you drink too much coffee," she said. "Maybe that's what's keeping you up nights."

The Boston Globe was spread between them on the small round table, a moisture ring from the yogurt container wrinkling the banner headline:

FBI: PROBE POSSIBLE LOCAL TERROR PLOT

Security heightened in high-rises, government buildings

He stabbed the paper with a stubby index finger. "See, that's what's keeping me up nights," he said. "The Nourwoods are keeping me up nights."

"Matt, it's too early."

"Fine," he said. "Just don't say I didn't warn you." He took a sip of coffee. "Why'd they move into the neighborhood, anyway?"

"What's that supposed to mean?"

"Was it for a job or something? Did they say?"

Kate rolled her eyes, in that way that always annoyed him. "He got a job at ADS."

"In Hopkinton?" ADS was the big tech company that used to be known by its full name. Andromeda Data Systems. They made—well, he wasn't sure what they did, exactly. Data storage, maybe. Something like that.

"That what he told you?"

She nodded.

"There you go. If he really got a job at ADS, why didn't they move somewhere closer to Hopkinton? That's the flaw in his cover."

She looked at him disdainfully for a long moment and then said, "Can you please just drop this already? You're just going to make yourself crazy."

Now he saw that he was upsetting her, and he felt bad. Softly, he said, "You ever hear back from the doctor?"

She shook her head.

"What's the holdup?"

She shook her head again, compressed her lips. "I wish I knew."

"I don't want you to worry. He'll call."

"I'm not worried. You're the one who's worried."

"That's my job," Matt said. "I worry for both of us."

The engineering firm where Matt worked was right in downtown Boston, in the tallest building in the city: a sleek sixty-story tower with a skin of blue reflective glass. It was a fine, proud landmark, a mirror in the sky. Matt, a structural engineer by training and an architecture nut by avocation, knew quite a bit about its construction. He'd heard stories about how, shortly after it was built, it would shed entire windowpanes on windy days like some reptile shedding its scales. You'd be walking down the street, admiring the latest addition to the Boston skyline, and suddenly you'd be crushed beneath five hundred pounds of glass, a hail of jagged shards maiming other passersby. You'd never know what hit you. Funny how things like that could happen, things you'd never in a million years expect. A flying window, of all things! No one was ever safe.

A Swiss engineer even concluded, years after it was built, that in certain wind conditions the tower might actually bend in the middle—might topple right over on its narrow base. How strange, he'd often thought, to be working in such a grandiose landmark, this massive spire so high above the city, and yet be so completely vulnerable, in a glass coffin.

He eased his big black Cadillac Escalade down the ramp into the underground parking garage. A couple of uniformed security guards emerged from their booth. This was a new procedure as of a few days ago, with the heightened security.

Matt clicked off the radio—his favorite sports-talk radio show, the host arguing with some idiot about the Red Sox bull pen—and lowered the tinted window as the older guard approached. Meanwhile, the younger one circled around to the back of the Escalade and gave it a sharp rap.

"Oh, hey, Mr. Parker," the gray-haired guard said.

"Morning, Carlos," Matt said.

"How about them Sox?"

"Going all the way this year."

"Division at least, huh?"

"All the way to the World Series."

"Not this year."

"Come on, keep the faith."

"You ain't been around here long enough," Carlos said. "You don't know about the curse."

"No such thing anymore."

"When you been a Sox fan as long as me, you're just waiting for the late-season choke. It still happens. You'll see." He called out to his younger colleague, "This guy's okay. Mr. Parker is a senior manager at Bristol Worldwide, on twenty-seven."

"How's it going?" the younger guard said, backing away from the car.

"Hey," Matt said. Then, mock-stern, he said, "Carlos, you know, you guys should really check everyone's car."

"Yeah, yeah," Carlos said.

Matt wagged his finger. "It only takes one vehicle."

"If you say so."

But it was true, of course. All someone had to do was pack a car—not even a truck; it wouldn't have to be any bigger than this Escalade—with RDX and park it in the right location in the garage. RDX could slice through steel support pillars like a razor blade through a tomato. Part of the floor directly above would cave right in, then the floor above that, and pretty soon, in a matter of seconds, the whole building would pancake. This was the principle of controlled demolition: The explosives were just the trigger. Gravity did the real work for you.

It always amazed him how little people understood about the fragility of the structures in which they lived and worked.

"Hey," Matt said, "you guys ever get the CCTV cameras at the Stuart Street entrance fixed?"

"Hell didn't freeze over, last I checked," said Carlos.

Matt shook his head. "Not good," he said. "Not in times like these."

The senior guard gave the Escalade a friendly open-handed pat as if sending it on its way. "Tell me about it," he said.

The first thing Matt did when he got to his cubicle was call home. Kate answered on the first ring.

"No word from the doctor yet?" he asked.

"No," Kate said. "I thought you were him."

"Sorry. Let me know when you hear something, okay?"

"I'll call as soon as I hear. I promise."

He hung up, checked his online office calendar, and realized he had ten minutes before the morning staff meeting. He pulled up Google and entered "license plate search," which produced a long list of websites, most of them dubious. One promised, "Find Out the Truth about Anyone!" But when he entered Nourwood's license plate number and selected Massachusetts, he was shuttled to another page that wanted him to fill out all kinds of information about himself and give his credit card number. That wasn't going to happen. Another one featured a ridiculous photo of a man dressed up to look like someone's idea of a detective, right down to the Sherlock Holmes hat and the big magnifying glass, in which his right eye was grotesquely enlarged.

Not very promising, but he entered the license plate number anyway, only to find that Massachusetts wasn't one of the available states. Another site looked more serious, but the fine print explained that when you entered a license plate and your own credit card information, you were "assigned" to a "private investigator." He didn't like that. It made him nervous. He didn't want to be exposed that way. Plus, it said the search would take three to five business days.

By then it would be too late.

He clicked on yet another website, which instantly spawned a dozen lewd pop-up ads that took over his whole screen.

And then Matt noticed his manager, Regina, approaching his cubicle. Frantically he looked for a power button on his monitor but couldn't find one. That was the last thing he needed—for Regina to sidle into his cubicle asking about the RFP, a Request for Proposal, he was late on and see all this porn on his computer screen.

But when she was maybe six feet away, she came to an abrupt halt, as if remembering something, and returned to her office.

Crisis averted.

As he restarted his computer, he found himself increasingly baffled: How could this guy, this "James Nourwood," not appear anywhere on the Internet? That was just about impossible these days. Everyone left digital grease stains and skid marks, whether it was phone numbers, political contributions, high school reunion listings, property sales, corporate websites . . .

Corporate websites. Now there was a thought.

Where was it that "Nourwood" worked again? Ah, yes. The big tech company ADS, in Hopkinton. Or so he had told Kate.

Well, that was simple to check. He found the ADS main phone number. An operator answered, "Good morning, ADS."

"I'd like to speak with one of your employees, please. James Nourwood?"

"Just a moment."

Matt's heart fluttered. What if Nourwood answered his own line? Matt would have no choice but to hang up immediately, of course, but what if his name showed up on Nourwood's caller ID?

Faint keyboard tapping in the background, and then absolute silence. He held his index finger hovered just above the plunger, ready to disconnect the call as soon as he heard Nourwood's voice.

Then again, if Nourwood really did answer the phone, then maybe it wasn't some cover name after all. Maybe there was some benign explanation for the fact that he couldn't be found on the Internet.

His finger hovered, twitched. He stroked the cool plastic of the plunger button, ready to depress it with the lightning reflexes of a sniper. There was a click, and then the operator's voice again: "How are you spelling that, sir?"

Matt spelled Nourwood for her slowly.

"I'm checking, but I don't find anyone with that name. I even looked under N-O-R-W-O-O-D, but I didn't find that either. Any idea what department he might be in?"

Matt's twitchy index finger couldn't be restrained anymore, and he ended the call.

After the staff meeting, he stopped by Len Baxter's office. Lenny was the head of IT in Bristol's Boston office, a bearded, gnomelike figure who kept to himself but had always been helpful whenever Matt had a computer problem. Every day, no matter the season, he wore an unvarying uniform: jeans, a plaid flannel shirt, and a Red Sox baseball cap, no doubt to conceal his bald spot. Everyone had something to hide.

"Mattie boy, what can I do you for?" Lenny said.

"I need a favor," Matt said.

"Gonna cost you." Lenny flashed a grin. "Kidding. Talk to me."

"Can you do a quick public-records search on LexisNexis?"

Lenny cocked his head. "For what?"

"Just a name. James Nourwood." He spelled it.

"This a personnel matter?"

"Oh, no. Nothing like that. He's just some sales guy at ADS who keeps trying to sell us a data recovery program, and I don't know, I get this funny feeling about him."

"I can't do that," Lenny said gravely. "That would be a violation of the Privacy Act of 1974 as well as the Gramm-Leach-Bliley Act."

Matt's stomach flipped over. But then Lenny grinned. "Just messing with you. Sure, happy to." He crunched away at his keyboard, squinted at the screen, tapped some more. "Spell it again?"

Matt did.

"Funny. Not coming up with anything."

Matt swallowed. "You're not?"

Lenny's stubby fingers flew over the keyboard. "Very peculiar," he said. "Your guy isn't registered to vote and never got a driver's license, hasn't purchased any property. . . . You sure he's not a figment of your imagination?"

"Know what? I must have gotten his name wrong. Never mind. I'll get back to you."

"No worries," Lenny said. "Anytime."

Matt was hardly a party animal. He disliked socializing, particularly with the neighbors. Wherever he lived, he preferred to keep a low profile. Plus, he didn't much like the Kramers. They had the biggest house in the neighborhood and a lawn like a golf course, and every year they resealed their driveway so it looked like polished onyx. They were throwing a party tonight to show off their latest renovation. Matt found this annoying. If you could afford to spend half a million dollars remodeling your house, the least you could do was keep quiet about it.

But this was one party that Matt was actually looking forward to. He wanted to ask the "Nourwoods" a few questions.

The party was already in full swing when he arrived: giddy, lubricated laughter and the smells of strong perfume and gin and melted cheese. He smiled at the neighbors, most of whom he didn't know, said hello to Audrey Kramer, and then caught sight of Kate chatting amiably with the Nourwoods. He froze. Why was she being so friendly to them?

As soon as Kate spied Matt, she waved him over. "Jimmy, Laura—my husband, Matt."

Nourwood was dressed in an expensive-looking blue suit, a crisp white shirt, and a striped tie. He looked prosperous and preening. His wife was small and blond and plain, solidly built, with small, pert features. Next to her husband she looked washed-out. They really didn't look like a married couple, Matt thought. They didn't seem to fit together in any way. Both of them smiled politely and extended their hands, and Matt noticed that her handshake was a lot firmer than her husband's.

"We've met," Nourwood said, his dark eyes gleaming.

"You have?" Kate said.

"Early this morning. He didn't tell you?" Nourwood laughed, showing very white, even teeth. "*Very* early this morning."

Kate flashed Matt a look of surprise. "No."

"Did you ever find your earring?" Nourwood asked Kate.

"Earring?" she said. "What earring?"

"The one Matt gave you—his first gift to you?"

Matt tried to intercept her with a warning look, but Kate gave him no chance. "This guy?" she said. "I don't think he's ever given me a pair of earrings the whole time I've known him."

"Ah," Nourwood said. His eyes bored right into Matt like an X-ray. "I misunderstood."

Matt's face went hot and prickly, and he wondered how obvious it was. He'd been caught in a transparent lie. How was he going to explain what he'd really been doing in Nourwood's driveway at five in the morning without sounding defensive or sketchy? And then he rebuked himself: This guy's a liar and an undercover operative, and *you're* acting like the guilty one?

The two women launched into a high-spirited conversation, like old friends, about restaurants and movies and shopping, leaving the two men standing there in awkward silence.

"My apologies," Nourwood said quietly. "I should have thought before I said anything. We

all have things we prefer to keep hidden from our spouses."

Matt attempted a casual chuckle, but it came out hollow and forced. "Oh no, not at all," he said. "I should have told you the whole story." He lowered his voice, confiding. "Those earrings were actually a surprise gift—"

"Ah," Nourwood said, cutting him off with a knowing smile. "Not another word. My bad."

Matt hesitated. Without further elaboration, his new, revised story made no sense: why the pointless lie, how had these imaginary earrings ended up on Nourwood's driveway, all that. But Nourwood either didn't need to hear more—or didn't believe him and didn't *want* to hear more.

Matt's Spidey Sense was tingling again.

Laura and Kate were laughing and talking a mile a minute. Laura was saying something about Neiman Marcus, Kate nodding emphatically and saying, "Totally. Totally."

Instead of trying to salvage a shred of credibility, Matt decided to change the subject. "So how do you like ADS?"

Nourwood stared at him blankly. "ADS?"

"Andromeda Data Systems. You don't work there?" Now he wondered whether Kate might have just heard wrong.

"Oh, right," Nourwood said, as if just now remembering. "It's fine. You know—it's a job."

"Uh-huh," Matt said. Maybe it was Nourwood's turn to get caught in a lie. "You just started there, right?"

"Right, right," Nourwood said vaguely, obviously not eager to talk about it.

"How's the commute?" Matt persisted, moving in for the kill. "You must, like, *live* on the turnpike."

"Not at all. It's not too bad."

There was no question about it: Nourwood didn't work at ADS at all. He was probably afraid to be asked too many questions about the company.

So Matt bore in. "What kind of work do you do?"

"Oh, you don't want to know, believe me," Nourwood said in an offhanded way. His eyes were roaming the room over Matt's shoulders, as if he was desperate for an escape from the grilling.

"Not at all. I'd love to know."

"Believe me," Nourwood said, feigning joviality, though there was something hard in his eyes. "Whenever I try to explain what I do, people fall asleep standing up. Tell me about yourself."

"Me? I'm an engineer. But we're not done with you." Then Matt flashed a mollifying grin.

"I guess you could say I'm an engineer, too," Nourwood said. "A project engineer."

"Oh, yeah? I know a fair amount about ADS," Matt lied. He knew nothing more than what he'd gleaned from a quick glance at their website this morning and skimming the occasional article in the *Globe*. "I'd love to hear all about it."

"I'm an independent contractor. On kind of a consulting project."

"Really?" Matt said, pretending to be fascinated. "Tell me about it."

Nourwood's restless eyes returned to Matt's, and for a few seconds seemed to be studying him. "I wish I could," he said at last. "But they made me sign all sorts of nondisclosure agreements."

Matt wondered whether Nourwood was a harmless king snake or a venomous prairie rattlesnake. "Huh," he said.

"It's just a short-term project anyway," Nourwood went on, his eyes gone opaque. "That's why we're renting."

Matt's stomach flipped over. A short-term project. That was one way of putting it. Of course it was short term. In a couple of days Nourwood's true mission would be finished. Matt cleared his throat, attempted another approach entirely. "You know, it's the weirdest thing, but you look so damned familiar."

"Oh?"

"I could swear I've met you before."

Nourwood nodded. "I get that a lot."

Matt doubted it. "College, maybe?"

"I don't think so."

"Where'd you go to college?"

Nourwood seemed to hesitate. "Madison," he said, almost grudgingly.

"You're *kidding* me! I've got a bunch of friends who went there. What year'd you graduate?"

He caught Kate giving him a poisonous look. She had this astonishing ability to talk and eavesdrop at the same time. In truth, Matt didn't know a single person who'd gone to the University of Wisconsin at Madison. But if Matt could get Nourwood to give him a year of graduation, he'd finally be able to unearth something on this guy.

Nourwood looked uncomfortable. "I didn't really socialize much in college," he said. "I doubt I'd know any of your friends. Anyway, I didn't—I didn't exactly graduate. Long story." A taut laugh.

"Love to hear it."

"But not a very interesting story. Maybe some other time."

"I'll take a rain check," Matt said. "We'd love to have you guys over sometime. What's your cell number?" Of course, Matt had no intention of inviting the Nourwoods over. Not in a million years. But there had to be ways to trace a cell phone number.

"I should have my new mobile phone in a day or two," Nourwood said. "Let me take yours."

Touché, Matt thought. He smiled like an idiot while he scrambled for a response. "You know, it's funny, I'm blanking on it."

"Is that your mobile phone right there, clipped to your belt?"

"Oh," Matt said, looking down, flushing with embarrassment.

"Your number's easy to find on the phone. Here, let me take a look."

Nourwood reached for Matt's phone, but Matt put his hand over it. Just then, Matt felt a painful pinch at his elbow. "Excuse us," Kate said. "Matt, Audrey Kramer needs to ask you something."

"Hope you find your earrings," Nourwood said with a wink that sent a chill down Matt's spine.

———

"What the *hell* do you think you were doing in there?" Kate said on the walk home.

Matt, embarrassed, snorted softly and shook his head.

"I don't *believe* you."

"What?"

"The way you were interrogating him? That was out-and-out rude."

"I was just making conversation."

"Please, Matt. I know damned well what you were doing. You might as well have put him under the klieg lights. That was way out of line."

"You notice how he was evading my questions?"

"Fine, so let it drop!"

"Don't you get it? Don't you get how dangerous this guy might be?"

"Oh, for God's sake, Matt. You're doing that *Rear Window* thing again. Laura seems perfectly nice."

"There you go: 'perfectly nice.' Like that milk that's about to go bad."

"The milk is fine," she snapped. "And I'm not even going to *ask* what you were doing in front of their house at five in the morning."

A moment passed. The scuff of their footsteps on the pavement. "You still haven't heard back from the doctor, have you?"

"Will you please stop asking?"

"But what's taking him so long?"

"Matt, we've been through this three times before."

"I know," he said softly.

"And we always come through just fine."

"There's always the first time."

"God, you're such a worrier."

"Better safe than sorry. I worry for both of us."

"I know," she said, and she linked arms with him and snuggled close. "I know you do."

The next morning, as Matt was backing the Escalade out of the garage, he glanced over and saw Nourwood getting into his tiny Toyota, and another idea came to him.

Halfway down the driveway, he stopped the car. For a minute or so he just sat there, enjoying the muted throb of the 6.2-liter all-aluminum V-8 engine with its 403 horsepower and its 517 foot-pounds of torque. He watched Nourwood back his crappy, holier-than-thou subcompact out into the street with a toylike whine and then proceed down Ballard to Centre Street.

James Nourwood was going to work, and Matt Parker was going to follow.

Let's see where you really work. Whoever you really are.

He called his manager, Regina, and told her he was having car trouble and would probably be a little late. She sounded mildly annoyed, but that was her default mode.

Matt kept his Escalade a few cars behind Nourwood's Yaris, so Nourwood wouldn't notice. At the end of Centre Street, Nourwood signaled for a right. No traffic light here, just a stop sign, and the morning rush hour was heavy. By the time Matt was able to turn, Nourwood was in the far left lane, almost out of sight, signaling left. That was the way to the Mass Pike westbound. The direction of Hopkinton and ADS headquarters. Maybe he really did work there after all.

Matt followed him around the curve, but then Nourwood abruptly veered into the right lane, onto Washington Street, which made no sense at all. This was a local road. Where was the man going?

When Nourwood turned into a gas station, Matt smiled to himself. Even those damned gas-sipping toy cars needed to fill up from time to time. Matt drove on past the gas station—he couldn't exactly follow him in—and parked along the curb fifty feet or so ahead. Far enough away that Nourwood wouldn't notice but close enough to see him leave.

But then Matt noticed something peculiar in his rearview mirror. Nourwood didn't pull up to a gas pump. Instead, he parked alongside another car, a gleaming blue Ford Focus not much bigger than his own.

Then Nourwood's car door opened. He got

out, looked around quickly, then opened the passenger's side door of the blue Ford and got in.

Matt's heart began to thud. Who was Nourwood meeting? The strong morning sun was reflected off the Ford's windows, turning them into mirrors, impossible to see in. Matt just watched for what seemed an eternity.

It was probably no more than five minutes, as it turned out, before Nourwood got out of the Ford, followed by the driver, a slender, black-haired young man in his twenties wearing khakis and a white shirt and blue tie. With crisp efficiency, the two men switched cars. Nourwood was the first to leave, backing the Ford out of the space, then hanging a left out of the gas station onto Washington Street, back the way he'd come.

Matt, facing the wrong way on Washington Street, didn't dare attempt a U-turn: too much oncoming traffic. There was nowhere to turn left. Frantic, he pulled away from the curb without looking. A car swerved, horn blasting and brakes squealing. Just up ahead on the right was a Dunkin' Donuts. Matt turned into the lot, spun around, and circled back. But the blue Ford was gone.

He cursed aloud. If only he had some idea which way Nourwood was headed. West on the turnpike? East? Or maybe not the turnpike at all. Furious at himself, he gave up and proceeded toward the Mass Pike inbound. He'd surely lost the last chance to flush the guy out: Tomorrow was the big day. In the morning, it would be too late.

As he drove onto the ramp and merged with the clotted traffic on the pike, his mind raced. Why had Nourwood switched cars? Why else except to elude detection, to avoid being spotted by someone who might recognize his vehicle?

The inbound traffic was heavy and sluggish, worse than usual. Was there an accident? Construction? He switched on his radio in search of a traffic report. "—According to a spokesman for the FBI's Boston office," a female announcer was saying. Then a man's voice, a thick Boston accent: "You know, Kim, if *I* worked in one of those buildings downtown, I'd take a personal day. Call

it a long weekend. Get an early start on my weekend golf game." Matt switched the radio off.

Just outside the city, the lines were long at the Allston/Brighton toll plaza, but not at the Fast Lane booths. Matt had never gotten one of those E-ZPass accounts, though. He didn't like the idea of putting a transponder on his windshield, an electronic dog tag. He didn't want Big Brother to know where he was at all times. Sometimes it amazed him how people gave up their right to privacy without a second thought. They just didn't think about how easily tyranny could move in to fill the vacuum. His brother, Donny, back in Colorado—he understood. He was a true hero.

As he glanced enviously over at the Fast Lane, he saw a bright blue car zipping past. The man behind the wheel had dark hair and a dark complexion.

Nourwood.

He was quite sure of it.

Miraculously, Matt had caught up with him on the highway—only to be on the verge of losing him again! Stuck in the slow lane, with three cars ahead of him. The driver at the booth seemed to be chatting with the attendant, asking directions or whatever. Matt honked, tried to maneuver out of the line, but there was no room. Then he remembered that even if he'd been able to get over to one of the Fast Lanes, he couldn't just drive through without a transponder. A camera would take a picture of his license plate and send him a ticket, and that was exactly the kind of trouble he didn't need.

By the time he handed the old guy a dollar bill and a quarter and cleared the booth, Nourwood was gone. Matt accelerated, moved to the left-hand lane—and then, like some desert mirage, caught a glimpse of blue.

Yes. There it was, not far ahead. Nourwood's cerulean blue Ford was easy to spot, because it was weaving deftly in and out of traffic, crazy fast, like Dale Earnhardt at Daytona.

As if he were trying to shake a tail.

Matt's Escalade had far more cojones than Nourwood's silly little Ford. It could do zero to sixty in 6.5, and its passing power wasn't too shabby either. But he had to be careful. Better to stay back, not draw Nourwood's attention. Or get pulled over by the cops: Now *that* would be ironic.

Just up ahead were the downtown exits. Matt normally took the first one, the Copley Square exit. He wondered—the thought dawned on him with a dread that seeped cold into the pit of his stomach—whether Nourwood was headed toward one of the city's skyscrapers to conduct surveillance, as these guys so often did when a terrorist operation was in the works.

Maybe even the Hancock.

Dear God, he thought. Not that. Of all buildings in Boston, not that.

Let Kate scoff at his paranoia. She wouldn't be scoffing when he flushed out this Nourwood, this man with a fake name and a contrived background and all his tricky driving maneuvers.

When Nourwood passed the Copley exit, Matt sighed aloud. Then, still changing lanes, speeding faster and faster, Nourwood passed the South Station exit, too.

Where, then, *was* he going?

Suddenly the blue Ford cut clear across three lanes of traffic and barreled onto an exit ramp. Matt was barely able to make the exit himself.

And when he saw the green exit sign with the white airplane symbol on it, he felt his mouth go dry.

He hadn't seen Nourwood load a suitcase into his car, or any other travel bags. The man was going to the airport, but without a suitcase.

Matt's cell phone rang, but he ignored it. No doubt the officious Regina calling from work with some pointless question.

As the blue Ford emerged from the Callahan Tunnel, a few car lengths ahead of Matt's Escalade, it veered off to the right, to the exit marked Logan International Airport. Nourwood passed the turnoffs for the first few terminals, stayed on the perimeter road, then took the turnoff for central parking. Now Matt was right behind him: living dangerously. If Nourwood happened to look in his rearview mirror, he'd see Matt's Escalade. No reason for Nourwood to suspect it was Matt. Unless, waiting in line to enter the garage, he glanced back.

So at the last minute, Matt swung his car away from the garage entrance and off to the side, letting Nourwood go on ahead. He watched the man's arm snake out—a charcoal gray sleeve, the dark-complexioned hand, the hairy wrist, and the expensive watch—and snatch the ticket. Then Matt followed him inside. He took the ticket, watched the lift gate rise. The ramp just ahead rose steeply: a 15% gradient, he calculated. Nourwood's blue Ford, once again, was gone.

Chill, Matt told himself. He's only going one way. You'll catch up to him. Or see his parked car. But as he wound steadily uphill, tires squealing on the glazed concrete surface, Matt saw no blue Ford. He marveled at the lousy design of this parking structure, all the wasted space under the grade ramps, the curtain walls and the horizontally disposed beams, the petrified forest of vertical columns taking up far too many bays. When he saw how enormous the garage was, how many possible routes Nourwood could have taken on each deck, he cursed himself for not taking the risk of staying right behind the guy. Now it was too late. How many times had he lost Nourwood this morning?

Half an hour later, having circled and circled the garage, up to the roof and back down, he finally gave up.

Matt slammed his fist on the steering wheel, accidentally hitting the horn, and the guy right in front of him at the exit, driving a Hummer, stuck out his tattooed arm and gave him the finger.

For the rest of the day, Matt could barely concentrate on his RFP. Who cared about it, anyway, with what was about to happen? At lunch he dodged an invitation from Lenny Baxter, the IT guy, to grab a sandwich at the deli, preferring to go off by himself and think.

As he finished his turkey club sandwich at Subway, crumpling the wrapper into a neat ball, his cell phone rang. It was Kate.

"The doctor called," she said.

"Finally. Tell me." His heart started racing again, but he managed to sound calm.

"We're fine," she said.

"Great. That's great news. So, how're you feeling?"

"You know me. I never worry."

"You don't have to," Matt said. "I do it for you."

Back at his cubicle, he found the website for the University of Wisconsin's office of the registrar. A line said, "To verify a degree or dates of attendance" and gave a number, which he called.

"I need to *verify*"—Matt deliberately used the word in order to sound official—"attendance on a job applicant, please."

"Of course," the young woman said. "Can I have the name?"

Matt was surprised at how easy this was going to be. He gave Nourwood's name, heard the girl tap at her keyboard. "All *righty*," she said, all corn-fed Midwestern hospitality. "So you should get a degree verification letter in two to three business days. I'll just need to get—"

"Days?" Matt croaked. "I—I don't have time for that!"

"If you need an immediate answer you can contact the National Student Clearinghouse. Assuming you have an account with them, sir."

"I—we're just—a small office here. And, um, the hiring deadline is today, or it's not going to go through, so if there's any way . . ."

"Oh," the woman said, full of genuine-sounding concern. "Well, let me see what I can do for you, then. Can you hold?"

She came back on the line a couple of minutes later. "I'm sorry, sir. I don't have a James Nourwood. I'm not finding *any* Nourwoods. Are you sure you've got the spelling right?"

At 6:45 P.M. Matt pulled into his driveway and noticed the blue Ford Focus parked next door. So Nourwood was home, too.

Turning his key in the front door, he realized it was already unlocked. He moved slowly, warily, through the living room, nerves a-jangle, listening, pulse racing. He thought he heard a female cry from somewhere in the house, though he wasn't sure whether it was Kate's or whether it was in fact a laugh or a cry, and then the hollow-core door to the basement came open, the one between the kitchen and the half bath, and James Nourwood loomed in the doorway, a twenty-pound sledgehammer in his hand.

Matt dove at Nourwood and tackled him to the floor. He could smell the man's strong aftershave, tinged with acrid sweat. He was surprised at how easily Nourwood went down. The sledgehammer slid from his grip, thudded onto the carpet. The guy barely put up a fight. He was trying to say something, but Matt grabbed his throat and squeezed it just below the larynx.

Matt snarled, *"You goddamned—"*

A shout came from somewhere close. Kate's voice, high and shrill. "Oh, my God! Matt, stop it! Oh, my God, Jimmy, I'm so sorry!"

Confused and disoriented, Matt relaxed his grip on Nourwood's throat and said, "What the hell's going on here?"

"Matt, get off of him!" Kate shrieked.

Nourwood's olive-complexioned face had gone a shade of purple. Then, unexpectedly, he laughed. "What you must have . . . thought," Nourwood managed to choke out. "I'm—so sorry. Your wife told me to just go down and grab . . . all my tools are in storage." He struggled, was finally able to sit up. "Laura's been nagging me for days to put up a fence around her tomato garden to keep out the chipmunks, and I didn't realize how—how much clay's in the soil here. You can't pound in the stakes without a decent sledgehammer."

Matt turned around, looked at Kate. She looked mortified. "Jimmy, it's all my fault. Matt's been on edge recently."

Now Laura Nourwood was there, too, ice clinking festively in a tumbler of scotch. "What's going *on* here? Jimmy, you okay?"

Nourwood rose unsteadily, brushed off his suit jacket and pants. "I'm fine," he said.

"What happened?" his wife said. "Was it the vertigo again?"

"No, no, no," Nourwood chuckled. "Just a misunderstanding."

"Sorry," Matt mumbled. "Shoulda asked before I jumped you."

"No, really, it's all my fault," Kate said later as they sat in the living room, drinks in their hands. Kate had heated up some frozen cheesy puff pastry things from Trader Joe's and kept passing around the tray. "Matt, I probably should have told you I'd invited them over, but I just saw Laura in her backyard planting out her tomatoes, and we started talking, and it turns out Laura's into heirloom tomatoes, which you know how much I love. And I was telling her that I thought it was probably too early to plant out her tomatoes around here, she should wait for last frost, and then Jimmy got home, and he asked if we had a sledgehammer he could borrow, so I just asked these guys over for a drink. . . ."

"My bad," Matt said, still embarrassed about how he'd overreacted. But it didn't mean his underlying suspicions had been wrong—not at all. Just in this one particular instance. Nothing else about the man had changed. None of his lies about his job or his college or what he was really doing.

"Tomorrow we'll all laugh about it," Kate said.

I doubt that, Matt thought.

"What do you mean?" said Nourwood. "I'm laughing now!" He turned to his wife, put his big ham hock hand over hers. "Just please don't ask our neighbors for a cup of sugar! I don't think I'm up to it." He laughed loud and long, and the women joined him. Matt smiled thinly.

"I was telling the ladies about my day from hell," Nourwood said. "So my sister Nabilah calls me last night to tell me she has a job interview in Boston and she's flying in this morning."

"Nothing like advance notice," said Laura.

Nourwood shrugged. "This is my baby sister we're talking about. She does everything last-minute. She graduated from college last May, and she's been looking for a job for months, and all of a sudden it's rush rush rush. And she asks can I pick her up at the airport."

"God forbid she should take a cab," Laura said.

"What is an older brother for?" Nourwood said.

"Nabilah's what you'd call a princess," said his wife.

"Really, I don't mind at all," said Nourwood. "But of course it had to be on the same day that my car's going into the shop."

"I think she planned it that way," Laura said.

"But the car dealership couldn't have been nicer about it. They were even willing to bring the loaner to a gas station on Washington Street. But I got a late start leaving the house, and then the kid had all kinds of paperwork he wanted me to fill out, even though I thought we'd gone over all of this on the phone. So there I am on the highway in this rented car, driving to the airport like a madman. Only I don't know where the turn signal is, and come to find out the parking brake is partly on, so the car's moving all jerky, like a jackrabbit. And I don't want to be late for Nabilah, because I know she'll freak out."

"God forbid she might have to wait a couple of minutes for her chauffeur," Laura said acidly.

"So right when I'm driving into the parking garage at Logan, my cell phone rings, and who should it be but Nabilah? She got an earlier flight, and she's been waiting at the airport for half an hour already, and she's freaking out, she's going to be late for the interview, and where am I, and all of this."

Laura Nourwood shook her head, compressed her lips. Her dislike for her sister-in-law was palpable.

"But I've already taken the ticket from the garage thingy, so I turn around, and I have to plead with the man in the booth to let me out without paying their minimum."

"What was it, like ten bucks, Jimmy?" said his wife. "You should have just paid."

"I don't like throwing away money," Nourwood replied. "You know that. So I race over to Terminal C and I park right in front of arrivals and get out of the car, and all of a sudden this state trooper's coming at me, yelling, and writing me a ticket. He says I'm not allowed to park in front of the terminal. Like I've got a car bomb or something. In this little rented Ford!"

"You do look Arab," his wife said. "And these days . . ."

"Persians are not Arabs," Nourwood said stiffly. "I speak Farsi, not Arabic."

"And I'm sure that Boston cop appreciates the distinction," Laura said. She looked at Matt and shrugged apologetically. "Jimmy hates cops."

Annoyed, Nourwood shook his head. "So as soon as I get back in the car to move it, Nabilah comes out, with like five suitcases—and she's not even staying overnight! So I race downtown to Fidelity, and then I have to floor it to get to Westwood because my eleven A.M. got moved up an hour."

"Don't tell me you got a speeding ticket," Laura said.

"When it rains, it pours," Nourwood said.

"Westwood?" Matt said. "You told me you work for ADS. They're in Hopkinton."

"Well, if you want to get technical about it, I actually work for Dataviz, which is a *subsidiary* of ADS. They just got acquired by ADS six months ago. And let me tell you, this isn't going to be an easy integration. They still haven't changed the name on the building, and they still answer the phone 'Dataviz' instead of 'ADS.'"

"Huh," Matt said. "And . . . your sister—did she go to UW too?"

"UW?" Nourwood said.

"Didn't you tell me you went to Madison?" Matt said. He added drily, "Maybe I misheard."

"Ah, yes, yes," Nourwood said. "James Madison University. JMU."

"JMU," Matt repeated. "Huh."

"That happens a lot," Nourwood said. "Not Wisconsin. Harrisonburg, Virginia."

Then that would explain why the University of Wisconsin had no record of any James Nourwood, Matt thought. "Huh," he said.

"And no, Nabilah went to Tulane," said Nourwood. "I guess we Nouris feel more comfortable in those southern colleges. Maybe it's the warmer climate."

"Nouris?"

"I married a feminist," Nourwood said.

"I'm confused," Matt said.

"Laura didn't want to take my name, Nouri."

"Why should I?" his wife put in. "I mean, how archaic is that? I was Laura Wood my whole life until we got married. Why shouldn't he change his name to James Wood?"

"And neither one of us likes hyphenated names," Nourwood said.

"This girlfriend of mine named Janice Ritter," Laura said, "married a guy named Steve Hyman. And they merged their names and got Ryman."

"That sounds a lot closer to 'Hyman' than to 'Ritter,'" Kate said.

"And the mayor of Los Angeles, Antonio Villar, married Corina Raigosa," Nourwood said. "And they both became Villaraigosa."

"That's brilliant," Kate said. "Nouri and Wood become Nourwood. Like Brad Pitt and Angelina Jolie become Brangelina!"

Nouri, Matt thought. Even if he had gone to the University of Wisconsin, they wouldn't have had a record of a Nourwood.

"Well, but that's just the tabloid nickname for them," Nourwood objected. "They didn't change their names legally."

"Neither did we," Laura Nourwood said.

"When you give me a son, we will," her husband said.

"*Give* you a son?" his wife blurted out. "You mean, when *we* have a *child*. *If* we have a child, I got news for you, Jimmy. You're not back in the old country. You've never even *been* to the old country."

Early the next morning, Matt was glugging the almost-spoiled milk down the sink drain when Kate entered the kitchen.

"Hey! What are you doing? That's perfectly good milk!"

"It tastes sort of suspicious to me," Matt said.

"Now you're getting paranoid about dairy products?"

"Paranoid?" He turned to face her, speaking slowly. "What if I'd been right about them?"

"But you weren't, you big goofball!"

"Okay, fine," Matt said. "We know that *now*. It's just that I couldn't quite shake the feeling that they were . . ."

"Undercover FBI agents?"

"They just had that vibe. And when I think about Donny, doing five consecutive life sentences in supermax back in Colorado just because he dared to fight for freedom on our native soil, you know? I just get the willies sometimes."

"Man, you're always jumping at shadows." She handed him a small red plastic gadget. "Here's the LPD detonator the doctor sent over. I told you he'd come through."

"I hope the doctor is absolutely certain this one's going to work. Remember Cleveland?"

"That won't happen again," she said. "The doctor wasn't running that operation. If there's one thing the doctor knows, it's explosives."

"What about the RDX?"

"The Escalade's already packed."

"Sweetie," Matt said, and he gave her a kiss. "How early did you get up?"

"Least I could do. You've got a long day ahead of you. You're taking the Stuart Street entrance, right?"

"Of course," he said. "All four of us are. No CCTV camera there."

"So, we'll meet up in Sayreville tonight?" Kate said.

"As planned."

"We're going to be Robert and Angela Rosenheim."

"That almost sounds like one of those blended names," Matt said.

"It's what the doctor gave us. We'd better get used to saying it. Okay, *Robert?*"

"Bob. No, let's make it Rob. Are you Angela or Angie?"

"Angie's okay."

"Okay." He paused. "But what if I *had* been right about the neighbors? Because one of these times I'm going to be. You know that."

"Well," Kate said, almost sheepishly. "I did take the precaution of letting the air out of their tires."

THE COLD WAR

BRENDAN DUBOIS

THE HARDWORKING and award-winning author Brendan DuBois (1959–   ) had his first Lewis Cole novel, *Dead Sand*, published in 1994. In the succeeding twenty-six years, he has written ten more books in the series, as well as eight stand-alone novels, three books in the science fiction, alien-invasion *Dark Victory* series, and three *Empire of the North* novels (available only as e-books). And, oh, yes, he has collaborated on two *New York Times* bestsellers with James Patterson, both published in 2019, *The First Lady* and *The Cornwalls Are Gone*.

It is as a short story writer that DuBois has excelled at an even greater level than his well-reviewed novels. With more than one hundred seventy stories to his credit, DuBois has earned numerous honors. "The Dark Snow," first published in the November 1996 issue of *Playboy*, was nominated for an Edgar and an Anthony and was selected for *The Year's Finest 25 Crime and Mystery Stories* (1997), *The Best American Mystery Stories 1997*, and *The Best American Mystery Stories of the Century* (2000). "A Ticket Out," first published in the January 1987 issue of *Ellery Queen's Mystery Magazine*, was included in *The Best American Noir of the Century* (2010). Two additional stories, "The Necessary Brother" and "Driven," have also been nominated for Edgars.

Out of the mystery genre, his big novel *Resurrection Day* (1999), which posited a different outcome to the 1962 Cuban missile crisis, has been published in eight countries and was named the Best Alternative History Novel of the Year at the 58th World Science Fiction Convention.

DuBois began his writing career as a journalist in New Hampshire, where he has lived his entire life.

He appeared on the television game show program *Jeopardy!*, where he was a one-time champion, and also won the game show *The Chase*.

"Old Soldiers" was originally published in the May 2000 issue of *Playboy*.

OLD SOLDIERS

BRENDAN DUBOIS

WHEN PERFORMING a boring chore like
splitting wood, you tend to dwell on trivia to pass
the time, such as the two distinct sounds you
encounter during the job. The first is a thump,
when the maul you're using makes a slight inden-
tation into the wood. The other is a sharp crack,
when you've started a major split that means you're
almost finished with that chunk of soon-to-be
firewood. Thoughts like these were going through
my mind as I was about an hour into my morning
woodcutting routine one spring Saturday.

Then a dark blue Ford LTD with government plates bumped its way up my dirt driveway, and I wasn't bored anymore.

And when Special Agent Cameron of the FBI
and a companion got out of the car, I momentarily wondered what kind of sound a maul
would make while being buried in the base of
someone's skull.

Cameron carried a slim leather briefcase and
his white hair was combed carefully over the
back of his head, as if he had just had his picture
taken for his official government ID. He had on a
charcoal gray suit, unlike his companion, about
twenty years younger, who wore blue jeans,
white polo shirt, and a dark brown leather jacket.

"Owen," Cameron said, as I rested near the
woodpile.

"I'd like to present Mr. . . . Smith. Mr. Smith
works for another government agency."

I stuck out my hand and as Smith came forward to shake it, I wiped it off with my handkerchief, and Smith paused, the slight grin on his
face steady under my insult. His dark brown hair
was cut short and his blue eyes were bright, brit-
tle and sharp. Underneath his polo shirt there
seemed to be hard muscles. He looked like a guy
who would spend his vacation in Europe, retracing Wehrmacht invasion routes through Poland
with a smile on his face.

"Really?" I said. "And would that government
agency be the GAO? Is your work being audited,
Agent Cameron?"

Cameron didn't look pleased. "No. And this
meeting has nothing to do with my previous visits. Mr. Smith has a matter to discuss with you,
in private. When the two of you are finished, I'll
take him back to Portland. That's it."

When the government pays your bills and
keeps you alive, year after year, after any competent actuary would have written you off as dead
long since, then I guess listening is the polite

thing to do. So I shrugged and said, "All right, why don't the both of you come in."

Smith spoke for the first time. "That sounds grand." He came forward, but Cameron shook his head. "No," he said. "I want no part of this."

So Smith followed me into the farmhouse as Cameron trudged back to the LTD.

In the kitchen, I poured myself a tall glass of lemonade, offering nothing to my uninvited guest, and we sat at the round oak table. Perhaps I was being childish, but Smith didn't seem to notice. He leaned back in his chair and rested his large hands on his flat stomach.

"Agent Cameron gave me a thorough briefing on the way over here," he said. "You certainly have a fascinating past, Mr. Taylor."

"Ain't I lucky," I said.

"And it's that past that has brought me here," he said. "Your talents. We want to use them, just for a short time."

"Sorry, I'm retired."

His smile was wide and merry. "Sorry, in return. You've been unretired and turned over to us. And if you don't care to cooperate, we can make your life quite miserable very quickly. I know what you've got here. In return for certain past services, you live here in total freedom, save for a few minor restrictions. Like staying within the town limits. Which brings me to my next point. Ever hear of Marion?"

Something seemed to wiggle around in my throat. "Maximum security prison."

He waved a hand in the air. "No, not maximum. Maximum is a dime a dozen. I'm sure even this rural wonderland has a maximum prison. No, Marion is the ultimate federal penitentiary.

"An inmate lives alone in a concrete cube eight feet in each direction. Once a week, you get out for an hour for some sunshine and fresh air. That's it. No radio, no television, newspapers and books strictly controlled, and the food is government-supplied. So. We reach an under-

standing here, everything's fine. If not, tomorrow at this time, you'll be staring at concrete."

I tried to stay calm. "Special Agent Cameron—"

"Look," he interrupted. "Some time ago Cameron made a mistake. A big one. In a little Texas town called Waco. Ever wonder why he's way out here in this area? Waco is why. And Waco is why Cameron cooperates. Which includes lending one of his charges for a while. So, Owen. What's it going to be?"

I put my hands under the table because they were clenching into fists so hard that I could feel fingernails starting to break skin. "What do you want?"

He waggled a finger in my direction.

"No, no, no. I want to hear the words from your mouth that you're on board. Then I will tell you what we have planned."

I nodded, and then said, "All right, I'm on board."

Smith's grin got wider. "Thanks. And I also won twenty bucks. Cameron bet me you'd say no. OK, here's the drill." He reached into his jacket and pulled out a small slip of paper and tossed it over. "There's a man named Len Molowski, lives up in Cardiff, about an hour north of here. He's in his mid-sixties, owns a small farm. That's his address."

I glanced at the paper. "And what's so special about Len Molowski?"

"What's special is that his real name is Leonid Malenkov. He's a Soviet military intelligence operative, placed here in deep cover almost four decades ago. You know those Jap soldiers who lived on in Guam and the Philippines, years after the war was over, who didn't give up? Same story, except they're here and they're Russian."

"So?"

I guess that wasn't the response Smith was looking for, as his smile faded. "Some old records we've kept over the years, we've managed to finally decode them. You'd be surprised what's for sale now over in Moscow. We found Len's name and a bunch of other names, all Soviet military intelligence, all placed into this country at about the same time, during the late fifties."

"And what was he going to do while in Maine? Burn down a forest?"

"Who knows and who cares," Smith said. "That he's still here is what counts. And that's why I'm here with you."

"At the risk of repeating myself, I'll do just that," I said. "So what? Hasn't the news gotten to you folks yet? The Cold War's over. They lost. We won. We have a hell of a budget deficit to pay, but they have McDonald's in Red Square, their nuclear subs are rusting and sinking at dockside, and their soldiers spend their time harvesting potatoes and trying to stay alive. What's the point of going after this guy?"

His eyes flashed at me. "The point is, we know we won the Cold War, but some people in Moscow haven't gotten the message. They don't like having NATO move in next door. They don't like having American fast food next to Lenin's tomb. They don't like American game shows on their TV. And we want to send them a message."

I picked up the paper again. "And how does Len become part of this message?"

Smith's gaze was steady, unblinking.

"We want you to go up to his farm. Pay him a visit. Confirm his background. And then handle it."

I was suddenly aware of how tired I was, from chopping all that wood and from talking to this awful young man. "Handle it how?"

"Don't play wedding night virgin with me, Owen. I've read your record, know your background. You know exactly what I meant by handle it."

I slowly nodded. "So I do. *Mokrie dela*, right? Russian for wet work. After all, blood is wet and tends to get on your shoes and clothing. A nice piece of euphemism from Department V of the old KGB. And by handling an old man who's probably clipping newspaper coupons and wondering how to pay for fertilizer this spring, this is going to do just what for you and your friends?"

"A message," Smith said slowly. "A demonstration. By retiring this old network of theirs,

we make an effective demonstration to the right people with a minimum of fuss. More efficient and cheaper than flying over the Secretary of State to talk about trade issues or some other goddamn nonsense."

I crumpled up the paper. "And part of the minimal fuss is me, right? Deniability in case anything goes wrong. If I'm caught, I'm a career criminal with mysterious ties who one day killed a Maine farmer for no good reason. Right?"

"Who says retirees are losing their marbles," Smith said.

I looked out the window at the parked LTD and the man inside. "Part of my agreement with the Department of Justice is that I—"

"I know, I know," he said. "You're not allowed to leave the confines of this lovely little town without express prior permission, blah blah blah. All taken care of. You have a week, Owen. Seven days from now we'll be back for results, or your bag better be packed. And that bag should contain a toothbrush and nothing else. The clock is running. Understood?"

"Understood."

Smith slapped his hands together and stood up. "Great. Glad we could reach agreement."

He walked out of the kitchen, and as he strolled to the LTD, I had a fantasy of running downstairs to retrieve one of my slightly illegal weapons and blowing away Mr. Smith before his hand reached the car door. I replayed it in my head as the car left my property.

There are negatives associated with life in a small town. The local cable provider thinks one channel from Boston is stretching its cultural limits. No bookstores. And the nearest supermarket has boiled ham and American cheese as the extent of its deli offerings.

But there are some advantages, too, and one of them owns and works at the Pinette General Store. Miriam Woods is my oldest and dearest friend in town, and she winked at me as I finished a late lunch of tomato soup and a BLT. She's a widow, several years younger than I am, with dark brown hair and even darker eyes that are lightly framed by wrinkles. She owns the store, she runs the town post office out of a storefront window off to the side, and she's also one of the town's three elected selectmen.

As she picked up plates, her son Eric was restocking shelves in one of the far aisles. She looked over at him and then at me and lowered her voice.

"This Tuesday," she said, "Eric has basketball practice and I was thinking of coming over to your place for dinner."

"Really?"

"Really. You supply the dinner and I'll supply the desserts. One of them will be in an ice cream container." She lowered her voice even more and winked again as she started wiping the counter.

I said slowly, "But I won't be home."

"Well, there's always Thursday night, because—"

"Miriam, I won't be home all next week."

She stopped wiping the counter.

"Oh?" And my dear Miriam was able to stuff about a ton of frost, disappointment, and inquiry into that little two-letter word.

"That's right. I have . . . I have business to attend to."

Her wiping cloth was clenched in a fist. "I see. What kind of business?"

"I'm sorry, I really can't say. It'll take less than a week and then I'll be back."

She managed a smile and shook her head and went over to the cash register, counting and recounting bills, all the while talking, as if talking to herself. "You've never once agreed to go away with me for a trip to somewhere, even if it's just Portland or Bar Harbor. You've always said you couldn't leave the town, that you wouldn't feel comfortable."

Then she looked at me and slammed the cash drawer shut. "Now you tell me you're leaving town for a week, and you can't tell me why. To hell with that and to hell with you."

She marched to the rear of the store and I followed, but she locked herself into her little post office cubicle. I suppose it would have taken me all of thirty seconds to get through the lock, but I knew I would pay for those thirty seconds for a very long time.

Instead, I went outside to my truck and was climbing in when I heard a familiar voice.

"Owen? Got a sec?"

I rolled down the truck's window as Eric approached in his white store apron. He's about as tall as I am but gangly, with the loose limbs of a fifteen-year-old. He shares his mother's hair and eyes, and those eyes were troubled now.

"Sure," I said. "More than a sec, whatever you need."

"Just wanted to see how you're doing with the Internet. Got any more questions for me?"

I did at that, and we talked techno speak for a while, him using phrases like HTML and links and hypertext with practiced ease, while I struggled along like a backwoodsman who's entered sixth grade at the age of forty. Eric had helped introduce me to the joys of cyberspace and was my own personal tech help line. I asked him a few questions and he gave me more than a few answers.

Then he nodded back toward the store. "I heard most of what went on back there, though I wish I hadn't."

"I wish I hadn't taken part in it, so don't worry."

Quick nod as he smoothed down the front of his store apron. "Mom gets like this, around this time every year. This is when dad died, and it bothers her still, though she never says a word."

"Does it bother you?" I asked.

He shrugged. "Not like it bothers her.

"I don't remember him that well. He spent most of his time either out in the woods or in a bar. Best memory I have is him lying on the couch, trying to balance a Coors can on his forehead and yelling at mom when she didn't move fast enough to get him another one. That's about it."

I started up the truck and he said, "Don't worry, she'll be fine in a bit."

"Honest?"

A wide smile. "Gosh, I don't know, Owen. I just thought that would make you feel better."

"Thanks," I said. "It did, just for a moment."

I then drove home, where I packed up and left the next morning to murder an old Soviet spy.

The day was warm, and I drove with the windows open, enjoying the wet smell of spring, of hidden whispers of trees and grass and crops ready to grow, ready to get back to life. As I drove out of town, I felt a tingle along my hands, as an old and deep part of me appreciated that I was leaving the reservation. Mysterious Mr. Smith had been correct. There were certain things I could not do as part of my agreement with the Department of Justice, and one of them was to cross the boundaries of the township of Pinette. Even thinking of the bad business ahead of me, I couldn't help grinning as I watched the miles roll up on the odometer. For at least this day, I was free to go where I wanted. It was a heady feeling, and if I had found the right tune, I would have been singing. But the only thing on the radio was a syndicated pop psychologist who seemed to gauge her success by seeing how many of her callers burst into tears.

About halfway to Cardiff, I pulled over at a mini-mall and bought a strawberry ice cream cone. I strolled inside, checking out the stores and the people moving about, young and old, families and single men and women of all ages and sizes. I sat on a bench and finished my cone, thinking about the pundits who carped about the "malling" of America. A serious problem, I'm sure, but on this spring day I was happy to be here, free to go into any one of half a dozen stores.

Which I did. I bought a dozen new hardcover books and put them in the truck, went into a computer store and picked up some software, and then went over to an electronics store where I acquired a digital camera and a nice cassette tape recorder. Elsewhere, I spent an obscene amount of money on clothes, and when I left the mini-mall, my credit card was almost smoldering at the unfamiliarity of so much use.

I continued north and came to a tiny county airport. A sign outside said FEARLESS FERN'S FLYING SERVICE and I had a neat little thought of renting Fern and his Flying Service and heading out to British Columbia. Instead, I kept on the job.

While the day had been warm, the night was cold indeed, and lying on the dirt and leaves in a copse of birch trees outside a Cardiff farmhouse was making my bones ache to the point where I wondered if they'd ache forever, or if a long hot bath would set things straight. I was wearing a "ghillie suit," a camouflage outfit with such varied colors and strips of netting and cloth that even in daytime I would melt against the backdrop of the forest. With a good ghillie suit and the patience to keep still, a hunter can be damn near invisible, even with the target standing next to him.

My target wasn't standing next to me, though. He was walking around in his old farmhouse about 100 feet from my hiding spot, alone except for an old collie dog that cowered whenever Len Molowski—or Leonid Malenkov—approached. The man appeared to be in his mid-sixties, with thick white hair combed to one side and black-rimmed glasses. His face was red and fleshy, and he wore a checked flannel shirt and brand-new blue jeans. I had been watching him since dusk, watching him cook and eat dinner by himself, toss a bag of trash on the porch, kick the dog when it got in his way, and then sit on a couch to pass a few hours in the ghastly blue light of the television.

There were some things I did not see.

I didn't see him cleaning a Kalashnikov AK-47 by lamplight. I didn't see a flag of the old Soviet Union flapping in the breeze from a flagpole. And I didn't see an Order of Lenin pinned to his thick chest.

I lifted my binoculars so I could scan the property. The farmhouse was larger than mine, with two stories and a wraparound porch that went around three sides of the house. There was a barn off to the right—also larger than mine, but I didn't have barn envy—and then what looked like a few dozen acres of fields beyond to the east. The nearest neighbor's house was about a half mile away. Everything on the property was neat but shabby, like he was doing all right but didn't want to show up the local populace.

I put the binoculars down, exchanging them for a handheld nightscope. The scenery flashed into pale green as I scanned. Two pickup trucks—one on cement blocks—and a tractor and other equipment in the barn. Nothing out of the ordinary—nothing, of course, except for me in the backyard, lying on the cold ground, 9mm Smith & Wesson Model 915 holstered to my side, water bottle, binoculars, nightscope, and some hard candies all within easy reach. If I had been younger and more eager, I suppose I could have handled this job immediately and been back home by morning.

But, among other things, I wasn't that person anymore. So I waited. The night air was still and it was so quiet that I could hear the drone of engines far off in the distance, and the murmuring of Len's television set. Eventually, Len got up from the couch and went upstairs. An upstairs light went on and I heard the flush of a toilet, and then all the lights went off and I stayed in the cold woods for another hour. Something rustled behind me, but I ignored it. I listened to the frantic hoo-hoo-hoo of an owl and heard a crash of wings and a squeaking noise as something was killed just a few yards from me.

And then I crept away, moving slowly.

Getting out is as important as getting in.

For the next couple of nights and days I kept watch on Len's house and discovered he had a pattern. He worked in the barn in the mornings or went out into the fields with a tractor, turning up the earth. At noon, he finished and went into town for lunch at the Cardiff Cafe. In the late afternoon, he spent his time around the house, and by the time evening rolled around it was the same routine: make dinner, kick the dog, watch television, and go upstairs.

I envied his bed and his home. I was living out of the back of my truck, for I wanted no record of my stay at any hotel or motel in the area. After my nights of surveillance outside his house, I slowly and carefully trekked my way back through the woods to my truck and drove to a place I'd picked out earlier. In these woods were many dirt paths and logging roads, and from one of these, a different one each night, I backed into the woods until I was sure I couldn't be spotted. Then I slept poorly in the rear of the truck on a foam mattress wrapped in a sleeping bag, and while Len had a cozy hot breakfast, I made do with coffee from a little camp stove and cold cereal. Fires mean smoke and smoke in the woods gets noticed, which is not what I planned for this little adventure.

His midday journeys into town, which I timed, each lasted more than an hour. On day three I waited till after he drove off and then I rose from my hiding spot. I shed the ghillie suit for what would pass for a disguise in these woods: a pullover jacket (the better to hide my holstered 9mm), a long-billed cap, binoculars around my neck and a Roger Tory Peterson bird book in my hand. I sauntered into Len's backyard as if I belonged there, went up to the rear door and in a few seconds I was inside. Len hadn't even bothered to lock the door.

Inside and off to the left was a large kitchen. The collie looked up from the kitchen floor, eyes curious, and thumped his tail as I murmured softly and rubbed his head. The tail thumped a few more times and he licked my hand and rolled over as I scratched his belly. Poor guy. Based on his treatment, I'm sure the collie would have helped me shift the furnishings into a moving van, but I had other plans.

I moved quickly, starting in the basement. It took just a few minutes to peg Len as a neat freak, his basement tidier than my kitchen. Boxes of clothing and canned food were stacked on the shelves, and there was an oil furnace that looked as if it had powered the 1939 World's Fair. Upstairs, the collie wagged his tail again as I went through the kitchen, the living room and the downstairs bathroom. Len had a few books, recent bestsellers, in the living room, and the usual news and sports magazines and newspapers. No *Khrushchev Remembers*. No *Gulag Archipelago*. No *History of the Communist Party of the Soviet Union*.

On the second floor, I found his bedroom and a spare room, and, besides neatly made beds, bureaus and closets filled with clothes, and a few more magazines, nothing else. I checked the time. I had been in the house about half an hour. Time to leave.

Downstairs, I gave the collie another belly scratch and went back to the woods to put on the ghillie suit. Forty-five minutes later, Len came home. As I waited for him, I thought about what I had not seen in the house. Quite a lot.

There were no family pictures on the walls or the bureaus.

No collections of letters or scrapbooks of photos.

No framed certificates of achievement from 4-H or the Grange or the Future Farmers of America.

In short, the things that should have been there, if Len were a usual Maine farmer.

From inside the house came the yelp of the collie, and I refocused my binoculars.

The next day I picked up a few groceries and made a quick phone call from a pay phone at a combination gas station and convenience store, a new one. I had not shopped at the same store twice, because I didn't want to be remembered, not even for a moment. When Miriam picked up the phone, she said, "Owen, I apologize."

"Oh," I said. "Very well. Apology accepted."

A sigh from the other end. "Don't you even want to know what I'm apologizing for?"

I turned and looked at a large AgriMark dairy truck rumbling by. "You're right. I should have asked."

Another sigh, but lighter than the first one. "Look, I was having a bad time the other day. Some old memories."

"I hear you."

"Of course you hear me, but I don't think you understand. When you said you were leaving and you couldn't tell me much—well, I don't like being left high and dry twice in the same decade."

"I understand."

I could hear voices in the background.

"Maybe you do, Owen. All right?"

"Absolutely, Miriam," and I was going to say something else when I heard a few more voices and then hers, saying, "Gotta go—bye" all in one breath as she hung up.

When Len next went back into town, I wandered around the reaches of his property in my bird-watcher's disguise. He had enough acreage for one man to farm, if he hired help in the spring and fall. Beyond the edge of one of the fields, I found a dump, where he had trashed a few appliances, a box spring, and some worn truck tires. When I walked up to investigate, a chipmunk jumped on a rusting washing machine and chattered at me.

"Oh, hush up," I said. "Don't you see I'm trying to uncover a dangerous Soviet spy?"

And I laughed.

Heading back, I saw something behind the barn that I hadn't noticed before, a worn path leading into the woods. I followed it, looking for a stream or a fishing hole, but instead it went deeper into the pine forest and then up a slight incline. The trail was old and well maintained, with branches and brush cleared away from the tree trunks. Last year's leaves crackled under my feet as I made my way. I stopped for a moment to note a red driveway reflector light nailed into a tree trunk. The nails were rust-red from being outside a long time. Farther up the trail were more reflectors. The trail was marked for someone traveling through here at night.

The climb got steeper and I rested for a few minutes, taking a swig of water from my bottle, before following the path through a series of switchbacks. After a few minutes of climbing that made my thighs twitch, I was on the top of the hill, breathing hard.

"Excelsior," I muttered, as I sat down on a fallen tree log.

The view was not what I expected. An airport was down there, with a long concrete runway that ran at an angle to the hill. A control tower and a number of hangars were in the distance, together with enough buildings for a small town. It was a much bigger airport than the one I had passed on the drive out, and also much bigger than such a remote and rural area would seem to need.

From the knapsack, I pulled out my binoculars and a map of the county. I scanned the few small private planes parked near the hangars. Those hangars were scaled for aircraft much bigger and faster than these Cessnas and Piper Cubs.

On the map, the marker for the town of Cardiff had a stylized aircraft symbol nearby. Below the cartoon plane were the words:

Raymond Air Force Base Strategic Air Command
(Closed and now available for civilian use)

Looking down at the old Air Force base as I sat there, the damn spring sun didn't warm me a bit.

That night in my ghillie suit, I watched Len go through his routine. Tonight was a bit different. At the kitchen table, he tossed down shot glass after shot glass of something from a clear bottle. Vodka was my guess. Then he started singing, a morose tune that I couldn't make out. It could have been in a foreign language, or it could have been that the breeze was blowing away from me, softening the sounds from the house. I waited for long hours as he gently placed his head on the kitchen table and fell asleep, and my hands and feet were trembling from cold before he woke to stagger upstairs.

The night after the drinking bout, after Len left for town, I stepped right up in my bird-watcher's outfit. I whistled as I walked through his yard and through the open sliding barn door. Ain't rural life grand, where people keep their outbuildings wide open for the benefit of would-be assassins?

A John Deere tractor was parked in the center of the barn, along with a collection of tills, spreaders, and harvesters. Everything looked to be in good working condition. There were a few bags of fertilizer and seed, and a ladder going up to the loft. I climbed it—wincing as a splinter dug into my hand—and on the second level found a collection of tools, leather harnesses, rolled blankets, and more bags of fertilizer. I went back down and outside past the tractor. Something was wrong, something was quite wrong.

I looked around, picking at the splinter on my hand. My internal alarm bells were jangling and everything felt odd, as though my inner ear balance had gone haywire. I squinted at the barn. It was bigger outside than it was inside.

I went back inside and paced the interior, counting off my steps, and then I came outside and repeated the process.

The dimensions were wrong. Something was hidden inside.

And it didn't take long to find. To the left as I went back in was an empty stable. I ran my fingers around the wood of its far wall and quickly located an eyebolt and heavy iron ring. I twisted and tugged and something went *click*, and I was able to swing the door open. Inside was a room with some boxes and a low table.

A faint light flickered from overhead, and I looked up to see a wire running from the fixture down to a car battery. A light that automatically came on whenever the door was opened. How convenient. The wooden table was built right up against the wall, and an old kitchen chair was slid underneath. On the wall were thumb-tacked photos, old black-and-white pictures that were curling at the edges, of Air Force aircraft: KC-135 and KC-10 tankers, and B-47 and B-52 bombers.

Squatting in the middle of the table was a dusty shortwave radio and receiver, about twenty or thirty years old, it looked like. Beside it was a desk calendar from 1979. Next to that was a small collection of books, cheap drugstore paperbacks. I opened one and saw rows of numbers, line after line. There were a few books in Russian, the Cyrillic writing looking odd in this place. There was also a small leatherbound note-book, which I scanned. The first brief entry was dated to 1959 and the last to 1981. The hand-writing was in Cyrillic, tight and nearly illegible.

Maybe it was the dust or the flickering light, but a headache, a powerful one, started throbbing at the base of my skull. To the left, leaning against the wall, was a large pack frame with webbed straps that looked as if it were designed to carry a heavy load, and next to the frame were four wooden boxes, about two feet deep, three feet wide and five feet long. The covers weren't nailed shut; they had fasteners that allowed the boxes to be opened quickly. I had a pretty good sense of what I would find when I opened the first box.

There, nestled in a dry and cracked Styro-foam casing, was a long dark green metal tube, with a handle about a third of the way from one end. There was also a sighting mechanism and a few other odds and ends, and a projectile with fins, about thirty inches long. More Cyrillic writing decorated the tubing.

I closed the cover.

And it was the creaking floor that saved me.

I spun on my feet, ducking my head and raising my left shoulder, as Len Molowski charged in, swinging an ax. The blade bounced off my raised shoulder, sliced into my left ear and struck the wall. Len was shouting something incompre-hensible and I backed away, tripping over the kitchen chair and falling flat on my ass on the barn floor. With a triumphant bellow, he took three steps toward me, ax raised high in the air, eyes glaring, face red, mouth twisted in anger, and by then I had frantically dug under my coat and pulled out my 9mm.

I pointed it up at him, both hands tight in the approved shooting grip, and snapped back the hammer. The clicking sound seemed to echo in the tiny room and he paused, ax in midair, the portrait of a frustrated lumberjack.

My voice was calmer than I thought pos-sible. "Right now I'm bleeding, Len, and when I'm bleeding, I tend to get upset, and when I'm upset, my trigger finger gets shaky. So toss the ax out into the barn and I won't be upset any-more. Understand?"

He stood there for just a moment, puffing and breathing hard, face still red. Then he tossed the ax, where it clanged off the John Deere tractor, and said, "You're trespassing. You're on my prop-erty. You get the hell off before I call the cops."

"Sure," I said. "Sounds like a good idea. And when you tell them about the trespasser in your barn, I'll tell them about the Soviet mili-tary officer named Leonid Malenkov, who owns said barn with surface-to-air missiles and other delights, and who's been in this country illegally for about forty years. Care to guess who'd they be more interested in?"

His eyes flickered to me and then to the ax, and I knew he was regretting having tossed it. Then he collapsed. His face whitened, his shoul-ders slumped, and he nodded, a sharp little motion.

"So, you've come," he said. "CIA? FBI? What is your name? What do you want?"

I motioned to the kitchen chair. "The name is Owen. I want you to sit down on that chair. And then we'll talk. And please don't insult me by thinking I work for either of those agencies. Right now I'm an independent contractor who's feeling particularly ornery."

A couple of minutes later, I had sloppily tied my handkerchief to my left ear, which was throbbing and hurt like hell but offered the advantage of allowing me to focus my mind. Len sat in the chair, thick hands folded on his lap. I sat on the table next to the radio, gently swinging my legs beneath me as I kept my 9mm pointed in his direction.

"Bomber gap, right?" I asked.

He looked at me, brow furrowed, eyes unblinking. "I don't know what you mean."

"Look, this will go a hell of a lot easier if we don't play games, Len. I know your background, your real name." I waved my pistol in the general direction of the hill I had climbed earlier. "You've got half a dozen handheld surface-to-air missiles—they look like an experimental version of the SA-7 Grail, right? And you're living next door to a Strategic Air Command base, supposedly chock-full of nuclear-armed B-52 bombers, just waiting for the word to take off and head up over the Arctic Circle and incinerate your motherland."

I waggled the pistol back and forth.

"Deep cover mission, right? You and probably a couple of dozen comrades, you took up residence near Air Force bases in the US, maybe even Britain and Turkey and other places. You wait for the word, and when the word comes, and when those B-52s are rolling down those runways during an alert, you're ready for them. A couple of surface-to-air missiles later, you've got flaming B-52 wreckage everywhere. You and your comrades have taken care of the situation, right here in the enemy's backyard."

Len was quiet, but his head moved just a bit, as if he were nodding. "Bomber gap," I said. "Back in the fifties and early sixties, the US thought there was a bomber gap, that you folks had more and better bombers than we did. And you know what? There was a bomber gap, but on the other side. We had bigger and better bombers, and your leaders, they must have been scared. They must have looked for something to tip the balance in their favor. Something quick and dirty and cheap. And they came up with you, am I right?"

A quick, almost embarrassed nod, and then he talked rapidly, like he was finally glad to tell someone of what he had done. "Yes. We were young, committed, all volunteers. We were told it would be a long, hazardous mission. But we did what we had to do. You had us ringed with bases, your NATO, your missiles. Your generals boasted of destroying us in a fortnight."

He folded his arms and stared at the far wall. "We were sworn to secrecy and taken to a remote area in Soviet Asia, near Alma-Ata. We were trained and retrained on how to fire our missiles. We fired them in the air at first, and then at drones, and then . . ."

He looked up at me. "Hard to say now, even years later. Last, we fired them at aircraft piloted by real pilots. American pilots, captured during the Korean War a few years earlier. They were told that if they could fly these jets and survive, that they could go home."

A shrug. "None did, of course."

I touched the bloody handkerchief on my ear. "Of course. And so you were sent here, to wait. And wait some more. What was that like?"

"I lived as a Maine farmer, every day hating this place and its people. Bah. No culture, no sense of family, no real life. Just scratch a living out of this poor dirt and screw your neighbors."

"Why didn't you go home?"

"Home," he said, twisting his face as if the word itself was sour. "First, I have no money for such a trip." He looked up at me, fists clenched. "And what kind of home awaits me? The stupid bastards! They gave it all up. All of it! And without a fight."

"Miss the old Soviet Union, do you?" I asked.

Len glared at me. "What do you think, you fool? At one time we were the mightiest empire in the world. We started with nothing, nothing at all. A backward peasant country dismembered by war, and in less than a decade, we were making you and your allies tremble. We meant something. We were powerful, we strode across the world stage, and now . . ." He nearly spat out the words. "Then we gave it all up, and for what? We have a drunken clown as a president. We have whores in Red Square and the Mafia ruling our cities, and that is what we have as we leave this century."

I looked around at the old gear and the radio and said, "How long since you've had contact from home? Five years? Ten?"

A shrug. "That sounds about right."

"In case you haven't noticed, your target air base has been closed for some years now," I said. "And the country you worked for doesn't even exist. There are ways of getting money. Why in hell didn't you pack it up and leave?"

He folded his arms, jutted out his jaw.

"Because I am a Soviet soldier. I follow my orders. And my orders are to stay here and keep watch on this base. I cannot predict the future. The old Communists may come back into power. This air base may be used again by your Air Force. I am not a coward, and I do not shirk my duty. I stay here and follow my orders."

I shook my head. "You know, there's a guy I just met that you should talk with. You two would probably get along. Old soldiers from old empires, still fighting in the middle of the wreckage and debris."

"And you, you are not an old soldier?"

"At one time I was, but things have changed."

"Then why are you here? To arrest me? Bring me back to your superiors?"

I lowered my pistol, aimed in his direction. "You see, that's the problem. I was sent here to kill you."

And with that, I pulled the trigger of the 9mm twice.

Back at home and exhausted after my nights and days in the Maine woods, I slept late. After I unloaded the new clothing and toys I had bought up on my way to Cardiff, I went to my little upstairs office and my computer, and, remembering certain things that Eric had taught me, did a little research in the wild reaches of the world wide web.

Mr. Smith was as good as his word and arrived the next day. I watched from my upstairs office, flanked by my new toys, as the dark blue LTD bumped up the dirt driveway, and the two men started walking to the house. Old master and new master. They weren't very different.

I waited for the knock on the door before I wrapped some things up and went down to the kitchen. Special Agent Cameron and Mr. Smith stood at the door, the FBI man looking like he was on his way to the dentist, the government man with a large grin on his face.

"Am I being graced with both of you today?" I asked.

Cameron said, "I'll wait on the steps."

He sat down gingerly on the stone steps to my house as Smith came into the kitchen. We sat at the table and I said, "Later this morning someone's coming to pump out my septic tank, and I'd rather spend the time looking into my septic tank than at you, Mr. Smith, so let's make this quick."

He smiled, self-satisfied. "You did well. Very good."

I made a show of looking surprised.

"Surveillance. You guys were watching me."

A happy nod. "That we were."

"Your folks were good. Didn't notice a thing."

"They're the best."

"And what did they notice?" I asked.

Smith leaned back in the kitchen chair, the old wood groaning under the pressure. "They saw you conduct yourself well, performing a surveillance of the property for three days. They saw the target return early, and they heard two gunshots. They then saw you back up the target's pickup truck to the barn, stuff him in an old feed bag in the rear of the truck and then drive out at about midnight. On a bridge spanning the Queebunk River, you dumped your load, returned to the property. Then you left. Our team moved in, checked the bullet holes in the wall and the blood on the floor. We also found the evidence of the target's connection to Soviet military intelligence. Like I said, nicely done. There was even a typewritten note for the mailman, asking him to take care of the dog. You're an oldie and a softie, Owen."

I kept my hands steady on top of the table.

"So I did a good job for you and your government friends, killing an old man who's no longer a threat to this country?"

The chair came down with a *thunk*.

"Owen, in our little agency, we decide who's a threat or not. And then we decide what to do. And in this case, you did exactly as we asked by killing that old man. Very good."

"Really?" I asked.

"Not bad at all. In fact, we may extend our little agreement with you, have you perform a few other . . . unusual tasks."

My voice was flat. "In other words, you want to hire a killer."

"If you want to be blunt."

I looked down at the table, slowly shook my head. "Sorry. I'm not feeling well, and I have to go to the bathroom." I looked up and said, "Being retired and all, sometimes your body betrays you."

He waved a hand in the air. "Sure. You run along. We'll talk in a few minutes."

I got up from the kitchen table and went upstairs. Ten minutes later, I flushed the toilet and went to the head of the stairs. "Smith!" I called down. "Come up here for a moment, will you?"

I went into my office and was rummaging around in the closet as he came in and looked at my bookshelves and my humble computer, humming along on my desk. I came out of the closet with my 9mm and in one snap-quick motion, I inserted the barrel into his left ear.

"Hey!" he said, hands raised. With my free hand, I put a finger to my lips.

"Shush," I said. "Come over here and sit down. That's right, in front of the computer."

We moved slowly and I tried to keep everything focused, for I could feel something from him, a coiled sense of energy like a rattlesnake ready to strike. I said, "In less than five minutes, Smith, you'll be free to go, but if you try anything sneaky, anything at all, I'll blow your damn head off. Understand?"

"You'd be in a world of hurt," he said, no longer smiling.

"Not really," I said. "I don't think Special Agent Cameron would miss you that much, and in this county, I would only have to explain to the police and my neighbors and a couple of lawyers how I came to shoot a trespasser in my house. Perhaps I'd get a stretch, but in less than a month everything would be back to normal again, except that salesmen wouldn't dare come down that driveway. Have a seat."

He did, settling himself heavily into the chair. I pushed the pistol into his ear just a little more for emphasis, and I said, "Take hold of the mouse, and double-click on that little icon in the upper left-hand column."

Smith did, and through the connection of the pistol against his head, I felt his body tense up. "What the hell is this?" he demanded, his voice a step above a strained whisper.

"Oh, I'm quite proud of it," I said.

"This is my very first webpage. See the nice headline, about a government conspiracy to murder old Soviets? Pretty catchy, don't you think? And right below that are half a dozen little thumbnail pictures of you, Smith, as you came up to my house a while ago. Digital cameras are amazing, aren't they? You can process and download pictures instantly. And you'd be surprised at what you can do with a microphone, some long wire and a cassette recorder. See those little speaker icons on the bottom? Double-click on the left one, why don't you."

His hand moved grudgingly and after the little snap-snap of the mouse came Smith's voice, coming from my computer's twin speakers. "Owen, in our little agency, we decide who's a threat or not. And then we decide what to do. And in this case, you did exactly as we asked by killing that old man. Very good."

I took a deep breath, feeling that intoxicating rush of putting everything on the line against a dangerous foe. "To repeat something you said, first time we met, the clock is running. You don't have any time for arguing. This page is up and active. I've posted messages to a dozen Internet discussion groups, inviting them to check out my webpage. And every second you argue, every second you try to wiggle out of what's going on, that means dozens and hundreds and thousands of visitors are going to see your lovely face and hear your thoughtful words. Think your bosses will be impressed next time they do your employee evaluation?"

"What do you want?" he asked, and as his shoulders sagged, I knew I had won.

"I close down the webpage, and you leave here and never come back, and none of your friends ever bother me again. Agreed?"

"Agreed," he said with about as much enthusiasm as a man agreeing to have a toenail removed with a chisel.

"Oh," I said. "One more thing. Stop bothering Special Agent Cameron. He's no friend of mine, but I'm used to him."

I pulled the pistol out of his ear and stepped back. He stood up, his face mottled red, his fists clenched. "Agreed."

I went over to the computer, double-clicked that, downloaded this, and in a moment the screen was blank.

Smith said, "You bastard."

I smiled. "That's the nicest thing that you've ever said to me."

Outside, as Smith stomped his way over to the parked LTD, I said to Cameron, "A moment of your time, Agent Cameron."

He looked over at me with tired eyes, and for the first time since he had first come to check up on me, I felt sorry for him.

"Yes? What do you want?"

What I wanted was to sit him down in my kitchen and talk to him, to find out what he saw in his mind's eye, his memory of that awful time in Waco and what happened that caused the torching of scores of people, setting off fuses that killed hundreds of people more, and to find out how he made it through, day after day.

But I said, "You owe me."

A slow nod. "You may be right. What do you have in mind?"

I told him. He thought about it for a moment, cocked his head.

"You got a deal," he said.

The LTD's horn blew twice as Smith leaned over and hammered the steering wheel, and Cameron managed a wan smile as he walked away.

"I don't envy you the ride back," I called out.

"Actually, I'm looking forward to it," he said.

Two days later I was driving north, Miriam at my side, holding my hand. She said, "I know Eric's big enough to hold down the store and close it up by himself tonight, but damn it, I don't like being kept in the dark like this."

"In a few minutes, all will be revealed," I said, driving easily with one hand. "I have a secret plan, m'dear."

"You do?" she asked, eyes a touch playful. "And what's that?"

I squeezed her hand. "If I told you, it wouldn't be a secret, now, would it."

She shook her head, muttered "you" and looked out the window.

But she didn't take her hand away. After a while of driving, I turned right into the parking area of a small airport. The familiar sign said FEARLESS FERN'S FLYING SERVICE. She looked over at me, surprised. "What are we doing here?"

"You'll see soon enough," I said.

We got out of my truck and I grabbed her hand again as we walked around a small hangar. A Cessna was waiting, engine grumbling, propeller turning, and a bearded man standing under the wing nodded at me and I nodded back. Miriam tried to say something, but I pretended the noise of the engine was too loud. A few minutes later, seated in the rear and with earphones on and seat belts fastened, we were in the air, the bearded man piloting.

"Owen," she said to me, her voice static-filled over the intercom system. "What's this all about?"

I gently reached over and grasped her hand. "It means a number of things. It means you and

I are going to Portland tonight, for dinner and to see a musical. We'll also be spending the night at a beautiful bed-and-breakfast near the harbor."

And savoring the new agreement I had with Cameron, I added, "Why don't we plan on getting away at least once every month? And you can name the place."

She nodded, blinked hard a few times and then looked out the side window. She held my hand all the way until we landed.

Some nights later I was in my pickup, engine idling. Next to me, a small rucksack in his lap, sat Len Molowski—or Leonid Malenkov, if you prefer.

"My ears are still ringing from when you shot at me," he said, looking out across at the barn where he had lived in the upstairs loft for the better part of a week.

"You're a farmer. Ever hear the proverb of how a farmer gets a mule to pay attention?"

Even in the darkened truck cab, I could tell that he was grinning. "Yes, I have. You strike him over the head with a wooden plank."

"So consider those shots two whacks over the head, Len. I had to make you understand that you'd been noticed, and that the next guy to come to your farm wouldn't be as thoughtful or as charming as I was. Frankly, all that talk about being a good Soviet soldier was a bit boring."

The man sighed. "Perhaps you are right. But after decades of keeping such a secret, I had to talk and talk, and I had to convince you and myself that what I did was right. I had to know that these years had a purpose. That they were not a waste."

"Did it work?"

Another sigh. "No, I do not think so. When you spread your blood on the floor, told me to play dead so you could put me in the truck in a feed bag, and when you dumped your camping gear in another feed bag and threw it into

the river, I was humiliated. A man who was supposed to be my enemy was trying to help me. Why did you do that?"

I rubbed at the steering wheel. "It was a long war, the Cold War. There had to be an end to it, the last two old soldiers coming to an understanding. It just made sense. That's all I can say."

I reached into my coat pocket, pulled out a thick envelope and passed it over. "Here. Inside's a goodly amount of cash. Pay me back whenever you can. About a half mile down this road is the center of town. There's a Greyhound bus station, bus leaves in an hour to Portland. From there . . . well, you can go anywhere you want. But if I were you, I might head to New York City. Go to a place called Brighton Beach. There's a lot of Russian emigres who live there. You might find a way to get home if you ask the right people."

"This money, this is charity, and I cannot—"

"Oh, shut up. You're still a marked man, and it's in both our interests that you get the hell out of here. All right? Now, get. Before you miss the bus."

Len waited for a moment, and then the envelope rustled as he packed it into his rucksack. He held out his hand to me. "I never forget. *Do svidaniya.*"

"*Do svidaniya* to you, too."

He got out of the truck, a stranger in an odd land, and I watched him as he walked down the road, rucksack on his back. I thought about what lay ahead of him. A bumpy bus ride to Portland. Then another long ride to New York, to a city full of strangers. Then . . . who knows. Perhaps he would try to make a living with the rest of the emigres in that crowded city. Perhaps he would go home, try to adjust to a motherland that had changed so much. It seemed inevitable that he would face poverty and loneliness, with no one to care where he went or where he stayed.

I started up my truck and headed back home.

God, how I envied him.

JAMES GRADY

AFTER GRADUATING from the University of Montana with a degree in journalism, James Grady (1949–   ), already interested in politics, attended several state conventions and then went to Washington, DC, to work on Montana senator Lee Metcalf's staff. He went on to work as a journalist, most significantly as a muckraking investigative reporter for columnist Jack Anderson for four years. While living on Capitol Hill, "the seeds of Condor got planted," he said in an interview.

The reference, of course, was to his most famous novel, *Six Days of the Condor* (1974), and the series character at the center of the iconic book and the 1975 film that was based on it, *Three Days of the Condor.* Directed by Sydney Pollack, it starred Robert Redford, Faye Dunaway, Cliff Robertson, and Max von Sydow.

Two ideas converged to give Grady the basis for the novel. His regular walking route in Washington took him past a townhouse that had a plaque in the front that sounded phony to him: American Historical Association. Having watched hundreds of noir films as a boy, he also had carried a dark thought: Suppose I returned from lunch and found that everyone in my office had been murdered? He combined the two; the entire secret division of the CIA located in a townhouse was wiped out while Condor was away on a lunch run, and the rest is essentially a chase novel when the killers realize he escaped the massacre.

Six Days of the Condor, in addition to being an exceptional thriller, and a famous one, is also historically significant as the first major American work to portray the country's own security agency as the villain.

In Grady's CIA, "Condor" is a generic coded appellation that has been assigned to several different characters. The young man in his first novel does not appear to be the same fellow portrayed in the present story, who is also young but now is the protagonist in a story set more than four decades later.

"Condor in the Stacks" was originally published in the Mysterious Bookshop's *Bibliomystery* series (New York, The Mysterious Bookshop, 2015); it was first collected in *Condor: The Short Takes* (New York, Mysterious Press, 2019).

CONDOR IN THE STACKS

JAMES GRADY

"ARE YOU TROUBLE?" asked the man in a blue pinstripe suit sitting at his D.C. desk on a March Monday morning in the second decade of America's first war in Afghanistan.

"Let's hope not," answered the silver-haired man in the visitor's chair.

They faced each other in the sumptuous office of the Director of Special Projects (DOSP) for the Library of Congress (LOC). Mahogany bookcases filled the walls.

The DOSP fidgeted with a fountain pen.

Watch me stab that pen through your eye, thought his silver-haired visitor.

Such normal thoughts did not worry that silver-haired man in a blue sports jacket, a new maroon shirt, and well-worn black jeans.

What worried him was feeling trapped in a gray fog tunnel of numb.

Must be the new pill, the green pill they gave him as they drove him away from CIA headquarters, along the George Washington Parkway, and beneath the route flown by 9/11 hijackers who slammed a jetliner into the Pentagon.

The CIA car ferried him over the Potomac. Past the Lincoln Memorial. Up "the Hill" past three marble fortresses for Congress's House of Representatives where in 1975, he'd tracked a spy from U.S. ally South Korea who was working deep cover penetration of America by posing as a mere member of the messianic Korean cult that provided the last cheerleaders for impeached President Nixon.

The ivory U.S. Capitol glistened across the street from where the CIA car delivered Settlement Specialist Emma and silver-haired *him* to the Library of Congress.

Whose DOSP told him: "I don't care how 'classified' you are. Do this job and don't make trouble or you'll answer to me."

The DOSP set the fountain pen on the desk.

Put his hands on his keyboard: "What's your name?"

"Vin," said the silver-haired stranger.

"Last name?"

Vin told him that lie.

The DOSP typed it. A printer hummed out warm paper forms. He used the fountain pen to sign all the correct lines.

"Come on," he told Vin, tossing that writing technology of the previous century onto his desk. "Let's deliver you to your hole."

He marched toward the office's mahogany door.

Didn't see his pen vanish into Vin's hand.

That mahogany door swung open as the twenty-something receptionist yawned, oblivious to the pistol under her outer office visitor Emma's spring jacket. Emma stood as the door opened, confident she wouldn't need to engage her weapon but with a readiness to let it fill her hand she couldn't shake no matter how long it had been *since*.

The DOSP marched these *disruptions* from another agency through two tunnel-connected, city block–sized library castles to a yellow cinderblock walled basement and a green metal door with a keypad lock guarded by a middle-aged brown bird of a woman.

"This is Miss Doyle," the DOSP told Vin. "One of ours. She's been performing your just-assigned functions with optimal results, *plus* excelling in all her other work."

Brown bird woman told Vin: "Call me Fran."

Fran held up the plastic laminated library staff I.D. card dangling from a lanyard looped around her neck. "We'll use mine to log you in."

She swiped her I.D. card through the lock. Tapped the keypad screen.

"Now enter your password," said Fran.

"First," CIA Emma told the *library-only* staffers, "you two: please face me."

The DOSP and Fran turned their backs to the man at the green metal door.

Vin tapped six letters into the keypad. Hit ENTER.

The green metal door clicked. Let him push it open.

Pale light flooded the heavy-aired room. A government-issue standard metal desk from 1984 waited opposite the open door. An almost as ancient computer monitor filled the desk in front of a wheeled chair. Rough pine boxes big enough to hold a sleeping child were stacked against the back wall.

Like coffins.

"Empty crates in," said Fran, "full crates out. Picked up and dropped off in the hall. It's your job to get them to and from there. Use that flatbed dolly."

She computer clicked to a spreadsheet listing crates dropped off, crates filled, crates taken away: perfectly balanced numbers.

"Maintenance Operations handles data entry, except for when you log a pick-up notice. They drop off the Review Inventory outside in the hall." Fran pointed to a heap of cardboard boxes. "From closing military bases. Embassies. Other . . . secure locations.

"Unpack the books," said Fran. "Check them for security breaches. Like if some Air Force officer down in one of our missile silos forgot and stuck some secret plan in a book from the base library. Or wrote secret notes they weren't supposed to."

Vin said: "What difference would it make? You burn the books anyway."

"Pulp them," said the DOSP. "We are in compliance with recycling regulations."

CIA Emma said: "Vin, this is one of those eyeballs-needed, *gotta-do* jobs."

"Sure," said Vin. "And you'll know right where I am while I'm doing it."

The DOSP snapped: "Just do it right. The books go into crates, the crates get hauled away, the books get pulped."

Vin said: "Except for the ones we save."

"Rescuer is not in your job description," said the DOSP. "You can send no more than one cart of material *per week* to the Preserve stacks. You're only processing fiction."

The DOSP checked his watch. "A new employee folder is on your desk. We printed it out. Your computer isn't printer or Internet enabled."

"Security policy," said CIA Emma. "Not just for you."

"Really." The DOSP's smile curved like a scimitar. "Well, as your Agency insisted, this is the only library computer that accepts his access code. A bit isolating, I would think, but as long as that's *security policy* and not *personal*."

He and brown bird Fran adjourned down the underground yellow hall.

Vin stood by the steel desk.

Emma stood near the door. Scanned her Reinsertion Subject. "Are you OK?"

"That green pill wiped out whatever OK means."

"I'll report that, but *hey*: you've only been out of the Facility in Maine for—"

"The insane asylum," he interrupted. "The CIA's secret insane asylum."

"Give yourself a break. You've only been released for eleven days, and after what happened in New Jersey while they were driving you down here . . .

"Look," she said, "it's your new job, first day. Late lunch. Let's walk to one of those cafes we saw when we moved you into your house. Remember how to get home?"

"Do you have kids?"

Her stare told him *no.*

"This is like dropping your kid off for kindergarten," said Vin. "Go."

Emma said: "You set the door lock to your codename?"

"Yeah," he said. *"Condor."*

His smile was wistful: "Can't ever get away from that."

"Call you Vin, call you Condor, at least you have a name. Got my number?"

He held up his outdated flip-phone programmed by an Agency tech.

She left him alone in that subterranean cave.

Call him Vin. Call him Condor.

Ugly light. The toad of an old computer squatting on a gray steel desk. A heap of sagging cardboard boxes. The wall behind him stacked with wooden crates—*coffins.*

Thick heavy air smelled like . . . basement rot, paper, stones, old insulation, cardboard, tired metal, steam heat. A whiff of the coffins' unvarnished pine.

He rode the office chair in a spin across the room. Rumbled back in front of the desktop computer monitor glowing with the spreadsheet showing nine cases—*pinewood coffins*—nine cases delivered to this Review Center. He clicked the monitor into a dark screen that showed his reflection with seven coffins stacked behind him.

Only dust waited in the drawers on each side of the desk's well. The employee manual urged library staffers to hide in their desk wells during terrorist or psycho attacks. *Like the atom bomb doomsday drills when I was a—*

And *he remembered!* His CIA-prescribed handful of daily pills didn't work perfectly: he could *kind of* remember!

Tell no one.

He slid open the middle desk drawer. Found three paperclips and one penny.

From the side pocket of the blue sports jacket he fetched the stolen fountain pen.

Sometimes you gotta do what you do just to be you.

He stashed the stolen pen in his middle desk drawer.

Noticed the monitor's reflection of seven coffins.

WAIT.

Am I crazy?

YES was the truth but not the answer.

He turned around and counted the coffins stacked against the back wall: *Seven.*

Clicked open the computer's spreadsheet to check the inventory delivery: *Nine.*

Why are two coffins missing?

The CIA's cell phone sat on his desk.

This is your job now. No job, no freedom.

Condor put the cell phone in his shirt pocket over his heart.

Suddenly he didn't want to be there because *there* was where *they* brought him, *transporting* him like a boxcar of doomed books. He counted the coffins: *still seven.* Walked out the door, pulling it shut with a click as he switched out the light.

The wide yellow-bricked hall telescoped away into distant darkness to his left. To his right, the tunnel ran about thirty steps until it T'ed at a brick wall.

He turned left, the longest route that let him look back and see where he'd been. Floated each stepping foot out in front of him empty of weight like Victor'd taught him in the insane asylum: aesthetically correct *T'ai chi* plus a martial arts technique that foiled foot-sweeping ninjas and saved you if the floor beneath your stepping shoe vanished.

Footsteps! Walking down that intersecting tunnel.

He hurried after those sounds of someone to ask for directions.

The footsteps quickened.

Don't scare anybody: cough so they know you're here.

The footsteps ran.

Pulled Condor into running, his heart jack hammering his chest.

Go right—*no left*, twenty steps until the next juncture of tunnels.

Whirr of sliding-open doors.

Dashing around a yellow brick walled corner—

Elevator—doors *closing!* He thrust his left arm into the doors' chomp—they bounced open and tumbled him into the bright metal cage.

FIST!

Without thought, with the awareness of ten thousand practices, his right forearm met the fist's arm, not to block but to blend with that force and divert it from its target.

The fist belonged to a woman.

And in the instant she struggled to recover her *diverted* balance, the palm of Condor's left hand rocketed her up and back so she bounced off the rear wall of the elevator as those metal doors closed behind him.

The cage groaned toward the surface.

"Leave me alone!" she yelled.

"You punched me!"

His attacker glared at him through black-framed glasses. Short dark hair. A thin silver loop pierced the right corner of her lower lip. Black coat. Hands clenched at her sides, not up in an on-guard position. She had the guts to fight but not the know-how.

"You chased me in here!" she yelled. "Don't deny it! I finally caught you! Stop it! You keep watching me! Doing things!"

"I don't do things!"

"Always lurking. Hiding. Sneaking. Straightening my reading room desk. KNOCK IT OFF! Weeks you've been at this, not gonna take it next time I'll punch—"

"Weeks?" he interrupted. "I've been doing *whatever* for weeks? Here?"

The elevator jerked to a stop.

Doors behind Condor slid open.

He loomed between the glaring woman and the only way out of this cage.

The elevator doors whirred shut.

The cage rumbled upwards.

He sent his right hand inside his sports jacket and she let it go there, confirming she was no trained killer. Pulled out his Library of Congress I.D. Showed it to her.

"Activation Date is today, my first day here. I can't be the one who's been stalking you."

The elevator jerked to a stop.

The doors behind Condor slid open.

"Oh." She nodded to the open elevator doors. He backed out the cage. She followed him into a smooth walled hall as the elevator doors closed. *"Um*, sorry."

"No. You did what you could to be *not* sorry. Smart."

"Why were you chasing me?"

"I'm trying to find an exit."

"This is a way out," she said and led him through the castle. "I'm Kim."

He told her he was Vin.

"You must think I'm nuts."

"We all have our own roads through Crazytown."

She laughed at what she thought was a joke, but couldn't hold on to happy.

"I don't know what to do," said Kim. "Sometimes I think I'm imagining it all. I feel somebody watching me, but when I whirl around, nobody's there."

"Chinese martial arts say eyes have weight," Vin told her.

"I'm from Nebraska," she said. "Not China."

Kim looked at him, *really looked* at him.

"You're probably a great father." She sighed. "I miss my dad and back home, though I wouldn't want to live there."

"But why live here?"

"Are you kidding? Here I get to be part of what people can use to make things better, have better lives, be more than who they were stuck being born."

She frowned: "Why do you live here?"

"I'm not ready to die," he said. "Here or any-where."

"You're a funny guy, Vin. Not funny *ha-ha*, but not *uh-oh* funny either."

They walked past a blue-shirted cop at the metal detector arch by the entrance. The cop wore a holstered pistol of a make Vin knew he once knew.

Just past the security line waited a plastic tub beneath an earnest hand-inked sign:

OLD CELLPHONES FOR CHARITY!

Funny guy Vin pictured himself tossing the CIA's flip-phone into that plastic bin. A glance at the dozen cellphones awaiting charitable recycling told him that would be cruel: His flip-phone was so uncool ancient that all the other phones would pick on it.

Condor and *not* his daughter stepped out into March's blue sky chill.

She buttoned her black cloth coat. "Would you do me a favor? You're new, so you can't be *whoever* it is. Come by my desk in the Adams reading room around noon tomorrow. Go with me to my office. See what I'm talking about, even if it's not there."

Standing in that chilly sunshine on a Capitol Hill street, Condor heard an echo from the DOSP: "Rescuer is not in your job description."

Sometimes you gotta do what you do just to be you.

"OK," said Condor.

Kim gave him her LOC business card,

thanked him and said goodbye, walked away into the D.C. streets full of people headed some-where they seemed to want to go.

"Remember how to get home?" Emma'd said.

An eleven-minute walk past the red brick Eastern Market barn where J. Edgar Hoover worked as a delivery boy a century before. Condor strolled past stalls selling fresh fruit and aged cheese, slabs of fish and red meat, flowers. He found himself in line at the market grill, got a crab cake sandwich and a lemonade, ate at one of the tall tables and watched the flow of mid-day shoppers, stay-home parents and nannies, twenty-somethings who worked freelance laptop gigs to pay for bananas and butchered chickens.

Where he lived was a blue brick townhouse on Eleventh Street, N.E., a narrow five rooms, one-and-a-half baths rental. No one ambushed him when he stepped into the living room. No one had broken the dental floss he'd strung across the stairs leading up to the bed he surfed in dreams. A flat-screen TV reflected him as he plopped on the couch, caught his breath in this new life where nothing, *nothing* was wrong.

At 8:57 the next morning, he snapped on the lights in his work cave.

Counted the coffins: *Seven.*

Checked the computer's spreadsheet: *Nine.*

Crazy or not, that's still the count.

Sometimes crazy is the way to go.

Or so he told himself when he'd flushed the green pills down the blue townhouse's toilet at dawn. Emma'd report his adverse reaction, so probably there'd be no Code Two Alert when that medication wasn't seen in Condor's next urine test.

His thirteen other pills lined up on his kitchen counter like soldiers.

Condor held his cooking knife that looked like the legend Jim Bowie carried at the Alamo. Felt himself drop into a deep stance, his arms curving in front of his chest. The Bowie knife twirled until the spine of the blade pressed against the inside of his right forearm and the razor-sharp cutting edge leered out like he'd been taught decades before by a Navy SEAL in a Lower East Side of Manhattan black site.

Condor exhaled into his here-and-now, used the knife to shave powder off five pills prescribed to protect him from himself, from seeing or feeling or thinking that isn't part of officially approved *sensible* reality. Told himself that a shade of unapproved crazy might be the smart way to go, because standing in his office cave on the second morning of work, it didn't make sense that the approved coffin count was (still) off by two.

He muscled a cardboard box full of books onto a waist-high, brown metal cart, rolled the burdened cart over to the seven empty coffins and lost his virginity.

His very first one. The first book he pulled from that box bulging with books recycled from a closed U.S. air base near a city once decimated by Nazi purification squads and then shattered by Allied bombers. The first volume whose fate he decided: *The List of Adrian Messenger* by Philip MacDonald.

Frank Sinatra played a gypsy in the black and white movie.

That had to make it worth saving, *right*? He leafed through the novel. Noted only official stamps on the pages. Put that volume on the cart for the Preserve stacks.

Book number two was even easier to save: a ragged paperback. Blue ink cursive scrawl from a reader on the title page: *You never know where you really are.* That didn't seem like a code and wasn't a secret, so no security breach. The book was Kurt Vonnegut's *Slaughterhouse Five.* Sure, gotta save that on the cart.

And so it went. He found a bathroom outside his cave, a trip he would have made more often if he'd also found coffee. Books he pulled out of shipping boxes got shaken, flipped through and skimmed until the Preserve cart could hold no more.

All seven pine wood crates were still empty, coffins waiting for their dead.

Can't meet Kim without dooming— *recycling*—at least one book.

The black plastic bag yielded a hefty novel by an author who'd gone to a famous graduate school MFA program and been swooned over by critics. That book had bored Condor. He plunked it into a blond pine coffin. Told himself he was just doing his job.

Got out of there.

Stood in the yellow cinderblock hall outside his locked office.

If I were a spy, I'd have maps in my cell phone. I'd have a Plan with a Fallback Plan and some Get Out of Dodge *go-to.* If I were a spy, an agent, an operative, somebody's asset, my activation would matter to someone who cared about me, someone besides the *targets* and the *rip-you-ups* and the *oppo*(sition), none of whom should know I'm real and alive and *on them.* If I were still a spy, I'd have a mission.

Feels like 40 years since I was just me.

Terrifying.

No wonder I'm crazy.

Outside where it would rain, the three castles of the Library of Congress rose across open streets from Congress's Capitol dome and the pillars of the Supreme Court because knowledge is clearly vital to how we create laws and dispense justice.

And *yes*, the swooping art deco John Adams castle where Condor worked is magnificent with murals and bronze doors and owls as art everywhere.

And *true*, the high-tech concert hall James Madison LOC castle that looms across the street from the oldest fortress of the House of Representatives once barely kept its expensively-customized-for-LOC-use edifice out of the grasp of turf-hungry Congressmen who tried to disguise their grab for office space as *fiscally responsible.*

But *really*, the gem of the LOC empire with its half-billion-dollar global budget and 3,201 employees is the LOC's Thomas Jefferson building: gray marble columns rising hundreds of feet into the air to where its green metal cupola holds the "Torch of Learning" copper statue and cups a mosaic sky over the castle full of grand marble staircases, wondrous murals and paintings, golden gilt and dark wood, chandeliers, a main reading room as glorious as a cathedral, and everywhere, *everywhere*, books, the words of men and women written on the ephemera of dead trees.

Down in the castle's sub-basement of yellow tunnels, Condor walked beneath pipes and electrical conduits and wires, past locked doors and lockers. He rode the first elevator he found up until the steel cage dinged and left him in a cavern of stacks—row after row of shelves stuffed with books, books in boxes in the aisles, books everywhere.

He drifted through the musty stacks, books brushing the backs of both his hands, his eyes blurred by the lines of volumes, each with a number, each with a name, an identity, a purpose. He circled around one set of stacks and saw *him* standing there.

Tom Joad. Battered hat, sun-baked lean Okie face, shirt missing a button, stained pants, scruffy shoes covered with the sweat dust of decades.

"Where you been?" whispered Condor.

"Been looking. How 'bout you?"

"Been trying," said Condor.

A black woman wearing a swirl of color blouse under a blue LOC smock stepped into the aisle where she saw only Condor and said: "Were you talking to me?"

The silver-haired man smiled something away. "Guess I was talking to myself."

"Sugar," she said, "everybody talks to somebody."

He walked off like he knew what he was doing and where he was going, saw a door at the end of another aisle of books, stepped through it—

BAM!

Collision hits Condor's thighs, *heavy* runs over *hurts* his toes—*Cart!*

A metal steel cart loaded with books slams into Condor as it's being pushed by . . .

Brown bird Fran. Pushing a metal cart covered by a blue LOC smock.

"Oh, my Lord, I'm so sorry!" Fran hovered as Condor winced. "I didn't see you there! I didn't expect anybody!"

She blinked back to her balance, sank back to her core. Her eyes drilled his chest.

"*Vin*, isn't it? Why aren't you wearing your I.D.? LOC policy requires visible issued I.D. The DOSP will not be pleased."

She leaned closer: "I won't tell him we saw each other if you won't."

"Sure," he said. *And thus is a conspiracy born.*

"That's better." She straightened the blue smock over the books it covered on her cart. "You should wear it anyway. If you're showing your I.D., you can go anywhere and do darn near anything. For your job, I mean."

He fished his I.D. from inside the *blah* blue sports jacket issued him by a CIA *dust master* who costumed America's spies. Asked her how to get to the reading room.

"Oh, my: you're a floor too high. There's a gallery above that reading room back the direction I came. You can't miss it." She tried to hook him with a smile. "How soon will you out-process the next shipment of inventory?"

"You mean pack books in the coffins to be pulped? It's only my second day."

"Oh, dear. You really must keep on schedule and up to speed. There are needs to be met. The DOSP has expectations."

"Must be nice," said Condor. "Having expectations."

He thanked her and headed the direction she said she'd come.

Went through the door labeled "Gallery."

That door opened to a row of taller-than-him bookshelves he followed to one of six narrow slots for human passage to the guardrail circling above the reading room with its quaint twentieth-century card catalog and research desks.

Nice spot for recon. Sneak down any slot. Charlie Sugar (Counter Surveillance) won't know which slot you'll use. Good optics. Target needs to crank his or her head to look up. Odds are, you spot that move in time to fade the half-step back to not be there.

Condor moved closer to the balcony guardrail. His view widened with each step.

Kim sat at a research desk taking notes with an iPad as she studied a tan book published before a man in goggles flew at Kitty Hawk. Kim wore a red cardigan sweater. Black glasses. Silver lip loop. A glow of purpose and focus. She raised her head to—

Condor eased back to where he could not see her and thus she did not see him. He walked behind bookshelves, found the top of a spiral steel staircase.

You gotta love a spiral steel staircase.

That steel rail slid through his hand as the world he saw turned around the axis of his spiraling descent. The reading room. Researchers at desks. Kim bent over her work. A street op named Quiller from a novel Condor'd saved loitered by the card catalog with a bespectacled mole hunter named Smiley. The stairs spiraled Condor toward a mural, circled him around, but those two Brits were gone when he stepped off the last stair.

Kim urged him close: "He's here! I just felt him watching me!"

"That was me."

"Are you sure?"

"Two tactical choices," he answered. Her anxious face acquired a new curiosity at this silver-haired man's choice of words. "Maintain status or initiate change."

"Change how?"

Condor felt the cool sun of Kabul envelop him, an outdoor marketplace cafe where what was supposed to happen hadn't. Said: "We could move."

Kim led him into the depths of the Adams building and a snack bar nook with vending machines, a service counter, a bowl of apples. They bought coffee in giant paper cups with snapped-on lids, sat where they could both watch the open doorway.

"Oh, my God," whispered Kim. "That could be him!"

Walking into the snack bar came a man older and a whiff shorter than her, a stocky man with shaggy brown hair and a mustache, a sports jacket, and shined shoes.

"I don't know his name," whispered Kim. "I think he tried to ask me out once! And maybe he goes out of his way to walk past where I am! When I feel eyes on me, he's not there, nobody is, but it could be, *it must be* him."

The counterwoman poured hot coffee into a white paper cup for Mustache Man. He sat at an empty table facing the yogurt display case. At the angle he chose, the refrigerated case's glass door reflected blurred images of Condor and Kim.

Life or luck or tradecraft?

Condor told her: "Walk out. Go to your office. Wait for my call."

"What if something happens?"

"Something always happens. Don't look back."

Kim marched out of the snack nook.

Mustache Man didn't follow her.

Call him Vin. Call him Condor.

He thumb-popped the plastic lid loose on his cup of hot coffee.

Slowed time as he inhaled from his heels. Exhaled a fine line. Unfolded his legs to rise away from the table without a sound, without his chair scooting on the tiled floor.

Condor carried the loose-lid cup of hot coffee out in front of him like a pistol.

Mustache Man was *five*, *four*, *three* steps away, his head bent over a book.

Condor "lurched"—jostled the coffee cup he held.

The loose lid popped off the cup. Hot coffee flew out to splash Mustache Man.

He and the stranger who splashed him yelped like startled dogs. Mustache Man jumped to his feet, reached to help *some older gentleman* who'd obviously tripped.

"Are you all right?" said Mustache Man as the silver-haired stranger stood steady with his right hand *lightly* resting on the ribs over Mustache Man's startled heart.

"I'm sorry!" lied Condor.

"*No, no*: it was probably my fault."

Vin blinked: "Just sitting there and it was your fault?"

"I probably moved and threw you off or something."

"Or something." The man's face matched the I.D. card dangling around his neck.

Mustache Man used a napkin to sponge dark splotches on his book. "It's OK. It's mine, not the library's."

"You bring your own book to where you can get any book in the world?"

"I don't want to bother Circulation."

Vin turned the book so he could read the title.

Mustache Man let this total stranger take such control without a blink, said: "Li Po is my absolute favorite Chinese poet."

"I wonder if they read him in Nebraska."

Now came a blink: "Why Nebraska?"

"Why not?" said Condor.

The other man shrugged. "I'm from Missouri."

"There are two kinds of people," said Condor. "Those who want to tell you their story and those who never will."

"Really?"

"No," said Vin. "We're all our own kind. I didn't get your name."

"I'm Rich Bechtel."

Condor told Mustache Man/Rich Bechtel—same name on his I.D.—that he was new, didn't know the way back to his office.

"Let me show you," volunteered Rich, right on cue.

They went outside the snack nook where long corridors ran left and right.

"Either way," Rich told the silver-haired man whose name he still hadn't asked.

"Your choice," said Condor.

"Sorry, I work at CRS." *CRS*: the *Congressional Research Service* that is and does as it's named. "I'm used to finding options, letting someone else decide."

"This is one of those times you're in charge," lied Condor.

He controlled their pace through subterranean tunnels. By the time they reached Condor's office, he knew where Rich *said* he lived, how long he'd been in Washington, that he loved biking. Loved his work, too, though as a supervisor of environmental specialists, "seeing what

they deal with can make it hard to keep your good mood."

"Is it rough on your wife and kids?" asked Condor.

"Not married. No family." He shrugged. "She said *no*."

"Does that make you mad?"

"I'm still looking, if that's what you mean. But *mad*: How would that work?"

"You tell me." He stuck out his right hand. Got a return grip with strength Rich didn't try to prove. "My name is Vin. Just in case, could I have one of your cards?"

That card went into Vin's shirt pocket to nestle beside Kim's that Condor fished out as soon as he was inside his soundproof cave. He cellphoned her office.

Heard the click of *answered call*. No human voice.

Said: "This is—"

"Please!" Kim's voice: "Please, *please* come here, see what—*Help me!*"

Condor snapped the old phone shut. Grabbed the building map off his desk.

Couldn't help himself: counted the stacked coffins.

Still seven where there should be nine.

Time compressed. Blurred. Rushing through tunnels and hallways. Stairs. An elevator. Her office in a corridor of research lairs. Don't try the doorknob: that'll spook her more. Should be locked anyway. His knock rattled her door's clouded glass.

Kim clacked the locks and opened the door, reached to pull him in but grabbed only air as he slid past, put his back against the wall while he scanned her office.

No ambusher. Window too small for any ninja. Posters on the walls: a National Gallery print of French countryside, a Smithsonian photo of blue globed earth, a full-face wispy color portrait of Marilyn Monroe with a crimson lipped smile and honesty in her eyes. Kim's computer glowed. A framed black-and-white photo of a Marine patrolling some jungle stood on her desk: *Father? Grandfather? Vietnam?*

"Thought I was safe," babbled Kim. "Everything cool, you out there dealing with it and I unlocked the office door. It was locked—swear it was locked! Looked around and . . . My middle desk drawer was open. Just a smidge."

Kim's white finger aimed like a lance at a now wide-open desk drawer.

Where inside on its flat-bottomed wood, Condor saw:

HARLOT

Red lipstick smeared, gouged-out letters in a scrawl bigger than his hand.

Kim whispered: "How did he get in here? Do that? Weren't you with him?"

"Not before. And you weren't here then either."

A tube of lipstick lay in the desk drawer near the graffiti, fake gold metal polished and showing no fingerprints. Condor pointed to the tube: "Yours?"

She looked straight into his eyes. "Who I am sometimes wears lipstick."

"So he didn't bring it and he didn't take it. But that's not what matters."

"Look under the lipstick," he said. "Carved letters. Library rules don't let anybody bring in a knife, so somebody who does is serious about his blade."

"I'm going to throw up."

But she didn't.

"Call the cops," said Condor.

"And tell them what? Somebody I don't know, can't be sure it's him, he somehow got into my locked office and . . . and did *that*? They'll think I'm crazy!"

"Could be worse. Call the cops."

"OK, they'll come, they'll care, they'll keep an eye on me until there's no more nothing they'll have the time to see and they'll go and *then what*? Then more of this?"

She shook her head. "I'm an analytic researcher. That's what I do. First we need to find *more* to verify what we say for the cops to show we're not crazy!"

"First call the cops. Then worry about verifying. Crazy doesn't mean wrong."

"What else you got?" Her look scanned his scars.

"Grab what you need," he said. "Work where I found you, the reading room, in public, not alone. I don't know about afterwards when you go home."

"Nothing's ever . . . felt wrong there. Plus I've got a roommate."

"So did the heroine in *Terminator*."

"Life isn't science fiction."

"Really?" Condor rapped his knuckles on her computer monitor.

Made her take cell phone pictures of HARLOT and email them to herself before he shut that desk drawer. "Got a boyfriend or husband or any kind of ex?"

"The last somebody I had was in San Francisco and he dumped me. No husband, ever. Probably won't be. Evidently all I attract are psycho creeps. Or maybe that's all that's out there. Why can't I find a nice guy who doesn't know that's special?"

"Do you like mustaches?"

"Hey, I wear a lip ring."

"Have you ever mentioned mustaches to anybody?"

She shook her head *no*.

"Then maybe he's had it for a long time."

Kim shuddered.

He escorted her back to the same reading room desk.

Left her there where her fellow LOC employees could hear her scream.

Took the spiral steel staircase up and went out the Gallery door, walked back the way he first came, through the stacks, row after row of shelved books. Down one aisle, he spotted a shamus wearing a Dashiell Hammett trenchcoat and looking like Humphrey Bogart before he knew his dream was Lauren Bacall.

Condor called out: "What's my move?"

The shamus gave him the long look. Said: "You got a job, you do a job."

His job.

Back in the sub-basement cave. Alone with the *still only seven* coffins. Alone with the cart piled high with the few books he could save from *the DOSP's expectations.*

Anger gripped him. Frenzy. Cramming books into the coffins. Filling all seven pine crates, plopping them on the dolly, wheeling it out of his office, stacking the coffins against the yellow cinderblock wall, pushing the empty dolly back into his cave, logging PICK UP in the computer, snapping off the lights, locking the door, home before five with a day's job done and the shakes of not knowing what to do.

Shakes that had him walking back to work before dawn. His I.D. got him inside past cops and metal detectors, down the elevator to the subterranean glow around the corner from his office and into the unexpected rumble of rolling wheels.

Condor hurried around the corner . . .

. . . and coming towards him was a dolly of pinewood coffins pushed by a barbell-muscled man with military short blond hair and a narrow shaved face. The blond muscle man wore an I.D. lanyard and had deep blue eyes.

"Wait!" yelled Condor.

The coffin-heavy dolly shuddered to a jerked stop.

"What are you doing?" said Condor. "These are my coffins—crates."

Couldn't stop himself from whispering: *"Nine."*

Looked down the hall to where yesterday he'd stacked *seven* coffins.

The barbell blond said: "You must be the new guy. I heard you were weird."

"My name is Vin, and you're . . . ?"

The blue-eyed barbell blond said: *"Like,* Jeremy."

"Jeremy, you got it right, I'm new, but I got an idea that, *like,* helps both of us."

Rush the grift so Jeremy doesn't have time to, like, make a wrong reply.

"I screwed up, *sorry,* stuck the wrong book in a crate, so what we need to do, what *I* need to do, is take them all back in my cave, open 'em

up, and find the book that belongs on the rescue cart. Then you can take the crates away."

"I'm doing that now. That's my job. And I say *when.*"

"That's why this works out for us. Because you're who says *when.* And while I'm fixing the mistake, you go to the snack bar, get us both—I don't know about you, but I need a cup of coffee. I buy, you bring, and by then I'll be done with the crates."

"Snack bar isn't open this early. Only vending machines."

Don't say anything. Wait. Create space for the idea to fall into.

"Needing coffee is weak," said Jeremy.

"When you get to my age, weak comes easy."

Jeremy smiled. "They might have hot chocolate."

"I think they do." Vin fished the last few dollar bills from the release allowance out of his black jeans. "If they got a button for cream, push it for me, would you?"

Jeremy took the money. Disappeared down the yellow cinderblock hall.

Vin rolled the dolly into his cave. Unlatched the first coffin, found a frenzied jumble of books, one with a ripped cover so the only words left above the author's name were: ". . . LAY DYING."

Remember that, I remember that.

The second crate contained another jumble that felt familiar, all novels, some with stamps from some island, Paris Island. *Yeah, this is another one I packed, one of the seven.* So was the third crate he opened, and the fourth.

But not number five.

Neatly stacked books filled that pinewood box. Seventy or more books.

But only three titles.

Delta of Venus by Anaïs Nin. *Never read it, maybe a third of this coffin's books.*

The rest of the renegade coffin's books were editions of *The Carpetbaggers* by Harold Robbins, many with the jacket painting of a blond woman in a lush pink gown and the grip of a fur stole draped round her shoulders as some man towered behind her.

I remember it! A *roman à clef* about whacky billionaire Howard Hughes who bought Las Vegas from the Mob, but what Vin remembered most about the book was waiting until his parents were out of the house, then leafing to *those pages.*

Now, that morning in his locked cave in a basement of the Library of Congress in Washington, D.C., Vin rifled through the coffin of discarded volumes of *The Carpetbaggers* and found nothing but those books, stamped properties of public libraries from New Mexico to New Jersey, nothing hidden in them, nothing hidden under them in the pinewood crates, nothing about them that . . .

What smells?

Like a bloodhound, Vin sniffed all through that coffin of doomed novels.

Smells like . . . Almonds.

He skidded a random copy of each book across the concrete floor to under his desk and closed the lid on the coffin from which they came.

The sixth crate contained his chaos of crammed-in books, but crate number seven revealed the same precise packing as crate five, more copies of Anaïs Nin and *The Carpetbaggers,* plus copies of two other novels: *The Caretakers* that keyed more memories of furtive page turning and three copies of *Call Me Sinner* by Alan Marshall that Vin had never heard of. Plus the scent of almonds. He shut that crate. The last two coffins held books he'd sent to their doom and smelled only of pine.

Roll the dolly piled high with coffins back out to the hall.

This is what you know:

Unlike the books that filled seven of the *there-all-along* coffins, the volumes in *where'd-they-come-from* two coffins were precisely packed, alphabetically and thus systematically clustered C and D titles, and all, *well,* erotic.

And smelled like almonds.

Remember, I can't remember what that means.

Jeremy handed Condor a cup of vending machine coffee. "You find what you were looking for?"

"Yeah," said Condor, a truth full of lies.

Jeremy crumpled his chocolate-stained paper cup, tossed it on top of the crates.

"I'll come with you." Vin fell in step beside the man pushing the heavy dolly.

"You are weird. Push the button for that elevator."

A metal cage slowly carried the two men and the coffin dolly up, up.

"Do you see many weird people down here?" asked Condor.

"Some people use this way as a shortcut out to get lunch or better coffee."

Rolling wheels made the only sounds for the rest of their journey to the loading dock. Jeremy keyed his code into the dock's doors, rolled the dolly outside onto a loading dock near a parked pickup truck.

An LOC cop with a cyber tablet came over, glanced at the crates, opened one and saw the bodies of books, as specified on the manifest. He looked at Condor.

"The old guy's with me," said Jeremy.

The cop nodded, walked away.

The sky pinked. Jeremy lifted nine crates—*nine*, not *seven*—dropped them into the pickup truck's rear end cargo box for the drive to the recycling dump.

"This is as far as you go," Jeremy told the weird older guy.

Condor walked back inside through the loading dock door.

The rattling metal grate lowered its wall of steel.

Luminous hands on his black Navy SEAL watch ticked past seven A.M. Condor stalked back the way he'd come, as if retracing geography would let him remake time, go back to *when* and do it right. When he got to the stacks where he'd been lost before, down the gap between two book-packed rows, he spotted a mouse named Stuart driving a tiny motorcar away in search of the north that would lead him to true love.

Condor whispered: "Good luck, man."

Voice behind you! "Are—"

Whirl hands up and out sensing guard stacks spinning—

Woman brown clothes eyes widening—

Fran, sputtering: "I was just going to say '*Are you talking to yourself?*'"

Condor let his arms float down as he faded out of a combat stance.

"Something like that."

"Sorry to have interrupted." She smiled like a woman at a Methodist church social his mother once took him to. Or like the shaved-head, maroon-robed Buddhist nun he'd seen in Saigon after that city changed its name. "But nice to see you."

Condor frowned. "Wherever I go, there you are."

"Oh, my goodness," twittered Fran. "Doesn't that just seem so? And good for you being here now. The early bird gets the worm. Believe you me, there are worms. Worms everywhere."

Flick—a flick of motion, something—*somebody* ducking back behind a shelf in an aisle between those stacks way down where Stuart drove.

"By the way," he heard Fran say: "Good job. The DOSP will be pleased."

"What?"

"Your first clearance transfer."

"How did you know I was sending out a load of coffins?"

Her smile widened. "Must have been Jeremy."

Amidst the canyons of shelves crammed with books, Condor strained to hear creeping feet beyond the twittering brown bird of a woman.

"Just walking by his shop in the basement, door must have been open, I mean, I used to have your job working with him."

Prickling skin: Something—*someone*—hidden from their eyes in the canyons of stacks moved the air.

"Vin, are you feeling OK?"

"'Just distracted."

"Ah." Fran marched away, exited through a door alone.

Alone, Condor telepathed to whoever hid in this cavern of canyons made by rows of shelved books. Just you and me now. All alone.

Somewhere waited a knife.

Walk between close walls of bookshelves crammed with volumes of transcribed RAF radio transmissions, 1939–1941. He could hear the call signs, airmen's chatter, planes' throbbing engines, bombs, and the clattering machine guns of yesterday.

Today is what you got. And what's got you.

What got him, he never knew—a sound, a tingling, a corner-of-his-eye motion, *whatever*: he whirled left to that wall of shelved books, slammed his palms against half a dozen volumes so they shot back off their shelf and knocked away the books shelved in the next aisle, a gap blasted in walls of books through which he saw . . .

Mustached and eyes startled wide Rich Bechtel.

"Oops!" yelled Condor. "Guess I stumbled *again*."

He flowed around the shelf, a combat ballet swooped into the aisle where Rich—suit, tie, mustache—stood by a jumble of pushed-to-the-floor books.

Condor smiled: "Surprised to see me here?"

"Surprised, why . . . ?"

"Yes, *why* are you here?"

The mustached man shrugged. "It's a cut-through to go get good coffee."

"Did you cut through past the balcony of the reading room?"

"Well, sure, that's a door you can take."

"So why were you hiding back here?" said Condor.

Rich shrugged. "I was avoiding *call me* Fran."

Confession without challenge: *As if we were friends*, thought Condor.

"A while back," continued Rich, "I was over here in Adams working on a Congressional study of public policy management approaches. One of the books I had on my desk was a rare early translation of the *Dao De Jing*, you know, the . . ."

"The Chinese Machiavelli."

"More than that, but *yes*, a *how power works* manual that Ronald Reagan quoted. Fran mistook it for something like the Koran. She walked by my research desk, spotted the title and went off on me about how dare I foster such thought. Things got out of hand. She might have pushed my books off the desk, could have been an accident, but . . ."

"But what?"

"I walked away. When I see her now, I keep walking. Or try not to be seen."

Condor said: "Nobody could make up that story."

The caught man frowned. "Why would I make up any story?"

"We all make up stories. And sometimes we put real people in the stories in our heads. That can be . . . confusing."

"I'm already confused enough." Rich laughed. "What are you doing?"

"Leaving. Which way are you headed?"

Rich pointed the way Condor'd come, left with a wave and a smile.

The *chug chug chug* of a train.

One aisle over, between walls of books, railroad tracks ran through a lush green somewhere east of Eden, steel rails under a coming this way freight train and sitting huddled on top of one metal car rode troubled James Dean.

Condor left that cavern of stacks, walked to the Gallery where he could see the empty researchers' desks on the floor of the reading room below. Checked his watch. Hoped he wouldn't need to pee. Some surveillances mean no milk cartons.

What does it mean when you smell almonds?

Don't think about that. Fade into the stacks. Be part of what people never notice.

On schedule, Kim with her silver lip loop and a woman wearing a boring professional suit walked in to the reading room. The roommate left. Kim settled at her desk. He gave the countersurveillance twenty more minutes, went to his office. No coffins waited outside against the yellow wall from a delivery by Jeremy: *Watch for that.*

So Condor left his office door open.

Sank into his desk chair.

Footsteps: outside the open door in the hall, hard shoes on the concrete floor of the yellow underground tunnel. Footsteps clacking louder as they came closer, closer . . .

She glides past his open door in three firm strides, strong legs and a royal blue coat. Silver-lined dyed blond hair floats on her shoulders, lush mouth, high cheekbones. Cosmic gravity pulls his bones and then she's gone, her *click click click* of high heels turning the basement corner, maybe to the elevator and out for mid-morning coffee.

Don't write some random wondrous woman into your story.

Don't be a stalker.

But he wasn't, wouldn't, he only looked, ached to look more, had no time to think about her, about how maybe her name was Lulu, how maybe she wore musk—

Almonds.

Up from behind his desk, out the lock-it door and *gone*, up the stairs two at a time, past the guards on the door to outside, in the street, dialing *that number* with the CIA cell phone. A neutral voice answered, waltzed Condor to the hang-up. He made it into his blue townhouse, stared at his closed turquoise door for nineteen minutes until that soft knock.

Opened his door to three bullet-eyed *jacket men*.

Emma showed up an hour later, dismissed them.

Sat on a chair across from where Condor slumped on the couch.

Said: "What did you do?"

"I called the cops," answered the silver-haired man who was her responsibility.

"Your old CIA Panic Line number. Because you say you found C4 plastic explosives. But you don't know where. You just smelled it, the almond smell."

"In the Library of Congress."

"That's a lot of *where*. And C4's not as popular as it used to be."

"Still works. Big-time boom. Hell of a kill zone."

"If you know how to get it or make it and what you're doing."

"You ever hear of this thing called the Internet?"

She threw him a change up: "Tell me about the dirty books."

"You know everything I know because I told those *jacket men*, they told you. Sounds crazy, right? And since I'm crazy, that's just about right. Or am I wrong?"

Emma watched his face.

"They aren't going to do anything, are they? CIA. Homeland Security."

"Oh, they're going to do something," said Emma. "No more Level Five, they're going to monitor you Level Three. Increase your surprise random home visits. Watch me watching you in case I mess up and go soft and don't recommend a Recommit in time to avoid any embarrassments."

"How did you keep them from taking me away now?"

"I told them you might have imbibed early and contra-indicated with your meds."

"Imbibed?"

"Tomorrow's St. Patrick's day." She shook her head. "I believe *you believe.* But you're trying to be who you were then. And that guy's gone into who you are now."

"Vin," he said. "Not Condor."

"Both, but in the right perspective."

"Ah," said Condor. "Perspective."

"What's yours? You've been free for a while now. How is it out here?"

"Full of answers and afraid of questions."

She softened. "How are the hallucinations?"

"They don't interfere with—"

"—with you functioning in the real world?"

"*The real world.*" He smiled. "I'll watch for it. What about Kim's stalker?"

"If there's a stalker, you're right. She should call the cops."

"Yeah. Just like I did. That'll solve everything."

"This is what we got," said Emma.

"One more thing we got," said Vin. "At work, I can't take it, packing coffins."

"Is it your back?" said Emma. "Do you need—"

"I need more carts to go to Preserve. I need to be able to save more books."

Emma probed. *Therapist. Monitor. Maybe friend.* "Those aren't just books to you. The ones at work. The novels."

Condor shrugged. "Short stories, too."

"They're things going to the end they would go to without you. You act like you're a Nazi working a book-burning bonfire. You're not. Why do you care so much?"

"We sell our souls to the stories we know," said Condor. "The more kinds of stories, the bigger we are. The better or truer or cooler the story . . ."

His shrug played out the logic in her skull.

"I'll see what I can do," said Emma. "About the cart."

"Carts," corrected Condor.

"Only if we're lucky."

She walked out of his rented house.

Left him sitting there.

Alone.

Sometimes you gotta do what you do just to be you.

Next morning, he dressed for war.

Black shoes good for running. Loose black jeans not likely to bind a kick. His Oxford blue shirt might rip if grabbed. He ditched the *dust master*'s sports coat for the black leather zip-up jacket he bought back when an ex-CIA cocaine cowboy shot him in Kentucky. The black leather jacket let him move, plus it gave the illusion of protection from a slashing knife or exploding bomb.

Besides, he thought when he saw his rock-and-roll reflection walking in the glass of the Adams building door, *if I'm going down, I'm going down looking like me.*

Seven pine wood crates waited stacked against the yellow wall outside his cave.

Condor caressed the coffins like a vampire. Inhaled their essence. Lifted their lids to reveal their big box of *empty*: smooth walls, carpentered bottoms of reinforcing slats making a bed of rectangular grooves for books to lie on and die. His face hoovered each of those seven empty coffins, but only in one caught a whiff of almonds.

He tore through his office. The computer said nine coffins waited outside against his wall. Desk drawers: still empty, no weapons. The DOSP's fountain pen filled his eyes. *Use what you got.* He stuck the pen in his black leather jacket.

Two women working a table outside the Adams building reading room spotted a silver-haired man coming their way. They wore green sweaters. The younger one's left cheek sported a painted-on green shamrock. She smiled herself into Condor's path.

"Happy St. Patrick's Day! You need some holiday green. Want to donate a dollar to the Library and get a shamrock tattoo? Good luck *and* keeps you from getting pinched. How about one on your hand? Unless you want to go wild. Cheek or—"

The silver-haired stranger pressed his trigger finger to the middle of his forehead.

"Oh, cool! Like a third eye!"

"Or a bullet hole."

Her smile wilted.

He stalked into the reading room. Clerks behind the counter. Scholars at research desks. *There*, at her usual place, sat Kim.

She kept her cool. Kept her eyes on an old book. Kept her cell phone visible on her desk, an easy grab and a *no contact necessary* signal. He kept a casual distance between where he walked and where she sat, headed to the bottom of a spiral staircase.

Playing the old man let him take his time climbing those silver steel steps, a spiraling ascent that turned him through circles to the sky. His first curve toward the reading room let him surveil the head tops of strangers, any of whom could be the oppo. The stairs curved him toward the rear wall that disappeared into a black and white Alabama night where a six-year-old girl in a small town street turns to look back at her family home as a voice calls "*Scout*." Condor's steel stairs path to the sky curved . . .

Fran.

Standing on the far side of the reading room. Condor felt the crush of her fingers gripping the push handle of a blue smock covered cart. Saw her burning face.

As she raged across the room at silver lip-ringed Kim.

You know crazy when you see it. When crazy keeps being where crazy happened.

Obsession. Call it lust that Fran dared not name. Call it fearful loathing of all that. Call it outrage at Kim's silver lip loop and how Kim represented an effrontery to The Way Things Are Supposed to Be. Call it envy or anger because that damn still young woman with soft curves Fran would never be asked to touch got to do things Fran never did. Or could. Or would. Got to feel things, have things, be things. Lust, envy, hate: complications beyond calculation fused into raging obsession and made Fran not a twittering brown bird, made her a jackal drooling for flesh and blood.

For Kim.

Kim sat at her desk between where Fran seethed and where Condor stood on spiral silver stairs to the sky. Kim turned a page in her book.

Fran's eyes flicked from her obsession—spotted Vin. Saw him see the real her. Snarled, whirled the cart around and drove hard toward the reading room's main doors.

Cut her off! You got nothing! She's got a knife!

Condor clattered down the spiral steel stairs, hurried across the reading room. He had no proof. No justifiable right to scream "HALT!" or call the cops—and any cops would trigger *jacket men* to snatch him away to the secret Maine hospital's padded cell or to that suburban Virginia crematorium where no honest soul would see or smell his smoke swirling away into the night sky.

He caught his breath at Kim's desk: "Not a mustache, a her!"

Kim looked to the main door where he'd pointed, but all she saw beyond Vin charging there was the shape of someone pushing a cart into the elevator.

Vin ran to the elevator, saw its glowing arrow: ↓

Over there, racc down those stairs, hit the basement level—

He heard *rolling wheels* from around that corner.

Rammed at Condor came the blue smocked cart.

That he caught with both hands—pulled more. Jerked Fran off balance. Pushed the book cart harder than he'd ever pushed the blocking sled in high school football. Slammed her spine against a yellow cinderblock wall. Pinned her there: *Stalker had a knife and a woman like Fran with knife-tipped shoes once almost killed James Bond.*

Condor yelled: "Why Kim?"

"She doesn't get to be her! Me, should be her, have her, stop her!"

The fought-over cart shook between them. Its covering blue smock slid off.

Books tumbled off the cart. Books summoned from heartland libraries to our biggest cultural repository where they disappeared on *official business.* Condor registered a dozen versions of the same title banned in high schools across America *because.*

"You filled the coffins! Tricked libraries all over the country into sending their copies of certain titles here to the mothership of libraries! You murdered those books!" Condor twisted the cart to keep Fran rammed against the wall. "You're a purger, too!"

"Books put filth in people's heads! Ideas!"

"Our heads can have any ideas they want!"

"Not in my world!" Fran twisted and leveraged the cart up and out from under Condor's push. The cart crashed on its side. He flopped off his feet, fell over it.

Wild punches hit him and he whirled to his feet, knocked her away.

Yelled: "Where are the coffins?! Where's the C4?!"

"I see you!" She yelled as the book she threw hit his nose.

Pain flash! He sensed her kick, closed his thighs but her shoe still slammed his groin. He staggered, hit the stone wall, hands snapping up to thwart her attack—

That didn't come.

Gone. Jackal Fran was gone, running down the basement tunnel.

Cell phone, pull out your cell phone.

"Kim!" he gasped to the woman who answered his call. "Watch out, woman my age Fran and she's not a brown bird, she's the jackal after you!"

"Don't talk! Reading room, right? Stay in plain sight but get to the check-out counter . . . Yes . . . The library computer . . . Search employee data base—No, not Fran *anybody*, search for Jeremy *somebody*!"

A ghost of Fran whispered: "*I used to have your job working with him.*"

Over the phone came intel: an office/shop door number, some castle hole.

The DOSP's pen tattooed that number on the back of his left hand.

He hung up and staggered through the underground tunnel.

Scan the numbers on the closed doors, looking for numbers with an SB prefix whatever that—*Sub-basement! Like my office!* One more level down.

At a stairwell, he flipped open his ancient phone and dialed another number: "Rich it's Vin, you gotta go help somebody right now! Protect her. Tell her I sent you. In Adams Reading Room, named Kim, silver lip loop . . . I thought you'd noticed her! And that's all right, you just . . . OK, but when you couldn't find the right words you walked on, right? Go now! . . . Don't worry, nobody knows everything. Play it with what you've got."

He jogged through yellow tunnels like he was a rat running a maze, *I'm too old for this*, staggering to a closed brown metal door, its top half fogged glass.

Condor caught his breath outside that door. The door handle wouldn't turn. He saw a doorbell, trigger-fingered its button, heard it buzz.

The click of a magnetic lock. The door swings open.

Come on in.

Jeremy stands ten steps into this underground lair beside a workbench and holding a remote control wand. The door slams shut behind Condor.

"What do you want?" said a caretaker of this government castle.

Caretaker, like in the novel Fran tried to murder, some story about sex and an insane asylum and who was crazy. *Stick to what's sane.* Condor said: "The coffins."

"They're here already?"

Scan the workshop: no sign of the two missing coffins. A refrigerator. Wall sink. Trash tub of empty plastic water bottles. The back of an open laptop faced Condor from the workbench where the tech wizard of this cave stood. Jeremy tossed the remote control beside an iPhone cabled to the laptop.

"Oh," said Jeremy. "You meant the crates for the books."

He took a step closer. "Why do you care?"

"There's something you don't know you know."

"I know enough."

Off to Jeremy's left waited the clear plastic roller tub holding half a dozen cell phones and its color printer sign proclaiming OLD TELEPHONES FOR CHARITY!

One heartbeat. Two.

"I didn't know you were the one collecting charity phones."

"What do you know?" Jeremy eased another step closer.

Sometimes crazy is the way to go.

Jeremy's blue eyes narrowed, his hands were fists.

Feel the vibe. See the movie.

Sunny blue sky behind the white dome of the U.S. Capitol. Across the street rises a castle with a green metal top and giant gray concrete walls of columns and grand staircases, windows behind which people work, a fountain out front where bronze green statues of Greek gods flirt and pose their indomitable will.

Tremble/rumble! The Library of Congress's Jefferson building shudders, sprays out exploded concrete dust like 9/11, like Oklahoma City. Fireballs nova through castle rooms of wood panels, wood shelves, books that no one would see again. Those walls crumble to rubble. The last moment of the castle's cohesion is a cacophony of screams.

You'll never make it to the door. Locked anyway. And he's between you and its remote control on the workbench by the computer umbilical corded to an ultra phone.

Make it real: "You and Fran."

"She's just a woman," said Jeremy. "More useful than a donkey, not as trainable. Like, deluded. Like all women in this Babylon where they don't know their place."

"Oh, I like all the places they will go," said Condor, quoting the book he'd heard read a million billion times to a frightened child traveling beside his mother on a bus through a dark Texas night. "Where'd Fran take those two coffins—*crates* that you and her use to smuggle in C4?"

"Somewhere for her stupid crusade."

For *her* stupid crusade. Not *our.*

A lot of roads run through Crazytown.

Jeremy took a step closer.

Condor flowed to walk a martial arts *Bagua* circle around him.

Almonds, a strong whiff in the air of what had been stockpiled down here.

"She even bribed you," guessed Condor as Jeremy turned to keep the silver-haired man from circling behind him.

"She funded the will of God."

"Fran thought the only God she was funding was hers. Didn't know about yours."

"My God is the only God."

"That's what all you people say."

Why is there a floppy flat empty red rubber water bottle on the floor?

Condor feinted. Jeremy flinched: he's a

puncher, maybe from a shopping mall *dojo* or hours watching YouTubes of jihad stars showing their wannabe homegrown brothers out there the throat-cutting ways of Holy warriors.

"Slats!" said Condor. "On the inside bottom of the crates. Reinforcing slats, they make a narrow trough. Somewhere outside, after you dump the books, you mold C4 into those slats—cream color, looks like glue on the wood if the guard outside checks. Odds are the guard won't check all the crates every time, you only use two, and even if somebody checks, nobody notices.

"Fran paid you to cut her out a couple crates before you delivered them. That gave you time with the crates in here to peel out what you hid, pass them on to her, she gives them back full of what you don't care about to fold back into the coffin count."

"Way to go, cowboy." Jeremy had that flat accent born in Ohio near the river. "You get to witness the destruction of the Great Satan's temple of heretical thought."

"Wow, did they email you a script?"

"You think I'd be so careless as to let the NSA catch me contacting my true brothers in the Middle East before I proved myself—"

Lunge, Jeremy lunged and Condor whirled left—whirled right—snake-struck in a three-beat *Hsing-i* counter-charge to—

Pepper spray burned Condor's face.

Breathe can't breathe eyes on fire!

The Holy warrior slammed his other fist into the silver-haired man's guts.

Condor was already gasping for air and flooding tears because of pepper spray. The barbell muscled punch buckled and bent him over, knocked him toward the workbench, teetering, stumbling—crashing to the floor.

Get up! Get up! Get to your knees—

The blue-eyed fanatic slapped Vin, a blow more for disrespect than destruction.

Condor saw himself flopping in slow motion. Kneeling gasping on the hard floor. His arms waving at his sides couldn't fly him away or fight his killer.

White cable connects the laptop to iPhone: Jeremy rips that cord free.

Whips its garrote around the kneeling man's neck.

Gurgling clawing at the cord cutting off blood to brain air to lungs, pepper-sprayed eyes blurring, a roar, a whooshing in his ears, can't—

BZZZZ!

That doorbell buzz startles the strangler, loosens his pull.

Blood rush to the brain, air!

BZZZZ!

Strangler jerks his garrote tight.

GLASS RATTLES as someone outside bangs on that door.

Can't scream gagging here in here help me in here get in here!

Jeremy spun Condor around and slammed him chest-first into the workbench.

Hands, your hands on the workbench, claw at—

Seven seconds before blackout, he *saw*.

The remote for the door. Wobbling on the workbench. *Flop reach grab—*

The jihad warrior whirled the gurgling apostate away from the high-tech gear.

Thumb the remote.

The door buzzes—springs open.

Fran.

Screaming charging rushing *IN!*

Jeremy knees Condor, throws him to the floor and the garrote—

The garrote goes loose around Condor's neck *but won't unwrap itself from the strangler's hands*, holds his arms trapped low.

"Stop it!" Fran screams at the treasonous pawn who's trying to steal her destiny. "He's mine to kill!"

Down from heaven stabs her gray metal spring-blade knife confiscated from a tourist, salvaged from storage by an LOC staffer who could steal any of the castle's keys.

Fran drove her stolen blade into Jeremy's throat.

Gasping grabbing his hands to his neck/what sticks out of there.

Wide eyed, his hands grab GOT HER weakness percolates up from his feet by the prone Vin, up Jeremy's legs, he's falling holding on to Fran, death grips her blouse that rips open as the force of his pull multiplied by his fall jerks her forward—

Fran trips over sprawled Condor.

Swan dives through the air over the crumpling man she stabbed.

Crashes *cracks* her skull on the workbench's sharp corner.

Spasms falls flat across the man she stabbed whose body pins Condor to the floor.

Silence. Silence.

Crawl out from under the dead.

Hands, elbows, and knees pushing on the concrete floor, straining, pulling . . .

Free. Alive. Face down on the floor, gasping scents of cement and dust, sweat and the warm ham and cabbage smell of savaged flesh. A whiff of almonds.

Jackhammer in his chest:

No heart attack, not after all this. Come on: a little justice.

Condor flopped over onto his back.

Saw only the castle's flat ceiling.

Propped himself up on his elbows. Sat. Dizzy. Sore from punches, getting kneed, strangled. Pepper-spray, tears, floor dirt, sweat: his face was caked. Must look like hell.

Nobody will let you walk away from this.

Almonds, C4: where's the C4?

The workbench, the laptop, glowing screen full of . . .

A floor plan. The LOC jewel, the main castle Jefferson Building.

A pop-ad flashed over the map, a smiling salesman above a flow of words:

"Congratulations on your new cell phone basic business plan. Now consider moving beyond mere networked teleconferencing to—"

The white computer cord garrote lay on the floor like a dead snake.

A snake that once connected the laptop computer to an iPhone.

An iPhone capable of activating all cell phones on its conferenced network.

A *for charity* tub that gobbles up donated old cell phones from our better souls.

The iPhone screen glowed with the LOC castle map and its user-entered red dots.

Dizzy: he staggered toward the wall sink, splashed water on his face, empty plastic water bottles in a tub right by that weird red rubber bag that doesn't belong here.

Vision: Jeremy smiling his Ohio smile, walking through the metal detectors with the baggy crotch of his pants hiding a red rubber bottle full of goo that's not water.

Grab the roller tub for donated cell phones. Close the laptop, put it in the tub beside the iPhone. The phone glowed the map of the castle.

The crisscrossed corpses on the floor kept still.

How long before anyone finds you?

Thumb the remote, the door swings open. Push the plastic tub on wheels into the hall. Condor pulled his blue shirt out of his waistband, used it to polish his fingerprints off the remote, then toss it back through the closing door into the basement shop, plastic skidding along the concrete floor to where the dead lay.

Go!

Race the rumbling plastic tub on wheels through the tunnels of the Adams building to the main castle of Jefferson, down into its bowels and follow the map on the iPhone screen to a mammoth water pipe. Gray duct tape on the inflow water pipe's far side: a cellphone wired as a detonator into a tan book-sized gob of goo.

Boom and no water for automatic sprinklers to fight fire.

Boom and water floods an American castle.

Pull the wires out of the gob of C4. Pull them from the phone. Pull the phone's battery. Toss the dead electronics into the tub.

What do you do with a handful of C4?

A shot bullet won't set it off. And C4 burns. Only electricity makes it go *Boom!*

Squeeze the C4 into a goo ball, shove it into your black jacket's pocket.

Condor charged the plastic tub on wheels to the next map number on the iPhone: bomb against a concrete weight-bearing wall. The iPhone led him to three more bombs. Each time he ripped away the electronics and squeezed the goo into a shape he could hide in his jacket pockets, and when they were full, he stuffed C4 goo inside his underpants.

Boom.

Run, catch that elevator, roll in with the tub. A man and a woman ride with you. He's a gaudy green St. Patrick's Day tie. She looks tired. Neither of them cares about you, about what happens in your crotch if the elevator somehow sparks static electricity.

Next floor plan in the iPhone.

Stacks, row after row of wooden shelves and burnable books and *there*, under a bookshelf, another cell phone–wired goo ball. Rubber bands bind this apparatus to a clear plastic water bottle full of a gray gel that a bomb will burst into a fireball.

Lay the bottle of napalm atop the cell phones in the wheeled tub.

Your underpants are full.

Cinch the rubber bands from that bomb around the ankles of your pants. Feed a snake of C4 down alongside your naked leg in the black jeans.

Roll on *oh so slowly.*

Hours, it takes him hours, slowed more by every load of C4 he stuffs in his pants, inside his blue shirt, in the sleeves of his black leather jacket.

Hours, he rolls through the Jefferson building for hours following iPhone maps made by an obsessed fanatic. Rolls past tours of ordinary citizens, past men and women with lanyard I.D. Rumbles down office corridors, through the main reading room with its gilded dome ceiling, until the final red X on the last swooped-to page of the iPhone's uploaded maps represents only another pulled-apart bomb.

In an office corridor, a door: MENS ROOM.

Cradle all the napalm water bottles in your arms.

The restroom is bright and mirrored, a storm of lemon ammonia.

And empty.

Lay screwed open water bottles in the sink so they *gluck gluck* down that drain.

One bottle won't fit. Shuffle it into the silver metal stall.

Can't stop, exhausted, drained, slide down that stall wall, slump to sitting on the floor, hugging the toilet like some *two beers too many* teenager.

The C4 padding his body makes it hard to move, but he drains the last non-recyclable water bottle into the toilet. That silver handle pushes down with a *whoosh.*

The world does not explode.

He crawled out of the stall. Made sure the water bottles in the sink were empty. Left them there. Left the tub of cellphones and wires in the hall for janitors to puzzle over. Dumped Jeremy's laptop in a litter barrel. Waddled to an elevator, a hall, down corridors and down the tunnel slope to the Adams building toward his own office.

Kept going.

Up, main floor, the blonde went this way, there's the door to the street, you can—

Man's voice behind Condor yells: "You!"

The blue pinstripe suit DOSP. Who blinks. Leans back from the smell of sweat and some kind of nuts, back from the haggard wild-eyed man in the black leather jacket.

"Are you quite all right, Mister . . . *Vin?*"

"Does that matter?" says this pitiful excuse for a government employee foisted on the DOSP by another agency.

Who then unzips his black leather jacket, fumbles inside it, pulls out—

A fountain pen Vin hands to the DOSP, saying: "'Guess I'm a sword guy.'"

Vin waddled away from his stricken silent LOC boss.

Stepped out into twilight town.

They'll never let you get away with this.

Capitol Hill sidewalk. Suit and ties with briefcases and work-stuffed backpacks, kids on scooters. That woman's walking a dog. The cool air promises spring. An umbrella of night cups the marble city. Some guy outside a bar over on Pennsylvania Avenue sings *Danny Boy.* Budding trees along the curb make a canopy against the streetlights' shine and *just keep going, one foot in front of the other.*

Go slow so nothing shakes out of your clothes.

Talking heads blather from an unseen TV, insist *this*, know *that*, sell *whatever.*

Waves of light dance on that three story high townhouse alley wall. Music in the air from the alley courtyard's flowing light. Laughter.

Barbecue and green beer inspired the St. Paddy's Day party thrown by the *not-yet-thirty* men and women in that group house. They did their due diligence, reassured their neighbors, *come on over*, we're getting a couple of kegs, buckets of ice for Cokes and white wine, craft or foreign beers for palates that had become pickier since college. There was a table for munchies. Texted invites blasted out at 4:20 before "everybody" headed out to the holiday bars after work. Zack rigged his laptop and speakers, played DJ so any woman who wanted a song had to talk to him and his wingman who was a whiz at voter precinct analyses but could never read a curl of lipstick.

Bodies packed the alley.

Everybody worked their look, the *cool* stance, the way to turn your face to scan the crowd, the right smile. Lots of cheap suits and work ensembles, khakis and sports jackets, jeans that fit better than Condor's bulging pants. Cyber screens glow in the crowd like the stars of a universe centered by whoever holds the cellphone. Hormones and testosterone amidst smoke from the two troughs made from a fifty-gallon drum sliced lengthwise by a long-gone tenant of yore. Those two barbecue barrels started out the evening filled by charcoal briquettes and a *Whump!* of lighter fluid. By the time Condor'd eased

his way to the center of the churning crowd, a couple guys from a townhouse up the street had tossed firewood onto the coals so flames leapt high and danced shadows on the alley courtyard's walls. The crowd surged as Zack turned up the volume on a headbanger song from the wild daze of their parents.

Who were Condor's age.

Or younger.

Hate that song, he thought.

He reached the inner edge of the crowd who amidst the flickering light tried not to see the *getting there* debts pressing down on them or the pollution from the barrel fires trapping tomorrow's sun. They'd made it here to this city, this place, this idea. They worked for the hero who'd brought them to town, for Congress *of course that would matter*, so would the group/the project/the committee/the caucus/the association/the website they staffed, the Administration circus ring that let them parade lions or tigers or bears, *oh my*, the downtown for dollars firm that pulled levers, the Agency or Department they powered with their sweat and so they could, *they should* sweat here, now, in the flickering fire light of an alley courtyard. Swaying. Looking. Hoping for a connection—heart, mind, flesh, community: get what you can, if nothing else a contact, a move toward more. The music surged. An American beat they all knew pulsed this crowd who were white and black, Hispanic and Asian, men and women and maybe more, who came from purple mountains' majesty and fruited plains to claim the capital city for this dream or that, to punch a ticket for their career, to get something done or get a deal, *to do* or *to be*—that is this city's true question and they, *oh they*, they were the answer *now.*

Near the burning barrels, a dozen couples jumped and jived to their generation's music blaring out of the speakers. Glowing cellphones and green dotted the crowd—bowlers, top hats. Over there was a woman in green foil boa. That woman blew a noisemaker as she shuffled and danced solo—not alone, no, she was not alone, don't anyone dare think that she was alone. She saw him, a guy old enough to be her father, all battered face lost in space, heard herself yell the question you always ask in Washington: *"What do you do?"*

He felt the heat of the flames.

"Hey old guy!" yelled Zack, DJ earphones cupped around his neck like the hands of a strangler. "This one's for you. My dad loves it."

Zack keyboarded a YouTubed live concert, Bruce Springsteen blasting *Badlands.*

Cranked up the volume as elsewhere in this empire city night, silver lip looped Kim shyly thanked a man with a mustache for being the knight by her side, for dinner, for *sure*, coffee at work tomorrow morning, for however much more they might have.

But in that alley, in that pounding drums and crashing guitars night, lovers like that became just part of the intensity of it all, like individual books in the library stacks of stories stretching into our savage forever.

Call him Vin. Call him Condor.

His arms shot toward the heaven in that black smoked night and he shuffled to the music's blare, arms waving, feet sliding into the dancing crowd.

A roar seized the revelers. A roar that pulled other arms toward heaven, a roar that became the whole crowd bopping with the beat, the hard driving invisible anthem.

"Go old guy!" shouts someone.

A silver-haired frenzy in black leather and jeans rocks through the younger crowd to the burning barrels, to the fire itself, reaches inside his jacket, throws something into those flames, something that lands with a shower of sparks and a sizzle and crackles and on, on he dances, pulling more of that magic fuel out of his jacket, out of its sleeves, out his—*Oh My God! He's pulling stuff out of his pants and throwing it on the fire!* Every throw makes him lighter, wilder, then he's dancing hands free in the air, stomping feet with the crowd bouncing around him. "Old guy! Old guy!" Cop cruisers cut the night with red and blue spinning lights. The crowd throbs. "Old guy! Old guy!" Burning almonds and fireplace wood, barbecue and *come hither* perfume, a reckless whiff of rebel herb that will become legal and corporate by the decade's end. "Old guy! Old guy!" There are bodies in a basement, mysteries to be found, questions clean of his fingerprints, books to be treasured. There are lovers sharing moments, dreamers dancing in the night, madmen in our marble city, and amidst those who are not his children, through the fog of his crazy, the swirl of his ghosts, the weight of his locked-up years, surging in Condor is the certainty that this *oh this*, this is *the real world.*

MISS BIANCA

SARA PARETSKY

THE ASCENT OF FEMALE mystery writers in the last quarter of the twentieth century is one of the era's most significant changes in the genre, and no one has played a bigger hand in that movement than Sara Paretsky (1947–). Not only has her tough private eye character, Victoria Iphigenia (generally and understandably known as V. I., but called "Vic" by her friends) Warshawski, been one of the most famous and popular fictional detectives in America for more than three decades, but Paretsky was the guiding force in the creation of Sisters in Crime, the highly successful organization devoted to getting more attention for women crime writers.

Her education indicated a political or sociological career (she received a BA in political science from the University of Kansas, a PhD in history from the University of Chicago, and an MBA, also from Chicago), and she performed community service in Chicago before turning to writing mystery fiction. The first V. I. Warshawski novel, *Indemnity Only*, was published in 1982 and Paretsky has written more than twenty books since then, all but two featuring her hard-boiled PI.

V. I. earned a law degree and worked for a short time as a public defender but soon went out on her own to become a private investigator specializing in white-collar crimes that frequently turn violent. She is physically fearless, with a background in karate and street fighting (not to mention her Smith & Wesson automatic) developed in her early years in a tough neighborhood on the south side of Chicago.

Among Paretsky's numerous honors are three lifetime achievement awards: the Cartier Diamond Dagger, given by the (British) Crime Writers' Association in 2002; the Grand Master Award, presented by the Mystery Writers of America in 2011; and the Bouchercon's Anthony Award in 2011.

"Miss Bianca" was originally published in *Ice Cold* (New York, Grand Central, 2014).

MISS BIANCA

SARA PARETSKY

ABIGAIL MADE HER TOUR of the cages, adding water to all the drinking bowls. The food was more complicated, because not all the mice got the same meal. She was ten years old, and this was her first job; she took her responsibilities seriously. She read the labels on the cages and carefully measured out feed from the different bags. All the animals had numbers written in black ink on their backs; she checked these against the list Bob Pharris had given her with the feeding instructions.

"That's like being a slave," Abigail said, when Bob showed her how to match the numbers on the mice to the food directives. "It's not fair to call them by numbers instead of by name, and it's mean to write on their beautiful fur."

Bob just laughed. "It's the only way we can tell them apart, Abby."

Abigail hated the name Abby. "That's because you're not looking at their faces. They're all different. I'm going to start calling you Number Three because you're Dr. Kiel's third student. How would you like that?"

"Number Nineteen," Bob corrected her. "I'm his nineteenth student, but the other sixteen have all gotten their PhDs and moved on to

glory. Don't give the mice names, Abby: you'll get too attached to them, and they don't live very long."

In fact, the next week, when Abigail began feeding the animals on her own, some of the mice had disappeared. Others had been moved into the contamination room, where she wasn't supposed to go. The mice in there had bad diseases that might kill her if she touched them. Only the graduate students or the professors went in there, wearing gloves and masks.

Abigail began naming some of the mice under her breath. Her favorite, number 139, she called "Miss Bianca," after the white mouse in the book *The Rescuers*. Miss Bianca always sat next to the cage door when Abigail appeared, grooming her exquisite whiskers with her little pink paws. She would cock her head and stare at Abigail with bright black eyes.

In the book, Miss Bianca ran a prisoner's rescue group, so Abigail felt it was only fair that she should rescue Miss Bianca in turn, or at least let her have some time outside the cage. This afternoon, she looked around to make sure no one was watching, then scooped Miss Bianca out of her cage and into the pocket of her dress.

"You can listen to me practice, Miss Bianca," Abigail told her. She moved into the alcove behind the cages where the big sinks were.

Dr. Kiel thought Abigail's violin added class to the lab, at least that's what he said to Abigail's mother, but Abigail's mother said it was hard enough to be a single mom without getting fired in the bargain, so Abigail should practice where she wouldn't disturb the classes in the lecture rooms or annoy the other professors.

Abigail had to come to the lab straight from school. She did her homework on a side table near her mother's desk, and then she fed the animals and practiced her violin in the alcove in the animal room.

"Today Miss Abigail Sherwood will play Bach for you," she announced grandly to Miss Bianca.

She tuned the violin as best she could and began a simplified version of the first sonata for violin. Miss Bianca stuck her head out of the pocket and looked inquiringly at the instrument. Abigail wondered what the mouse would do if she put her inside. Miss Bianca could probably squeeze in through the F hole, but getting her out would be difficult. The thought of Mother's rage, not to mention Dr. Kiel or even Bob Pharris's, made her decide against it.

She picked up her bow again, but heard voices out by the cages. When she peered out, she saw Bob talking to a stranger, a small woman with dark hair.

Bob smiled at her. "This is Abby; her mother is Dr. Kiel's secretary. Abby helps us by feeding the animals."

"It's Abigail," Abigail said primly.

"And one of the mouses, Abigail, she is living in your—your—" the woman pointed at Miss Bianca.

"Abby, put the mouse back in the cage," Bob said. "If you play with them, we can't let you feed them."

Abigail scowled at the woman and at Bob, but she put Miss Bianca back in her cage. "I'm sorry, Miss Bianca. Mamelouk is watching me."

"Mamelouk?" the woman said. "I am thinking your name 'Bob'?"

Mamelouk the Iron-Tummed was the evil cat who worked for the jailor in *The Rescuers*, but Abigail didn't say that, just stared stonily at the woman, who was too stupid to know that the plural of "mouse" was mice, not "mouses."

"This is Elena," Bob told Abigail. "She's Dr. Kiel's new dishwasher. You can give her a hand, when you're not practicing your violin or learning geometry."

"Is allowed for children working in the lab?" Elena asked. "In my country, government is not allowing children work."

Abigail's scowl deepened: Bob had been looking at her homework while she was down here with the mice. "We have slavery in America," she announced. "The mice are slaves, too."

"Abigail, I thought you liked feeding the animals." Dr. Kiel had come into the animal room without the three of them noticing.

He wore crepe-soled shoes which let him move soundlessly through the lab. A short stocky man with brown eyes, he could look at you with a warmth that made you want to tell him your secrets, but just when you thought you could trust him, he would become furious over nothing that Abigail could figure out. She had heard him yelling at Bob Pharris in a way that frightened her. Besides, Dr. Kiel was her mother's boss, which meant she must never EVER be saucy to him.

"I'm sorry, Dr. Kiel," she said, her face red. "I only was telling Bob I don't like the mice being branded, they're all different, you can tell them apart by looking."

"*You* can tell them apart because you like them and know them," Dr. Kiel said. "The rest of us aren't as perceptive as you are."

"Dolan," he added to a man passing in the hall. "Come and meet my new dishwasher— Elena Mirova."

Dr. Dolan and Dr. Kiel didn't like each other. Dr. Kiel was always loud and hearty when he talked to Dr. Dolan, trying too hard not to show his dislike. Dr. Dolan snooped around the lab looking for mistakes that Dr. Kiel's students made. He'd report them with a phony jokiness, as if he thought leaving pipettes unwashed in the sink was funny when really it made him angry.

Dr. Dolan had a face like a giant baby's, the nose little and squashed upward, his cheeks round and rosy; when Bob Pharris had taken two beakers out of Dr. Dolan's lab, he'd come into Dr. Kiel's lab, saying, "Sorry to hear you broke both your arms, Pharris, and couldn't wash your own equipment."

He came into the animal room now and smiled in a way that made his eyes close into slits. Just like a cat's. He said hello to Elena, but added to Dr. Kiel, "I thought your new girl was starting last week, Nate."

"She arrived a week ago, but she was under the weather; you would never have let me forget it if she'd contaminated your ham sandwiches— I mean your petri dishes."

Dr. Dolan scowled, but said to Elena, "The rumors have been flying around the building all day. Is it true you're from Eastern Europe?"

Dolan's voice was soft, forcing everyone to lean toward him if they wanted to hear him. Abigail had trouble understanding him, and she saw Elena did, too, but Abigail knew it would be a mistake to try to ask Dr. Dolan to speak more slowly or more loudly.

Elena's face was sad. "Is true. I am refugee, from Czechoslovakia."

"How'd you get here?" Dolan asked.

"Just like your ancestors did, Pat," Dr. Kiel said. "Yours came steerage in a ship. Elena flew steerage in a plane. We lift the lamp beside the golden door for Czechs just as we did for the Irish."

"And for the Russians?" Dolan said. "Isn't that where your people are from, Nate?"

"The Russians would like to think so," Kiel said. "It was Poland when my father left."

"But you speak the lingo, don't you?" Dolan persisted.

There was a brief silence. Abigail could see the vein in Dr. Kiel's right temple pulsing. Dolan saw it also and gave a satisfied smirk.

He turned back to Elena. "How did you end up in Kansas? It's a long way from Prague to here."

"I am meeting Dr. Kiel in Bratislava," Elena said.

"I was there in '66, you know," Dr. Kiel said. "Elena's husband edited the Czech *Journal of Virology and Bacteriology* and the Soviets didn't like their editorial policies—the journal decided they would only take articles written in English, French, or Czech, not in Russian."

Bob laughed. "Audacious. That took some guts."

Abigail was memorizing words under her breath to ask her mother over dinner: perceptive, editorial policies, audacious.

"Perhaps not so good idea. When Russian tanks coming last year, they putting husband in prison," Elena said.

"Well, welcome aboard," Dr. Dolan said, holding out his soft white hand to Elena.

She'd been holding her hands close to her side, but when she shook hands Abigail saw a huge bruise on the inside of her arm: green, purple, yellow, spreading in a large oval up and down from the elbow.

"They beat you before you left?" Dr. Dolan asked.

Elena's eyes opened wide; Abigail thought she was scared. "Is me, only," she said, "me being— not know in English."

"What's on today's program?" Dr. Kiel asked Abigail abruptly, pointing at her violin.

"Bach."

"You need to drop that old stuffed shirt. Beethoven. I keep telling you, start playing those Beethoven sonatas, they'll bring you to life." He ruffled her hair. "I think I saw your mother putting the cover over her typewriter when I came down."

That meant Abigail was supposed to leave. She looked at Miss Bianca, who was hiding in the shavings at the back of her cage. *It's good you're afraid*, Abigail told her silently. *Don't let them catch you, they'll hurt you or make you sick with a bad disease.*

Rhonda Sherwood's husband had been an account manager for a greeting card company in town. His territory was the West Coast. When he fell in love with a woman who owned a chain of gift shops in Sacramento, he left Rhonda and Abigail to start a new life in California.

It was embarrassing to have your father and mother divorced; some kids in Abigail's fifth-grade class made fun of her. Her best friend's mother wouldn't let her come over to play any more, as if divorce were like one of Dr. Kiel and Dr. Dolan's diseases, infectious, communicable.

When her husband left, Rhonda brushed up on her shorthand and typing. In May, just about the time that school ended, she was lucky enough to get a job working for Dr. Kiel up at the university. Rhonda typed all his letters and his scientific papers. Over dinner, she would make Abigail test her on the hard words she was learning: *Coxiella burnetii, cytoblasts, vacuoles.* Rhonda mastered the odd concepts: gram staining, centrifuging. Dr. Kiel was not a kind man in general, Rhonda knew that, but he was kind to her, a single mom. Dr. Kiel let Rhonda bring Abigail to the lab after school.

There were eight scientists in Dr. Kiel's department. They all had graduate students, they all taught undergraduate classes at the university, but Abigail and Rhonda both knew that none of the other scientists worked as hard as Dr. Kiel. He was always traveling, too, to different scientific conventions, or overseas. Rhonda hadn't been working for him when he went to Czechoslovakia three years ago, but she was making travel arrangements for him now. He was going to Washington, to San Francisco, and then to Israel.

Even though Dr. Kiel had an explosive temper, he had a sense of camaraderie that his colleagues lacked. He also had an intensity about his work that spilled over into the lives of his students and staff. His students and lab techs were expected to work long hours, do night shifts, attend evening seminars, but he took a personal interest in their families, their hobbies, took his male students fishing, brought his female students records or books for their birthdays. When he went to New York in August, he brought Rhonda back a scarf from the gift store in the Metropolitan Museum of Art. Dr. Kiel had a wife and five lumpy, sullen children: Abigail met them when Dr. Kiel had everyone in the department out to his house for a picnic right after school started. He never seemed to think about his children the way he did about his staff and students.

It was Dr. Kiel who suggested that feeding the animals might make Abigail feel that she was part of the team. He seemed to sense her loneliness; he would quiz her on her classes, her music. He knew better than to tease a ten-year-old girl about boys, the way Dr. Dolan did.

When Rhonda worried about the diseases the animals were infected with, Dr. Kiel assured her that Abigail would not be allowed in the contamination room. "And if some Q fever germ is brave enough to come through the door and infect her, we keep tetracycline on hand." He showed Rhonda the bottle of orange pills in one of his glass-doored cabinets. "I've had it, and so has Bob Pharris. Watch out for a high fever and a dry cough, with aching joints; let me know if either of you starts having symptoms."

"High fever, dry cough," Abigail repeated to herself. Every day when she went in to feed the animals, she checked Miss Bianca for a fever or a cough. "Do your joints ache?" she would ask the mouse, feeling her head the way Rhonda felt her own head when she was sick.

Elena Mirova's arrival unsettled the lab. She was quiet, efficient, she did whatever was asked of her and more besides. She worked with Bob and Dr. Kiel's other two graduate students, often giving them suggestions on different ways to set up experimental apparatus, or helping them interpret slides they were studying.

"Czech dishwashers know more science than ours in America," Bob said one day when Elena flipped through the back pages of the *Journal of Cell Biology* to show him an article that explained apoptosis in *Rickettsia prowazekii*.

Elena turned rigid, her face white, then hurriedly left the room, saying she heard the autoclave bell ringing.

"It's the communists," Rhonda explained to her daughter, when Abigail reported the episode to her.

"It was so weird," Abigail said. "It was like she thought Bob was accusing her of a crime. Besides, she was lying, the autoclave bell didn't ring."

"The Russians put her husband in prison," Rhonda said. "She's afraid that they'll try to find her here."

That frightened Abigail. Everyone knew how evil the communists were; they wanted to take over America, they wanted to take over the whole world. America stood for freedom and the communists wanted to destroy freedom.

"What if they come to the lab to get Elena and kill you instead?" she asked Rhonda. "Are the mice safe? Will they want the mice?"

Dr. Dolan came into Dr. Kiel's office at that moment. "Of course they want the mice; the mice are our most important secret."

Abigail rushed down to the animal room to make sure Miss Bianca was still safe. The mouse was nibbling on a piece of food, but she came to the front of the cage as soon as Abigail arrived. Abigail was about to take her out when she saw that Bob was in the contamination room.

Instead, she stroked the mouse's head through the cage door. "I wish I could take you home, Miss Bianca," she whispered.

When Bob came out and went into the back room to scrub himself down in the big sink, Abigail followed him.

"Do you think Elena is a communist spy?" she demanded.

"Where do you come up with these ideas, short stuff?" Bob asked.

"Dr. Dolan said the communists want our mice, because they're our most important secret."

"Dr. Dolan talks a lot of guff," Bob said. "There's nothing secret about the mice, and Elena is not a communist. She ran away from the communists."

"But she lied about the autoclave. She didn't like you saying how smart she was."

Bob stopped drying his arms to stare at her. "You're as small as the mice, so we don't notice you underfoot. Look: there's nothing secret about our mice. We get a grant—you know what that is? Money. We get money from the Army, so we do some work for the Army. The disease Dr. Kiel works with can make people very sick. If our soldiers got sick in Vietnam, they wouldn't be able to fight, so Dr. Kiel and I and his other students are trying to find a way to keep them from getting sick."

"But he has that drug, he showed my mom," Abigail said.

"That's great if you're already sick, but if you're in the middle of a battle, it would be better not to get sick to start with. It would be hard for the Army to get enough of the drug to our soldiers out in the jungles and rice paddies while the Vietcong were firing rockets at them."

"Oh," Abigail said. "You're trying to make a shot, like for polio."

"And the mice are helping us. We give them some of Dr. Kiel's disease, and then we study whether we've learned any way to prevent them from getting sick."

After Bob went back to the lab, Abigail took Miss Bianca from the cage and let her sit in her pocket, where she had a lump of sugar. "Even if the mice can help win a war with the communists, I think it would be better if you didn't get sick."

She practiced her violin for half an hour. The scratchy sounds she got from the strings sounded more like the squeaks the mice made than Bach, but neither she nor the animals minded. When she finished, she took Miss Bianca out of her pocket to ride on her shoulder. When she heard voices outside the animal room door she crouched down, holding Miss Bianca in her hand.

"Mamelouk is here," she whispered. "Don't squeak."

It wasn't Mamelouk, it was Dr. Kiel with Elena. Elena's face was very white, the way it had been when she first came into the lab. She fumbled in her handbag and produced a jar with something red in it that Abigail was sure was blood.

"I hope is sterile. Hard job doing self. *Myself*," Elena said.

Abigail bent her head over her knees, so Miss Bianca wouldn't have to see such a dreadful sight. After Dr. Kiel and Elena left the animal room, she stayed bent over for a long time, but finally went up to the floor where the labs and offices were.

Her mother wasn't in the outer office, but the typewriter was still uncovered, which meant she was either taking dictation from Dr. Kiel or in the ladies' room. The door to Dr. Kiel's inner office wasn't shut all the way; Abigail walked over to peer through the crack.

Dr. Dolan was there. He had a nasty look on his face. The vein in Dr. Kiel's forehead was throbbing, always a bad sign.

"I got the library to order copies of the Czech *Journal of Virology and Bacteriology*, and no one named Mirov is on the editorial pages," Dr. Dolan said.

"I didn't know you could read Czech, Patrick," Dr. Kiel said. "I thought you moved your lips when you read English."

Abigail wanted to laugh, it was such a funny insult. Maybe she could use it the next time Susie Campbell taunted her about her parents' divorce.

"Don't try to change the subject, Kiel," Dr. Dolan said. "Are you or aren't you harboring a communist here? What kind of background check did you do on your protégée before you let her into a lab doing sensitive work for the government?"

"I met her husband in Bratislava three years ago," Dr. Kiel said coldly. "We were correspondents until the tanks rolled in last year and the Soviets put him in prison as an enemy of the state. Elena came here in danger of her life."

"Correspondents? Or lovers?" Dr. Dolan sneered.

Abigail put a hand over her mouth. Lovers, like her father and the new Mrs. Sherwood out in California. Was Elena going to turn Mrs. Kiel into a single mom for the five lumpy Kiel children?

"Maybe you grew up in a pigsty," Dr. Kiel said. "But in my family—"

"Your communist family."

"What are you, Dolan? A stooge for HUAC?"

"The FBI has a right to know what you were really doing in Bratislava three years ago. You work with a weapons-grade organism, you speak Russian, you travel—"

"The operative word here being *work*," Dr. Kiel said. "If you worked on *listeria* as energetically as you do on spying on my lab you'd have won the Nobel Prize by now."

Mother came into the outer office just then and dragged Abigail to the hall. "Since when do you eavesdrop, young lady?" she demanded.

"But, Mom, it's about Elena. She's lying all the time, her husband didn't work for that magazine in Czechoslovakia, Dr. Dolan said. He says she's stealing Dr. Kiel away from Mrs. Kiel, like that lady who stole Daddy from us. And Elena just gave Dr. Kiel something funny in the animal room. It looked like blood, but maybe it's a magic potion to make him forget Mrs. Kiel."

Rhonda stared down at her daughter in exasperation, but also in sadness. "Abigail, I'm not sure it's such a good idea for you to come here after school. You hear things that are outside your experience and then you get upset by them. Elena is not going to break up Dr. Kiel's marriage, I promise you. Let's see if I can find someone to stay with you after school, okay?"

"No, Mom, no, I have to come here, I have to look after Miss Bianca."

Elena came into the hall where they were standing. She'd been in the lab but they hadn't seen her. Rhonda and Abigail both flushed.

"Sorry," Elena murmured. "I making all lives hard, but I not understanding, why is Dr. Dolan not like me?"

Rhonda shook her head. "He's jealous of Dr. Kiel, I think, and so he tries to attack the people who work for Dr. Kiel. Try not to pay attention to him."

"But Dr. Dolan said your husband's name wasn't in—in the Czech something, the magazine," Abigail piped up, to Rhonda's annoyance.

Elena didn't speak for a moment; her face turned white again and she clutched the door jamb for support. "No, he is scientist, he reading articles, deciding is science good or not good? He telling editor, but only editor have name in journal, not husband."

Dr. Dolan stormed out of Dr. Kiel's office, his round cheeks swollen with anger. "You were quite a devoted wife, Elena, if you studied your husband's work so much that you understand rickettsial degradation by lysosomal enzymes," he said sarcastically.

"I married many years, I learning many things," Elena said. "Now I learning how live with husband in prison. I also learn acid rinse glassware, forgive me."

She brushed past Dolan and went down the hall to the autoclave room, where the pressure machine washed glassware at a temperature high enough to kill even the peskiest bacterium.

Over the weekend, Bob and the other graduate students took care of the animals. On Monday, Abigail hurried anxiously back to the lab after school. Bob was in the animal room with a strange man who was wearing a navy suit and a white shirt. None of the scientists ever dressed like that: they were always spilling acids that ate holes in their clothes. Even Mother had to be careful when she went into the lab—once Bob accidentally dripped acid on her leg and her nylons dissolved.

"But she has access to the animals?"

Bob was shifting unhappily from one foot to the other. He didn't see Abigail, but she was sure the man in the suit was talking about her. She crept behind the cages into the alcove where the big sinks stood.

Bob was putting on a mask and gloves to go into the contamination room, but the man in the suit seemed to be afraid of the germs; he said he didn't need to go into the room.

"I just want to know if you keep it secure. There are a lot of bugs in there that could do a lot of damage in the wrong hands."

"You have to have a key to get in here," Bob assured the man, showing him that the door was locked.

When the two men left, Abigail went out to the cages. Miss Bianca's cage was empty. Her heart seemed to stop. She had the same queer empty feeling under her ribcage that she'd felt when Daddy said he was leaving to start a new life in California.

A lot of the cages were empty, Abigail realized, not just Miss Bianca's. Bob and Dr. Kiel had waited until the weekend so they could steal Miss Bianca and give her a shot full of germs while Abigail wasn't there to protect her.

Dr. Kiel had given Mother a set of keys when she started working for him. Abigail went back up the stairs to Dr. Kiel's lab. Mother was working on Dr. Kiel's expense report from his last trip to Washington. Abigail pretended to study Spanish explorers in the 1500s, sitting so quietly that people came and went, including Bob and the man in the suit, without paying attention to her.

Dr. Kiel was in his lab, talking to Elena as they stood over a microscope. The lab was across the hall; Abigail couldn't hear what anyone said, but suddenly Dr. Kiel bellowed "Rhonda!" and Mother hurried over with her shorthand notebook.

As soon as she was gone, Abigail went to the drawer where Mother kept her purse. She found the keys and ran back down to the animal room. She didn't bother about gloves and masks. At any second someone might come in, or Mother would notice her keys were missing.

There were so many keys on the key ring it took five tries before she found the right one. In the contamination room, it didn't take long to find Miss Bianca: slips of paper with the number of the mouse and the date of the injection were attached to each cage door. *139. Miss Bianca.* The poor mouse was huddled in the back of her cage, shivering. Abigail put her in her pocket.

"I'll get you one of those special pills. You'll feel better in a jiffy," Abigail promised her.

When she got back upstairs, Mother and Dr. Kiel were inside his office. He was talking to her in a worried voice. Elena and Bob were in the lab. Abigail got the bottle of pills from the cabinet. The bottle said four a day for ten days for adults, but Miss Bianca was so tiny, maybe one tablet cut into four? Abigail took ten of them and put the bottle away just as Mother came out.

While Mother was preparing dinner, Abigail made a nest for Miss Bianca in a shoebox lined with one of her t-shirts. She took a knife from the drawer in the dining room to poke air holes into the box, then used it to cut the pills into four pieces. They were hard to handle and kept slipping away from the knife. When she finally had them cut up, she couldn't get Miss Bianca to take one. She just lay in the shoebox, not lifting her head.

"You have to take it or you'll die," Abigail told her, but Miss Bianca didn't seem to care.

Abigail finally pried open the mouse's little mouth and shoved the piece of pill in. Miss Bianca gave a sharp squeak, but she swallowed the pill.

"That's a good girl," Abigail said.

Over dinner, Abigail asked her mother who the man in the suit had been. "He was with Bob in the animal room," she said. "Is he spying on the animals?"

Rhonda shook her head. "He's an FBI agent named Mr. Burroughs. Someone sent an anonymous letter telling the FBI to look at Dr. Kiel's lab."

"Because Elena is a communist spy?" Abigail said.

"Don't say things like that, Abigail. Especially not to Agent Burroughs. Elena is not a spy, and if Dr. Dolan would only—" she bit her lip, not wanting to gossip about Dolan with her daughter.

"But she did give Dr. Kiel a potion," Abigail persisted.

"Whatever you saw was none of your business!" Rhonda said. "Clear the table and put the dishes in the machine."

If Mother was angry, she was less likely to notice what Abigail was doing. While Mother watched *It Takes A Thief*, Abigail cleaned up the kitchen, then brought a saucer from her doll's tea set into the kitchen and put some peanut butter in it. Before she went to bed, she stuck some peanut butter onto another piece of the pill and got Miss Bianca to swallow it. When she brushed her teeth, she filled one of her doll's teacups with water. The mouse didn't want to drink, so Abigail brought in a wet washcloth and stuck it in Miss Bianca's mouth.

She quickly shoved the shoebox under her bed when she heard Mother coming down the hall to tuck her in for the night.

Abigail didn't sleep well. She worried what would happen when Dr. Kiel discovered that Miss Bianca was missing from the lab: she should have taken all the mice, she realized. Then the FBI might think it had been a communist, stealing their secret mice. What would happen, too, when Mother realized one of Abigail's t-shirts was missing.

In the morning, she was awake before Mother. She gave Miss Bianca another piece of pill in peanut butter. The mouse was looking better: she took the pill in her little paws and licked the peanut butter from it, then nibbled the tablet. Abigail took her into the bathroom with her and Miss Bianca sipped water from the tap in the sink.

All this was good, but it didn't stop Abigail feeling sick to her stomach when she thought about how angry Dr. Kiel would be. Mother would lose her job; she would never forgive Abigail. She put the mouse on her shoulder and rubbed her face against its soft fur. "Can you help me, Miss Bianca? Can you summon the Prisoner's Aid society now that I've saved your life?"

The doorbell rang just then, a loud shrill sound that frightened both girl and mouse. Miss Bianca skittered down inside Abigail's pajama top, trying to hide. By the time Abigail was able to extricate the mouse, she was covered in scratches. If Mother saw them—

The doorbell rang again. Mother was getting up. Abigail ran back to her bedroom and put Miss Bianca into the shoebox. She peeped out of her room. Mother was tying a dressing gown around her waist, opening the front door. Dr. Kiel was standing there, the vein in his forehead throbbing.

"Did you do this?" he demanded, shaking a newspaper in Mother's face.

Mother backed up. "Dr. Kiel! What are you—I just got up—Abigail! Put some clothes on."

Abigail had forgotten to button her pajama top. She slipped back into her room, her heart pounding. Dr. Kiel had come to fire Mother. Her teeth were chattering, even though it was a warm fall day.

She flattened herself against the wall and waited for Dr. Kiel to demand that Mother turn her daughter over to the police. Instead, Mother was looking at the newspaper in bewilderment.

"'Reds in the Lab?' What is this about, Dr. Kiel?"

"You didn't tell the paper that the FBI was in the lab yesterday?" he demanded.

"Of course not. Really, Dr. Kiel, you should know you can trust me."

He slapped the paper against his hand so hard that it sounded like the crack of a ball against a bat. "If Bob Pharris did it—"

"Dr. Kiel, I'm sure none of your students would have called the newspaper with a report like this. Perhaps—" she hesitated. "I don't like to say this, it's not really my place, but you know Dr. Dolan has been concerned about Elena Mirova."

Dr. Kiel had been looking calmer, but now his jaw clenched again. "Elena is a refugee from communism. She came here because I thought she could be safe here. I will not let her be hounded by a witch hunt."

"The trouble is, we don't know anything about her," Mother said. "She seems to know a great deal about your work, more than seems possible for a dishwasher, even one whose husband was a scientist."

Dr. Kiel snarled. "Patrick Dolan has been sharpening his sword, hoping to stick it into me, since the day he arrived here. He's not concerned about spies, he's studying the best way to make me look bad."

He looked down the hall and seemed to see Abigail for the first time. "Get dressed, Abigail; I'll give you a ride to school."

Dr. Kiel drove a convertible. Susie Campbell would faint with envy when she saw Abigail in the car. When she started to dress, Abigail realized her arms were covered with welts from where Miss Bianca had scratched her. She found a long-sleeved blouse to wear with her red skirt. By the time she had combed her hair and double-checked that Miss Bianca had water, Mother was dressed. Dr. Kiel was calmly drinking a cup of coffee.

Abigail looked at the newspaper.

The FBI paid a surprise visit to the University of Kansas campus yesterday, in response to a report that the Bacteriology Department is harboring Communists among its lab support staff. Several members of the department work on micro-organisms that could be used in germ warfare. The research is supposed to be closely monitored, but recently, there's been a concern that a Soviet agent has infiltrated the department.

The newspaper and the FBI both thought Elena was a spy. Maybe she was, maybe she really had given Dr. Kiel a magic potion that blinded his eyes to who she really was.

"Rhonda, we're going to have every reporter in America calling about this business. Better put your war paint on and prepare to do battle," Dr. Kiel said, getting up from the table. "Come on, Abigail. Get to school. You have to learn as much as you can so that morons like this bozo

Burroughs from the FBI can't pull the wool over your eyes."

Abigail spent a very nervous day frightened about what would happen when she got to the lab and Bob Pharris accused her of stealing Miss Bianca. She kept hoping she'd get sick. At recess, she fell down on the playground, but she only skinned her knees; the school nurse wouldn't let her go home for such a trivial accident.

She walked from school to the bacteriology department as slowly as possible. Even so, she arrived too soon. She lingered at the elevator, wondering if she should just go to Dr. Kiel and confess. Bob Pharris stuck his head out of the lab.

"Oh, it's you, short stuff. We've been under siege all day—your mom is answering two phones at once—someone even called from the BBC in London. A guy tried to get into the animal room this morning—I threw him out with my own bare hands and for once Dr. Kiel thinks I'm worth something." He grinned. "Number 19 cannot get a PhD but he has a future as a bouncer."

Abigail tried to smile, but she was afraid his next comment would be that he'd seen that Number 139 was missing and would Abigail hand her over at once.

"Don't worry, Abby, this will blow over," Bob said, going back into the lab.

Dr. Kiel was shouting; his voice was coming up the hall from Dr. Dolan's lab. She crept down the hall and peeked inside. Agent Burroughs, the bozo from the FBI, was there with Dr. Kiel and Dr. Dolan.

"What did you do with her?" Dr. Dolan said. "Give her a ticket back to Russia along with your mouse?"

Abigail's heart thudded painfully.

"The Bureau just wants to talk to her," said Agent Burroughs. "Where did she go?"

"Ask Dolan," Dr. Kiel said. "He's the one who sees Reds under the bed. He probably stabbed her with a pipette and threw her into the Kansas River."

Agent Burroughs said, "If you're hiding a communist, Dr. Kiel, you could be in serious trouble."

"What is this, Joe McCarthy all over again?" Dr. Kiel said. "Guilt by association? Elena Mirova fled Czechoslovakia because her husband was imprisoned. As long as she was in Bratislava, they could torture him with the threat that they could hurt his wife. She was hiding here to protect her husband. Your jackbooted feet have now put her life in danger as well as his."

"There was no Elena Mirova in Czechoslovakia," Burroughs said. "There are no Czech scientists named Mirov or Mirova."

"What? You know the names and locations of everyone in Czechoslovakia, Burroughs?" Dr. Kiel snapped. "How did you get that from the comfort of your armchair in Washington?"

"The head of our Eastern Europe bureau looked into it," Burroughs said. "The Bratislava institute is missing one of their scientists, a biological warfare expert named Magdalena Spirova; she disappeared six weeks ago. Do you know anything about her?"

"I'm not like you, Burroughs, keeping track of everyone behind the Iron Curtain," Dr. Kiel said. "I'm just a simple Kansas researcher, trying to find a cure for Q Fever. If you'd go back to the rat hole you crawled out of, I could get back to work."

"Your dishwasher is gone, whatever her name is, and one of your infected mice is gone," Burroughs said. "I'm betting Mirova-Spirova is taking your germ back to Uncle Ivan and the next thing we know, every soldier we have below the DMZ will be infected with Q Fever."

Abigail's bookbag slipped out of her hand and landed on the floor with an earth-ending noise. The men looked over at her.

Dr. Kiel said, "What's up, Abigail? You think you can be David to all us angry Sauls? Play a little Bach and calm us down?"

Abigail didn't know what he was talking about, just saw that he wasn't angry with her for standing there. "I'm sorry, Dr. Kiel, I was worried about the mouse."

"Abigail is the youngest member of my team," Dr. Kiel told Burroughs. "She looks after our healthy animals."

The FBI man rounded on Abigail, firing questions at her: Had she noticed Elena hanging around the contamination room? How hard was it to get into the room? How often did Abigail feed the mice? When did she notice one of the mice was missing?

"Leave her alone," Dr. Kiel said. "Abigail, take your violin down and play for the mice. We have a lab full of fascists today who could infect you with something worse than Q Fever, namely innuendo and smear tactics."

"You signed a loyalty oath, Dr. Kiel," Agent Burroughs said. "Calling me names makes me wonder whether you really are a loyal American."

Dr. Kiel looked so murderous that Abigail fled down to the animal room with her violin and her bookbag. She felt guilty about taking Miss Bianca, she felt guilty about not rescuing the other mice, she was worried about Miss Bianca alone at home not getting all the pills she needed. She was so miserable that she sat on the floor of the animal room and cried.

Crying wore her out. Her head was aching and she didn't think she had the energy to get to her feet. The floor was cool against her hot head and the smells of the animals and the disinfectants were so familiar that they calmed her down.

A noise at the contamination room door woke her. A strange man, wearing a brown suit that didn't fit him very well, was trying to undo the lock. He must be a reporter trying to sneak into the lab. Abigail sat up. Her head was still aching, but she needed to find Bob.

The man heard her when she got to her feet. He spun around, looking scared, then, when he saw that it was a child, he smiled in a way that frightened Abigail.

"So, Dr. Kiel has little girls working with his animals. Does he give you a key to this room?"

Abigail edged toward the door. "I only feed the healthy mice. You have to see Bob Pharris for the sick mice."

As soon as she'd spoken, Abigail wished she hadn't; what if this man wrote it up in his newspaper and Bob got in trouble?

"There aren't any foreigners working with the animals? Foreign women?"

Even though Abigail was scared that Elena was a spy, she didn't feel right about saying so, especially after hearing Dr. Kiel talking about witch hunts.

"We only have foreign witches in the lab," she said. "They concoct magic potions to make Dr. Kiel fall in love with them."

The man frowned in an angry way, but he decided to laugh instead, showing a gold tooth in the front of his mouth. "You're a little girl with a big imagination, aren't you? Who is this foreign witch?"

Abigail hated being called a little girl. "I don't know. She flew in on her broomstick and didn't tell us her name."

"You're too old for such childish games," the man said, bending over her. "What is her name, and what does she do with the animals?"

"Mamelouk. Her name is Mamelouk."

The man grabbed her arm. "You know that isn't her name."

Bob came into the animal room just then. "Abby—Dr. Kiel said he'd sent you—what the hell are you doing here? I thought I told you this morning that you can't come into the lab without Dr. Kiel's say-so and I know damned well he didn't say so. Get out before I call the cops."

Bob looked almost as fierce as Dr. Kiel. The man in the brown suit let go of Abigail's arm.

He stopped in the doorway and said, "I'm only looking for the foreign woman who's been working here. Magdalena, isn't it?"

Abigail started to say, "No, it's—" but Bob frowned at her and she was quiet.

"I *thought* you knew, little girl. What is it?"

"Mamelouk," Abigail said. "I told you that before."

"So now you know, Buster. Off you go."

Bob walked to the elevator with Abigail and called the car. He stood with a foot in the door until the man got on the elevator. They watched the numbers go down to "1" to make sure he'd ridden all the way to the ground.

"Maybe I should go down and throw him out

of the building," Bob said. "He was here when I opened for the day. Elena took one look at him and disappeared, so I don't know if he's someone who's been harassing her at home, or if she's allergic to reporters."

He looked down at Abigail. "You feeling okay, short stuff? You're looking kind of white—all the drama getting to you, huh? Maybe Dr. Kiel will let your mom take you home. She didn't even break for lunch today."

When they got to the office, Bob went in to tell Dr. Kiel about the man in the animal room, but Rhonda took one look at Abigail and hung up the phone mid-sentence.

"Darling, you're burning up," she announced, feeling Abigail's forehead. "I hope you haven't caught Q Fever."

She went into Dr. Kiel's office. He came out to look at Abigail, felt her forehead as Rhonda had, and agreed. "You need her doctor to see her, but I can give you some tetracycline to take home with you."

Rhonda shook her head. "Thank you, Dr. Kiel, but I'd better let the pediatrician prescribe for her."

Mother collected the bookbag and violin where Abigail had dropped them on the floor of the animal room. "I never should have let you work with the animals. I worried all along that it wasn't safe."

In the night, Abigail's fever rose. She was shivering, her joints ached. She knew she had Q Fever, but if she told Mother, Mother wouldn't let her stay with Miss Bianca.

Mother put cold washcloths on her head. While she was out of the room, Abigail crawled under the bed and got the mouse. Miss Bianca needed more of her pills, but Abigail was too sick to feed her. She put Miss Bianca in her pajama pocket and hoped she wouldn't make the mouse sick again.

Mother came and went, Abigail's fever rose, the doorbell rang.

Abigail heard her mother's voice, faintly, as if her mother were at the end of the street, not the end of the hall. "What are you doing here?

I thought it would be the doctor! Abigail is very sick."

An even fainter voice answered. "I sorry, Rhonda. Men is watching flat, I not know how I do."

She was a terrible spy; she couldn't speak English well enough to fool anyone. Abigail lay still, although her head ached so badly she wanted to cry. She couldn't sleep or weep; Mother might need her to call the cops.

"You can't stay here!" Mother was saying. "Dr. Kiel—the FBI—"

"Also KGB," Elena said. "They wanting me. They find me now with news story."

"The KGB?"

"Russian secret police. I see man in morning, know he is KGB, wanting me, finding me from news."

"But why do the KGB want you?"

Elena smiled sadly. "I am—oh, what is word? Person against own country."

"Traitor," Rhonda said. "You are a traitor? But—Dr. Kiel said you had to hide from the communists."

"Yes, is true, I hiding. They take my husband, they put him in prison, they torture, but for what? For what he write in books. He write for freedom, for liberty, for those words he is enemy of state. Me, I am scientist, name Magdalena Spirova. I make same disease that Dr. Kiel make. Almost same, small ways different. Russians want my *Rickettsia prowazekii* for germ wars, I make, no problem. Until they put husband in prison."

Rhonda took Elena out of the doorway into the front room. Abigail couldn't hear them. She was freezing now, her teeth chattering, but she slid out of bed and went into the hall, where she could hear Elena.

Elena was saying that when she learned the authorities were torturing her husband, she pretended not to care. She waited until she could take a trip to Yugoslavia. She injected herself with the *Rickettsia* she was working on right before she left Bratislava to go to Sarajevo. In Sarajevo, Elena ran away from the secret police who were watching her and hitchhiked to Vienna. From Vienna, she flew to Canada. In Toronto, she called Dr. Kiel, whom she had met when he came to Bratislava in 1966. He drove up to Toronto and hid her in the backseat of his car to smuggle her to Kansas. He gave her tetracycline tablets, but she didn't take them until she had extracted her infected blood to give to Dr. Kiel. That was the magic potion Abigail had seen in the animal room; that was why her arm was all bruised—it's not easy to take a blood sample from your own veins.

"Now, Dr. Kiel have *Rickettsia prowazekii*, he maybe find vaccine, so biological war not useful."

The words faded in and out. Miss Bianca had a bad Russian germ, now Abigail had it, maybe she would die for thinking Elena-Magdalena was a communist spy.

The front door opened again. Abigail saw the brown suit. "Look out," she tried to say, but her teeth were chattering too hard. No words would come out.

The brown legs came down the hall. "Yes, little girl. You are exactly who I want."

He put an arm around her and dragged her to her feet. Mother had heard the door; she ran into the hall and screamed when she saw the brown suit with Abigail. She rushed toward him but he waved an arm at her and she stopped: he was holding a gun.

He shouted some words in a language that Abigail didn't understand, but Elena-Magdalena came into the hall.

"I am telling Dr. Spirova that I will shoot you and shoot the little girl unless she comes with me now," the man said to Rhonda. His voice was calm, as if he was reading a book out loud.

"Yes, you putting little girl down." Elena's voice sounded as though her mouth were full of chalk. "I go with you. I see, here is end of story."

Elena walked slowly toward him. The man grinned and tightened his grip on Abigail. It took Rhonda and Elena a moment to realize he was going to keep Abigail, perhaps use her as a hostage to get safe passage out of Kansas. Rhonda darted forward but Elena shoved her to the ground and seized the man's arm.

He fired the gun and Elena fell, bleeding, but he had to ease his chokehold on Abigail.

"Miss Bianca, save us!" Abigail screamed.

She dropped the mouse down the man's shirtfront. Miss Bianca skittered inside in terror. The man began flailing his arms, slapping at his chest, then his armpits, as the mouse frantically tried to escape. He howled in pain: Miss Bianca had bitten him. He managed to reach inside his shirt for the mouse, but by then, Rhonda had snatched the gun from him. She ran to the front door and started shouting for help.

Abigail, her face burning with fever, fought to get the mouse out of his hand. Finally, in despair, she bit his hand. He punched her head, but she was able to catch Miss Bianca as she fell from his open fist.

The police came. They took away the KGB man. An ambulance came and took Elena to the hospital. The doctor came; Abigail had a high fever, she shouldn't be out of bed, she shouldn't be keeping mice in dirty boxes under her bed, he told Rhonda sternly, but Abigail became hysterical when he tried to take Miss Bianca away, so he merely lectured Rhonda on her poor parenting decisions. He gave Abigail a shot and said she needed to stay in bed, drink lots of juice, and stay away from dirty animals.

The next morning, Dr. Kiel arrived with a large bouquet of flowers for Abigail. Rhonda made Abigail confess everything to Dr. Kiel, how she had stolen Miss Bianca, how she had stolen tetracycline out of his office. She was afraid he would be furious, but the vein in his forehead didn't move. Instead, he smiled, his brown eyes soft and even rather loving.

"You cured the mouse with quarters of tetracycline tablets dipped in peanut butter, hmm?" He asked to see the pieces Abigail had cut up. "I think we're going to have to promote you from feeding animals to being a full-fledged member of the research team."

A few months later, Dr. Dolan left Kansas to teach in Oklahoma. Later still, Bob did get his

PhD. He was a good and kind teacher, even if he never had much success as a researcher. Magdalena recovered from her bullet wound and was given a job at the National Institutes of Health in Washington, where she worked until the fall of the Iron Curtain meant her husband could be released from prison.

Miss Bianca stayed with Abigail, living to the ripe old age of three. Although Rhonda continued to work for Dr. Kiel, she wouldn't let Abigail back in the animal lab. Even so, Abigail grew up to be a doctor working for Physicians for Social Responsibility, trying to put an end to torture. As for the five lumpy Kiel children, one of them grew up to write about a Chicago private eye named V. I. Warshawski.

BETRAYED

RONALD G. SERCOMBE

A SHORT STORY WRITER known for his mystery and adventure tales, Ronald George Sercombe (1893–1965) produced short fiction for both pulp magazines and what became known as the "slicks" because of the high-quality, shiny paper used.

Sercombe wrote stories for *Argosy* and *Liberty* (the popular series featuring Bessie Arbruster; in one story, the charming young lady goes fishing and catches a German submarine) and more than two dozen stories for *The Saturday Evening Post*, one of the most popular and high-paying magazines of the twentieth century.

Sercombe also provided the story for "Four Hours in White," an episode of the highly regarded television series *Climax!*. Directed by Buzz Kulik, it was a one-hour program that aired on CBS on February 6, 1958. The well-received drama is set in a hospital where a surgeon and a hospital administrator engage in a battle pitting two powerful figures against each other in a situation involving ethics, risk-taking, humaneness, cowardice, and bravado.

Identical twins have been in a serious accident in which one is largely unscathed while the other is almost certainly doomed unless one brother agrees to a kidney transplant for the other—a relatively new and still-dangerous procedure in 1958—which would also put his life at risk. The surgeon wants to proceed while the administrator prefers the safer, more conservative approach of doing nothing.

It is understandable that this program was made in what is often termed the Golden Age of television because it is well written, well directed, and featured such stars as Dan Duryea (as the principled surgeon), Ann Rutherford, and Steve McQueen (who played both twins).

"Betrayed" was originally published in the April 1964 issue of *Argosy*.

BETRAYED

RONALD G. SERCOMBE

THE CONSTELLATION, weary and a little wobbly after a thirteen-hundred-mile flight from New York with only a brief respite at Miami for fuel, fairly brushed the begonia-bowered peak of Blue Mountain, pushing through misty spirals nearly a mile and a half above the barren flatlands of Jamaica. Then it began a bumpy, ear-congesting descent to Palisadoes Airport. "There it is," Arthur Anders said, nudging the right elbow of his slumbering wife, Linda. "There's Jamaica—land of glistening ferns and eternal sunshine. Yonder lies Kingston." She opened her eyes briefly. They were a too-bright blue, set in a disingenuous face topped by a disheveled mop of tinted red hair. She yawned. "I couldn't care less," she said. "I wanted Rio. I still want Rio." Arthur Anders sighed. "How many times must I explain? Rio would have meant identification papers, passports, reams of red tape. Probably a clattering teletype message or a phone call to Central Intelligence." He spoke softly. The softness was appropriate because his eyes were soft brown, his face a soft tan and even his hair a softening gray. Few would suspect he possessed Q-clearance for atomic security. But this was quite in keeping with the policy of Central Intelligence—to select apparent nonentities for top security jobs.

The monstrous bird with the glistening wings nosed toward a landing strip. It bounced twice on macadam and its tires shrieked as they left a puffy wake of acrid, smoldering rubber. Like a beaten eagle, the plane taxied to a rolling ramp, trembled, spluttered, and whined as its four propellors ceased beating the air.

Parked near the airdrome were half a dozen old taxicabs. Salt, sun, and dust had long since removed their gloss—with one exception. Dudley's 1942 Chevrolet looked almost as bright as the day it had left the factory. The reason was obvious. Even now, as sweat dripped from his forehead, Dudley applied wax and vigorously polished the glabrous hood of the old car. In the trunk, he had several cans of touch-up paint, bottles of heavy oil, cans of grease, and plastic containers of water. The Chevrolet, purchased from a tourist in 1947 for two hundred hard-earned banana-picking pounds—or about five hundred and sixty American dollars—was his pride and joy. As he rubbed, Dudley sang softly, rhythmically:

Carry me ackee gone o' Linstead Market,
Not a quattie wort' sell;
Lard, what a night, not a bite,
What a Saturday night!

He counted passengers as they stepped down the ramp. There were forty-seven. More than half of them were obviously tourists, which made this a very good flight indeed for an off-season August day. The passengers looked uncomfortable as they emerged from an air-conditioned cabin into a ninety-degree furnace, donning sun glasses and mopping foreheads.

Dudley shaded his eyes with the palm of a hand. The noontime sun, reflecting on concrete paving, magnified the red texture of his dark skin. He was humbly proud of that color because it marked him as a true Jamaican, a descendant of Arawaks and a member of the proud but obsessively primitive Maroon tribe. Dudley, however, contrary to the mores of most of his friends and kin, had chosen to face civilization and its complex problems rather than retreat to the weird mountain fastnesses near Accompong.

Now the passengers were claiming their baggage and most of the cab drivers, their eyes gleaming like freshly minted Yankee silver dollars, were eagerly bargaining with tourists, offering "special" hourly, daily or weekly rates.

Not so Dudley. He merely stood stiffly at attention beside his shining car, which had two doors open. He smiled and nodded at all new arrivals who came within nodding range but he refused—as always—to take any part in the mad scramble for fares.

The mild-mannered man who elbowed his way through the crowd, clinging to an arm of a woman with reddish hair and blue eyes, spotted the gleaming cab. The man carried a leather attaché case.

"You free?" he inquired, glancing quickly at Dudley.

"Yes, sir," Dudley said courteously. "Climb right in, sir. Where are your bags?" He spoke with a distinct British accent.

"Over on the rack," the man said. "Two large brown suitcases. On each of them are the initials A. A."

Dudley reached out a hand for the attaché case but the man shook his head. "This I carry with me—always. Remember that."

Dudley got the bags and deposited them in the trunk of the cab. He closed the curb-side doors, climbed behind the driver's seat, pressed the foot starter, and the engine purred smoothly.

"The Myrtle Bank Hotel, sir?" Dudley asked, glancing over his right shoulder. Virtually all tourists checked in at the Myrtle Bank Hotel in Kingston to freshen up and arrange itineraries.

"It's hot as hell," the woman said irritably. "Get moving."

Dudley started driving as the man replied, "Just tour around Kingston for a while until we make up our minds. We neglected to make reservations. Do you suppose there are any vacancies in good mountain lodges—about three thousand feet up—above the heat and mosquito level?"

Dudley nodded. "I daresay, sir. This morning I brought down four departing guests from the Casa Carib. It is about four thousand feet up in the Blue Mountains. The accommodations are excellent, the food is very fine, and the view is beautiful. The temperature averages about sixty-six degrees. It is an ideal place for a man and a woman to get lost."

"What do you mean—lost?" The man sounded startled.

Dudley gestured laconically with his left hand. "Lost from all this, sir. The crowds, the traffic, the police whistles and horns."

"You speak very good English." Now the man sounded relieved. "You must have attended school."

Dudley nodded and his chest expanded. "Thank you, sir. My parents were quashies—peasants. They had nothing. It is very unpleasant, having nothing."

"So you decided to do something about it?" the man asked.

"Yes, sir. As a child, I used to drive out to the

airport with a friendly cab driver. I did many odd jobs. When the University of the West Indies was founded in 1949 I became a charter member of night-school classes." Dudley chuckled. "I also became the charter janitor."

The woman, glancing out of the cab window onto crowded Harbour Street, said icily, "Through these islands entered integration. I suppose you belong to the country club, too."

Dudley spoke quietly. "Hardly, mistress."

"Don't call me mistress!" the woman said belligerently, holding out her right hand. A diamond sparkled. "We've been duly wed for seven stupid years."

"Easy, Linda," the man said. "It's an island custom. Married women are known as mistresses."

She spoke harshly. "Damn the island customs! Damn the island, too! Now what do we do? Go and sit on top of a mountain and twiddle our thumbs for a couple of months?"

Arthur Anders, observing the veins bulging in Dudley's neck, said softly but firmly, "Perhaps you'd prefer to be laundering at Leavenworth. I warn you again, Linda—be careful what you say. You are on British soil, and Jamaicans, for the most part, are highly loyal subjects. I am sure you possess enough intelligence to realize that, as my hostess and confidential secretary, you are involved as an accessory before and after."

Dudley cleared his throat. "Excuse me, sir— mistress. We are now driving past the government buildings on Duke Street. Over yonder, where the coconut palms grow high, are the offices of the United States consular representative. Almost next door are the offices of the Cuban and Colombia consular representatives."

"Interesting," Arthur Anders said. He chuckled. "And tell me, where is the Khrushchev Club?"

"Jamaica," Dudley replied, "does not have consular headquarters for the Russians, so far as I know, sir."

Again Anders chuckled. "So you play cards with Fidel but Nikita is merely a kibitzer? 'Twas ever thus."

"I fear I do not understand."

"What is your name?" Anders asked.

"Dudley, sir."

"Dudley what?"

"Quashies rarely have second names, sir. It makes little difference. Sometimes they adopt the name of the owner of the banana or sugar cane plantations where they work. In my case, my parents and I worked for Sir Edward Dudley."

"I see." Anders hesitated. "Dudley, you might be helpful to me. We expect to be here for six weeks. What would you charge to serve as our private chauffeur, on a round-the-clock basis?"

"Fifteen pounds a week, sir. Plus fuel and room and board in servants' quarters wherever you lodge."

"I like to work in round figures," Anders replied, "without so many extra shillings for this and farthings for that. I'll pay you fifty American dollars a week for six weeks. Is it a deal?"

"That will be quite satisfactory, sir."

"The name is Anders. Arthur Anders."

"Yes, sir, Mr. Anders. Now would you and Mistress Anders like, perhaps, to visit the straw market or enjoy tall planter's punches at one of the better pubs?"

Linda spoke spitefully. "Take us out of this stinking town and up into the mountains. Now!"

"Yes, mistress." Dudley spoke quietly. "You will pardon me, please, but the town does not stink. Our island, as a whole, is a poor one. There is great poverty and much unemployment. But our people are clean and decent. Patient, too, I daresay."

"Take us up to the Casa Carib, Dudley," Anders ordered. "Mrs. Anders is tired and nervous. We had a bumpy flight."

Dudley made a quick left turn on to a blacktop road. He drove rapidly but professionally through the city, resting an elbow on the horn button at every intersection. Twice Anders closed his eyes and clenched his fists as he waited for a crash.

Then he came to realize that it was the driver with the loudest horn and fastest pick-up who managed to navigate successfully in Kingston.

They passed through several small, squalid villages. The black-top road ended abruptly and now they were climbing sharply up the mountain over a winding limestone road so narrow that no two cars could pass except at intervals of about a mile where the trail would widen briefly. Now and then, they would speed through dark tunnels, tropically and splendidly beautiful with the lush vegetation from alluvial pockets, and they could hear the wild, weird, rhythmic sound of water cascading over towering cliffs.

"Yonder," Dudley said, pointing to a magnificent tree with decorative hanging clusters of capsular fruits, "is one of our Ackee trees. Very good fruit. Mashed with beef, pork, and onions, it makes very good soup."

"How much further?" the woman asked.

"Four, perhaps five miles, mistress. The Blue Mountains are very steep. We must wind around and up."

Half an hour later, they emerged into a level clearing where the air was cool and invigorating and the view of Kingston and its busy harbor fairly breathtaking. Dudley braked the car to a halt at the steps of a structure that was architecturally British yet which resembled a stateside split-level ranch house built into the side of a mountain.

A tall, thin, agile man, carrying an armful of late-blooming cassias, stepped blithely down the steps from a wide verandah and greeted his new guests.

"Harry Chalmers, at your service," he said cheerfully, opening a car door. "Welcome aboard. Had my binoculars on you as you wound up the trail. Sorry Mrs. Chalmers is not with me. A bit under the weather, you know."

He helped Linda out of the car and presented her with the bouquet. She murmured her thanks. Then he shook hands firmly with Anders,

who said, "My wife, Linda, Mr. Chalmers. I am Arthur Anders. I trust you have a vacancy."

Chalmers nodded vigorously. "Oh, yes. Yes, indeed. Off season, you know. Four guests departed this morning. Only two other couples here. Honeymooners." Chalmers chuckled. "We see very little of them. We have a nice chalet overlooking the city, with twin beds, a tub and facilities for preparing snacks. Dudley, take their luggage over to the Mango Chalet. The door is open. Mrs. Anders, Mr. Anders, follow me. I shall order a fresh pot of tea while you register."

"Dudley," Anders said sharply, "the attaché case. I'll take it. It always stays with me. Remember?"

"Yes, sir," Dudley said.

Linda yawned. "I don't like tea. I really think I need a drink and a shower. I'll go with Dudley."

Chalmers looked apologetic.

"Shower?" he said. "I regret we have never installed showers. What a pity. But I shall have Matilda, our house girl, draw you a warm tub immediately."

"You got a swimming pool?" Linda asked irritably.

Chalmers nodded. "Yes, indeed. A charming pool. Fed by mountain springs." He smiled. "A bit on the coolish side for you statesiders. About sixty degrees. But invigorating. Most definitely."

"I'll bet," Linda said, trailing after Dudley. "Invigorating like an ice cube down your back."

"Don't mind her," Anders said, as Linda and Dudley vanished around a corner. "Long flight. Bumped into some squalls—all that sort of business."

"I understand," Chalmers said pleasantly. "Understand perfectly, old man. Sudden changes of altitude, too, you know. Such things are sometimes temporarily bothersome to newcomers. Tomorrow, she'll feel like a new woman. . . . Here—over this way. Here is the registry book. The rate for the Mango Chalet, double occupancy, is ten pounds a day. This includes dinner at sevenish each evening in the Manor House.

Most guests prepare their own breakfasts. You'll find the refrigerator adequately supplied. Then they tour the island, visiting our historic spots, and return for dinner."

Anders merely grunted. He was registering with care. At a New York hotel, he had made the dangerous mistake of signing correctly, "Mr. and Mrs. Andrew Anderson."

"I'll pay you two weeks in advance," Anders said crisply, laying four one hundred dollar bills on the desk. Chalmers studied his signature, counted the bills twice, and gave him eight American dollars in change.

"Now for a spot of tea, Mr. Anders?" Chalmers suggested, rubbing his hands together briskly. "Or perhaps you might prefer scotch and soda?"

Anders shook his head. "Thanks. I'll take a rain check."

Chalmers looked bewildered.

"I mean," Anders said, laughing, "I'll accept the invitation after I have freshened up and discussed plans with my wife."

"Most certainly," said Chalmers. "Delighted to have you, any time. By the way, Mango Chalet is so named because it rests beneath a large mango tree. If, during the night, you hear thumps on the roof, do not be alarmed. Occasionally, when breezes gust, mangoes drop."

"Glad it's not a coconut tree," Anders said jovially.

A bland-faced, uniformed Jamaican maid was leaving the chalet as Anders entered. She bowed her head.

"The mistress is in the tub, sir," she said. "Dudley has gone to the servants' quarters. On the table in the breakfast nook are two hand bells. All you need do for service is step out on the verandah, ring the small bell for me, the larger one for Dudley."

"Thank you," Anders said, admiring her figure as she left. Inside the chalet, he heard Linda splashing in the tub and singing. The words were slightly slurred. Anders suspected she had company in the tub: a bottle. In recent years, her capacity for alcohol had numbed her boudoir

bounteousness not to mention her executive reliability. They were heading, Anders often thought, for the point of no return.

"Linda," Anders called. "Are you all right? It's Arthur."

He heard her giggle. "Isn't it a crying shame. I thought maybe it was Dudley. He *does* look like Belafonte, doesn't he?"

"I want to talk to you," Anders said.

"Come on in. Bring Belafonte and Mr. Chalmers and Matilda. We'll have a hootenanny."

Angrily, Anders opened the bathroom door. The place was quaintly decorated, to put it mildly. Someone had converted an old rum vat into a tub. Linda was sitting in the tub, well lathered with suds and bourbon. A half-empty bottle rested precariously on the edge of the bathtub.

"On top of Old Smokey," she sang. "All covered with booze . . ."

"Damn it, Linda! Are you going to start this nonsense again?"

She looked at him with innocent blue eyes and blew an alcoholic bubble. "What else is there to do, darling—on top of Old Smokey? Twiddle our thumbs or pick pineapples or peel bananas? You tell me."

"Look," he said, swallowing his anger, "we've almost got it made. This is a nearly perfect hideout. About a month from now, after I'm sure we haven't been tailed, we'll fly to Caracas."

"Caracas," she said, imitating him. "Polly want a Caracas. But Linda wants out—back to New York where the lights are brighter and the martinis dryer."

"You'll like Caracas," he said quietly. "Lots of life and laughter. And from what I gather, by the time we get there, the Commies will be running the show in Venezuela. I'll be on top. We'll take vacations in Mexico City and Acapulco."

"Have you gathered anything else—like dough?" Linda demanded in a bitter voice.

"I'm moving cautiously. Our money—one hundred thousand dollars—lies just four thousand feet below us in the vault of the Bank of

Nova Scotia. Within the next few days, I'll contact Señor Cabrera of the Cuban consulate. I'll turn the papers over to him. He'll present them to the Soviet agent. We'll get our money, and after a cooling off period, we'll be on our way to South America."

She pouted. "Linda doesn't like Jamaica. Linda doesn't want South America. Linda wants New York—and out."

"You're in too damn deep to ever get out," he said savagely.

She laughed and wagged a pink finger at him. "Arthur's been a naughty boy," she said. "What would they say on Pennsylvania Avenue if Linda went back and told them how naughty?"

Anders shrugged. "It's as I told you. If you like the idea of laundering at Leavenworth, go on back to the states. You're hooked good. Don't forget it."

He walked out of the bathroom.

"Don't stumble over any cliffs, darling," he heard Linda call out, and simultaneously, someone knocked softly on the front door. He opened it abruptly.

"Pardon me, sir," Dudley said, handing him a fur neckpiece. "The mistress left this in the car."

"Thanks," Anders said ungraciously. He tossed the neckpiece on a chair. But as Dudley started to leave, he spoke again. "Dudley, I understand there are some mountain trails for tourists around here. Would you show me where they start?"

"Gladly, sir. Just follow me."

They walked behind the chalet and through a forest of mango and ebony trees. They reached a narrow limestone trail which afforded a spectacular view of the British cantonment, Newcastle, high in the mountains. The trail snaked perilously close to a precipice and a portion of it was sturdily fenced off with lignum vitae wood. Anders rested his arms on the fence.

"So it's a little hard making ends meet in this country?" he asked Dudley.

"It is not simple, sir."

"Here," Anders said, digging in a pocket. "I'll pay you three weeks in advance." He handed

Dudley three crisp fifty dollar bills and thought he detected a gleam in the eyes of the Jamaican.

"It is not necessary, sir. I trust you."

"Good. I trust you, too. So take the money. . . . Now, how'd you like to make another five hundred dollars?"

"Very much, sir. My automobile is rapidly deteriorating."

Anders cleared his throat. "All right. As I said, I trust you. And I think we understand each other." He gestured back toward the chalets. "Mrs. Anders has become very difficult. Impossible, in fact. She is a confirmed inebriant." Anders withdrew a wallet from his jacket. He extracted five one-hundred-dollar bills. "These trails are treacherous. I suspect that right now we are looking across a gorge that is at least a thousand feet deep. Could there not be an accident?" He handed the bills to Dudley.

Dudley glanced over both shoulders. His face was impassive as he accepted and pocketed the bills.

"Such things, I do not do myself, sir. But this does not eliminate the possibility of hiring an— ah—trustworthy assistant."

Anders smiled. "Good. One other thing. Are you acquainted with Señor Cabrera at the Cuban consulate?"

Dudley nodded. "Many times I have been his chauffeur."

Again, Anders smiled. "This afternoon, you will drive down to Kingston. I will write a note. In this note, I will advise the *señor* that I wish to meet him in a secluded spot to deliver some important papers. Do you know of such a spot?"

Dudley nodded. "The Harbour House. There is a back entrance to private rooms."

"Fine. Give me a report tomorrow."

"Very good, sir," Dudley said. He walked rapidly away and vanished in greenery—*almost,* Anders thought, *like an Indian.*

Anders expected, upon his return to the chalet, to find Linda passed out on a bed. Instead, the warm bath and relaxation apparently had had a sobering effect.

"Hi," she said nonchalantly. "I feel like stepping out. I'd like to take a ride to the top of Old Smokey."

"Go ahead," Anders said flatly. "I want to bathe, shave, and sack out. Ring the big bell and Dudley will appear."

She laughed. "You trust me alone with Belafonte?"

"I trust you alone with no one."

"Diplomat, where is your charm?"

"It stumbled over a cliff, darling."

"Too bad it left you behind." She walked out the front door.

Five minutes later, as the old Chevrolet struggled up a steep incline, Dudley said to Linda, "The road does not entirely reach the peak of the mountain, mistress. It becomes too hazardous. The last half-mile must be on foot."

"That's all right," Linda said. She was sitting on the front seat beside him. "You can stop right here, Dudley." She smiled.

"I beg your pardon, mistress?"

"I said to stop here."

He complied.

"How would you like to make a thousand dollars, Dudley?"

He shrugged. "Money is always useful."

She reached into a pocket of her shorts and withdrew five one-hundred-dollar bills. She handed them to Dudley.

"Arthur, my husband, will ask you to drive him down to Kingston in a day or two. After a conference, he will expect to return here with his attaché case loaded with money. However, he won't return here. There will be—well—some sort of an accident. You will return with the attaché case and receive an additional five hundred dollars. Agreed?"

"Such things," Dudley said, accepting the bills, "I do not do myself, mistress. But I feel confident it can be arranged."

"Good. Now take me back to the chalet. I need a drink."

Late that afternoon, Dudley drove alone down to Kingston. He parked in front of the Cuban consulate. Then he walked, slowly and carefully, using several back alleys, to the United Kingdom trade commissioner's office in the Royal Mail Building. He entered by a back door and walked up a flight of stairs. In a private-room, he filed a report with a middle-aged man who had guileless blue eyes set in a rare-roast-beef-red cherubic face.

"Describe the attaché case, Dudley," the man ordered.

Dudley did so. The man strolled over to a locker, extracted an attaché case and showed it to Dudley.

"Something like this one?"

"Almost identical, Mr. Bartlett."

"Good." Mr. Bartlett stuffed the case with newspapers and locked it. He smiled as he lit a cigar.

"Late tonight, Dudley," Mr. Bartlett said, "you will make a substitute. How is your problem. Then bring Anders's attaché case here. I will advise the United States consular representative and we shall meet here about midnight. Thus far, Dudley, good show."

"Thank you, sir."

People rarely locked their windows or doors in the chalets at Casa Carib because the night breezes were soothing and the establishment had an excellent reputation. It was comparatively simple for barefooted Matilda to exchange attaché bags while Anders and his wife were sleeping that night. However, as she closed the door, it made a slight thump and she heard Linda say in startled tones, "Arthur, Arthur—wake up! I heard something."

Anders muttered, "Go back to sleep. It's the mangoes. They fall on the roof."

At exactly midnight, British and United States Government authorities opened and examined the contents of Anders's attaché case while Dudley stood by.

"By Jove!" Bartlett said at one point. "Have

a look at this. An authentic Pentagon report on the exact positions of all your Minutemen silos, latest developments on your Titan, Atlas, Hound Dog, and Sergeant missiles, the operational data of SAC, the positions of your ocean-bottom radar detectors, the most recent report on deployment and positions of Polaris-equipped submarines, the areas covered by your picket ships—and more. Gad!"

"It is highly disturbing," the man from state-side said.

"Good work, Dudley," Mr. Bartlett said. "We'll take it from here, never fear."

Dudley fumbled in a pocket. "I have the thousand dollars for you—the money they gave me for destroying one another."

Mr. Bartlett smiled. "Put it in the bank. I have discussed that matter with Scotland Yard. We all agree you've earned it."

"Thank you very much indeed, sir."

About nine the next morning, Dudley reported to the Anders' chalet.

"Good morning, Dudley," Anders said. He appeared to be in excellent humor. "Mrs. Anders and I have decided to do a little island hopping. Preferably off the beaten tourist tracks. Can do?"

"I'll have the car ready in half a mo', sir," Dudley replied.

They drove for nearly an hour over wild and wonderful mountain trails and finally reached a weird, barren area, out of which rose fantastic pyramids and cones of limestone and thick forests.

"We are in Maroon country," Dudley explained quietly. "This is known as the Cockpit country of Trelawny, near Accompong. It is said the Maroons were originally slaves who fled from their Spanish masters. They have their own government and tribal chief. They are rarely seen, even by our natives."

"Are they dangerous?" Anders asked.

Dudley smiled a little. "It all depends. They seek peace. But the Maroons are most perceptive. They instinctively recognize evil and deal with it in accordance with their own laws."

He stopped the old car and opened the doors. "Come," he said. "I will show you the oldest and largest cotton tree on the island. Few tourists have seen it."

They trailed him up a sharp incline, through a forest of cassias, coconut palms, and cedars. Anders, who was puffing, glanced at his wrist watch. They had been walking for about forty-five minutes. He looked at Linda. She, too, was breathing hard.

"Dudley," Anders said sharply. "I think we . . ."

He looked all around. Dudley had vanished.

"Me Jane, you Tarzan," Linda said.

"Very un-funny," Anders said. "Sit down. I'm tired."

The following midnight, Dudley met again with the British and United States Government men in the back room of the Royal Mail House. Mr. Bartlett spoke severely.

"Somehow, Mr. and Mrs. Anders have escaped from the island," he said. "You should have contacted me immediately, Dudley."

Dudley smiled. "They have not escaped. The Maroons have them."

Mr. Bartlett frowned. "We shall have to go after them."

Dudley shook his head. "I would not advise it, sir. The *kill backra* is blooming near Accompong. It is said the Maroons have an epidemic among them."

"Good God, man!" Mr. Bartlett said. "If yellow fever is rampant among the Maroons, we must send them medical aid."

Dudley shook his head. "A doctor might not return, sir. Nor would our medicines be used. The Maroons have their own medicine men. And betrayal, sir, deserves betrayal."

"Highly irregular," Mr. Bartlett said, coughing. "You should have advised me. What about their landlord, Mr. Chalmers?"

"I have advised Mr. Chalmers," Dudley said evenly, "that Mr. and Mrs. Anders were suddenly recalled stateside. I shall bring their baggage to your office, sir."

Mr. Bartlett arose. He addressed his friends. "Insofar as I am concerned," he said, "this confidential matter is closed. I assume, of course, that a coded cablegram will be sent to the Pentagon. That will be all for now, Dudley."

Back in his old cab, Dudley sang a song as he drove up the mountain:

Down the way where the lights are gay,
And the sun shines daily on the mountaintop . . .

After a night's rest and a day's relaxation he would take Matilda to Montego Bay for a dancing date in the Square. They might even attend the cinema. There was a stateside film showing which he had long wished to see. It was entitled "Counterespionage."

FOR YOUR EYES ONLY

IAN FLEMING

CBS, AFTER IT HAD ENJOYED so much success with a television adaptation of *Casino Royale* (1953) for an episode of the series *Climax!* in 1954, made contact with Ian Lancaster Fleming (1908–1964) in an attempt to get him to create a series based on his James Bond character, asking him to write thirty-two episodes over a two-year period. Fleming came up with seven new story ideas plus recycled episodes based on his previously published novels. However, stating that he didn't want to have to go under contract to "writing episodes or otherwise slaving," the series never came to fruition.

Later in the year, apparently having difficulty coming up with plots for new books, Fleming pulled the ideas from original episodes together for a collection of stories; "For Your Eyes Only" was one of them. For the TV series, it had been tentatively titled "Rough Justice" but, when adapted for print, it was first called "Death Leaves an Echo," then "Man's Work," before Fleming settled on the current title. The red "Eyes Only" stamp that appears internally and on the dust jacket of the first edition, lifted straight from the author's naval intelligence experience, was used on secret documents.

Fleming, born in London, began his career as a journalist and, while officially a correspondent in Moscow for the London *Times*, he unofficially worked for the Foreign Office. Although he wrote other books, notably the children's classic *Chitty Chitty Bang Bang* (1964), it is for the creation of James Bond, the most famous spy in literature and probably the most famous literary creation of the twentieth century, that he is best known. He wrote twelve books about the charismatic 007, beginning with *Casino Royale*, and enjoyed modest but not spectacular success until President John F. Kennedy publicly expressed his fondness for the books.

"For Your Eyes Only" was originally published in the June 1, 1960, issue of *Weekend* magazine; it was first collected in *For Your Eyes Only* (London, Jonathan Cape, 1960).

FOR YOUR EYES ONLY

IAN FLEMING

THE MOST BEAUTIFUL BIRD in Jamaica, and some say the most beautiful bird in the world, is the streamer-tail or doctor humming-bird. The cock bird is about nine inches long, but seven inches of it are tail—two long black feathers that curve and cross each other and whose inner edges are in a form of scalloped design. The head and crest are black, the wings dark green, the long bill is scarlet, and the eyes, bright and confiding, are black. The body is emerald green, so dazzling that when the sun is on the breast you see the brightest green thing in nature. In Jamaica, birds that are loved are given nicknames. *Trochilus polytmus* is called "doctor bird" because his two black streamers remind people of the black tail-coat of the old-time physician.

Mrs. Havelock was particularly devoted to two families of these birds because she had been watching them sipping honey, fighting, nesting, and making love since she married and came to Content. She was now over fifty, so many generations of these two families had come and gone since the original two pairs had been nicknamed Pyramus and Thisbe and Daphnis and Chloe by her mother-in-law. But successive couples had kept the names, and Mrs. Havelock now sat at her elegant tea service on the broad cool veranda and watched Pyramus, with a fierce "tee-tee-tee" dive-bomb Daphnis who had finished up the honey on his own huge bush of Japanese Hat and had sneaked in among the neighbouring Monkeyfiddle that was Pyramus's preserve. The two tiny black and green comets swirled away across the fine acres of lawn, dotted with brilliant clumps of hibiscus and bougainvillaea, until they were lost to sight in the citrus groves. They would soon be back. The running battle between the two families was a game. In this big finely planted garden there was enough honey for all.

Mrs. Havelock put down her teacup and took a Patum Peperium sandwich. She said: "They really are the most dreadful show-offs."

Colonel Havelock looked over the top of his *Daily Gleaner*. "Who?"

"Pyramus and Daphnis."

"Oh, yes." Colonel Havelock thought the names idiotic. He said: "It looks to me as if Batista will be on the run soon. Castro's keeping up the pressure pretty well. Chap at Barclay's told me this morning that there's a lot of funk money coming over here already. Said that Belair's been sold to nominees. One hundred and fifty thousand pounds for a thousand acres of cattle-tick

and a house the red ants'll have down by Christmas! Somebody's suddenly gone and bought that
ghastly Blue Harbour hotel, and there's even talk
that Jimmy Farquharson has found a buyer for
his place—leaf-spot and Panama disease thrown
in for good measure, I suppose."

"That'll be nice for Ursula. The poor dear
can't stand it out here. But I can't say I like the
idea of the whole island being bought up by
these Cubans. But Tim, where do they get all the
money from, anyway?"

"Rackets, union funds, Government money—
God knows. The place is riddled with crooks and
gangsters. They must want to get their money out
of Cuba and into something else quick. Jamaica's
as good as anywhere else now we've got this con-
vertibility with the dollar. Apparently the man
who bought Belair just shovelled the money on to
the floor of Aschenheim's office out of a suitcase. I
suppose he'll keep the place for a year or two, and
when the trouble's blown over or when Castro's
got in and finished cleaning up he'll put it on the
market again, take a reasonable loss, and move off
somewhere else. Pity, in a way. Belair used to be a
fine property. It could have been brought back if
anyone in the family had cared."

"It was ten thousand acres in Bill's grandfather's day. It used to take the busher three days
to ride the boundary."

"Fat lot Bill cares. I bet he's booked his passage to London already. That's one more of the
old families gone. Soon won't be anyone left of
that lot but us. Thank God Judy likes the place."

Mrs. Havelock said "Yes, dear" calmingly
and pinged the bell for the tea things to be
cleared away. Agatha, a huge blue-black Negress
wearing the old-fashioned white headcloth that
has gone out in Jamaica except in the hinterland,
came out through the white and rose drawing-
room followed by Fayprince, a pretty young qua-
droon from Port Maria whom she was training
as second housemaid. Mrs. Havelock said: "It's
time we started bottling, Agatha. The guavas are
early this year."

Agatha's face was impassive. She said: "Yes'm.
But we done need more bottles."

"Why? It was only last year I got you two
dozen of the best I could find at Henriques."

"Yes'm. Someone done mash five, six of
dose."

"Oh dear. How did that happen?"

"Couldn't say'm." Agatha picked up the big
silver tray and waited, watching Mrs. Havelock's
face.

Mrs. Havelock had not lived most of her
life in Jamaica without learning that a mash is
a mash and that one would not get anywhere
hunting for a culprit. So she just said cheerfully:
"Oh, all right, Agatha. I'll get some more when I
go into Kingston."

"Yes'm." Agatha, followed by the young girl,
went back into the house.

Mrs. Havelock picked up a piece of petit-point
and began stitching, her fingers moving automatically. Her eyes went back to the big bushes
of Japanese Hat and Monkeyfiddle. Yes, the two
male birds were back. With gracefully cocked
tails they moved among the flowers. The sun was
low on the horizon and every now and then there
was a flash of almost piercingly beautiful green.
A mocking-bird, on the topmost branch of a
frangipani, started on its evening repertoire. The
tinkle of an early tree-frog announced the beginning of the short violet dusk.

Content, twenty thousand acres in the foothills
of Candlefly Peak, one of the most easterly of the
Blue Mountains in the county of Portland, had
been given to an early Havelock by Oliver Crom-
well as a reward for having been one of the signa-
tories to King Charles's death warrant. Unlike so
many other settlers of those and later times the
Havelocks had maintained the plantation through
three centuries, through earthquakes and hurricanes and through the boom and bust of cocoa,
sugar, citrus, and copra. Now it was in bananas
and cattle, and it was one of the richest and best
run of all the private estates in the island. The
house, patched up or rebuilt after earthquake or
hurricane, was a hybrid—a mahogany-pillared,
two-storeyed central block on the old stone foun-
dations flanked by two single-storeyed wings with
widely overhung, flat-pitched Jamaican roofs of

silver cedar shingles. The Havelocks were now sitting on the deep veranda of the central block facing the gently sloping garden beyond which a vast tumbling jungle vista stretched away twenty miles to the sea.

Colonel Havelock put down his *Gleaner*. "I thought I heard a car."

Mrs. Havelock said firmly: "If it's those ghastly Feddens from Port Antonio, you've simply got to get rid of them. I can't stand any more of their moans about England. And last time they were both quite drunk when they left and dinner was cold." She got up quickly. "I'm going to tell Agatha to say I've got a migraine."

Agatha came out through the drawing-room door. She looked fussed. She was followed closely by three men. She said hurriedly: "Gemmun from Kingston'm. To see de Colonel."

The leading man slid past the housekeeper. He was still wearing his hat, a panama with a short very upcurled brim. He took this off with his left hand and held it against his stomach. The rays of the sun glittered on hair-grease and on a mouthful of smiling white teeth. He went up to Colonel Havelock, his outstretched hand held straight in front of him. "Major Gonzales. From Havana. Pleased to meet you, Colonel."

The accent was the sham American of a Jamaican taxi-driver. Colonel Havelock had got to his feet. He touched the outstretched hand briefly. He looked over the Major's shoulder at the other two men who had stationed themselves on either side of the door. They were both carrying that new holdall of the tropics—a Pan American overnight bag. The bags looked heavy. Now the two men bent down together and placed them beside their yellowish shoes. They straightened themselves. They wore flat white caps with transparent green visors that cast green shadows down to their cheekbones. Through the green shadows their intelligent animal eyes fixed themselves on the Major, reading his behaviour.

"They are my secretaries."

Colonel Havelock took a pipe out of his pocket and began to fill it. His direct blue eyes took in the sharp clothes, the natty shoes, the glistening fingernails of the Major and the blue jeans and calypso shirts of the other two. He wondered how he could get these men into his study and near the revolver in the top drawer of his desk. He said: "What can I do for you?" As he lit his pipe he watched the Major's eyes and mouth through the smoke.

Major Gonzales spread his hands. The width of his smile remained constant. The liquid, almost golden eyes were amused, friendly. "It is a matter of business, Colonel. I represent a certain gentleman in Havana"—he made a throw-away gesture with his right hand. "A powerful gentleman. A very fine guy." Major Gonzales assumed an expression of sincerity. "You would like him, Colonel. He asked me to present his compliments and to inquire the price of your property."

Mrs. Havelock, who had been watching the scene with a polite half-smile on her lips, moved to stand beside her husband. She said kindly, so as not to embarrass the poor man: "What a shame, Major. All this way on these dusty roads! Your friend really should have written first, or asked anyone in Kingston or at Government House. You see, my husband's family have lived here for nearly three hundred years." She looked at him sweetly, apologetically. "I'm afraid there just isn't any question of selling Content. There never has been. I wonder where your important friend can possibly have got the idea from."

Major Gonzales bowed briefly. His smiling face turned back to Colonel Havelock. He said, as if Mrs. Havelock had not opened her mouth: "My gentleman is told this is one of the finest estancias in Jamaica. He is a most generous man. You may mention any sum that is reasonable."

Colonel Havelock said firmly: "You heard what Mrs. Havelock said. The property is not for sale."

Major Gonzales laughed. It sounded quite genuine laughter. He shook his head as if he was explaining something to a rather dense child. "You misunderstand me, Colonel. My gentleman desires this property and no other property in Jamaica. He has some funds, some extra funds, to invest. These funds are seeking a home in Jamaica. My gentleman wishes this to be their home."

Colonel Havelock said patiently: "I quite understand, Major. And I am so sorry you have wasted your time. Content will never be for sale in my lifetime. And now, if you'll forgive me. My wife and I always dine early, and you have a long way to go." He made a gesture to the left, along the veranda. "I think you'll find this is the quickest way to your car. Let me show you."

Colonel Havelock moved invitingly, but when Major Gonzales stayed where he was, he stopped. The blue eyes began to freeze.

There was perhaps one less tooth in Major Gonzales's smile and his eyes had become watchful. But his manner was still jolly. He said cheerfully, "Just one moment, Colonel." He issued a curt order over his shoulder. Both the Havelocks noticed the jolly mask slip with the few sharp words through the teeth. For the first time Mrs. Havelock looked slightly uncertain. She moved still closer to her husband. The two men picked up their blue Pan American bags and stepped forward. Major Gonzales reached for the zipper on each of them in turn and pulled. The taut mouths sprang open. The bags were full to the brim with neat solid wads of American money. Major Gonzales spread his arms. "All hundred dollar bills. All genuine. Half a million dollars. That is, in your money, let us say, one hundred and eighty thousand pounds. A small fortune. There are many other good places to live in the world, Colonel. And perhaps my gentleman would add a further twenty thousand pounds to make the round sum. You would know in a week. All I need is half a sheet of paper with your signature. The lawyers can do the rest. Now, Colonel," the smile was winning, "shall we say yes and shake hands on it? Then the bags stay here and we leave you to your dinner."

The Havelocks now looked at the Major with the same expression—a mixture of anger and disgust. One could imagine Mrs. Havelock telling the story next day. "Such a common, greasy little man. And those filthy plastic bags full of money! Timmy was wonderful. He just told him to get out and take the dirty stuff away with him."

Colonel Havelock's mouth turned down with distaste. He said: "I thought I had made myself clear, Major. The property is not for sale at any price. And I do not share the popular thirst for American dollars. I must now ask you to leave." Colonel Havelock laid his cold pipe on the table as if he was preparing to roll up his sleeves.

For the first time Major Gonzales's smile lost its warmth. The mouth continued to grin but it was now shaped in an angry grimace. The liquid golden eyes were suddenly brassy and hard. He said softly: "Colonel. It is I who have not made myself clear. Not you. My gentleman has instructed me to say that if you will not accept his most generous terms we must proceed to other measures."

Mrs. Havelock was suddenly afraid. She put her hand on Colonel Havelock's arm and pressed it hard. He put his hand over hers in reassurance. He said through tight lips: "Please leave us alone and go, Major. Otherwise I shall communicate with the police."

The pink tip of Major Gonzales's tongue came out and slowly licked along his lips. All the light had gone out of his face and it had become taut and hard. He said harshly. "So the property is not for sale in your lifetime, Colonel. Is that your last word?" His right hand went behind his back and he clicked his fingers softly, once. Behind him the gun-hands of the two men slid through the opening of their gay shirts above the waistbands. The sharp animal eyes watched the Major's fingers behind his back.

Mrs. Havelock's hand went up to her mouth. Colonel Havelock tried to say yes, but his mouth was dry. He swallowed noisily. He could not believe it. This mangy Cuban crook must be bluffing. He managed to say thickly: "Yes, it is."

Major Gonzales nodded curtly. "In that case, Colonel, my gentleman will carry on the negotiations with the next owner—with your daughter."

The fingers clicked. Major Gonzales stepped to one side to give a clear field of fire. The brown monkey-hands came out from under the gay shirts. The ugly sausage-shaped hunks of metal spat and thudded—again and again, even when the two bodies were on their way to the ground.

Major Gonzales bent down and verified where the bullets had hit. Then the three small men walked quickly back through the rose and white drawing-room and across the dark carved mahogany hall and out through the elegant front door. They climbed unhurriedly into a black Ford Consul Sedan with Jamaican number plates and, with Major Gonzales driving and the two gunmen sitting upright in the back seat, they drove off at an easy pace down the long avenue of Royal Palms. At the junction of the drive and the road to Port Antonio the cut telephone wires hung down through the trees like bright lianas. Major Gonzales slalomed the car carefully and expertly down the rough parochial road until he was on the metalled strip near the coast. Then he put on speed. Twenty minutes after the killing he came to the outer sprawl of the little banana port. There he ran the stolen car onto the grass verge beside the road and the three men got out and walked the quarter of a mile through the sparsely lit main street to the banana wharves. The speed-boat was waiting, its exhaust bubbling. The three men got in and the boat zoomed off across the still waters of what an American poetess has called the most beautiful harbour in the world. The anchor chain was already half up on the glittering fifty-ton Chriscraft. She was flying the Stars and Stripes. The two graceful antennae of the deep-sea rods explained that these were tourists—from Kingston, perhaps, or from Montego Bay. The three men went on board and the speed-boat was swung in. Two canoes were circling, begging. Major Gonzales tossed a fifty-cent piece to each of them and the stripped men dived. The twin diesels awoke to a stuttering roar and the Chriscraft settled her stern down a fraction and made for the deep channel below the Titchfield hotel. By dawn she would be back in Havana. The fishermen and wharfingers ashore watched her go, and went on with their argument as to which of the film-stars holidaying in Jamaica this could have been.

Up on the broad veranda of Content the last rays of the sun glittered on the red stains. One of the doctor birds whirred over the balustrade and hovered close above Mrs. Havelock's heart, looking down. No, this was not for him. He flirted gaily off to his roosting-perch among the closing hibiscus.

There came the sound of someone in a small sports car making a racing change at the bend of the drive. If Mrs. Havelock had been alive she would have been getting ready to say: "Judy. I'm always telling you not to do that on the corner. It scatters gravel all over the lawn and you know how it ruins Joshua's lawn-mower."

It was a month later. In London, October had begun with a week of brilliant Indian summer, and the noise of the mowers came up from Regent's Park and in through the wide open windows of M.'s office. They were motor-mowers and James Bond reflected that one of the most beautiful noises of summer, the drowsy iron song of the old machines, was going for ever from the world. Perhaps today children felt the same about the puff and chatter of the little two-stroke engines. At least the cut grass would smell the same.

Bond had time for these reflections because M. seemed to be having difficulty in coming to the point. Bond had been asked if he had anything on at the moment, and he had replied happily that he hadn't and had waited for Pandora's box to be opened for him. He was mildly intrigued because M. had addressed him as James and not by his number—007. This was unusual during duty hours. It sounded as if there might be some personal angle to this assignment—as if it might be put to him more as a request than as an order. And it seemed to Bond that there was an extra small cleft of worry between the frosty, damnably clear, grey eyes. And three minutes was certainly too long to spend getting a pipe going.

M. swivelled his chair round square with the desk and flung the box of matches down so that it skidded across the red leather top towards Bond. Bond fielded it and skidded it politely back to the middle of the desk. M. smiled briefly. He seemed to make up his mind. he said mildly: "James, has it ever occurred to you that every man in the fleet knows what to do except the commanding admiral?"

Bond frowned. He said: "It hadn't occurred to me, sir. But I see what you mean. The rest only have to carry out orders. The admiral has to decide on the orders. I suppose it's the same as saying that Supreme Command is the loneliest post there is."

M. jerked his pipe sideways. "Same sort of idea. Someone's got to be tough. Someone's got to decide in the end. If you send a havering signal to the Admiralty you deserve to be put on the beach. Some people are religious—pass the decision on to God." M.'s eyes were defensive. "I used to try that sometimes in the Service, but He always passed the buck back again—told me to get on and make up my own mind. Good for one, I suppose, but tough. Trouble is, very few people keep tough after about forty. They've been knocked about by life—had troubles, tragedies, illnesses. These things soften you up." M. looked sharply at Bond. "How's your coefficient of toughness, James? You haven't got to the dangerous age yet."

Bond didn't like personal questions. He didn't know what to answer, nor what the truth was. He had not got a wife or children—had never suffered the tragedy of a personal loss. He had not had to stand up to blindness or a mortal disease. He had absolutely no idea how he would face these things that needed so much more toughness than he had ever had to show. He said hesitantly: "I suppose I can stand most things if I have to and if I think it's right, sir. I mean"—he did not like using such words— "if the cause is—er—sort of just, sir." He went on, feeling ashamed at himself for throwing the ball back at M.: "Of course it's not easy to know what is just and what isn't. I suppose I assume that when I'm given an unpleasant job in the Service the cause is a just one."

"Dammit," M.'s eyes glittered impatiently. "That's just what I mean! You rely on *me*. You won't take any damned responsibility yourself." He thrust the stem of his pipe towards his chest. "I'm the one who has to do that. I'm the one who has to decide if a thing is right or not." The anger died out of the eyes. The grim mouth bent sourly. He said gloomily: "Oh well, I suppose it's what I'm paid for. Somebody's got to drive the bloody train." M. put his pipe back in his mouth and drew on it deeply to relieve his feelings.

Now Bond felt sorry for M. He had never before heard M. use as strong a word as "bloody." Nor had M. ever given a member of his staff any hint that he felt the weight of the burden he was carrying and had carried ever since he had thrown up the certain prospect of becoming Fifth Sea Lord in order to take over the Secret Service. M. had got himself a problem. Bond wondered what it was. It would not be concerned with danger. If M. could get the odds more or less right he would risk anything, anywhere in the world. It would not be political. M. did not give a damn for the susceptibilities of any Ministry and thought nothing of going behind their backs to get a personal ruling from the Prime Minister. It might be moral. It might be personal. Bond said: "Is there anything I can help over, sir?"

M. looked briefly, thoughtfully at Bond, and then swivelled his chair so that he could look out of the window at the high summery clouds. He said abruptly: "Do you remember the Havelock case?"

"Only what I read in the papers, sir. Elderly couple in Jamaica. The daughter came home one night and found them full of bullets. There was some talk of gangsters from Havana. The housekeeper said three men had called in a car. She thought they might have been Cubans. It turned out the car had been stolen. A yacht had sailed from the local harbour that night. But as far as I remember the police didn't get anywhere. That's all, sir. I haven't seen any signals passing on the case."

M. said gruffly: "You wouldn't have. They've been personal to me. We weren't asked to handle the case. Just happens," M. cleared his throat: this private use of the Service was on his conscience, "I knew the Havelocks. Matter of fact I was best man at their wedding. Malta. Nineteen-twenty-five."

"I see, sir. That's bad."

M. said shortly: "Nice people. Anyway, I told Station C to look into it. They didn't get anywhere with the Batista people, but we've got a good man with the other side—with this chap Castro. And Castro's Intelligence people seem to have the Government pretty well penetrated. I got the whole story a couple of weeks ago. It boils down to the fact that a man called Hammerstein, or von Hammerstein, had the couple killed. There are a lot of Germans well dug in in these banana republics. They're Nazis who got out of the net at the end of the War. This one's ex-Gestapo. He got a job as head of Batista's Counter Intelligence. Made a packet of money out of extortion and blackmail and protection. He was set up for life until Castro's lot began to make headway. He was one of the first to start easing himself out. He cut one of his officers in on his loot, a man called Gonzales, and this man travelled around the Caribbean with a couple of gunmen to protect him and began salting away Hammerstein's money outside Cuba—put it in real estate and suchlike under nominees. Only bought the best, but at top prices. Hammerstein could afford them. When money didn't work he'd use force—kidnap a child, burn down a few acres, anything to make the owner see reason. Well, this man Hammerstein heard of the Havelocks' property, one of the best in Jamaica, and he told Gonzales to go and get it. I suppose his orders were to kill the Havelocks if they wouldn't sell and then put pressure on the daughter. There's a daughter, by the way. Should be about twenty-five by now. Never seen her myself. Anyway, that's what happened. They killed the Havelocks. Then two weeks ago Batista sacked Hammerstein. May have got to hear about one of these jobs. I don't know. But, anyway, Hammerstein cleared out and took his little team

of three with him. Timed things pretty well, I should say. It looks as if Castro may get in this winter if he keeps the pressure up."

Bond said softly: "Where have they gone to?"

"America. Right up in the North of Vermont. Up against the Canadian border. Those sort of men like being close to frontiers. Place called Echo Lake. It's some kind of a millionaire's ranch he's rented. Looks pretty from the photographs. Tucked away in the mountains with this little lake in the grounds. He's certainly chosen himself somewhere where he won't be troubled with visitors."

"How did you get on to this, sir?"

"I sent a report of the whole case to Edgar Hoover. He knew of the man. I guessed he would. He's had a lot of trouble with this gun-running from Miami to Castro. And he's been interested in Havana ever since the big American gangster money started following the casinos there. He said that Hammerstein and his party had come into the States on six months visitors' visas. He was very helpful. Wanted to know if I'd got enough to build up a case on. Did I want these men extradited for trial in Jamaica? I talked it over here with the Attorney General and he said there wasn't a hope unless we could get the witnesses from Havana. There's no chance of that. It was only through Castro's Intelligence that we even know as much as we do. Officially the Cubans won't raise a finger. Next Hoover offered to have their visas revoked and get them on the move again. I thanked him and said no, and we left it at that."

M. sat for a moment in silence. His pipe had died and he relit it. He went on: "I decided to have a talk with our friends the Mounties. I got on to the Commissioner on the scrambler. He's never let me down yet. He strayed one of his frontier patrol planes over the border and took a full aerial survey of this Echo Lake place. Said that if I wanted any other co-operation he'd provide it. And now," M. slowly swivelled his chair back square with the desk, "I've got to decide what to do next."

Now Bond realized why M. was troubled, why he wanted someone else to make the decision. Because these had been friends of M. Because a personal element was involved, M. had worked on the case by himself. And now it had come to the point when justice ought to be done and these people brought to book. But M. was thinking: is this justice, or is it revenge? No judge would take a murder case in which he had personally known the murdered person. M. wanted someone else, Bond, to deliver judgement. There were no doubts in Bond's mind. He didn't know the Havelocks or care who they were. Hammerstein had operated the law of the jungle on two defenceless old people. Since no other law was available, the law of the jungle should be visited upon Hammerstein. In no other way could justice be done. If it was revenge, it was the revenge of the community.

Bond said: "I wouldn't hesitate for a minute, sir. If foreign gangsters find they can get away with this kind of thing they'll decide the English are as soft as some other people seem to think we are. This is a case for rough justice—an eye for an eye."

M. went on looking at Bond. He gave no encouragement, made no comment.

Bond said: "These people can't be hung, sir. But they ought to be killed."

M.'s eyes ceased to focus on Bond. For a moment they were blank, looking inward. Then he slowly reached for the top drawer of his desk on the left-hand side, pulled it open, and extracted a thin file without the usual title across it and without the top-secret red star. He placed the file squarely in front of him and his hand rummaged again in the open drawer. The hand brought out a rubber stamp and a red-ink pad. M. opened the pad, tamped the rubber stamp on it and then carefully, so that it was properly aligned with the top right-hand corner of the docket, pressed it down on the grey cover.

M. replaced the stamp and the ink pad in the drawer and closed the drawer. He turned the docket round and pushed it gently across the desk to Bond. The red sanserif letters, still damp, said: FOR YOUR EYES ONLY.

Bond said nothing. He nodded and picked up the docket and walked out of the room.

Two days later, Bond took the Friday Comet to Montreal. He did not care for it. It flew too high and too fast and there were too many passengers. He regretted the days of the old Stratocruiser—that fine lumbering old plane that took ten hours to cross the Atlantic. Then one had been able to have dinner in peace, sleep for seven hours in a comfortable bunk, and get up in time to wander down to the lower deck and have that ridiculous B.O.A.C. "country house" breakfast while the dawn came up and flooded the cabin with the first bright gold of the Western hemisphere. Now it was all too quick. The stewards had to serve everything almost at the double, and then one had a bare two hours snooze before the hundred-mile-long descent from forty thousand feet. Only eight hours after leaving London, Bond was driving a Hertz U-drive Plymouth saloon along the broad Route 17 from Montreal to Ottawa and trying to remember to keep on the right of the road.

The Headquarters of the Royal Canadian Mounted Police are in the Department of Justice alongside Parliament Buildings in Ottawa. Like most Canadian public buildings, the Department of Justice is a massive block of grey masonry built to look stodgily important and to withstand the long and hard winters. Bond had been told to ask at the front desk for the Commissioner and to give his name as "Mr. James." He did so, and a young fresh-faced R.C.M.P. corporal, who looked as if he did not like being kept indoors on a warm sunny day, took him up in the lift to the third floor and handed him over to a sergeant in a large tidy office which contained two girl secretaries and a lot of heavy furniture. The sergeant spoke on an intercom and there was a ten minutes' delay during which Bond smoked and read a recruiting pamphlet which made the Mounties sound like a mixture between a dude ranch, Dick Tracy, and *Rose Marie*. When he was shown in through the connecting door a tall youngish man in a dark blue suit, white shirt, and black tie turned away from the window and came towards him. "Mr. James?" the man smiled thinly. "I'm Colonel, let's say—er—Johns."

They shook hands. "Come along and sit down. The Commissioner's very sorry not to be here to welcome you himself. He has a bad cold—you know, one of those diplomatic ones." Colonel "Johns" looked amused. "Thought it might be best to take the day off. I'm just one of the help. I've been on one or two hunting trips myself and the Commissioner fixed on me to handle this little holiday of yours," the Colonel paused, "on me only. Right?"

Bond smiled. The Commissioner was glad to help but he was going to handle this with kid gloves. There would be no comeback on his office. Bond thought he must be a careful and very sensible man. He said: "I quite understand. My friends in London didn't want the Commissioner to bother himself personally with any of this. And I haven't seen the Commissioner or been anywhere near his headquarters. That being so, can we talk English for ten minutes or so—just between the two of us?"

Colonel Johns laughed. "Sure. I was told to make that little speech and then get down to business. You understand, Commander, that you and I are about to connive at various felonies, starting with obtaining a Canadian hunting-licence under false pretences and being an accessory to a breach of the frontier laws, and going on down from there to more serious things. It wouldn't do anyone one bit of good to have any ricochets from this little lot. Get me?"

"That's how my friends feel too. When I go out of here, we'll forget each other, and if I end up in Sing-Sing that's my worry. Well, now?"

Colonel Johns opened a drawer in the desk and took out a bulging file and opened it. The top document was a list. He put his pencil on the first item and looked across at Bond. He ran his eye over Bond's old black and white hound's-tooth tweed suit and white shirt and thin black tie. He said: "Clothes." He unclipped a plain sheet of paper from the file and slid it across the desk. "This is a list of what I reckon you'll need and the address of a big second-hand clothing store here in the city. Nothing fancy, nothing conspicuous—khaki shirt, dark brown jeans, good climbing boots or shoes. See they're comfortable. And there's the address of a chemist for walnut stain. Buy a gallon and give yourself a bath in the stuff. There are plenty of browns in the hills at this time and you won't want to be wearing parachute cloth or anything that smells of camouflage. Right? If you're picked up, you're an Englishman on a hunting trip in Canada who's lost his way and got across the border by mistake. Rifle. Went down myself and put it in the boot of your Plymouth while you were waiting. One of the new Savage 99Fs, Weatherby 6×62 'scope, five-shot repeater with twenty rounds of high-velocity .250–3.000. Lightest big game lever action on the market. Only six and a half pounds. Belongs to a friend. Glad to have it back one day, but he won't miss it if it doesn't turn up. It's been tested and it's okay up to five hundred. Gun licence," Colonel Johns slid it over, "issued here in the city in your real name as that fits with your passport. Hunting-licence ditto, but small game only, vermin, as it isn't quite the deer season yet, also driving-licence to replace the provisional one I had waiting for you with the Hertz people. Haversack, compass—used ones, in the boot of your car. Oh, by the way," Colonel Johns looked up from his list, "you carrying a personal gun?"

"Yes. Walther PPK in a Burns Martin holster."

"Right, give me the number. I've got a blank licence here. If that gets back to me it's quite okay. I've got a story for it."

Bond took out his gun and read off the number. Colonel Johns filled in the form and pushed it over.

"Now then, maps. Here's a local Esso map that's all you need to get you to the area." Colonel Johns got up and walked round with the map to Bond and spread it out. "You take this route 17 back to Montreal, get on to 37 over the bridge at St. Anne's and then over the river again on to 7. Follow 7 on down to Pike River. Get on 52 at Stanbridge. Turn right in Stanbridge for Frelighsburg and leave the car in a garage there. Good roads all the way. Whole trip shouldn't take you more than five hours including stops. Okay? Now this is where you've got to get things right. Make it that you get to Frelighsburg around three A.M. Garage-hand'll be half asleep and you'll be able to get the gear out of the boot and move off without him noticing even if you were a double-headed Chinaman." Colonel Johns went back to his chair and took two more pieces of paper off the file. The first was a scrap of pencilled map, the other a section of aerial photograph. He said, looking seriously at Bond: "Now, here are the only inflammable things you'll be carrying and I've got to rely on you getting rid of them just as soon as they've been used, or at once if there's a chance of you getting into trouble. This," he pushed the paper over, "is a rough sketch of an old smuggling route from Prohibition days. It's not used now or I wouldn't recommend it." Colonel Johns smiled sourly. "You might find some rough customers coming over in the opposite direction, and they're apt to shoot and not even ask questions afterwards—crooks, druggers, white-slavers— but nowadays they mostly travel up by Viscount. This route was used for runners between Franklin, just over the Derby Line, and Frelighsburg. You follow this path through the foothills, and you detour Franklin and get into the start of the Green Mountains. There it's all Vermont spruce and pine with a bit of maple, and you can stay inside that stuff for months and not see a soul. You get across country here, over a couple of highways, and you leave Enosburg Falls to the west. Then you're over a steep range and down into the top of the valley you want. The cross is Echo Lake and, judging from the photographs, I'd be inclined to come down on top of it from the east. Got it?"

"What's the distance? About ten miles?"

"Ten and a half. Take you about three hours from Frelighsburg if you don't lose your way, so you'll be in sight of the place around six and have about an hour's light to help you over the last stretch." Colonel Johns pushed over the square of aerial photograph. It was a central cut from the one Bond had seen in London. It showed a long low range of well-kept buildings made of cut stone. The roofs were of slate, and there was a glimpse of graceful bow windows and a covered patio. A dust road ran past the front door and on this side were garages and what appeared to be kennels. On the garden side was a stone flagged terrace with a flowered border, and beyond this two or three acres of trim lawn stretched down to the edge of the small lake. The lake appeared to have been artificially created with a deep stone dam. There was a group of wrought-iron garden furniture where the dam wall left the bank and, halfway along the wall, a diving-board and a ladder to climb out of the lake. Beyond the lake the forest rose steeply up. It was from this side that Colonel Johns suggested an approach. There were no people in the photograph, but on the stone flags in front of the patio was a quantity of expensive-looking aluminium garden furniture and a central glass table with drinks. Bond remembered that the larger photograph had shown a tennis court in the garden and on the other side of the road the trim white fences and grazing horses of a stud farm. Echo Lake looked what it was—the luxurious retreat, in deep country, well away from atom bomb targets, of a millionaire who liked privacy and could probably offset a lot of his running expenses against the stud farm and an occasional good let. It would be an admirable refuge for a man who had had ten steamy years of Caribbean politics and who needed a rest to recharge his batteries. The lake was also convenient for washing blood off hands.

Colonel Johns closed his now empty file and tore the typewritten list into small fragments and dropped them in the wastepaper basket. The two men got to their feet. Colonel Johns took

Bond to the door and held out his hand. He said: "Well, I guess that's all. I'd give a lot to come with you. Talking about all this has reminded me of one or two sniping jobs at the end of the War. I was in the Army then. We were under Monty in Eighth Corps. On the left of the line in the Ardennes. It was much the same sort of country as you'll be using, only different trees. But you know how it is in these police jobs. Plenty of paper-work and keep your nose clean for the pension. Well, so long and the best of luck. No doubt I'll read all about it in the papers," he smiled, "whichever way it goes."

Bond thanked him and shook him by the hand. A last question occurred to him. He said: "By the way, is the Savage single pull or double? I won't have a chance of finding out and there may not be much time for experimenting when the target shows."

"Single pull and it's a hair-trigger. Keep your finger off until you're sure you've got him. And keep outside three hundred if you can. I guess these men are pretty good themselves. Don't get too close." He reached for the door handle. His other hand went to Bond's shoulder. "Our Commissioner's got a motto: 'Never send a man where you can send a bullet.' You might remember that. So long, Commander."

Bond spent the night and most of the next day at the KO-ZEE Motor Court outside Montreal. He paid in advance for three nights. He passed the day looking to his equipment and wearing in the soft ripple rubber climbing boots he had bought in Ottawa. He bought glucose tablets and some smoked ham and bread from which he made himself sandwiches. He also bought a large aluminium flask and filled this with three-quarters Bourbon and a quarter coffee. When darkness came he had dinner and a short sleep and then diluted the walnut stain and washed himself all over with the stuff even to the roots of his hair. He came out looking like a Red Indian with blue-grey eyes. Just before midnight he quietly opened the side door into the automobile bay, got into the Plymouth and drove off on the last lap south to Frelighsburg.

The man at the all-night garage was not as sleepy as Colonel Johns had said he would be.

"Goin' huntin', mister?"

You can get far in North America with laconic grunts. Huh, hun, and hi! in their various modulations, together with sure, guess so, that so?, and nuts! will meet almost any contingency.

Bond, slinging the strap of his rifle over his shoulder, said "Hun."

"Man got a fine beaver over by Highgate Springs Saturday."

Bond said indifferently "That so?," paid for two nights and walked out of the garage. He had stopped on the far side of the town, and now he only had to follow the highway for a hundred yards before he found the dirt track running off into the woods on his right. After half an hour the track petered out at a broken-down farmhouse. A chained dog set up a frenzied barking, but no light showed in the farmhouse and Bond skirted it and at once found the path by the stream. He was to follow this for three miles. He lengthened his stride to get away from the dog. When the barking stopped there was silence, the deep velvet silence of woods on a still night. It was a warm night with a full yellow moon that threw enough light down through the thick spruce for Bond to follow the path without difficulty. The springy, cushioned soles of the climbing boots were wonderful to walk on, and Bond got his second wind and knew he was making good time. At around four o'clock the trees began to thin and he was soon walking through open fields with the scattered lights of Franklin on his right. He crossed a secondary, tarred road, and now there was a wider track through the woods and on his right the pale glitter of a lake. By five o'clock he had crossed the black rivers of U.S. highways 108 and 120. On the latter was a sign saying ENOSBURG FALLS 1 MI. Now he was on the last lap—a small hunting-trail that climbed steeply. Well away from the highway, he stopped and shifted his rifle and knapsack round, had a cigarette and burned the sketch-map. Already there was a faint paling in the sky and small noises in the forest—the harsh, melancholy cry of a bird he did not know and the rustlings of small animals. Bond visualized the house deep down in the little valley on the other side of the mountain ahead of him. He saw the blank curtained windows, the crumpled sleeping faces of the four men, the dew on the lawn, and the widening rings of the early rise on the gunmetal surface of the lake. And here, on the other side of the mountain, was the executioner coming up through the trees. Bond closed his mind to the picture, trod the remains of his cigarette into the ground, and got going.

Was this a hill or a mountain? At what height does a hill become a mountain? Why don't they manufacture something out of the silver bark of birch trees? It looks so useful and valuable. The best things in America are chipmunks, and oyster stew. In the evening darkness doesn't really fall, it rises. When you sit on top of a mountain and watch the sun go down behind the mountain opposite, the darkness rises up to you out of the valley. Will the birds one day lose their fear of man? It must be centuries since man has killed a small bird for food in these woods, yet they are still afraid. Who was this Ethan Allen who commanded the Green Mountain Boys of Vermont? Now, in American motels, they advertise Ethan Allen furniture as an attraction. Why? Did he make furniture? Army boots should have rubber soles like these.

With these and other random thoughts Bond steadily climbed upwards and obstinately pushed away from him the thought of the four faces asleep on the white pillows.

The round peak was below the tree-line and Bond could see nothing of the valley below. He rested and then chose an oak tree, and climbed up and out along a thick bough. Now he could see everything—the endless vista of the Green Mountains stretching in every direction as far as he could see, away to the east the golden ball of the sun just coming up in glory, and below, two thousand feet down a long easy slope of tree-tops broken once by a wide band of meadow,

through a thin veil of mist, the lake, the lawns and the house.

Bond lay along the branch and watched the band of pale early morning sunshine creeping down into the valley. It took a quarter of an hour to reach the lake, and then seemed to flood at once over the glittering lawn and over the wet slate tiles of the roofs. Then the mist went quickly from the lake and the target area, washed and bright and new, lay waiting like an empty stage.

Bond slipped the telescopic sight out of his pocket and went over the scene inch by inch. Then he examined the sloping ground below him and estimated ranges. From the edge of the meadow, which would be his only open field of fire unless he went down through the last belt of trees to the edge of the lake, it would be about five hundred yards to the terrace and the patio, and about three hundred to the diving-board and the edge of the lake. What did these people do with their time? What was their routine? Did they ever bathe? It was still warm enough. Well, there was all day. If by the end of it they had not come down to the lake, he would just have to take his chance at the patio and five hundred yards. But it would not be a good chance with a strange rifle. Ought he to get on down straight away to the edge of the meadow? It was a wide meadow, perhaps five hundred yards of going without cover. It would be as well to get that behind him before the house awoke. What time did these people get up in the morning?

As if to answer him, a white blind rolled up in one of the smaller windows to the left of the main block. Bond could distinctly hear the final snap of the spring roller. Echo Lake! Of course. Did the echo work both ways? Would he have to be careful of breaking branches and twigs? Probably not. The sounds in the valley would bounce upwards off the surface of the water. But there must be no chances taken.

A thin column of smoke began to trickle up straight into the air from one of the left-hand chimneys. Bond thought of the bacon and eggs that would soon be frying. And the hot coffee.

He eased himself back along the branch and down to the ground. He would have something to eat, smoke his last safe cigarette, and get on down to the firing point.

The bread stuck in Bond's throat. Tension was building up in him. In his imagination he could already hear the deep bark of the Savage. He could see the black bullet lazily, like a slow flying bee, homing down into the valley towards a square of pink skin. There was a light smack as it hit. The skin dented, broke, and then closed up again leaving a small hole with bruised edges. The bullet ploughed on, unhurriedly, towards the pulsing heart—the tissues, the blood-vessels, parting obediently to let it through. Who was this man he was going to do this to? What had he ever done to Bond? Bond looked thoughtfully down at his trigger-finger. He crooked it slowly, feeling in his imagination the cool curve of metal. Almost automatically, his left hand reached out for the flask. He held it to his lips and tilted his head back. The coffee and whisky burned a small fire down his throat. He put the top back on the flask and waited for the warmth of the whisky to reach his stomach. Then he got slowly to his feet, stretched and yawned deeply, and picked up the rifle and slung it over his shoulder. He looked round carefully to mark the place when he came back up the hill and started slowly off down through the trees.

Now there was no trail and he had to pick his way slowly, watching the ground for dead branches. The trees were more mixed. Among the spruce and silver birch there was an occasional oak and beech and sycamore and, here and there, the blazing Bengal fire of a maple in autumn dress. Under the trees was a sparse undergrowth of their saplings and much dead wood from old hurricanes. Bond went carefully down, his feet making little sound among the leaves and moss-covered rocks, but soon the forest was aware of him and began to pass on the news. A large doe, with two Bambi-like young, saw him first and galloped off with an appalling clatter. A brilliant woodpecker with a scarlet head flew down ahead of him, screeching each time Bond caught up with it, and always there were the chipmunks, craning up on their hind feet, lifting their small muzzles from their teeth as they tried to catch his scent, and then scampering off to their rock holes with chatterings that seemed to fill the woods with fright. Bond willed them to have no fear, that the gun he carried was not meant for them, but with each alarm he wondered if, when he got to the edge of the meadow, he would see down on the lawn a man with glasses who had been watching the frightened birds fleeing the tree-tops.

But when he stopped behind a last broad oak and looked down across the long meadow to the final belt of trees and the lake and the house, nothing had changed. All the other blinds were still down and the only movement was the thin plume of smoke.

It was eight o'clock. Bond gazed down across the meadow to the trees, looking for one which would suit his purpose. He found it—a big maple, blazing with russet and crimson. This would be right for his clothes, its trunk was thick enough and it stood slightly back from the wall of spruce. From there, standing, he would be able to see all he needed of the lake and the house. Bond stood for a while, plotting his route down through the thick grass and golden-rod of the meadow. He would have to do it on his stomach, and slowly. A small breeze got up and combed the meadow. If only it would keep blowing and cover his passage!

Somewhere not far off, up to the left on the edge of the trees, a branch snapped. It snapped once decisively and there was no further noise. Bond dropped to one knee, his ears pricked and his senses questing. He stayed like that for a full ten minutes, a motionless brown shadow against the wide trunk of the oak.

Animals and birds do not break twigs. Dead wood must carry a special danger signal for them. Birds never alight on twigs that will break under them, and even a large animal like a deer with antlers and four hooves to manipulate moves quite silently in a forest unless he is in flight. Had these people after all got guards out?

Gently Bond eased the rifle off his shoulder and put his thumb on the safe. Perhaps, if the people were still sleeping, a single shot, from high up in the woods, would pass for a hunter or a poacher. But then, between him and approximately where the twig had snapped, two deer broke cover and cantered unhurriedly across the meadow to the left. It was true that they stopped twice to look back, but each time they cropped a few mouthfuls of grass before moving on and into the distant fringe of the lower woods. They showed no fright and no haste. It was certainly they who had been the cause of the snapped branch. Bond breathed a sigh. So much for that. And now to get on across the meadow.

A five-hundred-yard crawl through tall concealing grass is a long and wearisome business. It is hard on knees and hands and elbows, there is a vista of nothing but grass and flower stalks, and the dust and small insects get into your eyes and nose and down your neck. Bond focused on placing his hands right and maintaining a slow, even speed. The breeze had kept up and his wake through the grass would certainly not be noticeable from the house.

From above, it looked as if a big ground animal—a beaver perhaps, or a woodchuck— was on its way down the meadow. No, it would not be a beaver. They always move in pairs. And yet perhaps it might be a beaver—for now, from higher up on the meadow, something, somebody else had entered the tall grass, and behind and above Bond a second wake was being cut in the deep sea of grass. It looked as if whatever it was would slowly catch up on Bond and that the two wakes would converge just at the next tree-line.

Bond crawled and slithered steadily on, stopping only to wipe the sweat and dust off his face and, from time to time, to make sure that he was on course for the maple. But when he was close enough for the tree-line to hide him from the house, perhaps twenty feet from the maple, he stopped and lay for a while, massaging his knees and loosening his wrists for the last lap.

He had heard nothing to warn him, and when the soft threatening whisper came from only feet away in the thick grass on his left, his head swivelled so sharply that the vertebrae of his neck made a cracking sound.

"Move an inch and I'll kill you." It had been a girl's voice, but a voice that fiercely meant what it said.

Bond, his heart thumping, stared up the shaft of the steel arrow whose blue-tempered triangular tip parted the grass stalks perhaps eighteen inches from his head.

The bow was held sideways, flat in the grass. The knuckles of the brown fingers that held the binding of the bow below the arrow-tip were white. Then there was the length of glinting steel and, behind the metal feathers, partly obscured by waving strands of grass, were grimly clamped lips below two fierce grey eyes against a background of sunburned skin damp with sweat. That was all Bond could make out through the grass. Who the hell was this? One of the guards? Bond gathered saliva back into his dry mouth and began slowly to edge his right hand, his out-of-sight hand, round and up towards his waistband and his gun. He said softly: "Who the hell are you?"

The arrow-tip gestured threateningly. "Stop that right hand or I'll put this through your shoulder. Are you one of the guards?"

"No. Are you?"

"Don't be a fool. What are you doing here?" The tension in the voice had slackened, but it was still hard, suspicious. There was a trace of accent—what was it, Scots? Welsh?

It was time to get to level terms. There was something particularly deadly about the blue arrow-tip. Bond said easily: "Put away your bow and arrow, Robina. Then I'll tell you."

"You swear not to go for your gun?"

"All right. But for God's sake let's get out of the middle of this field." Without waiting, Bond rose on hands and knees and started to crawl again. Now he must get the initiative and hold it. Whoever this damned girl was, she would have to be disposed of quickly and discreetly before the shooting-match began. God, as if there wasn't enough to think of already!

Bond reached the trunk of the tree. He got carefully to his feet and took a quick look through the blazing leaves. Most of the blinds had gone up. Two slow-moving coloured maids were laying a large breakfast table on the patio. He had been right. The field of vision over the tops of the trees that now fell sharply to the lake was perfect. Bond unslung his rifle and knapsack and sat down with his back against the trunk of the tree. The girl came out of the edge of the grass and stood up under the maple. She kept her distance. The arrow was still held in the bow but the bow was unpulled. They looked warily at each other.

The girl looked like a beautiful unkempt dryad in ragged shirt and trousers. The shirt and trousers were olive green, crumpled and splashed with mud and stains and torn in places, and she had bound her pale blonde hair with golden-rod to conceal its brightness for her crawl through the meadow. The beauty of her face was wild and rather animal, with a wide sensuous mouth, high cheekbones and silvery grey, disdainful eyes. There was the blood of scratches on her forearms and down one cheek, and a bruise had puffed and slightly blackened the same cheekbone. The metal feathers of a quiver full of arrows showed above her left shoulder. Apart from the bow, she carried nothing but a hunting-knife at her belt and, at her other hip, a small brown canvas bag that presumably carried her food. She looked like a beautiful, dangerous customer who knew wild country and forests and was not afraid of them. She would walk alone through life and have little use for civilization.

Bond thought she was wonderful. He smiled at her. He said softly, reassuringly: "I suppose you're Robina Hood. My name's James Bond." He reached for his flask and unscrewed the top and held it out. "Sit down and have a drink of this—firewater and coffee. And I've got some biltong. Or do you live on dew and berries?"

She came a little closer and sat down a yard from him. She sat like a Red Indian, her knees splayed wide and her ankles tucked up high under her thighs. She reached for the flask and drank deeply with her head thrown back. She handed it back without comment. She did not smile. She said "Thanks" grudgingly, and took her arrow and thrust it over her back to join the others in the quiver. She said, watching him closely: "I suppose you're a poacher. The deer-hunting season doesn't open for another three weeks. But you won't find any deer down here. They only come so low at night. You ought to be higher up during the day, much higher. If you like, I'll tell you where there are some. Quite a big herd. It's a bit late in the day, but you could still get to them. They're up-wind from here and you seem to know about stalking. You don't make much noise."

"Is that what you're doing here—hunting? Let's see your licence."

Her shirt had buttoned-down breast pockets. Without protest she took out from one of them the white paper and handed it over.

The licence had been issued in Bennington, Vermont. It had been issued in the name of Judy Havelock. There was a list of types of permit. "Non-resident hunting" and "Non-resident bow and arrow" had been ticked. The cost had been $18.50, payable to the Fish and Game Service, Montpelier, Vermont. Judy Havelock had given her age as twenty-five and her place of birth as Jamaica.

Bond thought: "God Almighty!" He handed the paper back. So that was the score! He said with sympathy and respect: "You're quite a girl, Judy. It's a long walk from Jamaica. And you were going to take him on with your bow and arrow. You know what they say in China: 'Before you set out on revenge, dig two graves.' Have you done that, or did you expect to get away with it?"

The girl was staring at him. "Who are you? What are you doing here? What do you know about it?"

Bond reflected. There was only one way out of this mess and that was to join forces with the girl. What a hell of a business! He said resignedly: "I've told you my name. I've been sent out from London by, er, Scotland Yard. I know all about your troubles and I've come out here to pay off some of the score and see you're not bothered by these people. In London we think that the man in that house might start putting pressure on you, about your property, and there's no other way of stopping him."

The girl said bitterly: "I had a favourite pony, a Palomino. Three weeks ago they poisoned it. Then they shot my Alsatian. I'd raised it from a puppy. Then came a letter. It said, 'Death has many hands. One of these hands is now raised over you.' I was to put a notice in the paper, in the personal column, on a particular day. I was just to say, 'I will obey. Judy.' I went to the police. All they did was to offer me protection. It was people in Cuba, they thought. There was nothing else they could do about it. So I went to Cuba and stayed in the best hotel and gambled big in the casinos." She gave a little smile. "I wasn't dressed like this. I wore my best dresses and the family jewels. And people made up to me. I was nice to them. I had to be. And all the while I asked questions. I pretended I was out for thrills—that I wanted to see the underworld and some real gangsters, and so on. And in the end I found out about this man." She gestured down towards the house. "He had left Cuba. Batista had found out about him or something. And he had a lot of enemies. I was told plenty about him and in the end I met a man, a sort of high-up policeman, who told me the rest after I had," she hesitated and avoided Bond's eyes, "after I had made up to him." She paused. She went on: "I left and went to America. I had read somewhere about Pinkerton's, the detective people. I went to them and paid to have them find this man's address." She turned her hands palm upwards on her lap. Now her eyes were defiant. "That's all."

"How did you get here?"

"I flew up to Bennington. Then I walked. Four days. Up through the Green Mountains. I kept out of the way of people. I'm used to this sort of thing. Our house is in the mountains in Jamaica. They're much more difficult than these. And there are more people, peasants, about in them. Here no one ever seems to walk. They go by car."

"And what were you going to do then?"

"I'm going to shoot von Hammerstein and walk back to Bennington." The voice was as casual as if she had said she was going to pick a wild flower.

From down in the valley came the sound of voices. Bond got to his feet and took a quick look through the branches. Three men and two girls had come on to the patio. There was talk and laughter as they pulled out chairs and sat down at the table. One place was left empty at the head of the table between the two girls. Bond took out his telescopic sight and looked through it. The three men were very small and dark. One of them, who smiled all the time and whose clothes looked the cleanest and smartest, would be Gonzales. The other two were low peasant types. They sat together at the foot of the oblong table and took no part in the talk. The girls were swarthy brunettes. They looked like cheap Cuban whores. They wore bright bathing-dresses and a lot of gold jewellery, and laughed and chattered like pretty monkeys. The voices were almost clear enough to understand, but they were talking Spanish.

Bond felt the girl near him. She stood a yard behind him. Bond handed her the glass. He said: "The neat little man is called Major Gonzales. The two at the bottom of the table are gunmen. I don't know who the girls are. Von Hammerstein isn't there yet." She took a quick look through the glass and handed it back without comment. Bond wondered if she realized that she had been looking at the murderers of her father and mother.

The two girls had turned and were looking towards the door into the house. One of them called out something that might have been a greeting. A short, square, almost naked man came out into the sunshine. He walked silently past the table to the edge of the flagged terrace facing the lawn and proceeded to go through a five-minute programme of physical drill.

Bond examined the man minutely. He was about five feet four with a boxer's shoulders and hips, but a stomach that was going to fat. A mat of black hair covered his breasts and shoulder blades, and his arms and legs were thick with it. By contrast, there was not a hair on his face or head and his skull was a glittering whitish yellow with a deep dent at the back that might have been a wound or the scar of a trepanning. The bone structure of the face was that of the conventional Prussian officer—square, hard and thrusting—but the eyes under the naked brows were close-set and piggish, and the large mouth had hideous lips—thick and wet and crimson. He wore nothing but a strip of black material, hardly larger than an athletic support-belt, round his stomach, and a large gold wrist-watch on a gold bracelet. Bond handed the glass to the girl. He was relieved. Von Hammerstein looked just about as unpleasant as M.'s dossier said he was.

Bond watched the girl's face. The mouth looked grim, almost cruel, as she looked down on the man she had come to kill. What was he to do about her? He could see nothing but a vista of troubles from her presence. She might even interfere with his own plans and insist on play-ing some silly role with her bow and arrow. Bond made up his mind. He just could not afford to take chances. One short tap at the base of the skull and he would gag her and tie her up until it was all over. Bond reached softly for the butt of his automatic.

Nonchalantly the girl moved a few steps back. Just as nonchalantly she bent down, put the glass on the ground and picked up her bow. She reached behind her for an arrow, and fitted it casually into the bow. Then she looked up at Bond and said quietly: "Don't get any silly ideas. And keep your distance. I've got what's called wide-angled vision. I haven't come all the way here to be knocked on the head by a flat-footed London bobby. I can't miss with this at fifty yards, and I've killed birds on the wing at a hun-dred. I don't want to put an arrow through your leg, but I shall if you interfere."

Bond cursed his previous indecision. He said fiercely: "Don't be a silly bitch. Put that damned thing down. This is man's work. How in hell do you think you can take on four men with a bow and arrow?"

The girl's eyes blazed obstinately. She moved her right foot back into the shooting stance. She said through compressed, angry lips: "You go to hell. And keep out of this. It was my mother and father they killed. Not yours. I've already been here a day and a night. I know what they do and I know how to get Hammerstein. I don't care about the others. They're nothing without him. Now then." She pulled the bow half taut. The arrow pointed at Bond's feet. "Either you do what I say or you're going to be sorry. And don't think I don't mean it. This is a private thing I've sworn to do and nobody's going to stop me." She tossed her head imperiously. "Well?"

Bond gloomily measured the situation. He looked the ridiculously beautiful wild girl up and down. This was good hard English stock spiced with the hot peppers of a tropical childhood. Dangerous mixture. She had keyed herself up to a state of controlled hysteria. He was quite cer-tain that she would think nothing of putting him out of action. And he had absolutely no defence. Her weapon was silent, his would alert the whole neighbourhood. Now the only hope would be to work with her. Give her part of the job and he would do the rest. He said quietly: "Now listen, Judy. If you insist on coming in on this thing we'd better do it together. Then perhaps we can bring it off and stay alive. This sort of thing is my profes-sion. I was ordered to do it—by a close friend of your family, if you want to know. And I've got the right weapon. It's got at least five times the range of yours. I could take a good chance of killing him now, on the patio. But the odds aren't quite good enough. Some of them have got bathing things on. They'll be coming down to the lake. Then I'm going to do it. You can give supporting fire." He ended lamely: "It'll be a great help."

"No." She shook her head decisively. "I'm sorry. You can give what you call supporting fire if you like. I don't care one way or the other. You're right about the swimming. Yesterday they were all down at the lake around eleven. It's just as warm today and they'll be there again. I shall get him from the edge of the trees by the lake. I found a perfect place last night. The bodyguard men bring their guns with them—sort of tommy-gun things. They don't bathe. They sit around and keep guard. I know the moment to get von Hammerstein and I'll be well away from the lake before they take in what's happened. I tell you I've got it all planned. Now then. I can't hang around any more. I ought to have been in my place already. I'm sorry, but unless you say yes straight away there's no alternative." She raised the bow a few inches.

Bond thought: "Damn this girl to hell." He said angrily: "All right then. But I can tell you that if we get out of this you're going to get such a spanking you won't be able to sit down for a week." He shrugged. He said with resignation: "Go ahead. I'll look after the others. If you get away all right, meet me here. If you don't, I'll come down and pick up the pieces."

The girl unstrung her bow. She said indifferently: "I'm glad you're seeing sense. These arrows are difficult to pull out. Don't worry about me. But keep out of sight and mind the sun doesn't catch that glass of yours." She gave Bond the brief, pitying, self-congratulatory smile of the woman who has had the last word, and turned and made off down through the trees.

Bond watched the lithe dark green figure until it had vanished among the tree-trunks, then he impatiently picked up the glass and went back to his vantage-point. To hell with her! It was time to clear the silly bitch out of his mind and concentrate on the job. Was there anything else he could have done—any other way of handling it? Now he was committed to wait for her to fire the first shot. That was bad. But if he fired first there was no way of knowing what the hot-headed bitch would do. Bond's mind luxuriated briefly in the thought of what he would do to the girl once all this was over. Then there was movement in front of the house, and he put the exciting thoughts aside and lifted his glass.

The breakfast things were being cleared away by the two maids. There was no sign of the girls or the gunmen. Von Hammerstein was lying back among the cushions of an outdoor couch reading a newspaper and occasionally comment-

ing to Major Gonzales, who sat astride an iron garden chair near his feet. Gonzales was smoking a cigar and from time to time he delicately raised a hand in front of his mouth, leant sideways, and spat a bit of leaf out on the ground. Bond could not hear what von Hammerstein was saying, but his comments were in English and Gonzales answered in English. Bond glanced at his watch. It was ten-thirty. Since the scene seemed to be static, Bond sat down with his back to the tree and went over the Savage with minute care. At the same time he thought of what would shortly have to be done with it.

Bond did not like what he was going to do, and all the way from England he had had to keep on reminding himself what sort of men these were. The killing of the Havelocks had been a particularly dreadful killing. Von Hammerstein and his gunmen were particularly dreadful men whom many people around the world would probably be very glad to destroy, as this girl proposed to do, out of private revenge. But for Bond it was different. He had no personal motives against them. This was merely his job—as it was the job of a pest control officer to kill rats. He was the public executioner appointed by M. to represent the community. In a way, Bond argued to himself, these men were as much enemies of his country as were the agents of SMERSH or of other enemy Secret Services. They had declared and waged war against British people on British soil and they were currently planning another attack. Bond's mind hunted round for more arguments to bolster his resolve. They had killed the girl's pony and her dog with two casual sideswipes of the hand as if they had been flies. They . . .

A burst of automatic fire from the valley brought Bond to his feet. His rifle was up and taking aim as the second burst came. The harsh racket of noise was followed by laughter and hand-clapping. The kingfisher, a handful of tattered blue and grey feathers, thudded to the lawn and lay fluttering. Von Hammerstein, smoke still dribbling from the snout of his tommy-gun, walked a few steps and put the heel of his naked foot down and pivoted sharply. He took his heel away and wiped it on the grass beside the heap of feathers. The others stood round, laughing and applauding obsequiously. Von Hammerstein's red lips grinned with pleasure. He said something which included the word "crackshot." He handed the gun to one of the gunmen and wiped his hands down his fat backsides. He gave a sharp order to the two girls, who ran off into the house, then, with the others following, he turned and ambled down the sloping lawn towards the lake. Now the girls came running back out of the house. Each one carried an empty champagne bottle. Chattering and laughing they skipped down after the men.

Bond got himself ready. He clipped the telescopic sight on to the barrel of the Savage and took his stance against the trunk of the tree. He found a bump in the wood as a rest for his left hand, put his sights at 300, and took broad aim at the group of people by the lake. Then, holding the rifle loosely, he leaned against the trunk and watched the scene.

It was going to be some kind of a shooting contest between the two gunmen. They snapped fresh magazines on to their guns and at Gonzales's orders stationed themselves on the flat stone wall of the dam some twenty feet apart on either side of the diving-board. They stood with their backs to the lake and their guns at the ready.

Von Hammerstein took up his place on the grass verge, a champagne bottle swinging in each hand. The girls stood behind him, their hands over their ears. There was excited jabbering in Spanish, and laughter in which the two gunmen did not join. Through the telescopic sight their faces looked sharp with concentration.

Von Hammerstein barked an order and there was silence. He swung both arms back and counted "Uno . . . Dos . . . Tres." With the "tres" he hurled the champagne bottles high into the air over the lake.

The two men turned like marionettes, the guns clamped to their hips. As they completed the turn they fired. The thunder of the guns split the peaceful scene and racketed up from the water. Birds fled away from the trees

screeching and some small branches cut by the bullets pattered down into the lake. The left-hand bottle disintegrated into dust, the right-hand one, hit by only a single bullet, split in two a fraction of a second later. The fragments of glass made small splashes over the middle of the lake. The gunman on the left had won. The smoke-clouds over the two of them joined and drifted away over the lawn. The echoes boomed softly into silence. The two gunmen walked along the wall to the grass, the rear one looking sullen, the leading one with a sly grin on his face. Von Hammerstein beckoned the two girls forward. They came reluctantly, dragging their feet and pouting. Von Hammerstein said something, asked a question of the winner. The man nodded at the girl on the left. She looked sullenly back at him. Gonzales and Hammerstein laughed. Hammerstein reached out and patted the girl on the rump as if she had been a cow. He said something in which Bond caught the words "una noche." The girl looked up at him and nodded obediently. The group broke up. The prize girl took a quick run and dived into the lake, perhaps to get away from the man who had won her favours, and the other girl followed her. They swam away across the lake calling angrily to each other. Major Gonzales took off his coat and laid it on the grass and sat down on it. He was wearing a shoulder holster which showed the butt of a medium-calibre automatic. He watched von Hammerstein take off his watch and walk along the dam wall to the diving-board. The gunmen stood back from the lake and also watched von Hammerstein and the two girls, who were now out in the middle of the little lake and were making for the far shore. The gunmen stood with their guns cradled in their arms and occasionally one of them would glance round the garden or towards the house. Bond thought there was every reason why von Hammerstein had managed to stay alive so long. He was a man who took trouble to do so.

Von Hammerstein had reached the diving-board. He walked along to the end and stood looking down at the water. Bond tensed himself and put up the safe. His eyes were fierce slits. It would be any minute now. His finger itched on the trigger-guard. What in hell was the girl waiting for?

Von Hammerstein had made up his mind. He flexed his knees slightly. The arms came back. Through the telescopic sight Bond could see the thick hair over his shoulder blades tremble in a breeze that came to give a quick shiver to the surface of the lake. Now his arms were coming forward and there was a fraction of a second when his feet had left the board and he was still almost upright. In that fraction of a second there was a flash of silver against his back and then von Hammerstein's body hit the water in a neat dive.

Gonzales was on his feet, looking uncertainly at the turbulence caused by the dive. His mouth was open, waiting. He did not know if he had seen something or not. The two gunmen were more certain. They had their guns at the ready. They crouched, looking from Gonzales to the trees behind the dam, waiting for an order.

Slowly the turbulence subsided and the ripples spread across the lake. The dive had gone deep.

Bond's mouth was dry. He licked his lips, searching the lake with his glass. There was a pink shimmer deep down. It wobbled slowly up. Von Hammerstein's body broke the surface. It lay head down, wallowing softly. A foot or so of steel shaft stuck up from below the left shoulder blade and the sun winked on the aluminium feathers.

Major Gonzales yelled an order and the two tommy-guns roared and flamed. Bond could hear the crash of the bullets among the trees below him. The Savage shuddered against his shoulder and the right-hand man fell slowly forward on his face. Now the other man was running for the lake, his gun still firing from the hip in short bursts. Bond fired and missed and fired again. The man's legs buckled, but his momentum still carried him forward. He crashed into the water. The clenched finger went on firing the gun aimlessly up towards the blue sky until the water throttled the mechanism.

The seconds wasted on the extra shot had given Major Gonzales a chance. He had got behind the body of the first gunman and now he opened up on Bond with the tommy-gun. Whether he had seen Bond or was only firing at the flashes from the Savage he was doing well. Bullets zipped into the maple and slivers of wood spattered into Bond's face. Bond fired twice. The dead body of the gunman jerked. Too low! Bond reloaded and took fresh aim. A snapped branch fell across his rifle. He shook it free, but now Gonzales was up and running forward to the group of garden furniture. He hurled the iron table on its side and got behind it as two snap shots from Bond kicked chunks out of the lawn at his heels. With this solid cover his shooting became more accurate, and burst after burst, now from the right of the table and now from the left, crashed into the maple tree while Bond's single shots clanged against the white iron or whined off across the lawn. It was not easy to traverse the telescopic sight quickly from one side of the table to the other and Gonzales was cunning with his changes. Again and again his bullets thudded into the trunk beside and above Bond. Bond ducked and ran swiftly to the right. He would fire, standing, from the open meadow and catch Gonzales off-guard. But even as he ran, he saw Gonzales dart from behind the iron table. He also had decided to end the stalemate. He was running for the dam to get across and into the woods and come up after Bond. Bond stood and threw up his rifle. As he did so, Gonzales also saw him. He went down on one knee on the dam wall and sprayed a burst at Bond. Bond stood icily, hearing the bullets. The crossed hairs centred on Gonzales's chest. Bond squeezed the trigger. Gonzales rocked. He half got to his feet. He raised his arms and, with his gun still pumping bullets into the sky, dived clumsily face forward into the water.

Bond watched to see if the face would rise. It did not. Slowly he lowered his rifle and wiped the back of his arm across his face.

The echoes, the echoes of much death, rolled to and fro across the valley. Away to the right, in the trees beyond the lake, he caught a glimpse of the two girls running up towards the house. Soon they, if the maids had not already done so, would be on to the State troopers. It was time to get moving.

Bond walked back through the meadow to the lone maple. The girl was there. She stood up against the trunk of the tree with her back to him. Her head was cradled in her arms against the tree. Blood was running down the right arm and dripping to the ground, and there was a black stain high up on the sleeve of the dark green shirt. The bow and quiver of arrows lay at her feet. Her shoulders were shaking.

Bond came up behind her and put a protective arm across her shoulders. He said softly: "Take it easy, Judy. It's all over now. How bad's the arm?"

She said in a muffled voice: "It's nothing. Something hit me. But that was awful. I didn't— I didn't know it would be like that."

Bond pressed her arm reassuringly. "It had to be done. They'd have got you otherwise. Those were pro killers—the worst. But I told you this sort of thing was man's work. Now then, let's have a look at your arm. We've got to get going—over the border. The troopers'll be here before long."

She turned. The beautiful wild face was streaked with sweat and tears. Now the grey eyes were soft and obedient. She said: "It's nice of you to be like that. After the way I was. I was sort of—sort of wound up."

She held out her arm. Bond reached for the hunting-knife at her belt and cut off her shirtsleeve at the shoulder. There was the bruised, bleeding gash of a bullet wound across the mus-cle. Bond took out his own khaki handkerchief, cut it into three lengths and joined them together. He washed the wound clean with the coffee and whisky, and then took a thick slice of bread from his haversack and bound it over the wound. He cut her shirtsleeve into a sling and reached behind her neck to tie the knot. Her mouth was inches from his. The scent of her body had a warm animal tang. Bond kissed her once softly on the lips and once again, hard. He tied the knot. He looked into the grey eyes close to his. They looked surprised and happy. He kissed her again at each corner of the mouth and the mouth slowly smiled. Bond stood away from her and smiled back. He softly picked up her right hand and slipped the wrist into the sling. She said docilely: "Where are you taking me?"

Bond said: "I'm taking you to London. There's this old man who will want to see you. But first we've got to get over into Canada, and I'll talk to a friend in Ottawa and get your passport straightened out. You'll have to get some clothes and things. It'll take a few days. We'll be staying in a place called the KO-ZEE Motel."

She looked at him. She was a different girl. She said softly: "That'll be nice. I've never stayed in a motel."

Bond bent down and picked up his rifle and knapsack and slung them over one shoulder. Then he hung her bow and quiver over the other, and turned and started up through the meadow.

She fell in behind and followed him, and as she walked she pulled the tired bits of goldenrod out of her hair and undid a ribbon and let the pale gold hair fall down to her shoulders.

THE RED, RED FLOWERS

M. E. CHABER

LIKE SO MANY OTHER pulp writers, Kendell Foster Crossen (1910–1981) was hugely prolific, with about two hundred fifty short stories to his credit along with more than forty novels. But it was the number of radio and television scripts—more than four hundred—that is truly impressive, with scriptwriting credits on such popular shows as *The Saint*, *77 Sunset Strip*, and *Perry Mason*.

Born in Ohio, he played football at Rio Grande College, was an amateur boxer, and worked a variety of colorful jobs, including carnival barker and insurance investigator—the career of his best-known detective character, Milo March, who appeared in more than twenty novels written under one of his numerous pseudonyms, M. E. Chaber. The martini-loving March also worked as a private investigator and frequently became involved in government matters, including espionage cases for the CIA. He is a tough guy, though he dislikes violence, and is a hedonist who likes good restaurants, an extravagant expense account, and at least one beautiful woman per book.

In addition to writing for the pulps, Crossen also worked as the editor of *Detective Fiction Weekly*, one of the top pulp magazines of the day.

Crossen's most successful protagonist was Jethro Dumont, who spent ten years in Tibet learning the secrets of Eastern meditation. He then returned to New York to fight crime using the superpowers that he could bring forth with a magical chant that turned him into the Green Lama. His adventures ran in *Double Detective* in the 1940s under his Richard Foster byline, which spawned a comic book superhero series in 1940 in *Prize Comics*. The crime fighter became so popular that he got his own comic book, *The Green Lama*, which inspired a 1949 radio program that lasted only eleven episodes.

"The Red, Red Flowers" was originally published in the February 1961 issue of *Blue Book*.

THE RED, RED FLOWERS

M. E. CHABER

IT WAS ONE of those mornings when nothing was going right. I reached the office early because I was expecting a phone call. It still hadn't come. The mail hadn't been delivered, so I was reading the morning paper. The Giants had lost the day before. The Yankees had won a doubleheader from Boston. When it's that kind of day, everything goes wrong. In disgust, I turned to the front pages. Things weren't any better there. The Russians had caught a second U-2 pilot and his plane, and were promising a quick trial for the pilot. I put the paper down and stared malignantly at the phone that didn't ring.

The name is March. Milo March. I'm an insurance investigator. At least that's what it says on my license and on the door of my Madison Avenue office. Which means that if you kill your wife, hoping to collect her insurance to spend on that blonde you met the other night, I'll probably be around looking for you. That's the general idea anyway. But everyone must have been on a temporary goodness jag. I hadn't had a job in two weeks.

The mail arrived. All bills. So it was still the same kind of day. Then the door opened and there was another mailman, this one with a registered letter. I signed for it and he went away.

I opened the letter and the day was complete. It said that Major March, US Army Reserve, was recalled to active duty. I was to report to an address in Washington. It was that same day. The time was sixteen hundred, or four o'clock. Which meant that I had about six in which to make it.

I thought of ignoring the whole thing, pretending I had never gotten the letter. But it had been registered, and when the Army wants you, they only give you two choices. You can walk in or be dragged in. So I made arrangements with another investigator to handle anything that came in for me, and notified my answering service to route the calls to him. Then I went downtown to my apartment in Greenwich Village. I dug out my uniform and discovered it didn't need anything but a pressing. I took it into the tailor, and went to the Blue Mill for a couple of martinis while being pressed.

At two o'clock that afternoon, looking every inch the well-dressed Army officer, I was at LaGuardia Field boarding a plane for Washington. An hour later I was telling a Washington cab driver where to take me, but I didn't give him the address in the orders, but a street corner nearby. When I got out of the cab I still had about a half hour to spare. I spent it in the nearest gin mill over another martini. I believe that Regulations state that an officer shouldn't drink while on duty, but then I wouldn't really be on duty until after I reported. Finally I walked down the street, looking for the address. There were three vacant lots in the middle of the block where builders had just begun to excavate. Beyond them were several old brownstone houses of the type which in recent years have been taken over by government bureaus. I walked past the vacant lots and reached the first building. I looked at the number. It was too high. I turned and retraced my steps. But after a few steps I realized that the number in my orders, if it had ever existed, had been where one of the vacant lots was now. I cursed to myself. If I'd had any doubts before about who was responsible for my return to active duty, they were gone.

I heard steps on the sidewalk while I was still standing there with the orders in my hand. I looked around. A pleasant-faced young man was strolling toward me. I almost ignored him, but then I took another look. There was something a little too studied about his casualness, and I knew I was right. I turned back to the vacant lot and stared at it innocently.

"Pardon me, Major," the young man said as he reached me, "is there anything wrong?"

I turned my innocence on him. "Why," I said, "I seem to have been given the wrong address."

"Perhaps I can help you," he said. "I know the neighborhood rather well. What address are you looking for?" He moved in slightly behind me as though to look over my shoulder. Out of the corner of my eye, I caught a slight movement of his right arm and I heard the scrape of something against cloth.

"This one," I said, holding up the paper.

I knew that the movement would catch his eyes for at least a couple of seconds. I lifted my left foot and brought it down hard on his right instep. There was a gasp of pain from him. I dropped the paper and pivoted, sending a right to his stomach just hard enough to bend him over. I chopped across his neck with the edge of my left hand and he dropped. He was unconscious—which was the way I wanted him. A slender blackjack was lying on the sidewalk next to him. I left him and the blackjack where they had fallen. I picked up my orders, folded the paper, and put it back in my pocket. Fortunately the street was still empty, so there was no one to raise a cry about the man on the street. I walked back to the first house beyond the lots. It seemed like the logical place.

This time I looked in. There was a tiny vestibule with an inner door, but there were no mailboxes, nameplates, or bells in it. Beyond the second door, I could see a long corridor with doors on either side. About halfway down the corridor there was a soldier, obviously standing guard. I could have just gone in and presented my orders and he probably would have escorted me into the office. But I was sore and I didn't want it that way.

I stepped back out on the street. The young man was still lying on the sidewalk. I skirted around the side of the brownstone and went to the back. There was a parking area there with four cars in it. One was an Army car with three stars on it. That proved I was right.

I hunted around the back until I found a greasy cloth that had been used on one of the cars. I slipped up to the rear door and tried it. It was locked, but it took me only a moment to pick it. I opened the door just enough to slip the rag, bunched up, in between it and the sill at the bottom. I struck a match and held it to the cloth. As soon as it began to smolder, I hurried back to the front of the house. I slipped into the vestibule, against the wall, and watched the soldier on guard. After a few seconds he began to sniff and look around. He caught a glimpse of smoke trickling in through the back door and hurried toward it.

The minute he moved, I had the second door open and was going quietly down the hall behind him. He was bending over the burning rag as I reached the door he'd been guarding. I opened the door silently and stepped inside. I was in a small, empty office. There was an open door leading into another, larger office. There were voices coming from that other office.

"I don't see why you had to do it this way," a man was saying. "We know March's work well enough. Why didn't you just have him come straight here and get it over with?"

"I like to test men before I give them assignments," said another voice. It was one I knew all too well. He chuckled. "O'Connor should be here with him any minute. It'll be worth a lot to see March's face when he comes here in the office."

I lit a cigarette and went to stand in the doorway. "You don't have to wait that long," I said. "Take a good look now."

The three men in the room whirled to look at me. I knew all three of them. One of them was George Hillyer, the civilian head of the Central Intelligence Agency. The other civilian was Philip Emerson, his assistant. And the third man was a big, red-faced Army officer with three bright shining stars on his collar. Lieutenant General Sam Roberts. The two civilians were quickly over their surprise, and I noticed they were both grinning but being careful to hide the fact from the General. He was still staring at me with his mouth open, but his face was beginning to get redder.

"Old Tricky Roberts," I said. "You haven't changed since the days when you couldn't steal a chicken without being caught." During the fracas that was known as World War II, General Roberts and I had been in OSS together, working behind the German lines. But he'd been a colonel then.

"You're talking to a superior officer, Major March," the General said. His voice was as stiff as an over-starched collar. "I could break you for that."

"Anyone who'll talk to a superior officer ought to be broken," I retorted. "Don't give me that malarkey, General. I know you since you were a chicken colonel, polishing those eagles until they screamed. You're in trouble, or I wouldn't have been recalled to active duty. You break me and who'll pull your chestnuts from the fire?"

His face was a deep purple. "Silence," he roared. "How the hell did you get in here?

O'Connor—" He broke off. "Anyway, Sanders was just outside the door with orders not to let anyone in," he finished.

There was an interruption. The outer door opened and two men came into the office. The first one was the soldier who had been on guard. He was followed by the young man I'd met in the street. He was limping and rubbing his neck.

"I beg your pardon, General," the soldier said, "but the back door was unlocked and somebody had stuffed an oily rag in it and set it on fire. But I didn't see anybody around."

The General glared at me and I gave him a sweet smile. He swung back to the two men. "What kind of an outfit is this?" he said angrily. "Can't anyone carry out a simple order without fouling it up?"

"The only one who's goofed around here," I said, "is a certain three-star general. First you send me orders with a phony address on them. Then you send a pet bird dog out to point me into a trap. Just so you can get a belly laugh when I'm dragged in by the heels."

"Well," the General said lamely, "I just wanted to see if civilian life had softened you up." He glanced at the two men in the doorway. "How about it, O'Connor?"

It was the young man who answered. "I'd say it hadn't, sir. I was in back of him, but I never had a chance."

"All right, go home, O'Connor. Take a couple of days off. Sanders, go back and wait in the car for me." The General swung his gaze back to me. "So right away you come in and beat up one of my best men, then you pick the lock on the back door, shove in a burning rag—which could have burned down the building—to draw away the guard just so you can make a grandstand play by breaking in here?"

"You want to play games," I said, "that's what you'll get. You never saw the day you could outsmart me. You tried it plenty of times when we were behind the lines together."

Any mention of the war always relaxed him. He leaned back in his chair and beamed at me. "It was a great war, wasn't it, Milo?"

"Save it for your memoirs," I said. "What kind of trouble are you in that you have to drag me back into this monkey suit?"

"You're right about its being trouble, Major," George Hillyer said. "The three of us discussed it and decided you were the best man for the job. . . . Yesterday the Russians got another of our U–2 planes."

"I read about it in the paper this morning," I said. "I thought those were the planes that flew so high no one could shoot them down. Do the Russians have a new type of gun?"

"No," the General growled. "The first plane had a jet flame-out and went down to thirty thousand feet. They couldn't have touched him at seventy thousand. The second plane had gone down to twenty thousand feet, under orders, when the Russians hit his plane."

"Why so low?"

"To make a drop," Hillyer said. "The pilot was supposed to drop ammunition, money, and information to a resistance group inside Russia. They got him before he succeeded in making the drop."

"What does this have to do with me?" I asked.

It was Hillyer who answered. "You've heard of Narodno Trudovoi Soyuz, Major?"

I nodded. "The National Alliance of Russian Solidarists. It's a group of anti-Communist Russians."

"Right. Their headquarters are in West Germany, but they have thousands of agents inside Russia. No one but Russians are permitted in the group. They have been very successful, mostly because of what they call the molecule system. It's something like the old Communist cell. Each group of agents in Russia consists of three persons, and those three do not know any other group. If one is captured and tortured, he can only inform on two other members. These NTS people have been very valuable to us in providing information. In return we have supplied them with money and materials. Our pilot was making a drop to an American agent in Russia who was then to contact a number of these underground molecules."

"Wasn't it dangerous having a man there who knew the different groups?"

"He didn't know them. The drop included a coded message to him giving him the location of the groups. The message was concealed behind a map of Russia, which would be part of a regular U-pilot's equipment. If anything had happened to the plane and pilot, we wanted the Russians to think it was a regular flight."

"Did they?"

"So far they have. But the map is one of the things they have on display in the Hall of Columns in Moscow. And the pilot knows there's a message on the back of the map. We don't believe he's being brainwashed or anything like that, but there's always a chance that he may try to use the information during his trial or later in prison to make a trade. If the Russians get the message, hundreds of agents will die, and we will lose a valuable source of information."

I was beginning to get the idea and I didn't like it. "You mean you want the pilot and the message snatched out of the Russians' hands?"

"Exactly."

"I could smell that one coming," I said. "I don't like it. You know, I've been in East Germany twice and Russia once. They have my fingerprints and considerable information about me. It won't be easy even to get into the country."

"We have that problem licked," the General said. It was the first time he'd spoken for several minutes.

"How?"

"It is not yet known," he said, "but we have a U–3 plane. Same as the U–2 but it will carry two men. We fly you over Russia at seventy thousand feet and you parachute in. Perfectly safe."

"For everybody except me," I said.

"It's fairly safe," Hillyer said. "We have a few days' time. We're going to have you brush up on your Russian and see that you get all the other information you need. We're providing you with clothes and identification, everything you need to prove that you're a Russian. We know you speak Russian well enough to fool them. We can give you one more bit of help. There will be one underground molecule—that is, three persons—who will assist you and be under your orders. For the rest you will be on your own."

"From fourteen miles up in the air?" I said. "That's really being on your own."

When the Army gets an idea, that's it. You'd think ideas were invented at West Point. Anyway, it went the way they said. I spent the next several days polishing my Russian. I took special classes each day and even went to sleep at night plugged into sleep lessons. In between I was fitted out for a pressure suit for the parachute jump, and given a complete set of clothes that had been made in Russia. I was given all kinds of identification cards, including a Party card and proof that I was a worker from Rostov who was spending two weeks in Moscow. I was even provided with a short-handled shovel, to bury the pressure suit after I landed; the shovel also had been made in Russia. Five days after reporting for duty, I was on an Army plane headed for Pakistan.

Three more days went by after we landed there.

I was introduced to the pilot who would fly me over Russia—a tall, blond boy from Indiana—and stuffed into a pressure suit. I felt, and probably looked, like an invader from Mars. I was led out to the plane, a stubby-winged, sleek-looking black plane with a needle nose. I climbed into the rear seat and hooked my helmet into the intercom. I checked to be sure that I had the knapsack that was going to parachute in with me.

"You plugged in, Major?" the pilot asked. His voice coming through the earphones in the helmet had a hollow sound.

"I seem to be," I said.

"All set, Major?"

"As much as I'll ever be," I grunted. "But I have a feeling that this is one thing which will never become habit-forming with me."

"There's nothing to it," he said cheerfully. "You don't even have to pull a ripcord. Your chute will open automatically when you've fallen about eight miles."

"They didn't tell me that jokes were a part of this, or I wouldn't have come," I said. "Where are you dropping me?"

"About ten miles southeast of Moscow. That'll give you the rest of the night to walk into the city."

"How can you be sure that's where you'll drop me?"

"Major, in this weather, I could drop you from this height and make you land on a dime. I don't even have to do any guessing about it. The whole thing's worked out mathematically."

We flew along in silence the next few minutes. Then he spoke again. "Better start getting ready, Major. Be sure you've got everything you want to take with you. It's hard coming back after something you forgot. There's a lever in front of you. See it?"

"Yeah."

"When I tell you to go, disconnect your communication cord and pull that lever. It'll drop you through the bottom of the ship and you'll be on your way. Okay?"

"Okay," I muttered, but I wasn't sure it was. I felt the way I had the first time I had a serious date with a girl—lightheaded. I checked to be sure the knapsack was fastened to my shoulders. I would have liked to check the rest of my equipment but I didn't know anything about it, so I waited.

"Go ahead, Major," the pilot said quietly. "And good luck."

"Thanks," I said. I reached up and pulled the cord from my helmet. I took a deep breath and pushed the lever in front of me.

After what seemed a very long time, I felt the tug of the parachute as it opened. After that, I was vaguely aware of swinging like a pendulum from it, but it was a pleasant sensation. Then, almost before I knew it, the ground came up to meet me and I went tumbling across it until the chute collapsed. I managed to unbuckle it and then take my helmet off. There was a gentle breeze and the smell of earth, but there were no lights.

I rested for a couple of minutes, then took the knapsack off my back. I removed my gloves and opened the pack. There was a small flashlight at the very top. Shielding the light, I looked around. I was in the middle of a plowed field.

I took the other clothes from the knapsack, and quickly undressed and put them on. I took the shovel and dug a hole in the field. I gathered up the parachute and folded it, dropping it and the pressure suit into the hole. I checked the knapsack to be sure that everything was out of it, then dropped it in too and shoveled the dirt back. When I was sure that the spot looked like the rest of the field, I used the light to check my compass and headed off in the direction of Moscow. About a mile on the way, I threw the shovel into a ditch, after first wiping the handle clean so there would be no fingerprints on it.

It was just four o'clock in the morning when I approached the edge of the city. I had already decided it would be foolish to start marching through the streets at that hour in the morning, so I found a field with some bushes in it and curled up and went to sleep.

It was shortly after eight when I awakened. Now there was some traffic on the road, mostly trucks. No one paid any attention to me as I walked into the city. I soon reached a bus stop, where several workers were waiting for a bus, and I joined them. I was dressed a little better than the other men—because I was, after all, on my vacation—but no one looked at me twice. I rode the bus into the center of Moscow and began to breathe a little easier.

It didn't take me long to find the address I'd been given. It was one of the new apartment buildings on the Kotelnicheskaye Embankment. It was in block D, entrance C. I worked my way through the corridors until I found the apartment. I knocked on the door and hoped someone was home.

The door was opened by a girl. She was small, dark-haired, and pretty. Even the loose-fitting clothes couldn't conceal that she had a full figure.

"Dobroe utro," I said. *"U vas est mesto dlae mene?"* It was part of a recognition code.

"Prikhodite v luboe vremae," she answered. "It is lovely in Moscow this time of year."

"Yes," I said. "I have been admiring the red, red flowers that grow around the Kremlin."

She smiled and stepped back, opening the door wider. "Come in," she said.

I entered the apartment and she closed the door. I looked around. There were two rooms, small but attractive. I turned back to the girl.

"We were expecting you today," she said. "I am Natasha Naristova."

"I'm Milo March," I said, "but here I will be known as Mikhail Mikhailovich." I showed her my identification.

"It is well done," she said, after looking at the papers. "You had no trouble in finding the apartment?"

"No. I've been in Moscow before."

"I know," she said. "I remember reading about the capitalist spy Milo March. But your country proved that you couldn't have been here, didn't they?"

I nodded. "Do you live here alone?"

"No, with my brother. He is one of us. He is at work now."

"You don't work?"

"Oh, yes. I am on the staff of *Pravda*. This is my day off. What are your plans? All we were told was to expect an agent, and to give him any help he needed."

"I want to go to the opening of the trial of the American pilot tomorrow. I have to get him and part of his possessions out of the country. Both are a threat to your group."

"That will be difficult," she said gravely. "I do not see how it can be done by only four of us."

"I will try to do most of it myself," I told her. "I don't want to risk you more than I have to."

"We will do what is needed. Tonight the third member of our group will be here and it can be discussed. You will stay here as long as you need to. Is there anything you would like now?"

"Some sleep," I said. "I had only three or four hours in a field this morning."

She led the way into the second room and indicated the two beds. I stretched out on one and was soon asleep.

I was awake by the middle of the afternoon. The girl was in the other room, reading. She made tea, and we spent the rest of the afternoon talking. At about five o'clock, her brother arrived. He was a big, blond fellow about my own age. His name was Ilya. He seemed even more pleased than his sister to learn that I was an American agent. During dinner, which Natasha cooked, he plied me with questions about America.

Shortly after dinner, there was a knock on the door. Ilya went and opened it. The man who entered was short and dark, with what seemed to be a perpetually scowling face. He was introduced to me as the third member of their NTS molecule. His name was Yuri Mogilev. Natasha brought out a bottle of vodka and filled four glasses. When they were passed around, she lifted her own.

"To a free Russia," she said, and we all drank. Then she brought out a chessboard and set it up between her brother and Yuri. They began to put the pieces on the board.

"We always bring out the chessboard," Natasha said. "Everyone believes that is the reason Yuri visits us so often. So if anyone comes while we are having a meeting, there is only a chess game."

The men moved the pieces around a few times and then settled back. "Now," said Ilya, "we are ready to discuss your problems. You have papers?"

I nodded. "I am Mikhail Mikhailovich, from Rostov. There I am a minor clerk in the offices of Internal Affairs. I have a two weeks' vacation, which I am spending in Moscow. I have all the necessary papers."

"Good. You will stay here, of course. If there are any questions, you and I were in the army together and that is why you are visiting me." He turned to Yuri. "You know the American pilot who goes on trial tomorrow? The task is to get him out of the country."

Yuri pursed his lips and scowled even more. "It is a big order. They will make the most of him for propaganda, and he will be well guarded. You have a plan?"

I shook my head. "I'll try to make it up as I go along. Will I have any trouble getting into the trial tomorrow?"

"No. That will be open to the public."

"Do any of you know where the pilot is being held prisoner?"

Ilya glanced at Yuri, who nodded. "The Voldovna Prison. It is where they take important political prisoners before their trials."

"Can I get any sort of rough plan of the prison, and the location of the pilot's cell?"

"I can get that for you," Ilya said. "By tomorrow night, I think. Anything else?"

"I don't think so. . . . I have considerable money with me, most of it in American dollars. I'll probably need to spend most of it in getting out. Will the dollars be better for bribes?"

"I do not think so," Ilya said. "I think you should change the dollars in the black market. Yuri can take care of it."

The four of us sat up talking late into the night, mostly about America, before we finally went to sleep. When I awakened the next morning I was alone in the apartment. There was a note from Natasha telling me where to find things for breakfast and how to get to the Hall of Columns. I had some rolls and tea, and left.

A crowd was already gathering for the trial. I entered the building with three or four others dressed pretty much as I was. Out in the corridor, there was a long, glass-covered case and a uniformed MVD man on guard. We filed by and looked at the things that had been taken from the captured pilot. There were a good many guns with ammunition, several watches, a big stack of ruble notes, a small bottle with a card identifying it as poison, all of the pilot's personal things, and the map. The latter was all I was interested in. Under the guise of gaping at the collection, I studied the case. It was locked as well as being guarded.

I followed the others into the large room that had once been the grand ballroom of the old Noblemen's Club, where the trial was to be held. It was flooded with lights, and there were several television cameras set up. About half the room was filled with newspapermen, many of them from the Western countries, including America. Fortunately, I didn't see any who might recognize me. Not that they might anyway, for this was going to be a big show and all eyes would be riveted on it.

The trial was quickly called to order, and the prosecutor faced the prisoner. "What is your name?" he asked.

"James Cooper," he said when the question had been translated into English.

"What is your nationality?"

"American."

"What is your profession?"

"Pilot."

There followed the reading of a long indictment of his crimes against the Soviet Union. I breathed a little easier when I realized that it contained no mention of his intending to contact the underground. It did list the guns and ammunition but merely charged that he'd had them in case of crashing inside Russia. When the indictment was finished, Cooper asked how he pleaded.

"Guilty," he said in a firm voice.

Lieutenant General Borisoglebsky, the presiding judge, leaned forward. "Weren't you aware that flying over Russia was a hostile act?" he asked.

"I didn't think about it," Cooper said.

"Didn't you realize your action might bring about a war?"

"Things like that were for the people who sent me to worry about."

And so it went throughout the day, the questions and answers droning on evenly. Cooper wasn't volunteering any information, although it seemed to me that he was being more cooperative than he had to be. But then, he may have been ordered to do so in case of capture.

Ilya and Natasha were already at the apartment when I got there. We had dinner together, and shortly afterwards Yuri arrived. He brought a newspaper with him and we took turns reading the story of that day's trial. They were milking it for everything they could.

Ilya had brought a hand-drawn map of Voldovna Prison, with the location of Cooper's cell marked on it. I examined it carefully, but the more I looked at it, the more impossible the job seemed. There were three outer doors to penetrate before reaching the cell blocks, and each one of those doors was locked and guarded.

"It looks difficult," I admitted finally.

"I think it is impossible," Natasha said. She'd been leaning over my shoulder, looking at the map with me. "We are told that even a regular visitor, with an official pass to visit a prisoner, must go through questioning by the three guards, and each guard communicates with the next one before you pass through the door. It is almost certain that they will be even more careful with an American prisoner."

"The biggest problem is time," I muttered. "How long do you suppose the trial will last?"

"Exactly two more days," Natasha said.

"Exactly? How do you know that?" I wondered.

"The hall is reserved for only two more days. And the writers and cameramen from *Pravda* are assigned for that time. They already have other assignments for the third day from now."

"At least it lets us know how much time we have," I said. "There is one other way. I don't like it, but maybe we have no choice. Ilya, is there any way we can get complete details on the transportation of Cooper to and from the trial? I mean routes, time, method of taking him, and the number of guards."

"I think so," he said slowly. "There is a man with whom I sometimes play chess at lunchtime. He would know, and I think he could be bribed."

"I'll give you the money," I said. "Try to get it tomorrow. Can you take extra time at lunch or take the afternoon off?"

"I can take the afternoon off."

"Then bring whatever you get here, and I'll meet you. There are a couple of other things I want to ask you about, but first there is something I want to do. I'll be back soon."

"Where are you going?" Natasha asked.

"Out," I said with a smile.

"Let me go with you," she said. "I can be of help."

"Not this time," I told her firmly. "I'll be back within an hour." I smiled at her and left.

It was still early in the evening, but there wasn't much traffic. I hit the small side streets and began walking and looking. I'd been searching for more than a half hour before I found what I was looking for. I was on a narrow, dimly lit street. There were two or three small restaurants and a few shops along it, and the rest were apartment houses. There was a man walking ahead of me; as he reached a streetlight I saw he was wearing an MVD uniform. I quickened my step.

I timed it carefully so as not to get too near until he was in between streetlights. He started to cross a narrow street angling off to the left, and I hurried forward.

"Comrade," I called, just loud enough to reach him but not enough to attract the attention of anyone in the apartment houses.

He hesitated and looked back, peering at me. "What is it?" he called. He sounded irritable.

"I need help," I said. I was almost up to him.

"I am off duty," he said, his tone clearly indicating that he didn't want to be bothered.

"It will take only a minute," I said. I reached him and looked around. There was no one on the street within two blocks of us. "It is only that I need some advice about something I found on the street."

"What is it?" he asked.

I reached into my pocket and pulled out a piece of paper. I held it out. "This," I said.

He took the paper and held it up, trying to get enough light on it to see it. I chopped my hand across his neck as hard as I could. He grunted deep in his throat and started to fall. I caught him and dragged him into the deep shadows of the alley. I went back to retrieve the paper I'd handed him. Then I went back and quickly stripped off his uniform. I rolled it up into a ball with the gun inside, and tucked the whole thing under my arm. It had taken no more than three or four minutes, and he was still unconscious as I stepped back to the street and walked away.

The uniform looked like any bunch of clothes under my arm, and I didn't draw a second glance from any of the few people I met on the way back to the apartment. Even so, I felt better when Natasha opened the door in answer to my knock. I stepped inside and she closed the door.

"I am glad you are back," she said. "What do you have there?"

I unrolled the uniform and smiled at the surprise on all three faces.

"What is it for?"

"I also have to do something to repatriate that paper Cooper was carrying before they find out about it. That comes before anything else tomorrow. I won't need help. This will either work simply and quickly—or not at all. Let's return to the second operation. If Ilya can get the information tomorrow, I will need two things. One will be easy, the other not."

"What do you want, Milo?" Natasha asked quietly.

"First, some old clothes. They should be working clothes, and the older the better."

"We have some of Ilya's that should fit you," Natasha said.

"Any way they could be traced to him if anything happens?" I asked.

She shook her head. "They came from the government store here, and there must be millions like them in Russia."

"All right. Now the hard one. I want to know where I can steal a car. But not any car. This should be an old one that looks as if it's about to fall apart. Maybe the kind of car that a man who was a good mechanic could recover from a junk heap and fix up."

"That's Yuri's department," Ilya said.

The short, dark man was lost in thought for a minute. Then he smiled. It was only the second time I'd seen him smile. "I know just the car," he said. "It would even be well if it were traced later, for the man who owns it is an informer on his neighbors. I can steal it any evening."

"Tomorrow evening? Or tomorrow afternoon?"

He scowled. "Tomorrow evening for certain.

Perhaps in the afternoon. Sometimes he is home by three o'clock."

"All right," I said. "We'll see what happens. Everything will depend on the information Ilya gets tomorrow. If it looks possible, then tomorrow afternoon you will show me where the car is, and I will steal it and make the try."

"If you try to rescue the pilot tomorrow," Natasha said, "what do we do?"

"You will have already done it," I told her. "The plans, the car, advice, that's about it."

They all three started to protest.

"Wait," I said. "I was sent to do this job. The way I'm planning it, everything will have a better chance if I do it alone. More people would only make them suspicious and we might even get in each other's way. And there's another thing. The three of you have important work to do here. My orders are to use your assistance as much as I have to, but not to risk you unduly. But there is one other thing you can be putting your minds to."

"What?"

"If I succeed in rescuing Cooper, I'll need someplace to hide him until we can make a break for it."

"We could keep him here," Natasha said.

I shook my head. "Too dangerous, unless we have no choice. It should be somewhere else."

"There might be another place," she said. "There is a girl I know slightly, who has a one-room apartment on the next floor. She is away on vacation now. If we could get into her apartment in some way . . ."

"I can get in," I said. "So that's settled."

"But how will you get him out of Russia?" Ilya asked.

I grinned. "More theft," I said. "My idea is to try to get to some field where we can steal a plane. A fast one. Then Cooper can fly us out. It's risky, but probably safer than anything else. Once I've gotten him, you can be sure of one thing—the bloodhounds will be over every inch of Russia."

"I like the way you think," Yuri exclaimed. "Perhaps I could go with you."

"No, Yuri," I said. "Your job is here, and, believe me, it's a much tougher one."

"Milo is right, Yuri," Natasha said.

"But in the meantime," I said, "you can be thinking about where we might have the best chance of getting a plane, and the best way to reach it."

Yuri nodded, trying not to show his disappointment.

We talked generally for another hour or so, then Yuri left, and the three of us went to sleep.

I was up early the next morning, and back at the trial as soon as the building was open. While I was waiting for everyone to file into the trial room, I took another look at the case the MVD man was guarding. The map was still there. I didn't want to attract attention by too much interest in the case, so I strolled around the building. There were several offices around at the other end of it, mostly filled with either MVD men or what seemed to be Russian VIPs. I got a couple of questioning glances and soon retreated to the trial room.

The hearing was much the same as the day before. It was clear that they were more bent on making the United States look guilty than in bringing out anything on Cooper.

Just before the midday recess, the defense attorney got up to answer one of the prosecutor's blasts. He painted a glowing picture of Cooper as a simple Midwestern boy, with an honest, peace-loving family, who never knew what he was getting into. He said that these were the kind of Americans the Russians understood and liked. And he wound up by saying, "To show the world the true meaning of socialist humanitarianism, this boy's father and two brothers are on their way to Russia right now as guests of the government. They will arrive in Moscow tonight, and be here by his side tomorrow when he once more faces this court."

There was a burst of applause from the audience, and then court was adjourned until afternoon. I hurried back to the apartment. Ilya was already there. To my surprise, so was Natasha.

"I decided to take the afternoon off, too," she explained. "It is not difficult in my job."

I nodded and turned to Ilya. "How did you make out?"

"Fine," he said. He brought a piece of paper from his pocket. "But it cost fifteen thousand rubles."

"It's worth it," I said. "Let's see."

The three of us bent over the sheet of paper. Ilya had made a crude drawing of the route between the prison and the Hall of Columns, with all the streets marked. The time of departure, both morning and afternoon, was written down, and the other information I had wanted. He was transported in an official MVD car with three guards, one of whom drove. The driver was an MVD man, and the other two were KGB. That made it a little tougher, but it still looked possible.

"I think I can do it," I said. "We'll talk more about it when I come back."

The three of us had lunch, and then I went into the other room and changed into the MVD uniform.

By the time I reached the Hall of Columns, the trial was already underway—which was what I wanted. The corridor was empty except for the glass-covered case and the solitary guard. I entered the building from the other side and walked down the corridor to the front. This time no one paid any attention to me as I passed the offices, I was only another uniform.

The guard at the case looked up in curiosity as I approached. "What is this?" he asked. "Am I being relieved early?"

"For a few minutes," I said. "I will stay here until you return—if you do."

"What do you mean by that?"

I shrugged. "Perhaps they will give you another assignment. All I know is that I was called into the office and ordered to come here. You are to report there at once to Colonel Sergeiev."

"Who the devil is Colonel Sergeiev?" he demanded.

"From the Komitet Gosudarstvennoy Bezopasnosti," I said.

He paled at the mention of the KGB. "What do they want to talk to me about?"

"How should I know?" I retorted. "Do you see any decorations on my uniform that they should take me into their confidence? I only follow orders as you do. And yours are to go at once to the office and see Colonel Sergeiev. I will guard the spy's things. Although I do not think he will be trying to get them back."

"That is true," he said, but his mind was on other things. "Well, I suppose I should be going . . ."

"I think so," I agreed solemnly.

He started off with a worried look on his face, then looked back. "What is your name, Comrade?"

"Chernicov," I said. "Good luck, Comrade."

He nodded absent-mindedly and walked on. I watched impatiently for him to disappear around the bend in the corridor. Then I would have two minutes, three at the very most, before he discovered there was no Colonel Sergeiev, no Chernicov, and no orders for him to report at the office. And within one minute after that there would be several men pounding down the corridor looking for me.

He moved out of sight. There was no time for niceties such as picking the lock. I lifted my gun and smashed the butt down on the glass. It broke with a crash. I reached through the jagged spears of glass and grabbed the map. I moved swiftly toward the front entrance, stuffing it into my pocket. Even as I went through the door, I thought I heard a shout somewhere back in the corridor.

I went down the steps to the street level and looked around. Immediately in front of the hall a number of Zim limousines were parked with no one in them. Farther down to the left a Pobeda, something like a small Chevrolet, was parked in front of a tobacco store. A man was sitting behind the wheel. I turned and strode quickly down to it.

"Move this car out of here," I ordered, "and make it fast."

"But I'm waiting for someone in there," he said, gesturing toward the Hall of Columns.

"I don't care who you're waiting for," I snapped. "Khrushchev is arriving here any minute, and the street is to be cleared. Drive out of here as fast as you can—or I may take you off the street myself."

He looked startled, but he obeyed. He started the car and pulled away, gunning the motor as much as he could. I turned and stepped into the tobacco shop. And none too soon. As I stood at the counter, I saw seven or eight men come running out of the Hall of Columns. They stopped to look around and caught sight of the Pobeda speeding away. They all piled into a Zim and gave chase as soon as they could get it started.

I bought a package of cigarettes, walked down to the first block, and turned left. Another block away, I caught a bus. I rode it for about fifteen blocks and got off. I caught another bus going the opposite way and stayed on for five blocks. Then I took a taxi.

Yuri was already with Ilya and Natasha when I reached the apartment. They all three looked relieved as I came in.

"You got it?" Natasha asked excitedly as she closed the door.

"Yes," I said. I took the map from my pocket and went immediately to the stove. I took a dish from the cupboard above and then held a match to the map.

"Give me another minute," I told them. I went into the other room and changed back to my own clothes. I returned to them carrying the uniform.

"This must be destroyed as quickly as possible," I said.

"There is an incinerator in the building," Natasha said. "Just down the hall. I'll put it in there."

"Good girl," I said, handing the uniform to her. She took it and hurried out the door. She was back within a couple of minutes.

"The gun may still be a risk," I said, "but I'm going to need it, so I'll take that one. I think I got away all right, but they're going to start a big hunt, and I think I may have made one mistake."

I told them about the taxi I'd taken, and they confirmed my guess. MVD men usually did not pay when they wanted to ride in cabs.

"But it may be all right," Yuri said. "The driver may be so pleased at getting paid that he will keep his mouth shut. And you did leave the taxi three blocks away."

"Maybe," I said. "But once he hears about the search for a phony MVD man, he may be frightened enough to report it. But the time it will take for that to happen may be long enough. What about the car, Yuri?"

"It is there," he said. "To take it will be easy."

"And the clothes?" I asked Natasha.

"In the other room. I should have told you so you wouldn't have to change twice."

"It's all right," I said. "I have a little time. Ilya, describe the streets on that route again."

"Yuri knows them even better than I do," he said.

We brought out the diagram that Ilya had made, and Yuri looked at it. He then gave me a minute, almost photographic description of the route of the car as it would take Cooper back to the prison. I finally settled on what looked like the best place, the last six blocks before the prison. From Yuri's description, it sounded narrow enough for what I had in mind. Yuri had said that two cars could barely pass. I put my finger on what looked to be about halfway along that stretch.

"What is along here, Yuri?" I asked.

"Workers' apartments," he said. "Perhaps one or two small stores. That is all."

"Are the people who live there apt to interfere?"

"If they see uniformed men fighting with another man, they'll lock the doors and pull the blinds down. They know that in such a case it is better to be completely ignorant."

"In this case, I approve," I said. "Well, we'll leave in about an hour and a half." I went into the other room and got the gun. I wanted to check it over thoroughly and be sure that everything was in perfect working order before I started.

"You will shoot the three guards?" Yuri asked eagerly.

"I don't know," I confessed. "I hope I don't have to shoot, but I may not be able to avoid it. I'll have to see how it works out."

I think Yuri looked disappointed, but we turned to other details. Natasha had checked and verified that the girl upstairs was still on her vacation. I would bring Cooper back to this apartment, then go up and pick the lock and move him there. Yuri had looked into airfields not too far from Moscow and thought he'd found a small one that had possibilities. He was going to try to find out more. Ilya suggested that the best way of getting to the airfield would be to buy a small car on the black market and drive as near there as possible. He thought that mere boldness might get us through, especially if we used a popular small car that many families used for their vacations. All the suggestions sounded possible, and we still had some time to decide on the best.

I changed into the old clothes, and transferred my papers and other possessions. Then Yuri and I left. We took a bus, transferred to another one, and finally ended up in a section of Moscow I had never seen before. We walked three blocks after getting off the second bus. Yuri finally stopped on a street corner and pointed in the direction we were facing.

"There it is," he said proudly.

There was only one car parked on the street, so there was no chance of making a mistake. Yuri had certainly followed my instructions to the letter. I had never seen an older or shabbier car. It evidently dated from the time when the Russians were copying our Fords, and it looked as if they had also copied the idea of repairing it with baling wire.

"Are you sure it will run?" I asked.

"Oh, it runs very good," Yuri said. "You want me to go show you?"

"I'll steal my own cars, Yuri," I said. "Where is the owner?"

"On the next block. Drinking vodka. He will be there for two hours or more. Nobody else will pay any attention. They hate him. So much that

if the car doesn't start at once, they may rush out and give you a push."

"Now, how do I get to Nevka Street?"

His face lit up. "You see, I told you that you need me. The way is very complicated, but I will show you."

"All right," I said, giving in. "But as soon as we're near the place, you'll have to get out."

He grinned, and we started down the street. We reached the car and climbed in. I hadn't really believed Yuri, but certainly no one made an outcry or paid any attention to us. I reached under the instrument panel, disconnected the ignition wires, and wired them together. I stepped on the starter. I don't think I expected anything to happen, but the motor started at once. It didn't sound too bad. I put it in gear and we moved off.

We reached a spot near my destination without mishap. I stopped the car and told Yuri to get out. He put up a little argument, but finally did.

"I'll see you back at the apartment," I told him, and drove off. I had a few minutes to spare and drove slowly. I finally reached the spot about fifteen minutes before the car with Cooper was due to arrive there. Yuri had described the street perfectly. By turning and backing I finally got the car directly across the street. There was no room for another car to get by on either side. I killed the motor and got out.

I went around to the front and lifted the hood. Then I reached down and ripped the wires from the carburetor. While I was at it, I got some grease, and smeared it around on my hands and a little on my face. I put the hood down and went back to sit behind the wheel. I waited until I knew the car was about due, then began stepping on the starter.

I was aware when the car arrived, but I didn't look up. The starter whirred with a dismal sound. The horn blew on the other car. I looked up, waved hopelessly at the car, and continued to press the starter.

The driver leaned out of the window. "Get out of the way," he ordered.

"I can't," I said. "It will not start."

"Then push it out of the way," he said.

I shrugged, and gave up with the starter. I made sure the hand brake was partly set, and climbed out. I got behind the car and pushed, but nothing happened. I saw the men in the car exchanging words, then the driver got out and came over to me.

"Come on," he said roughly. "We have to get this junk pile out of the street. We are on government business."

I gave him a sickly smile and gestured futilely at the car again. He muttered under his breath but put his own shoulder against it. We both pushed, but I didn't work too hard and the car still didn't move. We struggled for a couple of minutes and finally the driver straightened up, looked at the other car, and shrugged. There was some more conversation there, while I held my breath, then the rear door of the car opened and one of the KGB men got out. He left the door open. Inside I could see the other guard and Cooper.

The KGB man came over and scowled at me. "This time we'd better get this car out of the way or we will arrest you. Understand?"

"Yes, sir," I said.

One of them got on either side of me and put his shoulder to the car. I did the same, facing the one who had his back to me. As I pushed, I reached for my gun.

The car began to move slowly despite the brakes. I straightened up, and turned to face the man back of me. The gun barrel raked across his forehead before he even knew what was happening. Without waiting to see him fall, I whirled on the other one. He had already guessed that something had happened, and he was trying to turn and get his gun out at the same time. But he was at a disadvantage. He was off balance, and his back was toward me. Before he could make it, I brought the gun down on his head. He grunted and collapsed.

Two down, I muttered to myself, and looked at the car. The other KGB man had his gun out and was lining it up on me. I dropped to the ground behind the MVD man. The other gun went off, and I heard the bullet over my head. By then I had him in my sights. I pulled the trigger

gently, and saw him slump back against the seat. His gun dropped out of the car.

I jumped to my feet and ran over. The guard wasn't dead, or even unconscious. He was leaning against the back of the seat, one hand clutching his shoulder, the blood coming out between his fingers. He glared at me and tensed his body.

"Don't try it," I told him in Russian. "I can't miss you this close."

He struggled with himself and lost the battle. He stayed where he was, watching me closely. I turned my attention to Cooper. He was sitting there, looking as if he didn't believe what he saw.

"What is this?" he said as though he didn't expect an answer.

"It's what they used to call the arrival of the US Cavalry," I told him in English. "A modern version of an old-fashioned rescue. Come on, Cooper, let's get out of here, fast!"

"I don't believe it," he said. "You read stuff like this in books, but it doesn't happen. I'm only a sky jockey. Nobody is going to send the Cavalry to rescue me."

"Somebody did," I said impatiently. "Come on, we don't have all day. This place will be swarming with cops any minute."

He was shaking his head. "It was mighty nice of you to make the effort, but I'm not going with you!"

I had expected almost anything but this. "What?" I asked.

"I'm not going with you," he repeated.

"Why in the hell not?" I demanded.

"My dad and two brothers are landing here tonight," he said slowly. "What do you think would happen to them if I escaped?"

"They wouldn't dare do anything to them," I said.

He was shaking his head again. "I ain't going to risk it. My lawyer says I won't get more than seven years. I can do that and still find my family alive when I get home."

I looked at him with speculation.

"You can't do it," he said, guessing what I was thinking. "If you try to knock me out and drag me, you'll never make it. . . . You may not anyway unless you leave at once."

He was right. I knew it, but I hated to be cheated after everything that had been done. But I didn't have any time. I kicked the guard's gun under the car and looked at the other two guards. They were still out. I turned and ran.

"Give my regards to the Statue of Liberty when you see her," Cooper called after me.

I didn't bother to answer. I knew I was going to have my hands full for the next few minutes, at least until I could get back to the apartment and change clothes. I ran swiftly for two zigzag blocks, then slowed down to a fast walk. I threw the gun away. I wanted to keep it, but it would be too damning as evidence if it was found. Two more blocks away, I saw a small car parked with no one around it. I slipped into it, tore out the ignition wires, and put them together. Then I drove away. As I left the curb I heard a shout behind me but ignored it.

I left the car at the curb a good ten blocks away from the apartment house, and went the rest of the way on foot, keeping a sharp eye out for cops. I was about two blocks away from the apartment when I suddenly saw Natasha on the street ahead of me. At the same time she saw me, and started for me as fast as she could walk. Her face was white with tension and I knew something had happened.

"What's wrong?"

"We can't stand here. We must walk away from here." She led the way along the first cross street. "They arrested Ilya and Yuri. A half hour ago."

"Who?"

"KGB, I think. I was out and came back just in time to see them being led out into the streets."

"Do you know why?"

"No. One never knows. We may have been on a suspicion list, or someone may have made a report about us. Anything. And there are still guards on the apartment. Did you leave your papers there?"

"No."

"Then you can get away. That's why I waited on the street. I hoped I would see you before they found me."

"They won't find you now," I said.

"They will," she said. "No one can live in Russia without papers, and now I have no papers I can use."

"We'll find a way," I said. "But first we've got to hole up somewhere. There's probably already a description of me around. Do you know of a hotel where they don't frown on a girl visiting a man in his room?"

"The Molenka, I think. I believe I heard Yuri talking about it once."

"All right. First, let's go somewhere where I can buy clothes."

We took the subway, getting off at a stop Natasha knew. She led the way to a small clothing store and I succeeded in buying a suit that wasn't too bad. I bought a few other things and some clothes for her. There was no place for me to change there, but we went back to the subway and I changed in the men's room. I stuffed the old clothes under some paper in a trash basket and we went on to the hotel.

She was right about the hotel. The clerk looked at my papers and I signed the register. I explained that the girl wasn't staying long, and for a minute I thought he was going to wink at me.

"We'll be safe here for a while," I told her when we were in the room, "but we'd better not stay too long. The hunt for me will probably be overshadowed by the one for you, but there's always a chance someone will want to see your papers. And in the hunt for me, they may eventually get down to checking all the guests in hotels. I'll be all right until they make a call to Rostov. So we'd better put our minds to getting out of Moscow."

"How can I get out?" she asked. "And where would I go if I did get out?"

"To America, with me," I said.

"America?"

"Why not? You're a member of the Russian underground, and you should be very welcome. You'll probably get a job right away. You could be valuable."

"You think so?" she exclaimed. Then her face fell. "It is awful to think that I might get out just when Ilya and Yuri have been caught."

"I don't think we can do anything about that," I said gently. "If I hadn't created such an uproar, I might have been able to—but not now. We'll have to go, Natasha. I'm sure that Ilya and Yuri would agree."

Then she came into my arms and cried until she was exhausted.

We stayed in the hotel for two days, while I thought up ways of escaping and discarded them. The search was too big for either a black market car or another stolen one. The papers were full of the story of the American agent who had tried to rescue Cooper, and it had even started Khrushchev off on another tirade of threats against America. In the meantime, everyone there had denied knowing anything about an agent.

Finally I hit on an idea I thought might work. Leaving Natasha in the hotel room, I spent two nights down at the trucking center in Moscow. Most of it was spent in little cafés, drinking vodka and listening to the truck drivers.

The third night we both went down. By this time I was familiar with which trucks were which. Standing in the shadows, we watched a big six-wheeler being loaded for Leningrad. When it was loaded, the two drivers went into the café for a last drink. We slipped out of our shadow and quickly climbed in the back. We made ourselves as comfortable as we could on the boxes, and a few minutes later we were on our way.

All through the night the big truck roared along, and well into the next day. I had been watching the time, and when it seemed we should be nearing Leningrad, I slipped to the rear and began to watch through the tarpaulin. When we finally reached Leningrad, we looked for our chance, and as the truck went around a sharp corner, we dropped off.

In Leningrad we took a trolley to the center of the city, and I found a bus terminal. I bought two tickets to Tallinn, south of Leningrad, getting them one at a time and from different windows just in case someone wanted to see papers. But nothing happened and we were soon on the bus heading south.

Tallinn was a little more of a problem. We were there two days and nights and getting a little nervous, before I found a fisherman I could bribe to take us across the narrow neck of the Baltic to Finland. It wasn't the most ideal place to go, but I had little choice. That night the fisherman took us, and a couple of hours later we were at the American Embassy.

It took a little more doing to get them to awaken the Ambassador, but it was finally accomplished, and a handsome, gray-haired man in a fancy bathrobe was peering at us curiously.

"I'm a major in the United States Army," I told him. "For security reasons, I can't tell you any more than that at the moment. I want to make a phone call to General Sam Roberts, in Washington."

He must have heard of the General, but he didn't even blink. "That's a most unusual request, Major. Would you mind if the call was made in my presence?"

"No, sir."

"Then come on," he said. He led the way to his office and indicated the phone. I picked it up and put in the call. It took a while for it to get through, but finally there was General Roberts on the other end.

"General," I said, "this is your favorite chestnut puller. Have you been keeping up with your reading?"

"I'll say I have," he said. "We were worried about you, boy. I see where things didn't go quite right. How bad is it?"

"Not too bad. The first problem went off fine; the second didn't because the prize pupil didn't want to play."

He whistled. "Where are you now?"

"The American Embassy in Finland. And I'm homesick. Incidentally, you remember the three friends I was to look up?"

"Yes."

"One of them is with me. The young lady. The other two were unable to make it."

"I see," he said. He was silent for a minute. "I guess maybe the best way is the simplest. Less possible complications. Tell the Ambassador to expect a call from the State Department. We'll see you soon. Got any money left?"

"Enough to get back on."

"Okay, boy. Goodbye."

He hung up, and I told the Ambassador about the expected call. He had some brandy brought in, and we all sat and waited together. The call came in a half hour. I don't know what he was told, but it seemed to cheer him up. "Well, Major," he said, slapping me on the back when he'd finished, "why didn't you just tell me your troubles? No problem at all. We'll find a couple of rooms for you and the young lady, and everything will be fixed up in the morning."

I didn't know what he meant by that, but I kept my mouth shut. And I found out in the morning. Right after breakfast, we were handed two passports good for passage one way from Finland to America. The names on them weren't ours, but obviously the Ambassador didn't know that.

"Anybody can lose his passport, Major Johnson," he said. "No need to call Washington about that."

"I'm the cautious type," I said, and let it go at that.

That afternoon Natasha and I boarded a regular jetliner for America. When we'd unbuckled our seatbelts and leaned back, I lit a cigarette. "Well, honey," I said, "you'll soon be in America."

"I know," she said. She sounded excited. "Will I see you again after we are there?"

"Definitely."

"It will be wonderful. Still . . . I think I may miss Moscow in the spring."

"And the red, red flowers?" I asked, quoting from the password I had used when I first met her.

"Well, there will still be flowers blooming there, and maybe one day the whole country will bloom."

She smiled and put her head on my shoulder. A few minutes later she was asleep.

JEFFERY DEAVER

A WORLDWIDE BESTSELLER and one of the most consistently excellent suspense writers in the world, Jeffery Deaver (1950–) was born outside Chicago and received his journalism degree from the University of Missouri, becoming a newspaperman, after which received his law degree from Fordham University, practicing for several years. A poet, he wrote his own songs and performed them across the country.

He is the author of more than two dozen novels and four short story collections. His work has been translated into twenty-five languages and is a perennial bestseller in America and elsewhere. Among his many honors are seven nominations for Edgar Allan Poe Awards (twice for Best Paperback Original, five times for Best Short Story), three Ellery Queen Reader's Awards for Best Short Story of the Year, the 2001 W. H. Smith Thumping Good Read Award for *The Empty Chair* (2000), and the 2004 Ian Fleming Steel Dagger Award from the (British) Crime Writers' Association for *Garden of Beasts* (2004); he also won a Dagger for best short story. In 2009, he was the guest editor of *The Best American Mystery Stories of the Year*.

He has written about a dozen stand-alone novels, but is most famous for his series about Lincoln Rhyme, the brilliant quadriplegic detective who made his debut in *The Bone Collector* (1997), which was released on film by Universal in 1999 and starred Denzel Washington and Angelina Jolie. Other Rhyme novels are *The Coffin Dancer* (1998), *The Empty Chair* (2000), *The Stone Monkey* (2002), *The Vanished Man* (2003), *The Twelfth Card* (2005), *The Cold Moon* (2006), *The Steel Kiss* (2016), and *The Cutting Edge* (2018). His nonseries novel *A Maiden's Grave* (1995) was adapted for an HBO movie titled *Dead Silence* (1997) and starred James Garner and Marlee Matlin. His suspense novel *The Devil's Teardrop* (1999) was a 2010 made-for-television movie of the same name.

"Comrade 35" was originally published in *Ice Cold* (New York, Grand Central, 2014).

COMRADE 35

JEFFERY DEAVER

TUESDAY

To be summoned to the highest floor of GRU headquarters in Moscow made you immediately question your future.

Several fates might await.

One was that you had been identified as a counter-revolutionary or a lackey of the bourgeoisie imperialists. In which case your next address would likely be a gulag, which were still highly fashionable, even now, in the early 1960s, despite First Secretary and Premier Khrushchev's enthusiastic denunciation of Comrade Stalin.

Another possibility was that you had been identified as a double agent, a mole within the GRU—not proven to be one, mind you, simply *suspected* of being one. Your fate in that situation was far simpler and quicker than a transcontinental train ride: a bullet in the back of the head, a means of execution the GRU had originated as a preferred form of execution, though the rival KGB had co-opted and taken credit for the technique.

With these troubling thoughts in mind and his army posture well in evidence, Major Mikhail Sergeyevich Kaverin strode toward the office to which he'd been summoned. The tall man was broad shouldered, columnar. He hulked, rather than walked. The Glavnoe Razvedyvatelnoe Upravlenie was the spy wing of the Soviet Armed Forces; nearly every senior GRU agent, including Kaverin, had fought the Nazis one meter at a time on the western front, where illness and cold and the enemy had quickly taken the weak and the indecisive. Only the most resilient had survived.

Nothing culls like war.

Kaverin walked with a slight limp, courtesy of a piece of shrapnel or a fragment of bullet in his thigh. An intentional gift from a German or an inadvertent one from a fellow soldier. He neither knew nor cared.

The trek from his present office—at the British Desk, downstairs—was taking some time. GRU headquarters was massive, as befitted the largest spy organization in Russia and, rumors were, the world.

Kaverin stepped into the ante-office of his superior, nodded at the aide-de-camp, who said the general would see him in a minute. He sat and lit a cigarette. He saw his reflection in a nearby glass-covered poster of Lenin. The Communist Party founder's lean appearance was in marked contrast to Kaverin's: He thought himself a bit squat of face, a bit jowly. The comrade major's thick black hair was another difference, in sharp contrast to Lenin's shiny pate. And while the communist revolutionary and first Premier of the Soviet Union had a goatee that gave him— with those fierce eyes—a demonic appearance, Kaverin was clean shaven, and his eyes, under drooping lids, were the essence of calm.

A deep pull on the cigarette. The taste was sour and he absently swatted away glowing flecks of cheap tobacco that catapulted from the end. He longed for better, but couldn't spend the time to queue endlessly for the good Russian brands and he couldn't afford the Western smokes on the black market. When the cigarette was half smoked, he stubbed it out and wrapped the remainder in a handkerchief, then slipped that into his brown uniform jacket.

He thought of the executions he'd witnessed— and participated in. Often, a last cigarette for the prisoner. He wondered if he'd just had his.

Of course, there was yet another fate that might await, having been summoned to this lofty floor of headquarters. Perhaps he was being *rewarded*. The Comrade General, speaking for the Chairman of the GRU or even the Presidium itself—the all-powerful Politburo—could be recognizing him for furthering the ideals of communism and the glory of the Union of Soviet Socialist Republics. In which case he would receive not a slug from a Makarov pistol, but a medal or commendation or perhaps a new rank (though not, of course, a raise in pay).

Then, however, his busy mind, his *spy*'s mind, came up with another negative possibility: The KGB had orchestrated a transgression to get him demoted or even ousted.

The Soviet civilian spy outfit and the GRU hated each other—the KGB referred to their military counterparts contemptuously as "Boots," because of the uniforms they wore in their official capacity. The GRU looked at the KGB as a group of effete elitists, who trolled for turncoats among the Western intelligentsia, men who could quote Marx from their days at Harvard or Cambridge but who never lived up to their promise of delivering nuclear secrets or rocket fuel formulas.

Since neither the KGB nor the GRU had exclusive jurisdiction in foreign countries, poaching was common. On several occasions in the past year Kaverin had run operations in England and the Balkans right under the nose of the KGB and turned an agent or assassinated a traitor before the civilian spies even knew he was in country.

Had the pricks from Lubyanka Square somehow put together a scandal to disgrace him?

But then, just as he grew tired of speculation, the door before him opened and he was ushered into the office of the man who was about to bestow one of several fates.

A train trip, a bullet, a medal, or—another endearing possibility in the Soviet Union— perhaps something wholly unexpected.

"You may smoke," said the general.

Kaverin withdrew a new cigarette and lit it, marshaling more escaping sparks. "Thank you, sir."

"Comrade Major, we have a situation that has arisen. It needs immediate attention." The general was fat, ruddy and balding. The rumors were that, once, he had set down his rifle and chosen to strangle, rather than shoot, a Nazi who came at him with a bayonet on the outskirts of Berlin in 1945. One look at his hands and you could easily believe that.

"Yes, sir, whatever I might do."

So far, this did not seem like a death sentence.

"Did you know Comrade Major Rasnakov? Vladimir Rasnakov?"

"Yes, I heard he suffered a heart attack. Died almost instantly."

"It should be a lesson to us all!" The general pointed his cigarette at Kaverin. "Take the baths, exercise. Drink less vodka, eat less pork."

The man's rasping voice continued, "Comrade Rasnakov was on a very sensitive, very important assignment. His demise has come at a particularly inconvenient time, Comrade Major. From reading your dossier, you seem like a perfect replacement for him. You can drive, correct?"

"Of course."

"And speak English fluently."

"Yes."

This was growing more intriguing by the moment.

The general fixed him with a fierce gaze of appraisal. Kaverin held the man's eyes easily. "Now, let me explain. Comrade Rasnakov had a job that was vital to the cause of communist supremacy. He was in charge of protecting the lives of certain people within the United States— people who we have deemed indispensable to our interests."

Because they were all trained soldiers, GRU agents often served as undercover bodyguards for valuable double-agents in enemy countries.

"I will gladly take over his tasks, sir."

The vodka bottle thudded onto the middle of the desk. Glasses were poured and the men drank. Kaverin was moderate with alcohol— which put him in the minority of men in Russia. But, just like not uttering certain thoughts aloud, you never declined the offer to share a drink with a superior officer. Besides this was real vodka, good vodka. Made from corn. Although as a soldier and a member of the GRU, Kaverin had some privileges, that meant simply potatoes without frostbite, meat once a week instead of every other, and vodka that, while it didn't poison you, came in a corked bottle with curious flecks afloat. (Unlike the KGB, whose agents, even those in the field, had the best liquor and food and never had to queue.)

The general's voice diminished nearly to a whisper. "Intelligence was received from a trusted source in America about a forthcoming occurrence there. It is necessary that the man behind this event remains alive, at least until he completes what he intends."

"Who is this person? An agent of ours? Of another service?"

The general stubbed out his cigarette and lit another. Kaverin noted he left a good inch and a half unsmoked. The ashtray was filled with such butts. Together they must have made up a full pack.

"No . . ." His voice was even softer now. And—astonishing—the comrade generally actually seemed uneasy. He tapped the top secret file before him. "As you'll see in here, this man— Comrade Thirty-five, the code name we've given him—is not motivated by any overt desire to help the Soviet Union but that's exactly what the effect of his actions will be—*if* he succeeds in his mission." The general's eyes were far more intense than his whispered voice as he said, "And it is up to you to make sure that he remains alive to do so."

"Of course."

"Now, Comrade Rasnakov learned that there are two men who intend to take the life of our American comrade by week's end. That cannot happen. Now, read this file, Comrade Major. Study it. But make sure it does not leave the building. It is for your eyes only. It is perhaps the most sensitive document you will ever come in contact with."

"Of course."

"Learn all you can about Comrade Thirty-five and the two men who wish to harm him. Then make plans to leave immediately for America. You'll meet with Comrade Colonel Nikolai Spesky, one of our GRU agents in place. He can provide weapons and updated intelligence."

"Thank you for this opportunity, Comrade General." Kaverin rose and saluted. The general saluted in return then said, "One more thing, Comrade Major."

"Yessir."

"Here." The man handed him a packet of French cigarettes. "You must learn to smoke something that will not set fire to the carpet of your superior officers."

Kaverin returned to his own small office, which offered a partial view of the airport; he would sometimes sit and look at airplanes on final approach. He found this relaxing.

He opened the file and began to read. He got no more than halfway through the first paragraph, however, then sat up with a start, electrified as he read what the mission would entail and who was involved.

Oh, my God . . .

Kaverin lit a cigarette—one of the new ones—and noted that for the first time in years his thick fingers were actually shaking.

But then, soldier that he was, he put aside his emotions at the momentous consequences of the assignment and got to work.

WEDNESDAY

The flights were carefully planned to arouse the fewest suspicions of the enemy intelligence services.

For the trip Kaverin was dressed Western—a black fedora, a fake bespoke suit and white shirt and narrow black tie, like a funeral director, he thought. Which in a macabre way seemed appropriate. His route took him from Moscow to Paris on an Aeroflot TU-124, then to Heathrow. He connected there to a Trans-Canada Air Lines DC-8 bound for Montreal. Finally he flew from Canada into the United States, first port of call, Idlewild Airport in New York City.

Four hours later he disembarked in Miami.

Whereas New York had seemed hard as steel, edged and unyielding, the Floridian metropolis was soft, pastel, soothed by balmy breeze.

Kaverin walked from the airport terminal, inhaling deeply the fragrant air, and hailed a taxi.

The car—a huge Mercury—bounded into the street. As they drove, Kaverin stared at the palm trees, the bougainvillea, and plants he'd never seen. He blinked to observe a flamingo in the front yard of a small bungalow. He'd seen the birds in Africa and believed they were water dwellers. He laughed when he realized the creature was a plastic decoration.

He regretted that dusk was arriving quickly, and soon there was nothing to see but lights.

In a half hour he was at the address he sought, a small, one-story office building, squatting in a sandy lot filled with unruly green groundcover. On the front window was a sign.

East Coast Transportation Associates.
Nick Spencer, Prop.

As good a cover as any for a spy operation, he reflected. After all, the company *did* do some transporting: stolen secrets and occasional bodies. And the proprietor's pseudonym was a reasonable tinkering with the real name of the GRU agent who worked out of the facility.

Kaverin found the door locked and knocked. A moment later it flew open and there stood a round, broad-shouldered man in a short-sleeved beige shirt—with black vertical stripes of a chain design—and powder blue slacks. His shoes were white.

"Ah, Comrade!" Nikolai Spesky cried, warmly pumping his hand.

Kaverin frowned at the word, looking around at the other office buildings nearby.

Ushering him inside and locking the door behind them, Spesky laughed, and wrinkles rippled in his tanned face. "What are you worried about, Comrade? Microphones? It's a different world here."

"I suppose I am."

"No, no, no. See here, to eavesdrop, the government must get the courts to approve it."

"Which they surely do."

"Ah, Comrade, not necessarily. You'd be surprised. And, what's more, the CIA has no jurisdiction here."

Kaverin shrugged. He took off his heavy jacket—the temperature was about 75 degrees.

"Sit!" Spesky said jovially.

The men lit cigarettes. Spesky seemed delighted Kaverin was the agent chosen to take over for Comrade Rasnakov. "You are quite famous," Spesky said, though without the awe that would have made his comment awkward. "The vile traitor Penkovsky . . . The people owe you quite a debt, Comrade."

Penkovsky was a GRU agent who spied for the

British and Americans, his most valued contribution being providing information that helped Kennedy stand up to the Russians during the Cuban Missile Crisis in 1962. He was, as Kaverin had learned, less motivated by ideology than by a desire to lead a decadent life in the West. Which he had—until caught by the Soviets and executed.

"I was merely one of a number of people who found the traitor."

"Modest, modest . . . a good trait for a spy. We must remain unseen, anonymous, subtle. Only in that way can the exultant cause of Mother Russia and the ideology of *Herren* Marx and Engels, as espoused by our noble progenitor Comrade Lenin, be furthered for the glory of our cause and the people!"

Kaverin remained silent at this pronouncement. But then, as if he could not control himself, Spesky exploded with laughter. "I do a very good impersonation of the Premier, do I not?"

Khrushchev was notorious for his bombastic speeches, but Kaverin wouldn't think of answering the question affirmatively, though Spesky was in fact spot on.

The man scoffed good-naturedly. "Ah, relax, relax, Comrade! We are field agents. The rules don't apply to us." His smile faded. "It's a dangerous job we do and we are to be entitled to some indulgence, including poking fun at the people and the institutions taken far too seriously at home." He patted his large belly. To Kaverin it resounded like a timpani. "I missed my lunch today, Comrade. I must eat something." Squinting at his guest, the man asked, "Now, do you know of CARE packages?"

"Yes, indeed. They were a propaganda tool created by the West after the War for the purpose of exploiting the unfortunate and winning them to the cause of capitalism and imperialism."

Spesky waved his hand impatiently. "You must learn, Comrade Major, that in this country not every comment is an invitation to a political statement. I was merely inquiring if you know the concept. Because I have received a CARE package, of sorts—from my wife in Moscow, and I have been waiting for your arrival to indulge." He lifted onto his desk a large cardboard carton, labeled "Accounting forms," and, with a locking-blade knife, sliced open the lid. He removed a bottle of good vodka—Stolichnaya—and tins of paté, smoked fish and oysters. He unwrapped a loaf of dark bread and smelled it. "Not bad. Not too moldy yet."

They drank the vodka and ate the bread and paté, both of which were excellent. The bread didn't taste the least moldy to Kaverin, and he had quite some intimate knowledge of bread in its final stages.

Tossing down a third small glass of vodka, Spesky said, "I will tell you the details of this assignment." His face clouded over. "Now, our Comrade Thirty-five, the man you are to protect, is not a particularly likable fellow."

"So I have read."

"He acts impulsively, he speaks out when he should listen. Frankly I believe he is a cruel man and may be unstable. Accordingly he has made enemies."

"The Comrade General told me there are two men who present an immediate threat."

"Yes, that's correct. They are U.S. citizens, though of Latin American extraction. Comrade Rasnakov learned that they plan to kill him sometime on Friday." He slid a slim file across the battered desk. "Your job is to intercept them. Then communicate with them."

"Communicate?"

"Yes, exactly. With one of these." Spesky removed two pistols from his desk, along with two boxes of ammunition.

"You're familiar with these?"

One was a Colt Woodsman, a small caliber, .22, but very accurate, thanks to the long barrel. The other was a large 1911-style Colt .45. "And you will need a car, Comrade," Spesky told him. "I understand you can drive?"

A nod.

"Good. In the file you will find an address, an abandoned house. There's a garage behind it, off an alley—'garage' they say here to mean not a repair station but a separate place to keep your car in, like a stable."

"I'm aware of that."

"In the garage is a Chevrolet Bel Air. The keys are hidden up under the front seat . . . Ah, I see you know not only guns but automobiles too, Comrade."

Spesky had apparently noticed that Kaverin was smiling at the mention of the Bel Air.

"Now these are your targets." Spesky opened the file and tapped the documents.

Kaverin read through the file carefully, noting facts about the two men whose mission was to kill Comrade 35—Luis Suarez and Carlos Barquín, both in their mid-thirties. Dangerous men, who were former prisoners. They had murdered before. Their round faces—both bisected with thick mustaches—looked sullen, and Barquín gave the impression of being stupid.

Kaverin, though, knew it was a mistake to underestimate your enemy; he'd seen too many soldiers and agents die because they had done just that. So he read carefully, learning every fact he might about the men.

According to Rasnakov's sources, the two were presently traveling—whereabouts unknown—but would arrive in Texas day after tomorrow. The plan was to kill Comrade 35 that day. Spesky explained that Rasnakov had planned to lie in wait and kill them when they arrived at the boardinghouse. This would be Kaverin's job now. He pushed the file back and placed the guns and ammunition in his attaché case.

Spesky then handed him an envelope. It contained one thousand dollars U.S. and another airline ticket. "Your flight's tomorrow morning. You'll stay at a hotel near the airport tonight."

After calling for a taxi, Spesky poured more vodka and they ate the rest of the paté and some smoked oysters. Spesky asked about life back in Moscow and what were the latest developments at GRU headquarters. There was gossip about who had become nonpersons and an affair at a very high level, though Kaverin was careful not

to mention any names. Spesky was delighted nonetheless.

Neither man, however, had any hesitation in sharing stories about the latest KGB cock-ups and scandals.

When the taxi arrived, Spesky shook Kaverin's hand. Suddenly the brash spy seemed wistful, almost sad. "You will enjoy certain aspects of life here, Comrade. The weather, the food, the plenty, the women, and—not the least—the absence of spies and informers dogging you everywhere. Yet you will also find such freedom comes at a price. You will be alone much, and you will feel the consequences of that solitude in your soul. There is no one to look out for you, no one above to care for you. In the end, you will long to return home to Mother Russia. I know this for a fact, Comrade. I have eight months left here and yet already I am counting the days until I can fly back to her bosom."

THURSDAY

The flight the next morning, on a propeller-driven DC-7, was turbulent as the plane fought its way west through strong winds. The journey was so bad that the stewardesses, who were quite beautiful, could not serve breakfast. Kaverin, more irritated at that fact than scared, at least had managed to secure a vodka and he took comfort in sipping the drink and smoking nearly half a pack of Chesterfield cigarettes, which were marvelous, during the flight.

The weather broke and, as they descended, he could look down and see flat sandy earth for miles and miles, grass bleached by the season, occasional groves of trees. Cattle, lots of cattle.

The aircraft landed uneventfully and the passengers disembarked.

He took his attaché case, containing his guns and ammunition, from the plane's overhead bin and walked down the stairs onto the tarmac.

Pausing and inhaling the petrol- and exhaust-laced air, Mikhail Sergeyevich Kaverin found himself content. Here he was in a country very different from that portrayed by the great propaganda mill of the Soviet empire. The people were friendly and courteous, the food and cigarettes plentiful and cheap, the workers content and comfortable, not the least oppressed by greedy capitalist robber barons. And the weather was far nicer than in Russia this time of year. And nearly everyone owned an automobile!

Kaverin strode into the lobby of Love Field in Dallas, Texas. He glanced at the front page of today's morning newspaper, Thursday. November 21, 1963.

KENNEDY TO VISIT DALLAS TOMORROW

President and First Lady Join Governor
for Fund-Raiser at Dallas Trade Mart

Feeling the weight of the guns and ammunition in his case, Kaverin now felt an unabashed sense of pride to think that he alone had been selected for this critical mission of helping the USSR extend its reach throughout the world and further the glorious goals of communism.

As he waited for his bus, at a weedy stop in Dallas, Lee Harvey Oswald was troubled.

People had been following him. He knew this for a fact.

People who wanted to do him harm.

The skinny, dark-haired man, in his mid-twenties, looked around him again. Was there someone watching him? Yes!

But no. It was just a shadow. Still, he wished he had brought his pistol with him.

He awakened early in his boardinghouse on Beckley Avenue in Oak Cliff and taken a bus to a stop near the Dobbs House Restaurant for breakfast. The food had been bad and he'd complained. He wondered why he kept going back there. Maybe I'm a creature of habit, he reflected. He'd heard the phrase on a TV show.

Was it *Ozzie and Harriet*? He'd wondered. He liked that show, partly because it echoed his nickname in the Marines. *Ozzie Rabbit*.

When he thought this, he remembered his days in the service and recalled the fight he'd gotten into with a sergeant and that made him angry once more.

As angry as he'd been with the waitress over the food.

Why do I keep going back there? he thought again. Looked around once more. He didn't see any overt threats but he still had to be careful. Considering what he had planned for tomorrow. And considering that he knew people were after him, smart people. Ruthless ones.

The bus arrived and Oswald boarded it and rode to the place he worked, the Texas Book Depository on Elm Street and North Houston, across from Dealey Plaza. He climbed off the bus, and gazed about him once more, expecting to see one of the sullen faces of the men who he was sure were following him.

FBI maybe. Those bastards had been harassing Marina and their friends again.

Oh, he'd made some enemies in his day.

But in morning glare—it was a beautiful autumn day—he saw only housewives with perambulators and a few salesmen, a retired couple or two. Ranchers. Some Hispanic men . . .

Killers?

It was possible. Oswald grew alarmed and leapt into the shadows of the depository building to study them. But they showed no interest in him and strolled slowly to a landscaping truck, pulled out rakes and headed into the park across the street.

Despite the bristling of nerves up and down his back, Oswald noted that no one seemed to have much interest in him. He shivered again, though this was from the chill. He was wearing only a light jacket over his T-shirt, and he had a slight frame with little natural insulation.

Inside the depository he greeted fellow workers, nodding and smiling to some of them. And he got to work. It was while he was filling out paperwork for a book order that he happened to look down at a scar on his wrist. He was thinking of his attempt to become a Soviet citizen several years before. He was about to be deported but had intentionally cut himself to prolong his stay after his visa expired, and convince the Russians to accept him.

Which they had and they welcomed him as a comrade. But there was a lot of important work to do in this hemisphere and, with his Russian wife, he'd returned to the United States, where he'd resumed his procommunist and anti-American activities. But now, he wanted to return to Russia, for good, with Marina and their two baby girls.

There'd been a setback, though. An incident had occurred that had put his plans—and his life—at risk. After he finished his task tomorrow he wanted to go to Cuba for a while and then back to Russia. Just last month he'd gone to the Cuban consulate in Mexico City to get a visa to allow him to travel to Havana, but the bastards had given him the runaround. The officials had looked over his records and said he wasn't welcome in Cuba. Go away. None of them understood what an important man he was, more important than his five-foot-nine, 135-pound frame suggested. None of them understood his great plans.

The rejection in Mexico City had sparked his terrible temper, and he'd said and done some things he shouldn't have. The Cuban security force had been called and he'd fled the capital and eventually made his way back home.

Stupid, he told himself, making a scene like that. Like fighting with the waitress at the diner. He'd lost control and made a spectacle of himself.

"Stupid," he raged aloud.

He shivered once more, this time from pure fury, not fear or from the chill. And gazed out the window of the depository, looking for people spying on him.

Fucking Cubans!

Well, start being smart now. He decided it wouldn't be safe to go back to the boardinghouse. Usually he spent weekdays at the boardinghouse.

Tonight he'd return to the Paines in Irving, stay the night. Considering what he was about to do tomorrow, he couldn't afford any complications at the moment.

His serenity returned—thanks largely to a memory of his time in the Marines in 1954, specifically the day his firearms instructor had looked over his score on the rifle range and given him a nod (the man never smiled). "You did good, Ozzie. Those scores? You just earned yourself the rank of sharpshooter."

Anthony Barter swung his slim frame out of the car.

He stretched.

The thirty-one-year-old was tempted to light a Winston, *needed* one bad, but his employer wouldn't approve. It wasn't like drinking—that was wholly forbidden—but even taking a fast drag could get you in hot water.

So he refrained.

An old Martin 4-0-4 roared overhead and skewed its way onto the runway at Love Field.

He straightened his narrow tie and his dark gray felt fedora, from which he'd long ago removed the green feather—very bad form, that.

Barter looked around, oriented himself and went to the Eastern Airlines luggage claim area. His long hands formed into fists, relaxed and contracted once more.

He found a supervisor, a heavyset, balding man, sweating despite the pleasantly cool temperature. He displayed his identification.

The man drawled, "Oh. Well. FBI."

Barter was from New England: he'd been assigned to Texas, though, for ten years and recognized an accent from much further south, probably El Paso.

He explained he needed to find out about a passenger who'd arrived that morning from Miami. The supervisor almost seemed amused at the idea that luggage handlers could recognize a passenger, but he went off to gather his employees.

The Bureau's New York field office had informed their colleagues in Dallas-Fort Worth that a man believed to be a Russian military intelligence agent had arrived in the country yesterday or today and continued on to Dallas. There'd been debate in New York and Washington about the purpose of the agent's trip, if he was indeed an agent.

There was, of course, the question of Presidential security. Kennedy was coming to town tomorrow, and lately the threats against him had been numerous—thanks largely to the U.S.'s aiding Cuban rebels at the Bay of Pigs invasion, as well as Kennedy's and his brother's support for civil rights. (He'd kicked some Soviet ass last year, too, of course, with the missile blockade, but no one in national security believed that the Russkies were stupid enough to attempt to assassinate the President.)

No, more likely the spy's mission was pure espionage. The GRU was the intelligence organ specializing in stealing technology secrets—specifically those dealing with nuclear weapons and rocket systems—and Texas was home to a number of defense contractors. Barter's boss, the special agent in charge of the office here, immediately assigned him to the case.

The only lead was a photograph of the purported spy, entering the country as a Polish businessman. All individuals coming in from Warsaw Pact countries were surreptitiously photographed at Customs at Idlewild Airport. The image was crude but functional. It depicted a sullen man, blond and large, wearing a fedora not unlike Barter's. The man was about forty years of age.

After viewing the picture of the Russian, however, the baggage handlers reported that they hadn't noticed anyone resembling him.

Barter thanked them and stepped outside into the low November morning sun. Speaking to the cabbies was more productive. It took him only a half hour of canvassing to find the Prompt Ride taxi driver who recognized the man in the photo. He'd taken him to a boardinghouse off Mockingbird. The man remembered the number.

Barter climbed back into his red and white Ford Galaxie. He headed in the direction of the place and parked up the block. He approached cautiously but noted it was abandoned. Barter found a neighbor, a retiree, it seemed, who was washing his car. He showed his ID and asked about the house.

After the typical blink of surprise at the credentials, the man said, "Yessir, been closed up for months now. Bankruptcy. Foreclosed on. Damn banks. All respect."

Barter stifled a frown of frustration, fists clenching and relaxing. "Well, I'm trying to find someone who might've been here several hours ago." He displayed the picture.

"Yup. Saw him. Got outa a taxi cab. I was impressed. Them cost money. Taxis. Anyway, that fella picked up a car from the garage and drove off."

"Car?" Barter's heart beat a little faster.

But the man had only heard the engine, not seen the make or model.

They walked to the small detached structure. Barter opened the unlocked door. The place was empty.

"Sorry I can't be more help."

Barter sniffed the air and bent down to examine the floor of the garage.

"You've been plenty helpful, sir."

"So was I right? Bank robber? He looked plum like one."

"You have a good day, sir."

Mikhail Kaverin had checked into the Dallas Rose Motel, left his luggage and was enjoying piloting the Chevrolet Bel Air through the spacious streets of Dallas.

What a wonderful car this was!

A Bel Air! How Kaverin loved cars. He'd always wanted one, though in truth not a Russian make. For one thing, you waited forever and then you had to take whatever the government had on hand to sell you—for an exorbitant price (where was communism when you needed it?). And the best you could hope for was a temperamental, boxy AZLK or the slightly more stylish and popular GAZ Volga (whose manufacturer's hopes for a handsome income stream by sales to the West never materialized—since the vehicle's sole decoration was a big red Soviet star).

Guided by the map, and instructions from a helpful service station attendant, Kaverin found the Old East Dallas portion of town. The neighborhood was filled with private residences close together, many with front porches dotted with rockers and from whose roofs hung swings. He noted too inexpensive shops and a few small companies. He parked in front of the boardinghouse where Luis Suarez and Carlos Barquín would arrive tomorrow on their mission to track down and kill Comrade 35. It was a one-story, nondescript place, just a notch above shabby. He carefully studied doors and windows and sidewalks. And which neighbors seemed to be home now, during the day—potential witnesses.

He planned out the shootings. He would be waiting here in front of the house when they pulled up, with the trunk of the Bel Air open, pretending to be changing a tire. When they climbed out of their own car, he would shoot them and throw the bodies and their luggage in the trunk.

He drove slowly up and down the street, scanning, scanning. A spy's primary weapon is the power of observation. His first handler at the GRU, a man who later became a nonperson under Stalin, had insisted that Kaverin and he take long walks through the streets of Moscow. After they returned to headquarters the mentor would interrogate the younger agent about what he'd noted. The initial trips yielded a half dozen vague observations. The later ones, hundreds of impressions, all rendered in acute detail.

Sergei had been pleased. Kaverin pictured the man's unsmiling yet kind face and could almost feel the affectionate arm on his young shoulders. Then he tucked the hard thought away.

The peculiar circumstances of this assignment made Kaverin particularly cautious. He drove through the neighborhood again, looking for anyone who might be a threat. After fifteen minutes,

he was satisfied he had a good sense of the place and of the risks he might face. He piloted the expansive Chevy out of this part of town and onto a main road. In ten minutes he pulled into the parking lot of a large grocery store. As he climbed out and walked toward the front door he thought: This place has the most ridiculous name I've ever heard of in a retail establishment.

The Russian spy was shopping in a Piggly Wiggly.

FBI Special Agent Anthony Barter sat in his Galaxie, which was parked in the far end of the lot, and watched the spy walk toward the store.

Picking up the spy's trail had been less daunting than he'd expected. He'd deduced by smell and an examination of the significant oil slick on the garage's floor that the spy was driving a car that leaked and burnt oil. So Barter had driven to the nearest gas station, a Conoco, and flashed a picture of the man. Sure enough, the attendant said that the man, who spoke English fine, but with an accent, had come in driving a bright turquoise Chevy Bel Air, bought a couple quarts of Pennzoil.

The Russian had also picked up a map of the area. He'd asked about the best way to get to Old East Dallas, then motored off in that direction in his oil-guzzler.

Barter had headed over to that neighborhood himself and cruised the streets until he found the Bel Air, which was paused at a stoplight. It was hard to tell for certain, but he believed the driver was the man in the surveillance photograph.

The FBI man almost smiled as he watched the spy stop in his tracks at the entrance of the grocery store—probably astonished by the multitude of plenty spreading out in the aisles. When he disappeared inside, Barter climbed out of his car and, hoping that the Russian would spend some time browsing the aisles, hurried to the Bel Air.

The vehicle was registered to a company in Plano, which Barter suspected would be phony. The Russian's jacket and hat were sitting in the back seat. In the pocket of the sport coat he found a key to room 103 of the Dallas Rose

Motel, on East Main Street in Grand Prairie, about ten miles away.

Barter returned quickly to his Galaxie and pulled out of the lot before the Russian left the store. He knew this was a gamble but he was worried about continuing to follow his subject. J. Edgar Hoover had required all the agents in the bureau to study communist spies. The message was that the GRU operatives were the best of the best. Barter was afraid he'd be spotted. So he left and drove to the parking lot of a gas station across the street from the Dallas Rose Motel.

He waited nervously. What if the spy had checked out of the motel, and simply forgotten to return the key? What if it wasn't even his jacket? Had Barter lost his only lead?

If he ever needed a cigarette, it was now.

But he managed to refrain, nervously clenching and unclenching his sweaty hands.

Five minutes passed.

Ten.

Ah, thank you . . .

The brashly colored Bel Air rocked into the driveway and pulled up in front of room 103.

Barter's car was parked facing away from the motel and he was hunkered down, observing through his rearview mirror.

The Russian climbed out, looked around suspiciously but not Barter's way. He lifted a large grocery sack from the floor of the passenger seat. He disappeared through the door of his room.

Barter went to a pay phone and called his office. He asked a fellow agent about the company to which the Bel Air was registered. The man called back five minutes later. Yes, it was fake. Barter then ordered a surveillance team put together.

In twenty minutes, four FBI agents arrived, in two cars—personal ones, as Barter instructed. One vehicle pulled in front and one in the rear of the motel.

Whatever the Russian's game might be, it was now doomed to failure.

Kaverin was truly enjoying his time in the motel, which was a word that he had never heard before. It was, charmingly, a hybrid of "motor" and "hotel." How very clever.

While the décor was rough around the edges, the place was a million times better than the "posh" resorts on the Black Sea—those unbearably shabby shacks, featuring useless plumbing, stinking carpet, dirty sheets, and the worst examples of cheap furniture Russian factories could disgorge.

Yet here? The linens were clean, the air fragrant, towels plentiful. The soap was even wrapped; it wasn't decorated with body hairs from prior guests. No vermin prowled the floors.

And in the middle of the room was a television set! He flicked it on.

He opened his attaché case, removed the guns and cleaned them, eyes shifting from the screen to weapon and back.

A handsome newscaster was speaking into the camera.

"President Kennedy will arrive at Love Field in Dallas around noon tomorrow to attend a sold-out luncheon at the Dallas Trade Mart. More than two hundred thousand people are expected to greet the President as his motorcade makes its way through the city. Governor and Mrs. John Connelly will accompany the President and the lovely first lady, Jacqueline."

She is indeed lovely, Kaverin reflected, noting a film clip of her waving to people outside the White House.

He put the weapons away and perused the menu card on the bedside table. He lifted the beige receiver of the phone, reflecting how curious it was to make a call—even one as innocuous as this—and not worry about being listened to.

He smiled as he tried to understand the cheerful but heavily accented voice of the woman who took his order. He chose a large T-bone steak, a "Texas-sized" baked potato and a double helping of green beans. To drink, a large glass of milk.

It was decadent, yes, but Mikhail Kaverin had learned that as a spy—in the field or even at home—you could never be sure if any given meal was your last.

FRIDAY

At 6 A.M. Special Agent Anthony Barter pulled his Galaxie into the far end of the Dallas Rose's parking lot.

More or less refreshed after three hours' sleep, he climbed out of the car and walked casually toward the sedan containing the FBI surveillance team. Crouching, he asked the agent on the passenger side, "Anything?"

"Nup," drawled the man. "Nobody came or went."

"Any outside calls, in or out?"

That too was negative. Nor had the spy used the pay phone in the lobby. He hadn't left his room since his return from Piggly Wiggly.

Barter found his hands making fists, then relaxing. He looked over at the Bel Air.

"What do we do, Tony?"

"We wait till he exits, then follow him to see who he's rendezvousing with."

Barter's hope was that the spy was working with employees of LTO Inc. or one of the other big defense contractors here, whose engineers were designing sophisticated weaponry for the army and air force. He was hoping to bring down a whole cell of traitors spying for the Soviets.

He returned to his Galaxie, blinking as he noted a black sedan speed toward him and skid to a stop nearby. Barter was irritated; the Russian wouldn't have a view of this spot from his window but the squealing stop might have put him on his guard.

The driver leapt out and sprinted through traffic.

"The hell're you—?" Barter got no further than that. The young agent from his office was thrusting a telex into his hand.

TOP SECRET

Urgent.
Russian who entered country illegally two days ago identified as Mikhail Kaverin, GRU agent. Specialty reported to be close-in assassination of double agents and other enemies.

Hell! He's not a spy. He's a killer!

And Barter suddenly understood why Kaverin had come to town—not to steal secrets, but to assist in an assassination attempt. It was too much of a coincidence that a trained GRU killer was here just prior to the President. True, the Soviets would never risk an international incident by being directly involved in an assassination. But one of their agents could easily have come here to protect someone *else* whose mission was to kill Kennedy, someone private, without a direct connection to Russia, most likely a U.S. citizen.

Oh, Jesus Christ . . .

He explained his thinking: "Kaverin's here to back up an assassin. Maybe he's providing guns or acting as a bodyguard for the trigger man, or helping him with escape routes. I don't care if we break every bone in his body but we're going to find out who he's helping. Move *now*!"

With guns drawn, the agents ran to the door of Kaverin's room and kicked their way in.

Somehow, in his heart, Barter wasn't very surprised to find that the room's sole occupant was a bag of untouched groceries from Piggly Wiggly.

Nor was it any shock that the back window was unlocked.

Kaverin looked out the window of his room in the Skyline Motel, in north Dallas.

The parking lot and road were clear. The agents who'd been on his trail were, of course, still at the first motel he'd checked into, the Dallas Rose in Grand Prairie.

He'd become aware of a possible tail yesterday as he'd driven through the neighborhood of Old East Dallas, assessing risks, looking for anyone who might be unusually interested in him. He'd noted a Ford Galaxie—red body and white top. The car had been driving the opposite direction when he'd first seen it, but moments later it reappeared, following him.

Kaverin had left that area immediately and driven along commercial roads until he found the Piggly Wiggly and pulled in. The Galaxie followed. It too parked and the driver sat there alone, not smoking, not reading. All he was doing was ostentatiously *not* looking toward the Bel Air.

Clearly, this was suspicious: A man alone in a grocery store parking lot, who was not waiting for his wife?

He'd decided to find out the identity of his pursuer. So Kaverin left his jacket, containing the Dallas Rose room key, on the backseat and had gone into the grocery store and he'd slipped out the back, circling around to the parking lot. Yes, there was the man who'd been tailing him, wearing a suit—an official-looking one. He'd sidled up to the Bel Air and, looking around casually, too casually, eased the door open and went through the interior.

Kaverin himself had hurried to the man's Ford Galaxie—and found the registration. Anthony Barter. He found nothing of the man's affiliation but he'd hurried back to the Piggly Wiggly and used one of the store's pay phones, which—unlike in Russia—actually worked. He had had to make only three calls—to the Dallas Police, to the Texas Rangers, and to the FBI, asking for an Anthony Barter. The secretary at the last of the three had started to put him through to Special Agent Barter's office. He'd hung up, bought a sack's worth of random groceries and returned to his Bel Air.

The agent had left by then but when Kaverin had returned to the Dallas Rose he saw that, yes, the Galaxie was parked across the street. Kaverin had taken the groceries, gone inside, put on the TV and then quickly gathered his belongings and climbed out the back window. He'd made his way through a field to a bus stop and had ridden a mile then gotten off near a car dealership. He'd bought a four-year-old DeSoto Firedome coupe, huge and with impressive rear fins, with some of the thousand dollars Spesky had given him in Miami. He'd driven north until he found another motel, the Skyline. It was here that he'd spent the night, watching television, cleaning his weapons again and enjoying the sumptuous steak dinner.

Now, it was time to complete his mission. According to Rasnakov, Luis Suarez and Carlos Barquín would be arriving at the boardinghouse soon, to prepare for the killing of Comrade 35. Kaverin left the hotel and was at the boardinghouse in twenty minutes. He parked the DeSoto across the street, slipped the smaller of the guns—the Colt .22—into his waistband. He got out and opened the trunk, set the jack and tire iron on the grass beside the car and rested the spare tire against the bumper.

And he waited.

Fifteen minutes later a yellow Chrysler pulled slowly down the street, two men in the front seat. Men with mustaches and observant eyes.

Yes, they were his targets.

Kaverin's hand eased into his jacket, gripped the handle of his pistol. It didn't make much noise, just a pop, like a bigger gun with a silencer, but it was much more accurate.

He was breathing steadily, focusing on finding that unique place within you where you had to tuck your soul away when you took a human life. He murdered for his country, for the cause of what was just, for communism, for his own self-preservation. He was efficient at this dark task, even if he didn't enjoy it.

He knew he was ready. And flicked the safety catch off the gun as he crouched down, watching the Chrysler in the reflection of his car's chrome bumper.

It was then that a voice from behind startled Kaverin.

"Need some help there, sir?"

Still facing the Chrysler, he looked back to see a Dallas police officer standing on the sidewalk. Hands on his hips.

"I'm sorry?" the spy asked evenly.

"Have a flat? Need some help?"

"No, I'm doing fine, thank you, Officer." Kaverin was speaking over his shoulder, with his back to the officer. His jacket was open and the pistol obvious.

"Don't mind helping, really," the man drawled.

Kaverin casually fixed buttons, but as he did he looked across the street and saw his two targets staring his way. Perhaps they thought the police and he were working together, looking for them. Or maybe the officer's voice had simply caught their attention and they'd seen the pistol. In any event, the driver—it was Luis Suarez—aborted the parking maneuver, put the car in forward and eased into the street. He didn't speed away—not just yet. But once the Chrysler turned the corner, Kaverin heard the big engine accelerate fast.

He turned back to the policeman and gave an appreciative smile. "I've gotten everything taken care of, Officer. Thank you, though."

"Any time," the man said and returned to his beat.

At around 8:30 A.M., Lee Harvey Oswald was being driven to work at the Texas Book Depository by a friend. He often did this, bummed rides. He didn't have a license and, in fact, didn't enjoy driving.

He had mixed feelings about his decision to spend the night at the Paines' house in Irving. It was smart because it provided a good hiding place from those bastards who wanted to kill him. He'd looked forward to seeing Marina and their two daughters, one of whom was only a month old; they were staying permanently with the Paines. But that turned out to be a disappointment. He'd hoped to reconcile with Marina after a recent fight but it hadn't happened. The bickering resumed, the night had turned to shit and he was upset.

"Whatcha got back there?" his friend asked as they nosed through morning traffic. He was nodding toward the long, paperwrapped bundle in the backseat.

"Just some curtain rods."

"Ah."

Oswald continued to be cautious, shifting his gaze around the surrounding streets and sidewalks. Yes, some people seemed to be watching him, wary, suspicious, as if they knew exactly what he was going to do today. He reflected that he had told too many people about his contempt for Kennedy. And, hell, he'd just written an angry letter to the FBI, warning them to leave his family alone . . . That wasn't too bright.

And *curtain rods*?

Jesus. No, it's a 6.5-mm Carcano model 91/38 rifle. That's what was wrapped up in the paper. How could anybody believe the bulky package was curtain rods? You need to think better. Be smarter.

And be cautious. He had a sense that his enemies were getting closer and closer.

He had the chance to make an indelible mark on history. He'd be famous forever. He had to make absolutely sure nothing would prevent that.

He looked around the streets of central Dallas, partially deserted now. There'd be crowds later, that was for sure, right there along Elm Street. Thousands of people. He knew this because the local newspaper had conveniently reported the exact route the President's motorcade would take. The vehicles would come west on Main, then north briefly on Houston, then turn west again on Elm, passing right under the windows of the Texas Book Depository where he would be waiting in a sixth-floor window.

"You okay there, Lee?" his friend asked as he eased to a stop at a light.

"What's that?"

"You didn't hear me, I guess. I just asked if you'd be needing a ride back to the Paines' tonight?"

Oswald didn't answer for a minute. "No. I'll probably just take the bus."

"There. That's a good place to shoot," Luis Suarez said.

Carlos Barquín was examining the intersection where his partner was pointing—the sidewalk in front of the side door to the Texas Book Depository. "Looks like the *only* place to shoot. Good or bad, we don't have any choice. Where else could we do it?" He seemed impatient.

Suarez nodded, though he didn't much care for the man's attitude. "Not very private, though."

"Well, we don't have the luxury of private. Not with a paranoid asshole like him."

They had parked their Chrysler on North Record Street in downtown Dallas and were looking over the sidewalk in front of the Texas Book Depository. The morning was chill but they kept their jackets buttoned up because of the guns in their waistbands.

"I think it'll work. All the buildings, they'll cover the sounds of the shots."

"Cover them?" Barquín asked.

"I mean the sounds'll bounce around. Nobody will know where they came from."

"Oh."

"Nobody'll know it was us. We'll shoot him, drop the guns, and walk back to the car. Walk slowly." The pistols were wrapped in a special tape that didn't hold fingerprints.

Barquín said defiantly, "I know what to do. I've done this before."

Suarez didn't say anything. He and Barquín shared both a certain ideology and a love of liquor. They'd even shared the same woman once or twice. He really didn't like the man, however.

As they continued through the cool morning, Barquín asked, "That man, back there at the boardinghouse? In the suit, talking to the cop. He was police too, you think?"

"I don't know." Suarez had pondered who he'd been. He'd been armed and had been talking to that patrolman but it would have been odd for a cop to be there changing the tire of his own unmarked car—and an old DeSoto? No, the man was trouble but he couldn't figure out how he fit into the picture.

They had some effects back at the boardinghouse, which they'd stashed there last week, but they'd have to abandon them now. Not that it mattered; they could pick up whatever they needed on the road as the Underground spirited them out of the country and back to Havana.

As they walked up Houston toward Elm, they passed a dim alley. A car was parked there, rear end facing them, the engine running and the trunk open. What was familiar about it?

"That car, haven't we—?"

And Suarez realized it was the same DeSoto parked in front of the boardinghouse earlier when they'd seen that man changing the tire. The big, blond man. It was his car! Which meant—

He turned quickly, Barquín too. And both instinctively reached for their weapons, but the man was approaching fast from across Houston Street, already aiming his own gun at them.

The two Cubans froze.

Without a hesitation, without a blink, without breaking stride, the hulking blond man fired twice, hitting Barquín in the forehead.

Pop, pop.

He dropped to the ground like a discarded doll.

Suarez decided there was no choice. He continued to draw his gun, and hoped he could get a round off in time.

The weapon wasn't even out of his waistband when he saw a tiny flash, then felt a tap between his eyes, a burning.

Which lasted less than a second.

Kaverin got the bodies into the trunk of the DeSoto quickly.

This was effortless. They were slight, weighing half what he did.

He fired up the DeSoto—he liked the Bel Air better—and pulled into Houston Street and then made his way out of downtown.

The search to find the men had been tense, though he'd known in general where they would be going—the most likely place to shoot down Comrade 35. Once there, central Dallas, he'd cruised the streets, looking for a yellow Chrysler. Finally he'd spotted it, near North Record

Street. Suarez and Barquín were just getting out and walking south.

There were too many people to kill them there but Kaverin had noted the route they were taking and he'd pulled into an alley several blocks ahead of them. Once again he'd opened the trunk, then slipped into a doorway across Houston Street and waited. The men strode up the avenue and when their attention turned to the DeSoto he'd stepped across the street, drawing his gun.

Pop, pop . . .

Kaverin now drove out of the downtown area, parked, and walked up the street to the Western Union office he'd located earlier.

There the spy spent some moments with a cipher pad writing a telegram reporting his success. He sent it to a safe house in Washington, D.C., where someone with the Russian consulate was waiting.

In fifteen minutes the response came back. It referred to shipments of wheat and truck allotments. But after deciphering:

> *Have submitted to the Special Council of the Presidium the report regarding your successful elimination of the threat to Comrade 35. Please proceed to any locations where the two counterrevolutionaries had contact in Dallas and secure any helpful information. The people of the Soviet Union thank you.*

Kaverin returned to the boardinghouse in the Old East Dallas part of town, opened the trunk of the DeSoto after making sure no one could see him—and no beat police officers were nearby—and emptied the pockets of the men he'd just shot. He found a fob containing the key to the front door of the boardinghouse and one to room number 2. He walked slowly up to the front door, checked to make sure he was alone, and then entered their room.

The men had not been inside that morning—after the scare with the police—but they had apparently stored some things there: several suitcases, containing clothes, money, ammuni-

tion, binoculars and Spanish to English dictionaries. He pulled out a penknife and began to look for secret compartments. He found none.

At about 12:45, he heard a commotion from the hallway, voices speaking urgently. He thought at first it might be the police, that he'd been tracked here, or that someone had seen an unidentified man entering the boarders' room.

His hand on his pistol, he walked to the door, leaned close and listened.

"Did you hear? Did you hear?" a woman was calling, the words sliced by hysteria. "The President's been shot! They think he's dead!"

"No! Are you sure?" A man's voice.

Someone began to sob.

Kaverin released his grip on the Colt, looked around the room and walked to the television set. He turned it on and sat in a creaking chair to wait for the device to warm up.

SATURDAY

The time was 2 A.M., the day after the worst day of his life.

Special Agent Anthony Barter was trudging along the sidewalk to his apartment in Richmond, Texas. He'd been up for nearly twenty-four hours and he needed a little sleep—just a nap, really—and then a shower.

Then he'd return to the hunt for Lee Harvey Oswald's assistant or savior or bodyguard or whatever he was: the Russian spy, Mikhail Kaverin.

The fallout was bad. Barter had kept his own superiors at the FBI and the Secret Service informed of every fact he'd learned about the spy from the moment he'd gotten the report from New York. But it was finger-pointing time now and Washington wanted to know exactly, minute by minute, what he knew and when he knew it and why he wasn't more vocal about the threat to Kennedy.

"Because it wasn't a threat at first," he'd explained to the assistant director of the FBI in

Washington. "We thought he was after classified weapons information. His behavior was suspicious but he didn't seem dangerous."

The assistant director had barked, "Well, the President of the United States is now *suspiciously* dead, Barter. I thought you were tailing him."

Barter had sighed. "I was. He evaded me."

He didn't say "us." Barter didn't shift blame.

"Jesus Christ." The man told him that J. Edgar Hoover personally would be calling him at some point tomorrow. And slammed the phone down. At least that's what Barter imagined. He heard only a click, then static.

So this is what the demise of a career looks like, he thought. His heart clutched. Being a special agent was the only job that had ever appealed to him, the only job he'd ever wanted. His passion for the FBI went back to seeing newsreels about G-Men, to reading comic books about Elliot Ness, to watching movies like *Gang Busters* over and over again at Saturday afternoon matinees, while munching popcorn and sipping fizzy grape soda pop.

But his future wasn't the first thing in his mind at the moment. All he cared about was finding Lee Harvey Oswald's accomplice, finding Kaverin. For a moment he was flushed with anger and he hoped that, if he found the man, the Russian resisted arrest so Barter could put a bullet in his head. Even as he thought this, though, he knew it was an unreasonable, passionate reflex; the reality was that he would arrest the man, following procedure to a T and interrogate him firmly but respectfully.

The problem, of course, was *finding* him. Since he'd been Oswald's protector, and the assassin was now in custody, Kaverin was probably long gone. Barter guessed he was probably on a steamer headed back to Russia. Still, Barter was doing everything possible to find the man. The instant he'd heard of the shooting, he had sent the Russian's picture to every law enforcer in Texas and neighboring states and made sure the nearby airports and the train and bus stations were being watched. The automobile rental

agencies too (ironically the Texas Book Depository was crowned with a huge Hertz billboard, touting Chevrolets). Roadblocks were set up, as well, and the docks along the Texas coastline were being searched by local police, FBI, and the Coast Guard.

As every minute passed without word of a sighting, Barter grew more and more angry with himself. Oh, hell, if he'd only done more digging! Oswald had been under investigation by agents in his own office! The man had tried to defect to Russia, he was actively procommunist and had recently been in Mexico trying to get visas to Cuba and Russia. If that investigation had been better coordinated, Barter might have put the pieces together.

Now approaching his apartment, Anthony Barter paused, fished out his keys and stepped to his door, thinking: Okay, I'll have one Lone Star beer. Yes, agents were not supposed to drink. But considering that tomorrow Mr. Hoover would tell him that he was soon to be an *ex*-agent, liquor was one vice that he wouldn't have to worry about keeping secret any longer.

Barter walked inside, closed the door and locked it. He was reaching for the light switch when he heard, behind him, a floorboard creak. Special Agent Anthony William Barter's shoulders slumped. He thought of his failure to the Bureau, to his country—and to his President. He was almost relieved when the Russian agent's pistol muzzle touched the back of his head.

"How the hell did you find me?" Anthony Barter asked.

Mikhail Kaverin briefly studied the FBI agent, whose hands were shackled with his own cuffs. The Russian was impressed that the man seemed merely curious, not afraid. He returned to his task, which was using a penknife to slice open the lining of his attaché case.

Barter noted this surgery but seemed uninterested in it. His gaze was fixed ruthlessly on his visitor.

"How did I find you," Kaverin mused, slicing away. He explained about observing the agent's surveillance at the grocery store.

"You saw me?"

"Yes, yes, we're trained to notice that. Aren't you?"

"Not many people follow FBI agents. It's usually the other way around."

This made some sense.

He explained about his ruse at the Piggly Wiggly. The FBI man squinted his eyes shut in disgust. Then he sighed. "Okay, you didn't kill me," Barter said evenly. "So you're going to kidnap me. Negotiate my life for safe passage out of the country." He then said in a low, defiant voice, "But that isn't going to work, my friend. We don't negotiate with scum like you. Assassination's the most cowardly act imaginable. You and your countrymen're despicable and whatever you do to me, that won't stop our entire law enforcement apparatus from finding you and making sure you're arrested—and executed. And there'll be sanctions against your country, you know. Military sanctions." He shook his head in seeming disbelief. "Didn't your superiors think through what would happen if the President was killed?"

Kaverin didn't respond. He turned his attention to the agent. "We have not made introductions. I am Major Mikhail Kaverin of the Glavnoe Razvedyvatelnoe Upravlenie."

"I know who you are."

Kaverin wasn't surprised. He said, "Well, Special Agent Barter, I have no intention of kidnapping you. Nor of killing you, for that matter. I found it necessary to come up behind you and relieve you of your weapon so that you would not act rashly—"

"Shooting an enemy of the country, a spy, is not acting rashly."

Kaverin said, "No, but shooting an *ally* would be."

"Ally?"

"Agent Barter, I am going to tell you some things you will undoubtedly find incredible—

though they are true. Then, after we make some formal arrangements, I will give you your gun back and I will give you my gun and I will surrender to you. May I proceed?"

Warily Barter said, "Yes, all right." His eyes shifted from the pistol to the documents extracted from the lid of the attaché case.

"Earlier this week I was called into the office of my superior at GRU headquarters. I was given an assignment: to protect an individual in the United States who would further the interests of the Soviet Union. A man we have code named Comrade Thirty-five."

"Yeah, yeah, that son of a bitch, Lee Harvey Oswald."

"No," Kaverin said. "Comrade Thirty-five was our code name for John Fitzgerald Kennedy."

"What?" Barter squinted at him.

"'Thirty-five,'" Kaverin continued, "because he was the thirty-fifth President of the United States. 'Comrade' because he shared certain interests with our country." The Russian pushed forward the documents he'd extracted from his case. "Can you read Russian?"

"No."

"Then I will translate."

"They're fake."

"No, they are quite real. And I will prove to you they're real in a moment." Kaverin looked down and scanned the documents. "'To Comrade Major Mikhail Kaverin. Intelligence received from sources in Washington, D.C., has reported that in October of this year President John Fitzgerald Kennedy signed an executive order, initiating the reduction of American advisory and military forces in Vietnam.'"

"Vietnam?" Barter was frowning. "That's that country near China, right? A French colony or something. Sure, we've sent some soldiers there. I read about that."

Kaverin continued his reading. "'Our sources have reported that Charles de Gaulle told President Kennedy that it would be very detrimental for the United States to become enmeshed in the politics of Southeast Asia. Kennedy went against the advice of his generals and established the goal to have all American troops out of Vietnam and neighboring countries by 1964. After the Americans are gone, the communist regimes in Vietnam, Laos, and Cambodia will surge south through Malaysia and Singapore, establishing governments with true Marxist values throughout Southeast Asia. Our Premier and the Politburo will form an alliance with that bloc. Together we will stand firm against the wrong-minded Maoist cult in China.'

"'If anything were to happen to Kennedy, our intelligence assessment is that his successor, Lyndon Johnson, will drastically *increase* the U.S. military presence in the region. This would be disastrous for the interests of the USSR.'"

He put down the documents, shook his head and sighed. "You see, Agent Barter, the mission of the agent who preceded me and of myself was to do whatever we could to uncover any threats to your President Kennedy and stop them. Our job was to protect him."

Barter snapped, "That's bullshit! You knew about Oswald but you didn't report it! If you'd really been concerned, you—"

"No!" Kaverin replied angrily. "We knew *nothing* of Oswald. That's not why I was sent here. There was *another* threat to your President. Completely unrelated to the assassin. Do you know of Luis Suarez and Carlos Barquín?"

"Of course, we've been on the look-out for them for months. They're Cuban Americans under orders from Fidel Castro to kill Kennedy because of the Bay of Pigs invasion. We haven't been able to find their whereabouts."

"I can produce them."

"Where are they?"

"They're in the trunk of my car."

"Are you joking?"

"Not at all. *That* was my assignment. To find and eliminate them. We knew they were going to attempt to assassinate Kennedy, possibly on his visit here. When I shot them they were on Houston Street—at a place where your President's

motorcade would pass by. Undoubtedly they were looking for vantage points to shoot from. Both of them were armed."

"Why didn't you tell us that you had a lead to them?"

Kaverin scoffed. "What would you have done?"

"Arrested them, of course."

"For what? Have they committed a crime?"

Barter fell silent.

"I thought not. You would have put them away for a few months for threatening the President or for having a weapon. Then they would have been released to try to assassinate him again. My solution was far more efficient and . . . far more permanent." Kaverin grimaced. He said passionately, "No one was more shocked and upset than I to hear the terrible news today of your President's fate."

Kaverin fell silent, noting that Barter, who until now had been looking him straight in the eye, had grown evasive. The Russian said, in a whisper, "You knew about Oswald."

No answer for a moment. Then: "I'm not at liberty to talk about investigations."

Kaverin snapped, "You *knew* he was a threat and yet you were not watching him constantly?"

"We have . . . limited resources. We didn't think he'd be a threat."

Silence flowed between the men. Finally Kaverin asked softly, "Well, do you believe me, Special Agent Barter?"

After a moment the FBI man said, "Maybe I do. But you haven't told me what you want out of all this."

Kaverin gave a laugh. "It's obvious, no? I want to defect. I have failed in my mission. If I return home I will become a nonperson. I will be killed and my name and all record of my existence expunged. It will be as if I never existed. I had hoped to marry, even at this age, to have a son. That is a possibility if I remain here." He gave a faint smile. "Besides, I must tell you, Agent Barter. I've been in this country for only several days but I already find it rather appealing."

"What's in it for us?"

"I can give you a great deal of information. I have been a GRU officer for many years. And I can offer something more. Something to, as your card players here say, sweeten the pot."

Barter said, "And what's that?"

"What I can offer you, Agent Barter—excuse me, *Special* Agent Barter—is a real, living, breathing KGB agent."

"KGB?"

"Indeed. You can arrest him and interrogate him. Or your CIA could run him as a double agent. You Americans *love* KGB spies, do you not? Why, your citizens know nothing of the GRU or the Stasi. But the KGB? Pick up a James Bond novel or go to the cinema. Wouldn't it be a fine national security coup to land a fish like that?"

Kaverin put just the right tone into his voice to suggest that the arrest would be fine for Barter's career personally too.

"Who is this man?"

"He is in Miami, operating undercover as the head of a transportation company. His real name is Nikolai Spesky. He purports to be a GRU agent, but in fact his employer is the KGB."

"How d'you know that?"

"For one thing, because of your presence on my trail."

"Me?"

Kaverin said, "I assume you learned of me through an anonymous tip, correct?"

"Yes, that's right. Received by our New York office."

"Perhaps *through* New York, but it originated from Comrade Spesky in Miami. He informed on me. You see, neither Customs officials or any airline in New York knew that my final destination was Dallas. Only Spesky did. I didn't receive my ticket until I was in Florida. In fact, I wasn't wholly surprised when you appeared; I was suspicious of Spesky from the beginning. That is one of the reasons I was looking for surveillance—and spotted you."

"Why did you suspect him?"

"Top-brand vodka and paté and smoked oysters and bread with very little mold."

Barter shook his head.

Kaverin continued, "Spesky told me his wife had sent him such gifts from Moscow. No GRU field agent's wife would ever be able to afford such delicacies, only the wife of a KGB agent could."

"But why would he betray you? Wouldn't the KGB have the same interest you would—to keep the President alive so he'd withdraw the troops from Vietnam?"

Kaverin smiled again. "Logic would suggest that, yes. But in truth the essential interest of the KGB is in furthering the interest of the KGB. And that cause is advanced every time the GRU fails."

"So your security agencies spy on each other, for no other purpose than sabotaging their rivals?" Barter muttered, his tone dark.

Kaverin fixed him with a piercing look. "Yes, shocking, isn't it? Something that could *never* happen here. Fortunately you have Mr. J. Edgar Hoover to uphold the moral integrity of your organization. I know he would *never* illegally wiretap politicians or civil rights leaders or members of other governmental agencies."

Anthony Barter offered his first smile of the evening. He said, "I can't make any deals myself. You understand that?"

"Of course."

"But I think you're telling the truth. I'll go to bat for you. You know what that means?"

Kaverin gave a broad frown. "Please. I am a fan of the New York Mets."

Barter laughed. "The Mets? They had close to the worst season in major league history this year. Couldn't you pick a better team?"

Kaverin waved his hand dismissively. "It was their second year as a team. Give them some time, Agent Barter. Give them time."

The Russian then slid the photographs of the top-secret documents toward the agent, along with the keys to the DeSoto. He uncuffed the agent and, without a moment's hesitation, handed over both of the pistols.

"I'm going to make some phone calls, Major Kaverin. I hope you won't mind if I put the handcuffs on *you*."

"No, I perfectly understand."

He slipped them on, albeit with Kaverin's hands in front of him, not behind his back. Before he reached for the phone, though, he asked, "Would you like to have a beer?"

"I would, yes. In Russia we have vodka but we don't have beer. Not good beer."

The agent rose and went to the refrigerator. He returned with two bottles of Lone Star, opened them, and handed one to the spy.

Kaverin lifted his. "*Za zdorovie!* It means, 'To our health.'"

They tapped bottles and both took long sips. Kaverin enjoyed the flavor very much, and the FBI agent regarded the bottle with pleasure. "I'm not supposed to be doing this, you know. Mr. Hoover doesn't approve of drinking liquor."

"No one will ever know, Special Agent Barter," Kaverin told him. "I'm quite good at keeping secrets."

TUESDAY

TOP SECRET

NOVEMBER 26, 1963
FROM: OFFICE OF THE SECRETARY OF DEFENSE, THE PENTAGON, ARLINGTON, VIRGINIA
TO: SECRETARY OF THE ARMY
SECRETARY OF THE NAVY
SECRETARY OF THE AIR FORCE
SECRETARY OF THE JOINT CHIEFS OF STAFF

Be advised that President Lyndon Baines Johnson today issued National Security Action Memorandum 273. This order reverses NSAM 263, issued by the late President Kennedy in October of this year, which ordered the withdrawal of U.S. troops from Vietnam and the transfer of responsibility in countering communist insurgency in Southeast Asia to the Vietnamese and neighboring governments.

NSAM 273 provides for maintenance of existing U.S. troop strength in Vietnam and sets forth a commitment to increased American military and advisory presence in combating communism in the region.

THE SPY WHO CLUTCHED A PLAYING CARD

EDWARD D. HOCH

ALTHOUGH HE WROTE a few slim novels, including *The Shattered Raven* (1969), *The Transvection Machine* (1971), and *The Fellowship of the Hand* (1973), all largely forgotten today, Edward Dentinger Hoch (1930–2008) was a rare exception to the accepted wisdom that it is virtually impossible to earn a living writing short stories exclusively. He produced about nine hundred stories in his career, approximately half of them published in *Ellery Queen's Mystery Magazine*, beginning in 1962. In May 1973, Hoch started a remarkable run of publishing at least one story in every issue of *EQMM* until his death—and beyond, as he had already delivered additional stories.

Readers have never been able to decide which of Hoch's series characters was their favorite as he created numerous protagonists, including the bizarre Simon Ark, who claims to be two thousand years old and was the central character of his first published story, "Village of the Dead" (1955); Nick Velvet, the thief who steals only such innately worthless objects as the water in a swimming pool and the dust from an otherwise empty room (the first Velvet story was "The Theft of the Clouded Tiger," 1966); and Dr. Sam Hawthorne, who specializes in solving locked room and other impossible crimes and made his first appearance in 1974 in "The Problem of the Covered Bridge." Hoch also produced stories pseudonymously as Stephen Dentinger, Pat McMahon, Mr. X, and R. L. Stevens. He also ghostwrote an Ellery Queen novel, *The Blue Movie Murders* (1972).

Among Hoch's creations that appeared most prolifically was Jeffery Rand, the Double-C Man whose genius as a counterespionage agent, specializing in codes and ciphers, elevated him to be the head of the Department of Concealed Communications, a division of British Intelligence; during the course of the series, he resigns to work as a freelancer.

"The Spy Who Clutched a Playing Card" was originally published in the February 1968 issue of *Ellery Queen's Mystery Magazine*.

THE SPY WHO CLUTCHED A PLAYING CARD

EDWARD D. HOCH

DURING FEBRUARY and March the Gulf of Finland was always icebound, and this winter proved to be no exception. The flat stretch of snow which covered the ice sparkled in the afternoon sun, broken only occasionally by the tracks of a passing patrol vehicle or the irregular trail of some winter creature.

Near one shore, in an area where man rarely ventured during these frozen months, a single frost-crusted truck rested silently on great balloon snow tires. At the back of the truck a man dressed in white worked at a sort of drill that was boring through the snow and frozen earth toward some unseen goal. He worked quickly in the cold, glancing now and then at the distant white horizon as if fearing interruption.

Finally, deciding somehow that he was nearing his goal, he slowed the drill and carefully withdrew it from the hole. From the rear of this truck he pulled a coil of wire and some insulated tools. He was stooping over the hole, intent on his work, when the single shot came, a flat echoing sound that swept quickly over the terraces of snow and then was gone.

No other sound followed, and there was nothing to confirm its passing, except that the figure in white no longer worked by his truck. Now he was crumbled to the ground, and already the shifting snow—like desert sand or lazy waves—was beginning to lap and pull at his body . . .

Hastings had phoned Rand just after nine, asking him to see a certain Mr. Greene from Washington. When the visitor entered the office of Concealed Communications a half hour later, Rand needed only a single glance to know that the man was from the C.I.A. He hoped that the Americans were a bit more circumspect in their choice of agents for other countries. Rand had never yet met one in London who didn't seem to shout his profession with all the reticence of a screeching peacock.

Mr. Greene was no exception. Tall, angular, vaguely handsome—the sort who'd gone through college on the debating team and worked out Saturday afternoons in the school gym. He'd be married with three children, because that was the proper number to have these days, and his wife wouldn't object to his work because on this level it was no more risky than selling insurance.

"You're Rand," he said, holding out his hand. "They think very highly of your work in Washington."

"I'm pleased to hear that," Rand said, not believing a word of it. The man obviously wanted a favor.

"We've had an odd sort of report from the Scandinavian area. Washington thought that in the interests of time you might be able to give us some help at this end."

Rand smiled slightly and offered the man a cigarette. "Anything I can do . . ."

"A man named Alfred Penny was killed two days ago near the Gulf of Finland. He was shot by a high-powered rifle from some distance away."

"Alfred Penny? I don't know the name."

"He's had many names—Glaz, Blanco, Marrigal, to name a few. He was a specialist, an expert in all sorts of electronic listening devices, telephone taps, things like that."

"An expert for whom—the Russians or our side?"

Greene leaned back in his chair. "Neither side, surprisingly. He was a British subject, originally—which is one of the reasons we're getting you into it—but for the past five years he's worked for an organization called SPAD. Ever hear of them?"

"Of course," Rand replied. SPAD was a private intelligence organization headquartered in Paris and West Berlin, named after a popular French fighter plane of the First World War. Supposedly working for the West, it had been accused on occasion of supplying information to the highest bidder—East or West.

"We don't know who killed him, but we do know what he was up to out there. He was tapping into the hot line between Washington and Moscow."

"What!" Rand came forward in his chair. "Why in hell would he be doing that?"

Greene shrugged. "We're questioning SPAD about that right now. They claim his mission wasn't authorized, but we're not so certain."

Rand was frowning at the ceiling. "But what would he gain by tapping into the hot line? The thing is never used. It's for the ultimate emergency. The day the hot line has to be used, people like Penny and the rest of us will be beyond caring."

"Are you familiar with its operation, Mr. Rand? The hot line is not a voice connection as so many people seem to believe. It's a teletype, actually, with a one-time tape system to encipher messages."

Rand nodded. The one-time system had been perfected in 1918 by an officer of the U.S. Army Signal Corps. It used a teletypewriter tape perforated with a patternless, nonrepetitive series of holes to add electrical pulses to the plaintext message. Decipherment was absolutely impossible unless the receiver had an identical tape at his end. After being used once, that section of tape was destroyed. Germany had used the system in the 1920s, and Russia in the 1930s, but the necessity for having a disposable tape as lengthy as the messages prevented its universal use, especially on battlefields. A few Russian agents like Rudolf Abel and the Krogers had used variations of the one-time system, and it was presently well-regarded by the United Nations, the International Monetary Fund, and a number of other groups. Since both the U.S. State Department and the Russian government were users, it was a natural selection for the hot line link.

"So even if Penny tapped the line, he couldn't decipher it," Rand observed. "He'd be listening to a line that carried no messages, and he couldn't have understood them if it had. So why did he try to do it?"

Greene shrugged again. "I thought you might have some ideas, being the head of Double-C. Though actually that was only one reason for my visit. When they noticed something amiss with the line and went to investigate, they found Penny's body. He had a list of names on him."

"Foolish!" Rand snorted.

"Not so foolish. They were apparently a list of contacts. The list was hidden in the heel of his boot."

"Do people still do that sort of thing?" Rand marveled.

"They do. Here's the list."

He passed Rand a folded slip of paper. It was headed, *London*, and there followed three names: *Geoffrey Crayon, Hal Whitehood, Leo Vandor.*

"Interesting," Rand commented. "A list of contacts, you think?"

"What else?"

"Well, I can think of a number of things. For instance, perhaps Penny's killer planted the list on his body."

"No chance. As near as we can tell from the footprints, the killer went nowhere near the body. We mainly wanted your help with these names—any chance they're not what they seem? Of course Vandor is the Red spy awaiting trial, and Whitehood is the well-known movie star, but what about Crayon? The only one I know is in Washington Irving."

Rand smiled at the man. "I didn't realize the C.I.A. was so literary. Oh, I doubt very much that this is the Geoffrey Crayon of *The Sketch Book*, despite the fact that the book first appeared in London. No, I rather think that this is Geoffrey Crayon, the contract bridge expert. He plays often in tournaments around London, and he writes a weekly column in the *Express.*"

"Could any of these people be linked to an organization like SPAD?"

"Well, Leo Vandor is a known agent. I suppose he'd be the most likely."

Greene frowned out the window, where the winter sun was making one of its too-brief appearances. "Since this is primarily a communications matter, and could possibly involve the use of cipher, we were wondering if you could talk to these three men—question them about Alfred Penny."

"I'd be glad to," Rand replied. "But you don't usually learn much from spies by formal questioning."

"You don't learn much, but you just might force the hand of one of them."

"If there's a hand to be forced," Rand observed. "If the whole thing isn't just a coverup for something bigger."

"What could be bigger than the hot line?"

It was Rand's turn to stare out the window. "I don't know. I wish I did know sometimes what the other side's thinking."

When Rand went to see Whitehood the following morning, he took Parkinson with him. Parkinson was the youngest and most promising of Rand's half dozen assistants in Double-C—a sandy-haired cipher expert just three years out of Cambridge, who always called his superior "sir."

"Have you seen any of Whitehood's films, Parkinson?" Rand asked while they waited in the studio's reception room for the actor to appear.

"Those spy things, sir. They're really wild—wilder than the Bonds!"

"Do you think he could possibly be living his role off the screen?"

"I hope not, sir—not a woman in London would be safe!"

When he finally appeared, Whitehood was brisk and bristling. He looked much like the press release photos which Rand had studied, except that the boyish smile was nowhere in evidence. "Make it fast," he said. "I'm due back on the set."

Rand introduced them and said, "This matter concerns a man named Alfred Penny, who lived here in London for a number of years. Did you know him?"

"Never heard the name." The actor was impatient, restless in his chair. "Is that all?"

"He died recently. Your name was found on the body."

"Perhaps he was a fan," Whitehood said with an unconcerned shrug.

"I doubt that very much."

"Well, I don't know your Mr. Penny, and I really have no further time to spend with you."

"Just one more question," Rand said, "and then we'll let you go. Are you familiar with SPAD?"

"Who?"

"S-P-A-D."

"Airplane, wasn't it?" the actor said, but Rand thought he caught a fleeting spark of something—fear?—in the man's eyes.

"I think that's all for now," Rand said, getting to his feet. "Thank you for seeing us."

"Always glad to help the government," Whitehood said, and disappeared quickly through swinging doors.

When they were outside, Parkinson asked, "What do you think, sir? Was he telling the truth?"

"I don't know. I don't even know what Greene expected me to find." Rand bit pensively at his lower lip for a moment and then took out a pack of American cigarettes. "Look, call ahead and see if we can talk with Leo Vandor. He had to be in court for his arraignment this morning, and they weren't certain what time he'd be back in his cell."

Rand stood by the car, smoking his cigarette, marveling at the second straight day of winter sunshine. The temperature was still a frosty 35, but he thought it might warm up by afternoon.

Parkinson came running from the corner phone booth a moment later, his face flushed with excitement. Rand's heart skipped a beat and he threw away the cigarette. "What is it, Parkinson?"

"Vandor, sir! He's escaped—broke away from the guards while they were taking him to court!"

Leo Vandor had been arrested just before Christmas for violating the Official Secrets Act. Although the actual details of his espionage had only been vaguely reported thus far in the public press, Rand knew the outline of the case quite well. Vandor was an East European who'd come to England ten years earlier as a refugee from the Russians. He'd lived a quiet life as the managing editor of a small-circulation poetry magazine, apparently acting as a Russian agent during all this time.

His technique for receiving and passing on secrets was simplicity itself. Russian agents in the United States and other countries submitted poems to Vandor's magazine—poems with intricate messages hidden in the text, by cipher or microdot. These poems were "rejected" by Vandor, who simply put them in return envelopes addressed to cover addresses behind the Iron Curtain. Even if a mail check was being maintained, it showed only that certain people in both the United States and Russia submitted manuscripts to the same poetry magazine in London.

But the method had finally been detected, and somehow American and British counter-intelligence agents had been tipped off. Vandor was arrested, and in his possession at the time they found a mass of figures that translated into the orbits of a number of supersecret American satellites.

"And now he's escaped," Parkinson said.

Rand had a rare twinge of uncertainty. It was hard to believe that Vandor's escape was tied into the death of Penny, and yet . . . He got on the phone and spoke briefly with Hastings, arranging another meeting with Greene, the C.I.A. man. Then he rejoined Parkinson.

"There's a third name on that list," he said grimly. "I think we'd better pay a fast visit to Mr. Geoffrey Crayon, the contract bridge expert."

Crayon lived high above the London streets in one of the tallest and newest of urban apartment buildings. There were two stone lions by the front door, but once inside everything was chrome and glass, including the silent elevator that lifted them toward the top-floor penthouse.

Rand pushed the buzzer and waited. Presently a peephole opened in the massive oak door and a voice said, "Yes. State your business."

"I'm Rand, Department of Concealed Communications. Here's my identification. We'd like a word with you, sir—that is, if you're Geoffrey Crayon."

"I'm Crayon."

"Would you open the door, please?"

"What's it about?"

"It's a matter of national security."

"I'll be with you in a moment."

They stood waiting, and nothing happened. After a few moments Rand pushed the buzzer again. Still there was nothing. "Is there a back way out of here, Parkinson?"

"Just those stairs by the elevator, I'd imagine, sir. He didn't go down those."

"Think we can break down this door?"

"It's oak, sir."

Rand's heart was beating faster. "I'm afraid something's wrong."

"Maybe he's getting dressed."

The elevator doors slid open and a uniformed bobby emerged. "What's going on here?" he asked.

Rand flashed his identification. "We're trying to see Mr. Crayon, officer."

"That so? Well, you'd better come downstairs with me, then. Mr. Crayon just leaped to his death from the penthouse terrace."

It was after dark, but Rand was still in his little office overlooking the Thames, sitting with a cold cup of coffee and a copy of the late evening paper. The story had made a stop-press box on page one, beneath a headline which read: *Bridge Expert Dies Clutching Ten of Clubs.*

Rand tossed the paper aside as the C.I.A. man entered the office. "You've had a busy day," Greene said, sitting in the same chair he'd occupied before.

"Yes, I have. I was planning to see three people. The actor knew nothing, the spy escaped from custody, and the bridge expert committed suicide. I'd say I scored an absolute zero."

"No, no, not at all. At least you started things moving. What about Crayon? Any chance he was murdered?"

Rand shook his head. "None whatsoever. He thought we were coming to arrest him and he took the quickest way out. But what interests me is that on the way to his death he paused long enough to go through a deck of cards and select a ten of clubs to clutch in his hand."

"Interesting," Greene admitted. "Any idea why?"

"A message of some sort. But what? And to whom?"

The C.I.A. man shifted in his chair. "I have someone who may be able to help us there. We're holding a woman who was Alfred Penny's mistress. Want to see her?"

Rand hesitated, but only for a moment. He had the feeling he was already into this thing more deeply than he should be, more deeply than his official position called for. Still, something was afoot, and it might be crucial.

"All right," he agreed. "Let's go."

Her name was Marsha Mills, and she might have been a fashion model in her sleek miniskirt that seemed all wavy lines and garish colors; the sleeveless style of her blouse revealed a bruised right shoulder. Rand hadn't believed that girls really dressed like that, even in London. He'd preferred to view the entire thing as some wishful fantasy on the part of the fashion industry.

But here was one in the flesh, who sat with crossed knees, was nonchalantly smoking a cigarette, and telling them she was a schoolteacher.

"A progressive girls' school, you know."

"Of course," Rand said.

"And I can't understand why this man—" a motion toward Greene, "should hold me here. Am I under arrest or something?"

The place was a little office on Lower Thames Street, not far from the Billingsgate Market, in an area of the city hardly expected to harbor the London headquarters of the C.I.A. Greene was present, and so was another man who didn't speak. They were obviously waiting for Marsha Mills to start talking, and she knew it.

"You're not under arrest," Greene told her. "We just want you to tell us about Alfred Penny."

"I haven't seen him in months."

The C.I.A. man smiled. "Correction. You flew to Finland with him just last week. And when he was killed a few days ago you were registered at the New Helsinki Hotel as Mrs. Alfred Penny. Does that refresh your memory?"

She stubbed out her cigarette and avoided

their eyes. "What do you want to know? Can we work out a deal?"

"Maybe. Tell us why he went there," Greene prodded.

"I don't know."

"Was it a mission for SPAD?"

"Who?"

"I don't think you're really trying, Miss Mills. You can end up in a lot of trouble, you know."

She seemed to decide then. "All right, I'll give it to you straight, if you'll just let me go. A deal?"

"A deal."

"Alfred was one of the top men in SPAD—I don't have to tell you about them. He had access to more inside information about double agents than many of you people. A while back, he decided to strike out on his own. He had some big scheme that involved the flight to Finland and then contacting three men in London."

Rand was now interested. "Who were the three men?" he asked.

"I don't know their names. One was Russian, one British, and the third was a SPAD man. Alfred was going to offer them something, and make a huge amount of money."

"You mean he would sell something to the highest bidder?"

"I don't know the details."

"Did he tell anyone else he was going to Finland?"

"No. No one. I'm sure of that."

Greene took Rand aside and asked, "What do you think?"

"She was much too willing to talk. But you can't hold her. I suggest releasing her and watching where she goes. It just might prove interesting."

"All right," the American agreed.

They left the little office after Greene had given quick instructions to the other man. In the car back to Rand's building Greene said, "At least it tells us something, since we have those three names. We know Vandor is the Russian, and Crayon couldn't have been the British agent

or he wouldn't have killed himself when you came to question him."

Rand agreed. "So Crayon was the man from SPAD, and that leaves Whitehood as our own man. I'll check for confirmation."

"It doesn't explain why Crayon killed himself clutching a playing card."

"I have an idea about that," Rand said.

"A code of some sort?"

"More in the nature of a dying message, I think. An improvised code."

"Directed to SPAD?"

"Possibly," Rand said. But the whole thing bothered him. There were too many pieces in the puzzle—three separate espionage organizations, a murder, a suicide, an escape, a dying message. Too many pieces.

Back in his office, Rand tried unsuccessfully to reach Hastings in Internal Security. Finally he coded a quick message that read: *Urgent know if Whitehood is our own man.* He sealed it in an envelope and gave it to young Parkinson. "Find Hastings and get me a quick answer on this," he said.

"Where will you be, sir?"

"I'm going back to see Whitehood again. He's the only one of the three that's left."

This time the actor seemed more friendly and willing to talk. He sat in a relaxed posture against a vivid green sofa and said, "It's good to see you again, Mr. Rand. I am sorry if I appeared a bit brisk earlier. We were filming, you know. I'm always more relaxed here in my apartment."

Rand gave him a smile, trying to match the open friendliness. "It's about Alfred Penny again, I'm afraid. Since I saw you last, there've been some rather startling developments. A Russian spy named Vandor has escaped from custody; and a man named Crayon has committed suicide."

"Should I know either of them?" he asked blandly.

"Their names were with yours on Alfred Penny's body."

"Oh?"

Rand decided to wait no longer. "Look, Whitehood, I have reason to believe we're on the same side in this thing. I've asked for official confirmation that you're one of us. So let's not beat about the bush."

"What do you want to know?"

"That's more like it." Rand paused, then hurried on, feeling more sure of himself. "The man named Crayon died clutching a playing card—ten of clubs. Mean anything to you?"

The actor shrugged. "In some fortunetelling systems it means gambling. Perhaps this Crayon frequented the gambling clubs around London."

"A possibility," Rand agreed. And one he hadn't thought of. "But I look at it this way. Crayon wasn't just anybody—he was a well-known contract bridge expert. In his final moment of life, if he had to get a message to his people—to SPAD, for instance—he would realize that a playing card clutched in his hand would certainly make news. As it happened, the papers headlined the fact. Somewhere, someone noted that fact and read the message."

The telephone buzzed and Whitehood answered it. He listened for a moment, then passed it to Rand. "It's for you."

"Rand here."

"This is Parkinson, sir. I have the reply from Hastings."

"Good. You can give it to me clear, but no names."

"Hastings says he's not one of us, sir."

"What?" Rand wasn't sure he'd heard correctly.

"He's not ours, sir. They think he's SPAD."

Rand hung up the phone and turned to face the pistol held firmly in Whitehood's hand.

"You want to hear about it?" Whitehood asked. "All right, I'll tell you the whole thing." He smiled slightly. "Before I kill you, that is."

"You're SPAD, of course."

"Of course. I was Penny's partner until he got this crazy scheme and struck out on his own."

"Then Crayon was the Russian. And Vandor—"

"Vandor is a British double agent. He was allowed to escape. Penny and I uncovered the fact quite by accident. It was Vandor himself who tipped off the British to raid his own office and find the information on the American space satellites. And that of course is the key to the whole filthy business."

"How?"

"The Americans have launched several satellites from Vandenberg Air Force Base in California. These satellites, in the Discoverer, Samos, Midas, and Vela Hotel series, are designed to detect nuclear explosions and rocket launches. The satellite launches are usually reported without detail, in the public press, but the exact mission of each satellite is highly classified."

"So?"

"Last year the Americans launched a new satellite with a superior television eye. It can detect anything on the ground even through clouds. The Russians have obtained the orbits of all current satellites, but they do not know which one carries the powerful new lens."

"What good would it do if they did know?"

"They could move or hide the secret equipment when they know that particular satellite is passing overhead. Because of the rotation of the earth, it passes over the same spot only twice a month."

"So they needed to know—what?"

"A date, only a date. The date the satellite was launched by the Americans. When they know which one it is, they will then know its orbits."

"The information was sent to Vandor?"

"Yes, but of course he was a British agent. Unfortunately, it was also sent to Geoffrey Crayon of SPAD—I believe it was passed to him during a bridge game."

"So the ten of clubs must stand for a date. The tenth of some month?"

"Whatever it is, the Russians have it by now."

"*If* they correctly read the message of the card."

Whitehood steadied the pistol in his hand.

"I'll let the Russians worry about that. I've talked too much already."

"Why do you think you have to kill me?"

"Because I'm taking over where Penny left off. I might even take over with his mistress, too. I can't have you or the C.I.A. holding me in London while you try to solve this satellite thing."

"Did you kill Penny?"

"Of course not. But since he's dead, I can't let the chance to get all that money go to waste. Goodbye, Mr. Rand." And his finger tightened on the trigger.

"Wait! At least you can tell me what Penny was up to out there. Why was he tapping the hot line?"

Whitehood smiled. "You really don't know, do you?"

"No."

"He wasn't going to intercept messages. He was going to send his own. He was going to use the hot line as an exclusive espionage reporting service directly to the heads of state in Washington or Moscow—whichever would pay more. With his contacts from SPAD he would have a foolproof system—no middlemen, no chance of the messages going astray."

"That's fantastic! No government would agree to it."

"More fantastic than satellites in the sky? More fantastic than double agents like Vandor? I think not, Mr. Rand. In fact, I am going to try it myself."

It was then that young Parkinson came crashing through the window behind Whitehood. He landed on the spy's back and toppled him to the floor just as the gun exploded. Then, gasping, bleeding from glass cuts, he looked up and said, "I thought you might need some help, sir."

Just before dawn the next morning Rand found himself shaking hands with Leo Vandor at a Thames River dock. The C.I.A. man was there, too, and Hastings from Internal Security. Vandor was a big man who looked exactly like his pictures.

"Pleased to meet you, Mr. Rand," he said. "Even the Russians speak highly of you."

"I'm the one who should be pleased," Rand said. "You're slipping back behind the Curtain?"

"Of course. That is my job."

"If SPAD knows you're on our side, the Russians might know it too."

The tall man only shrugged. "That is the chance I have always taken."

Greene shifted his feet. "We must know if the Russians correctly read the message of the playing card. If so, the satellite with the special lens is useless."

Vandor smiled slightly. "I understand Mr. Rand has deduced the card's meaning."

Rand nodded absently. He'd explained it all a half dozen times already that night. "The date of a satellite launching last year from Vandenberg Air Force Base. Well, it's doubtful if they ever launch more than one satellite a week, so all Crayon really had to convey was the week that particular satellite went up. Now, there's one thing a deck of cards has in common with the calendar year—52 cards, 52 weeks. And in contract bridge the 52 cards have a specific rank—four suits, the highest spades, the lowest clubs. In order of rank you start with the ace of spades and go down to the two; then the same with hearts, diamonds, and clubs in that order. The ace of spades, therefore, is card number one in the deck, making the two of clubs card number 52."

"Making the ten of clubs card number 44," Greene said.

Rand nodded. "Last year, the 44th week was the week of October 30th. And that's when the special satellite went up."

"Do you think the Russians got the message?"

"If I figured it out, I'm sure they did too," Rand said.

Vandor shook hands once more. "My launch is waiting. I must say goodbye."

Rand watched him go, thinking that he might be seeing the last of a very brave man. Then, as he went back through the dawn mist to the warmth of the waiting car, he heard Greene say,

"We still don't know who killed Alfred Penny at the beginning of this whole affair. Was it SPAD or the Russians or who?"

Rand settled back in the seat as the car started. "I doubt if any of them would have bothered. Why kill a man bent on such a foolish mission? Besides, no one knew he was there."

"But someone did kill him!" Greene insisted.

"I think it's out of our territory," Rand said. "I think the motive was private rather than political. It's no sort of evidence, but you might have noticed that Marsha Mills had a bruised right shoulder—the kind of bruise the recoil of a high-powered rifle might leave. She was in Helsinki with him, and it wouldn't be the first time a woman killed her lover."

Greene's mouth dropped open. "I never thought of that."

Rand smiled and closed his eyes. It had been a long day, and a long night.

ROBERT ROGERS

LITTLE COULD BE DISCOVERED about Robert Rogers. In addition to "Affair in Warsaw," the only published work to come from his pen appears to be a nonfiction article, "The Undeclared War in Guatemala," written in collaboration with Ted Yates, for the June 18, 1966, issue of *The Saturday Evening Post*.

It is unfortunate that Rogers either stopped writing or stopped being published as his lone work of fiction is a first-rate Cold War thriller with well-drawn characters in the American marine and the lovely Polish girl with whom he falls in love.

"Affair in Warsaw" was originally published in the May 1962 issue of *Argosy*.

AFFAIR IN WARSAW

ROBERT ROGERS

LIKE ALL THE ONCE-GAY capitals of eastern Europe, Warsaw after midnight becomes a ghost town, where the silence is broken only by the frigid winds whistling down from the Baltic and the muffled tread of police patrols circulating endlessly through the snow-blanketed streets.

Standing in the darkness of the tiny, one-room apartment, Ray Claffey drew deeply on his cigarette and shivered. He was clad only in a pajama shirt, a far cry from the knife-creased uniform he wore during the day as captain in command at the Marine Guard detachment at the United States Embassy. Wiping the condensation from the window pane, he peered at the street below. The wind dragged a tattered newspaper through the patch of snow illuminated by the single street lamp. Otherwise, the street was empty.

Claffey smiled grimly, thinking of the frustration his Polish "tail" would be feeling at being shaken again. It was common knowledge that every member of the embassy staff was shadowed by a Polish agent, or tail. When Claffey had first arrived in Warsaw three years before, he had found the whole business highly entertaining. He enjoyed leading the agents on long, aimless walks through rain and sleet and blizzards. Then, as he grew familiar with the city, it became a contest. In civilian clothes, he would duck through department stores, in and out of taxis, timing himself as to how long it took to lose his pursuers. Despite his six-foot frame, Claffey was agile and smart. Inside a year, he could shake all but the most expert shadowers within a quarter of an hour. It was an amusing game he played to break the monotony of life within a hostile state. At least, it had been nothing but a game until he met Katrina. Since then, it had become a deadly serious business.

Crushing out his cigarette, he approached the bed where the girl lay sleeping, her delicate features faintly visible in the moonglow. Tenderly tucking the blankets about her tousled blond head, he seated himself wearily on the bed. His thoughts were cheerless as the winter night outside. By this time tomorrow, he would be in Paris. And without Katrina.

Don't get involved with a Polish female! It can lead to nothing but grief. This warning was constantly repeated to all members of the Embassy staff. It was drummed into them by lectures, pamphlets, meetings. But security lectures are one thing; a man's heart quite another. And from the day Katrina had walked into the embassy and hesitantly inquired about a job in the cafeteria, Claffey's heart had been involved. It was months before she agreed to go with him on a date to the opera. It was still more months before she shyly led him up the steep and narrow stairs to her room.

Now, a year had passed since that magic night and Claffey was hopelessly in love. At thirty, he was old enough to know that something like Katrina happened but once in a lifetime, and then only to the most fortunate of men. Katrina, with her innocent, love-filled eyes, her shy, slow-bursting smile that made his heart somersault, her slender, willing body, just ripening into womanhood. The thought of life without her was bone-chilling, like thinking of himself as dead and buried. Whatever happened, he could not lose her.

With a sigh, he lit another cigarette. In the flare of the match, he noticed the girl was awake, watching him with tender concern.

"Raymond," she said softly. "You must get back to the embassy before dawn. You should try to sleep."

"I'm thinking, sweetheart."

Her fingers traced the outline of his firm chin, then moved to his crew-cut black hair. "You must not worry so, darling," she whispered. "I promise you I will be careful."

Reaching up, he clasped her small, warm hand. His own hands were large, square, and capable. Capable enough to have won him the Navy Cross on the road from Chosin Reservoir.

"Katrina," he said, "I just can't go off and leave you here. There must be some way we can be married, some way you can leave Poland with me."

"Raymond, I have explained it so many times to you. I am an orphan, a ward of the State. Until I am twenty-one, I must have the State's permission to marry. You know they would not permit me to marry an American officer. Not these days."

"We could at least try," he said.

"That would make it worse. Then they would have me watched," she said. "No, it is better if you go first and wait for me in France. I will escape and join you there within thirty days."

"It's too risky, Katrina. Especially since they've put up that miserable wall in Berlin," he told her.

"There are other routes to the West," she interrupted softly. "Many Baltic fishing boats are in the black-market trade. For a price, they will carry a passenger to Denmark. With the money you have given me, it will be quite simple."

"It's still too dangerous."

Suddenly the girl sat bolt-upright. "Did you hear a noise?" she whispered.

Claffey listened. But there was only the sound of the wind clawing its way into the cracks and crannies of the poorly constructed building. He shook his head.

The girl relaxed. "Probably Madame Hruska's cat," she said.

Claffey nodded. Madame Hruska occupied the only other room on the top floor. She was a prostitute, blond and blowzy and past her prime. But she was a cheerful soul, and always had a friendly smile for Claffey when they chanced to meet upon the stairs. Of course, she had no idea that Katrina's boy friend was an American Marine.

"Come to bed now, darling," Katrina pleaded. "You will catch cold."

Before Claffey could reply, something heavy crashed against the door. With the sound of splintering wood, it burst open. Claffey sprang to his feet just as a flash bulb went off in a blinding burst of brilliance. Circles of colored lights danced before his eyes as he stumbled forward. Shadowy figures seemed to be pouring into the room. Male voices jabbered in Polish. Katrina screamed and another flash bulb exploded.

Lashing out blindly, Claffey's fist connected with flesh and bone. He was poised to strike again when a blunt object thudded into the back of his skull. The voices seemed to grow distant. He felt his knees buckling, then nothing.

———

He awoke, face down on the cold floor boards. Katrina, clad in her bathrobe, was hovering over him. Tears welled from her anxious eyes.

"I'm okay, sweetheart," he mumbled, climbing slowly to his feet.

A diminutive man in a brown, double-breasted suit was lounging against the dressing table. He had thin, colorless hair, a sharp, ferretlike face, and the icy eyes of a born assassin. An evil-smelling cigarette dangled from his lips.

"Who the hell are you?" Claffey said, starting forward.

"Vopek!" the little man barked.

Another man stepped into view through the open door. He was blond, half a head taller than Claffey, and had shoulders like a bull. His broad, pugilist's face was split by a grin which revealed a solid row of gold teeth. He looked impregnable as a tank, even without the big Czech pistol he held pointed at Claffey's midsection.

"Please do not tempt Vopek into shooting you, Captain Claffey," the little man said in English.

"What's this all about?" Claffey demanded angrily.

"Permit me to introduce myself," the little man said, with a mocking bow. "I am Major Satenz of the State Security Police. Surely you did not think you could keep this little love nest a secret from us. We have been watching you and the young lady for some weeks now."

"You took pictures?" Claffey ventured.

Major Satenz smiled a thin, unpleasant smile, like a razor cut before the blood comes. "Of course. They are being developed at this very moment. They should be charming photographs. A lovely girl in bed, and a muscular Marine in his pajama shirt. By the way, Captain Claffey, perhaps you would like to put on your trousers?" Satenz asked.

Flushing angrily, Claffey shrugged into his bathrobe. Katrina was slumped in a chair, staring sadly at her hands. He patted her shoulder reassuringly, then turned to Satenz. "I hate to spoil your fun, Mac," he said. "But if you think you're going to blackmail me, you've wasted your film.

I'm not married, and the Marine Corps already knows I sleep with girls. Most Marines do."

"As a servant of the People's Republic, I do not deal in blackmail," Satenz snapped. "The photographs will be used as evidence. I am arresting this girl for violation of the people's laws against prostitution."

"Watch your mouth, Mac," Claffey said. "Katrina and I are going to be married."

"That is not very likely," said Satenz. Turning, he surveyed the poorly furnished but immaculate room. His gaze lingered on a pinch-bottle of Scotch on the dresser, then moved to a nearby carton of American cigarettes: "Possession of black-market goods is also a serious offense."

"That stuff belongs to me," Claffey explained.

"Silence!" Satenz commanded. "It is quite obvious this girl is sleeping with you and receiving payment in black-market merchandise. She is guilty of crimes against the People's Republic." Uncapping the whiskey, he poured a glass half full and took a healthy swallow. "Ah," he said, smacking his lips. "I must admit you are a man of excellent tastes, Captain Claffey. In women as well as whiskey. The girl is pretty. Therefore, since her morals are already corrupted, she will be sentenced to a military brothel, where her many charms will be made available to our gallant soldiers."

Claffey felt a cold, helpless sensation spreading through his stomach. He glanced questioningly at Katrina.

Her blue eyes wide with horror, she was staring at Satenz like a bird mesmerized by a serpent. Slowly she nodded. "He speaks the truth, Raymond. In Poland these days, there is no justice, only the Security Police."

"But this is supposed to be a civilized country," Claffey exploded. Fists clenched, he took a step toward Satenz, then grimaced in pain as a pistol barrel was jabbed in his kidney. Whirling, he glared at Vopek. "Some day, I'm going to try you on for size, Mac."

"Captain Claffey." Satenz interrupted. "I suggest you return to your embassy immediately."

"Leave?"

"That is correct," Satenz said. "You are protected by diplomatic immunity, and I have no intention of detaining you. I trust, when you are in America, you will meditate occasionally on the misfortune you have brought to this poor Polish girl. But she must pay for her crimes. Unless, of course . . ."

"Unless what?" Claffey said warily.

With a faint smile, Satenz selected a pack of American cigarettes from the dresser, lit one, and slid the rest into his pocket. "As you know, Captain Claffey," he said, "the People's Republic is ever anxious to lessen tensions between our countries. We desire the friendship of Americans, including yourself. Also we would prefer to see our beautiful Katrina happy. Though she has violated the law, she is young, and the People's Republic could find it in its heart to let her become your bride. Provided you could offer some small proof of your friendship toward us."

"What sort of proof?" Claffey said.

Satenz shrugged. "In your position at the embassy, you have access to many things which would be of interest to us. Documents, codes, anything which would suitably demonstrate your gratitude to the People's Republic."

Treason, Claffey thought. He was being asked to commit treason. His lips moved angrily, but somehow he could not speak the refusal that would condemn Katrina to a horrible life.

"Don't listen to him, Raymond," Katrina said. "I would rather let them take me than have you ruin your life."

Claffey's shoulders slumped wearily. He felt a million years old. His duty to his country was clear, but what of his duty to Katrina? He needed time to think.

"I'm leaving on the midnight flight to Paris," he said. "Can you have her exit visa ready by then?"

"But of course," Satenz said, smiling. "Provided you cooperate with us."

Claffey took a deep breath. "What do you want me to do?"

An hour later, Claffey trudged slowly through the silent streets, his shoes throwing up tiny spurts of powdered snow. The sun, just rising, created odd, angular shadows in a group of ruined buildings left from World War II. Beyond the ruins, he could see the *Palac Kultury i Nauki*, the Palace of Culture and Science, Warsaw's only skyscraper. Previously, it had reminded him of a poor imitation of the Woolworth Building. But now it seemed to loom against the sky like a gigantic tombstone.

In his pocket was an East German camera resembling a cigarette case. It was an ingenious device for use indoors without special lighting. Satenz had instructed him in its operation. Claffey was to photograph documents at the embassy and return the camera to the Polish major that evening. In exchange, he would receive Katrina's exit visa.

Claffey paused to light a cigarette. The thought of abandoning Katrina was like a bayonet thrust. But how could he betray the country he loved and was sworn to defend? Even if he photographed only valueless, outdated documents, it would merely be the beginning. Using his first act as a lever, the Poles would follow him forever, forcing him deeper and deeper into the quicksand of treason. And there was no one to turn to for help.

He had to make up his mind. He had to choose between his country and the girl he loved. Flinging the cigarette in the gutter, he set off for the embassy. . . .

At eight o'clock that evening, Claffey approached the apartment building. The camera in his pocket was still unused. He could not stomach treason, not even to save Katrina. Also in his pocket were two tickets for the midnight flight to Paris. He had resolved somehow to get Katrina aboard that plane.

The street was empty except for a shiny black Zis sedan. Obviously, Major Satenz had already arrived. There was a faint odor of gas in the corridor, which grew stronger as Claffey mounted the steps two at a time. Through the open door, he saw Katrina. She was sprawled on the bed, clad in the pale blue dress he had given her for her twentieth birthday. Her eyes were closed. Bending over her, his hand on her breast, was Vopek.

In two strides, Claffey was beside the bed. His fist crashed into Vopek's jaw. The big Pole went tottering backwards across the room and came to rest against the wall, a confused look on his face.

Kneeling beside the girl, Claffey touched her wrist. Her pulse seemed steady. Her face was pale but peaceful: there was a tiny smile on her lips. Then he was brought to his feet by the click of a safety catch being thumbed behind him.

In Major Satenz's hand was a small Degtyareau automatic. "Calm yourself, Captain Claffey," he said with an amused expression. "The girl will be all right. She tried to commit suicide. Fortunately, the woman next door smelled the gas."

Claffey barely heard the rest. He was staring at the unconscious girl, stunned by the realization she had tried to destroy herself to save him. A growl from Vopek interrupted his thoughts. The giant Pole was coming out of it, and there was murder in his eye.

"I believe you owe Vopek an apology, Captain Claffey," Satenz said. "He was simply feeling the girl's heartbeat."

"Tell him to try her wrist next time."

Satenz's eyes narrowed. "An apology, Captain. Quickly!"

"All right," Claffey said. "Tell the ape I'm sorry. Also tell him the next time he lays his filthy paws on her, I'm going to break them off and feed them to him, finger by finger."

"Do not try my patience too far, Captain," Satenz warned him. "You have the pictures?"

"The camera is in my pocket. Where's the visa?"

"Here," said Satenz, producing a single sheet of paper with an official seal. "Stay where you are," he barked, as Claffey strolled toward the dresser.

Ignoring him, Claffey hefted the whiskey bottle. "Do you mind if I have a sip of my own whiskey."

Katrina stirred and sat up. Satenz's gaze flickered toward the bed. In that instant, Claffey flung the heavy pinch-bottle. Satenz, struck full in the forehead, collapsed like a sack of dirty laundry.

Vopek was tugging the big pistol from his coat when Claffey's shoulder drove into his midsection. The pistol skidded across the floor. Vopek lunged forward, his massive hands closing around Claffey's throat. Desperately, the American struggled to break the grip, but Vopek's wrists were like iron bars. Claffey's eyeballs bulged as the sausagelike fingers dug into his windpipe. With all his remaining strength, he buried his right fist, wrist deep, in his opponent's solar plexis. Vopek grunted and stepped back, giving Claffey space to bring up the heel of his hand in a smashing uppercut. The Pole's head struck the floor and he lay still.

Gasping for breath, Claffey snatched the visa from Satenz's limp hand. Unloading the big pistol, he shoved it under the mattress. The Degtyareau he slid into his pocket. He turned to Katrina, who had gotten to her feet.

"Are you all right, sweetheart?"

"Yes, Raymond, but what—"

"There's no time to talk. I need some rope to tie these characters."

"That would be a fatal mistake, Captain Claffey," Satenz said, painfully hoisting himself erect. There was an angry red knot on his forehead, but his eyes gleamed with triumph. "I anticipated you might attempt to take the girl by force. My men at the airport have instructions to shoot her, unless *I* escort her to the plane."

Claffey's jaw tightened. "Then you're going to escort her."

"Perhaps," said Satenz, smiling. "But what good will that do you? It will be a simple matter to have the plane turned back by fighters before it reaches the frontier. Your situation is hopeless, Claffey. Despite all your exertions, the girl will remain in Poland. Now give me that pistol and we will discuss things. It is still possible we will permit her to leave sometime in the future, *if* you obey my instructions. You can be useful to us in America, Claffey. You have the camera . . ."

"You can take your camera and shove it," Claffey said, but his voice was lifeless. He had failed Katrina.

Just then, a frizzled blond head appeared in the doorway. Claffey recognized the plump, over-rouged face of Madame Hruska, the prostitute from next door. Her mascaraed eyes blinked at the sight of Vopek on the floor. "Oh, please to excuse me," she mumbled in Polish. "I heard a noise and thought perhaps little Katrina—" She started to back out.

An idea glimmered in Claffey's mind. "Please do come in, madame," he said in careful Polish. "You must excuse the noise. Just a small quarrel between my friends here. One of them has gone to sleep." He pointed to the whiskey bottle and winked.

Chuckling understandingly, Madame accepted a cigarette. Claffey turned to Katrina. "Wait outside in the hall, sweetheart." The girl gave him a puzzled look but obeyed, closing the door behind her.

"Now, Madame Hruska," Claffey said politely. "I would like to engage your professional services. Please take off your clothes."

"You mean here, now?" the woman stammered, then glanced at the thick wad of bills Claffey thrust in her hand. Smiling, she commenced wiggling out of her dress.

Slipping his hand into the pocket containing the pistol, Claffey approached Satenz. "Unless you do exactly as I say, I'm going to kill you," he said softly.

"You're bluffing," Satenz replied. "You haven't got a chance."

"Then I have nothing to lose by killing you," Claffey said grimly. "Strip down to your underpants."

"Are you insane?" Satenz said. He looked at the menacing bulge in Claffey's pocket. Swallowing nervously, he slowly began unbuttoning his shirt.

Ten minutes later, Claffey removed the expended film from the cigarette-case camera. He scribbled a hasty note, while Madame Hruska, who was already dressed, watched in complete bewilderment. "Madame, please take this film to the American Embassy," he said. "Give it to Sergeant Donnelly of the Marine Guard. When he reads the note, he will give you three thousand *zlotys*."

"Three thousand!" she exclaimed. "But you have already paid me too much. And just for posing for a few silly pictures with your funny little friend here."

"You have been very kind to help us in our little joke," Claffey said. "Now please hurry, madame. Our joke will be spoiled unless you reach the embassy within fifteen minutes."

"I will be there in five minutes," she said, and departed quickly, her fleshly hips swaying happily.

Satenz's fingers were trembling with rage as he knotted his tie. "What is the meaning of this?" he demanded.

"Simply returning a favor," Claffey said. "You took my picture, I took yours."

"The girl will suffer for your insolence, swine. Nothing can save her now."

"You will save her, Major," Claffey said. "Because unless Katrina and I reach Paris tonight, my friend, Sergeant Donnelly, will turn those negatives over to the Central Intelligence Agency. CIA will know what to do with photographs of the fearsome Major Satenz in his drawers, with a fat whore on his lap and black-market whiskey and cigarettes beside him. They'll spread them all over Europe, along with a story of how you were outwitted by a twenty-year-old girl. The Polish Security Police will become a laughing stock. Your superiors might not like that, Major Satenz. They might even make you Prisoner Satenz. They might even liquidate you."

A twitch appeared in Satenz's left cheek.

"Calm yourself, Major," Claffey said.

"It doesn't have to be that bad. Once Katrina is safe in Paris, I promise you I'll burn the negatives. No one but you and I will ever know what a chump you are."

"What proof have I you won't use the pictures anyway?"

"Only my word of honor. That's more than you deserve."

Suddenly Vopek came awake. Scrambling to his feet, he looked around blankly.

"Have a good sleep, comrade?" Claffey said. "You're just in time to join us for a nice ride to the airport. Isn't that right, Major Satenz?"

After a moment's hesitation, Satenz nodded glumly. "Yes, that is right," he said. "Vopek, go down and start the car. We are driving Captain Claffey and his fiancée to the airport."

Dawn was breaking as the silver Constellation swung low over the suburbs of Paris on its way to Orly field.

Katrina turned from the window. "Raymond, it is like a beautiful dream. Can we really be married this morning?"

He squeezed her hand. "It will take a few days to push the paper work through, sweetheart."

Eyes sparkling, she leaned toward him. "But in the meantime, we might begin the honeymoon, yes?"

Her lips were warm, and very willing.

THE END OF THE STRING

CHARLES McCARRY

IT BECAME SO COMMON in reviews of his books to call Charles McCarry (1930–2019) "the American John le Carré" that it became a standing joke between him and his publisher. When he was called to be told of a major review, he would often ask, "Am I the American le Carré again?" and, mostly, he was. Arguably the greatest novelist of espionage fiction that America ever produced, McCarry disliked being identified as an author limited by a single genre. Instead, he declared that, like other serious novelists, he wrote about such universal themes as "love, death, betrayal and the American dream."

Most of his novels (he wrote only three short stories) are international espionage tales, mainly featuring his series character Paul Christopher, but he also wrote political novels, such as *Lucky Bastard* (1998), which humorously depicts an amoral politician who, though married, has a relentless penchant for seduction. Largely reviewed as a caricatured portrayal of Bill Clinton, it had, in fact, taken John F. Kennedy as its model (as the author discussed with me on several occasions). McCarry's science fiction novel, *Ark* (2011), is almost absurdly prescient in its descriptions and warnings of climate change and other catastrophes, all of which are based on sound science. He had previously anticipated suicide bombers in *The Better Angels*, published in 1979. Four years later, *The New York Times* reported on the apparent first instance of such terrorist acts occurring in real life. The same novel described terrorists on a suicide mission using an airplane filled with innocent passengers, first realized on September 11, 2001.

In addition to his (justly) venerated fiction, McCarry also was a highly successful writer of nonfiction, notably the ghostwritten *For the Record: From Wall Street to Washington* (1988) by Donald Regan; *Inner Circles: How America Changed the World: A Memoir* (1992) by Alexander Haig; and *Caveat: Realism, Reagan, and Foreign Policy* (1984), also by Haig. When he wrote his biography of Ralph Nader, McCarry averred that learning about his subject was one of the great disappointments of his life.

The events in the present story take place in Africa, one of the places to which McCarry was assigned during his years as a deep cover agent in the CIA; that assignment undoubtedly informed at least some elements of the tale.

"The End of the String" was first published in *Agents of Treachery*, edited by Otto Penzler (New York, Vintage, 2010).

THE END OF THE STRING

CHARLES McCARRY

I FIRST NOTICED the man I will call Benjamin in the bar of the Independence Hotel in Ndala. He sat alone, drinking orange soda, no ice. He was tall and burly—knotty biceps, huge hands. His short-sleeved white shirt and khaki pants were as crisp as a uniform. Instead of the usual third-world Omega or Rolex, he wore a cheap plastic Japanese watch on his right wrist. No rings, no gold, no sunglasses. I did not recognize the tribal tattoos on his cheeks. He spoke to no one, looked at no one. He himself might as well have been invisible as far as the rest of the customers were concerned. No one spoke to him or offered to buy him a drink or asked him any questions. He seemed poised to leap off his bar stool and kill something at a moment's notice.

He was the only person in the bar I did not already know by sight. In those days, more than half a century ago, when an American was a rare bird along the Guinea coast, you got to know everyone in your hotel bar pretty quickly. I was standing at the bar, my back to Benjamin, but I could see him in the mirror. He was watching me. I surmised that he was gathering information rather than sizing me up for robbery or some other dark purpose.

I called the barman, put a ten-shilling note on the bar, and asked him to mix a pink gin using actual Beefeater's. He laughed merrily as he pocketed the money and swirled the bitters in the glass. When I looked in the mirror again, Benjamin was gone. How a man his size could get up and leave without being reflected in the mirror I do not know, but somehow he managed it. I did not dismiss him from my thoughts, he was too memorable for that, but I didn't dwell on the episode either. I could not, however, shake the feeling that I had been subjected to a professional appraisal. For an operative under deep cover, that is always an uncomfortable experience, especially if you have the feeling, as I did, that the man who is giving you the once-over is a professional who is doing a job that he has done many times before.

I had come to Ndala to debrief an agent. He missed the first two meetings, but there is nothing unusual about that even if you're not in Africa. On the third try, he showed up close to the appointed hour at the appointed place: two A.M. on an unpaved street in which hundreds of people, all of them sound asleep, lay side by side. It was a moonless night. No electric light, no lantern or candle, even, burned for at least a mile in any direction. I could not see the sleepers, but

776

I could feel their presence and hear them exhale and inhale. The agent, a member of parliament, had nothing to tell me apart from his usual bagful of pointless gossip. I gave him his money anyway, and he signed for it with a thumbprint by the light of my pocket torch. As I walked away I heard him ripping open his envelope and counting banknotes in the dark.

I had not walked far when a car turned into the street with headlights blazing. The sleepers awoke and popped up one after another as if choreographed by Busby Berkeley. The member of parliament had vanished. No doubt he had simply lain down with the others, and two of the wide-open eyes and one of the broad smiles I saw dwindling into the darkness belonged to him.

The car stopped. I kept walking toward it, and when I was beside it, the driver, who was a police constable, leaped out and shone a flashlight in my face. He said, "Please get in, master." The British had been gone from this country for only a short time, and the locals still addressed white men by the title preferred by their former colonial rulers. The old etiquette survived in English, French, and Portuguese in most of the thirty-two African countries that had become independent in a period of two and a half years—less time than it took Stanley to find Livingstone.

I said, "Get in? What for?"

"This is not a good place for you, master."

My rescuer was impeccably turned out in British tropical kit—blue service cap, bush jacket with sergeant's chevrons on the shoulder boards, voluminous khaki shorts, blue woolen knee socks, gleaming oxfords, black Sam Browne belt. A truncheon dangling from the belt seemed to be his only weapon. I climbed into the backseat. The sergeant got behind the wheel, and using the rearview mirror rather than looking behind him, backed out of the street at breathtaking speed. I kept my eyes on the windshield, expecting him to plow into the sleepers at any moment. They themselves seemed unconcerned, and as the headlights swept over them they lay down one after the other with the same precise timing as before.

The sergeant drove at high speed through backstreets, nearly every one of them another open-air dormitory. Our destination, as it turned out, was the Equator Club, Ndala's most popular nightclub. This structure was really just a fenced-in space, open to the sky. Inside, a band played highlife, a kind of hypercalypso, so loudly that you had the illusion that the music was visible as it rose into the pitch-black night.

The music was even louder. The air was the temperature of blood. The odors of sweat and spilled beer were sharp and strong. Guttering candles created a substitute for light. Silhouettes danced on the hard dirt floor, cigarettes glowed. The sensation was something like being digested by a tyrannosaurus rex.

Benjamin, alone again, sat at another small table. He was drinking orange soda again. He, too, wore a uniform. Though made of finer cloth, it was a duplicate of the sergeant's, except that he was equipped with a swagger stick instead of a baton and the badge on his shoulder boards displayed the wreath, crossed batons, and crown of a chief constable. Benjamin, it appeared, was the head of the national police. He made a gesture of welcome. I sat down. A waiter placed a pink gin with ice before me with such efficiency, and was so neatly dressed, that I supposed he was a constable, too, but undercover. I lifted my glass to Benjamin and sipped my drink.

Benjamin said, "Are you a naval person?"

I said, "No. Why do you ask?"

"Pink gin is the traditional drink of the royal navy."

"Not rum?"

"Rum is for the crew."

I had difficulty suppressing a grin. Our exchange of words sounded so much like a recognition code used by spies that I wondered if that's what it really was. Had Benjamin got the wrong American? He did not seem the type to make such an elementary mistake. He looked down on me—even while seated he was at least a head taller than I was—and said, "Welcome to my country, Mr. Brown. I have been waiting for you to come here again, because I believe that you and I can work together."

Brown was one of the names I had used on previous visits to Ndala, but it was not the name on the passport I was using this time. He paused, studying my face. His own face showed no flicker of expression.

Without further preamble, he said, "I am contemplating a project that requires the support of the United States of America."

The dramaturgy of the situation suggested that my next line should be, "Really?" or "How so?" However, I said nothing, hoping that Benjamin would fill the silence.

Frankly, I was puzzled. Was he volunteering for something? Most agents recruited by any intelligence service are volunteers, and the average intelligence officer is a sort of latter-day Marcel Proust. He lies abed in a cork-lined room, hoping to profit by secrets that other people slip under the door. People simply walk in and for whatever motive, usually petty resentment over having been passed over for promotion or the like, offer to betray their country. It was also possible, unusual though that might be, that Benjamin hoped to recruit me.

His eyes bored into mine. His back was to the wall, mine to the dance floor. Behind me I could feel but not see the dancers, moving as a single organism. Through the soles of my shoes I felt vibration set up by scores of feet stamping in unison on the dirt floor. In the yellow candlelight I could see a little more expression on Benjamin's face.

Many seconds passed before he broke the silence. "What is your opinion of the president of this country?"

Once again I took my time answering. The problem with this conversation was that I never knew what to say next.

Finally I said, "President Ga and I have never met."

"Nevertheless you must have an opinion."

And of course I did. So did everyone who read the newspapers. Akokwu Ga, president for life of Ndala, was a man of strong appetites.

He enjoyed his position and its many opportunities for pleasure with an enthusiasm that was remarkable even by the usual standards for dictators. He possessed a solid gold bathtub and bedstead. He had a private zoo. It was said that he was sometimes seized by the impulse to feed his enemies to the lions. He had deposited tens of millions of dollars from his country's treasury into personal numbered accounts in Swiss banks.

Dinner for him and his guests was flown in every day from one of the restaurants in Paris that had a three-star rating in the Guide Michelin. A French chef heated the food and arranged it on plates, an English butler served it. Both were assumed to be secret agents employed by their respective governments. Ga maintained love nests in every quarter of the capital city. Women from all over the world occupied these cribs. The ones he liked best were given luxurious houses formerly occupied by Europeans and provided with German cars, French champagne, and "house-boys" (actually undercover policemen) who kept an eye on them.

"Speak," Benjamin said.

I said, "Frankly, chief constable, this conversation is making me nervous."

"Why? No one can bug us. Listen to the noise."

How right he was. We were shouting at each other in order to be heard above the din. The music made my ears ring, and no microphone then known could penetrate it. I said, "Nevertheless, I would prefer to discuss this in private. Just the two of us."

"And how then will you know that I am not bugging you? Or that someone else is not bugging both of us?"

"I wouldn't. But would it matter?"

Benjamin examined me for a long moment. Then he said, "No, it wouldn't. Because I am the one who will be saying dangerous things."

He got to his feet, uncoiled would be the better word. Instantly the sergeant who had brought me here and three other constables in plain clothes materialized from the shadows.

Everyone else was dancing, eyes closed, seemingly in another world and time. Benjamin put on his cap and picked up his swagger stick.

He said, "Tomorrow I will come for you."

With that, he disappeared, leaving me without a ride. Eventually I found a taxi back to the hotel. The driver was so wide awake, his taxi so tidy, that I assumed that he, too, must be one of Benjamin's men.

The porter who brought me my mug of tea at six A.M. also brought me a note from Benjamin. The penmanship was beautiful. The note was short and to the point: "Nine o'clock, by the front entrance."

Through the glass in the hotel's front door, the street outside was a scene from Goya, lepers and amputees and victims of polio or smallpox or psoriasis, and among the child beggars a few examples of hamstringing by parents who needed the income that a crippled child could bring home. A tourist arrived in a taxi and scattered a handful of change in order to disperse the beggars while he made his dash for the entrance. Clearly he was a greenhorn. The seasoned traveler in Africa distributed money only after checkout. To do so on arrival guaranteed your being fondled by lepers every time you came in or went out. One particularly handsome, smiling young fellow who had lost his fingers and toes to leprosy caught coins in his mouth.

At the appointed time exactly *Was I still in Africa?* Benjamin's sergeant pulled up in his gleaming black Austin. He barked a command in one of the local languages, and once again the crowd parted. He took me by the hand in the friendly African way and led me to the car.

We headed north, out of town, horn sounding tinnily at every turn of the wheels. Otherwise, the sergeant explained, pedestrians would assume that the driver was trying to kill them. In daylight when everyone was awake and walking around instead of sleeping by the wayside, Ndala sounded like the overture of *An American in Paris.* After a hair-raising drive past the brand-new government buildings and banks of downtown, through raucous streets lined with shops and filled with the smoke of street vendors' grills, through labyrinthine neighborhoods of low shacks made from scraps of lumber and tin and cardboard, we arrived at last in Africa itself, a sun-scorched plain of rusty soil, dotted with stunted bush, stretching from horizon to horizon. After a mile or so of emptiness, we came upon a policeman seated on a parked motorcycle. The sergeant stopped the car, leaped out, and leaving the motor running and the front door open, opened the back door to let me out. He gave me a map, drew himself up to attention, and after stamping his right foot into the dust, gave me a quivering British hand salute. He then jumped onto the motorcycle behind its rider, who revved the engine, made a slithering U-turn, and headed back toward the city trailed by a corkscrew of red dust.

I got into the Austin and started driving. The road soon became a dirt trail whose billowing ocher dust stuck to the car like snow and made it necessary to run the windshield wipers. It was impossible to drive with the windows open. The temperature inside the closed vehicle (airconditioning was a thing of the future) could not have been less than one hundred degrees Fahrenheit. Slippery with sweat, I followed the map, and after making a right turn into what seemed to be an impenetrable thicket of rubbery bushes, straddled a footpath which in time opened onto a clearing containing a small village. Another car, a dusty black Rover, was parked in front of one of the conical mud huts. This place was deserted. Grass had grown on the footpaths. There was no sign of life.

I parked beside the other car and ducked into the mud hut. Benjamin, alone as usual, sat inside. He wore national dress—the white toga-like gown invented by nineteenth-century missionaries to clothe the natives for the benefit of English knitting mills. His feet were bare. He seemed to be deep in thought and did not greet me with word or sign. A .455-caliber Webley revolver lay beside him on the floor of beaten earth. The light was dim, and because I had come into the shadowy interior out of intense sunlight, it was some time before I was able to see his face well enough to be absolutely certain that the mute tribesman before me actually was the chief constable with whom I had passed a pleasant hour the night before in the Equator Club. As for the revolver, I can't explain why I trusted this glowering giant not to shoot me just yet, but I did.

Benjamin said, "Is this meeting place sufficiently private?"

"It's fine," I replied. "But where have all the people gone?"

"To Ndala, a long time ago."

All over Africa were abandoned villages like this one whose inhabitants had packed up and left for the city in search of money and excitement and the new life of opportunity that independence promised. Nearly all of them now slept in the streets.

"As I said last night," Benjamin said, "I am thinking about doing something that is necessary to the future of this country, and I would like to have the encouragement of the United States government."

"It must be something impressive if you need the encouragement of Washington."

"It is. I plan to remove the present government of this country and replace it with a freely elected new government."

"That *is* impressive. What exactly do you mean by 'encouragement'?"

"A willingness to stand aside, to make no silliness, and afterwards to be helpful."

"Afterwards? Not before?"

"Before is a local problem."

The odds were at least even that afterward might be a large problem for Benjamin. President Ga's instinct for survival was highly developed. Others, including his own brother, had tried to overthrow him. They were all dead now.

I said, "I recommend first of all that you forget this idea of yours. If you can't do that, then you should speak to somebody in the American embassy. I'm sure you already know the right person."

"I prefer to speak to you."

"Why? I'm not a member of the Ministry of Encouragement."

"But that is exactly what you are, Mr. Brown. You are famous for it. You can be trusted. This man in the American embassy you call 'the right person' is in fact a fool. He is an admirer of President for Life Ga. He plays ball with President Ga. He cannot be trusted."

I started to answer this nonsense. Benjamin showed me the palm of his hand. "Please, no protestations of innocence. I have all the evidence I would ever need about your good works in my country, should I ever need it."

That made me blink. No doubt he did have an interesting file on me. I had done a good deal of mischief in his country, even before the British departed, and for all I knew his courtship was a charade. He might very well be trying to entrap me.

I said, "I'm flattered. But I don't think I'd make a good assistant in this particular matter."

Something like a frown crossed Benjamin's brow. I had annoyed him. Since we were in the middle of nowhere and he was the one with the revolver, this was not a good sign.

"I have no need of an assistant," Benjamin said. "What I need is a witness. A trained observer whose word is trusted in high places in the U.S. Someone who can tell the right people in Washington what I have done, how I have done it, and most of all, that I have done it for the good of my country."

I could think of nothing to say that would not make this conversation even more unpleasant than it already was.

Benjamin said, "I can see that you do not trust me."

He picked up the revolver and cocked it. The Webley is something of an antique, having been designed around the time of the Boer War as the standard British officer's sidearm. It is large and ugly but also effective, powerful enough to kill an elephant. For a long moment Benjamin looked deeply into my eyes and then, holding the gun by the barrel, handed it to me.

"If you believe I am being false to you in any way," he said, "you can shoot me."

It was a wonder that he had not shot himself, handling a cocked revolver in such a carefree way. I took the weapon from his hand, lowered the hammer, swung open the cylinder, and shook out the cartridges. They were not blanks. I reloaded and handed the weapon back to Benjamin. He wiped it clean of fingerprints, my fingerprints, with the skirt of his robe and put it back on the floor.

In the jargon of espionage, the recruitment of an agent is called a seduction. As in a real seduction, assuming that things are going well, a moment comes when resistance turns into encouragement. We had arrived at the moment for a word of encouragement.

I said, "What exactly is the plan?"

"When you strike at a prince," Benjamin said, "you must strike to kill."

Absolutely true. It did not surprise me that he had read Machiavelli. At this point it would not have surprised me if he burst into fluent Sanskrit. Despite the rigmarole with the Webley, I still did not trust him and probably never would, but I was doing the work that I was paid to do, so I decided to press on with the thing.

"That's an excellent principle," I said, "but it's a principle, not a plan."

"All the right things will be done," Benjamin said. "The radio station and newspapers will be seized, the army will cooperate, the airport will be closed, curfews will be imposed."

"Don't forget to surround the presidential palace."

"That will not be necessary."

"Why?"

"Because the president will not be in the palace," Benjamin said.

All of a sudden, Benjamin was becoming cryptic. Frankly, I was just as glad, because what he was proposing in words of one syllable scared the bejesus out of me. So did the expression on his face. He was as calm as a Buddha.

He rose to his feet. In his British uniform he had looked impressive, if slightly uncomfort-able. In his gown he looked positively majestic, a black Caesar in a white toga.

"You know enough now to think this over," he said. "Do so, if you please. We will talk some more before you fly away."

He ducked through the door and drove away. I waited for a few minutes, then went outside myself. A large black mamba lay in the sun in front of my car. My blood froze. The mamba was twelve or thirteen feet long. This species is the fastest-moving snake known to zoology, capable of slithering at fifteen miles an hour, faster than most men can run. Its strike is much quicker than that. Its venom will usually kill an adult human being in about fifteen minutes. Hoping that this one was not fully awake, I got into the car and started the engine. The snake moved but did not go away. I could easily have run over it, but instead I backed up and steered around it. Locally this serpent was regarded as a sign of bad luck to come. I wasn't looking for any more misfortune than I already had on my plate.

After dinner that evening I spent an extra hour in the hotel bar. I felt the alcohol after I went upstairs and got into bed, and fell almost immediately into a deep sleep. Cognac makes for bad dreams and I was in the middle of one when I was awakened by the click of the latch. For an instant I thought the porter must be bringing my morning tea and wondered where the night had gone. But when I opened my eyes it was still dark outside. The door opened and closed. No light came in, meaning that the intruder had switched off the dim bulbs in the corridor. He was now inside the room. I could not see him but I could smell him: soap, spicy food, shoe polish. *Shoe polish?* I slid out of bed, taking the pillows and the covers with me and rolling them into a ball, as if this would help me defend myself against the intruder who I believed was about to attack me in the dark with a machete.

In the dark, the intruder drew the shade over the window. An instant later the lights came on. Benjamin said, "Sorry to disturb you."

He wore his impeccable uniform, swagger stick tucked under his left arm, cap square on his head, badges and shoes and Sam Browne belt gleaming. The clock read 4:23. It was an old-fashioned windup alarm clock with two bells on top. It ticked loudly while I waited until I was sure I could trust my voice to reply. I was stark naked. I felt a little foolish to be holding a bundle of bedclothes in my arms, but at least this preserved my modesty.

Finally I said, "I thought we'd already had our conversation for the day."

Benjamin ignored the Bogart impersonation. "There is something I want you to see," he said. "Get dressed as quick as you can, please." Benjamin never forgot a please or a thank you. Like his penmanship, Victorian good manners seemed to have been rubbed into his soul in missionary school.

As soon as I had tied my shoes, he led the way down the back stairs. He moved at a swift trot. Outside the back door, a black Rover sedan waited with the engine running. The sergeant stood at attention beside it. He opened the back door as Benjamin and I approached and, after a brief moment as Alphonse and Gaston, we got into the backseat.

When the car was in motion, Benjamin turned to me and said, "You seem to want to give President Ga the benefit of the doubt. This morning you will see some things for yourself, and then you can decide whether that is the Christian thing to do."

It was still dark. As a usual thing there is no lingering painted sunrise in equatorial regions; the sun, huge and white, just materializes on the rim of the earth, and daylight begins. In the darkness, the miserable of Ndala were still asleep in rows on either side of every street, but little groups of people on the move were caught in our headlights.

"Beggars," Benjamin said. "They are on their way to work." The beggars limped and crawled according to their afflictions. Those who could not walk at all were carried by others.

"They help each other," Benjamin said. He said something to the sergeant in a tribal language. The sergeant put a spotlight on a big man

carrying a leper who had lost his feet. The leper looked over his friend's shoulder and smiled. The big man walked onward as if unaware of the spotlight. Benjamin said, "See? A blind man will carry a crippled man, and the crippled man will tell him where to go. Take a good look, Mr. Brown. It is a sight you will never see in Ndala again."

"Why not?"

"You will see."

At the end of the street an army truck was parked. A squad of soldiers armed with bayoneted rifles held at port arms formed a line across the street. Benjamin gave an order. The sergeant stopped the car and shone his spotlight on them. They had not stirred or opened their eyes as when the sergeant drove down this same street the night before. Whatever was happening, these people did not want to be witnesses. The soldiers paid no more attention to Benjamin's car than the people lying on the ground paid to the soldiers.

When the beggars arrived, the soldiers surrounded them and herded them into the truck. The blind man protested, a single syllable. Before he could say more, a soldier hit him in the small of the back with a rifle butt. The blind man dropped the crippled leper and fell down unconscious. The soldiers would not touch them, so the other beggars picked them up and loaded them into the truck, then climbed in themselves. The soldiers lowered the back curtain and got into a smaller truck of their own. All this happened in eerie silence, not an order given or a protest voiced, in a country in which the smallest human encounter sent tsunamis of shouting and laughter through crowds of hundreds.

We drove on. We witnessed the same scene over and over again. All over the city, beggars were being rounded up by troops. Our last stop was the Independence Hotel, my hotel, where I saw the beggars I knew best, including the handsome, smiling leper who caught coins in his mouth, being herded into the back of a truck. As the truck drove away, gears changing, the sun appeared on the eastern horizon, huge and entire, a miracle of timing.

Benjamin said, "You look a little sick, my friend. Let me tell you something. Those people are never coming back to Ndala. They give our country a bad image, and two weeks from now hundreds of foreigners will arrive for the Pan-African Conference. Thanks to President Ga, they will not have to look at these disgusting creatures, so maybe they will elect him president of the conference. Think about that. We will talk when you come back."

In Washington, two days later at six in the morning, I found my chief at his desk, drinking coffee from a chipped mug and reading the *Wall Street Journal*. I told him my tale. He knew at once exactly who Benjamin was. He asked how much money Benjamin wanted, what his time-table was, who his coconspirators were, whether he himself planned to replace the abominable Ga as dictator after he overthrew him, what his policy toward the United States would be—and, by the way, what were his hidden intentions? I was unable to answer most of these questions.

I said, "All he's asked for so far is encouragement."

"Encouragement?" said my chief. "That's a new one. He didn't suggest one night of love with the first lady in the Lincoln bedroom?"

A certain third world general had once made just such a demand in return for his services as a spy in a country whose annual national product was smaller than that of Cuyahoga County, Ohio. I told him that Benjamin had not struck me as being the type to long for Mrs. Eisenhower.

My chief said, "You take him seriously?"

"He's an impressive person."

"Then go back and talk to him some more."

"When?"

"Tomorrow."

"What about the encouragement?"

"It's cheap. Ga is a bad 'un. Shovel it on."

I was cheap, too—a singleton out at the end of the string. If I got into trouble, I'd get no help from the chief or anyone else in Washington. The old gentleman himself would cut the string.

He owed me nothing. "Brown? *Brown?*" he would say in the unlikely event that he would be asked what had become of me. "The only Brown I know is Charlie."

The prospect of returning to Ndala on the next flight was not a very inviting one. I had just spent eight weeks traveling around Africa, in and out of countries, languages, time zones, identities. My intestines swarmed with parasites that were desperate to escape. There was something wrong with my liver: the whites of my eyes were yellow. I had had a malaria attack on the plane from London that frightened the woman seated next to me. The four aspirins I took, spilling only twenty or so while getting them out of the bottle with shaking hands, brought the fever and the sweating under control. Twelve hours later I still had a temperature of 102; I shuddered still, though only fitfully.

To the chief I said, "Right."

"This time get *all* the details," my chief said. "But no cables. Your skull only, and fly the information back to me personally. Tell the locals nothing."

"Which locals? Here or there?"

"Anywhere."

His tone was nonchalant, but I had known this man for a long time. He was interested; he saw an opportunity. He was a white-haired, tweedy, pipe-smoking old fellow with a toothbrush mustache and twinkling blue eyes. His specialty was doing the things that American presidents wanted done without actually requiring them to give the order. He smiled with big crooked teeth; he was rich but too old for orthodontia. "Until I give the word, nobody knows anything but us two chickens. Does that suit you?"

I nodded as if my assent really was necessary. After a breath or two, I said, "How much encouragement can I offer this fellow?"

"Use your judgment. Take some money, too. You may have to tide him over till he gets hold of the national treasure. Just don't make any promises. Hear him out. Figure him out. Estimate his chances. We don't want a failure. Or an embarrassment."

I rose to leave.

"Hold on," said the chief.

He rummaged around in a desk drawer and after examining several identical objects and discarding them, handed me a large bulging brown envelope. A receipt was attached to it with Scotch tape. It said that the envelope contained one hundred thousand dollars in hundred-dollar bills. I signed it with the fictitious name my employer had assigned to me when I joined up. As I opened the door to leave, I saw that the old gentleman had gone back to his *Wall Street Journal.*

Benjamin and I had arranged no secure way of communicating with each other, so I had not notified him that I was coming back to Ndala. Nevertheless, the sergeant met me on the tarmac at the airport. I was not surprised that Benjamin knew I was coming. Like all good cops, he kept an eye on passenger manifests for flights in and out of his jurisdiction. After sending a baggage handler into the hold of the plane to find my bag, the sergeant drove me to a safe house in the European quarter of the city. It was five o'clock in the morning when we got there. Benjamin awaited me. The sergeant cooked and served a complete English breakfast—eggs, bacon, sausage, fried potatoes, grilled tomato, cold toast, Dundee orange marmalade, and sour gritty coffee. Benjamin ate with gusto but made no small talk. Air conditioners hummed in every window.

"Better that you stay in this house than the hotel," Benjamin said when he had cleaned his plate. "In that way there will never be a record that you have been in this country."

That was certainly true, and it was not the least of my worries. I was traveling on a Canadian passport as Robert Bruce Brown, who had died of meningitis in Baddeck, Nova Scotia, thirty-five years before at age two. Thanks to the sergeant, I had bypassed customs and passport control. That meant that there was no entry stamp in the passport. In theory I could not leave the country without one, but then again, I was carrying one hundred thousand American dollars in cash in an airline bag, and this was a

country in which money talked. If I did disappear, I would disappear without a trace. One way or another, so would the money.

"There is something I want you to see," Benjamin said. Apparently this was his standard phrase when he had something unpleasant to show me. After wiping his lips on a white linen napkin, folding it neatly, and dropping it onto the table, he led me into the living room. The drapes were drawn. The sun was up. A sliver of white-hot sunlight shone through. Benjamin called to the sergeant, who brought his briefcase and pulled the curtains tighter. Before leaving us he started an LP on the hi-fi and turned up the volume to defeat hidden microphones. Sinatra sang "In the Still of the Night."

Benjamin took a large envelope from the briefcase and handed it to me. It contained about twenty glossy black-and-white photographs—army trucks parked in a field; soldiers with bayonets fixed; a large empty ditch with two bulldozers standing by; beggars getting down from the truck; beggars being tumbled into the ditch; beggars, hedged in by bayonets, being buried alive by the bulldozers; bulldozers rolling over the dirt to tamp it down with their treads.

"The army is very unhappy about this," Benjamin said. "President Ga did not tell the generals that soldiers would be required to do this work. They thought they were just getting these beggars out of sight until after the Pan-African Conference. Instead the soldiers were ordered to solve the problem once and for all."

My throat was dry. I cleared it and said, "How many people were buried alive?"

"Nobody counted."

"Why was this done?"

"I told you. The beggars were an eyesore."

"That was reason enough to bury them alive?"

"The soldiers were supposed to shoot them first. But they refused. This is good for us, because now the army is angry. Also afraid. Now Ga can execute any general for murder simply by discovering the crime and punishing the culprits in the name of justice and the people. The generals have not told the president that the soldiers refused to follow his orders, so now they are in danger. If he ever finds out he will bury the soldiers alive. Also a general or two. Or more."

I said, "Who would tell him?"

"Who indeed?" asked Benjamin, stone-faced. I handed the pictures back to him. He held up a palm. "Keep them."

I said, "No, thank you."

The photos were a death warrant for anyone who was arrested with them in his possession.

Benjamin ignored me. He rummaged in his briefcase and handed me a handheld radio transceiver. Technologically speaking, those were primitive days, and the device was not much smaller than a fifth of Beefeater's, minus the neck of the bottle. Nevertheless, it was a wonder for its time. It was made in the U.S.A., so I supposed it had been supplied by the local chief of station, the man who played ball with Ga, as a trinket for a native.

Benjamin said, "Your call sign is Mustard One. Mine is Mustard. This is for emergencies. This, too." He handed me a Webley and a box of hollow-point cartridges.

I was touched by his concern. But the transceiver was useless—if the situation was desperate enough to call him. I would be a dead man before he could get to me. The Webley, however, would be useful for shooting myself in case of need. Shooting anyone else in this country would be the equivalent of committing suicide.

Benjamin rose to his feet. "I will be back," he said. "We will spend the evening together."

When Benjamin returned around midnight, I was reading Sir Richard Burton's *Wanderings in West Africa*, the only book in the house. It was a first edition, published in 1863. The margins were sprinkled with pencil dots. I guessed that it had been used by some romantic Brit for a book code. Benjamin was sartorially correct as usual—crisp white shirt with paisley cravat, double-breasted naval blazer, gray slacks, gleaming oxblood oxfords. He cast a disapproving eye on my wrinkled shorts and sweaty shirt and bare feet.

"You must wash and shave and put on proper clothes," he said. "We have been invited to dinner."

Benjamin offered no further information. I asked no questions. The sergeant drove, rapidly, without headlights on narrow trails through the bush. We arrived at a guard shack. The guard, a very sharp soldier, saluted and waved us through without looking inside the car. The road widened into a sweeping driveway. Gravel crackled under the tires. We reached the top of a little rise, and I saw before me the presidential palace, lit up like a football stadium by the light towers that surrounded it. The flags of all the newborn African nations flew from a ring of flagstaffs.

The soldiers guarding the front door, white belts, white gloves, white bootlaces, white rifle slings, came to present arms. We walked past them into a vast foyer from which a double staircase swept upward before separating at a landing decorated by a huge floodlit portrait of President Ga wearing his sash of office. A liveried servant led us up the stairs past a gallery of portraits of Ga variously uniformed as general of the army, admiral of the fleet, air chief marshal, head of the party, and other offices I could not identify.

We simply walked into the presidential office. No guards were visible. President Ga was seated behind a desk at the far end of the vast room. Two attack dogs, pit bulls, stood with ears pricked at either side of his oversize desk. The ceiling could not have been less than fifteen feet high. Ga, not a large person to begin with, was so diminished by these Brobdingnagian proportions that he looked like a puppet. He was reading what I supposed was a state paper, pen in hand in case he needed to add or cross something out. As we approached across the snow-white marble floor, our footsteps echoed. Benjamin's were especially loud because he wore leather heels, but nothing, apparently, could break the president's concentration.

About ten feet from the desk we stopped, our toes touching a bronze strip that was sunk into the marble. Ga ignored us. The pit bulls did not. Ga pressed a button. A hidden door opened behind the desk, and a young army officer in dress uniform stepped out. Behind him I could see half a dozen other soldiers, armed to the teeth and standing at attention in a closet-like space that was hardly large enough to hold them all.

Wordlessly, Ga handed the paper to the officer, who took it, made a smart about-face, and marched back into the closer. Ga stood up, still taking no notice of us, and strolled to the large window behind his desk. It looked out over the brightly lit, shadowless palace grounds. At a little distance I could see an enclosure in which several different species of gazelle were confined. In other paddocks—too many to be seen in a single glance—other wild animals paced. Ga drank in the scene for a long moment, then whirled and approached Benjamin and me at quick-march, as if he wore one of his many uniforms instead of the white bush jacket, black slacks, and sandals in which he actually was dressed. Benjamin did not introduce me. Apparently there was no need to do so, because Ga, looking me straight in the eye, shook my hand and said, "I hope you like French food, Mr. Brown."

I did. The menu was a terrine of gray sole served with a 1953 Corton Charlemagne, veal stew accompanied by a 1949 Pommard, cheese, and grapes. The president ate the food hungrily, talking all the while, but only sipped the wines.

"Alcohol gives me bad dreams," he said to me. "Do you ever have bad dreams?"

"Doesn't everyone, sir?"

"My best friend, who died too young, never had bad dreams. He was too good in mind and heart to be troubled by such things. Now he is in my dreams. He visits me almost every night. Who is in your dreams?"

"Mostly people I don't know."

"Then you are very lucky."

During the dinner Ga talked about America. He knew it well. He had earned a degree from a Negro college in Missouri. Baptist missionaries had sent him to the college on a scholarship. He graduated second in his class, behind his best friend who now called on him in dreams.

When Ga spoke to his people he spoke standard Africanized English, the common tongue of his country where more than a hundred mutually incomprehensible tribal languages were in use. He spoke to me in American English, sounding like Harry S. Truman. He had had a wonderful time in college: the football games, the fraternity pranks, the music, the wonderful food, homecoming, the prom, those American coeds! His friend had been the school's star running back; Ga had been the team manager; they had won their conference championship two years in a row. "From the time we were boys together in our village, my friend was always the star, I was always the administrator," he said. "Until we got into politics and changed places. My friend stuttered. It was his only flaw. It is the reason I am president. Had he been able to speak to the people without making them laugh, he would be living in this house."

"You were fond of this man," I said.

"Fond of him? He was my brother."

Tears formed in the president's eyes. Despite everything I knew about his crimes, I found myself liking Akokwu Ga.

Servants arrived with coffee and a silver dessert bowl. "Ah, strawberries and crème fraîche!" said Ga, breaking into his first smile of the evening.

After the strawberries, another servant offered cigars and port, discreetly showing me the labels. Ga waved these temptations away like a good Baptist. I did the same, not without regret.

"Come, my friend," said Ga, rising to his feet and suddenly speaking West African rather than Missouri English, "it is time for a walk. Do you get enough exercise?"

I said, "I wish I got more."

"Ah, but you must make time to keep up to snuff," said Ga. "I ride horseback every morning and walk in the cool of the evening. Both things are excellent exercise, and also, to start the day, you have the companionship of the horse which never says anything stupid. You must get a horse. If you are too busy for a horse, a masseur. Not a masseuse. They are too distracting. Massage is like hearty exercise if the masseur is strong and has the knowledge. Bob Hope told me that. Massage keeps him young."

By now we were at the front door. The spick-and-span young army captain who had earlier leaped out of the closet behind Ga's desk awaited us. Standing at rigid attention, he held out a paper for Ga. Benjamin immediately went into reverse, walking backward as he withdrew from eyeshot and earshot of the president, while the latter read his document and spoke to his orderly. I followed suit.

Staring straight ahead and barely moving his lips, Benjamin muttered, "He is charming tonight. Be careful." These were the first words he had uttered all evening. Throughout dinner, Ga had ignored him entirely, as if he were a third pit bull lying at his feet.

Outside, under the stadium lights. Ga led the way across the shadowless grounds to his animal park. Three men walked in front, sweeping the ground in case of snakes. As I knew from rumor and intelligence reports, Ga had a morbid fear of snakes. Another bearer carried Ga's sporting rifle, a beautiful weapon that looked to me like a Churchill, retail in London, £10,000.

The light from the towers was so strong that everything looked like an overexposed photograph. Ga pointed out the gazelles, naming them all one by one. "Some of these specimens are quite rare," he said, "or so I am told by the people who sell them. I am preserving them for the people of this nation. Most of these beasts no longer live in this part of Africa, but before the Europeans came with their guns and killed them for sport, we knew them as brothers."

Ga was a believer in raising a mythical African past to the status of reality. The public buildings he had built during his brief reign featured murals and mosaics depicting Africans of a lost civilization inventing agriculture, mathematics, architecture, medicine, electricity, the airplane, even the postage stamp. In his mind it was only logical that the ancients had also lived in peace with the lion, the elephant, the giraffe—everything but the serpent, which Ga had exiled from his utopia.

We tramped on a bit, to an empty paddock. "Now you will see something," he said. "You will see nature in the raw."

This paddock was unlighted. Ga lifted his hand, and the lights went on. Standing alone in the middle of the open space was an animal that even I was able to recognize as a Thomson's gazelle from its diminutive size, its lovely tan and white coat, the calligraphic black stripe on its flank. This one was a buck, just over three feet tall, a work of art like so many other African animals.

"This type of gazelle is common," Ga said. "There are hundreds of thousands of them in herds in Tanganyika. They can outrun a lion. Watch."

The word *suddenly* does not convey the speed of what happened next. Out of the blinding light in which it had somehow been concealing itself as it stalked the Tommy, a cheetah materialized, moving at sixty miles an hour. A cheetah can cover a hundred meters in less than three seconds. The Tommy saw or sensed this blur of death that hurtled toward him and leaped three or four feet straight up into the air, then hit the ground running. The Tommy was slightly slower than its predator, but far more nimble. When the cheetah got close enough to attack, the little gazelle would make a quick turn and escape. This happened over and over again. The size of the paddock or playing field, as Ga must have thought of it—was an advantage to the Tommy, who would lead the cheetah straight to the fence, then make a last-second turn. Once or twice the cheetah crashed into the wire.

"This is almost over," Ga said. "Usually it lasts only a minute or so. If the cat does not win very quickly, it runs out of strength and gives up."

A second later, the cheetah won. The gazelle turned in the wrong direction, and the cat brought it down. A cheetah is not strong enough to break the neck of its prey, so it kills by suffocation, biting the throat and crushing the windpipe. The Tommy struggled, then went limp. The cheetah's eyes glittered. So did Ga's.

Beaming, he threw an arm around my shoulders. He said, "Wonderful, eh?"

I smelled the food and wine on his breath, felt his excited heart beating against my shoulder. Then, without a good night or even a facial expression. Ga turned on his heel, and, surrounded by his snake sweepers and his gun beater, marched away and disappeared into the palace. The evening was over. His guests had ceased to exist.

We lost no time in leaving. Minutes later, as we rolled toward the wakening city in Benjamin's Rover, I asked a question.

"Is he always so hospitable?"

"Tonight you saw one Ga," Benjamin said. "There are a thousand of him."

I could believe it. In this one evening I had seen him in half a dozen incarnations, Mussolini redux, gourmet, Joe College, tender friend, zoologist, mythologist, and a fun-loving god who stage-managed animal sacrifices to himself.

The Rover purred along a smoothly paved but deserted road, bush to the left and right, the sticky night dark as macadam. Headlights appeared behind us and approached at high speed. The sergeant switched off the Rover's lights and pulled off the road. The tires bit into soft dirt. Benjamin and I were slammed together hip and shoulder. We were being overtaken by a motorcade. A Cadillac, the lead car, swept by at high speed, then a Rolls-Royce, then another Cadillac as chase car.

"The president," Benjamin said calmly when the Rover stopped bouncing. "He always has a woman or two before the sun rises. He is quick with them, never more than fifteen minutes, then he goes back to the presidential palace. He never goes to the same woman twice in the same month."

"He keeps thirty-one women?"

"More, in case one of them is not clean on a certain night."

"How does he choose which one?"

"Each woman has a number. Each month Ga receives from somebody in St. Louis, Missouri, what is called a dream book. It is used in America to play the numbers game. He uses the number in the dream book for the day."

I said, "So if you want to find him on any given night, you match the woman's number to the number for that particular day in the dream book."

"Yes, if you know the address of every woman, that is the key," Benjamin said.

He smiled and placed a hand on my shoulder, pleased as a proud father with the quickness of my mind.

For the next several days there was no sign of Benjamin. I was not locked up, but as a practical matter this meant that I was confined to the safe house during daylight hours. There was nowhere to go at night. Like any other prisoner I invented ways to pass the empty hours. Solitude and time-wasting did not bother me; I was used to them; both were occupational hazards. I was concerned by the lack of exercise, because I did not want to run out of breath in case I had to make a run for it. This seemed a likely outcome. How else could this situation end?

I jogged in place for an hour every morning, and in the afternoon ran the 100- and the 220-yard dashes, also in place but flat out. I did push-ups and sit-ups and side-straddle hops. I punched and karate-chopped the sofa cushions until I had beaten every last mote of dust from them. I jitterbugged in my socks to cracked 78 rpm records I found in a closet, Louis Armstrong, the Harmonica Rascals, the Andrews Sisters. Satchmo's "Muskrat Ramble" and the sisters' "Boogie Woogie Bugle Boy of Company B" provided the best workouts.

The sergeant stopped by every day to cook lunch and dinner and wash up afterward. He brought quality groceries, and he was a good cook, specializing in curries and local piripiri dishes loaded with cayenne pepper that made the heart beat in the skull. I asked him to bring me books. He refused money to pay for them or the groceries—apparently I was covered by a budget in secret funds—and came back from the African market the next day with at least one Penguin paperback by every writer I had named and a few more besides. The books were dog-eared and food- and coffee-stained, and most were missing pages.

I was in bed, reading a W. Somerset Maugham short story about adulterers in Malaya, when Benjamin finally showed up. As usual he chose the wee hours of the morning for his visit. He was as stealthy as he had been when he visited me in the hotel, and I heard no car or any other sound of his approach.

All the same I felt his presence before he materialized out of the darkness. He seemed to be alone. He carried a battered leather valise, the kind that has a hinged top that opens like a mouth when the catch is released. The valise seemed to jump in his hand, as if it contained a disembodied muscle. I rationalized this by thinking that he must be trembling for some reason. Maybe he had had a bout of fever and was not quite recovered. That would explain why I hadn't seen him for a week.

Then, at the instant when I realized that there was something alive inside the valise and it was trying to get out, Benjamin held the bag upside down over my bed and pressed the catch. The bag popped open and a huge blue-black mamba uncoiled itself from within. It landed on my legs. With blinding speed it coiled and struck. I felt the blow, a soft punch but no sting, on my chest just above the heart. I knew that I was a dead man. So apparently did the mamba. It stared into my eyes, waiting (or so I thought) for my heart to stop, for the power of thought to switch off. No more than a second had passed. Already I felt cold. An ineffable calm settled upon me. The laboring air conditioner in the window was suddenly almost silent. My hearing seemed to be going first. Next, I thought, the eyes. I felt no pain. I thought, Maybe after all there is a God, or was a God, if the last moment of life has been arranged in such a kindly and loving way.

Dreamily I watched as Benjamin's hand, black as the mamba, seized the snake behind the head. The serpent struggled, lashing its body and winding itself around Benjamin's arm. The sergeant appeared, stepping out of the darkness and into the light of my reading lamp just as Benjamin had done. It took the combined strength of these two powerful men to stuff the thing back into the valise and close it. They did so without the slightest sign of fear. In the half-light, with their faces close together, they looked more than ever like brothers. How strange it was, I thought, that this surreal scene in this misbegotten place should be the last thing I would ever see. Benjamin handed the valise to the sergeant. It jumped violently in his hand. The sergeant produced a key and, with a perfectly steady hand, locked the valise. His eyes were fixed on me. He was grinning in what I can only describe as total delight. Make that unholy delight.

To me, an unsmiling Benjamin said, "You must be wondering why you are not dead yet."

He was not grinning. The sergeant, watching me over Benjamin's shoulder, did it for him, big white teeth reflecting more light than there seemed to be in the room.

Up to this point I had not looked at my fatal wound. In fact, I had not moved at all since the snake had struck me. Something told me that any movement might quicken the action of the venom and rob me of whatever split seconds of life I might have left. Besides, I did not want to see the wound that I imagined, twin punctures made by the mamba's fangs, perhaps a drop or two of blood, and most horribly, venom oozing from the holes in my skin. Finally I found the courage to glance at my chest. It was unmarked.

I leaped out of bed, dashed into the bathroom, and examined my sweating torso. I stripped off my boxer shorts, the only garment I was wearing, and twisted and turned in the stingy light, looking for what I still feared was a mortal wound. But I saw no break in my skin, no bruise, even. The symptoms of death I had been feeling—the light-headedness, the shortness of breath, and a sense of loss so intense that it felt like the shutdown of the heart—went away.

Without bothering to put my shorts back on. I went back into the bedroom.

"Look at him!" the sergeant chortled, pointing a finger at me.

At first I thought he was making fun of my nakedness. I had spent time on a beach in South Africa, and the part of me formerly covered by my shorts was dead-white. I soon realized that he was laughing at something other than my tan line. I was the victim of the most sadistic practical joke since Harry Flashman was kicked out of Rugby College, and these two were the jokers. There is no mirth like African mirth, and both Benjamin and the sergeant were doubled over by it. They howled with laughter, their eyes were filled with tears, they gasped for breath, they hugged each other as they danced a jig of merriment, they lost their balance and staggered to regain it.

"Look at him!" they said over and over again. "Look at him!"

The locked valise had been placed on the bed. The contortions of the infuriated six-foot-long muscle that was trying to escape from it caused it to skitter across the sheets. I tried to get around the helpless men, but they kept lurching into my path, so I was not able to reach the Webley, Benjamin's gift to me, that was stashed under the mattress. My plan was to empty the revolver, if I could get my hands on it, into the pulsating valise. I was in no way certain that I could stick to this plan if I actually had the gun in my hands and this comedy team at point-blank range.

Breath by breath, I got hold of myself. So did Benjamin and the sergeant, though it took them a little longer. It was obvious what had happened. Some juju man had captured the snake and removed its fangs and venom sac. Knowing Benjamin—and by now I felt that I knew him intimately despite the brevity of our friendship—he had commissioned the capture and the veterinary surgery. Knowing also how terrified President Ga was of snakes, I could only surmise that the defanged mamba was going to be a player in the overthrow of the tyrant. Maybe, if the coup succeeded, Benjamin would make the mamba part of

the flag, as an earlier group of patriots had done a couple hundred years ago with another poisonous snake in another British colony.

Benjamin offered no explanations for the prank. I was damned if I was going to ask him any questions. I was by no means certain that I could control my voice. By now the joke had cooled off. Benjamin had stopped smiling. His grave dignity had returned. He made a minimal gesture. The sergeant picked up the valise.

Benjamin said, "I will be back soon."

With a scratchy throat, I said, "Good."

The two of them let themselves out the front door. I locked it behind them, and as I tried to put the key into my pants pocket I remembered that I was stark naked. Nakedness was deeply offensive to christianized Africans like Benjamin. Maybe that was why he had stopped laughing before the joke had really worn off.

I reached under the mattress and pulled out the Webley and cocked it. It is a very heavy weapon, weighing almost three pounds when fully loaded, and when I felt its heft in my hand I began to tremble. I could not stop. I was afraid that the gun might go off, but I had so little control over my muscles that I could not safely put it down. Teeth chattering, my body chilling in a room in which the temperature was not less than ninety degrees, I understood fully and for the first time just what a brilliant son of a bitch Benjamin was.

Two days later, at five in the morning, he showed up at the safe house for breakfast. He said he had been up all night. There was no outward sign of this. He was fresh from the shower, his starched uniform still smelled of the iron, and he sat up straight as a cadet in his chair. But he was not his usual masked self. There was an air of excitement about him that he did not bother to conceal.

He ate the yolks of his fried eggs with a spoon, then touched the corners of his mouth with his napkin. "The president of the republic is very upset," he said.

He spoke in a low tone. It was difficult to hear him because a Benny Goodman record was playing on the phonograph—the usual precaution against eavesdroppers—and Harry James and the rest of the trumpet section were playing as if their four or five horns were a single instrument.

I said, "Upset? Why?"

"He has discovered the fangs and the poison sac of a black mamba on his desk."

"Goodness," I said. "No wonder he's upset."

"Yes. He found these things when he came back from one of his women last night. They were right in the center of the blotter, in his coffee cup. If someone had poured coffee into the cup he might well have drunk it absentmindedly. He said so himself."

I could think of nothing to say. Certainly Benjamin needed no encouragement to go on with his story.

He said, "He flew off the handle and called me immediately. He screamed into the telephone. He was surrounded by traitors, he said. How could anyone have gained access to his office in his absence, let alone smuggled in the coffee cup? How could no one have noticed this coffee cup and what was in it? There are soldiers everywhere in the presidential palace. Or were."

"They are there no longer?"

"Naturally he has dismissed them. How could he trust them after this? He also ordered the arrest of the army chief of staff. His order has of course been carried out."

"The army chief of staff is in your custody?"

"For the time being, yes. It gives us an opportunity to talk frankly to each other."

"Who is handling security if not the army?"

"The national police. This is an honor, but it is a strain on our manpower, especially with the Pan-African festival beginning the day after tomorrow. Thousands will flood into Ndala, including twenty-six heads of state and who knows how many other dignitaries and nobodies. But of course the safety of our own head of state and government is the number-one priority."

"You are investigating, of course."

"Oh, yes," Benjamin said. "Suspects, some of them of very high rank, are being interviewed, quarters are being searched, every safe in the nation is being opened, information is being gathered, fingerprints and other physical evidence have been assembled, all the usual police procedures are in place, but on a much larger and more urgent scale than usual. The presidential palace is off-limits to everyone except the president and the police."

He was in complete control of his voice and his facial muscles. But underneath his unflappable behavior, he glowed with joy. He was within reach of something that he wanted very much indeed.

"The fangs and so on are not all that we have to worry about," Benjamin went on. "The president for life has also received an anonymous letter, mysteriously placed under his pillow by an unknown hand, stating that a sample of his bodily secretions has been given to a famous juju man in the Ivory Coast."

This was momentous news. Playing the naïf, my assigned role in this charade, I said, "Bodily secretions?"

"We believe they were obtained from one of Ga's women. He is deeply concerned. This can only mean that a curse has been put upon him by an enemy. The curse can be reversed only if we can find the culprit who hired the juju man."

Imparting this news, he remained impassive. No smile, no equivalent of a wink, no expression of any kind came to the surface. Benjamin himself had, of course, engineered everything he was reporting to me: the fangs, the venom, the anonymous letter with its chilling message. But he described these things as if he had no more idea than the man in the moon who was responsible for tormenting President Ga.

The juju curse was the keystone of the plot. I had known Africans, one of them an agent of mine who possessed a first-class degree from Cambridge, who had withered and died from witchcraft. The bodily secretion was the vital element in casting a juju spell. Some product of the victim's body was needed to invoke a truly effective curse, a lock of hair, an ounce of urine, a teaspoon of saliva, feces. The more intimate the product, the greater its power. Nothing could be a more effective charm than a man's semen. No wonder Ga was beside himself. And no wonder that he was now in Benjamin's power.

By now, more than thirty African heads of state had flown into Ndala for President Ga's Pan-African Conference. This was the day on which they would all ride through the city in their Rolls-Royces and Mercedes Benzes and Cadillacs, waving to the vast crowd that had been assembled to greet them. Whether any of these spectators had the faintest idea who the dignitaries were, or what they were doing in Ndala, were separate questions. Whole tribes had been bused or trucked or herded on foot into the city from the interior. Many were dancing. Chiefs had brought warriors armed with shields and spears to protect them against enemies, wives to service them, dwarves to keep them entertained. Every single one of these human beings seemed to be grunting or shouting or singing or, mostly, laughing, and the noise produced by all those voices, added to the beating of drums and the sound of musical instruments and the tootling of automobile horns, made the air tremble. Palm wine and warm beer flowed, and the spicy aroma of stews and roasting goats rose from hundreds of cook fires.

At last the sergeant found the exact spot he had been looking for, an empty space in front of the parliament building, and parked the car in the shadow of a huge baobab tree. A couple of constables were already on hand, and they cleared away the crowd so that we had an unobstructed view.

"They will come soon," the sergeant said.

It was a little before five in the afternoon. The parade was already about ninety minutes behind schedule, but there was no such concept as "on time" in Ndala or any other place in Africa. Maybe forty minutes later, we heard the faraway, warped sound of a brass band playing "The British Grenadiers." The music grew

louder, and the band marched by, drum major brandishing a baton that was as tall as he was, every musician's eye seemingly fixed on the Austin as the marching men turned eyes left on the parliament and the flags of the African nations that flew from its circle of flagpoles. A battalion of infantry then marched smartly by, drenched in sweat, arms swinging, boots kicking up powdery dust. The infantry were followed by several tanks and armored cars and howitzers. Finally came a platoon of bagpipers, tartan kilts, and sporrans swinging, "Scotland the Brave" splitting the sun-scorched air. If the Brits had taught these people nothing else in a century of colonialism, they had taught them how to organize a parade.

"Now come the presidents," the sergeant said. "President for Life Ga will be first, then the others." Then, even though we were alone in the car with the windows rolled up, he dropped his voice to a whisper and added, "Watch very carefully the road ahead of his car."

Ga's regal, snow-white Rolls-Royce materialized out of the dust. There were a few grunts from onlookers but no ululations or other such behavior. The masses merely watched this strange alien phenomenon, and no doubt they would have reacted in the same way if a spaceship had been landing among them. Not that the occasion was wholly lacking in ceremony. The soldiers posted along the street at ten-foot intervals came to present arms. The sergeant leaped out of the car, and he and the two constables stood to attention, saluting. I got out, too. No one paid the slightest attention to me. But then, only a few of the onlookers were paying very much attention to President Ga. The Rolls-Royce continued its stately approach, flags flying, headlights blazing. The crowd stirred and muttered.

Then, without warning, the crowd suddenly broke and began to run in all directions, men, women, children, the decrepit old borne aloft by their sons and daughters, everyone except the dancers, who had by now fallen into a collective trance and went right on dancing, oblivious to the panic all around them. Everyone else scattered as fast as their legs would carry them. The presidential Rolls-Royce slammed on its brakes and stood on its nose. Inside it, President Ga or one of his doubles, dressed in a white uniform, was thrown about like a rag doll.

It was impossible not to see Benjamin's hand in all this. A single thought filled my mind: assassination. He was going to kill this man in full view of thirty other presidents for life.

I leaped onto the hood of the Austin, then scrambled to the roof. From that vantage point I saw what all the fright was about. A black mamba at least ten feet long was slithering with almost unbelievable swiftness across the road in the path of the white Rolls-Royce. Suddenly half a dozen brave fellows, half-naked all of them, leaped out of the crowd and attacked the serpent with pangas, cutting it into pieces that writhed violently as if trying to reconnect themselves into a living reptile. The crowd uttered a loud, collective basso grunt. This was a huge yet subdued sound, like a whisper amplified to the power of ten thousand on some enormous hi-fi speaker yet to be invented.

The Rolls-Royce, Klaxon sounding, sped away. The sergeant said, "Get into the car. We must go."

I did as he ordered. Inside the sweltering, buttoned-up Austin, I asked if the mamba crossing President Ga's path on his day of triumph would be seen as a bad omen.

"Oh, yes," the sergeant said, grinning into the mirror. "*Very* bad. No one who saw will ever forget."

Darkness fell. The sergeant did not take me home but drove me to a different safe house on the outskirts of the city. As soon as we were inside I switched on the English-language radio. The opening ceremonies of the Pan-African Conference were now in progress at the soccer stadium. Announcers shouted to be heard above the blare of bands and choirs, the boom of fireworks, and the noise of the crowd. Needless to say, not a word was uttered over the airways about the meeting between the mamba and Ga's

white Rolls-Royce. Everyone knew all about it anyway by word of mouth or talking drum or one of the many Bantu tongues that could be signed or whistled as well as spoken.

In all those minds, as in my own, the questions were: What happens next and when will it happen? I left the radio on, knowing that the first word of the coup would come from its speakers. Second only to the capture or murder of the prince, the broadcasting station was the most important objective in any coup d'état. Obviously Benjamin and his coconspirators, assuming that he had any, must strike tonight. Never again would he have such an opportunity to destroy the tyrant before the very eyes of Africa. He would want to kill Ga in the most humiliating way possible. He would want to show him as weak, impotent, and alone, without a single person willing or able to defend him.

Promptly at eight o'clock, the sergeant carried a cooler into the house, rattled pots and pans in the kitchen, and served my dinner, all five courses at once. The food was French. "This is the same food that all the presidents will be eating at the state dinner," the sergeant said. I ate only the heated-up entrée, medallions of veal in a cream sauce that had separated because the sergeant had let it boil.

Around two in the morning, the sergeant's walkie-talkie squawked. He lifted it to his ear, heard what sounded to me like a single word, and replied with what also seemed to be a single word. The conversation lasted less than a second. He said, "Come, Mr. Brown. It is time to go."

We drove through a maze of streets but on this night of revelry saw no sleepers by the wayside. Everybody was still celebrating. Oil lamps and candles glowed in the blackness like red and yellow eyes, as if the entire genus *carnivora* was drawn up in a hungry circle on the outskirts of the party. Music blared from loudspeakers, people danced, thousands of shouted conversations stirred the stagnant, overheated air. The city had become one enormous, throbbing Equator Club.

The sergeant maneuvered the Austin through the pandemonium with one hand on the steering wheel and the other on the hooter, constantly beeping to let people know that he wasn't trying to sneak up on them and kill them. Not since Independence Night, I thought, could there have been so many witnesses awake at this hour, ready to observe whatever Benjamin was going to do next.

At last we drove out of the crowd and into the European quarter. Through the rear window I could see the distorted, smoky-red glow of the city. I imagined I could feel the earth quivering in rhythm to the innumerable bare feet that were pounding it in unison a mile or so away. The music and the shouting were very loud even at such a distance.

The sergeant drove at his usual brisk pace, lights off as usual. He parked the car and switched off the engine. By now my eyes had adjusted, and I could see another police car parked a few yards away. We were parked on a low hilltop, and the red glow of the city caught in the mirror-shine of its metal. Soon a third car drove up and parked close beside us. It was Benjamin's Rover, identifiable by the baritone throb of its engine. The driver's cap badge caught a little light. A large man who might have been Benjamin sat in the backseat alone.

Moving swiftly, Benjamin got into the backseat with me. The dome light blinked. He wore the dress uniform I supposed he had worn to the state dinner—long pants, white shirt with necktie, short epauletted mess jacket that the Brits call a bum freezer, decorations. Benjamin smelled as usual of starch, brass polish, soap, his own musk.

Headlights swept up the hill, turned sharp left into the street that paralleled the one on which our own cars were parked, then stopped. Car doors slammed, men moved quick-time, a key turned in a lock, a door squeaked as it was opened, a scratchy Edith Piaf LP played five or six bars of "Les amants de Paris."

We were parked behind the house into which Ga had gone to keep his rendezvous for tonight.

Jumpy light showed in an upstairs window, dim and yellowish, as if filtering down a hallway from another room. The back door opened. A flashlight blinked. The Rover's headlights flashed in reply.

"Come," Benjamin said. He got out of the car and strode into the darkness. I followed. The sergeant got something out of the trunk, then slammed the lid. Behind me I heard his brogans at a run. We went through the open door. Inside the house, the record changed on the hi-fi, and Piaf began to sing "Il Pleut." Benjamin, entirely at home, strode down a hallway, then up a stairway. At the top, in half-shadow outside a half-open bedroom door, a policeman stood at attention as if he did not quite know exactly what was expected of him or what would happen next.

In a mirror I saw a man and a woman engaged in vigorous coitus and heard the woman's moans and outcries. The sergeant marched into the room. Benjamin gave me a little push, and I marched in behind him. The room was full of burning candles. The smell of incense was strong. Smoke hung in the air. The woman shouted something in what sounded to me like Swedish. She was quite small. President Ga, lying on top of her, covered her completely. Her legs were wound around his waist, ankles crossed, feet in gilt shoes with stiletto heels. I looked into the mirror in hope of seeing the girl's face. My eyes met Ga's. The candlelight exaggerated the size of his startled, wide-open eyes. His face twisted into a mask of furious anger, and he rolled off the woman, knocking off one of her shoes. Now I saw her face, smeared lipstick, and tousled hair. She was a cookie-cutter blonde, as flawless as a dummy in a store window.

I knew what was coming next, of course. The sergeant took one step forward. In his outstretched hands he held the valise that I remembered so well. Evidently that was what he had retrieved from the trunk of the Austin. The snap of brass latches sounded like the metallic *one-two* of the slide of an automatic pistol. The sergeant opened the valise and turned it upside down.

The mamba flowed out of the bag with the same unbelievable swiftness, as if it were coming into being before our eyes. I tried to leap backward, but Benjamin stood immediately behind me, blocking the way. President Ga and the blonde froze as if captured in a black-and-white photograph by the flash of a strobe light.

The snake, a blur as it attacked, struck at the nearest target, President Ga. He grunted as if a bullet had entered his body. His mouth opened wide and he shouted in English. "Oh, Jesus, Sweet Jesus!" It was a prayer, not a blasphemy. In the same breath he uttered a tremendous sob. Between these two primal sounds, the woman, screaming, threw her body over the foot of the bed. Somehow she landed behind us on all fours in the hallway. Still shrieking, still wearing one gilt shoe, she sprinted down the hallway. The constable in the hall pursued her for a step or two, picked up the shoe after she kicked it off, and caught her by the hair, which was very long. Her head jerked back, but she kept going, leaving the constable with a handful of blond threads in his hand. He stared at these in puzzlement, then blew his whistle. At the head of the stairs the woman was captured by a second constable, a man almost as large as Benjamin. He carried her, squirming, kicking, screaming, back toward the bedroom. Her skin was so white that I half-expected powder to fly from it. She bit his face. He twisted her jaw until she let go, and when he saw his own blood on her teeth he slammed her twice against the wall, then let go of her, throwing his hands wide in disgust that a woman should have attacked him, should have *bitten* him. Her limp, unconscious body slid to the floor. She landed with a thump on her round bottom, her back against the wall, her head lolling inside its curtain of hair. She twitched as if dreaming, and I wondered if her spine was broken. She had shapely breasts, pretty legs, peroxided delta, and it looked as though she had lipsticked her nipples. For some reason, maybe because this touch of perversity was so unimaginative, so innocent, such a learner's trick, my heart went out to her, if only for a moment.

Behind me I heard a gunshot. In the confined space of the bedroom it sounded like an artillery round going off. The stink of cordite mingled with the incense. Benjamin stood over the bed with a smoking Webley in his hand. The headless snake in its death throes whipped uncontrollably over the bed, spraying blood on Ga and the sheets. With his hands protecting his genitals, Ga scooted rapidly backward over the bed to escape the serpent, even though he must have known that it was now harmless. What a seed God planted in the human mind on the day that Adam ate the apple! From the look on Ga's face it was clear that he believed that he himself was dying almost as fast as the snake had just done, but his instincts, from which he could not escape, instructed him to cover his nakedness and flee for his life.

Ga's eyes were now fixed on Benjamin. The question in them was easy to read: Had Benjamin murdered him or rescued him? Benjamin made a gesture to Ga: *Come.*

Ga, strangling on the words, said, "Doctor!"

Benjamin ignored him. Silently he pointed a finger first at the sergeant, then at Ga. Then he whirled on his heel and left the room. The sergeant picked up the writhing snake and threw it into the hallway, then grasped Ga's left arm, turned him onto his stomach, and expertly cuffed his hands behind him.

Surprised, then outraged, Ga shouted, "I order you—"

The sergeant punched him hard in the kidney. Ga shrieked in pain and subsided, gasping. The sergeant shouted an order in his own language. Two constables—the one who had been posted in the hallway all along and the one the blonde had bitten—came into the room, pulled Ga to his feet, and marched him naked down the hallway, past the headless mamba, past the crumpled blonde, and out the back door. The mamba, still twitching, would be the first thing the girl would see when she opened her eyes.

In the bedroom the hi-fi played the last words of the Piaf song that had begun as we entered the house. It had taken Benjamin three minutes and twenty seconds to carry out his coup d'état.

Outside, Ga struggled with the two constables who were trying to stuff him into the trunk of Benjamin's Rover. He kicked, squirmed, butted. One of the constables struck him on the hip bone with his baton. Ga collapsed like a marionette whose strings had been cut. The constables heaved him into the trunk and slammed it shut. One of them locked it, and then in his jubilation, knocked on it to make a little joke. The sergeant spoke an angry word to him.

Benjamin had already taken his place in the backseat of the Rover. I expected to be put into another car or to be left behind, but the sergeant opened the door for me, and I got in and sat beside Benjamin. We heard Ga in the trunk behind us—groans, childlike sobs, whisperings, appeals to Jesus, an explosive shout of Benjamin's name, so throat-scraping in its loudness that I imagined spit flying from Ga's mouth. If Benjamin derived any satisfaction from these proofs that his enemy was entirely in his power, he did not show it by sign or sound. He sat at attention in his Victorian dress uniform—silent, unmoving, eyes front.

The sergeant's Austin, driven by one of the constables, tailgated us as we rolled through the wide-awake city. It was just as noisy as before but more drunken, more out of control. What must Ga be thinking as he lay in pitch-darkness, folded like a fetus, naked and in shackles? Ten minutes ago he had been the most powerful man in Africa. Not now. He was silent. Why? Did he fear that the crowd would discover him and drag him out of the trunk and parade him naked through the howling mob? Did he imagine photographs and newsreels of this appalling humiliation being seen by the entire world?

We arrived at a darkened building I did not recognize. Somewhere above us a red light pulsed, and when I got out of the car I looked upward and realized that it was the warning beacon on the tower of the national radio transmitter. I made out the silhouettes of an armored car and maybe a dozen men in uniform.

The constables hauled Ga out of the trunk. He struggled and shouted words in a language I did not understand. A door opened and emitted a shaft of light. To my eyes, which had seen nothing brighter than a candle flame all evening, it was blindingly bright. We went through the door, a back entrance, into a cramped stairwell. A young chief inspector came to attention and saluted. He looked and behaved remarkably like the spick-and-span army captain I had met at the presidential palace. Other constables were posted on the stairway, one man on every other step. Incongruously for men who dressed like British bobbies and were trained to behave like them, each was armed with a submachine gun. I wondered what would happen if they all started shooting at once in this concrete chamber.

Ga screamed a question: "Do you know who I am?"

No one answered.

In a different, commanding tone, Ga said, "I am the president of this republic, elected by the people. I have been kidnapped by these criminals. I order you to arrest them at once."

Ga sounded like his newsreel self, voice like a church bell, and in spite of his abject state, looked like that old self, blazing eyes, imperious manner. However, the reality was that two large policemen had hold of his arms. He was naked and in chains and spattered with the blood of the mamba. A string of spittle hung from the corner of his mouth. The constables gave him a shove in the direction of the stairs. He stubbed his naked toes on the concrete step and sucked a sharp breath through his clenched teeth. This sound turned into a sob of frustration. The men to whom he was giving orders would not look at him.

I wondered if the next event in this Alice in Wonderland scenario might involve sitting Ga down at the microphone and ordering him to tell the nation that he had been removed from power. But no, he was frog-marched up the stairs and into the control room by his escorts. I remained with Benjamin and the sergeant in the studio. The control room was brightly lit. It was strange to gaze through the soundproof glass and see the wild-haired, glaring, unclothed Ga looking like one of his ancestors from the Neolithic.

The engineer switched on his mike and said, "Ready when you are, chief constable."

Into the open mike Ga shouted, "You will die, all of you! Your families will die! Your tribes, all of you will die!"

The engineer, quaking with fear, switched off the microphone, but Ga's mouth kept moving until the bigger constable put his hand over it, gagging him. Eyes rolling, chest heaving as he fought for breath, he kept on shouting. The constable pinched his nostrils shut, and the dumb-show noise behind the soundproof glass ceased.

Detecting movement near at hand, I shifted my gaze. A man in nightclothes was seated at the microphone. He was at least as nervous as the engineer. Benjamin handed him a sheet of paper. It was covered by Benjamin's perfect penmanship. Benjamin, a man who delegated nothing except, apparently, the most important announcement ever made over Radio Ndala, gave the engineer a thumbs-up signal. The engineer counted off seconds on raised fingers. He pointed to the announcer, who began reading in mellifluous broadcaster's English.

"Pay attention to this message from the high command of Ndala to all the people of our country," he said, voice steady but head twitching and hands trembling. "The tyrant Akokwu Ga is no longer the president of Ndala. He has been charged with mass murder, with treason, with corruption, and with other serious crimes and will be tried and punished according to the law. The functions of the government have been assumed for the time being by the high command of the armed services and the national police. The United Nations and the embassies of friendly nations have been informed of these developments. The people are to remain calm, obey the police, and return to their homes at once. An election to select a new head of state will be held in due course. The people are safe. The nation is safe. Investments by foreign nationals are safe. The treasure stolen by Akokwu Ga from the people is being recovered. All guests

in our country are safe, and they are at liberty to remain in Ndala or leave Ndala whenever they wish. Additional communiqués will be issued from time to time by the high command. Long live Ndala. Long live independence and freedom. Long live justice. Long live democracy."

As the announcer read, Ga, listening intently, became very still, very attentive, his gaze fixed on what must have been a loudspeaker inside the control room. He might have been a child listening to a bedtime story about himself, so complete was his absorption in what was being said. His eyes were wide, his face bore a look of wonder, his mouth was slightly open. A police photographer took several pictures of him. Ga drew himself up and posed, head thrown back, one shackled foot advanced, as if he were wearing one of his resplendent uniforms.

After that, he was marched back to the Rover and again dumped into its trunk. He did not struggle or make a sound. The camera, it seemed, had given him back his dignity.

Roadblocks manned by soldiers had been erected on the road to the presidential palace. At the approach of Benjamin's Rover they opened the barricades and saluted as we passed. We were a feeble force—two ordinary sedans not even flying flags, four police constables, and an American spy with a defective passport, plus the prisoner in the trunk of the car who was the reason for the soldiers' awe.

The palace came into view, illuminated as before by the megawatts that flooded down from the light towers. A dozen stretch limousines, seals of high office painted on their doors, were parked in the circular drive of the presidential palace. The palace doors were guarded by police constables armed with Kalashnikovs. On the roof of the palace, more constables manned the machine guns and antiaircraft guns that they had taken over from the army.

Benjamin waited for the constables in charge to haul Ga from the trunk, then he got out of the car. He gave me no instructions, so I followed along as he strode into the palace with his usual lack of ceremony. We climbed the grand stairway. All busts and statues and portraits in oil of Ga in his many uniforms had been removed. Less than an hour before, he had walked down these stairs as President of the Republic for Life. Now he climbed them as a prisoner dragging chains. There was a dreamlike quality to this scene, as if we did not belong in it or deserve it, as if it were a reenactment of an event from the life of some other tyrant who had lived and died in some other hour of history. Did Caesar as he felt the knife remember some assassinated Greek who had died a realer death?

A courtroom of sorts had been organized in Ga's vast and magnificent office. His desk and all his likenesses had been removed from this room, too. The Ndalan flag remained, flanked by what I took to be the flags of the armed forces and other government entities, but not by the presidential flag. The presidential conference table, vast and gleaming and smelling of wax, stood crosswise where Ga's desk had formerly been. Through the window behind it Ga's antelopes and gazelles could be seen, bathed in incandescent light as they bounded across the paddocks of his game park. Half a dozen grave men in British-style army, navy, and air force uniforms sat at the table like members of a court-martial. They were flanked by a half dozen others in black judicial robes and white wigs, clearly members of the supreme court, and a handful of other dignitaries wearing national dress or European suits.

All but the military types seemed to be confused by the entrance of the prisoner. In some cases this was obviously the last thing they had expected to see. Some if not all of them probably had not been told why they were there. Maybe some simply did not recognize Ga. Who among them had ever imagined seeing in his present miserable state the invulnerable creature the president of the republic had been?

If in fact there were any doubts about his identity, Ga removed them at once. In his unmistakable voice he shouted, "As president for life of the republic, I command you, all you generals, to arrest this man on a charge of high treason."

He attempted to point at Benjamin but of course could not do so with his wrists chained to his waist. Nevertheless, it was an impressive performance. Ga's voice was thunderous, his eyes flashed, he was the picture of command. For an instant he seemed to be fully clothed again. He gave every possible indication that he expected to be obeyed without question. But he was not obeyed, and when he continued to shout, the large constable did what he had done before, at the radio station. He clapped a hand over Ga's mouth and pinched his nostrils shut, and this time prolonged the treatment until Ga's struggle for breath produced high-pitched gasps that sounded very much like an infant crying.

The trial lasted less than an hour. Some might have called it a travesty, but everyone present knew that Ga was guilty of the crimes with which he was charged, and guilty, too, of even more heinous ones. Besides that, they knew that they must kill Ga now that they had witnessed his humiliation, or die themselves if he regained power. The trial itself followed established forms. Benjamin, as head of the national police, had prepared a bundle of evidence that was presented by a prosecutor and objected to by a lawyer appointed to defend Ga. Both men wore barrister's wigs. Witnesses were duly sworn. They testified to the massacre of the beggars. The immaculate young captain testified that Ga had embezzled not less than fifty million American dollars from the national treasury and deposited them in secret accounts in Geneva, Zurich, and Liechtenstein. The court heard tape recordings of Ga, in secret meetings with foreign ambassadors and businessmen, agreeing to make certain high appointments and award certain contracts in return for certain sums of money. Damning evidence was introduced that Ga had ordered the death of his own brother and had perhaps fed him alive to hyenas in the game park.

Without retiring to deliberate, the court returned a unanimous verdict of guilty on all counts. Benjamin, who was not a member of the court-martial, did not join the others at the table and was not called to testify. He spoke not a single word during the proceedings. When Ga, who had also been silent, was asked if he had anything to say before the sentence was pronounced, he laughed. But it was a very small laugh.

The prisoner was delivered to Benjamin for immediate execution. After this the court-martial reconvened as the Council of the High Command, and in Ga's presence—or, more accurately, as if Ga no longer existed and had been rendered invisible—elected the chief of staff of the army as acting head of state and government. Benjamin kept his old job, his old title, his old powers, and presumably, his pension.

I wish I could tell you for the sake of symmetry that Ga died the kind of barbarous death that he had decreed for others, that Benjamin fed him like a Thomson's gazelle to the cheetahs or gashed his flesh and set a pack of hyenas on him under the stadium lights. But nothing of the sort happened.

What happened was this. The generals and admirals and justices and the others got into their cars and drove away. Ga, Benjamin, the sergeant, the two constables, and I went outside. We walked across the palace grounds, Ga limping in his chains, away from the palace, over the lawns. Animals in the zoo stirred. Something growled as it caught our scent. Only the animals took an interest in what was happening. The constables guarding the palace stayed at their posts. The servants had vanished. Looking back at the palace I had the feeling that it was completely empty.

When we came to a place that was nearly out of sight of the palace—the white mansion glowed like a toy in the distance—we stopped. The constables let go of Ga and stepped away from him. Ga said something to Benjamin in what sounded to me like the same language that

Benjamin and the sergeant spoke to each other. Benjamin walked over to Ga and bent his head. Ga whispered something in his ear.

Benjamin made a gesture. The sergeant vanished. So did the two constables. I made as if to go. Benjamin said, "No. Stay." The stadium lights went out. The sun was just below the horizon in the east. I could feel its mass pulling at my bones, and even before it became visible, its heat on my skin.

We walked on, until we could no longer see the presidential palace or light of any kind no matter where we looked. Only moments of darkness remained. Ga sank to his knees, with difficulty because of the chains, and stared at the place where the sun would rise. Briefly, Benjamin placed a hand on his shoulder. Neither man spoke.

The rim of the sun appeared on the horizon. And then with incredible buoyancy and radiance, as if slung from the heavens, the entire star leaped into view. Benjamin stepped back a pace, pointed his Webley at the back of Ga's head, and pulled the trigger. The sound was not loud. Ga's body was thrown forward by the impact of the bullet. Red mist from his wound remained behind, hanging in the air, and seemed to shoot from the edge of the sun, but that was a trick of light.

Benjamin did not examine the corpse or even look at it. I realized he was going to leave it for the hyenas and the jackals and the vultures and the many other creatures that would find it.

Benjamin said to me, "You have seen everything. Tell them in Washington."

"All right," I said. "But tell me why."

Benjamin said, "You know why, Mr. Brown."

He walked away. I followed him, not sure I could find my way out of this scrubby wilderness without him but not sure, either, whether he was going back to civilization or just going back.

ANDREW KLAVAN

BORN IN NEW YORK CITY as one of four sons of the popular liberal talk-show host Gene Klavan, who cohosted *Klavan and Finch* and then hosted *Klavan in the Morning*, Andrew Klavan (1954–) grew up and identified himself early in life as a liberal and a Jew, both of which changed as he grew older. He described himself as an agnostic for some years before converting to Christianity, and he is now an active writer and blogger with libertarian conservative views. He hosts *The Andrew Klavan Show*, a satirical political podcast on *The Daily Wire*. He also is a contributing editor to *City Journal* and his essays have appeared in *The Wall Street Journal*, *The New York Times*, and the *Los Angeles Times*, among other places.

As a mystery writer, Klavan has enjoyed both popular and critical success, with five Edgar Allan Poe nominations, two of which were winners: *Mrs. White* (1983), coauthored with his brother Laurence under the pseudonym Margaret Tracy, which was the basis for *White of the Eye*, a film released in 1987 starring David Keith and Cathy Moriarty, and *The Rain* (1988), under the pseudonym Keith Peterson.

In 1992, he was nominated for an Edgar in the Best Novel category for *Don't Say a Word*, which later became a 2001 film that starred Michael Douglas, Sean Bean, and Brittany Murphy. His novel *True Crime* (1995) was filmed and released four years later with Clint Eastwood as director and star, featuring Isaiah Washington, LisaGay Hamilton, and James Woods. Klavan wrote the screenplays for the Michael Caine vehicle *A Shock to the System* (1990), a mystery based on the novel by Simon Brett, and the horror film *One Missed Call* (2008). He also wrote the story and cowrote the screenplay for *Gosnell: The Trial of America's Biggest Serial Killer* (2018), which featured Michael Beach, Dean Cain, Janine Turner, and Nick Searcy, who also directed.

Demonstrating his versatility, Klavan has written a series of thrillers for young adults called The Homelanders, including *The Last Thing I Remember* (2009), *The Long Way Home* (2010), *The Truth of the Matter* (2010), and *The Final Hour* (2011).

"Sleeping with My Assassin" was originally published in *Agents of Treachery* (New York, Vintage, 2010).

SLEEPING WITH MY ASSASSIN

ANDREW KLAVAN

I KNEW WHY she had come—of course I did—but I fell for her anyway—of course. That was what she'd been designed for and who I was, who they'd made me. I didn't even question it much, to be honest. I'd come to hate philosophizing of that sort by then. Endless discussions about nature versus nurture or fate versus free will. In the end, what are you even talking about really? Nothing: the way words work, the way the human brain puts ideas together—what we're capable of conceiving, I mean, not the real, underlying truth of the matter. I'm sure there's some logic to a person's life and all that. Some algorithm of accident and providence and inborn character that explains it. Maybe God can work it out, if he exists and has a calculator handy. Maybe even he shrugs the whole thing off as a pain in the celestial ass.

But for me, in the event, it was more poetry than philosophy or math. I saw her and I thought, "Ah, yes, of course, that's who they *would* send, isn't it?" She was death and the past and my dreams incarnate. And I fell for her, even knowing why she'd come.

―――――――

I had premonitions of the end as soon as I read about the train wreck. I saw it on the *Drudge Report* over my morning coffee and suspected right away it was one of ours. A computer glitch on the D.C.–New York corridor. A head-on collision, twenty-seven dead, no one, seemingly, to blame. They were still digging bodies from the smoking wreckage when the FBI announced it wasn't terrorism. A likely story. Of course it was terrorism. By afternoon and through the two days following, various Islamist groups were claiming credit by way of various YouTube videos featuring various magi with greasy beards and colorful noses and utterly ridiculous hats. That was a likely story, too. Those hate-crazy clowns—they didn't have the network for it, not in this country.

Which meant it was a genuine riddle. Because we *did* have the network, but we had no cause.

I worried at it for a day or two, trying to sort out the possibilities. Stein was our man on the eastern railways, and I suppose, after so many decades of silence and unknowing, he might have just flipped and pressed the button. But he was always a stolid character, unlikely to go rogue. And anyway, instinct told me this was something else, something more disturbing. It had the smell of geniune catastrophe.

Finally, the anxiety got to be too much for me. I decided to take a risk. I couldn't contact Stein himself, of course. If we weren't active, it would be a useless danger. If we were, it would mean death to us both. Using my cover, I called a contact at the Agency instead—a threat analyst in the New York office—and he and I took a lunchtime stroll around the hole in the ground where the World Trade Center used to be.

There was nothing particularly strange about this. There are plenty of gabby spooks around. You'd be surprised. A lot of these guys are just overeducated bureaucrats playing *Spy vs. Spy*. They graduate with an ideology and maybe some computer skills but no real sense of evil whatsoever. Secrecy doesn't mean that much to them. Gossip is the only real talent they have— and the only real power they have—and they know you have to give to get. Buy them a drink and they'll spill state secrets like your Aunt May talking about Cousin Jane's abortion: all raised eyebrows and confidential murmurs and theoretically subtle hints you'd have to be an idiot not to understand.

But Jay—I'll call him Jay—was different. He'd been in Afghanistan, for one thing. He'd seen the sort of things people do to one another on the strength of bad religion or through the logic of misguided ideas or just out of plain monkey meanness. He knew the moral universe was not a simple machine in which you pour goodness in one end and goodness reliably comes out the other. All this made him better at his job than the academic whiz kids, more circumspect, more paranoid and thoughtful, less likely to make an easy trade for information. Subtlety, in fact, was the whole point for him. The unsaid thing that left open a world of possibilities. Which was his world—because the way Jay saw it, you never really knew.

We were on the walkway beside the wreckage pit, moving in slow, measured steps amid a quick, jerky, time-lapse lunch crowd. We were shoulder to shoulder, our eyes front. Both of us in overcoats, both of us with our hands in our pockets. It was a biting October day.

Jay made the slightest gesture with his head toward the damage. Not dramatic at all—barely perceptible. But just enough to answer my objections to blaming the *jihadis*, just enough to say, *They did* that, *didn't they?*

"That was different," I said. Muttering, tight-lipped. "Primitive. Plus they got lucky. Plus we were stupid then."

"Oh, we're stupid now," he said with a laugh. "Believe me."

"Still."

He looked at me as we walked along—looked until I turned and read his eyes. I saw that he was puzzled, too; he smelled catastrophe, too.

"You know something?" he asked me.

I shrugged. I didn't. "There was some chatter before the fact," I said. "They knew it was on the way."

This was just a guess, but I felt sure it was a good one. It was the only reason I could think of why the YouTube wise men in their absurd hats should have had any measure of credibility with Jay at all. I could tell by his reaction that I'd gotten it right. There *had* been chatter. They *had* known.

Jay pursed his lips and let out a breath, a whispered whistle. We both faced front again. I saw him nodding from the corner of my eyes, confirming my suspicions.

"So why are there no fingerprints?" he wondered aloud.

Well, exactly. That was the question. Because the Arabs leave fingerprints. They pretty much have to. They pretty much *want* to, but even if they didn't, they would. Because they don't have the network. They aren't implanted, integrated, invisible the way we are. How could they be? Think of our preparation, the time we had to establish ourselves here. Time enough, in fact, so that the whole point and purpose of us passed away.

Which brought me right back where I'd started. They had the cause but not the network. We had the network but not the cause. I couldn't make any sense of it, and it had me worried. I kept circling around it in my mind as I walked uptown on Broadway toward my office.

It was a long walk in the brisk, wistful weather. Soon enough, the useless round of reasoning wore itself out, and I wasn't thinking at all anymore but had drifted instead into daydreams.

I'd always been like that, a dreamer, all my life. Lately, though, the quality of the dreams had changed. There was an aspect of compulsion to them, maybe even of addiction. They'd acquired a disturbing and ambient realism, too. I was there sometimes almost more than I was here. I *wanted* to be there more. I found a kind of peace when I was dreaming that I never had otherwise.

It was always about the Village. Always about Centerville. Not memories of my childhood, mind you. I had those, too, but the daydreams were something different, something more pathetic really, when you consider it. In the daydreams, I was in my hometown again but as a man in his early thirties, say, a man some quarter century younger than I am now but some fifteen years older than I was when I left the Village for good. I suppose, if you wanted to get psychological about it, you could say I was imagining myself at my father's age, the age my father was when I was little. But I think, more to the point, I was dreaming about myself at an age when I was still romantic but not unrecognizably young, more like myself than a seventeen-year-old but vigorous enough to play the handsome hero of a love story.

That's what they were, my daydreams: love stories. Their plots are too childish and embarrassing to go into at length, but a few details give their flavor. The setting played a major role: Centerville's green lawns and trim clapboard houses, the Stars and Stripes waving above the verandas, the bikes and trikes rattling along the sidewalks. Churches, parks and ponds, and elm-shaded walkways. And the school, of course, the gray-shingled, all-American elementary school. The world of my boyhood, in other words.

She—the girl, the love interest—was variously named Mary or Sally or Jane. Smith was always her last name. Mary or Sally or Jane Smith. She was always very prim and proper—sometimes shy, sometimes warm and outgoing, but always proper and modest as good women were back there, back then. That, I think, was the heart of what I pined for. Not the Village's peaceful lawns and houses—or not *only* its lawns and houses and tree-lined walks—but the sweetness of its women, their virginity or at least their virtue or at least what I had thought as a boy was their virtue and had so admired and desired and loved.

The rest of the daydream—the plot—was, as I say, all nonsense. I would be some romantic figure just home from some war or adventure, usually with a dashing scar on my cheek to show for it. There would be misunderstandings and separations, physical heroism sometimes and finally reconciliation, even marriage, even, if I was dreaming at leisure in the solitude of my apartment, a wedding night. Insipid, adolescent scenarios, I know, but it would be difficult to overstate how engrossed I could become in them, how soothing it was to me to return in my mind to the innocence and peace of that American small-town setting, circa 1960, to reexperience the virtue and propriety of women in the days before radicalism and feminism and sex on demand. That old and innocent America, all gone now, all forever gone.

Walking home from Ground Zero that day, I was so immersed, in fact, that I reached the middle of Washington Square Park before I came back to myself—and then I woke to my surroundings with a sort of breathless rush, a threatening flutter of panic. I stood still by the dry, leaf-littered fountain. I stood with my hands in my pockets and scanned swaths of landscape to the right and the left of the marble arch. Then I turned around and scanned the paths behind me. I had the unnerving sense that I was being followed or watched. I was almost sure of it. My eyes went over the faces of the few people sitting on the benches, the few sitting on the rim of the fountain, and the several others passing on the walks beneath the naked trees. I had the feeling that I had seen someone I knew or recognized, that it was that that had jolted me out of my day-dreaming fugue state.

But there was no one. After another moment or two, I moved on. I was rattled, but uncertain what to make of it. On the one hand, my spycraft had grown rusty from long disuse, and I was doubtful it could be trusted. On the other hand, I hated even to entertain the thought that this train wreck and its riddles might mark a return to the paranoia of the bad days.

The bad days, as I still thought of them, came in the early nineties, after the system collapsed and the wall came tumbling down. Communication with our controls, always infrequent, had ceased entirely and, forbidden to make contact with one another, we were completely in the dark. Sleepers—any undercover operatives, but sleepers especially—are always in danger of losing their sense of purpose, of becoming so immersed and identified with the culture they've infiltrated that they become estranged from their motherland and their mission. But now our purpose was lost *in fact*; our motherland and mission were gone well and truly. What's the point of a Soviet pretending to be an American once the Soviet Union no longer exists?

That little conundrum was inner hell enough, believe me, but then the deaths began. Three of us in the space of a year and a half. David Cumberland, the movie director, collapsed on top of a terrified starlet after he or she or his dealer or personal assistant or someone, the investigators never determined who, misjudged the ratio of morphine to cocaine in one of his speedballs.

Then Kent Sheffield went out the window of a Paris hotel in the wake of rumors he'd embezzled some of his clients' investments. And finally, Jonathan Synge, one of the first of the Internet billionaires, went down with his twenty-six-foot sailboat in the choppy waves outside the Golden Gate. All of which could have been coincidental or could have meant that the network was blown and the Americans were mopping up or that our own masters were getting rid of us, covering their tracks in light of the new situation. The uncertainty only added to the terror of it.

And the terror, I will not lie, was awful. There was no information, no contact, nothing but the deaths and the waiting. I was rudderless and ceaselessly afraid. My discipline collapsed. I started drinking. My marriage, such as it was, unraveled into a series of affairs and violent arguments and "discussions" that were even more vicious arguments in disguise. I couldn't tell Sharon the truth, of course, so our fights were always off the point and only served to increase my isolation.

"It was bad enough when you were just cold and silent, but now you're disgusting," she said to me. I was coming through the door in the dark of first morning. She was standing in the bedroom doorway in a pink nightgown, her arms hugged tight beneath her breasts. Her face was haggard and grim. She was a competent, sophisticated woman, but anger made her look weak and humorless. As long as we'd been minimally civilized with each other, her company—the mindless conformity of her expectations, the low normalcy of her social-climbing ambitions, just her reliable, undemanding presence day to day—had been some sort of comfort to me. Now even that was gone.

"Let me at least close the door," I said. "The whole building doesn't have to hear you."

"Jesus. I can smell her on you from here."

"So you wash the smell of them off first. What does that make you? The Virgin Mary?" Naturally, it wasn't what I wanted to say. I wanted to tell her about the never-ending fear and silence and the loneliness that made the fear and silence worse. I wanted to cry out to her that my whole purpose in life was gone and that I had known it was gone for years, but now that I could read all about it on the front page there was no denying it to myself any longer. I wanted to fall on my knees and bury my face in her belly and cling to her like a stanchion in high winds and tell her oh, oh, oh, I didn't want to die, not now when it had all become so useless and not like this, hustled into the center of some drab tabloid scenario by a pair of deadpanned experts in faked suicides and accidents, my extermination just another job.

"Oh, and don't give me that look," I said to her instead—even though she had turned her face away now to hide her crying. "We don't even make any sense anymore, do we? I mean, what's the point? Why shouldn't I cheat? What the hell am I getting out of it? It isn't as if you keep house or bring me my drinks and slippers. You're not the mother of my children. . . ."

"Whose fault is that?" she said raggedly, in a tearful rage.

"You work, you make as much money as I do. It isn't as if you need me the way a man wants to be needed. Women . . ." I waved a hand in the air, too drunk to form the thought I wanted, something about the way it used to be, what women were like, what marriage was like in the good old days. "You're just a roommate with a vagina," I finished finally. "As if that's supposed to count for everything. Well, I like a different vagina from time to time, if that's all it comes down to, so sue me. . . ."

The phone rang, interrupting this learned disquisition on modern social mores. Both Sharon and I reared up and stared at the instrument, indignant, as if it were some underling who had dared to break in on important business between us. If a couple can't rip each other to shreds in peace at four in the morning, what's the world coming to?

It rang again. Sharon said, "Go on and talk to your whore." Then she whirled in her pink nightgown and stormed back into the bedroom, slamming the door behind her.

"My whore doesn't have our number," I said—but only softly, because Sharon was no longer there to be hurt by it. Meanwhile, I was thinking *What the hell?* A wrong number? A neighbor complaining about the noise? The signal to set off a disaster or a harbinger of my own assassination? What? I was trying to talk myself out of the less pleasant scenarios, but it was no good. When the phone rang again, I tasted fear, chemical and sour, in the back of my throat.

I stepped to the lampstand by the sofa, took up the handset. Listened without a word.

"I can't stand it anymore," a terrified voice said at once.

"Who is this?" But I already knew—I could guess anyway.

"I don't care about the protocol." He was whining shamelessly. I could practically hear him sweat. "What good is protocol to me? We can't just sit here and be picked off one by one. We have to do something."

"You have the wrong number," I said.

I hung up. I stood in the center of the room and stared at nothing and swallowed the sour taste in my mouth. I was suddenly fully sober.

That was almost—was it possible?—yes, almost twenty years ago. And that night—that was the worst of it. Whatever their cause, the deaths among us stopped at three. As time went by with no contact and no further disasters, the paranoia faded almost away.

Twenty years. Twenty years of silence and unknowing, the network an orphan, the regime that spawned it gone. The mission? It became a vestigial habit of thought, like some outmoded quirk of inclination or desire acquired in childhood but useless to or even at odds with adult life. I went on as I was trained to go on *because* I had been trained and for no other reason. What had once been the purpose of my every movement became more like a neurotic superstition, an obsessive compulsion like repeatedly washing the hands. I maneuvered my career and cultivated my contacts with an eye to sabotage, positioned myself where I could do the most damage. But there was no damage to do, and no point in doing it. And I didn't want to anyway. Why would I? Why would I hurt this country now?

Don't get me wrong. It wasn't that I had come to love America. I didn't love America. Not this America, weak and drab and stagnant. Its elites in a self-righteous circle jerk and its fat farm fucks muttering "n———" and its n———s shrunken to bug-eyed skeletons on the watery milk of the government tit. Corrupt politician-alchemists spinning guilt and fear into power. Depraved celebrities with no talent for anything but self-destruction. And John Q. Public? Turn on the television and there he was, trying to win a million dollars on some hidden-camera game show by wallowing in the slime of his own debauchery. That was entertainment now—that was culture—that was art. And then the women. Go out on the street and there they were, barking *fuck* and *shit* into their cell phones. Working like men while their men behaved like children, playing video games and slapping hands and drinking beers with their baseball caps on sideways, then trudging sheepishly home with a "yes, dear," to their grim, sexless fuck-and-shit mommy-wives. There was no spirit in the land. No spiritual logic to lead anyone to love or charity. Nothing for the soul to strive for but welfare bread and online circuses. A Rome without a world worth conquering. I did not love this America; no. If I was loyal to anything, it was the country I had known in childhood. The innocent small-town community with its flags and churches and lawns. The women in their virtue and their skirts below the knee. The fathers in their probity and suits and ties. I loved the pride in liberty back then—not the liberty of screwing whom you wanted and cursing whatever curses—but the liberty born of self-reliance and self-control. The Village—I loved the Village. I loved Centerville. And Centerville was gone.

All the same—all the same, what was left of it—what was left of this country here and now—was still a relative paradise of comfort and convenience. What else was there left to care

about but that? Revolution? Whatever came of revolution but slavery and blood? No. I had my routines, I had my successful business, the restaurants I enjoyed, my golf games, my sports on TV, my occasional women. Why—in the name of what forsaken cause?—would I do damage to such a pleasant ruin of a place to live and die in as this?

So when I sensed our hand in the train wreck, I just felt my comforts threatened, frankly. I was unnerved—worried almost to the point of panic—to think that I might lose my easy, pleasant life.

What else was I supposed to feel, given the realistic possibilities?

I spent the next several days after my meeting with Jay in virtual isolation in my apartment, trolling the Internet obsessively, searching for answers. Stein had been put in charge of the internal investigation now, so there was nothing like trustworthy information from any of the official sources. But there were clues. At least I thought there were. I thought I sensed traces of the truth lying right out in the open, right there in the daily news. A resurgence of Russian arrogance despite plummeting oil prices. A cat-and-canary silence in the Middle Eastern capitals despite all the outlying wise men beating their breasts. It all made for a sort of faint, wispy, curling smoke trail of reasoning if you knew how to see it, how to follow it. The implications were too horrible for me to face directly, but I must've understood them at some subconscious level all the same, because my anxiety grew more unbearable every day. Protocol or no, the impulse to try to contact Stein himself was almost irresistible.

I might've done it, too, if I hadn't remembered Leonard Densham.

It was Densham who had called me that early morning twenty years ago—that morning of my fight with Sharon. His was the whining, sweaty voice on the phone: *I can't stand it anymore. We have to do something.* He had always been the weak link, always, even when we were boys back in Centerville. The last to take a dare, the first to seize on an excuse for cowardice. He should've been eliminated then, but he had peculiar aptitudes when it came to rockets and satellites and so on, the big things at the time. In fact, he had ended up at the Department of Defense, working on the global navigation satellite system. But he was a weak link all the same. He should have been left behind.

As the days went by—those obsessive, anxiety-ridden days in my apartment, at my computer—I became convinced that he—Densham—was the one who had been following me in Washington Square Park. It made sense. If there was danger, uncertainty, anxiety, it made sense that Densham would be the first to break, the first to make contact, now as before. I became convinced that I had actually seen him in the park and subconsciously recognized his face, that it was that that had brought me out of my reverie.

Assuming I was right, I didn't think he would be hard to find. If he was following me, he must've been looking for a chance to make a safe approach. All I needed to do was give him the opportunity.

I chose a place called Smoke—a small smoking club amid the old brick warehouses on the lower west side. Nothing but two rows of cocktail tables in a narrow room of red carpet and red walls and black curtains with no windows behind them. The light was low and the music was loud: impossible to wire, difficult to observe. I went there three days running, arriving in the early evening before the crowds. I sat at the table nearest the back, where I could see everyone who came and went. Each day, I smoked one long Sherman and had one glass of malt and left.

On the third day, just as my smoke burned down to the nub, Densham pushed through the door and came hurrying down the center aisle toward my table.

Once upon a time, I would have said he had gone mad. No one really uses that word anymore. There are syndromes now and pathologies. Schizophrenia and bipolar disorder and this disorder and that. I suppose the notion that someone could just lose touch with reality is problematic in an age when no one is quite certain reality even exists. But Densham was something, all right: delusional, paranoid, anxiety-ridden, fevered, a raging whack job—make up your own diagnosis.

You only had to look at him to see it. It was bone-cold outside—there were snow flurries—and the club was poorly heated. I had sat through my drink with my overcoat on. But Densham? The sweat was gleaming on his face when he came in. His hair was limp and shiny with it. His eyes burned. His fingers worked constantly. He sat across from me at the small round table, bent over, rocking slightly with his fingers working so that he seemed to be playing an invisible clarinet in the empty air.

The waitress was a pretty young thing in a white blouse and black skirt and black stockings, but he barely glanced at her. He brushed her away at first, in fact, with those fiddling fingers, and only called her back to him and ordered a beer as an afterthought—so as not to look suspicious, I guess. Likewise, he shook his head when I opened my box of Shermans to him—and then quickly held my wrist before I could withdraw it. He took a cigarette and leaned into my plastic lighter so that, even through the smell of smoke, I caught a whiff of something on him, some vintage feminine perfume that touched me somehow.

"Calm down," I murmured to him as I held the flame. "You'll only draw attention to yourself. Just calm down."

I lit a fresh cigarette for myself as well, and we both sat back and drew smoke. Densham tried frantically to smile and seem relaxed. It just made him look even crazier.

"You understand what they've done, don't you? Can you see it?" The moment he spoke, the clues and my suspicions began to fall into place. But before I could put them all together, he leaned forward again, hot-eyed and urgent, his fingers drumming the table spasmodically. And he said, "They've sold us. They've sold the network."

My stomach dropped and my thoughts became clear. "To the Arabs."

"Of course, to the Arabs! Who else would . . . ?"

The waitress brought his beer, and he fell back against his chair, sucking crazily on his cigarette until he choked and coughed. I watched the girl's skirt retreating. Then, more calmly than I felt, I said, "That's ridiculous, Densham. Pull yourself together. Look at you. You're falling apart."

"Of course I'm falling apart! I didn't come here to blow things up for a bunch of camel-fucking madmen!"

"Quiet! For God's sake."

He clapped his cigarette hand to his mouth as if to hush himself.

"It doesn't make sense," I said. "What would they sell us *for*?"

Densham gave a jerky shrug, his hand fluttering up into the air now like a butterfly on a string, the cigarette trailing smoke behind. "Oil. What else? The price of oil. That's all they have left now, after all the fine philosophy they fed us. They need a lift in the price of oil—and fast. And what do they have to sell in return that the Arabs want? Us! The network."

I laughed, or tried to make a noise like laughter. "You're crazy. You're making this up."

"I'm not making it up. I deduce it."

"You can deduce anything. It may just be a train crash, Densham. For God's sake."

He stared at me, searched me with that peculiar power of insight crazy people have. "You know it. You know I'm right, don't you?"

I hid behind my drink. "Ah! Things go through your mind when you're on edge. It happens to all of us."

"I think Stein must have gone over."

"What? Gone over to whom?"

"The Americans!" he hissed. "Else why haven't they killed him like they did Cumberland and the others? Or arrested him at least?"

I didn't bother to answer him this time. I saw how it was with him now. He had sat at home in whatever life he had these twenty years and stewed in his terrors and suspicions, and now every outlandish theory seemed like the plain truth to him, every worst-case scenario seemed the obvious fact of the matter. He was like one of those people who call into radio shows at night to talk about flying saucers and government conspiracies. He saw it all clearly and everyone else was blind. He was mad, in other words.

"You'll see. You'll see," he said. "We're activated. Activated *and* blown. In a week, a month, a year, we'll each get the call to serve the jihad. Refuse it, and our masters hurl us out a window. Accept it, and the Americans run us down with a car in some alley. We're dead either way." He laughed bitterly.

I'd had enough. I reached for my wallet. "You're out of your mind. You've been stewing in your own juices. You need to get out more. Get a good psychiatrist. Whatever you do, don't come near me again."

"I'm not going to do it! You understand? Camel-fucking madmen. I won't do it. That's not what I agreed to."

I shrugged. "We were children. None of us ever agreed to anything."

"Maybe the Americans can use me," Densham went on. "*They'll* spare me. Why not? They spared Stein, didn't they? Americans have always been sentimental that way. They'll see how it is. They'll see I have something to live for now. Finally. Something to live for . . ."

"Shut up. Would you shut up? Pull yourself together. Damn it!"

I threw some cash down on the table and stood. Densham looked up at me as if he only now remembered I was there. He nibbled at the end of his cigarette like a squirrel nibbling on a nut. He seemed small and furtive and ashamed.

"Do you ever miss it?" he said.

"What are you talking about?" I said irritably. I stood there, buttoning my overcoat. "Miss what?"

"The Village. Centerville. *I* miss it sometimes. I miss it a lot."

I looked away from him, embarrassed. It was as if he'd read my daydreams. "Don't be ridiculous," I said. "There's nothing to miss."

"There is to me." He gave another pathetic little laugh, a sob almost. "I loved it. It's the only thing I ever did love really."

"We all . . . idealize our childhoods."

"No. No," he repeated earnestly. "That life, that way of life. That's what we should've been fighting for all along."

I felt my face go hot. I stared down at him as if he were saying something incredible, something I hadn't thought myself a thousand times. "Fighting for?" I said, trying to keep my voice down. "How could we fight for it? It wasn't even real."

"It was real to me."

I sneered, disgusted by him—disgusted because he seemed just then to me to be my own pathetic Inner Man made flesh.

"Get yourself some help, Densham," I said.

He laughed or sobbed again. I left him there and strode across the room to the door.

His death made the news, small splashes on the inside pages of the tabloids, likewise small but more stately obituaries in the broadsheets, and then, inevitably, links online. Instapundit was where I found it. They linked to a *New York Post* story: *Satellite Pioneer in Shocking SM Suicide.* Densham had been found hanging from the clothes rod in his closet strangled with his own belt and dressed in bizarre leather corsetry and other paraphernalia. A fatal wardrobe malfunction during an otherwise quiet evening of autoerotic asphyxiation—so said the local constabulary.

As murder, it was art—if it *was* murder. That was the genius of it. How could you know for sure? But I knew. At least, I thought I knew. I read the story with my stomach in a tailspin. I recognized it right away as the end of peace of mind for me, the end of what was left of my peace of mind. What sort of mental breakwater would

stand against the flood of paranoia now? No. There was no getting away from it: The bad days had returned.

How awful suspense is! Worse than any actual catastrophe. How often have you heard a cancer patient tell you, "The worst part was waiting for the test results." Worse than the cancer itself: the waiting, not knowing, afraid. Awful. And there were days of it now, weeks of it, months.

Maybe that was also part of the reason I fell in love with her. Not just what she looked like and how she behaved and what she represented. That was all in the mix, of course. But maybe I was also just grateful—so grateful—that she had finally arrived.

By then, the dark, snowy winter had given way to a spring so mild it seemed a kind of silent music. I forced myself to go out of doors just to experience it, just to feel the air. The wistful air. Truly, just like a strain of half-remembered music. Even in New York with the heat of its traffic, its noises and smells, you couldn't feel that air without a softness opening in you, a sense of longing for the past—whatever past it was you happened to long for. I, of course, walked the city streets and dreamed of Centerville, dreamed myself into love stories set in the Village. It was the only relief I had from the suspense, the heavy winter cloud of waiting, unknowing and afraid.

I was lost in those dreams even as she approached me. I was in a coffee shop, at the window counter, my hand limp around the cardboard cup as I gazed unseeing at the storefront glass.

"Do you mind if I sit here?" she said. She had a beautiful voice. I noticed it right away. It was clear and mellow with diction at once flowing and precise. It was the way that women used to speak when they thought about how they *should* speak, when they trained themselves to speak like ladies.

I looked up and she was lovely. Maybe twenty years younger than I, in her thirties. Poised, but not with that brusque, mannish confidence I so often see in women today. Consciously grace-ful rather, as if her grace was a thing she did for people, a gift she gave them. Her whole style was graceful and vaguely old-fashioned in a sweet, pretty way. Shoulder-length blonde hair in a band. A blue spring dress wide at the shoulders, nipped at the waist, and ending modestly over the knee. I caught the scent she was wearing, and it was lovely, too, graceful and old-fashioned, too. I thought I knew it from somewhere but couldn't remember where.

"Do you mind if I sit here next to you?"

"Not at all," I said to her—but at the same time, my eyes swept the room and I saw there were plenty of tables open, plenty of other places she could sit.

She saw my eyes, read my thoughts. "There was a man outside," she told me. "Following me, making remarks. I thought if I sat next to you, if it seemed as if we knew each other . . ."

What happened next happened very quickly, my brain working things out, my emotions responding, all in a cascading flash. My first reaction was instinctive, automatic. An attrac-tive woman had asked for my protection: I was warmed and immediately alert to the possibil-ity of romance. But in the next moment—or in the next segment of that moment—it was all so quick—I remembered where I'd smelled that perfume before. It was the same scent I'd caught coming off Densham in the club when he had leaned toward me so I could light his cigarette. *I have something to live for now*, he had told me. *Finally. Something to live for.*

My eyes went to her eyes—her pale blue eyes—and I thought, *Ah, yes, of course, that's who they* would *send, isn't it?* And what was, I sup-pose, horrible—horrible and yet mesmerizing somehow—was that I saw she saw my thought, I saw she saw that I understood everything, and I saw that *she* understood, understood that it didn't matter to me, that it was to her advantage, in fact, because I wanted her, welcomed her.

She was death and the past and my dreams incarnate, and I was in love with her already. I always had been.

You would think what followed would have been more or less bizarre, but it wasn't. Not to me. Every lover at the start is in a kind of fiction anyway. The restraint, the things held back, the best foot forward. Even this latest generation of whores and boors must have some courting ritual or other before they go at it like monkeys and then wander off to nurse their hangovers. Every mam-mal has its manners, its method of approach.

So the fact that she and I never acknowl-edged the reality of our situation didn't seem to me as strange as all that. We dined together and went to the movies and took long walks in Cen-tral Park and took drives into the country to see the spring scenery, just like anyone. We talked more or less at random about what we enjoyed and what we'd seen and what we ought to do. I told her about my business, which offered secure storage and online backup for the computer files of major corporations and government agencies. She told me about teaching English as a second language to visitors and immigrants. That was a nice touch: I was a wealthy entrepreneur, and she was a do-gooder, just getting by. It gave me all kinds of opportunities to take care of her, to play the man. She liked that, being taken care of. She liked for me to open the door for her and stand when she entered a room and hold her chair when she sat down. She accepted these tokens of gentlemanly respect with grace but also with gratitude. She had a way of nestling in my kindnesses, of luxuriating in my protection and the vulnerability it allowed her. She had a way of looking up at me in expectant deference when there was a decision to be made so that I felt helpless to make any decision but the one that would ultimately please and shelter her. She was all softness and beauty, and I found myself tending to her as if she were the last flower left in an otherwise stony world.

As for the past—as for talking about the past: We shared only fragments of it in those first days, fragments at intervals now and then, and if my memories were distortions and hers were lies, how different were we from anyone in the early stages of attraction?

We became lovers in the prettiest way, the gentlest and most graceful way, only after weeks and weeks of courtship and subtle seduction and slow surrender. I wish I had the words to describe the sweetness of her reticence, her modesty, and the measured yielding of her modesty to her passions and to mine. You want to tell me it was all inauthentic? False? A performance? As the kids say nowadays: Whatever! Have such things ever been anything *other* than a kind of performance, a kind of dance? An art form, if you will. And what's art but a special sort of falsehood, a falsehood by which we express the inexpressible truth about ourselves and about the human condition?

Well, that was the way I thought about it anyway—as a kind of art, a kind of story we were telling with our lives, a kind of lovely dance. Right up until the moment of climax, right up until the moment I came, holding her naked in my arms and thanking God—really, thanking God—for the late-life blessing of her. And then it all crumbled in my mind to ashes. What is it, I wonder, about the male orgasm that vaporizes every standing structure of sentiment and enchantment?

An hour later I sat bitterly in the dark, smoking a Sherman by the open window, staring balefully at the shape of her asleep on the bed. The taste of the cigarette brought my meeting with Densham back to me. His squirrelly, nervous voice beneath the smoke and music . . . *We're activated. Activated* and *blown. In a week, a month, a year, we'll each get the call to serve the jihad. Refuse it, and our masters hurl us out a window. Accept it, and the Americans run us down with a car in some alley. We're dead either way.*

She stirred in the shadows and murmured my name. Then, finding me there at the window framed by the relative light of the night city, she propped herself up on an elbow. "Are you all right, sweetheart?"

"Which was it?" I said to her. "Did he take the mission or refuse it?"

"What? Who?"

"Densham. He said he was going to turn them down and trust in the protection of the Americans. But I don't think he would have had the courage in the end. Once he was actually confronted with the choice, it would've been easier just to go along." The words came out of me in a low, tumbling rush. "He would've told himself that he was all wrong about the Americans, that they had no clue about us, that that's why Stein had gone along and gotten away with it scot-free. He could've convinced himself of anything if he thought it meant being with you. You were all he wanted, what he was living for. And there you were, all the while, waiting patiently, watching to see what he knew, who he spoke to, which way he'd turn. Just like you're doing with me."

She didn't answer. She didn't say, *I don't know what you're talking about.* It was chilling. She didn't even bother to pretend.

"I suppose that means that you *are* with the Americans," I said. "He took the mission and you had to stop him. . . . Or, who knows, maybe you're one of ours. Maybe he *did* refuse and that's why you did it. . . ."

"What time is it?" she murmured. "I'm sorry—I'm still asleep. Whatever it is, we can talk in the morning. Come back to bed and be with me."

Eventually, the mood passed and I did.

Strangely, as much as I was expecting the final call, it came unexpectedly. Because I was that lost in her, that immersed in the living dream of our romance. Hours and days at a time, I would forget the call was coming, though I always knew. When it finally did come, nothing could have been further from my mind.

We were in the park. It was an early summer's day. We were eating lunch at the café overlooking the lake. I was telling a funny story about a website I had sold to a teenage millionaire who had dropped out of high school and had all the money in the world but no manners whatsoever. She was laughing in the most charming and flattering way, graciously covering her mouth with one hand. I was thinking how lovely, how truly lovely she was and what a joy.

The phone in my jacket pocket began to vibrate. Normally, of course, I wouldn't have answered during lunch, but this was the third time it had gone off in as many minutes.

"Excuse me," I said to her. "It might be an emergency at my office." I believed it, too. That was how completely submerged I was in our fairy tale.

I fetched out the cell phone and held it to my ear and even then, even when I heard the cantata in the background, it was a moment before I understood. Bach 140: the first part of the signal. And then a voice said, "George?" which was the other part.

"I'm sorry, you have the wrong number," I responded automatically.

"Oh, sorry, my mistake," the man said. The music was cut short as he hung up.

I slipped the phone back into my pocket, my eyes on her the whole time now.

"Wrong number?" she said finally. Just like that, completely natural, completely believable.

And in the same way, the same tone, almost believing it myself, I answered, "Yes. Sorry. Now what was I saying?"

As we walked back to my apartment, I found myself saddened more than anything, saddened that it was over. Though the light of the summer day stayed bright through the late afternoon, it had acquired, I noticed, an aura of emotional indigo, a brooding border of darkness that I remembered seeing in my college days when I had walked a lover to the train station for what I knew to be the last time. Now I held her cool hand in mine and glanced down from time to time at her fresh, upturned face and listened to that flowing, ladylike diction as she chattered about this or that future plan—and I ached for every passing minute, every minute that brought us closer to the end.

"Why don't you pour us some wine?" I said, as I helped her with her coat in the foyer. "I just have to check my e-mail for a moment."

I went into the study, consciously cherishing the domestic noises she made moving around the kitchen. I switched on the computer.

Our procedures had last been updated more than twenty years ago. They still included quaint arrangements like drop points and locker keys and corner meetings. I doubted that sort of thing was operational anymore and, as it turned out, I was right. They had sent the material straight to my computer: an untraceable packet that simply appeared as an icon on the desktop when I turned the machine on. I didn't read the whole code. Just enough to see what it was. A virus I could spread through my backup apparatus so that my clients would lose some of their files. Then, when they went to restore the files through my service, they would be rewritten with instructions that would plant minor, undetectable but ultimately devastating glitches throughout entire systems. It was, in other words, a cyber time bomb that would hobble key security responses at essential moments and render the nation helpless to defend against . . . whatever it was our camel-fucking friends were planning to do. At a glance, the business seemed quite elegant and devastating. But I think what struck me most about it was its clinical and efficient realism. It was as devoid of romance as a bad news X-ray. It pushed the whole notion of romance out of my mind.

Maybe that's why I seemed to see her afresh when I walked back into the living room. There she stood now in the center of the floor with our wineglasses, one in each hand. Wearing a pleated skirt and a buttoned blouse and a pearl necklace against her pink skin. It was the first time she seemed simply fraudulent to me. Beautiful, but fraudulent. Like a satire of a fifties housewife. Not even that. A satire of a television program about a fifties housewife. The sight of her brought a bitter taste of irony into my mouth and into my mind, and as I took a glass from her,

I smirked into those wonderful eyes—while they regarded me with nothing I could detect but wide, blue innocence.

I sat in my favorite easy chair. She sat on the rug at my feet. That, too, in my suddenly prosaic mood, struck me as somewhat overintentional: a patent construct, a cynical tableau of a woman modest in her youth doting on a somewhat older man in his authority.

All the same, I held my glass down to hers and she lifted hers to mine and we clinked them together. I sipped and sighed.

"I was raised," I said, "in a town called Centerville." I don't know why I felt I had to tell her this, but I did. It was the last act of the play, I guess. The only way I could think to keep it going just a little longer.

She did her part as well. She put her head on my knee and gazed up at me dreamily as I stroked her hair. "Yes," she said. "You've mentioned it. In Indiana, you said."

"Yes. Yes. It was supposed to be in Indiana, a small town in Indiana. But, in fact, of course, it was in the Ukraine somewhere. Surrounded by these vast wheat fields. Quite beautiful really. Quite typically American. They wanted us to grow up as typical Americans. That's what the place was made for. Even as they trained us for what we were going to do, they wanted us to develop American habits of manner and mind so we could be slipped into the places they prepared for us, so we wouldn't stand out, you know, wouldn't give ourselves away."

She was very good. Quiet and attentive, her expression unreadable. She could've been thinking anything. She could've simply been waiting for the sense of it to be made clear.

"The problem was, of course, that our intelligence services . . . well, let's say they never had much of a sense of nuance. Or a sense of humor, for that matter." I laughed. "No, never a lot in the way of humor, that's for sure. They constructed the place out of self-serious field reports and magazine articles they accepted without question and programs they saw on TV.

Especially the programs they saw on TV, those half-hour situation comedies that were so popular in the fifties, you know, about small-town family life. They developed the whole program around them. Trained our guardians and teachers with them. Reproduced them wholesale in their plodding, literal Russian way, as the setting for our upbringing. As a result, I would say now, we grew up in an America no actual American ever did. We grew up in the America America wanted to be or thought of itself as or . . . I don't know how you would express it exactly. It was a strange dichotomy, that's for sure. Brutal psychologically, in some ways. We were planted as children in the middle of the American Dream and then taught that it was evil and had to be destroyed. . . ."

I sipped my wine. I stroked her hair. I gazed into the middle distance, talking to myself more than anything now, musing out loud, summing up, if you will. "But it was . . . my childhood. You know? I was a boy there. There were, you know, friends and summer days and snowfalls. Happy memories. It was my childhood."

"You sound as though you miss it," she said.

"Oh, terribly. Almost as if it had been real." I looked down at her again. Her sweet, gentle, young and old-fashioned face. "As I love you. As if *you* were real."

She sat up. She took my hand. "But I *am* real." I was surprised. It was the first lie she'd ever told me—aside from everything, I mean. "You see me, don't you? Of course I'm real."

"I'm not going to do it," I told her. "You can tell whoever sent you. I've already deleted the code." Now, again, she simply waited, simply watched me. I stroked her cheek fondly with the back of my hand. "I've given it a lot of thought. It was difficult to know how to approach it actually. Should I try to outguess you, determine what would activate your protocol? Or try to figure out the right and wrong of the matter—though I suppose it's a little late for that. In the end, though . . . in the end, you know what it was? It was a matter of *authenticity*. Of all things. But really, I mean it. When I was younger, I tried to figure out: Who am I? Who was I meant to be? Who *would* I have been if none of this had ever happened? But what good is any of that? Thinking that way? We all have histories. We all have childhoods. Accidents, betrayals, cruelties that leave their scars. We're none of us how we were made. So I thought, well, if I can't be who I am, let me at least be what I seem. Let me be loyal to my longings, at least. Let me be loyal to the things I love. Even if they are just daydreams, they're mine, aren't they? Let me be loyal to my dreams."

She didn't answer. Of course. And the look on her face remained impossible to decipher. I found myself appreciating that at this point. I was grateful for it, though her beauty broke my heart.

I took a final sip of wine and set the glass down on a table and stood. I touched her face a final time, my fingers lingering, then trailing across the softness of her cheek as I moved away.

I didn't turn to her again until I reached the bedroom doorway. And then I did stop and turn and I looked back at her. She made a nice picture, sitting on the rug, her feet tucked under her and her skirt spread out around her like a blue pool. She had followed me with her eyes and was watching me, and now she smiled tentatively.

"Look at you," I said, full of feeling. "Look at you. You were never more beautiful."

And as I turned again to leave the room, I added tenderly, "Come to bed."

PERMISSIONS ACKNOWLEDGMENTS